DIE WITH ME

DIE WITH ME

Elena Forbes

Quercus

First published in Great Britain in 2007 by

Quercus
21 Bloomsbury Square
London
WC1A 2NS

A CIP catalogue record for this book is available from the British Library

ISBN (HB) 1 84724 156 5
ISBN-13 978 1 84724 156 6
ISBN (TPB) 1 84724 157 3
ISBN-13 978 1 84724 157 3
ISBN (SP) 1 84724 227 8
ISBN-13 978 1 84724 227 3

10 9 8 7 6 5 4 3 2 1

Printed and bound in Great Britain
by Clays Ltd, St Ives plc.

For Clio and Louis

1

The tombstone was nearly six feet tall, weathered and mottled with lichen. A pair of fat-cheeked cherubs framed the inscription: 'How short is life, how soon comes death.' Soon comes death. So very true. She was late, his bride, his partner 'til death do us part. More than ten bloody minutes late, he noticed, checking his watch yet again. Had she no sense of occasion? Didn't she care that he was standing there in the cold, waiting for her? Soon it would be dark. People would start leaving work to go home and they would miss their chance.

He glanced towards the entrance to the churchyard, his breath a pale cloud blown away by the wind. Still nothing. Stamping his feet hard on a horizontal grave slab for warmth, hands jammed deep in the pockets of his overcoat, he backed into the recess of the church porch. For ceremony's sake he had thought of pinning a flower in his buttonhole but had decided against it. Too noticeable. Besides, he hated flowers.

Where the hell was she? Maybe she had never meant to come. Maybe she had just been stringing him along all the time. Digging his nails into his palms at the thought, he jerked his head over his shoulder and spat on the ground, imagining what he would do to her if she stood him up. Telling himself not to worry, he examined the thick skeins of cobwebs that stretched like gauze between the pillars of the porch, focusing on a fat, dead fly imprisoned in the sticky mesh. She'd be here. She had to come. She wouldn't dare let him down.

He caught a movement out of the corner of his eye and swung round to face the road. Framed by the wrought iron archway at the end of the path, she stood at the top of the steps looking up towards him, eyes startled. Her white face, curtained by long waves of hair, seemed like a full moon, featureless. Sweat pricked his palms and a swell of excitement swept over him, tingling down his back, making the hairs on his neck stand on end. He exhaled sharply. Moistening his lips with his tongue, he smoothed down his hair with his fingers, watching as she came through the gate and walked towards him up the path. Her movements were jerky, like a little bird, nervous, hesitating, never taking her eyes off him. She was younger than he had imagined, no more than fourteen or fifteen. His maiden, his bride. She was perfect. The breath caught in his throat and he was unable to speak.

Dressed in nothing but black, as he had insisted, she was wearing an old raincoat, several sizes too large, that looked as though it had been borrowed or bought in a second-hand shop. Beneath it peeped the uneven fringe of a long skirt and heavy boots with a strap and silver buckle at the ankle. He noticed all the details, pleased that she had done as she was told.

She stopped a few feet away as if unsure, peering short-sightedly at him. 'Are you Tom?'

Her voice was pitched high, her enunciation childlike. He detected a slight accent but couldn't place it. Trying to contain his excitement, he stepped out of the shadows and smiled, reaching out his arm to welcome her.

'Gemma.'

Trembling, tentative, she offered him a small hand from beneath the rolled-up coat sleeve. Her fingers were icy and limp as he pressed them briefly to his lips. As he touched her skin, he caught the faint smell of Pears soap, kindling old, unpleasant memories. He let her hand drop a little too quickly and she looked away, embarrassed, folding her arms tightly and hugging herself. Gently, he took her by the elbow and pulled her towards him.

'Dear Gemma. You're so beautiful, you know. Much more than I'd imagined. Much, much more. So very beautiful.'

Still gazing at her feet, she flushed, giving a shy wriggle of pleasure. No doubt it was the first time anyone had ever said those words to her.

'You're sure you want to do this?' he said.

She glanced up at him, her pale-lashed eyes searching his face, looking for reassurance, maybe, or something else. Did she like what she saw? Did she find him handsome? Of course she did. He could see it in her eyes. He was everything she had hoped for, and more. He had filled her dreams for so long and now here he was, Prince Charming, standing in front of her, flesh and blood.

On a hot summer's night, would you offer your throat to the wolf with the red roses? Why did that bloody song keep popping up in his mind? *Will he offer me his mouth? Yes. Will he offer me his teeth? Yes. Will he offer me his jaws? Yes. Will he offer me his hunger? Yes. And will he starve without me? Yes.* The hunger. The yearning. So difficult to control. *And does he love me? Yes.* He had said that he loved her.

He bent down to kiss her properly. Again that foul whiff of Pears. Had she scrubbed herself all over with it? He tried to block it out, watching as she gave a little sigh, screwing her eyelids tight shut as she yielded, her lips in a tight moue, like a child's kiss. He was surprised at her inexperience. Most girls her age were little better than whores.

He kissed her again, allowing his lips to linger for a moment, touching her mouth ever so lightly with his tongue, feeling her soften beneath his grasp as he observed her, the un-plucked eye-brows, the fine golden down on her cheeks, the faded dusting of freckles on her nose. The winter light bleached the colour from her face, giving her a deathly pallor. He was sure she was a virgin, although that had no special appeal for him.

After what he considered to be long enough, he stepped back and she opened her eyes. They were a clear blue, without doubt her best feature. Trusting eyes, soft and innocent. She really was perfect. He smiled at his good fortune, showing her his beautiful white teeth.

'You're really sure? You're not just wasting my time?'

3

She looked away as if his gaze burnt her, fingers fiddling with a thread hanging from the end of her coat sleeve.

'I'm serious about this, you know,' he said, watching her closely. 'You're not going to let me down?'

She shook her head slowly but he was unconvinced. He touched her lightly under the chin, making her look up at him again.

'Come on. We're in this together. *Together, forever, you and I.*'

The words came from another song but it was the sort of trite thing she liked. Easily pleased, she had lapped up the poetry he had sent her, all about love and about death. It seemed to touch a chord, opening a floodgate of confession and neediness. The pain, the loneliness, the sad catalogue of neglect and unhappiness. He understood her so well. He was her soul mate, her first and only love.

'Us. Together. Never parted. It's what you wanted, isn't it? It's what you said.' He stared at her, trying to inject warmth into his expression, trying to tamp down his impatience. 'We don't belong in this world. You know it's the only way.'

Gulping, she nodded slowly, tears welling.

'Good. I've got everything we need in here.' He patted his rucksack and swung it over his shoulder. Bending forward, he kissed her quickly again. 'Come, my darling. It's time.' Clamping an arm around her, he marched her into the dimly-lit interior of the church.

The air was stale; damp mingling with the stench of rotting flowers from various stands of wilted white roses and chrysanthemums placed at intervals along the aisle. He couldn't imagine why anyone would choose this church to be married in. There was no atmosphere, nothing remarkable about the bare, cavernous interior with its marble plaques, war memorials and anonymous rows of brown pews, nothing to attract tourists or other casual visitors. It was a neglected place, unloved and unfrequented. Security was also extraordinarily absent, although there was nothing worth taking. He had done his research and chosen it carefully. Weekday mid-afternoons were a void time, perfect for what lay ahead.

Gemma stood transfixed, gazing up at the round stained-glass window at the end of the nave above the altar, its jewel colours illuminated by the dim light from outside. The martyrdom of St Sebastian, early nineteenth century, he remembered reading in the church pamphlet. St Catherine or St Joan would have been a more appropriate backdrop but female martyrs were thin on the ground in London.

He jerked her by the elbow. 'Come on. Someone could come along any minute and we can't risk being disturbed.'

She allowed herself to be propelled towards the heavy-curtained archway near the pulpit. Behind was a long flight of stairs leading to the organ and the empty gallery high above the nave. As he pulled back the curtain, she stopped and peered up into the dark area above.

'It's so high,' she said, drawing out the word 'high' as if it were something shocking.

He knew he was going to have trouble. He wanted to say that 'high' was the whole point, as she damn well knew. 'High' was what it was all about. They'd discussed everything at length. Now was not the time for doubts. For a moment, he pictured her wheeling above him, spinning through the air, her black raincoat fanning out behind her like the wings of a huge crow. He could hear the sound of it flapping and he felt almost feverish.

'Come on, I'm with you. Just a little further now.' He took hold of her wrist and started to drag her up the first flight of stairs.

She tried to pull her arm away. 'You're hurting me.'

He caught the puzzled look in her eyes and let go. 'Sorry, my darling. I'm just feeling nervous, that's all. I've waited so long for this. For you. I'll follow you, shall I?'

He watched as she stumbled up the stairs. At the top, she wavered, then collapsed in a heap on the landing. Putting her head in her hands, she bent over double, her hair falling over her face and down her legs like a sleek, brown cloak. Half choking, she started to sob.

Shit. This was all he needed. Even though the sound was

muffled, somebody might hear. He wanted to jam his hand over her mouth but he mustn't alarm her. He knelt down on the stair below her, holding her knees, which were clamped tightly together. He would do anything if it would only make her shut up. Slowly, he started to massage her thighs through the thick woollen layers of her skirt.

'It's going to be OK. If you don't want to do it, we don't have to.' He cupped his hands around her head and kissed her hair over and over again, feeling almost high with worry. 'Please stop crying. Really, it's OK. I'm just so glad I met you.' If only she would look at him, he was sure he could win her around. 'We don't have to do it. We don't have to, you know.' He took her tiny hands in his and peeled them away from her face, forcing her to raise her head, eyes still tight shut. 'Look at me, Gemma. We'll do whatever you want. Really... I mean that. I love you.'

Slowly she opened her eyes and he rewarded her with one of his softest smiles, brushing her wet, sticky hair off her face, using the edge of her coat sleeve to wipe away the slime around her nose and lips.

'I don't want to,' she whispered, trembling as she gazed at him. 'I don't want to...' She couldn't finish the sentence. Die. Die with me. Be mine forever. That's what he had said.

He rose, went over to her and sat down on the step beside her. Wrapping his arm tightly around her, he pulled her into him, cradling her head against his shoulder.

'Nor do I, my darling, nor do I.' Stroking her soft hair, he kissed the top of her head. 'Not now I've met you, anyway. Do you feel that too?'

She nodded, pressing her head hard into his coat sleeve.

'You've saved me, you know. You're so very special. My little Gemma. Shall we do the ceremony anyway? I have everything ready. Shall we exchange rings as we planned?' She gave a squeak of assent, burying deep into him, nuzzling his shoulder like a kitten. 'Very special,' he said, still stroking her hair, trying to soothe her. 'So very special.'

She started as if stung by something, her hand flying to her mouth as she looked up at him.

'What's the matter?'

'The note. I left a note like you told me. What happens when Mum finds it?'

Was that all? He smiled with relief. 'Don't worry. We can either get it back or...' he let the sentence hang before continuing, 'you can come and stay with me. Then it won't matter. You don't have to go home, if you don't want to. There's no way they'll find us. No way at all.'

She blushed, glancing at him out of the corner of her eye as she returned the smile. For a moment, in spite of her swollen eyes and blotchy face, she looked almost pretty.

'Come on then. I think you'll like the gallery. It's very private, a really special place. Nobody will bother us there.'

He stood up and helped her to her feet, patting down the folds of her coat and brushing away the dust and fluff from the floor. Barely able to contain himself, he took her by the hand and kissed it one last time, closing his eyes briefly as he pictured again what was to come. She was his. All his. He was sure.

2

There was no justice in life. DI Mark Tartaglia gazed through the glass porthole of the door to the intensive care room where his boss, DCI Trevor Clarke, was stretched out in bed, at the centre of a spaghetti junction of wires and tubes. Apart from the dark strip of moustache visible beneath the oxygen mask, Clarke was unrecognisable. He'd been in a coma ever since the accident, his head held fast in a clamp to protect his injured spine, with his shattered pelvis and legs surrounded by a metal cage. Thank God he'd been wearing a helmet and proper clothing when he came off his motorbike. But the prognosis wasn't good.

Sally-Anne, Clarke's fiancée, sat by the bed, head bowed, one of Clarke's huge hands cupped in hers. She was dressed in a bright pink and white checked suit, her long, blonde hair pulled back in a ponytail tied with a gold ribbon. Tartaglia had just missed her the day before when he had called by and he didn't relish seeing her now. For a moment he thought about coming back later. But sod it, Clarke was one of his best mates; he had every right to be there too. He rapped on the glass panel, opened the door and went in.

Sally-Anne looked round briefly. Her eyes were red, rimmed with mascara. He wasn't sure if she was crying for Clarke or for herself. Any woman who could up sticks and leave two small kids and a husband for another man, even if it was someone as nice as Clarke, had to be selfish beyond belief. And it had all happened so fast. Impulsive as always, Clarke never did things by halves. One minute she was just the new bit of squeeze, brought along for the occasional drink or bite to eat. Next thing, she was living in his flat in Clapham, he'd put her name on his mortgage and bank account and now that her divorce had come through, they were talking about getting hitched. But that was before the accident. Maybe Tartaglia was being harsh, but he couldn't imagine Sally-Anne looking after a paraplegic for the rest of her life.

'Any progress?' Tartaglia asked, walking over to the foot of the bed. He'd already heard from Clarke's nurse that there was none but he didn't know what else to say. The longer Clarke stayed in a coma, the worse the likely outcome.

Sally-Anne shook her head, stroking the top of Clarke's hand with her long pink nails, gazing fixedly at what could be seen of his face as if she were willing him to open his eyes or speak. Tartaglia wondered how long she had been there and what was going through her mind. Conversation seemed pointless and he stood behind her, feeling awkward, the silence punctuated by the bleeping of the monitors around the bed and the episodic shushing of the ventilator.

After a moment, Sally-Anne muttered something to Clarke that sounded like 'see you later', carefully placed his hand back on top of the sheet, patted it and stood up. Straightening her short skirt, she picked up her handbag and turned to Tartaglia, tears in her eyes.

'I hate hospitals. I hate the smell. It reminds me of having my appendix out when I was a kid and I feel so bloody useless. What's the point of coming? What good can I do? I mean, he doesn't even know I'm here.'

Avoiding her gaze, Tartaglia shrugged and stuffed his hands in his pockets. He was there because he cared about Clarke, because he wanted to see him, poor bastard. Of course it wouldn't do Clarke any good, in the state he was in. But that wasn't the point. Even if it was a pretty empty gesture, it was a mark of their friendship, of respect.

She took a tissue out of her bag and blew her nose. Her eyes fastened onto the motorbike helmet under Tartaglia's arm. 'Stupid prat. Why did Trevor have to go and buy that wretched bike? He hasn't ridden one in years.'

Her tone was bitter and Tartaglia wondered if somehow she held him personally to blame, as he was close to Clarke and the only other member of the murder team to ride a motorbike. For a moment he thought of the gleaming red Ducati 999 in the hospital car park and felt almost guilty. But if Sally-Anne thought he'd led Clarke astray, she was wrong. Mid-life crisis was the phrase that came to mind. At least, that was the joke around the office. Six months, almost to the day, after Clarke's wife left him for her yoga teacher, he'd started WeightWatchers and joined the local gym. Next came the motorbike, the contact lenses, the garish shirts and the leather jacket. What with the seventies-style moustache he refused to shave off, he was starting to look like one of the Village People. Just when they were all wondering if Clarke was going to come out of the closet, along came Sally-Anne, almost young enough to be his daughter, and his brief second stint as a single man was over. Clarke was well aware of what his work mates thought but he didn't seem to mind. He was just happy and at peace with the world. That should have been all that mattered but Tartaglia couldn't help worrying that Clarke would end up getting hurt.

Sally-Anne was still staring at Tartaglia, arms clasped tightly around her handbag. 'You know, I just keep hoping he's going to open his eyes. That's all I want. Just to know that he's still all there, up top, I mean. Anything else, we can learn to cope with together.'

The way she spoke sounded genuine and he felt a little surprised. Had he been wrong about her? Did she really love Clarke after all?

'Have you thought about playing him some music?' he said, feeling embarrassed, wanting to appear helpful if nothing else. 'You know, something he'll recognise. They say it sometimes works.'

'That's not a bad idea. I suppose anything's worth a try, given the state he's in. But a Walkman's definitely out.' Gulping, she gave a wry smile in Clarke's direction. 'I mean, where would you put the headphones?'

She had a point. You could barely make out Clarke's eyes, let alone his ears. 'What about one of those portable machines with speakers?'

She nodded slowly, as if he had said something important. 'We've got one in the kitchen at home. I'll bring it in this evening with some CDs. Trev really loves Celine Dion, for some weird reason. Maybe the sound of her voice will wake him up, even if mine won't.'

Tartaglia grimaced. 'God, I'd forgotten he has such crap taste in music. If I were you, I'd try and find something he really hates, like Eminem or 50 Cent. He's such an ornery bastard, you should play it really loud right next to him and see what happens. That'll do the trick, if anything will.'

She gave him a wistful smile. 'I can just imagine him shouting at me to turn it off. That would be good, wouldn't it?'

She looked up into his eyes for reassurance. Although her face had brightened momentarily, tears were still not far away. In spite of the make-up and sophisticated clothes, she looked like a young girl. She hesitated, head slightly to one side as if there was something else she wanted to say. But after a second she just touched his arm and walked past him, her impossibly high heels squeaking on the linoleum.

Opening the door, she glanced back at him. 'Maybe see you tomorrow. If there's any change before then, I'll let you know.'

As the door closed behind her, Tartaglia's mobile rang. In spite of the hundreds of notices plastered around the hospital, he had forgotten to switch it off. He flipped it open and heard the smooth tones of Detective Superintendent Clive Cornish, at the other end.

'Are you with Trevor?'

'Yes, but I'm about to leave.'

'Any progress?'

'None, I'm afraid,' Tartaglia said, turning away and whispering into the mouthpiece, as if Clarke might somehow be able to hear him. 'But at least he's still alive.'

Cornish gave a heavy sigh. Clarke was well liked and respected by everybody, even Cornish, a man not normally known for warmth or feelings of compassion towards anyone. 'That's something, I suppose. Anyway, I need you over in Ealing right away, at a church called St Sebastian's. It's on South Street, just off the main drag. I've told Donovan to meet you there. There's been a suspicious death. With Trevor out of action for the foreseeable future, you're now the acting SIO.'

St Sebastian's was set back a little above the road in a leafy residential area, a high wall with iron railings forming the boundary. Bathed in bright winter sunshine, the church was plain, with simple, graceful lines and tall stone pillars flanking the entrance. Georgian, Tartaglia thought, from the little he knew of architecture. It seemed at odds with the endless criss-cross streets of ornate Edwardian redbrick terraced houses that surrounded it, as if it had been taken from somewhere else and plonked down in the middle of Ealing by mistake.

DS Sam Donovan stood huddled by the main gate, hands jammed in her coat pockets, eyes watering and nose red from the cold.

'You took your time,' she said, shivering. 'It's bloody freezing out here and I'll probably catch my death now.'

Tiny and slim, with brutally short, spiky brown hair that framed an otherwise pretty, regular-featured face, she was wearing a purple coat, baggy trousers and Doc Martens, her chin tucked into the thick folds of a long, woolly, lime green scarf, wrapped several times around her neck.

'Sorry. The traffic was bad. I've been over at St Mary's, seeing Trevor.'

'How is he?' she asked, ducking under the crime scene tape and leading the way up the steps to the churchyard.

'Unfortunately, no change. But I'll fill you in later.' They started to walk together slowly up the long path that curved towards the church door. 'Cornish said we've got an unexplained death.'

She nodded, taking a crumpled paper tissue from her pocket

and blowing her nose loudly, as if she was trying to make a point. 'I've had a full briefing with DI Duffey from the on-call MIT. The victim's a fourteen-year-old girl called Gemma Kramer. She fell from the organ gallery inside the church two days ago. Ealing CID initially assumed it was an accident or suicide.'

'Was there a note?'

'No. But they didn't find anything suspicious about her death and, after what sounds a pretty cursory forensic exam of the ground floor, the crime scene was released.'

'Released?' he said, pausing in the middle of the path and turning to her.

'Afraid so. Apparently there'd been some pressure from the vicar and some locals to reopen the church for a christening.'

Shaking his head, he moved on again, Donovan at his side. Manning a cordon around a crime scene twenty-four hours a day was an expensive business and with resources stretched, as always, it wouldn't be the first time such a thing had happened.

'So what changed their minds?'

'Just after the church was cleaned up and re-opened for business, a witness materialises out of the woodwork saying she saw the girl going into the church with a man a couple of hours before her body was found. Somebody then has the sense to ask for a full tox analysis and when the report comes back, it's panic stations. The girl had traces of alcohol and GHB in her system.'

'GHB? Was she sexually assaulted?'

'Not according to DI Duffey. The crime scene was re-sealed immediately and a thorough forensic investigation was carried out of the whole church. It was only a cursory clean, hopefully not much damage was done.'

'We should be thankful for small mercies, I suppose,' he said, stopping again for a moment and glancing around the churchyard, wanting to get his bearings.

The graves were so crowded together that the whole area was almost entirely paved, with hardly a blade of grass to be seen. The stones were deeply weathered and most of the inscriptions barely readable. It seemed that nobody had been buried there for many years. He pulled out a Marlboro red from a pack in his pocket and turned his back to the wind to light it, letting the sun warm his face for a moment.

'Is the girl local?' he asked, taking a long, deep drag and watching the smoke gust away on the cold air.

'No. She's from Streatham. Nobody has a clue what she was doing around here.'

'Tell me about the witness.'

'I've just been to see her. She's called Mrs Brooke. She's in her late sixties or early seventies and lives a couple of streets away. Don't be put off by her age,' she added, no doubt seeing the sceptical look on his face. 'She used to be a ladies fashion buyer for Selfridges and has quite an eye for detail. She seemed pretty reliable to me.'

He smiled. 'OK. I'll take your word for it. What time was all this?'

'Just after four in the afternoon. She was going out to tea with a friend and was sitting in the shelter across the road, waiting for a bus.'

Turning, he saw an old-fashioned bus shelter about twenty yards away, partially obscured by a tight row of tombstones and an ancient yew tree.

'According to Mrs Brooke, Gemma came from that direction,' Donovan continued, pointing across him to the left. 'The Tube's that way, so we assume that's how she got to Ealing. Gemma crossed the road and went up the steps into the churchyard. The next time Mrs Brooke looked over, she was kissing some bloke just over there, in front of the porch. She said she felt a bit shocked as Gemma looked very young and the man was quite a bit older. Then they went into the church together.'

'Mrs Brooke saw all of this from where she was sitting?'

'So she says.'

Tartaglia strode up the path to the porch and wheeled round. 'According to her, they were standing here?'

'That's right.'

He looked back across the churchyard to the road in front. At four in the afternoon it would have been getting dark but the line of sight to the bus stop was relatively clear and he felt reassured that Mrs Brooke would have had a good view.

'How old did she say the man was?' Tartaglia asked, taking another pull on his cigarette as Donovan caught him up.

'She thought he was in his thirties or possibly early forties, but she couldn't be sure. He was a lot taller than Gemma, as he had to bend right down when he kissed her. Although, given that Gemma was apparently about my height, that's not saying much.' Donovan smiled. She was not much over five foot and proud of it.

He glanced back again at the shelter. Even at this time of day, the interior was shadowed. From where he was standing, it was almost impossible to see if anyone was inside. Maybe Gemma and her friend had been unaware that they were being observed, or maybe they didn't care.

'Do we have a description of the man?'

'White, with dark hair, wearing a dark coat or jacket. He must have been waiting in the churchyard for Gemma, as Mrs Brooke didn't see him arrive.'

'Did she see him leave?'

Donovan shook her head. 'After a few minutes, the bus came along and she got on. She didn't think anything more about it until she saw the CID boards appealing for witnesses. So far, she's the only person to come forward.'

'What have forensics turned up?'

'Just the usual condoms, sweet papers and cigarette butts in the churchyard. But don't get too excited. None of it's recent.'

'With the weather we've been having, I'm not surprised.'

'I didn't know cold weather was ever a deterrent,' she said with a wry grin. 'Anyway, I'm going to catch my death out here. Can we go inside?'

He nodded, stubbed out his cigarette and pushed open one half of the heavy panelled door, Donovan slipping under his outstretched arm.

The interior of the church was barn-like, with a high, vaulted ceiling. Light flooded in through various ornate stained glass windows, casting a kaleidoscope of colours and patterns on the walls and the black and white marble floor. The temperature was almost as cold as outside, and an unpleasant musty smell hung in the damp air, coupled with a strange sourness. Decay, he thought. Things rotting away. The smell of neglect and penny pinching. Like so many English churches, the place was redolent of the past, a past with little relevance or connection to the present, the brass work tarnished, the embroidered kneelers threadbare and disintegrating, the memorial plaques that plastered the walls commemorating people long since dead and forgotten.

Although born and brought up a Catholic in Edinburgh, his Catholicism was well lapsed and not a matter that caused him any loss of sleep. But the churches of his youth were places of warmth, much frequented and loved, an integral part of family life and the community, very different to St Sebastian's. The last time he'd set foot inside a church had been at least a year before, when his sister, Nicoletta, had dragged him along to Sunday mass at St Peter's, the Italian church in Clerkenwell, before one of her marathon family-and-friends lunches. The atmosphere in the church had hummed: the air thick with the smell of incense; the rows of crystal chandeliers shimmering; every surface waxed and gleaming; and the metalwork polished within an inch of its life. The pews had been packed, with everyone in their Sunday best. It was a riot of colour and richness. Afterwards, hundreds of people thronged the pavement outside, gossiping and stopping at one of the many local bars and cafés for an espresso or grappa. Looking around the drab interior of St Sebastian's, he couldn't imagine such a scene. It felt unused and uncared for. A sad and lonely place for a young girl to die.

He followed Donovan down the nave, stopping in front of a large dark green stain that spread messily outwards across the marble floor.

'This is apparently where the girl fell.'

In order to pinpoint the spot where Gemma Kramer had died, the forensic team had used the chemical LMG to reveal the original blood traces. Around the outside, spatters and tracks from a mop and some sort of brush used to scrub the floor were easily visible, the wash of green fading into a pale verdigris at the edges, shot with bright blue and yellow light from one of the huge, arched windows. Tartaglia gazed up at the wide gallery that spanned the full width of the nave high above, an ornately carved balustrade running along the edge. The thought of the girl plummeting down from such a height made him shiver. Short of a miracle, no one could survive that fall.

'What time was the body found?' he asked, still staring up into the dark space of the gallery, the tall gilt pipes of the organ just visible at the back.

'Just after six, when someone came to tidy up for the evening service. They have Holy Communion at seven-fifteen on a Wednesday.'

'So nobody came in here between four and six?'

She shook her head. 'According to Duffey, the vicar leaves the main church unlocked for prayer but it's usually empty in the afternoon. I don't think they get many worshippers or visitors.'

Finding it extraordinary that it was left unsecured, particularly given its apparent state of disuse, Tartaglia wondered what had brought the girl to such a place. Was it by chance? Or had she and the man known that the church was left unlocked?

'How do we get up to the gallery?' he said.

'Follow me.' She walked over to a narrow archway to one side of the pulpit. As she pulled back the heavy red velvet curtain that hung across it, a cloud of dust flew up into the air, the particles dancing in a shaft of sunshine from above. She fumbled around behind the curtain, switching on a series of lights and illuminating the staircase and gallery.

Tartaglia started up the long, steep flight of stairs, Donovan making heavy weather just behind him.

'You know, you really should give up the fags,' he said to her when she finally reached the top.

She smiled, still out of breath. 'You're hardly one to talk. Anyway, I've been trying the patches but I think I've become addicted to them too.'

'They didn't work for me either.' Instinctively he felt in his pocket for his cigarettes.

She gave him a withering look.

He turned away, glancing around the gallery. Apart from the organ and the rows of stalls for the choir, it was empty. He walked over to the balustrade and gripped the heavy wooden rail with his hands, trying to see if there was any give. But the whole thing felt solid as stone. It was also a good four feet high. There was no way the girl could have fallen over it by accident. He stared down at the wide green stain way below. The area was now streaked with deep red and gold light and for a moment he pictured her lying there, a small, dark form, broken on the marble paving. Whatever had happened, it was a violent and horrible death.

He turned back to Donovan. 'Are there any signs of a struggle?'

She nodded. 'They found several clumps of long hair near the edge of the balcony which may belong to Gemma. The hair was pulled out at the root, so they'll be able to compare the DNA. They also found traces of candle wax and incense and what looks like red wine spilt on the floor.'

He shrugged. 'We are in a church, after all. Are they sure it's recent?'

'There was choir practice on Monday night but the floor was apparently cleaned on Tuesday morning. The vicar says nobody's been in the gallery since. Samples have gone off for analysis and we should get the results back soon.'

The combination of incense, candle wax and wine instantly conjured up the idea of a mass or some other sort of ritual. Maybe it was black magic or a form of New Age ceremony, he thought. A young girl and an older man. Even though there appeared to be no evidence of sexual assault, the presence of the

GHB in Gemma's system rang alarm bells. The drug, like Rohyp-
nol, was becoming increasingly common in date rape cases. He
wondered if the choice of a church as the location was significant
in some way. Had Gemma been a willing participant in whatever
had gone on, or had she been forced? Had the man dragged her or
held her down by her hair for some reason? Had she struggled?
Hopefully the post mortem results would reveal more. The main
question now was what had become of the man?

'If you've seen enough, we ought to be going,' Donovan said,
checking her watch. 'We've got a meeting with the pathologist in
just over half an hour, in Victoria.'

'Who did the PM?' he asked, as they started to walk back
together towards the stairs.

'Dr Blake.'

Tartaglia tensed, glancing quickly over at Donovan. But there
wasn't a glimmer of anything untoward in her expression. Being
realistic, there was no way she could know what had been going
on. No way any of them could. At least he hoped so. He sighed.
Shit. Shit. Why did it have to be Fiona Blake?

3

The last time Tartaglia had seen Fiona Blake, she'd been lying naked next to him in his bed. That had been about a month ago and he'd barely spoken to her since.

Today she was dressed in a prim grey suit, auburn hair scraped back tightly in a bun, white blouse buttoned up tight to the collar, as if she was trying to hide any hint of femininity or softness.

'There's no sign of sexual assault,' she said in her usual precise tone. 'In fact, Gemma Kramer was a virgin.'

She stared at him across her desk as if they were total strangers and for a moment he had to remind himself of the intensity he had so recently felt. She had kept him and Donovan waiting outside in the corridor for nearly half an hour. He was sure it was deliberate and it made him feel even more awkward and nervous of seeing her in an official capacity, particularly with Donovan there too. But he felt grateful that Donovan was sitting beside him now, a protective shield, her presence inhibiting any possibility of a more personal conversation.

'I understand you found traces of GHB in her system,' Donovan said.

'Yes, and alcohol. There was a small amount of red wine in her stomach. Both were ingested shortly before death.'

'GHB's not known as Easy Lay for nothing,' Tartaglia said. 'Are you sure she wasn't assaulted in some way?'

Blake gave him a piercing look. 'As I said, Inspector, I found no evidence of any form of sexual activity.'

The use of his title felt like a slap in the face. Although why she should be feeling angry was beyond him. It had been good, better than good, if he was honest, for the short while it had lasted. It had only come to a sudden halt when he had found out accidentally from someone else that she had a long-term boyfriend called Murray, a fact that she had never bothered to mention. He remembered the last terse phone call when, ignoring the subject of Murray, as if it made no difference to anything, she'd suggested that they meet up as usual. He'd shouted at her, told her to leave him alone, to stop calling. Angry with himself as much as with her, he'd slammed the phone down before she could say anything else. Finally he had understood why she could only see him at odd hours, why they only ever met at his flat and why her mobile was invariably switched off late at night and at weekends.

'I suppose there's no way of telling if it was mixed with the wine and then drunk, or if they were taken separately?'

She shifted in her chair, and looked away towards the window. 'I can see what you're thinking, but I can't help you. Maybe the wine was spiked, but it's impossible to tell. People do take GHB recreationally, you know.'

He shook his head. 'The girl was barely fourteen, and a church seems a pretty strange place to choose, if all you want to do is get high.' As he spoke, he noticed a large, single diamond on Blake's ring finger. It looked like an engagement ring. Perhaps conscious of his gaze, she slid her hands off the table and folded them in her lap behind the desk.

'Would she have been aware of what was going on around her?' Donovan asked.

Blake gave her a tight smile. 'Like someone a little drunk.'

'No more than that?'

'With the right dose, the effects are placidity, sensuality and mild euphoria. Anxieties dissolve into a feeling of emotional warmth, well-being and pleasant drowsiness.'

'You mean she would lose her inhibitions,' Donovan said, glancing at Tartaglia for confirmation. They were obviously thinking along the same lines.

He nodded. 'And fear.'

'It produces a heightening of the sense of touch, increased sexual enjoyment and performance for both men and women,' Blake continued, ignoring where they were going with this.

'Which is why I keep coming back to a sexual motive,' Tartaglia said, rapping his fingers lightly on the edge of the desk. 'Picture this. Gemma was with a much older man. She met him outside the church – clearly they had arranged to meet there. They kiss, so we know he's not a stranger, then they go inside together. The church is empty, nobody about at that time of day, and it's more than likely they knew it would be. This all smells to me of careful preparation. They go upstairs to the gallery and sit or lie on the floor. They light candles, burn incense and drink wine, all of which they would have had to bring with them. Then the girl falls to her death and the man disappears.'

'What do you want me to say, Inspector?' Blake asked, her face expressionless.

She was still missing the obvious, as far as he was concerned. Pathologists were so literal, so clinical. Just deal with the bald facts, never try to interpret them, let alone use your imagination.

'Look, we're talking about a fourteen-year-old girl,' he insisted, holding her gaze. 'A virgin, according to you. This was all pre-meditated, not something that just happened by chance. Why go to all this trouble, unless there's something specific you want to get out of it? The girl's the follower in all of this, the innocent victim. And now she's dead, with GHB in her system. Don't tell me there was no sexual purpose.'

Blake shook her head slowly. 'This is pure speculation. There is absolutely no physical evidence to suggest a sexual encounter.'

Exasperated with not getting the answer he wanted, he exhaled, leaning back in the chair so violently that it made a loud crack beneath him. 'You looked for signs of a struggle? Grazing, bruis-ing, scratches? You checked her fingernails?'

Blake looked affronted. 'Of course. I did the PM myself but I found nothing suspicious. The details are all in my report, which you'll have in the morning.'

She cleared her throat and folded her arms as if that was the end of the matter. For a moment he pictured her, white-skinned, full-breasted and bleary eyed, her hair fanned out on the pillow. But that was history and he felt furious with himself again for allowing his thoughts to wander in that direction.

'OK, going back to the GHB,' he said, forcing himself back into the present. 'What sort of quantities are we dealing with here?'

'Nothing especially high, nothing more than a couple of grams. Although even a small amount of alcohol would intensify the sedative effect. Gemma would have been in quite a happy and relaxed state, but she may have had trouble staying awake.'

'How quickly would it have taken effect?' Donovan asked.

'It depends on the dosage and the purity of the drug. But for someone Gemma's size, on an empty stomach, I'd say fairly quickly, particularly with the alcohol. Probably no more than ten to fifteen minutes at most.'

'Might she have wanted to jump off the balcony? You know, like someone on a bad trip?'

Blake shook her head. 'GHB doesn't make you hallucinate.'

'Would she have been capable of climbing over the balcony on her own in that state?'

'Remind me how high the balcony is?'

'About four feet,' Tartaglia said. 'And very solid.'

Blake seemed thoughtful, running a finger over her lips for a moment before folding her hands tidily in front of her. 'In my opinion, it's highly unlikely. She wasn't much over five feet tall and she would be feeling very dizzy standing up, maybe even a little nauseous because of the combined effect of the drug and the alcohol. She would increasingly have lost control over her movements. I don't think she would have had the coordination to climb over anything that high, either aided or unaided.'

For a moment, his thoughts turned back again to the church and the dark balcony high above the nave where something very strange had gone on. What was the point of the drug if there was no sexual motive? None of it made any sense. The only certainty was that Gemma's death had been no accident.

He stood up to go and Donovan followed suit. As he picked up his jacket, he noticed a couple of framed photographs sitting on top of the filing cabinet. One showed a broad-shouldered man with a deeply tanned face, wearing sunglasses and ski gear, grinning broadly against a snowy mountain backdrop. He was in his late thirties or early forties, with the thick, white-blond hair of a Scandinavian. The one next to it was of the same man, his face paler this time, in one of those stupid wigs and gowns barristers wore. Fucking Murray, he thought. Christ, she'd made such a fool of him.

He glanced over at her and caught her eye. He knew she had seen him looking at the photographs and he forced a smile and leaned over the desk towards her.

'Is there anything else you think I should be aware of, Dr Blake? Something important that I may have missed or maybe forgot to ask you? Every little detail's important. That's where the devil is, as they say.'

She coloured, a flicker of emotion crossing her face. Surprised but gratified that he had got some sort of a reaction, he was suddenly aware of Donovan's presence in the room and cursed himself for having said anything.

'I understand what you're getting at,' Blake said quietly. 'Everything's in my report. But there is something that perhaps I should draw to your attention, in the light of the scene you describe, it may or may not be significant. A lock of the girl's hair had been cut off.'

'Lengths of hair were found at the crime scene, but according to the crime scene manager, it was pulled out at the root,' Donovan said.

Blake shook her head. 'This is different. I've no idea when it was done, although it must have happened very recently. It was sliced off right at the scalp. The section was about two inches wide and whoever did it used a sharp blade.'

'Where was this?' Tartaglia asked.

'Just at the base of her neck. We only noticed it by accident when we were turning her over.'

Outside, Tartaglia turned to Donovan. 'I'll head straight back to Barnes and brief the team. You go and see Gemma's parents. The man's clearly someone she knew and we've got to find him.'

Before Donovan could reply, he turned on his heel and strode off towards his motorbike, which was parked further down the road.

Bristling with pent-up curiosity, Donovan unlocked her car and climbed in. Mark Tartaglia and Dr Fiona Blake. She was amazed. Tartaglia always played his cards close to his chest but she usually managed to find out eventually if he was seeing someone. She would never have guessed in a million years that he would have gone for Blake. Blake wasn't bad looking, she had to admit grudgingly. But she was one of those irritating women who thought themselves above everyone else, just because they held a clutch of degrees. Men were unfathomable. They defied all common sense, suckers for any pretty face, never mind the person inside.

She pulled out her A-Z from the glove compartment and looked up Gemma's parents' address. It would take her no more than half an hour to get to Streatham, she reckoned. Switching on the ignition, she let the car idle for a minute, waiting for the heater to kick in. Her thoughts drifted back to Tartaglia and Blake. Their affair had to be recent, as she was pretty sure from conversations she had had with Tartaglia that there'd been no woman in his life a couple of months before. Of course, however much she instinctively disliked Blake, she couldn't blame her for going for Tartaglia. He was bloody gorgeous. It was unfair that any man should be made like that, with those brooding, dark looks and that lovely generous mouth. At times, he could look so serious, so intense. But when he smiled, his whole face lit up. The only consolation was that he seemed generally unaware of the effect he had on others. Thank God he'd never realised what she thought.

In the early days, she had taken great pains not to let her feelings show and now that they'd got to know each other much better, she'd stopped hankering after him. They were mates. Good mates. Not a relationship she wanted to put at risk for something she knew couldn't last. Anyway, he was impossible, too independent and single-minded, which would make her feel insecure. Also, who in their right mind would want to have a relationship with a detective on a murder team, on call all hours, having to drop everything when a new case came along, working all day and night and weekends? No sane person would bother for long.

But what had happened between Tartaglia and Blake? There'd definitely been a row of some sort; you could have cut the atmosphere in the room with a knife. At first she'd assumed that they'd had some sort of professional spat, pathologists being bloody awkward creatures at the best of times. But then it had all got very tense just as they were leaving and it was clear that there was something else going on, something personal. Tartaglia had leant over towards Blake and said something. Although she couldn't quite remember what it was, it had sounded pretty innocuous. But the reaction on Blake's face was instantaneous and she looked as though she had been hit.

Trying to replay the conversation in her mind, so as to pin down the exact words, Donovan slipped Maroon 5's *Songs About Jane* into the CD player, tabbing to her favourite song, 'She Will Be Loved'. She let the music and lyrics wash over her for a moment. Of course Tartaglia could trust her. She wouldn't tell anyone, if that's what he was worried about. But she was buggered if she was going to let him think he could pull the wool over her eyes, try and pretend that there was nothing going on. Not after what she'd witnessed.

4

Getting to Streatham took longer than Donovan had imagined but she found the Kramers' address without trouble and pulled up on a yellow line outside. The house was modern, semi-detached with a neat strip of lawn to one side and a straight, paved path leading between two tidy flowerbeds to the front door. A black taxicab, which she assumed belonged to Gemma's father, was parked in the driveway in front of the garage, and she could see lights on behind the drawn curtains.

Thank goodness she wasn't there to break the news to the family. That was the part of the job she'd always hated most, particularly when a child was concerned. But it was bad enough having to talk to the parents now, knowing that Gemma's death hadn't been either a suicide or a simple accident. Unlike several of her colleagues, she found it difficult to cut herself off, found it impossible not to empathise with those affected by the death of a loved one. She had often asked herself why she had ever joined Clarke's murder team, and could only suppose that it was for the satisfaction of catching the person responsible, justice and retribution the only compensation for all the pain.

She took a deep breath and pressed the doorbell. The man who answered the chimes was wearing combats, trainers and a T-shirt, with a gold Star of David hanging from a heavy chain around his neck. His head was shaved, which emphasised the roundness of his face, and he looked to be in his early forties. Short, squat and barrel-chested, with the beginnings of a beer gut, he reminded her of a bulldog as he stood planted in the middle of the doorway as if he were guarding it.

'Mr Kramer? I'm DS Donovan.' She held out her ID. 'I'm with the team looking into Gemma's death.'

He stuffed his hands into his pockets as if he didn't know what to do with them and gazed vaguely at the warrant card before moving aside, almost grudgingly, to let her pass.

'I'm Dennis Kramer, her stepdad. You'd better come in.' His voice was a deep, throaty growl, his accent instantly recognisable as south London.

The DI at Ealing had said nothing about a stepfather. Stepfathers were prime suspect material in such a case. But whatever the relationship, if Mrs Brooke's description was accurate, Kramer could be ruled out immediately on physical grounds. Although he could have shaved off his hair in the last couple of days, he was still nothing like the man the old lady had described.

'Is Gemma's mother at home?'

'Mary's lying down upstairs. Seeing Gemma's body at the...' he struggled for the word then grunted. 'I said I'd do it but she insisted on going. It more or less finished her off.'

'I hope you don't mind, but I've some questions I need to ask. Is the family liaison officer here?'

He shook his head. 'She was getting on my nerves so I sent her off. No point in her hanging around all day and night like a spare penny. The doctor's pumped Mary full of stuff and she's out for the count now so she can't talk to anyone. If you want to ask questions, you'll have to make do with me. I've just put the kettle on. Fancy a cup of tea?'

'Please. White, no sugar,' she said, suddenly aware of the familiar ache in the pit of her stomach. What with being tied up with Ealing CID all morning and then with Tartaglia, she had completely forgotten about lunch. Thank goodness she'd managed a proper breakfast, although it was now a distant memory. It was always like this with a new investigation. Adrenalin and coffee were the main things keeping you going and you had to make a conscious effort to remember to eat, grab a sandwich or a takeaway somewhere on the run if you were lucky. It was going to be a battle keeping off the fags.

'The lounge is just there, on your left,' Kramer said, waving his hand vaguely towards the door. 'Make yourself comfortable and I'll be with you in a sec.'

She pushed open the door and walked into a small, cream-coloured room, with thick wall-to-wall carpet and a dark leather three-piece suite. She assumed that Gemma's mother had chosen the decor, as she couldn't picture Kramer selecting the fawn and maroon striped curtains with their neat tiebacks, let alone the line of reproduction botanical prints, which hung on one of the walls. An expensive-looking TV on a glass and chrome stand took pride of place opposite the sofa, next to it a tall shelf unit with a couple of limp-looking pot plants, a collection of DVDs and a series of gilt-framed photographs.

She walked over, her eye drawn by a photo of a pretty young girl with long, glossy brown hair. It was a school photograph, the girl dressed in a navy blue cardigan over a blue and white checked blouse, her hair held back by an Alice band. The photo bore the title 'Convent of the Sacred Heart' at the bottom with the previous year's date. Gemma, she assumed. She looked no more than twelve, her smile innocent and open like a child's, with nothing of the self-consciousness of a teenager. Donovan remembered how she herself had hidden from the camera from puberty onwards, pulling faces to disguise her embarrassment whenever she was caught, knowing that she would hate the end result.

She had just turned her attention to a photo of a pair of cheeky-looking little boys, when Kramer came into the room with a mug of tea in each hand.

'That's Patrick and Liam,' he said, passing her a mug and taking his own over to the sofa, where he sank down heavily, crossing his feet under the small glass coffee table. 'They're my kids, Gemma's half-brothers. I've had to ship them off to their nan's until Mary's better. She can't cope with anything at the moment.'

Donovan settled herself in one of the comfortable-looking armchairs and took a notebook and pen out of her bag. 'Just for formality's sake, could you tell me where you were on Wednesday afternoon?'

He looked instantly affronted. 'What, me? What's it got to do with me?'

'Just a routine question, Mr Kramer. You know how it is. We have to dot the "i"s and cross the "t"s.' She took a sip of tea. It was good, strong stuff and she instantly felt better.

He nodded slowly, grudgingly appearing to accept the explanation. 'I was at Gatwick till about five. Had to pick up a regular, but his flight was delayed coming in.'

He gave her the client's name and phone number, which she noted down.

'Perhaps you can start by giving me a little background info. You said you're Gemma's stepfather.'

'That's right.'

'Are you Irish?' she asked, hoping to ease him into things.

'Do I bloody sound it?'

'It's just that Patrick and Liam...' she said, wondering why he was being so prickly.

He shook his head, interrupting. 'That's down to Mary. She's from Cork but she come to London when she was ten. I was born and brought up in Elephant and Castle.'

'What about Gemma's father? Her biological father, I mean.'

'Mick? Yeah, he's bloody Irish. Him and Mary were childhood sweethearts but he didn't stop long once she got pregnant. Mary was just eighteen and he run off a couple of months before Gemma was born.'

'Do you know how we can contact him?'

He shrugged. 'No idea where the bugger is. Turns up like a bad penny from time to time when he wants money, when he knows I'm out at work. Mary's always a soft touch where he's concerned. Caught him nosing round here about a year ago. I'd come home early and we had a right punch-up. He'll think twice about stopping by again, I can tell you.'

The bitterness was unmistakable and Donovan suspected that behind the protectiveness for his wife, he was jealous. She wondered how Gemma fitted into the triangle. 'What about Gemma? Did she have any contact with him?'

He shook his head. 'Wasn't interested. From what I hear, he's fathered a whole litter of kids with various women, in between being in and out of the nick, that is.'

'He's in prison?'

'Well, we haven't heard from him in a while. It's either that, or the chinning I give him last time he come round.' A flicker of pleasure crossed his face. 'His full name's Mick Byrne, if you want to check him out. That's B-Y-R-N-E. He's bound to be on one of your computers, given his record.'

Donovan made a note. It would be easy to find out if the father was in prison. 'What's his form?'

'Got sticky fingers. Can't keep his hands off other people's things. He's a bit of a conman, but nothing violent, if you know what I mean.'

'Is it possible that Gemma might have seen him secretly, given how you felt about him?'

Kramer's eyes bulged angrily and he clenched his lips. 'No way. She never kept anything from us. Gemma was a good girl. I've brought her up from the age of five.' He paused, swallowing hard. 'I was her dad, as far as she was concerned. Her only dad. Why are you interested in Mick?'

'Gemma was seen with a man shortly before she died. He looked to be in his thirties or forties, tall with dark hair. We need to find him.'

He grimaced. 'Well, that can't be Mick. Last time I saw him, he was nearly as bald as me and not 'coz of a Number One. All his hair dropped out last time he was inside. Alopecia, I think they call it. Serves him bloody right for all the trouble he's caused.'

'Gemma was with some man. As I said, we need to find out who it is. That's the main reason I'm here.'

He stared at her for a moment, looking puzzled. 'What do you mean "with some man"?'

Donovan took a deep breath. 'Gemma was seen kissing this man outside the church where she died. She must have known him pretty well.'

'Kissing?' The word shot out of his mouth like a bullet. 'You've got it wrong. Gemma wasn't interested in boys.'

'This was a man, not a boy, Mr Kramer.'

'Gemma didn't know any men,' he said emphatically. He bit his lip and looked away, his eyes fixing on one of the flower prints that hung over the TV. 'Course, she was pretty. Takes after her mum. But she wasn't a slag, like a lot of girls her age.' For a moment, his thoughts seemed to drift elsewhere.

'I'm only telling you what the witness saw. It's very important that we find this man. He may be able to shed some light on how Gemma died.'

He put his mug down and leaned forwards towards her, hands flat on his knees. 'Gemma couldn't have been with a man. She was a good girl, Sergeant. A really good girl.' He jerked a stubby finger at the photo on the shelf. 'See that? It was only taken last autumn. You wouldn't know she was fourteen, would you? She looks so young.'

Wondering why he was trying so hard to convince her, she wanted to say that youth had never stopped a young girl from pursuing her dreams or doing something stupid. And parents, however good and caring, were often the last to know. If he wanted to ignore reality, that was his business but she needed to confront him with the facts. It was easily possible that he knew the man in some capacity.

'Mr Kramer, Gemma was seen by a witness kissing a man much older than herself. We're talking proper kissing, not a peck on the cheek. They then went into the church together.'

He was shaking his head. 'Not Gemma. Like I said, you got it wrong.'

'The pathologist found traces of the drug GHB in her system. We come across it sometimes in cases of date-rape.'

He frowned. 'She wasn't...' his voice trailed off.

'No. She wasn't sexually assaulted. But it's pretty clear that she knew the man she was with. Maybe she got the drug from him. We've got to find him and I was hoping maybe you could help.'

The words seemed to wash over him and he bent forward and put his face in his hands, closing his eyes and rubbing his temples. He seemed more shocked by the presence of the man than by the fact that Gemma had been drugged, still failing to understand or acknowledge Gemma's death as suspicious. But if he didn't want to join up the dots, it wasn't for her to do it for him. 'What about relatives or family friends?'

He looked up and slammed his fist on the table, making the mugs rattle. 'What are you saying? You think one of my friends has been messing around with Gemma behind my back?'

'She must have met the man somewhere, Mr Kramer. I'm going to need a list of everyone you know who Gemma's been in contact with recently.'

He sighed and sank back in the sofa, staring hard up at the ceiling, shaking his head slowly. 'I don't believe what I'm hearing. You didn't know Gemma. She wasn't that way.' His scalp was shiny with sweat, small beads starting to run down his cheeks. 'She should've been at school,' he said, closing his eyes again and pinching the bridge of his thick nose with his fingers, his face red.

'I'll need that list as soon as possible. In the meantime, who are her close friends? Maybe they would know who she was seeing.'

He took a crumpled handkerchief out of the pocket of his combats, dabbed at his head and face and blew his nose. 'She didn't have any close friends. She's only been at the convent since last Easter. Before that, she was at the local comprehensive.'

'There must be someone she's close to, someone her own age who she would confide in.'

He shook his head and blew his nose again.

'Why did she change schools?'

'They was bullying Gemma. She was a bright girl, really sensitive. Had a heart of gold, used to work at the local animal shelter in the holidays.'

'What happened?'

He gave her a weary look. 'The usual stuff. The school wasn't on top of things. They give the kids a good talking-to a few times but it didn't change nothing. They just went out and picked on her again. We had to get her out of there. It's lucky I earn a decent living and we could do something about it. I pity the poor kids who are stuck in a place like that.'

'Why did you choose the convent?'

'Mary's Catholic. As I said, Gemma was a bright girl and we thought she'd do well there. Also, we didn't want her growing up too fast.'

That was the real reason, Donovan thought, wondering why they were so protective of Gemma. Had she given them cause for concern before? The innocent picture he presented didn't square with what had happened at St Sebastian's, or what she knew of other young girls of Gemma's age. Either he was hiding something, or Gemma had led a secret life.

'Had she made any friends since moving schools?'

'She's come home a few times with a girl called Rosie. Spent the night at her place once or twice, I think.'

'Do you have her number?'

'It'll be in her diary.'

'May I see it?'

He shrugged and got slowly to his feet. 'It's one of them electronic things. It's upstairs in her desk.'

'What about a phone?' she said, following him out the door, interested to see Gemma's room. A search team would have to go over it properly but she wanted to take a look for herself.

Kramer shook his head. 'No point. Mary walked her to and from school and she didn't have many friends to call.'

Most girls Gemma's age were allowed to walk to school on their own. They also had cell phones; it was odd that her parents hadn't given her one and Donovan wondered if Gemma had minded, if she had felt the odd one out in her peer group.

'What about a computer? Did Gemma have access to the internet?'

He nodded. 'Used it for her schoolwork. It's all in her room upstairs.'

'You'd better show me.'

The stairs were narrow and Kramer seemed out of scale as he lumbered up them, holding on so tight to the thin banister that it creaked and wobbled beneath his grasp. Following behind, Donovan passed a half-open door on the first floor landing, glimpsing through it the dark shape of Gemma's mother in bed, deeply asleep judging by the sound of heavy breathing coming from the room. Thank God she didn't have to go through all this with her.

Gemma's bedroom was on the top floor at the front of the house. Kramer hesitated on the landing, staring down at the floor as if he couldn't bring himself even to look at the door.

'Do you mind going in by yourself? I can't bear seeing her things.'

'Of course, Mr Kramer,' she said. 'I'll come and find you downstairs, shall I? I won't be long.'

She waited until he disappeared from view then she pushed open the door and walked in.

Light streamed in from the street outside, casting long shadows across the floor. Thinking that someone in one of the houses opposite might be looking out, she moved to close the curtains before switching on the light at the wall. The bed was made, not even a wrinkle in the duvet or pillows, which were patterned with tiny rosebuds and bows. A purple cardigan hung over the back of a chair and a pair of flat black shoes peeped out from under the bed next to a pair of pink slippers. It was as if she had walked into a bubble, separate from the real world, and it brought a knot to her throat. The room was frozen in time, the clock stopped on the day Gemma died, the child never coming home. Having your child die before you must be one of the most terrible things in the world, she had often thought, a scar that would never heal which tainted everything and poisoned the future. She wondered what Kramer and his wife would do with Gemma's room. Would they leave it just as it was or would they change it? Perhaps they would find it impossible to continue living in the house with all its memories.

Looking around, almost everything in the room was pink: walls, curtains, carpet, bed covers, even the string of fairy lights in the shape of little angels hanging in an arc over the bed. It was a little girl's bedroom. Donovan wouldn't have been caught dead with a room like that at the age of fourteen. Six, maybe, when you had no choice in the matter, but never fourteen. Her walls had been papered with posters and photos, but apart from a gilt-framed print of a girl jumping a fence on a pony, Gemma's were totally blank.

Although Gemma's development seemed to be arrested, no expense had been spared in kitting out the room. Along with a new-looking laptop, Gemma had her own TV and mini hi-fi system. The small collection of CDs, mainly boy bands and similar, were anodyne, nothing to give her parents cause for worry. She remembered Kramer's words: 'We didn't want her growing up too fast', wondering what it was that they were trying to protect her from. On the surface at least, the poor kid had had no choice but to remain a child, wrapped in this pastel-pink cocoon. She wondered how Gemma had felt about it, whether she had resented it at all. Maybe what she had been doing in that church had been an attempt to escape.

A small desk stood in a corner of the room, inside the single drawer a collection of coloured pens and pencils, stationery, a mini iPod and a PDA, with a Barbie logo on the front. But there were no letters or cards, no journal or any other personal items of interest. Putting the iPod and PDA in her bag to examine later, she tried the chest of drawers, feeling around amongst the neat piles of clothing. But there was nothing hidden there.

The bookshelf above the desk was packed with a mixture of children's classics, what looked like a full set of Harry Potters and Georgette Heyers, as well as *The Hobbit*, a gift set of the Narnia books and *Artemis Fowl*. Apart from a child's encyclopaedia and a few factual books on horses and riding, fantasy seemed to be the predominant theme. Donovan was surprised to see that Gemma was a reader, given the lack of books in her parents' sitting room downstairs.

A copy of *Wuthering Heights* lay on the low table next to the bed. The paperback was well thumbed and fell open as she picked it up. Flicking through, she noticed several passages heavily underlined in purple, some with a star inscribed in the margin. Wondering if perhaps Gemma was studying it at school, she skimmed through some of the highlighted chunks. They all seemed to be about Heathcliff, a physical description of him on one page accompanied by several exclamation marks and a small inked heart. It instantly struck a chord. For a moment Donovan remembered the acute feeling of teenage longing, the wanting to belong to another world, far removed from family and friends. Heathcliff, the dark and dangerous lover who had filled her dreams too. He had seemed so real for a while. How could the smelly, spotty, greasy-haired youths she had known at school ever measure up? Heathcliff had blighted any opportunities for adolescent romance and she was forced to admit that a part of her still hankered after him even now.

Glancing at her watch, she realised that it was past seven o'clock. She went over to the desk, unplugged the laptop and tucked it under her arm. Checking the room one last time to make sure she hadn't missed anything obvious, she switched off the light and went downstairs. She would send a team over in the morning to go through the rest of Gemma's things more thoroughly.

Downstairs, Kramer walked her to her car, putting the laptop onto the back seat while she wrote out a receipt for the items she was taking. He held the door open for her as she climbed behind the wheel, then handed her a folded piece of paper.

'That's the list you wanted,' he said. 'I've written down a couple of names but I can't believe any of them would...' He shook his head, clenching his lips, unable to finish the sentence.

She gave him a reassuring smile. 'Thank you, Mr Kramer. We just have to check every angle you know. We wouldn't be doing our job properly otherwise.'

He nodded slowly as if he accepted this, resting his arm heavily on the edge of the door as if he wanted to keep her there. 'So, Sergeant. What do you think happened to our Gemma? It was an accident, right?'

'It's too early to tell, Mr Kramer,' she said, noncommittally, hoping he'd let her leave without probing any further. Kramer was still a suspect, even though in her heart she didn't believe he had had anything to do with it. She started the engine but he was still holding on to the door as if he wasn't finished.

'You know, they thought it was suicide,' he said leaning towards her and speaking in a whisper, as if he was worried that someone might overhear. 'But I told them it can't be. Gemma would never do that. It would break her mum's heart, it would.'

'It's not suicide, Mr Kramer. You can be sure of that,' she replied, surprised again that he seemed unable to understand that Gemma's death was suspicious.

He nodded once more, looking strangely relieved, and stepped back from the car. Something about his reaction didn't feel right and she was aware of him watching her as she closed the door. Turning to reach for her seatbelt, she glanced over at him again and caught a glimmer of something on his face that puzzled her. He looked like someone who had just pulled off a trick, although for the life of her, she couldn't figure out what it was.

5

It was evening and the investigation into Gemma Kramer's death was well under way. Tartaglia yawned and locked his fingers in front of him, cracking his knuckles and stretching his neck forward to ease the tiredness that had suddenly overwhelmed him. There had been the team to assemble from various other on-going cases, actions to be assigned and a further debriefing and file handover with the DI at Ealing CID. Until he heard back from Donovan, the priority was St Sebastian's. Everyone who was available had gone over to Ealing to conduct interviews, starting with the vicar and the people who used the church regularly, and going on to knock on doors in the area. Local CCTV footage was being checked, although in such a residential district, cameras were few and far between, and the tube station was their main hope. Somehow, they had to try and come up with more witnesses and get a better description of the man seen with Gemma.

As acting SIO, Tartaglia had decided to move out of the cramped quarters he normally shared with Gary Jones, the other DI on Clarke's team. It wasn't an issue of his new seniority. He needed a quiet place where he could gather his thoughts and think through things clearly without interruption.

Standing in the doorway of Clarke's office, he wondered how long it would take him to sort out the mess of papers, files and miscellaneous possessions Clarke had left behind. He felt a pang of sadness as he thought about Clarke lying motionless in his hospital bed but he couldn't work in such chaos. How Clarke had ever managed so effortlessly was beyond him.

The room was little more than a shoebox at the front of the

building, the single grimy window facing onto the road that led from Barnes Pond to the common, opposite the backs of a row of expensive period houses, with neat gardens; suburban Barnes in all its glory. Judging by the icy temperature, the heating was on the blink again. Nothing in the bloody building ever worked properly. But at least he didn't have to put up with Jones's BO any longer, the lovey-dovey phone calls to the wife and the smell of the home-made tuna and onion sandwiches which Jones seemed to eat at all hours of the day.

Barnes Green wasn't supposed to be a permanent location for the two murder squads it currently housed. When Tartaglia had joined Team Five of Homicide West, Clarke had jokingly told him not to bother unpacking his things. The low-built early seventies block was past its sell-by date and they'd all be relocating soon. But nearly three years on, there was no sign of a move and they had learned to live with the cramped and shabby working conditions, sandwiched on the first floor between part of the Flying Squad above and a child protection unit on the ground floor below. It was a far cry from the offices up in Hendon, at the Peel Centre, where five of the other murder teams worked in relative luxury.

Feeling hungry, he decided to make some coffee to fill the gap while he sorted out somewhere to put his things in Clarke's office. There was no canteen in the building and he'd have to go out later for something to eat. He walked down the corridor to a tiny internal room, once used for storage, which served as the kitchen for the entire first floor. Functional was the only positive word to describe it; a health hazard was probably more accurate and he used it as little as possible, preferring to get his coffee and food from one of the many fancy delis that peppered the area. He opened the door of the fridge but couldn't see any milk, just an ancient looking tub of margarine and an already opened tin of tomato soup. However, he didn't have time to go out so he boiled the kettle and made a strong brew of instant black coffee. Disgusted at the predictable state of things, he carried the mug back into Clarke's office where he struggled to find a safe place to put it down. He swept a variety of papers and files into a couple of rough piles and helped himself to an unopened Kit-Kat which he found marking a place inside a folder.

He pulled up the saggy brown corduroy chair that Clarke had brought in from somewhere and sat down at the desk to go through the papers. As he stretched out his legs, he kicked against something hard at the back. Digging around underneath, he pulled out a large cardboard box containing two pairs of ancient, mud-encrusted trainers, a humane mousetrap and a blow heater. Wedged behind the box was a rolled-up sleeping bag, which he remembered Clarke using for all-night sessions. At least Tartaglia wouldn't be needing that. His flat in Shepherd's Bush was only a fifteen-minute motorbike ride away. After trying the blow heater, which seemed to be broken, he put everything back in the box, stuffing the sleeping bag on top and dumped it all in the corridor to take away later.

He was about to sit down again at the desk when his mobile rang: it was Donovan.

'I'm on my way back. I've just seen Gemma's stepdad, Dennis Kramer.'

'Stepfather?'

'Don't get excited. He doesn't fit the witness description and if his alibi checks out, he's in the clear. I've got Gemma's computer with me. Is Dave around?'

DC Dave Wightman had a degree in something to do with computers and was regarded as the in-house expert on most things technical.

'He's just come back from Ealing.'

'Tell him I'll drop it off in about ten minutes. It needs to go over to Newlands Park for analysis but he's so good with computers. I was hoping he could have a quick look at it first. There was nothing else in her room of any interest. In the meantime, a couple of friends of Kramer's want checking out.' She gave him the names and addresses, which he noted down. 'I'm going to see a girl called Rosie Chapple later on. She seems to be Gemma's only friend.'

'Did you see Gemma's mother?'

She gave a long, wheezy sigh. 'No. She was out for the count in bed. Can I tell you the rest once I get a bite to eat? I missed lunch and I'll pass out if I don't get something now.'

He looked at his watch, realising that he had also had little to eat that day. It would be a while before everyone was back from Ealing and there should be time to nip out for a quick bite. It would probably be the only break he'd get for a while. 'I'll see you in the Bull's Head in twenty minutes. I'll order for you. What do you fancy?'

'Don't mind. Just make it large.'

Stopping off in the main office outside to tell DC Dave Wightman about the computer, Tartaglia grabbed his jacket from his old office and went downstairs. He walked through the car park at the back of the building and out of the main gate onto the street. It was close to freezing and a mist was rolling up in thick drifts from the Thames. The air was wet on his face and smelled of rotting leaves mixed with wood smoke, someone burning a proper fire nearby. As he turned down Station Road, he could just make out the black wilderness of Barnes Common in the distance, a long string of orange streetlights marking the perimeter.

When he'd first come down to London from Edinburgh shortly after graduating from university, he had felt swamped by its size, lack of cohesion and frenetic pace of life. He remembered having an argument in a pub with some jolly Londoner who had tried to persuade him that the city was really only a friendly series of villages joined together. Having lived in Edinburgh all his life, it was something he failed to see, there being no village-like qualities about Hendon, where he'd done his training as a police cadet, or Oxford Street and its environs, where he had walked his first beat. London seemed just a grey, filthy, sprawling, unfriendly mass and he wondered whether he had made a mistake leaving home. Gradually, as he got to know the city better, he started to realise that most areas had their own distinct personality and community, which made life more tolerable. Nowhere was this more true than in Barnes, picture-postcard pretty and so rural that it could almost be in the country, even though it was only a few miles from the centre of town.

He passed the village green with its pond, barely visible in the mist, a couple of ducks quacking from somewhere near the edge of the water, and followed the road around into the narrow, brightly-lit high street. Unusually for London, it was free of chain stores and retained an old-fashioned feel, offering instead an exotic range of small shops, expensive boutiques and restaurants, along with the myriad of estate agents, reflecting the fact that it was a popular, if expensive, place to live. Cut off from central London by the river Thames, Barnes seemed to be in a world of its own. If the wealthy local clientele, which included several well-known faces from theatre and television, wanted something functional like a pair of socks or underpants, they had to make the trip over Hammersmith Bridge into the smoke.

Approaching the river, the fog became dense and he could barely see in front of him. Swathed in a veil of white, The Bull's Head sat at the end of the High Street, overlooking the river embankment, next door to what had once been Barnes Police Station, the old building now converted into expensive flats.

Walking into the large, open-plan bar, Tartaglia was greeted as usual by loud music coming from the back room. The pub was famous for its daily sessions of live jazz, occasionally boasting musicians even he had heard of, such as Humphrey Lyttelton and George Melly. Jazz wasn't his cup of tea in any shape or form and often the music was so loud it was difficult to hold a conversation. But tonight the sounds drifting into the bar were half decent, someone with a voice like John Lee Hooker singing the blues, accompanied by a guitar. There were worse places to drink and it was certainly a lot better than the watering holes around Hendon.

He bought a pint of Youngs Special for himself and a half of their ordinary bitter for Donovan, who tended to prefer something a little less strong. They might still be officially on duty but he didn't give a damn. It had been a long day and he had the feeling that it wasn't anywhere near over yet. He was supposed to have been seeing his cousin Gianni for beer and pizza in front of the TV with the DVD of *Downfall*, but that plan had had to be shelved and, as far as the weekend was concerned, he could kiss goodbye to that too. He ordered two large helpings of lasagne and salad and settled himself at a table in the far corner by one of the windows. He had just started on his pint when Donovan appeared through the main door, pink-faced and out of breath, her hair damp from the air outside. She swung her satchel onto the floor and stripped off several layers of clothing, down to a pair of baggy black trousers, held up with braces, and a red and black striped T-shirt that reminded him amusingly of Dennis the Menace. He liked the way she dressed; it suited her, even if it was rarely ever feminine. She could usually pass for a pretty young boy.

Donovan quickly rubbed her hair with the edge of her scarf, making it stand up in short tufts, then flopped down in the chair opposite him. 'That's better. Cheers,' she said, taking a gulp of bitter and wiping her top lip with the back of her hand. 'God, I needed that.'

'We're checking on Kramer's two mates. They both live close together, which makes it easy.' He glanced at his watch. 'Should hear back soon. What time are you seeing the girl?'

'Not for a while. Her mother said she wouldn't be home before ten at the earliest, as it's Friday night.' She took another large sip, then leaned back in her chair, legs stretched out in front of her. 'This isn't going to be easy,' she said, thoughtfully. 'I think Gemma was leading a secret life and I don't think her parents had a clue.' She told him about her conversation with Kramer and her initial impressions of Gemma.

He listened carefully, asking the odd question here and there. When she'd finished, he sipped his pint in silence for a moment. Although there had been a few famous cases over the years, stranger killings were rare in London. Usually the killer was to be found within the victim's close circle of family, friends and colleagues and the majority of murders were relatively straight-forward to solve, with the main challenge being to get sufficient proof for a conviction. From what Mrs Brooke had said, Gemma had seemed to know the man she met outside the church, so hope-fully it was only a matter of time before they'd find out who he was.

'What do you make of Kramer?' he asked, after a minute. 'I know you say he doesn't fit the description but…'

'He's an odd bloke and really overprotective. But unless he's a brilliant actor, I think he genuinely cared about Gemma. What's strange is that he seemed unable to grasp the fact that her death is suspicious. It's as if he'd already made up his mind about what had happened.'

'Or knew what had happened?'

'No. I don't think he would have harmed her, or knowingly let any of his friends mess about with her.'

He gave her a searching look. He could tell from her expression that there was something else. 'What is it?'

She cradled her nearly empty glass in her hands, swilling the brown liquid around the sides before taking a last gulp of bitter. 'I'm pretty sure he's holding something back. I just don't have a clue what it is. I've been over and over in my mind what we talked about but there's nothing I can pin it on, nothing in particular that he said or did that struck a wrong note. Until, that is, just after we'd said goodbye. I was about to drive off and he'd relaxed, thinking I was going. I saw something, just a glimmer in his expression, nothing more than that. He looked as though he'd gotten away with something.' She drained her glass and grimaced. 'Maybe I'm reading too much into it.'

He shook his head. Her instincts were usually spot on. 'I doubt it. Let's get him in. Make it formal and turn up the temperature.'

'He sees himself as a tough guy, real hardboiled on the surface. Maybe he thought, because I'm a woman, he could pull the wool over my eyes. I just don't see why, if he loved Gemma, he would want to protect someone who had harmed her.' She gave a weary sigh and stood up. 'Another pint?'

Tartaglia shook his head and watched her move towards the bar. Kramer wouldn't have been the first to underestimate her. Her physical size and looks gave a misleading impression of innocence and fragility. But what was she to do? High heels and red lipstick were hardly the answer. He respected her for getting on with things as if none of it mattered, even though he knew she found it irritating at times. Apart from what had happened with Kramer, she seemed a little on edge, although he couldn't pinpoint why. He wondered if she had picked up the vibes between him and Blake earlier on. The last thing he needed was to be the centre of office gossip, particularly when there was nothing going on anyway. At least Donovan wasn't one to gossip, unlike some. He knew little about her personal life other than that there'd been some man called Richard around for a while. But she had stopped mentioning him and Tartaglia hadn't wanted to appear nosey by asking. Perhaps giving up smoking was making her feel on edge.

Donovan returned after a moment and sat down, a glass with ice and lemon and a slimline tonic in her hand. 'Thought I'd better go for something soft. Otherwise I'll be under the table, given the little I've had to eat today.' She poured the tonic into the glass and took a large gulp.

'What's bothering you?'

She smiled. 'According to Kramer, Gemma had no private life. He said she wasn't interested in boys. I got the impression he really believed what he was telling me, that he wasn't spinning me a yarn.'

'Your point is?'

'I was just thinking back to what Mrs Brooke said. She's absolutely positive about what she described. As I told you, she seemed pretty sharp for someone her age. I also checked her out with the vicar, as apparently she's a regular at St Sebastian's. He says she's reliable.'

'So, Gemma met the guy in secret. She wouldn't be the first, particularly given how you describe Kramer.'

She nodded. 'Maybe Gemma's friend Rosie knows something. The man has to be somebody Gemma trusted. She kissed him, after all, and, from what I can tell about her, I don't see her picking up just anybody in the street or in some internet chat room. This girl was a real romantic, I tell you.'

As she finished speaking, their food arrived. Tartaglia had just picked up his knife and fork when his phone rang. He answered it, listened for a moment, then snapped it shut.

'Damn,' he said, getting to his feet, staring down for a second at the untouched plate of lasagne, the smell unbearably good. 'That was Dave. He's found something on her computer. Says it's really weird. We'd better go back to the office right away.' He saw the look of desperation on Donovan's face. 'Look, you have yours. Then catch me up. Perhaps you can get them to put mine in a doggy bag.'

6

Twenty minutes later, Donovan rushed into the main open-plan
office. At that hour, the long, low-ceilinged room, which housed
the majority of the thirty-odd detectives who made up Clarke's
team, was uncharacteristically empty and quiet. Crammed with
desks, phones and computers, it buzzed during the day with noise
and activity and closely resembled a battery-hen shed. But with
less pressing cases in hand, those not in Tartaglia's immediate
team had gone home for the night.

Tartaglia was perched on a desk at the front, next to the white
board, chewing on a pen, reading some papers. He had taken off
his jacket and tie, unbuttoned the top few buttons of his shirt and
rolled up his sleeves as if he was settling in for the night. He
looked troubled and Donovan wondered what exactly Wightman
had discovered on Gemma's laptop. Wightman stood beside him,
methodically sorting a thick wedge of papers into several separate
piles and stapling them together. Short, fresh-faced and thickset,
Wightman was in his late twenties, although he looked barely
eighteen and was the newest recruit to the team.

DCs Nick Minderedes and Karen Feeney came into the room
immediately behind Donovan, having just got back from knocking on doors in Ealing.

'Sit down, everybody,' Tartaglia said, looking up. 'We'll be
ready in a minute.'

Donovan deposited the bag containing Tartaglia's takeaway on
a filing cabinet behind him and pulled up a chair between
Minderedes and Feeney. Feeney sneezed three times in succession,
took a tissue out of her pocket and blew her nose loudly. Her eyes

were watering and she looked bedraggled, sitting there wrapped up in her limp mackintosh.

'You OK?' Donovan asked.

'Just tired,' Feeney said. 'Nothing knackers you like tramping the streets for hours at this time of year. And one of my shoes has sprung a leak.' Her voice was thick and nasal and it sounded to Donovan as though she was getting a cold. Feeney took a small mirror out of her bag and peered into it, dabbing her pale cheeks and wiping away the shadow of mascara from under her eyes. 'Will you look at my hair,' she said, turning her attention to her frizz of bright red curls. 'Just takes a drop of rain to ruin a good blow-dry. Thank Christ I wasn't planning on doing anything exciting later.'

'That makes two of us,' Donovan replied. 'I had a hot date lined up with Jonathan Ross but I'm sure he'll understand.'

'Sorry you ladies lead such dull lives, but I really did have something on for tonight,' Minderedes muttered gloomily. 'And it's the third bloody time I've had to cancel this chick because of work. She's going to give up on me at this rate.'

Hunched in his overcoat, he took a stick of gum out of the pocket, peeled off the wrapper and put it into his mouth, chewing vigorously as if to compensate for what he was missing. Small and wiry, with thinning dark hair, his eyes were an unusual shade of green, almost yellow, and he had a permanently hungry, restless look, as if never satisfied with anything for long.

'Anyone I know?' Donovan asked, unravelling her scarf and unbuttoning her coat, feeling hot and a little sweaty from her brisk walk back to the office.

'The new barmaid at the Bull's Head. You know, the one with short dark hair. Polish, with big...' He gestured, cupping his hands in front of his chest.

'But she barely speaks English,' Feeney said, raising her eyebrows.

He grinned, still chewing hard. 'What's that got to do with anything?'

Donovan shook her head wearily. Minderedes's success with women was beyond her. He had the emotional maturity of a teenager, although he knew how to turn on the charm in a crude sort of way when it suited him. She prided herself on being one of the few single women in the office who had never succumbed. She wasn't quite sure where Feeney stood in that respect.

As Wightman started to pass around a set of papers to each of the assembled group, DC Yvette Dickenson came into the room, carrying a mug of something hot.

Tartaglia looked round at Dickenson. 'Anyone else coming?'

'No, sir,' she said. 'They're out checking the names Mr Kramer gave us.' She walked over to where Donovan, Feeney and Minderedes were sitting, pulled out a chair from a nearby desk and eased herself down onto it carefully. Yawning, she took off her glasses, rubbed her eyes and started to polish the thick lenses on the edge of her shirt. Nearly eight months pregnant, she seemed to be finding most things at work a strain, although she wasn't due to go on maternity leave for another few weeks. Donovan wondered if she would last the course.

'Right,' Tartaglia said, clapping his hands to get everyone's attention. 'Let's get started now. Dave's found gold on Gemma Kramer's computer. There'll be a full briefing in the morning but I want your views straight away.' He turned to Wightman.

Wightman cleared his throat. 'The copies I've just given you are from Gemma Kramer's email store. I've only had time for a quick look, as the laptop's going off shortly to Newlands Park for full analysis. But I think I've picked up most, if not all, of the interesting stuff. As you'll see, there are nearly fifty messages going back over the last three months between Gemma and a man called Tom.'

'The last email in the sequence from Tom was sent the day before Gemma died,' Tartaglia added. 'Judging from what's in it, he's the man she was seen with at the church.'

As the group started to read through the sheets, the coughs, sniffs and rustling of paper turned to a hushed silence, leaving behind only the sound of underwater gurgling coming from Gemma's laptop, which lay open on one of the desks with a screensaver of brightly coloured tropical fish swimming up and down a reef.

'Turn the bloody sound off, will you?' Tartaglia said, after several minutes, glancing up at Wightman. 'Can't hear myself think.'

Wightman reached over, fiddled with something on the keyboard and the screensaver disappeared, leaving behind a visual of one of the emails.

For a moment, Donovan gazed blankly at the screen, the words she had just been reading swilling like smoke in her mind. Hearing Gemma Kramer's voice coming off the printed page, she felt sick. Gemma talked of her sense of isolation, how she was being bullied at school, how nobody seemed to understand her, how her mother and stepfather didn't care about her. The language was childish, the tone pathetic and moving. By contrast, the responses from the man called Tom were chilling.

The wooing, the grooming, was subtle and progressive, with layer upon layer of delicate persuasion. Donovan looked back at one of the sheets in her hand, eyes focusing on some lines from one of Tom's emails to Gemma that sounded as if they came from some rubbish pop song. Even if it was cringe-makingly awful, it was exactly the sort of thing calculated to appeal to a naïve young girl. Tom seemed to use anything to touch Gemma and worm his way deeper into her psyche. He orchestrated everything carefully, always in control. Like a piece of music, the emotional intensity of his emails rose and fell, sometimes powerful and dramatic, sometimes quiet, restrained and almost courtly, the concept of love and death and suicide running through them all as a leitmotif. They were two star-crossed lovers, like Romeo and Juliet, with the cruel world set against them. He understood Gemma's psychology perfectly and played her like a master.

Many teenagers had a fascination with death. But what had started out as an abstract idea on Gemma's part, the wish to kill herself little more than a child's cry from the heart, had been inexorably turned into a reality by Tom. It was evil in its purest form.

Although just the wrong side of thirty, Donovan could still recall the sense of alienation and despair of being a teenager, although in her case it had been nowhere as strongly felt as Gemma's. She remembered a girl called Annette who had lived next door to her in Twickenham, where she had grown up. One day, without warning, Annette had gone into her bedroom, closed the door and hanged herself. The shockwaves reverberated around the immediate community but nobody seemed to have any explanation for why Annette had done it. One minute she appeared to be a perfectly normal, happy fourteen-year-old, with everything to look forward to; the next, she was gone. And Donovan, then aged twelve, couldn't make sense of it either. But for months afterwards, the image of Annette haunted her, with her long, fair hair and heavy fringe, hanging dead in her room like some bizarre rag-doll.

Skimming through the last few pages of Gemma's emails, Donovan came to the final one in the sequence, sent by Tom the day before Gemma died.

Darling Gemma
Everything is ready and love is impatient. I thought of phoning you at home, even knowing how risky it is and how I could blow everything. I wanted to reassure you, to tell you how much I want you. Just don't worry. It will all be fine, you'll see. Trust me. I'll be waiting for you by the door of the church at four o'clock. Don't be late and don't forget to bring the ring – I have a beautiful one to give you in return. It was my mother's. We will exchange them when we say our vows. Also, don't forget the note for your mother – you have the wording I sent you. Just copy it out in your best handwriting but don't leave it anywhere too obvious. We don't want her finding it before we're done.

Trust me, there is no other way, not if you want me. When we meet, I'm sure I can make your fears melt away. Until then, remember one thing. This isn't a world worth living in. There can be no future for us here. Think what would happen to you (and me) if they found out. They would never allow us to be together. Just focus on that and I will take care of the rest. As Shakespeare wrote: 'If I must die, I will encounter darkness as a bride' and you will be the most beautiful bride. I hardly deserve you.
Die with me, my darling, and we will never be parted.
Your loving bridegroom,
Tomxx

As she read it, she shivered, imagining the high, dark gallery of the church, Gemma and the man called Tom, going through some sort of mock wedding ceremony, incense and candles burning. Poor Gemma. She hadn't stood a chance.

Donovan didn't know much about computers, but for Tom to have been so explicit in writing about his intentions, he must believe that he could never be traced. She had friends in the police who had worked on breaking paedophile rings and she knew that it was easily possible for someone to disappear into thin air if they knew what they were doing.

Feeney and Dickenson were still reading but Minderedes turned to Donovan, having finished.

'I thought I'd seen everything,' he whispered, shaking his head. 'It makes me sick to read this shit. It's unbelievable.'

She nodded in reply, just as Tartaglia got to his feet.

'Hendon are checking out the email addresses that Tom used,' he said. 'Although I'm sure none of them will be traceable. I'm also bloody sure that the fucker's name isn't Tom.'

He walked over to the window, smacking the side of a filing cabinet hard with the palm of his hand as he passed, and stared out for a moment. Then he turned round, frowning, stuffing his hands in his pockets. In the overhead strip-light, his eyes were in deep shadow but he looked as though he wanted to hit someone, lay them out cold.

'We've got to find out how he came across Gemma,' he said quietly.

'What about chat rooms?' Feeney asked, looking up from her papers.

'And suicide websites,' Dickenson added, with a half-stifled yawn. 'I saw a programme on telly recently about strangers meeting up on the internet to commit suicide together. Apart from the odd phone call, the people had never spoken or met before.'

'I saw that programme too,' Minderedes said.

The whole thing was sick, Donovan thought, remembering the programme, which had been on only a few weeks before. But there was fuck-all the police could do about it. The Suicide Act, which dated back over forty years, hadn't envisaged the opportunities of the internet. For the moment, most of what the sites were doing and the information they were providing to assist would-be suicides was not illegal. Calls to strengthen the law and ban suicide sites had so far fallen on deaf ears, which she found extraordinary. Total strangers meeting to jump off a bridge holding hands, or dying together in a car filled with carbon monoxide was bad enough. But at least there was no compulsion or coercion involved. They were adults and could make up their own minds, although to Donovan, the idea of wanting company when you were going to kill yourself seemed bizarre. But children and teenagers, with over-fertile imaginations, were so vulnerable and easily influenced. They needed protecting from such concepts and material, let alone being exposed to somebody who might use it to do them harm.

'I haven't found any trace of her visiting any chat rooms, let alone suicide websites,' Wightman said. 'All the places she logged onto were educational or the usual kids' games and stuff.'

Donovan flipped through the sheets to the beginning. 'However Gemma and Tom met, I don't think they were strangers at the time the emails started.'

'How do you work that one out?' Dickenson said, pushing her heavy-rimmed glasses up her nose and peering at Donovan bleary-eyed. 'They could have just been chatting on the net. No matter what Dave says, I still fancy that theory until we hear back from Newlands Park.'

Donovan held up the copy of the first email in the sequence. 'Here, take a look at Tom's first email. He asks her how she is, if she's feeling any better. He asks her if what he said, referring to sometime before, made sense. The tone is intimate, as if he's talking to a lover or a close friend. He certainly doesn't sound like a complete stranger to me.'

'That's right,' Feeney said, scanning the sheets and nodding slowly. 'She also says in one of the emails right at the beginning that she found his voice reassuring.'

'And she asks him if she can call him again,' Donovan replied. 'According to her stepfather, Gemma didn't have a mobile, so maybe she spoke to Tom from home.'

'We're checking the phone records now,' Tartaglia said quietly, as if he was only half-listening. He turned away towards the window and stared out, his thoughts clearly somewhere else.

'He's got to be someone she knows well,' Feeney said. 'Gemma seems so comfortable pouring out her feelings to him.'

Donovan shook her head. 'I'm not sure. All that comes across is that she thinks he understands her better than anyone else. That's intoxicating for any young girl and he bloody knows it. But if he is someone she knew, someone in her close circle of family or friends, or perhaps someone she knew from school or her neighbourhood, surely there would be references in the emails. But there aren't any. He talks about her family but only in general terms. I don't get the impression of familiarity from anything he says.'

'Maybe he's someone she knows but she doesn't realise it,' Wightman said. 'Maybe his email identity is a cover.'

'Then why doesn't she recognise his voice?' Feeney asked. 'Surely if she knew him, he wouldn't be able to disguise himself for long.'

Donovan was on the point of agreeing when Tartaglia wheeled around.

'Karen,' he said, clicking his fingers and striding back to the front of the room, a sudden urgency in his voice. 'Can you go and get the exhibits book? He talks about this sham ceremony in the email and giving her a ring. Run through the list of personal effects and see if a ring was found on her body.' As Feeney got up and went out of the room to find the file, he turned to Minderedes. 'Nick, I want you and Dave to start checking the Coroners' records for suicides of young women in London over the last couple of years.'

Minderedes looked aghast. 'But sir...' He stopped short when he saw Tartaglia's expression.

Wightman coloured, raising his pale eyebrows. 'All suicides, sir?'

'All suicides,' Tartaglia said emphatically.

A half-stifled groan went up from Minderedes and Wightman simultaneously. Donovan sympathised. There was no central record of suicides, each case being dealt with and recorded at a local level by the Coroner for that district. The only way of searching was to go to each office and examine the registers individually by hand. Also, as the business of the Coroner was only to establish the victim's identity, where and when they died and the cause of death, the records were not at all comprehensive. It was going to be a Herculean task and she couldn't see the point of it. There were no grounds so far to think Gemma's death was anything other than a one-off.

'Look,' Tartaglia said, staring hard at Minderedes. 'I know this is going to involve a lot of work and I'll speak to Superintendent Cornish immediately and see if we can get some extra help. But we must check everything thoroughly.'

'But why, sir?' Minderedes said, still looking sceptical. 'Surely you don't think he's done it before?'

Before Tartaglia had a chance to reply, Feeney came back into the room with the file.

'A gold ring is listed amongst the effects,' she said. 'The girl was wearing it on her third finger, left hand.'

'I want it fingerprinted immediately,' Tartaglia said. 'And the hallmark and manufacturer checked. According to the emails, they exchanged rings. I presume the other ring wasn't found at the crime scene?'

Feeney studied the list of exhibits and shook her head. 'There's no mention of it.'

'Then we must assume Tom has it.' He paused, catching Donovan's eye. 'Along with the lock of hair he cut from Gemma's head. Sam, you remember what Dr Blake said, don't you?'

Puzzled, she gazed at him for a moment. 'God, you're right,' she said, thinking back to what Blake had said. She had been so wrapped up in what had been going on at the time between Tartaglia and Blake that she had forgotten all about it.

Tartaglia turned to Minderedes. 'Think about this, Nick. It appears that Tom took a ring from Gemma. It also appears, from what the pathologist told us, that he cut off a lock of her hair from the back of the head, where it would least likely be spotted. Unless you have a better idea, they sound like souvenirs to me, which has bad connotations. It's possible he's done this thing before and nobody's picked it up because the death was wrongly recorded as a suicide.'

'Which is what almost happened with Gemma,' Donovan added, almost shouting. 'CID had more or less closed the case.'

'Just one thing, sir,' Wightman said, looking down at one of the sheets. 'In the last email, where Tom talks about the rings, he tells Gemma to leave a note for her mother. But there wasn't one, was there?'

'There's definitely no mention of a note anywhere in the files, sir,' Feeney said.

As Feeney spoke, something clicked into place and Donovan jumped to her feet. 'I've got it. Now I know what Kramer was holding back. He was so bloody relieved when I said that Gemma's death wasn't a suicide. I bet there was a note and he's either destroyed it or hidden it. It also explains why he wasn't remotely curious about what I was doing there and the fact that Gemma's death was suspicious. He thought he knew for sure what had really happened. He thought Gemma had killed herself and he didn't want that stigma attached to his daughter.'

Tartaglia's face creased into a broad smile. 'Well done, Sam. Let's pull Kramer in and see what he's got to say.' He turned to Feeney. 'Call his local nick and get them to send a car to pick him up. Tell them we'll be over shortly. Also, we'd better see if he recognises the ring, although I think we know what the answer will be.' He looked at Donovan. 'Do you want to come?'

With a quick glance at her watch, she shook her head and stood up. 'I've got to go and see Rosie Chapple, Gemma's school friend. I'm already late.'

Poor Kramer. She actually felt sorry for him and was glad to have an excuse not to be there. She had seen the wording in one of the emails that Tom had told Gemma to copy. Although the text was brief and quite innocuous, not laying the blame at any particular door, she thought of Kramer's pain, what he must have felt on finding the note, believing that Gemma had killed herself. From the little she knew of Kramer, her gut instinct told her that he had taken it to protect his wife, Mary. Better for a mother to think that her daughter had died in an accident or even in suspicious circumstances than to learn that she had chosen to take her own life, abandoning those who loved her. Donovan wondered how the Kramers would cope once they learned the truth about what had happened. For a moment she pictured Kramer's face earlier that evening as he fought back the tears and the inert shape of Gemma's mother lying in her bed. The loss of their daughter would be something they would never get over, something they would carry with them for the rest of their life.

Kramer would have to be hauled over the coals for what he had done but really they should be thanking him. If he hadn't appropriated the note, nobody would have bothered to request a special post mortem and there would have been no toxicology report revealing the presence of GHB in Gemma's system. Apart from the witness, who easily might have been disregarded, there would have been nothing to arouse suspicion. Gemma Kramer's death would have been recorded as a suicide and Tom would have been home and dry. Case closed.

7

Tom unlocked the faded navy-blue front door of the small terraced house and went inside. There was a chill in the air, coupled
with an unpleasant, mouldy odour. But he was in a hurry and
there was no time to turn on the heating and air the rooms. He
switched on the lights, ran up the two short flights of stairs to his
grandfather's dressing room on the first floor and pushed open the
door.

Even though his grandfather had been dead for over three years,
the room still held the familiar medicinal smell mixed with stale
tobacco that he'd associated with him since childhood. He went
over to the tall mahogany chest of drawers, turned on the lamp
and helped himself to the bottle of Trumper's Limes, which stood
on the small tray, along with the hair pomade, mouthwash and
wooden-backed brushes. As he rubbed some of the cologne on his
fingers and patted it on his face, his eye ran along the row of
brown-tinted army photographs that hung above on the wall. The
old bugger. What glory now? It amused him to use his grandfather's aftershave, to think how angry he would be if he were still
alive. Personally, Tom preferred something more modern and
musky, a bit more exotic and provocative. But Limes went perfectly with the role he was playing. Tonight he was the dapper
young ex-major, and old-fashioned restraint was the keyword.
The woman he had met at the bridge club was taking him to the
theatre, followed by dinner. It was a nice treat and she was tolerable company. But he hoped she wasn't expecting a fuck at the end
of it. If so, she'd be disappointed.

He brushed his hair until it gleamed, then exchanged his cheap
cufflinks for a pair of old gold monogrammed ones from the

small brown leather box on a tray that contained a variety of ancient studs and collar stiffeners. Almost done, he did up his top button and opened the small wardrobe door, selecting a sober regimental tie from the rack. The tie reeked of mothballs and he sprinkled several drops of Limes on it before knotting it carefully and washing his hands at the small basin under the window.

On his way downstairs he passed his grandmother's room. Automatically, he paused outside the closed door, careful where he put his feet for fear of making one of the floorboards creak. It had been a while since he had lived in the house but he still felt nervous, like a small boy caught out of bed, creeping along the landing to listen to the grown-up conversation going on below. He almost expected to hear the peremptory tinkle of the little bell she used to summon him when she wanted something. But there was nothing this time, not even the tap-tap of her cane as she crept around inside the room. Even so, the silence failed to reassure him. She was still there. He had seen her many times, sometimes no more than a shadow, semi-transparent and rippling like mist in the air, sometimes more tangible so that he could see every wrinkle and age spot that marked her withered skin. She liked to surprise him, catch him unawares. But he was past being frightened of her.

For a moment, his hand lingered near the door handle. He wondered whether, if he opened it quickly, he might catch a fleeting glimpse of her inside. Maybe she would be tucked up in bed listening to the radio – the wireless, as she insisted on calling it – or sitting at her dressing-table in her voluminous nightgown, studying her reflection in the mirror as she smoothed down her long white hair with one of her silver brushes. Ghosts weren't supposed to have a reflection, but she had one and the room still stank of her, no matter how often he cleaned and scrubbed it. It emanated partly from the rows of ancient clothes that hung like discarded skins in her wardrobe. But it also clung to the air she had once breathed. The cloying smell, a mixture of sweet, gardenia perfume, face powder and sour old woman, had worked itself into every corner and crevice, impregnating the very walls. It made him sick every time he went inside. He had thought about selling the house after she died, thinking that perhaps then she would leave him alone. He could do with the cash, but he knew he couldn't rid himself of her that easily. What's more, he didn't want people asking questions, poking around and nosing into their things; his things. Above all, the house was his secret place.

He waited a couple more moments, listening for some sort of sound from inside the room. But there was nothing and he carried on down the stairs. The portrait of his grandfather in the hall, dressed in full military regalia, glowered at him and he gave it a mock salute. The old fucker looked as humourless as ever, with his eye-patch and moustache. Puffed up like a peacock and arrogant as always, so bloody sure of himself, with so little right to be. But that was then. Tom was the master now.

Tom. He'd have to stop thinking of himself as Tom, although he saw himself more as Tom than any of the others. He was currently Matt or George or Colin, depending on who was at the receiving end. The names were ordinary but it was easier that way. Before Tom, he'd been Alain, after watching Alain Delon in some old film. But the stupid girl couldn't spell and kept calling him Alan, a name he loathed, reminding him of a nasty, fat-faced bully of a boy he'd once known at school. Yes, plain and simple was best. Besides, he couldn't see himself as a Brad or Russell or Jude. It just wasn't him and every detail was important. Any false note and they'd smell a rat.

He opened the door to the small sitting room, turned on the overhead light and went over to the small display cabinet by the French windows that housed his grandmother's collection of snuffboxes and tea caddies. They were her little treasures and she had shared them with no one, taking them out lovingly each week and dusting them, allowing him only to look through the glass but never to touch.

He found the small silver key in its hiding place on the ledge at the back, unlocked the glass door and took out a caddy made in

the shape of a pear. It was his favourite. As a child, it had particularly fascinated him, so life-like, carved from a single piece of
wood. He had liked stroking its smooth, yellow-brown curves
when his grandmother had gone out to play cards. Once, when
she came home early, she caught him at the cabinet and beat him
hard, sending him to bed without his tea. After that, she had
hidden the key but he had always found it. Didn't matter where
she put it, he was always one step ahead of the old bag. Always.
He glanced at the pair of matching black urns on the mantelpiece. It was strange to think of all that energy and loathing
reduced to nothing but a few handfuls of grey dust. There were
times when he wanted to pour them both down the toilet. But it
was better to have them there where he could see them, where he
could reassure himself with the tangible evidence that they were
both really dead.

He opened the lid of the caddy and took out the signet ring
Gemma had given him. Made of old pink gold, it was engraved
with someone's initials, the edges smooth from years of wear.
Perhaps she had bought it from an antique market stall or maybe
it belonged to a relative. Not bad, he thought, given that she was
only fourteen. The little bitch had had taste. He slipped it on his
finger and took out the long lock of hair he had cut from her head
as she lay on the floor of the gallery, semi-comatose. Stupidly, he'd
overdone the dose, which had quite spoiled things, and the silly
cow hadn't been aware of anything by that point. He twined the
long silky strands of brown hair around his finger and closed his
eyes, catching its delicate scent and stroking it rhythmically
against his cheek as he replayed in his mind what had happened.

She was surprisingly heavy, for such a slip of a girl. A real dead
weight, he remembered thinking with a smile, as he lifted her up
and carried her to the edge of the balcony. As he looked at her for
the last time, her eyes had rolled back in their sockets and for a
moment he thought she was going to be sick. At least she was past
struggling. Holding her in his arms, he peered down into the dim
area below. He savoured that knife-edge moment. It made him

high. If only he could prolong it, make it last forever. But the rushing urgency overcame him as before and he couldn't stop himself. With an almighty heave, he had hurled her high into the air, for a second a flapping bundle of black. He thought she gave a little gasp as she fell. Maybe she realised what was happening. But it was all over too quickly and he was left with the aching emptiness again.

He opened his eyes, twisted the hair into a coil and returned it with the ring to the caddy, locking it away in the cabinet, making sure to hide the key. If the shade of his grandmother came rummaging around for it, she'd be out of luck, he thought with satisfaction, as he walked over to the large gilt mirror that hung above the fireplace. Taking a silk handkerchief from his jacket pocket, he wiped the fine layer of dust from the centre and studied his reflection. He flicked a speck from his shoulder, made a final adjustment to his tie and, moistening a finger with his tongue, smoothed down each of his fine brows as he checked his shining white teeth. Perfect. He was ready.

8

Rosie Chapple lived not far from Gemma in a two-storey Victorian cottage set back behind a small, untidy front garden. Donovan rang the bell and, after a moment, a tall, gangly woman with wild, frizzy, greying hair answered the door. Her eyes were kohl-rimmed and she looked like a gypsy, with dangly earrings, coloured bangles and a long, flowing patchwork dress.

'Detective Sergeant Donovan,' Donovan said, showing her ID. 'I phoned earlier. Is Rosie back?'

'I'm Sarah Chapple, her mother,' the woman said, with a jingle of bangles as she held out her hand. 'She's just got in. You'd better come with me.'

Donovan caught a waft of sandalwood as she followed Sarah inside, down a narrow corridor into an open-plan kitchen at the back. A pale-faced girl with a halo of black, curly hair sat at the small scrubbed pine table, shovelling rice crispies into her mouth. She looked up and gave Donovan a weary look, before continuing to eat.

The room was painted a dark rust and had a homely feel, with an old dresser on one side, every shelf heaving with china and books, the walls crammed with photographs and colourful pictures.

'This is Rosie,' Sarah said, patting her daughter's hand as she sat down next to her and gestured Donovan to the scuffed wooden chair opposite. 'I know you've come about Gemma's death. How can we help?'

'We're trying to piece together what happened. Gemma...'

'It was at a church, wasn't it?' Sarah interrupted.

'Yes. Gemma was seen outside with a man before she died. We're trying to find out who he is.'

Sarah looked surprised. 'Do you mean a boyfriend?'

Donovan nodded. 'Although he was considerably older than Gemma.'

'Gemma never mentioned anyone,' Sarah said, with a quick glance towards Rosie, who was noisily scraping up the last few mouthfuls of cereal and milk, apparently oblivious to what was being discussed around her.

'It's very important we find him,' Donovan said, as Rosie clanked her spoon down in the empty bowl, pushed it away and stared down at the table, shoulders hunched.

'What's the man got to do with it?' Sarah asked. 'The school said Gemma had a fall. I thought it was an accident.'

'It's not as simple as that,' Donovan said, looking at Rosie, who was picking at a patch of candle wax stuck on the table. Was she feeling uncomfortable because of her mother being there, or because Donovan was a policewoman? Or was there another reason? 'Do you know anything about this man?' she said, trying to catch Rosie's eye.

Sarah shook her head. 'I told you, I haven't heard anything about Gemma having a boyfriend.'

Donovan tried to contain her irritation. 'Thank you, Mrs Chapple. But I need to ask Rosie.' She wanted to ask Sarah Chapple to leave, but as Rosie was a minor, that was out of the question. She stared hard at Rosie, willing her to look up. 'Did Gemma tell you about a man? I really need to know.'

Rosie sniffed and looked away, focusing on a distant point on the far wall.

'Please, Rosie,' Donovan said. 'He may have had something to do with Gemma's death.'

Sarah gasped. 'Oh my God! Are you saying she was murdered?'

At the word 'murdered', Rosie looked round, and Donovan saw tears in her eyes.

'We're treating her death as suspicious, Mrs Chapple. Which is why I need Rosie to tell me if she knows anything.'

Sarah turned to Rosie, clamped an arm around her shoulder

and leaned towards her. 'Come on, sweetheart. If you know something, you'd better tell the sergeant. There's no point in keeping secrets if Gemma was murdered.'

Rosie bowed her head, pulled down the sleeves of her baggy black jumper over a set of bitten fingernails, and hugged herself. 'She didn't talk about him much,' she said, in a small, high-pitched voice, which Donovan could barely hear. 'I thought he was just one of her fantasies.'

A look of horror crossed Sarah's face. 'Is he a paedophile? Was Gemma assaulted?'

Exasperated, Donovan glared at her. If only the woman would shut up and let her daughter speak. 'No, Mrs Chapple. She wasn't assaulted. Please let Rosie continue.' She turned back to Rosie. 'Do you have any idea where she met him?'

Rosie shook her head. 'She never said.'

'Please think, Rosie. There must be something else. Every little detail is important. We must find him.'

Rosie appeared confused, looking first at her mother, then back at Donovan. 'Talked about him like he was real special, like some sort of pop star or actor or something. We all thought she was telling porkies and we teased her.' Tears were streaming down her cheeks. 'I feel so bad now,' she said, burying her face in her arms.

Sarah rubbed her shoulders and stroked her head. 'It's all right, sweetheart. You mustn't feel guilty about it.' Putting her arm protectively around Rosie, she turned to Donovan. 'Gemma was an odd girl, Sergeant. The sort who invited teasing, if you know what I mean. I teach art at the school and I've got three daughters, so I know what girls can be like. Gemma was good at heart but she was full of stories. It was difficult to know what to believe, sometimes. I put it down to a lack of confidence and the fact that her mum should have spent more time with her.' She gave Rosie a little squeeze and kissed the top of her head. 'Girls need their mums, even at this age. But Gemma's brothers were a handful and they took up all Mary's energy, from what I could see.'

'I'm sorry if this is distressing for you,' Donovan said, peering down at Rosie. 'Nobody's going to blame you for anything. It would just help if you could tell me what you know.'

Rosie looked up, gulped, wiped her nose with the back of her hand. 'She said she was going to run away with him.'

'Did she ever mention suicide?' Donovan asked.

Sarah put her hands to her mouth. 'Suicide? Goodness, I thought you said her death was suspicious?'

'Please answer the question, Rosie,' Donovan said, ignoring Sarah. 'Did Gemma ever talk about suicide?'

Rosie nodded. 'Everyone thought she was just trying to get attention for herself, just trying to be different. That's why nobody liked her.'

'But you did?'

Rosie sniffed and nodded. 'When she wasn't making up stuff, she could be really nice and I felt sorry for her.'

'Did she have any interests outside school that you know of? Any clubs or societies?'

'She belonged to a swimming club, I think,' she said, rubbing her eyes with her fingers and pushing her springy dark curls off her face.

'Surely you can get all that from her parents?' Sarah asked.

'Gemma kept a lot hidden from them, Mrs Chapple. She met this man somehow and we must find the connection. Is there anything else you can tell me, Rosie?'

Rosie sighed and looked at her for a moment before speaking. 'So, he is real?' she said doubtfully, as if she was still trying to take it all in. 'You mean she wasn't lying about him?'

'He's real enough,' Donovan said. It was almost as if the news was a relief to Rosie and she had the feeling that there was more to come. 'Please tell me what you know.'

Rosie paused for a moment before replying. 'She called me on Wednesday.'

Sarah gave her a sharp look. 'What, the day she died? You didn't tell me.'

'My phone was out of juice and I only picked up the message yesterday. When I listened to it, they'd already told us at school that she was dead. It was really weird, hearing her voice.'

'What did she say?' Donovan asked.

Rosie shrugged. 'I thought it was just another one of her silly stories. She said she was meeting this bloke Tom at a church and that they were going to be married. She said it would be the last time I'd hear from her, but that I should be happy for her.'

'What else?'

Rosie wiped away another tear with the back of her hand. 'She said she was late and had seen him standing by the church door, waiting for her. But he hadn't seen her. She sounded really excited. She said she just had to call me quickly to tell me and to say goodbye.'

'Where was she calling from?' Donovan asked.

'Must have been a call box,' Rosie replied. 'Her stupid parents wouldn't allow her a mobile and I could hear traffic in the background.'

They would have to check the caller number on Rosie's phone but it sounded plausible. 'Is there anything else?'

Rosie hesitated and looked at Donovan uncertainly.

'Go on,' Sarah said, firmly. 'What else did she say?'

Rosie sighed. 'It seemed sort of weird. But she said he looked just like Tom Cruise in *Interview with the Vampire*.'

After checking in with Tartaglia and telling him about her conversation with Rosie, Donovan wearily drove the short distance home to the small house she shared with her sister, Claire, in Hammersmith. There was nothing more to be done that night and Tartaglia had told her to go home and get some sleep, ready for the next day. A big glass of wine and a hot, deep bath would sort her out, she thought, letting herself in quietly through the front door. Claire was in, her bag and keys dumped on the hall table, next to a pile of half-opened mail, her briefcase and shoes discarded at the bottom of the narrow flight of stairs. As a solicitor in one of the City law firms, she worked long hours and would have been tucked up in bed hours ago.

Donovan went into the kitchen and checked the answer machine but there were no messages and no note either from Claire to say that anyone had called. Disappointed, although not surprised, she dropped her keys onto the table and poured herself a glass of white wine from an open bottle in the fridge. It wasn't very nice but it was all there was and at least it was cold. She and Claire never had time to do any shopping. Resisting the urge to light a cigarette, she took her wine upstairs and tiptoed past Claire's bedroom door into the bathroom where she turned on the taps and helped herself to a large dollop of Claire's Body Shop Orange Blossom Bath Essence. She undressed quickly and sank back into the bath, feet up on either side of the taps, letting the rising water wash over her shoulders and neck as she sipped her wine.

Logic told her that she shouldn't expect to hear from Richard again. Newly promoted to DI, Richard had recently joined one of the murder teams in south London and was working all hours. It had got to the point where they rarely ever saw each other. He had half-suggested she put in for a transfer to somewhere closer to where he worked. But why should she move? She hadn't known him that long and she was enjoying working on Clarke's team. There had never been much of a sparkle about Richard. A small part of her hoped he might get over his pride or inertia and call her. But what then? She needed something different. Someone different. More than anything she wanted some fun for a change and perhaps some excitement.

It was past midnight by the time Tartaglia got home – a ground floor flat in a terraced house off Shepherd's Bush Road. He pushed his motorbike up the short tiled path that led from the street to the front door, parking it out of sight behind the high hedge, by the dustbins. He'd bought the flat with some money left to him by his grandfather a few years before. The place had been a tip, with wiring, plumbing and fixtures dating back to the seventies. It had taken him, his cousin Gianni, and a couple of the lads from Gianni's building firm several weekends to transform it, painting the walls white, sanding the floorboards and putting in a modern kitchen and bathroom. The flat was the first place he had ever owned and it would take a lot to get him to move again.

As he put his key in the lock, Henry, the Siamese cat belonging to his upstairs neighbour Jenny, twisted around his legs, meowing to be brought in. Judging by the dark windows and drawn curtains on the floor above, Jenny had gone to bed. As he opened the front door and let himself into his flat, Henry slipped through his legs, weaving his way into the sitting room. He wasn't keen on cats, generally; their hair made him sneeze. But Henry had become a frequent visitor, thick-skinned to all efforts to exclude him, and Tartaglia had grown fond of him, often leaving the kitchen window at the side of the house ajar so that Henry could come and go.

He went into the sitting room, switched on the light and drew the shutters across the window, blocking out the orange glare of the streetlamp just outside. He flung his jacket onto the sofa and checked the answer machine. Apart from a bleep where somebody had hung up, there were two messages, one from Sally-Anne saying that there was no change in Clarke's condition and one from his sister, Nicoletta, asking him over for Sunday lunch. She said there was someone she wanted him to meet, no doubt another of her hopeless, single female friends. For once, he was relieved to be working all weekend, with an excuse that even Nicoletta would be forced to accept.

He knew he should try and get some sleep. There was the briefing at seven that morning and it was going to be another long day. But he felt wired, thoughts buzzing in his head. He undid his tie and top button and went into the kitchen for a drink. What was it with women? Not content just to get married themselves, once they'd done that, they spent their whole time matchmaking everybody else. Nicoletta seemed obsessed with getting him hitched and his cousin Elisa, Gianni's sister, was almost as bad. They kept reminding him that he was only a few years away from being forty, a point they viewed as some sort of a watershed, although it meant nothing to him. Why couldn't they understand that he was happy as he was and leave him alone?

Happy? Well, not unhappy, he thought, opening the bottle of Sicilian Nero d'Avola that Gianni had given him for his birthday, and pouring himself a large glass. Seeing Fiona Blake that morning had caused all sorts of uncomfortable feelings to surface. Why was he attracted to complicated women, women he couldn't quite pin down? Why was he never interested in nice, straightforward women like Donovan?

The wine was a deep, black purple and smelled heady and full of spice. He took a large draught, letting it swill around his mouth, enjoying the pungent flavour. Christ, it was good, he thought, taking another long swig. Gianni really knew a thing or two about wine. Perhaps he had been a bit hard on Fiona but he'd been angry. Screw Murray. Even though it was late, he felt like calling her. Maybe he'd apologise for what had happened earlier. It would be nice to hear her voice. Then he remembered the ring on her finger. No point. She had made her choice and he had to put her out of his mind.

He went into the sitting room, put REM's *Around the Sun* on the CD player and dimmed the lights. He sank down into the middle of the large, comfortable sofa, shoes off, feet up on the glass coffee table, and closed his eyes momentarily. Henry appeared from nowhere and jumped onto his lap, purring loudly, settling himself down into a tight pale beige coil. Tartaglia took another slug of wine and lit a cigarette, trying to lose himself in the music, watching the smoke snake up towards the ceiling. The sound was good. Like his motorbike, the player had been an extravagance, but well worth it. Thank God, he had nobody to dictate how he spent his money.

Donovan had called to tell him about her meeting with Rosie Chapple and he had spoken to Superintendent Cornish to brief him about what they had discovered. Not a man to show emotion easily, Cornish had sounded a little rattled as Tartaglia outlined his theory that Gemma's death might be part of a series. Cornish had refused to give him extra resources to help search the records for matching suicides, saying that he couldn't justify such a thing on the basis of a 'pure hunch'. But he had promised to come down to Barnes for the next day's morning meeting, clearly wanting to keep closer tabs on things, considering what Tartaglia had said. Tartaglia hoped that that was going to be the limit of his hands-on input. Unlike Clarke, Cornish had almost no murder experience, having risen through the ranks in other departments, almost entirely on the uniform side. Cornish could handle the media, for all he cared, and he would keep him fully briefed, but he wanted to be left in overall day-to-day charge of the case.

He could still feel the reheated lasagne from the pub sitting in his stomach, and wondered whether he'd be able to sleep. He shouldn't have had it, but he was so hungry after seeing Kramer that he would have eaten almost anything. Kramer, the hard man, had gone to pieces once he discovered that they knew about the suicide note. Tartaglia felt deeply sorry for the man. Kramer had handed over the note, written on flowery paper in Gemma's childish handwriting, folded neatly in a pink envelope with her mother's name on the front. But it had revealed nothing new, the wording being identical to what Tom had ordered Gemma to write. Kramer and his two friends' alibis had checked out and they had let him go with a severe bollocking for withholding evidence. Kramer was a dead end. They would have to look for Gemma's killer elsewhere.

9

Monday, six thirty a.m., and Tartaglia sat at Clarke's desk in his large, comfortable corduroy chair, struggling to focus on the file in front of him, a half-drunk mug of lukewarm black coffee at his side. He had had no sleep in the previous twenty-four hours and was finding staying awake a challenge. Contrary to Tartaglia's initial hopes, Cornish had continued to refuse to give him any additional resources to scour the registers at the coroners' offices in the various London districts. It wasn't clear whether this was because he doubted Tartaglia's instincts or whether he feared what might be found, although Tartaglia suspected it was a combination of both. In the end, Tartaglia's team had spent the last couple of days painstakingly going through the books page-by-page, clocking up hundreds of man-hours, complaining vociferously that it was all a complete waste of time. Eventually, they had turned up two suicides that appeared to fit the pattern. The case files had been retrieved from central records and, after Tartaglia had read through the documents in detail, Donovan and Dickenson had been immediately dispatched to interview the families.

Laura Benedetti, aged fifteen, had fallen to her death eight months before in a church in Richmond, her body found by a local woman coming in to change the flowers. Laura lived in a council flat in Islington, several miles away, very close to Tartaglia's sister, Nicoletta's house. According to Donovan, Laura was the only child of a couple from Sardinia who seemed to work all hours of the day and night, the mother cleaning houses in the smarter streets of the area, the father a head waiter in the restaurant of a West End hotel. The photo Tartaglia had seen of Laura reminded him instantly of Nicoletta at the same age, oval face, soft brown eyes and long, dark hair, although there was something dreamy about Laura's expression which was very different to Nicoletta's. Donovan had told Tartaglia how Laura's father had wanted to return home to Sardinia immediately after the tragedy but her mother had so far refused. She was unable to leave the country where her daughter had died, making a shrine of Laura's tiny bedroom and visiting her grave almost daily. Donovan seemed more than usually affected by what she had heard, stating with glistening eyes how some people found it impossible to move on in any way from such a tragedy.

The other girl, Elinor Best, known as Ellie, had died four months after Laura in similar circumstances in a church in Chiswick, her body discovered by a tramp taking refuge inside during a storm. Ellie had lived several miles away in a prosperous residential part of Wandsworth with a younger brother and sister. Her father was a solicitor, her mother a journalist, and her background couldn't have been more different to Gemma and Laura's. Aged sixteen, with reddish-brown hair, a rash of freckles and a pert, turned-up nose, she had been a budding violinist, chosen a few weeks before her death to play in one of the London youth orchestras. Her parents had recently separated and Donovan and Dickenson had only been able to see the mother so far, who was living alone with her two remaining children in the house in Wandsworth, apparently blaming the father for what had happened to Ellie.

But most striking of all had been the fact that both girls had left brief suicide notes and the wording was almost identical to the note left by Gemma Kramer. No doubt they too had been dictated by Tom. There were no witnesses to either Laura or Ellie's death and with nothing to arouse suspicion, no further investigation had seemed necessary. The local coroners had duly recorded verdicts of suicide. With the deaths happening in two different areas, there had been no chance of anyone spotting the similarities and linking the two cases.

At the time the parents of both girls had adamantly refused to believe that their daughters had any reason to kill themselves. However, the local CID investigation had revealed that both Laura and Ellie had been badly bullied at school, echoing what Tartaglia's team already knew about Gemma. Like her, the two girls seemed to be misfits. Laura, small for her age, uncommunicative and sensitive, had been teased about her poor English, whilst Ellie had been overweight and lacking in self-confidence. Struggling academically, music had been her only area of achievement. According to the case notes, Ellie had been prescribed anti-depressants by her GP. Whilst a visit from the police several months later must have been intensely painful for the families, Tartaglia took some comfort from the fact that both Laura's parents and Ellie's mother seemed relieved to learn that their daughters' deaths were being looked into again.

Ellie Best had been cremated. But Laura Benedetti had been buried. Her exhumation had taken place a little after three a.m. that day in an anonymous North London cemetery. Tartaglia and Feeney had attended, together with Alex James, the crime scene manager, Dr Blake, and an annoying middle-aged man from the Coroner's Office who had a streaming head cold and seemed purely concerned with the inconvenience of missing a night's sleep. None of them wanted to be standing there in the middle of the night huddled together around the grave, listening to the rain drumming on the sides and roof of the forensic tent while the undertakers did their work. But the cover of darkness was necessary in order to reduce the chance of anyone finding out what they were doing. The last thing they needed were the prying eyes of local residents, let alone the press. Laura's remains had been taken away to the mortuary for a post mortem and Tartaglia was due there in a couple of hours to see what Blake had found.

He got up from the desk, about to head for the kitchen to make some fresh coffee, when his mobile rang. As he answered it, he caught sight of himself in the small round mirror on the wall, which Clarke used for the occasional morning shave. He looked like shit, with a day's growth of beard and deep, dark circles under his eyes. He ran his fingers quickly through his hair in an attempt to smooth it down, and heard Superintendent Cornish's voice muffled at the other end.

'Has the exhumation taken place?'

'Yes, and the post mortem's being done as we speak.' Tartgalia cradled the phone under his ear as he pushed aside a packing case full of Clarke's things, which Sally-Ann was due to collect at some point. He closed the door firmly against the background noise coming from the main office opposite and tried to focus on what Cornish was saying.

'When do you expect to get the results?' Cornish said.

'They're rushing them through, so hopefully within the next twenty-four hours. I'm on my way over shortly to see the pathologist.'

The pathologist. The words had a nice, detached ring to them, the opposite of what he really felt, if he was honest. Glancing again in the mirror, he rubbed the thick black stubble on his chin with his fingers. With the morning meeting due to start shortly, there'd be no time to go back home for a shower, a shave and a change of clothes before meeting Fiona Blake later at the mortuary. Clarke's electric razor was in one of the many boxes in the hall but it looked like a health hazard and he preferred a wet shave anyway. Sod it, he thought, smiling at his own vanity. Why should he care about pleasing Fiona? She would just have to take him as she found him. He turned away and sank down in the chair, putting his feet up heavily on the desk.

'The press haven't got wind of anything, I hope?' Cornish said, chewing something loudly as he spoke.

Tartaglia heard the clatter of china and the sound of a woman's voice in the background. Cornish must be at home having breakfast. Knowing Cornish, it would be muesli, granary toast with a low-fat spread and a pot of a particular brand of Earl Grey tea. According to Clarke, the muesli and tea travelled with Cornish everywhere, even when he went away for a work conference. He was a creature of habit in everything he did, imagination not being his strong point.

'Not as far as I know,' Tartaglia replied, aware that he didn't have Cornish's full attention.

'Did you find the rings?' Cornish's mouth was still full, the final word sounding like 'wings'.

There were few things Tartaglia found more irritating than trying to have a conversation with someone who was eating, particularly when he'd been up all the night and had had no breakfast. Trying to stifle his annoyance, he replied: 'Laura Benedetti's mother thinks she was wearing one but she's not a hundred per cent certain. If there was a ring, nobody knows where it is.'

Cornish made a dissatisfied grunt at the other end. 'What a pity.'

'But Ellie Best was wearing one when she died and her mother kept it. It's identical to Gemma Kramer's, plain gold, eighteen carat, same hallmark. It looks like Tom bought a job lot. We're still trying to trace the manufacturer.'

'When do we hear back about the girls' computers?'

'Again, it's being treated as a priority,' Tartaglia said. 'But they couldn't give me a precise time.'

The computers had been retrieved from other family members, who had been using them, and sent off for analysis. But even if the emails could be recovered, they were unlikely to be much help in finding the killer. According to the experts at Newlands Park, it had proved impossible to trace Tom from Gemma's computer.

'You're sure there are only two deaths that fit the pattern?' Cornish asked, taking a slurp of what Tartaglia assumed was tea.

'As I told you last night, there's one other death we're looking into. But it's not an instant fit. Marion Spear was single, just turned thirty, so she's quite a bit older than the others. She fell from the top storey of a car park nearly two years ago, just within the time frame we've been searching. There was an investigation at the time as there were no witnesses and no suicide note. But in the end, short of any conclusive evidence to the contrary, the coroner recorded an open verdict.'

'Why are you bothering with her?'

'Purely on the basis of location. The car park was just down the road from where Gemma died.'

Cornish coughed as if something had gone down the wrong way. Tartaglia heard the sound of a chair being scraped back, followed by running water. Growing increasingly impatient as Cornish spluttered and cleared his throat, he stood up and started to pace around the small room.

'What about a ring?' Cornish gasped, after a moment.

'We're checking to see if she was wearing one. If not, I think there's no reason to get an exhumation order at this point.'

'So, apart from her, you think we have three victims?'

'Subject to confirmation from the pathologist on Laura, yes. First Laura, then Ellie and then Gemma.'

'Just the three?'

'As far as we can tell.' Of course, there was no way to be a hundred per cent certain but they'd trawled the records as thoroughly as possible, given limited time and resources. The phrase needles and haystacks came to mind. 'Would you like me to widen the search, maybe start looking outside the London area?' As he said this, he knew what the answer would be.

Cornish took another noisy gulp of something and cleared his throat again. 'It's too much of a long shot and we haven't got the manpower. Also, I don't want to risk a leak and have the press crawling all over us before we're ready. Call me when you've seen the pathologist.'

Holding a handkerchief over his nose to dampen the overpowering stench of decay, Tartaglia stared down at the shrivelled, greenish-black remains of Laura Benedetti stretched out before him on the steel gurney. Eight months in a London cemetery had reduced her to something barely recognisable as human and with a momentary pang he remembered the photo of her he had seen.

Thanks to the ring, they were sure about Ellie Best. But he needed some sort of confirmation from Fiona Blake that Laura

Benedetti was also part of the series. However, Blake was taking her time. He had only just arrived at the mortuary when she had rushed out of the room to the corridor outside to take a call on her mobile. Judging from the peal of what sounded like flirtatious laughter that echoed through the doors, it was personal and he'd put money on it being a man at the other end.

He was on the point of going out to insist that she come back and talk to him, when the double doors swung open and she strode briskly back into the room as if nothing had happened, shoes squeaking on the lino, her white coat hugging her hips as she walked towards him.

'We should get the tox results back by tomorrow,' she said matter-of-factly, coming over to where he was standing, hands in the pockets of her coat. 'But they're unlikely to tell us much, as you know.'

He hadn't expected anything else, given the state of decomposition of Laura's body and the time it had spent in the ground.

'Are you telling me then that there's nothing suspicious about her death?' he said levelly, removing the handkerchief temporarily and trying not to inhale. His stomach churned and he hoped this wasn't going to take long.

'The girl died from a fall onto a hard surface, just as it says in the coroner's report. Nothing wrong there. But there is one thing,' she said, catching his eye. 'It's useful that I saw the last victim. I knew what I was looking for.'

As she brushed past him and went over to the gurney, putting on a fresh pair of surgical gloves, he caught a faint, fleeting whiff of her perfume and found himself momentarily wanting to reach out and touch her hair, stroke the soft skin of her neck.

Using both hands, she gently shifted the remains of the head to one side, then looked round at him. 'Look. Here, by the base of her scalp.' She pointed with a finger.

Clamping the handkerchief back over his mouth and nose, he stepped forward and peered down at the blackened mess of flesh, trying to see what she was indicating. It was almost impossible to make out anything meaningful. Then, peering even closer, he saw the razor-sharp line, dark against an even darker mass.

'He's taken a lock of hair?' he guessed, excitement starting to bubble up.

'Yes,' she said, with a satisfied smile, as if she had just given him a wonderful present. 'It's easy to miss because of the decomposition and the colour of her hair. But do you see here?' As she ran her finger over the spot she met his eye again. For a second, he wondered again who she had been speaking to on the phone.

'A chunk of hair has been removed,' she said, still holding his gaze. 'It's been cut off cleanly with a sharp blade, exactly like the other girl.'

10

'Islington, Wandsworth, Streatham, Richmond, Chiswick and Ealing.' Tartaglia pointed with a pen at the large map of Greater London that Wightman had fixed to the white board in the main office, the locations marked with drawing pins. 'That's where Laura, Ellie and Gemma lived and died. Marion Spear also lived and died in Ealing. Is there any connection we can make at this point?'

There was a long pause before Wightman replied: 'The scale of the map makes the locations look quite close together but it's actually an enormous area. Doesn't make much sense to me.'

'Me neither,' Donovan added. 'Laura from Islington ends up dead in Richmond; Ellie, from Wandsworth, in Chiswick; and Gemma, from Streatham, in Ealing. Apart from the fact that he's killing the girls a good few miles from where they each live, I can't see any pattern either.'

The only response from Dickenson was a loud, throaty sigh. It was late afternoon and Donovan and Wightman were perched on a bank of empty desks near the board. Dickenson sat to one side on a chair, feet stretched out in front of her, toes resting on the rail of another chair. Her hands were clasped awkwardly over her stomach and she looked as if she had only had a few hours of sleep, eyes struggling to focus, yawning intermittently. Tartaglia wondered whether it wouldn't be better to send her home, although he knew she'd bite his head off if he suggested any such thing.

All his team's efforts so far had concentrated on researching the victimology of the three girls, trying to find a link between them, be it their schools, clubs, doctors, dentists, and suchlike. It was early days, but so far they had uncovered nothing to suggest that the three girls' paths had crossed during the previous two years. There had to be a link but they were missing it.

'Have any of you come across geographical profiling?' Tartagalia asked.

'We used a profiler once for a rape case when I was in Lewisham,' Dickenson said, stifling another yawn. 'He had some really interesting things to say.'

'You mean, like Cracker, sir?' Wightman asked.

Tartaglia shook his head. 'You're talking about psychological profiling. Geographical profiling is totally different.' He tapped the map with his pen. 'This isn't anything like the real thing. Nowadays it's all done on a computer and you need a minimum of five locations for proper analysis. But it's still worth visualising where the victims lived and where they died, in case something leaps out. Also, the location of a crime's a hard fact. It's not open to interpretation and it tells us a lot about the criminal.'

'You mean why Tom chose the places he killed the three girls?' Donovan asked. 'Local knowledge, that sort of thing?'

'Exactly. All three murders took place in the general west London area. The churches were all pretty disused and perfect for his purpose. Given what we know of him from the emails, the places weren't chosen at random. Which means he either knows them or spent time finding them.'

'For what it's worth, the churches are all close to tube stations on the District Line,' Dickenson said. 'Perhaps that's how he's getting around.'

Tartaglia nodded. 'Maybe. Another thing that's interesting is that all three killings happened during the week, in the mid to late afternoon. This also applies to Marion Spear's death. Our killer must be somebody who is either unemployed or who has a relatively flexible working arrangement. He can take time off without it being noticed. It's possible he avoids the weekend because he himself has commitments, a family maybe.'

'Or else, because there are fewer people around on weekday afternoons,' Wightman said.

Donovan nodded. 'And the girls are less likely to be missed by their families. They were all supposed to be at school when they went to the churches.'

'What about the fact that all three crime scenes are churches?' Wightman asked. 'Maybe the whole church thing turns him on.'

Tartaglia shrugged. 'The church is certainly part of the whole theatrical ritual which he used to lure the girls to him. But at this stage, I'm not reading anything more into it.'

'You don't think the churches mean something special to him?' Dickenson asked, looking surprised.

'Anything's possible,' he replied, with a shrug. 'But sitting here, how can we possibly tell? If we start wondering about his psychological motivation, we get into the realms of fairytales. Anyway, even if churches have some sort of special significance for him, how does it help us find him?'

'You don't have much time for psychological profiling, then?' Dickenson asked, looking sceptical.

'As far as I'm concerned it's an arcane art and its predictions are about as scientific as a tabloid horoscope.' He gazed at her tired face for a moment, feeling a combination of frustration and sympathy for her. 'We'd all like to have a magic bullet and I wish I could tell you that it worked. But you only have to look at the screw-ups that have taken place in some well-known cases to see that it can be very misleading.'

'Won't you be consulting a psychological profiler?' Donovan asked, with a wry glance in Dickenson's direction.

'At some point, maybe,' he said, noncommittally. He knew he would probably be forced to bring one on board eventually, if only to satisfy his superiors that he'd ticked all the right boxes. But as far as he was concerned, any decent, experienced detective could add as much value as a psychological profiler, although it wasn't fashionable to say so.

'But surely they can help in narrowing the field of focus,' Dickenson said, irritably, refusing to give up.

'That's the theory. But like everything, it depends on the quality of the input. Garbage in, garbage out.'

Tartaglia sighed, wishing that Dickenson hadn't pushed him. But he might as well be honest, even if word of his heresy somehow filtered back to Cornish, who was a staunch believer. 'Look, I'll give you a perfect example. The bloke we used on the North London Strangler case was worse than useless, even though he's got a list of degrees the length of your arm and is reckoned to be one of the top profilers in this country. He...'

'But there've been some fantastic books on profiling,' Dickenson interrupted. 'Surely, they can't all be rubbish.'

'I'm not saying they are, although many of the case studies have been rewritten with the benefit of hindsight. My point is that we don't need the distraction. Going back to the North London Strangler case, the profiler, or Behavioural Investigative Analyst, as we're supposed to call them now, as if it makes them sound more scientific, was way off the mark. He wasted a lot of our time. He told us that the man we were looking for – a violent rapist-turned-murderer – was in his early to mid-twenties, sexually dysfunctional, lived alone and had difficulty making friends. In fact, Michael Barton was in his late thirties, popular with his mates and a right Jack-the-Lad with the ladies. His wife was so happy with his performance in the sack that she didn't question what he got up to late at night, when he supposedly took the dog out for a walk.'

'But you caught him,' Donovan said.

'No thanks to the profiler. If we'd followed his advice, we'd still be looking for the murderer and, no doubt, there would have been further victims.'

'How did you get him, then?' Wightman asked.

'The area of the attacks was very small, which was striking. Most murderers don't have unlimited time. They need to feel comfortable with the territory, know where's safe, where they're unlikely to be disturbed and how to make a quick getaway. With Barton, we drew our own conclusions, based on common sense. We focused on all locals, irrespective of age and background, with previous convictions for assault, particularly of a sexual nature. Barton popped up on the radar screen as he had been arrested several years before on two separate charges of attempted rape, although both victims refused to go to court and the charges were dropped, which was why there was no record of his DNA. It was before the change in the law.'

Dickenson still looked doubtful. 'But Gemma Kramer, Ellie Best and Laura Benedetti are all under twenty. Surely, that tells us something about the killer?'

Tartaglia shook his head. 'Not necessarily. Tom may be targeting all sorts of women. But the only ones he's successful in luring to their deaths happen to be in that age group. Perhaps they're self-selecting.'

'You mean because they're young, naïve and easily suggestible,' Donovan added, appearing to agree with what he had said. 'They were also in a vulnerable state of mind. We know that all three were being bullied at school and one was on Prozac. People like that aren't thinking straight. How else can he con them into believing that they should go and top themselves with him?'

Tartaglia nodded. 'Maybe we're just seeing the tip of the iceberg. For every victim, how many failures, and what's the profile of each of the failures? Maybe he goes after older women too but they don't buy his story. It's too early to jump to conclusions, we don't have enough information yet, which is why I'm keeping an open mind on Marion Spear.'

'A woman in her late twenties or early thirties, like Marion Spear, wouldn't fall for his crap. And she'd be more likely to report him,' Dickenson said emphatically, shifting in her chair and folding her arms tightly across her chest. 'Why would he take the risk?'

Donovan shook her head. 'We know nothing about her yet. Maybe there's a reason.'

'But the way Marion Spear died is different to the other three,'

Dickenson said sharply. 'And there was no suicide note. The verdict was accidental death.'

'I agree,' Tartaglia said. 'But she fell to her death from a high place and lived and died in Ealing, only a few blocks away from where Gemma was killed. Personally, I find that interesting. Certainly worth a closer look.'

As he spoke, he knew it sounded flimsy. But it was impossible to explain gut feeling to most people. All he had to pin it on were a couple of lines in one of the emails to Gemma that kept niggling at him. Tom had asked Gemma if she found high places exciting, if she got a thrill looking down from a tall building or a cliff. Still trying to justify to himself why he felt Marion Spear's death worth looking into, Tartaglia had re-read the email earlier that morning after coming back from the cemetery.

Do you feel the attraction of the void? Do you feel the pull as you look over the edge of a high place, knowing that you're only a second away from death if you choose?

'Are you going to exhume Marion Spear?' Wightman asked, interrupting Tartaglia's train of thought.

He shook his head. 'We need to find out a lot more about her background. For now, let's concentrate on the three confirmed victims. What about where the girls lived?' He glanced over at Donovan. 'Sam, any thoughts?'

She stared at the board for a moment, ruffling her hair with her fingers. 'Well, Gemma only lived a couple of miles away from Ellie, which is a coincidence. But I can't see any link with Islington.'

'Maybe he has a job where he travels around London,' Wightman said.

'Or maybe he met them over the internet and where they live is irrelevant,' Dickenson added, still sticking doggedly to her original theory.

'But I told you, he didn't meet Gemma over the internet,'

Donovan replied, with an exasperated look in Dickenson's direction. 'At least not according to what was on her computer. There was some other connection, wasn't there? I mean, what holds true for her, may also hold true for the others.'

'We'll know for sure once we get the results back from the analysis of Laura and Ellie's computers,' Tartaglia said, just as Cornish's tall, slim figure appeared in the doorway. He was carrying a shiny black leather briefcase, which Tartaglia had never seen before, and looked sleek as a Savile Row tailor's dummy in a well-cut, silver-grey suit.

'Mark, sorry to interrupt. I need a word.'

Cornish's manner was tense. He rarely made the trip from Hendon down to Barnes and Tartaglia felt instantly wary. Leaving the group still speculating about possible interpretations of the locations, Tartaglia followed Cornish out of the room and down the corridor to Clarke's office.

Cornish shut the door behind them and gestured towards Clarke's chair. 'Have a seat.'

'I'm fine here,' Tartaglia replied, feeling even more suspicious. 'You take the chair. They're like gold-dust in this office.'

He rolled the chair over towards Cornish and perched himself on the edge of the desk. Cornish studied it with distaste before brushing the seat with his hand and sitting down gingerly. He opened the briefcase and thrust a folded copy of the *Evening Standard* at Tartaglia. 'You'd better read that.'

As Tartaglia unfolded it and saw the front-page headline, he felt his stomach knot. 'Metropolitan Police Hunt Serial Killer'. How on earth had they found out so quickly? It was incredible how journalists managed to worm their foul tentacles into the most unlikely places. Spite and jealousy often played a part and some people would do anything for a bung or a free lunch. But it would be almost impossible to trace the source. Wherever the truth lay, for the press to have discovered what was going on at such an early stage was very bad news.

'I'm sure the leak's not from here,' he said, quickly scanning the first few paragraphs. 'None of the team would...'

'Of course not,' Cornish snapped, although his expression was less than convincing. 'But it's definitely someone on the inside. They've got all the bloody details.'

Tartaglia searched down the page again. 'Except for the lock of hair and the GHB.'

'That's something, I suppose,' Cornish said bitterly. He snatched back the paper, shoved it in his briefcase and flipped the locks several times, as though he was securing a top-secret document. Dumping the case down on the floor, he stood up and started to pace the small room, hands stuffed in his trouser pockets. 'But they know about the rings and the fake marriage ceremony. That's far too much, in my book.' He turned back momentarily to Tartaglia with a pained look. 'And they've given him a bloody moniker. "The Bridegroom", I ask you.'

'That's how the killer signed himself in the final email.'

'Exactly. Which means they've talked to someone who's seen the emails. We're leaking like a bloody sieve.' Cornish paused in front of Clarke's mirror and made a minute adjustment to the knot of his pale blue silk tie.

The gesture almost made Tartaglia smile. Trust Cornish to be worrying about his appearance at such a time. 'You know how difficult it is keeping such things out of the press, sir. It's not the first time...'

'They're even speculating about the number of victims,' Cornish continued, as if he hadn't heard. 'They're wondering how many suicides have been misdiagnosed, wondering if we have another Shipman on our hands.' Cornish stared into the mirror, smoothing his sleek, silver hair with a palm, as if to calm himself.

'That's ludicrous.'

'Of course it is.' Cornish suddenly swung around, expression startled. 'We are sure about the third, aren't we?'

Tartaglia nodded. 'Dr Blake confirmed it. The tox results are unlikely to tell us anything, but a lock of hair is definitely missing, same as with Gemma Kramer.'

'But how the hell do they know about number three? You only dug her up this morning.'

'As I said, sir, this is not the first time there's been a leak.' He had to make the point even though he knew that Cornish wasn't listening.

Cornish shook his head slowly. 'This is exactly what I didn't want to happen. How do they expect us to do our jobs with this sort of pressure, under a bloody microscope, all the details out there for any Tom, Dick or Harry to pick over?'

'You've spoken to the press office?'

'Of course, but there's nothing they can do now. The genie's out of the bottle and there's no putting it back. Damage limitation's our main objective. I'm doing a briefing in time for the evening news.' He paused, deep in thought for a moment, then turned to Tartaglia, rocking back on his heels, hands back in his pockets, looking uncomfortable. 'Look, Mark. This has forced my hand, I hope you understand.'

'Meaning?'

'Well, I'm going to have to ask you to step down as SIO.'

'What? You can't blame me for this?'

Cornish pursed his lips. 'Of course I don't. But this is all getting out of control. With Trevor in hospital, I have no choice.'

'So you're taking over?'

Cornish shook his head and folded his arms defensively. 'Can't do that. Haven't got the time. I'm bringing someone experienced in.'

Tartaglia felt a jolt of anger and the blood rise to his face. He stared hard at Cornish who looked suddenly embarrassed. 'But I'm experienced, sir. You could come in as SIO and handle the press. I could still report directly to you.'

'Can't do, Mark. We have a linked series on our hands. It's big news and I must make sure everything's properly handled.'

'But I've worked two serial cases in the last two years, both with a successful conviction.'

'I know. But Clarke headed up the team.'

Fists clenched behind his back, nails digging deep into his palms, Tartaglia shook his head, still not quite believing what was happening. 'We worked together. He'd tell you the same if he were here.'

Cornish forced a smile. 'Look, Mark, I'm not doubting that. You're bloody good at what you do. That's why I asked you to step up as SIO in the first place.'

'Yes, and I'm the one who's found out that there's a serial killer at work. I can handle the investigation. You don't need to bring in someone from outside.'

'I must, given what's happened, given that things are now a lot more...' Cornish paused, searching for the word then shrugged his shoulders apologetically. 'Well, complicated, shall we say, and high profile. It's very delicate, don't you see? I need someone very experienced on the ground in Barnes to take overall charge.'

'I could carry on reporting to you,' Tartaglia continued, almost shouting. 'It's been done before.'

Cornish blinked, speaking slowly between clenched his teeth. 'I told you, I haven't got the time.'

Or the experience, Tartaglia thought, bitterly. That's what was at the root of it all. The other superintendents and chief superintendents up in Hendon wouldn't think twice about stepping in and taking charge, leaving Tartaglia as SIO. But not Cornish. He didn't feel secure enough, just in case he screwed up. It was fucking unfair. This should have been Tartaglia's big break, an important stepping-stone in the path to becoming a DCI himself. He had done all the spadework. He had found out about the other girls. Now, just because Cornish wasn't up to it, someone else was going to come in, steal his thunder and take over.

'So, who is it?' Tartaglia said, trying to contain his desire to punch Cornish.

Cornish spoke quietly. 'DCI Carolyn Steele. Maybe you've come across her.'

Carolyn Steele. Although Tartaglia had never had any direct dealings with her, he knew who she was by sight. There weren't that many female DCIs heading up murder teams, certainly not half-decent looking ones. In her early forties, he guessed, Steele was short and shapely in an athletic sort of way, with dark hair, almost luminously pale skin and a pair of striking green eyes. She'd been working up in Hendon for a while and had a good enough reputation, although that didn't make it any better. Before that, he thought she'd been running one of the murder teams based in East London.

Another thought occurred to Tartaglia and made him even more furious. 'When did you decide this? It wasn't today, was it? You're not just doing this because of the leak?'

Cornish shook his head, avoiding his eyes as he picked at a tiny thread from his jacket sleeve. 'Once it was clear that we were looking at a series, I had to do something. As I said, I'm very busy. It's just a shame it couldn't be managed in a more gradual way.'

Before Tartaglia had a chance to reply, there was a knock and Carolyn Steele put her head around the door.

'They told me you were in here, sir,' she said to Cornish. 'Are you ready for me?'

Cornish nodded. 'Come in Carolyn. This is Mark Tartaglia.'

Steele closed the door behind her and turned abruptly to Tartaglia. She held out a small, firm hand that was cold to the touch, studying him in a way that instantly irritated him.

'Hello, Mark. I'm looking forward to working with you. It's an interesting case we've got here.'

11

Carolyn Steele sat in Clarke's office, reading through the files. Tartaglia had given her a full debriefing and, so far, she couldn't fault anything that he had done in the investigation or the conclusions that he had drawn. Before coming, she had checked him out with various people up in Hendon. He was generally well thought of, although very much Clarke's man, with a reputation for being a little headstrong. But stepping into that small, claustrophobic office and meeting him for the first time, arrogant and cock-sure were the words that came to mind. The air almost hummed with it, the antagonism in his eyes blinding. She was taken aback by the strength of his reaction. After all, she was just following orders. It wasn't her fault she had been parachuted in over his head.

Was it because she was a woman, perhaps? Anyone who thought sexism in the Met was a thing of the past had his or her head in the sand. Perhaps Cornish had prepared the ground badly or, worse still, had deliberately said something to undermine her. It wouldn't be the first time, she thought, remembering a previous investigation where, for reasons of his own, the waters had been poisoned by her superior. Cornish had seemed even more awkward than usual and he had scuttled out of the room and back to Hendon almost immediately as if he seemed embarrassed or had something to hide. She had never worked directly for him before and found his behaviour hard to read. Perhaps he was the kind who liked to light the touch paper, step back and watch what happened.

It had been particularly awkward asking Tartaglia to vacate Clarke's office; yet another slap in the face. But there was no available alternative, the facilities at Barnes being even more cramped and dilapidated than she had been led to believe, with barely room to swing a mouse, let alone a cat. She had made the mistake of parking her car in the building's small underground car park, only to be told that it was for the exclusive use of the robbery squad on the second floor. She had to take her chances with the rest of them, fighting for a free space in the open back yard, in the end blocking someone in and having to leave a note. For the first time, she actually thought with some fondness of her glass box of an office up in Hendon. Hopefully she wouldn't have to be away for long, although with a case like this, anything was possible.

She had left Tartaglia and his team in charge of the Gemma Kramer investigation, continuing to research the girl's background, checking phone records, the places she visited every day, the people she saw, trying to find a link with the other victims. The other DI, Gary Jones, and his team were doing the same for Laura Benedetti and Ellie Best. Unfortunately, Clarke's team was even more stretched than Cornish had led her to believe, with only two DIs rather than the usual three, and even lighter in the lower ranks. The issue was common throughout the Met. Of course, there were the usual explanations; several members of the team had moved on elsewhere, yet to be replaced, one was off on long-term sick leave, one on maternity leave, and another about to join her shortly. But with a high profile case like this one, it didn't help. Not for the first time, she wondered if she had been handed a poisoned chalice.

She glanced at her watch. Cornish would have just finished the media briefing. Following on from that, the press office had managed to get her a last-minute slot on *Crimewatch* the next day. She knew they were likely to be inundated with calls, all of which would have to be followed up whether helpful or not, taking up valuable time and manpower. But there was no alternative. With little to go on, they urgently needed more information. Once the calls started coming in, it would be vital to narrow the field of focus as far as possible. The next step was to call in a profiler.

As usual, neither of the Met's two in-house profilers was available. Looking down the handful of other names on the National Crime Faculty approved register, a few were familiar. However, she was unlikely to have the luxury of choice. Although she wanted input right away, it was going to be difficult finding anybody immediately who had time to spare. Scattered all over the country, they were usually tied up with academic or clinical matters and she knew from experience that you could wait weeks, or even months, before getting an opinion, by which time it was often of no use.

A particular name kept leaping out at her from the list. Although she tried to avoid looking at it, her eyes couldn't help returning to it. He was the obvious solution. He was based in London and, if anyone was likely to do her a favour and drop everything, he would. But should she ask him? Was it wise? Probably not. Shoes off, stockinged feet up on the edge of the desk drawer, she swivelled slowly from side to side, weighing up the pros and cons, Clarke's ancient chair squeaking worryingly beneath her. No, it wasn't wise but who else was there? Besides, it was the right thing for the case. She would worry about the consequences later. She swung her feet onto the floor, feeling for her shoes with her toes as she stretched for the phone and dialled his number. It was disturbing that she could still remember it by heart.

'It's an unusual case, don't you think?' Steele said, pretending to focus on her bitter lemon, swirling the ice around in the glass, as she studied Dr Patrick Kennedy's reaction out of the corner of her eye. Although he was doing his best to appear only casually interested in what she had told him, she could tell he was intrigued. It amused her that with all his knowledge of psychology he could sometimes be so transparent, as well as unaware of the fact. She looked up at him and smiled sweetly. 'Naturally, your name came to mind because of the book you're writing on serial killers. I thought you'd find the case particularly interesting so I haven't spoken to anyone else about it yet.'

'I appreciate that,' he said, after taking a swig of sauvignon blanc, a broad grin on his boyish face. 'You've only given me a brief outline, but I can see all sorts of fascinating aspects about the case already.'

They were sitting at the back of a half-empty wine bar in South Kensington, around the corner from where Kennedy worked in the Unit for Forensic Psychology, part of London University. Kennedy was well known within the Met and she had suggested somewhere near him, rather than Barnes, as she didn't want any of her new team seeing them together until he was officially on board. She was now regretting leaving the choice to him. Although it was late afternoon, the air was still thick with the smell of fried food and cigarette smoke, left over from the lunchtime crowd. Her hair and clothes would reek of it afterwards and she hoped she would-n't have to stay long.

As usual, Kennedy was looking good. Dressed casually for a change in a leather jacket, shirt and jeans, his broad face was almost unlined and his thick, wavy brown hair devoid of any grey. Although just over forty, according to the brief biographical infor-mation on his website that she had re-checked earlier, he could easily be taken for one of his postgraduate students. It had been a stroke of luck bumping into him the previous week at the Peel Centre in Hendon, where she normally worked. Kennedy had just given a lecture on Behavioural Investigative Analysis, the new buzzword for profiling, at the Met's Crime Academy. He was trying to find his way around the huge, sprawling complex to one of the canteens but had lost his way. It had been a while since they had last seen each other and he seemed uncharacteristically hesitant, almost embarrassed, as he asked her to join him for a coffee. But she was late for a meeting and they agreed to catch up sometime soon for a drink. He had left a couple of messages on her answer machine a few days later, suggesting a couple of dates, but feeling suddenly wary, she had failed to return the calls. At least he didn't seem to be holding it against her now.

'So, Patrick, what do you think? Do you have time to look at it?'

She caught his eye, trying to gauge his reaction. He pursed his lips and took a large mouthful of wine, spinning it out. He knew he was her best option at such short notice, that nobody else would be likely to make space for her immediately. Calling in personal favours was not something she liked to do, as a rule, but what other choice did she have? She needed input right away. And from his perspective, it wasn't often that such a case came along. Surely, he wouldn't say no.

He put his glass down with a shrug. 'I'm very busy at the moment, but what's new.'

'So, can you help?' she said, wanting to hurry things along, desperate to get his agreement and get out of that foul-smelling, airless place.

'From the little you've told me, it's certainly intriguing. I'd need to juggle a few things.' He let the sentence hang, studying her carefully in a way that was suddenly intimate and made her feel uncomfortable. She had the impression that there was something he wanted to say and she hoped he wasn't going to allude to what had happened between them before. Then he nodded slowly and smiled. 'It's good of you to ask me, Carolyn. And I'm very pleased to see you again, even if you don't return my calls.'

'Well?' she asked, ignoring the comment. 'Will you help?'

He nodded slowly. 'Yes, I think I can. It's a shame the press have got involved quite so early and that the source seems to be so accurate. But, in a funny way, that may be to our advantage.'

'How?'

'Because it buys us some time. The reptile will have to go to ground for a while. No blushing young virgin's going to march up the aisle with him now, are they? When can I see the files?'

'I'll get copies sent over to you straight away.' She scribbled down the Barnes address on the back of a business card and passed it to him. 'This is where I'm based for the moment.'

As she stood up to go, he put his hand on her arm. 'Surely you don't have to rush off? Stay and finish your drink.'

She smiled, shaking her head. 'Gotta go. They'll be wondering where I am. I'll see you tomorrow morning, my office at eight a.m. OK?'

He returned her smile, although he looked disappointed, and gave her a mock salute.

'Ay, ay, ma'am. Anything you say. As always.'

Early the next morning, Tartaglia headed down the corridor towards the office he was once again sharing with DI Gary Jones. On his way in, he had picked up a bacon sarni and a cup of good, strong cappuccino from the local deli, looking forward to tucking into both of them at his desk undisturbed before the morning briefing. Jones was out until lunchtime and he would have the room to himself, for a change. Approaching Clarke's office, he heard voices and laughter coming from inside. The door was half-open door and he saw Steele sitting behind the desk, talking to someone hidden from view. As he passed by, Steele turned and caught his eye.

'Mark, there you are. Can you come in here for a minute?'

Tartaglia pushed back the door and saw a familiar figure in an expensive-looking suit lounging casually against the windowsill next to Steele. The man gave him a wide grin.

'Hi there, Mark. How are you these days?'

Fuck. Dr Patrick Kennedy. The profiler who had nearly screwed up the Barton case. Feeling instantly suspicious, Tartaglia waited in the doorway for Steele to say something.

'Patrick's just been telling me that you've worked together before on another case.'

Kennedy was still grinning. 'Yes, Mark and I are old friends.'

'Patrick's going to assist us with this one,' Steele said, seemingly unaware that anything was wrong.

Unable to trust himself to reply, Tartaglia said nothing, staring hard at Kennedy. He hadn't changed at all. Glossy and smug, with his thick mane of hair – an indecent amount of hair for a real man, according to Clarke, who was thinning on top – Kennedy looked more like a game show host than a university professor, particularly inappropriate in the context of Clarke's dingy, threadbare office. Had Steele brought Kennedy in herself? Or was the decision down to Cornish, something that wouldn't surprise him at all?

'Patrick needs to see the places where the girls died,' she continued. 'Can you give him the guided tour?'

'I was supposed to be trying to track down Marion Spear's family this morning,' he said as levelly as possible.

'Get someone else to do it. Patrick's part of the team now and you're the best person to bring him up-to-date.'

'I don't have a car.' It was a lame excuse but he couldn't think of anything better.

Kennedy pulled out a set of keys from his jacket pocket and jangled them at Tartaglia. 'Let's take mine. I'll drive; you navigate. You can fill me in on the way.'

Increasingly impatient and angry, Tartaglia sat in the passenger seat of Kennedy's old, dark green Morgan, which was parked in front of St Sebastian's, the scene of Gemma Kramer's murder. Kennedy had been gone for almost three quarters of an hour. There was little to see inside the church and Tartaglia was sure he must be deliberately spinning it all out in some pathetic show of power. The car radio was out of commission, the aerial snapped off, and the only cassettes Tartaglia could find were the soundtracks to *Phantom of the Opera* and *Les Misérables*, both of which would be torture. Short of making pointless calls or playing games on his mobile, he had nothing to do. Perhaps he should have gone with Kennedy into the church but he had already had more than enough of Kennedy's company and comments on the case.

Everything about Kennedy grated. He was so self-seeking, so arrogant, so unashamedly sure of himself. Earlier, a small posse of photographers and reporters had been hanging around outside the gates of the car park in Barnes. Instead of ignoring them and driving away like any sensible person, Kennedy had stopped and rolled down the window to talk to them, also waving cheerily at a well-known actor who lived next door who had come out to walk his dog. Whether or not the actor had a clue who Kennedy was, the reporters lapped it up. When asked by one of them if he was now engaged on profiling 'The Bridegroom' case, Kennedy winked and smiled enigmatically, with a 'no comment' that any decent reporter would take as absolute confirmation. Remembering how Kennedy had courted publicity in the Barton case, Tartaglia wondered if Kennedy had actually tipped them off. Whether true or not, photos of Kennedy's mug would be plastered all over the evening papers. It was amusing to think what Cornish, who hated any form of publicity, would make of that.

Outside, the temperature was only a few degrees above freezing and Tartaglia had been forced to switch on the engine to keep warm and to stop the windows from misting up completely. The car idled noisily, white smoke gusting from the exhaust. In spite of the gleaming paintwork and chrome trimmings, it felt as though it was on its last legs. Clunking and jerking, it had gasped its way around the tour of the two other London churches where the other girls had died. Every time Kennedy changed gear, it made alarming grinding sounds and it had nearly expired behind the car park where Marion Spear had fallen to her death. No doubt it spent a lot of time in an expensive repair shop, as Tartaglia couldn't see Kennedy getting his manicured hands dirty under the bonnet.

Above the noise of the engine, Tartaglia heard the sound of someone singing. He looked up to see Kennedy sauntering down the church path towards him, swinging his briefcase back and forth like a child with a new toy.

'Let's grab a bite to eat. I'm absolutely famished,' Kennedy said cheerfully, levering himself in through the driver's door and automatically passing his briefcase to Tartaglia to hold. He slid down into the leather bucket seat and slammed the gear into first. As he tried to pull away, the car lurched forward and stalled.

He grunted. 'Like all women, she's a trifle temperamental.'

Tartaglia stared at him aghast. 'She?'

Kennedy patted the steering wheel and grinned as he tried the ignition again. 'Daisy, my motor. Mark, this is Daisy,' he said, waving his hand expansively towards the rattling bonnet of the car as if he were making a formal introduction.

Tartaglia closed his eyes momentarily, stifling a groan. 'We ought to head back to Barnes,' he said, trying to ignore the pangs of hunger in his stomach. Even though it was almost two o'clock and he'd had nothing to eat since early that morning, starvation was preferable to another hour in Kennedy's company.

'I've got to eat,' Kennedy replied emphatically, in the manner of someone not used to skipping a meal. 'I'm sure Carolyn will understand if we're not back pronto. I know a decent little tapas bar just around the corner. I'll put it on expenses,' he added, as if that was all that was needed. He clunked the car into gear again and they juddered away from the pavement.

Carolyn. It wasn't the first time Kennedy had dropped her Christian name into the conversation and it felt as though he was trying to make a point. Steele had also used Kennedy's Christian name and it appeared that she and Kennedy were already on pretty friendly terms, something that Tartaglia had been feeling increasingly annoyed about all morning.

The tapas bar was in a small parade of shops facing Ealing Green. Kennedy seemed to be a valued customer, the Spanish manager greeting him like a long-lost friend and offering them drinks on the house. Feeling churlish, Tartaglia insisted on a glass of tap water while Kennedy accepted a jumbo glass of house Rioja. Tartaglia wasn't averse to the odd drink at lunchtime but he was buggered if he was going to relax and make merry with Kennedy. While they waited for two portions of mixed tapas, Tartaglia reached into his jacket pocket for a cigarette to calm himself and fill the silence. As he pulled out his lighter and packet of Marlboro reds, Kennedy shook his head, smiling and pointing at the small 'No Smoking' sign immediately behind Tartaglia on the wall. Inwardly seething, Tartaglia zipped away the pack and took a long sip of water. Such a stance was surprising, given most

Spaniards' love of good, strong, tobacco anywhere and at any time of day. But there were puritans in every race. This was what it would soon be like, once the smoking ban came into force. Sanctimonious pricks like Kennedy would have a field day.

'Aren't you interested to know what I think?' Kennedy asked.

'Of course,' Tartaglia said, as politely as possible. He might as well listen. Steele would be getting the full story when they got back to Barnes and it would be important to be prepared. 'I just know how you experts like to take your time, consider everything carefully, before you give us an opinion.'

Kennedy relaxed back in his chair. 'Sure. I've only got the barest of details at the moment. But I can give you some off-the-cuff comments... which might help you. I've been up all night reading the files and it's pretty fascinating stuff.' He raised his eyebrows meaningfully, as if waiting for some sort of encouragement.

Tartaglia steeled himself. 'So, what have you found out?'

Kennedy sucked in his breath and was silent for a moment as if he was considering the question carefully. The mannerism was something Tartaglia remembered from the past. It had seemed a put-on then and it still seemed fake, but he said nothing. After a moment, Kennedy leaned forwards, planted his elbows on the table and clasped his hands in front of him. 'Well, the locations, the churches are particularly interesting.'

'What about the car park?'

Kennedy shook his head. 'I think we can forget that one. It doesn't fit in any respect.'

'But Marion Spear fell to her death like the others and it's just around the corner from where Gemma Kramer died. Surely that warrants closer investigation?'

'What's the point?' Kennedy shrugged.

'I was hoping you'd tell me, Dr Kennedy. You're the one with the imagination.'

Kennedy smiled. 'Psychological insight, you mean. Think of Cinderella. If the shoe don't fit, no amount of trying it on will change things.'

Tartaglia looked away for a moment, resisting the impulse to smack him. The fact that Kennedy was prepared to dismiss Marion Spear's death so categorically was enough to give him fresh hope. Kennedy had been wrong in the past and there was a good chance he was wrong now. Even before hearing his view, Tartaglia had been determined to carry on looking into what had happened to her, at least until they had strong evidence to rule her out. He had managed to get hold of her mother's phone number and, whatever Kennedy said, he was going to call her as soon as he got back to the office. He just hoped Kennedy wouldn't try and queer the pitch with Steele.

'I just think it's worth following up,' he said quietly, meeting Kennedy's gaze. 'That's all.'

Kennedy shook his head. 'Square pegs and round holes. Don't waste your time on it.'

Tartaglia glanced away again, watching the manager unload what looked like their food from the dumb waiter behind the bar. Just sit back and listen, don't argue, Tartaglia told himself, as the manager came bustling over with the assorted plates of tapas. It wasn't worth risking World War Three at this point.

'Let's go back to the three confirmed victims,' Kennedy said, loading his plate with slices of ham and more than his fair share of hot squid in tomato sauce without waiting for Tartaglia. Taking a large bite, Kennedy pronounced the squid delicious. 'The fact that they all died in churches has a particular significance for our killer. Let's call him Tom, although of course that's not his real name.' He shovelled more squid into his mouth.

'You don't think it's just part of the act, the way he attracts the girls, making them think they're going through some sort of religious ceremony?'

Kennedy shook his head, struggling to speak, mouth still full. 'No. I think... actually... it means something particular to him... maybe some sort of "V" sign at the church and the establishment. I'm sure he had a religious upbringing and I think the profanity appeals to him. It's a sort of personal joke.'

Tartaglia's personal theory was that Tom had chosen churches because they were places that would lull the girls into a false sense of security, but Kennedy's idea was interesting and not implausible. He spooned some prawns in garlic sauce onto his plate and waited for Kennedy to continue.

'Look, we have three girls, all roughly the same age,' Kennedy said, between mouthfuls. 'We have to ask ourselves, why does he choose *them*? What makes them vulnerable? Why are they falling prey?'

Tartaglia shrugged, helping himself to a few small slices of cured ham and olives. 'You tell me.'

Kennedy was silent for a moment as if he was formulating the theory. 'It's sexual, of course. All about control and dominance. These poor little darlings are easy pickings. No doubt he believes they deserve their fate. Although he doesn't sexually assault them per se, killing them, watching them die, is his equivalent. He may even achieve orgasm when he does it, although my guess is that he's impotent.'

'No trace of semen was found at the crime scene.'

'It doesn't matter. Whether he has a wank or not, it's still sexual. He's like those perverts who watch snuff movies. Only, he wants it live. And now he's got a taste for it, he's going to keep going back for more, possibly developing his little fantasy as he perfects his skills. I'm sure he thinks he's so clever that he won't be caught.'

'Really?' Tartaglia said flatly, trying what little Kennedy had left of the ham. Kennedy was spouting the usual serial killer stuff that you could find in any station bookshop.

'He's also bloody ballsy,' Kennedy said, stabbing the air with his knife. 'I'll give him that. He's taking a big risk that he won't be disturbed, although that possibly adds to the excitement. This is a highly organised individual, someone calm and methodical in everything he does. He plans the killings down to the last detail. He's also a good communicator and highly literate, judging from the emails. He pitches them just right for each girl.'

Annoyingly, Tartaglia found himself agreeing with Kennedy again, although he would rather be punched in the face than say so. 'Maybe he has had a good education. But how does that help us find him? What about his age, background, formative life experiences, shoe size and inside leg measurement? That's what you profilers are so good at working out. What do you see in your crystal ball?'

'No need to be facetious, Mark. You and I are old friends. We can both take credit for catching Michael Barton.'

Tartaglia shook his head in disbelief. 'You really think you can take credit for Barton?'

'Naturally,' Kennedy replied, with a disingenuous smile, using his napkin to wipe a trace of tomato sauce from his lips. 'I know we've had our little disagreements but we were all part of the winning team that caught the reptile.' Noting Tartaglia's expression, he added: 'Anyway, let's not waste energy raking over history. Regarding this case, I'll need some time to put together a full profile on Tom. But you're looking at a very different type of individual to Barton. Our Tom's a classic psychopath.'

Tartaglia sighed. 'Yes, yes. He feels no remorse or empathy with the victim. They are just a means to an end and he has no conscience. Tell me something I don't know.'

Kennedy forced an indulgent smile, looking like a teacher trying to deal with a difficult pupil. 'Well, judging from the emails, I'd say this one was a grammar school boy or possibly privately educated. That should help you narrow the search when you eventually find some suspects.'

'That's an interesting theory,' Tartaglia said flatly. He finished what was left of the ham and added some butter bean salad to his plate, trying to block out Kennedy from his consciousness, wishing he had allowed himself a glass of wine to go with it and dull the pain.

'Look, it's always about resources, isn't it?' Kennedy continued, oblivious. 'Once Carolyn does *Crimewatch* tonight, you're going to be inundated. You know what it's like? Too much information, most of it useless, and not enough manpower or hours in the day. You're going to have to focus. I'm telling you, don't waste your time on the car park girl.' He wagged his finger at Tartaglia, with a knowing grin. 'I know you. You haven't given up on her, have you? Just stick with the three girls and find out what they have in common, how it was Tom came across them.'

'That's what we're already doing,' Tartaglia said, scraping up some beans from his plate, trying not to let Kennedy rile him further.

'There have got to be similarities,' Kennedy said emphatically. He tossed back his wine and waved his empty glass in the air until he caught the manager's attention. 'Sure you won't join me?' he asked Tartaglia, as the manager came over with the bottle.

Tartaglia shook his head. 'You shouldn't either. You're driving.'

'Lighten up, Mark. One more won't hurt. I'm a big guy and I can take it.' Kennedy patted his chest with satisfaction as he watched the manager fill the glass to the brim.

As the manager moved away, Tartaglia could hold back no longer. 'You know Tom's going to try and do it again, don't you? I'm sure he's got several prospects lined up.'

'Hang on a minute,' Kennedy said, tipping the remains of the little bowls of tapas onto his plate. 'With all the publicity, what girl in her right mind is going to go along with him now?'

Tartaglia slapped down his knife and fork on his plate. 'But they're NOT in their right mind, are they? That's why they're such easy prey.'

'He's been outed. Nobody's going to fall for the suicide pact rubbish now.'

'What do you think he's going to do? Give up and go back to the day job? He's a chameleon. He'll adapt. Tom's got a taste for killing. He's going to have to satisfy the craving again somehow, even if he has to change the game.'

'But as we know, most serial killers are creatures of habit.'

'This man's cleverer than most. Think about it. These young girls are just a piece of piss for him; they're too easy. He'll soon want something more challenging. The press hype may be the catalyst.'

'If you're right, that gives us an opportunity. He may screw up.'

'Let's hope so. I'm afraid I don't think you're going to have long to wait.'

12

Tom stared at the TV screen, smiling. Detective Chief Inspector Carolyn Steele was doing well, her husky voice hitting just the right note of gravity mixed with emotion, as she appealed for witnesses. Shame though about the boxy jacket and plain white blouse. They weren't flattering. Maybe she thought it made her look business-like, but a uniform would have been better, if that was the image she wanted. There was also something about a woman in uniform that was a real turn-on. For a moment he pictured Carolyn slowly undoing the buttons and peeling off the layers to music, down to stockings and suspenders and a skimpy black bra and thong.

It reminded him of a stag night he'd been to a few years before. There had been three strippers dressed up as WPCs with handcuffs and truncheons, two bottle-blondes and a brunette, all clapped-out slags, well past their sell-by date. Having taken off their clothes to indiscriminate drunken applause, the brunette had made a beeline for him, slithering her stinking, sweat-slippery body down onto his lap, asking if he wanted extras. She tried to cuff him to a chair but he smacked her hard and shoved her off him, throwing her onto the floor. She hit her face on something, drawing blood, and started screaming hysterically, threatening to call the cops. Everyone was roaring with laughter, even the other whores joined in. But in the end, he'd been forced to give the slag a whacking great tip to shut her up and leave him alone. The reek of her cheap perfume had stayed in his nose for days.

But there was nothing cheap about Carolyn Steele. She was a class act, just the sort of woman he liked. Her sleek black hair framed her broad face nicely and the make-up artist had dolled her up to look as good as Fiona Bruce. Better, in fact.

The camera cut to a crime scene reconstruction. A young girl, posing as Gemma Kramer, stood outside St Sebastian's talking to a man dressed in a dark overcoat. It took him a few seconds to realise that the man was supposed to be him. What a joke. While the girl bore a passing resemblance to Gemma, the man was nothing like him. Wrong hair, wrong clothes, wrong build. Even his body language was wrong as he talked to Gemma, bending forwards to kiss her as if he actually enjoyed it. The fucking plods were way off the mark there. Couldn't they get anything right? Details were so important. Details were what mattered.

The camera retreated, showing a panoramic view of the church. It was just as he recalled it, although he had never bothered to admire it from that angle. A head and shoulders photograph of Gemma appeared on the screen. She was wearing school uniform and looked even younger than he remembered. The sight of her sent a shiver of pleasure through him, taking him straight back. He closed his eyes, struggling to block out the droning commentary, trying to focus. What he would give to live each exquisite moment again. He could picture the real flesh and blood Gemma so clearly, he could almost touch her, smell her. The long brown hair, the fine down on her cheeks, the creamy skin with its sprinkling of freckles. Soon she would fade, details blurring, then bleaching into nothingness, like an old photograph, until she was of no use to him. As with the others, he would have to replace her. But for the moment, she was still fresh enough. In his mind, she looked at him with her clear blue eyes and held out her hand, enticing him forward. He smiled, and this time she smiled back. She wanted it as much as he did, the little bitch. He took her hand, feeling it cold in his, but she was still smiling, egging him on. As he drew her slowly into the dark interior of the church, he felt the rush of blood once again.

13

Donovan pulled up outside Tartaglia's flat in Shepherd's Bush and killed the engine. She had been busy all day and had hardly set foot in the office. The only time she had caught sight of Tartaglia was on his way up the stairs, coming in from the trip with Kennedy as she made her way out of the building to follow up on what had proved to be another dead end. Pausing briefly on the half-landing, he had hurriedly sketched out what happened with Kennedy and they arranged to meet after work at his flat for a late drink, when they would have time to talk uninterrupted.

Although she was not on Clarke's team at the time of the Barton investigation, she couldn't help agreeing with Tartaglia: Kennedy seemed very pleased with himself. Somehow, he made them all feel as though they had a celebrity in their midst and Yvette Dickenson seemed particularly impressed, asking Kennedy to sign her copy of his latest book on profiling. He lapped it up as if it were his due, flashing his mouthful of brilliant white teeth and scribbling down a dedication in huge, loopy handwriting, with Yvette gazing at him like a teenage girl, even in her state. It was sick-making. However, Kennedy seemed to be oblivious to the stir he was causing, Steele being the prime focus of his attentions. Donovan couldn't fathom the precise nature of their relationship but had decided that it definitely went beyond the purely professional, although Steele treated Kennedy more like an old friend than a lover. Perhaps she hadn't noticed the way Kennedy looked at her. Maybe she wasn't interested. It was going to be worth keeping a close watch on the pair.

Lights glimmered through the crack at the top of the shutters in Tartaglia's sitting room but there was no response when she rang the bell. When she dialled his home number from her mobile, the answer machine clicked on. Maybe he'd given up on her or nipped out for a pint of milk or a quick drink on his own. But she was sure he'd be back. He wasn't the type to forget an arrangement. A fine drizzle had set in and she climbed back into her car and turned on the engine to keep warm, eyes scanning the road in front while she waited.

Tartaglia had seemed more than usually on edge when she had seen him earlier. No doubt the hours spent with Kennedy had had something to do with it. But she sensed there was more to it than that. The tension between him and Steele was obvious to everyone, the atmosphere unpleasant and heavy like before a storm. Although they both went out of their way to be polite, each deferring almost unnecessarily to the other, they reminded her of a pair of dogs, hackles up, skirting warily around each other, spoiling for a fight. She just hoped for Tartaglia's sake that he would be able to keep his temper under control and not do anything stupid.

Everything was Cornish's fault and she didn't blame Tartaglia for a second for feeling so bitter – no one did, certainly not those in Tartaglia's immediate team. There had been no need to bring in Steele. But Cornish hadn't the balls to oversee things himself and to let Tartaglia carry on running things. Self-preservation was Cornish's motto and he had made sure that Steele's neck was on the line, not his. If she succeeded in finding the killer, he would take ultimate credit for it. If she failed, he would step back and she would be the one blamed. Donovan wondered if Steele knew this, if she had had any choice in the matter.

She waited a few more minutes and was on the point of leaving a note and driving off when she caught sight of Tartaglia briefly illuminated under a street lamp, jogging around the corner at the far end of the road. Climbing out of the car, she popped the locks and sheltered under her umbrella as she watched him slog along the pavement towards her. As he spotted her, he waved.

'Good thing I was late,' she said, when he came up to her, panting. Hair soaked, water running down his face, he was wearing running shorts, trainers and a white T-shirt that stuck to his skin. Bloody hell, he looked great, even like that, she thought, hoping he couldn't read her mind.

'Sorry,' he said, in between deep breaths, plastering his hair back off his face with his hand and stretching his legs. 'Thought you'd been held up, so I went out for a run. Helps clear the mind.'

She followed him up the path to the front door. 'Wouldn't it be better if you gave up the fags?'

He turned round and grinned, still out of breath. 'What, like you, you mean? I saw you having a quick one in the car park this morning. Thought you'd stopped?'

'Don't give me a hard time. I need it at the moment. Look, I've brought you a present.'

'What is it?' he said, eyeing the plastic bag in her hand as he fumbled in his pocket for his keys.

'A tape of this evening's appeal on *Crimewatch*. I went by my flat to collect it. In spite of what you said earlier, I thought you might like to see it.'

He gave her a withering look as they went inside. 'Just what I've always wanted.' He unlocked the door to his flat and held the door open for her.

'Steele did a good job. Came across really well.'

'I just hope it shakes out some new information,' he said, closing the door behind them. 'I'm going to take a shower. If the phone rings, can you answer it? It may be Sally-Anne.'

'Any news?'

'Sorry, I should have told you. She called earlier to say that Trevor came round a couple of hours ago.'

'Thank God,' she said, feeling an instant surge of relief. 'That's fantastic news.'

He was grinning at her. 'And guess what, Sally-Anne played Eminem really loudly in his ear and after ten minutes he opened his eyes.'

She laughed, trying to picture the scene. 'Typical Trevor. Did he yell at her to turn it off?'

'Probably. It's about the only fucking chink of light in the last twenty-four shitty hours. Sally-Anne said she'll call back once she's found out when I can visit.' He waved vaguely in the direction of the sofa as he walked towards the door to the inner hall. 'Put on some music and make yourself at home. I think there's a bottle of decent white open in the fridge, or some red in the rack next to the sink. I won't be long. Then maybe we can get something to eat. I'm starving.'

She put the package down on the glass and chrome coffee table, took off her coat and went into the kitchen, where she found an open bottle of Italian Gavi in the fridge. Pouring herself a glass, she took it back into the sitting room where she examined Tartaglia's extraordinary music collection, which ranged from obscure Italian opera to hip-hop, finally selecting an old Moby CD. She slid it into the player and sat down on the comfortable leather chair by the window.

Gradually starting to unwind, she gazed around the room, searching for the slightest trace of female occupation. She hadn't forgotten the scene in Dr Blake's office. But there were no telltale signs. No signs of anything interesting at all. As usual, the flat was absurdly tidy, with none of the usual haphazardness, unconscious or deliberate, which she associated with other male colleagues and friends. Everything had a place and a function, from the long lines of DVDs, CDs and books grouped alphabetically on the shelves, to the neat rows of glasses, crockery, drinks and cooking ingredients in the kitchen cupboards. Compared to the over-flowing, cosy house she shared with her sister, Tartaglia's flat was clinical. No family photos, personal knick-knacks, objects of a sentimental nature brought home from a holiday or marking a particular relationship. Knowing him, it wasn't that he couldn't be bothered to make a home. It was a matter of deliberate choice.

Although the lack of clutter was alien to her, she liked the bare, white walls and the large black and white photograph over the fireplace. It was the only picture in the entire room. She got up, glass in hand, to take a closer look. It was simple but evocative. A young woman strolled down a sun-drenched, cobbled street, sweeping a lock of dark hair off her face. She seemed preoccupied by something, unaware of the photographer. Behind her was a high arched doorway, the name 'Bar Toto' hanging in large neon letters above it, some words in what looked like Latin carved deep into the stone to one side. Judging from the woman's clothing and shoes, it had been taken sometime in the late fifties or early sixties. It reminded her of *La Dolce Vita*, the only Italian film she had ever seen. Apart from the fact that the picture was of somewhere in Italy, she had no idea why Tartaglia had chosen it, although the image was very striking.

As she continued to stare at it, losing herself in the scene, imagining a story behind it, the phone rang. She picked it up, hoping to hear Sally-Anne's voice at the other end.

'Is Mark there?' a woman asked, in a light Scottish accent.

'He's taking a shower,' she replied, instantly curious. Definitely not Fiona Blake.

There was a pause. 'Will he be long?'

'I don't know. He's just come back from a run. I'm Sam Donovan. I work with him,' Donovan said, something in the woman's tone compelling her to explain.

'Ah.' The woman sounded a little disappointed. 'I'm Nicoletta, his sister. Could you please just let him know that I called and that we're expecting him for lunch this Sunday. Tell him, no arguments. John and the kids want to see him and Elisa and Gianni and some friends are coming over. It's all arranged.'

Wondering what Tartaglia's reaction would be to such an order, Donovan put down the phone just as Tartaglia reappeared, barefoot, wearing jeans and a loose, open-necked shirt, vigorously rubbing his hair dry with a towel. Donovan relayed the message.

'Shit,' he said, lobbing the towel into the small hall, which led to the rest of the flat. 'I've been with the murder squad for nearly three years and, whatever I say, Nicoletta still doesn't get it. As far as she's concerned, the case can get fucked. Sunday is sacrosanct and nothing stops a family get-together, not even somebody lying dead in a mortuary. I need a bloody drink.'

He went into the kitchen, returning with the bottle of wine and a large, full glass. He sank down in the middle of the sofa, exhaling loudly as he put his bare feet up heavily on the coffee table. 'God, it's been a bugger of a day. It's only a matter of time before I'll be having to take orders from that prick, Kennedy.'

He looked rougher than she had seen him for a while, with dark shadows under his eyes, almost like bruises. Judging by the thick stubble on his chin, he hadn't shaved since early morning. Perhaps all he needed was a few good nights of sleep, although there was little chance of that in the foreseeable future. She hoped that was all that was wrong with him.

She sat down again, kicking off her shoes and leaning forward to massage her tired feet. 'You said Kennedy wanted to stop you looking into Marion Spear's death.'

He nodded. 'According to the expert, she doesn't fit his victim profile. But I don't give a flying fuck what he thinks. I still think it's worth pursuing.'

'How can you be so sure?'

'In here and here,' he said, pounding his heart and stomach with his fist. 'Something a spineless idiot like Kennedy wouldn't have a clue about.'

She was taken aback by the strength of the emotion in his dark eyes. She had never seen him like this before and she wasn't sure why he cared so much. Tartaglia's instincts were usually good but the policeman who solved a case on gut feel was a cliché reserved for detective novels. Maybe he was letting his hatred of Kennedy cloud his judgment. 'Have you found out anything more?'

'I've finally tracked down Marion's mum. She's still living up in Leicester, where Marion came from. She gave me some stuff on Marion's background, although most of it I already knew from the file. Apparently, Marion had come down south to work as an estate agent, first in Acton and then in Ealing. On the day she died, she had taken a client to visit a flat. After that, nobody saw her again. The flat was quite close to the car park where she fell.'

'Don't tell me it's another Mr Kipper.'

Tartaglia shook his head. 'The bloke was traced at the time and crossed off the list. But I'd still like to talk to him again and to the people in the estate agent's. Reading through the file, the investigation seems pretty cursory to me. According to Marion's mum, Marion didn't know many people and had been feeling lonely living in London. When she died, she was thinking of going back home to Leicester.'

'You really think she's worth looking into?'

He nodded. 'We're grubbing around in the dark. Ellie Best's computer was wiped clean and the only way to link her to the other deaths is the ring. Copies of the emails recovered from Laura Benedetti's computer came in this afternoon but they tell us nothing. Surprise, surprise, they are almost identical to what we found on Gemma Kramer's computer, although the killer called himself Sean instead of Tom. We have no clue how he got to the girls or who he is. We have fucking nada.'

'Maybe *Crimewatch* will do the trick.'

He shrugged. 'The response is usually great but with a complicated case like this it isn't always straightforward. Take the Barton case. Loads of calls came in after Trevor appeared on TV and we spent a huge amount of time sifting through all the information and following it up. But in the end, none of it helped catch Barton.'

She started to feel a little depressed. 'I still don't see why you think it's worth considering Marion Spear?'

He took a large gulp of wine, put the glass down on the table and folded his arms wearily. 'It's simple. Laura Benedetti wasn't necessarily Tom's first attempt at killing.'

'She was the first that fits the pattern that we know of.'

'Tom didn't spring from nowhere as a fully-fledged psychopath. He must have killed, or tried to, before. There's usually an escalation in what happens.'

'But we've searched the records.'

'We don't know what we're searching for. Take Michael Barton. He started off as a petty burglar who turned to rape.'

'Are you saying Barton killed a woman by mistake?'

'Although Barton's attacks were becoming increasingly violent, when he set out that night I personally doubt he had murder in mind. He didn't mean to strangle Jane Withers but she wouldn't do what he wanted. Unlike the others, she kept screaming and struggling. We know from her autopsy that she fought hard. He had to subdue her and silence her, otherwise he risked being caught. In the process, he got carried away and what was supposed to be rape, turned into murder.'

'But I understand he killed four more women. They can't all have been accidents.'

'We don't know what went on in his mind – the bastard won't talk. But probably somewhere in the middle of throttling the life out of poor Jane, he discovered that killing turned him on in a whole new way. A lot of what he did to her was post mortem. Perhaps he wasn't aware at that point if she was alive or dead.'

Donovan was silent for a moment as she finished her wine. 'Why are you so anti Dr Kennedy? I agree he's a prick but there are enough of those around and we all make mistakes. Also, he has had some successes.'

Tartaglia shook his head. 'Maybe. But to Kennedy, the Barton case was just another academic puzzle. He forgot he was dealing with real people, flesh and blood, who had families, husbands, children...' His voice tailed off for a moment before he continued. 'It was all a game to him,' he said bitterly. 'His refusal to believe that he might be wrong wasted valuable time and, in my view, cost the last two victims their lives.'

'You didn't have to listen to him.'

'No. But it's difficult to filter out the noise, particularly when it's coming from a so-called expert. It makes you doubt your own instincts. Also, what if we'd been wrong? We'd have had a job explaining to the powers-that-be why we ignored him.'

'Everything's easy to see with the benefit of hindsight.'

'Of course, but Trevor and I blame ourselves. If we hadn't paid so much attention to Kennedy, I'm sure we would have found Barton sooner. That's why I intend to follow my nose this time. If Trevor were here, he'd back me up, I know.'

'You really think Marion Spear could be an early victim?'

'To be honest, I've no idea. But at the moment, she's all we've got. We must find the early victims, the botched attempts before Tom perfected his act. Unless something lands in our lap, it's our best chance of catching him.'

'We've only been looking in London. Maybe Tom started killing somewhere else.'

'It's possible. But you know how difficult it's been to search thoroughly without a central log. As it is, I'm not convinced we've found all the victims. But extending the search outside London is impossible. We haven't got the resources nor is there any reason to justify doing it at the moment. Perhaps *Crimewatch* will do the job for us. We'll soon hear if there's been anything similar going on in other parts of the country.'

'Do you think he's killing them in different parts of London to make it difficult for someone to spot?'

'The thought had occurred to me. At least now, with all the publicity, he won't get away with it again so easily.'

She sank back in her chair and closed her eyes, rubbing her temples with her fingers, feeling suddenly out of her depth. In the short space of time she'd been on Clarke's team, she'd had to deal with a number of murders. Although grisly and upsetting, they had usually been cases of domestic violence gone wrong, or someone with a grievance against a member of their family, friend or work colleague. Nothing she had seen so far had prepared her for something like this.

'He's not going to stop, is he?' she said, softly, after a moment.

Tartaglia shook his head. 'The clock's ticking. Unless we can establish the connection between Laura, Ellie and Gemma, our only other means of catching him is to wait for him to do it again. If so, let's just hope with all the media pressure, he fucks up.'

As he reached for his glass, the phone rang and he got up to answer it. Donovan realised almost immediately from Tartaglia's tone of voice that it wasn't Sally-Anne at the other end. After a brief exchange, he grabbed a pencil and a piece of paper from the table, jotted something down, then slammed the phone into its cradle.

Stretching his arms in the air, he yawned and came back to the sofa. 'That was the blessed Carolyn. Sounded pretty chuffed with her performance on TV.'

'Was that all she wanted?'

'Some bloke's phoned in to say that he thinks he saw Gemma's killer steaming out of the church late that afternoon. The timing checks out, so hopefully we may get a better description of the man.'

'You're going round to see him now?'

He shook his head. 'Thank God, no. It's been fixed for tomorrow morning, eight a.m. at Ealing nick. Apparently, the caller lives nearby. I'd like you to be there too.'

She nodded, grateful that it wasn't six or seven a.m. The description of Gemma's killer released on *Crimewatch* had been kept deliberately vague and it would be interesting to see if what the caller had seen tallied with Mrs Brooke's statement.

'That should tie in nicely with following up on Marion's Mr Kipper and the local estate agent,' he said, rubbing his hands together, smiling. 'Meantime, I *have* to eat something. Let's order a takeaway and watch effing Carolyn on film. Maybe she'll be nominated for an Oscar.'

He was about to reach for the phone when the doorbell rang.

Donovan gave him an enquiring look. 'Expecting someone?'

'I'm not expecting anyone.'

As surprised as Donovan, he went out of the flat and opened the front door to find a woman standing at the bottom of the steps in the middle of the path, sheltering from the rain under a large umbrella. It took him a moment to realise that it was Fiona Blake. He stared at her, not knowing what to say.

'I was just passing and saw your light on,' she said. There was a moment's hesitation before she added: 'May I come in?'

Her speech was a touch slurred. Although she said she was passing, she lived on the other side of town. Even though her face was in shadow, he could see that she was dressed up, lips shiny, just catching the light, hair sleek around her shoulders. He wondered what she was doing at that hour in his neighbourhood. Part of him would have given a great deal to invite her inside but he knew he shouldn't. He still felt bruised after everything that had happened, remembering the photographs in her office, the ring on her finger. Anyway, with Donovan just on the other side of the wall, the choice was made for him. Thank God, temptation was put out of his way.

'It's not a good time,' he said, instantly gauging from the tightening of her expression that he'd said the wrong thing. He saw her eyes focusing on his bare feet then moving to the half-drunk glass of wine in his hand. He was suddenly aware of the music drifting softly out the door behind him and realised how it all must look.

'I can see you're busy,' she said frostily.

'Work, I'm afraid.'

'Work? Of course. You're always working. Perhaps another time.'

She slipped her handbag over her shoulder and started to walk back down the path towards the street.

'Fiona, wait. It's not like that.' He felt stupid as soon as he'd said it.

She stopped by the front gate and turned, teetering a little on her very high heels as she stared hard at him. 'Not like what?'

'I've got a colleague with me. We're discussing the case.' He didn't see why he should have to explain himself to her but he found himself doing it anyway.

'I just thought we should talk, that's all,' she said, clearly not believing him. 'But as you say, it's not a good time. I'm sorry, I shouldn't have come.'

'I'd like to talk. Honestly, I would. But not now.'

She hesitated, shifting her weight awkwardly from one foot to another as if her shoes were uncomfortable. 'When?'

'I'll call you,' he said, hoping to placate her, although he wasn't sure if he would.

She shook her head slowly as if she didn't believe him and turned away without a word, walking off down the road.

Thoughts racing, feeling stupid and inept, he watched her go, listening to the clip of her heels on the wet pavement. He waited for a moment then went back inside, slamming the front door behind him, and then the door to the flat, as he tried to stifle the yearning to go after her.

Donovan was still sitting in the chair by the window, feet tucked up under her, a huge grin on her face. The walls in the house weren't thick and she must have heard part, if not all, of what had been said.

'Would you like me to go?' she asked, taking a sip of wine as if she had no intention of doing any such thing. 'I really don't want to be in the way...'

'You're not,' he said firmly, walking over to the table and topping up his glass. He felt suddenly relieved that Donovan was there and grateful for her company.

'Was it Dr Blake?' she asked after a moment.

He nodded.

She put down her glass, unfolded her legs and got to her feet. 'Really, I'm very happy to leave, if you want me to. Why don't you call her back?'

'Not a good idea.'

She sighed, shaking her head slowly as if she understood everything. 'Ah, Mark. Life's never simple, is it?'

He could tell what was going through her mind: he was thinking with his dick, and she was probably right. 'I don't want to talk about it,' he said firmly. 'Now let's order that sodding curry.'

A bitter wind gusted across Hammersmith Bridge, blowing with it a mist of icy rain. Kelly Goodhart stopped and closed her eyes for a moment listening to the sound as it whistled around the tall gothic towers, rushing through the ironwork structure high above. The air was so cold, she could barely feel her toes in her sodden boots, let alone her fingers. But none of that would matter soon. It was nearly midnight and she wouldn't have much longer to wait.

The last time she had stood there, almost on that very spot, had been with Michael. They had been for a long walk along the towpath, stopping on the bridge to watch the sun set. Afterwards, they had gone to The Dove in Hammersmith for a couple of drinks before returning home for supper. It was Sunday evening, late autumn and unusually warm for that time of year. They had sat out on the little terrace at the back overlooking the river, watching the rowing boats plough up and down, gazing content-edly at the darkening outline and playing fields of St Paul's school opposite, where Michael had studied as a boy.

Hearing the perennial drone of an aeroplane somewhere above, she opened her eyes and leaned back against the wrought iron balustrade, peering across the water. She could just make out the pub amongst the stretch of old houses on the opposite shore, its lights still shining even at that hour. The memory of happier times brought tears to her eyes, which mingled with the rain. It all seemed so distant now.

Not wanting to think about it anymore, she turned away into the wind and looked down-river, holding tight onto the wooden handrail as she gazed at the glittering modern office buildings and warehouse conversions further along, silhouetted against the cloudy night sky. The river ran high up against the wall, the sodium lights along the bank reflecting in the rippling black water, which looked deceptively calm from a distance. The river curved sharply away to the right, towards Fulham and Chelsea and the next string of bridges, which were hidden from view. The opposite bank was dark and it was almost impossible to make out where the river ended and land began, the only light glinting through the thick, swaying trees coming from the terrace of houses that backed onto the towpath.

The line of old-fashioned lamps along the bridge cast intermittent pools of pinkish-yellow light on the churning water immediately below, the current moving furiously along, carrying with it all manner of detritus. Gazing down, she spotted a small, uprooted tree or branch, reaching up like a bony outstretched hand, momentarily caught in an arc of light before being swept away beneath the bridge. It was as if it was beckoning to her and she felt the invisible pull of the water, inviting her, drawing her down towards it. Thank God the darkness that had enveloped her for so long would soon be over.

She heard the rattle of wheels on the bridge as a car sped towards her, the headlamps momentarily blinding, and she turned away, retreating into the shadow of one of the huge buttresses, stuffing her hands in her pockets for warmth. At that hour there was hardly any traffic and it was only the fourth car she had counted in the past ten minutes, along with a single pedestrian, an elderly man out walking a Labrador, who was so bundled up in hat and coat against the weather that he didn't even look at her as he went past.

Finding it impossible to stand still, as much from nerves as the cold, she started to walk back across the bridge, listening to the hollow thud of her footsteps on the path. She went over her checklist again in her mind: the note and money for her cleaner, ready on the kitchen table along with the keys to her car and the letter for her brother, containing details of her bank accounts and other assets, her will with its short list of bequests and the instructions for her burial. So many loose ends that needed to be carefully tied up. But everything was in order, she reassured herself. She had forgotten nothing.

Drowning was supposed to be a pleasant way to go, according to what she had read. As your lungs filled with water, you experienced a high, a feeling of euphoria and floatiness. On a night like this, if you didn't drown instantly, you would die of hypothermia, the effects of which weren't very different. She wasn't a good swimmer so she would probably drown, although she had no strong feelings either way. All that mattered was that it happened tonight.

She looked at her watch. It was now just past midnight. He said he would be coming by tube and she stopped and scanned the length of the bridge towards Hammersmith, eyes straining to catch any movement. But there was none. He was only a few minutes late but every minute counted and already she started to feel anxious. When they had spoken that morning, he had given her his word that he would be there, that he wouldn't fail her. She rubbed her wedding ring with her thumb, turning it round and round her finger in her pocket as she worried about what she would do if he didn't come. She knew she couldn't go through with it on her own but the thought of living another day was unbearable. Surely he wouldn't let her down.

Trying to calm herself, she started to walk again, stamping hard on the path to keep warm. She was almost on the other side when her eyes caught a movement in the distance and she noticed the small, dark, bobbing shape of someone coming along the pavement below towards her, just before the foot of the bridge. Hesitant, she stopped again and squinted into the distance, her breath catching in her throat. It looked like a man. It could be him. As he slowly approached, she struggled to make out his features in the orange streetlight but she was sure she recognised the tall, broad-shouldered outline and the long, loping gait that was so distinctive. Tears in her eyes, she exhaled sharply, gasping from sheer relief, and hugging herself tightly. She had been foolish to worry. He had come as he had promised and with a surge of elation, she watched him draw near.

14

Tartaglia strode into room three at Ealing Police Station, where a youngish-looking man and Donovan were seated opposite each other at the table, engrossed in conversation.

'Sorry to keep you waiting,' Tartaglia said, banging the door closed with his heel.

Donovan gave Tartaglia an enquiring look but the man smiled and shrugged good-humouredly as if he had all the time in the world.

'Not a problem,' the man said. 'Sergeant Donovan has been taking good care of me. I was in the middle of explaining what happened.'

'This is Adam Zaleski,' Donovan said. 'He's just been telling me about the man he saw running away from the church where Gemma Kramer died.'

Zaleski gave Donovan another easy smile and leant back in his chair, pushing his small, steel-rimmed glasses up his nose. Young, slim, with very short dark hair, wet from the rain outside, he was dressed in a sober grey suit and plain, navy tie, clearly on his way in to the office.

Tartaglia dumped his helmet and gloves on the floor in the corner and fumbled to unzip his soaking jacket. It was a relief to take it off for a while and he shook it energetically a few times to get rid of the water clinging to the surface, before hanging it on the coat rack behind the door. In spite of the waterproofs, he felt as though the freezing rain outside had penetrated right through to his skin. His cheeks smarted in the stuffy warmth of the small room, his hands still like blocks of ice.

The day had started badly. For some reason he had overslept, waking with a churning stomach and a thick head. No doubt the greasy takeaway he had shared with Donovan the previous evening was something to do with it, as well as the half bottle of Barolo he had polished off on his own after she had gone, trying to obliterate Fiona Blake from his thoughts. To make matters worse, it had been raining heavily when he left the flat this morning. Still dark outside, the roads were slick as a skidpan, and the traffic was much heavier than normal.

He hated being late; hated others being late too. It was unforgivable. But as he came back to the table, he saw from the clock by the door that it was worse than he had imagined. He should have been there nearly three-quarters of an hour ago. He sighed and shook his head, angry with himself, as he sat down next to Donovan opposite Zaleski. He felt unfocused and out of control, desperate now for a large cup of strong, black coffee, a cigarette or three and something to eat. But that would have to wait until they finished with Zaleski. Hopefully the interview wouldn't take long.

He took out a notebook and pen from his pocket, more for formality's sake than anything else, as he could see that Donovan had been taking copious notes. As he did so, Zaleski stood up.

'I hope you don't mind if I remove my jacket. It's like the Sahara in here.' His voice was flat and accentless, the tone a little husky, as if he was getting over a cold.

Draping the jacket carefully over the back of his chair, Zaleski sat down again and folded his hands in front of him on the table, ready for business. He looked more muscular without the jacket, a pristine white shirt taut across his chest and upper arms.

Zaleski might be dying of heat but Tartaglia was still freezing. Rubbing his hands together to get his circulation going, Tartaglia leaned across the table. 'Please can you take me through what you've already told Sergeant Donovan?'

'Sure. It's pretty simple, really,' Zaleski said, shrugging again, giving Tartaglia a pleasant smile. 'I was walking along Kenilworth

Avenue. Just as I was passing St Sebastian's, this bloke comes down the steps and out of the gate. He wasn't looking where he was going and he nearly walked straight into me.'

'You say "nearly". Did he touch you at all?'

Zaleski looked puzzled. 'Touch me?'

'If this man proves to be the person we're looking for and he had physical contact with you, we'll need the clothes you were wearing for forensic examination.'

Zaleski nodded. 'Oh, I see. No, he didn't touch me. He just glared at me for a second, almost angry, as if it was my fault. Then he turned and walked off. After a moment, I heard a car engine start up further along the road and it drove away. I didn't see anyone else around, so I presume it was his car.'

Zaleski spoke in a quiet, considered manner as if aware of the importance of each detail. He would come across well in court, if it ever came to that.

'Did you see the car?'

'Only its taillights disappearing. It was too dark.'

'You said you thought it was a car, not a van,' Donovan said.

'That's right. At least it didn't sound like a van, if you know what I mean.'

'But you got a good look at the man?' Donovan prompted.

Zaleski nodded. 'I'd say so. He was very close and there's a streetlamp right by the entrance to the church. He's white, clean-shaven, round about my age.'

'Which is?'

'Thirty-six.'

Tartaglia studied Zaleski. He was usually good at judging someone's age but Zaleski looked barely thirty.

'What about height?'

Zaleski paused for a moment, rubbing his chin thoughtfully. 'I don't know. I'm about five ten. I'd say he was possibly a bit taller but I really can't be sure. You see, it all happened so quickly.'

'What about hair colour?'

'Brown. Thick, I think, and longish.'

'Brown?'

'Well, certainly lighter than mine, although the streetlamp was one of those orange ones so it's difficult to be precise.'

Tartaglia nodded. Although Zaleski seemed to have good recall of what had happened, orange street lighting made it almost impossible to read colours accurately. Mrs Brooke had described the man as having dark hair but then she had seen him from a distance in fading daylight. Some sort of mid-to-dark-brown was probably the best they could do for the moment.

'You said you saw his face clearly. I don't suppose you have any idea about eye colour?'

Zaleski considered for a moment, picking at a loose thread attached to his cuff button.

'I'd say they were pale.'

'Pale?' Donovan said, checking her notes and scribbling something down.

'Well, I think if he had dark eyes they would have stood out, even under the streetlamp. But now you ask, I'm not so sure.'

'Of course, you only saw him briefly,' Tartaglia said, aware that he'd pushed Zaleski too far. Sometimes, in a misguided effort to be helpful, witnesses remembered things that they hadn't actually seen. Zaleski seemed eager to please and he realised he would have to tread more carefully.

'Do you happen to remember what he was wearing?'

Zaleski grimaced. 'It's funny, but I really only remember his face, the way he looked at me. That's what sticks in my mind. The rest is a bit of a blur, although I think he was dressed in a coat, the way you had him in the reconstruction, with his hands in the pockets. I haven't a clue about the trousers or shoes. It all happened so quickly, you see. One minute he's there, the next he's gone.'

Although Zaleski seemed to feel that he should have remembered things more clearly, they were making progress. Mrs Brooke hadn't been able to see the man's features from where she was standing, whereas Zaleski had seen him up close, albeit for only a few seconds.

'That's perfectly understandable. Do you think you saw him well enough to help us put together an e-fit?'

'I could certainly try.'

'Assuming the car you heard was his, which way did he go?'

'South.'

Donovan checked her notes. 'You said, towards Popes Lane.'

'That's right.'

'What time was this?' Tartaglia asked.

'Definitely after five. Maybe about five-fifteen. I was on my way over to pick up my car from the garage. It was there for a service and an MOT. They shut at half past and I was in a bit of a rush to get there in time, as I needed it that evening. I've given Sergeant Donovan the details, if you want to check it out. They may be able to remember exactly what time I arrived.'

They would check as a matter of course but the time fitted perfectly. Without doubt, Zaleski had seen Tom. Hopefully, he would be able to pick him out of a line-up if they ever found him.

'Why didn't you come forward sooner?' Donovan asked. 'Didn't you see the witness appeal boards? They were dotted all around the streets close to the church.'

Zaleski shook his head. 'I don't normally go that way. I live right on the other side of Ealing and I work in South Ken. I only found out about what had happened when I watched *Crimewatch* last night.'

Tartaglia closed his notebook and slipped it into his pocket. 'What do you do for a living, Mr Zaleski?'

'I'm a hypnotist.'

'Stage shows, you mean?' Tartaglia barely stifled his surprise. There was nothing showy or theatrical about Zaleski, qualities he imagined were par for the course for a hypnotist, which, in his view, was tantamount to being a fairground conjurer. If anything, Zaleski looked like a drone accountant or lawyer in one of the big City firms.

Zaleski grinned, clearly having come across such a reaction before. 'Nothing glamorous like that. I'm not Paul McKenna. I just have a small practice. Perhaps I should be more ambitious, but I enjoy what I do and it pays the bills, so my bank manager's happy.'

Tartaglia struggled to imagine how anybody could earn a living from such a profession. 'What sort of things do you do?'

'My main area of interest is in treating people with phobias and addictions. Claustrophobia, fear of flying, things like that. Most of the people who come to see me simply want to lose weight or stop smoking.' He glanced at Donovan and smiled as if they shared some secret. 'That's my bread and butter. Luckily, there's a lot of demand and I usually get good results. It normally only takes a few sessions.'

'It's that easy?' Tartaglia said sceptically, acutely aware of the half-empty packet of cigarettes in his pocket and suddenly craving a smoke again.

'It certainly works for some people,' Donovan said, a little defensively, he thought, as she tucked away her notebook and pen in her bag. 'A friend of mine's company paid for all the smokers in the office to be hypnotised in order to get them to give up. She used to smoke twenty a day and she hasn't touched one since.'

Tartaglia looked back at Zaleski, still unconvinced. 'You really could make me give up smoking or drinking?'

Zaleski was smiling. 'You'd have to want to give up. Real-life hypnosis is nothing like you see in films. I can't make you do anything you don't want to do. I can't take control of your mind.'

'Then how does it work?'

'Through suggestion. I just help you along the path you've already chosen.' Zaleski reached behind into his jacket pocket for his wallet, plucked out a business card and handed it to Tartaglia. 'Why don't you try it some time?'

'Maybe. If ever I find there's something I can't deal with myself. In the meantime, I think we've covered everything for now.' He stood up, Zaleski and Donovan following suit. 'I'll get someone from my team to contact you later this morning about the e-fit.

We'll also need you to make a formal statement. Nowadays, we have to record these things both on video and audio.'

He walked Zaleski to the door and pointed him in the direction of the front desk and the way out. Once he was out of sight, Tartaglia crumpled up Zaleski's business card and aimed it at the bin in the corner. Annoyingly, it landed just short.

'You're just like my father,' Donovan said, walking over and scooping it up to drop it in the bin. 'He never picks up anything.'

From what he remembered, Donovan's father was an over-weight, grey-bearded former English teacher in his early sixties. Only a few years older than Donovan, Tartaglia felt stung by the remark. 'I can't believe I'm anything like your father.' He unhooked his jacket from the rack, where it had been dripping onto the lino, creating a small pool, and gave it a vigorous shake to get rid of the last few drops of water. 'And you're hardly Miss Tidy. Your house looked like a gypsy encampment last time I saw it.'

'Well, I do try, but Claire totally defeats me. Don't worry. You're not really like Dad,' she said, patting his arm and smiling as if she knew what he had been thinking.

He walked to the door and held it open for her impatiently. 'There's a Starbucks on the High Street just down the road from the estate agents where Marion Spear worked. If we get a move on, we've time for a quick breakfast before the estate agent opens.'

15

After several strong coffees and a plate of stodgy croissants, Tartaglia left Donovan to interview the owner of Grafton Estate Agents while he went to find Harry Angel, the man to whom Marion Spear had been showing a flat and the last person known to have seen her alive. The driving rain had slowed to a drizzle and the cold, wet air felt pleasantly fresh on his face after the fug of the café, helping to clear his head as he walked the few blocks to the bookshop where Angel worked.

From what he could tell from the slim case file, the local CID investigation into Marion Spear's death had been cursory. Given the usual issues of finite resources and heavy workload, it wasn't surprising. Harry Angel had been interviewed several times. But he had stuck to his story about leaving Marion Spear outside a flat in Carlton Road, Ealing. With no witnesses to contradict him, no apparent motive and nothing to link him to the crime scene, they had eventually given up on him.

No evidence of foul play had emerged. Marion had either fallen to her death by accident, which seemed unlikely owing to the height of the car park walls, or she had committed suicide. Although no note had been found, he could see why suicide had seemed the most plausible conclusion, with significant weight being attached to statements from both Spear's mother and a flatmate, who said that Marion was unhappy and was finding it difficult to make friends in London. Nobody had looked beyond this fact, to consider how a lonely young woman like Marion might easily fall prey to something sinister.

Thinking of the photograph of Marion in the file, he wondered if he was right. She was attractive, in an unthreatening, girl-next-door way, young-looking for her thirty years, with shoulder-length, dark blonde hair and a wistful, sweet expression in her eyes. Perhaps he was reading too much into it, but she looked sad. She must have had admirers; someone would have taken an interest, surely. But according to the statements, Marion kept herself to herself and rarely went out. Kennedy was wrong about her not fitting the victim profile. Even if Marion Spear was a lot older than Gemma, Ellie and Laura, even if she had died in a different way, there was a common strand. They were all lonely, all isolated, all vulnerable in their different ways. Had Marion somehow caught Tom's attention?

The bookshop where Angel worked was in the middle of the parade facing onto Ealing Green, a few doors along from the tapas bar where Tartaglia and Kennedy had lunched the day before. Sandwiched between a bright, organic food shop and a fancy French coffee bar, the bookshop seemed out of place, the front painted with several uneven layers of ancient-looking black gloss, the name 'Soane Antiquarian Books' written in faded gold lettering across the top.

He peered briefly through the partially misted-up window at the display of second-hand books on architecture and history of art, then tried pushing the door. It was locked and he noticed from the sign on the door that the shop wasn't due to open for another half hour. But he could see a light on towards the back of the dim interior and somebody moving around inside. After trying the bell a few times, he gave up and rapped loudly on the door. A minute later, a tall, rangy man appeared out of the gloom. Studying Tartaglia suspiciously, he pointed at the sign, mouthing in slow motion, as if for an idiot, the words, 'We're closed.' Tartaglia mouthed back the word 'Police', holding up his warrant card to the glass. The man hesitated, deciding what to do, then slowly unlocked the door, opening it a few inches and scanning the warrant card through the crack.

'What do you want?' he said.

'Are you Harry Angel?'

The man hesitated again then nodded.

'I'm Detective Inspector Mark Tartaglia. May I come in? I'm sure you wouldn't want me to discuss things with you from the pavement.'

With a grudging look, Angel threw open the door and let him pass, a small bell attached to the door jingling violently.

The interior was cramped and barely warmer than outside, the dark red walls lined with shelves of hardbacks, some of them leather-bound. Some sort of strident modern opera was playing in the background and Tartaglia could smell freshly brewed coffee.

'What's this about?' Angel asked, hands on hips. He was a couple of inches taller than Tartaglia, well over six foot, with large feet encased in a pair of ancient velvet slippers with a gold crest on the front. Dressed in faded jeans and a baggy dark green pullover, Angel was older than he had initially appeared, perhaps in his late thirties or early forties, with a pale, bony face and a sweep of floppy, dark reddish-brown hair. Although his height was a possible stumbling point, he just about matched Zaleski's description of the man seen running from St Sebastian's. It was a wild leap of imagination, Tartaglia knew, with nothing whatsoever to link the two, but he couldn't help feeling a twinge of excitement.

'It's about Marion Spear. I understand you were one of the last people to see her alive.'

'Marion Spear?' Angel looked doubtful, as if he had never heard the name before, but Tartaglia had noticed a flicker of recognition cross his face.

'Yes, Marion Spear. She fell to her death from a car park quite close to here, shortly after she had taken you to see a flat in Carlton Road. It was barely two years ago. Surely you haven't forgotten?'

'Shit.' Angel wheeled around and bounded off out of sight towards the back of the shop.

The smell of something burning suddenly filled the air.

Tartaglia followed him through the ranks of shelves to a long, narrow kitchen, built in an extension overlooking a small, overgrown garden. Angel was busy mopping up what appeared to be milk from the top of an old electric cooker, an expression of distaste puckering his thin lips. The lime green units and brown lino looked vintage seventies but the room was tidy and spotlessly clean, surprisingly at odds with Angel's scruffy appearance.

'Come on, Mr Angel. Marion Spear. I'm sure you remember who she is.'

Angel turned and glared at him. 'Look, of course I remember, Inspector. I just don't know what I can add to what I told you lot last time.' He rinsed the cloth under the tap and went back to wiping the surface of the cooker until all traces of milk had disappeared.

'I'd like to hear it for myself, if you don't mind.'

Angel slapped the cloth down on the worktop. 'Why are you bothering about her now?'

'Because we're looking into her death again.'

Angel tossed the milk pan into the sink and filled it with water. 'That was the last of the bloody milk,' he said, as if Tartaglia were to blame. 'If you want to share my coffee, it'll have to be black.'

'Thanks, but I can manage without,' Tartaglia said, eyeing the small glass cafetiere of muddy-looking brown liquid next to the stove. The stuff at Starbucks had been like dishwater and Angel's looked no better. Angel reached for a mug from the plate rack above the sink and poured a full cup. Taking a large gulp, he smacked his lips, then leaned back against the sink, cradling his mug. 'OK. What can I tell you?'

'Let's start with how you knew Marion Spear.'

Angel sighed deeply as if it were all a waste of time. 'I didn't know her, per se. She just took me around a few flats.' He took another mouthful of coffee before adding: 'It wasn't my fault that she chose to top herself straight after an appointment with me.'

'Top herself? Why do you say that?'

Angel shrugged. 'That's what everyone thought at the time, if I remember correctly. Although, as I told your boys in blue, she seemed perfectly normal when I left her. Quite chirpy, actually.' Angel scratched his beaky nose. 'You think it was an accident?'

'It's possible, although unlikely.'

'Yes, it didn't seem right to me,' he said, emphatically. 'I know that car park. The walls are really high. All these new safety regulations, you know what it's like. They build walls so you can't even bloody see over them, let alone fall over them.' He let the sentence hang then turned to Tartaglia with a look of surprise. 'You think her death is suspicious?'

'Let's say, for the moment we're keeping an open mind.'

'Are you re-opening the case?'

'We're just taking a fresh look.'

'You've got new evidence?'

'I didn't say that, Mr Angel. I'm just checking things over, kicking the tyres, that's all.'

Angel clearly didn't believe him, raising his eyes to the ceiling and smiling. 'Ah, I see where this is going. Muggins here was one of the last people to see her alive so you think I may have had something to do with it. It's just like last time. You lot have no imagination.'

'Naturally, I need to talk to you, which is why I'm here.'

Angel shook his head reprovingly. 'As I said, I've been through those hoops before. Surely you can do better than that? I mean, what's my motive? Or perhaps I'm just a psycho?' He widened his eyes and bared his teeth, in a Norman Bates impersonation. 'They couldn't find anything on me last time, so why are you bothering?'

Although Angel seemed to think he'd been given a tough time, from what Tartaglia had seen of the file, there were many unanswered questions. Also, there hadn't been a thorough check on Angel's background or any real attempt to find a link between him and Marion beyond the obvious. No doubt, as the suicide theory gained credence, it hadn't seemed necessary.

For the moment, he wanted to allay Angel's suspicions. 'It's early days, Mr Angel. Before we jump to conclusions, perhaps you can tell me what you remember about Marion Spear.'

'Look, I made a statement at the time and I've nothing new to add.'

'I've read your statement but I'd like to hear what happened myself.'

Still grinning, as if it were all a bad joke, Angel took a large gulp of coffee then shrugged. 'All right. From what I remember, she was a nice girl, a cheerful sort. I think she was relatively new to the job and eager to please. Not like some of the jaded old trouts in the estate agents around here who can't be bothered to get off their fat arses. She took me to see a lot of flats but none of them was quite right.'

'You said she seemed perfectly normal that day?'

He nodded. 'She showed me a couple of new things that had just come on the books. That was it. Business as usual. First time I know something's wrong is when one of your lot comes calling a couple of days later.'

Angel's casual manner seemed a little forced and Tartaglia was sure he was hiding something. 'Didn't she mention where she was going next after seeing you? Didn't she say anything?'

'Why should she? I mean, I was just a client.'

'Where did you think she was going?'

Angel gave another deep sigh, as if the whole subject bored him. 'Search me. I assumed she was either going back to the office or to meet another client. Surely, you can check her diary.'

'There were no further entries until late that afternoon. She should have gone straight back to the office but she didn't.' He studied Angel for a moment. 'So, you had absolutely no idea where she went?'

Angel drained his mug and banged it down on the counter. 'Of course not.'

'Your relationship was purely professional?'

'I'd hardly call it a relationship. The lady took me to see some flats, that's all.'

'You never saw her socially?'

There was a second's hesitation. 'We might have bumped into each other in the street. Maybe she came into the bookshop once or twice. But nothing more than that.'

Tartaglia hid the little stab of excitement he felt at hearing this. According to Angel's original statement, Marion Spear had never set foot in the bookshop. They had only ever met at the estate agents where she worked or at a flat that she was showing him. Angel had been adamant on that point but he wasn't going to remind him. 'Was she interested in second-hand books on architecture?' he asked, casually.

'Amazing though it may seem, Inspector, a lot of people are. Anyway, we stock a wide variety of books.'

'But I'm talking about Marion Spear. Why would she come in here?'

'I seem to remember she liked reading.'

'You discussed books together?'

'Maybe.'

'So, she came in to buy a book?'

'Probably. It's what people do.'

'Or was it to see you, for some reason?'

Angel's expression hardened and he folded his arms defensively. 'Look, I really don't remember. Maybe she didn't come here.'

Tartaglia was sure he was lying. 'But you just said that she did.'

'I said that she might have done. I just don't remember her doing so. Clear?' Angel's voice went up a tone.

'It's curious. You remember some things so very clearly, and other things, not at all.' Angel puckered his lips but said nothing. Reminding himself that even if Angel had lied, it wasn't evidence of anything, he decided to leave it for the moment. 'Do you have a computer, Mr Angel?'

Angel looked surprised. 'Yes, why?'

'Is it here or at home?'

'This is my home. I live upstairs.'

'Where's your computer?'

'Down in the basement, where we pack up all the books we send out. We do a lot of business over the net.'

'May I see it?'

Angel stared at him for a moment, then shrugged. 'Be my guest. Although, I can't see why it's of any interest.'

Angel seemed almost relieved, which was puzzling. Maybe it was an act or maybe the subject of the computer didn't bother him.

He followed Angel down a narrow flight of stairs to a low-ceilinged, windowless room that ran the full length of the shop. While the ground floor had the air of an old-fashioned library, the basement operation was modern and streamlined. Boxes full of books were neatly stacked and labelled in rows on the floor, with a shelving unit along one wall housing business stationery and thick rolls of bubble wrap and brown paper. Three cheap, pine trestle tables were lined up against the other wall for the actual packing. Judging by the number of books waiting to be wrapped and sent, the internet was an important source of business and the operation looked efficient. A new-looking Apple Mac sat on a small table in a corner, its screen dead. Short of asking Angel to turn it on and let him scan the hard drive, there was little Tartaglia could do without a warrant and there wasn't sufficient grounds for that yet. Angel still seemed curiously relaxed. Maybe he had another computer elsewhere.

'Very impressive,' Tartaglia said, turning away and gazing at a tower of full jiffy bags and neatly wrapped parcels waiting to be posted out, the top one addressed to somewhere in Canada. 'You send books all over the world?'

Angel nodded. 'Thanks to the internet. We wouldn't be able to survive without it.'

'You keep saying 'we'. Do you have a business partner?'

Angel shook his head. 'Force of habit. The business used to belong to my grandfather and we worked together. But he's dead now.'

'So, you take care of this entirely on your own?' There had been no mention of anyone else in the file but, judging by the scale of the operation, he felt sure that Angel had help of some kind. Angel hesitated. 'If you don't want to tell me,' Tartaglia continued, 'I can find out.'

Angel looked annoyed. 'Look, I've nothing to hide. A woman comes in to help a couple of days a week. That's all.'

'Could you give me her details?'

'What's she got to do with Marion Spear?'

'I'll be the judge of that,' Tartaglia said, curious that Angel seemed reluctant to give it to him.

Angel sighed. 'She's called Annie Klein. She's only been helping me out in the last few months. Surely you don't need to bother her?'

'Probably not, but I'd like her details all the same.'

Angel scribbled something down on a piece of paper and thrust it at Tartaglia. 'Is there anything else or can we go back upstairs? I should be opening up soon and I haven't even had my breakfast.'

'Thank you. I've seen enough for now.'

Tartaglia led the way back upstairs. At the top, he turned to face Angel. 'Just a couple more things. Could you tell me what you were doing between four and six last Wednesday afternoon?'

'Why on earth do you want to know about that?'

'Please answer the question, Mr Angel.'

It took a moment for Angel to answer as if he were debating in his mind whether he needed to. 'I was here, of course.'

'Can anyone corroborate that?'

'Now what's this about?'

'Please answer the question, Mr Angel.'

'Nobody was here apart from me. Annie doesn't usually work Wednesdays.'

'What about customers coming into the shop? Might someone have seen you here during that time?'

'Weekday afternoons are usually quiet but I really can't remember.'

'Perhaps you can check your records.'

'Look, what's all this got to do with Marion Spear?'

'Absolutely nothing at the moment.' He let the words sink in before adding: 'But we're investigating a murder which took place at St Sebastian's, just around the corner from here.'

It took a second for the significance of the words to penetrate. Angel's eyes widened. 'What, that young girl? You think...' He put his hands on his hips and stared at Tartaglia, his face turning red, his expression a mixture of anger and indignation. He was either a good actor or the reaction was genuine. 'Now look here, Inspector. I've tried to be helpful and I've answered all your questions. But if you start trying to join up the dots and make a cat look like a horse, I'm going to have to call a lawyer.'

'Calm down, Mr Angel. You're a local. It's just a routine question. I'm sure you'll be able to prove that you were here at that time.'

Before Angel could reply, the sound of someone knocking loudly on the shop front door made Tartaglia turn around. Donovan was standing on the step, nose pressed to the glass.

'Can't she bloody see we're closed,' Angel muttered, looking round in the direction of the door.

'That's my Sergeant. One last question; do you have a car, Mr Angel?'

Angel turned back and glared at him, arms still folded. 'A van. Before you get any ideas, I use it for book-buying trips.'

Tartaglia smiled. 'What sort of ideas would those be?'

Angel said nothing, biting his lip.

'What sort of a van?'

'A VW camper. Now, if that's all, I've got work to do.'

'Thank you, Mr Angel,' Tartaglia said, unlocking the door and opening it wide, letting a gust of freezing, damp air blow inside. 'I'll get someone to call you later about last Wednesday. Perhaps you can give them the licence number of the van at the same time. Just for the record.'

Without waiting for a response, Tartaglia went out, slamming the door behind him, the little bell jangling furiously. Aware that Angel was watching from the window, he and Donovan walked down the street until they were out of sight, sheltering under a shop awning from the rain while he gave her the gist of his conversation with Angel.

'I want you to go and see this woman right away.' He handed Donovan the paper with Annie Klein's details and explained what Angel had said. 'When you've done that, can you check with the shops on either side of Angel's. See if they remember him going out at all last Wednesday afternoon.'

'Will do.'

'There's also Marion's ex-flatmate, Karen Thomas. She works somewhere near here.' He passed her another slip of paper. 'Did you get anything interesting from Angela Grafton?'

She was about to reply when her mobile rang. Answering it, she listened for a moment before speaking. 'Yes, he's here. I'll tell him. Right away, I understand.' She snapped her phone shut and turned to Tartaglia looking excited. 'That was Steele. She's been trying to get hold of you but you're not answering your pager and your mobile's apparently switched off.'

'Damn.' In his hurry to get out the door that morning, he'd left his pager in his other jacket pocket and he had forgotten to turn on his phone after the interview with Zaleski. 'What does she want?'

'A woman was seen struggling with a man late last night on Hammersmith Bridge. The woman fell in and the man ran away. They can't find her body but she's probably dead. Local CID called us right away and Yvette's been briefed. She'll meet you at the rendezvous point on the Hammersmith side of the bridge.'

16

'Where did it happen?' Tartaglia asked, ducking under the tape that marked the inner cordon on the north side of Hammersmith Bridge.

'About three quarters of the way along, on the Barnes side, sir,' Yvette Dickenson said.

Out of breath, her over-sized, overstuffed handbag constantly slipping off her shoulder, she had been struggling to keep up with him from the rendezvous point. Stifling impatience, he held the tape up high for her to step through. Although the rain had stopped temporarily, the wind had picked up and was whipping her thick brown hair across her face, strands catching on the edges of her glasses, which were spattered with rain. She made a couple of futile attempts to restrain her hair with a gloved hand, then seemed to give in to the forces of nature. Bundled up in a large grey overcoat, which barely met around her stomach, her eyes were red, nose streaming, and she looked miserable. Tartaglia wondered why Steele couldn't have let her stay behind in the warmth of the office and sent someone else to brief him instead. Also, why Dickenson wasn't tucked up at home enjoying the last month or so of her pregnancy in relative tranquillity was beyond him. But he knew it was her choice and not a subject she liked to discuss.

Scanning the length of the bridge, he could just make out the flapping white material of the forensic tent, tucked away behind one of the tall towers that held up the bridge. He crossed the bridge on his motorbike every day on his way to work but he had long since stopped noticing it. With the pressure of daily life, of getting from A to B as quickly as possible, it had faded into the general background, like so much of London. However, on foot it seemed much more substantial and garish. In his view, whoever was responsible for painting it that particular shade of goose-shit green should be taken out and shot. But it was still handsome in a solid, Victorian sort of way, with ornate ironwork picked out in gold and four tall towers, each looking like a mini replica of Big Ben. It formed the gateway between urban Hammersmith and rural Barnes and was a favourite spot for couples watching the sun set over the river, as well as suicides. More extraordinarily, it had survived three separate terrorist attacks, although why anyone should target it was beyond him. There were far more famous and important bridges along the Thames to choose.

Dickenson had fallen behind and he stopped for a moment, turning away from the icy wind, hands stuffed in his pockets. The sky was ominously dark, with only a glimmer of light on the horizon. After the heavy rain, the swollen river below was the colour of milky coffee, awash with debris and flowing particularly fast around the pontoons of the bridge. On the south side, it was so high that it skimmed the bank, almost at the level of the towpath. Anyone going over, particularly at night, would have stood little chance.

'They were standing just over there, sir,' Dickenson said, out of breath as she caught up with him, gesturing ahead towards an area at the foot of one of the towers where the footway had been taped off by the forensic team.

Just at that point, the path looped outwards around the tower, forming a balcony overlooking the river. He remembered standing close to the spot with friends a few years before, watching the Oxford and Cambridge boat race. The area was covered with scaffolding and a makeshift tent to protect it from the elements, bright lights shining inside and the shadows of the SOCOs moving around.

He turned to Dickenson. 'Where was the witness when she saw the couple?'

'On the other side of the road, sir. She said the man and woman were standing very close together. She first thought they were kissing but when she went past she heard them arguing.'

'What time was this?'

'Just after midnight. She lives in Barnes and was on her way home.'

'Could she hear what they were they saying?'

'Not the exact words, what with wind and the noise of the river. But she said the woman was crying and seemed to be pleading with the man. She thought the woman sounded American, although she couldn't be sure. The witness was nearly on the other side when she heard the woman scream. She turned around and saw the woman struggling with the man; he then pushed her over the bridge.'

'He pushed her? She's sure?'

'That's what she said. She thought she heard a splash and ran to the other side of the bridge but the water was so dark, she couldn't see the woman at all.'

'What about the man?'

'He was bending right over the edge looking down. For a moment, she worried that he might fall in too. He seemed to be talking to himself, totally unaware of her presence and she thought maybe he was high on something. After a moment, he ran off towards Hammersmith.'

'Do we have a description?' The bridge was quite well lit at night and visibility should have been good.

'Pretty basic, I'm afraid. Tall, slim build, and scruffily dressed. He was wearing a coat or jacket with a hood, which was pulled up over his head so the witness couldn't see his face clearly. The woman was older and quite smartly dressed. She said they looked an odd pair.'

He couldn't help feeling a little disappointed that the description of the man was so vague. 'What about forensics?'

'The SOCOs have found some scuffmarks on the railings and a whole load of fingerprints, although some are badly smudged.'

He nodded. 'It's a popular place to stand and admire the view.'

Although there was a lot of pedestrian traffic on the bridge, if the man had held onto the rail as he looked over, they might get some prints. But if it was Tom, why had he taken the woman there? With the previous three murders, Tom had chosen quiet, private places where there was little risk of interruption and where he could control the environment. The bridge, with cars, cycles and pedestrians going by even late at night, was very public and to kill someone there would require a degree of improvisation. Yet Tom's previous killings seemed to have been so carefully planned and staged, down to the last detail, the ritual seemingly important. In Tartaglia's view, it didn't feel right. Hypersensitive, given all the publicity, Cornish had insisted that they look at any possible crime that could be linked. But Tartaglia cursed the tenseness of a situation which had brought him there simply because a woman had been pushed from a high place.

'I assume there's no sign of the body yet?' he asked, knowing the answer. It could take days, sometimes weeks, for a body to surface from the murky depths of the Thames. Given the current, it was probably half way down the river by now, somewhere near Greenwich.

Dickenson shook her head. 'The River Police have been alerted and the local uniforms are searching the banks on either side. Maybe she managed to swim away.'

'Unlikely. The current's particularly strong at this time of year. Unless she was a very strong swimmer, she would have been pulled under almost immediately. Have you checked to see if anyone's reported her missing?'

'Nothing's come in so far. I'm liaising with DS Daley at Hammersmith, who's in charge of the case for the moment.'

'What about CCTV footage?'

'DS Daley's dealing with that now. It's lucky the bloke went off Hammersmith way. The area around the Broadway's littered with cameras.'

Tartaglia looked over the bridge again at the swirling water

146

below. His instincts told him that they were wasting their time. But one thing held him back from saying so outright. The incident had happened on Hammersmith Bridge, right on the doorstep of the Barnes murder investigation team, almost like a direct challenge. But if Tom was responsible, he had changed his MO. They would have to wait for the body to surface to discover more. In the meantime, the priority was to find the man.

He turned and started to walk back towards Hammersmith, Dickenson stumbling along beside him. 'How much longer is the bridge going to stay closed?' he asked, after a moment.

'The crime scene manager thinks it may be another few hours, sir. I just hope it's open before I have to go home.' She sighed, every step an effort. He considered offering her his arm but thought better of it. Knowing Dickenson, she would misinterpret the gesture as patronising or a reminder of the fact that she was finding it difficult doing her job in the last few months of her pregnancy. 'I had quite a time getting into work this morning,' she continued, irritably. 'I had to go all the way over to Putney Bridge to get across. The traffic was a ruddy nightmare, I can tell you.'

He nodded sympathetically. Despite the fact that the Barnes office was straight over the bridge, only a quarter of a mile away, he was going to have to make a lengthy detour to get there. Thank God he had his bike. 'It's a bugger having to go all the way around. Hopefully, it won't be for much longer. I'll bet the worthy burghers of Barnes are up in arms.'

She gave him a weak smile. 'There've been no end of complaints and it's barely lunchtime. It's as if they think we've done it deliberately to ruin their day.'

He shook his head. You couldn't win. When the bridge had been closed for over two years for structural work and refurbishment, the doctors, dentists, writers, musicians, actors and other solidly middle class residents on the Barnes side had campaigned militantly to keep it permanently closed to cars, so as to preserve their nice little village haven from commuter traffic. But close it for a day and everyone was screaming blue murder. It mattered not a jot that some poor woman might have died, let alone been killed.

Donovan slid Coldplay's *X&Y* into the CD player and shoved the car into gear. According to the A-Z, Annie Klein lived about a ten-minute drive away from Soane Antiquarian Books, close to the M4 motorway. Hopefully, she'd get there before Harry Angel had a chance to call Klein and prime her. Although there was no evidence that Marion Spear had been murdered, let alone anything to link her death with that of the other three girls, she agreed with Tartaglia. Angel definitely merited closer investigation.

Inching along in heavy traffic, she thought back to the conversation earlier that morning with Angela Grafton, Marion Spear's former boss. Grafton, a large-boned, red-faced woman in her late fifties, with a helmet of lacquered, bottle blonde hair, had been forthright and helpful. Chain-smoking, planted behind her large desk, she tipped a long tube of ash into a saucer and said: 'Marion may have been nearly thirty but she had as much nous as a sixteen-year-old. Or less so, given what sixteen-year-olds are like these days.'

In full flow, hardly needing any prompting from Donovan, she spoke emphatically, her opinions not open to question. 'Of course, it's not surprising when you understand Marion's background.' She gave Donovan a knowing look as if to say that she'd seen much of the world and understood all its ins and outs. 'Only child, with Dad running off at a young age, leaving Mum to cope on her own. I certainly remember the mum, silly goose of a woman; always on the phone, fussing and fretting, never letting Marion be, whining about how lonely she was without her. Passive aggressive, I think they call that type nowadays. She wanted Marion to throw in the towel and go home to Leicester. Poor Marion, I remember thinking on more than one occasion, what a waste it was. She was a decent girl but there was something about her that made you feel sorry for her, and want to take her under your wing. But there's only so much you can do.'

Sighing deeply, as if Marion had been an accident waiting to happen, she had added that Marion had been popular with clients but that she didn't remember anyone in particular ringing up or coming around to see her at the office. 'I certainly don't recall her talking about a boyfriend or admirer. But then why would she mention it to me?' She shrugged her broad shoulders. 'Marion wasn't the type to confide. She was a pretty little thing but she didn't stand a chance, with her god-awful mother. A woman like that would make anyone secretive, don't you think?'

The traffic was still creeping along and Donovan heard a siren in the distance. With the roads still slick from the rain, she wondered if maybe there had been an accident up ahead. Worrying that Angel would be calling Klein any minute now, Donovan took the next turning off the main road and started to cut through the side streets and onto Popes Lane, where things were moving faster. Stopping once outside the gates of Brentford Cemetery to consult the A-Z, five minutes later she turned into the road where Klein lived.

Although not much more than half a mile from Ealing Green, the area had a different feel, paint peeling, front gardens untidy, estate agent boards scattered everywhere, interspersed with the odd sign offering B&B accommodation. Klein's address was in the middle of a long row of tall, ramshackle semi-detached houses. Stepping around a collection of kids' bikes that had been abandoned in a pile in the middle of the path, the owners probably having gone off home for lunch, Donovan walked up to the front door and peered at the intercom. 'Klein' was scrawled in biro on a piece of tape stuck against the top bell. She pressed the buzzer several times until a sleepy female voice answered.

'Who is it?'

'I'm looking for Annie Klein. I'm Detective Sergeant Donovan.'

'Police?'

Donovan heard the alarm in the woman's voice. Used to the

reaction, even from completely innocent members of the public who weren't accustomed to dealing with the police, she tried to sound as friendly as possible. 'Nothing to worry about, I assure you. I just need a quick word concerning Harry Angel.'

There was silence followed by the screech of a sash window being hauled open somewhere above. Donovan craned her neck upwards and saw a woman with long, bright red hair peering down at her.

'I'm Annie. Is Harry OK?'

'He's absolutely fine. May I come up?'

'Are you really a policewoman?' She sounded a little sceptical.

Donovan held out her warrant card, although at that distance it was just a token gesture.

'It's all right, I believe you,' Annie said. 'Here, catch this.' A couple of Yale keys on a key ring landed at Donovan's feet. 'The buzzer's not working. Top floor, just follow the stairs.'

Annie appeared to have a trusting, accommodating nature. At least it seemed as though Angel hadn't yet warned her to expect a visit from the police.

The hall floor was awash with unopened post, directories still in their plastic wrappings piled haphazardly in a corner. With its stale smell, threadbare carpet and tatty green paint, the place reminded Donovan of her university digs. Panting, pausing for breath on each narrow landing, she laboured up the steep stairs to the fourth floor. She really must do something about the ciggies. She was only thirty-three and, according to the drivel she read in magazines on the rare occasions she found time to go to the hairdresser, she ought to be in her prime, ought to be able to gallop up the stairs like a thoroughbred and make wild, passionate love to some good-looking bloke waiting for her at the top. Pigs might fly, she thought, as she turned up the final flight of stairs.

Annie Klein stood in the open doorway, barefoot, wearing a frayed, embroidered silk dressing gown and little else. Bleary-eyed, she yawned and folded her arms, pulling the dressing gown tightly around her tall, skinny frame.

'I was right,' she said, smiling, staring down at Donovan. 'You don't look at all like a policeman. Not that I'd know much about that, apart from watching *The Bill*.'

She looked to be in her late twenties or early thirties. Her voice was pleasant, quite deep, with a transatlantic twang that sounded a little fake. The dark, petrol blue of her dressing gown set off her pale skin and long, curly copper-coloured hair. Her eyes were a startling dark brown. She was at least six foot tall, Donovan realised, following her inside, wishing that she hadn't chosen to wear flat boots that morning, not that heels would have made much difference. Usually her lack of height didn't bother her but for some reason suddenly she felt at a disadvantage.

'Do you feel like a cup of tea?' Annie asked. 'I was just about to make some when you rang the bell.'

'Please.' Donovan sat down in a deep, saggy armchair covered with a sparkly orange throw. After all the coffee she'd drunk that morning, she was buzzing. Tea would make a welcome change.

The large room was light, with sloping eaves and two windows, the walls painted a bright pink. A mirror hung above the small fireplace, decorated with gold-painted scallop shells, and a large, professional-looking black and white photograph of a young woman covered most of the wall next to it. It took Donovan several seconds to realise that the picture was of Annie, the make-up, clothes and lighting completely transforming her.

Watching her make tea in the tiny kitchen area in the corner of the room, Donovan was intrigued. Annie seemed far too exotic a creature to be working for Angel packing books.

'Do you model?' she asked, as Annie came over with two full mugs.

'I used to. But I'm more interested in acting these days.' She grimaced. 'Sadly, it's not that interested in me.' She sat down on the sofa opposite, gracefully swinging her long legs up underneath her and tucking the folds of her dressing gown tightly around her feet.

'I understand you work part-time at Soane Books.'

Annie hesitated, taking a sip of tea. 'Well… not officially. What I mean is, Harry pays me cash and I don't declare it.'

Donovan smiled, hoping to put her at ease. 'Don't worry. I'm not interested in that. How long have you worked there?'

'Just a few months. The internet business has really taken off and Harry can't cope on his own.'

'Do you know if he had any help in the shop a couple of years ago?'

Annie shook her head. 'I don't think so, but you'd better ask him. Anyway, why do you want to know?'

'We're investigating the death of a woman called Marion Spear.'

Annie looked doubtful. 'What's this got to do with Harry?'

'Mr Angel was one of her clients. I just need to get some basic details so that we can eliminate him from our enquiries.'

'Harry knows you're here?'

'Oh, yes. He gave us your name and address.' It was stretching the truth but Annie didn't seem the suspicious type. By the time she found out that Angel wasn't at all keen for her to talk to the police, it would be too late.

Annie seemed easily reassured and smiled. 'Well then, I suppose there's no harm my talking to you.'

'As I said, I just want a bit of background, that's all. Perhaps you can start by telling me how often you work at the shop?'

'It depends. I've got a lot of free time at the moment and Harry's pretty laid-back about when I come and go.'

'You're there most days?'

'On and off if it's busy, when I haven't got auditions.'

It seemed a cosy arrangement and Donovan got the impression that Harry Angel was more of a friend than a boss. 'Have you known each other long?'

Annie smiled and took another sip of tea. 'A few years, actually.'

'You had a relationship?' Donovan asked, catching a certain look in her eyes and reading between the lines.

'Well, I wouldn't really call it that. We went out a few times but it didn't work out.'

'Why was that?'

Annie took refuge in her tea. 'Look. I don't want to talk out of school. Harry's a decent guy.'

'But it didn't work out.'

Annie sighed and shook her head. 'No.' She took a long sip of tea and, after a moment, added: 'Harry's a bit intense. Gets carried away too quickly and I wasn't after anything serious.'

'Intense?'

Annie brushed away a long lock of hair that had fallen across her face. 'Yeah. You know how guys can be.'

Apart from a spotty fifth-form admirer who haunted the school gates waiting for her to come out, Donovan had little personal experience of such things. Somehow, since then, she'd failed to inspire intensity in any man. But, thinking about it, maybe that was no bad thing. Obsession was unhealthy, particularly when it was one-way. Give her a normal, down-to-earth bloke any day. Although they seemed to be pretty thin on the ground and, thinking of Richard, her ex, 'normal' didn't exactly make the earth move.

'Can you be more specific?' Donovan asked.

Annie hesitated. 'Well, he used to leave little notes and poems at night under the windscreen wiper of my car. I had a car in those days, you see.'

'Anonymous notes, you mean?'

Annie nodded. 'I'd come out the next morning and find them waiting for me. Of course, I knew they were from him, even though he wouldn't admit it.'

'You think he was checking up on you? Watching you?'

Annie shrugged as if she didn't mind. 'Maybe. I hadn't really thought of it like that.'

'What did the notes say?'

'Oh, they were just a few lines. Sort of... well...' she furrowed her brow, searching for the word, '...sort of enigmatic.'

'They weren't threatening?'

Annie looked surprised at the idea. 'No way. I think they were supposed to be kind of romantic.'

'Did he do anything else?'

She giggled. 'He left a dollar bill under the wiper once but I never worked out what he meant by it.'

Any initial disadvantage she had felt when first meeting Annie swiftly evaporated. Annie might have the advantage in terms of height and looks but she seemed out of touch with reality. Even if she hadn't found Angel's behaviour peculiar, let alone threatening, in Donovan's book he had all the makings of a stalker. Also, although she had only glimpsed Angel briefly, she had to agree with Tartaglia. In poor light, Angel might easily fit the description given by Zaleski.

'So, you called a halt to things?'

'Yeah. He kept ringing me for a while but eventually he got the message.'

'How did you get back in touch?'

'I was looking for some part-time work and I answered an ad he'd put in the local paper. I thought twice about it when I realised who it was, I can tell you. But I needed the money and he seemed pretty cool about things.' She giggled again, looking down at her mug. 'Actually, I get the feeling he's still pretty keen on me.'

'And that doesn't bother you?' Donovan asked, finding it impossible to fathom Annie's attitude. Her manner was so ridiculously open and easy-going, so trusting. It reminded Donovan of the way Marion Spear had been described and she felt increasingly concerned.

Annie's eyes opened wide. 'Why should it? Harry's a sweetie, really, and I can handle it.' She uncoiled herself from the sofa and stood up. 'Would you like another cup of tea?'

Donovan shook her head and put her mug down on the floor beside her chair. It was still almost full, the tea so weak it was little more than water mixed with milk and now lukewarm. 'What about family and friends? Who does Mr Angel see regularly?'

'I honestly don't know,' Annie said, walking over to the kitchen area and switching on the kettle. 'He never talks about his family or anyone in particular. He's real private.'

'But surely he gets phone calls at work.'

'I'm stuck down in the basement most of the time and I can't hear anything. There's an answer-machine upstairs, so there's no need to take messages.'

'So, you don't know if he's got a girlfriend?'

Annie turned back to Donovan with a smile. 'If he has, it sure isn't anything serious. Anyway, he wouldn't tell me. I mean, it'd spoil his chances, wouldn't it?'

Donovan waited while Annie finished making her tea and came back to the sofa. 'Just to recap; you've never heard him mention Marion Spear.'

Annie shook her head, sitting down again. 'You said this woman died. What happened?'

Donovan decided to give her the bare facts. It might give Annie a much-needed jolt and help her to remember things more clearly. If nothing else, it was worth putting her on her guard about Harry Angel.

'She fell to her death from the top storey of a car park near where she worked. It's quite close to the bookshop. The coroner recorded an open verdict but we're now looking into it again.'

Annie looked blank. 'You haven't told me what Harry's got to do with any of this.'

'We're trying to trace Marion Spear's final movements. He was one of the last people to see her on the day she died. She showed him a flat in Carlton Road in Ealing but we don't know where she went after that.'

Annie looked puzzled. 'Harry looking at flats? Are you sure?'

'Why does that surprise you?'

Annie seemed embarrassed, as if she had said the wrong thing, coiling a long strand of hair around her finger. 'Well, when his granddad died, he left Harry the shop. The upstairs rooms had been used for storage and were in quite a state. But Harry cleaned the place out, gave it all a lick of paint and moved in.'

'When was this?'

'I'm not sure, but Harry was already living there when I first met him. I think he had moved in quite recently, as I remember the smell of the paint. It was overwhelming.'

According to the file, Harry had given the shop address when Marion Spear died. 'Maybe he decided he wanted a change.'

Annie shook her head. 'He's never talked about wanting to move. I mean, why would he? The space over the shop is enormous and all he has to do is roll downstairs to work in the morning. I wish I had it that easy.'

Feeling increasingly impatient, Donovan realised she was going to have to spell it out for Annie. 'An hour after the appointment with Mr Angel, Marion Spear was dead.'

Annie stared at her. 'Surely you can't think Harry had anything to do with it? I know he's a bit eccentric but he means well.' She started to chew one of her long fingernails, shaking her head slowly as she mulled it over. 'I don't know what he was doing, going to see a flat with that woman, but I know he wouldn't harm a fly.'

'I'm sure you're right,' Donovan said. She'd done her best and there was no point in pushing Annie further, as she clearly refused to entertain any suspicions about Angel. She stood up to go. 'Just one more question. Were you working at the shop last Wednesday afternoon?'

Annie paused for a moment, thinking back, then shook her head. 'Not Wednesday. I had an audition in Hammersmith.'

'So, you didn't see Mr Angel at all on Wednesday?'

'No.'

'If you're not there, what does he do if he has to go out?'

'He normally puts a note up on the door saying "Back in five minutes". It's a bit of a con because he's usually gone longer than that, but it means that people tend to come back.'

Donovan picked up her bag, took out a card and handed it to

Annie. 'Thanks for being so helpful. If you remember anything else, would you give me a call?'

Annie took the card with the delight of a child being handed a sweet. Clearly fond of Angel, she appeared to be unaware of the implications of some of the things she had said. Still wondering how a woman of roughly her own age could be such an ingénue, Donovan hoped Annie wouldn't be foolish enough to repeat the conversation verbatim to Angel and put him on his guard. Simple Annie might be, but she was right about one thing, Donovan was sure; Angel wasn't interested in looking at flats. He was personally interested in Marion Spear, something he'd successfully hidden from the previous investigation.

17

To: Carolyn.Steele@met.police.uk
From: Tom659873362@greenmail.com

Dear Carolyn,
I hope you don't mind first names but I hate formalities, don't you? Also, I feel I already know you, even though we haven't yet met – I certainly look forward to that pleasure one day very soon. For the moment, though, let me congratulate you on your performance last night on *Crimewatch*. You looked good and you struck just the right note, I thought. Well done for keeping just a few interesting details back from the public. We wouldn't want them knowing all our little secrets, would we? Just so you know it's me writing this and not some cheap imitation trying to get your attention, you could have mentioned Gemma's long, silky brown hair. I think of her every time I stroke that lovely lock. She's very dear to me, you know. But hey, I'm a fickle sort of guy. You know that already, don't you? I think you understand me. Perhaps to you, I'd be true. Perhaps. But we can talk about that another time – when we meet. I'm straying from the point. Getting back to the show last night, people should be praised when they do something well. You deserve to be kissed for it, by a man who knows how. I, too, deserve praise, don't you think? I'm very good at what I do; I'm getting away with murder!
With fondest wishes
Yours (dare I say, your?)
Tom

Steele swivelled round in her chair to face Tartaglia, expressionless. 'So, what do you make of it?' Her tone was business-like, without any trace of emotion, as if she were asking his opinion about a run-of-the-mill communiqué.

It was early evening and she had called him into her office, taking care to shut the door behind them, which was unusual. She had never had anything private to discuss with him until now, never solicited his opinion about anything major so far and he felt surprised and a little bewildered that she had sought him out now. The email left him momentarily speechless, not sure what to say, other than the obvious platitudes. Angry on her behalf, feeling a spark of unaccustomed concern for her, he was amazed at the barefaced cheek of it. The cocky, sexual overtones were particularly revolting. He had no idea if Steele lived alone or if she had a partner. Notwithstanding the general resentment he felt for her, he was instantly worried, wondering how, as a woman, she was affected by it, whether or not she felt intimidated.

Even with all her years of experience with the Met, seeing the darker side of humanity on a daily basis, emails from a serial killer were not run of the mill. It had to touch her in some manner. She had to feel something. But she was giving nothing away, matter-of-factly treating what had happened as if it were all part of the normal workday routine. Although perhaps it was all an act for his benefit, trying to show how tough she could be.

She sat very upright, mouth taut, face a pale, blank canvas, looking at him, waiting for his response. He struggled to find the right words and failed. 'Did you mention in *Crimewatch* that he calls himself Tom?'

She nodded. 'I decided to do so, just in case either it really is his name or nickname, or might ring a bell with someone.'

'When did you receive the email?'

'About an hour ago. Of course it's untraceable.'

He put his hands in his pockets and leaned back against the wall, studying her closely. But there was still no sign of emotion in her eyes. An hour ago? She had been dealing with it on her own for a full hour, without saying anything to the members of her team in the room outside? How could she keep it all to herself? She was extraordinary. Clarke would have been out of his office like a rocket, hopping mad or excited, or both, wanting to share it, wanting to get everyone's view.

'I've spoken to the lads at Newlands Park. According to them, sending emails like this is a piece of piss. All Tom has to do is drive around with a laptop in his car and tap into any unsecured network. Apparently, there are thousands and thousands of official and unofficial wi-fi hotspots all over London.'

'What about the email address?'

'He's probably set up a sack-load of them especially for the purpose. There's no way of tracing him at all.'

He shook his head in disbelief. 'Are they sure?'

'That's what they said. Of course they'll have a go, but they told me not to expect anything.'

She sighed, stifling a yawn, again as if they were talking about something trivial. 'Apparently, if we knew where he was when he was online, we might be able to trace the signal back to the modem, then trace the modem back to the place where the computer was purchased. But even if the computer's not stolen, knowing our Tom, he's unlikely to have given his real details to the shop, don't you think? Anyway, if he's moving around, as they suspect, it won't work.'

'Have you told Cornish?'

She nodded. 'And I'm telling you and Gary, when he gets back. But nobody else needs to know. I can't risk another leak to the press.'

As if stiff from sitting at the desk too long, she bowed her head, leaning forward in her chair, locking her fingers and stretching her arms out in front of her. Slim and lithe, with her sleek dark hair and green eyes, she reminded him of a cat. Like all cats, she was inscrutable. She did her duty as a boss but kept him at arm's length wherever possible, as if she was wary of him.

He wasn't expecting her to treat him the way Clarke had done

– that easy, mutually rewarding relationship had been built up over several years. But he had expected something more of her. He'd heard good reports of her from people who had worked for her in the past, but as far as he could see, they were talking about a different person.

'Now, tell me about what happened on the bridge,' she said, tilting her chair back and putting her feet up on the bottom drawer of her desk, which was slightly open.

As he started to explain what had happened, he pictured the bridge in his mind, with the brown swelling water below, trying yet again to make sense of what had gone on. Was it really connected to the other girls? It was like trying to find your way in thick, drifting fog, he thought. Just when you managed to make out something familiar and got your bearings, another wave of fog would roll in and the landscape would become unrecognisable again. He wasn't sure what he thought about any of it anymore.

'So, there's nothing yet to link what happened to the killings?' she said once he had finished.

He shook his head. 'Not until we find the body.'

'Why did CID call us?'

'Some bright spark had been reading the papers and thought it wasn't worth taking any chances. If it turns out to be Tom, they'll deserve a medal.'

'But we only have the witness's word for what happened.'

'CCTV footage from the bridge confirms what she saw. Some sort of incident definitely took place, although we have no clear visual of the man's face. But I spoke to forensics and it seems as though they've retrieved some decent prints. Let's hope that at least one will belong to him.'

Steele looked thoughtful. 'The MO's very different. But I suppose we must keep an open mind. Tom's a clever sod and he's hardly going to get away with the same routine after all the stuff in the media.'

'But if Tom is responsible, why didn't he refer to it in the email to you? You'd think he'd be bragging about it.'

She shrugged, her eyes flicking back to the screen. 'The thought occurred to me, too, when I first read this shit,' she said, distractedly. He caught a slight tensing in her face, as if it pained her to look at it. Perhaps it had affected her in some way after all. 'But maybe he thinks we don't yet know about what happened on the bridge.'

She had a point. In normal circumstances, the local CID would handle the investigation until it was clear that the death was suspicious. Given their heavy workload and the lack of a body, it was unlikely the bridge would have been closed down so quickly, if at all. Perhaps Tom had been counting on that.

'But if it is him, why choose Hammersmith Bridge?' he said. 'Unless he *wants* us to find out about it?'

For a moment she said nothing, still staring at the screen, fingers steepled under her chin as if she was thinking it all through. Then she reached for the mouse, closed down the email and turned to face him. 'I'm going to get Patrick's opinion on it. Maybe he can shed some light on all this. Now, tell me about Ealing, this morning,' she said briskly, as if wanting to get off the subject of Kennedy. 'I hear the witness had some useful information.'

'Yes. He seems to have had a good look at the man and the e-fit should come out well.'

'I also hear you've been stirring things up with a man called Harry Angel. He's made a complaint to the Borough Commander. He claims you were harassing him.'

Surprised that Angel had taken things so far, so quickly, Tartaglia shrugged. 'He didn't like my line of questioning.'

'Is this to do with the Marion Spear case?'

He nodded.

'Why are you chasing after that, when we've so much on our plate already?'

'I've told you, I think she could be an early victim.'

'But Marion Spear doesn't fit the victim profile.'

It was as if Kennedy himself was talking. 'I haven't seen Dr

Kennedy's written report yet,' he said, trying to contain his resentment.

'Don't be pedantic, Mark. You know what he thinks.'

'Yes, and he's jumping to the wrong conclusion.'

She tensed as if he had criticised her personally. 'Tom goes for young girls. Marion Spear was thirty. She doesn't fit.'

'Maybe it's just a coincidence that the three victims we know about were all in their teens. Maybe there are others we don't yet know about who weren't so young.'

'There's no time to speculate about what he might have done. We've got to stick to what we know.'

'If he only goes for young girls, why did he write you that email?' He was clutching at straws but somehow he had to convince her.

She coloured and her expression hardened as if somehow he had touched a nerve. 'That's different. The email is just a wind-up, to prove how clever he is.'

'Let's hope so.'

'It doesn't change the profile.'

He sighed with frustration. 'OK. For argument's sake, let's take the three girls. I agree their age is a common factor. But there's another one, which the profile ignores: personality type. They were all loners, all apparently depressed. All three had a history of being bullied at school and it was so bad that Ellie Best was on anti-depressants. With that background, they were all vulnerable and open to the idea of suicide. We know Marion Spear was depressed and lonely too. Yes, she's older, but maybe her age is irrelevant or maybe he was less fussy before.'

'We're overloaded as it is, not even counting what's just happened on the bridge. We haven't got the resources to chase up every long shot.'

'How else are we going to find him? Unless any new leads come in from *Crimewatch*, we've got nowhere with the three girls. He's covered his tracks too well and we can't find the link. If Marion Spear is an early victim, maybe he made mistakes.'

'But you've got nothing, have you? Nothing concrete.'

'Not yet. But I want to keep trying. I have a hunch.' The minute the words were out of his mouth, he knew he'd made a mistake.

She shook her head. 'That's not enough. Look, Mark. If you insist on following this up, it will have to be in your own time.'

He was about to reply that he would do just that when there was a knock and the door swung open to reveal Kennedy.

'Sorry I'm late,' he said, grinning broadly. 'With the bridge closed off, I had to go all around the houses via Putney to get here. Hope I'm not interrupting.'

'Of course not, Patrick,' Steele said, getting to her feet. 'Mark and I had just finished.'

After the talk with Steele, Tartaglia had retreated to his office to try and finish the day's paperwork. But he was soon forced to give up. It was useless. The heating was working overtime for a change and the room was like an oven. He couldn't concentrate, as he thought about their conversation. To make matters worse, Gary Jones had just got back from following up a fruitless set of calls that had come in from *Crimewatch*. Several new 'witnesses' had come forward, claiming to have seen Gemma with Tom, not just at the church in Ealing but at various locations dotted all over the city. Some of them were cranks and time-wasters, some just wishful-thinkers, wanting to appear helpful. But none of the reports held water even at the most basic of levels. In addition, half of London, with a teenage daughter who used the internet, now seemed convinced that they might have come across Tom in a chat room somewhere. However loony some of the callers appeared, each call had to be properly investigated. But so far there were no genuine fresh leads. At least none of the calls had thrown up any evidence that Tom had been active outside the London area.

Sweating, feet up on the desk, shoes off, Jones was on the phone to what sounded like his brother, letting off steam at top volume about some rugby match or other. Built like a prop-forward gone to seed, with a thinning thatch of short fair hair, Jones dominated the cramped space with his sheer physical presence. Tartaglia felt hemmed in, almost claustrophobic, and he couldn't hear himself think over the rich, booming voice. He got up from his desk and started to change into waterproofs, thinking of going to see Clarke on his way home, although he had no idea yet about whether Clarke would be fit to see him. As he picked up his keys and helmet, Donovan appeared in the doorway.

'I've just got in. Fancy a drink? It's on me, this time.'

Ten minutes later, they were sitting in a corner of The Bull's Head, each with a pint of Young's Special, trying to ignore the buzz of speculation around them about what had happened on the bridge the night before.

'Fucking Rasputin. I'll bet he's giving her more than just professional advice.' Tartaglia gave Donovan a meaningful look and took a large swig of bitter.

'Ignore him.'

'Easier said than done.'

She watched him light a cigarette.

As the smoke coiled in her direction, she was amazed to find she had no desire to follow suit. On a moment's impulse, she had retrieved Adam Zaleski's card from the bin that morning, making an excuse to Tartaglia, as they left to go to the café, that she had left something behind in the meeting room. Zaleski had managed to fit her in for a quick half-hour session of hypnosis before she was due back in Barnes. Knowing Tartaglia's views on such things, she thought it best not to mention it. Zaleski was a witness and, strictly speaking, she shouldn't have sought him out. But she admitted to herself that she found him quite attractive. He had told her that she would only need another couple of sessions and she felt calm, almost serene, and in control. Perhaps that was what meditation was all about.

Drawing hard on his cigarette, Tartaglia leaned towards her. 'Am I mad to think that the Marion Spear case could be related?'

She smiled, unused to seeing him so full of self-doubt. 'Listen.

From what I've heard today, it's well worth pursuing. That's what I wanted to talk to you about.' She told him about her chat with Annie.

Tartaglia looked a little disappointed. 'So, Angel wasn't interested in looking at flats but was after Marion. We can't hang him for that.'

'But Annie practically admitted he'd been stalking her. And the fact that he went out of his way to hide his interest in Marion, is suspicious.'

He shook his head. 'Lying doesn't add up to murder. People lie to us all the time, even innocent ones. You know that.'

'I still think it's worth following up. If he's innocent of anything other than fancying Marion, why doesn't he come clean? Knowing we're taking a second look is an ideal opportunity for him to set the record straight, particularly when he also knows that we're investigating the other murders.'

She paused, studying him closely as she took a sip of her beer, noting the doubt and strain in his face. If only Clarke was still around, he would know what to do. The news from the hospital had been positive since he had come out of the coma, but it seemed that recovery was going to be slow. Nobody in the office, let alone Tartaglia, had dared yet voice the thought that Clarke might never be coming back. It was as if by not talking about it, and skirting around the subject, there was still a good chance that Clarke might, one day, stride in through the door, sweep Steele aside and take charge again with all of his old good humour and warmth. However, the likelihood was that Clarke would never be able to work again, certainly not take charge of a murder squad, with all the pressures and physical stresses the role entailed. In their hearts, they all knew it. But the moment wasn't right to talk to Tartaglia about it, although she sensed it wasn't far from his thoughts. Not for the first time, she felt how much he was in need of his mentor.

'This isn't like you, Mark,' she said, touching his hand gently. 'Don't listen to Steele and Kennedy. Just think what Trevor would

say if he were here. He'd tell you to follow your instincts, would-
n't he? He always trusted your judgement and backed you up.
You've got to remember that, keep hold of it, and trust yourself.
I certainly do.'

His face creased into a tired smile. 'Thanks.'

'Don't look so depressed. I may have something else. After I
saw Annie, I went to see Marion Spear's flatmate, Karen.'

'The one who made the statement when she died?'

'Yes. She gave me the same spiel about Marion being lonely
and wanting to go back up north to be with her Mum. She said
she tried many times to get her to go out with her and the gang
but apparently Marion preferred to stay in and watch TV. To be
honest, given what I know about Marion and having met Karen,
it doesn't surprise me. I think I'd prefer to stay in and watch *Big
Brother* too.'

'What about Angel? Does Karen remember him?'

'No. Doesn't remember any particular bloke hanging around
Marion. But Karen said that she was often out, staying over at her
then boyfriend's flat. However, when I pressed her, she mentioned
another girl, called Nicola, who had been living in the flat temporarily. Karen said that although Nicola wasn't there for long,
she and Marion became quite chummy. Apparently they occasionally used to go out to the pub or to see a film together.'

'There's no mention of this Nicola woman in the file.'

'What's new? Nicola was only there for a month or so and she
moved on before Marion died. Karen has no idea if she and
Marion even stayed in touch after Nicola left. Maybe CID
thought that Karen's statement was enough to determine
Marion's state of mind or maybe they didn't bother to find out if
there'd been anybody else living in the flat.'

'We must find her.'

'Don't worry, I'm onto it and I won't say anything to Steele.
Karen isn't sure where Nicola's gone but she's given me the land-
lord's number. Maybe Nicola left a forwarding address. I'll check
it out first thing in the morning.'

Somebody passed behind her carrying drinks to one of the tables and Donovan caught the words 'fucking marvellous' and 'about bloody time' accompanied by a round of raucous cheers and applause. Listening for a moment, she gathered that the bridge had reopened.

'That's a relief,' she said, turning back to Tartaglia. 'I thought it was going to take me several hours to get home.'

Tartaglia downed the remainder of his pint. 'Going back to Angel, what about last Wednesday afternoon? Do any of his neighbours remember what he was up to?'

She shook her head. 'I checked with several of the shops on either side of him and nobody noticed whether he was in or out. However, they told me that he tends to keep odd hours. Reading between the lines, they think he's a bit eccentric. I've left my card in case somebody remembers something.'

He sighed, running his fingers through his hair. 'Angel's a bloody long shot but we've got to keep checking. Maybe Nicola will remember him, if only you can find her. At the moment, she's our best bet.'

'Our only bet, you mean.'

18

'Well, he's playing with you, isn't he?' Kennedy said, helping himself to the mound of gnocchi alla gorgonzola which Steele had left almost untouched on her plate. 'Cat and mouse. Showing you who's in control, who's boss. Thinks he's so bloody clever. He's deliberately belittling you, of course, treating you as a sex object. But then he sees all women as objects. Some just suit his purposes better than others.' He scooped up another large forkful of gnocchi.

Steele watched him silently, amazed that he kept so svelte, given how much he seemed to eat. She had no appetite, the words in the email still swimming around in her mind. They had been to Hammersmith Bridge for a cursory look and she had waited patiently for nearly half an hour in the warmth of Kennedy's car while he paced up and down, talking into a dictaphone as he examined every detail of the bridge and the immediate surrounding area. When he was done, he had confirmed that it was far too early to make any pronouncements as to whether what had happened might possibly fit the pattern. On the one hand, the MO had changed. On the other, he agreed that the proximity to the murder team's office was striking, almost like a direct challenge. Hungry and irritated at being kept waiting for so long for so little result, she bit back the desire to tell him that Tartaglia had already arrived at the same conclusions.

Kennedy seemed to be taking it all blithely in his stride, back in the car talking nineteen to the dozen, in a state of professional elation about the email. She found it impossible to be so detached. She felt shaken, somehow dirtied by having received it and she wanted to punch fucking Tom, get him on the ground and take a pair of heavy boots to his head. How dare he. How fucking dare he. She knew she was an obvious target but it still got to her, eating away at her in every quiet moment. The thought that he knew, or had somehow guessed, that she lived on her own was particularly unnerving.

Kennedy stretched his arm across the table and patted her hand. 'Carolyn, you're not upset, are you?' Wary of giving him any encouragement, she slid her hand away and reached for her glass, taking a sip of wine to hide her confusion.

'You mustn't let it get to you,' he continued, thick-skinned as ever, ignoring the small rejection.

'I'm not,' she said firmly.

'It's what he wants. He's trying to get under your skin. He has a very high opinion of himself and it's a game to him, nothing more. You've got to try and remember that.'

She took another sip of wine. 'Thanks. I'll bear it in mind.'

Was there any point in keeping up the pretence? Part of her wanted to tell him how she really felt, get it off her chest. Maybe she'd feel better. But if she opened up, she knew he would use it to his advantage, draw closer to her, and it would be impossible to push him away again. She had to keep a distance between them. The easiest policy was to let him talk, not interrupt the flow, and try and let it wash over her, as if none of it mattered.

He gave her his usual warm smile. 'You know, it might have been better if you'd got one of the blokes to do *Crimewatch*. On the other hand, maybe it's good to get a dialogue going.'

'Dialogue? Is that what you call it? I hardly have the right of reply, do I? The bastard's untraceable.'

'Of course. He's calling the shots and that's how he likes it,' he said, eyeing her kindly, if a little questioningly, as he drained his glass. He grabbed the half-empty bottle, poured himself some more wine and topped up hers at the same time. 'He conforms perfectly to type, you know. Organised, with a grandiose sense of self-worth, as well as being manipulative and devious. He's incapable of feeling empathy, guilt or remorse. Other people are only objects to serve his purpose. Although labels aren't really helpful to you, he's your classic charismatic psychopath.'

'Charismatic? You're joking.'

'It's a clinical sub-group. He has the ability to be engaging, charming, slick and verbally facile, as we've seen in his emails to the girls, as well as this one to you. He also needs excitement, likes taking risks and living dangerously, which is why he emailed you. He's upped the temperature and thinks he's invincible.'

She took a gulp of wine and smacked the glass down hard on the table. 'He's bloody evil, that's what he is.'

'Maybe, but the more risks he takes, the more chance we have of catching him.' He put on a pair of half-moon reading glasses and unfolded the copy of the email, studying it again carefully. She had never seen him in glasses before and he looked different, suddenly older and more scholarly. She found it strangely endearing, as if it made him more approachable and human.

'It's interesting how he's changed his style,' he said, still scanning the page. 'He was much more flowery when he was writing to the girls. But with you, of course, he's pitching to a different audience. He's quite a chameleon, don't you think?'

'What the hell does it matter?'

Wishing that she could be as logical and dispassionate, she stared down at the table, trying to clear her mind and press down on the anger she felt. But it was impossible. She didn't usually drink much and her head was spinning, thoughts whirling uncontrollably, unable to obliterate the email from her mind. She felt out of control and feared that she might burst into tears at any minute.

Misinterpreting what she was thinking, he added: 'You're not his type. So I shouldn't worry.'

She looked up at him, not sure whether to laugh or cry. 'Yes. He likes young flesh, doesn't he?'

'It's not just that. Of course, you're very attractive. But you're far too strong and together for him. He picks weak victims because underneath it all, in spite of his bravura, he's not up to a real challenge. He can manipulate these poor little girls and do what he wants with them, although he despises them all the more for it. In sending you that email, he's trying to make you one of them. But he can't. He knows you're not like that. It's interesting that his seeing you on the TV is the trigger for the email. He probably hates strong women even more than weak ones. Probably had a domineering, bullying mother at home, bossing him, controlling him, smothering him, forcing him to escape into the fantasy world in his head. It was the only place where he was in control, where he could be himself and play out his games without interference.'

'Lots of people were fucked up as children. But they don't turn into murderers.'

He smiled serenely, ignoring her. 'I'll put my money on his being an only child, or the youngest child, with a big gap between him and the next sibling. I also expect he was a real weed and bullied at school. But I'll give you chapter and verse on all of that when I finish my report.'

She folded her arms, leaning back in her chair until she felt the edge touch the wall behind her. 'I don't give a stuff about what happened in his childhood. All that matters is that he's evil.'

He shrugged. 'Maybe. Whatever the reality, the simple fact is that he's angry. He's been made to feel inadequate all his life and, as I think I told you, I'm pretty sure he's impotent. That only adds to the anger and violence he feels inside. In killing, he's taking back the power. It's all about control. You may think his background is only of academic interest to people like me, but he's targeting you specifically because you're a woman. A man in charge of the case wouldn't have got the same reaction, I'm positive. Like it or not, you may have to deal with him in the near future, so you need to bear in mind his psychology.'

She looked at him aghast. 'Deal with him? What do you mean?'

He looked surprised. 'He's going to contact you again, of course. Maybe he'll try and get you to respond.' Perhaps sensing her revulsion, he added: 'I wouldn't worry. I don't think he actually wants to see you face to face. It's just a little fantasy of his, all part of the game, kidding himself that he has the ability to form a relationship with you, if he so chooses.'

'It's a fucking sick fantasy,' she said, as the waiter took away the plates and left them with dessert menus.

Kennedy gave his a cursory look and slapped it down on the table. 'Panna cotta for me. What about you?'

She shook her head. 'Nothing, thanks. I'm just not hungry.'

He took off his glasses and tucked them away in his breast pocket. A moment passed before he said: 'You *are* going to tell your whole team what's happened, aren't you?'

'Only Mark and Gary. I don't think it's a good idea for the rest of them to know.'

'What are you worried about? The email's an important piece of the puzzle.'

'What if the press get to hear of it?'

'I still think it's a risk worth taking. Why don't you break the news at the morning meeting tomorrow and I'll come and give them a profile update?' Sensing her hesitation, he added: 'You're ashamed of the way he's written to you, aren't you? You find all the personal stuff an affront.'

'Damn right I do,' she said bitterly, suddenly finding it a relief that Kennedy seemed to understand.

'But it's not about you, it's about him. Put yourself in his shoes. By treating you like all the others he's actually de-personalising you.'

'Well, it doesn't come across that way.'

'I understand why you feel that but...'

'Don't give me all that psychologist crap, Patrick. You have no idea what it feels like.'

He nodded sympathetically, as though he was dealing with a fractious child, which made her feel even angrier. 'Naturally, you're upset...' he said, looking concerned.

'Upset? Of course I'm bloody upset. But this is all just a job to you, isn't it?'

The room suddenly felt very hot. She stood up, wanting to dash to the ladies to get away from his gaze, splash some water on her face. But he caught hold of her hands and forced her back down in her chair.

'Please listen to me, Carolyn. Of course the case fascinates me. I'd be an out and out liar to say otherwise. But I only took it on because you asked me to. I'm not you, I don't know exactly what you're feeling but I can imagine. Bloody furious, I expect. Absolutely livid. You also feel vulnerable, don't you? And that's not a comfortable feeling for someone like you, is it?'

Embarrassed by the warmth in his eyes, she tugged her hands away and folded her arms tightly across her chest again. 'I don't need analysing, thanks.'

'It doesn't help that you feel isolated within your own team. I can see what's happening with Tartaglia. He's an arrogant, headstrong sod and he hates the fact that you've been brought in over his head. I'll bet he's trying to undermine you at every possible opportunity, maybe even turn the whole team against you. It's all that latin machismo stuff coursing in his veins. Probably doesn't like taking orders from a woman. You need support at a time like this, not gang warfare.' He paused, rubbing his lips thoughtfully with a finger before adding: 'I don't know how it works, but maybe if you have a word with Cornish, you can get him taken off the case or even transferred elsewhere. There must be some disciplinary issue you could get him on.'

She shook her head, not wishing to discuss the situation any further. It pained her to think about it. Like it or not, what Kennedy said about Tartaglia rang uncomfortably true and she felt threatened. But she knew she would get no sympathy from Cornish. Attitude and arrogance were not hanging offences and Tartaglia had a good stock of credit with the people who mattered up in Hendon. If she couldn't handle him, it would only reflect badly on her. With no solution to the case in sight, she was already on rocky ground.

She felt a headache coming on and closed her eyes, putting her hands to her face and massaging her temples and the bridge of her nose with her fingers, trying to fight back the tears. He was right about everything, of course. Too bloody right for comfort and she hated him seeing her that way. She must seem so pathetic and weak. The fact that he appeared to understand her, that he saw what was inside so clearly, made her feel ten times more vulnerable, drawing her towards him in spite of herself. There was nobody else she could talk to who understood and he seemed genuinely to care about her. But she wondered why he did, why he bothered. She felt all the old wariness surfacing again, suspicious of his motives for wanting to get close, questioning what it was that really interested him. Could she trust him?

'Going back to the email, you feel despoiled by it, don't you?' he said.

She nodded slowly, not able to meet his eye, focusing on the flickering flame of the candle in front of them.

'But that's exactly what Tom wants,' he continued. 'He wants to get to you, pollute your thoughts and dreams, play mind games with you. If you let him, he will be winning. Take a deep breath, clear your head and try and think straight.'

He reached over and took her hand again in his. His grasp felt cool and strong, his fingers gently stroking her skin. It felt so reassuring and this time she didn't pull away immediately, although she still found it impossible to look him in the eye.

'I'm with you on this, Carolyn. Trust me. I'll look after you and together we'll nail the bastard, I promise.'

Tartaglia said goodbye to Donovan and headed out to his motorbike, which was parked outside the pub by the embankment. A light wind was blowing and the night air was cold and damp, the sky almost cloudless with the moon rising just above the river. He put on his helmet and drove off down the High Street.

Nearing the intersection with Castelnau, he spotted what looked like Kennedy's Morgan, parked on a double yellow line on the wrong side of the road, in front of the parade of shops just before the crossroads. As he slowed to check, he saw Kennedy and Steele come out of one of the restaurants. They were walking close together, almost arm in arm, and appeared to be deep in conversation. He passed them and pulled up just around the corner, watching behind in his mirror. Kennedy escorted Steele over to the passenger side and unlocked the door, giving her his hand to help her into the low seat. Kennedy said something to her then, before closing the door, he tucked the trailing folds of her coat around her. The gesture struck Tartaglia as intimate and inappropriate. Fearing that his worst suspicions were being confirmed, he watched Kennedy walk around to the other side and climb in.

Even in the mirror, Tartaglia could see the smile on Kennedy's face. Like the cat with the proverbial cream, he thought. If they were having an affair, he'd go straight to Cornish. Cornish was notoriously intolerant of such things and in the current tense climate, fearful of the press getting wind of anything negative, he'd have Kennedy, and possibly Steele too, off the case in a flash. Determined to find out for sure what was going on, Tartaglia decided to follow them.

Kennedy drove along Castelnau, over the bridge and headed for Kensington, then Hyde Park and north up the Edgware Road. Although Tartaglia had no idea where either of them lived, they were going in the general direction of Hendon, probably making for Steele's place. Keeping a safe distance behind, each time they stopped at a set of lights he could see Kennedy through the small back window, gesticulating and nodding, as if engaged in a lively conversation. Kennedy was driving conspicuously slowly, possibly worried about being stopped and breathalysed and Tartaglia was tempted to call in his licence number. But with Steele in the car, he had to leave it. After another ten minutes, they turned off Kilburn High Road, past West Hampstead tube and forked right down a series of wide, residential side streets, eventually pulling over and double-parking in front of a large, semi-detached house set back from the street behind a low wall and a hedge.

Tartaglia stopped behind a small van under some trees on the opposite side of the road and killed the engine, waiting. After a moment, Kennedy got out, walked round to Steele's side and opened the door for her, again offering her his hand to help her out. They exchanged a few words on the pavement and pecked each other briefly on the cheek. As Steele turned to go, Kennedy seemed to catch hold of her hand again but she pulled away and walked up the path. Kennedy stood by the gate, watching as she put her key in the door and she gave him a brief wave before turning and going inside. Shortly after, lights came on at garden level and someone Tartaglia assumed was Steele drew the curtains across the large bay window at the front. Kennedy waited for a moment, staring at the front of the house, then got back in the car and started the engine, turning on the headlamps.

That appeared to be it. Tartaglia didn't know whether to feel disappointed or relieved. It certainly didn't look like an affair to him. From what he had seen, Kennedy was interested but Steele seemed to be treating him merely as a friend. The thought of Kennedy's ego receiving a bruising gave him a brief flicker of satisfaction. He waited in the shadows, not wanting to start up the bike until Kennedy had gone. But five minutes later, Kennedy was still sitting there in his car, engine idling. Perhaps Steele was coming out again after all. Perhaps he had misread the situation and she was getting some things and they were going to Kennedy's place for the night. Suddenly Kennedy's headlamps went out again and the engine stopped running.

A few seconds later, Kennedy got out of the car and walked up to Steele's front door, lingering by the steps for a moment as if wondering whether or not to ring the bell. Then he walked around to the front window where he stood, his head just visible over the top of the hedge, shifting from one foot to the other, as though he was trying to peer though a crack in the curtains. His movements were furtive. After a moment, he walked back to the front gate, peered up and down the street, then went down into the garden, disappearing around the side, presumably towards the rear of the house.

Kennedy was peeping. Almost unable to believe what he was seeing, Tartaglia's first instinct was to follow him and catch him red-handed. It would be a very sweet moment. But even as he thought about doing it, he stopped himself, knowing just what Kennedy would say, how he would lie through his teeth. Tartaglia could just imagine his tone of outrage: 'I was just making sure Carolyn's safe, that there's nobody lurking in her back garden.' The email she had received was ample justification for concern and Steele would believe Kennedy. Also, how on earth could Tartaglia explain his own presence there? As he wondered what to do, his mobile rang. He bent down, cradling it into his chest to dampen the noise, and saw Fiona Blake's name flash on the screen. After a second's hesitation, he flipped it open.

'Mark. It's me. Can we talk?' Her voice sounded husky and thick.

'When did you have in mind?' he whispered, his eyes on Steele's front garden, watching for any sign of movement.

'Is there something wrong with the line? I can barely hear you. I know it's late but what about now? Can I come and see you?'

'I'm not at home. I'm in the middle of something.'

'Oh.' She sounded disappointed. 'Tomorrow, then?'

'Maybe. I'll call you when I finish work. Got to go.' Seeing Kennedy re-emerging down the path, he hit the red button before she could reply.

With a last, lingering look over his shoulder in the direction of Steele's front window, Kennedy climbed back into his car and drove off. Tartaglia waited a few more minutes to make sure that Kennedy was not going to return, and then he switched on his engine. It was definitely going to be worth keeping a closer eye on Kennedy.

Carolyn Steele kicked off her shoes, tossed her coat over the back of the sofa in the sitting room and went from room to room closing the curtains and blinds, checking that all the windows and both the front door and the French windows at the back were securely locked. It was all because of that stupid email. Irrational fears were one of the penalties of choosing to live on your own, she told herself, but she was prone to them. 'Night fears' was what her dad used to call them when, as a child, she'd been unable to go to sleep or would wake up crying in the middle of the night. All to do with chemicals in the brain, she'd read in some magazine. But it didn't put a stop to them. Would the comfort of having some-body sleeping next to her drive them away? She doubted it.

She had lived in this flat for over ten years, spending time and money getting it exactly the way she wanted. Although the ceil-ings were low, it had large windows front and back, almost to ground level, and was light and airy during the day. She had gone to a lot of trouble to make it comfortable and welcoming, buying a colourful rug to brighten up the dull beige carpet and putting a gas log fire in the old marble fireplace, hanging an antique mirror above. She had built cupboards on either side, with a few rows of shelving above for her books, CDs and the few things which held any sentimental value, like the photos of her nephew and niece and the Victorian sewing box, inlaid with small diamonds of ivory, which used to belong to her grandmother.

She felt more at ease here than anywhere else. Even so, dark corners could open up and take her by surprise and occasionally she was forced to sleep with the light on. Perhaps she should have allowed Patrick to come in for coffee, just tonight. But he'd been quite pushy about it in the car, which she had found annoying. He was so bloody presumptuous and sure of himself and she resented feeling as though she was being manoeuvred into a corner. Maybe it would have been good to carry on talking, but she was worried that things wouldn't stop there. Better to seem rude than to do anything impulsive that she might regret later.

Her head was starting to throb and she grabbed a couple of Hedex from the cabinet in the bathroom and went into the galley kitchen. Searching in a cupboard for a tin of cocoa, she caught sight of a bottle of single malt whisky that an admirer had given her the Christmas before last. Designed to impress, it had a fancy label and looked expensive. She rarely drank spirits and it had stayed lurking at the back of the cupboard behind the baked beans ever since, untouched. Knowing that it was unlikely to make her feel any better, she cracked open the seal and poured herself a small measure, just for the hell of it. It tasted sharp and smoky in an unpleasant way but she was determined to drink it. Maybe if she got properly pissed she'd be able to forget about everything and sleep. She took the glass into the sitting room and sat for a moment in one of the large, deep chairs, flicking through the TV channels before switching off in disgust. As usual, there was nothing worth watching.

Gulping down the remainder of the whisky, she went into the bedroom and got undressed. She turned on the shower, stepped in and closed her eyes, letting the hot water wash over her. Patrick. Had she made a mistake in involving him in the case? Or was she silly to be so wary? Perhaps she should just stop worrying and let herself go. She had to admit that she still found him superficially attractive and the attention was flattering. It wasn't as if she was spoilt for choice. Beneath the bravado, he had a more serious side, almost steely at times, and he was rarely boring. But something kept holding her back, although she wasn't exactly sure what it was.

She knew little about his background, other than that he was a Catholic and had never been married. For a man the wrong side of forty, that was telling you something. Once he had said jokingly that he'd never married because he hadn't found the right woman. But she knew it was a load of rubbish. He was so self-absorbed, she couldn't imagine him caring deeply about anyone else, let alone ever really letting go and falling in love. Her good friend Lottie always seemed to pick men like that. She'd often watched the trajectory of Lottie's relationships, wondering why Lottie, who in other respects was a relatively sensible person, couldn't see what was in front of her nose. Some men were walking disasters and any woman who allowed herself to get involved with someone like that was just asking to get hurt. She was determined that it wouldn't happen to her. Although knowing it with one's head was one thing; physical attraction made even the sanest people do the silliest of things.

She thought back to that one drunken night they had spent together nearly a year before. The sex had been fine, at a basic functional level. But somehow she had been expecting more of a connection, more electricity. Something. The whole thing felt impersonal, disappointing and flat like a glass of champagne that had lost its fizz. It was as though she didn't matter; she could have been anybody. It was all about him and she realised she had made a mistake to let things go so far. Kennedy seemed blithely unaware of her reaction and had asked her to go away with him the following weekend. When she had refused, he had seemed very surprised, as if nobody ever turned him down, and had pestered her to have dinner with him again. But the more he persisted, the more her instincts told her to back off and she had avoided all contact with him on the work front until the phone calls finally stopped.

One thing that puzzled her was why, after everything that had happened, he still seemed drawn to her. Was it her independence, perhaps, and the fact that she hadn't succumbed easily to him? It was all about conquest, surely. She was unfinished business as far as he was concerned, a challenge. With all his psychological insight about others, had he any inkling of his own motivation? Had he any self-awareness at all? She doubted it. A relationship with such a man would be doomed. Every time she felt herself weaken, she must remember that and not allow sheer physical attraction and flattery to lead her astray. Even so, she felt as though she was struggling to keep her balance at the top of a slippery slope. A slope that probably had all sorts of unpleasant and potentially damaging things waiting at the bottom.

19

Café Montmartre was new and gleaming with fresh paint, fixtures and fittings. An attempt had been made to recreate the feel of the genuine French article. But with its lilac walls, dinky gilt mirrors and brass lights, it was a cheap parody, totally lacking in any kind of atmosphere. They had got all sorts of other details wrong too, Tom thought, spreading a large dollop of marmalade on his croissant. For starters, the French didn't eat marmalade, from what he could remember. Instead they made something unpleasantly sweet and gloopy out of oranges that had none of the tangy bitterness and bite of a decent English marmalade. At least this one came in its own small pot, safe from contamination by someone else's buttery knife or, worse still, toast crumbs. Grudgingly, he was forced to admit that it didn't taste too bad, although it couldn't hold a candle to his grandmother's. She cut her peel nice and thick and sometimes put brandy in it. Hers was the best he had ever tasted, made with Seville oranges when they came into season once a year just before Christmas. He remembered the pleasure of being allowed to lick the pan and spoon, if he had been good. Luckily, the old bat had made a new batch just before he'd throttled the life out of her and he had enough to last him a long while.

He took a bite of croissant. The butter was salted, of course, unlike real French butter, but although a bit chewy, the croissant was acceptable. Which was more than could be said for the coffee, which he'd had to send back twice. The waitress looked pretty pissed off, failing totally to understand what he was talking about and, when he'd insisted on hot milk, instead of cold, she seemed to think he was being difficult. From what he could tell, she was Russian or from some unsophisticated, Central European shithole. It wasn't surprising she hadn't a clue. But her attitude left a lot to be desired. She wouldn't be getting a tip from him and if she had the gall to try and add service to his bill, he'd strike it off.

Something about her, smilingly oblivious each time she spoke to the way she murdered the English language, made him think of Yolanda. She was another of these stupid cunts who came over here and made no proper effort to get to grips with the native tongue. They were just there for a good time; slags, all of them. All thanks to the EU and the stupid British taxpayer. But in a way, that played nicely into his hands. The papers had tried to spoil things for him and the old routine wouldn't work any longer. But it was time for a change anyway and it would be fun to try something new. There was little Yolanda, totally unaware of what was going on in the big world around her, just ripe for the picking. He was amazed that anybody had employed her to look after their kids. Didn't parents have more care these days? Or were they so engrossed in their own work and lives that they didn't give a stuff? His talents were wasted on her but he wasn't going to pass up the opportunity. She was asking for it, stupid little bitch.

He glanced at the headlines in the café's newspaper, skim-reading the first few pages, then laid it down beside him on the red leatherette bench. There was nothing in it about him today, which was a little disappointing. Perhaps it was a deliberate ploy to try and make him feel unimportant. He didn't like the moniker they had given him. 'The Bridegroom'. It sounded rather limp, unless perhaps they were thinking of Death as a bridegroom. It certainly didn't have the same oomph as 'The Yorkshire Ripper' or 'The Night Stalker'. But maybe they'd come up with something more imaginative once they got to appreciate his talents a little better. So far, they didn't know the half of it.

The waitress slapped what looked like a cappuccino down in front of him. He took a sip through the nasty sprinkling of cocoa on the surface and pushed it away. It was an empty gesture, as the slag was already busy with another customer, taking down his order and giving him a cheap, flirty smile. Watching her, hating her, with her greasy, pudding-face and bleach-streaked hair, he felt on edge. Nasty, low-cut T-shirt and tight, short denim skirt which revealed an unappetising amount of shapeless leg – piano legs, as his grandmother would have called them. Nothing left to the imagination.

Seeing her stirred him up, rekindling the familiar desire. He closed his eyes and pictured taking her somewhere quiet, slamming her up against a wall, pressing hard against her, her hands forced behind her back, his hand tight like a clamp over her mouth and nose. He was so much stronger. He could see the panic in her eyes, kicking, thrashing, trying to bite him, her face turning pink and then purple as she struggled to breathe. Like a butterfly stuck with a pin, he would hold her there for as long as it took, waiting for her to finally weaken and go limp. That exquisite moment as the light was snuffed out. Then the look of surprise permanently frozen on her face as he slowly removed his hand. Just like that old witch, his grandmother. How he treasured that memory.

He'd been to confession that morning, the first time in weeks, and he'd seen her in one of the pews dressed in her black widows' weeds, like so many of the foul old women who infested the place as if they had nothing better to do with their day. She didn't look at him – as if she didn't care that he was there or what he might tell the priest. He ignored her in return, walking to the front to wait his turn by the confessional without giving her the satisfaction of looking back. When he came out later, she was gone. But back at the house, he found her sitting in her favourite red velvet armchair by the fireplace, arrogantly oblivious to the fact that the grate was empty and cold. Her image flickered, translucent like a candle flame and she turned her sour, yellow face slowly towards him, malice in her eyes as she mouthed something. Bastard. That was the word, he was sure. He'd gone out of the room and slammed the door on her. She could just fuck off. Bastard. The little bastard. That was what she had always called him. How he hated her. He would squeeze the life out of her again and again, if only he could.

The longing was back much sooner than before, aching, gnawing at him, pulsing like a heartbeat. The hunger, the deep gut-twisting desire. It was getting stronger. There was only one way to deal with it. He would have to change the setting, alter the script a little, but it was good to improvise and he was sure it would be just as satisfying. As he sketched out in his mind a scenario for little Yolanda, the policewoman's face rose inexplicably in his mind.

20

It was late afternoon when Tartaglia took the call from DI Mike Fullerton of Hammersmith CID.

'We know who the woman on the bridge was,' said Fullerton. 'Her name's Kelly Goodhart. She's an American lawyer living in London. She was in her early forties and lived alone in Kensington. Her boss reported her missing and when someone from her local station went over to her flat, they found a suicide note.'

'Have you checked her emails?'

'That's why I'm calling you. She made an agreement to top herself with some bloke. But there's more and it doesn't smell right. You'd better come and take a look.'

An hour later, Tartaglia sat opposite Fullerton in his small office, just off Hammersmith Broadway, pouring over copies of Kelly Goodhart's recent email correspondence. With a spreading gut and thinning sandy hair, Fullerton was due to retire at the end of the month and he seemed less than delighted to have such a case land in his lap.

His team had made a start by analysing the email traffic over the past three months, although there were several years' worth that might have to be gone through if Kelly's death turned out to be suspicious. Apart from the odd item of shopping on the net, or theatre ticket bookings, the majority of her emails were to family and friends in the US. But in the last month Kelly had exchanged over a dozen emails with someone calling himself Chris, culminating in an agreement to meet on Hammersmith Bridge to commit suicide together.

Tartaglia was struck by the difference in tone and style of Chris's emails to the ones Tom had exchanged with the three girls. Chris's emails to Kelly were short, almost businesslike. As they discussed the concept of suicide and arranged when and where to meet and how to go about killing themselves, they sounded like two people deciding on the best way of getting to the airport. There was no evidence of coercion on Chris's part and at face value, Chris sounded nothing like Tom. But maybe Tom was smart enough to change his modus operandi with someone like Kelly, who was clearly intent on killing herself without anyone's persuasion.

'Do you have any idea how they met?' Tartaglia asked.

Fullerton shook his head. 'It's not clear from what we have so far. But I assume it's down to one of these effing suicide websites. It's a bit like lonely hearts, putting total strangers together to top themselves. There are hundreds of the bloody things all over the world. They should all be closed down, in my opinion. They're evil, encouraging the poor, desperate sods, telling them how to do it and the like.'

Flicking through the emails, Tartaglia nodded agreement. Chris had pasted a DIY guide to suicide from one of the websites in an email, asking Kelly which method appealed to her. A rapid series of brief, matter-of-fact emails ensued.

Do you have any preference? At least sleeping pills are easy to get hold of.
I personally don't like the idea of hanging...

The barbecue tray in the car seems a pretty painless way to go. I suppose we would just drift off after a short while...

Perhaps we could put on some nice music, although we would have to decide what and I suspect we have different tastes. But if that idea appeals, I'm sure we could work it out...

Do you have a car? I sold mine a couple of months back...

Any ideas where we could go? I like the South Downs or maybe somewhere else by the sea. Or would you rather stay in London?

Honestly, I'm easy. Like you, I just want to get on with it.

It looked as though Hammersmith Bridge had been Kelly's idea, for 'sentimental reasons', which she didn't seem prepared to elaborate.

Fullerton took a pipe and pouch of tobacco from his jacket breast pocket. 'It's bloody weird, all this, don't you think?' he said, after adding a pinch of fresh tobacco to the bowl and lighting it. He blew several puffs of pungent smoke into the room.

The smell instantly reminded Tartaglia of his grandfather and namesake, who had smoked a pipe all his life, even on his deathbed. All the smoking paraphernalia that went with the habit, the racks, the collection of worn pipes and cleaners and the old-fashioned turned-wood jars where the pouches of tobacco were kept, was now cluttering up the mantelpiece of his father's small study in Edinburgh. Nobody had the heart to get rid of them.

'How's that?' Tartaglia asked.

'Well, I can understand someone getting so depressed that all they want to do is kill themselves. In my view, that's a person's right. But it beggars belief that they'd want company, particularly with someone they'd never met.'

'Perhaps they're worried that they'll bottle out if they try on their own. Perhaps they want moral support.'

'That's a bit weedy, don't you think? Imagine this,' Fullerton poked the air with the chewed tip of his pipe, 'I don't know if you've ever been on a blind date but it can be bloody awkward. You turn up at the place as arranged, then along comes the other person and they're not at all how they described themselves. You feel let down and maybe you take an instant dislike to them too. What do you do then? Tell them it's all a big mistake and go home?'

'Worse still, what if the other person turns out not to be interested in killing themselves but just wants to watch you die?'

Fullerton, who was trying to relight his pipe, stopped, holding it in mid-air. 'That's sick, that is,' he said, shaking his head in disgust.

'I agree. But that's what we could be dealing with here,' Tartaglia said, studying Kelly's most recent emails to Chris, written a couple of days before the incident on the bridge. He read out a few of the sentences.

Can I really trust you? How do I know that you are who you say you are, and that you're not lying to me? Forgive me for being blunt. I don't want to put you off if you're genuine.

I told you what happened before and you can understand why I'm wary. There are some very strange people out there. I just pray you're not one of them.

Is Chris your real name? Or are you Tony, trying to fool me again? Please call me and put my mind at rest. I really want to do this and I don't want to wait much longer.

'Chris, Tony, it's all a bit confusing, isn't it?' Fullerton said.

'Our guy uses many different names. It's too early to tell what's going on. I'm going to need to see some more of her emails.'

Fullerton sighed, and made a chuffing sound as he sucked on the pipe and puffed out some plumes of smoke. 'I was afraid you were going to say that. How much do you want?'

'Say, for the last year to start with. When do you think you can get it done?'

'We'll deal with it straight away, but we're short-staffed at the moment and I've only got a couple of people available. Can you spare us anyone?'

'We're very stretched too but I'll talk to DCI Steele and see if we can find someone to send over here. At least there's now a stronger case for our involvement,' Tartaglia said, looking at his watch. He would have to call Steele right away. He was due at the hospital in half an hour to see Trevor and there was no time to go back to Barnes. After that, he had reluctantly arranged to meet Fiona Blake for a drink. 'Any news from forensics?'

Fullerton shook his head. 'I'll give them another call to chase them. They know it's top priority but then so is everything these days.'

Tartaglia stood up and Fullerton followed suit, walking him to the door.

'What's Kelly Goodhart's background?'

'I spoke to her boss,' Fullerton said. 'He was the one who reported her missing. He sounded pretty upset, although he said he wasn't entirely surprised. According to him, Kelly had been depressed for quite a while and he thought she'd been receiving counselling. You see, she married another lawyer in her office. They went out to Sri Lanka for their honeymoon and got caught up in the Boxing Day tsunami. The husband was killed and his body was never found. Apparently, she couldn't get over it.'

It had taken Donovan most of the day to locate Nicola Slade. She had moved several times in the previous two years and was now settled in a flat-share on the ground floor of a wide terraced house in Cricklewood. She had just come in after finishing for the day at the local primary school, where she worked as a supply teacher. Plump and nearly as short as Donovan, she had thin, shoulder-length mid-brown hair and glasses, and looked to be in her late twenties or early thirties. She was dressed in a baggy purple jumper and a flared grey corduroy skirt that just skimmed the top of her thick-soled boots.

She offered Donovan tea and ginger biscuits and they sat down together in the shabby sitting room that overlooked the concrete patch of front garden, Donovan choosing the sofa, Nicola a large floor cushion, where she sat cross-legged, skirt draped over her lap like a rug. Festooned with a forest of pot plants in macramé containers, the room was gloomy, the only light coming from a single bulb hanging in the centre of the ceiling hidden by a Japanese paper lantern.

Nicola's manner was brisk and efficient once Donovan had explained the situation. 'Of course I remember Marion,' she said, offering Donovan the plate of biscuits before helping herself to one and taking a large bite. 'We were cooped up together in that tiny flat for weeks, neither of us knowing anyone in London. It's lucky we hit it off.'

'But you didn't know she was dead?'

Nicola shook her head. 'My fault as usual. I'm hopeless at keeping in touch. We saw each other a couple of times after I left Ealing but I'd moved down to Dulwich to be close to what I thought was a permanent job and it was quite a trek meeting up. You know what it's like, I'm sure. It's very easy to lose touch in this city, even with people you like. After that, we exchanged the odd phone call and Christmas cards, but that was about it. I feel guilty now, knowing she's dead.' Nicola shivered and pulled her knees tightly into her chest, hugging them and taking a sip of tea. 'Perhaps I should have made more of an effort to see her,' she added, after a moment.

'If it makes you feel any better, I don't think it would have made any difference to what happened.'

'You said at first everyone thought she had committed suicide.'

'Yes. We're still not sure what happened.'

'Well, she would never have killed herself. That much I know.'

'Really? Both Karen and Marion's mother made statements saying that she was very depressed.'

Nicola shook her head dismissively. 'You would be, too, if you had to live with that dreadful Karen. As for Marion's mother, I don't think she knew if it was morning or night half the time. She was a real basket case, from what I could gather. I had to speak to her on the phone many times when Marion was out and I was very pleased she wasn't my mum.'

'You're saying Marion wasn't depressed?'

'Look, everyone's lonely when they first come to London. Or at least most people are,' she said, nibbling the last chunk of her biscuit. 'What I'm saying is that it wouldn't matter how depressed Marion was, she wouldn't kill herself. Marion was into religion, big time. Went to the Catholic church around the corner at least twice a week. Along with sex before marriage, contraception and abortion, suicide's a mortal sin, according to them, isn't it?'

Donovan shrugged. She'd been brought up by atheist parents and had nothing more than a vague idea about Catholicism.

'Shame priests don't take the same view about paedophilia,' Nicola continued, helping herself to another biscuit and dunking it deep in her tea. 'They're such bloody hypocrites.'

Donovan finished her mug and put it down on the floor, there being no other obvious place. 'When did you last hear from Marion?'

'God. It's ages ago, I suppose. Well over two years. I've moved around a lot and changed my mobile a zillion times too. She probably had no idea where I'd gone. Even my mum has a job keeping up with me.'

'Going back to Ealing, did you and Marion go out a lot together?'

'Occasionally we went to the pub round the corner for a drink or to see a film. But usually we stayed in and watched the telly or read a book. Neither of us had much money, you see. Karen was rarely in, thank God, and we had great fun cooking, although Marion did most of the work. We'd watch one of those chef programmes like *Ready Steady Cook* and try out some of the recipes. Unlike me, Marion was a right little domestic goddess when she put her mind to it.'

'Do you remember Marion having any boyfriends?'

'Well, no one who turned up at the breakfast table, if that's what you mean. Although I doubt whether Marion would be on for that. But there was definitely the odd admirer. Marion was a pretty girl. Whenever we went out together, there was always some bloke coming over, trying to chat her up. I think some of her clients tried it on, but that's just an impression.'

'Was there anybody in particular?' Donovan said, wondering if she meant Angel.

Nicola thought hard. 'There was some bloke but it was all a bit strange. He made a real fuss over her, gave her some flowers and chocolates. She said he was really charming and different from the others.'

'Different?' Donovan gave her a questioning look.

Nicola grinned. 'Wasn't trying to get into her knickers on the first date.'

'When was this?'

'Just before I moved out.'

'This was a client?'

'Could be. But I'm not sure. Although how else was she likely to meet anyone?'

Donovan made a note. She didn't want to give Nicola the impression that they already had a suspect within their sights. For the sake of being thorough, it would also be worth checking with Grafton's to see who else, apart from Angel, they had on their books at the time.

'She went out with this man?' Donovan asked.

'At least twice, if not more. Of course, she was flattered by all the attention but I remember her saying he was out of her league.'

'What did she mean by that?'

'I don't know. For someone so pretty, Marion really lacked confidence. She wasn't at all full of herself, which is probably why she was so likeable.'

'Did you meet him?'

'No. He didn't come to the flat. They always met somewhere else, somewhere public like a pub or a bar. I thought it was really odd and it made me wonder if he had something to hide, like he was married or in a relationship, or something. Marion insisted he wasn't but she could be unbelievably naïve, particularly where men were concerned. Although she wasn't the sort to tell lies, I did wonder at first if maybe he was a figment of her imagination. You know, like the pretend boyfriends some girls had in school. That was until I saw him, of course.'

'You saw him?' Donovan said, matter-of-factly, not wanting to appear too excited.

'Once, by accident. I was on my way home and I spotted them standing together on the opposite side of the road. I think they were outside the cinema. They were facing each other and he was holding her hands, gazing into her eyes, saying something. It looked pretty romantic to me.'

'Did he see you?'

'Oh, no. He was very intent on Marion and she didn't see me either. They were so engrossed, I thought it best to leave them to it. Then they got into a car and drove off somewhere.'

'Can you describe him?'

'Good-looking. Quite flashy, I thought. Not at all Marion's type really. I sort of understood what she meant by out of her league, although she was lovely enough for any man.'

'What about height, hair colour, you know?'

'I'd say tall, but don't forget I was on the other side of the road. Dark hair, sort of longish but well cut, I think. God, it's all coming back to me now. I can just picture him standing there looking at her. He was smiling. He had a really cheesy smile. You know, gleaming and perfect like in a toothpaste ad.'

Although the description was quite general, it could easily fit Angel and Donovan felt very pleased with herself. It also tallied with the description given by the witnesses of the man seen at St Sebastian's. Hopefully, she had found the link between Marion and the other girls. If she was right, it would be one in the eye for Steele and Kennedy. Tartaglia would be over the moon.

'You're sure it's the same man Marion talked about?'

'Oh, yes. She came home about half an hour later and I made a point of asking her. She said it was him.'

'Do you know if she carried on seeing him after you moved out of the flat?'

Nicola took off her glasses, breathed on them and started to polish them with the hem of her skirt. 'She didn't seem to want to talk about him and I got the impression it had fizzled out for some reason, but she didn't say why.'

'Did he have a name?'

She put her glasses back on and shook her head slowly. 'David? Simon? Peter? I'm hopeless, aren't I? Memory like a sieve. I know she told me. It was something simple like that, nothing fancy like kids get called these days. Hopefully, it'll come back to me.'

'Do you have any idea where they met?'

'No. Marion was a bit coy about that, I seem to remember, as if she was embarrassed for some reason. That's one of the reasons why I first wondered if he really existed.'

'Do you know what sort of car it was?'

Nicola laughed. 'You're asking the wrong person. I can't tell one make from another. Anyway, I was far too busy looking at him.'

'Was it a saloon or a sports car?'

'No idea whatsoever, I'm afraid.'

'Could it have been a van?'

'Definitely not a van. That much I can tell you.'

Donovan wondered how long Angel had owned his camper van and if he also had had access to a car two years before. 'But you could identify him?'

Nicola hesitated then nodded. 'If I saw him again, I'm pretty sure I'd recognise him.'

21

Tartaglia returned from the bar with two glasses of wine and sat down at the small table opposite Fiona Blake. She was wearing a simple cream blouse and navy blue suit that set off her pale skin and hair, which she wore down, the way he liked it, full, just skimming her shoulders. She had got to the bar first. When he had kissed her lightly on the cheek before sitting down, he had smelt alcohol on her breath and assumed she had had a quick drink on her own before he arrived, although there was no glass in front of her. Perhaps she was feeling as nervous as he was. He still wasn't convinced that it was a good idea to meet, and he had thought about calling her and making an excuse. But in the end he couldn't help himself. He had to know why she wanted to see him.

They were in a basement wine bar close to where Blake worked. The long, narrow room was filling up quickly with people from the offices around and the buzz of conversation mingled with the background thud of music. The bar was Blake's regular haunt, where they had first met for a drink a couple of months before when it had all started. He wondered if she had suggested the place deliberately or had simply forgotten. Perhaps it wasn't important to her. By coincidence, they were even sitting at the same table. But he wasn't sentimental about such things, although it felt strange to be there with her again, after everything that had happened.

He lit a cigarette, watching as she picked up her full glass. She took a sip then put the glass down, folding her small hands neatly on the table in front of her, as though she had something important to say. He noticed instantly that she wasn't wearing her engagement ring. Maybe she and Murray had split up and that was what she wanted to tell him. But he checked himself, doubting that things could be so simple.

She took a deep breath. 'Look, Mark. I'm really very sorry about what happened.'

'What do you mean?'

'In my office and at the mortuary the other day. I just felt so awkward seeing you again and I handled myself badly. It was childish and I shouldn't have behaved like that. That's why I came round the other night. I wanted to apologise.'

'I felt awkward too,' he said. Still do, he wanted to say, although he had no wish to show her how much she affected him.

She gave him a nervous smile, flicking a long strand of copper hair away from her face. 'I'm sorry about everything really. I wanted to explain but you wouldn't see me. I know you think I haven't been straight with you...'

She looked at him intently, as if waiting for him to say something. The colour had come to her cheeks and her eyes were a fierce blue. He took a mouthful of wine, a pinot grigio and the best on offer. But it was thin and sharp and he put the glass down, taking another draw on his cigarette instead. What was he supposed to say? That she'd lied to him, deliberately led him up the garden path and humiliated him? He'd said it all before on the phone and there was no point in having another row face to face. Surely that wasn't why she'd asked him to come.

She sighed heavily. 'This is very difficult for me, Mark. I thought you knew how things stood.'

'How things stood?'

She shrugged. 'With Murray, I mean.'

He could feel the blood rise. 'How was I supposed to know? I'm not telepathic. I only found out by mistake, from someone else.'

She waved her hand vaguely in the air as if it was all something trivial. 'It's a complicated situation; you know how these things are. You and I barely knew one another and I didn't know how to explain.'

'It's pretty simple, Fiona. You just tell me you have a partner. End of story.'

She nodded slowly. 'Of course, I should have done. I see that now. Again, I'm sorry. Do you forgive me?' She was looking at him questioningly. However sweet her expression, he still couldn't help feeling bitter and he looked away, taking another deep pull on his cigarette. If she had told him about Murray, he would never have allowed things to go so far. And she knew it too, which was why she had said nothing. She still wasn't being honest either, with herself or with him.

'Can't we be friends again?' she said quietly.

Friends. She made it sound so simple but it felt like a slap in the face. 'Sure. I've no problem with that,' he said, biting his lip. The word was hollow, yet another lie. They had never been friends. Their brief relationship, such as it was, had been entirely sexual; the word 'friend' had never once entered his thoughts in those few heady weeks. Did 'friends' now mean that they were to act as if nothing had ever happened, that it could all be switched off at a touch, like a light? He certainly had never had that sort of control over his emotions, once they were engaged. Perhaps what had happened between them meant little or nothing to her after all. If so, why come round to his flat, why the late night call, why bother to see him now? It didn't make sense. But he'd never been very good at understanding women.

She smiled. 'Good. I'm glad you're OK about it. Now we've cleared the air, tell me about the case. Is it going well?'

He took a drag of smoke and shook his head, suddenly relieved that she had moved things onto a less emotional level. 'It's not going well at all,' he said, and proceeded to tell her about Kelly Goodhart. Blake seemed genuinely interested, listening quietly, asking a few pertinent questions. He gave her the basic run through, finding it good for a change to be able to talk to someone who was only involved on the periphery of the case. 'Even if someone else does the autopsy,' he added, 'I'd like you to examine her, once we find the body. You know exactly what we're looking for.'

'Delighted to help in any way I can. You really think she's another in the series?'

'It's too early to tell. But the stuff in the emails rang alarm bells.'

'How are you getting on with Carolyn Steele?'

'OK,' he said, noncommittally. 'Why?'

'Just wondered. I've come across her a few times before. She's quite attractive, don't you think?'

'Not my type,' he said, surprised. Women never understood what attracted men to other women, and vice versa. He was still baffled by what Fiona saw in the weak-mouthed, cotton-haired man in the photographs in her office.

'Any news on DCI Clarke?'

'He's making good progress, thank God.'

'When will he be able to come back to work?'

He shrugged. 'No idea, at the moment. He was very badly injured and it could be several months.' That was the official line anyway, although he knew deep down that there was little likelihood of Trevor coming back. Of course, it was still too early to be sure but when he'd spoken to Sally-Anne that morning, she had let slip something about moving to the seaside, once Trevor was out of hospital. It had sounded permanent, not like a holiday for recuperation.

'So, you may find yourself working for Carolyn Steele for a while?'

'I suppose so.' He stubbed out his cigarette, suddenly wondering if Cornish would ask Steele to take over permanently. There would be several other candidates for the job and Steele might not want it. However, the thought of Steele as his boss for the long term was a daunting prospect.

'The papers said you've got some sort of psychological profiler involved.'

He looked at her warily, wondering if perhaps office gossip had filtered as far as the pathology lab. 'Yes, Dr Patrick Kennedy.'

'He's quite well known, isn't he?'

'He's good at self-publicity, if that's what you mean.'

'I find the whole idea of psychological profiling very unscientific.'

'That depends,' he said, moving to light another cigarette. 'The FBI do a fantastic job but they have a lot more experience of serial killers than we do. Our approach is pretty ad hoc by comparison and, as you say, unscientific. We do have a few decent profilers in this country but they're like gold dust.'

She looked amused, smoothing back her hair from her face and tucking it behind her ears. 'Dr Kennedy's not one of them, I take it, judging by your expression.'

Tartaglia smiled. 'It's not my call, but he doesn't seem to be adding much value so far.'

There was another awkward silence and he wondered if he ought to make some sort of excuse and go. But she hadn't finished her glass of wine and he didn't want to appear rude. Again, he had the impression that she was waiting for him to say something. He just didn't know what it was. The whole situation seemed forced. He was suddenly reminded again of how they had never really talked before about anything other than work, never really engaged in normal, everyday conversation and he felt at a loss for words, not having a clue what to say to ease things along. He had no idea what she was interested in, didn't know much about her at all, and there was only one question he wanted to ask: was she still with that fucking barrister? But he couldn't bring himself to say it.

'Have you seen any good films lately?' she asked, after a moment.

He almost laughed, wondering if she was going through the same thought processes as he, struggling to find an area of commonality. 'Haven't had time. You know what it's like.'

She nodded sympathetically. He noticed a smear of lipstick on the edge of her lovely mouth and was tempted to reach across and wipe it away. But he held back, worried that she might misinterpret the gesture and not sure if he could trust himself to stop there.

'Do you know, Mark, it's really good to see you.'

'I'm glad,' he said, hiding his surprise at the warmth of her tone by forcing down a gulp of the awful wine. At least she had had the sense to ask for a glass of red.

'Perhaps we can go to a film or something next week. There are several things on I'd like to see.'

'A film? Maybe.' Without knowing why, he was sure they wouldn't have the same taste in films. 'What about Murray? Won't he mind?' He tried to keep the bitterness out of his voice.

She waved her hand dismissively. 'Oh, he's away on a case all next week.'

Well, that answered the only question he had wanted to ask. She and Murray were still together. 'Next week's no good for me,' he said, thinking that he really should make his excuses now and go. 'We're working all hours at the moment. I shouldn't really even be here now.'

She smiled. 'Then I appreciate your coming all the more.' Without warning, she leaned forward and started to stroke his cheek, running her fingers through his hair. 'I've missed you, you know. Can't stop thinking about you.'

Confused, he pulled away. He hadn't seen this coming at all. 'What are you doing?'

She looked surprised. 'What's wrong? I want to kiss you.'

'Look, Fiona. I don't think it's a very good idea.'

She was still smiling. 'Are you worried this is a public place? It didn't stop you before.'

'We were talking about friendship only a moment ago.'

'Friendship, of course. But I bloody fancy you. That's all. I had this dream about you...'

'You're engaged to another bloke, I seem to remember,' he said, trying to stifle the urgent desire to grab hold of her.

She took a sip of her wine and glanced away, squeezing her lips together as if she had tasted something sour. He lit another cigarette, hoping that maybe she would say something to contradict him. But she refused to meet his eye.

'You are still engaged to him, aren't you?' he said, when she didn't reply. Still no response. 'I'll take that as a "yes". So, we're back where we were before which, as far as I'm concerned, is nowhere that interests me. Why can't you just be honest?'

She banged her glass down on the table and stared at him angrily. 'You're so bloody puritanical, you know. Life's not black and white, at least mine isn't. Why can't we see each other again? What's wrong with it, if we both want to? And I know you do.'

'The way it was before?'

She frowned. 'Maybe not exactly like before.'

'But close enough, you mean? That doesn't work for me, as you well know. And what about Murray? You're supposed to be marrying the guy, for Christ's sake.'

She sighed heavily, looking down at her hands. 'If you must know, Murray and I aren't getting on.'

'Now, that's a surprise.' He reached over and touched her lightly under the chin, forcing her to look up at him. 'But you're still engaged to him. Yes? Why don't you just come out and say it?'

She glared at him. 'All right, then. For what it's worth, which is not a great fucking deal to me, I'm still officially engaged to Murray.'

Seeing tears not far away, he stubbed out his cigarette and reached over and took her hand. 'I'm sorry you're not happy, truly I am. But I've made my position clear.' He kissed her fingers gently and stood up to go. 'You've got to sort out your life, Fiona, and you've got to decide what you want. As that boring old saying goes, you can't have your cake and eat it.'

22

Tom was late. Deliberately so. Entrances were so important and he'd wanted to keep Yolanda waiting, make her feel insecure. He pushed open the door of the Dog and Bone and went inside. He'd first come there many years ago when it was called something else, when it had been down-at-heel and inhabited mainly by a contingent of smelly old men who had the knack of making a pint last most of the evening. Now it was part of the new wave of pubs sweeping across London, not an ounce of brass or etched glass to be seen anymore, the dark purple walls studded with dreadful modern oils, all for sale, sofas and chairs dotted about every-where, instead of old-fashioned fixed banquettes, and big, thick candles guttering on every available surface. It looked like a brothel. Already packed, the noise was deafening, music throb-bing through ceiling speakers, the air thick with smoke. He had chosen it carefully. Located in a seedy part of town on the Regent's Canal, it had no regular local clientele, the majority of drinkers being tourists from some of the nearby cheap hotels, or transients passing through London for a few months. He was sure he and Yolanda would go unnoticed.

He weaved his way through the dimly-lit interior, checking the faces until he eventually spotted what he assumed was Yolanda, the only girl on her own, occupying the centre of a large, brown leather sofa at the back. Her posture was upright, hands at her sides, legs carefully crossed in front of her as if she'd come for an interview. As he approached, her eyes flitted towards him and she smiled hesitantly. He saw she was smoking; something he couldn't bear. Thank God, if things went to plan, he wouldn't have to kiss her. He forced a broad smile to his face.

'Yolanda?'

She nodded, fumbling with her cigarette and putting it down in the filthy ashtray on the table in front of her. He noticed that her nails were bitten to the quick; something else that revolted him.

'Hi. I'm Matt,' he said. She gave him another shy smile in return, moving aside to make space for him next to her.

She had loved the two Jason Bourne films and he thought 'Matt' would do well enough for her, although he knew he looked nothing like Matt Damon. However, he could tell from her expression, she was pleased. And so she damn well should be. In the normal course of events she hadn't a hope in hell of having a drink, let alone anything else, with someone like him. Small, sallow-skinned and totally flat-chested, she was as plain as a sheet of cardboard, although her dark hair was nice and shiny – clean, he was pleased to note – and she had large, round brown eyes that looked as though they'd trust the devil. She was dressed demurely in a long-sleeved blue T-shirt that had gone through the wash a few too many times, and a knee-length cotton skirt, with thick black tights and boots beneath. There was nothing improperly tight or revealing, unlike the rest of the tarts in the room who were flaunting their flesh like pros. Yolanda was a mouse by comparison, with next to no make-up and an outbreak of spots on her chin, which she hadn't bothered to disguise. She looked a lot younger than twenty-one and he wondered if she had lied about her age, not that it mattered.

'Would you like another drink?' he said, noticing the half-empty glass of what looked like Coca-Cola. 'Maybe something stronger?'

'Please. Thank you.' She spoke so quietly, he could barely hear her.

'A glass of wine?'

She nodded, picked up the smouldering stub of her cigarette and started to pull on it again, as if every centimetre counted. Disgusted, he got up and shouldered his way to the bar where he ordered two large glasses of the cheapest plonk. No point wasting good money on her and he wasn't intending to drink much himself. While the barman uncorked a fresh bottle, Tom glanced over his shoulder through the crowd and saw her staring fixedly at him, mouth slightly open. Catching his eye, she ducked away out of sight. Wasn't she just the little blushing bride, although he wasn't bothering with all that crap tonight. She would do very well, he thought, making his way slowly back towards her with the wine, careful not to spill a drop.

Conversation was laboured and almost entirely one-way. He asked her about her work as an au pair, about her family back in Spain, her studies and all sorts of other trivial and tiresome questions. He was having to shout above the noise of the room, repeating himself several times before the stupid girl understood. Clutching her glass tightly as if she was afraid someone was going to take it from her, she nodded like one of those dogs some people have in the back of their car. From what he remembered, her English wasn't bad but she seemed stunned into near silence, her replies monosyllabic. The whole process was exhausting and he wondered how much more he was going to have to endure. At least the wine seemed to be working its magic. For such a whippet of a thing, she was knocking it back in a hearty manner, getting quite giggly and almost flirtatious, like a silly little schoolgirl, her round, cow eyes on him all the time, as if she couldn't believe her luck. If she carried on like this, the whole thing would be a piece of cake. The only difficulty was how to get her from A to B.

'Shall we go somewhere a bit quieter?' he shouted, after a while. 'I have a car and I know a really nice little place nearby where we can talk.'

'No car, thank you. I like here,' she said, frowning, after he had repeated himself three times.

She seemed to particularly disapprove of the mention of a car. He almost laughed. What did she think he was going to do with her in it? He'd rather jump out of a plane without a parachute than screw the pathetic little bitch. The very thought was absurd.

He stretched out his hand. 'Come on, Yolanda. It's too noisy.'

She shook her head looking mulish. 'No. Is OK here.'

Perhaps he was pushing too hard. Maybe she needed another injection of alcohol to loosen her up. He might even have to give it a few drops of GHB if she carried on being so fucking tricky. Although that might cock up the timing of what he had planned.

'Another drink? Yes?' he said, forcing a smile.

She nodded slowly, looking quite sulky, which angered him. She should be bloody grateful that he was paying her any attention at all, stupid fucking little bitch. He tipped the remainder of his wine into her glass and got up to buy another round.

Yolanda watched him as he threaded his way through the packed room towards the bar. The noise was so loud, she wanted to clamp her hands over her ears. She felt tired suddenly and very alone. London was a cruel place. Everything pressed in on her and she felt almost suffocated. London sucks the life out of you, her friend Dolores had said, before going back to Spain for good. Nobody cares. Nobody wants to know, everyone so tense, in a hurry, no time for anyone else. They don't even look at you as you pass them in the street, let alone say 'hello', as people do where she came from. A wave of homesickness flooded over her and she felt tears prick her eyes. What was she doing here with this man?

When they had spoken on the phone and exchanged all of those emails, she had felt he really understood her, that he felt the same way too. She had gone to the library each day to see if he'd sent her a message, feeling ecstatic when there was one, desperate when there was nothing. She hadn't expected him to be so good-looking or polished. She had pictured someone younger, sensitive, unsure, full of doubt and loneliness, trying to make sense of a difficult life. But this man wasn't like that. He was confident. Assured. In control. It showed in the way he held himself, in his every move and gesture. He couldn't disguise it. Everything about him made her want to retreat back inside herself away from him. Men had always made her feel that way, awkward, unattractive, cheapened by the occasional attention and, whatever they said, unworthy. They told such lies. All they wanted was one thing.

That's what her mother had always said, and this one was no different. He'd mentioned his car – she knew what that meant. All the stuff about understanding her had been a sham and, when he wasn't smiling – which he did a lot – the look in his eye frightened her.

She couldn't see him from where she was sitting. Hopefully, he couldn't see her either and it would take him a while to get their drinks. But he would be back. Then, what would she do? How in heaven would she get away? He wouldn't simply let her go. He'd follow her outside and she wouldn't be safe from him there. Wondering if she could attach herself to somebody, she looked around at the tables nearby but everyone was deep in conversation. Nobody looked as if they'd be going home for hours. And what would she say, anyway? Can I come with you? Can you see me home safely? They would probably think she was weird. The room was hot. She wasn't used to drinking – had done it to please him and to give herself courage – and her head was beginning to spin. He'd be back soon with their drinks and a rush of panic swept over her. She had to go now. Before he came back. Spotting an exit at the back of the room, she picked up her bag, slipped her jacket off the nearby rack and dashed outside.

The air was freezing but it was good to breathe after the sweaty smoky atmosphere of the pub. She ducked down as she passed in front of the windows until she was clear, then rushed as fast as she could, slipping, sliding, almost falling, down the short flight of damp steps to the canal. She remembered the way she had come earlier. It was the quickest way back to the tube and anyway there was no time to stop and look at her A-Z. If he found out she'd gone, she was sure he'd come after her. She had to press on. Put some distance between them. Hopefully, he wouldn't know which way she'd gone.

The path was so dark, the few lights widely spaced, casting strange intermittent pools of orange light on the ground. Eyes streaming from the cold, lips dry with fear, she ran on, the sound of her feet echoing on the concrete. The rank smell from the water was overpowering, making her feel sick, but she couldn't stop now. The path curved round to the left, following the course of the canal, tall buildings hugging it close on either side, only a few lights on in the windows, nobody around. As she rounded the bend, a dark shape was silhouetted against the light on the path in front of her. It looked like a man but she couldn't be sure. Was it him? Sweet Mary, mother of Jesus, had he found her? Heart pounding, gasping, she stopped, the scream rising from deep inside. She clamped her hands over her mouth before it could come out. It couldn't be him. She was being silly. Even if he had worked out which way she'd gone, he couldn't be out there in front of her. There hadn't been time. Perhaps this person would help. Take her to the tube and make sure she was safe.

'Please. I need help,' she called out. Her eyes adjusting to the half-light, she could see now that it was a man, the outline tall and broad-shouldered, the ragged edge of short hair catching the light. But he didn't move, planted in the middle of the path, legs slightly apart, arms at his side, his face in shadow. He stood so still, he might be a statue. Like the bronze ones of people walking, near the canal by Paddington Station. They had taken her by surprise when she'd first seen them, they were so lifelike. But she didn't remember any statue along this stretch, certainly nothing in the middle of the path. Would he help her? Should she tell him what had happened? As she went hesitantly towards him she heard the sound of running feet accelerating just behind her and she was thrown to the ground.

23

There was a crush of half-drunk Australians at the bar and it took a long while to be served. When Tom got back, he couldn't see Yolanda anywhere.

She must have gone to the loo. Not surprising, after all the drink she had put away. Her bag had gone, but women always took their bags with them when they went to have a pee. It was one of life's many mysteries why the bag had to go with them everywhere, like a security blanket. His grandmother was rarely to be parted from hers and she had been intensely proud of the fact that it was real crocodile skin, although it was so battered, the poor croc must have been slaughtered a good century before. It had a faceted crystal clasp the colour of a tiger's eye and it was rigid and upright in a strangely prim way. When he was naughty as a child, it had often been the first thing that came to hand; she had hit him over the head with it more times than he cared to remember, often drawing blood. The brass edges were like a wide, cruel mouth and he used to have nightmares about it opening its lips and gobbling him up into the red leather interior. He remembered discovering it sitting on the floor like an unwanted guest beside his grandmother when he was trying to work out what to do with her body.

He had been waiting for what seemed like a very long while indeed for Yolanda to return when a thickset man with a shaved head, shiny with sweat, plonked himself down beside him on the sofa.

'Excuse me, someone's sitting there,' Tom said.

'Someone's sitting here?' The man mimicked his tone, going

through the pretence of examining the seat cushion. 'You need glasses, mate. There's nobody here.' He threw his head back, opening his mouth wide and roared at his own wit. He was drunk, or certainly on his way there. Tom had learnt how to handle himself with bullies like this and it wouldn't take much to silence the cunt. But he couldn't risk a scene, couldn't risk anyone remembering him there.

'My friend's sitting here,' Tom said firmly. 'She's just gone to the ladies.'

The man laughed again, almost spilling his pint as he eased his bulk down into the seat cushion, trying to get comfortable. 'You mean the young bird with the black hair? She skipped out the door over there before you came back.' He jerked his head in the direction of the exit on the far side of the room. 'She's done a runner on you, mate,' he said, looping a muscular arm around a half-naked teenage slapper with a stud in her eyebrow and top lip, who appeared on his lap from nowhere. 'Must have rumbled your little game.'

Staring hard at the man for a second, Tom realised that there was no reason for him to lie. Yolanda had escaped. Furious, trying to keep tight control of his facial muscles, he got to his feet. Such a thing had never happened to him. No one had ever dared stand him up before.

'Thanks for telling me,' he said forcing a smile. 'She said she was feeling sick. I'd better make my way home.'

The man ignored him and started to bury his face in the slapper's tits, making her shriek with delight. Judging from his demeanour, the man was well pissed already. The night was still young and by the next morning, his memory of what had happened in the pub would be blurred or even totally forgotten.

Tom picked up his coat and disappeared quickly out the door into the cold night air. He had to find Yolanda. He had underestimated the little bitch, he realised. In spite of all her pathetic moaning and whingeing and her apparent air of vulnerability, there was a core of toughness. She wasn't sweet and pliant like the others. They would have done anything for him, but not this one. Her talk of suicide was just a sham to get his attention. She was a cunning, fucking whore and she had deceived him. The thought made him feel violent. He wanted to strangle the life out of her scrawny body, stamp her out then and there, put an end to her, whatever the risk. He couldn't afford to let her live. She mustn't get home.

The pub was perched on the side of a bridge overlooking part of the Grand Union Canal. The quickest way to the nearest tube was along the towpath and he had secretly observed Yolanda coming along that way earlier. It wasn't at all a nice place to walk alone at night, particularly if you were young and female. But half-drunk and new to London, he was sure she would have taken the same route back.

He walked down the steps on the far side of the bridge leading to the canal. The air was cold and damp and a light mist was rising from the water blurring the edge of the towpath. Hemmed in by buildings on either side, the canal curved away like a slick of black oil, reflecting the shimmering light of the moon, which was emerging from behind the office blocks on the horizon. As far as he could see, there was nobody around, the only noise coming from the traffic on the flyover close by.

He was walking fast, almost running. The path was amazingly poorly lit, the lamps casting pools of sickly light, which only seemed to accentuate the deep shadows around. The fishy, stagnant stench from the canal was almost unbearable and he held his coat sleeve to his nose as he went along. Still sure she had come this way – after all, the stupid girl had no imagination – he kept going until he heard a strange, whimpering sound up ahead. It sounded like a dog chained up alone. Wary of what might be in front of him, he slowed his pace, keeping close to the shadow of the high wall that ran alongside the canal. Peering into the gloom beyond, he made out the shape of someone sitting on the ground a little further along. He braced himself for something unpleasant. But as he cautiously drew nearer, he recognised her.

Yolanda. He felt a surge of excitement. Cowering against the wall, her face turning towards him, she stared at him like a small, frightened animal. He walked up to where she sat and looked down at her. She was trembling but he saw the relief on her face as she recognised him. She sat motionless on the bare ground, huddled in her jacket, hugging her knees and clutching her skirt tightly around her. As he looked closer, he noticed that her skirt was practically hanging off her, slit into long tails of fabric. Her tights were also ripped, exposing the pale flesh of her knees and a large part of her thighs. Looking quickly up and down the path to make sure that nobody was around, he knelt down beside her. Something was wrong with her face. As he reached over to touch a dark smear on her cheek, she flinched and cried out. Peering at her in the dim light, he could see what looked like blood running down her forehead and out of her mouth and nose.

'What happened?' he said, softly, although seeing no sign of her bag anywhere, he thought he could guess. Serve her bloody right for running off like that. Teach her a fucking lesson, it would.

For a moment she didn't reply and he repeated the question.

'Man, two man. He...' She looked away and started to cry again. 'They have...' she gasped, struggling for the word, '...knife.' She gestured as if holding it to her throat.

He wasn't sure from what she was saying what had happened, not that it mattered. But at least he had found her, although the sight of her revolted him. He had to quieten her down so as not to attract any unwanted attention. He had to get her out of there somehow before anyone came along and called the police.

Gritting his teeth, he reached forward and stroked her hand. It felt cold and disgustingly wet to the touch. 'Please don't cry, Yolanda. I'm here now and you're going to be OK.'

Whether or not she understood him, his tone seemed to calm her and she stopped crying and started to dab her eyes with the sleeve of her jacket. At least he'd found the stupid little bitch. It wasn't the way he'd planned things and he felt furious with her for trying to spoil everything. But at least he had her now. However disgusting she was, there was no way she would get away from him again.

'You were very silly to go off like that,' he said softly. 'What did you think you were doing?'

She shook her head and immediately vomited on the ground. He looked away until she had finished, wondering how he was going to get her to come with him. If push came to shove, he'd have to pick her up by force, but he didn't relish the thought of touching her again, let alone holding her.

'You have water? Please,' she mumbled, after a moment.

What did she think he was, a fucking packhorse? He shook his head. 'No water.' Then he had an idea. 'But I have brandy. You know, cognac.' He remembered that the Spanish word was similar to the French. He pulled out the large silver hipflask that had belonged to his grandfather and waved it in front of her, giving her his most warm and gorgeous smile. 'You want? Make you feel better.'

The smile, or possibly the prospect of more alcohol, seemed to do the trick and she nodded slowly.

'One minute. I can't see. I need some light.' Turning his back to her, he got up and walked over to the edge of the canal. Checking to make sure that they were still alone, he unscrewed the cap of the flask, took a little plastic container from his inside coat pocket and poured it into the flask. It was a shame to ruin decent brandy but there was no other way. Luckily, GHB was tasteless. He came back and knelt down beside her again, sliding off the oval cup from the bottom of the flask and pouring out a large measure of brandy. He put the cup to her lips and slowly tipped it towards her. The first sip made her splutter and cough and she cried out. No doubt it burnt like hell. But she seemed to like it and took the cup in her fingers, draining it in a few minutes.

'Want some more?'

She shook her head, still holding onto the cup as if her life depended on it. He prised it out of her fingers and shook any remaining drops on the ground. The cup would have her fingerprints on it and he would have to clean it very carefully when he got home. Drying it temporarily on his handkerchief, he clipped it back onto the bottom of the flask and tucked the flask away in his pocket. He must get a move on. He had done a number of experiments with GHB on himself and, when laced with something strong like brandy, the effect could be very quick, particularly on someone as small and thin as Yolanda.

He bent over her. 'We must go.'

'You call police, yes?' She had huddled back against the wall and looked as if she was prepared to stay there all night if necessary.

'Yes, but not now. Can't stay here. It's dangerous. Dangerous.' He repeated the word, hoping to instil some urgency into her.

'You think they come back?'

Noticing with pleasure the alarm in her eyes, he nodded. He watched as she struggled slowly to her feet, hugging her sides and leaning back heavily against the wall for support. She closed her eyes and groaned. Fearing that she was either going to faint or be sick again, he backed away. But after a moment, she seemed to pull herself together and took a few unsteady steps towards him before her legs crumpled and she fell forward, hitting the ground hard with her knees. He could see he was going to have to help, although the thought of touching her made him want to retch. He took her by the arm and hoisted her up onto her feet again.

'Come on, Yolanda. You can do it.'

'Where we go?'

'Back to the pub.'

'The pub?'

'Yes. We can get help there.'

She nodded as if this was acceptable, leaning her head heavily against him as she allowed him to steer her onto the path. She stank of vomit and brandy but he would have to put up with it for a short while.

It seemed to take an hour to cover a hundred metres. Looking down at her, as they passed under a streetlamp, he noticed with distaste that she had been slobbering all over the sleeve of his coat. No doubt she had got blood on it too. Fucking little bitch. What was she playing at? He tried to pull his arm away but she clung on tight, stumbling into him and giggling now. The GHB was beginning to take effect. He wouldn't be able to let go of her in case she tipped into the water by herself and ruined the whole damn thing. He would have to ditch his clothes in the morning, which was intensely annoying, but it would be worth it, he told himself. It would all be worth it. He'd make bloody sure it was.

As they rounded the bend, he could see the pub in the distance, overlooking the water. It wasn't far from there to his car but he doubted that she would make it. She was muttering something to herself in Spanish, eyes closed, head lolling, as he dragged her along, his arms locked around her to stop her falling. She was a dead weight and he was getting tired of supporting her. He could try picking her up properly and carrying her all the way to the car. If anyone saw them together they would probably assume she was drunk or ill, and he was helping her home. But there were too many bloody police crawling around the streets these days and he couldn't afford to take the risk.

Scanning the horizon, wondering what to do, he noticed the dark outline of a small pedestrian bridge half way along. Although not that high above the water, it would be better than nothing. As he tried to get her to take a step forward, she slipped through his arms and collapsed in an untidy heap on the ground, moaning quietly to herself. She was well gone now. It was all happening too quickly. Furious, he realised that he would have to pick her up and carry her after all. Tucking the remnants of her damp skirt tightly around her thighs, he picked her up in his arms and walked the short distance to the bridge. Why were they always so fucking heavy? God help him if he came across a six-footer.

He was almost half way across when he heard the sound of a bell and looked round to see a cyclist coming fast towards him along the towpath. Fuck. This was all he needed. Hoping that they wouldn't come across the bridge, he put Yolanda down, propping her against the iron rail for support. He wrapped his arms tightly around her, bent forwards and kissed her. He could taste the blood and vomit on her mouth and felt sick. He waited, listening, and after what seemed ages, he heard the wheels whoosh past on the path followed by another tinkle from the bell, now further on, as the cyclist speeded into the distance.

He straightened up, spat into the water and wiped his mouth on his sleeve. Still holding her, he gazed at the sky. Apart from a few wispy clouds, it was clear and full of stars. He felt his skin begin to tingle. He was so close now. He wanted to prolong the moment, capture it in his mind just like before. The moon was high in the sky and, as it came out from behind the veil of a cloud, the light illuminated the bridge like a spotlight. He looked down at Yolanda. Her eyes were tightly closed and her breathing almost imperceptible. She wasn't aware of anything around her now. The moonlight bleached her skin a strange bluey-white and she looked unreal, like a doll.

His blood was humming. He could barely contain himself. He was almost there. Almost. Just one last thing to do. He took his grandmother's old sewing scissors from his pocket. Resting Yolanda's head on his shoulder like a sleeping child, he snipped off a long, thick lock of hair then tucked it away with the scissors in his pocket. He was ready. He lifted her up and sat her on the edge of the bridge facing him, holding her tightly by her upper arms so that she wouldn't tip over just yet. Her head flopped forward and her hair fell over her face, spoiling everything. He had to see her face. Cradling the back of her head in his hand, he swept back her hair and gazed at her, almost unable to contain himself. He needed to freeze this last image in his mind. She was so still. Still as death.

Excitement rising like a tide, he closed his eyes, and breathed deeply for a second. He had the fleeting memory of heat and a garden in full summer. An intense, sweet smell filled his head. The scent of stocks, or was it gardenia? It was intoxicating. Just like the last time. He inhaled deeply again, high with yearning. After a moment, he half-opened his eyes and gazed at her once more.

He felt the rush of blood, the wave of heat from deep down and slowly loosened his grip on her arms, watching her topple backwards over the bridge. With a shudder, he gasped, closing his eyes again as he heard the splash.

24

Tartaglia got out of the car and watched Wightman nudge the Mondeo into an impossibly small parking space up against the railings, above the canal. It was late afternoon and would soon be dark. Mercifully, it had stopped raining, but the air was thick with damp and a wind was getting up. He had last been here in the heat of summer many years before, when he had first arrived in London and had taken a guided walk along the towpath of the Regent's Canal from Little Venice all the way to Camden Lock.

Gazing over the railings, the only thing that had changed was the horizon, now filled with the glittering cluster of office blocks that had sprung up around Paddington Basin. Immediately below, a strip of public gardens stretched down to the towpath and the canal. Beyond was the large triangle of dark water where three canals converged, known as Browning's Pool, after the poet Robert Browning who had once lived opposite. It was bordered by an incongruous mix of seventies housing on one side and rows of cream-coloured neo-classical villas, worth many millions, set back above the canal behind manicured hedges. A body was not what you expected to find on your doorstep in this part of town and he saw several people standing in the windows of the houses, watching the activities down below on the canal.

Wightman joined Tartaglia and they walked along the road to where a section had been cordoned off, just in front of where the mortuary van was parked. They showed their IDs to a uniformed PC from the local station and descended a steep, slippery set of stairs to the towpath and canal below.

At the bottom, Tartaglia stopped and looked across the water again, taking in the scene. Apart from the sound of the wind whipping through the trees and across the water, all he could hear was the squawking of geese from the small island in the middle. Even in summer, the pool had been a disturbing thick, browny-green soup. But close up, under a darkening sky, it looked poisonous and he pitied the divers who had had the task of retrieving the body.

Two large narrow boats were moored along that side of the bank, one a floating puppet theatre, the other somebody's home. Just beyond, the path was screened off and a small forensic tent was pitched on the paving next to an empty tourist boat. Gathered beside it, chatting, with takeaway cups of tea or coffee in their hands, were what he assumed were a couple of officers from the local CID, along with the mortuary van driver and his assistant. As they approached, a young man in a short, dark overcoat stepped forward from the group and introduced himself as DS Grant.

'We fished the body out a few hours ago from under the water bus, sir,' he said to Tartaglia, pointing at the tourist boat.

'I hear it's a young girl,' Tartaglia said.

Grant nodded. 'She got caught up on the propeller.' He pointed to the far end of the tourist boat. 'She's in a right state. Dr Blake's in the tent with her now.'

It was lucky that Blake had been on call when the body was found and he was grateful that she had made sure that he was called to the scene. He ducked in through the flap, leaving Wightman and Grant outside.

The body lay on the ground, already sheeted up, ready for removal to the mortuary. Blake was kneeling beside it, dictating something into a recorder. She looked up and gave him a fleeting smile.

'Oh, good. I'm glad you've got here. I was just finishing up.'

'I got your message. I hear there's a lock of hair missing.'

She nodded and got to her feet slowly, as if she was stiff from kneeling for a while. 'Just like the last two. That's why I insisted they call you right away. But there's one big difference. This girl's been beaten up and, from what I can see without examining her properly, she's also been sexually assaulted. Quite brutally, in fact.'

'Assaulted? He's never done that before.' Tartaglia rubbed his chin, surprised. Some killers stuck more or less to the same pattern. With others, like Michael Barton, there was a gradual progression of violence, as if they needed more and more to satisfy them, often leading them to make mistakes. It was usually what led to their being caught. But he had never heard of a change in MO as sudden or extreme as this. There hadn't been even a whiff of that kind of violence used against any of the other girls, let alone any form of sexual assault. He felt baffled.

She was looking at him inquiringly. 'Do you think it could be a copycat?'

He shook his head. 'Nobody knows about the locks of hair. It's one of the few details that wasn't leaked. Do you have any idea how long she's been in the water?'

'She's not in bad condition, so I'd say not long. Certainly less than twenty-four hours and probably closer to twelve.'

'That's very helpful. Was she already dead when she went in, or did she drown?'

'I'm not sure at the moment. I'll have to get her back to the lab and see how much water's in her lungs. However, she put up quite a fight and I'm hopeful, given the extent of her injuries, that we may get a DNA profile of your man.'

'What about a ring?' he said, thinking back to the other girls.

'Apart from a gold cross around her neck, she isn't wearing any jewellery.'

He stared down at the body, wishing, not for the first time, that the dead could speak. Maybe the ring had come off in the struggle or afterwards in the water. Or maybe there was no ring, in which case, was Tom the killer? It still didn't feel right. 'You're sure the hair's been deliberately cut off? Couldn't it have been caught up somehow in the propeller?'

Blake shook her head. 'Some of the injuries to the torso are definitely post mortem and caused by the propeller. But the head is undamaged, apart from some bruising to her face, which happened shortly before death, presumably when she was attacked.'

Still trying to puzzle it out, he said nothing for a moment. Seeing he was unconvinced, she added: 'If her hair had been caught up on something, it would have been pulled out at the root. However, this was done with a sharp blade, just like the other two I examined. I really wouldn't have troubled you otherwise. Do you want to see for yourself?'

He shook his head. 'I'll take your word for it. I suppose it has to be him then. But it's bizarre. He didn't assault the others in any way whatsoever. Why would he go and do this now? It makes no sense from a psychological point of view.'

She shrugged. 'That's for you to work out. I can only tell you what I find. I'll call you once I get her back to the lab and take a proper look. Maybe something else will turn up.'

He nodded and was about to go when she touched his arm.

'Mark, wait,' she said, peeling off her gloves. 'I just wanted to say you were right about what you said last night. About me, I mean. I know I need to sort things out. I just need a good kick up the arse.' She hesitated, then added: 'Thanks for being honest. That's all.'

He smiled, relieved that she wasn't angry. 'I didn't mean to be harsh.'

She shook her head with a rueful smile. 'I deserved it. Are we still friends?'

He nodded, although the word 'friends' again struck a false note. Perhaps it was a euphemism for something he didn't quite understand. Whatever she meant by it, he decided not to hold it against her. Before he said something he knew he would regret, he ducked out of the tent and walked over to where Wightman and Grant were standing together on the towpath talking.

'Do we know who she is?' Tartaglia asked Grant.

'It's possible she's a Spanish girl called Yolanda Garcia. She works as an au pair for a family called Everett in Paddington.

They reported her missing when she didn't come home last night and the physical description fits.'

'Last night? That ties in nicely with what Dr Blake has just told me about timing,' Tartaglia said. He turned to Wightman. 'Call Sam and ask her to go and see the family right away and get some background on the girl and a firm ID. If she lived in Paddington, she didn't have far to come. Also, ask Sam to see if the girl left any form of a suicide note.' As Wightman moved away to make the call, he turned to Grant. 'Do we have any idea where she went in?' From memory, that stretch of the canal was nearly two miles long. There was no point wasting time and resources knocking on doors and combing the canals for witnesses until they had a better idea of where it had happened.

Grant shook his head. 'Apparently, there's almost no current. So, I'm assuming it must be somewhere close by. But you're best off speaking to the skipper of the boat. He seems to be a walking encyclopaedia on these canals.'

'What about CCTV footage?'

'I've already spoken to someone at British Waterways and they'll let us have whatever there is. But there aren't many cameras along this part of the canal.'

'I don't suppose there were any reports of someone being pushed in last night?'

Grant shook his head. 'No such luck. It's been so cold, I guess everyone was inside.'

'Where's the skipper?'

'Last time I saw him, he was in the floating café over there, having a cup of tea and a piece of home-made cake.' Grant nodded in the direction of a narrowboat moored on the other side of the canal. 'He's pretty pissed off that he can't put his boat away and go home until we're done.'

Tartaglia grinned. 'Life's tough, isn't it. He should try our job for a change.'

*

Tartaglia found Ed Sullivan, the skipper of the tourist boat, huddled in a corner of the café, nursing what looked like a fresh mug of tea. In his late forties, he was thin and wiry, with short, greying dark hair and the permanently tanned skin of somebody who spent most of his life out in the open. After being told again firmly that he wasn't going to be able to take the boat back to Camden for a while, Sullivan seemed resigned to his fate and relaxed into his seat to tell his story.

'I was just going under that bridge over there, when the engine stopped,' he said, taking a gulp of tea and pointing out the window towards the small bridge that spanned the entrance to the Regent's Canal. 'I opened the hatch to take a recce at the propeller and when I reached inside, I felt something soft and a bit mushy, sort of like a wet carpet. But I couldn't shift it so I had to let the boat drift to the bank over there. Then I got out and took a look. When I dug around underneath the platform with a boat hook, I found a foot. That's when I called you lot.' He took another mouthful of tea. 'Had a whole load of Russians on board. They got out and started taking pictures. Can you believe it? The ghouls. I couldn't bloody get rid of them and they had the cheek to demand their money back, even though we were practically home and all they had to do was walk across the ruddy bridge. I suppose we should be thankful nobody's slapped us with a lawsuit for emotional damage.'

Tartaglia shook his head in sympathy, although nothing surprised him any longer about human behaviour. 'You said that the body was under some sort of a platform?' he asked, knowing nothing about boats.

Sullivan nodded. 'See over there, on the left-hand side at the end.' He pointed to one end of the tourist boat on the opposite side of the pool. 'The platform sits just on the water, in front of the engine room. It's where I stand and steer the boat. The girl was lying crossways, wedged in between the platform and the pro-peller.' Noticing Tartaglia's puzzled expression he added: 'Look,

I'll show you.' Sullivan took out a pen from his pocket and drew a diagram on the back of a paper napkin.

Tartaglia looked at the drawing for a moment. 'Thanks. That makes it much clearer.' He studied Sullivan's weather-beaten face, surprised at how unaffected he seemed by what had happened. 'You seem very calm. Are you all right?'

Sullivan waved his hand in the air nonchalantly. 'Oh, don't worry about me. This isn't the first time.'

'Really?'

Sullivan nodded matter-of-factly. 'I was working on a dredger on one of the Oxford canals and got another body jammed in the propeller. It was some poor student who had fallen off his bike into the water and drowned. He'd only been on the bottom of the canal a short time when the boat snagged him. They offered me counselling and everything but I've been fine about it. Can't let these things get to you, can you? Otherwise we'd all be nervous wrecks.'

'Quite,' Tartaglia said, glad that in addition to being apparently unaffected by what had happened, Sullivan seemed not in the least bit curious as to how the girl came to be in the water. No doubt he assumed it was another accident. 'You say the engine stopped when you went under that bridge over there. Is that where you think the girl fell in?'

Sullivan shrugged. 'Not necessarily. She *could* have been caught up on another boat first or maybe we picked her up somewhere else along the way. We were coming back from Camden and were nearly home when the engine stopped so she could have gone in anywhere along that stretch.'

Tartaglia shook his head wearily, struggling to understand it all. Blake had said that the body hadn't been in the water long. Decomposition had barely started and it would have been lying at the bottom of the canal, not floating on the surface. 'Explain one thing please, Mr Sullivan. How can a body lying at the bottom of a canal get caught up on a boat? Surely there's ample room for a boat to pass over.'

Sullivan gave him an indulgent look as if he was used to people unfamiliar with boats and canals. 'This is the boat, right?' he said, pointing at the drawing on the napkin. 'And here's the waterline.' He drew it in. 'There's the rudder, see? And the propeller and the platform we were talking about. The canals around here are no more than six feet deep and less than that in some places. Modern boats don't have much draft...'

'Draft?' Tartaglia interrupted.

'Depth in the water. The modern ones float over most things without a problem. But an old boat like this one, or the dredger I was working on in Oxford, they sit quite a bit lower in the water. There's not much between the bottom of the boat and the bottom of the canal. As you go along, the water underneath gets quite churned up, particularly if you're passing through somewhere narrow and enclosed, like under a bridge.'

'I see. So, you would have disturbed the body as you passed over it?'

Sullivan nodded. 'It's easy for all sorts of rubbish and stuff to get picked up and trapped in the propeller. I often have to stop and clear it out. It's bloody lucky we didn't break down in the Maida Tunnel. It's black as pitch and there's no towpath. In the olden days, the bargemen had to send the horses over the top and lie on their backs on the roof of their barge and push themselves along inside with their feet. Then they'd re-hitch the horses on the other side. It's where the expression "legging it" comes from,' he said with a smile. 'I wouldn't like to be stuck in there for long, particularly with all those Russian harpies and a dead body, I can tell you.'

'You clearly know these boats and canals like the back of your hand, Mr Sullivan. Can't you hazard a guess where she went in?'

Sullivan smiled, as if flattered to be consulted. 'My guess, and it's only a guess, mind, is that she fell in close to where we picked her up. It seems the most probable but don't hang me if you find out she fell in at Limehouse.'

'Can't you be more precise? I promise I won't hang you if you're wrong. It's very important we find out where she went in.'

Sullivan nodded thoughtfully and drained his mug, putting it down with a satisfied sigh. 'OK. Allowing time for her to get caught up under the boat and possibly moved along just a little way before she hit the propeller, that would put it on the stretch just before the Maida Tunnel. On the eastern side, around Lisson Grove.'

Donovan found the Everett family's address without a problem. They lived in a maisonette in a huge terraced house near Paddington Station, only ten minutes away from Little Venice. The call had been logged just after midnight and Judy Everett didn't seem in the least surprised when Donovan explained that a girl's body had been found, matching the description given of Yolanda.

'Of course it's a shock,' Judy Everett said, attempting to spoon the pink, mushy contents of a small jar into the mouth of a toddler, who was sitting in a high chair looking unenthusiastic. Seeing what was inside the jar, Donovan didn't blame him.

Tall and gawky, with a mass of unruly brown hair and a healthy, scrubbed complexion, Judy seemed to be taking things in her stride. Although the large, airy kitchen was in a state of chaos with paper and colouring pens littering the floor, the sink and draining board groaning with unwashed dishes and pans and plates of half-eaten food lying discarded on the counter.

'I knew right away that something had happened when Yolanda didn't come home,' Judy said, turning to Donovan hand on hip. 'She was always back well before midnight. It's one of our house rules and she'd never broken it before.'

'How long had she been living with you, Mrs Everett?'

'Oh, about five months.'

'So you know her quite well.'

'Not really. In fact, she was a complete mystery to me. I normally have some sort of a rapport going with the girls while they're here. They never stay long but I've become quite fond of many of them. They've really become like members of the family and we keep in touch.'

'But not Yolanda?'

Judy shook her head. 'I can't pretend, can I?' She sighed heavily. 'God, it's awful, if it is Yolanda. I feel really guilty now, not liking her. I mean, there was nothing wrong with her and she actually seemed to be quite bright. I never had to tell her anything twice. But she wasn't the sort of girl you immediately warm to. She was good with my two boys, though, which was all that really mattered.' She sighed again, rubbing her face with her hand and frowned. 'If it's her, I don't know what I'm going to tell Alex. He's my elder son and he's five. He was really fond of her.'

'Was she unhappy, do you think?'

Judy shrugged. 'To be honest, I don't know. She was such a serious little thing and she didn't have much of a sense of humour, although her English wasn't fantastic, so perhaps that's unfair. As I said, she did her job OK, so I had no complaints. I just have no idea what went on underneath.'

Red-faced, nose streaming, the child spat out the last spoonful of food and banged the side of his chair with a fat, grubby fist. Judy wiped his mouth and the tray in front of him quickly with some kitchen paper and offered him a child's beaker of what looked like juice, which he sucked for a moment then brandished in the air triumphantly as if it was the FA Cup.

'Had she worked somewhere else before coming to you?'

'No. This was her first time in this country and she didn't seem to know anybody. She didn't go out much, apart from her English classes. I felt sorry for her, but what can you do? I'm not her mother. I work four days a week and I haven't got time to look after the girls, as well as everybody else. They have to learn to fend for themselves.'

Her tone was a little defensive and Donovan wondered if maybe she was also feeling guilty after all for not having taken more of an interest. For a moment, thinking back to what people had said about Marion Spear, Donovan felt for Yolanda. Donovan had grown up in the leafy suburbs of St Margaret's, Twickenham, on the outskirts of London. She had a sense of belonging, a network of family and close friends, yet even she found London a cold and lonely place at times. How must it be for someone coming to it for the first time, trying to carve out a life for themselves on their own, with little or no support? It would make anyone vulnerable.

'Did Yolanda have access to the internet from here?' she asked.

The child threw the beaker onto the floor and Judy stooped to pick it up, handing it back to him without a glance. 'She wasn't allowed on our computer but I remember her going off to the local library sometimes to send emails home.'

'When did you last see her?' Donovan said, making a mental note to check the library computers if the body turned out to be Yolanda's.

'She gave the boys their tea yesterday, that would be about five-thirty. Alex is having tea at a friend's at the moment.' She glanced at her watch. 'Which reminds me, I ought to go and pick him up soon.'

'I won't take up much more of your time, Mrs Everett. But I need a rough idea of when Yolanda went out.'

Judy thought for a moment. 'That's a bit tricky. I came home from work and took over at about six, as it was her evening off. I didn't see her after that. She usually stays in her room and watches TV, even on her evenings off. We put one in the au pair's bedroom to keep them occupied. That way, we don't have them hanging around with us in the evening.'

'So, you didn't hear her go out?'

'No. But she creeps around like a mouse. I suppose it might have been when I was giving the boys a bath, but I can't be sure. The walls in these houses are so thick.'

'What time was that?'

'About seven. But it could have been any time after that. I didn't notice she'd gone out until Johnny came home, which was just before eight.' The toddler had thrown the cup onto the floor again and started to cry. Judy picked him up, balancing him on her hip and wiping his nose with a crumpled tissue, which she retrieved from the sleeve of her cardigan. 'So, what happens now?'

'We obviously need to make sure that the girl is Yolanda. Do you know if she has any family in this country?'

Judy shook her head. 'They're all in Spain. She came from somewhere in the north by the sea. I don't remember where, I'm afraid, but I can probably dig out an address or phone number somewhere if you want it.' Her eyes flitted briefly towards a small desk in the corner of the room, its surface covered in a sea of papers and books.

'I'll need that if it turns out to be her. Do you think your husband would be able to come and identify her?'

Judy gave a rasping laugh. 'I'm afraid it will have to be me. Johnny would pass out at the sight of a dead body. But I'm a GP so I'm used to these things. I'll make a phone call so that Alex can stay where he is, then I'll see if my mum can come and mind Toby. I imagine you want it done straight away.'

Donovan nodded. 'The sooner the better. If it is her, we'll also need to go through her things.'

With Toby happily perched on her hip, Judy walked Donovan to the front door of the flat. 'Assuming it is Yolanda, can you tell me what happened? Did she fall in?'

'We're not sure yet what happened,' Donovan said noncommittally. 'I don't suppose you found any sort of note?'

'You mean a suicide note?' Judy looked shocked. 'I can check her bedroom again but I didn't see anything when I went in there last night. She didn't even say goodbye when she went out. You really think she might have killed herself?'

'We don't know, Mrs Everett. The first step is to identify her.'

25

Tartaglia left Wightman beside the canal, waiting for backup from Barnes and some local uniforms to arrive in order to start the search for witnesses along the canal. Based on what Sullivan had said, they had decided to work their way east from the Maida Tunnel. He just hoped Sullivan's guess was a good one.

The course of a murder investigation rarely ran straight. Even with what looked superficially to be the simplest of cases, there were always ups and downs, twists and turns and, with the more complicated ones, often long periods when nothing seemed to give. He felt completely baffled by what he had seen at the canal. The missing lock of hair meant that it had to be Tom. But why had he attacked the girl? Why risk leaving his DNA at the scene? The more he thought about it, the less sense he was able to make of it.

He consoled himself with the thought that Steele would do no better. He was sure her first action, on hearing about what he had learned, would be to call in Kennedy. He gave her a minute, or five at the outside, from the moment he had spoken to her on his mobile beside the canal before she would be punching in Kennedy's number. Whatever was going on between them, they seemed to be joined at the hip. Kennedy would have a field day with all of this. Tartaglia could already picture him swaggering up and down her office, spouting his shit as if he were God. Just to save himself from the experience of having to hear it all, Tartaglia was tempted again to tell Steele what he had seen outside her flat. But what was the point? He'd been through all the pros and cons already and he knew she wouldn't believe him.

He found her a little intimidating, he had to admit. She was so bloody cold and unreadable. Cornish wasn't exactly cuddly either, but at least he was transparent and totally predictable, with all his silly little foibles and vanities. By comparison he was almost endearing. Whereas Steele had all the charm of an automaton. Fearing what she would say, Tartaglia still hadn't found the right moment to tell her what Donovan had learned from Nicola Slade about Marion Spear's secret lover. As far as he was concerned, even if there was nothing but a whisper of suspicion to link Harry Angel to any of the others, he was still in the frame for what Tartaglia was sure was Spear's murder. But he wanted Kennedy's cloud of heat and light to pass before he attempted to convince Steele to let him have another go with Angel. And there was no point in even attempting that, until they found out where the forensic trail would lead from the canal body. Hopefully, there would be news from Fiona Blake within the next forty-eight hours.

What worried him most was that he no longer trusted his instincts – almost felt as though he hadn't got any anymore. Everything was obscure and he wished again that Clarke was still around. He would know what to make of it all, if anyone would. St Mary's Hospital wasn't more than a stone's throw from Maida Vale and he decided to chance it and see if Clarke would be up to seeing him. It would also be a good idea to give Barnes a miss, at least until the morning. Hopefully, by then Kennedy would have been and gone.

'I thought if I was hypnotised I'd become a robot or do something stupid or embarrassing, you know, like you see in stage shows,' Donovan said.

Adam Zaleski grinned. 'That's just theatre. Those people you see taking their clothes off, or pretending to be chickens, do it because they want to. I can't make you do anything you don't want to do.'

They were sitting at a table in the ground floor bar of the Polish Club, just up the road from Zaleski's practice in South

Kensington. After Donovan's second hypnotherapy session early that evening, he had suggested going for a quick drink afterwards. He intrigued her and she had found it impossible to say no. After all, who could blame her for wanting a life outside work and how else was she ever going to meet anyone new who wasn't in the police?

With a twenty foot ceiling and huge windows overlooking Exhibition Road and part of Imperial College opposite, the room was an extraordinary mix of styles, with bits of sixties and seventies décor, together with chandeliers, large carved mirrors and faded gilt. The atmosphere evoked an earlier, grander era, somehow not entirely English. There were also elements of seediness, the carpet and curtains reminiscent of a cheap hotel, as if there hadn't been enough money around in recent years to maintain standards. Some sort of elevator jazz was playing in the background and the room was nearly full, everybody talking Polish. If it hadn't been for the view out the front, Donovan could have easily imagined herself in a foreign country.

Zaleski had insisted that they drink vodka and had ordered some special variety flavoured with rowanberries. He had also refused to let her pay for her drink, saying that this was his territory. Although he was not much older than she was, he had an old-fashioned charm that she found very appealing.

'The first time I was very conscious of what you were saying,' she said. 'But this time I found myself drifting off, as if I was asleep. I feel so incredibly relaxed now, it's amazing.'

'It's a bit like being in a trance,' he replied, as the waiter brought over two small shot glasses of clear liquid on a silver tray. 'But you're actually in a heightened state of awareness. Your conscious mind is suppressed and I'm talking to your inner-conscious mind.' He picked up his glass and clinked hers. '*Na zdrowie*. It means cheers.'

'Cheers.' She had never drunk neat vodka before and she took a sip warily. It was icy cold and viscous. Not unpleasant at all, in fact.

He downed his in one gulp. 'That's how you're supposed to drink it,' he said, smiling. 'But I'll let you off this time, as you're new to it.'

She took another sip, swilling it round on her tongue to get the full taste. It had much more flavour than the stuff you bought at the supermarket and she could now understand why it was drunk on its own. 'Why do I have to wear those headphones when you're hypnotising me?'

'I use a technique called Neuro-Linguistic Programming, or NLP, as we call it. You don't want all the science stuff, but basically wearing headphones maximises concentration, so all you hear is my voice and what I'm saying.'

'I still find it unbelievable that I'm sitting here having a drink and I don't even fancy a cigarette.'

'The most important thing is that you really want to make the change. It won't work otherwise.'

She took another, larger sip of vodka, feeling pleased with herself. If she finally cracked the smoking thing, it would be one in the eye for that sceptic, Tartaglia. 'Tell me about the club,' she said after a moment. 'Has it been here for long?'

'Donkey's years. It goes back at least to the Second World War, when the Polish government in exile used to meet upstairs. But it was dying on its feet until Poland joined the EU. It's still caught in a bit of a time warp but at least the average age of the members has come down by about four decades. You know, there are now more Poles living in the UK than in Warsaw.'

It was amazing how the EU had changed London, with the huge migration of immigrants from Eastern Europe and other countries. The Brits had at last become a bit more diluted, which was so much for the better in her opinion, the huge cultural mix being one of the many reasons she liked living and working in London.

She drained her glass with a final sip. 'Do you come here a lot?'

He nodded. 'It's a funny old place, but I'm rather fond of it. It's got a terrace out at the back, which is quite nice in summer, and I do like a shot or two of vodka after a hard day at work. Speaking of which, would you like another?' he said, noticing her empty glass. 'They're very small, after all, and one barely touches the sides, I find.'

'Please.' It was already giving her a deliciously warm feeling but she was sure she could handle one more. 'Are we supposed to throw our empty glasses into the fireplace?'

He laughed. 'Only in the movies or in Russia. I think if you tried it here, you'd give one of the older members a heart attack. It's safer to let the waiter take them.' He gestured for the waiter who appeared almost immediately.

'Who are they?' she asked, looking up at the many portraits on the walls, after the waiter had removed the glasses and taken their order.

'They're pretty hideous, aren't they? I suppose they're all Poles. But apart from Rula Lenska, I don't recognise any of them, although the blokes in the berets over the bar must be war heroes. However, I don't think there's much logic to it, as there's a huge picture of the Duke of Kent over the fireplace in the dining room and I doubt whether he even has a Polish maid.'

She laughed and, still looking around, said: 'It's quite a collection. But I'm not sure if I'd give any of them wall space, myself.'

'I imagine somebody bequeathed them to the club – I'd put good money on it being the artist – and I expect the old biddies on the committee were too polite to refuse.'

'What about that gold eagle over there, with the crown?'

'It's the national emblem and it's supposed to be a white eagle. The communists removed the crown from the emblem when they came to power. But of course this one here still has his.'

Their drinks arrived. 'How do you say "cheers" again in Polish?' she said, raising her glass.

'*Na zdrowie.*'

It sounded so lovely when he said it and she tried to copy him. She had never had much of an ear for languages at school but it seemed to trip off the tongue quite easily. 'It sounds so much nicer than cheers.'

'Let alone "down the hatch" or "bottoms up",' he said, smiling. 'English vocabulary can be very functional and un-poetic, particularly when it comes to drinking or romance.'

She felt her cheeks turn pink. She wasn't sure if it was the vodka or the way he was looking at her.

'Do you speak Polish fluently?' she asked.

'I was born and brought up over here but we always spoke it at home.' He downed his vodka and smiled at her. 'Now, it's your turn.'

'In one, you mean? OK. Here goes.'

He watched as she knocked it back. It was ice cold and made the back of her throat burn. But it tasted even better than the first.

'That one's called Jebrowska,' he said. 'It means Bison Grass. Are you up for trying another one? They have a lemon vodka which is quite delicious. Or maybe you've had enough. It can be quite powerful when you're not used to it.'

She hesitated. She was supposed to be cooking supper for Claire, although she hadn't even got around to buying it yet. Luckily there was a Tesco just round the corner from their house which was open late. It wouldn't do to arrive home pissed. But what the hell. She felt so relaxed, sitting there with him, that she wanted to postpone the inevitable moment of departure. 'OK. Just one more and then I really must go.'

The waiter was nowhere to be seen and Zaleski went up to the bar to order the final round.

'You know, you're not at all what I imagine a policewoman to be like,' he said, sitting down again a few minutes later with their drinks.

She laughed. 'Really?'

'I hasten to add that I haven't met any. Not up close, anyway, apart from some bloke who did me for speeding once.'

'The murder squad's a bit different to traffic,' she said, hoping he wasn't going to ask her about the case.

'I can imagine. What's your background? I mean, why did you join the police in the first place? You don't seem the type.'

She shrugged. 'There's no type, really, particularly these days. I've got a degree in English but that's not much use for anything, unless you want to teach, like my parents did. My father's a card-carrying *New Statesman* reader and joining the police was probably the only way I could shock him, other than becoming a Young Conservative.'

He smiled. 'What I really meant when I said you didn't look the type was that you're very feminine and petite.'

'Short, you mean?'

'No, petite. I chose the word carefully.'

'Don't worry, it doesn't bother me. I'm very happy the way I am and luckily these days there's no minimum height requirement. Anyway, for what I do, I don't need to be physically strong.'

'No. I suppose detecting is all about brain power.' They clinked glasses. 'Here's to you, Sam, and good detecting.' He smiled and downed his vodka. Then he said something in Polish.

'What does that mean?'

He grinned. 'I said you have beautiful eyes.'

She felt herself colour again. Why did such things always sound so much nicer in a foreign language? She thought of Jamie Lee Curtis being turned on by Russian in *A Fish Called Wanda*. But Polish was just as sexy, particularly when spoken by Adam. He had the quiet sort of looks that grew on you. If he took off his nerdy glasses and wore his hair a little longer, he'd almost give Tartaglia a run for his money. He could also do with sharpening up his clothes. But she liked the fact that he didn't bother or didn't seem to be aware that he was attractive.

'Sorry. I should be behaving more professionally,' he said, still smiling. 'You are my client but at least you've only one more session to go.'

'Do you really think I won't ever want a cigarette again?'

'We'll see. But that's usually all that's needed. Your last session's on Friday, isn't it?'

She nodded.

'I'm pretty sure you're my last appointment, like today. Why don't I take you out to dinner afterwards to celebrate?'

She didn't want to appear too keen but there was nothing she wanted to do more. 'That would be lovely. Shall we come here again?'

He shook his head with a smile. 'All Poles eat is pig, cabbage and potatoes. I think we can do a little better than this funny old place. Leave it to me.'

26

To: Carolyn.Steele@met.police.uk
From: Tom837920ixye8785@hotmail.com

My Dear Carolyn,
Have you missed me? I know you've been thinking of me and
I've certainly been thinking of you. Loads, and in ways that
you can't even begin to picture. What is it about you that
draws me to you? Is it your lovely, silky dark hair and your
white, white skin? I love your eyes, they're like a cat's and
cats are such sensual, playful animals. But it's so much more
than that. I'm not superficial, truly I'm not. It's not about
looks, is it? You have something really special. Has anyone
ever told you? I'm sure they have, I'm not so green that I
believe I'm the first. But nobody will appreciate you quite like
me. You know that, don't you? Does it excite you to think of
me? Does it make you yearn for me? Do I fill your dreams?
I'm the lover you've always longed for, the one who'll never
leave you. Shall I come and see you? Would you like that?
I don't want to be impatient. I don't want to push it until
you're ready. But I know it's going to be *so good*, I can hardly
wait. When you're alone in your bed tonight, close your eyes
and think of me there with you. I'm very, very good. The best
you'll ever have. Just close your eyes and imagine. The reality
will be so much better.
Tomxxx

p.s. Have you found little Yolanda yet? She was nothing
compared to you.

Steele stared at the screen, the words swimming in front of her. She felt sick, deeply shaken by what she had read. She had tried to get hold of Cornish but he had left the office and hadn't arrived home yet. He also wasn't answering his mobile and she left a message asking him to call her urgently. Tartaglia and Jones were out on the road somewhere but there was no point in speaking to them until they could see what she had in front of her. Besides, she was afraid her voice would give her away. She didn't want either of them to know how she really felt.

The mention of Yolanda's name was yet another pinprick. Her body had been officially identified earlier by her employer and her parents in Spain were being contacted. A search of Yolanda's room had revealed nothing of interest and, unlike the previous girls, no suicide note of any shape or form could be found in the flat. Perhaps the routine had changed or perhaps, thinking about the canal scene Tartaglia had described, something had gone wrong. The two computers in Yolanda's local library had been removed and sent away for analysis but Steele held out little hope of their providing much new information, let alone a link to Tom. He covered his tracks too well. He was untouchable.

She stood up and walked over to the window, gazing for a moment at the street below. It was dark outside and people were hurrying home from Barnes Station up the road, briefcases and shopping bags in hand. Lights were on in most of the houses opposite and where people had forgotten to close their curtains, she could see happy little domestic scenes, children playing or watching television, somebody cooking supper, somebody else arriving back from work. She felt as though she was somewhere remote, looking at another world that had nothing to do with her.

Somehow Tom knew how to press all the right buttons. But how could he? Was she so transparent to him, so typical of a woman of her age and background? Was it perhaps a lucky guess, had he hit the bull's-eye by accident or had he talked to someone who knew her? She shivered. She felt that he was getting closer, moving nearer, in ever decreasing circles. He was toying with her, playing with her, but would he really come? Should she ask Cornish for protection? Or did Tom only want to frighten her? She was sure that he would know that he had got to her, that this is how she would react. Maybe he would be gloating, picturing her state of mind. She felt furious at the thought and impotent. But however much she tried to fight it, stop it getting to her, it was useless. The bastard knew where she was vulnerable.

Feeling close to tears, she walked over to the door, made sure it was properly closed, and locked it. She couldn't risk anybody coming in at the moment. Flopping back down in her chair, she squeezed the bridge of her nose with her fingers, squeezed until it hurt and all she could focus on was the pain. She *would not* let herself cry, would not let them all see her like that. But she had to tell someone. She needed to talk and there was only person she could trust. Taking several deep breaths to calm herself, hoping that her voice wouldn't give her away, she picked up the phone and punched in Kennedy's number.

'You're in a right pickle, aren't you, Mark?' Clarke said, his face creasing into an awkward smile, clearly delighted that Tartaglia had come to seek his advice.

'Nice of you to care. But you know me, I never like things easy.'

Clarke sighed heavily. 'No, you're a demanding bugger…even at the best of times.'

Tartaglia was perched next to Clarke's bed on a small, hard chair, which he had had to carry in from a nearby waiting room, there being no chairs for visitors in the ward. Clarke lay beside him, flat on his back, attached to a drip, which Tartaglia presumed was to kill the pain, the lower half of his body still imprisoned under the large protective cage. Surrounded by a sea of cards, flowers and untouched baskets of fruit still in their cellophane, Clarke seemed in good spirits, considering everything. But his eyes were bloodshot and his long, boney face looked grey. He had been a big man but he had lost a considerable amount of weight, almost shrivelling overnight, and he had aged at least ten years. Tartaglia hoped that the shock on his face, when he'd first caught sight of Clarke, hadn't shown.

A huge, fluffy pink teddy bear was tucked up under the sheets next to Clarke, a tag with the words: 'Darling Trevor, I love you' pinned to a silk bow around its neck. It was such a funny, incongruous sight that, if it wasn't also so incredibly sad, Tartaglia would have been tempted to take a photo with his mobile for the team to see.

Although Clarke didn't have his own room any longer, they had at least put him in a small ward, with only four beds, one of which was empty, and given him the end bay by one of the windows. Tartaglia had thought of pulling the curtains around the bed for privacy, but as the man next door was out for the count and snoring loudly and the one opposite seemed deeply engrossed in listening to something on a set of headphones, there didn't seem much point.

'So Trevor, what do you think?' Tartaglia said, after a moment.

Clarke was silent, staring hard at the ceiling, as he pretended to give the matter further consideration. But Tartaglia wasn't fooled. He had seen Clarke's eyes light up as he recounted, blow by blow, the details of what had happened. Clarke was rarely slow to make up his mind, usually having a flash of insight or inspiration that usually took everybody by surprise and cut straight to the chase. But here he was, lying almost immobile in the bed, just savouring the moment and enjoying keeping Tartaglia dangling. Some things never changed.

'Y'know, I wish they'd put an effing flatscreen up there,' Clarke said. 'I'm getting fed up with the view.' His voice was laboured, words coming out a touch slurred and slower than his usual machine gun fire delivery. Tartaglia wondered if he had been wrong to come, wrong to trouble him with all of this.

'I'm surprised Sally-Anne hasn't rigged one up. She'd do anything for you, wouldn't she?'

Clarke half smiled. 'Yeah, I'm a lucky sod, aren't I. Way more than I deserve. You should stop messing about. Get yourself a good woman like that.'

'Quit fooling around, Trevor, and tell me what you think?'

Clarke turned his head slowly and glanced over at him. 'You mean about Carolyn Steele?'

'Stop teasing, Trevor, and spill the beans. I can see right through you.'

'OK. OK. We'll sort out the little matter of Carolyn later. What do I bloody think? Well... Other than I'd kill for a fag, and that I miss this flaming lark like nobody's business... I think... you're not looking in the right place.'

'Are you sure you're up to this, Trevor? I can easily come back another time.'

'Don't you bloody dare,' Clarke growled. 'This, and Sally-Anne, is all I got to keep me going.' He paused and smacked his lips. 'As I said, you've got it wrong somewhere.'

'Tell me something I don't know.'

'Fucking sod's law I smash m'self up when something interest-ing like this comes along.' He sighed and reached over with his huge hand and patted Tartaglia's knee. 'Nice of you to come and see me, though. I was wondering how you were all getting on without me.' He shifted his shoulders stiffly in the bed in prepa-ration and pursed his lips. 'Well, let's start with Marion Spear. You're dead right to link her to the others.'

Hearing Clarke say it brought instant relief. At least Clarke, the wisest of them all, didn't think he was mad. 'But there's no real reason.'

'Yeah there is, and you know it. If you want reminding or convincing again, she fell from a high spot and she matches the personality type. Just don't give me all that crap that bloody Kennedy said. He talks the talk and walks the walk but you know he don't know his arse from his elbow. What a fucking wanker he is.' Clarke paused before going on. 'Tell me this: why would a sweet girl like Marion Spear throw herself from a car park? She had her mum. She had a decent job. And she had a lover. Even if he is a fucking psycho, she didn't know that.'

'Maybe he dumped her.'

'Maybe. Maybe she was so gutted she wanted to top herself. Although from what you say, I think she'd have gone for something that takes less courage... like pills or something that makes less of a mess. And good girls like her... with a mum like that... they would have left a note, see? She was an only child. Stands to reason she's not going to make her final exit without telling her dear old mum why.'

'What about the lover?'

Clarke gave a glimmer of a smile. 'I'd put good money on him being Tom.'

'You make it sound so simple.'

Clarke winced and shook his head slowly, taking his time before he replied. 'It's not rocket science. I just have a fresh pair of eyes, that's all. It's what Steele should be doing for you. Keeping her distance so she can give you that.'

'She's keeping her distance, all right.'

Clarke sighed. 'Sam's done a good job finding that flatmate. You tell her so from me.' He reached over again and squeezed Tartaglia's hand. 'I miss you lot, you know.'

Tartaglia puckered his lips, fighting hard not to show how sad he felt, wondering if Clarke knew that he would probably never be coming back. He had heard from Sally-Anne that morning that although Clarke wasn't paralysed, thank God, his legs were so damaged that the rest of his life was likely to be spent in a wheelchair or, at best, on crutches, unless the drugs and physio worked a miracle.

'You mentioned any of this to Carolyn?' Clarke said, after a moment.

'No. I haven't found the right moment.'

'Yeah, she's not listening is she... with that pussy Kennedy buzzing around... whispering sweet nothings in her ear. I can just imagine what he's saying 'bout you and me. Won't be pretty.'

'You think I should tell her? I'd like to get Angel in and see if either Nicola Slade or Adam Zaleski can identify him.'

Clarke was momentarily silent again, rubbing his thick moustache slowly with his fingers as if it was good to still feel it there. 'Don't think you need to rush it. Even if she agrees...which she may well not, way things are going. Say one of them picks him out of a line up. What's it going to give you? OK, so you now know he's the one...and he's effing guilty. What are you going to do about it? You're not going to bang him to rights without proper...hard evidence, are you? He's unlikely to go all wimpy and confess. You need something more. But I'm buggered if I know what.'

'But if he was IDd, we'd have grounds for a search warrant.'

Clarke shook his head and closed his eyes.

'Really, Trevor. I think I should come back another time,' Tartaglia said after a moment.

Clarke jerked his head round, looking at Tartaglia out of the corner of his eye. 'Fuck off with that, will you? If you bleeding bugger off...I'll never speak to you again. I swear.'

His tone and expression was so fierce that Tartaglia decided to let it go. He could see that it meant more to Clarke than anything at that moment.

'What were you saying?' Clarke said, a minute later.

'About the search warrant.'

Clarke grunted. 'So what if you persuade Steele and some frigging judge to let you have a go? You know me, always like to assume the worst and work backwards. What if you search his flat... and shop... and find nothing? Where are you then? From what you say, this Tom's a right clever bastard. He's not going to leave stuff lying around willy nilly for you to find. He'll have it stashed away. Safe. Somewhere not at his main address. Nah, I think you're going to have to sit tight... bide your time for a little longer. 'Til you see what comes out of this canal business.'

Tartaglia stifled a sigh. Clarke was right, of course. To move things forward, they needed some sort of a break but he had no idea where, or in what shape, it was going to come.

'What about Kelly Goodhart, the woman on Hammersmith Bridge?' Tartaglia said.

'Like you... I'm pretty sure our Tom was in touch with her at some point. If you're lucky... and you've always had the luck of the devil... not like me... he may even turn out to be the bloke who ran away. Don't suppose the body's turned up?'

'Not yet.'

'Typical. Father bloody Thames having fun with us as usual. But see here. You're so wrapped up in all this. You're forgetting about the three girls.'

'Hardly.'

Clarke shook his head. 'Yeah you are. You've gotta go back to square one. Go over your tracks again. See what you've missed.'

'We've checked everything, over and over, the schools, the clubs they belonged to, their friends, everything.'

'Leave it out Mark, it's not good enough and you know it. You have to keep doing it... 'til you find the link... deliverymen... taxi drivers who may've taken them somewhere... dentists... doctors... all of that. You know the stuff. Even down to what bloody perfume and shampoo they used.'

'You really think there's a link?'

'Course there is. Has to be.' Clarke closed his eyes, wincing. He was sweating heavily and Tartaglia wondered if he should call a nurse. But he knew what Clarke's response would be. At least Clarke was still alive and his mind was all there. Tartaglia sat back in his chair as far as he could, so that Clarke couldn't see his face.

'He's not picking them at random... out of the phone book... is he?' Clarke continued, almost in a whisper. 'Ask yourself again what they all have in common. Forget age. I agree with you. It's about personality. The sort of girls they were. What put them in his way. They all were depressed, for starters. Weren't they? At least three of them wanted to top themselves with him. If it wasn't on the internet…where do people like that meet one another?'

'We've tried the Samaritans but according to the phone records, Kelly Goodhart's the only one who ever called them.'

'What about all the public phone boxes round where they lived? They may not have wanted to call from home.'

Tartaglia groaned. With everything else on their plate, the job of checking the records going back over the last couple of years was the last thing they needed. They were still grappling with following up all the calls that had come in from *Crimewatch*. 'True. But if so, they could have called from anywhere, near their school, near the tube, near a friend's house, et cetera, et cetera.'

'C'mon, Mark. I know it's a long shot, but what else you got? Talk to Carolyn at least. See if she can persuade Cornish to give you more manpower.'

'She won't pay any attention to me, I know.'

Clarke exhaled loudly, his breath rasping. 'Listen, mate, what's happened to you? This isn't the old Mark talking. What do you do with a woman? You, of all people, should know that.'

Tartaglia smiled. 'Try not to lose my temper, with this one at any rate.'

'That would be nice for starters. But you've got to work on her… charm her… haven't you? They've all got their little ways. I know she's your boss and you're pissed off because she came in and stole the bloody case from under you. But that was that prick Cornish's doing. Problem is… you don't fancy her… so you can't be arsed to make peace. But you've got to swallow your pride 'n' have a go. You know I'm right.'

'Easier said than done. She's as warm and approachable as a rattlesnake.'

Clarke waved a hand slowly in the air dismissively. 'That tough stuff's just an act. Believe me. Women are all the same underneath… 'part from the bloody muff divers, of course. Even your charm would be lost on them, I agree. But I'm pretty sure Carolyn doesn't bat for their side.'

'Trevor, you're not listening. She's really taken against me, for some reason.'

'She told you that, did she? Nah, didn't think so. You just need your heads knocking together, you two. She probably thinks... like the rest of us... that you're a smartarse... arrogant... prick... who believes he's God's gift. But you do have another side to you. When you can be fucked. That's why we all love you.'

'That's nice. I'll try and remember that, when Steele has me out on my ear.'

'As I said, you've got to try and charm the lady. Like that wanker Kennedy's been doing. He knows which side his bloody bread is buttered. Carolyn's not a bad sort underneath. You need to try and patch things up. Get her on your side.'

'You think I should tell her that I saw Kennedy peeping?'

Clarke thought for a moment before shaking his head slowly. 'Don't waste your time. But you ought to be keeping tabs on him. See what *he's* up to. The pansy deserves a good chinning, if you ask me. If he does it again, shop him to Cornish. Just make sure it's not you that sees him doing it. Going back to the case. My gut feel is that it's a botched job so far. There's no case on earth where there aren't clues. Believe me. You're either blind... and it's staring you in the bloody face... or you've been barking up the wrong tree.'

'Thanks, Trevor. You've made my day.'

Tartaglia was about to tell Clarke that it was time for him to go when his mobile rang. As usual, he'd forgotten to follow hospital instructions to switch it off. He saw from the screen that it was Steele. He flipped it open and listened to what she had to say. When he had finished he turned back to Trevor.

'Yes!' Tartaglia punched the air.

Clarke craned his head round to look at him. 'Fucking cat that's got the cream now, eh? So, what's up?'

'We may have a breakthrough at last. We've got a fingerprint match from Hammersmith Bridge. It's a bloke called Sean Asher and he fits the description of the man seen with Kelly Goodhart.

They're taking him in for questioning to his local nick and I've got to get over there right away.'

Clarke sighed. 'Bugger me. Forget everything I've just said. Lady Luck loves you, mate, even if Carolyn Steele doesn't. Maybe... sodding devil that you are... you're going to be bailed out. I'll be expecting an instant update, mind.'

Tartaglia drew in his breath with a whistle and shook his head. 'Sorry, Trevor. Looks like I'm going to be very busy for a while. Don't know when I'll find the time to drop by and see you again.'

Clarke narrowed his eyes and gave him a lopsided grin. 'You sod. Here's me in my state 'n' you're sat there winding me up. Thought you was interested in *me* and not this friggin' case. Now bugger off. Don't come back until you've made some progress. If not... I'll get Sally-Anne to wheel me in my bed straight down to Barnes. I'll sort you idle plonkers out and there'll be blood on the carpet, I warn you.'

27

Sitting in meeting room three at Paddington Green Station, half-drunk cups of cold coffee littering the table in front of them, tape and camera still running after nearly two hours, it occurred to Tartaglia that he'd been bowled yet another googly. It was proving to be a long and frustrating night and the pressure of knowing that Steele and Kennedy were watching in another room on the video link, along with Dave Wightman, didn't help.

Sean Asher had been arrested on suspicion of murder but was proving impervious to any of the usual tactics. He seemed quite resigned to sitting there all night, if need be. Whatever Tartaglia and Nick Minderedes threw at him, he refused to admit to having killed Kelly Goodhart. He spoke quietly and emphatically and refused to raise his voice. He had even politely told his brief to shut up when she had tried to intervene at one point. Considering everything, Asher seemed extraordinarily calm and in control of himself. It was as if none of it mattered. He was innocent and he didn't need anybody to look out for him. He had all the self-right-eousness of a martyr.

The room was hot and airless and beneath his jacket, Tartaglia could feel his shirt sticking to his skin, the collar uncomfortably tight. He wondered how much longer Asher would hold out. Asher sat calmly opposite, upright in his chair, dressed like a student in torn, faded jeans, trainers and a short-sleeved black T-shirt which showed off a muscular pair of arms. Judging by the smell coming from Asher's corner, he hadn't washed in days. He was in his early thirties, tall and well-built, with very short spiky brown hair that looked recently cut. Apart from the length of his hair, he fitted the general description of the man seen with Gemma Kramer. However, there was something soft, almost girlish about his round face, which was at odds with his muscular physique, and the nails of his nicotine-stained fingers were bitten to the quick, indicating a nervous, self-destructive disposition. He was not how Tartaglia had pictured Tom.

Asher's fingerprint had popped up on the system because he had been arrested for a minor affray during an anti-Iraq war demonstration a few years before. There was nothing else on the system and it was hardly a textbook background for a serial killer. It didn't feel right. Tom didn't seem the type to waste time with ideals. Tartaglia couldn't see him waving the flag for anybody other than himself and if he had, he certainly wouldn't be so stupid as to get arrested for something so trivial.

Before the interview had started, Steele had shown Tartaglia a copy of the most recent email from Tom. She was matter-of-fact about it, but he sensed beneath that cool exterior that it was getting to her and, thinking back again to the lines in the email, he felt full of doubt. He just couldn't square the tone and vocabulary of what he had read with the weak-faced man sitting in front of him.

The brief, Harriet Wilson, was a tired-looking woman in her mid-forties, with a mess of sandy hair threaded heavily with grey. She sat silently beside Asher, fanning her face with a notebook, eyes focused on a far corner of the room while Asher went through the answers for the umpteenth time. Yes, he had gone to Hammersmith Bridge with Kelly Goodhart. Yes, they had made a suicide pact to jump off the bridge together. But no, he hadn't tried to kill her. She had tried to take him with her instead. The witness was either lying or blind. The one thing he wouldn't volunteer was why he had wanted to kill himself in the first place.

'You really expect me to believe that she tried to pull you over with her? What a load of crap,' Minderedes said, throwing his eyes up to the ceiling and shaking his head as if he couldn't stomach such a lie.

Asher shrugged. 'Why not? It's the truth. She was in a right state, I can tell you. Didn't want to do it on her own.' His voice was surprisingly high pitched for a tall man, nasal, almost reedy, and he had a light northern accent.

'But according to you, you let her.'

'Couldn't help it. As I said, when I got there, I bottled out. Found I couldn't go through with it.'

'You say you changed your mind,' Tartaglia said, cutting in. 'You still haven't told us why.'

Asher raised his thin brows. 'Why? I got cold feet, like. It's allowed, isn't it? Hadn't signed a ruddy contract.'

Late at night, forty feet up on a freezing, windy bridge, with a total stranger, Tartaglia could almost sympathise. But Tom was a clever bastard and it was the only story that made sense, other than genuine innocence.

Minderedes leaned across the table with his hard man face. He too was sweating heavily, his usually fluffy dark hair plastered back on his skull. With his strange yellow-green eyes and beetley black brows, he actually looked quite menacing.

'Pull the other one, Tom. It's got bells on it,' he said.

'Why do you keep calling me Tom? My name's Sean.'

'Silly me. I'm the one who's confused again,' Minderedes said. 'You told her your name was Chris, didn't you?'

'Right. I explained that.'

'You said you didn't want her to know who you really were, in case she was some sort of nutter.'

'That's right.'

'But you're the nutter, aren't you?'

Asher shook his head. 'Christ, you people are so cynical. It's sad.'

'Goes with the job. If you saw what we see every day... but there, I'm forgetting that you do.'

Asher's expression hardened. 'If I want to do away with myself, that's my business. Nobody else's. And it don't make me a nutter.'

'It does, when you try to involve someone else.'

'I didn't "try to involve her", as you say. She was acting under her own free will. That's not against the law, is it, or is Big Brother already onto that little loophole? Fuck free will. Just do what you're told. Is that it?'

'You think it's a loophole, persuading people to kill themselves in front of you, pushing them off when they don't want to do it? In our book, it's murder.'

Asher shook his head slowly as if he found the question incredible. 'I didn't push her and I didn't have to persuade her. It was what she wanted to do. How many more times do I have to say it?'

Minderedes banged the table with his fist and stood up. 'As many as it will take until you tell us the truth, matey.'

'I give up. You folk are worse than on the box.' Asher folded his arms tightly in front of him, clamping his lips shut as if there was nothing more to be said. He was mistaken if he thought they were going to let it go at that.

'I've had enough of your fucking stories,' Minderedes said, and turned his back on Asher, striding over to the tiny barred window in the corner and appearing to look out. It was a good dramatic gesture until you knew that there was only the car park outside.

Tartaglia had so far taken a back seat for most of the proceedings and let Minderedes have his head. He was an excellent detective and generally good at interviews, usually because he knew how to get up the interviewee's nose to the point where they let something slip out of sheer annoyance. But Asher seemed impervious. It was time for a more subtle approach.

'OK, Sean. Let's say we believe you for a moment. We've read the emails between you and Kelly Goodhart. Why was she so wary of you? What was she scared of?'

'I told you, she thought I was someone else.'

'Who?'

'Search me.'

'You obviously said something to reassure her when you spoke on the phone, otherwise she would have never agreed to meet you.'

'Don't remember.'

'That's not good enough, you know. Unless you can convince us otherwise, we're looking at a charge of murder here.'

The brief sprang to life. 'Hang on a minute. We're going round in circles here. You don't even have a body.'

'Come on, Mrs Wilson,' Tartaglia said. 'Don't get technical. You don't think Kelly Goodhart would have survived, do you?' Wilson stared blankly at him. 'It's only a matter of time before her body turns up.'

She sighed. 'OK, Inspector. Say it does. Even in your wildest dreams, you can't turn this into a charge of murder.'

'Can't we? The witness saw him struggle with Mrs Goodhart. She said she thought he pushed her over.'

'Inspector, I don't want to teach my grandmother to suck eggs but you know there's all the difference in the world between someone thinking something might have happened and it actually happening. All you have is suspicion.'

'Yes, reasonable suspicion in the circumstances.'

Wilson shook her head. 'As I see it, we have a set of circumstances here which can be interpreted at least two ways.'

Tartaglia stifled a sigh, wiping his brow with the back of his hand. Wilson was right, of course. Somehow, just by articulating it, she had managed to deflate even the smallest bubble of hope. They had nothing at that juncture that would even get past the CPS, unless of course Asher confessed, and it looked very unlikely that he was going to oblige.

'My client is trying to be helpful, Inspector,' Wilson continued. 'But if you insist on pushing this murder lark without any proper evidence, I'm going to have to advise him to stop talking to you.'

Tartaglia continued to look at Sean, who was staring down at the table in front of him, expression fixed as if he was no longer engaged in the conversation.

'Help me, Sean, and I'll help you.' He waited for a moment, studying Asher's blank moon of a face, wondering what was going on in his mind. 'See here, Sean, we're looking for somebody who was in contact with Kelly Goodhart and wanted to watch her die. Sick though that is, he wouldn't just leave it there. If she got cold feet, like you say happened to you, he'd damn well make sure she did it, whether she wanted to or not.' There was still no reaction from Asher. 'How would you feel if somebody had forced you to go through with it? Not because they wanted company in the last moments of their life, like Mrs Goodhart, but because they're warped and twisted and get turned on by it. This bloke is sick. He gets his kicks from watching innocent people die.' Asher looked up, an almost imperceptible softening about the corners of his eyes. 'If you're not this man, as you say you're not, we need to find him.' Still watching Asher, Tartaglia let the sentence hang before continuing. 'We know he's done it before. Not with mature women like Mrs Goodhart, who were sure about what they were doing, but with young, defenceless, depressed little girls.'

'Don't start trying to shift the ground, Inspector,' Mrs Wilson said. 'We're here to talk about only one thing and that's what happened on Hammersmith Bridge.'

'This is the bloke in the papers, right?' Asher said, ignoring her, looking puzzled.

'We think so,' Tartaglia said. 'Please try and remember what Kelly Goodhart told you. It's very important.'

Asher scratched his bottom lip. For a moment it looked as if he was about to come out with something meaningful. Then he shook his head. 'I don't remember, I'm sorry.'

Tartaglia sighed. He didn't believe him for a second. 'OK. Let's take a break here. Interview suspended at ten fifty p.m.'

He wanted to give Asher time to reflect. He had seen the hesitation in his eyes, the slight unbending as though he had finally caught his interest. Hopefully, what he had said had struck a chord. On a more practical note, he also needed a pee, some fresh air and some more coffee to keep him going. And if he was lucky, he'd also be able to nip out back for a quick fag before Steele caught him.

*

'So, we've got nothing so far,' Steele said, in an almost accusatory voice looking from Tartaglia to Minderedes and back again.

'Certainly nothing to hold him on,' Minderedes said, shrugging. 'Unless we turn up something juicy when we search his flat, that is.'

They were in another meeting room along the corridor from where Asher was being held. Steele, Tartaglia, Wightman and Minderedes were grouped around the small table, coffee and a half-eaten plate of stale sandwiches from the canteen in front of them. Kennedy stood behind, as if he wanted to separate himself from proceedings, leaning against the wall, hands in pockets, his expression unreadable.

The room was just as airless and stiflingly hot, thick with the sour smell of stale sweat and tired bodies, the occasional whiff of aftershave coming from Minderedes whenever he leaned across for his coffee or a sandwich. It was enough to give anyone a headache. Still dying for a smoke, Tartaglia wondered how much longer Steele would keep them there, pointlessly going round and round in circles. He wanted to get back to Asher. He knew he had something interesting to say.

The only surprising thing was how silent Kennedy was. Never one normally to hold back with his opinions, it almost seemed as if he wasn't there. Either he was deliberately trying not to intrude, which was uncharacteristic, or he was stumped and didn't want to admit it.

Steele turned to Tartaglia. 'Mark?'

Tartaglia was fast coming to the conclusion that Asher wasn't Tom but there was no point in telling them that. Gut feel counted for nothing in that room and he could already hear what Steele would say: 'Give me facts, not feelings'. Everything was black and white to her.

'I agree with Nick,' Tartaglia said, trying to focus on concrete matters, things that could be explained in a few simple words. 'We've all seen the emails. Kelly Goodhart wanted to kill herself. Asher just happened to be there for the ride, according to him, and we can't prove otherwise. The witness was quite far away when she saw the struggle. She thought she saw him push Mrs Goodhart over the bridge. But she isn't a hundred per cent sure. It won't stand up to cross-examination, if it ever gets that far, which is unlikely. No, whether Asher really is Tom or not, if he sticks to his story he'll be home and dry.'

'Dave? Have you got anything to add?'

Wightman shook his head. It had all been said already.

'What about you, Patrick,' Steele asked, looking over her shoulder at Kennedy. 'What do you think?'

Kennedy frowned and pursed his lips, running his fingers through his thick hair for a moment, as if giving the matter deep consideration. 'Well, it's tricky,' he said slowly. 'Given what I've just seen, Asher's not the type to respond to pressure. I watched him closely. If anything, strong-arm tactics seemed to reinforce his statement of innocence. Now, you could read that two ways: either he's a tough nut, who's worked out that if he sticks to the story, you have nothing on him; or he's probably telling the truth.' It was stating the obvious but somehow Kennedy made it sound as if he had invented it.

'Do you think this is our man?' Steele asked, still looking at Kennedy as if she was hoping for something more.

Again Kennedy paused for thought, then shook his head. 'Impossible to tell. It's all academic anyway, if you can't hold him.'

Steele sighed, locked her fingers and stretched her arms out in front as if her shoulders were stiff. 'We can't let him go yet,' she said. 'He's all we've got. If he doesn't want to talk, we'd better search his flat and see if we can turn something up. Can you sort it out, Nick?'

Minderedes was about to reply when there was a knock and Harriet Wilson put her head around the door, catching Tartaglia's eye.

'Mr Asher would like to talk to you, Inspector. Off the record.'

'Off the record, what does he think this is?' Steele said. 'A blooming free session of counselling?'

Wilson shrugged. 'Don't shoot the messenger. I don't even know what it is he wants to say. But he's said he will only speak to the Inspector alone.'

'Just me?' Tartaglia asked.

'Yes,' she said. 'Doesn't even want me there. I think he's actually trying to be cooperative,' she added, seeing Steele shaking her head. 'If you assume innocence for a change rather than instant guilt, why don't you give it a whirl?'

'Why should we?' Steele said flatly. 'He's in here on suspicion of murder. We're not at his beck and call.'

'I know it's nothing to do with me,' Wilson said. 'But what have you got to lose? The time's ticking away and you know that you've got nothing to hold him here.'

'We haven't searched his flat yet.'

'If he's innocent, like he says, you won't find anything and I doubt whether he'll want to speak to you anymore after that.' She looked around the room at the watching faces. 'Look, what harm can it do, just a few minutes of the Inspector's time. If you don't learn anything, you can always go back to plan A, that is if you have a plan A.'

After a bit of bartering they had compromised. No tape and no video, but Tartaglia, now sitting opposite Asher, alone in the room, was allowed to make notes. If, in the end, he was wrong and Asher turned out to be Tom, it would be the strangest of games. He had brought Asher a sandwich and a cup of coffee, both of which sat on the table untouched.

'We spoke on the phone a couple of times,' Asher said quietly. 'At first she was very wary, kept trying to catch me out. I began to think that it wasn't worth the ticket. But gradually she came round a bit.'

'Why do you think that was?'

Asher paused for a moment, as if he was trying to think back. 'Well, she said my voice was different, for starters.'

'In what way different?'

'Don't know. Different tone maybe. I got the feeling the other bloke spoke posh, like the people who read the news on the telly. She thought I was putting on my accent at first.'

'You persuaded her you weren't?'

'Not to start with. Asked me where I come from and all sorts of other things like that, family, school, you know. It was like being interviewed for a bloody job. I had to tell her my name's not Chris. That put her off for a bit. Then she rang me again with some more questions.'

'Did she tell you anything about herself?'

'Said she was a lawyer. That didn't surprise me, the way she kept asking the bleeding questions. Really pissed me off, it did. But when she told me her husband had died in the tsunami, I felt sorry for her. Then she told me about the other bloke and I understood why she had to check me out.'

'This was all on the phone?'

Asher nodded.

'For someone who was so wary to start off with, it sounds as if she was easily convinced, don't you think? How did she know that you weren't the other man?'

'Gut feel, I suppose,' Asher said, almost a little too quickly. 'You just make your mind up about someone.'

Tartaglia stared hard at him, making Asher look away. 'There's more, isn't there, Mr Asher?'

Asher was silent for a moment before replying. 'Yeah. It's what I didn't want to say before.' He looked up at Tartaglia. 'Do you have a fag?'

In spite of the no smoking sign on the wall, Tartaglia offered him one and lit one himself. Asher took the first pull as if it were his last, then leaned back hard against his chair, making it creak. He sighed heavily. 'I suppose you'd better know. She wouldn't meet me at all, until I told her why I wanted to top myself.'

Again Asher was silent, as if something was weighing heavily on his mind. His face was slack, mouth half open, eyes vacant as if he were somewhere else.

'Well?' Tartaglia said.

Asher looked up. 'I used to be a PE teacher, until recently, that is. My last job was at a posh girls' school out in Surrey.' He paused, filling his lungs with more smoke. 'I made the stupid mistake of falling for one of the girls. It was nothing smutty,' he added quickly, catching the look on Tartaglia's face. 'Nothing like that, Inspector. I'm not a paedophile. Really I'm not. All we did was a bit of kissing and cuddling, that's all.'

'I've heard that before.'

'I can see what you're thinking but you're wrong. They were all wrong. Her name's Sarah and I loved her, you see. I really loved her and wanted to marry her when she was old enough. She was fifteen going on twenty-five. A beautiful young thing with a wise head on young shoulders. She was a lot wiser than me, I can tell you.'

Asher took another deep drag on the cigarette, blowing the smoke into rings, which curled up towards the strip light above. 'To cut a long story short, her parents found out, went to see the bloody headmistress and I was sacked. It's not fair, is it?'

'What, being sacked?'

'No. I didn't mind about that so much. What's unfair is you can't choose who you love, can you?'

Tartaglia saw the pain in Asher's eyes and nodded. How right Asher was. The pursuit of love, nothing sensible or reasoned about it, something that, try as you might, was impossible to control: the madness; the highs; the terrible lows. He thought back, remembering all those stupid mistakes and errors of judgement that he'd made, the time and energy wasted, hope burning strong, followed by disillusionment, finding that he'd been chasing after a fantasy. The cold light of day that flooded in afterwards was always so harsh and unforgiving. But he had never been totally desperate and without hope. He had never lost all sense of himself or his trust in the goodness of life and the future. Perhaps he had never let himself go to the brink, never completely put himself on the line. Some people were just more highly tuned than others. Although he wasn't like Sean Asher, he could still feel for him and pity his pain.

'You wanted to kill yourself because of her?' Tartalia asked.

Asher nodded, nibbling hard at a piece of loose skin around one of his nails. His finger was bleeding but he didn't seem to care. 'Her parents took her away from school and sent her abroad for the summer. She got over it quickly but I didn't. Still haven't,' he added after a moment.

'We'll have to check this out, you know.'

Asher shrugged. 'Be my guest. I've nothing to hide now. I thought she still loved me, you see, that it was only a matter of time before we could be together. Then...'

'Then?'

Asher sighed. 'Then she wrote to me. They call it a Dear John letter, don't they? Except mine was addressed to Dear Sean. It was horrible, like another person talking, someone I didn't know. Maybe her mother made her write it but she signed it. And it was her writing. It did me in, I can tell you. When Kelly asked to see proof of why I wanted to top myself, to see that I was genuine, like, I sent her the letter. Then she understood.'

'We didn't come across anything like that in her flat when we went through her things.'

'She sent it back to me, didn't she. I've still got it and I can show you, if you want.'

'Please. Why didn't you tell us this before?'

'None of you were listening, were you? Too busy trying to make me confess to something I hadn't done. I thought you wouldn't understand about Sarah, thought you'd judge me, call me a fucking paedophile and lock me up. Anyway, it's private. It's my business, nobody else's.'

Asher was probably right about how they might have reacted earlier. Tartaglia couldn't help respecting his reasons for wanting to keep quiet, relieved that at least he now appeared to be telling the truth. 'So, getting back to Kelly Goodhart. You managed to convince her that you were genuine.'

Asher nodded.

'Do you remember anything else she may have said about the other man who contacted her?'

'I know she never met him. But she said she thought she could trust him and he proved her wrong.'

'Those were her exact words?'

'Maybe I haven't got it quite right but something along those lines. We'd met up, you see. She said she wanted to see me, face to face, like. It was the last hurdle she put me through. We went to a café just off the North End Road. I showed her my passport, just so she'd know I was who I said I was. She said the other bloke had freaked her out. She said he'd been playing with her, egging her on, messing with her head. She could see I wasn't into that sort of thing.'

From what Asher had said, it sounded like Tom had tried to get to Kelly Goodhart. 'Did she tell you how he was doing this?'

'No.'

'Is there anything else you can tell me about him?'

'Sorry, no.'

'Was there anything else she said?'

'She told me she'd been born and brought up a Catholic and she asked me if I was religious. When I said I'm not, haven't been to church since I was a kid, she seemed relieved. Said that religion was a disguise for all sorts of evil things. That people use it to get what they want. It was just after we'd been talking about the other bloke but I don't know if it had anything to do with him.'

'You're sure there's nothing else?'

Asher took a final drag on his cigarette, which was almost down to the butt, and dropped it into his cup of coffee, where it hissed momentarily. 'I've told you everything, I swear. She was a sharp lady, Inspector. Real brainy and nice. I'm sorry she's gone, truly I am.'

'Why didn't you try and talk her out of it?'

'Because I understood her. I knew what she were feeling, what she was going through. She wanted to end it and I respected that. I could see that the light had gone out for her and it were how I felt at the time too. She just had a darn sight more courage than me.'

They would still have to search Asher's flat just to make sure, but Tartaglia was convinced by now that nothing would come of it. At least in the meantime, whatever Steele and Kennedy thought, he knew somehow he had made progress.

Dave Wightman drew up along the road from the address in West Hampstead that Tartaglia had given him, and killed the engine. They had let Sean Asher go just before midnight and Wightman had driven quickly over from Paddington Green so that he was ready and waiting for Steele when she arrived home. If Kennedy was with her, Tartaglia had told him to keep watch and take notes. If not, he could go home. When Tartaglia had explained the situation and told him what Clarke had said to him earlier in the hospital, Wightman was only too happy to be involved and trusted with the task. If that's what the boss wanted, that's what he would do, no questions asked. He respected both Clarke and Tartaglia more than anybody and he had no liking for Kennedy. He seemed so full of himself and there was also something rather odd about him, although he couldn't put his finger on exactly what it was. However, he wasn't entirely surprised to find that Kennedy was a bloody peeping Tom. In his view, all perverts deserved to be outed. Never mind that Steele would be hopping mad if she found out. She had a real blind spot where Kennedy was concerned and if something peculiar was going on, it needed to be exposed.

Wightman looked at his watch. It was well past midnight. Luckily, he had nobody waiting at home for him, apart from his mum, and she was used to his erratic hours and would have been in bed, asleep, long ago. He listened to Heart FM for about ten minutes, until he saw Steele's car coming down the road and switched off the radio. He ducked down as she passed and waited for her to get out. She was on her own and he watched her park a little further along the road, walk to the front door and go in.

Tartaglia had left Paddington Green before any of them and in ten minutes he was home. He felt wired, thoughts buzzing in his mind. Even though it would be an early start next morning, there was no point in trying to go to sleep yet. He switched on the music system, not bothering to check what CD was in the machine, opened a bottle of Gavi which had been chilling in the fridge, and poured himself a large glass. It tasted a little sharp but he didn't care. Unbuttoning his shirt, he walked around the room with his glass of wine, thinking about Sean Asher. Something Asher had said kept niggling at him but try as he might, he couldn't think what it was. He tried replaying the interview in his mind, word by word, seeing Asher sitting in front of him, picturing his expressions and reactions. But it still wouldn't come. From experience he knew not to try and winkle it out, no point in trying to force it. It would come when it was ready, if at all.

There was only one message on the answer machine, from Nicoletta, again insisting that he come to lunch. He was positive now that she was hatching a plot and, irritated by her persistence, he deleted the message, went into the bathroom, turned on the shower and got undressed. As soon as the water was hot, he stepped in, turned the tap on full to get maximum pressure and moved the temperature gauge up a little until the heat was almost unbearable. The cubicle filled with steam almost immediately and he took several deep breaths, shutting his eyes, trying to clear his thoughts.

Thinking of the second email that Steele had received that day, he wondered how she was feeling, going back to her flat on her own. He couldn't believe that the words had left her untouched, that she wouldn't be worried. But there was no point in offering help where it wasn't wanted. He grabbed a bottle of shampoo from the rack and massaged a small amount into his scalp. It felt good and he stood rubbing it in, thanking his lucky stars that his thick hair showed no signs of thinning as he got older, unlike his brother-in-law John, Nicoletta's husband, who had lost most of his hair in the space of five years.

When he had finished, he got out and had just started to dry himself when he heard his mobile ringing in the sitting room. He picked it up just before voicemail kicked in and heard Wightman's voice at the other end.

'I did what you said, sir,' Wightman said. 'She came home on her own and went inside. I waited, like you asked me to, and about ten minutes later, Kennedy showed. He hung around for a bit in the street and then went round the back, just like you said. Her lights were still on and he was gone a good quarter of an hour. Then he came out again and drove off.'

'You wrote all of this down?'

'Yeah, with the exact times. I waited a bit, just to make sure he wouldn't come back and, when he didn't, I thought I'd go and take a look round the back. There's a gate halfway down the side passage but the lock's broken, so anyone can go through. Her bathroom and kitchen's down there. She'd left the lights blazing all over the place. The blind was drawn in the bathroom but I could see right into the kitchen.'

'What about her bedroom?'

'It's round the back. She had the curtains drawn but they don't quite meet and I could see her quite clearly lying in bed. I think she had the telly on because I could hear the noise in the background. He must have stood there, watching her.'

'Good work. I had a feeling he'd go there again, particularly after seeing her this evening. He just can't resist.'

'What are you going to do, sir?'

'I'd like you to do the same tomorrow night and I think you should take somebody with you. If Kennedy does it again, I want you to call me and we'll bring him in. No point in messing about any longer.'

'No, and he bloody deserves what's coming.'

28

Tom pushed away the remains of his smoked chicken and avocado salad and sipped his glass of wine, watching the tail-end of the lunchtime crowd from his seat in the far corner of the wine bar. Most of the men were dressed in badly cut suits, with loud ties and gallons of hair gel. The women looked even more ridiculous, perched on stools around the small high tables, their short skirts hugging their fat thighs, tits pushed up and out, the heels of their shoes so high they could barely walk. Faces lathered in slap, they had 'fuck me' written all over them. It was all so bloody obvious, so fake and nasty, but the men seemed to be gagging for it like stupid, bouncy little puppies, lapping up every giggle, every cheap sideways glance and calculated flick of the dyed hair. In the normal course of events, he'd have been long gone. But he had more important things to think about.

The fever had passed and he felt calm again, satiated for the moment. He'd been stupid with Yolanda, although he reminded himself how much worse it might have been if the little bitch had lived to tell the tale. Nobody must ever be allowed to get away. No point in beating himself up about it now but he must never do something so risky and badly thought out again. He'd been up for most of the past night, unable to sleep. He'd watched part of a war film on TV and then, when that was over, listened to some music, until the fucking arsehole of an estate agent who lived next door had banged on the wall and shouted so loudly that he was forced finally to turn it off.

He felt tired today but at least he had come to a decision. It was time to go away for a bit, take a long holiday until things quietened down. There were places in the world where you could live cheaply, where life was cheap, where nobody would notice if you were there one day and gone the next. It would be a different game but it might be amusing for a while. Certainly different. Variety was the spice of life, according to someone in the know and it was time for a change. Lots of people took sabbaticals these days, so why shouldn't he? Anyway, he had a fair bit of money put by in the bank and he could afford it. He would find a safe place for his little treasures and then he would be off somewhere exotic and hot. It would be good to lounge around on a beach, drink margaritas and get a tan, somewhere where there were lots of backpackers and tourists coming and going, lots of slags looking for a bit of tawdry romance and a quick shag, where the police were crass amateurs at the game.

Just thinking about it got the old buzz going again. It would be a new beginning and he would reinvent himself. Like a magician, he would disappear in a puff of smoke and leave the London lot chasing their arses, with nothing to find. The thought made him feel warm inside and there was no point in hanging about, now he'd made up his mind. His grandmother could rattle around in the old house on her own as much as she liked once he'd gone. He didn't give a flying fuck what she thought and it would serve her bloody right.

She was showing herself more frequently now, for some reason. Last night when he'd gone over to put Yolanda's hair in one of her little tea caddies, she had appeared on the first floor landing, peering down angrily at him over the banister as if questioning his right to be there. He had every fucking right. It was his house, not hers any longer, he had shouted. But she ignored him as usual. She was wearing her favourite navy and cream spotted silk dress, the one which she usually put on when friends came round for bridge, and he could see the bright spots of rouge on her cheeks and the hard line of crimson lipstick on her shrunken lips. Even down in the hall, he was aware of her cloying scent and she seemed so solid for a change that he was tempted to rush upstairs and try and touch her. That would give the old bag a fright and put the wind up her. But before he had the chance, she disappeared like smoke in the wind as if she had never been there at all.

The bitch would get a shock once she realised that he had gone and he decided to look on the net for tickets that afternoon. It wouldn't take long to pack his things. But first there were some other practical issues to deal with and he took a pen from his pocket and started to make a short list on the back of an envelope. Along with all the boring mundane items, there was that one last thing he had to take care of. In the normal course of events he wouldn't have bothered. It was also highly risky, but what the hell. He wrote down the bullet point, underlining it and marking it with a large question mark. But he knew that he had to do it. The plan had been taking shape in his mind over the last few days and it would be so, so simple, like taking candy from a baby. He saw it as his final curtain call, his swan song. It would be good to go out with a bang.

29

Growing increasingly annoyed, Tartaglia paced up and down the towpath alongside the Regent's Canal, near the spot where they now knew Yolanda Garcia had been assaulted. It was past four o'clock in the afternoon and Steele and Kennedy were nearly twenty minutes late. Steele had called him earlier to say that she and Kennedy wanted to view the scene and he had no choice but to wait, although what earthly purpose it would serve was beyond him. So far, Kennedy had drawn little meaningful conclusion from the other crime scenes he had visited and Steele only echoed whatever he said. If they didn't turn up soon, it would be dark and there would be next to nothing to see.

Samples taken from Yolanda's body had been rushed through as a priority and the computer had come up with two DNA matches: Lee O'Connor and Wayne Burns, eighteen and nineteen respectively, both with form as long as your arm for a whole range of crimes, including burglary, mugging and assault. They had been arrested and questioned, each crumbling like a house of cards in the face of the overwhelming forensic evidence, each blaming the other for what had happened. Apart from that, the important details of their stories more or less matched. They explained how, high on a cocktail of alcohol and drugs, they had found Yolanda wandering along the towpath and given her what, in their view, she was looking for. However, they both vehemently denied having had anything to do with her death. At least one piece of the puzzle solved. It had never seemed psychologically probable to Tartaglia that Tom had raped Yolanda before killing her.

The spot where Tartaglia was standing was only about half a mile from where Yolanda's body had turned up. But it might have been in another city. Unlike the area around Little Venice, with its expensive houses, tall trees and glossy, colourful houseboats, this stretch of the canal was seedy and barren, surrounded by the backs of tall office buildings and dilapidated council housing. The few houseboats moored along the bank were patched and tatty, some barely habitable. A series of small bridges intersected the canal at irregular intervals and the towpath seemed to be primarily used as a local cut-through by a mixture of cyclists, dog-walkers and joggers. Even in the fading daylight it was forbidding. Wondering why anyone dared to venture along it after dark, he sighed at the thought of a young girl, on her own and new to the city, trying to get home that way.

Tartaglia was almost on the point of giving up, when he spotted Steele, walking along the towpath towards him in the gloom. She seemed to be on her own.

'Sorry I'm late,' she said briskly, coming up to where he was standing. 'The traffic was horrendous and I had trouble finding a place to park.'

'I thought Dr Kennedy was gracing us with his presence,' he said, failing to keep the sarcasm out of his voice.

'I decided to come alone,' she replied curtly, offering no further explanation for the change in plan.

'Are we sure this is where she was attacked?' she asked, looking towards the area along the path where the SOCOs were working.

'According to O'Connor and Burns. They live nearby and seem to know the towpath pretty well.'

She sighed heavily, as if imagining what had happened. 'Pretty grim, isn't it?'

'Not where I'd choose to die, certainly.'

'Are you sure we can't do the pair of them for her murder?'

He shook his head. 'A lock of her hair's missing and there's GHB in her system. Who else could it be? Newlands Park have the computers from the library where she sent her emails. They're treating it as a priority and I expect they'll show she was in contact with Tom, like the others.'

She nodded, as if convinced. 'But we still have no idea how Tom had originally come across any of them.'

'No.'

'Nor how he found Yolanda?'

'No,' he replied again. 'Neither O'Connor nor Burns saw anybody, although given the state they had been in, they might not have noticed someone watching from afar.'

'But Tom killed her along here?'

'It can't be far and it's got to be towards Maida Vale. O'Connor and Burns ran off the other way and they say they didn't see anybody.'

Steele followed his eye then turned and gazed in the opposite direction. 'Perhaps she was killed where her body turned up? I know that stretch with all the houseboats, it's…'

'Unlikely,' Tartaglia interrupted before any further speculation. 'This section of the towpath stops at the Maida Tunnel, further along there.' He jerked his head in the general direction. 'To reach the other side, you have to go up some very steep steps and walk across a series of roads. I don't see Tom risking that with her, do you?'

Steele frowned, as if irritated and didn't reply.

'We'd better get a move on, otherwise there'll be nothing to see,' he said impatiently, noticing how quickly the light was dimming.

They walked together in silence towards the barrier of the inner cordon. She seemed lost in thought, perhaps regretting having come. He had no idea why she had bothered to make the journey. Maybe she just wanted an excuse to get out of the office.

'What was Tom doing down here?' she said quietly, as if talking to herself. 'It doesn't make any sense. All the other crime scenes have been places he could control.' She stopped and folded her arms, going through the motions of studying the scene in front of her. 'So, the girl's attacked over there, O'Connor and Burns run off and leave her, and along comes Tom to murder her. It's all a bit coincidental, don't you think?' She turned to Tartaglia with a sceptical look.

'I don't believe in coincidences either,' he said, a little sharply. 'I'm sure he wasn't coming along here by chance. He must have known where to find her.'

She nodded slowly, her eyes focusing on a distant point further down the canal as if lost in thought. 'Which way's the tube?' she asked, after a moment.

'Over there.' He pointed behind them. 'O'Connor and Burns say she was heading that way when they met her.'

She rubbed her lips thoughtfully. 'So, she wasn't going to meet Tom. She was on her way home.'

'That's what we think. We know that she left her employer's house between seven and a quarter to eight. If O'Connor and Burns are to be believed, it was close to ten when they came across her down here. Which gives her ample time to have met Tom.'

She looked at him questioningly. 'So what's your theory?'

Surprised that she actually seemed to want his opinion, Tartaglia said: 'From what we know, Tom plans his killings very carefully. There's nothing opportunistic in the way he chooses his victims. So it's fair to assume that Yolanda was the intended victim, that Tom had selected her in his usual way and that the contact followed a similar pattern to the other girls.'

She gave him a curt nod of agreement. 'That seems logical.'

'Let's say she had agreed to meet him somewhere near here. I imagine the choice of location will be his. It's a pretty seedy area and...'

'Low risk from his point of view,' she added.

'Yes. It's pretty transient and people are unlikely to remember him, or at least that's what he was hoping. The meeting place would have to be somewhere very close to the canal for her to con- sider coming this way. She had a considerable amount of alcohol in her bloodstream so we're checking all the pubs and bars in the area.'

She didn't say anything for a moment, as if she were thinking it all through very carefully. 'But why was she coming along here without Tom? If they had met, I'm amazed he let her out of his sight.'

It was the one thing that had puzzled Tartaglia too. As he gazed at the scummy, dark brown slick of water, he had a flash of inspiration and turned to Steele. 'Maybe he was late. Or she got cold feet for some reason, either before they met or after.'

She raised her eyebrows. 'The one that got away, you mean?'

'It's the only thing that stacks up, given what we know about him.'

She looked thoughtful. 'That would have made him very angry indeed. Very, very angry. He would be panicking as well, worrying about failing and also worrying about leaving a trail. He would have to find her and finish her off somehow.'

'If she twigged what he was up to and was trying to get away, she'd have been in a blind panic, not thinking straight. It may also explain why she was desperate enough to come along here after dark.'

Steele nodded, as if that was what she was thinking too. 'He has to find her. He can't let her get away…'

'Whatever his motivation, he must have worked out which way she went. He either found her after she had been attacked or it's possible that he even watched, waiting for his moment.'

She sighed. 'If he saw her being attacked, it would mean nothing to him. Someone like him has no concept of mercy. It's all just a despicable game.'

He looked at her a little surprised. He could tell from the bitterness in her tone that she wasn't just thinking of Yolanda but of the emails and she seemed to be taking what had happened by the canal personally. If so, it was a brave move to come down there and try to get close to what had happened. If she wasn't careful, it would end up haunting her. Sometimes it was vital to keep a distance but after everything that had gone between them, he bit back the desire to say so.

She folded her arms and turned to him. 'So where do you think he killed her?

He looked along the ribbon of water again, towards the dark entrance of the Maida Tunnel. 'I don't think he'd have gotten far with her. According to the post mortem results, she had a significant amount of GHB in her system and there was very little water in her lungs. So she must have been unconscious, or almost unconscious, when she was put into the canal. My guess is that she was killed somewhere very close to where we're standing now.'

Steele followed his gaze, her expression distant as if she were picturing it all in her mind. 'I agree with you,' she said quietly, after a moment. 'He probably had something entirely different planned for her but he ran out of options and was forced to improvise.'

He agreed. 'I think there's a very good chance that somebody saw something. If so, we'll find them.'

'You say Harry Angel was out all that Wednesday afternoon?' Donovan asked, trying to contain her excitement.

'Most definitely.' Jenny Evans gave an emphatic toss of her small, round head. 'I've been off sick with the flu, otherwise I'd have called you sooner.'

Donovan was sitting at the small bar at the back of Wild Oats, an organic food shop immediately next door to Harry Angel's bookshop in Ealing. The shop smelled deliciously of a mixture of coffee and freshly baked bread and Jenny had just presented her with a large cappuccino on the house. With short, fluffy grey hair, Jenny looked to be in her mid-fifties. Her pink checked shirt-sleeves were rolled up and she wore a spotless white apron over a calf-length brown tweed skirt and flat slip-on shoes. Her manner was reassuringly precise and down-to-earth and she reminded Donovan of an old-fashioned school matron.

Taking a sip of rich coffee through the thick layer of froth, Donovan asked: 'You are sure about this? That it was *that*

Wednesday afternoon, I mean. When I came in here before, nobody remembered anything.'

Jenny planted a plump, bare forearm on the slate counter and gave a sideways glance at the scrawny, scantily dressed young girl standing at the front of the shop, helping a customer to some cheese. 'They wouldn't, would they? It's not their shop and half the time their mind's on other things, usually boys and pop music. All I can say is that it's a jolly good thing the till does all the adding and working out the change for them, otherwise I don't know where we'd be. At least someone had the sense not to throw away your card and to leave it on my desk for when I came back.'

'Do you remember what time Mr Angel went out, Mrs Evans?'

Jenny gave her a brisk smile. 'It's Miss Evans, but please call me Jenny. Everyone does. Harry came in and got a sandwich and a coffee about one o'clock and said he was popping out for a bit. He asked if we could keep an eye on things.'

'What did he mean by that?'

'He gets deliveries from time to time. I was fond of his grand-father, even though he was a tricky old sod, and I don't mind sign-ing for things and taking them in if we're not too busy. Although I draw the line at being expected to mind the shop, without even being asked, for the whole afternoon, like that Wednesday.'

'So, he was gone a long time?' Donovan said, amazed that Angel had had the gall to pretend otherwise when Tartaglia had questioned him. Perhaps he thought that they wouldn't bother to check.

'Yes. I remember distinctly, he didn't come back until well after five. I was hopping mad by then. He hadn't told me he'd be gone long and I had a constant stream of his customers coming in here all afternoon, asking if we knew where he was. Naturally, think-ing he'd be back soon, I told them to wait or come back later. Some of them seemed to imagine I was stringing them along on purpose, trying to con them into buying something.'

'Do you know where he'd been?'

She shook her head. 'He didn't even have the courtesy to let me

274

know when he got back. He just slipped in and removed the sign. Once I found out he was there, I jolly well went round and gave him a piece of my mind. He was cool as a cucumber, even had the nerve to pretend he'd been there for quite a while. When he saw that wouldn't wash, he just thanked me for minding the shop and showed me the door in no uncertain terms.'

'Did you ask where he'd been all that time?'

'I didn't bother. He wouldn't tell me. But I've a pretty good idea what he was up to.'

Donovan gave her an enquiring look. 'I promise to be discreet, Jenny.'

'Well...' Jenny opened her small, round brown eyes in a conspiratorial fashion and leaned towards Donovan across the counter, speaking in a half-whisper. 'It's sex, isn't it? Has to be. I'll wager he's got some lady on the go and pops round for a session of nooky in the lunch hour, only this one went on till teatime.'

'You really think so?' Donovan asked, stifling a giggle and making a quick note.

'Oh, yes. Harry's always chasing after every bit of skirt that comes in his shop. His grandfather was just as bad, even in his eighties. Maybe it's genetic or perhaps it comes from living amongst all those musty old books.'

'Is there any particular woman that you can think of?'

Jenny sighed as if she didn't know where to begin. 'Take young Saffron over there,' she jerked her head in the direction of the young girl at the front of the shop. 'He was after her for a while and he was really persistent, even though she gave him absolutely no encouragement. Sadly for him, she thinks anything over twenty-five is ancient and books aren't her thing anyway. In the end, he got the message.'

'He made a nuisance of himself?'

'Certainly he did. But then that new assistant of his came along and we haven't seen him for dust.'

'Annie Klein, you mean? Tall, lots of red hair?' Donovan added for clarification, seeing the name meant nothing to Jenny.

Jenny wagged a stubby finger in the air. 'That's the one. I didn't remember her name, although she comes in for coffee and stuff quite a lot. Yes, he seems very keen on her now, so Saffron's off the hook.'

'But you think he may have someone else as well?'

'His sort always does. They can't go without.'

'Does Mr Angel often leave the shop unattended?'

'Quite often, once or twice a week maybe. If he's on one of his book-buying trips, he can be gone for the whole day. At least then he puts a proper note in the window saying he's out. But if he's only out for a short while, he leaves a note that says "Back soon" or something like that. It's a bit of a cheek, I think, making people wait around when you're actually not going to be back soon. I sometimes wonder if he's trying to cover his back for some reason.'

'That's all very useful background information,' Donovan said, noting the look of intense curiosity in Jenny's eye. No doubt, like everyone who fancied themselves as an amateur detective, she would be watching Angel's every move from now on, which was not a bad thing. 'Would you be prepared to sign a statement saying that Mr Angel was out all that Wednesday afternoon?'

Jenny smiled. 'Of course, I'd be delighted, if that's what you need. I believe in speaking the truth. Has Harry done anything wrong?' It was clear from her expression that she wouldn't be at all surprised if he had and would love to know what it was. Luckily, she seemed to have no idea just how serious the matter was.

Donovan smiled. 'I'm just making routine enquiries at the moment. There's really nothing to worry about. But thank you very much for being so frank. I'll send somebody over to see you later and take down your statement.'

30

'This is ridiculous,' Angel said, glaring at Tartaglia across the small table, arms folded. 'You're just clutching at straws.'

Tartaglia shrugged. 'Maybe. But when I came to see you, you told me you were in your shop all that Wednesday afternoon. We now learn otherwise. As you know, we've since obtained a signed statement from a witness who says that you weren't where you said you were at the time in question.'

They were sitting in a meeting room in Ealing Police Station where Angel had been brought in for questioning. Clutching at straws was an accurate description. There was as yet no hard evidence to link Angel to any crime and Steele had taken some convincing about the need to interview Angel again. However, Kelly Goodhart's body had been fished out of the Thames that morning, after the police had been alerted by the skipper of a passing barge. Her body had been taken by water to the small mortuary on the river at Wapping and a cursory examination had revealed that although she was wearing a wedding ring, there was no missing lock of hair. The ring would need to be identified by her family and a full toxicology report had been ordered to make sure that there was no GHB or similar substance in her system. But with the finding of her body, any residual suspicion that Sean Asher might be Tom had evaporated. Angel was the only suspect they had, the only one with a link, however tenuous, to both Marion Spear and, due to the location of his shop, the killing of Gemma Kramer. Once Donovan had outlined to Steele what Nicola Slade and Jenny Evans had both said, Steele had finally agreed to Tartaglia's request to bring him in.

Initially shocked and resistant when two uniformed officers had appeared at his shop to escort him to the local station, Angel had caved in once he had learned of the witness statement and agreed to cooperate. Wightman had been sent to fetch Adam Zaleski to see if he could identify Angel as the man he had seen running away from the church where Gemma Kramer had died. Separately, Donovan had gone off to North London to find Nicola Slade in the hope that she might recognise Angel as Marion Spear's mystery lover.

Angel's expression hardened. 'You say you have a witness. Who is it?' He waited a moment for Tartaglia to respond before adding: 'Is it Annie?' Guilt was written all over his face.

Tartaglia shook his head. 'I can't tell you that at the moment, Mr Angel. But in my book, your not being where you say you were that afternoon looks suspicious. Why did you lie? According to the witness, you didn't get back until well after five. As you know, we're in the middle of a murder investigation and...'

Angel interrupted, looking outraged at the implication. 'But I never even met that girl. How can you think I had anything to do with that?'

'All you need to do is explain what exactly you were doing during the time in question. It's very simple.'

'I was *with* someone. Know what I mean?' Angel raised his eyebrows and leaned towards him, adopting a man-to-man tone, as if his word in such matters should be sufficient.

'What, all afternoon? I find that difficult to believe.'

Angel shrugged. 'Well, you know how these things are. It started off as lunch but one thing led to another...'

'All I'm interested in is eliminating you from our enquiries but I can't until I can prove your alibi.'

Angel looked at him wearily. 'See here, the lady's married. I'll give you her name but I can't have your lot wading over there with their size twelves upsetting her, not to mention what her husband would do to both of us if he finds out what's been going on. He's a really nasty piece of work.'

'I appreciate all of that, Mr Angel. Really I do. But you give me no option unless you cooperate.'

Angel slumped back in his chair and waved his hand in the air as if he was swatting a fly. 'OK, OK. You can talk to her, but please, please tell your boys to be discreet.'

'Of course we will. If the lady confirms what you say, there'll be no need for her husband to hear of it,' Tartaglia said, although as far as he was concerned, lover's alibis were rarely worth the paper they were printed on.

Angel raised his eyes to the ceiling for a moment, as if he could just picture the disaster about to fall down around him, then leaned forward again, giving him a name and address in a whisper, as if he imagined that the walls had ears. 'And don't go round there before nine in the morning or after six at night,' he added. 'That's when the rottweiler's home.'

'Thank you,' Tartaglia said, noting down the details and ignoring the instructions on timing. They would go when it suited them and if Angel got into trouble for his philandering, it was what he deserved. 'You've been very cooperative, Mr Angel. Now, what about the identity parade?'

Angel sighed heavily. 'I suppose I have no problems with that. Maybe then you'll believe me when I say I never went near that bloody church.'

Just after nine o'clock that evening, Donovan arrived at Ealing Police Station with Nicola Slade. Nicola had been out having a drink with some friends in a nearby pub when Donovan reached her on her mobile and they had arranged for Donovan to pick her up outside the pub and drive her over to Ealing.

As they came into the reception area of Ealing Police Station, they met Tartaglia and Adam Zaleski emerging from the back, deep in conversation. Feeling suddenly embarrassed, Donovan turned to Nicola, explaining who Tartaglia was. Still talking, Zaleski gave her nothing more than a brief smile of recognition as he walked out the main door into the street with Tartaglia. Thank goodness Zaleski knew how to be discreet. The only person that she'd told, apart from her sister, was Yvette Dickenson. At least from past experience, she could be trusted to keep her mouth shut. Anyway, why should she tell Tartaglia? Nothing was going on between her and Zaleski and Tartaglia had hardly been forthcoming about his affair, or whatever it was, with Fiona Blake. Two could play at that game.

Donovan escorted Nicola into one of the meeting rooms where she was to wait until the line-up was ready. Nicola looked tired, dumping her bag down on the floor and sitting down heavily in a chair, not even bothering to undo her coat.

'It's strange being back in this part of town,' she said with a sigh, scraping her wispy hair off her face with a hand. 'It brings it all back, what happened to Marion, I mean. I still remember the way she looked that day, when I saw her with that man. She seemed really happy, positively glowing. I still can't believe she's dead.'

'Let's hope we've got the right man,' Donovan said.

Nicola nodded. 'Me too. I've been thinking about nothing else since you came to see me.'

Donovan patted her on the shoulder. 'Don't torture yourself. There's nothing you could have done. Would you like a cup of coffee? I saw a vending machine in the hall.'

'Please. Black with two sugars. I need something to pep me up.'

The vending machine along the corridor was new and not a type Donovan was used to, offering an extraordinary array of options. As she was working out whether to go for a 'double espresso' type coffee for Nicola, or to simply choose 'normal with extra strength', Tartaglia appeared beside her.

'How are you getting on?' he asked.

'She's in one of the meeting rooms,' Donovan said, deciding to go for the large espresso. 'They'll be ready for her in a minute. What about you?' She didn't trust herself to mention Zaleski by name. 'Any luck?'

He shook his head wearily. 'Zaleski didn't identify Angel. There was no doubt in his mind. The man he saw running out of the church wasn't in the identity parade.'

'That's a shame. What about Mrs Brooke? Do you think it's worth asking her to take a look?'

'Dave's bringing her in now but I don't hold out a great deal of hope. Zaleski got a much better view of the man and he was positive he didn't see him in the line-up. Angel's still in the frame for Marion Spear but there's nothing now to link him to Gemma Kramer.'

Donovan sighed. 'Well, maybe we have to face the fact that the two deaths aren't related after all.'

He nodded. 'Let's see what Nicola Slade comes up with first.'

Sipping her coffee, Nicola gazed through the one-way glass at the ten men lined up in front of her on the other side. She walked up and down then stopped in front of Harry Angel.

'He looks familiar,' she said, pushing her glasses up her small, turned-up nose and peering at him closely. 'I've definitely seen him somewhere.'

'Do you remember where?' Donovan said, trying not to sound too interested.

She shook her head then turned to Donovan who was standing behind her. 'I just don't know. He looks familiar, as I said, but he's not the man I saw that day with Marion.'

'You're sure? Please take your time.'

She sighed, staring hard again at the glass, biting her lip, as if she were forcing herself to remember something. Then she added: 'I'm sorry. I'm really sorry.' She bowed her head and started to cry, taking a tissue out of her bag and blowing her nose loudly, dabbing at her eyes with the back of her hand. 'I wanted to do this for Marion and I've failed.'

'Nothing to be sorry about.' Donovan put an arm around her, feeling disappointed that Nicola hadn't been more categorical about Angel. If only she could remember where she had seen him and if it was anything related to Marion Spear. But memory worked in funny ways and it was pointless putting pressure on her.

'That's the way it goes sometimes,' Donovan said, steering her towards the door. 'But it was worth a try. I'll take you home when you're ready. Maybe something will come back to you later.'

Steele slammed the door to her flat shut and double locked it, dumping her briefcase and umbrella down in a corner, kicking off her sodden shoes and throwing her coat over the back of the sofa, where it could dry by the radiator. It had been blowing a gale outside, sheets of almost horizontal rain coming down and she had got completely soaked on the walk from her car. At least the flat was warm and welcoming but she felt ragged, barely able to hold it together any longer. The orange glow from the streetlamp outside flooded the room and she drew the curtains quickly before switching on the light. She turned on the TV, flicking through the channels until she found a news programme and let it buzz away in the background, the noise making her feel less alone.

The answer machine was showing four messages and she hit the replay button. Twice the caller hung up. Then she heard Patrick Kennedy's voice.

'Carolyn, are you there? I've tried your mobile but it's switched off. Sorry not to speak to you today but things have been a bit busy. It's about eight. If you get home soonish, give me a call and let's have a drink. I can pop over to you if you like.'

The fourth message was also from Kennedy, the message recorded about half an hour before and he sounded either tired or a bit drunk or possibly both, his words a little slurred.

'It's Patrick. Give me a call when you get home. I'm at the flat. I'll be up till quite late. Gotta lot of papers to mark. It would be nice to talk.'

Talk? Men never wanted to talk, at least not when you needed them to, when you actually wanted to know what was going on in their peculiar minds. Patrick was more in touch with his feminine side than most, but what did they have to talk about? If it was the case, it could wait until morning. If it was about things more personal, she had no desire to talk at all. The less said about that the better, as far as she was concerned. He was trying to get closer to her, force his way in and she wanted to knock him back, make him go away. There was something about him that unnerved her, his keenness maybe, the fact that he was so thick-skinned, so sure about things that he wouldn't take no for an answer.

Affairs at work were par for the course when you did such long hours, when you had little or no personal life. How the hell did you ever meet anyone outside, someone who would understand the pressures and put up with them? Until Patrick came along and she was taken in by his swagger and intelligence, she had never so much as allowed herself a kiss, let alone anything more, with someone she worked with. She never wanted to put herself in such a position of weakness, give anyone that power over her. The fear of wagging tongues and knowing glances stopped her in her tracks before anything ever had a chance to get started. Patrick had been the only lapse. Perhaps underneath it all, he was bitter and was looking to exact some sort of revenge. She certainly should have realised that he wouldn't let go of her that easily and she felt furious with herself for ever having brought him in on the case.

She deleted the messages and went into the kitchen. After hunting around in the fridge and cupboards, she found a pack of vegetarian moussaka in the freezer compartment and stuck it in the microwave. It was the last thing she felt like eating but there was nothing else in the flat and she felt far too tired to go out again. She looked at the half-full bottle of red wine standing on the counter. In the old days, the days before Barnes, she rarely ever had a drink in the evening. But it was becoming a habit. Sod it. She had to unwind somehow. She pulled out the stopper and poured herself a large glass, taking it with her into the bathroom, where she turned on the shower and started to undress.

If only she could get a few decent hours of sleep she'd be OK but she knew it was unlikely and she was dreading the battle ahead of her that night. Some people, who were not prone to worries, or perhaps with no conscience, seemed to fall asleep instantly. It was like a light being switched out. One minute they were talking and fully conscious, the next, they lay there completely comatose, as if they had been drugged. It was so unfair. Falling asleep had always been a struggle for her but it had got much worse since taking on this case. She'd been waking at around three in the morning, tied up in knots, thoughts spinning, unable to get back to sleep again until nearly five, when it was almost too late to bother. No wonder she felt so out of control, her emotions ebbing and flowing uncomfortably close to the surface. Just touch her and she'd bleed. It was all to do with those bloody emails. She could hear the unknown voice, imagine it whispering to her: *Do I fill your dreams? I'm the lover you've always longed for, the one who'll never leave you.* However hard she tried to block them out, the nasty little words kept wriggling their way back into her mind.

She showered quickly, put on a dressing gown and went into the kitchen, where the moussaka was steaming and bubbling in the microwave. She could smell it through the door and realised suddenly just how hungry she was. Turning it out onto a plate, burning the tips of her fingers as she did so, she topped up her wine, prepared a tray and carried it all into the sitting room, where *Sea of Love*, starring Al Pacino, was just starting on the TV. She'd seen it before but it didn't matter. Anything would do. She sank into a chair, feet up on the coffee table, gazed at the flickering screen and wolfed down the moussaka, wishing suddenly that she'd bought a larger pack. Just as she finished, the phone rang.

If it was bloody Patrick again, she'd scream. She let it ring until the answer machine kicked in. She heard her message play over the speaker, followed by the click as the person at the other end hung up. Curious, she got up and dialled 1471 but the voice said that the caller's number was withheld. It was bloody Patrick. Of course it was. It had to be. Who else would be calling her at that hour, not leaving a message, withholding their number? She knew what he was up to. He was checking up on her, trying to see if she had come home. How dare he. How fucking dare he. She put her hands to her face, biting back the tears.

Tartaglia was at home, about to get ready to go to bed, when Wightman called just before midnight.

'There's no sign of Kennedy, sir. I don't know what it's like with you, but it's raining cats and dogs up here. Perhaps he got put off.'

'Maybe he has other plans,' Tartgaglia said, listening to the sound of the rain beating against his sitting-room window, wondering why Kennedy hadn't shown. 'What a shame. I was looking forward to your bringing him in. How long have you been there?'

'The best part of two hours, sir. She came home just after ten. She was on her own and nobody's been there since. Do you want us to wait a little longer?'

'Is she still up?'

'She's just switched off the lights in the front room. She's probably on her way to bed. Do you want me to go round the back and check?'

'No. You and Nick go home and get some sleep. We'll try again tomorrow.'

Steele lay in bed in the dark. Ignoring instructions on the packet, she had taken two Nytol half an hour before, washed down with the last inch of wine from the bottle. But drowsiness seemed far away. She still felt tense, muscles tight, thoughts buzzing around. When would the pills start to take effect? The wind was making a terrible noise outside, rattling the old sash window in her bedroom as if some invisible hand was shaking it. She would never get to sleep with that racket going on and she got up, found some tissues in the bathroom and wedged them down the sides until there was no possible movement or sound.

As she climbed back into bed, she heard the slam of the main front door of the house, followed by the heavy tread of her neighbour who lived in the flat on the ground floor, above. She listened as his footsteps moved around and, after a few minutes, the floorboards immediately overhead creaked as he went into his bedroom. Her curtains didn't quite meet in the middle and, through the gap, she saw the light go on upstairs, illuminating the garden at the back like a floodlight. She waited for him to close his blinds and go to bed but after a moment, she heard the tramp of his feet out of the room again. After a minute, there was the distant sound of music from the front of the house.

She was never going to be able to sleep like this. She got out of bed and tried to pull the curtains shut but when she forced them together in the middle, she was left with a gap at either side, which seemed to let in even more light. They were pale cream and more decorative than practical. Her mother had made them for her as a Christmas present a couple of years before but had somehow got the measurements a little wrong. They were also thinly lined. It had never really bothered her quite as much as it did now but something would have to be done. She hadn't the heart to replace them and maybe a set of blackout blinds behind the curtains would do the trick. Perhaps she could measure the window and order them over the phone. She certainly wouldn't have a free moment to go into a shop for a while.

She climbed back into bed and stared at the light outside, willing it to go out, listening to the heavy bass beat coming from upstairs. It sounded like some sort of rap, relentlessly repetitive and she wondered how much longer she should give him before going up there and asking him to turn the bloody thing off. She was just on the point of getting out of bed when she saw a shadow cross the window. There was no mistaking it. Somebody was in the back garden.

For a moment she froze then got up and grabbed her dressing gown, which was lying across the end of her bed. Slipping it on quickly, she crept towards the window to take a look. She peered hard through the gap but saw nothing. Trembling, standing just behind the curtains, she waited in the dark listening. *Shall I come and see you? Would you like that?* Was he really out there? Would he try and break in? There were all sorts of strange noises coming from outside but it was impossible to tell what might be a footstep or what was the wind.

Her fingers felt for the window catch, checking that it was secure, that both stops were also in place. She waited for several minutes, wondering if someone was really standing out there on the other side. If she saw the shadow again, she'd dial 999. But there was nothing. Perhaps she had imagined it. Maybe her state of mind was making her jumpy. The shadow could have been cast by the trees outside, blowing in the wind. Perhaps. She went over to the bed, pulled her duvet off and wrapped it tightly around her. After checking that all of the other windows in the flat were secure, she went into the sitting room and curled up in a tight ball on the sofa, listening.

31

The morning started badly. Still raining, the road was as slippery as grease and, as Tartaglia curved through the traffic around Hammersmith Broadway, a large, battered black 4x4 cut him up, accelerating and changing lanes without indicating, making him swerve and nearly come off the bike. He chased after it, swearing pointlessly into his visor, catching up with it again at the next set of lights and pulling alongside. He was about to rap his fist on the window and give the driver a piece of his mind when he saw that a young woman was at the wheel, a car-full of children in the back. As he glared at her through the streaming glass, she glanced over and gave him a sweet, fleeting smile, clearly unaware of what she'd done. As the light changed to green, she accelerated away into the distance, leaving him with a rankling sense of impotence.

He felt like that Greek who was forced to push a boulder up a hill every day only to have it fall back on him and roll down to the bottom each night. Nothing was giving, nothing going his way. With neither Zaleski nor Nicola identifying Angel, they had been forced to let Angel go and the look of smug triumph on Angel's face as he got up to leave was burned on his mind. Predictably, the lover had provided an alibi. They would keep prodding but he didn't hold out much hope of her altering her story for the moment, as she seemed quite smitten with Angel, for some inexplicable reason. As for Kennedy, it was sod's law that he had decided on an evening in for a change.

As Tartaglia crossed the bridge and passed the spot where Kelly Goodhart had jumped to her death, he slowed and said a silent prayer for her, adding one for Sean Asher. At least for him, there was still hope.

He parked his bike in the car park at the back of the office and walked up the stairs to the first floor. Shaking the rain off his helmet, he pushed open the door to find Cornish hovering awkwardly in the corridor beyond, hands in pockets.

'There you are, Mark. I was looking out of the window and saw you drive in. Do you mind coming into Carolyn's office for a minute?' He sucked in his lips, looking embarrassed for some reason.

'Sure. What's the problem?' he asked, wondering if perhaps Steele had made a complaint about him.

'There's been another email.' Cornish lowered his voice to a whisper, talking out of the corner of his mouth as they walked together towards her office. 'Between you and me, I think she's a bit upset. I thought you might know what to say. You know her better than I.'

Tartaglia was tempted to tell him that he didn't know her at all but there wasn't much point. The subtleties of relationships were beyond Cornish.

They found Steele sitting behind her desk reading through some papers. As they entered the room, she glanced up briefly. She looked even paler than usual, her eyes bloodshot and puffy as if she hadn't slept for days.

'What do you make of this,' Cornish said, picking up a piece of paper from the corner of the desk and passing it to Tartaglia.

To: Carolyn.Steele@met.police.uk
From: slwewxnsehTom98342@hotmail.com

My dearest Carolyn,
I came to you last night while you were asleep. You looked really beautiful, your dark head on the pillow, breathing deeply. You were like a child, so innocent and fragrant, I wanted to wrap myself around you and bury my face in your neck and breasts. Were you dreaming of me? I'm sure you were. I watched you for a while. I couldn't resist kissing your cheek. I just had to taste your skin, touch it with my teeth,

ever so gently, I promise. You were so soft and you smelt of something sweet and heady. Is it roses? You must have felt my touch, as you stirred and gave a little moan. I didn't want to wake you, so I crept away. Our time will come very, very soon, my darling. Not much longer for us to wait now.
Your Tomxxx

Anybody, any woman receiving such vile, repellent rubbish would feel furious, if not threatened. Studying the taut lines of Steele's face, looking beyond her lack of open reaction, Tartaglia saw finally how much it had touched her and how shaken she was by it. Had Tom really gone to her flat? Surely, if he had been there, actually got inside by the sound of things, she would know. It seemed far-fetched, possibly nothing more than another wind-up. He suddenly wondered if Kennedy had had anything to do with it.

'Of course it may all be made up,' Cornish said matter-of-factly, trying to make light of the matter for Steele's benefit. 'But we've sent a forensic team over to Carolyn's flat to go through everything, inside and out. Perhaps you can stay with friends until this is over.'

'Over?' she said, her voice hoarse as if she'd been talking a lot. 'And when will that be? I have no intention of being scared out of my flat.'

The muscles of her face were rigid, her mouth drawn into a hard, thin line as if it was the only way she could control it. Tartaglia wanted to tell her that nobody would think badly of her if she let herself go, everybody would understand and sympathise. But she would only misinterpret his motives, particularly with Cornish there, looking unperturbed and immaculate in his dark suit as if the stains of life never touched him.

Tartaglia glanced out the window for a moment, watching the rain run down the glass, Clarke's words coming back to him. Charm her, get her on your side. But it was far too late for that.

'There's something you both need to know,' he said. There was no better time. Slowly and carefully he told them about Kennedy and what he and Wightman had witnessed outside Steele's flat. As he spoke, he saw Steele's expression harden. The colour returned to her face until she had a fierce patch of red on each cheek as though she had been slapped.

'You've been spying on me,' she said, her voice catching in her throat. Her eyes swivelled to Cornish. 'Did you know about this?'

'He knew nothing about it,' Tartaglia said, before Cornish could reply. 'I was going to tell him if it happened again.'

'Happened again?'

'Dr Kennedy didn't appear last night. Dave and Nick waited for a couple of hours...'

She looked horrified. 'You involved Dave and Nick in this?'

'Like me, they just wanted to know you were safe.'

'So, that's who was round the back of my flat, in the garden last night.'

'Somebody was in your back garden last night? You didn't mention this, Carolyn,' Cornish said, a little accusatorily.

Steele compressed her lips tightly and didn't reply.

'Nobody went round the back,' Tartglia said. 'They just kept an eye from the road. You can ask them, if you want.'

'Well somebody was there,' she said. 'I'm positive. Didn't they see anyone?'

Tartaglia shook his head. 'It has to be Dr Kennedy. They must have missed him somehow.'

Although clearly shocked, it was interesting that she wasn't trying to defend Kennedy or deny that he could have done such a thing.

'So, when did all this start?' she said, her voice betraying the emotion beneath.

'After the first two emails. I was concerned for your safety.'

'No you bloody weren't.'

'Come, come Carolyn,' Cornish said, with a little embarrassed cough. 'We're all under a lot of pressure at the moment. I agree it's not orthodox and Mark should have checked with me first but...'

Steele ignored him, eyes fixed on Tartaglia. 'You were just out to spy on Patrick... Dr Kennedy and me. Weren't you? It's got nothing to do with the bloody emails.'

Tartaglia shook his head. 'As I said, I was concerned about you and it's a very good thing I did. If I hadn't, we'd have no idea what Dr Kennedy gets up to after hours. Have you considered for a moment that he might be behind the emails?'

'Patrick?' She stared at him dumbfounded then gave a small, strangled laugh. 'Oh, he's Tom, is he? Is that what you really think? Dr Patrick Kennedy, a well-respected forensic psychologist, just happens to be a psycho in his spare time. That's a bloody laugh.'

'Even if he isn't Tom, he could still have written the emails. Ask yourself, why are you being targeted? What are the emails designed to do? The writer wants to shake you up, make you feel vulnerable. Maybe it is Tom. But maybe it's somebody else, trying to use the situation to try and get closer to you. That's what Kennedy wants, isn't it?'

'Is that true, Carolyn?' Cornish asked.

She was shaking her head slowly in disbelief. 'I can't believe he'd do such a horrible thing.'

'The emails were written by somebody who knows the details of the case,' Tartaglia added, meeting her eye. 'Somebody who also thinks he knows you and understands how to get to you. Who better than Dr Kennedy, with all his psychological insight?'

'I still can't believe it,' she said, almost gasping.

Cornish rubbed his chin thoughtfully. 'I agree it sounds a little far-fetched. But Dr Kennedy's certainly familiar with the emails that Tom sent the other girls.'

'Yes,' Tartaglia said. 'And he's more than clever enough to fake his style.'

Cornish nodded. 'And of course, there have been other hoaxes before. Just think of the Yorkshire Ripper.'

Steele said nothing, as if she didn't trust herself to speak.

'Coming back to this morning's email,' Tartaglia said. 'He talks about watching you while you were asleep. The night before last, Dave saw Dr Kennedy peering through a gap in your bedroom curtains. Your light was on at the time, according to Dave. Now I don't know what Dr Kennedy might see if he did that but you can picture it. Perhaps Dr Kennedy also watched you when you were asleep.'

'If it's true, I'll string him up myself,' Steele said quietly. She closed her eyes momentarily and gave a deep sigh, as if it was all too much for her. Then she bent down and searched in her handbag for a tissue, blowing her nose loudly. Her eyes were red and Tartaglia could see that she was close to tears.

Tartaglia turned to Cornish. 'What are we going to do, sir?'

'It's awkward. Dr Kennedy's a very well-respected academic. It's hard to believe that someone like him would have sent the emails.'

'I agree. But he's definitely been peeping. Perhaps we should get him in for questioning.'

'He'll deny it,' Steele said, looking up at Tartaglia. 'He'll just say he had my welfare at heart, just like you.' Her tone was bitter. But she was right. Even if confronted with what they had seen outside Steele's flat, Kennedy would laugh it all away. They hadn't yet sufficient grounds for a warrant to search his home and take away his computer to see if he had actually sent the emails.

'But we have to do something, sir,' Tartaglia said, turning to Cornish. Sensing his hesitation, Tartaglia added: 'I don't believe that Kennedy is Tom. But he's definitely been up to no good and I still think he could have sent the emails. If we do nothing, it could backfire on us badly.'

Cornish folded his arms and appeared to consider the matter, no doubt picturing how he might end up with egg on his face. 'You're right, Mark,' he said, after a moment. 'We have to do something. We'd better run a background check on Dr Kennedy, see if he's done anything like this before. And I want a proper external surveillance team on Carolyn's flat for the next few nights, with cameras and a full alarm system with a panic button. After this last email, it's the only thing to do if Carolyn wants to stay there. I'll go and get it sorted right away.'

As soon as Cornish had left the room, Steele stood up slowly and walked over to where Tartaglia was standing. She was trembling and her knuckles were white as she clenched her fists at her side. For a second he thought she was going to slap him.

'Why didn't you tell me what you were doing? Didn't you trust me?'

'If I'd come to you and told you what I'd seen that first night, you would never have believed me.'

'But what made you go there in the first place?'

Tartaglia hesitated. How was he to explain the impulse that had led him to her flat? He had been angry and he had wanted to catch her and Kennedy out. It now seemed a nasty, shabby thing to have done, even in the light of what he had discovered. But she was right. He didn't trust her, certainly not enough to tell her the truth now. 'I had a suspicion. Nothing more than that.'

She raised her eyebrows. 'One of your famous hunches, I suppose?'

'It's a good thing I did follow it up,' he said, ignoring the sarcasm in her voice.

'Maybe, but you should have told me first.'

'I needed further proof. That's why I involved Dave and Nick.' He gazed at her angry, pale face for a moment then added: 'There was no point in coming to you. You're blind as far as Dr Kennedy is concerned.'

He saw the words hit home. 'Perhaps I have been blind,' she said, after a moment. 'But as your superior, I find your behaviour inexcusable.'

He realised that on top of everything that had happened to her, he had humiliated her and he felt deeply sorry. 'I didn't mean to embarrass you and I wish that this all hadn't had to come out in front of Superintendent Cornish. But you must understand that I couldn't keep quiet after seeing that email.'

She walked over to the door and held it open. 'Please go now. I want to be on my own.'

It was nearly two o'clock in the afternoon when Gary Jones rolled into the small office he shared with Tartaglia. He'd been out at the Old Bailey all morning, where he had been called to give evidence in an old case. Slapping down a wadge of papers in front of his computer, he sidled over to where Tartaglia was sitting, pushed aside some files and a stack of new CDs that had just arrived from Amazon in the morning post, and eased his broad girth onto a corner of the desk.

'How'd it go?' Tartaglia said, chewing on the last mouthful of avocado and bacon ciabatta sandwich he'd bought from the deli down the road and wiping his fingers on a paper napkin.

Jones stretched his short arms up in the air and yawned. 'I wasn't needed after all. The arsehole's changed his plea to guilty.'

'Wish they were all as easy.'

'Hear you've got Cornish on the warpath about Dr Kennedy. Do you think Steele'll press charges?'

'I guess it depends what forensics and surveillance come up with. At the moment, it's only our word against his. It would be really nice to catch it all on camera.'

'Yeah, but just think what a meal the press would make of it if there's a court case. My money's still on her letting it drop.'

Tartaglia nodded. He wouldn't blame her if she let it go. He had seen how fragile she was underneath. Having her private life exposed in public was probably a step too far, even if it was what Kennedy deserved. 'You know, Steele was furious when she found out that we had seen what was going on with Kennedy. It's amazing. You'd think she'd be pleased.'

Jones shook his head. 'She's a bloody woman isn't she? Logic's not their strong point.'

'I don't think I'd be thinking straight either if I were in her shoes.'

Jones shrugged, as if he couldn't be bothered to think about it any longer and picked up the wrapper from Tartaglia's sandwich. He examined the ingredients label. 'You ought to make your own, mate,' he said. 'Never know what rubbish they put in them.'

'Thanks. I'll remember that, when I have five seconds at home to cut up sandwiches.'

'Get yourself a partner,' Jones said, balling the wrapper and lobbing it into the bin. 'They take care of all that business.'

'More trouble than it's worth,' Tartaglia said, thinking of Jones's wife, who was high maintenance, on the phone to Jones all day long, whatever they were working on in the office. Anyway, none of the women he was ever interested in seemed to have time for the domestic stuff, although it wasn't something that bothered him. Better to have an independent mind and a sense of humour than somebody who could iron and cook supper, which was something he could do himself.

Jones's eye lit on the pile of CDs sitting on the desk beside him. 'Got yourself some new music? Planning an evening in, are you?'

'That OK by you?'

'You're always buying stuff. You must have quite a large collection by now.'

Jones picked the top two CDs off the pile, scanned the front covers then flipped them over. 'Charlie Parker and Humphrey Lyttelton? Don't tell me you're getting into jazz now.'

'I'll be forty in a few years. Thought I'd give it a whirl. I like to be broad-minded.'

'Broad-minded? You're certainly that, in spades from what I hear.' Jones raised his pale eyebrows and gave Tartaglia what was supposed to be a knowing look, although Tartaglia had no idea what he meant by it. 'You can't go wrong with "Best of", in my book,' Jones continued.

'Knowing you, that figures. You're now making me regret buying them.'

'And here's Verdi's Requiem. That's a nice piece.' Jones peered at the front cover and pointed a stubby finger at one of the photographs on the front. 'You know, this chappie here looks just like you.'

Tartaglia glanced over. 'Ildebrando D'Arcangelo. He's a baritone from Pescara.'

'Well, he's your dead ringer, is all I can say. It's incredible. Sure you haven't got a twin?'

'That's very flattering. Sadly, I haven't got his voice.'

Jones nodded sympathetically. 'I love a bit of opera myself. I've been in the choir since I was a nipper. What do you think of our boy Bryn? He's the best, isn't he?'

'I've only seen him once but he was fantastic. Wish I could afford to go more often.'

Jones continued leafing slowly through the stack, examining each box as if it were some peculiar, rare specimen. 'Who's Ornella Vanoni when she's at home?'

'Italian singer from the sixties.'

'And Matchbox Twenty? And The Editors? Am I missing something?'

'Just stick to your Eagles cover versions and don't worry your pretty little head about it,' Tartaglia said, feeling increasingly irritated and hemmed in by Jones's physical presence. He grabbed the CDs out of Jones's hands and put them on the far side of the desk. 'Now piss off, Jonesey, and leave me alone. I've got work to do.'

Jones shrugged and got to his feet, plodding over to his rucksack and pulling out a thermos and a wrapped pack of thick home-made sandwiches. 'You sure have catholic tastes, Mark,' he said, sitting down heavily in his desk chair and peeling off the foil. Within seconds of his taking his first huge bite, the usual smell of tuna fish and onion filled the air.

'I'm a Catholic, so that's not surprising.' Tartaglia wheeled his chair backwards to try and avoid the smell.

Jones shook his head knowingly. 'I forgot you're a left-footer.

Catholic by name, catholic by nature. Does it apply to women, by any chance?' He took another bite of his sandwich, again the same mischievous look in his small brown eyes.

'Only to music…' Tartaglia said, with a sudden idea where this might be leading. It was amazing how even the most private of things didn't stay private for long. If Donovan had talked, he'd murder her. He was about to add something else, when a word snagged in his mind. Catholic. A shaft of light penetrated the darkness. That's what Sean Asher had said about Kelly Goodhart. She was a Catholic.

'What about female pathologists?' Jones said between mouthfuls. 'Ones with red hair and…'

'Shut up for a minute, Gary.' Tartaglia waved him away with a hand, barely hearing him, mind racing, as things started to fall into place. 'I've got something. Catholic. You said Catholic.'

'What about it?' Jones said, mouth full again.

Tartaglia squeezed his eyes tight shut for a moment, trying to blot out Jones. 'I've just remembered. Kelly Goodhart was a Catholic. So was Marion Spear. I'll bet Yolanda Garcia and Laura Benedetti were too. Maybe Gemma and Ellie were as well. We've got to check. I think it's the connection and we've fucking missed it. How can we be so fucking stupid?'

Before Jones could reply, Tartaglia had swung off his seat and rushed out of the room, running down the corridor to the open plan office, where Yvette Dickenson was at her desk, eating the remains of her lunch.

'Where's everyone?'

She shrugged. 'Most of them are still down by the canal, doing the house to house. Why?'

'Call them back, whoever you can get hold of. Right away. Wait, before you do that,' he said, as she reached for the phone. 'Do we know if either Gemma Kramer or Ellie Best were Catholics?'

Dickenson looked at him blankly. She probably thought he'd gone mad. 'I don't know about Gemma but I think Ellie was. I vaguely remember her mum saying something about it. Why, is it important?'

'I'll put money on Gemma being a Catholic too. I think I've worked out what the connection is. Tom's victims are all Catholic. Call the girls' families. Get the names of any religious associations or choirs they may have belonged to.'

She looked doubtful. 'But we've been through all the clubs and stuff like that, sir. There was no link.'

He sighed. Perhaps it wasn't quite so simple. But he was sure he was on the right track. 'If the only thing that the girls had in common was that they were all Catholic, it has to be to do with that.'

'Could Tom be a priest, sir?'

He shook his head. 'They lived in different parts of London. They wouldn't have had the same one.' He stuffed his hands in his pockets, staring into the middle distance as he tried to work it all through. Then he turned back to Dickenson. 'Look, if you're young and lonely and depressed, what do you do?'

'You have to talk to someone, or at least that's what I'd do.'

'Exactly. But if you can't speak to your parents, and maybe you don't want to speak to your priest, where else do you go?'

'We checked the Samaritans and there was no connection.'

Tartaglia shook his head impatiently. 'I know. But maybe there's somewhere like that... perhaps somewhere specifically Catholic and we've missed it for some reason.' He sighed heavily. It would-n't be the first time. 'Get me the names and addresses of the churches the girls went to. I'm going to talk to one of their priests.'

32

The familiar sweet smell of incense and candle wax greeted Tartaglia as he walked through the heavy doors of St Peter's Italian Church on Clerkenwell Road, where they had discovered that Laura Benedetti had once worshipped. Although the large original Italian community in Clerkenwell had long since dispersed, it was still one of the main focal points for Italians living in London and he knew it well. It was where his cousin Elisa had been married and Nicoletta and her husband John, living in Islington not far away, had christened both children there a few years before.

He gazed around momentarily at the ornate nineteenth century interior, with its rows of tall pillars and Roman arches. It was a riot of colour with painted panels depicting the saints, gold leaf and coloured marble everywhere and hundreds of candles burning in the small side chapels. He was struck again by how different it was to the Anglican churches where Gemma, Laura and Ellie had died. It occurred to him that maybe Tom had deliberately chosen places that were very different in feel to what the girls had been used to, places that would have no resonance of family, friends and their communities.

The next mass was not due to start for over an hour. Apart from a few elderly ladies scattered around the pews close to the altar, heads bowed in prayer, there was nobody to be seen. He had called Nicoletta before coming. Shouting over the background screams of his young nephew and niece, who were fighting as usual, she had given him the name of her priest, Father Ignazio, extracting in return a promise that he would come to lunch the following Sunday, whatever happened with 'the bloody case'.

Given that 'the bloody case' looked to be hotting up again, he bit his lip and said nothing. No point in having another row and he would worry about what excuse to make, if need be, nearer the time.

He walked out of the church and round the corner to the entrance of the parish office, which was in a small side street. An old lady showed him into a small, airless waiting room on the ground floor and told him that Father Ignazio would see him shortly. The room had a high ceiling and was painted white, with bare, dark wood floors. A massive bookcase, full of leather-bound religious works in Latin and Italian, ran the length of one wall, the only other furniture being a refectory table and a set of mahogany chairs. A large crucifix hung at one end of the room and a picture of St Vincent Pallotti, the founder of St Peter's, with two of its Fathers, decorated the other.

After a few minutes, Father Ignazio entered the room.

'I hear you want to see me,' he said, gesturing for Tartaglia to sit down at the table opposite him.

His face was tanned and almost unlined. He looked not much older than Tartaglia, although his black hair was showing the first signs of grey at the temples. Tall and thin, he had a slight stoop and wore heavy-rimmed glasses with thick lenses that magnified his dark eyes. Tartaglia introduced himself, watching Father Ignazio's face break into a broad, warm smile when he mentioned the family connection. As Father Ignazio spoke of Nicoletta and her family, whom he seemed to know well, he switched to his native Italian, talking in a heavy Neopolitan accent, which Tartaglia found difficult to follow at first.

'Unfortunately, I'm here on police business,' Tartaglia said, reverting to English, once Father Ignazio had finished. As Tartaglia explained what he was after and the connection with Laura Benedetti, Father Ignazio frowned and, sighing heavily, crossed himself.

'Of course, I read about the case in the papers. You really think there's a connection to our church somehow?'

'Indirectly, possibly. It's the only thing we can find that all the victims have in common.' He gave a brief background profile of the three young girls, leaving out Marion Spear and Kelly Goodhart. There seemed no point in complicating the picture.

'You think the murderer is a Catholic?' Father Ignazio said, after Tartaglia had outlined the situation.

'Probably, or at least working for some sort of Catholic organisation. As the girls lived in different parts of London, my feeling is that it isn't at a local level.'

Father Ignazio nodded, apparently reassured by this.

'They were all depressed, possibly suicidal, although they were coerced in that direction,' Tartaglia continued. 'At some point they may have sought counselling. Given that, for some reason, they may not have wanted to talk to their priests, I wondered...'

Father Ignazio nodded again. 'Yes, I understand. They were very young. It's natural. You're wondering if there may be some other place where they would go.'

'Exactly, either by phone or in person, where they could be anonymous, where there would be no chance of their family finding out.'

'The Samaritans perhaps?'

'We've looked at that. I was thinking of something specifically Catholic which the girls could find out about, possibly through their local churches or communities.'

Father Ignazio stroked his chin thoughtfully. 'Well, there are several small organisations that I know of, all run on a voluntary basis, of course. Come with me. I think there are some leaflets that may interest you, at the front of the church.'

He got to his feet and Tartaglia followed him out into the hall and through a small door, which led directly into the church. They walked down the aisle and across to the main entrance doors where Father Ignazio stopped in front of a wooden rack filled with a variety of information pamphlets.

'There are a quite a few here,' he said, gathering together a handful of leaflets from the rack. He studied them carefully, then put several back before handing one to Tartaglia. 'Maybe this is what you're looking for. It's the only one that really fits what you've told me. They're like the Samaritans, only Catholic.'

Tartaglia looked at the leaflet. The organisation called themselves 'CHA: the Catholic Help Association'. 'We treat your calls in total confidence,' the blurb said. There was no office address, only a phone number. He had never heard of the organisation but reading quickly through the blurb, it seemed genuine and, as Father Ignazio had said, very similar in vein to the Samaritans in what they were offering. He could just picture it now, the girls calling in, feeling depressed, Tom answering the phone at the other end. It all made sense. They had gone through the girls' home phone records very carefully and had checked for any contact with well-known organisations like the Samaritans. But perhaps out of ignorance or human error they had missed the significance of any calls to 'CHA'. It was equally possible that the girls had gone somewhere else to phone, like a friend's house or a public call box.

'This looks like it,' he said, turning to Father Igazio. 'Thank you. Do you have any idea where they're based?'

Father Ignazio shook his head. 'All I know is they're in London. I've seen their leaflets in other churches too. I'm not sure if they have a presence elsewhere.' He walked with Tartaglia out of the main door and down the steps to the street. 'It's a terrible, terrible thing to contemplate, somebody abusing such a position of trust, such a…' Father Ignazio's voice trailed off. He gazed down at the pavement for a moment, shaking his head slowly, and then looked back at Tartaglia with a heavy sigh. 'Of course, there are evil people in all walks of life. No doubt you see more of them than I do.'

Tartaglia nodded. 'I imagine so. Thank you very much for your help. I'll let you know if we find anything.'

Father Ignazio smiled, took Tartaglia's hand in both of his and gave it a hearty shake, clasping it warmly as he met his eye. 'It would be nice too to see you here one day, Inspector, come along and join the rest of your family.'

Tartaglia smiled back, thinking it was probably something long overdue. 'I promise you I will, Father. Very soon.'

After leaving the church Tartaglia called the office and found Yvette Dickenson still at her desk. No doubt, with her impending maternity leave, she was grateful for all the extra overtime, although, in his view, she should have been at home long ago, putting her feet up. He gave her the details from the pamphlet to check.

'Call this number and find out where they're based. Then get someone over there right away. If they're not cooperative, tell them we'll get a warrant. I want a list of anyone who's worked for them over the last couple of years, in any capacity. But I'm particularly interested in anyone who's been manning the phones. We'll need access to their phone records. While we're at it, we'd also better check the other churches and see if they have the same or anything similar. Then call me back.'

'I've had Nicola Slade on the phone, sir. She's rung several times to speak to Sam. She's quite insistent.'

'Why can't Sam deal with it?'

There was a pause at the other end. 'She went home a little early.' He could tell that Dickenson was being evasive.

'What did Nicola Slade want?'

'She wouldn't say. Just said she had to speak to Sam.'

'Well, where is Sam?'

There was another pause before Dickenson spoke. 'She's got a date.' There was another second's hesitation before she added, as if in justification: 'She's allowed a personal life, isn't she?'

A date? This was the first he knew of Donovan having anybody around. Last thing he'd heard was her moaning about a total absence of attractive men. 'Of course she's allowed a personal life, but what a time to pick. We're in the middle of a bloody investigation.' He wasn't sure whether he felt angrier from a professional point of view or from a personal one. Now was hardly the time to go out on hot dates. Also, Donovan usually let slip most things about her private life, such as it was, even asking for his advice sometimes. Why hadn't she told him about this? There had been ample opportunity.

'It's just tonight,' Dickenson said a little sharply, as if trying to excuse her.

'OK, OK. Point taken,' he replied irritably. There was no gain in antagonising Dickenson and getting the sisterhood in the office up in arms against him for trying to stop one of their tribe from having a bit of fun. He would have words with Donovan in the morning. 'Give me Nicola Slade's number and I'll ring her now.' He took down the details and hung up. He was about to call Nicola when his mobile buzzed, Wightman at the other end.

'Sir, we've got something,' he said. 'I'm over at the canal and we've found a pub where Yolanda went the night she was attacked. There's a bloke here who recognises her picture. He says she was in here drinking with a man and it sounds like Tom.'

He paused for a moment, trying to calm himself and collect his thoughts. Things were starting to happen. He could feel it. What was that old saying about buses? You're standing there in the cold but nothing comes along. You're almost on the point of giving up and then suddenly three of the damned things appear. Life was often like that and investigations were no different. This was what he had been waiting for.

'Give me the address,' he said, trying to contain his excitement. 'I'll be over there right away.'

The Dog and Bone was perched on the corner of a bridge overlooking the Regent's Canal, close to the stretch of water where Tartaglia had met Steele the other day. The bar was full, the air thick with smoke and sweat, loud music pumping through ceiling speakers above. The majority of the clientele seemed to be tourists, with a large, loud contingent of Australians or New

Zealanders gathered close around the bar, although he couldn't tell which they were from the accents. Judging by the merriment and the general look of things, they'd been in there a while and had already put away several beers.

He found Wightman perched on a stool in a corner at the far end, talking to a burly man in his mid-thirties, with a shaved head and tattoos covering every inch of what could be seen of his arms. Pint in hand, legs stretched out in front of him, he lounged against some cushions in the middle of a large velvet sofa with the air of someone who owned the place.

Tartaglia pulled up a stool from another table and sat down next to Wightman, opposite the man.

'Mr Stansfield was here the other day,' Wightman said, turning to Tartaglia. 'He remembers seeing Yolanda in here with a man.'

'That's right,' Stansfield said, taking a large gulp of bitter and wiping his mouth with the back of his hand. 'They was sat right here. Where I am now. And I was standing over there where Paul and Mick are.' Stansfield jerked his head towards a couple of men who looked like clones of himself, grouped around a cigarette machine, on the opposite side of the room.

'Do you remember if they came in together?' Wightman asked.

'She was here on her own for a bit then he appeared, this poncey git.'

'Poncey? What do you mean?' Tartaglia asked.

'Fancied himself, didn't he? Right flash so-and-so, he was.'

'Early to mid-thirties, short dark hair, medium height and build...' Wightman read from his notes. 'Sounds like our man, all right.'

'Yeah? Well he spoke real proper.'

'You spoke to him?' Wightman asked, looking up surprised.

'I was just getting round to telling you that when the Inspector arrived,' Stansfield said, taking a slurp of beer. 'They was talking for a while, him and the young girl.'

'Was the pub full?' Tartaglia asked.

'Yeah, more or less.'

'If you were standing over there with your mates, how come you noticed what they were doing?'

Stansfield jabbed his thumb at the table. 'This 'ere's my place, see. It's where me and me mates sit. We're working over the road and we're in most nights. When I come in and see the young lady sat here, I thinks to myself, OK, not a problem. She doesn't know. But I keeps an eye on it, see. She don't look much of a drinker to me, she'll be on her way soon, I thinks. But then this bloke turns up and they sit here having a right old chinwag, at least he's doing most of the wagging. And he keeps nipping off to the bar to buy her drinks, trying to get her pissed, know what I mean? Next minute I look over and see her hop it, out that door there.' Stansfield jerked his head in the direction of one of the exits. He raised his almost non-existent eyebrows. 'Can't blame her, can you, poor girl.'

'So, she left the pub without him? On her own?'

'Yeah, picks up her jacket and bag and legs it while he's at the bar. I thought it was dead funny.'

'Nobody else followed her out?'

Stansfield shook his head. 'Then the plonker comes back and sits here waiting for her, twiddling his thumbs. Made me laugh again, it did. Well, she's not coming back is she? So I move over here and I sits down in her place. "Someone's sitting there" he says, all hoity toity.' Stansfield screwed up his face and mimicked the voice. 'Told him he needs flamin' glasses. Nobody's sat here, are they? Takes a minute for him to work it out and he doesn't look best pleased when the penny drops and he sees she's gone and buggered off.'

'Did he say anything else?'

Stansfield thought hard for a minute, draining his pint and putting down his empty glass with a loud clunk as if making a point. He cleared his throat as if something was catching in it.

'Another pint, Mr Stansfield?' Wightman said, smiling.

Stansfield nodded. 'Don't mind if I do, particularly if you're buying, mate. Sure is nice to take one off the old Bill for a change.'

'So, what did he say, Mr Stansfield?' Tartaglia asked, as Wightman got up to go to the bar.

Stansfield stretched his short muscular arms out wide along the back of the sofa as if he was settling in. 'Well, he comes up with some cock and bull story about her being sick, or something. But it was clear as bleedin' daylight what'd happened. She don't fancy the poncey toad, does she?'

'What happened next?'

'He fucks off, he does. Out of here like greased lightning.'

'Which way did he go?'

Stansfield shook his head. 'Dunno. Tanya'd come over, hadn't she? She's my bird. I don't remember nothing after that.' He gave Tartaglia a wide, toothy grin, showing several large gaps.

'We'll need you to make a formal statement, Mr Stansfield, and we'll also need your help putting together an e-fit of the man. It sounds like you got a very good look at him.'

'No problem.' The smile suddenly disappeared and Stansfield frowned. 'You telling me this is the bird what was killed down by the canal a few days ago?' he said. 'The one who was sat right here?'

Tartaglia nodded.

'Bleedin' hell. You think this bloke I saw did it?'

'We're at an early stage of the investigation, Mr Stansfield.'

Stansfield gave him a knowing look and shook his head. 'Yeah, yeah. Pull the other one. It's got bells.' He gave a heavy sigh, examining a food stain on his T-shirt as if he'd only just noticed it. 'The minute I clapped eyes on him, I knew he was a wrong 'un. Poor, bleedin' girl, that's what I say. Poor little thing.' He met Tartaglia's eye. 'I hope you string him up right and proper when you find him. Prison's too good for his sort.'

'I agree,' Tartaglia said, getting to his feet. Stansfield didn't know the half of it.

33

'Have you lived all your life in this country? Donovan asked.

Adam Zaleski nodded. 'London born and bred, although I've never felt at all English. Never really felt I belong here, or anywhere else for that matter.'

They were sitting at a table in the window of a little French restaurant in Ealing, near where Adam Zaleski lived. They had eaten oysters, followed by turbot with hollandaise sauce, Zaleski choosing the same things as Donovan, something that she found strangely reassuring. It was nice to know they had the same taste in food, at least. She thought she had never had anything quite so delicious, but perhaps it was his company making everything seem gilded and amazingly heady. He was so easy to talk to, so relaxed and interesting. There was nothing that grated or felt awkward and he seemed genuinely interested in her, not like some men who only wanted to talk about themselves. Her course of hypnosis being finished, Zaleski had bought a bottle of champagne to celebrate and it tasted wonderful. And the incredible thing was, she didn't crave a cigarette at all. When someone at the table behind them lit up, she felt almost sick.

The waiter appeared at the table and they ordered dessert: sorbet made with fruit and some sort of plum brandy for Donovan, Zaleski preferring the cheese.

'Are both your parents Polish?' she asked, taking a sip of champagne once the waiter had moved away.

'My mother was, but she's dead. Died when I was very young and I was brought up by her parents. Zaleski's their name. I've never known my father. He dumped her when he found out she was pregnant.'

'Oh.' The word sounded stupid but she didn't know what else to say.

'She was only seventeen and they weren't married,' he continued, appearing not to mind.

He spoke matter-of-factly but she wondered how he really felt inside. 'Have you never wanted to get in touch with him?'

His face hardened and he shook his head, pausing momentarily before answering. 'I never want to see him. Ever. From what I know, he was a right sod. I'd scrub his genes away, if only I could. Apparently I look just like him, which is ironic, given how I feel about him.'

She gazed at him inquiringly, wondering if she should change the subject. But curiosity got the better of her. 'You said your mother died?'

He nodded slowly, swirling his champagne around in the glass until little bubbles fizzed angrily around the edge.

'She killed herself. It's the ultimate abandonment, isn't it? I was only three, luckily too young to remember her, although I've got photographs.'

'I'm sorry.'

He sighed. 'It's OK. I'm old enough now to feel detached, or at least have some perspective. Most of the time I try not to think about it. I mean, what's the point? What's done is done. Luckily, someone was there to look after me.'

He took off his glasses, dropping them on the table, and rubbed his face with his hands. Then he looked up at her and she noticed for the first time what nice eyes he had. They were hazel, neither green nor brown but somewhere in between. He reached across and took her hand, his face creasing into a smile. 'Let's talk about more cheerful things. Tell me about you. Where do you come from?'

Her hand felt so small in his and although the touch was lovely, she felt awkward and suddenly shy. 'Like you, I'm a Londoner, born and bred. I was brought up in Twickenham. My parents are both teachers, although they're now retired.'

'Do you have any brothers and sisters?'

'One sister, Claire. She's two years older than me. She's a solicitor for one of the big City firms.'

'Are you close?'

She nodded, pulling her hand gently away on the pretext of reaching for her glass of champagne. 'We're very different, very, very different but we get on most of the time. We share a house together.'

'Hammersmith, you said?'

'That's right. It's Claire's house but I contribute to the mortgage.'

'Does she look at all like you?'

Donovan laughed. 'Not at all. Nobody would even guess we're sisters. She's tall, nearly five nine, with dark, curly hair. Takes after my father. And, as for me, well...' She shrugged.

'I think you're lovely,' he said, looking her in the eye and taking her hand again, stroking it gently with his fingers. 'Really lovely. Your skin feels so smooth and soft.'

She could feel the colour rising to her cheeks but before she had time to say anything silly, the waiter appeared with her sorbet and Zaleski's cheese.

Tartaglia was on his way out of The Dog and Bone when his phone rang. He heard a woman's voice saying something faintly at the other end.

'Who's that?'

'Is that DI Mark Tartaglia?' the voice repeated, louder this time.

'Hang on a minute,' he said. 'Can't hear anything in here.' He went outside, sheltering in the doorway from the rain, the phone cradled tightly against his ear.

Speaking quickly, in a breathy voice, the woman announced herself as Nicola Slade and he realised he had forgotten to call her back.

'I spoke to the lady at your office and she said you'd be calling me,' she continued. 'When you didn't, she gave me your number. I hope it's OK.'

'Of course it's OK. I'm sorry. I would have got back to you sooner but I've just been interviewing someone.'

'I really wouldn't have bothered you but this is important and I can't get hold of DS Donovan. You know the man I said I saw with Marion? The one she was keen on? Well, he was at Ealing Police Station. I didn't realise it was him until afterwards,' she said, almost chatty, not knowing the impact of her words. 'I had a dream last night about Marion and... well, it only hit me late this afternoon. He looks so different now, you see. He's changed his appearance and things.'

'You mean the man in the line-up?'

'No. I told you it wasn't him. It was the bloke you were with, when I was standing at reception with DS Donovan. You and the man went outside together. Do you remember?'

As she spoke, he felt as though a wave of freezing air had blown over him and he shuddered. The answer had been lying in front of them all of the time. Everything clicked into place now. Horribly so, and they'd been so stupid. So bloody stupid. Marion Spear. Laura Benedetti. Ellie Best. Gemma Kramer. Yolanda Garcia. It all made sense. Perhaps there were others that they knew nothing about.

'You are absolutely sure that it's the same man, Miss Slade? It's easy to make mistakes.'

'He really looks different,' she added, trying to justify why she hadn't recognised the man before. 'But I'm sure it's him now. I'm positive. I wouldn't have called you otherwise.'

When they got outside the restaurant, Zaleski took Donovan by the hand again, looking down at her smiling. 'If you're tired, I could take you home.' He paused. 'Otherwise, I've got some very good Polish vodka in the freezer at my place, if you fancy a night-cap.'

'That would be lovely,' she said, with a giggle. 'I don't feel in the least bit tired.'

'Good. It's only about five minutes away.' He kissed her lightly on the cheek and they walked hand in hand down the road.

Even the frosty night air couldn't bring her down. She felt elated, on a high. It was as if she were playing hookey, mobile switched off, pager at home, and all the cares of the job left behind for a while. She damn well deserved some fun for a change and Adam was so nice. Tartaglia would be furious if he found out, but she didn't care. He wasn't her keeper.

The route took them past the parade with Angel's bookshop. As they walked past, she glanced in through the window. The shop was in darkness, but looking up she saw lights blazing on the first floor, curtains wide open, and she saw what looked like Angel and some blonde-haired woman moving around in the room. She stopped, listening to the distant strains of opera that drifted down, wondering who the woman was and what Angel was up to.

'You OK?' Zaleski said.

'Fine,' she replied, still distracted, wondering if perhaps she should give Nicola Slade another call now and see if anything had come back to her. Maybe she should tell Zaleski that she'd skip the vodka this evening. He was sure to understand and if he was interested, he'd call her again.

'Come on then,' he said, pulling her gently by the hand. 'We'll catch our death standing around out here.'

She hesitated, not knowing what to do. Something was telling her to call Nicola Slade.

'What's the matter?' he said, his tone a little impatient. He followed her gaze to the window above. 'Is that someone you know?'

She looked back at him and smiled. 'No, not really... it's just that, well, we've got so much on at the moment, I'm a bit preoccupied. Perhaps I should be getting home.'

He took both her hands in his, looking at her quite seriously, almost offended. 'Are you having second thoughts?'

'Of course not.' She was being stupid. Why ruin the evening with Zaleski because of the bloody case? It was late and Nicola would probably be in bed by now.

'Let's go, then,' he said, taking her firmly by the arm.

With a last lingering look up at Angel's window, she allowed herself to be steered away. There was no point worrying about all of that stuff now. It could wait until the morning, when she got into work, hopefully not too late or hung-over. She'd give Nicola a bell then.

They crossed the main road, walking for a minute along the green.

'That's Pitshanger Manor,' he said, as they passed a large eighteenth century house, set back from the road behind wrought iron railings and a wide drive. 'It used to belong to the architect Sir John Soane. Sadly, it's now owned by the council and there's nothing worth seeing.'

She nodded, the name meaning nothing to her, other than the connection with Angel's bookshop. Angel. Why couldn't she stop thinking about him? She felt suddenly tired and it occurred to her that she really ought to go home. Even if it was too late to call Nicola Slade, it might be a good idea to get some sleep. She also felt that in her state of mind, she'd be better off on her own.

She stopped walking and turned to him. 'Look, Adam, would you mind very much if I went home?'

'What's troubling you?'

'Work, that's all. I'm sorry. I just can't seem to switch off.'

'You're sure that's all?'

She saw the disappointment in his eyes and suddenly felt guilty for having mentioned anything. Bloody work. It was always getting in the way. 'I promise. I've had a lovely evening. Thank you.'

'If you want to go home, that's fine,' he said. 'But I haven't said anything wrong, have I?'

She smiled, hoping to reassure him. 'Not at all. Really, it's just the case. I'm just a bit preoccupied, that's all.'

He nodded slowly. 'I understand. Your work's obviously very

important to you and it must be difficult to put it aside for the evening.'

Important? It was important. But she felt so silly letting it intrude like this.

'What about just a quick one?' he said, before she had time to reply. 'My house really isn't far from here and then I'll call you a cab.'

She hesitated, seeing the anxious look on his face, and nodded. 'OK. Just one would be lovely.'

He took her by the hand again and they walked along the side wall of what looked like a large garden attached to Pitshanger Manor, threading their way through a series of residential streets beyond, with rows of low-built Edwardian redbrick houses, some terraced, some semi-detached in neat, matching mirrored pairs.

The area was strangely deserted and the only person they saw was a stout, middle-aged woman, bundled up in a bulky anorak, out walking a small brown and white Jack Russell. As they passed her, the little dog ran up to Zaleski, running in circles around his feet, jumping and yapping as if it wanted to play. They were forced to stop.

'Can't you keep your dog under control?' Zaleski shouted at the woman, who had walked on, stabbing at the dog with his foot, trying to keep it at bay. 'It should be on a lead.'

'Sorry,' the woman said, rushing back to where they were standing. She picked up the wriggling dog in her arms. 'Fred's not usually like this.' She sounded affronted, clearly thinking that it was Zaleski's fault. She turned on her heel and strode away, the dog, still fighting for freedom, tucked tightly under her arm.

'I hate dogs,' he said, vehemently, once the woman had gone, brushing the legs of his trousers as if to remove any trace, before taking Donovan's hand again and walking on.

'That one's certainly very energetic,' she said, wanting to diffuse the tension.

It was interesting how both dogs and cats could sense people who didn't like them. Donovan loved dogs, all animals in fact, and she found Zaleski's reaction a little extreme and off-putting. But there was no point in getting into an argument about it. Perhaps he hadn't been brought up with any animals.

Zaleski gave her a tight smile in reply and they walked on together in silence. Two minutes later, Zaleski stopped outside a low-built semi-detached house, that looked like all the others, and pushed open a small white wooden gate, holding it open for her. The woodwork looked as though it could do with several licks of paint but the small strip of garden was neat and tidy, bins tucked under a shelter, a high, clipped hedge at the front, separating it from the road.

'Here we are,' he said, leading her by the hand up the short path to the front door. 'This is my house.'

As soon as Tartaglia had hung up on Nicola Slade, he called Dickenson's mobile.

He could hear the sound of traffic as she answered.

'I need you to check a name for me,' Tartaglia said.

'I'm just crossing Hammersmith Bridge. I'm on my way home.'

It was late and, in her condition, he couldn't blame her. But now was not the time to be going home. 'Is anyone else in the office?'

'Dave and Nick just got back. They're following up on the info you gave me. I'm sorry, I thought it was OK to go.'

'Look, this is urgent. I think Tom is Adam Zaleski. Call them and get them to check if he works at the CHA in some capacity.'

There was a second's silence at the other end. 'Zaleski! You mean the witness? The hypnotist?'

'Of course,' he said sharply, no time to explain.

'Shit! Sam's having dinner with him now.'

He felt his heart miss a beat. 'She's having dinner with Adam Zaleski? How the hell... Where?'

'I don't know. Oh my God!'

'Get onto Dave and Nick immediately. I need Zaleski's address. NOW. It's somewhere in Ealing. Should be in the file. And get a

team over there with a warrant. We've got to find him before...'
His voice trailed off as he thought about what might happen.
Thank Christ he had his bike. He could be in Ealing in twenty
minutes. Fifteen if he was lucky.

34

Donovan watched as Zaleski unlocked the door and followed him inside, waiting while he switched on the hall lights. The interior smelt of damp and something musty but it was pleasantly warm after the cold night air. The first thing she noticed was a large oil painting of a man, wearing a beret, in military uniform, hanging in the hallway by the door. It looked like the ones she'd seen in the Polish Club.

'That's my grandfather,' he said, just behind her. 'He was quite a hero in his day.'

She turned around. 'He doesn't look at all like you. In fact, he looks very fierce.'

He smiled grimly. 'He certainly was. But he's dead now, thank God. So's my grandmother. This was their house. It's where I grew up.'

He took her coat and hung it up on a rack nailed high on the wall, made of dark varnished wood and what looked like some sort of small animal horns for hooks. It had a brass plaque in the middle with an inscription, which she was too far away to read.

He led her into a small sitting room at the front. 'Make yourself at home. I'll be back in a minute with the vodka.'

She sat down on the sofa feeling suddenly uncomfortable. Her family house in Twickenham, where she had lived all her life until going to university, was similar to Zaleski's architecturally. But the atmosphere was so completely different: noisy, chaotic and cheerful, full of animals, people coming and going, with all the resultant mess and the feel of things permanently in a state of flux. Here everything was so formal, from the hard back and curved arms of the sofa, covered in what appeared to be some sort of expensive-looking red damask, which wouldn't last a second in her home, to the faded chintz curtains with the tight pelmet and the ornate gilt mirror hanging over the mantelpiece, way too large for the small room, as if it was meant for a much bigger house. A clock ticked quietly from a mahogany card table in the corner and, in the dim light, she felt as though she had stepped back in time, into another world that wasn't entirely English. The house was like a museum, a place for show, not for use, and she couldn't picture Zaleski, either as a small boy or as a man, living there.

After a few minutes, he reappeared with a small wooden tray. A bottle of vodka, with a bright yellow label, nestled in a silver ice bucket, two shot glasses beside it, already full, the sides misted from the cold liquid inside. He put down the tray on a long, low wooden stool. The seat was covered in needlework, faint shades of blue and red the predominant colours, the design some sort of crest, possibly belonging to his family. He passed her a glass and sat down beside her, resting his arm lightly on the back of the sofa behind her. She felt suddenly excited by his closeness, wondering when, if, he would kiss her.

'Na zdrowie,' he said, raising his glass and clinking hers. 'Here's to you, Sam Donovan.'

She smiled, managing to knock back half the glass, this time prepared for the burning sensation, actually beginning to enjoy it. She sipped the rest slowly, waiting for the wave of warmth that would follow.

'I know I shouldn't ask, but I was wondering how the case is going?' he said in an off-hand manner. 'That man you wanted me to identify, is he the one you're after?'

He was looking at her inquiringly, waiting for her reply.

'Yes,' she replied, after a second's hesitation. 'Or, at least, we think so.'

She knew she shouldn't have said anything but he'd never asked before and he was so nice to be with. Good-looking too. Afraid that he could read her thoughts, she tried to focus on something else. She was beginning to feel a little giddy, must try to keep a check on things, just give him the bare minimum and change the subject.

She drained the final drop of vodka and put the glass down on the tray.

'Unfortunately, we haven't got anything so far to put him at the crime scene. It's all a bit disappointing.'

'I'm sorry I couldn't help,' he said, shrugging. 'I just didn't recognise the man, I'm afraid.'

'That's fine. You can only say what you saw. It's just that… well, we think we can link him to two of the murders.' She found herself saying it without meaning to.

'What about the latest one? I read in the papers about a murder down by one of the canals. Are they linked?'

'Yes. Yes, they are.' She took a deep breath, surprised that he'd made the connection. As far as she was aware, the press hadn't yet. Stop there. Don't say anymore. Change the subject, but she couldn't think of what to say next. Her mind was feeling a little hazy.

He took the small bottle of vodka from the ice bucket. 'One more for the road?'

She hesitated, then passed him her glass. 'Why not?'

'You're getting a taste for it, aren't you? That's good,' he laughed, topping up both glasses and passing one over to her. He clinked her glass. 'Now, down in one this time.'

She did as she was told, although she was suddenly beginning to feel quite drunk. As she stretched forward to put her empty glass back on the tray, she missed and knocked it over. 'Sorry.'

He righted the glass for her. 'Don't worry about it.'

For some reason it was affecting her far more than usual. Had she really had a lot to drink? She didn't think so. Vodka on top of champagne. That was it. Silly thing to do. No more vodka. Perhaps she should ask him to call a taxi now. But she felt such a fool. He'd think she was no better than a schoolgirl who was unable to hold her drink. Perhaps if she waited a minute, she'd feel better, maybe ask for some coffee or water.

She could feel his fingers gently stroking her shoulder.

'So, if you can't find anything, what do you do?' he said. 'Do you just keep an eye on him?'

She nodded, concentrating on keeping her eyes open and the muscles of her face under control. He was studying her closely. Perhaps he had guessed she was drunk. She hoped he wouldn't think badly of her. What was strange was he'd had roughly the same amount to drink. Although he was a man. Much bigger. It was all about body mass.

'What evidence do you have on him?' he asked.

She answered automatically. 'That's the problem. Well... we haven't got much to go on.' She could hear herself slurring.

He shook his head slowly and took off his glasses, folding them carefully, and putting them down next to him on the sofa. 'No, I suppose you haven't.'

Gazing down at her toes, she giggled. Somehow, even though there wasn't anything funny, she couldn't help herself. 'No, we've got fuck all, sweet FA.'

He stared at her for a moment then said: 'You lot haven't got a clue, have you?'

It wasn't just the words that penetrated, making her raise her eyes again slowly to look at him. It was the change in his voice. His tone was cold and unfamiliar and she frowned, struggling to focus. She saw a different person in front of her. A stranger. Somehow his face had transformed, morphed into something unrecognisable. What she saw frightened her.

'A clue?'

'Yeah. The answer was staring you in the face all the time and you haven't got a fucking clue.'

Through the thickening fog in her mind, she realised what was happening.

'It's you... isn't it?' she said, barely able to get the words out. 'You're Tom.' She tried to get up but her arms and legs wouldn't work properly.

She felt him grip her wrists and push her down in her seat.

'Save your energy. You're not going anywhere.'

She knew she couldn't fight him. She felt as though she'd been anaesthetised, no control over her body, eyelids heavy as lead. Somehow she had to stay awake. She had to. He was going to kill her. Mustn't let him. Try and work something out. 'How come you're not...'

He smiled. 'Drunk or drugged, like you? You're feeling it now, aren't you? We've both had two glasses but I'm still sober. What a riddle. To be nice, I'll tell you the answer, as I can see you'd have problems working it out on your own and you won't be conscious for much longer.'

His words sounded distant. Echoing. Her head lolled back heavy on his arm; she couldn't help it. The room was spinning. She wanted to be sick. 'Drug...'

He grabbed her face with his hand and forced her to look at him, digging his fingers into her cheeks. Although she was aware of what he was doing, it felt as though it was happening to someone else.

'Yes, GHB, what a lovely little substance it is. Once in the system, particularly taken with alcohol, it takes no time to work. It was in your first glass. There's some in the bottle too, for good measure. You're so far gone, you didn't notice that I didn't drink mine. Look, here it is.' He held the full glass in front of her eyes, moving it slowly from side to side like a pendulum. 'Can you still hear me?'

'Why?' She mouthed the word, not even sure if any sound came out. Keep awake. Try and keep awake. 'Why...'

He pushed her face away and she slid off the sofa onto the floor, head knocking against the stool.

'Why? Why did I kill all those sad little girls?' He got up and came and stood over her. His face looked so far away, distant, staring down at her from high above. 'There is no "why". Things just are the way they are.'

It was the last thing she heard.

*

Tartaglia was nearly in Ealing when he felt the vibration of his phone in his inside breast pocket. He pulled over to the side of the road, looked at the caller ID and rang Dickenson straight back.

'The address is in South Ken, sir,' she said, her voice high-pitched and full of alarm. 'I called you before to tell you but you were probably on the road.'

'South Ken?'

'Yes. Gary and the team are over there now but there's no sign of Zaleski. No sign of anyone, in fact. It looks like it's some sort of office building and everyone's gone home.'

'Check the file again. Zaleski definitely lives in Ealing.'

'I have, sir. But this is the address he gave.'

Heart pounding, he tried to calm himself, think clearly, remember back to what Zaleski had said when he had first interviewed him. He distinctly remembered him saying he lived in Ealing, which was why he was there when Gemma Kramer had died. Think. Think. For fuck's sake try and remember. What had Zaleski been doing? Why was he there? What had he said? He was on his way home. Yes, on his way home and he was dropping his car at a garage... no, collecting it, that was it, when...

'I've got it!' he shouted. 'Zaleski was collecting his car from a garage. I know we checked it out to corroborate the timing. The licence number should be on file. Run it through the system and call me back immediately with Zaleski's address.'

35

Tartaglia stood outside the gate of number 89 Beckford Avenue. Upstairs the house was dark but a light was on in the ground floor front room, just visible behind the curtains. For a moment, he wondered what to do. Maybe they were still out at dinner. Maybe Sam was safely at home in bed by now. But if not... Should he ring the bell, see what would happen? If Sam was in there, Zaleski might do something desperate. Surprise was his only advantage, coupled with the fact that Zaleski didn't know that he knew.

The house was semi-detached with a tall gate at the side leading, he assumed, to the back garden. He tried the gate but it was locked. He took off his helmet, heavy jacket and gloves, dumping them out of sight under the hedge, then jumped, catching hold of the top of the frame of the gate and hauling himself up and over it, landing almost silently on the other side. Shadowed from the light coming from the street, the narrow side-passage was almost black and he could barely see in front of him. He felt his way along the brick wall of the house, no lights showing through any of the side windows, and into the back garden where visibility was a little better, a general dull light reflected from the sky above. He could just make out a small stretch of lawn, flowerbeds and a paved area by the house, a few shrubs in large tubs lined up along the edge. There were no lights on except in a room at the very top of the house and there was no sound or movement coming from inside. Watching for a moment, he saw a shadow cross the top floor window, which he hoped was Zaleski, although he had no idea whether Zaleski lived there on his own or not.

Two doors gave out onto the garden, one a pair of French windows, the other half-glazed, leading out from a small side extension. He tried the French windows first but they were locked, the curtains drawn tightly against them. The other door was also locked and, pressing his face to the glass, he peered into the dim interior, just making out a table or desk with a computer, the screensaver giving off a flickering glimmer of light. Maybe someone had left a key in the lock. If not, he wasn't sure what he would do.

Looking round for something hard to use, he found a sturdy-looking trowel sticking out of the earth in one of the pots near the door. He took off his pullover and, wrapping it around the handle of the trowel to deaden any noise, he aimed the handle at the glass. It took several blows before the corner of the glass shattered with a muffled tinkle. He chipped away at the small hole with the edge of the trowel until it was big enough to put his hand through and, hand now wrapped in the pullover, reached inside, feeling for the key, praying that it would be there.

He felt its cold edge. Thank God. He turned the lock, opened the door and stepped gingerly through, over the glass, into the dark study. A door led into the hall and he opened it carefully, listening. Apart from the distant buzz of traffic several roads away, everything was silent. Light filtered in from the street outside through the stained glass panels which framed the front door. Beside it sat a plastic petrol can and a small suitcase. Was Zaleski going away somewhere? Was he even there? Was Sam? The house was so quiet.

Two doors led off the hall, one he presumed going into the room with the French windows on the garden side, the other, at the front, had a strip of light showing through the crack at the bottom. Perhaps they were in there, although he couldn't hear the sound of anyone talking. As he crept towards the door, trying to deaden the sound of his boots on the tiled floor, he heard a step behind him and felt the edge of something cold and hard pressed like a finger against the back of his neck.

'Don't turn around. This is a gun.'

Tartaglia recognised Zaleski's voice instantly. A light was switched on, illuminating the hall.

'Oh, I see it's you, Inspector,' Zaleski said from behind. 'What are you doing breaking into my house?' He kept the gun pinned to Tartaglia's neck.

'Where's Sam? She's here, isn't she?'

'She's upstairs powdering her nose. Why, are you doing the jealous lover bit? Is she your girlfriend?' Zaleski prodded Tartaglia's neck with the nose of the gun. 'I'd have thought you'd go for something a bit more raunchy.'

'Sam's my friend.'

'What, you'd risk your life for a friend?'

Risk his life? It struck him for the first time that that was what he was doing but he felt strangely calm. 'Yes. Yes I would.'

'There's no accounting for taste. I'm surprised that you care about her that much. She seems quite an ordinary little tart to me. Really nothing special.'

'Is she OK?' Tartaglia said levelly, refusing to give Zaleski the satisfaction of a reaction. Was the gun real or a replica? Not worth taking a punt on it, though, given what he knew of Zaleski.

'Depends what you mean by OK. She got a bit out of control, so I had to calm her down, get her into the right state of mind. That's what it's all about, with women.'

'You mean drug them so you can do what you want?'

'Stop trying to be provocative, Inspector. It doesn't suit you. Do you like guns? I'll bet you're a good shot, aren't you?' he said, when Tartaglia didn't respond. 'This one's a Luger and it's got a nice history to it. My grandfather took it off a dead German in the Second World War. That's after he killed him, of course. He used to love telling me about it when I was a child. Apparently, it was quite gruesome, the killing, I mean. I don't have the stomach for blood and gore, myself. But guns give you a real sense of power, don't they?'

'I wouldn't know,' Tartaglia said, firmly, wondering what the hell he was going to do, wondering also if it explained why Zaleski had thrown the girls to their deaths rather than killing them outright. He hadn't wanted to get his hands dirty. He wanted to distance himself from the mess and physical foulness of death. A gun was arm's length too...

'Yeah, a real sense of power,' Zaleski continued. 'It goes like this. I'm the one with the gun, so you're going to do what I want. You're going to jump when I tell you to jump. Have you got that? Now open that door in front of you... push it wide open, that's right... now, put your hands on your head, walk in slowly, and go and sit down on the sofa. Don't try anything silly,' he added, seeing Tartaglia hesitate in the doorway, as he wondered if he had time to slam it shut in Zaleski's face and barricade himself in until help arrived.

'The Luger may be an antique but it still works and I'm a bloody good shot.'

Tartaglia turned the handle and walked inside, his eyes flicking around the room, looking for a means of defence or escape. But there was none. It was a peculiar place, full of horrible old-fashioned, brown furniture and knick-knacks, a strange, dusty smell hanging in the air as if the room wasn't often used or aired. As he turned round and sat down, he saw Zaleski for the first time, standing by the fireplace, gun in hand pointed straight at Tartaglia's heart.

Zaleski was wearing a dark overcoat, scarf and leather gloves. He looked as if he was on his way out. The bag by the door. The petrol. What was Zaleski going to do with the petrol, if that's what it was? He had removed his glasses and he looked different, a lot tougher and much more confident, his face hard and drawn, lines more pronounced. He was a little shorter than Tartaglia, possibly not as fast or as fit. In the normal course of events, Tartaglia wouldn't baulk at taking him on. But there was the gun. And Sam.

Where was Sam? Why had she allowed herself to be drawn in by Zaleski? Single women with too much imagination and too much time to think about things were a danger to themselves and other people. If only she'd said something. If only. But what would he have done? Reprimand her? Tell her not to see Zaleski? It wouldn't have worked. Sam had a mind of her own and would have told him to get lost. At least, if Zaleski was here, hopefully she was still alive. Maybe upstairs somewhere.

'It's a shame you've butted in and tried to spoil my plans like this.' Zaleski's manner was suddenly more urgent. 'Just when Sam and I were getting down to business.'

'She's alive?'

'Don't waste your time worrying about her.' Zaleski smacked his lips, studying Tartaglia, gun still pointed at his chest. 'Now, what the fuck am I going to do with you? It's very inconvenient, you see, your turning up like this. I'm going to be late...late for a very important date. Miss Donovan's waiting and I don't want to disappoint her.'

It was a pointless question but Tartaglia wanted to string things out, keep Zaleski there as long as possible. 'You work for CHA, don't you? That's how you found them all, isn't it? You're one of their helpline volunteers.' He noted the surprise in Zaleski's eyes.

'My, my. We have been a busy little bee. Well done for finding the connection. You're more on the ball than I thought.'

'They came to you needing help and support and you killed them. Why?'

'Why does everyone want to know why? It's like nature. When you're hungry, you have to eat.'

'That's shit and you know it.'

'They wanted to die with me. They were begging me, gagging for it. I just helped ease things along.'

'You'll be put away for life for this.'

'Can't hang a bloke for being helpful. Anyway, what evidence do you have? If you bother to read the emails the girls sent me, they all wanted to die.'

'Not Sam.'

'Tarts like that are accidents waiting to happen. They only have themselves to blame and I'm doing her a favour.'

'Marion Spear didn't want to die.'

Again there was a flicker of surprise on Zaleski's face. 'Christ, Inspector. I'm really impressed. I'll admit little Marion was a bit different but let's not get pedantic. She was one of those foul clingy types who won't leave a bloke alone. She made me feel claustrophobic. I had to do something.'

'You killed her straight out. None of this fake suicide crap.'

'Like the others she wanted to die, I can assure you. If she couldn't have me, she wanted to end it all. That's what she said. The whining cunt's better off where she is.'

'You're sick.'

'Enough chitchat. I haven't got time. Stay right where you are and don't move.'

Zaleski walked quickly over to a small table in the corner, eyes fixed on Tartaglia, unblinking. A tray with an ice bucket stood on the table and Tartaglia watched as Zaleski took a bottle of clear liquid out of the bucket and filled a shot glass to the brim. Gun still pointed at Tartaglia, he put the glass down on a stool in front of the sofa, pushing it gently towards Tartaglia with his foot.

'Drink it,' he said. 'NOW,' he shouted when Tartaglia didn't move.

What on earth was he to do? No doubt the drink was drugged. If only Zaleski would come a little closer, maybe he'd have a chance. But Zaleski had moved away again, standing with his back to the fireplace, his head reflected in the mirror behind. Play for time; that was the only thing left. Play for time. Hopefully, the team would be there soon.

Tartaglia leaned forward slowly and picked up the glass. It was cold and wet to the touch. As he held it up, he saw a trace of lipstick on the edge and wondered if it was Sam's.

'Fucking drink it,' Zaleski shouted again. 'I haven't got time to waste watching you pussy around.'

Tartaglia put the glass to his lips and tasted the ice-cold liquid with the tip of his tongue. Some sort of vodka, with a slightly aromatic smell. GHB was tasteless. No point in speculating how much was in it.

'Now, knock it back. In one,' Zaleski said. 'That's how we Poles do it, you know.'

Should he throw it in Zaleski's face, aim for the eyes and blind him momentarily while he lunged and took the gun? But Zaleski didn't look away, not for a second and there was nothing to distract him with. If the gun really was loaded and in working order, Tartaglia knew he wouldn't stand a chance. But if he didn't do something, if he drank the vodka and passed out, what would become of Sam? Zaleski would kill her for sure. Kill both of them. Stall. Play for time. It was the only option.

'What were the emails about, the ones to Carolyn Steele?'

'You mean the policewoman? The one on *Crimewatch*?'

'Yeah. You emailed her.'

Zaleski shook his head, looking genuinely surprised. 'Not me. Why would I? She's not my type.'

If it wasn't Zaleski, then it had to be Kennedy, although whether he would ever live to make sure Kennedy got his comeuppance, was another matter. 'Sam's not your type either. Let her go.'

Zaleski laughed. 'My type? That's an interesting question. I hadn't really thought about it before. But I don't actually think I have a type, you know.'

'Yeah, you do. You like them weak and vulnerable, so lonely and depressed they'll do whatever you want. It's a bit like the gun. Makes you feel in control, doesn't it? More like a real man.'

Zaleski's face hardened and he stabbed the air with the Luger. 'Shut up about the fucking girls and drink.'

'You're just a coward. A fucking, spineless, dickless wimp who...'

'Fucking shut up and drink.' Zaleski shouted, his voice rising to a shriek.

'If you want me to drink it, you'll have to come and make me.'

'Oh, tough guy, are you now? Been watching too many cop films. But we're not in the movies. This is real life and you are going to die.'

Zaleski watched him for a moment, as if deciding what to do next, then kicked the stool away from in front of him.

'Put the glass down and get on your knees, hands on your head.' He pointed at the floor in front of him. Hands on head, kneeling. Execution style. Tartaglia realised he had nothing left to lose.

'GET DOWN ON THE FLOOR,' Zaleski screamed.

Now. Now was the moment. Head bowed, eyes locked on Zaleski's legs, he sighed and slowly made as if to kneel down. Then he lunged, hurling himself in mid-air across the small room. Zaleski fell back, crashing hard against something behind and the gun went off. Tartaglia felt a sharp pain on the side of his head and everything went black.

'Well, you two've certainly been having a lively time without me,' Clarke said light-heartedly from his horizontal position in the hospital bed.

'Yeah, life was getting dull without you so we thought we'd liven things up a bit,' Tartaglia replied.

It was Sunday morning, two weeks later, and Tartaglia and Donovan had dropped in to see Clarke on their way to Nicoletta's for lunch. He was looking a lot better than the last time Tartaglia had seen him, over two weeks before. The colour had come back to his face and he seemed to have more energy and interest in life, even though he was still barely able to move his head. Tartaglia had borrowed two rickety chairs from another ward and he and Donovan sat by Clarke's bedside, Tartaglia recounting everything that had happened, Donovan listening quietly, head bowed, barely adding anything to the flow.

'It's nice you can both make light of it,' Donovan said, sharply. 'Particularly you, Mark. I'm surprised at you.'

'Sorry,' Tartaglia said, reaching over and patting her hand gently. He could kick himself for being so insensitive. She gave him a tight, grudging smile and stared back at the floor, her fingers tightly clenched in her lap.

Make light of what had happened? What else could they do? It had been a complete balls-up from start to finish. He... they... were both lucky to be alive. And Zaleski had got away, no trace anywhere. When the team arrived at Zaleski's house in Ealing, they found the house on fire, filled with smoke and petrol fumes, flames licking the front door. If they had got there even fifteen minutes later, it would have been too late for Tartaglia and Donovan.

Discovering Tartaglia's motorbike parked outside and his jacket and helmet by the hedge in the front garden, Gary Jones had insisted on going in, refusing to wait for the fire brigade to come. He and Nick Minderedes had kicked in the front door, jackets wrapped around their faces, and had found Tartaglia and Donovan lying together side by side on the floor in the front living room, seemingly lifeless.

Still comatose, Tartaglia and Donovan had been taken to hospital. Apart from smoke inhalation and a deep gash to the side of Tartaglia's head, which had been caused by the ricochet of the bullet when Zaleski's gun had gone off, there was no serious, lasting physical damage to either of them. Although, when Donovan came round six hours later, she complained of the worst hangover of her life. They were both kept in for a couple of days for observation and then released.

But that wasn't the end of it. He found himself replaying in his mind over and over again what had happened, picturing Zaleski standing there, smiling, gun pointed at his chest, remembering Zaleski's words so clearly. 'It's like nature. If you're hungry, you have to eat.' It was probably the best explanation they would ever get, if they needed one. If only the bullet hadn't grazed his head, he would have had Zaleski, no question about it. He would have overpowered him, smashed his face in and held him there until help came. But there was no point in torturing himself about what might have been. Things hadn't happened that way. If nothing else, attacking Zaleski had bought them a little time and saved his and Donovan's life. It was probably the best rugby tackle he'd ever made, although that was small consolation for the fact that Zaleski had got away.

For Donovan, too, the nightmare was still going on. It was as though a dark cloud had enveloped her, letting in no light or air. She had turned down all offers of professional counselling for the moment and seemed to have retreated inside herself, uncharacteristically subdued. Under pressure from Claire and her colleagues, she had taken a week off work but had insisted on coming back after only three days, even though everybody could see she wasn't ready. But it was worse being at home, she said, particularly when there was nothing physically wrong with her. In a quiet moment she had confided in Tartaglia how she dreaded being on her own, dreaded going to sleep, fearful of the dreams that she knew would come. Although it was painful watching her go through the bare motions of life, coming to work, going home, lost in her own world, he understood why she preferred to keep going. Illogically, she blamed herself for everything that had happened, even for Zaleski's getting away, and nothing that he, or anyone else, could say made it any better. All he could do was to try and keep her occupied, keep her mind off things and hope that, in time, she would heal.

At least the idea of seeing Clarke had brought some light to her face. Nor did she mind coming along with Tartaglia to Nicoletta's, as protection from whatever Machiavellian match-making scheme Nicoletta had up her sleeve. The idea actually seemed to amuse her and she seemed curious to meet Nicoletta. For the first time since the night at Zaleski's, she seemed to have made an effort with her appearance, putting on some make-up, dressed in a tight black polo-neck, short skirt, feet encased in impossibly high, purple suede wedge shoes that were held on by what appeared to be little more than a couple of straps. He'd never seen her in a skirt before and realised she had good legs. He wanted to tell her how nice she looked but something so trivial and superficial was probably the last thing she needed to hear.

'So, there's no trace of Zaleski,' Clarke said with a grunt.

'No,' Tartaglia replied. 'His name was on the passenger list of an Air France flight to Paris that night but he could be anywhere by now.' He glanced over at Donovan. She was still staring fixedly at the floor, mind far away.

'Once the fire was put out, we searched the house in Ealing, as well as another small flat which we discovered he was renting nearby,' he continued. 'We also searched his office in South Ken. But we found nothing. Whatever computer he used to send the emails was gone and there were no trophies, no locks of hair or rings or anything to directly link him to any of the girls' murders, other than the fact that he did voluntary part-time work as a counsellor for CHA. Although it's clearly how he came across them, we've been through the girls' phone records again and there's no direct evidence that any of the girls called or even spoke to him there. We assume they must have used a public phone, or someone else's phone, to call. Kelly Goodhart is the only one who we know called the helpline and as she used her office line, it took us a while to trace.'

'So, you've got nothing on him?' Clarke said, sighing heavily.

'We're just scratching the tip of the iceberg. There are probably other girls we don't know about and I suspect he probably killed his grandparents too. But there's no proof. I'm afraid that attempted murder of two police officers is the best we can do.'

Before Clarke could say anything else, a well-built, middle-aged nurse bustled into the room and came over to the bed.

'Won't be a minute, will we, Mr Clarke?' she said, briskly drawing the curtains around Clarke, without any further explanation. She had a thick Irish brogue and something about her manner and general physique, as well as the unforgiving glint in her eyes, instantly reminded Tartaglia of a nun who had once taught him his catechism, rapping his knuckles with a ruler every time he made a mistake.

'Time for my morning ablutions,' Clarke groaned from behind the screen of green. 'It's the high spot of my day.'

Donovan excused herself to find the ladies and Tartaglia waited patiently by the side of Clarke's bed, listening to all sorts of strange rustling and slapping sounds, accompanied by further groans and sighs from Clarke.

'Have you made your peace with your new DCI?' Clarke asked, after a few moments.

'Sort of,' Tartaglia replied, thinking back to the previous Friday when Cornish had paid a flying visit to Barnes and announced to the assembled team that Steele would be taking over permanently from Clarke. It came as no surprise to anybody but it was clear from the hushed silence that greeted the announcement that few were pleased. 'Thinking of what you said, I took her some flowers when I heard the news. I thought it might help build a bridge or two.'

'There you go, you're learning, mate. They love flowers.'

'She had the decency to thank me for them and she didn't gloat. I don't know what I was expecting but at least she was polite. I said I hoped we could put everything behind us and she said she did, too, in that clipped tone of voice she uses when she's not interested and wants to hurry you along.'

'So, that's that, then. Everything in the garden's rosy.'

'Funny you should mention roses. When I went into her office later to talk to her about something else, they were stuffed in the bin, still in their wrapping. Cost me a fortune, they did.'

Clarke gave a wheezing laugh from behind the curtain. 'There's bloody women for you. Ungrateful cows, the lot of them. The nicer you are, the worse they behave. At least you made the effort.'

'I guess she's still upset about the emails and everything that happened with Kennedy. Even though she wouldn't press charges for the peeping, he's looking at a jail sentence for sending the hoax emails.'

'She's a strange one.'

'Yeah, she knew I'd seen what she'd done with the flowers but she said nothing. When I went into her office the next morning, there were the flowers sitting in a vase on her desk as if nothing had happened.'

'You see? I told you Carolyn's got a sensitive side to her.'

'Possibly,' Tartaglia said, nodding slowly. He hadn't realised quite how badly everything had affected her, how personally she took it. He was never very good at working out what went on in women's minds and he found Steele's impenetrable. Not for the first time he wondered if maybe he had misunderstood her all along and that maybe he was more than half to blame for all the problems that had gone on between them. 'I think the cleaners took pity on my poor roses and fished them out and Steele hadn't the guts to throw them away again.'

'No, Mark. My money's on Carolyn having second thoughts. Like all women, she's just bloody complicated and tricky and she knows how to yank your chain. Ouch,' he shouted suddenly. 'That hurts. Can't you be more bleeding careful, Nurse Mary?'

Outside, it was a dazzling winter day, the sky a piercing blue with barely a cloud, the air cold, a slight breeze ruffling the bare branches of the trees. Tartaglia got out of Donovan's car along the street from Nicoletta's house in Islington and stood on the pavement waiting for her, warming his face in the weak sunshine. She was busy scrabbling around in the back of the car trying to pick up the contents of her handbag, which had fallen off the seat onto the floor when she took a corner too fast.

His phone rang. Thinking it might be Nicoletta, wondering where they were, he took it out of his pocket and saw from the caller ID that it was Fiona Blake. He let it ring, waiting for voice-mail to pick up. Donovan was now busy checking her face in the mirror, applying some lipstick or something. Wary, wondering what Blake wanted, he dialled 121 and listened to her message.

'Mark, it's Fiona. I probably shouldn't call. Just wanted you to know I've broken up with Murray.' The tone was hesitant, voice soft. After a long pause she added: 'Maybe we could meet for a drink. Give me a call. If you want to, that is. I hope you do.'

The last time he'd seen her or spoken to her was in the forensic tent beside the canal, standing beside Yolanda's body. Assuming that it really was all over between them, he had come round to thinking that it was probably better that way. She was no good for him, not what he needed, whatever that was. But knowing it didn't make it any better. Hearing her message reawakened the longing and, not for the first time, he felt powerless to stop himself doing what he knew he shouldn't. Inevitably he would call her.

For the moment, he switched off his phone and turned to Donovan, who was climbing out of the car, bag in hand. She locked the doors and he walked her to the small wrought iron gate of Nicoletta's house.

'I apologise in advance for the mess,' he said, holding the gate open.

'What on earth for?'

'You'll see. Carlo and Anna are three and five and the house is usually in chaos. Nicoletta doesn't seem to care and my brother-in-law, John, just turns a blind eye. Anything for the sake of peace, as far as he's concerned.'

'You know me,' she said quietly. 'I'm used to a bit of chaos on the home front.'

'Oh yes, I was forgetting. But you won't have seen anything like this. Just watch where you sit. There's bound to be something sticky or sharp on the seat.'

Just before he pressed the bell, she touched his arm lightly, and he turned to her.

'You know, you're asking a lot,' she said.

'Look, we don't have to go, if you don't want to. I can easily tell Nicoletta that you feel ill or something. After everything that's happened, she'll understand.'

She shook her head, her expression serious. 'I didn't mean that. I'm happy to come with you to the lunch. It's good to keep my mind off things and it's kind of you to ask me. It's just... well... I've never had to *play* at being somebody's girlfriend before.'

He looked at her and smiled. 'Thanks. I appreciate the effort. But then it's not everyone who gets to save your life. I must be special to you.' There he was making light of things again but it was what came naturally.

She shrugged, as if none of it mattered and he looped an arm around her, pulling her into him and giving her shoulder an affectionate squeeze. 'I'm very fond of you, Sam. I hope you know that.'

She looked up at him and smiled back for the first time in a while. 'Yes, I do and it means a lot.'

'Thought I'd lost you there for a moment.'

'You very nearly did.'

He bent down and kissed the top of her head. 'Are you ready? Are you sure you're OK with this?' She nodded and he took her by the hand. 'Right, let's go.'

37

Adam Zaleski climbed out of the small plane onto the tarmac and was greeted by a wave of searing heat and humidity. Even through his dark glasses, the sky was an electric blue, not a cloud to be seen. Bag in hand, he waved goodbye to the pilot and followed behind the two other passengers towards the airport buildings at the end of the short, dusty runway. They were no better than a collection of shabby, prefabricated huts, a herd of strange-looking, scrawny cattle plucking at the scrub in front, everything reassuringly far removed from the Western world. Even the air smelt different. He felt like skipping for joy, jumping up and down for the sheer fucking fun of it. He was free. Totally free. He had got away with everything.

He had picked up an English paper along the way and read about how Donovan and Tartaglia had been rescued in the nick of time. It was the only thing that grated and it made him angry just to think about it. He should have poured the petrol over their fucking bodies. But no point in crying over spilt milk. He was long gone and the photograph of him, printed in the paper, was a dud. Nobody would recognise him as he was now, tanned, with short, dyed blonde hair and a light beard. If anything, he looked a bit like David Beckham, although his eyes were the wrong colour. Anyway, he was now well out of reach of English newspapers.

Sam Donovan's small face swam into his thoughts again, all lipsticked, rouged and perfumed, ready for death and cradled in his arms as he carried her back downstairs before dumping her beside the other policeman. He had dressed her in one of his grandmother's favourite silk numbers but she was such a scrawny

340

little thing, it kept gaping open and he'd had to tie the belt around her twice to make her decent. Sam. The dirty stain on an otherwise glorious chapter. He thought of her as she was before, sitting on the sofa beside him, eyes half closed, mumbling, struggling to keep her mind together, failing dismally. 'Why?' she had asked. Why? Why? Why? The question still hung in the air, nagging at him, screaming at him just like his fucking grandmother. Even though he hadn't actually seen *her* for a while, her voice was still there, whining and wailing in his ear like a fucking banshee. He'd thought about it a lot since, tried to come up with an answer to silence the witch once and for all, make the old whore go back to her grave along with all the rest of them. Why does anybody do anything? Why? Because they want to. That's why, stupid cow, stupid fucking bitch. *Because they can.* It's that fucking simple.

Little Sam. The one who had wriggled away. The only one. He didn't care about the other stupid wanker of a policeman. He was nothing. But Sam mattered, she mattered all right and the thought was eating away at him until he had no peace. He'd been greedy to go for her, plain greedy and he deserved a ticking off, a firm, hard rap over the knuckles. He should have called it quits after Yolanda. But along came the little whore, gagging for it, offering herself to him on a plate, poor fucking, pathetic tart. It would have been churlish to refuse, although it had cost him dear. At least they had nothing on him to link him to any of the others. No forensic trail. Sweet fuck all, in fact. Still, it was a pity she had lived to tell the tale. She was unfinished business. He couldn't rid himself of her, her face, her voice, her smell. That awful smell of gardenias from his grandmother's old scent bottle. Sam was taunting him, laughing at him. The one that got away. But not for long. As he crossed the short stretch of tarmac, he promised himself that he'd find her again. One day soon. Then he'd make the little bitch rue the day she first tasted Polish vodka.

ACKNOWLEDGEMENTS

Thanks are due to a number of people for their expert advice, as well as apologies for my having ignored it on occasion in the interest of fiction. Any errors are entirely mine. From the Metropolitan Police, Consultant Senior Investigating Officer David Niccol and Tracy Alexander of the Forensic Directorate deserve a particular mention for their invaluable assistance and good humour. I also would like to thank Detective Chief Superintendent Andy Murphy, Detective Chief Inspector David Little and Detective Superintendent Jill McTigue for their help. Thanks go to Jeremy Silewicz, Wayne Kenward and George Andraos for enlightening me on the subjects of Polish vodka, Italian motorbikes and Wi-Fi hotspots, and to my friends and fellow crime writers at Criminal Classes: Margaret Kinsman, Gerry O'Donovan, Richard Holt, Keith Mullins, Cass Bonner, Nicola Williams, and particularly Kathryn Skoyles. Special thanks are due to my agent Sarah Lutyens, to my editor Sue Freestone, and to everyone at Quercus, as well as to Lisanne Radice for words of wisdom. Lastly, I am indebted to Stephen Georgiadis and Jeanne Scott-Forbes for their support and input along the way.

MULTIMEDIA OVER IP AND WIRELESS NETWORKS

MULTIMEDIA OVER IP AND WIRELESS NETWORKS

COMPRESSION, NETWORKING, AND SYSTEMS

Edited by

Philip A. Chou
Microsoft Corporation

Mihaela van der Schaar
University of California, Los Angeles

ELSEVIER

AMSTERDAM • BOSTON • HEIDELBERG • LONDON
NEW YORK • OXFORD • PARIS • SAN DIEGO
SAN FRANCISCO • SINGAPORE • SYDNEY • TOKYO

Academic Press is an imprint of Elsevier

ACADEMIC
PRESS

Academic Press is an imprint of Elsevier
30 Corporate Drive, Suite 400, Burlington, MA 01803, USA
525 B Street, Suite 1900, San Diego, California 92101-4495, USA
84 Theobald's Road, London WC1X 8RR, UK

This book is printed on acid-free paper. ⊚

Library of Congress Cataloging-in-Publication Data
Application submitted

British Library Cataloguing-in-Publication Data
A catalogue record for this book is available from the British Library.

Multimedia over IP and wireless networks : compression, networking, and systems / edited by Philip A. Chou, Mihaela van der Schaar.
    p. cm.
  ISBN-10: 0-12-088480-1
  ISBN-13: 978-0-12-370856-4
  1. Multimedia communications. 2. Computer networks. 3. Multimedia systems. I. Chou, Philip A. II. Schaar, Mihaela van der.
  TK5105.15.M95 2007
  006.7–dc22

                                        2007003425

ISBN 13: 978-0-12-088480-3
ISBN 10: 0-12-088480-1

For information on all Academic Press publications
visit our Web site at www.books.elsevier.com

Transferred to DIgital Printing in 2011.

Table of Contents

About the Editors   vii

About the Authors   ix

Part A Overview   1

Chapter 1   Multimedia Networking and Communication: Principles
and Challenges   3
Mihaela van der Schaar and Philip A. Chou

Part B Compression   11

Chapter 2   Error-Resilient Coding and Decoding Strategies for Video
Communication   13
Thomas Stockhammer and Waqar Zia

Chapter 3   Error-Resilient Coding and Error Concealment Strategies
for Audio Communication   59
Dinei Florêncio

Chapter 4   Mechanisms for Adapting Compressed Multimedia to
Varying Bandwidth Conditions   81
Antonio Ortega and Huisheng Wang

Chapter 5   Scalable Video Coding for Adaptive Streaming Applications   117
*Béatrice Pesquet-Popescu, Shipeng Li, and
Mihaela van der Schaar*

Chapter 6   Scalable Audio Coding   159
Jin Li

Part C IP Networking   185

Chapter 7   Channel Protection Fundamentals   187
*Raouf Hamzaoui, Vladimir Stanković, Zixiang Xiong,
Kannan Ramchandran, Rohit Puri, Abhik Majumdar, and
Jim Chou*

Chapter 8 Channel Modeling and Analysis for the Internet 229
Hayder Radha and Dmitri Loguinov

Chapter 9 Forward Error Control for Packet Loss and Corruption 271
Raouf Hamzaoui, Vladimir Stanković, and Zixiang Xiong

Chapter 10 Network-Adaptive Media Transport 293
Mark Kalman and Bernd Girod

Part D Wireless Networking 311

Chapter 11 Performance Modeling and Analysis over Medium Access Control Layer Wireless Channels 313
Syed Ali Khayam and Hayder Radha

Chapter 12 Cross-Layer Wireless Multimedia 337
Mihaela van der Schaar

Chapter 13 Quality of Service Support in Multimedia Wireless Environments 409
Klara Nahrstedt, Wanghong Yuan, Samarth Shah, Yuan Xue, and Kai Chen

Part E Systems 451

Chapter 14 Streaming Media on Demand and Live Broadcast 453
Philip A. Chou

Chapter 15 Real-Time Communication: Internet Protocol Voice and Video Telephony and Teleconferencing 503
Yi Liang, Yen-Chi Lee, and Andy Teng

Chapter 16 Adaptive Media Playout 527
Eckehard Steinbach, Yi Liang, Mark Kalman, and Bernd Girod

Part F Advanced Topics 557

Chapter 17 Path Diversity for Media Streaming 559
John Apostolopoulos, Mitchell Trott, and Wai-Tian Tan

Chapter 18 Distributed Video Coding and Its Applications 591
Abhik Majumdar, Rohit Puri, Kannan Ramchandran, and Jim Chou

Chapter 19 Infrastructure-Based Streaming Media Overlay Networks 633
Susie Wee, Wai-Tian Tan, and John Apostolopoulos

Index 671

ABOUT THE EDITORS

Mihaela van der Schaar received her Ph.D. degree from Eindhoven University of Technology, Eindhoven, The Netherlands, in 2001. She is currently an Assistant Professor in the Electrical Engineering Department at UCLA. Prior to this, between 1996 and June 2003 she was a senior researcher at Philips Research in the Netherlands and the USA, where she led a team of researchers working on multimedia coding, processing, networking, and streaming algorithms and architectures. She has published extensively on multimedia compression, processing, communications, networking, and architectures and holds 28 granted U.S. patents and several more pending. Since 1999, she has been an active participant to the ISO Motion Picture Expert Group (MPEG) standard, to which she made more than 50 contributions and for which she received three ISO recognition awards. She chaired the ad hoc group on MPEG-21 Scalable Video Coding for three years, and also co-chaired the MPEG ad hoc group on Multimedia Test-bed. She is a senior member of IEEE, and was also elected as a Member of the Technical Committee on Multimedia Signal Processing (MMSP TC) and Image and Multidimensional Signal Processing Technical Committee (IMDSP TC) of the IEEE Signal Processing Society. She was an Associate Editor of IEEE Transactions on Multimedia and SPIE Electronic Imaging Journal from 2002 to 2005. Currently, she is an Associate Editor of IEEE Transactions on Circuits and Systems for Video Technology and an Associate Editor of IEEE Signal Processing Letters. She served as a General Chair for the Picture Coding Symposium (PCS) in 2004. She received the NSF CAREER Award in 2004, the IBM Faculty Award in 2005, the Okawa Foundation Award in 2006, and the Best Paper Award for her paper published in 2005 in the IEEE Transactions on Circuits and Systems for Video Technology.

Philip A. Chou received a B.S.E. degree from Princeton University, Princeton, NJ, in 1980, and an M.S. degree from the University of California, Berkeley, in

1983, both in electrical engineering and computer science, and a Ph.D. degree in electrical engineering from Stanford University in 1988. From 1988 to 1990, he was a Member of Technical Staff at AT&T Bell Laboratories in Murray Hill, NJ. From 1990 to 1996, he was a Member of Research Staff at the Xerox Palo Alto Research Center in Palo Alto, CA. In 1997, he was the manager of the compression group at VXtreme in Mountain View, CA, before it was acquired by Microsoft in 1997. From 1998 to the present, he has been a Principal Researcher with Microsoft Research in Redmond, Washington, where he currently manages the Communication and Collaboration Systems research group. Dr. Chou also served as a Consulting Associate Professor at Stanford University from 1994 to 1995, an Affiliate Associate Professor at the University of Washington since 1998, and an Adjunct Professor at the Chinese University of Hong Kong since 2006. Dr. Chou's research interests are data compression, information theory, communications, and pattern recognition, with applications to video, images, audio, speech, and documents. Dr. Chou served as an Associate Editor in source coding for the IEEE Transactions on Information Theory from 1998 to 2001 and as a Guest Associate Editor for special issues in the IEEE Transactions on Image Processing and the IEEE Transactions on Multimedia in 1996 and 2004, respectively. From 1998 to 2004, he was a Member of the IEEE Signal Processing Society's Image and Multidimensional Signal Processing Technical Committee (IMDSP TC). He served as Program Committee Chair for the inaugural NetCod 2005 workshop, and he currently serves on the organizing committee for ICASSP 2007. He is a Fellow of the IEEE, a member of Phi Beta Kappa, Tau Beta Pi, Sigma Xi, and the IEEE Computer, Information Theory, Signal Processing, and Communications Societies, and was an active member of the MPEG committee. He is the recipient, with Anshul Seghal, of the 2002 ICME Best Paper award, and he is the recipient, with Tom Lookabaugh, of the 1993 Signal Processing Society Paper award.

ABOUT THE AUTHORS

John Apostolopoulos received his B.S., M.S., and Ph.D. degrees in EECS from Massachusetts Institute of Technology (MIT). He joined Hewlett-Packard Laboratories in 1997, where he is a Principal Research Scientist and Project Manager for the Streaming Media Systems Group. He also teaches and conducts joint research at Stanford University, where he is a Consulting Assistant Professor in EE. He received a Best Student Paper Award for part of his Ph.D. thesis, the Young Investigator Award (Best Paper Award) at VCIP 2001 for his paper on multiple description video coding and path diversity for reliable video communication over lossy packet networks, and in 2003 was named "one of the world's top 100 young (under 35) innovators in science and technology" (TR100) by Technology Review. He contributed to both the U.S. Digital Television and JPEG-2000 Security (JPSEC) standards. His research interests include improving the reliability, fidelity, scalability, and security of media communication over wired and wireless packet networks.

Kai Chen received his Ph.D. degree in Computer Science from the University of Illinois at Urbana-Champaign in 2004. He received his M.S. and B.S. degrees from University of Delaware and Tsinghua University, respectively. He is currently working at Google Inc.

Jim Chou received B.S. and M.S. degrees in electrical engineering from the University of Illinois at Urbana-Champaign in 1995 and 1997, respectively. He received the Ph.D. degree in electrical engineering from the University of California, Berkeley in 2002. He has worked at TRW, Bytemobile, and Sony Research in the past. Jim holds two U.S. patents and has several patents pending. Currently, Jim is a Video Architect at C2 Microsystems. His research interests include coding theory, wireless video transmission, digital watermarking, and estimation and detection theory.

Philip A. Chou is Principal Researcher and Manager of the Communication and Collaboration Systems group at Microsoft Research. He also holds affiliate professor positions at the University of Washington and the Chinese University of Hong Kong. Prior to coming to Microsoft, Dr. Chou was Compression Group Manager at VXtreme (a startup company acquired by Microsoft) in 1997, a Member of Research Staff at the Xerox Palo Alto Research Center from 1990 to 1996, a Consulting Associate Professor at Stanford from 1994 to 1995, and a Member of the Technical Staff at AT&T Bell Laboratories from 1988 to 1990. Dr. Chou received a Ph.D. from Stanford University in 1988, an M.S. from the University of California, Berkeley, in 1983, and a B.S.E. from Princeton University in 1980. His research interests include data compression, information theory, communications, and pattern recognition, with applications to video, images, audio, speech, and documents. Dr. Chou is a Fellow of IEEE.

Dinei Florêncio received B.S. and M.S. degrees from the University of Brasília, Brazil, and a Ph.D. degree from the Georgia Institute of Technology, Atlanta, all in electrical engineering. He has been a researcher in the communication and collaboration systems group at Microsoft Research since 1999. From 1996 to 1999, he was a Member of Research Staff at the David Sarnoff Research Center. From 1994 to 1996, he was an Associated Researcher with AT&T Human Interface Lab (now part of NCR), and an intern at the (now defunct) Interval Research in 1994. He is a Senior Member of the IEEE. He has published over 25 referred papers, has been granted 20 U.S. patents, and has received the 1998 Sarnoff Achievement Award.

Bernd Girod is Professor of Electrical Engineering and (by courtesy) Computer Science in the Information Systems Laboratory of Stanford University, California. He was Chaired Professor of Telecommunications in the Electrical Engineering Department of the University of Erlangen-Nuremberg from 1993 to 1999. His research interests are in the areas of video compression and networked media systems. Prior visiting or regular faculty positions include the Massachusetts Institute of Technology, Georgia Institute of Technology, and Stanford University. He has been involved with several startup ventures as founder, director, investor, or advisor, among them Vivo Software, 8x8 (Nasdaq: EGHT), and RealNetworks (Nasdaq: RNWK). Since 2004, he has served as the Chairman of the new Deutsche Telekom Laboratories in Berlin. He received an Engineering Doctorate from University of Hannover, Germany, and an M.S. degree from Georgia Institute of Technology. Professor Girod is a Fellow of IEEE.

Raouf Hamzaoui received an M.Sc. degree in mathematics from the University of Montreal, Canada, in 1993, the Dr. rer. nat. degree from the Faculty of Applied Sciences of the University of Freiburg, Germany, in 1997, and the Habilitation degree in computer science from the University of Konstanz, Germany, in 2004.

From 2000 to 2002, he was an Assistant Professor with the Department of Computer Science of the University of Leipzig, Germany. From 2002 to August 2006, he was an Assistant Professor with the Department of Computer and Information Science of the University of Konstanz. Since September 2006, he has been a Professor for Media Technology in the School of Engineering and Technology at De Montfort University, Leicester, United Kingdom. His research interests include image and video compression, multimedia communication, channel coding, and algorithms.

Mark Kalman received a B.S. in Electrical Engineering and a B.Mus. in Composition from Johns Hopkins University in 1997. He completed his M.S. and Ph.D. degrees, both in Electrical Engineering, at Stanford University in 2001 and 2006, respectively. He is currently with Pure Digital Technologies, Inc., in San Francisco, California.

Syed Ali Khayam received his B.E. degree in Computer Systems Engineering from National University of Sciences and Technology (NUST), Pakistan, in 1999 and his M.S. degree in Electrical Engineering from Michigan State University (MSU) in 2003. He received his Ph.D. from MSU in December 2006. He worked at Communications Enabling Technologies from October 2000 to August 2001. His research interests include analysis and modeling of statistical phenomena in computer networks, network security with emphasis on detection and mitigation of self-propagating malware, cross-layer design for wireless networks, and real-time multimedia communications.

Yen-Chi Lee received a B.S. and M.S. degrees in Computer Science and Information Engineering from National Chiao-Tung University, Hsinchu, Taiwan, R.O.C., in 1997 and 1999, respectively, and a Ph.D. degree in Electrical and Computer Engineering from Georgia Institute of Technology, Atlanta, in 2003. In 2003, he joined Nokia Research Center, Irving, TX, as a research engineer, where he conducted research on video teleconferencing over GSM GPRS/EGPRS networks. He has been with Qualcomm Inc., San Diego, CA, as a video system engineer since 2004. His current research focuses on the areas of video compression techniques and real-time wireless video communications; particularly, error-resilient video coding and error control, low-delay video rate control, and channel rate adaptation. Yen-Chi has published 16 research papers and currently holds 14 pending patent applications.

Jin Li is currently a Senior Researcher at Microsoft Research (MSR) Redmond. He received his Ph.D. from Tsinghua University in 1994. Before moving to Redmond, he worked at the University of Southern California, the Sharp Laboratories of America, and MSR Asia. Since 2000, Dr. Li has also served as an adjunct professor at Tsinghua University. Dr. Li has more than 80 referred conference and journal papers in a diversified research field of media compression and communication and peer-to-peer content delivery. He holds 18 issued U.S. patents, with many more pending. Dr. Li is an Area Editor for the Journal of Visual Communication and Image Representation (Academic Press) and an Associate Editor of IEEE Transactions on Multimedia. He is a Senior Member of IEEE. He was the recipient of the 1994 Ph.D. Thesis Award from Tsinghua University and the 1998 Young Investigator Award from SPIE Visual Communication and Image Processing.

Shipeng Li received B.S. and M.S. degrees from the University of Science and Technology of China (USTC), Hefei, China, in 1988 and 1991, respectively, and a Ph.D. degree from Lehigh University, Bethlehem, PA, in 1996, all in electrical engineering. He was with the Electrical Engineering Department, USTC, from 1991 to 1992. He was a Member of Technical Staff with Sarnoff Corporation, Princeton, NJ, from 1996 to 1999. He has been a Researcher with Microsoft Research Asia, Beijing, China, since May 1999 and has contributed to some technologies in MPEG-4 and H.264. His research interests include image/video compression and communications, digital television, multimedia, and wireless communication.

Yi Liang's expertise is in the areas of networked multimedia systems, real-time voice and video communication, and low-latency media streaming over wire-line and wireless networks. Currently holding positions at Qualcomm CDMA Technologies, San Diego, CA, he is responsible for the design and development of video and display system architecture for multimedia handset chipsets. From 2000 to 2001, he conducted research with Netergy Networks, Inc., Santa Clara, CA, on voice-over-IP systems that provide superior quality over best-effort networks. From 2001 to 2003, he led the Stanford-Hewlett-Packard Labs low-latency video streaming project, in which he and his colleagues developed error-resilience techniques for rich-media-communication-over-IP networks at very low latency. In the summer of 2002 at Hewlett-Packard Labs, Palo Alto, CA, he developed an accurate loss-distortion model for compressed video and contributed in the development of the pioneering mobile streaming media content delivery network (MSM-CDN) that delivers rich media over 3G wireless. Yi Liang received a Ph.D. degree in Electrical Engineering from Stanford University in 2003 and a B.Eng. degree from Tsinghua University, Beijing, China, in 1997.

Dmitri Loguinov received a B.S. degree (with honors) in computer science from Moscow State University, Russia, in 1995 and a Ph.D. degree in computer science from the City University of New York in 2002. Since 2002, he has been an Assistant Professor of Computer Science with Texas A&M University, College Station. His research interests include peer-to-peer networks, Internet video streaming, congestion control, topology modeling, and Internet traffic measurement.

Abhik Majumdar received a B.Tech. degree from the Indian Institute of Technology (IIT), Kharagpur, and M.S. and Ph.D. degrees from the University of California, Berkeley, in 2000, 2003, and 2005, respectively, all in Electrical Engineering. He is currently with Pure Digital Technologies, San Francisco, CA. His research interests include multimedia compression and networking and wireless communications. Dr. Majumdar was awarded the Institute Silver Medal from I.I.T. Kharagpur for outstanding achievement in the graduating class of 2000.

Klara Nahrstedt is a Full Professor at the University of Illinois at Urbana-Champaign, Computer Science Department. Her research interests are directed toward multimedia distributed systems, quality of service (QoS) management in wired and mobile ad hoc networks, QoS-aware resource management in distributed multimedia systems, QoS-aware middleware systems, quality of protection in multimedia systems, and tele-immersive applications. She is the co-author of the widely used multimedia book *Multimedia: Computing, Communications and Applications*, published by Prentice Hall in 1995, and the multimedia book *Multimedia Systems*, published by Springer-Verlag in 2004. She is the recipient of the Early NSF Career Award, the Junior Xerox Award, and the IEEE Communication Society Leonard Abraham Award for Research Achievements. She is the Editor-in-Chief of the ACM/Springer Multimedia Systems Journal, and the Ralph and Catherine Fisher Professor. Klara Nahrstedt received her B.A. in mathematics from Humboldt University, Berlin, in 1984, and an M.Sc. degree in numerical analysis from the same university in 1985. She was a research scientist in the Institute for Informatik in Berlin until 1990. In 1995, she received her Ph.D. from the University of Pennsylvania in the Department of Computer and Information Science. She is a Member of ACM and a Senior Member of IEEE.

Antonio Ortega received the Telecommunications Engineering degree from the Universidad Politecnica de Madrid, Spain, in 1989 and the Ph.D. in Electrical Engineering from Columbia University, New York, NY in 1994. His Ph.D. work was supported by a Fulbright Scholarship. In 1994, he joined the Electrical Engineering-Systems department at the University of Southern California, where he is currently a Professor and Associate Chair of the Department. He is a Senior Member of IEEE, and a Member of ACM. He has been Chair of the Image and Multidimensional Signal Processing Technical Committee (IMDSP TC) and a member of the Board of Governors of the IEEE SPS (2002). He was the Technical Program Co-chair of ICME 2002 and has served as Associate Editor for the IEEE Transactions on Image Processing and the IEEE Signal Processing Letters. He received the National Science Foundation (NSF) CAREER award, the 1997 IEEE Communications Society Leonard G. Abraham Prize Paper Award, and the IEEE Signal Processing Society 1999 Magazine Award. His research interests are in the areas of multimedia compression and communications. His recent work focuses on distributed compression, multiview coding, compression for recognition and classification applications, error-tolerant compression, and information representation for wireless sensor networks.

Béatrice Pesquet-Popescu is an Associate Professor at ENST Paris, where she is currently the leader of the Multimedia Group. Her current research interests are in scalable and robust video coding, adaptive wavelets, and multimedia applications. EURASIP gave her a Best Student Paper Award in the IEEE Signal Processing Workshop on Higher-Order Statistics in 1997; in 1998, she received a Young Investigator Award granted by the French Physical Society, and she received, together with D. Turaga and M. van der Schaar, the 2006 IEEE Circuits and Systems Society CSVT Transactions Best Paper Award for the paper "Complexity Scalable Motion Compensated Wavelet Video Encoding." She has authored more than one hundred book chapters, journal articles, and conference papers in the field and holds more than 20 patents in wavelet-based video coding. She is a Member of the IEEE Multimedia Signal Processing Technical Committee, an elected EURASIP AdCom Member, and a Senior Member of IEEE.

Rohit Puri received a B.Tech. degree from the Indian Institute of Technology, Bombay, the M.S. degree from the University of Illinois at Urbana-Champaign, and a Ph.D. degree from the University of California, Berkeley, in 1997, 1999, and 2002, respectively, all in electrical engineering. From 2003 to 2004, he was with Sony Electronics Inc., San Jose, CA. He was then with the EECS Department, University of California, Berkeley, as a Research Engineer. He is currently a Senior Video Architect at PortalPlayer Inc., San Jose, CA. His research interests include multimedia compression, distributed source coding, multiple descriptions coding, and multi-user information theory. Dr. Puri was awarded the Institute Silver Medal by the Indian Institute of Technology, Bombay, for outstanding achievement in the graduating class, in 1997. He was a recipient of the 2004 Eliahu I. Jury Award at the University of California, Berkeley, for the best doctoral thesis in the area of systems, signal processing, communications, and controls.

Hayder Radha is a Professor of Electrical and Computer Engineering at Michigan State University (MSU). He received his Ph.M. and Ph.D. degrees from Columbia University in 1991 and 1993, an M.S. degree from Purdue University in 1986, and a B.S. degree (honors) from MSU in 1984 (all in electrical engineering). From 1996 to 2000, he worked for Philips Research as a Principal Member of Research Staff and Consulting Scientist in the Video Communications Research Department. From 1986 to 1996, he worked at Bell Labs in the areas of digital communications, image processing, and broadband multimedia networking. He served as Co-chair and Editor of the Broadband and LAN Video Coding Experts Group of the ITU-T. He was a Philips Research Fellow, and he is a recipient of the Bell Labs Distinguished Member of Technical Staff, AT&T Circle of Excellence, College of Engineering Withrow Distinguished Scholar, and the Microsoft Research Content and Curriculum Awards.

Kannan Ramchandran received M.S. and Ph.D. degrees from Columbia University in Electrical Engineering in 1984 and 1993, respectively. From 1984 to 1990, he was a Member of Technical Staff at AT&T Bell Labs in the telecommunications R&D area. From 1993 to 1999, he was on the faculty of the Electrical and Computer Engineering Department at the University of Illinois at Urbana-Champaign and was a Research Assistant Professor at the Beckman Institute and the Coordinated Science Laboratory. Since fall 1999, he has been an Associate Professor in the Electrical Engineering and Computer Sciences department, University of California, Berkeley. His current research interests include distributed algorithms for signal processing and communications, multi-user information theory, wavelet theory and multiresolution signal processing, and unified algorithms for multimedia signal processing, communications, and networking. Dr. Ramchandran was a recipient of the 1993 Eliahu I. Jury Award at Columbia University for the best doctoral thesis in the area of systems, signal processing, and communications. His research awards include the National Science Foundation (NSF) CAREER award in 1997, ONR and ARO Young Investigator Awards in 1996 and 1997, and the Okawa Foundation Award at the University of California, Berkeley, in 2000. In 1998, he was selected as a Henry Magnusky Scholar by the Electrical and Computer Engineering department at the University of Illinois, an honor that recognizes excellence among junior faculty. He is the co-recipient of two Best Paper Awards from the IEEE Signal Processing Society, has been a Member of the IEEE Image and Multidimensional Signal Processing Committee and the IEEE Multimedia Signal Processing Committee, and has served as an Associate Editor for the IEEE Transactions on Image Processing.

Samarth Shah received his B.E. degree in Computer Science and Engineering from the University of Madras, India, in 1998 and completed his Ph.D. in Computer Science at the University of Illinois at Urbana-Champaign in 2005. Since 2005, he has been working at Motorola Inc. in Libertyville, Illinois, in the area of VoIP-over-WiFi.

Vladimir Stanković received the Dipl.-Ing. degree in electrical engineering from the University of Belgrade, Serbia, in 2000, and the Dr.-Ing. degree from the University of Leipzig, Germany, in 2003. From 2002 to 2003, he was with the Department of Computer and Information Science, University of Konstanz, Germany. From June 2003 to February 2006, he was with the Department of Electrical and Computer Engineering at Texas A&M University, College Station, first as a Postdoctoral Research Associate and then as a Research Assistant Professor. In February 2006, Dr. Stanković joined the Department of Communication Systems, Lancaster University, Lancaster, United Kingdom, as a lecturer. His research focuses on multimedia networking, network information theory, and wireless communications.

Eckehard Steinbach (IEEE M'96) studied Electrical Engineering at the University of Karlsruhe, Germany, the University of Essex, United Kingdom, and ESIEE in Paris. From 1994 to 2000, he was a member of the research staff of the Image Communication Group at the University of Erlangen-Nuremberg (Germany), where he received an Engineering Doctorate in 1999. From February 2000 to December 2001, he was a Postdoctoral Fellow with the Information Systems Laboratory of Stanford University. In February 2002, he joined the Department of Electrical Engineering and Information Technology of Munich University of Technology, Germany, where he is currently an Associate Professor for Media Technology. His current research interests are in the area of networked and interactive multimedia systems.

Thomas Stockhammer has been working at the Munich University of Technology, Germany and was visiting researcher at Rensselear Polytechnic Institute (RPI), Troy, NY and at the University of San Diego, California (UCSD). He has published more than 80 conference and journal papers, is member of different program committees, and holds several patents. He regularly participates and contributes to different standardization activities, such as JVT, IETF, 3GPP, ITU, and DVB, and has co-authored more than 100 technical contributions. He is acting chairman of the video ad hoc group of 3GPP SA4. He is also co-founder and CEO of Novel Mobile Radio (NoMoR) Research, a company working on the simulation and emulation of future mobile networks. He is working as a research and standardization consultant for Siemens Mobile Devices and now consults for Digital Fountain, the leading provider for forward error correction. His research interests include video transmission, cross-layer and system design, forward error correction, content delivery protocols, rate–distortion optimization, information theory, and mobile communications.

Wai-Tian Tan joined Hewlett-Packard Laboratories in December 2000, where he is a member of the Streaming Media Systems Group. He received a B.S. degree from Brown University in 1992, an M.S.E.E. degree from Stanford University in 1993 and a Ph.D. degree from the University of California, Berkeley, in 2000. He worked for Oracle Corporation from 1993 to 1995. His research focuses on adaptive media streaming, both at the end-point and inside the delivery infrastructure.

Chia-Yuan (Andy) Teng was born in Taipei, Taiwan, China, in 1964. He received a college diploma from National Taipei Institute of Technology, Taipei, Taiwan, in 1984, a M.S. degree in Electrical Engineering from National Sun Yat-Sen University, Kaoshiung, Taiwan, in 1989, and a Ph.D. degree in Electrical Engineering and Computer Science from the University of Michigan, Ann Arbor, in 1996. In 1989, he was with the Industrial Technology Research Institute (ITRI), Hsinchu, Taiwan. From 1990 to 1992, he was a Faculty Member of the Department of EE, Chien-Hsin Institute of Technology, Chunli, Taiwan. From 1996 to 1998, he was with the Corporate Research, Thomson Multimedia, where he participated in the standardization and research of digital TV, satellite, and cable systems. From 1998 to 2004, he was with the San Diego R&D Center, Nokia Mobile Phones, where he was a Technical Team Leader in DSP entity and involved in the development and design for multimedia, streaming, and DSP firmware. Dr. Teng joined Qualcomm Corporation in Aug. 2004, where he is currently a Staff Engineer/Manager in the Video Systems Group. His research interests include video/image coding, video/image processing, multimedia streaming, Internet protocols, and video telephony.

Mitchell Trott received B.S. and M.S. degrees in Systems Engineering from Case Western Reserve University in 1987 and 1988, respectively, and a Ph.D. in electrical engineering from Stanford University in 1992. He was an Associate Professor in the Department of Electrical Engineering and Computer Science at the Massachusetts Institute of Technology (MIT) from 1992 until 1998, and director of research at ArrayComm from 1997 through 2002. He is now a member of the Streaming Media Systems Group at Hewlett-Packard Laboratories. His research interests include streaming media systems, multi-user and wireless communication, and information theory.

Mihaela van der Schaar is currently an Assistant Professor in the Electrical Engineering Department at UCLA. She has published extensively on multimedia compression, processing, communications, networking, and architectures and holds 28 granted U.S. patents. Since 1999, she has been an active participant to the ISO Motion Picture Expert Group (MPEG) standard, to which she made more than 50 contributions and for which she received three ISO recognition awards. She was an Associate Editor of IEEE Transactions on Multimedia and SPIE Electronic Imaging Journal and is currently an Associate Editor of IEEE Transactions on Circuits and System for Video Technology and of IEEE Signal Processing Letters. She received the NSF CAREER Award in 2004, the IBM Faculty Award in 2005, the Okawa Foundation Award in 2006, and the Best Paper Award for her paper published in 2005 in the IEEE Transactions on Circuits and Systems for Video Technology.

Huisheng Wang received the B.Eng. degree from Xi'an Jiaotong University, China, in 1995 and the M.Eng. degree from Nanyang Technological University, Singapore, in 1998, both in electrical engineering. She is currently pursuing her Ph.D. degree in the Department of Electrical Engineering-Systems at the University of Southern California, Los Angeles. From 1997 to 2000, she worked in Creative Technology Ltd., Singapore as a R&D software engineer. She was also a research intern at La Jolla Lab, ST Microelectronics, San Diego, CA, and at HP Labs, Palo Alto, CA. Her research interests include signal processing, multimedia compression, networking, and communications.

Susie Wee is the Director of the Mobile and Media Systems Lab in Hewlett-Packard Laboratories (HP Labs). She is responsible for research programs in multimedia, networked sensing, next-generation mobile multimedia systems, and experience design. Her lab has activities in the U.S., Japan, and the United Kingdom, and includes collaborations with partners around the world. Wee's research interests broadly embrace the design of mobile streaming media systems, secure scalable streaming methods, and efficient video delivery algorithms. In addition to her work at HP Labs, Wee is a Consulting Assistant Professor at Stanford University. She received Technology Review's Top 100 Young Investigators Award in 2002, served as an Associate Editor for the IEEE Transactions on Image Processing and IEEE Transactions on Circuits, Systems, and Video Technologies. She is currently a Co-Editor of the JPEG-2000 Security standard (JPSEC). Wee received her B.S., M.S., and Ph.D. degrees in electrical engineering from the Massachusetts Institute of Technology (MIT).

Zixiang Xiong received a Ph.D. degree in Electrical Engineering in 1996 from the University of Illinois at Urbana-Champaign. He is currently an Associate Professor in the Department of Electrical and Computer Engineering at Texas A&M University, College Station. His research interests are network information theory, code designs and applications, networked multimedia, and genomic signal processing.

Yuan Xue received her B.S. in Computer Science from Harbin Institute of Technology, China in 1998 and her M.S. and Ph.D. in Computer Science from the University of Illinois at Urbana-Champaign in 2002 and 2005, respectively. Currently, she is an Assistant Professor at the Department of Electrical Engineering and Computer Science of Vanderbilt University. She is a recipient of the Vodafone fellowship. Her research interests include wireless and sensor networks, peer-to-peer and overlay systems, QoS support, and network security. She is a Member of the IEEE and ACM.

Wanghong Yuan received his B.S. and M.S. degrees in 1996 and 1999, respectively, from the Department of Computer Science, Beijing University, and his Ph.D. degree in 2004 from the Department of Computer Science, University of Illinois at Urbana-Champaign. He is a software engineer at Microsoft Corporation. Before joining Microsoft, he was a research engineer at DoCoMo USA Labs from 2004 to 2006. His research and development interests include operating systems, networks, multimedia, and real-time systems, with an emphasis on the design of energy-efficient and QoS-aware operating systems.

Waqar Zia received his B.Sc. degree in electrical engineering from the University of Engineering and Technology, Taxila, Pakistan in 2000. He worked on embedded digital video processing for three years in Streaming Networks Ltd., Islamabad, Pakistan. He received his M.Sc. degree in Information and Communication Systems from Hamburg University of Technology, Germany, in 2005. He then started working on his Ph.D. under the supervision of Prof. Klaus Diepold and Thomas Stockhammer at the Technical University of Munich, Germany. His work focuses on complexity-constrained error-robust video communication on handheld devices. He has also actively participated in recent 3GPP standardization and has co-authored several technical contributions along with pursuing his research work.

PART A

OVERVIEW

CHAPTER   1   Multimedia Networking and Communication: Principles and
              Challenges
              (Mihaela van der Schaar and Philip A. Chou)

1

Multimedia Networking and Communication: Principles and Challenges

Mihaela van der Schaar and Philip A. Chou

In case you haven't noticed, multimedia communication over IP and wireless networks is exploding. Applications such as BitTorrent, used primarily for video downloads, now take up the lion's share of all traffic on the Internet. Music file sharing, once on the legal cutting edge of massive copyright infringement on college campuses around the world, has moved into the mainstream with significant legal downloads of music and video to devices such as the iPod and numerous other portable media players. Multimedia podcasting to client computers and portable devices is a phenomenon exploding in its own right. Internet radio, pioneered in the late 1990s, is now being joined in a big way by peer-to-peer television such as CoolStreaming and PPLive. Audio and video on demand over the Internet, also available since the late 1990s on the Web sites of well-funded organizations such as CNN.com and MSNBC.com, are now at the core of a multitude of new music and video businesses from Napster to iTunes to MTV's Urge service, and will be expanding imminently to full-length movie delivery on demand. Moreover, Web sites such as YouTube have made publishing videos on demand available to anyone with a home video camera, which these days is nearly everyone with a mobile phone. Indeed, most mobile phones today can actively download *and upload* both photos and videos, sometimes in real time. Internet telephony is exploding, with popular applications such as Skype and others enabling wideband voice and video conferencing over the Internet. In general, voice over IP (VoIP) is revolutionizing the telecommunications industry, as circuit-switched equipment from PBX to long haul equipment is being replaced by soft IP switches. Enhanced television is also being delivered into the living room over IP networks by traditional telephone providers through DSL.

Once inside the home, consumer electronics manufacturers, and increasingly, the computer industry and its partners, are distributing audio and video over WiFi to monitors and speaker systems around the house. Now that the analog-to-digital revolution is nearly complete, we are undergoing an all-media-over-IP revolution, with radio, television, telephony, and stored media all currently being delivered over IP wireline and wireless networks. To top it all off, brand new types of media, such as game data for interactive gaming over the Internet, are strongly emerging.

Despite having unleashed a plethora of new multimedia applications, the Internet and wireless networks provide only limited support for multimedia. The Internet and wireless networks have inherently unpredictable and variable conditions. If averaged over time, this variability may not significantly impact delay-insensitive applications such as file transfer. However, variations in network conditions can have considerable consequences for real-time multimedia applications and can lead to unsatisfactory user experience. Multimedia applications tend to be *delay sensitive, bandwidth intense, and loss tolerant*. These properties can change the fundamental principles of communication design for these applications.

The concepts, theories, and solutions that have traditionally been taught in information theory, communication, and signal processing courses may not be directly applicable to highly time-varying channel conditions, adaptive and delay-sensitive multimedia applications, and interactive multiuser transmission environments. Consequently, in recent years, the area of multimedia communication and networking has emerged not only as a very active and challenging integrative research topic across the borders of signal processing and communication, but also as a core curriculum that requires its own set of fundamental concepts and algorithms that differ from those taught in conventional signal processing and communication courses.

This book aims at providing the reader with an in-depth understanding of the theoretical foundations, key design principles, algorithms, and existing standards for multimedia communication and networking.

This introductory chapter provides motivation for studying the topic of multimedia communication, the addressed applications, and associated challenges. Subsequently, a road map of the various chapters is provided. A suggested use for graduate instruction and self-study is also provided.

1.1 DIMENSIONS OF MULTIMEDIA COMMUNICATION

1.1.1 Multimedia Communication Applications

The emergence of communication infrastructures such as the Internet and wireless networks enabled the proliferation of the aforementioned multimedia applications. These applications range from simple music downloading to a portable device, to watching TV through the Internet on a laptop, or to viewing movie trailers posted on the Web via a wireless link. Some of these applications are new to the Internet revolution, while others may seem more traditional, such as sending VoIP to an apparently conventional telephone, sending television over IP to an apparently conventional set top box, or sending music over WiFi to an apparently conventional stereo amplifier.

An obvious question that comes to mind when considering all the aforementioned applications is how to jointly discuss these applications. What do they have in common and how do they differ? To provide an answer to this seemingly simple question, we will discuss the various dimensions of these multimedia communication applications.

1.1.2 Streaming Versus Downloading

Conventional downloading applications (e.g., file transfer such as FTP) involve downloading a file before it is viewed or consumed by a user. Examples of such multimedia downloading applications are downloading an MP3 song to a portable device, downloading a video file to a computer via BitTorrent, or downloading a podcast. (Despite its name, podcasting is a "pull" technology with which a Web site is periodically polled for new multimedia content.) Downloading is usually a very robust way to deliver media to a user. However, downloading has two potentially important disadvantages for multimedia applications. First, a large buffer is required whenever a large media file (e.g., an MPEG-4 movie) is downloaded. Second, the amount of time required for the download can be relatively large, thereby requiring the user to wait minutes or even hours before being able to consume the content. Thus, while downloading is simple and robust, it provides only limited flexibility both to users and to application designers.

An alternative to downloading is streaming. Streaming applications split the media bit stream into separate chunks (e.g., packets), which can be transmitted independently. This enables the receiver to decode and play back the parts of the bit stream that are already received. The transmitter continues to send multimedia data chunks while the receiver decodes and simultaneously plays back other, already received parts of the bit stream. This enables low delay between the moment data is sent by the transmitter to the moment it is viewed by the user. Low delay is of paramount importance for interactive applications such as video conferencing, but it is also important both for video on demand, where the user may desire to change channels or programs quickly, and for live broadcast, where the content length is unbounded a priori, but the delay must be finite. Another advantage of streaming is its relatively low storage requirements and increased flexibility for the user, compared to downloading. However, streaming applications, unlike downloading applications, have deadlines and other timing requirements to ensure continuous real-time media playout. This leads to new challenges for designing communication systems to best support multimedia streaming applications.

1.1.3 Streaming Media on Demand, Live Broadcast, and Real-Time Communication

Multimedia streaming applications can be partitioned into three classes by delay tolerance. Interactive audio and video telephony, teleconferencing, and gaming have extremely low delay tolerance, usually no more than 200 ms of end-to-end delay for comfortable interaction. In contrast, live broadcast applications (e.g., Internet radio), which typically have no interactivity, have a large delay tolerance, say up to 30 s, because the delay cannot be detected without interactivity and without a reference, such as a neighbor who is listening to a conventional radio. (Cheers coming from a neighbor's apartment 30 s before a goal can certainly ruin the surprise!) Intermediate in terms of delay tolerance is the application of streaming media on demand, which has only moderate interactivity requirements, such as channel changing and VCR-like control. The differences in delay tolerance among these three classes of multimedia applications have profound effects on their design, particularly with respect to error recovery. Low-delay, low bit rate applications such as telephony can afford only error-resilience techniques, whereas high-delay or high bandwidth applications can afford complete error recovery using either forward error correction or retransmission-based techniques.

It is worth noting here that although applications in all three classes play out multimedia in real time, the phrase "real-time communication" is commonly used only for the first application, that is, audio and video telephony, conferencing, and gaming, whereas the phrase "streaming" is often associated only with the latter two applications.

1.1.4 Online Versus Off-Line Encoding

Another essential difference between multimedia communication applications is whether the content is encoded online, as in the case of real-time communication or live broadcast applications, or is encoded off-line, as in the case of streaming media on demand. The advantage of online encoding is that the communication channel can be monitored and the source and channel coding strategies can be adapted correspondingly. For instance, the receiver can inform the transmitter of the information that is lost and the encoder can adjust correspondingly. The advantage of off-line encoding is that the content can be exhaustively analyzed and the encoding can be optimized (possibly in nonreal time over several passes of the data) for efficient transmission.

1.1.5 Receiver Device Characteristics

The constraints of the receiver devices on which the various applications are consumed by the end user also have an important impact on multimedia communication. In particular, the available storage, power, and computational capabilities of the receiving device need to be explicitly considered when designing complete multimedia communication solutions. For instance, the design of multimedia compression, scheduling, and error protection algorithms at the receiver should explicitly consider the ability of the receiver to cope with packet loss. Also, receiver-driven streaming applications can enable the end device to proactively decide which parts of the compressed bit streams should be transmitted depending on the display size and other factors.

1.1.6 Unicast, Multicast, and Broadcast

Multimedia communication can be classified into one of three different categories: unicast, multicast, and broadcast, depending on the relationship between the number of senders and receivers. Unicast transmission connects one sender to one receiver. Examples of such applications include downloading, streaming media on demand, and point-to-point telephony. A main advantage of unicast is that a back channel can be established between the receiver and the sender. When such a back channel exists, the receiver can provide feedback to the sender about experienced channel conditions, end-user requirements, end-device characteristics, and so on, which can be used accordingly to adapt compression, error protection, and other transmission strategies.

Multicast transmission connects the sender to multiple receivers that have elected to participate in the multicast session, over IP multicast or application level multicast. Multicast is more efficient than multiple unicasts in terms of network resource utilization and server complexity. However, a disadvantage of multicast compared to unicast is that the sender cannot target its transmission toward a specific receiver.

Broadcast transmission connects a sender to all receivers that it can reach through the network. An example is broadcast over a wireless link or a shared Ethernet link. As in multicast, the communication channel may be different for different receivers. In this book, when we refer to the live broadcast application, we are usually talking about a solution in which a live signal is actually multicast over the network.

1.1.7 Metrics for Quantifying Performance

Unlike conventional communication applications, multimedia communication applications cannot be simply evaluated in terms of the achieved throughput, packet loss rates, or bit error rates, as these applications are delay sensitive and not all the various transmitted bits are "created equal," that is, have the same importance. Instead, multimedia performance needs to be quantified in terms of metrics such as the perceived quality or objective metrics such as the Peak Signal-to-Noise Ratio (PSNR) between transmitted and received media data. Hence, the importance of each bit or packet of multimedia data depends on its delay requirements (i.e., when it needs to be available at the receiver side) and impact on the resulting PSNR. These new evaluation criteria fundamentally change the design principles for multimedia communication systems compared to communication systems for traditional delay-insensitive, loss-intolerant applications.

1.2 ORGANIZATION OF THE BOOK

This book aims at providing an in-depth understanding of the theoretical foundations, key design principles, algorithms, and existing standards for the aforementioned multimedia networking and communication scenarios. The book is divided into five major parts.

The first part of the book discusses how multimedia data can be efficiently compressed to enable optimized transmission over the Internet and wireless networks. Unlike traditional compression techniques such as MPEG-2, which were designed solely for storage (e.g., on DVD disks) or transmission over error-free networks with relatively large and guaranteed bandwidth, compression schemes that enable efficient multimedia communication over the Internet and wireless networks need to have the ability to cope with different channel conditions, characterized by different bit error rates, packet loss rates, access bandwidths, or time-varying available bandwidths. Chapter 2 discusses error-resilient techniques for video transmission over such error-prone networks, while Chapter 3 presents algorithms and solutions for error-resilient audio transmission. To cope with the changes in bandwidth, Chapter 4 provides a thorough analysis of the various mechanisms for bandwidth adaptation, as the network often offers heterogeneous, time-varying channel conditions. To effectively cope with adaptive streaming applications or multicasting applications, where a variety of receivers would like to simultaneously access the same multimedia content, Chapter 5 introduces existing and emerging scalable video coding algorithms, while Chapter 6 discusses scalable audio coding.

The second part of the book focuses on efficient solutions for bit stream transmission over IP networks. Chapter 7 introduces the fundamentals of channel protection needed to insulate bit streams from the error-prone nature of the channels over which they are transmitted. Chapter 8 discusses how to effectively model and characterize the complex communication channels within networks such as the Internet. Having an accurate model of the channel becomes paramount when finding an efficient trade-off between the bit rates allocated to source and channel protection. Chapter 9 focuses on Forward Error Correction (FEC) mechanisms aimed at effectively protecting multimedia bit streams at the application layer. These solutions can successfully exploit the available knowledge of the multimedia bit streams. Chapter 10 focuses on the corresponding retransmission-based mechanisms. Unlike FEC mechanisms, retransmission-based mechanisms can be instantaneously adapted to each channel realization. However, the retransmission-based algorithms are not well suited to the multicast case or the live broadcast scenario, where many receivers are connected to a single sender. FEC mechanisms must be used here instead.

The third part of the book focuses on multimedia transmission over wireless networks. Chapter 11 discusses MAC-centric channel models characterizing the specific behavior of wireless networks, thereby offering insights into the challenges associated with multimedia streaming over such networks. Chapter 12 shows how to cope with these challenges, how the various layers of the protocol stack can collaborate to ensure efficient wireless multimedia communication, and how the cross-layer design deployed at one station influences multiuser interaction and fairness in such environments. Chapter 13 provides various solutions for providing the necessary quality of service guarantees in such wireless environments.

The fourth part of the book discusses efficient multimedia system design, which is essential for ensuring that the streaming solutions are efficiently optimized and deployed. Chapter 14 presents approaches to streaming media on demand as well as live broadcast, while Chapter 15 presents approaches to real-time communication applications such as telephony and conferencing. To ensure the continuous playout of multimedia despite packet loss and jitter, Chapter 16 exploits the "time elastic" behavior of these applications by discussing the concept of adaptive media playout.

The final part of the book presents several advanced topics on multimedia communication. Chapter 17 discusses how multimedia compression and transmission algorithms can take advantage of the multipath diversity existing in the Internet and wireless networks. Chapter 18 presents distributed video coding principles, algorithms, and their applications to, for example, low-cost encoding for multimedia streaming. Chapter 19 introduces the capabilities, architectures, and design principles of building overlays on top of the existing Internet and wireless infrastructures for enhanced support to multimedia applications.

1.3 SUGGESTED USE FOR GRADUATE INSTRUCTION AND SELF-STUDY

This book is intended as a textbook for a graduate-level course on multimedia networking and communication or as reference text for researchers and engineers working in the areas of multimedia communication, multimedia compression, multimedia systems, wireless communication, and networking. This book can be used for either a semester-length course or a quarter-length course if some of the advanced topics are left for self-study or as part of a research project associated with the class.

One of the best ways to understand the challenges and theory for multimedia communication and networking discussed in this book is through the completion of a multimedia-related project. This is because the importance of the various principles and techniques taught in such a course, as well as their interrelationships, become apparent when solving "real" multimedia communication problems. Students should be encouraged to choose a project topic related to their interests and/or research backgrounds. The summary and further reading sections concluding the various chapters can be used as a starting point for defining relevant class projects. For instance, students having a background on wireless communication can choose a project topic on cross-layer wireless multimedia transmission or multimedia transmission over multihop wireless networks, students having interests on information theory can select projects on joint source-channel coding or distributed source coding, and students with a background on signal, speech, or image processing can investigate topics related to robust multimedia compression, scalable coding, error concealment, or adaptive media playout.

1.4 SUPPLEMENTARY MATERIAL FOR THE BOOK

Supplementary material for this book can be found at `http://books.elsevier.com/companions/0120884801`. This includes an additional chapter to this book, Chapter 20, which presents state-of-the-art techniques for multimedia transmission over peer-to-peer networks. Also, the Web page contains slides, exercises, and additional material for the various chapters, which can be used by potential instructors for a class on multimedia communication and networking. For feedback about the book or the material posted on this Web site, the reader can contact the coeditors of this book, Mihaela van der Schaar (mihaela@ee.ucla.edu) and Phil Chou (pachou@microsoft.com).

ACKNOWLEDGMENTS

The coeditors acknowledge the contributions by our incredibly talented team of chapter authors. We also acknowledge Hyunggon Park, Yiannis Andreopoulos, Andres I. Vila Casado, Cong Shen, Miguel Griot, Jonas B. Borgstrom, and Nicholas Mastronarde, all graduate students in the Electrical Engineering Department at UCLA, for reading initial drafts of the book and providing constructive feedback. We acknowledge the patience and careful editorial work of Chuck Glaser, Rick Adams, Rachel Roumeliotis, and the staff at Elsevier. In addition, Mihaela van der Schaar would like to thank her husband for his help and support, as well as for the many discussions they had on this book.

PART **B**

COMPRESSION

CHAPTER   2   Error-Resilient Coding and Decoding Strategies for Video
              Communication
              (Thomas Stockhammer and Waqar Zia)

CHAPTER   3   Error-Resilient Coding and Error Concealment Strategies for
              Audio Communication
              (Dinei Florêncio)

CHAPTER   4   Mechanisms for Adapting Compressed Multimedia to Varying
              Bandwidth Conditions
              (Antonio Ortega and Huisheng Wang)

CHAPTER   5   Scalable Video Coding for Adaptive Streaming Applications
              (Béatrice Pesquet-Popescu, Shipeng Li, and
              Mihaela van der Schaar)

CHAPTER   6   Scalable Audio Coding
              (Jin Li)

2

Error-Resilient Coding and Decoding Strategies for Video Communication

Thomas Stockhammer and Waqar Zia

2.1 INTRODUCTION

Video is becoming more and more popular for a large variety of applications and networks. Internet and wireless video, especially, has become part of our daily lives. However, despite many advances in terms of bandwidth and capacity enhancements in different networks, the data transmission rate will always be a scarce resource due to physical limitations, especially for high quality high bit rate applications. Therefore, good compression is as important as ever. Furthermore, real-time delivery of multimedia data is required for several application scenarios, such as conversational applications, streaming, broadcast, or video-on-demand services. Under such real-time constraints, unfortunately the Quality-of-Service (QoS) available in current and next generation networks is in general not sufficient to guarantee error-free delivery to all receivers. Therefore, in addition to the capability of easy integration into existing and future networks, video codecs must provide means of dealing with various transmission impairments. In communication environments, standardized solutions are desirable at terminals to ensure compatibility. That is why video coding standards such as MPEG-4 and H.264/AVC have become popular and attractive for numerous network environments and application scenarios. These standards, like numerous previous standards and more recent standards such as VCI, use a hybrid coding approach, namely Motion Compensated Prediction (MCP). MCP is combined with transform coding of the residual. We will focus on MCP-coded video in the remainder of this chapter and mainly concentrate on tools and features integrated in the latest video coding standard H.264/AVC [19,45] and its test model software JM.

We will focus on specific tools for improved error resilience within standard-compliant MCP-coded video. More advanced error-resilience features, such as multiple description coding, distributed video coding, and combinations with network prioritization and forward error correction, are left to the remaining chapters of this book and the references therein. It is assumed that the reader has some basic knowledge of the encoding and decoding algorithms of MCP-coded video, for example, as discussed in [14].

2.2 VIDEO COMMUNICATION SYSTEMS

2.2.1 End-to-End Video Transmission

Figure 2.1 provides an abstraction of a video transmission system. In order to keep this work focused, we have excluded capturing and display devices, user interfaces, and security issues; most computational complexity issues are also ignored. Components that enhance system performance, for example, a feedback channel, will also be introduced later in this chapter. In contrast to still images, video frames inherently include relative timing information, which has to be maintained to assure perfect reconstruction at the receiver's display. Furthermore, due to significant amounts of spatiotemporal statistical and psychovisual redundancy in natural video sequences, video encoders are capable of reducing the actual amount of transmitted data significantly. However, excessive lossy compression results in noticeable, annoying, or even intolerable artifacts in the decoded video. A trade-off between *rate* and *distortion* is always necessary. Real-time transmission of video adds additional challenges. According to Figure 2.1, the video encoder generates data units containing the compressed video stream, which is stored in an

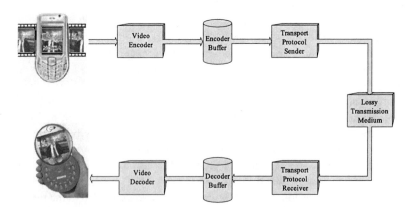

FIGURE 2.1:   Simplified lossy video transmission system.

encoder buffer before the transmission. The transmission system may delay, lose, or corrupt individual data units. Furthermore, each processing and transmission step adds some delay, which can be fixed, deterministic, or random. The encoder buffer and the decoder buffer compensate for variable bit rates produced by the encoder as well as channel delay variations to keep the end-to-end delay constant and to maintain the time line at the decoder. Nevertheless, in general the initial playout delay cannot be too excessive and strongly depends on the application constraints.

2.2.2 Video Applications

As discussed in Chapter 1, digitally coded video is used in a wide variety of applications, in different transmission environments. These applications can operate in completely different bit rate ranges. For example, HDTV applications require data rates in the vicinity of 20 Mbit/s, whereas simple download-and-play services such as MMS on mobile devices might be satisfied with 20 Kbit/s, three orders of magnitude less. However, applications themselves have certain characteristics, which are of importance for system design. For example, they can be distinguished by the maximum tolerable end-to-end delay and the possibility of online encoding (in contrast to the transmission of pre-encoded content). In particular, real-time services, such as broadcasting, unicast streaming, and conversational services, come with significant challenges, because generally, reliable delivery of all data cannot be guaranteed. This can be due to the lack of a feedback link in the system or due to constraints on the maximum end-to-end delay. Among these applications, conversational applications with end-to-end delay constraints of less than 200 to 250 ms are most challenging for the system design.

2.2.3 Coded Video Data

In contrast to analog audio, for example, compressed digital video cannot be accessed at any random point due to variable-length entropy coding as well as the syntax and semantics of the encoded video stream. In general, coded video can be viewed as a sequence of data units, referred to as access units in MPEG-4 or network abstraction layer (NAL) units in H.264. The data units themselves are self-contained, at least on a syntactic level, and they can be labeled with data unit-specific information; for example, their relative importance for video reconstruction quality. However, on a semantic level, due to spatial and temporal prediction, the independent compression of data units cannot be guaranteed without significantly harming compression efficiency. A concept of directed acyclic dependency graphs on data units has been introduced in [6], which formalizes these issues. The data units themselves are either directly forwarded to a packet network or encapsulated into a bit or byte stream format containing unique synchronization codes and then injected into a circuit-switched network.

2.2.4 Transmission Impairments

The process of introduction of errors and its effects are markedly different in IP and wireless-based networks. For wireless networks, fading and interference cause *burst errors* in the form of multiple lost bits, while congestion can result in lost packets in an IP network. Nowadays, even for wireless networks, systems include means to detect the presence of errors on physical layer segments and the losses are indicated to higher layers. Intermediate protocol layers such as the User Datagram Protocol (UDP) [32] might decide to completely drop erroneous packets and the encapsulated data units.

Furthermore, video data packets are treated as lost if they are delayed more than a tolerable threshold defined by the application. Hence for the remainder of this chapter we will concentrate on the effects of entire data units lost and present means to deal with such losses in video applications. Detailed description of the processes of introduction of losses in IP and wireless-based networks will be given in Chapter 8 and Chapter 11, respectively.

2.2.5 Data Losses in MCP-Coded Video

Figure 2.2 presents a simplified yet typical system when MCP video is transmitted over error-prone channels. Assume that all macroblocks (MBs) of one frame s_t are contained in a single packet $\mathcal{P}_t$, for example, in an NAL unit in the case of H.264/AVC. Furthermore, assume that this packet is transmitted over a channel that forwards correct packets to the decoder, denoted as $\mathcal{C}_t = 1$, and perfectly detects and discards corrupted packets at the receiver, denoted as $\mathcal{C}_t = 0$.

In case of successful transmission, the packet is forwarded to the regular decoder operation. The prediction information and transform coefficients are re-

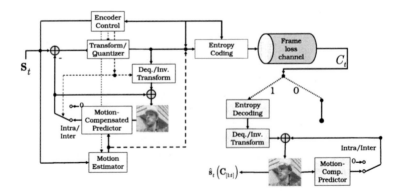

FIGURE 2.2:   Simplified lossy video transmission system.

trieved from the coded bit stream to reconstruct frame $\hat{s}_{t-1}$. The frame is forwarded to the display buffer and also to the reference frame buffer to be used in the MCP process to reconstruct following inter-coded frames, for example, $\hat{s}_t$. In the less favorable case that the coded representation of the frame is lost, that is, at our reference time $t = 0$, $C_t = 0$, so-called *error concealment* is necessary. In the simplest form, the decoder just skips the decoding operation and the display buffer is not updated, that is, the displayed frame is still $\hat{s}_{t-1}$. The viewer will immediately recognize the loss of fluent motion since a continuous display update is not maintained.

However, in addition to the display buffer, the reference frame buffer is also not updated as a result of this data loss. Even in case of successful reception of packet $\mathcal{P}_{t+1}$, the inter-coded frame $\hat{s}_{t+1}$ reconstructed at the decoder will in general not be identical to the reconstructed frame $\tilde{s}_{t+1}$ at the encoder. The reason is obvious, as the encoder and the decoder refer to a different reference signal in the MCP process, resulting in a so-called reconstruction *mismatch*. Therefore, there will again be a mismatch in the reference signal when decoding $\hat{s}_{t+2}$. Hence it is obvious that the loss of a single packet $\mathcal{P}_t$ affects the quality of all the inter-coded frames $\hat{s}_{t+1}, \hat{s}_{t+2}, \hat{s}_{t+3}, \ldots$. This phenomenon, present in any predictive coding scheme, is called *error propagation*. If predictive coding is applied in the spatial and temporal domains, it is referred to as *spatiotemporal error propagation*.

Therefore, for MCP-coded video, the reconstructed frame at the receiver, $\hat{s}_t$, not only depends on the actual channel behavior C_t, but on the previous channel behavior $C_{[1:t]} = \{C_1, \ldots, C_t\}$ and we write $\hat{s}_t(C_{[1:t]})$. An example for error propagation is shown in Figure 2.3. The top row presents the sequence with perfect reconstruction; in the bottom row only packet $\mathcal{P}_t$ at time $t = 0$ is lost. Although the remaining packets are again correctly received, the error propagates and is still visible in decoded frame $\hat{s}_{t=8}$. At time $t = 9$, the encoder transmits an intra-coded image, and since no temporal prediction is used for coding this image, temporal error propagation is terminated at this time. It should be noted, however, that even

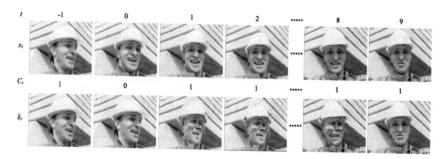

FIGURE 2.3:   Example for error propagation in a typical hybrid video coding system.

with inter-coded images, the effect of a loss is reduced with every correct reception. This is because inter-coded frames might consist of intra-coded regions that do not use temporal prediction. An encoder might decide to use intra-coding when it finds that temporal prediction is inefficient for coding a certain image region.

Following the intra image at $t = 9$, the decoder will be able to perfectly reconstruct the encoded images until another data packet is lost for $t > 9$.

Therefore, a video coding system operating in environments where data units might get lost should provide one or several of the following features:

1. means that allow completely avoiding transmission errors,
2. features that allow minimizing the visual effects of errors in a frame, and
3. features to limit spatial as well as spatiotemporal error propagation in hybrid video coding.

In the remainder of this chapter we restrict ourselves to forward predictive MCP video coding, although most of the concepts generalize to any kind of dependencies. A formal description of packetized video with slice structured coding and error concealment, as well as the extension of operational encoder control for error-prone video transmission, are discussed in Section 2.3.

2.3 ERROR-RESILIENT VIDEO TRANSMISSION

2.3.1 System Overview

The operation of an MCP video coding system in a transmission environment is depicted in Figure 2.4. It extends the simplified presentation in Figure 2.2 by the

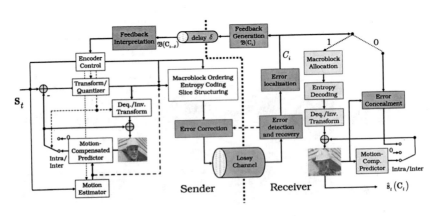

FIGURE 2.4: MCP video coding in packet lossy environment: Error-resilience features and decoder operations.

addition of typical features used when transmitting video over error-prone channels. However, in general, for specific applications not all features are used, but only a suitable subset is extracted. Frequently, the generated video data belonging to a single frame is not encoded as a single data unit, but MBs are grouped in data units and the entropy coding is such that individual data units are syntactically accessible and independent. The generated video data might be processed in a transmission protocol stack and some kind of error control is typically applied, before the video data is transmitted over the lossy channel. Error control features include Forward Error Correction (FEC), Backward Error Correction (BEC), and any prioritization methods, as well as any combinations of those. At the receiver, it is essential that erroneous and missing video data are detected and localized. Commonly, video decoders are fed only with correctly received video data units, or at least with an error indication, that certain video data has been lost. Video data units such as NAL units in H.264 are self-contained and therefore the decoder can assign the decoded MBs to the appropriate locations in the decoded frames. For those positions where no data has been received, error concealment has to be applied. Advanced video coding systems also allow reporting the loss of video data units from the receiver to the video encoder. Depending on the application, the delay, and the accurateness of the information, an online encoder can exploit this information in the encoding process. Likewise, streaming servers can use this information in their decisions. Several of the concepts briefly mentioned in this high-level description of an error-resilient video transmission system will be elaborated and investigated in more detail in remaining sections.

2.3.2 Design Principles

Video coding features such as MB assignments, error control methods, or exploitation of feedback messages can be used exclusively or jointly for error robustness purposes, depending on the application. It is necessary to understand that most error-resilience tools decrease compression efficiency. Therefore, the main goal when transmitting video goes along the spirit of Shannon's famous separation principle [38]: Combine compression efficiency with link layer features that completely avoid losses such that the two aspects, compression and transport, can be completely separated. Nevertheless, in several applications and environments, particularly in low delay situations, error-free transport may be impossible. In these cases, the following system design principles are essential:

1. *Loss correction below codec layer*: Minimize the amount of losses in the wireless channel without completely sacrificing the video bit rate.
2. *Error detection*: If errors are unavoidable, detect and localize erroneous video data.
3. *Prioritization methods*: If losses are unavoidable, at least minimize losses for very important data.

4. *Error recovery and concealment*: In case of losses, minimize the visual impact of losses on the actually distorted image.
5. *Encoder–decoder mismatch avoidance*: In case of losses, limit or completely avoid encoder and decoder mismatch to avoid the annoying effects of error propagation.

This chapter will focus especially on the latter three design principles. However, for completeness, we include a brief overview on the first two aspects. The remainder of this book will treat many of these advanced issues.

2.3.3 Error Control Methods

In wireless systems, below the application layer, error control such as FEC and retransmission protocols are the primary tools for providing QoS. However, the trade-offs among reliability, delay, and bit rate have to be considered. Nevertheless, to compensate the shortcomings of non-QoS-controlled networks, for example, the Internet or some mobile systems, as well as to address total blackout periods caused, for example, by network buffer overflow or a handoff between transmission cells, error control features are introduced at the application layer. For example, broadcast services make use of application-layer FEC schemes. For point-to-point services, selective application layer retransmission schemes have been proposed. For delay-uncritical applications, the Transmission Control Protocol (TCP) [31,40] can provide QoS. The topics of channel protection techniques and FEC will be covered in detail in Chapter 7 and Chapter 9, respectively. We will not deal with these features in the remainder of this chapter, but concentrate on video-related signal processing to introduce reliability and QoS.

2.3.4 Video Compression Tools Related to Error Resilience

Video coding standards such as H.263, MPEG-4, and H.264 only specify the decoder operation in case of reception of an error-free bit stream as well as the syntax and semantics of the video bit stream. Consequently, the deployment of video coding standards still provides a significant amount of freedom for encoders and decoding of erroneous bit streams. Depending on the compression standard used, different compression tools are available that offer some room for error-resilient transmission.

Video compression tools have evolved significantly over time in terms of the error resilience they offer. Early video compression standards, such as H.261, had very limited error-resilience capabilities. Later standards, such as MPEG-1 and MPEG-2, changed little in this regard, since they were tailored mostly for storage applications. With the advent of H.263, things started changing dramatically. The resilience tools of the first version of H.263 [18] had only marginal improvements over MPEG-1; however, later versions of H.263 (referred as H.263+ and H.263++, respectively) introduced several new tools that were tailored specifically for the purpose of error resilience and will be discussed in this section. These tools resulted in a popular acceptance of this codec; it replaced H.261 in most video communication applications. In parallel to this work, the new emerging standard MPEG-4 Advanced Simple Profile (ASP) [17] opted for an entirely different approach. Some sophisticated resilience tools, such as Reversible Variable Length Coding (RVLC) and resynchronization markers, were introduced. However, despite their strong concept, these tools did not gain wide acceptance. One of the reasons for this is that these tools target to solve the issues of lower layers in the application layer, which is not a widely accepted approach. For example, RVLC can be used at the decoder to reduce the impact of errors in a corrupted data packet. However, as discussed in Section 2.2.4, errors on the physical layer can be detected and lower layers might discard these packets instead of forwarding them to the application.

Up to date, the final chapter in error-resilient video coding is H.264/AVC. This standard is equipped with a wide range of error-resilience tools. Some of these tools are modified and enhanced forms of the ones introduced in H.263++. The following section gives a brief overview of these tools as they are formulated in H.264/AVC and the concepts behind these. Considering the rapid pace of evolution of these tools, it is also important to know the origin of these tools in previous standards.

Some specific error-resilience features such as error-resilient entropy coding schemes and arbitrary slice ordering will not be discussed. The interested reader is referred to [43,60]. It is also worth considering that most features are general enough to be used for multiple purposes rather than being assigned to a specific application. Some of the tools have a dual purpose of increased compression efficiency along with error resilience, which seems to be contradictory initially, but this ambiguity will be resolved. In later sections of this chapter, we will present some of these tools in action in different applications and measure their impact on system performance.

Slice Structured Coding

For typical digital video transmission over networks, it is not suitable to transmit all the compressed data belonging to a complete coded frame in a single data packet for a variety of reasons. Most importantly, variations are expected in the sizes of such data packets because of a varying amount of redundancy in different frames of a sequence. In this case the lower layers have to subdivide the packet to make it suitable for transmission. In case of a loss of a single such division, the decoder might be unable to decode an entire frame with only one synchronization point available for an entire coded frame.

To overcome this issue, *slices* provide spatially distinct resynchronization points within the video data for a single frame (Figure 2.5). A number of MBs are grouped together; this is accomplished by introducing a slice header, which contains syntactic and semantic resynchronization information. The concept of slices (referred to as group of blocks [GOB] in H.261 and H.263) exists in different forms in different standards. Its usage was limited to encapsulate individual rows of MBs in H.263 and MPEG-2. In this case, slices will still result in variable sized data units because of the varying amount of redundancy in different regions of a frame. Slices take their most flexible and advanced form in H.264/AVC. The encoder can select the location of the synchronization points at any MB boundary. Intra prediction and motion vector prediction are not allowed over slice boundaries. An arbitrary number of MBs can be assigned to a slice, which results in different modes of operation. For example, the encoder can decide to allocate either a fixed number of MBs or a fixed number of bits to a slice. The later mode of operation, with a predefined data size of a slice, is especially useful from a network perspective, since the slice size can be better matched to the packet size supported by the network layer. In this case, a loss of a data unit on network layer will result in a loss of a discrete number of slices, and a considerable portion of a picture might remain unaffected by the loss.

Hence in H.264/AVC, slices are the basic output of the video encoder and form an independently accessible entity. Provision of access to those units is provided either by the use of unique synchronization markers or by the appropriate encapsulation in underlying transport protocols. The details of slice structured coding modes and the implications are discussed in Section 2.4.2.

FIGURE 2.5:   A sketch of a picture divided into several slices, demarcated by gray boundaries.

Flexible MB Ordering

In previous video compression standards, such as MPEG-1, MPEG-2 and H.263, MBs are processed and transmitted in raster–scan order, starting from the top-left corner of the image to the bottom right. However, if a data unit is lost, this usually results in the loss of a connected area in a single frame.

In order to allow a more flexible transmission order of MBs in a frame in H.264/AVC, Flexible Macroblock Ordering (FMO) allows mapping of MBs to so-called *slice groups*. A slice group itself may contain several slices. For example, in Figure 2.6, each shaded region (a slice group) might be subdivided into several slices. Hence *slice group* can be thought of as an entity similar to a picture consisting of slices in the case when FMO is not used. Therefore, MBs may be transmitted out of raster–scan order in a flexible and efficient way. This can be useful in several cases. For example:

- Several concealment techniques at the decoder rely on the availability of correctly received neighbor MBs to conceal a lost MB. Hence a loss of collocated image areas results in poor concealment. Using FMO, spatially collocated image areas can be interleaved in different slices. This will result in a greater probability that neighboring MB data is available for concealing the lost MB.
- There might exist a Region Of Interest (ROI) within the images of a video sequence, for example, the face of the caller in a video conferencing system. Such regions can be mapped to a separate slice group than the background to offer better protection against losses in the network layer.

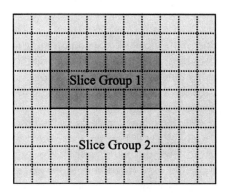

FIGURE 2.6: MBs of a picture (dotted lines) allocated to two slice groups. Light-gray MBs belong to one slice group, and dark-gray MBs belong to the other.

A description of different modes and specific applications of FMO are given in Section 2.4.2.

Scalability

Scalable coding usually refers to a source coder that simultaneously provides encoded version of the same data source at different quality levels by extracting a lower quality reconstruction from a single binary description. Scalable coding can be realized using *embedded bit streams*, that is, the bit stream of a lower resolution is embedded in the bit stream of higher resolution. Unlike one-dimensional sources such as speech or audio, where usually the quality levels are defined by the quantization distortion, for video the quality can be changed in basically three dimensions, namely spatial resolution, temporal resolution or frame rate, and quantization distortion. Scalable video coding is realized in standards in many different variants and will be extensively treated in Chapter 5. Commonly, scalability is synonymously used with a specific type of scalability referred to as *successive refinement*. This specific case addresses the view point that information is added such that the initial reproduction is refined. In this case, the emphasis is on a good initial reproduction.

Data Partitioning

The concept of *data partitioning* originates from the fact that loss of some syntax elements of a bit stream results in a larger degradation of quality compared to others. For example, the loss of MB mode information or motion vector (MV) information will, for most cases, result in a larger distortion compared to loss of a high-frequency transform coefficient. This is intuitive, since, for example, MB mode information is required for interpreting all the remaining MB information at the decoder.

In the case of data loss in the network, data partitioning results in the so-called *graceful degradation* of video quality. Graceful degradation targets the reduction of perceived video quality that is, to some extent, proportionate to the amount of data lost. In this case, the emphasis is on a good final reproduction quality, but at least an intermediate reconstruction is possible.

The concept of categorizing syntax elements in the order of their importance started with MPEG-4 and H.263++. For these standards, video coded data was categorized into header information, motion information, and texture information (transformed residual coefficients), listed here in the order of their importance. Figure 2.7 shows the interleaved structure of data when using the data partitioning mode. For example, combining this concept with that of RVLC and resynchronization markers, it could be possible to retrieve most of header and MV information even for the case of data lost within the transform coefficients partition.

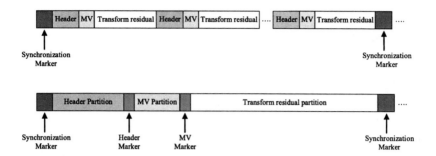

FIGURE 2.7: The layout of a compressed video data without using data partitioning (top) and with data partitioning (bottom) in H.263++. A packet starts with a synchronization marker, while for the data partitioning mode, two additional synchronization points are available, such as the header marker and the MV marker.

In the H.264/AVC data partitioning mode, each slice can be segmented into header and motion information, intra information, and inter texture information by simply distributing the syntax elements to individual data units. Typically, the importance of the individual segments of the partition is in the order of the list. In contrast to MPEG-4, H.264/AVC distinguishes between inter- and intra-texture information because of the more important role of the latter in error mitigation. The partitions of different importance can be protected with Unequal Error Protection (UEP), with the more important data being offered more protection and vice versa. Due to this reordering only on the syntax level, coding efficiency is not sacrificed, but obviously the loss of individual segments still results in error propagation with similar but typically less severe effects as those shown in Figure 2.3. Some detailed investigations of synergies of data partition and UEP can be found in [13,24,42].

Redundant Slices

An H.264/AVC encoder can transmit a redundant version of a normally transmitted slice using possibly different encoding parameters. Such a *redundant slice* can be simply discarded by the decoder during its normal operation. However, in the case when the original slice is lost, this redundant data can be used to reconstruct the lost regions. For example, in a system with frequent data losses, an H.264/AVC encoder can exploit this unique feature to send the redundant, coarsely quantized version of an ROI along with the regular representation of it. Hence the decoder will be capable of displaying the lost ROI, albeit at a lower quality. It is worthwhile to notice that this will still result in an encoder–decoder mismatch of reference pictures, since the encoder being unaware of the loss uses the original slice as a reference, but this effect will be less severe compared to the case when this tool is not used.

Flexible Reference Frame Concept

Standards such as H.263 version 1 and MPEG-2 allow only a single reference frame for predicting a P-type frame and at most two frames for predicting a B-type frame. However, there is a possibility of significant statistical dependencies between other pictures as well. Hence using more frames than just the recent frame as reference has a dual advantage: increased compression efficiency and improved error resilience at the same time. Here we focus on the latter effect exclusively. This concept has been recognized as especially useful for transmission over error-prone channels.

In prior codecs, if the encoder is aware of the only reference picture being lost at the decoder, the only available option to limit error propagation was to transmit intra-coded information. However, intra-coded data has significantly large size compared to temporally predicted data, which results in further delays and losses on the network. H.263+ and MPEG-4 proposed tools, such as the Reference Picture Selection (RPS), allows flexible selection of a reference picture on a slice or GOB bases. Hence temporal prediction is still possible from other correctly received frames at the decoder. This results in improved error resilience by avoiding using corrupted picture areas as reference. In H.264/AVC, this restrictive concept has been generalized to allow reference frames to be selected in a flexible way on an MB basis (Figure 2.8). There is also the possibility of using two weighted reference signals for MB inter prediction. Frames can be kept in short-term and long-term memory buffers for future reference. This concept can be exploited by the encoder for different purposes, for compression efficiency, for bit rate adaptivity, and for error resilience.

Flexible reference frames can also be used to enable *subsequences* in the compressed stream to effectively enable temporal scalability. The basic idea is to use a subsequence of "anchor frames" at a lower frame rate than the overall sequence frame rate, shown as P frames in Figure 2.9. Other frames are inserted in between these frames to achieve the overall target frame rate, shown as P' frames in Figure 2.9. Here, as an example, every third frame is a P frame. These P' frames can use the low frame rate P frames as reference, but *not* the other way around. This is shown by the chain of prediction arcs in Figure 2.9. If such a P' frame is lost, the error propagates only until the next P is received. Hence P frames are more important to protect against error propagation than P' frames, and some prioritization techniques at lower layers can make use of this fact. This concept is similar to using B frames in prior standards, except that a one-directional predic-

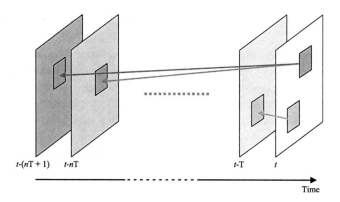

FIGURE 2.8:   A sketch of an H.264/AVC inter-predicted frame at a given time t, with different MBs referencing different frames. The frame interval in this sketch is T.

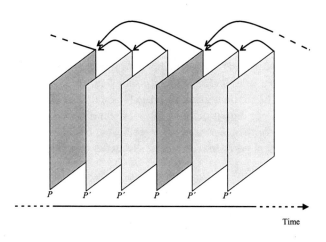

FIGURE 2.9:   H.264/AVC inter prediction with subsequences. Arcs show the reference frame used for prediction.

tion chain avoids any buffering overhead as with the bidirectionally predicted B pictures.

Some use cases of the flexible concept specifically for error-resilience purposes are presented in Section 2.5. More details on this mode can be studied in Subsection 2.5.4 and [9,63,64,69].

Intra Information Coding

Even though temporal redundancy might exist in a frame, it is still necessary to have the possibility of switching off temporal prediction in hybrid video coding. This feature enables random access and also provides error robustness. Any video coding standard allows encoding image regions in *intra mode*, such as without reference to a previously coded reference frame. In a straightforward way, completely intra-coded frames might be inserted. These frames will be referred to as "intra frames" in the remainder of this chapter. In H.264/AVC, the flexible reference frame concept allows the usage of several reference frames; not limited to just the temporally preceding frame. Hence in H.264/AVC, intra frames are further distinguished as Instantaneous Decoder Refresh (IDR) frames and "open GOP" intra frames, whereby the latter do not provide the random access property as possibly frames "before" the intra frame are used as reference for "later" predictively coded frames (Figure 2.10).

In addition, intra information can be introduced for just parts of a predictively coded image. Again most video coding standards allow encoding of single MBs for regions that cannot be predicted efficiently or due to any other case the encoder decides for nonpredictive mode. H.264/AVC intra-coded MBs gain significant compression by making use of spatial prediction from neighboring blocks. To limit error propagation, in H.264/AVC this intra mode can be modified such that intra prediction from inter-coded MBs is disallowed. In addition, encoders can also guarantee that MB intra updates result in Gradual Decoding Refresh (GDR), that is, entirely correct output pictures after a certain period of time. Some advanced techniques for the purpose of error resilience, based on intra updates, and their impact on system performance will be discussed in Section 2.5.3.

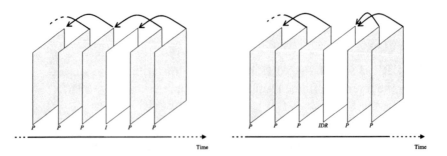

FIGURE 2.10: Inter prediction with open GOP intra "*I*" (left) and *IDR* (right). Temporal prediction (shown by arcs) is not allowed from the frames coded before an IDR frame.

Switching Pictures

H.264/AVC includes a feature that allows applying predictive coding even in the case of different reference signals. This unique feature is enabled by introducing Switching-Predictive (SP) pictures for which the MCP process is performed in the transform domain rather than in the spatial domain and the reference frame is quantized—usually with a finer quantizer than that used for the original frame—before it is forwarded to the reference frame buffer. These so-called primary SP (PSP) frames, which are introduced to the encoded bit stream, are in general slightly less efficient than regular P-frames but significantly more efficient than regular I-frames. The major benefit results from the fact that this quantized reference signal can be generated mismatch free using any other prediction signal. In case that this prediction signal is generated by predictive coding, the frames are referred to as secondary SP (SSP) pictures, which are usually significantly less efficient than P-frames, as an exact reconstruction is necessary. To generate this reference signal without any predictive signal, so-called Switching Intra (SI) pictures can be used. SI pictures are only slightly less inefficient than common intra-coded pictures and can also be used for adaptive error-resilience purposes. Further details on this unique feature within H.264/AVC are covered in Chapter 4 and [22].

2.4 RESYNCHRONIZATION AND ERROR CONCEALMENT

2.4.1 Formalization of H.264 Packetized Video

By the use of slices and slice groups as introduced in Section 2.3, video coding standards, particularly H.264/AVC, provide a flexible and efficient syntax to map the N_{MB} MBs of each frame s_t of the image sequence to individual data units. The encoding of s_t results in one or more data units $\mathcal{P}_i$ with sequence number i. The video transmission system considered is shown in Figure 2.4. Assume that each data unit $\mathcal{P}_i$ is transmitted over a channel that either delivers the data unit $\mathcal{P}_i$ correctly, indicated by $C_i = 1$, or loses the data unit, that is, $C_i = 0$. A data unit is also assumed to be lost if it is received after its nominal Decoding Time Stamp (DTS) has expired. We do not consider more complex concepts with multiple decoding deadlines, also referred to as Accelerated Retroactive Decoding [11, 21], in which late data units are processed by the decoder to at least update the reference buffer, resulting in reduced long-term error propagation.

At the receiver, due to the coding restriction of slices and slice groups, as well as with the information in slice headers, the decoder is able to reconstruct the information of each correctly received data unit and its encapsulated slice. The decoded MBs are then distributed according to the mapping $\mathcal{M}$ in the frame. For all MBs positions, for which no data has been received, appropriate error concealment has to be invoked before the frame is forwarded to the reference and display buffer. The decoded source $\hat{s}_t$ obviously depends on the channel behavior for all the data units $\mathcal{P}_i$ corresponding to the current frame s_t, but due to the predictive coding and error propagation in general, it also depends on the channel behavior of all previous data units, $\mathcal{C}_t \triangleq \mathcal{C}_{[1:i_t]}$. This dependency is expressed as $\hat{s}_t(\mathcal{C}_t)$.

Due to the bidirectional nature of conversational applications, a low-delay, low-bit rate, error-free feedback channel from the receiver to the transmitter, as indicated in Figure 2.4, can be assumed, at least for some applications. This feedback link allows sending some back channel messages. These messages make the transmitter aware of the channel conditions so that it may react to these conditions. These messages are denoted as $\mathcal{B}(\mathcal{C}_t)$. The exact definition and applications of such messages are described in Section 2.5. In our framework we model the feedback link as error free, but the feedback message delay is normalized to the frame rate such that $\mathcal{B}(\mathcal{C}_{t-\delta})$ expresses a version of $\mathcal{B}(\mathcal{C}_t)$ delayed by δ frames, with $\delta = 0, 1, 2, \ldots$. The exploitation of this feedback link and different types of messages having assigned specific semantics in the encoding process are discussed later.

2.4.2 Video Packetization Modes

At the encoder the application of slice structured coding and FMO allows limiting the amount of lost data in case of transmission errors. Especially with the use of FMO, the mapping of MBs to data units basically provides arbitrary flexibility. However, there exist a few typical mapping modes, which are discussed in the following.

Without the use of FMO, the encoder typically can choose between two slice coding options: one with a constant number of MBs, $N_{\mathrm{MB/DU}}$, within one slice resulting in an arbitrary size, and one with the slice size bounded to some maximum number of bytes $S_{\max}$, resulting in an arbitrary number of MBs per slice. Whereas with the former mode, the similar slice types as present in H.263 and MPEG-2 can be formed, the latter is especially useful for introducing some QoS, as commonly the slice size and the resulting packet size determine the data unit loss rate in wireless systems. Examples of the two different packetization modes and the resulting locations of the slice boundaries in the bit stream are shown in Figure 2.11. With the use of FMO, the flexibility of the packetization modes is significantly enhanced, as shown in the examples in Figure 2.12. Features such as slice interleaving, dispersed MB allocation using checkerboard-like patterns, one or several foreground slice groups and one left-over background slice groups, or subpictures within a picture are enabled. Slice interleaving and dispersed MB allocation are especially powerful in conjunction with appropriate error concealment, that is, when the samples of a missing slice are surrounded by many samples of

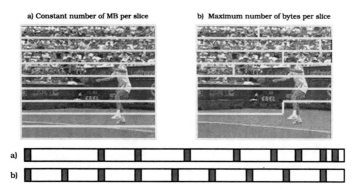

FIGURE 2.11:   Different packetization modes: (a) constant number of MBs per slice with variable number of bytes per slices and (b) maximum number of bytes per slice with variable number of MBs per slice.

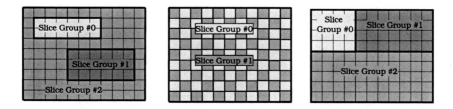

FIGURE 2.12:   Specific MB allocation maps: foreground slice groups with one left-over background slice group, checkerboard-like pattern with two slice groups, and subpictures within a picture.

correctly decoded slices. This is discussed in the following section. For dispersed MB allocation typically and most efficiently checkerboard patterns are used, if no specific area of the video is treated with higher priority.

Video data units may also be packetized on a lower transport layer, for example, within RTP [59], by the use of aggregation packets, with which several data units are collected into a single transport packet, or by the use of fragmentation units, that is, a single data unit is distributed over several transport packets.

2.4.3 Error Concealment

With the detection of a lost data unit at the receiver, the decoder conceals the lost image area. Error concealment is a *nonnormative* feature in any video decoder, and a large number of techniques have been proposed that span a wide range of performance and complexity. The basic idea is that the decoder should generate a representation for the lost area that matches perceptually as close as possible to the lost information without knowing the lost information itself, within a manageable complexity. These techniques are based on *best effort*, with no guarantee of an optimal solution. Since the concealed version of the decoded image will still differ from its corresponding version at the encoding end, error propagation will still occur in the following decoded images until the reference frames are synchronized once again at the encoder and the decoder. This subject will be addressed in detail in Section 2.5.4.

Most popular techniques in this regard are based on a few common assumptions:

- Continuity of image content in spatial domain; natural scene content typically consists of smooth texture.
- Temporal continuity; smooth object motion is more common compared to abrupt scene changes and collocated regions in image tend to have similar motion displacement.

Such techniques exploit the correctly received information of the surrounding area in the spatial and temporal domains to conceal the lost regions. Here we mainly focus on the techniques that conceal each lost MB individually and do not modify the correctly received data.

To simplify the discussion in this section and unless specified otherwise, "data loss" refers to the case that *all* the related information of one or several MBs is lost, for example, MB mode, transformed residual coefficients, and MVs (for the case of inter-coded MBs). This assumption is quite practical as typically a corrupted packet will be detected and discarded before the video decoder.

There exists an exhaustive amount of literature proposing different error concealment techniques. However, only a few simple schemes are commonly used in practical applications. We will put emphasis on error concealment with some practical relevance, but provide reference to other important error concealment methods. In general, error concealment needs to be assessed in terms of performance and complexity.

Spatial Error Concealment

The spatial error concealment technique is based on the assumption of continuity of natural scene content in space. This method generally uses pixel values of surrounding available MBs in the same frame as shown in Figure 2.13. Availability refers to MBs that either have been received correctly or have already been concealed. We consider the case of loss of a 16×16 MB. The most common way of determining the pixel values in a lost MB is by using a weighted sum of the closest boundary pixels of available MBs, with the weights being inversely related to the

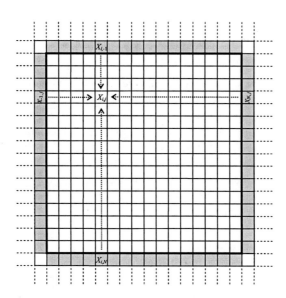

FIGURE 2.13:   Pixels used for spatial error concealment (shaded pixels) of a lost MB (thick frame), $M = N = 16$.

distance between the pixel to be concealed and the boundary pixel. For example, at a pixel position i, j in Figure 2.13, an estimate $\hat{X}_{i,j}$ of the lost pixel $X_{i,j}$ is

$$\hat{X}_{i,j} = \alpha\{\beta X_{i,-1} + (1 - \beta)X_{i,16}\} + (1 - \alpha)\{\gamma X_{-1,j} + (1 - \gamma)X_{16,j}\}. \quad (2.1)$$

Here in this equation, α, β, and γ are weighing factors that will determine the relative impact of pixel values of vertical versus horizontal, upper versus lower, and left versus right neighbors, respectively. The top-left pixel of the lost MB is considered as origin. As discussed earlier, the weighing factors are set according to the inverse of the distances from the pixel being estimated. This technique as proposed in [33] is widely used in practice because of its simplicity and low complexity. Since this technique works on the assumption of continuity in spatial domain, discontinuity is avoided in concealed regions of the image. Obviously, this technique will result in blurred reconstruction of the lost region, since natural scene content is not perfectly continuous and lost details will not be recovered. Typically the spatial error concealment technique is never used alone in applications, rather it is combined with other techniques, as discussed in the following sections. It is worthwhile to note that since this technique heavily relies on the availability of horizontal and vertical neighbor pixels, decoders applying this technique can benefit from the application of FMO; for example, by the use of a checkerboard-like pattern.

More sophisticated methods with higher complexity have been proposed in the literature. These methods target to recover some of the lost texture. Some of them are listed in the following.

- In [66], a spatial error concealment technique is proposed that is based on an a priori assumption of continuity of *geometric structure* across the lost region. The available neighboring pixels are used to extract the local geometric structure, which is characterized by a bimodal distribution. Missing pixels are reconstructed by the extracted geometric information.
- Projection onto convex sets in the frequency domain is proposed in [47]. In this method each constraint about the unknown area is formulated as a convex set, and a possible solution is iteratively projected onto each convex set to obtain a refined solution.

Temporal Error Concealment

Temporal error concealment relies on the continuity of a video sequence in time. This technique uses the temporally neighboring areas to conceal lost regions.

In the simplest form of this technique, known as the Previous Frame Concealment (PFC), the spatially corresponding data of the lost MB in the previous frame is copied to the current frame. If the scene has little motion, PFC performs quite well. However, as soon as the region to be concealed is displaced from the corresponding region in the preceding frame, this technique will, in general, result in significant artifacts in the displayed image. However, due to its simplicity, this technique is widely used, especially in decoders with limited processing power.

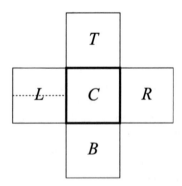

FIGURE 2.14:   Neighboring available MBs (T, R, B, and L) used for temporal error concealment of a lost MB C. MB L is encoded in 16×8 inter mode, and the average of its two MVs is used as a candidate.

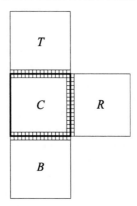

FIGURE 2.15: Boundary pixels of MB C used for the boundary-matching criteria.

A refinement of PFC attempts to reconstruct the image by making an estimate of the lost motion vector. For example, with the assumption of a uniform motion field in the collocated image areas, motion vectors of the neighboring blocks are good candidates to be used as displacement vectors to conceal the lost region. Good candidate MVs for this technique are the MVs of available horizontal and vertical inter-coded neighbor MBs. If a neighboring MB is encoded in an inter mode other than the inter 16×16 mode, one approach is to use the average of the MVs of all the blocks on the boundary of the lost MB. In general, more than one option for the application of displacement vectors exists; for example, using the horizontal neighbor, the vertical neighbor, the zero displacement vector, etc. To select one of the many candidates, a boundary-matching-based technique can, for example, be applied (Figure 2.15). In this case, from the set of all candidate MVs **S**, the MV $\hat{v}$ for temporal error concealment is selected according to

$$\varepsilon_T(v_i) = \sum_{m=0}^{15} \left(X_{x+m,y}(v_i) - X_{x+m,y-1} \right)^2,$$

$$\varepsilon_R(v_i) = \sum_{n=0}^{15} \left(X_{x+15,y+n}(v_i) - X_{x+16,y+n} \right)^2,$$

$$\varepsilon_B(v_i) = \sum_{m=0}^{15} \left(X_{x+m,y+15}(v_i) - X_{x+m,y+16} \right)^2,$$

$$\hat{v} = \arg\min_{v_i \in \mathbf{S}} \left(\varepsilon_T(v_i) + \varepsilon_R(v_i) + \varepsilon_B(v_i) \right). \tag{2.2}$$

Here, for each motion vector $v_i \in \mathbf{S}$, errors ε_T, ε_R, and ε_B are calculated for top, right, and bottom edges, respectively. The first term of error functions is the pixel recovered from the reference frame using the selected motion vector v_i, while the second element is an available boundary pixel of a neighboring MB. The upper-left pixel of the lost MB has a pixel offset x, y. Finally, the vector that results in minimum overall error is selected, since this vector gives a block that possibly fits best in the lost area. Obviously, it is possible that none of the candidate vectors are suitable and in such a case temporal error concealment results in fairly noticeable discontinuity artifacts in the concealed regions.

Several variants and refinements of the temporal error concealment technique have been proposed, usually with some better performance at the expense of sometimes significantly higher complexity. A nonexhaustive list is provided in the following:

- In [4], *overlapped block motion compensation* is proposed. In this case an average of three 16×16 pixel regions is used to conceal the missing MB. One of these regions is the 16×16 pixel data used to conceal the lost MB by the process described earlier, the second and third regions are retrieved from the previous frame by using the motion vectors of horizontal and vertical neighbor MBs, respectively. These three regions are averaged to get the final 16×16 data used for concealment. Averaging in this way can reduce artifacts in the concealed regions.

- In [2], it is proposed to use the median motion vector of the neighboring blocks for temporal concealment. However, the benefits of this technique have been relativized in, for example, [57].

- In [57], Sum of Absolute Differences (SAD) is used instead of Sum of Squared Differences (SSD) for the boundary-matching technique. This results in reduced computational complexity.

- A simpler variant is used in practice [3]: It is proposed to only apply the motion vector of top MB, if available, otherwise zero MV is used (i.e., PFC is used if top MB is not inter coded or is lost as well).

- In [30], a *multihypothesis* error concealment is proposed. This technique makes use of the multiple reference frames available in an H.264/AVC decoder for temporal error concealment. The erroneous block is compensated by a weighted average of correctly received blocks in more than one previous frame. The weighting coefficient used for different blocks can be determined adaptively.

- In [20], the idea presented in [30] is extended. In this proposal, temporal error concealment is used exclusively. However, two variants of temporal error concealment are available: the low-complexity concealment technique governed by (2.2) and the multihypothesis temporal error concealment. The decision as to which technique is used is based on the temporal activity (SAD) in the neighboring regions of the damaged block. For low activity, the low-complexity technique is used, while multihypothesis temporal error concealment is used for higher activity.

Also, the adaptive combination of spatial concealment with temporal error concealment is of some practical interest and will therefore be discussed in more detail in the following.

Hybrid Concealment

Neither the application of spatial concealment nor temporal concealment alone can provide satisfactory performance: if only spatial concealment is used, concealed regions usually are significantly blurred. Similarly, if only temporal error concealment is applied, significant discontinuities in the concealed regions can occur, especially if the surrounding area cannot provide any or not sufficiently good motion vectors. Hence to achieve better results, the hybrid temporal–spatial technique might be applied. In this technique, MB mode information of reliable and concealed neighbors can be used to decide whether spatial error concealment or temporal error concealment is more suitable. For intra-coded images only spatial concealment is used. For inter-coded images, temporal error concealment is used only if, for example, in the surrounding area more than half of the available neighbor MBs (shown in Figure 2.14) are inter coded. Otherwise, spatial error concealment is used. This ensures that a sufficient number of candidate MVs are available to estimate the lost motion information. We refer to this error concealment as Adaptive temporal and spatial Error Concealment (AEC) in the following.

Other techniques have been proposed to decide between temporal and spatial concealment mode:

- A simple approach in [57] proposes the use of spatial concealment for intra-coded images and temporal error concealment for all inter-coded images invariably.
- In [48], it is suggested that if the residual data in a correctly received neighboring inter-predicted MB is smaller than a threshold, temporal error concealment should be used.

Miscellaneous Techniques

In addition to the signal-domain MB-based approaches, other techniques have been proposed in the literature, for example,

- Model based or object concealment techniques, as proposed in [5,51], do not assume simple a priori assumptions of continuity as given earlier. These techniques are based on the specific texture properties of video objects, and as such are a suitable option for multiobject video codec, that is, MPEG-4.

An object-specific context-based model is built and this model governs the assumptions used for concealment of that object.

- Frequency-domain concealment techniques [16,29] work by reconstructing the lost transform coefficients by using the available coefficients of the neighboring MBs as well as coefficients of the same MB not affected by the loss. These initial proposals are specifically for DCT transform block of 8×8 coefficients. For example, in [16], based on the assumption of continuity of the transform coefficients, lost coefficients are reconstructed as a linear combination of the available transform coefficients. However, noticeable artifacts are introduced by this technique. As a more realistic consideration, in [29] the constraint of continuity holds only at the boundaries of the lost MB in spatial domain.

- In an extension to the spatial and temporal continuity assumptions, it is proposed in [34] that the frames of video content are modeled as a Markov Random Field (MRF). The lost data is suggested to be recovered based on this model. In [35] the authors proposed a less complex but suboptimal alternative to implement this model for error concealment. For example, for temporal error concealment, only the boundary pixels of the lost MB are predicted based on a MAP estimate, instead of predicting the entire MB. These predicted pixels are used to estimate the best predicted motion vector to be used for temporal error concealment. In [39], the MAP estimate is used to refine an initial estimate obtained from temporal error concealment.

Selected results

A few selected results from various important concealment techniques are presented in Figure 2.16. From left to right, a sample concealed frame when using PFC, spatial, temporal, and AEC is shown. PFC simply replaces the missing information by the information at the same location in the temporally preceding frame. Hence, it shows artifacts in the global motion part of the background as well as

PFC   Spatial only   Temporal only   AEC

FIGURE 2.16: Performance of different error concealment strategies: PFC, spatial concealment only, temporal error concealment only, and AEC.

in the foreground. Spatial error concealment based on weighted pixel averaging smoothes the erroneously decoded image and removes strange block artifacts, but also many details. Temporal error concealment relying on motion vector reconstruction with boundary-matching-based techniques keeps details, but results in strange artifacts in uncovered areas. Finally, AEC—a combination of temporal and spatial error concealment—keeps many details but also avoids strange block artifacts and is therefore very appropriate with feasible complexity. In the remainder of this chapter we will assume exclusively AEC, which reduces to PFC in the case that all MBs of a picture are transmitted in a single packet.

For a further detailed study of error concealment techniques, the reader is referred to [36,52,54,56] and the references therein.

2.4.4 Selected Performance Results for Wireless Test Conditions

To get an insight in error-resilient video coding for 3G mobile communication scenarios, we take a look at a few selected results. The simulated scenario is of a packet-switched conversational application and is specified in detail by 3GPP [8]. This application is characterized by its stringent low-delay and low-complexity requirements, since the processing has to be done in real time on hand-held devices. As a result, the maximum allowed buffering at the encoder is limited to 250 ms and only the first frame is encoded as intra, to limit any delays caused by buffering overheads. A simple random intra MB refresh technique is used, with 5% MBs of every frame coded in intra mode. The most recent frame is used for motion compensation to limit the complexity. With these limitations, we observe the impact of slice size on error resilience of the application. Two channel configurations are compared: one with moderate Radio Link Control (RLC) Packet Data Unit (PDU) loss rate of 0.5% and the other with a higher loss rate of 1.5%. The Radio Access Bearer (RAB) in this test supports transmission of 128 Kbps, with a radio frame size of 320 bytes. Here as an example we use the Quarter Common Intermediate Format (QCIF) sized test sequence *foreman* at 15 frames per second. The encoder is configured to match the maximum throughput of channel while taking into account packetization overheads. The criterion used here as a metric of perceived video quality is PSNR of luma (Y) signal.

Figure 2.17 compares the Y PSNR of the decoded video at a loss rate of 1.5% for two cases: transmitting an entire frame in a slice versus a fixed slice size of 150 bytes. At the given bit rate, a compressed frame has an average size of roughly 1000 bytes. The error-free performance for both cases is also plotted as a reference. Obviously, using a smaller slice size of 150 bytes results in typically lower PSNR in an error-free case because of two reasons: increased packetization overhead and prediction limitations on slice boundaries. However, this configuration outperforms in the case of lossy channel throughout the observed period. A few selected frames are also presented for comparison. The effects of losses already

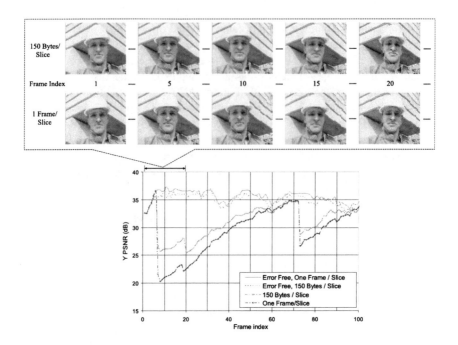

FIGURE 2.17: (Bottom) Plot of Y PSNR with two different slice modes. Results for an error-free case are given as a reference. (Top) A few selected frames for the two slice modes for comparison.

start appearing in the fifth frame. While transmitting one frame per slice results in loss of an entire frame for a lost RLC PDU, the loss affects only a small area of the image for fixed slice size. The spatiotemporal error propagation is much smaller in this case.

Figure 2.18 shows the comparative effects of various slice sizes for different channel loss scenarios. A single point on the curves is obtained by averaging the Y PSNR, denoted as $\overline{PSNR}$, for several channel realizations to achieve higher statistical significance. The error-free curve shows the effects of reduced compression and hence smaller $\overline{PSNR}$ for smaller slice sizes. However, at a loss rate of 0.5%, the drawbacks of using larger slice sizes become obvious. The advantage of using slice sizes smaller than 350 bytes does not sufficiently compensate for their overhead. However, increasing slice size beyond this results in a drop of $\overline{PSNR}$. This is because of a greater portion of a frame affected by a lost RLC

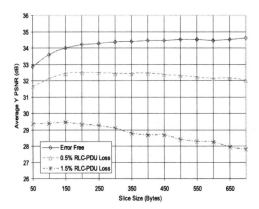

FIGURE 2.18: Plot of $\overline{\text{PSNR}}$ versus slice size with RLC PDU loss rate as a parameter.

PDU. The performance degradation is much more drastic for a loss rate of 1.5%, shown by a significant drop of $\overline{\text{PSNR}}$ for larger slice sizes.

2.5 ERROR MITIGATION

2.5.1 Motivation

As already discussed, error propagation is the major problem when transmitting MCP-coded video over lossy channels. Therefore, if the encoder is aware that the channel will likely be lossy or even knows that the decoder has experienced the loss of certain data units, it should change its encoding behavior, despite sacrificing some compression efficiency. To illustrate this, selected frames for different encoding strategies when transmitting over channels with the same bit rate and error rate constraints are shown in Figure 2.19. The first line, referred to as (a), shows the case where no specific error-resilience tools are applied. The already elaborated problem of error propagation is obvious in later frames. For the sequence in the second line, referred to as (b), the same bit rate and error statistics are applied, but the encoder chooses to select intra-coded MBs in a suitable way. It can be observed that the error propagation is less of an issue but that some residual artifacts are still visible. In addition, the error-free video has lower quality as its compression efficiency is reduced due to the increased amount of intracoding under an identical bit rate constraint. Error propagation can be completely avoided if interactive error control is used, as shown in the third row, labeled with (c). However, in this case also, compression efficiency is sacrificed, especially if necessary feedback of the decoder state is delayed. Details on the appropriate selection of

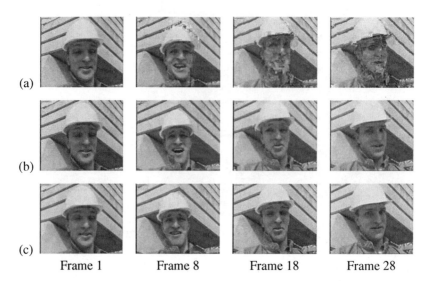

Frame 1   Frame 8   Frame 18   Frame 28

FIGURE 2.19: Selected frames of a decoded video sequence for a packet lossy channel with same bit rate and error constraints: (a) no error robustness, (b) adaptive intra updates, and (c) interactive error control.

MB modes in error-prone environments, especially taking into account the trade-off between quantization distortion and reduced error propagation, are discussed in the following.

2.5.2 Operational Encoder Control

The tools for increased error resilience in *hybrid* video coding, in particular those to limit error propagation, do not significantly differ from the ones used for compression efficiency. Features such as multiframe prediction or intra coding of individual MBs are not primarily error-resilience tools. They are mainly used to increase coding efficiency in error-free environments, although design freedom is left to the video encoder. The encoder implementation is responsible for appropriate selection of one of the many different encoding parameters, the so-called *operational coder control*. Thereby, the encoder must take into account constraints imposed by the application in terms of bit rate, encoding and transmission delay, complexity, and buffer size. When a standard decoder is used, such as an H.264/AVC compliant decoder, the encoding parameters should be selected by the encoder such that good rate–distortion performance is achieved. Since the encoder is limited by the syntax of the standard, this problem is referred to as *syntax-constrained rate–distortion optimization* [28]. In case of H.264/AVC, for example, the encoder must appropriately select parameters such as motion vectors, MB modes, quantization parameters, reference frames, or spatial and temporal resolution, as shown in Figure 2.20. This also means that bad decisions at the encoder can lead to poor results in coding efficiency, error resilience, or both. For compression efficiency, operational encoder control based on Lagrangian multiplier techniques has been proposed. The distortion d_{b,m_b} usually (at least in the H.264/AVC test model) reflects the SSD between the original MB s_b and the reconstructed version of the MB $\tilde{s}_{b,m}$ if coded with option m, that is,

$$d_{b,m} = \sum_i |s_{b,i} - \tilde{s}_{b,m,i}|^2, \qquad (2.3)$$

and the rate $r_{b,m}$ is defined by the number of bits necessary to code MB b with option m. Finally, the coding mode is selected for MB b as

$$\forall_b \quad m^*_b = \arg \min_{m \in \mathcal{O}} (d_{b,m} + \lambda_{\mathcal{O}} r_{b,m}), \qquad (2.4)$$

whereby $\mathcal{O}$ defines the set of selectable options, for example, MB modes. For the Lagrangian parameter $\lambda_{\mathcal{O}}$ it is proposed in [46] and [62] that if the SSD is applied as a distortion measure, then $\lambda_{\mathcal{O}}$ should be directly proportional to the square of the step size Δ of a uniform quantizer applied. The procedure in (2.4) can be applied to select motion vectors, reference frames, and MB modes. However, it is

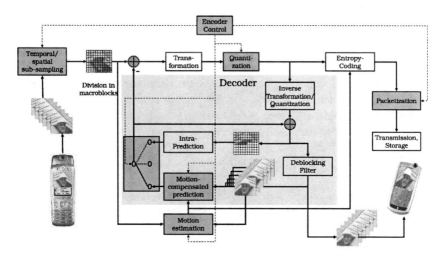

FIGURE 2.20: H.264/AVC video encoder with selectable encoding parameters highlighted.

obviously contradictory if the same decision procedure is applied to obtain good selections for compression efficiency and error resilience. This will be further discussed in the following.

2.5.3 Adaptive Intra Updates

In the presence of errors it has long been recognized that the introduction of more frequent nonpredictively coded image parts is of major importance. In early work on this subject, for example, [15,25,68], it has been proposed to introduce intra-coded MBs, regularly, randomly, or preferably in a certain pseudo-random update pattern. In addition, sequence characteristics and bit rate influence the appropriate percentage of intra updates.

Recognizing this, it has been proposed [67,7,61] to modify the selection of the coding modes according to (2.4) to take into account the influence of the lossy channel. When encoding MB b with a certain coding mode m_b, it is suggested to replace the encoding distortion $d_{b,m}$ by the decoder distortion

$$\tilde{d}_{b,m}(\mathcal{C}_t) \triangleq \left\| \mathbf{s}_{b,t} - \hat{\mathbf{s}}_{b,t}(\mathcal{C}_t, m) \right\|^2, \tag{2.5}$$

which obviously depends on the reconstructed pixel values $\hat{s}_t(\mathcal{C}_t, m)$ and therefore also on the channel behavior $\mathcal{C}_t$ and the selected coding mode m.

In general, the channel behavior is not deterministic and the channel realization $\mathcal{C}$, observed by the decoder, is unknown to the encoder. Thus it is not possible to directly determine the decoder distortion (2.5) at the encoder. However, we can assume that the encoder has at least some knowledge of the statistics of the random channel behavior, denoted as $\hat{\mathcal{C}}_t$. In a Real-Time Transport Protocol (RTP) [37] environment, the Real-Time Control Protocol (RTCP), for example, can use a feedback channel to send receiver reports on the experienced loss and delays statistics, which allow the encoder to incorporate these statistics into the encoding process. Assume that the statistics on the loss process are perfectly known to encoder, that is, $\mathcal{B}(\mathcal{C}_t) = \hat{\mathcal{C}}_t$, and assume that the loss process is stationary. Then, the encoder is able to compute the expected distortion

$$\overline{d}_{b,m} \triangleq \mathbb{E}_{\hat{\mathcal{C}}_t}\left\{ \tilde{d}_{b,m}(\hat{\mathcal{C}}_t) \right\} = \mathbb{E}_{\hat{\mathcal{C}}_t}\left\{ \left\| \mathbf{s}_{b,t} - \hat{\mathbf{s}}_{b,t}(\hat{\mathcal{C}}_t, m) \right\|^2 \right\}. \tag{2.6}$$

A similar procedure can be applied to decisions on reference frames and motion vectors. The selection of motion vectors based on the expected distortion has, for example, been proposed in [65]. The estimation of the squared expected pixel distortion in packet loss environment has been addressed in several contributions. For example, in [7,23], and [61], methods used to estimate the distortion introduced due to transmission errors and the resulting error propagation have been proposed. In all these proposals the quantization noise and the distortion introduced by the transmission errors (the so-called drift noise) are linearly combined. Since the encoder needs to keep track of an estimated pixel distortion, additional complexity and memory are required in the encoder. The most recognized method, the so-called Recursive Optimal per-Pixel Estimate (ROPE) algorithm [67], however, provides an accurate estimation for baseline H.263 and MPEG-4 simple profile-like algorithms, using simple temporal error concealment, by keeping track of the first and second moment of the decoded pixel value $\tilde{s}(\mathcal{C}_t)$, namely $\mathbb{E}\{\tilde{s}(\mathcal{C}_t)\}$ and $\mathbb{E}\{\tilde{s}^2(\mathcal{C}_t)\}$, respectively.

A powerful yet complex method has been proposed in [44] by applying a Monte Carlo–like method. An estimate of the decoder distortion $\overline{d}_{b,m}$ in (2.6) is obtained as

$$\overline{d}_{b,m}^{(N_C)} \triangleq \frac{1}{N_C} \sum_{n=1}^{N_C} \tilde{d}_{b,m}(\mathcal{C}_{n,t}) = \frac{1}{N_C} \sum_{n=1}^{N_C} \left\| s_{b,t} - \hat{s}_{b,t}(\mathcal{C}_{n,t}, m) \right\|^p, \qquad (2.7)$$

with $\mathcal{C}_{n,t}, n = 1, \ldots, N_C$, representing N_C independent realizations of the random channel $\hat{\mathcal{C}}_t$, and estimate of the loss probability at the receiver represented as p. An interpretation of (2.7) leads to a simple solution to estimate the expected pixel distortion $\overline{d}_{b,m}$. For more details we refer to [44]. To obtain an estimate of the loss probability p at the receiver, the feedback channel can be used in practical systems.

2.5.4 Interactive Error Control

The availability of a feedback channel, especially for conversational applications, has led to different standardization and research activities in recent years to include this feedback in the video encoding process. Assume that, in contrast to the previous scenario where only the statistics of the channel process $\hat{\mathcal{C}}$ are known to the encoder, in the case of timely feedback we can even assume that a δ-frame delayed version $\mathcal{C}_{t-\delta}$ of the loss process experienced at the receiver is known at the encoder. This characteristic can be conveyed from the decoder to the encoder by sending acknowledgment for correctly received data units, negative acknowledgment messages for missing slices, or both types of messages.

In less time-critical applications, such as streaming or downloading, the encoder could obviously decide to retransmit lost data units in case it has stored a backup of the data unit at the transmitter. However, in low-delay applications the retransmitted data units, especially in end-to-end connections, would in general arrive too late to be useful at the decoder. In case of online encoding, the observed and possibly delayed receiver channel realization, $\mathcal{C}_{t-\delta}$, can still be useful to the encoder, although the erroneous frame has already been decoded and concealed at the decoder. The basic goal of these approaches is to reduce, limit, or even completely avoid error propagation by integrating the decoder state information into the encoding process.

The exploitation of the observed channel at the encoder has been introduced in [41] and [12] under the acronym *Error Tracking* for standards such as MPEG-2, H.261 or H.263 version 1, but has been limited by the reduced syntax capabilities of these video standards. When receiving the information that a certain data unit—typically including the coded representation of several or all MBs of a certain frame $s_{t-\delta}$—has not been received correctly at the decoder, the encoder attempts to track the error to obtain an estimate of the decoded frame $\hat{s}_{t-1}$ serving as reference for the frame to be encoded, s_t. Appropriate actions after having tracked the error are discussed in [12,41,53,56,61]. However, all these concepts have in common that error propagation in frame $\hat{s}_t$ is only removed if frames $\hat{s}_{t-\delta+1}, \ldots, \hat{s}_{t-1}$ have been received at the decoder without any error.

Nevertheless, this promising performance when exploiting decoder state information at the encoder has been recognized by standardization bodies, and the problem of continuing error propagation has been addressed by extending the syntax of existing standards. In MPEG-4 [17, version 2] a tool to stop temporal error propagation has been introduced under the acronym New Prediction (NEW-PRED) [10,27,50]. Similarly, in H.263+ Annex N [18, Annex N] RPS for each Group-of-Blocks (GOB) is specified. If combined with slice structured mode as specified in H.263+ Annex K [18, Annex K], as well as Independent Segment Decoding (ISD) as specified in H.263+ Annex R [18, Annex R], the same NEW-PRED techniques can be applied within the H.263 codec family.

NEWPRED relies on the availability of timely feedback, online encoding, and the possibility that the encoder can choose other reference frames than the temporally preceding ones. In addition, it allows one to completely eliminate error propagation in frame $\hat{s}_t$ even if additional errors have occurred for the transmission of frames $\hat{s}_{t-\delta+1}, \ldots, \hat{s}_{t-1}$. Different encoder operation modes have been discussed in the literature [10], which can basically be distinguished in a mode where only acknowledged areas are used for reference and another mode, in which the operation is only altered when information is received that the decoder is missing some data units.

In H.263++ Annex U [18, Annex U], NEWPRED was introduced exclusively for the purpose of improving error resilience. In H.264/AVC, the extended syntax allowing selection of reference frames on an MB or even sub-MB basis has a dual impact: enhanced compression efficiency and, at the same time, ease of incorporating methods for limiting error propagation [61]. We will in the following introduce conceptual operation modes when combining decoder state information in the encoding process.

Therefore, we assume that at the encoder each generated data unit $\mathcal{P}_i$ is assigned a decoder state $\mathcal{C}_{\text{enc},i} \in \{\text{ACK}, \text{NAK}, \text{OAK}\}$, whereby $\mathcal{C}_{\text{enc},i} = \text{ACK}$ reflects that data unit $\mathcal{P}_i$ is known to be correctly received at the decoder, $\mathcal{C}_{\text{enc},i} = \text{NAK}$ reflects that data unit $\mathcal{P}_i$ is known to be missing at the decoder, and

$C_{enc,i} = \text{OAK}$ reflects that for data unit P_i the acknowledgment message is still outstanding and it is not known whether this data unit will be received correctly.

With feedback messages conveying the observed channel state at the receiver, that is, $B(C_t) = C_t$, and a back channel that delays the back channel messages by δ frames, we assume in the remainder that for the encoding of s_t, the encoder is aware of the following information:

$$C_{enc,i} = \begin{cases} \text{ACK} & \text{if } \tau_{\text{PTS},i} \leq \tau_{s,t-\delta} \text{ and } C_i = 1, \\ \text{NAK} & \text{if } \tau_{\text{PTS},i} \leq \tau_{s,t-\delta} \text{ and } C_i = 0, \\ \text{OAK} & \text{if } \tau_{\text{PTS},i} \geq \tau_{s,t-\delta}, \end{cases} \qquad (2.8)$$

where $\tau_{\text{PTS},i}$ is the Presentation Time Stamp (PTS) of P_i and $\tau_{s,t-\delta}$ is the sampling time of $s_{t-\delta}$.

This information about the decoder state $C_{enc,i}$ can be integrated in a modified rate–distortion optimized operational encoder control similar to what has been discussed in Subsection 2.5.2. In this case the MB mode m_b^* is selected from a modified set of options, $\hat{O}$, with a modified distortion $\hat{d}_{b,m}$ for each selected option m as

$$\forall_b \quad m_b^* = \arg \min_{m \in \hat{O}} (\hat{d}_{b,m} + \lambda_{\hat{O}} r_{b,m}). \qquad (2.9)$$

In the following we distinguish four different operation modes, which differ only by the set of coding options available to the encoder in the encoding process, $\hat{O}$, as well as the applied distortion metric, $\hat{d}_{b,m}$. The encoder's reaction to delayed positive acknowledgment (ACK) and negative acknowledgment (NAK) messages is shown in Figure 2.21, assuming that frame d is lost and the feedback delay is $\delta = 2$ frames for three different feedback modes.

Feedback Mode 1: Acknowledged Reference Area Only

Figure 2.21a shows this operation mode: Only the decoded representation of data units P_i that have been positively acknowledged at the encoder, that is, $C_{enc,i} = \text{ACK}$, are allowed to be referenced in the encoding process. In the context of operational encoder control, this is formalized by applying the encoding distortion in (2.9), that is, $\hat{d}_{b,m} = d_{b,m}$, as well as the set of encoding options that is restricted to acknowledged areas only, that is, $\hat{O} = O_{\text{ACK},t}$. Note that the restricted option set $O_{\text{ACK},t}$ depends on the frame to be encoded and is applied to the motion estimation and reference frame selection process. Obviously, if no reference area is available, the option set is restricted to intra modes only, or if no satisfying match is found in the accessible reference area, intra coding is applied. With this mode in use, an error might still be visible in the presentation of a single frame; however, error propagation and reference frame mismatch are completely avoided.

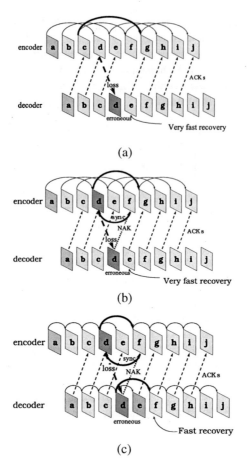

FIGURE 2.21:   Operation of different feedback modes. (a) Feedback Mode 1. (b) Feedback Mode 2. (c) Feedback Mode 3.

Figure 2.22a shows the performance in terms of average Peak Signal-to-Noise Ratio (PSNR), denoted by $\overline{\text{PSNR}}$, for feedback mode 1 with different feedback delays δ compared to the channel-adaptive mode selection scheme for *foreman*, error pattern 10 (as given in test conditions specified in [58]), AEC, and $N_{\text{MB/DU}} = 33$. The number of reference frames is $N_{\text{ref}} = 5$, except for $\delta = 8$ with $N_{\text{ref}} = 10$. The results show that for any delay this system with feedback outperforms the best system without any feedback. For small delays, the gains are significant and for the same average PSNR the bit rate is less than 50% compared to the forward-only mode. With increasing delay the gains are reduced, but compared with the

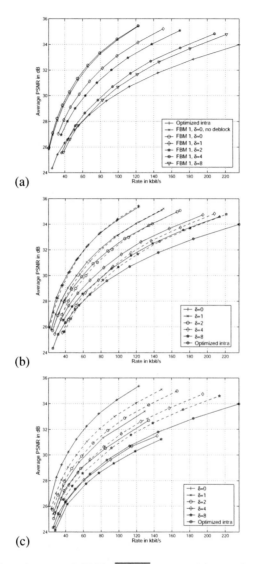

(a)

(b)

(c)

FIGURE 2.22: Average PSNR ($\overline{\text{PSNR}}$) versus bit rate for different feed-back modes for sequence *foreman*. (a) Average PSNR ($\overline{\text{PSNR}}$) versus bit rate for Feedback Mode 1. (b) Average PSNR ($\overline{\text{PSNR}}$) versus bit rate for Feedback Mode 2 (solid lines), Feedback mode 1 replotted for compari-son (dashed lines). (c) Average PSNR ($\overline{\text{PSNR}}$) versus bit rate for Feedback Mode 3 (solid lines), Feedback mode 2 replotted for comparison (dashed lines).

highly complex mode decision without feedback, this method is still very attractive. Obviously, these high delay results are strongly sequence dependent but for other sequences similar results have been verified.

Feedback Mode 2: Synchronized Reference Frames

Feedback mode 2 as shown in Figure 2.21b differs from mode 1 in that not only positively acknowledged data units but also a concealed version of data units with decoder state $C_{\text{enc},i} = \text{NAK}$ are allowed to be referenced. This is formalized by applying the encoding distortion in (2.9), that is, $\hat{d}_{b,m} = d_{b,m}$, but the restricted reference area and the option set in this case also include concealed image parts, $\hat{O} = O_{\text{NAK},t} \supseteq O_{\text{ACK},t}$. The critical aspect when operating in this mode results from the fact that for the reference frames to be synchronized the encoder must apply exactly the same error concealment as the decoder.

Figure 2.22b shows the performance in terms of average PSNR, denoted as $\overline{\text{PSNR}}$, for feedback mode 2 with different feedback delays δ compared to the curves in Figure 2.22a for the same parameters. The results for feedback mode 2 show similar results as for feedback mode 1. However, the advantage of feedback mode 2 can be seen in two cases: for low bit rates and for delays $\delta < N_{\text{ref}} - 1$. This is so because referencing concealed areas is preferred over intra coding by the rate–distortion optimization. For higher bit rates this advantage vanishes as the intra mode is preferred anyways over the selection of "bad" reference areas. For delay $\delta = 4$ with $N_{\text{ref}} = 5$, that is, only a single reference frame is available at the encoder, the gains of feedback mode 2 are more obvious, since for feedback mode 1, in case of a lost slice, the encoder basically is forced to use intra coding.

Feedback Mode 3: Regular Prediction with Limited Error Propagation

Feedback modes 1 and 2 are mainly suitable in cases of higher loss rates. If the loss rates are low or negligible, the performance is significantly degraded by the longer prediction chains due to the feedback delay. Therefore, in feedback mode 3 as shown in Figure 2.21c it is proposed to only alter the prediction in the encoder in case of the reception of a NAK. Again, the encoding distortion in (2.9) is applied, that is, $\hat{d}_{b,m} = d_{b,m}$, but the reference area and the option set in this case are altered only in case of receiving a NAK to already acknowledged image parts, that is, $\hat{O} = O'_{\text{ACK},t}$, or, as applied in our case to acknowledged and concealed image parts, $\hat{O} = O'_{\text{NAK},t}$. Areas that are possibly corrupted by error propagation are also excluded as references. This mode obviously performs well in cases of lower error rates. However, for higher error rates error propagation still occurs quite frequently.

Figure 2.22c shows the performance in terms of average PSNR for feedback mode 3 compared to channel-adaptive mode selection and feedback mode 2, again for the same parameters as in Figure 2.22a. Note that feedback mode 2 and feedback mode 3 are identical for zero feedback delay. However, surprisingly, for increasing delay, feedback mode 3 performs significantly worse than feedback mode 2. The error propagation, though only present for at maximum $\delta - 1$ frames, degrades the overall quality much more significantly; the gain in compression efficiency cannot compensate the distortion due to packet losses. Obviously, the performance depends on the sequence characteristics and especially on the loss rate. For lower rates it is expected (and shown later) that the differences between feedback modes 2 and 3 are less significant, but in general feedback mode 2 is also preferable over feedback mode 3 from the subjective performance.

Feedback Mode 4: Unrestricted Reference Areas with Expected Distortion Update

For completeness we present an even more powerful feedback mode, which extends feedback mode 3 to address error propagation with more intra updates. We also discuss its drawbacks and justify why it is hardly used. In [61] and [67] techniques have been proposed that combine the error-resilient mode selection with available decoder state information in the encoder. In this case the set of encoding options is not altered, that is, $\hat{\mathcal{O}} = \mathcal{O}$, but only the computation of the distortion is altered. Only for all data units with outstanding acknowledgment at the encoder, that is, $\mathcal{C}_{\text{enc},i} = \text{OAK}$, is the randomness of the observed channel state considered; for all other data units the observed channel state is no longer random. The expected distortion in this case is computed as

$$\hat{d}_{b,m} = \begin{cases} \mathbb{E}_{\{\hat{\mathcal{C}}_i\}}\{\tilde{d}_{b,m}(\hat{\mathcal{C}}_i)\} & \text{if } \mathcal{C}_{\text{enc},i} = \text{OAK}, \\ \mathbb{E}_{\{\mathcal{C}_i\}}\{\tilde{d}_{b,m}(\mathcal{C}_i)\} & \text{if } \mathcal{C}_{\text{enc},i} \neq \text{OAK}. \end{cases} \tag{2.10}$$

Compared to feedback modes 1 and 2, this method is especially beneficial if the feedback is significantly delayed. Compared to feedback mode 3, it reduces the unsatisfying performance in case of error propagation. Note that for $\delta \to \infty$ this mode turns into the mode selection without any feedback at all, and for $\delta = 0$ this mode is identical to feedback mode 2 and feedback mode 3. However, whenever the encoder gets information on the state of a certain data unit at the decoder, the statistics in the encoder have to be recomputed. Thus, the computational, storage, and implementation complexities are significantly increased [67].

2.5.5 Selected Performance Results for Internet Test Conditions

To verify the conclusions of the previous subsection at least partly for other error rates, bit rates, and test sequences we have evaluated selected error-resilience

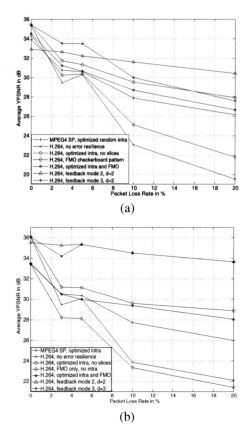

(a)

(b)

FIGURE 2.23:   Average PSNR ($\overline{\text{PSNR}}$) over packet error rate for *fore-man*, QCIF, with frame rate $f_s = 7.5$ fps and *paris*, CIF. MPEG-4 with optimized random intra updates is compared to H.264 in various configurations. (a) *foreman*, 64 kbit/s, (b) *paris*, 384 kbit/s.

tools as presented previously. Test cases as suggested in [58] have been used. That is, we evaluate performance on four IP packet loss traces with 3, 5, 10, and 20% average loss rates, respectively. Note that the 5% trace is especially bursty. Also, the Common Intermediate Format (CIF) test sequence *paris* encoded at frame rate $f_s = 15$ frames per second (fps) is evaluated. Figure 2.23 shows $\overline{\text{PSNR}}$ as a function of packet loss rate[1] for *foreman* at 64 kbit/s and *paris* at 384 kbit/s.

---

[1] The labels on the abscissa specify the corresponding error pattern rather than random packet loss rates. Note that the 5% error file is burstier than the others, resulting in somewhat unexpected results.

Various error-resilience tools in H.264/AVC are compared to the MPEG-4 simple profile with an optimized ratio of random intra updates. The results are consistent for both sequences. The significance of the difference between different schemes is mainly explained by different sequence characteristics. It is observed that for error-free transmission abandoning any error-resilience tools obviously results in the best performance. The performance gains in terms of compression efficiency of H.264 over the MPEG-4 simple profile is also visible. If feedback mode 2 is used, in our case with feedback delay $\delta = 2$, we have to sacrifice some compression efficiency as the prediction signal is in general worse as it is further in the past. This does not apply for feedback mode 3. However, the performance in an error-free transmission environment is less relevant for our investigations. With increasing loss rates it is obvious that any kind of error-resilience feature in general improves the performance. Thereby, it is again recognized that reducing error propagation is much more important than packetization modes such as FMO, in our case with a checkerboard pattern and two packets per frame. Again, with the average PSNR as the measure of interest, the best performance without any feedback is obtained using channel-adapted rate–distortion-optimized mode selection according to (2.4) with each packet containing an entire source frame. Additional significant performance improvements can be achieved by the introduction of decoder feedback information. Thereby, for lower error rates feedback mode 3 outperforms feedback mode 2, but feedback mode 2 provides very consistent results over a large variety of error rates.

From these results, as well as subjective observations, it can be concluded that avoiding error propagation is basically the most important issue in error-prone video transmission. If no feedback is available, an increased percentage of intra MBs, selected by channel-adapted optimization schemes, performs best. Whenever feedback is available, it is suggested that interactive error control be applied. For short delays or low error rates, it is suggested to modify the prediction only in case of the reception of NACK message. In all other cases, it is suggested to reference only those areas for which the encoder is sure that the decoder has exactly the same reference area.

2.6 SUMMARY AND FURTHER READING

This chapter provides some background when transmitting MCP-coded standard-compliant video over error-prone channels. It is important to understand that video can benefit significantly if the transmitter can be sure that the video will be delivered reliably. Typically, the introduction of error-resilience tools in the video coding layer is very costly in terms of compression efficiency. The overhead is in general much better spent in lower layers of the protocol stack. Nevertheless there exist applications in which errors are inevitable. If the video encoder is not aware of distortions on the transmission link, this in general leads to dramatic quality degradations due to instantaneous errors as well as spatial–temporal error propagation. Whereas the effect of instantaneous errors can be decreased by the use of specific packetization modes, the usually more severe effect of error propagation can be reduced by the application of more frequent intra information, interactive error control, or a combination of both. Preferably, for good overall performance, the selection of error-resilience tools is integrated in rate–distortion-optimized mode selection whereby the channel characteristics should be taken into account in this optimization. In general, standard-compliant decoders such as H.264/AVC can effectively operate even in harsh transmission environments if the encoder is appropriately designed for the transmission conditions and application constraints and the decoder includes some form of appropriate error concealment.

Additional literature on different subjects for error-resilient video transmission is plentiful; some work has already been discussed. In case of detailed interest in different subjects the reader is first of all encouraged to cover the remaining chapters of this book. Furthermore, magazines as well as journals have published special issues that deal exclusively with error-resilient video transmission, for example, [1,26,49,55,63], which provide a good starting point to dive into deep waters of error-resilient video transmission. Enjoy it!

REFERENCES

[1] J. Apostolopoulos. Reliable video communication over lossy packet networks using multiple state encoding and path diversity. In *Proceedings SPIE Visual Communications and Image Processing (VCIP)*, volume 4310, pages 392–409, San Jose(CA), USA, January 2001.

[2] E. Asbun and E. J. Delp. Real-time error concealment in compressed digital video streams. In *Proceedings Picture Coding Symposium*, Portland, Oregon, April 1999.

[3] G. Bjøntegaard. Definition of an error concealment model TCON. Doc. ITU-T/SG15/LBC-95-186, ITU-T, Boston, USA, June 1995.

[4] M.-J. Chen, L.-G. Chen, and R.-M. Weng. Error concealment of lost motion vectors with overlapped motion compensation. *IEEE Trans. on Circuits Syst. Video Technol.*, 7(3):560–563, June 1997.

[5] T. P.-C. Chen and T. Chen. Second-generation error concealment for video transport over error prone channels. In *Proceedings IEEE International Conference on Image Processing*, Rochester(NY), USA, September 2002.

[6] P. A. Chou and Z. Miao. Rate-distortion optimized streaming of packetized media. *IEEE Transactions on Multimedia*, 8(2):390–404, April 2006.

[7] G. Cote, S. Shirani, and F. Kossentini. Optimal mode selection and synchronization for robust video communications over error-prone networks. *IEEE Journal on Selected Areas in Communications*, 18(6):952–965, June 2000.

[8] Video adhoc group database for video codec evaluation. Technical Report S4-050789, 3GPP SA4 Video Adhoc Group, September 2005.

[9] A. Eleftheriadis, M. R. Civanlar, and O. Shapiro. Multipoint videoconferencing with scalable video. *Journal of Zhejiang University Science*, 7(5):696–706, May 2006.

[10] S. Fukunaga, T. Nakai, and H. Inoue. Error resilient video coding by dynamic replacing of reference pictures. In *Proceedings IEEE Globecom*, London, United Kingdom, November 1996.

[11] M. Ghanbari. Postprocessing of late cells for packet video. *IEEE Trans. on Circuits Syst. Video Technol.*, 6(6):669–678, December 1996.

[12] B. Girod and N. Färber. Feedback-based error control for mobile video transmission. *Proceeding of the IEEE*, 97:1707–1723, October 1999.

[13] J. Goshi, A. E. Mohr, R. E. Ladner, E. A. Riskin, and A. F. Lippman. Unequal loss protection for H.263 compressed video. *IEEE Trans. on Circuits Syst. Video Technol.*, 15(3):412–419, March 2005.

[14] B. G. Haskell, A. Puri, and A. N. Netravali. *Digital Video: An Introduction to MPEG-2*. Chapman & Hall, New York, USA, December 1996.

[15] P. Haskell and D. Messerschmitt. Resynchronization of motion-compensated video affected by ATM cell loss. In *Proceedings IEEE International Conference on Acoustics, Speech and Signal Processing*, volume 3, pages 545–548, 1992.

[16] S. Hemami and T. Meng. Transform coded image reconstruction exploiting interblock correlation. *IEEE Transactions on Image Processing*, 4(7):1023–1027, July 1995.

[17] ISO/IEC JTC 1. *Coding of audio-visual objects, Part 2: Visual*. Apr. 1999; Amendment 1 (version 2), Feb., 2000; Amendment 4 (streaming profile), January 2001.

[18] ITU–T. *Video Coding for Low Bit Rate Communication*, version 1, November 1995; version 2, January 1998; version 3, November 2000.

[19] ITU–T and ISO/IEC JTC 1. *Advanced Video Coding for Generic Audiovisual Services*, 2003.

[20] B. Jung, B. Jeon, M.-D. Kim, B. Suh, and S.-I. Choi. Selective temporal error concealment algorithm for H.264/AVC. In *Proceedings IEEE International Conference on Image Processing*, Singapore, October 2004.

[21] M. Kalman, P. Ramanathan, and B. Girod. Rate–distortion optimized streaming with multiple deadlines. In *Proceedings IEEE International Conference on Image Processing*, Barcelona, Spain, September 2003.

[22] M. Karczewicz and R. Kurceren. The SP and SI frames design for H.264/AVC. *IEEE Trans. on Circuits Syst. Video Technol.*, 13(7), July 2003.

[23] C. W. Kim, D. W. Kang, and I. S. Kwang. High-complexity mode decision for error prone environment. Doc. JVT-C101, Joint Video Team (JVT), Fairfax(VA), USA, May 2002.

[24] A. H. Li, S. Kittitornkun, Y. H. Hu, D. S. Park, and J. D. Villasenor. Data partitioning and reversible variable length codes for robust video communications. In *Proceedings Data Compression Conference (DCC)*, Snowbird(UT), USA, March 2000.

[25] J. Liao and J. Villasenor. Adaptive intra update for video coding over noisy channels. In *Proceedings IEEE International Conference on Image Processing*, volume 3, pages 763–766, October 1996.

[26] A. Luthra, G. J. Sullivan, and T. Wiegand. Special issue on the H.264/AVC video coding standard. *IEEE Trans. on Circuits Syst. Video Technol.*, 13(7), July 2003.

[27] T. Nakai and Y. Tomita. Core experiments on feedback channel operation for H.263+. Doc. LBC96-308, ITU-T SG15, November 1996.

[28] A. Ortega and K. Ramchandran. Rate–distortion methods in image and video compression. *IEEE Signal Processing Mag.*, 15(6):23–50, November 1998.

[29] J. W. Park, J. W. Kim, and S. U. Lee. Dct coefficients recovery-based error concealment technique and its application to the MPEG-2 bit stream error. *IEEE Trans. on Circuits Syst. Video Technol.*, 7(6):845–854, December 1997.

[30] Y. O. Park, C.-S. Kim, and S.-U. Lee. Multi-hypothesis error concealment algorithm for H.26L video. In *Proceedings IEEE International Conference on Image Processing*, pages 465–468, Barcelona, September 2003.

[31] J. Postel. DoD standard transmission control protocol. Request for Comments (standard) 761, Internet Engineering Task Force (IETF), January 1980.

[32] J. Postel. User datagram protocol. Request for Comments (standard) 768, Internet Engineering Task Force (IETF), August 1980.

[33] P. Salama, N. Shroff, E. J. Coyle, and E. J. Delp. Error concealment techniques for encoded video streams. In *Proceedings IEEE International Conference on Image Processing*, volume 1, pages 9–12, Washington DC, USA, October 1995.

[34] P. Salama, N. Shroff, and E. J. Delp. A Bayesian approach to error concealment in encoded video streams. In *Proceedings IEEE International Conference on Image Processing*, pages 49–52, Lausanne, Switzerland, September 1996.

[35] P. Salama, N. Shroff, and E. J. Delp. A fast suboptimal approach to error concealment in encoded video streams. In *Proceedings IEEE International Conference on Image Processing*, pages 101–104, Santa Barbara(CA), USA, October 1997.

[36] P. Salama, N. B. Shroff, and E. J. Delp. Error concealment in encoded video. In *Image Recovery Techniques for Image Compression Applications*. Kluwer Academic Press, Dordrecht, The Netherlands, 1998.

[37] H. Schulzrinne, S. Casner, R. Frederick, and V. Jacobson. RTP: A transport protocol for real-time applications. Request for Comments (standard) 3550, Internet Engineering Task Force (IETF), July 2003.

[38] C. E. Shannon. A Mathematical Theory of Communications. *Bell Systems Technology Journal*, pages 379–423, 623–656, 1948.

[39] S. Shirani, F. Kossentini, and R. Ward. A concealment method for video communications in an error-prone environment. *IEEE Journal on Selected Areas in Communications*, 18(6):1122–1128, June 2000.

[40] T. Socolofsky and C. Kale. A TCP/IP tutorial. Request for Comments (standard) 1180, Internet Engineering Task Force (IETF), January 1991.

[41] E. Steinbach, N. Färber, and B. Girod. Standard compatible extension of H.263 for robust video transmission in mobile environments. *IEEE Trans. on Circuits Syst. Video Technol.*, 7(6):872–881, December 1997.

[42] T. Stockhammer and M. Bystrom. H.264/AVC data partitioning for mobile video communication. In *Proceedings IEEE International Conference on Image Processing*, pages 545–548, Singapore, October 2004.

[43] T. Stockhammer, M. M. Hannuksela, and T. Wiegand. H.264/AVC in wireless environments. *IEEE Trans. on Circuits Syst. Video Technol.*, 13(7):657–673, July 2003.

[44] T. Stockhammer, T. Wiegand, and D. Kontopodis. Rate-distortion optimization for JVT/H.26L coding in packet loss environment. In *Proceedings International Packet Video Workshop*, Pittsburgh(PA), USA, April 2002.

[45] G. J. Sullivan and T. Wiegand. Video compression – from concepts to the H.264/AVC standard. *Proceeding of the IEEE*, 93(1):18–31, January 2005.

[46] G. J. Sullivan and T. Wiegand. Rate-distortion optimization for video compression. *IEEE Signal Processing Mag.*, 15(6):74–90, November 1998.

[47] H. Sun and W. Kwok. Concealment of damaged block transform coded images using projections onto convex sets. *IEEE Transactions on Image Processing*, 4:470–477, April 1995.

[48] H. Sun and J. Zedepski. Adaptive error concealment algorithm for MPEG compressed video. In *Proceedings SPIE Visual Communications and Image Processing (VCIP)*, pages 814–824, Boston(MA), USA, November 1992.

[49] R. Talluri. Error-resilient video coding in the ISO MPEG-4 standard. *IEEE Communications Magazine*, 36(6):112–119, June 1998.

[50] Y. Tomita, T. Kimura, and T. Ichikawa. Error resilient modified inter-frame coding system for limited reference picture memories. In *Proceedings Picture Coding Symposium*, Berlin, Germany, September 1997.

[51] D. S. Turaga and T. Chen. Model-based error concealment for wireless video. *IEEE Trans. on Circuits Syst. Video Technol.*, 12(6):483–495, June 2002.

[52] V. Varsa, M. M. Hannuksela, and Y.-K. Wang. Non-normative error concealment algorithms. Doc. VCEG-N62, ITU-T SG16/Q6 Video Coding Experts Group (VCEG), Santa Barbara(CA), USA, September 2001.

[53] W. Wada. Selective recovery of video packet losses using error concealment. *IEEE Journal on Selected Areas in Communications*, 7:807–814, June 1989.

[54] B. W. Wah, X. Su, and D. Lin. A survey of error concealment schemes for real-time audio and video transmissions over the internet. In *IEEE International Symposium on Multimedia Software Engineering*, pages 17–24, Taipei, Taiwan, December 2000.

[55] Y. Wang, S. Wenger, J. Wen, and A. G. Katsaggelos. Error resilient video coding techniques. *IEEE Signal Processing Mag.*, 17(4):61–82, July 2000.

[56] Y. Wang and Q. Zhu. Error control and concealment for video communication: A review. *Proceeding of the IEEE*, 86:974–997, May 1998.

[57] Y.-K. Wang, M. M. Hannuksela, V. Varsa, A. Hourunranta, and M. Gabbouj. The error concealment feature in the H.26L test model. In *Proceedings IEEE International Conference on Image Processing*, volume 2, pages 729–732, Rochester(NY), USA, September 2002.

[58] S. Wenger. Common conditions for wireline, low delay IP/UDP/RTP packet loss resilient testing. Doc. VCEG-N79, ITU-T SG16/Q6 Video Coding Experts Group (VCEG), Santa Barbara(CA), USA, September 2001.

[59] S. Wenger, M. M. Hannuksela, T. Stockhammer, M. Westerlund, and D. Singer. RTP payload format for H.264 video. Request for Comments (standard) 3984, Internet Engineering Task Force (IETF), February 2005.

[60] S. Wenger, G. Knorr, J. Ott, and F. Kossentini. Error resilience support in H.263+. *IEEE Trans. on Circuits Syst. Video Technol.*, 8:867–877, November 1998.

[61] T. Wiegand, N. Färber, K. Stuhlmller, and B. Girod. Error-resilient video transmission using long-term memory motion-compensated prediction. *IEEE Journal on Selected Areas in Communications*, 18(6):1050–1062, June 2000.

[62] T. Wiegand and B. Girod. Lagrangian multiplier selection in hybrid video coder control. In *Proceedings IEEE International Conference on Image Processing*, Thessaloniki, Greece, October 2001.

[63] T. Wiegand and B. Girod. *Multi-Frame Motion-Compensated Prediction for Video Transmission*. KL, KLADR, 2001.

[64] T. Wiegand, X. Zhang, and B. Girod. Long-term memory motion-compensated prediction. *IEEE Trans. on Circuits Syst. Video Technol.*, 9(1):70–84, February 1999.

[65] H. Yang and K. Rose. Source–channel prediction in error-resilient video coding. In *Proceedings IEEE ICME*, Baltimore(MD), USA, July 2003.

[66] W. Zeng and B. Liu. Geometric-structure-based error concealment with novel applications in block-based low-bit-rate coding. *IEEE Trans. on Circuits Syst. Video Technol.*, 9(4):648–665, June 1999.

[67] R. Zhang, S. L. Regunthan, and K. Rose. Video coding with optimal inter/intra-mode switching for packet loss resilience. *IEEE Journal on Selected Areas in Communications*, 18(6):966–976, June 2000.

[68] Q. F. Zhu and L. Kerofsky. Joint source coding, transport processing, and error concealment for H.323-based packet video. In *Proceedings SPIE Visual Communications and Image Processing (VCIP)*, volume 3653, pages 52–62, San Jose(CA), USA, January 1999.

[69] W. Zia and F. Shafait. Reduced complexity techniques for long-term memory motion compensated prediction in hybrid video coding. In *Proceedings Picture Coding Symposium*, Beijing, China, April 2006.

3

Error-Resilient Coding and Error Concealment Strategies for Audio Communication

Dinei Florêncio

3.1 INTRODUCTION

In this chapter we review the main techniques for error concealment in packet audio. As explained in Chapters 7–10, forward error correction (FEC) or repeat request solutions are often adequate for streaming media and broadcast. These can virtually eliminate information loss, guaranteeing that every bit is actually received at the decoder side. Nevertheless, these techniques will also require the introduction of additional delay, and the higher the protection level desired, the higher the delay required. Real-time communication (RTC) applications are very delay sensitive and will not be able to fully exploit these techniques to reduce 100% of the losses. For this reason, RTC needs are quite unique. We need error concealment, and we need FEC techniques that can be applied without excessive increase in delay. In this chapter we look at some of the techniques used in error concealment for speech and look at media-aware FEC techniques, with particular interest in RTC.

Compression and error concealment are tightly related. Compression tries to remove as much redundancy from the signal as possible, but the more redundancy is removed, the more important each piece of information is, and therefore the harder it is to conceal lost packets. More specifically, speech is a dynamic but slowly varying signal; the key way of compressing speech is by only transmitting signal *changes* in relation to the previous or expected state. Nevertheless, only transmitting these changes in a differential form means that if you lose some information (e.g., due to a packet loss), the decoder does not know the current state of the signal any more. It is always expected that the segment corresponding to the missing data will not be properly decoded. But with differential coding, subsequent frames may also be affected. Furthermore, it is easier to replace any missing speech segments if one has received the correct signal in the vicinity of the missing segment. For all these reasons, error concealment may significantly depend on the compression technology used.

We will start this chapter by looking at some of the basic ideas behind packet loss concealment for speech. With that objective, in Section 3.2 we introduce the basic concealment techniques used in nonpredictive speech codecs. The job of concealing losses becomes harder as the codec removes more and more redundancy from the signal. In Section 3.3, we discuss some of the techniques used to reduce the impact of the feedback loop in CELP (Codebook Excited Linear Prediction) and other predictive codecs. In Section 3.4, we present some recent results in loss concealment for transform coders, which are used both in speech and in audio applications. Finally, in Section 3.5 we discuss recent research in media-aware FEC techniques. Particular attention is paid to speech, due to its importance in RTC, but many of the recent advances in loss concealment techniques we will discuss apply also to audio. For example, the same principles used in the overlapped transform concealment techniques can be used for most audio codecs, and the media-aware FEC can be applied to most audio or video coders. We also point out that this chapter is closely related to the ideas presented in Chapters 15 and 16.

3.2 LOSS CONCEALMENT FOR WAVEFORM SPEECH CODECS

When digital systems started replacing analog equipment a few decades ago, processing power was scarce and expensive, and coding techniques still primitive. For those reasons, most early digital systems used a very simple coding scheme: PCM (Pulse Code Modulation). In this digital representation of speech, there isn't really any coding in the compression sense. The signal is simply sampled and quantized. More specifically, the speech signal is typically sampled at 8 KHz, and each sample is encoded with 8-bit precision, using one of two quantization schemes, usually referred to as A-law and μ-law. This gives a total rate of 64 Kbps. The PCM system used in telephony has been standardized by the ITU (International Telecommunication Union) in the standard G.711 [1]. For Voice over Internet Protocol (VoIP) or other packet network applications, the speech samples will be grouped into frames (typically 10 ms in duration) and sent as packets across the network, one frame per packet. Note that a *frame* corresponds to a data unit in the terminology of Chapter 2. Note that, since there is no real coding, there is no dependence across packets: packets can be received and decoded independently. When G.711 was first adopted, the main motivation was quality: A digital signal was not subject to degradation. At the same time, a 64-Kbps digital channel had a significant cost, and there was a strong push toward increased compression. With the evolution of speech compression technology, and increased processing power, more complex speech codecs were also standardized (e.g., [3–6]), providing better compression. Curiously, today, in many applications bandwidth is not necessarily a significant constraint any more, and we are starting to see basic PCM-coded speech increasing in usage again. Furthermore, many error concealment techniques operate in the time domain, and therefore are best understood as applying to PCM-coded speech. For this reason, in this section we review the basic concept of packet loss as applied to speech and look at some common techniques to conceal loss in PCM coded speech.

We assume speech samples are PCM coded and grouped in 10-ms frames before transmission. Since we assume packets are either received error free or not received at all, this implies that any loss incurred in the transmission process will imply a missing segment of 10 ms (or a multiple thereof). Figure 3.1 shows a segment of a speech signal. The signal is typical of a voiced phoneme. Figure 3.1(a) shows the original signal, whereas 3.1(b) shows a plot where 20 ms (i.e., two packets) is missing. As can be inferred from the picture, a good concealment algorithm would try to replace the missing segment by extending the prior signal with new periods of similar waveforms. This can be done with different levels of complexity, yielding also different levels of artifacts. We will now investigate a

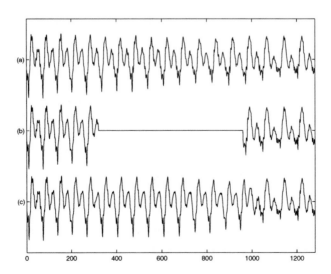

FIGURE 3.1: (a) A typical speech signal. (b) Original signal with two missing frames. (c) Concealed loss using Appendix I of G.711.

simple concealment technique, described in the Appendix I of Recommendation G.711 [2]. The results of applying that algorithm are illustrated in Figure 3.1(c).

3.2.1 A Simple Algorithm for Loss Concealment: G.711 Appendix I

The first modification needed in the G.711 decoder in order to allow for the error concealment is to introduce a 30 sample delay. This delay is used to smooth the transition between the end of the original (received) segment and the start of the synthesized segment. The second modification is that we maintain a circular buffer containing the last 390 samples (48.75 ms). The signal in this buffer is used to select a segment for replacing the lost frame(s).

When a loss is detected, the concealment algorithm starts by estimating the pitch period of the speech. This is done by finding the peak of the normalized cross-correlation between the most recent 20 ms of signal and the signal stored in the buffer. The peak is searched in the interval 40 to 120 samples, corresponding to a pitch of 200 to 66 Hz.

After the pitch period has been estimated, a segment corresponding to 1.25 periods is taken from the buffer and is used to conceal the missing segment. More specifically, the selected segment is overlap-added with the existing signal, with the overlap spanning 0.25 of the pitch period. Note that this overlap will start in the last few samples of the good frame (which is the reason we had to insert the 30 sample delay in the signal). The process is repeated until enough samples to fill the gap are produced. The transition between the synthesized signal and the first good frame is also smoothed by using an overlap-add with the first several samples of the received frame.

Special treatment is given to a number of situations. For example, if two or more consecutive frames are missing, the method uses a segment several pitch periods long as the replication method, instead of repeating several times the same pitch period. Also, after the first 10 ms, the signal is progressively attenuated, such that after 60 ms the synthesized signal is zero. This can be seen in Figure 3.1(c), where the amplitude of the synthesized signal starts to decrease slightly after 160 samples, even though the synthesized signal is still based on the same (preceding) data segment. Also, note that since the period of the missing segment is not identical to the synthesized segment, the transition to the new next frame may present a very atypical pitch period, which can be observed in Figure 3.1(c) around sample 1000.

The reader is directed to the ITU Recommendation [2] for more details of the algorithm. Results of the subjective tests performed with the algorithm, as well as some considerations about bandwidth expansion, can be found in [7]. Alternatively, the reader may refer to Chapter 16, which gives details of a related timescale modification procedure. For our purposes, it suffices to understand that the algorithm works by replicating pitch periods. Other important elements are the gradual muting when the loss is too long and the overlap-add to smooth transitions. These elements will be present in most other concealment algorithms.

By the nature of the algorithm, it can be easily understood why it works well for single losses in the middle of voiced phonemes. As expected, the level of artifacts is higher for unvoiced phonemes and transitions. More elaborate concealment techniques will address each of these issues more carefully, further reducing the level of artifacts, at the cost of complexity. One possibility is to use an LPC filter and do the concealment in the "residual domain" [8,9]. Note that this is unrelated to the concealment of CELP codecs (which we will investigate in the next section). Here we simply use LPC to improve the extrapolation of the signal; the coefficients are actually computed at the decoder. In CELP codecs, we have to handle the problem of *lost* LPC coefficients.

3.3 LOSS CONCEALMENT FOR CELP SPEECH CODECS

In the previous section we looked at error concealment for PCM coded speech. In PCM coded speech, each speech frame is encoded independently (in fact, each *sample* is encoded independently). For this reason, the loss of one packet does not impair the decoding of subsequent frames. However, since no redundancy is removed from the signal, toll quality speech using G.711 requires 64 Kbps. Many other codecs will remove more redundancy from the signal, and therefore require a lower rate. More recent codecs are actually quite aggressive in removing redundancy. For example, several flavors of CELP coding have been used in speech codecs standardized by the ITU, including G.728 [3], G.729 [4], and G.722.2 [6]. Other organizations have also standardized several other CELP codecs, including the European Telecommunications Standards Institute (ETSI), which standardized several GSM (Global System for Mobile Communications) codecs [10] and the 3GPP (Third Generation Partnership Project) AMR (Adaptive Multi-Rate) codec [11], as well as the US Department of Defense (DoD), which standardized one of the first LPC codecs, the DoD FS-1016 [12], and more recently a 2.4-Kbps mixed excitation linear prediction (MELP) codec, the MIL-STD-3005 [14].

While a full understanding of a CELP codec is outside the scope of this chapter, we will need a basic understanding in order to deal with the concealment techniques used in association with these codecs. We will now present a quick summary of important elements of a CELP codec.

Figure 3.2 shows a block diagram of a typical CELP decoder. The first important element in these codecs is the use of a Linear Prediction (LP) filter, indicated as "LPC Synthesis Filter" in the figure. The second element is the use of a codebook as the input to the filter (thus the name "code excited linear prediction, CELP"). We are mostly concerned with the decoding operation so that we

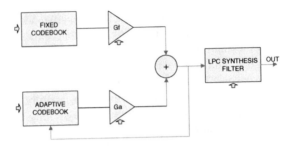

FIGURE 3.2:   Block diagram of a basic CELP codec.

can verify what will happen when a frame is lost. In Figure 3.2, the wide arrows indicate the places where data or parameters are received. We see that the decoder will receive information relating to the LP filter (possibly including a long-term predictor, based on pitch) and on what part of the codebook to use as excitation. Specific CELP codecs will vary in how the codebook is populated, if the codebook is adaptive or not, and on how the filter coefficients are encoded and transmitted. Other differences, less relevant to our problem, relate to how the search on the codebook is performed, how filter coefficients are interpolated, and so on. More details about CELP codecs can be obtained from several sources, for example, from [13].

To understand the key elements of loss concealment for CELP codecs, we will now take a look at the loss concealment technique used in G.729. This ITU codec is a typical CELP codec and operates at 8 Kbps. It uses 10-ms frames and two codebooks: a fixed algebraic codebook and an adaptive codebook (based on the recent past excitation signal). The LPC filter is transmitted by first converting from LPC coefficients to Line Spectral Pairs (LSP), which are then differentially encoded by a vector quantization scheme. When a frame is lost, the decoder will take four specific actions to conceal the loss:

- Repeat the synthesis filter parameters. Since the differential information from the lost frame is not available, the same parameters of last received frame are used.
- Attenuate the adaptive and fixed codebook gains. The fixed codebook gain is reduced by 2% at each 5-ms subframe. The adaptive codebook gain is attenuated by 10% at each subframe and is also limited to 0.9. Note that reducing these gains will decrease the output energy, helping to hide artifacts produced by the concealment.
- Generate the replacement excitation. Since no excitation is received regarding the lost frame, a replacement excitation needs to be generated. The way the excitation is generated depends on the periodicity classification of the previous frame. If the previous frame was classified as periodic, the excita-

tion is generated by the adaptive codebook only, and the pitch delay is set to the same as the previous frame. If more then one frame is lost, each lost frame will increment the pitch by one. However, if the previous frame was classified as aperiodic, the excitation is taken only from the fixed codebook. The entry of the codebook to be used as excitation is based on a pseudo-random algorithm.

- Attenuate the memory of the gain predictor. Since the gains are transmitted on a recursive basis, by using a predictor, the exact state of the predictor is lost when a frame is missing. That will imply that even if the next frame is received without errors, the gains will not be correctly decoded. To help alleviate this problem, the value of the gain predictor is updated with an attenuated version of the codebook energy.

Note that the first three actions are related to generating the signal segment corresponding to the lost frame. The fourth item is related to reducing the artifacts produced in future frames, due to the mismatch in the internal state of the decoder. Rosenberg [15] analyzed the behavior of G.729 under losses and concluded that the artifacts produced by the internal state mismatch are actually more significant (subjectively) than the artifacts introduced by synthesizing the lost frame per se. This parallels the findings for video detailed in the previous chapter. He also concluded that the artifacts due to the mismatch last for approximately 70 to 100 ms.

Error concealment algorithms for CELP codecs are generally very codec specific. The error concealment used in G.729 is relatively simple, but it is a good example of how error concealment for CELP codecs work. Because of the importance of mitigating the effects of the internal state mismatch, more elaborate concealment techniques are highly associated with the particular codec they apply to. Furthermore, many modern CELP codecs are already designed with error concealment in mind and provide an associated algorithm that usually performs well. An example of a more elaborate concealment technique is the one used in the Wideband Adaptive Multirate codec (AMR-WB). This codec is standardized as the 3GPP recommendation TS 26.190 and as ITU G.722.2 [6]. The error concealment algorithm is described in standards ITU G.722.2 Annex I and in 3GPP TS 26.191. It follows the same basic principles of the technique described earlier, but it increases the performance at higher loss rates by having several different procedures for each one of six different states. The states are essentially a measure of how reliable the current state of the codec is. The reader is directed to the specification for more details of the concealment algorithm [6].

3.4 LOSS CONCEALMENT FOR LAPPED TRANSFORM CODECS

Linear transforms are widely used in signal compression. They have the primary objective of concentrating the signal energy on a few coefficients, thus preparing the data for the subsequent quantization and entropy coding. Block transforms (e.g., the Discrete Cosine Transform, DCT) are convenient in that they make each block of data independent, constraining the effect of any error (either by quantization or by loss) to that single block of data. Nevertheless, by not exploiting correlation between adjacent samples in different blocks, they may often produce a structured noise (blocking artifacts), which is readily identifiable in the decoded signal as a buzzing sound. Overlapped transform coders occupy an important niche between block codes and fully predictive coders. They still limit the data to a certain block of samples, but their basis functions do not have discontinuities at block boundaries. Instead, basis functions spread over to (i.e., overlap) neighboring data blocks. This significantly reduces blocking artifacts, while preserving or even improving the compression qualities of the transform. For these reasons, overlapped transforms are used in numerous audio and speech codecs (e.g., MP3, Windows Media Audio [WMA], and ITU-G722.1).

A loss concealment technique based on exploiting the partial information available about certain samples has been recently introduced [16]. The technique can be used with essentially any linear transform where some of the coefficients are missing. Important cases include missing "frames" of overlapped transform (e.g., Modulated Lapped Transform, MLT) coefficients, or wavelet coefficients, or even single or multiple missing transform coefficients within a block of a block transform (e.g., DCT). However, since we are mostly interested in concealment of missing blocks in real-time speech and audio communication over packet networks, we will focus our discussion on the case of overlapped transforms.

When using an overlapped transform based codec, if a frame or block of coefficients is lost, partial information is available about the missing segment. While this information is not of enough quality to be used directly, it provides important clues about the missing segment. In this section we discuss ways in which to exploit this partial information to maximize the quality of the recovered signal. In particular, we apply some of the techniques to single-frame loss concealment on the ITU-G722.1 codec [5].

In order to better understand the scenario, let us take a look at how an overlapped transform is used for coding purposes. Figure 3.3a shows a one-dimensional signal. In this example, the signal is split into overlapping blocks of $2N$ samples, as shown in Figure 3.3b. Then, at each block, N transform coefficients are obtained by multiply/accumulate operations with the N basis functions constituting the transform. Figure 3.4 shows the first few basis functions of a typical transform. On the decoder side, the basis functions are scaled by the transform coefficients and added. Subsequent frames of the signal are then overlapped and added. Figure 3.3c shows the contribution of each overlapping block, before addition. Note that the recovered segments have the same length but are not identical to the original segments: the original signal is recovered only after adding the overlapping parts. Now, suppose the information about one of the blocks was

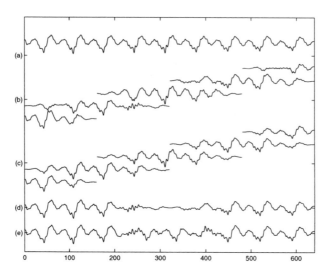

FIGURE 3.3: A sample speech signal. (a) Original signal. (b) Signal split into overlapping segments and windowed. (c) Corresponding segments after decoding. (d) Overlapped/added signal with one missing block. (e) Error concealment using simple block repetition.

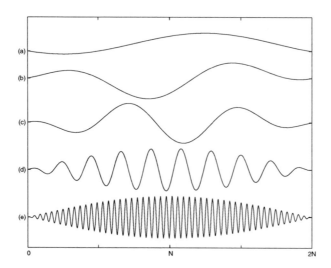

FIGURE 3.4: A few basis functions of the MLT transform. From top to bottom: 1st, 2nd, 3rd, 10th, and 50th basis functions.

lost. A total of $2N$ samples—spawning the lost block—cannot be reconstructed correctly. If we replace the lost coefficients with zeros, we would have the reconstructed signal indicated in Figure 3.3d. Note that in this example, although only N coefficients are missing, a total of $2N$ samples do not reconstruct correctly, due to the overlapping nature of the transform. Nevertheless, overlapped transforms like the MLT are critically sampled. This means that some partial information is available about the $2N$ incomplete samples. More specifically, a total of N linear equations are available regarding these $2N$ samples. We will now examine how this can be used to improve the loss concealment.

3.4.1 Speech Codecs

The ITU standard recommends that lost blocks be replaced with the previous block. While this technique is reasonable for low loss rates, artifacts are still present and become significant at loss rates that are common in the Internet. In particular, replication of coefficients does not take into account the alignment of pitch periods between past and lost frames. (See examples of speech codecs, G.722.1.)

In Section 3.2.1 we presented one of the main principles behind loss concealment for speech: pitch replication. As we will see, the algorithm presented in [16] can be seen as an elaborate pitch replication system. It uses the partial information available to synthesize a signal that has similar spectral characteristics and aligns well with the surrounding blocks.

The MLT transform can be decomposed into a windowing operation, followed by a folding and a DCT. Each block of coefficients can thus be written in matrix form as

$$m = dct(FJx), \tag{3.1}$$

where m is the $N \times 1$ vector of the resulting transform coefficients, F is the $N \times 2N$ fold-over matrix

$$F = \begin{bmatrix} 0 & 0 & & 1 & 1 & & 0 & 0 & 0 & 0 & \cdots & 0 & 0 & \cdots & 0 & 0 \\ \vdots & & & & & \ddots & \vdots & \vdots & \vdots & & & \vdots & \vdots & & \vdots & \vdots \\ 0 & 1 & & 0 & 0 & & 1 & 0 & 0 & 0 & \cdots & 0 & 0 & \cdots & 0 & 0 \\ 1 & 0 & \cdots & 0 & 0 & \cdots & 0 & 1 & 0 & 0 & \cdots & 0 & 0 & \cdots & 0 & 0 \\ 0 & 0 & \cdots & 0 & 0 & \cdots & 0 & 0 & 1 & 0 & \cdots & 0 & 0 & \cdots & 0 & -1 \\ 0 & 0 & \cdots & 0 & 0 & \cdots & 0 & 0 & 0 & 1 & \cdots & 0 & 0 & \cdots & -1 & 0 \\ \vdots & \vdots & & \vdots & \vdots & & \vdots & \vdots & \vdots & \vdots & \ddots & & & & \vdots & \vdots \\ 0 & 0 & \cdots & 0 & 0 & \cdots & 0 & 0 & 0 & 0 & & 1 & -1 & & 0 & 0 \end{bmatrix} \tag{3.2}$$

and J is a scaling matrix, that is, an $N \times N$ diagonal matrix with the windowing coefficients

$$J_{ij} = \begin{cases} \sin(\pi/2N(i+0.5)), & \text{if } i = j, \\ 0, & \text{otherwise.} \end{cases} \tag{3.3}$$

Furthermore, we will often need to refer to the signal before the DCT is applied. Let's call that z. So, we write

$$z = FJx. \tag{3.4}$$

Note that in (3.2) the nonzero elements of the folding matrix form two nonoverlapping subblocks. In other words, we can decompose F in four submatrices, where two of them are zero matrices:

$$F = \begin{bmatrix} F_1 & \mathbf{0} \\ \mathbf{0} & F_2 \end{bmatrix}. \tag{3.5}$$

Similarly, we write

$$J = \begin{bmatrix} J_1 & \mathbf{0} \\ \mathbf{0} & J_2 \end{bmatrix}, \quad x = \begin{bmatrix} x_1 \\ x_2 \end{bmatrix}, \quad z = \begin{bmatrix} z_1 \\ z_2 \end{bmatrix}, \quad \text{and} \quad y = \begin{bmatrix} y_1 \\ y_2 \end{bmatrix}. \tag{3.6}$$

Looking at the block diagonal structure of F and J, we can easily see that only the first half of the samples of x is used in computing the first half of the folded vector FJx (and similarly for the second half). That is, we can write

$$z_1 = F_1 J_1 x_1. \tag{3.7}$$

Therefore, if the next block of coefficients (which would also be using the second half of samples of x) is lost, we can use this partial knowledge about the samples to try to estimate x_2.

More specifically, suppose an isolated block is lost (i.e., both the preceding and the subsequent blocks to the missing block of coefficients are correctly received). The missing (incomplete) set of samples is $2N$ long. By computing the inverse DCT of the received data (but before applying the unfolding matrix), we have access to y. We can therefore write the following equation, applying to the first incomplete N samples:

$$z_2 = F_2 J_2 x_2. \tag{3.8}$$

Note that the x_1 and x_2 in (3.7) and (3.8) refer to different blocks. To avoid confusion, we will now add a time index to our notation. Namely to represent blocks at different time instants we will add a superscript index, indicating the block ordering. For example, x^n will mean the vector x and time instant n.

Assume the block at time n is missing, but both the previous and the subsequent blocks are correctly received. So, since block n is missing, but we have received blocks $n - 1$ and $n + 1$, we can write

$$\begin{bmatrix} z_2^{n-1} \\ z_1^{n+1} \end{bmatrix} = \begin{bmatrix} F_2 & \mathbf{0} \\ \mathbf{0} & F_1 \end{bmatrix} \begin{bmatrix} J_2 & \mathbf{0} \\ \mathbf{0} & J_1 \end{bmatrix} \begin{bmatrix} x_1^n \\ x_2^n \end{bmatrix}. \tag{3.9}$$

Note that the matrices containing F_1, F_2, J_1, and J_2 are now rotated in relation to the original F and J matrices. For simplicity, let's refer to these modified (block rotated) matrices in the aforementioned equation as G and H. We therefore write

$$\begin{bmatrix} z_2^{n-1} \\ z_2^{n+1} \end{bmatrix} = GHx^n. \tag{3.10}$$

Note that this is an underdetermined system of equations. We know z_2^{n-1} and z_2^{n+1}, and we are trying to estimate the $2N$ samples of x^n. This underdetermined system could be solved for the minimum energy vector x^n using the Moore–Penrose generalized inverse of GH. This would provide the minimum energy signal segment x that satisfies the received (partial) information. Nevertheless, simulations show that this is not a good choice for x, as the nature of the matrix J tends to concentrate the energy in the higher gain samples. A better choice is to find the solution minimizing the energy of the windowed signal Hx. This solution does distribute more evenly the energy across the samples of x. Nevertheless, it still does not use the information about the neighboring frames. Before proceeding to describe the best mode, let us introduce a small change in interpretation. Let us introduce an identity matrix I in (3.10), which becomes

$$\begin{bmatrix} z_2^{n-1} \\ z_2^{n+1} \end{bmatrix} = GHIx^n. \tag{3.11}$$

We now interpret I not as a simple identity matrix, but as a matrix whose columns form a basis for the space of x. In this context, the basis I consists simply of impulses at each sample location. Using the generalized inverse of GH would be minimizing the energy of the basis representation over these impulses. That takes into account the partial information about the missing samples, but it does not take into account all the prior information we have about the missing segment: the properly received signal segments just before (and possibly after) the missing segment. To fully exploit that information, we will reshape the aforementioned equation by introducing two small modifications. The first modification improves the signal continuity across frames by removing the no-excitation response. The second biases the reconstructed signal toward having the same spectrum and pitch as the neighboring segments.

To account for the signal continuity, we estimate the LPC filter corresponding to the previous block and compute the no-excitation response of the LPC filter into the missing segment, $\check{x}$. We then modify (3.11) to account for $\check{x}$ and write

$$\begin{bmatrix} z_2^{n-1} \\ z_2^{n+1} \end{bmatrix} - GH\check{x} = GHI\hat{x}^n, \tag{3.12}$$

where $\hat{x} = x - \check{x}$.

To account for the spectral continuity, we invoke our interpretation of I as a basis for the vector x (now $\hat{x}$) to claim we should not be minimizing the energy of x. Instead, we should be minimizing the energy of the representation of x under a basis whose functions have a spectrum corresponding to the desired LPC spectrum. To that end, we apply the LPC filter to the identity matrix, to obtain a new basis L, where each column of L corresponds to a time-shifted version of the impulse response of the LPC filter.

Finally, we compute an estimate of the periodicity and pitch period for the segment and apply that to the basis functions as well. Each column of L is now a series of "colored" pulses, each apart by the pitch period, each with the impulse response of the LPC filter, and each with decreasing amplitude, based on the estimated periodicity index. For simplicity, we still call this final basis matrix L. The representation on this new basis is not x any more, so let's call it r. We now have

$$\begin{bmatrix} z_2^{n-1} \\ z_2^{n+1} \end{bmatrix} - GH\check{x} = GHLr^n, \tag{3.13}$$

which is then solved by the pseudo inverse of GHL, that is,

$$r^n = (GHL)^\dagger \left(\begin{bmatrix} z_2^{n-1} \\ z_2^{n+1} \end{bmatrix} - GH\check{x} \right), \tag{3.14}$$

where $\dagger$ denotes the pseudo inverse. Note that this is the solution that minimizes the LPC residual of x, as we wanted. The final solution for x is obtained by simply computing

$$x^n = Lr^n + \check{x}. \tag{3.15}$$

Figure 3.5 shows a sample of the results obtained by the concealment algorithm. The first signal is the original, the second is the signal reconstructed using the proposed technique, and the third is the results of concealment by a pitch replication method. In both cases every third packet is lost.

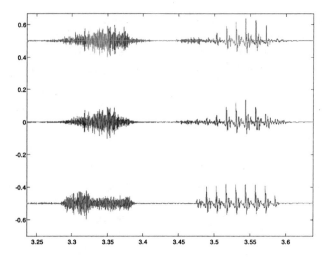

FIGURE 3.5: Sample results. (a) Original signal. (b) Concealed using the partial information method, after losing every third frame. (c) Concealed using the pitch replication method.

In this section, we presented an error concealment technique that exploits the partial information available for the missing segment of a signal encoded by an overlapped transform. The discussion was centered around a speech codec, simply because speech is of foremost importance for real-time communication. Nevertheless, the same principle can be applied to other overlapped transform codecs. In particular, the same ideas apply to error concealment in music, as long as we remove the conditions relating to pitch and introduce a higher order model to account for the harmonic nature of music.

3.5 FORWARD ERROR CORRECTION TECHNIQUES FOR SPEECH

In the previous sections, we discussed several error concealment techniques, targeted at alleviating the consequences of packet losses. Some of these techniques are reasonably effective and will provide quite adequate speech quality, especially at low loss rates. Nevertheless, as the loss rates increase, concealment becomes increasingly hard and is prone to leave a number of artifacts. For this reason, Forward Error Correction (FEC) is often used—either in isolation or as a complementary measure—against packet losses. FEC techniques can range from simple packet replication techniques to more elaborate schemes, including media-dependent FEC. In this section, we discuss media-dependent FEC and present a framework for optimum rate distortion bit allocation. We will also present a case study based on the AMR-WB codec [6]. More general FEC methods can be found in Chapters 7 and 9.

3.5.1 Delay and FEC

Generally speaking, FEC schemes allow the receiver to correctly decode a message, even if some of the packets are lost. This is done by adding redundant information to the stream. The information can be included in a separate packet, or appended to existing packets. For example, one could send a parity packet after every three data packets, as illustrated in Figure 3.6. In this scheme, if one of the three packets is lost, one can use the parity packet to recover the original information without loss. This increase in robustness is useful, but it also increases the bandwidth requirement by 33% (by sending one extra packet for every three original packets). Furthermore, there is also a delay cost: if the first of the three packets is lost, the receiver has to wait until receiving the parity packet before decoding the lost packet. In this example, this would add an extra two-frame delay. Partially to reduce this added delay, most FEC schemes for real-time communication simply repeat the packet. More information about standard FEC techniques will be discussed in Chapters 7 and 9. But for now, let's simply mention that using an FEC code that spreads over N blocks will essentially add up to N blocks delay. For this reason it is highly desirable for FEC codes to spread the smallest number of blocks possible.

3.5.2 Media-Dependent FEC

As we mentioned, it is desirable that the FEC technique introduces as little extra delay as possible. Ideally, we would like FEC codes that spread only a single block. Unfortunately, under the traditional FEC techniques, the only such "code" available is packet repetition. That happens because traditional FEC try to protect the *bits* of the message. When one is sending media, protecting individual bits is

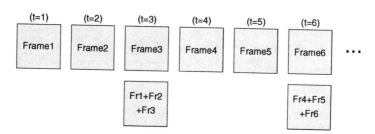

FIGURE 3.6: FEC example with a 4:3 redundancy. Each fourth block is an XOR of the previous three blocks.

not as important anymore, but instead, the idea is to protect the *signal*. In other words, a rate–distortion trade-off can now be applied. Looked at from this point of view, packet repetition is clearly suboptimal. For example, in a 10% loss scenario, the error correction information is only used 10% of the time and yet uses the same rate as the primary packet.

In traditional FEC codes, the sender inserts bit redundancy in the transmitted packets, and the receiver will either perfectly receive the frame or receive nothing. There is no rate–distortion trade-off. In media-dependent FEC methods, in contrast, the transmitter sends multiple descriptions of the same frame so that in case of packet loss, another packet containing the same data, albeit different quality, can be used to recover the loss. Hence, each packet will carry an appropriate representation of the current frame, along with a coarse representation of one or more previous frames. Clearly, there is a trade-off between attributing rate to redundant information instead of to the current frame. By increasing the amount of redundant information, we increase the probability and the quality of loss recovery while sacrificing from the quality of the most recent frame. An example of such media-dependent FEC schemes is the one presented in [17]. Earlier work includes the Robust Audio Tool [18], which limits the repeat packet to be the same as the original one. The problem can be formulated as follows. Given a model for the channel and a total transmission rate R (i.e., fixed packet size), what is the optimum partition of the bit budget between redundant and current frames such that a distortion measure D_T is minimized? We consider each frame as a signal segment and each packet may contain information units regarding one or more frames. The units can contain raw data or a representation of data derived by some compression algorithm (e.g., LPC coefficients, prediction errors). We model each packet as a collection of multiple units corresponding to different segments of the signal, each possibly having a different rate. For each packet, r_1 is the rate of the present segment and r_i is the rate of $(i-1)$th past segment. The number of these units and the rate of each unit can be either fixed by the optimization algorithm prior to transmission or adaptively changed based on the input signal. Figure 3.7 shows an example, with four consecutive packets, with each packet carrying information about the current frame, as well as lower fidelity information about the two previous packets.

Another point of interest is whether each unit is dependent on previous units (i.e., differential coding). We will analyze here the case in which each segment of data is processed independently. This would be the case, for example, of encoding video with all I-frames or encoding speech using G.722.1 ("Siren") or G.711 (PCM). The case of history-dependent algorithms, where each segment is sent as a unit, is handled in detail in [19].

We now analyze the optimization problem where each frame is encoded independently of neighboring frames. The optimal rate of each packet is chosen to minimize the average distortion given the loss model. We start our discussion with

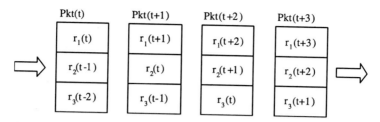

FIGURE 3.7: Media-aware FEC example with a factor of 3 redundancy. The current block carries the frame with full resolution and previous blocks with decreasing degree of accuracy.

the case where there is only a single–rate distortion function to be used, the bit rate allocation is fixed (i.e., independent of the actual signal), the loss model is i.i.d., and delay is ignored. This can then be extended to more complex scenarios.

Assume no inter-frame coding and a fixed rate–distortion function $D(r)$. The distortion $D(r)$ is the average distortion due to using rate r for a generic compression algorithm using only data in the current frame. As an example, suppose there are three units in each packet, as in Figure 3.7, and the packet loss is an i.i.d. Bernoulli process with loss probability p. Since the loss event is i.i.d., without loss of generality, we can restrict our decoder to use the first packet received, even though we may receive multiple units for the same segment. It follows automatically that the optimum solution requires $r_1 \geq r_2 \geq r_3$. Since the probability of a packet being received is $1 - p$, and since if we receive a packet we will use the r_1 contained in that packet for reconstruction of the corresponding frame, the distortion for this frame will be $D(r_1)$ with probability $(1 - p)$. However, there is a probability p that this packet is not received. In that case, we will wait for the next packet, which contains the same frame, but coded at rate r_2. That packet has itself probability $(1 - p)$ of being received. Therefore, the probability that we use the data contained in that packet is going to be $p(1 - p)$, and in that case the distortion is going to be $D(r_2)$. We can proceed similarly with the third packet to conclude that the distortion contributed by that packet is $p^2(1 - p)D(r_3)$. Finally, if none of the three packets containing information about this segment is received, we will use some other loss concealment technique, which we assume will itself induce a distortion K. The same computation will hold for any particular segment (frame) of the signal. Therefore, the expected distortion at any time is given by

$$D_T = (1 - p)D(r_1) + p(1 - p)D(r_2) + p^2(1 - p)D(r_3) + p^3 K. \qquad (3.16)$$

The distortion K directly depends on the loss concealment strategy, and we assume it to be comparable to $D(0)$. If we do not include any delay considerations,

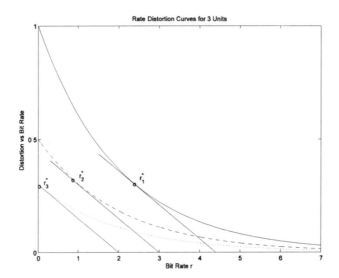

FIGURE 3.8: Optimization procedure. Each rate is used. The optimum solution is the one that implies the same derivative on each of the (scaled) curves.

the optimization problem can be formulated as

$$\min_{r_1, r_2, \ldots, r_N, N} D_T(r_1, \ldots, r_N), \quad \text{s.t.} \quad \sum_{i=1}^{N} r_i < R, \qquad (3.17)$$

where N is the total number of units to be used and R is the total rate. Since we assume no inter-frame coding, the R–D curves are the same for the first unit and for subsequent (FEC) units. This can be seen in Figure 3.8, which illustrates the contribution of each of the terms in (3.16). Note in the figure that the curve corresponding to each unit has the same shape, but has been appropriately scaled by the associated probability, as prescribed by (3.16). In this example, the total distortion D_T is the sum of the three different rate distortion curves, where each curve is simply the product of $D(r)$ and the respective probability coefficient coming from the channel model. Hence, given N, the problem (for convex rate–distortion functions) is formulated as an unconstrained optimization using Lagrange multipliers,

$$\min_{r_1, r_2, \ldots, r_N, N} D_T(r_1, \ldots, r_N) + \lambda \sum_{i=1}^{N} r_i, \qquad (3.18)$$

where λ is the Lagrange multiplier. The optimal configuration is reached when

$$\frac{\partial D_T}{\partial r_1} = \frac{\partial D_T}{\partial r_2} = \frac{\partial D_T}{\partial r_3}. \tag{3.19}$$

Since we assume the encoding of each unit is independent (no inter-frame coding), the partial derivatives are simplified to

$$\left.\frac{\partial D_T}{\partial r}\right|_{r1} = \left.\frac{\partial D_T}{\partial r}\right|_{r2} = \left.\frac{\partial D_T}{\partial r}\right|_{r3}. \tag{3.20}$$

In other words, the problem is now reduced to finding the optimum rate points $r_1^*, \ldots, r_n^*$ such that the slopes of the scaled–rate distortion curves are the same at each r_i^* and $\sum_{i=1}^{N} r_i^* \leq R$. This is illustrated in Figure 3.8.

Note that whenever N is not given a priori, it must be included as a parameter in the optimization. In principle, the induced delay is N, because to present the frames at a constant rate, the receiver has to wait for the N packets before decoding a frame. (However, we will see in Chapter 16 that adaptive playout can be used to keep the average delay below N.) Since (3.16) does not include any penalty for latency, the optimization in (3.20) will artificially favor a large N. Nevertheless, note that even if there is no penalty for latency, there is always a finite value of N such that the algorithm stops and favors the quality instead of error recovery. If we define ordered curves in the figure as $D_1, \ldots, D_i$ (e.g., for Figure 3.8, $i = 3$), then the number of units that would be included will be upper bounded by

$$N^* = \arg\max_N \sum_{i=1}^{N} \hat{D}_i^{-1}\left(\hat{D}_N(r = 0)\right) \leq R, \tag{3.21}$$

where $\hat{D}_i(r)$ is the derivative of the function $D_i(r)$ and $\hat{D}_i^{-1}(r)$ is the inverse of $\hat{D}_i(r)$. After getting an upper bound, N can be computed by decreasing N and recomputing the distortion until D_T starts to increase. Since N is generally small, this exhaustive search in N is usually not a problem.

This procedure will determine the optimum rate allocation to each packet and to each error correcting packet. Each subsequent (error correcting) packet will always be at the same or lower rate as the previous packet. If a packet is lost, but a subsequent packet containing the error correcting information is received, the decoder will replace the lost information with that contained in the correction packet. In other words, this can be viewed as a forward error correction technique where the objective is to recover the signal, not the bits. In the same way the original (source) encoding may have introduced signal distortions in order to optimize the channel utilization, the channel coding may also introduce its own distortion,

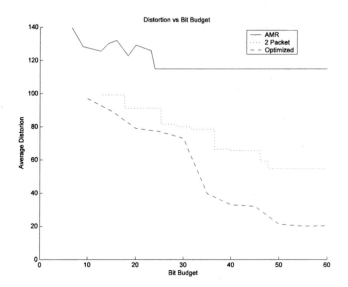

FIGURE 3.9:   Subjectively weighted SNR after decoding for several error rates. Top curve is for original (single packet) AMR, dotted line for repeat only, and lower (dashed line) results are for media-aware FEC, which typically selects a lower rate for correction packets.

also to optimize the channel utilization. Furthermore, the aforementioned method guarantees that both the channel and source coding are operating at optimal condition, therefore the name "combined source-channel coding."

The optimization procedure presented in this section assumed an intra-only coder, a fixed rate–distortion function, and an i.i.d. loss model. Each and all of these constraints can be removed under certain assumptions. Details can be found in [19], which also includes an example of applying this technology to a AMR-WB codec. Figure 3.9 shows a plot of final quality as a function of error rate when applying this technology and compares that to a repeat-only FEC strategy.

3.6 OTHER ERROR-RESILIENT CODING TECHNIQUES

In previous sections we looked at two main ways to alleviate the consequences of packet loss: concealment and FEC. In the first technique, we try to synthesize the missing information based on surrounding (i.e., received) blocks. The second technique sends some additional redundant information (FEC), which helps recover the missing information, either in its natural form or with reduced fidelity. A few other techniques fall somewhere between these two, in the sense that instead of adding redundancy, they will leave some redundancy in the signal at coding time. Ideally this is done in a well-planned way, leaving only the redundancy that will be most effective in recovering the lost packets. This is in contrast to some older techniques (e.g., G.711), where redundancy was left in the signals mostly to simplify computation. An example of such an error-resilient technique can be seen in the Siren codec (G.722.1), which intentionally does not use differential coding, to increase robustness to noise. A few other techniques used to improve error resilience include Multiple Description Coding (Chapter 17) and unequal error protection (Chapter 9), which can be used with standard codecs, but are particularly useful when used with scalable codecs (Chapter 6).

3.7 SUMMARY AND FURTHER READING

In this chapter we have looked at Error Concealment Strategies and Error Resilient Coding for Audio Communication. We looked at some of the basic techniques that are used in concealing packet losses, applied to several kinds of codecs, including frame-independent codecs, overlapped transform codecs, and fully predictive codecs. We looked at some of the techniques incorporated into international standards, and looked at a few additional techniques. We saw that many codecs are available and can be used for specific application. The particular choice of a codec will generally involve system design issues, for example, computational complexity, bandwidth availability, backward compatibility, and so on. Furthermore, commercial considerations often play a major role as well. These include existing intellectual property right, licensing terms, availability of source code, and so on. For example, many of the codecs mentioned were designed for a specific application. As a general rule, CELP codecs tend to perform well in terms of rate/distortion for most rates above 2400 bps, as long as encoding clean speech. For example, mostly all codecs used in cellular phone systems are CELP based. However, when coding music or when background noise becomes more prevalent, waveform codecs start to present good performance. Indeed, while the ITU and the GSM have standardized several CELP codecs to use at different rates, in telecommunication systems some of the primary VoIP systems use waveform-based codecs. For example, Microsoft Messenger uses Siren/G711.1 as the default codec. This can be partially attributed to the fact that bandwidth constraints on VoIP are not as severe as in cellular systems and partially to the fact that use of a close-talking microphone is not expected in the desktop environment.

The main objective of this chapter was to look at the different techniques available. A number of subsequent chapters will look at related topics, in particular about aspects related to FEC, scalable audio coding, and adaptive playout. These are techniques that are particularly important for speech communication.

REFERENCES

[1] ITU-T Recommendation G.711, *Pulse code modulation (PCM) of voice frequencies*, November 1988.

[2] ITU-T Recommendation G.711, Appendix I, *A high quality low-complexity algorithm for packet loss concealment with G.711*, September 1999.

[3] ITU-T Recommendation G.728, *Coding of speech at 16 kbit/s using low-delay code excited linear prediction*, September 1992.

[4] ITU-T Recommendation G.728, *Coding of speech at 8 kbit/s using conjugate-structure algebraic-code-excited linear prediction (CS-ACELP)*, March 1996.

[5] ITU-T Recommendation G.722.1, *Low-complexity coding at 24 and 32 kbit/s for hands-free operation in systems with low frame loss*, May 2005.

[6] ITU-T Recommendation G.722.2, *Wideband coding of speech at around 16 kbit/s using Adaptive Multi-Rate Wideband (AMR-WB)*, July 2003.

[7] R. V. Cox, D. Malah, and D. Kapilow, "Improving upon toll quality speech for VOIP," *Signals, Systems and Computers, 2004. Conference Record of the Thirty-Eighth Asilomar Conference*, vol. 1, pp. 405–409, November 2004.

[8] E. Gunduzhan and K. Momtahan, "Linear prediction based packet loss concealment algorithm for PCM coded speech," *IEEE Transactions on Speech and Audio Processing*, vol. 9, num. 8, pp. 778–785, November 2001.

[9] M. Elsabrouty, M. Bouchard, and T. Aboulnasr, "Receiver-based packet loss concealment for pulse code modulation (PCM G.711) coder," *Signal Processing*, vol. 84, pp. 663–667, 2004.

[10] K. Jarvinen *et al.*, "GSM enhanced full rate speech codec," *Proc. of ICASSP*, vol. 2, pp. 771–774, April 1997.

[11] 3GPP Recommendation TS 26.071, *AMR speech Codec; General description*, ver 6.0.0, December 2004.

[12] T. E. Tremain, "The Government Standard Linear Predictive Coding Algorithm: LPC-10," *Speech Technology Magazine*, pp. 40–49, April 1982.

[13] X. Huang, A. Acero, and H. Hon, *Spoken language processing: A guide to theory, algorithms and system development,*" Prentice Hall, 2001.

[14] "MELP vocoder algorithm: The new 2400 bps federal standard speech coder," Atlanta Signal Processors, Inc., available (as of August 2006) at http://www.aspi.com/tech/specs/pdfs/melp.pdf.

[15] J. Rosenberg, "Distributed Algorithms and Protocols for Scalable Internet Telephony," *Ph.D. thesis*, Columbia University, 2001.

[16] D. Florencio, *Personal notes about Siren codec packet loss concealment,* Microsoft, 2004.

[17] V. Hardman *et al.*, "Reliable audio for use over the Internet," *Proc. INET*, 1995.

[18] J.-C. Bollot and A. Vega-Garcia, "The case for FEC-based error control for packet audio in the Internet," *ACM Multimedia Systems*, 1996.

[19] S. Kozat and D. Florencio, "Media dependent FEC," Internal Report, Microsoft, 2003.

4

Mechanisms for Adapting Compressed Multimedia to Varying Bandwidth Conditions

Antonio Ortega and Huisheng Wang

4.1 INTRODUCTION

Most currently deployed networks provide no quality of service (QoS) guarantees. Thus it is clearly necessary for bandwidth adaptation mechanisms to be available in order for real-time multimedia delivery applications to be successful. These mechanisms allow applications to adjust gracefully to changes in available channel bandwidth. Without these adaptation tools, changes in available bandwidth will lead to significant quality degradation, leading occasionally to total service interruption. This is an even more pressing need when one considers the increasing heterogeneity of both networks and network access devices.

Consider, for example, a hypothetical application where a traveling user is interested in accessing video captured by a wireless home surveillance camera. This user gains remote access to the video feed using a wireless network device, such as a cell phone. In order to provide a smooth, constant quality playback, such a system would have to be robust to bandwidth fluctuations due to multiple causes; for example, variations in traffic within the home network, load of the cable modem access network, distance of the user to the nearest base station, and load in the wireless access network. This is in addition to traffic fluctuations along the relevant paths within the Internet backbone.

Clearly, one possible way to tackle the problem would be to engineer application and network resources so as to avoid altogether these bandwidth fluctuations, or at least reduce their amplitude. Indeed, in all the most successful deployments of digital video systems (cable and satellite broadcasting) some form of bandwidth reservation is in place so that each video transmission receives a fixed bandwidth. These systems are in fact (i) closed, so that a single service provider controls all the communication links and thus how many video transmissions occur at any given time, and (ii) reliable, so that, except for rare outages, bandwidth levels available to each video transmission remain constant.

While these applications have been very successful commercially, current interest is driven by multimedia applications that operate over open, heterogeneous and potentially unreliable networks. Witness, for example, the current growth in voice over IP (VoIP) systems. Interest in deploying other such applications (from video conferencing to video on demand) over these networks is considerable, but the technical challenges are very significant.

This chapter is devoted to tools and techniques that allow applications that involve transmission of multimedia streams to cope with significant changes in transmission bandwidth. We call these *bandwidth adaptation* mechanisms. Note that there are other tools available to improve the quality of multimedia delivery over these challenging network environments. In particular, techniques for multimedia resilience and error concealment allow the decoder to either eliminate the effect of losses or excessive delays (by introducing redundancy) or to "mask" their effect on the decoded media (using error concealment). In many cases these techniques are applied to a design based on worst case assumptions, for example, the designer may determine what the maximum packet loss rate for the system is likely to be and then select appropriate error-resilience techniques to ensure sufficient quality even at those loss rates.

Instead, our main focus is on *dynamic* adaptation: various components of the application actively monitor and react to changes in network behavior by making adjustments to the data being sent to the receiver.

Our simple traveling user example illustrates the importance of bandwidth adaptation mechanisms; in their absence variations in available bandwidth may lead to packet losses in the video stream and thus to very abrupt variations in video quality, and possibly to complete interruption of service. For example, if the surveillance camera is set to encode video at a certain rate regardless of network conditions, then usable video quality may not be available unless the minimum bandwidth encountered at all links along the network route exceeds the bandwidth required by the application. This example also indicates that there are many possible mechanisms for adaptation, such as the fact that, the two end applications could communicate with each other, or intermediate nodes of the network could modify the video stream (e.g., via transcoding) to make it conform to the available bandwidth. One of the goals of this chapter will be to describe alternative adaptation mechanisms and illustrate their relative merits. Note that bandwidth adaptation cannot guarantee loss-free transmission, so mechanisms to minimize the impact of losses and for error concealment may also be needed, as discussed in Chapters 2, 3, 8, 9, and 10.

All practical multimedia networking systems currently in use incorporate some form of bandwidth adaptation. For example, widely deployed commercial systems such as Windows Media Player and RealPlayer make use of adaptation technologies, namely Intelligent Streaming [6] and SureStream [19], respectively. In both systems, multiple redundant representations of the same content are created, with each version optimized for a specific transmission rate. During transmission, the streaming server dynamically adapts to the bandwidth changes by switching between these streams in such a way as to maximize the reconstructed video quality.

These systems, and alternative ones to be discussed in more detail in this chapter, operate by

(i) observing the characteristics of the network environment (e.g., bandwidth availability, packet loss rates) and

(ii) increasing/decreasing the rate of the multimedia stream so as to maximize quality available to the users.

The performance of these systems will depend on many factors, such as the type and accuracy of information that is available about the network state; where this information is acquired; and constraints on how the streaming rate can be adjusted.

Note that the multimedia codec being used is a very important factor in determining what forms of adaptation are feasible. Some media codecs are designed so as to facilitate bandwidth adaptation; for example, this is the case when scalable coding (described in Chapter 5) is used. With a scalable codec a media sequence is encoded into a number of layers, or as an embedded stream with fine granularity, such that the transmitter can easily select a subset of layers or bits to send based on the current channel condition.

This chapter provides a general overview of bandwidth adaptation mechanisms, focusing on **where** the adaptation occurs (e.g., at the sender end, or somewhere in the network), **who** decides how to adapt (e.g., sender- vs. receiver-driven adaptation is possible), **how** the adaptation is supported by various codecs (e.g., scalable vs. nonscalable systems), and the **trade-offs** in performing the adaptation with different options using a number of criteria (e.g., in terms of delay, latency, complexity, quality).

Note that our main goal is to provide an overview of various classes of techniques available for bandwidth adaptation and to summarize their relative merits. A more detailed and quantitative performance comparison falls outside of the scope of this chapter and, given the complexity of these systems, may indeed be difficult to develop. Note also that most of our discussions will be relevant to general streaming media systems, although often our specific examples (in partic-

ular our discussion of coding techniques) will focus on the case of video streaming.

4.1.1 A Simplified System—Definition of Major Components

To facilitate the discussion, in what follows we consider simplified systems with
three components. A *sender* provides the media data, which could be encoded
from a live media input or could be obtained from a pre-encoded stream. A *client*
initiates the request for a media stream and plays it back to the end user. A *proxy* is
an intermediate node of the network that facilitates the interaction between client
and sender. Note that in some cases a proxy contains all the information requested
by the client and thus in effect acts as the sender. Our focus in this chapter will
be on scenarios where the sender is the "main" source for the media stream, and
where the proxy plays an auxiliary role.

   More complex systems can be used in practice [4,11,41,52], for example, multiple proxies could play a role, or the content could be delivered from more than one
sender, to multiple users, through multiple network routes, etc. In recent years,
peer-to-peer (P2P) networks [45,54,57] have also been studied as alternatives to
traditional client–server architectures. However, a discussion of the simpler system is sufficient to understand the various bandwidth adaptation mechanisms.

4.1.2 Chapter Outline

The chapter is organized as follows. In Section 4.2, we first discuss how the
bandwidth variations affect the received multimedia quality, especially for delay-
constrained transmission. Here we introduce an important concept, namely that
of an end-to-end delay constraint for a multimedia communication system. Then
we provide a global overview of a bandwidth adaptation system architecture in
Section 4.3, discussing the trade-off and criteria to choose a particular adaptation
mechanism for a given application. In Section 4.4, we describe different coding techniques that can be used to adjust the coding rate of a multimedia source
to match the available bandwidth, and briefly review the optimization techniques.
Finally, Section 4.5 provides a summary of the main ideas introduced in this chapter.

4.2 IMPACT OF AVAILABLE BANDWIDTH ON MULTIMEDIA QUALITY

In order to understand bandwidth adaptation mechanisms for multimedia applications, it is necessary to understand first the impact of bandwidth variations on
received media quality.

4.2.1 Downloading and Streaming

In contrast to data communication or to simple media downloading, real-time media streaming is often subject to strict delay constraints. The main difference with respect to a download application is that *media playback starts as data is still being received, so that playback could be interrupted if the decoder ran out of data to decode.*

Typical streaming applications operate as follows:

1. **Data request**. A request is sent to the media sender so that data streaming to the receiver starts.
2. **Client buffer loading**. As data starts to reach the client, decoding does not start immediately. Instead the client waits to have "enough" data to start decoding.
3. **Playback**. Once there is sufficient data available at the client, playback starts and at that point only relatively minor adjustments in the playback timing are possible, so that the rate at which media is played back (e.g., the number of video frames per second) needs to remain nearly constant.[1] An example of playback adaptation can be found in [39] and in Chapter 16.

There are multiple strategies for clients to determine that enough data is available to begin decoding. For example, a target total number of bits may have to be buffered before playback starts. Alternatively, a predetermined time for buffering (e.g., a few seconds) could be chosen so that users always experience the same time latency before playback starts. Finally, a more practical approach may be to wait until the number of bits that represents a selected playback time has been received (e.g., the number of bits needed to encode a video segment with a predetermined duration). Details can be found in Chapter 14.

Note that the primary concern in many applications is playback latency, rather than storage at the receiver. Thus, in applications such as streaming to a computer, where there is plenty of memory available, the amount of data loaded before playback may still be kept small to limit the initial latency in the system. Note also that latency is particularly important when the user is expected to frequently switch media sources, as the latency penalty will be incurred every time the user switches.

Regardless of which technique is chosen to preload the buffer, at the time when playback starts, the decoder will have a certain number of bits available for decoding. This available data translates into a playback duration (e.g., if there are

---

[1] More precisely, the number of frames per second received needs to be consistent with what the receiver expects to play back. Thus, adaptation mechanisms that involve both transmitter and receiver are possible (e.g., so that fewer frames per second are transmitted and played back when bandwidth availability is reduced).

N compressed frames in the decoder buffer and K frames/second are decoded, then the decoder will be able to play from the buffer for N/K seconds). Thus the amount of data available in the decoder buffer at a given time tells us for how long playback could proceed, even if *no data was to be received* from the network.

4.2.2 Available Bandwidth and Media Quality

To understand the need for bandwidth adaptation, consider what would happen if reductions in channel bandwidth were not matched by reductions in the source coding rate. Assume a constant media playback rate, for example, a fixed number of frames per second in a video application. When network bandwidth becomes lower, if the number of bits per frame does not change, then the number of frames per second received is bound to decrease. Since the receiver continues playing frames at the same rate, eventually there will be no frames left for playback in the receiver buffer and thus playback will be interrupted. This will be a *decoder buffer underflow*.

Thus, as network bandwidth fluctuates, bandwidth adaptation is needed to ensure that playback is not interrupted. Roughly speaking, this requires that the number of frames/second provided by the network matches (on average) the number of frames/second consumed for playback at the receiver. The general goal of bandwidth adaptation mechanisms will be to manage the quality of the frames transmitted so that when the available bandwidth is reduced, the rate (and hence the quality) of transmitted frames is also reduced. In essence, the goal is to avoid service interruptions by lowering the media quality in a "graceful" manner.

We next provide a more detailed discussion of the delay constraints that are present in a real-time media communications system.

4.2.3 Delay-Constrained Transmission

Consider, as an example of delay-constrained transmission, a real-time video transmission system where all operations have to be completed within a predetermined time interval. The *end-to-end delay* from a video source to a destination contains the following five components, as illustrated in Figure 4.1:

- *Encoding delay* ΔT_e: the delay required to capture and encode a video frame.
- *Encoder buffer delay* ΔT_{eb}: the time the encoded media data corresponding to a given frame spends in the transmission buffer. Note that this delay could be zero if the channel bandwidth is higher than the bit rate produced by the encoder, that is, data transmission would start as soon as video data is placed in the buffer.

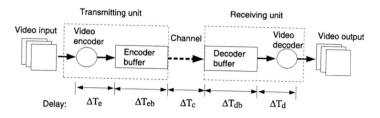

FIGURE 4.1:   Delay components of a communication system.

- *Transmission channel delay* ΔT_c: the delay for encoded data being transmitted through the network, caused by transmission, congestion, and possible retransmission over a lossy channel.
- *Decoder buffer delay* ΔT_{db}: the time for encoded data to wait in the decoder buffer for decoding. This delay allows smoothing out the variations in transmission delay and in rates across frames.
- *Decoding delay* ΔT_d: the delay for decoding process and final display.

Both encoding and decoding delays are usually fixed, so that we focus primarily on the remaining delay terms. Note that when considering pre-encoded media, the encoding delay is not considered as the video is already encoded off-line and ready for transmission. In this case we can consider that the encoding buffer is of infinite size and contains the complete encoded sequence.

In summary, the main constraint in the system is the status of the decoder buffer, that is, as long as the decoder buffer contains data, decoding can proceed. Thus bandwidth adaptation mechanisms should be designed with the objective of ensuring that the decoder buffer is not "starved" of data. In some cases, accurate and timely information about the decoder buffer state is available, which can then be used to make bandwidth adjustments (this would be the case, for example, if the client makes bandwidth adaptation decisions). In other cases, exact information may not be available, but the state of the buffer could be estimated using, for example, estimates of available bandwidth.

Different applications may have different delay requirements. For example, for live interactive video, a round-trip delay between 150 and 400 ms is usually required, while an initial play-out delay up to a few seconds is acceptable for noninteractive video streaming. Once selected, end-to-end delay requirements impose a constraint on the encoding rate for each frame.

4.3 OVERVIEW OF BANDWIDTH ADAPTATION ARCHITECTURES

We are now ready to define more precisely what we consider as *bandwidth adaptation mechanisms*: These are techniques that enable the rate of a media stream to be modified during a playback session (i.e., while a user is connected and receiving content for playback) in order to accommodate changes in the network (e.g., changes in available bandwidth, congestion, and packet losses).

In order to provide a rough classification of bandwidth adaptation architectures, note that defining a specific mechanism requires choosing:

- *Adaptation points*, that is, the locations in the network where the bit stream is adapted to match specific bandwidth requirements. For example, adaptation could take place at the sender, at a proxy, or even at the client application.
- *Decision agents*, that is, the component within the system where decisions about transmission rate changes are made. This decision could be made at the sender, a proxy, or the client, based on whatever information is available at that point in the network.
- *Coding techniques*, that is, the source coding techniques designed to facilitate bandwidth adaptation. Note that not every technique is appropriate for a certain combination of adaptation point and decision agent. These techniques are discussed in Section 4.4.

It is important to note that, in general, bandwidth adaptation decisions need *not* be made at the same point in the network where the adaptation itself takes place. A concrete example of this situation is client-driven techniques where each client evaluates the status and parameters of its own transmission link and requests to the sender changes to the streaming parameters; in this case bandwidth adaptation decisions are made by clients and put in place by the sender.

In general, the choice of adaptation point and decision agent for a particular system depends on what information is available to each component of the system (client, sender, or proxy if there is any), on available computational resources, and on the characteristics of the bit stream.

4.3.1 Trade-Offs

Before discussing specific architectures in detail it is useful to understand how operating at client, server, or proxy leads to different trade-offs.

First, note that adaptation decisions should be based on available information about (i) the state of the network (e.g., bandwidth availability) and (ii) the relative importance of information encoded in the media stream (e.g., how much degradation will result from dropping one of the layers in a scalable representation, or in general the rate–distortion characteristics of different parts of the stream).

Figure 4.2 illustrates that source-related information is likely to be known more accurately at the sender (which can analyze media as it encodes or extracts relevant information from an existing stream) than at the client (which must rely on information provided to it by the server). Similarly, more efficient adaptation

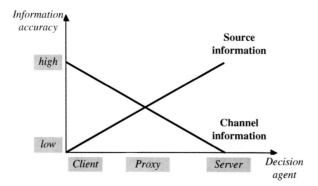

FIGURE 4.2:   Trade-off between the accuracy of source information and channel information available at various network locations.

decisions are possible when information about the state of the network is timely and accurate. Ideally, information should be available about the channel behavior observed by the client. Thus the client has access to more accurate information in a more timely way, as it observes packet arrival events. Figure 4.2 also illustrates that since the most accurate information is not available in a single place, some algorithms will entail information exchange between client and sender. Examples include where the client sends packet status feedback to the sender or where the sender provides the client with information about the source, such as an "RD preamble" [40].

Second, two major factors affect the performance of a bandwidth adaptation algorithm for a single client, namely (i) the granularity with which bandwidth can be adapted and (ii) the speed with which changes can be made to react to variations in network behavior.

Figure 4.3 illustrates that when actual adaptation (i.e., change in the rate at which data is sent to the client) is performed at the server, finer granularity can be achieved. Conversely, when adaptation takes place at the server the reaction time may be longer because packets resulting from adaptation will take longer to arrive at the client.

Third, it is often important to consider system-level trade-offs. Not only how a particular client's quality is affected by bandwidth adaptation, but rather how adaptation affects overall network performance. Figure 4.4 illustrates how system scalability and overall network utilization are affected by choices made in the bandwidth adaptation mechanism. If decisions on how to change the bandwidth, and even adaptation itself, are performed close to the client, the system will be easier to scale, since more of the computation cost will be borne by the clients. However, if bandwidth adaptation is performed close to the clients this will be to

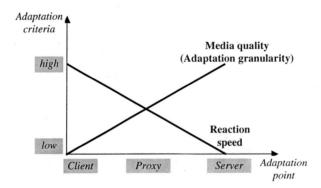

FIGURE 4.3: Comparison on bandwidth adaptation flexibility and reaction time to serve a single client.

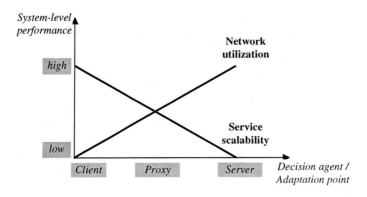

FIGURE 4.4: Comparison on service scalability and overall network utilization when serving multiple clients.

the detriment of overall network utilization, since data rate reductions will only reduce utilization close to the client.

4.3.2 Where Should the Adaptation Points Be?

As introduced earlier, an adaptation point is the system component where the bandwidth of the stream is physically changed. Each possible choice of location for the adaptation points has different advantages in terms of various performance metrics of interest.

4.3.2.1 Sender

The sender has the most flexibility in terms of compression format, since it can adjust the coding parameters in real time (in case live encoding to single users is performed), and can switch between several simultaneously produced streams (simulcast), etc. Moreover, the sender is typically least constrained in terms of storage and processing. Generally, then, adaptation at the sender provides the most flexibility from a source coding perspective. In practice, this means that when the sender performs bandwidth adaptation, this makes it possible to achieve finer grain bandwidth adaptation will be possible, as shown in Figure 4.3, with least penalty in terms of quality at the receiver.

There are several drawbacks in server-driven bandwidth adaptation. The sender is furthest away from the client; thus when congestion occurs in the network there may be a delay before the bandwidth adaptation can take effect (see Figure 4.3). Moreover, depending on where network information is being captured, this information may be unreliable. If bandwidth changes are requested by the client (see Section 4.3.3), and are thus based on more reliable information about the state of the network, letting the adaptation happen at the server means that the delay in reacting can be significant, which can reduce the effectiveness of bandwidth adaptation. If the sender itself is estimating the network state, it will be able to adapt faster, but may not have sufficiently accurate information about the network to be effective.

Adaptation at the server also presents problems in terms of *scalability* in cases where data is being broadcast to multiple clients. First, each server may be limited in the number of clients it can provide content to simultaneously, in particular if compression or bandwidth adaptation is computationally expensive. Second, the server may have to create separate versions of the same content for clients with different Internet access bandwidths, for example, one for 56K modem connections, and another for DSL, etc. This will in turn create a heavy traffic load in the local network around the server, which may also have a negative impact on other content being served.

Physical adaptation is closely related to the coding techniques applied in a particular application. Since the sender can access the source more flexibly, a number of adaptation techniques have been proposed. Such techniques include source rate control (i.e., adjusting coding parameters during the encoding process [29,76]), rate–distortion optimized packet scheduling [16,48], and switching between different bit streams or layers [19,67].

4.3.2.2 Client

Bandwidth adaptation at the client essentially means that the client does not decode all the content it receives. This would be beneficial only in terms of lowering the complexity of decoding or avoiding decoding of lower priority data that is likely to be corrupted. This type of adaptation in general requires a coding format that supports complexity scalability. The reconstructed quality is related to the complexity of the decoder used. For example, van der Schaar and de With [70] proposed to reduce the memory costs of an MPEG-2 decoder by re-compressing the I- and P-reference pictures prior to motion-compensated reconstruction. Transform coding and motion estimation algorithms with complexity scalability have also been studied [35,36,55]. In addition to the complexity-scalable modifications of existing decoders, recent research has also attempted to model the complexity based on the compressed source characteristics and the decoding platform capabilities [69]. Clearly, such a system would have no impact on the traffic being carried by the network, and thus would not contribute to reduced congestion.

4.3.2.3 Proxy

Proxies are a good compromise between server and client adaptation. A proxy is responsible for a smaller number of clients than a server, which improves scalability and traffic balancing, and is also closer to the clients so it can respond faster to changes that affect the client. Most often, the source information at the proxy is stored as a pre-encoded stream received from the original media server, and thus transcoding is widely employed for adaptation at this point. For example, Shen *et al.* [59] have proposed a transcoding-enabled proxy caching system to provide different appropriate video quality to different network environments.

4.3.3 Sender-, Client-, and Proxy-Driven Adaptation

Note that there are many situations where the changes in source coding rate are implemented at one point in the network, based on decisions made somewhere else. A particular case of interest is that where the client makes decisions about data to be transmitted and submits these to the server.

4.3.3.1 Client-Driven Decisions

Information about the status of decoded data is best when bandwidth adaptation decisions are made by the client, in particular when these decisions are based on accurate and fine grain information, for example, arrival or not arrival of individual packets. The client-driven approach can also help reduce the processing complexity at the server side, thus allowing the server to support more clients simultaneously.

Examples of this method include the Adaptive Stream Management (ASM) process of the SureStream technology used in RealSystem 8 [19]. Two major components involved in this process are a compressed media file, which contains multiple independently encoded streams of a given source, and an ASM rule book, which describes various forms of channel adaptation that involve selecting combinations of encoded streams as a function of the channel status (including bandwidth, packet loss, and loss effect on the reconstructed signal). The ASM rule book is sent to the client at the beginning of a session. During transmission, the client monitors the rate and loss statistics of arriving packets, and then instructs the server to subscribe to a rule, or combination of rules, to match the current channel behavior. Another example is that of receiver-driven adaptation in the context of multicast delivery [15,46].

A drawback is that, while the client makes the decisions, these need to be implemented in either a server or a proxy, as in the example given earlier. This is because bandwidth adaptation at the client can only help in reducing the complexity of decoding. Thus there will be some latency before the changes in bandwidth can be implemented. Another potential drawback is that some clients, such as low-power hand-held devices, may not have sufficient computation power to implement a complex decision process.

4.3.3.2 Proxy-Driven Decisions

In this type of system, proxies can estimate the state of the network (or get this information from the client) and then decide on appropriate changes to the bandwidth to be used by the media stream. For example, a proxy can select certain packets to be forwarded to the client, change transcoding parameters, or send instructions to the server so that the server can modify the information it transmits. Chakareski *et al.* [10] have proposed a rate–distortion optimized framework in the scenario of proxy-driven streaming. At any given time, the proxy determines which packets should be requested from the media server and which should be retransmitted directly from the proxy to the client in order to meet rate constraints on the last hop while minimizing the average end-to-end distortion. Approaches that have investigated the role of proxies in terms of both streaming and caching also include [50]. The proxy, usually located at the edge of a backbone network, coordinates the communication between the source server and the client, and can potentially achieve better bandwidth usage than a client- or server-driven system.

4.3.3.3 Server-Driven Decisions

Finally, in this scenario estimates of network state are provided to the server, which decides on data to be sent to each client. Feedback is often required for this approach. The server-based approach has the most information about the source (e.g., about possible rate–distortion operating points) and thus can work with a more flexible and efficient adaptation algorithm in terms of source coding. In addition, the server can regulate connections with different clients as a whole to improve overall bandwidth utilization. The main disadvantage of this approach is that the server may not have reliable or timely information about the state of the network near the client.

As an example, the work of Hsu *et al.* [29] performs source rate control by assigning quantizers to each of the video blocks under the rate constraints at the encoder, where the available channel rate is estimated by incorporating the channel information provided by the feedback channel and a priori channel model. Related work [30] shows that source rate control algorithms can also be applied for various types of network-related rate constraints. Intelligent transport mechanisms, such as optimal packet scheduling for a scalable multimedia representation [16,48], can also be performed at the server.

4.3.4 Criteria and Constraints

This section provides an overview of different criteria that can be applied to select a bandwidth adaptation mechanism for a given application. We emphasize that this is, by necessity, a qualitative discussion. Many of the techniques that are mentioned in this chapter have only been proposed in a research context and have not been fully tested in a more realistic network environment. Moreover, a quantitative comparison of the various methods is likely to be very complex, as should be clear given the number of criteria to be considered in general.

4.3.4.1 Media Quality

Clearly, the ultimate criterion to evaluate the performance of a bandwidth adaptation mechanism should be the resulting subjective media quality at the receiver in the presence of typical bandwidth variations. Some progress has been made in devising objective metrics that can capture the perceptual quality of media under various compression strategies [34,37,68]. These objective metrics are most advanced for the analysis of audio sources, somewhat less so for video applications. Approaches that can compare meaningfully different methods in the presence of variations in the network behavior (e.g., bandwidth fluctuations, packet losses) are not that readily available.

Service interruptions, such as those that might occur if no bandwidth adaptation is used, are obviously undesirable, and so one could, for example, compare different techniques in terms of their outage probability (the probability that perceptual quality over a given period of time drops below acceptable levels). A comparison would still be challenging: for example, an end user may deem two configurations with different, but nonnegligible, outage probability to be equally unacceptable.

Quality evaluation is also more complicated once a bandwidth adaptation mechanism is put into place because these mechanisms are dynamic in nature.

Thus, they operate only when the bandwidth falls below certain levels and lead to changes in the media quality (e.g., in the context of video, variations in frame rate, frame resolution, frame quality). In this situation, it is unclear whether users will base their quality assessment on the perceived "average" quality, the worst case quality level, the duration of the worst quality, etc.

Many currently deployed practical media streaming systems generally select one of multiple streams, that is, the one whose bandwidth best matches the bandwidth available to the end user; in many cases no adaptation is possible within a stream. Thus system designers only have a limited amount of real-life experience with bandwidth adaptation mechanisms. It also follows from this that the impact of various such mechanisms on perceptual media quality is not as well understood.

In summary, while progress has been made toward understanding subjective quality metrics for various types of media, challenges remain in addressing situations where quality adaptations (not to mention information losses) take place. For this reason, and also to facilitate bandwidth adaptation mechanisms, objective quality metrics, such as peak signal-to-noise ratio (PSNR), are often used. For example, authors have proposed optimizing average PSNR (e.g., [29]) or minimizing the loss in PSNR introduced by bandwidth adaptation, with respect to the PSNR achieved when the media stream transmitted at a given target bit rate (e.g., [16]).

4.3.4.2 End-to-End Delay, Reaction Time, and Latency

As discussed earlier, a longer end-to-end delay facilitates preserving a consistent quality level in the face of bandwidth fluctuations. Roughly speaking, a longer end-to-end delay leads to more multimedia units (e.g., video frames) being stored in the decoder buffer so that the application can absorb short-term variations in bandwidth.

When the end-to-end delay is not long, the reaction time of the adaptation system to changes in bandwidth becomes important. The system has to detect relevant variations in network behavior and then trigger the necessary changes in the media stream so as to best match bandwidth availability. Ideally, this should happen sufficiently fast so that the end user does not suffer from negative consequences of mismatch between network availability and stream requirements.

Note that this leads to interesting design trade-offs in the context of the adaptation architectures discussed earlier. For example, a faster reaction may be possible if the sender makes adaptation decisions, but these may suffer from a somewhat worse knowledge of network status at the client.

Long end-to-end delay is a practical solution only for one-way transmission applications. For two-way communications, a long delay will limit the interactivity. Even in the case of one-way communications, excessive end-to-end delays lead to higher initial latencies, which would be undesirable if the user switches multimedia streams frequently.

4.3.4.3 Complexity

An interesting challenge in architecting a bandwidth adaptation mechanism is that several components (client, proxy, and sender) can play a role. Thus, taking into account complexity requires identifying first which of these components is least constrained in terms of complexity.

While it may appear at first obvious that the server will be richer in computation resources, this may not be true in general. In particular, for applications such that each sender is responsible for multiple clients, overall computation power at the sender may be significant, but computation power for each client served may have to be limited in order to ensure scalability.

4.3.4.4 Storage

Storage constraints are unlikely to be of much importance, except for mobile applications. It is also worth mentioning the complexity implications of shared storage. While massive storage is often available at a very low cost, there may be significant computation costs involved in managing a large number of streams being produced out of a shared storage device. In this context, bandwidth adaptation tasks (e.g., switching between two pre-encoded versions of a media stream) may add to the complexity of the system.

4.3.4.5 Information Overhead

Consider existing digital video delivery systems (e.g., a digital cable system) and compare them with systems such as those we have discussed. In a digital cable system bandwidth is expected to be reliable and there is minimal interaction between receiver and sender.

Instead, proposed bandwidth adaptation architectures often require auxiliary information to be exchanged between client and sender. Examples of this extra information include estimates of channel state, acknowledgments of reception of information, and rate distortion "preambles."

4.3.5 Examples

Depending on the type of application, network characteristics, and optimization criteria, it is possible that different bandwidth adaptation architectures may be preferable. This section sketches some examples that allow us to discuss how particular choices of architecture can be made. Note that we are not proposing a concrete methodology for architecture selection. Moreover, there may be several architectures that are suitable for a given scenario. Thus, these examples are meant to illustrate possible approaches in the design process, rather than to claim optimality for any of the different approaches.

In the case of one-to-one interactive two-way communication, such as video conferencing, a relatively short end-to-end delay, usually between 150 and 400 ms, is required. Thus it may be preferable for the decision agent and the adaptation point to be located close to each other so as to avoid excessive delay before adaptation takes place. One possible solution is presented in Table 4.1. When a server receives feedback indicating a channel status change, it estimates the new available channel bandwidth [29] and then makes the corresponding adaptation decision. The adaptation can be as simple as skipping transmission of some of the packets to prevent video freezing or losing connections. More advanced techniques can also be applied, such as, for example, adjusting the video codec parameters to increase or decrease the encoding rate. However, the limited bandwidth and stringent delay requirement in this case may limit the potential performance gains achievable through adaptation.

In the case of one-to-one one-way streaming, a longer initial play-out delay, of up to a few seconds, is likely to be acceptable. A more appropriate solution for this case would then be client-driven streaming, such as the SureStream technology used in RealSystem [19]. During the streaming session, a client monitors the bandwidth and loss characteristics of its connection and makes decisions based on more accurate and fine grain channel information. Then it instructs the server to take certain actions, for example, switching to different streams, or selectively transmitting only the number of layers in a layered codec that the given link can support, such that the end-to-end distortion can be minimized over the current channel condition.

In the case of Internet broadcast or multicast, the traditional single-server-based delivery system faces several major problems, including service scalability and traffic load unbalance, as discussed in Section 4.3.2. To address these problems, today's content delivery networks employ multiple geographically dis-

Table 4.1: Examples of bandwidth adaptation architectures for different video communication applications

Application	Bandwidth estimator	Decision agent	Adaptation point
One-to-one interactive two-way communication	Server	Server	Server
One-to-one one-way streaming	Client	Client	Server
Internet broadcast	Client	Proxy	Proxy

tributed edge servers to either forward the incoming live content or deliver the on-demand content from their local cached storages to their local clients. It is possible to directly extend the client-driven server-adaptation technique to multicast delivery. However, it may be better if proxy servers can take a more active role in the bandwidth adaptation process, as the bandwidth limitations often occur in the access network, such as a DSL connection. This proxy-based architecture, as shown in Table 4.1, can reduce the reaction time, avoid congestion in the Internet, and provide appropriate qualities for clients with different connections.

4.4 CODING TECHNIQUES FOR BANDWIDTH ADAPTATION

Previous sections have discussed general bandwidth adaptation architectures under the assumption that a mechanism would be available to adjust the number of bits transmitted to represent multimedia sources. In this section we provide an overview of coding techniques that can be used in practice to adjust the coding rate of transmitted multimedia sources.

Many criteria can be used to compare different coding techniques. Since their primary goal is to enable representation of the sources at different rate levels, one primary concern is what reproduction quality is achievable at each of those rate levels. Thus, as for all coding techniques, it will be important to know the rate distortion (RD) characteristic of each possible operating point.

In addition, there are other criteria that are specific to bandwidth adaptation scenarios.

First, it will be useful to provide as many rate operating points as possible (i.e., so that fine grain adaptation is possible). Generally speaking, finer grain in the adaptation will come at the cost of increases in achievable distortion for a given rate.

Second, some coding techniques will only allow adaptation to take place at the encoder, while others will enable adaptation anywhere in the network. The latter model will typically also lead to some RD inefficiency.

Finally, adaptation granularity can be evaluated not only in terms of achievable rate points, but also in terms of temporal constraints. In some applications it may be desirable to adjust the rate of individual temporal components (e.g., frames in a video sequence), which again may come at the cost of reduced RD performance.

4.4.1 Rate Control

Rate control techniques are used *during the encoding process*. They rely on adjusting multiple coding parameters to meet a target encoding rate. We focus here on rate control techniques for video, as in both audio and speech coding variable bit rate encoding techniques (which tend to lead to more challenging rate control) are not as popular.

In the case of video, when the same coding parameters (e.g., quantization step size, prediction mode) are used throughout a video session, the number of bits per frame will change depending on the video content so that the output bit rate will vary from frame to frame. Thus, when video content is "easy" to encode (e.g., low motion and low complexity scenes) and a given quantization selection is chosen, the rate will tend to be lower than if the same combination of quantizers was used for a more complex scene. Even though the encoder and decoder buffers can help smooth the (short term) variations in the rate per frame, a rate-control algorithm is usually needed in order to allocate bits among all coding units (e.g., frame, macroblock, or others) to maximize the end quality subject to the rate constraint.

All major video coding standards provide mechanisms for flexible coding parameter selection, with the chosen parameters being communicated to the decoder as overhead. To illustrate the key concepts, here we concentrate on a hybrid video coding structure, which is an essential component of all major standards, and in particular on one based on block-based motion-compensated prediction and Discrete Cosine Transform (DCT) coding. In such a framework, a frame is divided into a number of macroblocks (MB), each containing a luminance block (of size 16×16) and two chrominance blocks (e.g., 8×8 Cb and 8×8 Cr).

A series of coding decisions have to be made in compressing each frame:

1. Type of frame (e.g., I-, P-, or B-frame) to be chosen or whether the frame is to be skipped, that is, not encoded at all.
2. Mode to be used for each MB, for example, Intra, Inter, Skip, etc.
3. If an MB is coded in INTRA mode,
   (a) What quantization step size (QP) should be used to code the DCT coefficients of each block?
   (b) If intra prediction is allowed, for example, in H.264, how to perform intra prediction; that is, how to generate the reference block from the neighboring blocks in the same frame.
4. If an MB is coded in INTER mode,
   (a) What motion compensation should be used, for example, with or without overlapping, reference frame selection, search range, and block size?
   (b) How to code the residual frame, for example, which QP should be chosen?

The options just listed are by no means exhaustive; they are intended to serve as an illustration of the range of coding mode choices available in modern video coders. Note that as the number of possible modes increases so does the complexity of the encoding process and the importance of selecting efficient rate control algorithms. In fact, one can attribute much of the substantial coding gains achieved by recent standards, such as H.264/MPEG-4 part 10 AVC [2], to the addition of several new coding modes combined with efficient mode decision tools based on RD criteria.

A very common approach to rate control is to modify the QP [29,65]. A large QP can reduce the number of encoded bits at the expense of an increased quantization error, and vice versa. However, changing QP only while keeping the other coding modes constant may not achieve the optimal performance. For example, coding in INTER mode is effective in most cases when changes in video content are due to the motion of objects in the scene. Instead, INTRA mode may be more appropriate in situations when there is a significant difference between coded and reference images, such as uncovered regions (part of the scene is uncovered by a moving object) or lighting changes. However, the optimal selection of INTER/INTRA coding for a given block may in fact be different at different QPs. More general rate-control algorithms should optimize different coding parameters as well, such as frame rate, coding modes for each frame and MB, and motion estimation methods [13,24,76].

Each combination of these coding parameters results in a different trade-off between rate and distortion. Thus efficient parameter settings will be those that are chosen based on rate–distortion optimized techniques. The typical problem formulation seeks to select the coding parameters that minimize the distortion under constraints on the rate (usually the average bit rate over a short interval). Many solutions have been proposed, with some based on heuristic approaches and others following well-known techniques such as Lagrangian optimization or dynamic programming. More details on this topic can be found in [53,65] and references therein.

The computation involved in the optimization approach mainly includes two parts: (1) collection of rate–distortion data, which may require to actually code the source with all different parameter settings, and (2) the optimization algorithm itself. Both parts can be computationally intensive but often the data collection itself represents the bulk of the complexity, which has led to the development of numerous approaches to model the R–D characteristics of multimedia data [20, 27,28,43]. Two main types of modeling approaches have been reviewed in [28]. One class of techniques [27] involves defining models for both the coding system and the source so that R–D functions can be estimated before actually compressing the source. The modeling accuracy depends on the robustness of the R–D model to handle different source characteristics. The second class of techniques requires actually coding the source several times and then processing the observed R–D data to obtain a complete R–D curve. Examples include the estimation algorithms proposed in [20,43]. These approaches are usually more computationally intensive, as well as more accurate, since they estimate the parameters from the actual coding results of the corresponding source.

In summary, the choice of an appropriate rate-control algorithm depends on the multimedia application, especially on whether it is delay constrained. For instance, a complicated approach can be used for off-line coding. However, heuristic approaches may be more practical for online live multimedia communications.

4.4.2 Transcoding

The term "media transcoding" is normally used to describe techniques where a compressed media bit stream format is converted into format. It is often used at either the server or the proxy when the source is only available as a pre-encoded stream so as to match limitations in transmission, storage, processing, or display capabilities of specific network, terminals, or display devices. Transcoding is one of the key technologies for end-to-end compatibility of two or more different networks or systems operating with different characteristics and constraints.

Because the transcoder takes as an input a compressed media stream, the decoded quality of the transcoder output is limited by the input stream, which has certain information loss compared to the original source. However, the transcoder has access to all the coding parameters and statistics, which can be easily extracted from the input stream. This information can be used not only to reduce the transcoding complexity, but also to improve the quality of the transcoded stream using a rate–distortion optimization algorithm.

A typical application of transcoding is to adapt the bit rate of a precompressed video stream to a reduced channel bandwidth. Clearly, we can first reconstruct video back to the pixel domain by decoding the input compressed bit stream and then re-encode the decoded video to meet the target bit rate. The rate control techniques described earlier can then be used at the encoding stage. However, the whole process (decoding and encoding) is very computationally expensive, and more efficient techniques have been developed that reuse information contained in the original input bit stream.

The main drawback of these more efficient transcoding techniques is the drift problem (which will also arise in some of the other coding techniques introduced in this chapter). Drift is created if the reference frame used for motion compensation at the encoder is different from that used at the decoder. This happens, for example, when the transcoder simply requantizes the residual DCT coefficients with a larger QP to reduce the output bit rate. When a decoder receives the transcoded bit stream, it reconstructs the frame at a reduced quality and stores it into the frame buffer. If this frame is used as prediction for future frames, the mismatch error is added to the residual of the predicted frame, leading to a degraded quality for all the following frames until the next I frame. Based on the trade-off between complexity and coding quality, we briefly describe two basic transcoding architectures, namely, open-loop and closed-loop transcoders.

Figure 4.5a shows an open-loop architecture based on a requantization approach [51]. The bit stream is dequantized and requantized to match the bit rate

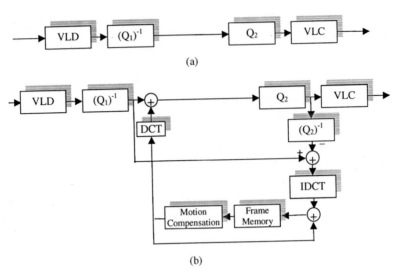

FIGURE 4.5: Transcoding architectures for bit-rate reduction [72]: (a) Open loop. (b) Closed loop.

target. Another open-loop approach is to discard the high-frequency DCT coefficients [22,66] to reduce the rate. All these operations work on the DCT coefficients directly, and thus the computation load is light but this architecture leads to drift.

A closed-loop architecture introduces an extra drift-compensation module, as shown in Figure 4.5b [7], to eliminate the mismatch between the reference frames at the encoder and decoder. The frame memory in the configuration holds a difference signal and is added to the residual component to compensate for the prediction mismatch. The additional DCT/IDCT can be removed by using DCT-domain MC [12,47,62]; several simplified DCT-domain transcoders are described in [8,42]. Compared to the straightforward approach with cascaded decoder and encoder, this approach usually requires less computation to achieve almost equivalent quality with the exception of slight inaccuracy due to nonlinearity introduced by clipping and rounding operations or floating point inaccuracies [79]. Even for the cascaded pixel-domain transcoder, the encoder can be simplified by reusing the motion vectors and other information.

Regardless of the transcoding architecture, a rate-control algorithm is applied to yield the desired bit rate. As discussed in [56], a two-pass rate-control approach typically performs better than a single-pass approach, since information obtained from the results of the first pass (e.g., selected RD operating points of all frames) can be used in the second pass of the algorithm to improve the quality. A transcoder can be regarded as a special two-pass approach [78], where the first pass creates the input compressed bit stream and the second pass creates the output compressed stream based on the results of the first pass. For example, bit allocation to each frame ideally depends on the frame complexity, which is not easy to estimate for real-time video encoding but can be obtained more accurately from the number of bits each frame spent in the input bit stream. Similarly, optimal requantization for transcoding [26,63,75] requires the knowledge of the original DCT coefficients statistics, which can be estimated from the input compressed bit stream as well.

In addition to being used for bit rate adaptation, video transcoding is also widely employed for spatial resolution and frame rate adaptation. More details on different transcoding techniques are well discussed elsewhere [72,78].

4.4.3 Scalable Coding

The coding methods discussed so far in this chapter aim to optimize the media quality for a fixed bit rate. This poses a problem when multiple users are trying to access the same media source through different network links and with different computing powers. Even in the case of a single user accessing one media source over a link with varying channel capacity, relying on an often complex rate-control algorithm to make rate adjustments in real time may not be practical (e.g., if the changes in rate have to occur in a very short time frame). Scalable coding is thus designed to facilitate bandwidth adaptation over a given bit rate range, as well as to provide error resilience for potential transmission errors.

Scalable coding, or layered coding [1,3,21,38,61], specifies a multilayer format in which a video sequence is coded into a base layer and one or more enhancement layers. The base layer provides a minimum acceptable level of quality, and each additional enhancement layer incrementally improves the quality. Thus, graceful degradation in the face of bandwidth drops or transmission errors can be achieved by decoding only the base layer, while discarding one or more of the enhancement layers. The enhancement layers are dependent on the base layer and cannot be decoded if the base layer is not received. A scalable compressed bit stream typically contains multiple embedded subsets, each of which represents the original video content in a particular amplitude resolution (called SNR scalability), spatial resolution (spatial scalability), temporal resolution (temporal scalability), or frequency resolution (frequency scalability or, in some cases, data partition). Scalable coders can have either coarse granularity or fine granularity. In MPEG-4 fine granularity scalability (FGS) [38], the enhancement-layer bit stream can be truncated at any point, where the reconstructed video quality increases with the number of bits received.

Unfortunately, all current scalable video coding standards suffer to some degree from a combination of lower coding performance and higher coding complexity, as compared to nonscalable coding. A key issue is how to exploit temporal correlation efficiently in scalable coding. It is well known that motion prediction increases the difficulty of achieving efficient scalable coding because scalability leads to multiple possible reconstructions of each frame [58]. In this situation either (i) the same predictor is used for all layers, which leads to either drift or coding inefficiency, or (ii) a different predictor is obtained for each reconstructed version and used for the corresponding layer of the current frame, which leads to added complexity. MPEG-2 SNR scalability with a single motion-compensated prediction (MCP) loop and MPEG-4 FGS exemplify the first approach. MPEG-2 SNR scalability uses the enhancement-layer information in the MCP loop for both base and enhancement layers, which leads to drift if the enhancement layer is not received. MPEG-4 FGS provides flexibility in bandwidth adaptation and error recovery because the enhancement layers are coded in "intra" mode, which results in low coding efficiency, especially for sequences that exhibit high temporal correlation. Some advanced approaches with multiple MCPs are described elsewhere [5,31,58,71,77]. In summary, the design goal in scalable coding is to minimize the reduction in coding efficiency while realizing the scalability to match the network requirements. More details on scalable video coding can be found in Chapter 5, and details on scalable audio coding can be found in Chapter 6.

An alternative to bandwidth adaptation and reliable communication is Multiple Description Coding (MDC) [25,74]. With this coding scheme, a video sequence is coded into a number of separate bit streams (referred to as descriptions) so that each description alone provides acceptable quality and incremental improvement can be achieved with additional descriptions. Each description is individually packetized and transmitted through separate channels or through one physical channel that is divided into several virtual channels by using appropriate time-interleaving techniques. Each description can be decoded independently to provide an acceptable level of quality. For this to be true, all the descriptions must have some basic information about the source, and therefore they are likely to be correlated. Some hybrid approaches have also been proposed recently to combine the advantages of layered coding and MDC [18,73].

Scalable coding techniques allow media servers to adapt to varying network conditions in real time. To do this, an intelligent transport mechanism is required to select the right packets (layers or descriptions) to send at a given transmission time to maximize the playback quality at the decoder. Some recent work has been focused on rate–distortion optimized scheduling algorithms for scalable video streaming [16,48]. In this case, each packet is not equally important due to different distortion contributions, playback deadlines, and packet dependencies caused by temporal prediction and layering. Runtime feedback information is employed to make the transport decisions based on the current network condition and decoder receiving status. See also Section 4.4.5.

4.4.4 Bit Stream Switching

Although scalable coding can potentially provide flexible bandwidth adaptation over unpredictable best-effort networks, current coding techniques still suffer from relatively low coding efficiency, especially when the bit rate range is large. As a result, bit stream switching techniques are widely used in many commercial video streaming systems [6,19] to create multiple versions of the same content at different bit rates and dynamically switch among them to accommodate the bandwidth variations. In this section, we introduce three major switching techniques, namely multiple bit rate coding, SP/SI pictures, and stream morphing.

4.4.4.1 Multiple Bit Rate (Simulcast) Coding

In this approach each media source is simply compressed into multiple independent nonscalable bit streams at different bit rates and qualities. During the transmission, the server switches to a particular bit stream whose transmission yields the minimum reconstructed distortion based on the estimation of actual channel bandwidth and loss characteristics. Ideally, once a change in network bandwidth is detected, the server will immediately switch to a more appropriate stream to reflect the change promptly. However, because of motion prediction, switching between bit streams at arbitrary locations, such as a P-frame, may introduce severe drift effects since the reference frames are different at the encoder and decoder.

The simplest way to achieve a drift-free switching is to insert I-frames periodically in each stream and let the switching from stream to stream occur only at those I-frames. Obviously, because adaptation requests only take effect when an I-frame is reached, this increases the latency of bandwidth adaptation. To provide more flexible adaptation, the frequency of I-frames has to be increased at a cost of significantly increased bit rates to achieve the same quality. Thus, allowing more effective stream switching comes at the cost of a decrease in video quality for a given target bit rate. In addition, the flexibility of bandwidth adaptation also depends on the number of different bit streams available, each coded at a different bit rate. The more bit streams are available, the more accurate and finer level bandwidth adjustments can be supported. The inefficiency of coding I-frames results in a much larger storage requirement on the media server when the number of supported bit streams is large. The trade-off between coding efficiency and switching flexibility thus becomes a main consideration on the design of a drift-free switching approach.

More efficient approaches for drift-free switching aim at removing the overhead associated with I-frames, which exists even for normal transmission without switching between bit streams. In order to facilitate switching at inter frames (i.e., P-/B-frames), an extra bit stream is created at each predefined switching point at

an increased rate cost when switching happens, while keeping the coding efficiency for normal transmission at the same or close to the one without supporting the switching functionality. One way is to encode the difference of reference
frames at the switching points and transmit this as an additional bit stream, which
can be used for drift compensation at the decoder. The mismatch can be removed
if lossless compression is applied. Another way is to introduce a specially encoded P-frame, called an S-frame [23], to achieve switching at the location of
inter frames. As illustrated in Figure 4.6a, to initiate switching from bit stream 1
to bit stream 2 at time t, an S-frame (frame $S_{12,t}$) is encoded as a P-frame with
the previously reconstructed frame at time $t - 1$ in bit stream 1 (frame $P_{1,t-1}$) as
the reference frame and the reconstructed frame at time t in bit stream 2 (frame

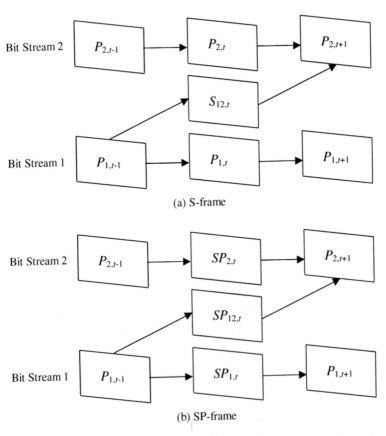

FIGURE 4.6:   Switching from bit stream 1 to bit stream 2 through specially encoded frames: (a) S-frame and (b) SP-frame.

$P_{2,t}$) as the target frame. This approach cannot completely eliminate the drift. However, by reducing the QP of the S-frame, the drift amount can be controlled and made relatively small. Another disadvantage of this approach is that the rate required for S-frames can be very large due to the small QP that is required. The SP-/SI-frames to be introduced in the next section provide an improved drift-free switching approach to the S-frames. In addition to switching between nonscalable bit streams, bit stream switching can also be performed for several independently coded scalable streams [67].

4.4.4.2 SP/SI Pictures

The extended profile of H.264/MPEG-4 part 10 AVC [2] introduces two new frame types referred to as SP-frames and SI-frames [33]. SP- and SI-frames facilitate switching between multiple independently coded bit streams and also provide "VCR-like" functionalities, such as random access, fast forward, fast backward, and so on.

Within each encoded bit stream, SP-frames are created at the switching points in two different types, namely primary SP-frame and secondary SP-frame (see Figure 4.6b). The primary SP-frame (frames $SP_{1,t}$ and $SP_{2,t}$ in Figure 4.6b) is created by motion-compensated prediction from the previously reconstructed frames in the same bit stream, while the corresponding secondary SP-frame (frame $SP_{12,t}$ as an example) is generated, with identical reconstructed values as the primary SP-frame (frame $SP_{2,t}$), by using the previously reconstructed values from another bit stream. A primary SP-frame is encoded with almost the same coding efficiency as the corresponding P-frame. The difference between SP- and P-/S-frames lies in that, due to the special encoding of the secondary SP-frame, the pair of SP-frames can be identically reconstructed even if they are predicted using different frames. Compared to I-frames, SP-frames can achieve same switching functionality with significantly fewer bits by exploiting motion-compensated predictive coding. An alternative to a secondary SP-frame is an SI-frame, using only intra prediction to produce identical reconstructed values as the corresponding primary SP-frame. It is mainly used when motion prediction is not efficient, such as switching between bit streams representing completely different video sequences, or for random access in which decoding of the current frame does not depend on any previous frames.

4.4.4.3 Stream Morphing

Stream morphing [44] has been introduced as an interesting alternative to scalable video coding and is related to techniques that have been proposed for efficient scalable DPCM coding [58,60,64]. Scalable coding schemes operate in the signal domain to separate an input into different layers. For example, in a closed loop system, the video sequence obtained from reconstructing the base layer is subtracted from the original video sequence, which is in turn compressed. Alternatively, an open loop system (e.g., one based on wavelet transforms) would directly separate the input sequence into "components" (e.g., subbands), compress these separately, and form the layers by grouping various of these components.

Stream morphing is based on the following observation. Consider a video sequence encoded with a nonscalable codec (say MPEG-2) at two different target rates. Clearly there will be some redundancy between the two bit streams since they represent the same sequence, albeit at different rates. For example, most blocks will have the same motion vectors at both rates, large DCT coefficients in the residual signal will tend to be in the same locations, etc. A stream morphing technique would use the low rate stream as the base layer. Then the enhancement layer will contain a bit stream with a special syntax that allows the decoder to reconstruct the high rate *bit stream* from the low rate *bit stream*. For example, this enhancement layer could include differential information with respect to the motion vectors included in the base layer. Note that this is a transformation between bit streams. Thus one of the principal differences between stream morphing and standard scalability tools is that *decoding the base layer is not needed to reproduce the signal at the highest quality*. Instead, the base layer bit stream is "morphed" into the high-resolution bit stream, on which a standard decoder is used (e.g., the MPEG-2 decoder in our example). Note also that the quality levels at the decoder are exactly determined by the two (or more) originally encoded versions.

4.4.5 Overview of Optimization Techniques for Bandwidth Adaptation

Recall that bandwidth adaptation requires (i) observing the state of the network, (ii) estimating or observing the state of the decoder, and then (iii) based on bandwidth availability and decoder state, deciding what information should be sent next to the decoder. In this section we discuss briefly this decision process. Our focus here is in highlighting the challenges involved and how these have to be addressed by proposed techniques.

Ideally the goal in deciding what information is sent to the decoder should be to maximize the expected quality at the decoder. Note that we consider expected quality because there is uncertainty about the actual quality available at the decoder; changes in bandwidth, packet losses, and so forth will affect the resulting quality.

To facilitate the discussion, in what follows we assume that information available for transmission has already been packetized. The role of the decision mechanisms under consideration is essentially to prioritize the transmission so that most "important" information is sent first.

Optimization of expected quality at the decoder is complex because of multiple factors:

- The expected distortion is hard to estimate.
- The candidate packets may depend on each other.
- At any given time there are many candidate packets.

Estimating the expected distortion at the transmitter requires first determining both the current "state" of the transmission channel and its expected behavior in the near future. Various types of channel models are considered in Chapters 7 and 11. The type of channel models available, for example, with memory [29] or without it [16,48], depends on the systems being considered. Observations may include packet receipt feedback, received power measurements, etc. While the accuracy of the models may be questionable, it is also likely that even an inaccurate model will provide enough information to improve on a system that makes no assumptions about the transmission channel.

In addition, estimations of expected distortion are based on the reconstruction quality achievable when different sets of packets are received. In cases where pre-encoded data is being transmitted it is possible, in theory, to quantify exactly achievable distortion in each scenario. In practice, however, techniques that require less computation and provide estimates of expected distortion may be preferable. For example, some methods may attach some importance to each packet, where the importance is based on some simplifications about the decoding process (e.g., frames that depend on frames received in error are not decoded, no error concealment is applied); see, for example, [16,48]. Then optimization techniques would seek to maximize the expected "importance" of packets received.

Most widely used video coding techniques make use of prediction across frames. This complicates distortion estimation, since a packet loss may affect multiple future frames. A very powerful technique used to capture the dependencies is that formalized by Chou and Miao [16], which leads to the creation of a directed acyclic graph to represent all the packets being transmitted. With this type of technique it is possible to attach more importance to packets from which multiple other packets depend. As we had indicated earlier for the channel model, even a rough model of these dependencies (which may not provide exact distortion values) is likely to provide better results than techniques that completely ignore the existence of these dependencies.

Optimization complexity should definitely be of concern. As has been demonstrated by various authors (see [9–11,14,16,17,32,48,49,73,80,81]) efficient techniques can be developed once knowledge of the structure of the media stream (including dependencies) and an estimate of the channel state are available. This can be done by estimating the expected distortions if several different candidate packets (not necessarily all available ones) were transmitted. This distortion can be estimated for one decision (the next packet to be transmitted) or more than one.

After this evaluation, the packet leading to a lower expected distortion is chosen, and this decision process is repeated for the next packet.

4.5 SUMMARY AND FURTHER READING

The heterogeneous and time-variant nature of today's networks imposes a number of challenges for real-time video communication. In this chapter, we have discussed alternative techniques for bandwidth adaptation and their relative merits. The main points made in this chapter are summarized as follows.

- We classify bandwidth adaptation architectures based on three basic design decisions, namely selection of adaptation points, decision agents, and source coding techniques. Bandwidth adaptation is made based on available source and channel information. The source-related information is known more accurately at the sender, while channel information is more accurate at the client. A proxy, located in the middle of the network, can achieve a good compromise between server and client adaptation.
- When the sender acts as the adaptation point, the highest degree of flexibility is possible in terms of source coding, which facilitates achieving finer granularity rate adaptation, reducing the quality penalty at the receiver. However, this may lead to a longer reaction time if network state information is provided by the receiver. Adaptation decisions may be inefficient if, instead, the sender itself has to estimate the state of the network without waiting for receiver feedback. Adaptation at the sender makes scaling to a large number of receivers more difficult, as it increases the computation load at the sender. Adaptation at the client can reduce decoding complexity, but will have no impact on the network traffic.
- If the sender is the decision agent, it will have access to more accurate source information, but may not have reliable or timely information about the network state near the receiver. This approach helps improve overall bandwidth utilization when multiple receivers are served by the sender. In contrast, if the client acts as the decision agent, there is potential for better adaptation decisions given the higher accuracy network and packet arrival information. However, when decisions made by the receiver have to be put in place by the sender, the latency involved can lead to lower adaptation efficiency.
- Rate control techniques are used during the encoding process to adjust coding parameters to meet a target encoding rate. Transcoding techniques, often used at either the server or the proxy, take a compressed media stream as an input and convert it to another compressed stream. Scalable coding provides flexible bandwidth adaptation over a given bit rate range rather than at a fixed bit rate. Different from the aforementioned techniques, bit

stream switching techniques encode the same media content into multiple versions at different bit rates and dynamically switch among them to accommodate the bandwidth variations. In this chapter we have discussed several switching techniques: multiple bit rate coding, SP/SI pictures, and stream morphing. The trade-off between coding efficiency (to reduce overhead) and switching flexibility is a main consideration on the design of various switching techniques.

Further details on many of the bandwidth adaptation techniques described in this chapter can be found in other literature, as well as in other chapters in this book. For example, Ortega and Ramchandran [53] and Sullivan and Wiegand [65] discuss rate–distortion optimization for image and video compression; Vetro *et al.* [72] and Xin *et al.* [78] provide overviews of transcoding; and Goyal [25] and Wang *et al.* [74] review state-of-the-art multiple description coding. For more details on rate–distortion-optimized streaming, the article by Chou and Miao [16] can serve as a starting point. Although this chapter focused on the fundamentals of bandwidth adaptation on a simple client–server system, there is considerable interest in more complex systems with multiple paths used for media transport, such as content delivery networks and P2P networks. The interested reader is referred to the work of Apostolopoulos *et al.* [4], Padmanabhan *et al.* [54], and Rejaie and Ortega [57].

REFERENCES

[1] ISO/IEC 13818-2. *Generic coding of moving pictures and associated audio, part-2 video*. November 1994.

[2] ISO/IEC 14496-10 and ITU-T Rec. H.264. *Advanced video coding*. 2003.

[3] ISO/IEC 14496-2/FPDAM4. *Coding of audio-visual objects, part-2 visual, amendment 4: streaming video profile*. July 2000.

[4] J. Apostolopoulos, T. Wong, W.-T. Tan, and S. Wee. On multiple description streaming with content delivery networks. In *Proc. Conf. Computer Communications (INFOCOM)*, June 2002.

[5] J. F. Arnold, M. R. Frater, and Y. Wang. Efficient drift-free signal-to-noise ratio scalability. *IEEE Trans. Circuits and Systems for Video Technology*, 10(1):70–82, February 2000.

[6] B. Birney. Intelligent streaming. http://www.microsoft.com/windows/windowsmedia/howto/articles/intstreaming.aspx, May 2003.

[7] P. Assunção and M. Ghanbari. Post-processing of MPEG2 coded video for transmission at lower bit rates. In *Proc. Int'l Conf. Acoustics, Speech, and Signal Processing*, volume 3, pages 1998–2001, May 1996.

[8] P. Assunção and M. Ghanbari. A frequency-domain video transcoder for dynamic bit-rate reduction of MPEG-2 bit streams. *IEEE Trans. Circuits and Systems for Video Technology*, 8(8):953–967, December 1998.

[9] J. Chakareski, J. Apostolopoulos, S. Wee, W. Tan, and B. Girod. Rate-distortion hint tracks for adaptive video streaming. *IEEE Trans. Circuits and Systems for Video Technology*, 15(10):1257–1269, October 2005.

[10] J. Chakareski, P. A. Chou, and B. Girod. Rate-distortion optimized streaming from the edge of the network. In *Proc. Workshop on Multimedia Signal Processing*, December 2002.

[11] J. Chakareski and B. Girod. Rate-distortion optimized packet scheduling and routing for media streaming with path diversity. In *Proc. Data Compression Conference*, March 2003.

[12] S.-F. Chang and D. G. Messerschmitt. Manipulation and compositing of MC-DCT compressed video. *IEEE J. Selected Areas in Communications*, 13(1):1–11, January 1995.

[13] M. C. Chen and A. N. Willson. Rate-distortion optimal motion estimation algorithms for motion-compensated transform video coding. *IEEE Trans. Circuits and Systems for Video Technology*, 8(2):147–158, April 1998.

[14] G. Cheung and W. Tan. Directed acyclic graph based source modeling for data unit selection of streaming media over QoS networks. In *Proc. Int'l Conf. Multimedia and Exhibition*, August 2002.

[15] P. A. Chou, A. E. Mohr, A. Wang, and S. Mehrotra. Error control for receiver-driven layered multicast of audio and video. *IEEE Trans. Multimedia*, 3(1):108–122, March 2001.

[16] P. A. Chou and Z. Miao. Rate-distortion optimized streaming of packetized media. *IEEE Trans. Multimedia*, 8(2):390–404, April 2006.

[17] P. A. Chou and A. Sehgal. Rate-distortion optimized receiver-driven streaming over best-effort networks. In *Proc. Int'l Packet Video Workshop*, volume 1, April 2002.

[18] P. A. Chou, H. J. Wang, and V. N. Padmanabhan. Layered multiple description coding. In *Proc. Int'l Packet Video Workshop*, volume 1, April 2003.

[19] G. J. Conklin, G. S. Greenbaum, K. O. Lillevold, A. F. Lippman, and Y. A. Reznik. Video coding for streaming media delivery on the internet. *IEEE Trans. Circuits and Systems for Video Technology*, 11(3):269–281, March 2001.

[20] W. Ding and B. Liu. Rate control of MPEG video coding and recording by rate-quantization modeling. *IEEE Trans. Circuits and Systems for Video Technology*, 6(1):12–20, February 1996.

[21] M. Domanski, A. Luczak, and S. Mackowiak. Spatio-temporal scalability for MPEG video coding. *IEEE Trans. Circuits and Systems for Video Technology*, 10(7):1088–1093, October 2000.

[22] A. Eleftheriadis and D. Anastassiou. Constrained and general dynamic rate shaping of compressed digital video. In *Proc. Int'l Conf. Image Processing*, volume 3, pages 396–399, October 1995.

[23] N. Farber and B. Girod. Robust H.263 compatible video transmission for mobile access to video servers. In *Proc. Int'l Conf. Image Processing*, volume 2, pages 73–76, October 1997.

[24] B. Girod. Rate-constrained motion estimation. In *Proc. Visual Communications and Image Processing*, pages 1026–1034, September 1994.

[25] V. K. Goyal. Multiple description coding: Compression meets the network. *IEEE Signal Processing Magazine*, 18(5):74–93, September 2001.

[26] Z. Guo, O. C. Au, and K. B. Letaief. Parameter estimation for image/video transcoding. In *Proc. Int'l Symp. Circuits and Systems*, volume 2, pages 269–272, May 2000.

[27] H.-M. Hang and J.-J. Chen. Source model for transform video coder and its application. *IEEE Trans. Circuits and Systems for Video Technology*, 7(2):287–311, April 1997.

[28] Z. He and S. K. Mitra. From rate–distortion analysis to resource-distortion analysis. *IEEE Circuits and Systems Magazine*, 5(3):6–18, 2005.

[29] C.-Y. Hsu, A. Ortega, and M. Khansari. Rate control for robust video transmission over burst-error wireless channels. *IEEE J. Selected Areas in Communications*, 17(5):1–18, May 1999.

[30] C.-Y. Hsu, A. Ortega, and A. Reibman. Joint selection of source and channel rate for VBR video transmission under ATM policing constraints. *IEEE J. Selected Areas in Communications*, 15(6):1016–1028, August 1997.

[31] H.-C. Huang, C.-N. Wang, and T. Chiang. A robust fine granularity scalability using trellis-based predictive leak. *IEEE Trans. Circuits and Systems for Video Technology*, 12(6):372–385, June 2002.

[32] M. Kalman and B. Girod. Rate-distortion optimized streaming of video with multiple independent encodings. In *Proc. Int'l Conf. Image Processing*, volume 1, October 2004.

[33] M. Karczewicz and R. Kurceren. The SP- and SI-frames design for H.264/AVC. *IEEE Trans. Circuits and Systems for Video Technology*, 13(7):637–644, July 2003.

[34] S. A. Karunasekera and N. G. Kingsbury. A distortion measure for image artifacts based on human visual sensitivity. In *Proc. Int'l Conf. Image Processing*, April 1994.

[35] K. Lengwehasatit and A. Ortega. Probabilistic partial distance fast matching for motion estimation. *IEEE Trans. Circuits and Systems for Video Technology*, 11(2):139–152, February 2001.

[36] K. Lengwehasatit and A. Ortega. Scalable variable complexity approximate forward DCT. *IEEE Trans. Circuits and Systems for Video Technology*, 14(11):1236–1248, November 2004.

[37] A. Leontaris and A. R. Reibman. Comparison of blocking and blurring metrics for video compression. In *Proc. Int'l Conf. Acoustics, Speech, and Signal Processing*, March 2005.

[38] W. Li. Overview of fine granularity scalalability in MPEG-4 video standard. *IEEE Trans. Circuits and Systems for Video Technology*, 11(3):301–317, March 2001.

[39] Y. J. Liang, N. Farber, and B. Girod. Adaptive playout scheduling and loss concealment for voice communication over IP networks. *IEEE Transactions on Multimedia*, 5(4), December 2003.

[40] Yi J. Liang and B. Girod. Prescient R-D optimized packet dependency management for low-latency video streaming. In *Proc. Int'l Conf. Image Processing*, September 2003.

[41] Yi J. Liang, E. Steinbach, and B. Girod. Multi-stream voice transmission over the internet using path diversity. In *Proc. ACM Multimedia*, September 2001.

[42] C.-W. Lin and Y.-R. Lee. Fast algorithms for DCT-domain video transcoding. In *Proc. Int'l Conf. Image Processing*, volume 1, pages 421–424, October 2001.

[43] L.-J. Lin and A. Ortega. Bit-rate control using piecewise approximated rate–distortion characteristics. *IEEE Trans. Circuits and Systems for Video Technology*, 8(4):446–459, August 1998.

[44] J. Macnicol, J. Arnold, and M. Frater. Scalable video coding by stream morphing. *IEEE Trans. Circuits and Systems for Video Technology*, 15(2):306–319, February 2005.

[45] N. Magharei and R. Rejaie. Adaptive receiver-driven streaming from multiple senders. *Proceedings of ACM Multimedia Systems Journal, Springer-Verlag*, 11(6):1–18, April 2006.

[46] S. McCanne, V. Jacobson, and M. Vetterli. Receiver-driven layered multicast. In *ACM SIGCOMM*, August 1996.

[47] N. Merhav. Multiplication-free approximate algorithms for compressed-domain linear operations on images. *IEEE Trans. Image Processing*, 8(2):247–254, February 1999.

[48] Z. Miao and A. Ortega. Expected run-time distortion based scheduling for delivery of scalable media. In *Proc. Int'l Packet Video Workshop*, volume 1, April 2002.

[49] Z. Miao and A. Ortega. Fast adaptive media scheduling based on expected run-time distortion. In *Proc. Asilomar Conf. Signals, Systems, and Computers*, volume 1, November 2002.

[50] Z. Miao and A. Ortega. Scalable proxy caching of video under storage constraints. *IEEE J. Selected Areas in Communications*, 20(7):1315–1327, September 2002.

[51] Y. Nakajima, H. Hori, and T. Kanoh. Rate conversion of MPEG coded video by requantization process. In *Proc. Int'l Conf. Image Processing*, volume 3, pages 408–411, October 1995.

[52] T. Nguyen and A. Zakhor. Multiple sender distributed video streaming. *IEEE Trans. Multimedia*, 6(2):315–326, April 2004.

[53] A. Ortega and K. Ramchandran. Rate-distortion methods for image and video compression. *IEEE Signal Processing Magazine*, 15(6):23–50, November 1998.

[54] V. N. Padmanabhan, H. J. Wang, and P. A. Chou. Resilient peer-to-peer streaming. In *Proc. Int'l Conf. Network Protocols*, November 2003.

[55] W. Pan and A. Ortega. Complexity-scalable transform coding using variable complexity algorithms. In *Proc. Data Compression Conference*, pages 263–272, March 2000.

[56] A. R. Reibman and M. T. Sun, editors. *Compressed Video over Networks*. "Variable bit rate video coding." Marcel Dekker, New York (NY), 2001.

[57] R. Rejaie and A. Ortega. Pals: Peer-to-peer adaptive layered streaming. In *Proc. Int'l Workshop on Network and Operating Systems Support for Digital Audio and Video (NOSSDAV)*, June 2003.

[58] K. Rose and S. Regunathan. Toward optimality in scalable predictive coding. *IEEE Transactions on Image Processing*, 10:965–976, July 2001.

[59] B. Shen, S.-J. Lee, and S. Basu. Caching strategies in transcoding-enabled proxy systems for streaming media distribution networks. *IEEE Trans. Multimedia*, 6(2):375–386, April 2004.

[60] R. Singh and A. Ortega. Erasure recovery in predictive coding environments using multiple description coding. In *IEEE Workshop on Multimedia Signal Processing*, 1999.

[61] I. Sodagar, H.-J. Lee, P. Hatrack, and Y.-Q. Zhang. Scalable wavelet coding for synthetic/natural hybrid images. *IEEE Trans. Circuits and Systems for Video Technology*, 9(2):244–254, March 1999.

[62] J. Song and B.-L. Yeo. A fast algorithm for DCT-domain inverse motion compensation based on shared information in a macroblock. *IEEE Trans. Circuits and Systems for Video Technology*, 10(5):767–775, August 2000.

[63] H. Sorial, W. E. Lynch, and A. Vincent. Selective requantization for transcoding of MPEG compressed video. In *Proc. Int'l Conf. Multimedia and Exhibition*, volume 1, pages 217–220, August 2000.

[64] N. Srinivasamurthy, A. Ortega, and S. Narayanan. Efficient scalable encoding for distributed speech recognition. *Speech Communication*, 48:888–902, 2006.

[65] G. J. Sullivan and T. Wiegand. Rate-distortion optimization for video compression. *IEEE Signal Processing Magazine*, 15(6):74–90, November 1998.

[66] H. Sun, W. Kwok, and J. W. Zdepski. Architectures for MPEG compressed bitstream scaling. *IEEE Trans. Circuits and Systems for Video Technology*, 6(2):191–199, April 1996.

[67] X. Sun, F. Wu, S. Li, W. Gao, and Y.-Q. Zhang. Seamless switching of scalable video bitstreams for efficient streaming. *IEEE Trans. Multimedia*, 6(2):291–303, April 2004.

[68] K. T. Tan and M. Ghanbari. A multi-metric objective picture-quality measurement model for MPEG video. *IEEE Trans. Circuits and Systems for Video Technology*, 10(7):1208–1213, October 2000.

[69] M. van der Schaar and Y. Andreopoulos. Rate-distortion-complexity modeling for network and receiver aware adaptation. *IEEE Trans. Multimedia*, 7(3):471–479, June 2005.

[70] M. van der Schaar and P. H. N. de With. Near-lossless complexity-scalable embedded compression algorithm for cost reduction in DTV receivers. *IEEE Trans. on Consumer Electronics*, 46(4):923–933, November 2000.

[71] M. van der Schaar and H. Radha. Adaptive motion-compensation fine-granular-scalability (AMC-FGS) for wireless video. *IEEE Trans. Circuits and Systems for Video Technology*, 12(6):360–371, June 2002.

[72] A. Vetro, C. Christopoulos, and H. Sun. Video transcoding achitectures and techniques: an overview. *IEEE Signal Processing Magazine*, 20(2):18–29, March 2003.

[73] H. Wang and A. Ortega. Robust video communication by combining scalability and multiple description coding techniques. In *Proc. Symp. Electronic Imaging*, volume 1, January 2003.

[74] Y. Wang, A. R. Reibman, and S. Lin. Multiple description coding for video delivery. *Proceedings of the IEEE*, 93(1):57–70, January 2005.

[75] O. Werner. Requantization for transcoding of MPEG-2 intraframes. *IEEE Trans. Image Processing*, 8(2):179–191, February 1999.

[76] T. Wiegand, M. Lightstone, D. Mukherjee, T. G. Campbell, and S. K. Mitra. Rate-distortion optimized mode selection for very low bit rate video coding and the emerging H.263 standard. *IEEE Trans. Circuits and Systems for Video Technology*, 6(2):182–190, April 1996.

[77] F. Wu, S. Li, and Y.-Q. Zhang. A framework for efficient progressive fine granularity scalable video coding. *IEEE Trans. Circuits and Systems for Video Technology*, 11(3):332–344, March 2001.

[78] J. Xin, C.-W. Lin, and M.-T. Sun. Digital video transcoding. *Proceedings of the IEEE*, 93(1):84–97, January 2005.

[79] J. Youn, J. Xin, and M.-T. Sun. Fast video transcoding architectures for networked multimedia applications. In *Proc. Int'l Symp. Circuits and Systems*, volume 4, pages 25–28, May 2000.

[80] R. Zhang, S. Regunathan, and K. Rose. Optimized video streaming over lossy networks with real-time estimation of end-to-end distortion. In *Proc. Int'l Conf. Multimedia and Exhibition*, volume 1, August 2002.

[81] R. Zhang, S. L. Regunathan, and K. Rose. Video coding with optimal inter/intra-mode switching for packet loss resilience. *IEEE J. Selected Areas in Communications*, 18(6):966–976, June 2000.

5

Scalable Video Coding for Adaptive Streaming Applications

Béatrice Pesquet-Popescu, Shipeng Li, and Mihaela van der Schaar

5.1 INTRODUCTION

The transmission of multimedia content over IP networks such as the Internet and wireless networks has been growing steadily over the past few years. Moreover, multimedia streaming and the set of applications that rely on streaming are expected to continue growing. Meanwhile, the current quality of streaming multimedia, in general, and video, in particular, can still be greatly improved. To achieve a higher level of quality and further proliferation of IP video, many technical challenges have to be addressed in the two areas of video coding and networking (streaming). A framework that addresses both the video coding and the networking challenges associated with IP-based video streaming is *scalability*. From a video coding point of view, scalability plays a crucial role in delivering the best possible video quality over unpredictable, "best-effort" networks. Bandwidth variation is one of the primary characteristics of "best-effort" networks, and current IP networks are a prime example of such networks. Video scalability enables an application to adapt the streamed video quality to changing network conditions (and specifically to bandwidth variation) and device complexities [40]. From a networking point of view, scalability is needed to enable a large number of users to view any desired video stream, at anytime, and from anywhere.

Scalable techniques try to avoid simulcast solutions, in which several encoders run in parallel. Simulcast solutions usually require knowledge of the network and decoder capabilities in advance in order to select the best encodings. To avoid network overload, the number of bit streams that can be simultaneously multiplexed

117

is limited. Even though point-to-multipoint connections are enabled by the simulcast solution, there is a clear loss in efficiency.

Consequently, any scalable video coding solution has to enable a very simple and flexible streaming framework, and hence, it must meet the following requirements.

1. The solution must enable a streaming server to perform only minimal real-time processing and rate control while outputting a very large number of simultaneous unicast (on-demand) streams.

2. The scalable video coding approach over IP networks has to be highly adaptable to unpredictable bandwidth variations due to heterogeneous access technologies of the receivers (e.g., analog modem, cable mode, xDSL, wireless mobile, and wireless LANs) or due to dynamic changes in network conditions (e.g., congestion events).

3. The video coding solution must enable low-complexity decoding and low-memory requirements to provide common receivers (e.g., set top boxes and digital televisions), in addition to powerful computers, the opportunity to stream and decode any desired Internet video content.

4. The streaming framework and related scalable video coding approach should be able to support both multicast and unicast applications. This, in general, eliminates the need for coding content in different formats to serve different types of applications.

5. The scalable bit stream must be resilient to packet loss events, which are quite common over IP networks.

These requirements are the primary drivers behind the design of the existing and emerging scalable video coding schemes.

5.2 SCALABILITY MODES IN CURRENT VIDEO CODING STANDARDS

5.2.1 Spatial, Temporal, and SNR Coding Structures

There are three basic types of scalability in scalable video coding: spatial, temporal, and quality (or SNR) scalabilities. In a spatial scalable scheme, full decoding leads to high spatial resolution, while partial decoding leads to reduced spatial resolutions (reduction of the format). In a temporal scalable scheme, partial decoding provides lower decoded frame rates (temporal resolutions). In an SNR scalable scheme, temporal and spatial resolutions are kept the same, but the video quality (SNR) varies depending on how much of the bit stream is decoded.

Current standards, such as H.263, H.264, MPEG-2, and MPEG-4 (both part 2 and part 10), are based on a predictive video coding scheme (see Figure 5.1).

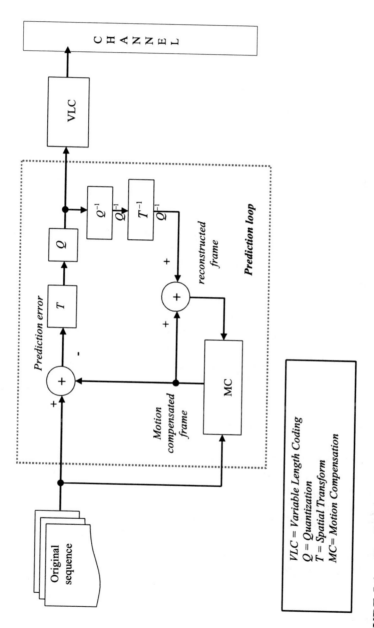

FIGURE 5.1: Predictive (hybrid) video coding scheme.

Although they were not initially designed to address these issues, current standards tried to upgrade their video coding schemes in order to include scalability functionalities. However, this integration generally came at the expense of coding efficiency (performance).

In a standard environment, scalability is achieved through *a layered structure*, where the encoded video information is divided into two or more separated bit streams corresponding to the different layers (see Figure 5.2).

- The base layer (BL) is generally highly and efficiently compressed by a nonscalable standard solution.
- The enhancement layer(s) (EL) encode(s) the residual signal to produce the expected scalability (it delivers, when combined with the base layer decoding, a progressive quality improvement in case of SNR scalability, a higher spatial resolution for spatial scalability, and a higher frame rate for temporal scalability).

To achieve *spatial scalability* in the hybrid scheme presented in Figure 5.3, the input video sequence is first spatially decimated to yield the lowest resolution layer, which is encoded by a standard encoder. A similar coding scheme is employed for the enhancement layer. To transmit a higher resolution version of the current frame, two predictions are formed: one is obtained by spatially interpolating the decoded lower resolution image of the current frame (spatial prediction) and the other by temporally compensating the higher resolution image of the predicted frame with motion information (temporal prediction). The two predictions are then adaptively combined for a better prediction and the residue after prediction is coded and transmitted. In Figure 5.3, a scheme with two resolution levels is depicted, but the same principle can be used to produce several spatial resolution enhancement levels. This solution corresponds to a Laplacian pyramid and is noncritically sampled, or redundant (the number of output samples is higher than the number of input samples).

The drawback of this approach is that the different encoding loops with their own motion estimation steps are used in parallel, at the encoder side, and several motion compensation loops are necessary at the decoder side, thus increasing the computational complexity both at the encoder and at the decoder. A possible advantage of this scheme is the flexibility in choosing the downsampling/upsampling filters, in particular for reducing aliasing at lower resolutions.

Related to the spatial scalability, there is the issue of *motion vector scalability*. Indeed, the different resolution levels will need motion vector fields with different resolutions and, possibly, accuracies. For the aforementioned Laplacian pyramid coding, the simplest approach is to estimate and encode the motion vectors, starting from the lowest resolution and going to the highest. From one layer to the other, the motion vector size needs to be doubled. Additionally, a refinement of the motion vector can be performed at higher resolutions. At this point, the pre-

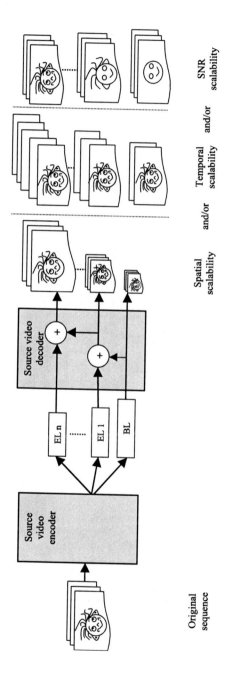

FIGURE 5.2: Global structure of a layered scalable video-coding scheme.

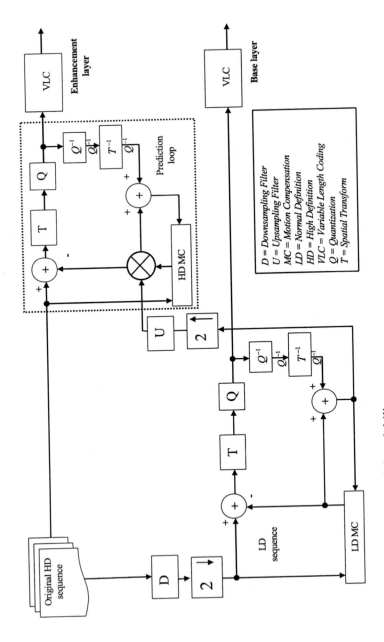

FIGURE 5.3: Layered spatial scalability.

cision and the accuracy of the motion can also be increased at higher levels. By precision we understand here the size of the block considered for motion estimation and compensation. When doubling the resolution, the dimensions of the block also double, and the motion representation loses in precision. Therefore, it may be convenient to split the block in smaller subblocks (two rectangular or four square ones) and look for refinement vectors in the subblocks. The decision to split or keep the lower resolution precision may be taken based on a rate–distortion criterion. Once the lowest resolution motion vector field is encoded, the next levels can be either encoded independently, with a possible loss in efficiency, or only the refinement vector(s) can be encoded in the refinement layer. The interested reader is referred to [22] for a more detailed discussion on motion vector scalability and its impact on the prediction complexity.

Temporal scalability involves partitioning of the group of pictures (GOP) into layers having the same spatial resolution. A simple way to achieve temporal scalability is to put some of the B frames from an IBBP ... stream into one or several enhancement layers. This solution comes at no cost in terms of coding efficiency. In a more general setting, the base layer may contain I, P, and B frames at the low frame rate, while the enhancement layers can only use frames from the immediately lower temporal layer and previous frames from the same enhancement layer for temporal prediction. Generally, temporal prediction from future frames in the same enhancement layer is prohibited in order to avoid reordering in the enhancement layers. An example with one enhancement layer is presented in Figure 5.4.

The layered solution can be seen as an upgrade of standard solutions in order to provide scalability. The main shortcoming of these schemes comes from the fact that the information redundancy between the different layers cannot be fully exploited. This functionality is thus achieved at the expense of implementation complexity and coding efficiency.

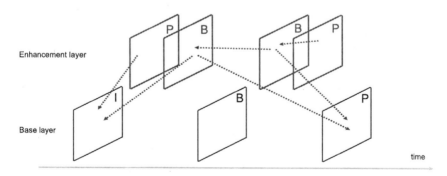

FIGURE 5.4: General framework for layered temporal scalability.

A general problem with introducing scalability in a predictive video coding scheme is the so-called *drift effect*. It occurs when the reference frame used for motion compensation in the encoding loop is not available or not completely available at the decoder side. Therefore both the encoder and the decoder have to maintain their synchronization on the same bit rate in the case of SNR scalability, resolution level for spatial scalability, and frame rate in the case of temporal scalability.

For *SNR scalability*, a layered encoder exploits correlations across subflows to achieve better overall compression: the input sequence is compressed into a number of discrete layers arranged in a hierarchy that provides progressive refinement. A strategy often used in the scalable extensions of current standards (i.e., in MPEG-2 and H263) is to encode the base layer using a large quantization step, whereas the enhancement layers have a refinement goal and use finer quantizers to encode the base layer coding error. This solution is illustrated in Figure 5.5 and is discussed in more detail later.

5.2.2 Successive Approximation Quantization and Bit Planes

To realize the SNR scalability concept discussed earlier, an important category of embedded scalar quantizers is the family of embedded dead zone scalar quantizers. For this family, each transform coefficient x is quantized to an integer

$$i_b = Q_b(x) = \begin{cases} \text{sign}(x) \cdot \left\lfloor \dfrac{|x|}{2^b \Delta} + \dfrac{\xi}{2^b} \right\rfloor, & \text{if } \dfrac{|x|}{2^b \Delta} + \dfrac{\xi}{2^b} > 0, \\ 0, & \text{otherwise}, \end{cases}$$

where $\lfloor a \rfloor$ denotes the integer part of a; $\xi < 1$ determines the width of the dead zone; $\Delta > 0$ is the basic quantization step size (basic partition cell size) of the quantizer family; and $b \in \mathbb{Z}_+$ indicates the quantizer level (granularity), with higher values of b indicating coarser quantizers. In general, b is upper bounded by a value $B_{\max}$, selected to cover the dynamic range of the input signal. The reconstructed value is given by the inverse operation,

$$y_i^p = Q_b^{-1}(i_b) = \begin{cases} 0, & i_b = 0, \\ \text{sign}(i_b) \cdot \left(|i_b| - \dfrac{\xi}{2^b} + \delta \right) 2^b \Delta, & i_b \neq 0, \end{cases}$$

where $0 \leq \delta < 1$ specifies the placement of the reconstructed value y_i^b within the corresponding uncertainty interval (partition cell), defined as $C_{i_b}^b$, and i is the partition cell index, which is bounded by a predefined value for each quantizer level (i.e., $0 \leq i \leq M_b - 1$, for each b). Based on the aforementioned formulation, it is rather straightforward to show that the quantizer Q_0 has embedded within it

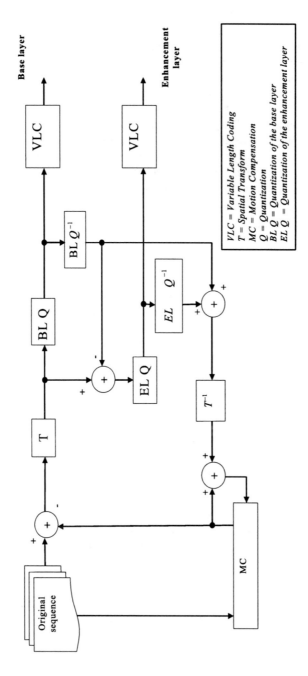

FIGURE 5.5: Layered SNR scalability.

all the uniform dead zone quantizers with step sizes $2^b \Delta$, $b \in \mathbb{Z}_+$. Moreover, it can be shown that, under the appropriate settings, the quantizer index obtained by dropping the b least-significant bits (LSBs) of i_0 is the same as that which would be obtained if the quantization was performed using a step size of $2^b \Delta$, $b \in \mathbb{Z}_+$ rather than Δ. This means that if the b LSBs of i_0 are not available, one can still dequantize at a lower level of quality using the inverse quantization formula.

The most common option for embedded scalar quantization is successive approximation quantization (SAQ). SAQ is a particular instance of the generalized family of embedded dead zone scalar quantizers defined earlier. For SAQ, $M_{B_{max}} = M_{B_{max}-1} = \cdots = M_0 = 2$ and $\xi = 0$, which determines a dead zone width twice as wide as the other partition cells, and $\delta = 1/2$, which implies that the output levels y_i^b are in the middle of the corresponding uncertainty intervals $C_{i_p}^b$. SAQ can be implemented via thresholding by applying a monotonically decreasing set of thresholds of the form

$$T_{b-1} = \frac{T_b}{2},$$

with $B_{max} \geq b \geq 1$. The starting threshold $T_{B_{max}}$ is of the form $T_{B_{max}} = \alpha x_{max}$, where x_{max} is the highest coefficient magnitude in the input transform decomposition, and α is a constant that is taken as $\alpha \geq 1/2$.

Let us consider the case of using a spatial transform for the compression of the frames. By using SAQ, the significance of the transform coefficients with respect to any given threshold T_b is indicated in a corresponding binary map, denoted by W^b, called the significance map. Denote by $w(\mathbf{k})$ the transform coefficient with coordinates $\mathbf{k} = (\kappa_1, \kappa_2)$ in the two-dimensional transform domain of a given input. The significance operator $s^b(\cdot)$ maps any value $x(\mathbf{k})$ in the transform domain to a corresponding binary value $w^b(\mathbf{k})$ in W^b, according to the rule

$$w^b(\mathbf{k}) = s^b(x(\mathbf{k})) = \begin{cases} 0, & \text{if } |x(\mathbf{k})| < T_b, \\ 1, & \text{if } |x(\mathbf{k})| \geq T_b. \end{cases}$$

In general, embedded coding of the input coefficients translates into coding the significance maps W^b, for every b with $B_{max} \geq b \geq 0$.

In most state-of-the-art embedded coders, for every b this is effectively performed based on several encoding passes, which can be summarized in the following:

Nonsignificance pass: encodes $s^b(x(\mathbf{k}))$ in the list of nonsignificant coefficients (LNC). If significant, the coefficient coordinates $\mathbf{k}$ are transferred into the refinement list (RL).

Block Significance pass: For a block of coefficients with coordinates $\mathbf{k}_{block}$, this pass encodes $s^b(x(\mathbf{k}_{block}))$ and $\text{sign}(x(\mathbf{k}_{block}))$ if they have descendant blocks (under a quad tree decomposition structure) that were not significant compared to the previous bit plane.

Coefficient Significance pass: If the coordinates of the coefficients of a significant block are not in the LNC, this pass encodes the significance of coefficients in blocks containing at least one significant coefficient. Also, the coordinates of new significant coefficients are placed into the RL. This pass also moves the coordinates of nonsignificant coefficients found in the block into the LNC for the next bit plane level(s).

Refinement pass: For each coefficient in the RL (except those newly put into the RL during the last block pass), encode the next refinement of the significance map.

5.2.3 Other Types of Scalability

In addition to the aforementioned scalabilities, other types of scalability have been proposed.

- Complexity scalability: the encoding/decoding algorithm has less complexity (CPU/memory requirements or memory access) with decreasing temporal/spatial resolution or decreasing quality [40].
- Content (or object) scalability: a hierarchy of relevant objects is defined in the video scene and a progressive bit stream is created following this importance order. Such methods of content selection may be related to arbitrary-shaped objects or even to rectangular blocks in block-based coders. The main problem of such techniques is how to automatically select and track visually important regions in video.
- Frequency scalability: this technique, popular in the context of transform coding, consists of allocating coefficients to different layers according to their frequency. Data partitioning techniques may be used to implement this functionality. The interested reader is referred to Chapter 2 of this book for more information on data partitioning.

Among existing standards, the first ones (MPEG-1 and H.261) did not provide any kind of scalability. H.263+ and H.264 provide temporal scalability through B-frames skipping.

5.3 MPEG-4 FINE GRAIN SCALABLE (FGS) CODING AND ITS NONSTANDARDIZED VARIANTS

5.3.1 SNR FGS Structure in MPEG-4

The previously discussed conventional scalable coding schemes are not able to efficiently address the problem of easy, adaptive, and efficient adaptation to time-varying network conditions or device characteristics. The reason for this is that they provide only coarse granularity rate adaptation and their coding efficiency often decreases due to the overhead associated with an increased number of layers.

To address this problem, FGS coding has been standardized in the MPEG-4 standard, as it is able to provide fine-grain scalability to easily adapt to various time-varying network and device resource (e.g., power) constraints [6,44]. Moreover, FGS can enable a streaming server to perform *minimal real-time* processing and rate control when outputting a very large number of simultaneous unicast (on-demand) streams, as the resulting bit stream can be easily truncated to fulfill various (network) rate requirements. Also, FGS is easily adaptable to unpredictable bandwidth variations due to heterogeneous access technologies (Internet, wireless cellular or wireless LANs) or to dynamic changes in network conditions (e.g., congestion events). Moreover, FGS enables low-complexity decoding and low-memory requirements that provide common receivers (e.g., set top boxes and digital televisions), in addition to powerful computers, the opportunity to stream and decode any desired streamed video content. Hence, receiver-driven streaming solutions can only select the portions of the FGS bit stream that fulfill these constraints [40,45].

In MPEG-4 FGS, a video sequence is represented by two layers of bit streams with identical spatial resolution, which are referred to as the base layer bit stream and the fine granular enhancement layer bit stream, as illustrated in Figure 5.6.

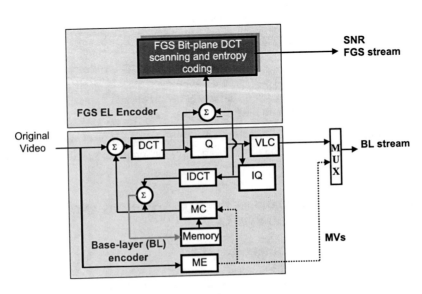

FIGURE 5.6:   MPEG-4 FGS encoder.

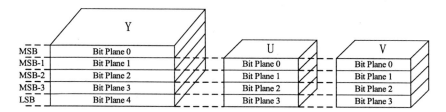

FIGURE 5.7:   The structure of bit planes of Y, U, and V components.

The base layer bit stream is coded with nonscalable coding techniques, whereas the enhancement layer bit stream is generated by coding the difference between the original DCT coefficients and the reconstructed base layer coefficients using a bit-plane coding technique [1,6,7]. The residual signal is represented with bit planes in the DCT domain, where the number of bit planes is not fixed, but is based on the number of bit planes needed to represent the residual magnitude in binary format. Before a DCT residual picture is coded at the enhancement layer, the maximum number of bit planes of each color component (Y, U, and V) is first found. In general, three color components may have different numbers of bit planes. Figure 5.7 gives an example of 5 bit planes in Y component and 4 bit planes in U and V components. These three values are coded in the picture header of the enhancement layer stream and transmitted to the decoder.

All components have aligned themselves with the least significant bit (LSB) plane. The FGS encoder and decoder process bit planes from the most significant bit (MSB) plane to the LSB plane. Because of the possible different maximum numbers of bit planes on Y, U, and V components, the first MSB planes may contain only one or two components. In the example given by Figure 5.7, there is only Y component existing in the MSB plane. In this case, bits for the coded block pattern (CBP) of each macroblock can be reduced significantly. Every macroblock in a bit plane is coded with row scan order.

Since the enhancement layer bit stream can be truncated arbitrarily in any frame (see Figure 5.8), MPEG-4 FGS provides the capability of easily adapting to channel bandwidth variations.

5.3.2 MPEG-4 Hybrid Temporal–SNR Scalability with an All-FGS Structure

As mentioned earlier, temporal scalability is an important tool for enhancing the motion smoothness of compressed video. Typically, a base layer stream coded with a frame rate f_{BL} is enhanced by another layer consisting of video frames that do not coincide (temporally) with the base layer frames. Therefore, if the enhancement layer has a frame rate of f_{EL}, then the total frame of both base and enhancement layer streams is $f_{BL} + f_{EL}$.

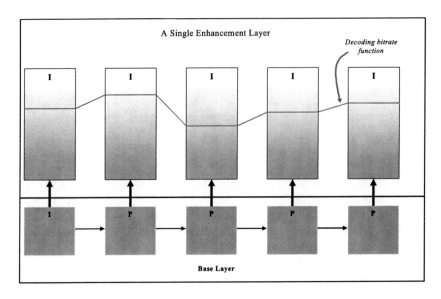

FIGURE 5.8:   An MPEG-4 FGS two-layer bit stream.

In the SNR FGS scalability structure described in the previous section, the frame rate of the transmitted video is *locked* to the frame rate of the base layer regardless of the available bandwidth and corresponding transmission bit rate. Since one of the design objectives of FGS is to cover a relatively wide range of bandwidth variation over IP networks (e.g., 100 kbps to 1 Mbps), it is quite desirable that the SNR enhancement tool of FGS be complemented with a temporal scalability tool. It is also desirable to develop a framework that provides the flexibility of choosing between temporal scalability (better motion smoothness) and SNR scalability (higher quality) at transmission time. This, for example, can be used in response to user preferences and/or real-time bandwidth variations at transmission time [44]. For typical streaming applications, both of these elements are not known at the time of encoding the content.

Consequently, the MPEG-4 framework for supporting hybrid temporal–SNR scalabilities building on the SNR FGS structure is described in detail in [44]. This framework provides a new level of abstraction between encoding and transmission processes by supporting *both* SNR and temporal scalabilities through a *single* enhancement layer. Figure 5.9 shows the hybrid scalability structure. In addition to the standard SNR FGS frames, this hybrid structure includes motion-compensated residual frames at the enhancement layer. These motion-compensated frames are referred to as FGS Temporal (FGST) pictures [44].

As shown in Figure 5.9, each FGST picture is predicted from base layer frames that do not coincide temporally with that FGST picture, and therefore, this leads

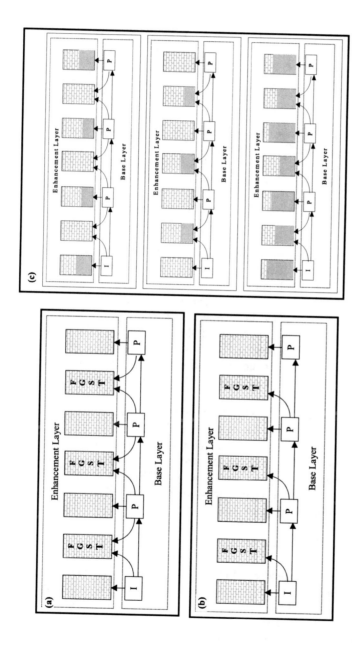

FIGURE 5.9: FGS hybrid temporal–SNR scalability structure with (a) bidirectional and (b) forward prediction FGST pictures and (c) examples of SNR-only (top), temporal-only (middle), or both temporal and SNR (bottom) scalability.

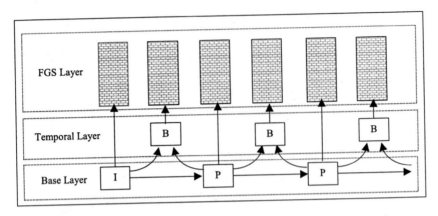

FIGURE 5.10:   Multilayer FGS–temporal scalability structure.

to the desired temporal scalability feature. Moreover, the FGST residual signal is coded using the same fine granular video coding method employed for compressing the standard SNR FGS frames.

Each FGST picture includes two types of information: (a) motion vectors (MVs) that are computed in reference to temporally adjacent base layer frames and (b) coded data representing the bit planes DCT signal of the motion-compensated FGST residual. The MVs can be computed using standard macroblock-based matching motion-estimation methods. Therefore, the motion-estimation and compensation functional blocks of the base layer can be used by the enhancement layer codec.

The FGST picture data is coded and transmitted using a data-partitioning strategy to provide added error resilience. Under this strategy, after the FGST frame header, all motion vectors are clustered and transmitted before the residual signal bit planes. The MV data can be transmitted in designated packets with greater protection. More details on hybrid SNR–temporal FGS can be obtained from [44]. Finally, these scalabilities can be further combined in a multilayer manner, and an example of this is shown in Figure 5.10.

5.3.3 Nonstandard FGS Variants

To improve the coding efficiency of FGS, various temporal prediction structures have been proposed. For example, in [8], an additional motion compensation loop is introduced into the enhancement layer using the reconstructed high-quality reference. Furthermore, an improved method is proposed in [9] where an estimation-theoretic framework is presented to obtain the prediction optimally considering both the reconstructed high-quality reference and the base layer information.

This optimization translates into consistent performance gains in compression efficiency at the enhancement layer. Nonetheless, the main disadvantage of such schemes is the high complexity due to the multiple motion estimation loops for the enhancement layer coding.

However, the FGS scheme can also benefit from temporal dependency at the FGS enhancement layer based on one prediction loop. Motion-Compensated FGS (MC-FGS) was first proposed to address this problem in [10]. A high-quality reference, generated from the enhancement layer, can be utilized in the motion compensation loop to get better prediction. However, in case there is a close-loop structure at the enhancement layer, it could induce drift errors when the enhancement layer cannot be guaranteed at the decoder side due to network bandwidth fluctuations. Several methods used to reduce the drift in the MC-FGS structure are discussed in [10].

To introduce temporal prediction into the FGS enhancement layer coding without severe drift errors, several alternative techniques have been proposed. Progressive FGS (PFGS) proposed in [12,13] explores a separate motion compensation loop for the FGS enhancement layer to improve the compression performance and provides means to eliminate the drift error as well. There are two key points in the PFGS coding. One is to use as many predictions from the enhancement reference layers as possible (for coding efficiency) instead of always using the base layer as in MPEG-4 FGS. The other point is to keep a prediction path from the base layer to the highest quality layer across several frames, for error recovery and channel adaptation. Such a prediction path enables lost or erroneous higher quality enhancement layers to be automatically reconstructed from lower layers gradually over a few frames. Thus, PFGS trades off coding efficiency for drift error reduction.

In [14], a robust FGS (RFGS) technique was presented by incorporating the ideas of leaky [10,15] and partial predictions to deal with the drift error. In RFGS, the high-quality reference used in the enhancement layer compensation loop is constructed by combining the reconstructed base layer image and part of the enhancement layer. A frame-based fading mechanism is introduced to cope with the mismatch error. Specifically, at each frame, a uniformly leaky factor between 0 and 1 is applied to the enhancement layer before adding to the base layer image to alleviate the error propagation. Moreover, an adaptive leaky prediction based on the RFGS is proposed in [16] where the leaky factor is determined for each bit plane of enhancement layer according to its significance and location to further improve the coding performance.

Furthermore, several techniques are proposed to achieve more flexible trade-off between drift errors and coding efficiency at the macroblock level rather than at the frame level. The macroblock-based PFGS (MPFGS) is one such scheme [17,18]. In MPFGS, three INTER modes, HPHR, LPLR, and HPLR, are proposed for the enhancement layer macroblock encoding (see Figure 5.11). In fact,

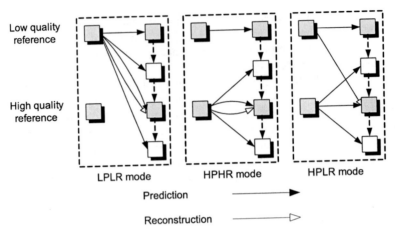

FIGURE 5.11: INTER modes for the enhancement macroblocks in MPFGS.

the HPHR mode is used to get high coding efficiency by using higher quality reference, while the HPLR mode is imposed to attenuate the drifting error by introducing the mismatch error into the encoding process. Assuming that the base layer is always available at the decoder, LPLR and HPLR modes help reset the drift errors potentially caused by the HPHR mode. A decision-making mechanism is presented in MPFGS to choose the optimal prediction mode for each enhancement layer macroblock by considering the error propagation effects and taking advantage of the HPLR mode to achieve a flexible trade-off between high coding efficiency and low drifting error. Another macroblock-based approach is presented in [19,20], called enhanced mode-adaptive FGS (EMFGS). Three predictors, the reconstructed base layer macroblock, the reconstructed enhancement layer macroblock, and the average of the previous two, are proposed in EMFGS. A uniformly fading factor, 0.5, is used to form the third predictor. Also, a mode-selection algorithm is provided to decide the encoding mode of the enhancement layer macroblock.

Another network-aware solution was presented in [45] to alleviate the FGS coding inefficiencies based on the available network conditions—video transcaling (TS), which can be viewed as a generalization of (nonscalable) transcoding. With TS, a scalable video stream that covers a given bandwidth range is mapped into one or more scalable video streams covering different bandwidth ranges. The TS framework exploits the fact that the level of heterogeneity changes at different points of the video distribution tree over wireless and mobile Internet networks. This provides the opportunity to improve the video quality by performing the appropriate TS process. An Internet/wireless network gateway represents a good candidate for performing TS, thus improving the performance of FGS-based compression schemes.

5.4 MOTION-COMPENSATED WAVELET VIDEO CODECS

As wavelets inherently provide a hierarchical representation of the analyzed content and also have proved very attractive for spatial and quality scalability in still image coding, an intense effort has been deployed since the late-1980s to extend these decompositions in the temporal direction. This can be done by considering the video sequence as a volume of pixels and applying the temporal transform on samples along the temporal dimension. Temporal subbands are then spatially transformed also using a wavelet transform.

5.4.1 Motion-Compensated Temporal Filtering (MCTF)

The idea of temporal extensions of subband decompositions appeared in the late 1980s, with the works of Karlsson and Vetterli [1] and Kronander [2]. In these works the classical temporal closed-loop prediction scheme was replaced by a temporal subband decomposition, which didn't take into account any motion compensation. Later it was shown that motion prediction was also important in these schemes [3] in order to reduce the detail energy subbands, thus leading to much better compression performance and visual quality, and ideally the temporal transform should be applied along the motion trajectories.

The simplest temporal wavelet transform is the Haar transform, performing sums and differences of pairs of frames to obtain respectively approximation and detail subbands. It is illustrated in Figure 5.12 on a group of frames (GOF) of eight frames, which allows performing a maximum of three levels of dyadic decomposition. A review of various MCTF structures for scalable video coding can be found in [42].

Due to the two-tap low-pass and high-pass filters and downsampling by a factor of 2, no boundary problems appear when decomposing a GOF of size 2^L into a number of up to L resolution levels.

Moreover, if motion estimation and compensation is performed between pairs of successive frames, without overlapping, the number of operations and the number of motion vector fields are the same as for coding the same number of frames in a predictive scheme (and equal to $2^L - 1$). However, as pairs of pixels have to be processed in successive frames in order to obtain the coefficients of the approximation and detail frames, the motion invertibility becomes a very important problem.

For example, in a block-based motion-compensated prediction, which is the most usual technique for temporal prediction, the same area in the reference frame

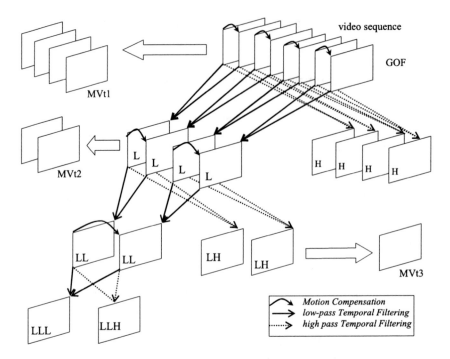

FIGURE 5.12:   Temporal Haar wavelet decomposition of a GOF.

can be used to predict several areas in the current frame, while parts of the reference frame are not used at all for prediction. This gives rise to multiple connected and unconnected pixels (see Figure 5.13) [3,4]. In order to avoid such problems, other motion models, such as *meshes*, can be employed [30].

Moreover, in order to take advantage of in-place calculations and guaranteed reversibility of the scheme even for nonlinear operations (such as the operations involving motion compensation), a lifting implementation of the wavelet filter bank was proposed [5,21]. This way, after splitting the input samples in odd and even indexed ones, theoretically any biorthogonal filter bank with finite impulse responses can be represented with a finite number of predict-update (see Figure 5.14) steps, possibly followed by multiplication with a constant.

In the case of temporal decomposition of the video, motion estimation is first performed between input frames, and the motion vector fields (denoted by v in Figure 5.15) are used for motion-compensated operations in both the predict and the update steps.

An important remark is that the predict operator can use *all* the even indexed input frames (denoted by x_{2t_i}) to perform the motion-compensated prediction of the odd indexed frames (denoted by $\{x_{2t+1}\}$), while the update operator can use

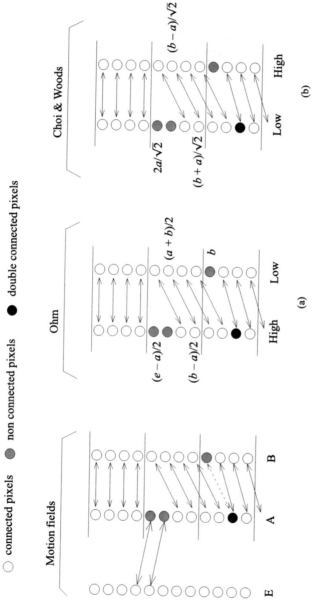

FIGURE 5.13:   Temporal MC Haar filtering: connected, unconnected, and multiple connected pixels.

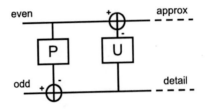

FIGURE 5.14: Basic steps of a lifting scheme.

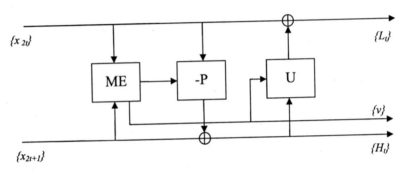

FIGURE 5.15: Spatiotemporal motion-compensated lifting scheme.

all the detail frames ($\{H_{t_t}\}$) thus computed to obtain the approximation subband frames ($\{L_{t_t}\}$). The predict and update operators then also involve the motion vectors used to match corresponding positions. Therefore, in the $t + 2D$ framework they actually become spatiotemporal operators:

$$H_t(\mathbf{n}) = x_{2t+1}(\mathbf{n}) - P\left(\left\{x_{2(t-k)}, v_{2t+1}^{2(t-k)}\right\}_{k \in T_k^p}\right), \quad \forall \mathbf{n} \in S,$$

$$L_t(\mathbf{p}) = x_{2t}(\mathbf{p}) + U\left(\left\{H_{t-k}, v_{2t}^{2(t-k)+1}\right\}_{k \in T_k^u}\right), \quad \forall \mathbf{p} \in S,$$

where v_i^j is the motion vector field used to predict the current frame i from the reference frame j, T_k^p (respectively T_k^u) is the support of the temporal predict (respectively update) operator, and the spatial position is denoted by $\mathbf{n}$ or $\mathbf{p}$.

In the simplest case of the Haar multiresolution analysis, the previous relations become

$$H_t(\mathbf{n}) = x_{2t+1}(\mathbf{n}) - x_{2t}\left(\mathbf{n} - v_{2t+1}^{2t}\right), \quad \forall \mathbf{n} \in S,$$

$$L_t(\mathbf{p}) = x_{2t}(\mathbf{p}) + H_t\left(\mathbf{p} + v_{2t}^{2t+1}\right), \quad \forall \mathbf{p} \in S.$$

However, from the temporal prediction viewpoint, it is better to make use of longer filters. The biorthogonal 5/3 filter bank has been most studied. In this case, both forward and backward motion vectors need to be used for a bidirectional prediction. The analysis equations have the form

$$H_t(\mathbf{n}) = x_{2t+1}(\mathbf{n}) - \frac{1}{2}\left[x_{2t}\left(\mathbf{n} - v_{2t+1}^{2t}\right) + x_{2t+2}\left(\mathbf{n} - v_{2t+1}^{2t+2}\right)\right], \quad \forall \mathbf{n} \in S,$$

$$L_t(\mathbf{p}) = x_{2t}(\mathbf{p}) + \frac{1}{4}\left[H_{t-1}\left(\mathbf{p} + v_{2t}^{2t+1}\right) + H_t\left(\mathbf{p} + v_{2t+1}^{2t+2}\right)\right], \quad \forall \mathbf{p} \in S.$$

Due to the fact that a bidirectional prediction is used in this structure, the number of motion vector fields is double compared with the Haar decomposition, and therefore the coding of this information may represent an important part of the bit stream at low bit rates. Efficient algorithms are needed to further exploit redundancies between motion vector fields at the same temporal decomposition level or at different levels [23].

To effectively deal with the problem of motion-compensated temporal wavelet filtering associated with fractional precision motion vectors, many-to-one mapping for the covered areas and nonreferred pixels for the uncovered areas [31], proposes a new and general lifting structure (see Figure 5.16) that unifies all the

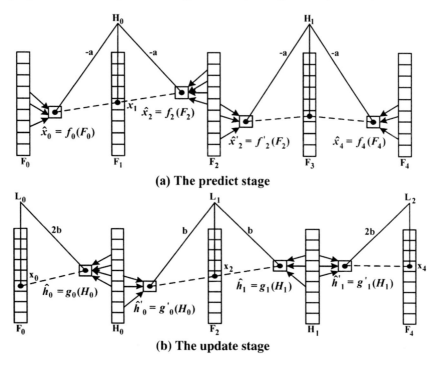

(a) The predict stage

(b) The update stage

FIGURE 5.16:   The Barbell lifting scheme.

previous works to solve this problem and enables any traditional motion compensation techniques in block-based motion prediction coding to be easily adopted in the MCTF framework. The core of this work is a so-called *Barbell lifting* scheme, in which instead of a single pixel value, a function of a set of pixel values is used as the input to the lifting step. The Barbell lifting scheme essentially moves any existing effective motion prediction schemes in traditional video coding to the MCTF frames.

A new update scheme, energy distributed update (EDU), is proposed in [32] to avoid a second set of motion vectors or complex and inaccurate inversion of the motion information used in the traditional update step. The idea is to update where predict is made by distributing high-pass signals to the low-pass frame. Meanwhile, it provides further coding efficiency gain.

5.4.2 Three-Dimensional (3D) Wavelet Coefficients Coding

After 3D (temporal and spatial) wavelet analysis, a video sequence will be decomposed into a certain number of 3D subbands. For example, in Figure 5.17, a three-level wavelet (motion compensated) decomposition is performed in the temporal direction, followed by a three-level 2D spatial dyadic decomposition within each of the resulting temporal bands.

The next step in 3D wavelet video coding is to encode the transformed 3D wavelet coefficients in each subband efficiently. Since the subband structure in 3D wavelet decomposition for video sequence is very similar to the subband structure

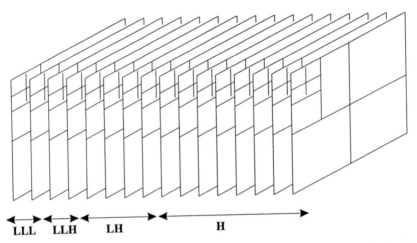

LLL   LLH   LH   H

FIGURE 5.17: Separable 3D wavelet transform. Three-level dyadic temporal (motion compensated) wavelet decomposition, followed by three-level 2D spatial dyadic decomposition.

in 2D wavelet decomposition for image, it is natural to extend many existing 2D wavelet-based image coding techniques, such as SPIHT [33], EBCOT [34], and EZBC [35], to the 3D case. As a matter of fact, almost all the existing 3D wavelet coefficients coding schemes use one form of these 3D extensions, such as 3D SPIHT [38], 3D ESCOT [36,37], and 3D EZBC [38,39].

Generally speaking, after 3D (motion compensated) wavelet decomposition, there is not only spatial similarity inside each frame across the different scale, but also temporal similarity between two frames at the same temporal scale. Furthermore, temporal linkages of coefficients between frames typically show more correlation along the motion trajectory. An efficient 3D wavelet coefficient coding scheme should exploit these properties as much as possible. Several algorithms for texture coding in 3D wavelet schemes have been developed.

5.4.2.1 3D SPIHT

3D SPIHT is an extension of the concept of SPIHT still image coding to 3D video coding. As we know, the SPIHT algorithm takes advantages of the nature of energy clustering of subband/wavelet coefficients in frequency and space and exploits the similarity between subbands. It utilizes three basic concepts: (1) searching for sets in spatial-orientation trees in a wavelet transform; (2) partitioning the wavelet transform coefficients in these trees into sets defined by the level of the highest significant bit in a bit plane representation of their magnitudes; and (3) coding and transmitting bits associated with the highest remaining bit planes first.

There is no constraint to dimensionality in the SPIHT algorithm itself, as pixels are sorted regardless of dimensionality. The 3D SPIHT scheme can be easily extended from 2D SPIHT, with the following three similar characteristics: (1) partial ordering by magnitude of the 3D wavelet transformed video with a 3D set partitioning algorithm; (2) ordered bit plane transmission of refinement bits; and (3) exploitation of self-similarity across spatiotemporal orientation trees.

For the 3D wavelet coefficients, a new 3D spatiotemporal orientation tree and its parent–offspring relationships are defined. For pure dyadic wavelet decomposition with an alternate separable wavelet transform in each dimension, a straight-forward extension from the 2D case is to form a node in 3D SPIHT as a block with eight adjacent pixels, two in each dimension, hence forming a node of $2 \times 2 \times 2$ pixels. The root nodes (at the highest level of the pyramid) have one pixel with no descendants and the other seven pointing to eight offspring in a $2 \times 2 \times 2$ cube at corresponding locations at the same level. For nonroot and nonleaf nodes, a pixel has eight offspring in a $2 \times 2 \times 2$ cube one level below in the pyramid. For nondyadic decomposition similar to the 2D wavelet packet decomposition case, the $2 \times 2 \times 2$ offspring nodes are split into pixels in these smaller subbands at the corresponding orientation in the nodes at the original level. For the common

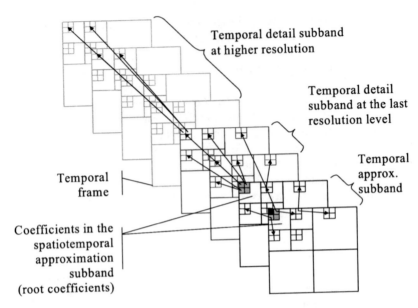

FIGURE 5.18: Parent–offspring relationship in a spatiotemporal decomposition.

$t + 2D$ type of wavelet decomposition the parent–offspring relationship is shown in Figure 5.18. With such defined 3D spatiotemporal trees, the coefficients can be compressed into a bit stream by feeding the 3D data structure to the 3D SPIHT coding kernel. The 3D SPIHT kernel will sort the data according to the magnitude along the spatiotemporal orientation trees (sorting pass) and refine the bit plane by adding necessary bits (refinement pass).

5.4.2.2 3D ESCOT

The 3D SPIHT coding scheme provides natural scalability in rate (quality). However, it is difficult to provide temporal or spatial scalabilities due to the inherent spatiotemporal tree structure. Even with extra effort, it can only provide partial temporal or spatial scalabilities by modifying the decoder or encoder [35]. However, 3D ESCOT [36,37] can provide full rate, temporal and spatial scalabilities by constraining the encoding of wavelet coefficients independently within each subband. Meanwhile, the R–D optimized bit stream truncation process after encoding guarantees a bit stream with the best video quality given a bit rate constraint.

The 3D ESCOT scheme is in principle very similar to EBCOT [34] in the JPEG-2000 standard, which offers high compression efficiency and other functionalities (e.g., error resilience and random access) for image coding. In extending the 2D EBCOT algorithm to 3D ESCOT, a different coding structure is used to form a new set of 3D contexts for arithmetic coding that makes the algorithm very suitable for scalable video compression. Specifically, each of the subbands is coded independently in the extended coding structure. The advantage of doing so is that each subband can be decoded independently to achieve flexible spatial/temporal scalability. The user can mix an arbitrary number of spatiotemporal subbands in any order to obtain the desired spatial or temporal resolution.

Unlike the EBCOT encoder [34] in JPEG2000, the ESCOT encoder takes a subband as a whole entity. There are two reasons for this. (1) Normally a video frame has lower resolution than a still image. Not splitting a subband further into many small 3D blocks brings better coding efficiency of the context-based adaptive arithmetic coder. (2) Taking a subband as a whole entity is also convenient for incorporating the possible motion model in the coding process, since within the same 3D subband, the motion vector may point from any coefficients on a temporal plane to any other coefficients on other temporal planes.

As in the 2D EBCOT case, the contexts for 3D ESCOT are also formed with immediate neighbors in the same subband. The difference is that the immediate neighbors are now in three directions instead of two: horizontal, vertical, and temporal (Figure 5.19). In addition, the temporal neighbors not only may be spatially collocated in different frames, but also may be neighbors pointed to by motion vectors across frames with a certain motion model [36,37].

The encoding of the 3D wavelet coefficients in the 3D ESCOT scheme is done bit plane by bit plane. For each bit plane, the coding procedure consists of three distinct passes: Significance Propagation, Magnitude Refinement, and Normalization, which are applied in turn. Each pass processes a "fractional bit plane." In each pass, the scanning order is along the horizontal direction first, the vertical direction second, and finally the temporal direction. In the Significance Propagation pass, samples that are not yet significant but have a "preferred neighborhood" are

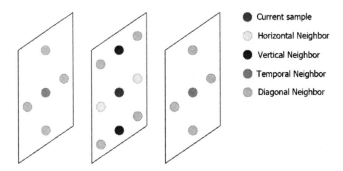

FIGURE 5.19:   Immediate neighbors of a sample in 3D ESCOT coding.

processed. A sample has a "preferred neighborhood" if and only if the sample has at least a significant immediate diagonal neighbor for a HHH (high frequency in three directions) subband or a significant immediate horizontal, vertical, or temporal neighbor for the other types of subbands. In the Magnitude Refinement pass, the samples that have been significant in the previous bit planes are encoded. In the Normalization pass, those samples that have not yet been coded in the previous two passes are coded.

In the previous stage, each subband is coded separately up to a specific precision and each forms an independent bit stream. The objective of optimal bit stream truncation is to construct a final bit stream that satisfies the bit rate constraint and minimizes the overall distortion. As in the EBCOT algorithm [34], the end of each pass at each "fractional" bit plane is a candidate truncation point with a precalculated R–D value pair for that subband. A straightforward way to achieve R–D optimized truncation is to find the convex hull of the R–D pairs at the end of each fractional bit plane and truncate only at the candidate truncation points that are on the convex hull.

To achieve quality scalability, a multilayer bit stream may be formed, where each layer represents a quality level. Depending on the available bandwidth and the computational capability, the decoder can choose to decode up to the layer it can handle. The fractional bit plane coding ensures that the bit stream is finely embedded. Since each subband is independently coded, the bit stream of each subband is separable. The encoder can choose to construct a bit stream favoring spatial scalability or temporal scalability. Also, the decoder can easily extract only a few subbands and decode only these subbands. Therefore, the implementation of resolution scalability and temporal scalability is natural and easy.

5.4.2.3 3D EZBC

3D EZBC is an extension of the EZBC image coder [35] to allow coding of three-dimensional wavelet coefficients. The concept of EZBC is inspired by the success of two popular embedded image coding techniques: zero-tree/-block coding, such as SPIHT [33], and context modeling of the subband/wavelet coefficients, such as EBCOT [34]. As discussed, zero-tree/-block coding takes advantage of the natural energy clustering of subband/wavelet coefficients in frequency and in space and exploits the similarity between subbands. Moreover, instead of all pixels, only a small number of elements in the lists [33] need to be processed in individual bit plane coding passes. Thus, processing speed for this class of coders is very fast. However, in the context model based coders [34], individual samples of the wavelet coefficients are coded bit plane by bit plane using context-based arithmetic coding to effectively exploit the strong correlation of subband/wavelet coefficients within and across subbands. Nevertheless, unlike zero-tree/-block coders, these algorithms need to scan all subband/wavelet coefficients at least once to

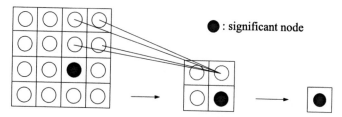

FIGURE 5.20:   Quad tree decomposition in 3D EZBC.

finish coding of a full bit plane, with an implied higher computation cost. The EZBC algorithm combines the advantages of these two coding techniques, that is, low computation complexity and effective exploitation of correlation of subband coefficients, using both ZeroBlocks of subband/wavelet coefficients and context modeling.

Similar to EZBC for image coding, 3D EZBC is based on quad tree representation of the individual subbands and frames. The bottom quad tree level, or pixel level, consists of the magnitude of each subband coefficient. Each quad tree node of the next higher level is then set to the maximum value of its four corresponding nodes at the current level; see Figure 5.20. In the end, the top quad tree node corresponds to the maximum magnitude of all the coefficients from the same subband. As in EZBC, 3D EZBC uses this quad tree-based zero-block coding approach for hierarchical set-partition of subband coefficients to exploit the strong statistical dependency in the quad tree representation of the decomposed subbands. Furthermore, to code the significance of the quad tree nodes, context-based arithmetic coding is used. The context includes eight first-order neighboring nodes of the same quad tree level and the node of the parent subband at the next lower quad tree level. Experiments have shown that including a node in the parent subband in the interband context model is very helpful in predicting the current node, especially at higher levels of a quad tree.

Like SPIHT and other hierarchical bit plane coders, lists are used for tracking the set-partitioning information. However, the lists in 3D-EZBC are separately maintained for nodes from different subbands and quad tree levels. Therefore, separate context models are allowed to be built up for the nodes from different subbands and quad tree levels. In this way, statistical characteristics of quad tree nodes from different orientations, subsampling factors, and amplitude distributions are not mixed up. This ensures a resolution scalable bit stream while maintaining the desirable low complexity feature of this class of coders.

5.4.3 Variants and Extensions: UMCTF, 3-bands

The concept of "unconstrained MCTF" (UMCTF) [10,43] allows very useful extensions of the MCTF. By selecting the temporal filter coefficients appropriately, multiple reference frames and bidirectional prediction can be introduced, such as in H.264, in the MC-wavelet framework. No update step is used, however, which makes this scheme comparable with an open-loop multiresolution predictive structure. We can adaptively change the number of reference frames, the relative importance attached to each reference frame, the extent of bidirectional filtering, and so on. Therefore, with this filter choice, the efficient compensation strategies of conventional predictive coding can be obtained by UMCTF, while preserving the advantages of conventional MCTF.

Other extensions of the temporal transform are aimed at providing nondyadic scalability factors. This can be achieved by M-band filter banks, for which a general framework was proposed in [25]. In particular, a three-band filter bank in lifting form was proposed in [24] and is illustrated in Figure 5.21. For simplicity, Figure 5.21 shows only predict and update blocks; however, as in the dyadic case, they involve motion estimation/compensation.

Following the notation in Figure 5.21, the analysis equations, which lead to one approximation and two detail subbands, are

$$
\begin{cases}
H_t^+(\mathbf{n}) = x_{3t+1}(\mathbf{n}) - P^+\big(\{x_{3t}\}_{t\in N}\big), \\
H_t^-(\mathbf{n}) = x_{3t-1}(\mathbf{n}) - P^-\big(\{x_{3t}\}_{t\in N}\big), \\
L_t(\mathbf{p}) = x_{3t}(\mathbf{p}) + U^+\big(\{H_t^+\}_{t\in N}\big) + U^-\big(\{H_t^-\}_{t\in N}\big).
\end{cases}
$$

Note that in this scheme all the frames indexed by multiples of three are used by the two prediction operators. For example, by choosing frames x_{3t} and x_{3t+3} for the prediction of frame x_{3t+1} and likewise choosing frames x_{3t-3} and x_{3t} for predicting frame x_{3t-1}, a structure similar to the classical IBBP ... structure can be obtained.

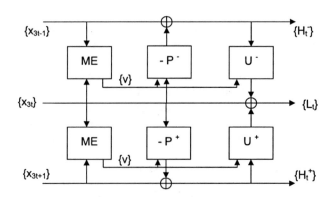

FIGURE 5.21:   Three-band lifting scheme.

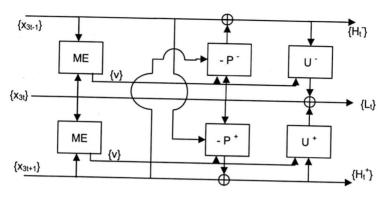

FIGURE 5.22:   A three-band lifting-like scheme.

However, the simplest choice, corresponding to a Haar-like transform, is to have identity predict operators and linear update operators. In this case, the analysis equations become

$$
\begin{cases}
H_t^+(\mathbf{n}) = x_{3t+1}(\mathbf{n}) - x_{3t}\left(\mathbf{n} - v_{3t+1}^{3t}\right), \\[2mm]
H_t^-(\mathbf{n}) = x_{3t-1}(\mathbf{n}) - x_{3t}\left(\mathbf{n} - v_{3t-1}^{3t}\right), \\[2mm]
L_t(\mathbf{p}) = x_{3t}(\mathbf{p}) + \dfrac{1}{4}\left(H_t^+\left(\mathbf{p} + v_{3t+1}^{3t}\right) + H_t^-\left(\mathbf{p} + v_{3t-1}^{3t}\right)\right).
\end{cases}
$$

More complex *lifting-like* schemes (as in Figure 5.22) have been proposed in [26], as well as other possible M-band motion-compensated temporal structures.

These structures allow a frame rate adaptation from 30 to 10 fps, for example, or from 60 to 20 fps. Flexible frame rate changes can be achieved by cascading dyadic and M-band filter banks.

Another direction for the extension of spatiotemporal transforms is to replace the 2D wavelet decomposition by other spatial representations, such as wavelet packets [27] or general filter banks [29], which also allow for more flexible spatial scalability factors [28].

5.4.4 Switching Spatial and Temporal Transforms

The interframe wavelet video coding schemes presented in the previous sections employ MCTF before the spatial wavelet decomposition is performed. Throughout the chapter we refer to this class of interframe wavelet video coding schemes as $t + 2D$ MCTF. Despite their good coding efficiency performance and low complexity, these types of MCTF structures have also several drawbacks.

1. *Limited motion-estimation efficiency.* $t + $ 2D MCTF are inherently limited by the quality of the matches provided by the employed motion estimation algorithm. For instance, discontinuities in the motion boundaries are represented as high frequencies in the wavelet subbands, and the "Intra/Inter" mode switch for motion estimation is not very efficient in $t + $ 2D MCTF schemes, as the spatial wavelet transform is applied globally and cannot encode the resulting discontinuities efficiently. Moreover, the motion estimation accuracy, motion model, and adopted motion estimation block size are fixed for all spatial resolutions, thereby leading to suboptimum implementations compared with nonscalable coding that can adapt the motion estimation accuracy based on the encoded resolution. Also, because the motion vectors are not naturally spatially scalable in $t + $ 2D MCTF, it is necessary to decode a large set of vectors even at lower resolutions.

2. *Limited efficiency spatial scalability.* If the motion reference during $t + $ 2D MCTF is, for example, at HD resolution and decoding is performed at a low resolution (e.g., QCIF), this leads to "subsampling phase drift" for the low resolution video.

3. *Limited spatiotemporal decomposition structures.* In $t + $ 2D MCTF, the same temporal decomposition scheme is applied for all spatial subbands. Hence, the same levels of temporal scalability are provided independent of the spatial resolution.

A possible solution for the aforementioned drawbacks is to employ "in-band temporal filtering" schemes, where the order of motion estimation and compensation and that of the spatial wavelet transform (2D-DWT) are interchanged, which we denote as $2D + t$ MCTF schemes. The spatial wavelet transform for each frame is entirely performed first and multiple separate motion compensation loops are used for the various spatial wavelet bands in order to exploit the temporal correlation present in the video sequence (see Figure 5.23). In contrast to the method of Figure 5.15, where spatial decomposition steps were interleaved with the temporal tree, MCTF can now also be applied to spatial high-pass (wavelet) bands. Subsequently, coding of the wavelet bands after temporal decorrelation can be done using spatial-domain coding techniques such as bit plane coding followed by arithmetic coding or transform-domain coding techniques based on DCT, wavelets, and so on.

5.4.5 Motion Estimation and Compensation in the Overcomplete Wavelet Domain

Due to the decimation procedure in the spatial wavelet transform, the wavelet coefficients are not shift invariant with reference to the original signal resolution. Hence, translation motion in the spatial domain cannot be accurately estimated and compensated from the wavelet coefficients, thereby leading to a significant

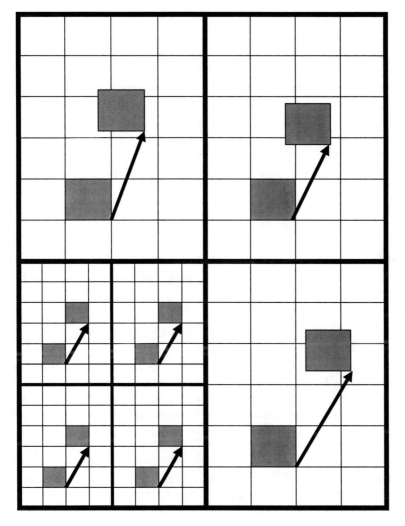

FIGURE 5.23:   Multiresolution motion compensation coder using "in-band prediction."

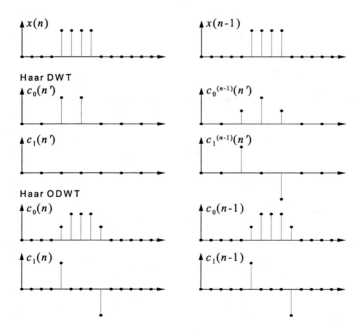

FIGURE 5.24: Shift variance of the Haar wavelet transform. Right signal shifted by one sample to the right, low-pass and high-pass coefficients in Haar DWT and Haar ODWT.

coding efficiency loss (see Haar 1D-DWT case in Figure 5.24). To avoid this inefficiency, motion estimation and compensation should be performed in the overcomplete wavelet domain rather than in the critically sampled domain (see Haar 1D-ODWT case in Figure 5.24). Overcomplete discrete wavelet data (ODWT) can be obtained through a similar process as the critically sampled discrete wavelet signals by omitting the subsampling step. Consequently, the ODWT generates more samples than DWT, but enables accurate wavelet domain motion compensation for the high-frequency components, and the signal does not bear frequency-inversion alias components.

Despite the fact that ODWT generates more samples, an ODWT-based encoder still needs to only encode the critically sampled coefficients. This is because the overcomplete transform coefficients can be generated locally within the decoder. Moreover, when the motion shift is known before analysis and synthesis filtering are performed, it is only necessary to compute those samples of the overcomplete representation that correspond with the actual motion shift.

The $t + 2D$ MCTF schemes (Figure 5.25a) can be easily modified into $2D + t$ MCTF (Figure 5.25b).

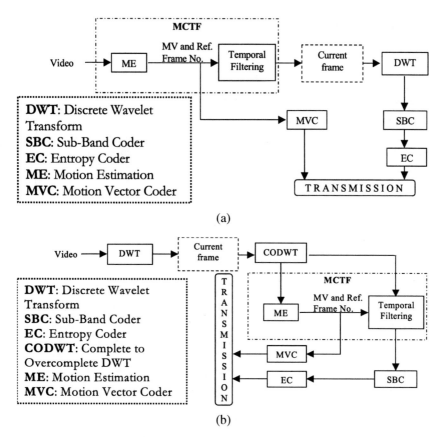

(a)

(b)

FIGURE 5.25: (a) The encoding structure that performs open-loop encoding in the spatial domain – $t + 2D$ MCTF. (b) The encoding structure that performs open-loop encoding in the wavelet domain (in-band) – $2D + t$ MCTF.

More specifically, in $2D + t$ MCTF, the video frames are spatially decomposed into multiple subbands using wavelet filtering, and the temporal correlation within each subband is removed using MCTF (see [19,20]). The residual signal after the MCTF is coded subband by subband using any desired texture coding technique (DCT based, wavelet based, matching pursuit, etc.). Also, all the recent advances in MCTF can be employed for the benefit of $2D + t$ schemes, which have been first introduced in [46–48].

5.5 MPEG-4 AVC/H.264 SCALABLE EXTENSION

As scalable modes in other standards, MPEG-4 AVC/H.264 scalable extension enables scalabilities while maintaining the compatibility of the base layer to the MPEG-4 AVC/H.264 standard. MPEG-4 AVC/H.264 scalable extension provides temporal, spatial, and quality scalabilities. Those scalabilities can be applied simultaneously. In MPEG-4 AVC/H.264, any frame can be marked as a reference frame that can be used for motion prediction for the following frames. Such flexibility enables various motion-compensated prediction structures (see Figure 5.26).

The common prediction structure used in the MPEG-4 AVC/H.264 scalable extension is the hierarchical-B structure, as shown in Figure 5.26. Frames are categorized into different levels. B-frames at level i use neighboring frames at level $i - 1$ as references. Except for the update step, MCTF and hierarchical-B have the same prediction structure. Actually, at the decoder, the decoding process of hierarchical-B and that of MCTF without the update step is the same. Such a hierarchical prediction structure exploits both short-term and long-term temporal correlations as in MCTF. The other advantage is that such a structure can inherently provide multiple levels of temporal scalability. Other temporal scalability schemes compliant with MPEG-4 AVC/H.264 have been presented in [25] and are shown to provide increased efficiency and robustness on error-prone networks.

To achieve SNR scalability, enhancement layers, which have the same motion-compensated prediction structure as the base layer, are generated with finer quantization step sizes. At each enhancement layer, the differential signals to the previous layer are coded. Basically it follows the scheme shown in Figure 5.26.

To achieve spatial scalability, the lower resolution signals and the higher resolution signals are coded into different layers. Also, coding of the higher resolution signals uses bits for the lower resolution as prediction. In contrast to previous coding schemes, the MPEG-4 AVC/H.264 scalable extension can set a constraint on

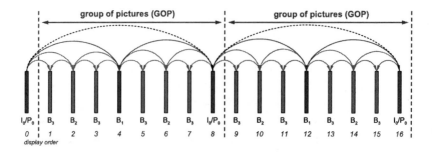

FIGURE 5.26:   Four-level hierarchical-B prediction structure.

the interlayer prediction among different resolutions in which only intra-coded macroblocks are reconstructed to predict the higher resolution, whereas for inter-coded macroblocks, only the motion-compensated residue signals are allowed to predict the corresponding residue signals at the higher resolution. The advantage of such a constraint is that it reduces the decoding complexity because the decoder does not need to do motion compensation for the lower layer. The drawback is that such constraint may have a coding performance penalty.

5.6 SPATIOTEMPORAL–SNR TRADE-OFFS FOR IMPROVED VISUAL PERFORMANCE

In [41], it was shown that performing trade-offs among spatial, temporal, and SNR resolutions as a function of content characteristics often results in a considerably improved user experience for multimedia applications. Nevertheless, this multidimensional flexibility also brings two major challenges. First, no objective measure exists that can quantify the impact on the video quality after multidimensional adaptation (MDA) operations in a synergistic manner, as each component of MDA affects the video quality in a very distinct way. Second, even with an acceptable quality measurement, effective methods for modeling the relationship between video quality and various adaptation operations are important for deciding the right MDA given a resource constraint. To solve this challenge, a general classification-based prediction framework was used successfully in [41] for selecting the preferred MDA operations based on subjective quality evaluation. For this purpose, domain-specific knowledge or general unsupervised clustering was first deployed to construct distinct categories within which the videos share similar preferred MDA operations. Thereafter, a machine learning-based method was applied where the low-level content features extracted from the compressed video streams are employed to train a framework for the problem of joint spatiotemporal–SNR adaptation selection.

5.7 SUMMARY AND FURTHER READING

New perspectives in video compression are reinforced by recent advances in scalable video coding. MCTF-based coders provide high flexibility in bit stream scalability across different temporal, spatial, and quality resolutions. In addition, they provide better error resilience than conventional (prediction based) coders. In fact, MCTF-based coders are better able to separate relevant from irrelevant information. The temporal low-pass bands highlight information that is consistent over a large number of frames, establishing a powerful means for exploiting multiple frame redundancies not achievable by conventional frame-to-frame or multiframe prediction methods. Moreover, noise and quickly changing information that cannot be handled by motion compensation appear in the temporal, high-pass bands, which can supplement the low-pass bands for more accurate signal reproduction whenever desirable, provided that a sufficient data rate is available. Hence, the denoising process that is often applied as a preprocessing step before conventional video compression is an integral part of scalable MCTF-based coders.

Due to the nonrecursive structure, higher degrees of freedom are possible for both encoder and decoder optimization. In principle, a decoder could integrate additional signal synthesis elements whenever the received information is incomplete, such as frame-rate up-conversion, film grain noise overlay, or other elements of texture and motion synthesis, which could easily be integrated as a part of the MCTF synthesis process without losing any synchronization between encoder and decoder. From this point of view, even though many elements of MCTF in the lifting interpretation can be regarded as extensions of proven techniques from MC prediction-based coders, this framework exhibits and enables a number of radically new options in video encoding. However, when a wavelet transform is applied for encoding of the low-pass and high-pass frames resulting from the MCTF process, the commonalities with 2D wavelet coding methods are obvious. If the sequence of spatial and temporal filtering is exchanged ($2D + t$ instead of $t + 2D$ wavelet transform), MCTF can be interpreted as a framework for further interframe compression of (intra frame restricted) 2D wavelet representations such as JPEG 2000. From this point of view, a link between the previously separate worlds of 2D wavelet coding with their excellent scalability properties and compression-efficient motion-compensated video coding schemes is established by MCTF. This shows the high potential for future developments in the area of motion picture compression, even allowing seamless transition between intra frame and inter frame coding methods, depending on the application requirements for flexible random access, scalability, high compression, and error resilience. Furthermore, scalable protection of content, allowing access management for different resolution qualities of video signals, is a natural companion of scalable compression methods.

Nevertheless, a number of topics can be identified that still require further research, but may also lead to even higher compression performance of this new class of video coding algorithms. These include

- Strategies for motion estimation and motion vector encoding, including consideration of prediction and update steps, bidirectional prediction, and update filtering, as well as combined estimation over different levels of the temporal wavelet tree.
- Application and optimization of nonblock-based motion compensation, which is more natural used in combination with spatial wavelet decomposition.
- Scalability of motion information.

- Optimum adaptation of the spatial/temporal decomposition trees, including consideration of integrated solutions of spatial/temporal filtering.
- Optimization of spatial/temporal encoding, including psychovisual properties.
- Rate–distortion optimum truncation of scalable streams, including the trade-offs at various rates.
- Creation of complexity-scalable video coding bit streams.

BIBLIOGRAPHY

[1] G. Karlsson and M. Vetterli. "Subband coding of video signals for packet switched networks," *Proc. Visual Commun. Image Process.*, SPIE vol. 845, pp. 446–456, 1987.

[2] T. Kronander. "Some aspects of perception based image coding," *Ph.D. Thesis*, Linköping University, 1989.

[3] J.-R. Ohm. "Three-dimensional subband coding with motion compensation," *IEEE Trans. Image Processing*, no. 3, pp. 559–571, 1994.

[4] S.-J. Choi and J. W. Woods. "Motion compensated 3D subband coding of video," *IEEE Trans. Image Processing*, vol. 8, pp. 155–167, 1999.

[5] B. Pesquet-Popescu and V. Bottreau. "Three-dimensional lifting schemes for motion-compensated video compression," *Proc. IEEE ICASSP*, pp. 1793–1796, Salt Lake City, USA, May 2001.

[6] H. Radha, M. van der Schaar, and Y. Chen. "The MPEG-4 Fine-Grained Scalable Video Coding Method for Multimedia Streaming over IP," *IEEE Trans. on Multimedia*, vol. 3, Issue 1, pp. 53–68, March 2001.

[7] W. Li. "Overview of Fine Granularity Scalability in MPEG-4 video standard," *IEEE Trans. Circuits and Systems for Video Technology*, vol. 11, no. 3, pp. 301–317, 2001.

[8] U. Horn, K. W. Stuhlmüller, M. Link, and B. Girod. "Robust internet video transmission based on scalable coding and unequal error protection," *Signal Processing: Image Commun.*, September 1999.

[9] K. Rose and S. L. Regunathan. "Toward optimality in scalable predictive coding," *IEEE Trans. Image Processing*, vol. 10, pp. 965–976, July 2001.

[10] M. van der Schaar and H. Radha. "Adaptive Motion-Compensation Fine-Granularity-Scalability (AMC-FGS) for Wireless Video," *IEEE Trans. on Circuits and Systems for Video Technology*, June 2002.

[11] M. van der Schaar and D. S. Turaga. "Unconstrained motion compensated temporal filtering framework for wavelet video coding," *Proc. IEEE ICASSP*, May 2003.

[12] F. Wu, S. Li, and Y.-Q. Zhang. "DCT-prediction based progressive fine granularity scalability coding," *Proc. IEEE ICIP 2000*, Vancouver, Canada, vol. 3, pp. 556–559, September 10–13, 2000.

[13] F. Wu, S. Li, and Y.-Q. Zhang. "A framework for efficient progressive fine granularity scalable video coding," *IEEE Trans. Circuits and Systems for Video Technology*, special issue on streaming video, vol. 11, no. 3, pp. 332–344, 2001.

[14] H. Huang, C. Wang, and T. Chiang. "A robust fine granularity scalability using trellis-based predictive leak," *IEEE Trans. Circuits and Systems for Video Technology*, vol. 12, no. 6, pp. 372–385, 2002.

[15] A. Fuldseth and T. A. Ramstad. "Robust subband video coding with leaky prediction," in *Proc. DSP Workshop*, Loen, Norway, pp. 57–60, September 1996.

[16] Y. Gao and L.-H. Chau. "An Efficient Fine Granularity Scalable Coding Scheme Using Adaptive Leaky Prediction," *Fourth International Conference on Information, Communications & Signal Processing and Fourth Pacific-Rim Conference on Multimedia (ICICS-PCM 2003)*, Singapore, December 2003.

[17] X. Sun, F. Wu, S. Li, W. Gao, and Y.-Q. Zhang. "Macroblock-based progressive fine granularity scalable video coding," *Proc. IEEE ICME*, Japan, August 2001.

[18] Feng Wu, Shipeng Li, Xiaoyan Sun, Bing Zeng, and Ya-Qin Zhang. "Macroblock-based progressive fine granularity scalable video coding," *International Journal of Imaging Systems and Technology*, vol. 13, Issue 6, pp. 297–307, 2003.

[19] W. H. Peng and Y.-K. Chen. "Mode-adaptive fine granularity scalability," *Proc. IEEE ICIP*, pp. 993–996, Greece, 2001.

[20] W.-H. Peng and Y.-K. Chen. "Enhanced Mode-Adaptive Fine Granularity Scalability," *International Journal of Imaging Systems and Technology*, vol. 13, no. 6, pp. 308–321, March 2004.

[21] L. Luo, J. Li, S. Li, Z. Zhuang, and Y.-Q. Zhang. "Motion compensated lifting wavelet and its application in video coding," *Proc. IEEE ICME*, Tokyo, Japan, August 2001.

[22] D. Turaga, M. van der Schaar, and B. Pesquet. "Complexity Scalable Motion Compensated Wavelet Video Encoding," *IEEE Trans. on Circuits and Systems for Video Technology*, vol. 15, no. 8, pp. 982–993, August 2005.

[23] J. Barbarien, Y. Andreopoulos, A. Munteanu, P. Schelkens, and J. Cornelis. "Coding of motion vectors produced by wavelet-domain motion estimation," *Proc. PCS 2003*, pp. 193–198, April 2003.

[24] C. Tillier and B. Pesquet-Popescu. "3D, 3-Band, 3-Tap Temporal Lifting for Scalable Video Coding," *Proc. IEEE ICIP 2003*, pp. 14–17, Barcelona, Spain, September 2003.

[25] C. Bergeron, C. Lamy-Bergot, G. Pau, and B. Pesquet-Popescu. "Temporal scalability through adaptive M-band filterbanks for robust H264/MPEG-4 AVC coding," Special issue on Video Analysis and Coding for Robust Transmission. *JASP*, 2006.

[26] C. Tillier, B. Pesquet-Popescu, and M. van der Schaar. "3-Band Temporal Structures for Scalable Video Coding," *IEEE Trans. on Image Processing*, vol. 15, Issue 9, pp. 2545–2557, September 2006.

[27] G. Pau and B. Pesquet-Popescu. "Comparison of Spatial M-Band Filter Banks for t+2D Video Coding," *Proc. of SPIE/IEEE VCIP 2005*, Beijing, China, July 2005.

[28] G. Pau, B. Pesquet-Popescu, and G. Piella. "Modified M-Band Synthesis Filter Bank for Fractional Scalability of Images," *IEEE Signal Processing Letters*, vol. 13, Issue 6, pp. 345–348, June 2006.

[29] M. Trocan, C. Tillier, and B. Pesquet-Popescu. "Joint wavelet packets for group of frames in MCTF," *Proc. SPIE*, San Diego, USA, July 2005.

[30] A. Secker and D. Taubman. "Highly Scalable Video Compression with Scalable Motion Coding," *IEEE Trans. on Image Processing*, vol. 13, no. 8, pp. 1029–1041, August 2004.

[31] R. Xiong, F. Wu, J. Xu, S. Li, and Y.-Q. Zhang. "Barbell lifting wavelet transform for highly scalable video coding," *Proc. Picture Coding Symposium 2004*, San Francisco, CA, USA, December 2004.

[32] Bo Feng, Jizheng Xu, Feng Wu, Shiqiang Yang, and Shipeng Li. "Energy distributed update steps (EDU) in lifting based motion compensated video coding," *Proc. IEEE ICIP 2004*, Singapore, October 2004.

[33] A. Said and W. A. Pearlman. "A new fast and efficient image codec based on set partitioning in hierarchical trees," *IEEE Trans. on Circ. and Systems for Video Techn.*, vol. 6, pp. 243–250, June 1996.

[34] D. Taubman. "High performance scalable image compression with EBCOT," *IEEE Trans. on Image Processing*, no. 9, pp. 1158–1170, 2000.

[35] S.-T. Hsiang and J. W. Woods. "Embedded image coding using zeroblocks of subband/wavelet coefficients and context modeling," *MPEG-4 Workshop and Exhibition at ISCAS 2000*, Geneva, Switzerland, May 2000.

[36] J. Xu, S. Li, and Y.-Q. Zhang. "A wavelet video coder using three dimensional embedded subband coding with optimized truncation (3D ESCOT)," *IEEE-PCM 2000*, Sydney, December 2000.

[37] J. Xu, Z. Xiong, S. Li, and Y.-Q. Zhang. "3D embedded subband coding with optimal truncation (3D-ESCOT)," *Applied and Computational Harmonic Analysis* 10, p. 589, May 2001.

[38] S.-T. Hsiang and J. W. Woods. "Embedded video coding using invertible motion compensated 3D subband/wavelet filter bank," *Signal Processing: Image Commun.*, vol. 16, pp. 705–724, May 2001.

[39] S.-T. Hsiang, J. Woods, and J.-R. Ohm. "Invertible temporal subband/wavelet filter banks with half-pixel accurate motion compensation," *IEEE Trans. on Image Processing* 13, pp. 1018–1028, August 2004.

[40] M. van der Schaar and Y. Andreopoulos. "Rate-distortion-complexity modeling for network and receiver aware adaptation," *IEEE Trans. on Multimedia*, June 2005.

[41] Y. Wang, M. van der Schaar, S. F. Chang, and A. Loui. "Content-Based Optimal MDA Operation Prediction for Scalable Video Coding Systems Using Subjective Quality Evaluation," *IEEE Trans. on Circuits and Systems for Video Technology*—Special issue on Analysis and Understanding for Video Adaptation, October 2005.

[42] J. R. Ohm, M. van der Schaar, and J. Woods. "Interframe wavelet coding: Motion Picture Representation for Universal Scalability," *EURASIP Signal Processing: Image Communication*, Special issue on Digital Cinema, 2004.

[43] D. Turaga, M. van der Schaar, Y. Andreopoulos, A. Munteanu, and P. Schelkens. "Unconstrained motion compensated temporal filtering (UMCTF) for efficient and flexible interframe wavelet video coding," *EURASIP Signal Processing: Image Communication*, 2004.

[44] M. van der Schaar and H. Radha. "A hybrid temporal-SNR Fine-Granular Scalability for Internet Video," *IEEE Trans. on Circuits and Systems for Video Technology*, March 2001.

[45] H. Radha, M. van der Schaar, and S. Karande. "Scalable Video TranScaling for the Wireless Internet," *EURASIP Journal of Applied Signal Processing* (JASP)—Special issue on Multimedia over IP and Wireless Networks, No. 2, pp. 265–279, 2004.

[46] Y. Andreopoulos, M. van der Schaar, A. Munteanu, J. Barbarien, P. Schelkens, and J. Cornelis. "Fully-Scalable Wavelet Video Coding using In-Band Motion-Compensated Temporal Filtering," *Proc. on IEEE International Conference on Acoustics, Speech and Signal Processing (ICASSP)*, 2003.

[47] J. Ye and M. van der Schaar. "Fully Scalable 3-D Overcomplete Wavelet Video Coding Using Adaptive Motion Compensated Temporal Filtering," *Proc. SPIE Video Communications and Image Processing (VCIP)*, 2003.

[48] Y. Andreopoulos, A. Munteanu, J. Barbarien, M. van der Schaar, J. Cornelis, and P. Schelkens. "In-band motion compensated temporal filtering," *EURASIP Signal Processing: Image Communication* (special issue on "Subband/Wavelet Interframe Video Coding"), vol. 19, no. 7, pp. 653–673, August 2004.

6

Scalable Audio Coding

Jin Li

6.1 INTRODUCTION

High-performance audio codecs bring digital music into practical reality. The most popular audio compression technology today is MP3 [8], which stands for layer III of the MPEG-1 audio compression standard. Developed in the early 1990s, MP3 does not perform very well in terms of compression efficiency. More advanced audio compression technologies have been proposed later, such as the MPEG-4 Advanced Audio Codec [1,10], Real Audio, and Windows Media Audio (WMA). The latter two are commercial audio coders developed by RealNetworks and Microsoft, respectively. Most existing audio codecs optimize only on a single target compression ratio, striving to deliver the best perceptual audio quality given the length of the bit stream or to deliver the shortest length of the bit stream given a constraint on playback quality. However, such a goal is far from enough, especially considering the unique characteristics of audio (as well as other media file) compression. Unlike data compression, where all content must be exactly preserved during the compression, audio compression is elastic and tolerates distortion. It is always possible to compress the audio a little more or a little less, with slightly more or less distortion. In fact, in many applications, it is difficult to foresee the exact compression ratio required at the time the audio is compressed. The ability to quickly change the compression ratio afterward has important applications and led to better user experience in audio storage and transmission. For example, if the compression ratio is adjustable, the compressed audio can be stretched to meet the exact requirements of the customer. We can build a stretchable audio recording device, which at first uses the highest possible compression quality (lowest possible compression ratio) to store the compressed audio. Later, when the length of the compressed audio at the highest quality exceeds the memory of the device, the compressed bit stream of the existing audio file can be truncated to leave memory for newly recorded audio content. A device with scalable audio compression technology can perform this stretch step again and again, continuously increasing the compression ratio of the existing media, and freeing up storage space to squeeze in new content. As discussed in Chapter 4, the ability to quickly adjust the compression ratio is also very useful in the media communication/streaming scenario, where the server and the client may adjust the size of the compressed audio to match the instantaneous bandwidth and condition of the network, and thus reliably deliver the best possible media quality over the network. Moreover, multiple description coding [9] may also be obtained from a scalable coded audio bit stream. The idea is to apply more protection (using an erasure code with more parity packets) toward the head of the bit stream and to apply less protection toward the tail of the bit stream. Thus, with any number of packet losses, a prefix of the compressed bit stream is always preserved. As a result, the quality of the delivered audio may degrade gracefully with an increase in packet loss probability.

The straightforward way of adjusting the compression ratio of a compressed audio file is to first decode the compressed media file and then re-encode it. The computational complexity involved in the decoding and re-encoding operation can be quite costly. Moreover, there is usually a performance penalty involved, as the re-encoded audio is usually lower quality compared with directly encoding the audio file at the target compression ratio. Transcoding technologies have been developed to adjust the compression ratio of traditionally compressed bit streams, such as MP3 bit streams. Compared with decoding and then re-encoding, transcoding achieves modest computation savings by skipping some of the compression operations, mainly the inverse and forward transform and (for video transcoding) motion estimation. Almost all existing transcoding techniques still need to perform the entropy decoding and re-encoding; therefore, the speed of the transcoding is not very fast, usually at least 25% of that of media encoding.

In comparison, scalable/embedded coders allow the compressed bit stream to be directly manipulated. Popularized by Shapiro in his embedded zerotree wavelet (EZW) [12] image coder, embedded coder has the attractive property that the high compression ratio bit stream is embedded in the low compression ratio bit stream. Increasing the compression ratio can thus be done very quickly by extracting from a master bit stream the subset of the bit stream that corresponds to the application bit stream. In the case of embedded image compression, this operation can be further simplified to truncating the existing bit stream. In the domain of image compression, it has been shown [4,11,13] that embedded coding cannot only achieve flexible bit stream adjustment, but also obtain state-of-the-art compression performance and reasonable computational complexity. In fact, the most recent image compression standard, JPEG-2000 [14], defines an embedded image coder.

It is a misconception that you have to pay for the scalable functionality with compression performance. Just as embedded image coding did not take off until highly efficient bit plane entropy coding was developed, highly efficient embedded audio coding needs unique technologies that suit its need for embedded coding. In this chapter, we develop an embedded audio coder (EAC) with performance that exceeds or matches that of the best available audio coders. The key technology that empowers EAC with such high performance is the use of implicit auditory masking and a high-performance subbit plane entropy coder.

6.2 SCALABLE AUDIO CODING FRAMEWORK

The embedded audio coder is a fully scalable audio waveform coder. There are three components of the EAC: an encoder, a decoder, and a parser. The encoder turns the input audio waveform into a compressed bit stream with the highest desirable bit rate, audio sampling rate, and number of audio channels. We call the compressed bit stream formed by the encoder the master bit stream, since all scaled bit streams (which we call application bit streams) will be formed by extracting subsets of bits from the master bit stream. The decoder turns the compressed bit stream, whether the master bit stream or the application bit stream, back into an audio waveform. The parser extracts a subset of the master bit stream to form an application bit stream with a reduced rate, reduced sampling rate, or reduced number of audio channels.

The framework of the EAC encoder is shown in Figure 6.1. The input audio waveform first goes through a channel mixer (MIX). Each channel of mixed audio is then separately transformed and quantized. After that, the transformed and quantized audio coefficients are split into sections, with each section of audio

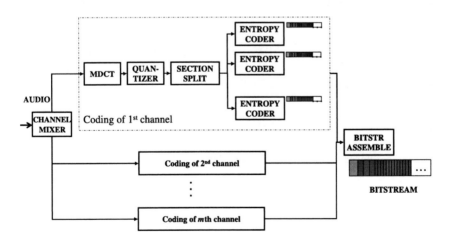

FIGURE 6.1:   Embedded audio coding framework.

coefficients corresponding to one mixed channel of a particular time span and frequency range. Next, an embedded entropy coder is applied to each section to encode the coefficients into an embedded bit stream. Each section bit stream can be truncated after compression to trade distortion versus coding rate. Finally, a bit stream assembler puts together the embedded bit streams of the sections to form the master bit stream of the compressed audio.

Because the master bit stream is formed by concatenating together separately coded section bit streams, the master bit stream may be reshaped in a number of ways. In fact, the EAC parser takes the master bit stream as input and outputs an application bit stream with a possibly reduced bit rate, reduced number of audio channels, reduced sampling rate, or a combination of all. To scale by number of audio channels or audio sampling rate, the EAC parser simply drops the sections that are not needed any more. To scale by bit rate, the EAC parser further truncates the embedded bit stream of each section. The reshaped bit streams of needed sections are then put together to form the application bit stream.

The EAC decoder simply reverses the operation of the EAC encoder. It first de-multiplexes the master bit stream or the application bit stream into a compressed bit stream for each section. Then, the compressed bit stream for each section is fed into a separate entropy decoder. The decoded coefficients are combined, in-verse quantized, and transformed. Finally, a channel remixer recovers the playable audio waveform.

In the following, we will describe in detail the components of the EAC en-coder: the channel mixer, the audio transform, the quantizer, the section splitter, the embedded entropy coder, and the bit stream assembler.

6.3 CHANNEL MIXER: SCALE BY NUMBER OF AUDIO CHANNELS

The channel mixer combines the input audio into a number of mixed channels. If the input audio is mono, the MIX simply passes through the audio. If the input audio is stereo, we may combine and mix the left (L) and right (R) audio channels into ch_1 and ch_2, as follows:

$$\begin{bmatrix} ch_1 \\ ch_2 \end{bmatrix} = \mathbf{M_1} \begin{bmatrix} L \\ R \end{bmatrix}, \tag{6.1}$$

where the mixing matrix $\mathbf{M_1}$ takes the form

$$\mathbf{M_1} = \begin{bmatrix} \frac{\sqrt{2}}{2} & \frac{\sqrt{2}}{2} \\ \frac{\sqrt{2}}{2} & -\frac{\sqrt{2}}{2} \end{bmatrix}. \tag{6.2}$$

If the input audio has more than two channels, a multichannel mixer will be used to mix the multichannel audio. For example, the operation to mix six input audio channels can be described as

$$
\begin{bmatrix} ch_1 \\ ch_2 \\ ch_3 \\ ch_4 \\ ch_5 \\ ch_6 \end{bmatrix} = \begin{bmatrix} \mathbf{M}_1 & & & 0 & & \\ & 1 & & & 0 & \\ 0 & & \ddots & & & \\ & 0 & & & 1 & \end{bmatrix} \mathbf{M}_2 \begin{bmatrix} L \\ R \\ C \\ LS \\ RS \\ LFE \end{bmatrix}, \tag{6.3}
$$

where the six input channels, Left Front (L), Right Front (R), Center Front (C), Low Frequency Enhancement (LFE), Left Surround (LS), and Right Surround (RS), are mixed into six output channels ch_i, in which i denotes the ith mixed channel. The matrix $\mathbf{M}_1$ is the stereo mixing matrix in (6.2), and $\mathbf{M}_2$ is the multi-channel to stereo fold-down matrix,

$$
\mathbf{M}_2 = \begin{bmatrix} 1 & & \alpha & \beta & & \chi \\ & 1 & \alpha & & \beta & \chi \\ & & 1 & & & \\ & & & 1 & & \\ & & & & 1 & \\ & & & & & 1 \end{bmatrix},
$$

where α, β and χ are constant fold-down parameters. Both mixing matrices $\mathbf{M}_1$ and $\mathbf{M}_2$ have the desirable properties that a small set of mixed audio channels may represent a scaled-down representation of the original multichannel audio. For example, ch_1 represents the audio component $L + R$ and may serve as a good mono representation of the stereo audio, should the playback device only support mono playback. ch_1 and ch_2 form a scaled-down stereo representation of the six-channel input audio. The MIX operation thus ensures that the compressed bit stream can be scaled by audio channels.

6.4 AUDIO TRANSFORM

After channel mixing, the waveform of each mixed audio channel is transformed by a modified discrete cosine transform (MDCT) or a modulated lapped transform (MLT) [5]. We switch the MDCT window between a long and a short window. The long window is used for homogeneous audio segments, while the short window is used for audio segments with large energy fluctuations to reduce the effect of pre-echoing. Assuming the input audio is sampled at 44.1 kHz, the size of the long MDCT window (W_l) is 2048 samples, while the size of the short MDCT window (W_s) is 256 samples.

The MDCT is defined

$$X(m) = \sqrt{\frac{2}{N}} \sum_{k=0}^{2N-1} w(k)x(k) \cos \frac{(2k+1+N)(2m+1)\pi}{4N}, \quad m = 0, \ldots, N-1,$$

(6.4)

where N is the length of the MDCT window (W_l or W_s), $X(m)$ is the value of the MDCT coefficient, $x(k)$ is the input audio samples, and $w(k)$ is the window function. The MDCT can be decomposed into two operations: windowing and time domain aliasing (TDA) and the discrete cosine transform of type IV (DCT-IV).

The windowing/TDA operation takes the form

$$\begin{pmatrix} x(k) \\ x(N-1-k) \end{pmatrix} \mapsto \begin{pmatrix} w(N-1-k) & w(k) \\ -w(k) & w(N-1-k) \end{pmatrix} \begin{pmatrix} x(k) \\ x(N-1-k) \end{pmatrix},$$

$$\text{for } k = 0, \ldots, N/2 - 1,$$

(6.5)

where $w(k)$ is a window function that fulfills the time domain aliasing cancellation (TDAC) condition

$$w(k)^2 + w(N-1-k)^2 = 1, \quad k = 0, \ldots, N/2 - 1.$$

(6.6)

One of the most widely used window functions in audio compression is the Sine window,

$$w(k) = \sin\left[\frac{\pi}{N}\left(k + \frac{1}{2}\right)\right].$$

(6.7)

Another popular window is the Kaiser–Bessel Derived (KBD) window, which does not have an analytic expression.

After the windowing/TDA operation, the DCT-IV is applied:

$$X(m) = \sqrt{\frac{2}{N}} \sum_{k=0}^{N-1} x(k) \cos \frac{(2k+1)(2m+1)\pi}{4N}, \quad m = 0, \ldots, N-1.$$

(6.8)

The DCT-IV can be implemented by a prerotation, an FFT, and a postrotation.

The operation of the MDCT with switching window is depicted in Figure 6.2. Each channel of mixed audio is separated into frames of length W_l (the size of the long window). Each frame can be occupied by a single long window or can be split into W_l/W_s (in the default configuration, 8) short windows. If two consecutive frames are both long windows, a long window TDA operation is applied between the frames. Between two short windows, or between a long and a short window, a short window TDA operation is applied. After the TDA operation, a DCT-IV operation is applied to the signal.

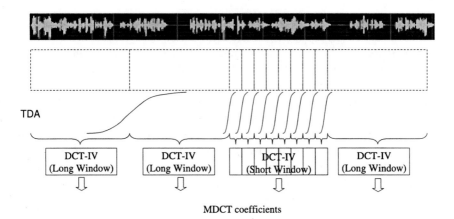

TDA

FIGURE 6.2:   MDCT with a switching window.

The MDCT operation can be easily inverted, as both the TDA and the DCT-IV operation can be inverted. The inverse TDA operation is

$$\begin{pmatrix} x(k) \\ x(N-1-k) \end{pmatrix} \mapsto \begin{pmatrix} w(N-1-k) & -w(k) \\ w(k) & w(N-1-k) \end{pmatrix} \begin{pmatrix} x(k) \\ x(N-1-k) \end{pmatrix},$$

$$\text{for } k = 0, \ldots, N/2 - 1, \tag{6.9}$$

and the inverse DCT-IV operation is

$$x(k) = \sqrt{\frac{2}{N}} \sum_{m=0}^{N-1} X(m) \cos \frac{(2k+1)(2m+1)\pi}{4N}, \quad k = 0, \ldots, N-1. \tag{6.10}$$

6.5 QUANTIZATION AND SECTION SPLIT

After the MDCT transform, all MDCT coefficients are uniformly quantized according to the rule

$$q(m) = sign\big(X(m)\big) \left\lfloor \frac{|X(m)|}{\delta} \right\rfloor, \tag{6.11}$$

where $X(m)$ is an MDCT coefficient, $q(m)$ is the quantization result, δ is the quantization step size, $sign(x)$ returns the sign of the coefficient x, and $\lfloor x \rfloor$ denotes the largest integer that is less or equal than x. The quantization process is conventional: uniform with a central dead zone twice the size of the quantization step size δ. However, the quantizer does not determine the ultimate quality of the encoded audio. Because the quantized coefficients will be encoded by a subbit plane-embedded entropy coder with a truncatable bit stream, additional distortion can be introduced by the entropy coding module and the bit stream assembler module. Thus, the main functionality of the quantization module is to map the co-efficients from a floating point representation to an integer representation so that they can be more efficiently processed by the entropy coding module. The default quantization step size in EAC is rather fine, for example, $\delta = 1/128$.

To improve the efficiency of the entropy coder, we group the quantized coef-ficients of a certain number of consecutive frames into a time slot. In the default configuration, a time slot consists of 16 frames, that is, 16 long MDCT windows or 128 short windows. A time slot therefore consists of 32,768 samples, which is about 0.74 second if the input audio is sampled at 44.1 kHz.

For sampling rate scalability, we may further split the coefficients in the time slot into a number of sections, each section covering the coefficients of a par-ticular frequency range. For example, for a possible $2\times$ and $4\times$ sampling rate reduction, we split the coefficients into three sections of 0–0.25π, 0.25π–0.50π, and 0.50π–1.00π. By throwing away the coefficients corresponding to 0.50π–1.00π, and inversely transforming by a MDCT with a half window size for both long and short MDCT windows, we can decode the bit stream into audio with a $2\times$ sampling rate reduction. Similarly, by throwing away the coefficients corre-sponding to 0.25π–0.50π and 0.50π–1.00π, and inversely transforming by an MDCT with a quarter window size, we can decode the audio with a $4\times$ sam-pling rate reduction. Such an audio sampling rate reduction can be considered as passing the audio waveform through a low-pass filter that first transforms the au-dio by MDCT, throws away half (or three-quarters) of the coefficients, and then inversely transforms the coefficients with an MDCT at half (or quarter) window size. It provides an effective means of sampling rate reduction of the compressed audio, which is very useful if the decoding device does not have a good high frequency response or it wants to save computational power.

6.6 EMBEDDED SUBBIT PLANE ENTROPY CODING

The section of the quantized coefficients in a time slot is encoded by an embedded subbit plane entropy coder, which is one of the most complicated components in EAC. We will explain in detail the working of the subbit plane entropy coder in the following. First, we review the human auditory system in Section 6.6.1. Then we explain the implicit auditory masking approach in Section 6.6.2. We discuss the embedded coding unit (ECU) and the subbit plane entropy coder in Sections 6.6.3 and 6.6.4, respectively. We describe the arithmetic entropy coding unit in Section 6.6.5.

6.6.1 Human Auditory Masking

A detailed description of the human auditory system is beyond the scope of this chapter. The interested reader may refer to [7]. However, it is worth noticing that the characteristic of the human auditory system that most affects audio compression is auditory masking.

The human auditory system can be roughly divided into 26 critical bands, each of which is a bandpass filter bank with bandwidth on the order of 50 to 100 Hz for bands below 500 Hz and up to 5000 Hz for bands at high frequencies. Within each critical band, there is an auditory masking threshold, also referred to as the psychoacoustic masking threshold or the threshold of the just noticeable distortion (JND) [2]. Audio waveforms with an energy level below the JND threshold will not be audible. The auditory JND threshold is highly correlated to the spectral envelope of the signal. This is in contrast to the JND threshold in the human visual system, where the masking of a weak visual signal by a nearby strong signal occurs only over a very short range, and the dominant visual sensitivity is the same for a certain frequency regardless of the input signal. Let the auditory JND threshold of a critical band k at time i be $TH_{i,k}$. The JND threshold can be calculated as the maximum of a quiet threshold and a masking threshold. The quiet threshold TH_ST_k dictates the sensitivity of the auditory system for critical band k without the presence of any strong audio signal. It can be calculated through an equal loudness curve, such as the Fletcher–Munson curve [7] shown as the solid line in Figure 6.3. According to the quiet threshold, the sensitivity

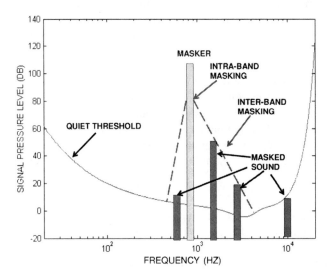

FIGURE 6.3:   Auditory masking threshold: simultaneous masking.

of the ear is nearly constant for a large range (1–8 kHz) and drops dramatically before 500 Hz and after 10 kHz. Nevertheless, in audio compression, the auditory JND threshold is largely shaped by masking, which is an effect by which a low-level signal (the maskee) can be made inaudible by a simultaneously occurring strong signal (the masker) as long as the masker and the maskee are close enough to each other in time and frequency. The auditory masking threshold consists of three components: the simultaneous intra-band mask, the simultaneous inter-band mask, and the temporal mask. The most basic form of auditory masking is simultaneous intra-band masking, where the maskee and the masker are at the same time instant and within the same critical band. The intra-band masking threshold $TH\_INTRA_{i,k}$ is directly proportional to the average spectral energy $AVE_{i,k}$ of the masker in critical band k at the same time instant i, and can be expressed in dB as

$$TH\_INTRA_{i,k}(\text{dB}) = AVE_{i,k}(\text{dB}) - R_{\text{fac}}, \qquad (6.12)$$

where R_{fac} is a constant offset value determined through the psychoacoustic experimentation. The second form of masking is simultaneous inter-band masking, where the maskee and the masker are at the same time instant, but at neighboring critical bands. The level of such inter-band masking $TH\_INTER_{i,k}$ can be formulated as

$$TH\_INTER_{i,k} = max(TH_{i,k-1} - R_{\text{high}}, TH_{i,k+1} - R_{\text{low}}), \qquad (6.13)$$

where R_{high} and R_{low} are the attenuation factors toward the high- and low-frequency critical bands, respectively. The higher frequency coefficients are more easily masked; thus the attenuation R_{high} is smaller than R_{low}. Combining quiet, intra- and inter-band auditory masking, the auditory masking threshold created by a strong audio signal identified as the "masker" is illustrated in Figure 6.3, where the auditory JND threshold is shown as the dashed line. Any signal below the JND threshold, for example, compression distortion, will not be audible by human ears.

The third form of masking is temporal masking, which dictates that a strong signal can also mask a weak signal in the same critical band, but in the immediate preceding or following time interval. The duration within which premasking applies is less than one-tenth that of the postmasking, which is in the order of 50 to 200 ms. The temporal masking threshold $TH\_TIME_{i,k}$ can be expressed as

$$TH\_TIME_{i,k} = max(TH_{i-1,k} - R_{\text{post}}, TH_{i+1,k} - R_{\text{pre}}), \qquad (6.14)$$

where R_{pre} and R_{post} are the attenuation factors for the preceding and following time intervals, respectively. A sample temporal masking generated by a masker is shown in Figure 6.4.

The combined auditory JND threshold is the maximum of the quiet threshold, the simultaneous intra- and inter-band masking, and the temporal masking threshold,

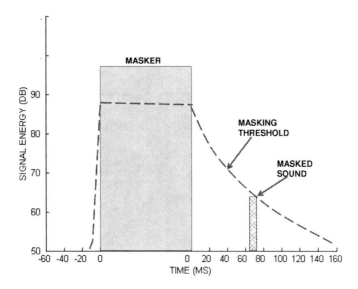

FIGURE 6.4:   Auditory masking threshold: temporal masking.

$$TH_{i,k} = max(TH\_ST_k, TH\_INTRA_{i,k}, TH\_INTER_{i,k}, TH\_TIME_{i,k}).   (6.15)$$

Calculation of the JND threshold requires the iteration of (6.13)–(6.15). Thus, if the input audio consists of several strong maskers, the combined JND threshold will be the maximum of the masking threshold generated by the individual masks.

6.6.2 Implicit Auditory Masking

Using the auditory masking effect, an audio coder can devote fewer bits to the coefficients that are less sensitive to the human ear and more bits to the auditorily sensitive coefficients, thus improving the quality of the coded audio. In EAC, the auditory masking module is integrated with the embedded entropy coding module. It is done in a unique way with two distinctive features. First, the auditory JND threshold is derived from the partially coded coefficients and does not need to be transmitted. Second, the auditory JND threshold is used to determine the order that the bits of the coefficients are encoded, rather than to change the coefficients (by adopting a different quantizing step size for different critical bands). We call the approach implicit auditory masking because the auditory JND threshold is implicitly derived during the coding process.

To illustrate this distinctiveness, we show the process of encoding using traditional auditory masking in Figure 6.5 and that of the implicit auditory masking

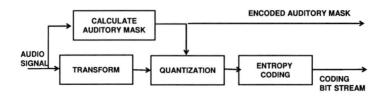

FIGURE 6.5:   Encoding using traditional auditory masking.

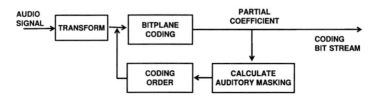

FIGURE 6.6:   Encoding using implicit auditory masking.

in Figure 6.6. In traditional auditory masking, the encoder calculates the JND threshold based on the spectral envelope of the input audio waveform. The JND threshold is then encoded as a part of the compressed bit stream and is transmitted to the decoder. The encoder also quantizes the transform coefficients with a step size proportional to the JND threshold, that is, the coefficients are quantized coarsely in the critical bands with a larger JND threshold and are quantized finely in those with a smaller JND threshold. The approach is simple and suits a nonscalable coder. In scalable audio coding, it is not efficient. First, sending the auditory JND threshold consumes a nontrivial number of bits, which can be as much as 10% of the total number of coded bits. Since the auditory masking module is applied before the entropy coding module, the JND threshold must be transmitted with the same precision regardless of the compression ratio. The JND threshold overhead thus eats significantly into the bit budget, especially if the compressed bit stream is later scaled to a low bit rate. Second, as shown in Section 6.6.1, the JND threshold is shaped by the energy distribution of the input audio, while the same energy distribution is revealed through the bit plane coding process of the embedded entropy coder. As a result, the information is coded twice, which wastes precious coding bits.

The framework of implicit auditory masking is shown in Figure 6.6. Compared to Figure 6.5, the auditory masking operation is now integrated into the loop of the entropy coding module and is performed as follows. We first set the initial auditory JND threshold to the quiet threshold. A portion of the transform coefficients, for example, the top bit planes, is then encoded. Afterward, an updated auditory JND threshold is calculated based on the spectral envelope of the partially coded transform coefficients. Since the decoder may derive the same auditory JND threshold from the same coded coefficients, the values of the auditory JND threshold need not be sent to the decoder. Using this implicitly calculated JND threshold, both the encoder and the decoder figure out which portion of the transform coefficients is to be encoded next. After the next portion of the coefficients has been encoded, the auditory JND threshold is updated again, which is then used to guide the coding order of the remaining portion of the coefficients. The process iterates among the operation of sending a portion of the quantized MDCT coefficients, updating the JND threshold, and using the updated JND threshold to determine the portions to be sent next. It only stops when a certain end criterion has been met, for example, the quantized coefficients have been encoded to the least significant bit plane (LSB), a desired coding bit rate has been reached, or a desired coding quality has been reached. By deriving the auditory masking threshold implicitly from the partially coded coefficients, bits normally required for the auditory JND threshold are saved. The saving can be especially significant at a low bit rate or when the coding bit stream is later truncated to a lower bit rate. Implicit auditory masking may thus significantly improve compression efficiency. Moreover, in all existing audio coders, the auditory JND threshold is carried as a header in the bit stream. In contrast, implicit auditory masking does not have an error-sensitive header. The EAC-compressed bit stream is thus less susceptible to transmission errors and therefore offers better error protection in a noisy channel, such as in a wireless environment. A third advantage of implicit auditory masking results from the fact that instead of coding the auditorily insensitive coefficients coarsely, the EAC encodes them at a later stage. By using auditory masking to govern the coding order, rather than to quantize the coefficients, the quality of the compressed audio becomes less sensitive to the accuracy of the JND threshold, as slight deviations in the threshold simply cause certain audio coefficients to be coded later.

6.6.3 Embedded Coding Unit

The section of quantized coefficients in a time slot is ultimately encoded by a subbit plane entropy coder. It encodes the audio coefficient bit by bit, and in a rate-distortion optimized order.

The subbit plane entropy coder of EAC is a general version of the simple bit plane coder, which works as follows. Let i index the time interval, j index the frequency component, and k index the critical band. Let $x_{i,j}$ be a coefficient at time interval i, frequency j, and $s_{i,k}$ be a critical band k at time interval i. Let each audio coefficient be represented in binary sign and magnitude form as

$$[\pm b_{L-1} b_{L-2} \cdots b_0], \tag{6.16}$$

where b_{L-1} is the most significant bit (MSB), b_0 is the least significant bit (LSB), and $\pm$ is the sign of the coefficient. A group of bits of the same significance from different coefficients forms a bit plane. For example, bits b_{L-1} of all coefficients form the most significant $L-1$ bit plane. The bit plane coder encodes the coefficients bit plane by bit plane: first the most significant bit plane, then the second most significant bit plane, and so on. This way, if the output-compressed bit stream is truncated, at least part of each coefficient can be decoded.

The subbit plane coder in EAC goes one step further in recognizing that bits in the same bit plane can be different in their rate and distortion contributions. First, the coefficients represented by the bits may have different JND thresholds that lead to vastly different subjective distortions even if the objective distortions are the same. Second, the bits can be statistically different considering their neighbor coefficients and coding histories. An illustration of subbit plane is shown in Figure 6.7. Since the coefficients in EAC are actually arranged in a 2D array indexed by the time interval i and frequency j, the actual bit array is 3D. However, it is difficult to draw a 3D bit array; therefore, we show a slice of the bit array in 2D in Figure 6.7. Note that the sign of the coefficient is also part of the bit array, as the 'plus' and 'minus' signs can be represented by 0 and 1, respectively. Let b_M be a bit in a coefficient x, which is to be encoded. If all more significant bits in the same coefficient x are 0s, the coefficient x is said to be insignificant (because if the bit stream is terminated right before bit b_M has been coded, coefficient x will be reconstructed as zero), and the current bit b_M is to be encoded in the mode of significance identification. Otherwise, the coefficient is said to be significant, and the bit b_M is to be encoded in the mode of refinement. We distinguish between significance identification and refinement because a significance identification bit

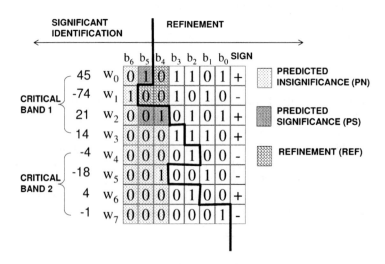

FIGURE 6.7:   Subbit plane-embedded entropy coding.

has a very high probability of being 0, while a refinement bit is usually equally distributed between 0 and 1. The sign of the coefficient only needs to be encoded immediately after the coefficient turns significant, that is, a first nonzero bit in the coefficient is encoded. For the bit array in Figure 6.7, the significance identification and the refinement bits are separated by a solid bar. For a critical band $s_{i,k}$, we call the band insignificant if all the coefficients in the critical band are insignificant. It becomes significant when at least one coefficient is significant. EAC defines three subbit planes in a bit plane: the predicted significance (PS), the refinement (REF), and the predicted insignificance (PN). The PS subbit plane consists of bits of coefficients that are insignificant but has at least one neighbor known to be significant. The REF subbit plane consists of bits of coefficients that are already significant, that is, in the refinement mode. The PN subbit plane consists of bits of coefficients that are insignificant with no neighbors known to be significant. The subbit plane design is motivated by previous work on image coding [4] and the JPEG 2000 standard [14], which show that bits in different subbit planes contribute different decreases in average distortion per coding bit spent. For the sample bit array in Figure 6.7, we show the subbit plane types with different shades for the first three bit planes of the bit array.

We call a subbit plane of a critical band as an embedded coding unit (ECU). ECU is the smallest unit in the EAC reordering operation. The coding orders of ECUs are determined by the instantaneous JND threshold of the critical band. First, the initial auditory JND thresholds are calculated by using the quiet threshold. Using the initial threshold, the coding order of the ECUs is determined, and a set of high-priority ECUs is encoded. After a number of ECUs have been encoded or after a certain update interval, the auditory JND threshold is recalculated by both the encoder and decoder based on the partially coded coefficients at the moment. The updated JND threshold is then used to determine the formation and the coding order of the remaining ECUs. The process iterates until a certain end condition is met.

Note that we deliberately chose to update the JND threshold infrequently rather than updating after the encoding of one ECU or even after encoding one bit. This is in order to reduce the computational cost required of updating the JND threshold. Because in EAC, a slightly outdated JND threshold only leads to a slightly nonoptimal coding order of the ECUs, its impact on compression performance is minimal.

We mark the identity of each ECU by the critical band the ECU resides in and an ID that identifies the subbit plane. The ID is a rational number whose integer part is just the bit plane index and whose fractional part is assigned according to the subbit plane class. Currently, the PS, REF, and PN subbit planes are assigned with fractional values 0.875, 0.125, and 0.0, respectively. As an example, the ID of the PS subbit plane of bit plane 7 is 7.875. The fractional value is designed with the consideration of the average rate-distortion contribution of each subbit plane class. Within each critical band, EAC encodes the ECUs according to the descending order of their IDs. For a critical band with a total of L bit planes, the first ECU to be encoded is the PN subbit plane of bit plane $L - 1$ (ID: $L - 1.0$) because all coefficients are insignificant at bit plane $L - 1$. The next three subbit planes to be encoded are the PS (ID: $L - 1.125$), REF (ID: $L - 1.875$), and PN (ID: $L - 2.0$) subbit planes of bit plane $L - 2$. Subsequently, the subbit planes of bit plane $L - 3$ are encoded. With the order of ECUs within a critical band already determined, the implicit auditory masking process only needs to determine the order of the ECUs among different critical bands. Conveniently, this can be done by determining the critical bands whose ECUs are next in line to be coded. We assign two important properties to each critical band: an instantaneous JND threshold and a progress indicator. The instantaneous JND thresholds are based on the partially reconstructed coefficient values of already coded coefficients, and the progress indicator records the ID of the next ECU to be encoded. It is the gap between the progress indicator and the instantaneous JND threshold that determines the coding order of ECUs. The coding process of the subbit plane entropy coder with implicit auditory masking can thus be described as follows.

1. Initialization.

    The maximum bit plane L of all coefficients is calculated. The progress indicators of all critical bands are set to the PN subbit plane of bit plane $L - 1$ (with ID: $L - 1$). The initial instantaneous JND threshold of each critical band is set according to the quiet threshold. We also mark all critical bands as insignificant.

2. Finding the current gap.

    For each critical band, we calculate a gap between its progress indicator and the instantaneous JND threshold. The gap is closely related to the level of the coding noise over the auditory JND threshold, the noise-to-mask ratio (NMR). The largest gap among all critical bands is defined as the current gap. The value of the current gap can be negative, which simply means that the coefficients with signal energy level below the auditory JND threshold are encoded. It can be easily proven that the instantaneous JND threshold is monotonically increasing and the progress indicator is monotonically decreasing. Therefore, the current gap shrinks in every iteration.

3. Encoding all critical bands with gap equal to the current gap.

    We encode all critical bands with gap value the same as the current gap in this iteration. Such a process leads to the encoding of the ECUs with the largest reduction of NMR per coding bit spent. This encoding step may further consist of the following substeps.

    (a) Critical band skipping.

        If a chosen critical band is insignificant (not a single coefficient is significant), a status bit is encoded to indicate whether the critical band turns significant after the coding of the current bit plane. This is an optional step. However, it speeds up the coding/decoding operation significantly, as large areas of zero bits can be skipped with this step.

(b) Encoding the ECU of the critical band.

We locate the ECU, that is, the subbit plane that is next in line to be coded for each critical band. For each bit in the subbit plane, its context is calculated and the string of bit and context pairs are then compressed by a modern context adaptive entropy coder. The process of context calculation and subbit plane entropy coding is detailed in Section 6.6.4.

(c) Moving the progress indicator.

After the subbit plane is encoded, the progress indicator moves forward to the ID of the next subbit plane to be encoded.

4. Recording rate-priority points.

After all critical bands of the current gap have been encoded, we record the current coding rate R_i and the current gap S_i. These will be used in the bit stream assembler stage for rate-distortion optimization.

5. Updating the instantaneous JND threshold.

The instantaneous JND thresholds of all critical bands are updated based upon the already coded ECUs. There are tricks so that the encoder and decoder can recalculate the JND thresholds very efficiently, using on average less than one arithmetic operation per coefficient. For details, please refer to [3].

6. Repeating steps 1–5.

The steps 1–5 are repeated until a certain end criterion is reached, for example, the desired coding bit rate/quality has been reached, or all bits in all coefficients have been encoded.

6.6.4 Subbit Plane Context Adaptive Entropy Coder

The significance identification bits, refinement bits, and sign bits are not statistically equivalent even within their own categories. Statistical analysis demonstrates that if an MDCT coefficient $x_{i,j}$ has a large magnitude, its neighboring coefficients in time and frequency may have a higher probability of having large magnitudes as well. Moreover, its frequency harmonics (at double and/or triple frequency) may have large magnitudes too. To account for such statistical differences, we entropy encode the significance identification bits, refinement bits, and sign bits with context, each of which is a number derived from the already coded coefficients in the neighborhood of the current coefficient. The bits within the same context are assumed to be independent identically distributed (i.i.d.). The subsequent entropy coding can then automatically gather statistics for bits within each context, that is, the probability of being one, and use the statistics for efficient entropy coding. Such technique is called context adaptive entropy coding and is frequently used in modern image/audio/video coding systems.

We first describe the contexts for the refinement bits and sign bits because they are simpler. The context for the refinement bits depends on the significance status of the four immediate neighbor coefficients, which for coefficient $x_{i,j}$ are the coefficients with the same frequency but for the preceding $(x_{i-1,j})$ and following $(x_{i+1,j})$ time intervals, and coefficients for the same time interval but at lower $(x_{i,j-1})$ and higher $(x_{i,j+1})$ frequencies. The refinement context is formed according to Table 6.1. Depending on the number of bit planes after significance identification, we assign the refinement bit to one of three refinement coding context categories: 10, 11, and 12. If one of the four neighbor coefficients is unreachable as it falls out of the current time slot or the current section or belongs to a frame with different window size, it is considered insignificant.

To determine the context for sign coding, we calculate a horizontal sign count h and a vertical sign count v. We separate the four neighbor coefficients into two pairs, a horizontal pair $(x_{i,j-1}$ and $x_{i,j+1})$ and a vertical pair $(x_{i-1,j}$ and $x_{i+1,j})$. For each pair, the sign count is calculated according to Table 6.2. The expected sign and the context of sign coding can thus be further calculated according to Table 6.3. Depending on the sign and significance status of the neighbors, the sign bit is assigned with one of five context categories: 13, 14, 15, 16, and 17. The context for the refinement and sign coding is designed with reference to the context used in the JPEG 2000 standard [14]. However, the significance identification context is specially tailored for audio coding. To calculate the context of the significance identification bit, we not only use the significance status of the four neighbor coefficients, but use the significance status of the half-harmonics $x_{i,j/2}$ and the MDCT window size. The use of the half-harmonic frequency is due to the fact that most sound-producing instruments produce harmonics of the base tone. Therefore, there is a strong correlation among the coefficient and its harmonics. The context used for the significance identification can be found in Table 6.4. De-

Table 6.1:   Context for the refinement bit.

Context	Description
10	Current refinement bit is the first bit after significance identification and there is at least one significant coefficient among the immediate four neighbors.
11	Current refinement bit is the first bit after significance identification and there is no significant coefficient in the immediate four neighbors.
12	Current refinement bit is at least two bits away from significance identification.

Table 6.2: Calculation of sign count.

Sign count	Description
−1	Both coefficients are negative significant or one is negative significant and the other is insignificant.
0	Both coefficients are insignificant or one is positive significant and the other is negative significant.
1	Both coefficients are positive significant or one is positive significant and the other is insignificant.

Table 6.3: Expected sign and context for sign coding.

Sign count	h	−1	−1	−1	0	0	0	1	1	1
	v	−1	0	1	−1	0	1	−1	0	1
Expected sign		−	−	+	−	+	+	−	+	+
Context		13	14	15	16	17	16	15	14	13

Table 6.4: Context for significance identification (S: significant, N: nonsignificant, *: arbitrary).

Context	MDCT window size	Significance status of coefficient			
		$x_{i,j-1}$	$x_{i-1,j}$	$x_{i+1,j}$	$x_{i,j/2}$
0	2048	N	N	N	N
1	2048	*	S	*	*
2	2048	S	N	*	*
3	2048	N	N	S	*
4	2048	N	N	N	S
5	256	N	N	N	N
6	256	*	S	*	*
7	256	S	N	*	*
8	256	N	N	S	*
9	256	N	N	N	S

pending on the significance status of the four neighbors and the half-harmonics, we classify the significance identification bit into one of 10 contexts: 0–9.

As a summary, a total of 18 contexts are used for embedded audio coefficient coding. Of these, there are 10 contexts for significance identification, 3 for refinement coding, and 5 for sign coding.

6.6.5 Context Adaptive Entropy Coder

Through the aforementioned process, the section of quantized audio coefficients is turned into a sequence of bits, each of which is attached with a context. All bits associated with the same context are assumed to be independently and identically distributed (i.i.d.). Let the number of contexts be N, and let there be n_i bits in context i, within which the probability of the bits to take value 1 is p_i. Using classic Shannon information theory, the entropy of such a bit-context sequence can be calculated as

$$H = \sum_{i=0}^{N-1} n_i \left[-p_i \log_2 p_i - (1 - p_i) \log_2 (1 - p_i) \right]. \tag{6.17}$$

The task of the context entropy coder is thus to convert the sequence of bit-context pairs into a compact bit stream representation with length as close to the Shannon limit as possible. Several coders are available for such task. The coders used in EAC include the adaptive Golomb coder [6] and the QM coder. It is observed that the adaptive Golomb coder has about the same compression efficiency as the QM coder, with roughly the same complexity.

In the following, we describe the implementation of the QM coder with focus on three key aspects: general arithmetic coding theory, fixed point arithmetic implementation, and probability estimation.

The Elias Coder

The basic theory of the MQ coder can be traced to the Elias Coder, or recursive probability interval subdivision. The process can be graphically illustrated in Figure 6.8. Let $S_0 S_1 S_2 \cdots S_n$ be a series of bits that is sent to the arithmetic coder.

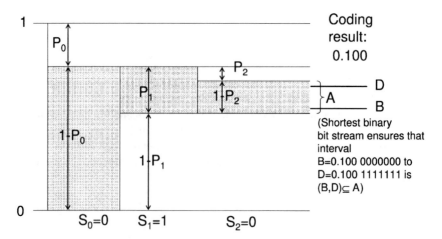

FIGURE 6.8: Elias coder: Probability interval subdivision.

Let P_i be the probability that the bit S_i is 1. We may form a binary representation (the coded bit stream) of the original bit sequence by the following process:

1. Initialization.
   Let the initial probability interval be $(0.0, 1.0)$. We denote the current probability interval as $(C, C + A)$, where C is the bottom of the probability interval and A is the size of the interval. After initialization, we have $C = 0.0$ and $A = 1.0$.
2. Probability interval subdivision.
   The binary symbols $S_0 S_1 S_2 \cdots S_n$ are encoded sequentially. For each symbol S_i, the probability interval $(C, C + A)$ is subdivided into two subintervals $(C, C + A(1 - P_i))$ and $(C + A(1 - P_i), C + A)$. Depending on whether the symbol S_i is 1, one of the two subintervals is selected. That is,

$$C = C, \qquad\qquad A = A(1 - P_i) \quad \text{for } S_i = 0, \quad \text{and}$$
$$C = C + A \cdot (1 - P_i), \quad A = A \cdot P \qquad \text{for } S_i = 1. \qquad (6.18)$$

3. Bit stream output.
   Let the final coding bit stream be referred to as $k_1 k_2 \cdots k_m$, where m is the compressed bit stream length. The final bit stream creates an uncertainty interval where the lower bound B and upper bound D can be expressed as

$$D = 0.k_1 k_2 \cdots k_m 111 \cdots,$$
$$B = 0.k_1 k_2 \cdots k_m 000 \cdots. \qquad (6.19)$$

As long as the uncertainty interval (B, D) is contained in the probability interval $(C, C + A)$, the coding bit stream uniquely identifies the final probability interval, and thus uniquely identifies each subdivision in the Elias coding process. The entire binary symbol string $S_0 S_1 S_2 \cdots S_n$ can thus be recovered from the compressed representation. It can be shown that it is possible to find a final coding bit stream with length

$$m \leq \lceil - \log_2 A \rceil + 2 \qquad (6.20)$$

to represent the final probability interval $(C, C + A)$, where $\lceil x \rceil$ returns the smallest integer that is larger than or equal to x. Notice A is the probability of the occurrence of the binary strings $S_0 S_1 S_2 \cdots S_n$, and the entropy of the symbol stream can be calculated as

$$H = \sum_{S_0 S_1 \cdots S_n} -A \log_2 A. \qquad (6.21)$$

The arithmetic coder thus encodes the binary string within 2 bits of its entropy limit, no matter how long the symbol string is. This is very efficient.

The Arithmetic Coder: Finite Precision Arithmetic Operation

Exact implementation of Elias coding requires infinite precision arithmetic, an unrealistic assumption in real applications. Using finite precision, Elias coding becomes arithmetic coding. Observing the fact that the coding interval A becomes very small after a few operations, we may normalize the coding interval parameters C and A as

$$C = 1.5 \cdot [0.k_1 k_2 \cdots k_L] + 2^{-L} \cdot 1.5 \cdot C_x,$$
$$A = 2^{-L} \cdot 1.5 \cdot A_x, \qquad (6.22)$$

where L is a normalization factor determining the magnitude of the interval A. The fixed-point integers A_x and C_x are fixed-point integers representing values between $(0.75, 1.5)$ and $(0.0, 1.5)$, respectively. Bits $k_1 k_2 \cdots k_L$ are the output bits that have already been determined (in reality, certain carryover operations have to be handled to derive the true output bit stream). By representing the probability interval with the normalization L and fixed-point integers A_x and C_x, it is possible to use fixed-point arithmetic and normalization operations for the probability interval subdivision operation. Moreover, since the value of A_x is close to 1.0, we may approximate $A_x \cdot P_i$ with P_i. The interval subdivision operation (6.18) may thus be calculated

$$\begin{array}{llll} C_x = C_x, & A_x = A_x - P_i & \text{for } S_i = 0, & \text{and} \\ C = C + A_x - P_i, & A_x = P_i & \text{for } S_i = 1, \end{array} \qquad (6.23)$$

which can be done quickly without any multiplication. The compression performance suffers a little, as the coding interval now has to be approximated with a fixed-point integer, and $A_x \cdot P_i$ is approximated with P_i. However, experiments show that the degradation in compression performance is less than 3%, which is well worth the saving in implementation complexity.

Probability Estimation

In the arithmetic coder it is necessary to estimate the probability P_i of being 1 for each binary symbol S_i. This is where context comes into play. Within each context, the symbols are coded as if they are independently distributed. We estimate the probability of the symbol within each context through observation of the past behaviors of symbols in the same context. For example, if we observe n_i symbols in context i, with o_i symbols being 1, we may estimate the probability that a symbol takes on the value 1 in context i through Bayesian estimation as

$$p_i = \frac{o_i + 1}{n_i + 2}. \qquad (6.24)$$

In the QM coder, probability estimation is implemented through a state-transition machine. It may estimate the probability of the context more efficiently and may take into consideration the nonstationary characteristic of the symbol string. Nevertheless, the principle is still to estimate the probability based on past behavior of the symbols in the same context.

6.7 BIT STREAM ASSEMBLER

Finally, a bit stream assembler module allocates the available coding bits among the time slots, channels, and sections, and produces the final compressed bit stream.

Recall from Section 6.6.3 that each section of quantized MDCT coefficients is compressed separately into an embedded bit stream. We record a rate and a priority value each time the current gap shrinks. Let $R_{t,c,s,i}$ and $S_{t,c,s,i}$ be the rate and priority value for time slot t, channel c, section s, and truncation point i. The main functionality of the bit stream assembler module is thus to find the proper truncation point for each section of bit stream and to generate a combined bit stream.

The bit stream assembly module may operate in a number of modes. It may operate in distortion controlled mode. In this case, the user may define a desired NMR S_{desired} for the compressed bit stream. The bit stream assembler module then truncates all segments with distortion smaller than the desired NMR away, and leaves only those segments with distortion greater than threshold. The truncation point i for time slot t, channel c, and section s can be expressed as

$$i = \arg \max_{k} (S_{t,c,s,i} > S_{\text{desired}}). \qquad (6.25)$$

The bit stream assembler may operate in rate controlled mode. The user defines a total bit rate R_{total} for the entire compressed audio file (for variable bit rate coding) or a bit rate R_s for each time slot (for constant bit rate coding). The bit stream assembler then searches for the right priority value S, which truncates the embedded section bit streams according to (6.25) and allows the total length of the truncated bit streams to stay just below the bit rate limit.

After the truncation points for each section are determined, the bit stream assembler combines the section bit streams into an EAC master bit stream. The bit stream syntax of the master bit stream is as follows. (It is also the syntax of the application bit stream that is derived from the master bit stream.) The EAC bit stream starts with a global header, which identifies the EAC bit stream and stores global codec information such as the parameters of the transform module and entropy coding module. The global header is then followed by the compressed bit streams of individual time slot. The time slot is again led by a header, which

FIGURE 6.9: EAC bit stream syntax (master and application bit stream).

records the lengths of the compressed bit streams in the time slot, and the lengths of the compressed bit streams of the individual sections. The time slot header is then followed by the truncated embedded bit stream of each section of each audio channel of that time slot. The syntax of the EAC master bit stream is shown in Figure 6.9.

Finally, the bit stream assembler generates a companion file that holds the structural information of the EAC bit stream. In EAC, the companion file stores the rate $R_{t,c,s,i}$ and priority $S_{t,c,s,i}$ value pairs of all sections up to the truncation points. The companion file is not necessary for decoding an EAC bit stream or scaling the EAC bit stream by the number of audio channels or audio sampling rate. If the compressed audio is scaled by channels, the compressed bit streams of the unused channels are removed from the bit stream. If the compressed audio is switched into a lower sampling rate, the compressed bit streams of the sections corresponding to higher sampling rate are dropped. When the EAC bit stream is scaled by bit rate, the companion file is used. In this case, the EAC parser reads both the EAC master bit stream and the associated companion file. Then, the bit stream assembler is called upon to redetermine the truncation points of the bit streams of each section based on the new desired bit rate. An application bit stream of a different coding bit rate can thus be generated.

6.8 SUMMARY AND FURTHER READING

The main objective of this chapter is to get the reader familiar with scalable audio coding technology. We looked at the concepts, framework, and fundamental building blocks of scalable audio compression. Using EAC, an embedded audio coder, as an example, we provided a framework for fine grain scalable audio coding. We studied the individual building blocks of EAC, including the channel mixer, the audio transform, the quantization and section split unit, the auditory masking module, the embedded subbit plane entropy coder, and the bit stream assembler. Throughout the chapter, we explained how scalable audio coding differs from nonscalable audio coding in terms of technology used. This knowledge should aid the reader in building and using scalable audio coding technologies in his or her own work.

Scalable audio coding is a very attractive feature for audio storage and transmission. We gave a brief description on how scalable coded audio can be used in storage applications in Section 6.1. Scalable coding is one of the fundamental aspects of advanced media transmission technologies. Examples of using scalable coding to improve quality of service in media delivery can be found extensively in Chapters 2, 4, 9, 10, and 14 of this book.

REFERENCES

[1] G. Grill. MPEG-4 general audio coder. In *AES International Conference on High Quality Audio Coding*, Firenze, September 1999.

[2] N. Jayant, J. Johnston, and R. Safranek. Signal compression based on models of human perception. *Proceedings of the IEEE*, 81(10):1385–1422, 1993.

[3] Jin Li. Embedded audio coding (EAC) with implicit auditory masking. In *ACM Multimedia*, pages 592–601, 2002.

[4] Jin Li and Shawmin Lei. An embedded still image coder with rate-distortion optimization. *IEEE Transactions on Image Processing*, 8(7):913–924, 1999.

[5] H. S. Malvar. Lapped transforms for efficient transform/subband coding. *IEEE Trans. Acoust., Speech, Signal Processing*, 38(6):969–978, 1990.

[6] H. S. Malvar. Fast adaptive encoder for bi-level images. In *Data Compression Conference*, pages 253–262, 2001.

[7] B. C. J. Moore. *An Introduction to the Psychology of Hearing*. Academic Press, 5th edition, 2003.

[8] G. Noll. MPEG digital audio coding. *IEEE Signal Processing Magazine*, pages 59–81, September 2001.

[9] V. N. Padmanabhan, H. J. Wang, and P. A. Chou. Resilient peer-to-peer streaming. In *ICNP '03: Proceedings of the 11th IEEE International Conference on Network Protocols*, page 16, Washington, DC, USA, 2003. IEEE Computer Society.

[10] S. R. Quackenbush. Coding of natural audio in MPEG-4. In *IEEE International Conference on Acoustics, Speech and Signal Processing*, pages VI:3797–3800, Seattle, Washington, 1998.

[11] A. Said and W. A. Pearlman. A new, fast, and efficient image codec based on set partitioning in hierarchical trees. *IEEE Transactions on Circuits and Systems for Video Technology*, 6(3):243–250, 1996.

[12] J. M. Shapiro. Embedded image coding using zerotrees of wavelet coefficients. *IEEE Transactions on Signal Processing*, 41(12):3445–3463, December 1993.

[13] D. Taubman. High performance scalable image compression with EBCOT. *IEEE Transactions on Image Processing*, 9(7):1158–1170, 2000.

[14] D. S. Taubman and M. W. Marcellin. *JPEG 2000: Image Compression Fundamentals, Standards and Practice*. Kluwer Academic Publishers, Norwell, MA, USA, 2001.

PART C

IP NETWORKING

CHAPTER 7   Channel Protection Fundamentals
(Raouf Hamzaoui, Vladimir Stanković, Zixiang Xiong,
Kannan Ramchandran, Rohit Puri, Abhik Majumdar, and
Jim Chou)

CHAPTER 8   Channel Modeling and Analysis for the Internet
(Hayder Radha and Dmitri Loguinov)

CHAPTER 9   Forward Error Control for Packet Loss and Corruption
(Raouf Hamzaoui, Vladimir Stanković, and Zixiang Xiong)

CHAPTER 10   Network-Adaptive Media Transport
(Mark Kalman and Bernd Girod)

7

Channel Protection Fundamentals

**Raouf Hamzaoui, Vladimir Stanković, Zixiang Xiong,
Kannan Ramchandran, Rohit Puri, Abhik Majumdar, and
Jim Chou**

7.1 INTRODUCTION

In many ways, the Internet (or a wireless network for that matter) can be regarded simply as a communication channel in a classical communication system. This chapter discusses the fundamentals of channel protection that lie beneath the error control techniques used to communicate multimedia over the Internet and wireless networks.

The goal of a classical communication system is to transfer the data generated by an information source efficiently and reliably over a noisy channel. The basic components of a digital communication system are shown in Figure 7.1: a source encoder, channel encoder, modulator, demodulator, channel decoder, and source decoder.

The source encoder removes the redundancy in the digital data produced by the information source and outputs an information sequence. If the information source is analog, its output must be digitized before it is processed by the source encoder. The channel encoder adds redundancy to the information sequence so that channel errors can be detected or corrected. The output of the channel encoder is a finite sequence of symbols called a channel codeword. The set of possible channel codewords is called a channel code. The modulator maps the channel codeword to a signal that is suitable for transmission over a physical channel. The demodulator converts the received signal into a discrete sequence of real numbers of the same length as the channel codeword. In hard decision decoding, each real number in the sequence is mapped to a channel code symbol before being processed by the channel decoder. When the real numbers are left unquantized or quantized to a number of levels that is greater than the size of the channel

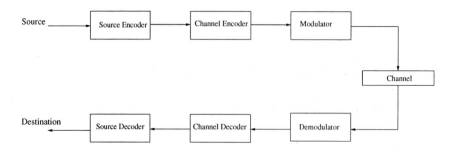

FIGURE 7.1:   Basic components of a digital communication system.

code alphabet, one speaks of soft decision decoding. The channel decoder tries to recover the input to the channel encoder from the output of the demodulator. Finally, the source decoder produces an estimate of the information sequence.

In this chapter, we look in detail at the basic constituents of a communication system. In Section 7.2, we briefly explain the notions of entropy of an information source, mutual information, rate–distortion function, and capacity of a channel. These notions are needed to introduce four fundamental theorems due to Claude Shannon: the noiseless coding theorem [45], the source coding theorem [46], the channel coding theorem [45], and the source-channel coding theorem [46]. Our exposition mainly follows that of McEliece [17], where proofs of the theorems can be found. For simplicity, we focus on discrete memoryless sources and channels. References are provided for extensions and generalizations. Shannon's coding theorems give an insight on what can be achieved by a communication system. Unfortunately, the theorems are not constructive. Optimal codes were shown to exist, but it was not explained how to construct them. The remainder of the chapter is dedicated to practical system design. Section 7.3 contains an overview of the most important channel codes. Section 7.4 reviews state-of-the-art modulation techniques, focusing on a promising method called hierarchical modulation. Section 7.5 considers communication systems where feedback information can be sent from the receiver to the transmitter. In this situation, error control based on error detection and retransmission (automatic repeat request [ARQ]) can be more efficient than error correction alone (forward error correction [FEC]). We review the most important ARQ techniques and discuss hybrid methods that combine ARQ and FEC.

7.2 SHANNON'S SOURCE AND CHANNEL THEOREMS

An information source is given by a sequence of random variables X_n, each of which takes values in an alphabet A. We say that the source is *discrete* if the alphabet A is finite or countable. We say that the source is *memoryless* if the random variables X_n are independent and identically distributed. For simplicity, a discrete memoryless source X_n will be denoted by a random variable X whose probability distribution $p(x)$ is the probability distribution common to all the random variables X_n.

Definition 7.1 (Entropy of a discrete memoryless source). Let X be a discrete memoryless source with alphabet A. The entropy of X is

$$H(X) = -\sum_x p(x) \log p(x),$$

where the sum is taken over all $x \in A$ for which $p(x) > 0$.

Any base of the logarithm can be used in the expression for the entropy. When this base is two, the entropy is measured in bits.

The entropy of a discrete memoryless source X measures the amount of uncertainty in the source. Since the entropy is completely defined by the probability distribution of X, we speak also of the entropy of the random variable X.

Given the discrete random variables $X, Y_1, \ldots, Y_n$, the *conditional entropy* $H(X \mid Y_1, \ldots, Y_n)$ is the average uncertainty remaining in X after observing $Y_1, \ldots, Y_n$. Formally, with $H(X \mid y_1, \ldots, y_n) = -\sum_x p(x \mid y_1, \ldots, y_n) \log p(x \mid y_1, \ldots, y_n)$, we set

$$H(X \mid Y_1, \ldots, Y_n) = \sum_{y_1, \ldots, y_n} p(y_1, \ldots, y_n) H(X \mid y_1, \ldots, y_n).$$

The difference $I(X; Y) = H(X) - H(X|Y)$ is known as the *mutual information* of the two random variables X and Y. It expresses the amount of information provided by Y on X.

7.2.1 Source Coding

A code $\mathcal{C}$ of size M over an alphabet B is a set of M words, possibly varying in length, made up of symbols from B. The words in $\mathcal{C}$ are called *codewords*. The length of a codeword $\mathbf{c}$ (i.e., the number of symbols in $\mathbf{c}$) is denoted $|\mathbf{c}|$. When all the codewords in $\mathcal{C}$ have the same length k, we say that $\mathcal{C}$ is a block code of length k.

7.2.1.1 Lossless Source Coding

To compress a discrete source X_n over alphabet A without information loss, one can use a lossless encoding scheme $(\mathcal{C}, f)$, which consists of a code $\mathcal{C}$ (known as a source code) and an injective map $f : A \rightarrow C$ (known as an encoder). A source code C is *uniquely decodable* if for all positive integers k and all codewords $\mathbf{c}_i, \mathbf{d}_i, i = 1, \ldots, k$, the equality $\mathbf{c}_1 * \cdots * \mathbf{c}_k = \mathbf{d}_1 * \cdots * \mathbf{d}_k$ implies that $\mathbf{c}_i = \mathbf{d}_i$ for all $i = 1, \ldots, k$. Here $*$ denotes concatenation.

The average codeword length of an encoding scheme (C, f) with respect to a discrete memoryless source X can be expressed $L = \sum_x p(x)|f(x)|$.

Shannon's noiseless coding theorem [45] says that the entropy of a discrete memoryless source X over alphabet A gives the smallest average number of code symbols (from the alphabet B) needed to losslessly represent one source symbol (from the alphabet A), when the base of the logarithm is $|B|$. Before stating the theorem more precisely, we must define the extension of a discrete source. The kth extension of a source X_n is the source $X_n^k = (X_{(n-1)k+1}, \ldots, X_{nk})$ obtained by blocking X_n into blocks of length k. Thus if X_n is a discrete memoryless source taking values in A, then X_n^k is a discrete memoryless source taking values in A^k, where A^k is the set of all words of length k over A.

Theorem 7.1 (Shannon's noiseless coding theorem). *Let X be a discrete memoryless source. Let X^k be its kth extension. Let L_k be the minimum average codeword length over all encoding schemes for X^k whose codes are uniquely decodable. Then*

$$H(X) \leq \frac{L_k}{k} \leq H(X) + \frac{1}{k}.$$

7.2.1.2 Lossy Source Coding

Suppose now that the symbols generated by a discrete memoryless source X over alphabet A are to be reproduced by symbols from a finite alphabet $\hat{A}$ called the reproducing alphabet. A single-letter distortion measure $d : A \times \hat{A} \rightarrow \mathbb{R}^+$ measures the distortion $d(x, y)$ when symbol $x \in A$ is reproduced as $y \in \hat{A}$. The distortion between a word $\mathbf{x} = (x_1, \ldots, x_k) \in A^k$ and a word $\mathbf{y} = (y_1, \ldots, y_k) \in \hat{A}^k$ is defined as $d(\mathbf{x}, \mathbf{y}) = \sum_{i=1}^{k} d(x_i, y_i)$.

A lossy compression scheme (C, k, M, f) for the memoryless source X is given by a block code C of length k and size M over the reproducing alphabet $\hat{A}$, and a mapping f from A^k to C. This compression scheme allows us to represent any sequence of k source symbols with $\lceil \log_2 M \rceil$ bits. Thus the *rate* of a block code of length k and size M is defined to be $(\log_2 M)/k$ bits per symbol.

Example 1. Let $A = \{0, 1\}$, $\hat{A} = \{0, 1\}$, and $C = \{00, 11\}$. Then the mapping $f : A^2 \rightarrow C$ given by $f(00) = 00$, $f(01) = 00$, $f(10) = 11$, $f(11) = 11$ defines a lossy compression scheme $(C, 2, 2, f)$ for the source X. By using the binary representation $00 \mapsto 0$ and $11 \mapsto 1$, any sequence of two source symbols can be represented by one bit.

The average distortion of the lossy compression scheme $(\mathcal{C}, k, M, f)$ with respect to the source X and the single-letter distortion measure d is

$$D(\mathcal{C}, k, M, f) = \frac{1}{k} \sum_{\mathbf{x} \in A^k} p(\mathbf{x}) d(\mathbf{x}, f(\mathbf{x})),$$

where for $\mathbf{x} = (x_1, \ldots, x_k)$, $p(\mathbf{x}) = \prod_{i=1}^{k} p(x_i)$.

Example 2. In Example 1, suppose that the distortion measure d is given by $d(x, y) = 0$ if $x = y$ and $d(x, y) = 1$, otherwise. Suppose also that $Pr\{X = 0\} = p(0) = p$, where $0 < p < 1/2$. Then the average distortion of the lossy compression scheme $(\mathcal{C}, 2, 2, f)$ is $p(1 - p)$.

Let Y be a random variable that is jointly distributed with X according to the joint probability distribution $p(x, y) = p(x)p(y|x)$ for some conditional probability distribution $p(y|x) = p_{Y|X}(y|x)$. As a function of the conditional probability distribution $p_{Y|X}$, the average distortion when X is reproduced as Y is thus

$$D(p_{Y|X}) = \sum_{x \in A, y \in \hat{A}} p(x) p(y|x) d(x, y).$$

Note that the smallest value that can be taken by $D(p_{Y|X})$ is

$$D_{\min} = \sum_{x \in A} p(x) \min_{y \in \hat{A}} d(x, y).$$

Definition 7.2 (Rate–distortion function). Let X be a discrete memoryless source over alphabet A, and let $\hat{A}$ be a reproducing alphabet. The rate–distortion function of the source X with respect to a single-letter distortion measure $d : A \times \hat{A} \to \mathbb{R}^+$ is the function

$$R(D) = \min_{p_{Y|X} : D(p_{Y|X}) \leq D} I(X; Y),$$

for all $D \geq D_{\min}$, where the minimum is taken over all conditional distributions $p(y|x)$ subject to the constraint $D(p_{Y|X}) \leq D$.

Henceforth we assume that the base of the logarithm in the mutual information is 2, so that $R(D)$ is measured in bits.

We can now state Shannon's source coding theorem [46].

Theorem 7.2 (Shannon's source coding theorem). *Let X be a discrete memoryless source over alphabet A, and let $\hat{A}$ be a reproducing alphabet. Let $R(D)$ be the rate–distortion function of the source X with respect to a single-letter distortion measure $d : A \times \hat{A} \to \mathbb{R}^+$. Then for any $D' > D$ and $R' > R(D)$, there exists a lossy compression scheme $(\mathcal{C}, k, M, f)$ such that $M \le 2^{\lfloor kR' \rfloor}$ and $D(\mathcal{C}, k, M, f) < D'$.*

The theorem roughly says that one can reproduce the source symbols with an average distortion that is smaller than D by spending no more than $R(D)$ bits per source symbol.

7.2.2 Channel Coding

A discrete channel takes at every time unit n a symbol from a finite input alphabet A_X and outputs symbols from a finite output alphabet A_Y.

Let X_n be the random variable that gives the nth input symbol of the channel and let Y_n be the random variable that gives the nth output symbol of the channel. We say that the channel is memoryless if $Pr\{Y_n = y \mid X_n = x\} = p(y|x)$ is independent of n for all $y \in A_Y$ and $x \in A_X$, the transition probabilities $p(y|x)$ satisfy $p(y|x) \ge 0$ and $\sum_{y \in A_Y} p(y|x) = 1$, and $Pr\{Y_1 = y_1, \ldots, Y_n = y_n \mid X_1 = x_1, \ldots, X_n = x_n\} = \prod_{i=1}^{n} p(y_i|x_i)$ for all n.

Definition 7.3 (Channel capacity). The capacity of a discrete memoryless channel with input alphabet A_X, output alphabet A_Y, and transition probabilities $p(y|x)$, $y \in A_Y, x \in A_X$ is

$$C = \max_{p_X} I(X; Y),$$

where X is a random variable that gives the input symbol to the channel and Y is a random variable that gives the corresponding output symbol according to the joint probability distribution $p(x, y) = p(x)p(y|x)$, for some source distribution $p(x) = p_X(x)$.

Since we assume that the base of the logarithm in the mutual information is 2, C is measured in bits.

Example 3. The binary symmetric channel (BSC) is a discrete memoryless channel with $A_X = A_Y = \{0, 1\}$ and transition probabilities $p(0|1) = p(1|0) = p$ and $p(0|0) = p(1|1) = 1 - p$. When a bit is sent over the BSC, it is either corrupted with probability p or correctly received with probability $1 - p$. It is easy to prove that the capacity of the BSC is $1 + p \log p + (1 - p) \log(1 - p)$ [15].

Example 4. The binary erasure channel (BEC) is a discrete memoryless channel with $A_X = \{0, 1\}$, $A_Y = \{0, 1, ?\}$ and transition probabilities $p(?|0) = p(?|1) = p$ and $p(0|0) = p(1|1) = 1 - p$. When a bit is sent over the BEC, it is either erased with probability p or correctly received with probability $1 - p$. The capacity of the BEC is $1 - p$ [15]. More details on the BEC are provided in Chapter 8.

We now consider the situation when the symbols generated by a discrete source U with source alphabet A are to be sent over a discrete channel with input alphabet A_X and output alphabet A_Y. To protect the source symbols against transmission errors, redundancy is added. For this, we use a channel code, which is a block code $\mathcal{C}$ of length n over A_X. We also use a channel encoding scheme, which is an injective function from A^k to $\mathcal{C}$. Using the channel encoding scheme, blocks $(u_1, \ldots, u_k)$ of source symbols of length k are mapped to channel codewords of length n. The channel codewords are then sent over the channel where errors may occur. Next, a function g from A_Y^n to $\mathcal{C}$ called a channel decoding scheme is used to map a received word $\mathbf{y} = (y_1, \ldots, y_n)$ to a channel codeword. Finally, this channel codeword is mapped to the corresponding source word $(\hat{u}_1, \ldots, \hat{u}_k)$ (since the encoding scheme is injective, this source word is unique when it exists). The rate of transmission of this system (or code rate of the code $\mathcal{C}$) is $\frac{k}{n}$. It characterizes the speed with which source information is transmitted over the channel or equivalently the redundancy introduced by the channel code.

An ideal channel decoding scheme for this system minimizes the probability of a word decoding error

$$P_e = \sum_{\mathbf{c} \in \mathcal{C}} \sum_{\mathbf{y} \in A_Y^n : g(\mathbf{y}) \neq \mathbf{c}} Pr\{\mathbf{Y} = \mathbf{y} \mid \mathbf{X} = \mathbf{c}\} Pr\{\mathbf{X} = \mathbf{c}\},$$

where $\mathbf{Y} = (Y_1, \ldots, Y_n)$ and $\mathbf{X} = (X_1, \ldots, X_n)$. This is realized with *maximum a posteriori decoding*, where the received word $\mathbf{y} = (y_1, \ldots, y_n)$ is mapped to a channel codeword $\mathbf{c} = (c_1, \ldots, c_n)$ that maximizes the probability $Pr\{\mathbf{X} = \mathbf{c} \mid \mathbf{Y} = \mathbf{y}\}$. In practice, however, one uses *maximum-likelihood decoding*, where $\mathbf{y}$ is mapped to a channel codeword $\mathbf{c}$ that maximizes the probability $Pr\{\mathbf{Y} = \mathbf{y} \mid \mathbf{X} = \mathbf{c}\}$. It is easy to see that maximum-likelihood decoding is equivalent to maximum a posteriori decoding when all channel codewords are generated with the same probability. Another important decoding scheme is known as *minimum distance decoding* where the received word $\mathbf{y} = (y_1, \ldots, y_n)$ is mapped to a channel codeword $\mathbf{c} = (c_1, \ldots, c_n)$ that has smallest Hamming distance to $\mathbf{y}$. Here the Hamming distance is defined as follows.

Definition 7.4 (Hamming distance). Let $\mathbf{x} = (x_1, \ldots, x_n)$ and $\mathbf{y} = (y_1, \ldots, y_n)$ be two words of the same length. The Hamming distance $d_H(\mathbf{x}, \mathbf{y})$ between $\mathbf{x}$ and $\mathbf{y}$ is equal to the number of indices $k \in \{1, 2, \ldots, n\}$ such that $x_k \neq y_k$.

Given a BSC with bit error probability p, we have

$$Pr\{\mathbf{Y} = \mathbf{y} \mid \mathbf{X} = \mathbf{c}\} = p^{d_H(\mathbf{c},\mathbf{y})}(1 - p)^{n - d_H(\mathbf{c},\mathbf{y})}. \tag{7.1}$$

If $0 < p < 1/2$, the probability in (7.1) is largest when $d_H(\mathbf{c}, \mathbf{y})$ is smallest. Therefore minimum distance decoding and maximum-likelihood decoding are equivalent for this channel.

An alternative to minimizing the probability of a word decoding error is to minimize the information symbol error rate p_e defined as $p_e = \frac{1}{k} \sum_{i=1}^{k} p_e^{(i)}$, where $p_e^{(i)} = Pr\{\hat{u}_i \neq u_i\}$. When the symbols are bits, the information symbol error rate is called the information *bit error rate* (BER). Note that $\frac{1}{k} P_e \leq p_e \leq P_e$. To minimize the information symbol error rate, the decoder uses the *symbol maximum a posteriori* (MAP) rule, where for $i = 1, \ldots, k$, the reconstructed information symbol $\hat{u}_i$ is computed as a symbol $u \in A$ that maximizes the a posteriori probability $Pr\{U_i = u \mid \mathbf{Y} = \mathbf{y}\}$. Here U_i is the random vector that corresponds to the information symbol u_i, $i = 1, \ldots, k$.

The channel coding theorem [45] states that the source information can be transmitted reliably over a noisy channel, provided the rate of transmission is below the capacity of the channel. In other words, any rate below the channel capacity is achievable.

Theorem 7.3 (Shannon's channel coding theorem). *Consider a discrete memoryless channel with input alphabet A_X and capacity C. For any positive number $R < C$ and $\varepsilon > 0$, there exists a channel code $C = \{\mathbf{c}_1, \ldots, \mathbf{c}_M\}$ of length n over A_X and a channel decoding scheme g such that*

1) $M \geq 2^{\lceil Rn \rceil}$.
2) *If codeword $\mathbf{c}_i$ is sent over the channel and word $\mathbf{y}$ is received, then $Pr\{g(\mathbf{y}) \neq \mathbf{c}_i\} < \varepsilon$ for all $i = 1, \ldots, M$.*

7.2.3 Source-Channel Coding

Suppose now that the output of the channel decoding scheme is mapped to a word of length k over a reproduction alphabet $\hat{A}$. The average distortion of the resulting transmission system is $\frac{1}{k} E[d(\mathbf{U}, \mathbf{V})]$, where the random vector $\mathbf{U}$ describes a word of k successive source symbols, the random vector $\mathbf{V}$ describes the corresponding word of k reconstructed symbols, and E denotes the expectation operator.

The source-channel coding theorem [46] says what a system can achieve in terms of average distortion and rate of transmission.

Theorem 7.4 (Shannon's source-channel coding theorem). *Given a discrete memoryless source characterized by rate–distortion function $R(D)$, a discrete* *memoryless channel characterized by capacity $C > 0$, any $D > D_{\min}$, and any $r < C/R(D)$, there exist for sufficiently large k and n an encoding scheme that maps source words of length k into channel words of length n and a decoder that maps channel output words of length n into reproduced words of length k such that the expected distortion is at most D and the transmission rate k/n is at least r.*

The encoding scheme promised by the theorem is a concatenation of a lossy compression scheme and a channel encoding scheme. The theorem is also known as the separation theorem because the lossy compression scheme and the channel encoding scheme can be designed independently.

7.2.4 Extensions

Shannon's theorems can be extended to more general information sources. For example, we say that a discrete source X_n is *stationary* if the random process X_n is stationary. The nth marginal entropy of a stationary source is $H_n = H(X_n \mid X_{n-1}, \ldots, X_1)$. One can show that when the source is stationary, the sequence H_n is decreasing and bounded below by zero. This allows us to define the entropy of a stationary source as follows.

Definition 7.5 (Entropy of a stationary source). Let X_n be a stationary source. The entropy of the source (also often called the entropy rate of the source) is defined $\bar{H} = \lim_{n \to \infty} H_n$.

With this definition, Shannon's noiseless coding theorem can be extended to stationary sources that satisfy the asymptotic equipartition property [3]. The source coding theorem can also be extended to sources with abstract alphabets, including the set of real numbers in particular [22].

Shannon's channel coding theorem can be extended to other channels, the most famous one being the *additive white Gaussian noise* (AWGN) channel. In the time-discrete AWGN channel, both the channel input alphabet A_X and the channel output alphabet A_Y are the set of real numbers $\mathbb{R}$. The relationship between the random variable X_n that gives the nth input to the channel and the random variable Y_n that gives the nth output of the channel is given by $Y_n = X_n + Z_n$, where $\{Z_n\}$ is a sequence of independent, identically distributed, Gaussian random variables with mean 0 and variance $N_0/2$. One can show [15] that for this channel reliable transmission is possible as long as the rate of transmission is smaller than the capacity

$$C = \frac{1}{2} \log_2 \left(1 + \frac{2P}{N_0} \right) \text{ bits per transmission,}$$

where P is a constraint on the expected value of the random variable X_n^2. If we denote by R the rate of transmission, by $E_s = P$ the symbol energy, and by $E_b = E_s/R$ the energy per bit, then the condition $R < C$ gives $E_b/N_0 > \frac{2^{2R}-1}{2R}$ for reliable transmission. Here E_b/N_0 is called the bit energy to noise spectral density ratio and $\frac{2^{2R}-1}{2R}$ is the Shannon bound. Since $R > 0$, we must also have $E_b/N_0 > \log_e 2$ or $10\log_{10} E_b/N_0 > -1.6$ dB, which is called the theoretical Shannon limit.

In the time-continuous AWGN channel, the relationship between the transmitted signal $s(t)$ (the output of the modulator) and the received signal $r(t)$ (the input of the demodulator) is $r(t) = s(t) + n(t)$, where $n(t)$ is a white Gaussian noise. The capacity of a band-limited AWGN channel is [15]

$$C = W \log_2\left(1 + \frac{P}{N_0 W}\right) \text{ bits per second,}$$

where W is the channel bandwidth in Hz, $N_0/2$ is the power spectral density of the noise, and P is a constraint on the average power. When P is much smaller than $N_0 W$, the channel is called a wideband AWGN channel. One can prove [11] that if binary modulation is used and the demodulated signal is sampled at a rate of $2W$, then E_b/N_0 must be larger than the practical Shannon limit of 0.2 dB to achieve a BER of 10^{-5} for a rate of transmission $R = 1/2$.

7.3 CHANNEL CODING AND ERROR CONTROL FOR BIT ERRORS AND PACKET LOSSES

Channel codes can be divided into two classes: linear and nonlinear. Linear codes are easier to implement and, as a result, have received a greater amount of attention historically. We will also confine our attention to linear codes in this section. We first describe linear block codes, including cyclic redundancy check (CRC) codes for error detection, Reed–Solomon codes, low-density parity-check (LDPC) codes, irregular repeat-accumulate (IRA) codes, tornado codes, digital fountain codes, and lattice codes. We then describe convolutional codes, rate-compatible punctured convolutional (RCPC) codes, and turbo codes. We discuss the properties of these codes and mention efficient algorithms for encoding and decoding, emphasizing their computational complexity. We also explain how the problem of burst errors (explained further in Chapter 8) can be alleviated with interleaving.

7.3.1 Linear Block Codes

In a linear block code, the codeword symbols are taken from a field. A formal definition of a field is beyond the scope of this text and may be found in a mathematics book on abstract algebra (see [12]). Informally, a field consists of a set of elements, together with two operations called addition and multiplication that must fulfill a given number of properties. Some examples of well-known fields are the set of real numbers and the set of rational numbers. These fields are known as infinite fields because they contain an infinite number of elements. Linear block codes, however, typically consist of elements from a finite field. In particular, consider the finite field $GF(2) = \{0, 1\}$. The addition operation for $GF(2)$ is modulo-2 addition and the multiplication operation is defined similarly to the multiplication operation for two binary numbers:

$$0 + 0 = 0 \quad 0 + 1 = 1 \quad 1 + 1 = 0$$
$$0 * 0 = 0 \quad 0 * 1 = 0 \quad 1 * 1 = 1.$$

Finite fields are also called Galois fields. The size of a Galois field must be a power of a prime. Conversely, for any prime power q, one can construct a Galois field of size q. Let $GF(q)$ be a finite field of size q and let n be a positive integer. Then it is easy to check that $[GF(q)]^n$ is a linear space over $GF(q)$. An (n, k) linear block code C over $GF(q)$ is a k-dimensional linear subspace of the linear space $[GF(q)]^n$. In particular, for any two codewords $c_1, c_2 \in C$, the sum of the codewords is also a codeword, $c_1 + c_2 \in C$. Since C is a k-dimensional linear space, we can find a set of k basis vectors so that every codeword can be expressed as a linear combination of the basis vectors. In vector-matrix notation, we can express every codeword c of C as

$$c = uG, \tag{7.2}$$

where u is a $1 \times k$ vector of field elements and G is a $k \times n$ matrix whose k rows are k basis vectors. The matrix G is known as a generator matrix and elementary row operations can be performed on G to form another matrix G' that will generate an equivalent code. If G is manipulated to be of the form $G = [I_k | P]$ where I_k is the $k \times k$ identity matrix and P is a $k \times (n - k)$ matrix, then G is said to be in systematic form and the first k symbols of the codeword c will be identical to the k symbols of u. The final $n - k$ symbols of c are referred to as parity symbols.

The performance of a block code is often measured by the number of errors that it can correct or the amount of noise that it can remove. The performance is usually dependent on two things: (1) the decoder that is used to decode a received word to a codeword and (2) the distance between each pair of codewords in the block code. Let us first consider the distance between a pair of codewords. For block codes, the Hamming metric or the Euclidean metric is usually used to measure the distance between pairs of codewords. The Hamming distance is useful for measuring the distance between two codewords whose symbols belong to a finite field. Sometimes in communications applications, however, each field element of the codeword is mapped to a real number. In such scenarios, it is useful to use a Euclidean metric to determine the distance between codewords. For example, if each codeword, $\mathbf{c}_i = (c_{i,1}, c_{i,2}, \ldots, c_{i,n})$, is mapped to a vector of real numbers, $\mathbf{r}_i = (r_{i,1}, r_{i,2}, \ldots, r_{i,n})$, then the Euclidean distance between two codewords $\mathbf{c}_i, \mathbf{c}_j$ may be defined as

$$d_E(\mathbf{c}_i, \mathbf{c}_j) = \sqrt{(r_{i,1} - r_{j,1})^2 + (r_{i,2} - r_{j,2})^2 + \cdots + (r_{i,n} - r_{j,n})^2}. \qquad (7.3)$$

Now, if we let $d_{\min}$ represent the minimum distance between any pair of codewords, and if an arbitrary codeword is transmitted over a noisy channel, then the codeword may be successfully recovered if the decoder decodes the received word to the closest codeword and the amount of noise is less than $d_{\min}/2$. Note that if the block code is linear, then the minimum distance $d_{\min}$ is simply the smallest weight of a nonzero codeword. Here the weight of a codeword is the number of its nonzero symbols.

For the Hamming distance, successful decoding translates into there being less than $d_{\min}/2$ changes to the symbols of the original codeword, where $d_{\min}$ represents the minimum Hamming distance between any pair of codewords. For the Euclidean distance, successful decoding translates into the magnitude of the noise being less than $d_{\min}/2$. For the aforementioned, we may visualize the correct decoding region of each codeword to be a sphere with radius $d_{\min}/2$ (as in Figure 7.2), and thus if a codeword is corrupted by noise, as long as the noise does not perturb the codeword to be outside of its correct decoding region, then suc-

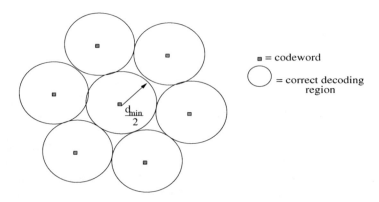

FIGURE 7.2: Example of a codebook that consists of several codewords with a minimum distance of $d_{\min}$. The correct decoding regions are shown as spheres centered around the codewords with a radius of $d_{\min}/2$.

cessful decoding will be guaranteed. It is apparent that for a given n and k, it is desirable to find a code that maximizes d_{min}.

Once a code with parameters n, k, and d_{min} is found, efficient encoding and decoding algorithms for generating the code are necessary to enable the code to be practical.

In general, if the minimum distance of a linear code is t, then the receiver can detect up to $t - 1$ transmission errors. However, by using minimum distance decoding, where the received word is decoded to a nearest codeword, a linear code of minimum distance t allows the correction of up to $\lfloor \frac{t-1}{2} \rfloor$ errors. It can be shown that a linear code of minimum distance t can simultaneously correct e_c errors and detect e_d errors if $e_c + e_d \leq t - 1$ with $e_c \leq e_d$. Moreover it can correct e_e erasures and e_c errors simultaneously if $e_e + 2e_c \leq t - 1$.

The minimum distance of an (n, k) linear code must be less than or equal to $n - k + 1$. Linear (n, k) codes whose minimum distance is equal to $n - k + 1$ are called maximum-distance separable (MDS) codes.

Linear codes can be simply modified to obtain new linear codes. Puncturing a linear code consists of removing a number of coordinate positions from each codeword. If an (n, k) linear MDS code is punctured, then the resulting code is an $(n - 1, k)$ linear MDS code. Shortening a linear code consists of keeping only codewords with the same symbol in a given position and then deleting this position. If an (n, k) linear MDS code is shortened by keeping only codewords with the zero symbol in a given position, then the resulting code is an $(n - 1, k - 1)$ linear MDS code.

The encoding scheme for an (n, k) linear code can be implemented in $O(n^2)$ time. However, there is no efficient way to decode a general linear code with maximum-likelihood decoding [8]. Usually one uses syndrome decoding. To explain syndrome decoding, we must introduce the parity check matrix. The parity check matrix $\mathbf{H}$ of an (n, k) linear code with generator matrix $\mathbf{G}$ is an $(n - k) \times n$ matrix whose rows are orthogonal to the rows of the generator matrix, that is,

$$\mathbf{GH}^T = \mathbf{0}. \tag{7.4}$$

The parity check matrix may be viewed as a generator matrix for a code that lies in the null space of $\mathbf{G}$. It is clear that for any codeword $\mathbf{c}$ that is generated by $\mathbf{G}$,

$$\mathbf{cH}^T = \mathbf{0}. \tag{7.5}$$

Now, if we add an error vector, $\mathbf{e}$ to $\mathbf{c}$, then

$$(\mathbf{c} + \mathbf{e})\mathbf{H}^T = \mathbf{0} + \mathbf{eH}^T = \mathbf{s}, \tag{7.6}$$

where we call $\mathbf{s}$ the syndrome of $(\mathbf{c} + \mathbf{e})$. If we let each syndrome correspond to an error vector, then the function of a syndrome decoder is to first compute the

Table 7.1: Standard array of a binary code. The first row contains all codewords of the code. Each following row is formed by taking a minimum weight vector, adding it to the first row, and then checking if the resulting addition is already part of the standard array. If the resulting addition is not part of the standard array, then it is added as a new row to the standard array. This process is continued until the standard array is filled.

$c_1 = 0$	c_2	...	c_{2^k}
e_1	$e_1 + c_2 \ldots$	...	$e_1 + c_{2^k}$
e_2	$e_2 + c_2 \ldots$	...	$e_2 + c_{2^k}$
e_3	$e_3 + c_2 \ldots$	...	$e_3 + c_{2^k}$
$\vdots$	$\vdots$	$\vdots$	$\vdots$
$e_{2^{n-k}-1}$	$e_{2^{n-k}-1} + c_2 \ldots$	...	$e_{2^{n-k}-1} + c_{2^k}$

syndrome of the received vector and then subtract the corresponding error vector from the received vector. Another way of viewing syndrome decoding is through a standard array [36]. A standard array of a binary code is formed by setting aside a $2^{n-k} \times 2^k$ array and populating the first row of the array with all 2^k possible codewords with the all-zero codeword occupying the first column of the first row. Next, we generate all possible weight 1 error vectors and add each error vector to the first row to generate another row. This process is continued by increasing the weight of the error vector and filling the rows until the entire array is populated as in Table 7.1. If the result of an addition of an error vector with the first row equals a row that is already in the standard array, then the error vector is skipped and the next error vector is used to generate further rows. The result will be an array, where each row corresponds a shift of all of the codewords by an error vector. The first column will contain the error vectors and each row may be indexed by the syndrome. Therefore, syndrome decoding may be viewed as indexing a row of the standard array and then adding the first element of the row to the received vector.

Example 5. Consider a (3, 1) binary repetition code. This block code consists of two codewords, {000, 111}. A generator matrix for the code is

$$\mathbf{G} = [1\ 1\ 1].\qquad(7.7)$$

The corresponding parity check matrix is

$$\mathbf{H} = \begin{bmatrix} 1 & 0 & 1 \\ 0 & 1 & 1 \end{bmatrix}.\qquad(7.8)$$

And we can tabulate the standard array as follows:

$$\left\{\begin{array}{ll} 000 & 111 \\ 001 & 110 \\ 010 & 101 \\ 100 & 011 \end{array}\right\}. \tag{7.9}$$

Notice that the minimum weight codeword is $(1, 1, 1)$ and therefore the minimum distance of the code is 3. This implies that one error may be *corrected* if a minimum distance decoder is used for decoding. Alternatively, up to two errors may be *detected*.

Since the decoding of general linear block codes is not efficient, special classes of linear codes with fast decoding algorithms were developed. The most popular of these is the class of cyclic codes. An (n, k) linear code is a cyclic code if for each codeword $(c_1, \ldots, c_{n-1}, c_n)$, the right shift $(c_n, c_1, \ldots, c_{n-1})$ is also a codeword.

7.3.1.1 CRC Codes

CRC codes are shortened cyclic binary codes used for error detection. Given a generator polynomial $g(x) = \sum_{i=0}^{r} g_i x^i$, $g_i \in \{0, 1\}$ of degree r, the codeword for a binary information sequence $\mathbf{u} = (u_1, \ldots, u_k)$ is the concatenation $\mathbf{u} * \mathbf{p}$ of $\mathbf{u}$ and the word $\mathbf{p}$ of length r associated to the polynomial $p(x) = x^r u(x) \bmod g(x)$. Here we use the unique correspondence between a word $\mathbf{w} = (u_1, \ldots, u_m)$ of length m and the polynomial $w(x) = w_1 + w_2 x + \cdots + w_m x^{m-1}$ of degree at most $m - 1$. Suppose that the codeword $\mathbf{u} * \mathbf{p}$ is sent over a binary symmetric channel and let $\mathbf{u}' * \mathbf{p}'$ be the received word. Here $\mathbf{u}'$ and $\mathbf{p}'$ are words having the same length as $\mathbf{u}$ and $\mathbf{p}$, respectively. Then the decoder computes $p''(x) = x^r u'(x) \bmod g(x)$ and declares an error if $p''(x)$ is not equal to $p'(x)$. Some of the most popular generator polynomials are the CRC-12 polynomial $1 + x + x^2 + x^3 + x^{11} + x^{12}$, the CRC-16 polynomial $1 + x^2 + x^{15} + x^{16}$, and the CRC-CCITT polynomial $1 + x^5 + x^{12} + x^{16}$. A CRC code with generator polynomial $g(x) = \sum_{i=0}^{r} g_i x^i$, $g_0 \neq 0, g_r \neq 0$ can detect any burst error of length $k \leq r$. Agarwal and Ivanov [2] provided an $O(nm2^{r+m})$ algorithm for computing the probability of undetected error for a CRC code of length n whose generator polynomial has degree r and m nonzero coefficients. The encoding and decoding of CRC codes can be efficiently implemented with shift register circuits.

7.3.1.2 Reed–Solomon Codes

Reed–Solomon codes are nonbinary linear block codes over a finite field $GF(q)$. Let α be an element of order n in $GF(q)$ [i.e., n is the smallest positive integer such that $\alpha^n = 1$, where 1 is the identity element for the multiplication in $GF(q)$]. Let $r \in \{1, \ldots, n\}$. The set of all vectors $(c_0, \ldots, c_{n-1})$ in $[GF(q)]^n$ such that $\sum_{i=0}^{n-1} c_i \alpha^{ij} = 0$, $j = 1, \ldots, r$, is called a Reed–Solomon code of redundancy r over $GF(q)$. This code is an $(n, n - r)$ cyclic code of minimum distance $r + 1$. Thus, Reed–Solomon codes are MDS codes. Therefore an (n, k) Reed–Solomon code can correct e_0 symbol erasures and e_1 symbol errors simultaneously if $e_0 + 2e_1 \le n - k$. In particular, in a channel where only erasures can occur, all codeword symbols of an (n, k) Reed–Solomon codeword can be correctly recovered if at least k symbols are received.

Reed–Solomon codes are suitable for the correction of burst errors. An (n, k) Reed–Solomon code can be decoded in $O(n^2)$ time with Berlekamp's iterative algorithm [7]. Guruswami and Sudan [23] developed a polynomial-time algorithm for Reed–Solomon codes that finds a list of all codewords within a distance $\lceil n - \sqrt{n(k-1)} - 1 \rceil$ from a received word. Thus, the algorithm is guaranteed to determine the list of all potentially sent codewords if at most $\lceil n - \sqrt{n(k-1)} - 1 \rceil$ errors occurred during transmission. The complexity of the algorithm is $O(n^{15})$ if exactly $\lceil n - \sqrt{n(k-1)} - 1 \rceil$ errors occurred and only $O(n^3)$ otherwise. The algorithm of Berlekamp [7] is a hard-decision decoding algorithm, which does not exploit all available information at the receiver when the demodulator allows soft decisions. Efficient soft-decision decoding algorithms for Reed–Solomon codes were proposed by Koetter and Vardy [28] and Jiang and Narayanan [26]. For example, the algorithm of Jiang and Narayanan [26] outperforms hard-decision decoding by up to 3.1 dB at decoding error probability 10^{-5} when decoding a $(15, 7)$ Reed–Solomon code over a binary-input AWGN channel.

7.3.1.3 LDPC Codes

LDPC codes were introduced by Gallager [21]. They have attracted increased interest since MacKay and Neal [34,35] reported their outstanding performance on a binary-input AWGN channel. An (n, k) LDPC code is a linear code with a sparse parity-check matrix $H = (h_{ij})$. It can also be described with a bipartite graph, called Tanner graph, whose set of nodes consists of variable nodes and check nodes. Variable nodes correspond to the n codeword symbols, while check nodes correspond to the $(n - k)$ equations defined by the parity-check constraint. A variable node is connected to a check node if the codeword symbol corresponding to the variable node is involved in the parity equation defining the check node. That is, check node i is connected to variable node j if $h_{ij} = 1$. In a regular LDPC code, each column has the same number d_v of ones and each row has the same number d_c of ones. Thus, in the Tanner graph of the code each variable node has degree d_v and each check code has degree d_c, as shown in Figure 7.3. In an irregular LDPC code, the degrees of the variable nodes and check nodes are chosen according to some nonuniform distribution. Efficient encoding of LDPC codes

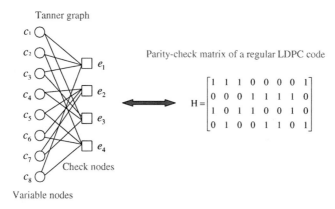

FIGURE 7.3:   Tanner graph of a regular LDPC code of length 8. The degree of the variable nodes is $d_v = 2$, and the degree of the check nodes is $d_c = 4$.

is discussed in [40], where it is shown in particular that some of the best LDPC codes can be encoded in $O(n)$ time with high probability. Because of the sparseness of their Tanner graph, LDPC codes can be decoded in $O(n)$ time with an iterative procedure known as probabilistic decoding [21], message passing, sum-product algorithm [49], or belief propagation [37]. These algorithms alternately pass information between adjacent variable nodes and check nodes to compute estimates of the a posteriori probabilities of the codeword symbols. The decoded codeword is based on the estimates obtained after convergence or if a maximum number of iterations is reached. Chung *et al.* [14] were able to design a rate-$\frac{1}{2}$ irregular LDPC code of length 10^7 bits that is only 0.04 dB away from the Shannon limit for a binary-input AWGN channel and a bit error rate of 10^{-6}.

7.3.1.4 IRA Codes

Irregular repeat-accumulate (IRA) codes were introduced by Jin and colleagues [27] as a generalization of the repeat-accumulate (RA) codes of [16]. IRA codes can be encoded in linear time. They are decoded with the sum-product algorithm, achieving on the binary-input AWGN channel a performance competitive with that of the best LDPC codes of comparable complexity.

7.3.1.5 Tornado Codes

Tornado codes [31,32] are (n, k) erasure codes that allow encoding and decoding with time complexity linear in the block length n. This speed-up over Reed–Solomon codes is obtained at the cost that slightly more than k encoding symbols are required to reconstruct all k information symbols. More precisely, Luby *et al.* [32] prove that for any $\varepsilon > 0$, one can construct a Tornado code that recovers all k information symbols from only $(1 + \varepsilon)k$ encoding symbols with probability $1 - O(n^{-3/4})$.

7.3.1.6 Digital Fountain Codes

Luby [30] recently introduced a new class of powerful erasure correcting codes called Luby Transform (LT) codes. LT codes are rateless in the sense that a potentially limitless stream of encoding symbols (or a digital fountain) can be generated for a given information sequence. Thus, in contrast to classical block codes, one need not design the code a priori for a fixed n. With LT codes, each encoding symbol can be generated from k information symbols in $O(\log k)$ time on average, and one can recover all k information symbols from $k + O(\sqrt{k} \log^2(k/\delta))$ encoding symbols with probability $1 - \delta$ in $O(k \log k)$ time, on average.

By concatenating an LDPC code as an outer code and an LT code as an inner code, Shokrollahi [47] was able to construct rateless codes called Raptor codes whose erasure correcting performance is similar to that of LT codes, but can be encoded and decoded in only $O(k)$ time.

7.3.1.7 Lattice Codes

Codes over finite fields can also be interpreted as codes over real numbers by mapping each element of the finite field to a real number. For example, in the binary $(3, 1)$ repetition code, the binary digit 0 can be mapped to the real value $-a$ and the binary digit 1 can be mapped to the real value $+a$ so that the two codewords are $(-a, -a, -a)$ and $(+a, +a, +a)$. Minimum distance decoding then means decoding the received vector to the codeword that is closest in Euclidean distance. In this section, we will consider a class of codes called lattice codes, which contain codewords that are amenable to Euclidean distance decoding instead of Hamming distance decoding.

Informally, a lattice Λ is an infinite regular array of points that covers an m-dimensional space uniformly. A lattice is defined by a set of basis vectors so that any point in the lattice can be represented as a linear combination of the basis vectors. More precisely, if the basis vectors are given as $\mathbf{v}_1 = (v_{1,1}, v_{1,2}, \ldots, v_{1,m})$, $\mathbf{v}_2 = (v_{2,1}, v_{2,2}, \ldots, v_{2,m}), \ldots, \mathbf{v}_n = (v_{n,1}, v_{n,2}, \ldots, v_{n,m})$ where $m \geq n$, then we can define a generator matrix, $\mathbf{G}$, to be a matrix that contains the basis vectors as the rows of the matrix and any lattice point can be written as

$$\lambda = \zeta \mathbf{G},$$

where ζ is an n-dimensional vector of integers [13]. For example, a generator matrix for the m-dimensional integer lattice (often written as $\mathbb{Z}^m$) is the m-

dimensional identity matrix. The lattice points of the m-dimensional integer lattice consist of all the possible m-dimensional vectors of integers.

The conventional method of using a lattice for channel coding is to take a finite subset of lattice points and define a one-to-one mapping between the lattice points and binary vectors that represent the information that is to be sent over a channel. The goal of using lattice codes for channel coding is to maximize the amount of information that can be conveyed over the channel for a given power constraint. As an example, consider the problem of sending bits over an AWGN channel. One method of addressing this problem is to choose a lattice and then map vectors of bits to a finite subset of the lattice. The lattice points will then represent the real values that are sent over the channel and corrupted by noise. The decoder will receive a noisy sequence of points and attempt to recover the bits by decoding the noisy values to the closest lattice points in Euclidean distance. The decoding region for each lattice point is often referred to as its *Voronoi region* and is defined to be the set of points whose Euclidean distance to the given lattice point is closer than that to any other lattice point.

To illustrate the above concepts, consider the hexagonal lattice defined by the generator matrix

$$ \mathbf{G} = \begin{bmatrix} 1 & 0 \\ \frac{1}{2} & \frac{\sqrt{3}}{2} \end{bmatrix} . $$

A pictorial representation of the lattice points that are generated by the aforementioned generator matrix is given in Figure 7.4, where a finite subset of the

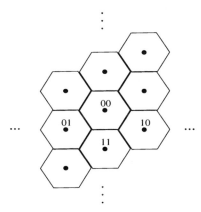

FIGURE 7.4: Example of a hexagonal lattice. A finite subset of the lattice points is shown, and the Voronoi region of each lattice point is a hexagon.

hexagonal lattice is shown. If we take four of the lattice points as our finite subset, then we can define a mapping of this subset to binary vectors of length two. In
Figure 7.4, we chose four lattice points and arbitrarily assigned two-dimensional
bit vectors to the lattice points. A transmitter may then parse a bit string into vectors of length two and map each vector to a lattice point. Each of the lattice points
represent a two-dimensional real vector that will be corrupted by additive white
Gaussian noise. The Voronoi region of each lattice point is shown as a hexagon.
Therefore, if the additive noise is not large enough to perturb a lattice point outside of its Voronoi region, then the decoder will be able to successfully decode
the bits sent by the encoder.

7.3.2 Convolutional Codes

A class of codes that are often used with both Hamming distance decoders and
Euclidean distance decoders are convolutional codes. For simplicity, we restrict
our description to binary convolutional codes. Like an (n, k) linear block code,
an (n, k) convolutional code maps length-k blocks of information symbols into
length-n blocks of output symbols, but each output block depends on the current
and previous information blocks. A convolutional code can in general be defined
by a linear finite state machine (LFSM). For a binary (n, k) convolutional code
of memory v, the LFSM can be expressed as v stages of k shift registers that are
connected by n different modulo-2 adders, as in Figure 7.5. At each time instant,
k bits are shifted in to the LFSM and n bits are output from the LFSM. The shift
registers in combination with the modulo-2 adders serve to constrain the possible
output sequences. The goal of designing a convolutional code is to constrain the
possible output sequences to be separated by a large distance. For example, if

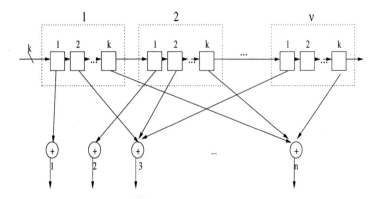

FIGURE 7.5:   A linear finite state machine representation of a convolutional code. There are k input bits, n output bits, and the memory is v.

the convolutional code is to be used with a Hamming distance decoder, then it is
desirable to design the convolutional code so that the possible output bit sequences
are separated by a large Hamming distance. However, if the convolutional code
is to be used with a Euclidean distance decoder, then a mapping between the
output bit sequences and vectors of real values must be defined and it is desirable
to design the convolutional code so that the possible vectors of real values are
separated by a large Euclidean distance. In general, better convolutional codes
can be found as the memory is increased.

As is common with LFSMs, it is often beneficial to express the LFSM as a
state transition diagram. The states represent the contents of the registers in the
LFSM, and the transitions between states are determined by the input bits. As an
example, consider the convolutional code shown in Figure 7.6a. The parameters
of the code are given as $v = 2$, $k = 1$, and $n = 2$. In the example, bits are shifted
into the registers one at a time and the input bit is represented as the variable u.
The contents of the registers that represent the state of the convolutional code are
given as variables s_1 and s_2. The output bits of the convolutional code are given
as variables c_1 and c_2. We can represent the convolutional code as a state diagram
by assigning a circle to each possible state (as in Figure 7.6b) and representing
the transitions between states with arrows. As can be seen from Figure 7.6 the
input bit, in combination with the current state of the convolutional code, will
determine the following state of the convolutional code. For example, if at a given
time instant the state of the registers is given as 01 and the input bit is 1, then 1
will be shifted out of the right-most register and the input bit will be shifted into
the left-most register. As a result, the following state of the convolutional code
will be 10.

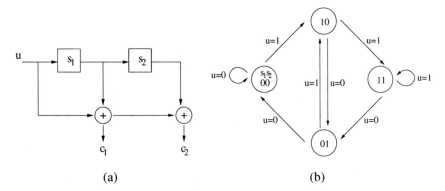

(a) (b)

FIGURE 7.6: (a) Convolutional code example with parameters $v = 2$,
$k = 1$, and $n = 2$. (b) State diagram representation of convolutional code.

Any convolutional code can also be expressed as a vector-matrix product

$$\vec{c}(D) = \vec{u}(D)\mathbf{G}(D), \tag{7.10}$$

where $\vec{c}(D) = [c_1(D), c_2(D), \ldots, c_i(D), \ldots, c_n(D)]$ is a row vector of n polynomials, with the ith polynomial representing the ith output bit sequence. A bit sequence, $\{b_0, b_1, \ldots, b_m\}$ can be represented as a polynomial $b_0 + b_1 D + \cdots + b_m D^m$ by weighting the ith bit in time by D^i where D is a variable representing delay. Similarly, $\vec{u}(D) = [u_1(D), u_2(D), \ldots, u_j(D), \ldots, u_k(D)]$ is a row vector of k polynomials, with the jth polynomial representing the jth bit sequence. The matrix $\mathbf{G}(D)$ is a $k \times n$ matrix that contains generator polynomials that specify the relationship between the input polynomials and the output polynomials. For example, consider the convolutional code shown in Figure 7.6a. The first output bit is the modulo-2 addition of the current input bit and the previous input bit in time. We can write a polynomial equation for the first output bit as

$$c_1(D) = u(D) + Du(D),$$

where the variable D represents delay. The second output bit is equal to the modulo-2 addition of the current input bit, the bit from the previous time instant, and the bit from two time instants ago. We can write a polynomial equation for the second output bit as

$$c_2(D) = u(D) + Du(D) + D^2 u(D). \tag{7.11}$$

Now, the two equations just given can be combined into the form of (7.10) where the generator matrix can be expressed as

$$\mathbf{G}(D) = \begin{bmatrix} 1 + D & 1 + D + D^2 \end{bmatrix}$$

and $\vec{c}(D) = [c_1(D), c_2(D)]$, $\vec{u}(D) = [u(D)]$. The aforementioned representation of a convolutional code is often useful for analyzing the performance characteristics of a code.

Another representation of a convolutional code is as a trellis. A pictorial representation of a trellis can be formed by aligning all of the possible states in a vertical column for each time instant and then connecting the states in accordance with the state transition diagram. The trellis representation of a convolutional code is particularly useful for decoding, as quick decoding algorithms such as the Viterbi decoding algorithm can be derived from the trellis representation. An example of a trellis representation of the convolutional code in Figure 7.6a is given in Figure 7.7, where the states are represented as dots and the transitions are labeled by the input bit that causes the transition and the resulting output bits.

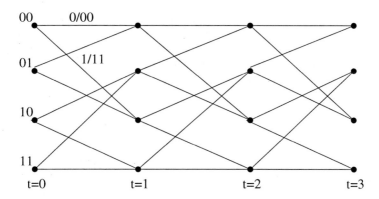

FIGURE 7.7: Trellis representation of convolutional code given in Figure 7.6a.

The goal of the decoder is to find the codeword from the convolutional code closest to the received sequence in either Hamming distance or Euclidean distance (if the output bits of the convolutional code are mapped to real values). This can be done efficiently by using the trellis diagram. If we let $y^{(i)}$ represent the received block (of length n) at time instant i and let $c^{(i)}_{u_i, s_i \to s_{i+1}}$ represent the output block (of length n) at time instant i corresponding to the transition between states s_i and s_{i+1} that results from input block u_i (of length k), then mathematically the goal of the decoder is to find the output sequence $\hat{c}$ that is closest in distance to the received sequence,

$$\hat{c} = \arg\min_{c \in C} \mathbf{d}(c, y).$$

In the equation just given, C represents the set of valid codewords, $c = \{c^{(0)}_{u_0, s_0 \to s_1}, c^{(1)}_{u_1, s_1 \to s_2}, \dots, c^{(m)}_{u_m, s_m \to s_{m+1}}\}$ represents a valid sequence of output blocks, and $y = \{y^{(0)}, y^{(2)}, \dots, y^{(m)}\}$ represents a sequence of received blocks. Furthermore, $\mathbf{d}(c, y)$ is the distance metric between the output sequence and the received sequence and can be written as a summation of distances between the received blocks and the output blocks at the various time instants,

$$\mathbf{d}(c, y) = \sum_{i=0}^{m} d\left(c^{(i)}_{u_i, s_i \to s_{i+1}}, y^{(i)}\right). \tag{7.12}$$

Assuming that the trellis starts in state zero (i.e., all of the registers of the convolutional code are cleared to zero), a naive approach to finding the codeword sequence that is closest to the received sequence would be to calculate the distance of the received sequence to each path in the trellis that starts in state zero and then declare the path that is closest to the received sequence as the decoded codeword. This method is inefficient because the amount of computation grows exponentially with the length of the sequence. A more efficient decoding algorithm can be realized by using the Viterbi algorithm. The Viterbi algorithm begins at the first stage of the trellis by calculating the distance between all branches of the trellis that emerge from state zero and the corresponding block in the received sequence (i.e., $d(c_{u_0,s_0 \to s_1}^{(0)}, y^{(0)})$). In general, there will be 2^k branches that emerge from any state, so the Viterbi algorithm starts by calculating 2^k distance metrics. For the next stage in the trellis, we can prune paths that end in the same state s_1. More specifically, for all paths that converge to the same state, we can keep the path that has the minimum distance up to that state and prune all other paths. This works because if multiple paths converge to the same state, then any path that may emerge from this state will have an associated distance that will be added to the distance associated with the path that ends in that state. Mathematically, we can break up the total distance metric for any path that goes through a state at time i as the distance metric from state 0 at time 0 to state s_i at time i and the distance metric from state s_i to state s_{m+1} at the end of the trellis:

$$\mathbf{d(c, y)} = \sum_{j=0}^{i-2} d\left(c_{u_j,s_j \to s_{j+1}}^{(j)}, y^{(j)}\right) + d\left(c_{u_{i-1},s_{i-1} \to s_i}, y^{(i-1)}\right)$$

$$+ \sum_{j=i}^{m} d\left(c_{u_j,s_j \to s_{j+1}}^{(j)}, y^{(j)}\right). \tag{7.13}$$

From (7.13), we see that all paths that merge at state s_i will have the same possible distances $\sum_{j=i}^{m} d(c_{u_j,s_j \to s_{j+1}}^{(j)}, y^{(j)})$ added to the existing distance of the path and therefore a path with a larger distance at state s_i cannot achieve a smaller overall distance than a path with a smaller distance at state s_i. As a result, we can prune the total number of paths to be no larger than the total number of states. In other words, at each time instant, at most 2^{vk} paths are kept (one path for each state). At time instant m, the minimum-distance path can be determined and traced back to state 0 at time instant 0. The output sequence associated with the minimum distance path is the decoded codeword.

Because the time complexity of the Viterbi algorithm is exponential in the memory order, faster but suboptimal sequential decoding algorithms (e.g., the Fano and Stack algorithms [50]) are used in many time-critical applications. A generalization of the standard Viterbi algorithm is the list Viterbi algorithm (LVA) [44,41], which finds the L most likely paths instead of only the most likely one.

Symbol MAP decoding (see Section 7.2.2) of convolutional codes can be done with soft-input soft-output algorithms. Two of the most prominent ones are the

BCJR algorithm of Bahl and colleagues [4] and the soft-output Viterbi algorithm of Hagenauer and Hoeher [25]. Both algorithms output for each information bit u_i, $i = 0, \ldots, km$, an a posteriori log-likelihood ratio (LLR)

$$\Lambda(u_i) = \log \frac{Pr\{U_i = 1 \mid \mathbf{Y} = \mathbf{y}\}}{Pr\{U_i = 0 \mid \mathbf{Y} = \mathbf{y}\}}$$

whose sign specifies the reconstructed source bit $\hat{u}_i$.

A family of convolutional codes can be generated from a single convolutional code, called a mother code, with rate $\frac{1}{n}$. Some output symbols of the mother encoder are punctured, which allows the construction of a family of codes with rates $\frac{p}{np}, \frac{p}{np-1}, \ldots, \frac{p}{p+1}$, where p is the puncturing period. To obtain RCPC codes [24], all protection symbols of the higher rate-punctured code are used by the lower rate codes (the higher rate codes are embedded into the lower rate codes). A nice feature of RCPC codes is that if a higher rate code does not provide enough protection, one can switch to a lower rate code simply by adding extra redundant symbols. Another good feature of RCPC codes is that the same Viterbi trellis can be used for all rates.

As mentioned earlier, a convolutional code may be used as either a Hamming distance code or a Euclidean distance code. If the convolutional code is used as a Euclidean distance code, then a mapping between the possible output bits at any given time instant and a set of real values must be defined. One method of defining a mapping is to first choose a constellation of real values such as a finite subset of lattice points and then define a bijective mapping between the lattice points and the possible output bit vectors. For example, the convolutional code shown in Figure 7.6a has two output bits, which can assume one of four possible two-bit combinations, so we can define a mapping between the four possible two-bit combinations and the four lattice points shown in Figure 7.4. Recall, however, that the goal of code design is to maximize the minimum distance between possible output sequences, and the aforementioned procedure may not maximize the minimum distance for a given convolutional code and a given set of constellation points. A proper Euclidean distance code design should jointly consider the convolutional code and the set of constellation points in defining the mapping between bits and constellation points. This concept was first introduced by Ungerboeck [48], and the resulting codes are often referred to as trellis-coded modulation (TCM) codes.

TCM codes are usually formed by letting a convolutional code index a partition of constellation points [48]. Forney [20] and Conway and Sloane [13] independently utilized this heuristic to define a set of codes that are derived from a convolutional code that indexes a lattice partition. More specifically, both Forney and Conway and Sloane showed that good trellis codes can be obtained by partitioning a well-known lattice and then searching for a convolutional code to index the partition. In this chapter, we will denote a lattice partition as Λ/Λ', where Λ' is a sublattice of Λ and partitions Λ into *cosets* of Λ'. A coset of Λ' is formed by choosing a lattice point, $\lambda \in \Lambda$, and adding this element to all of the lattice points in Λ'. We denote the coset as $\Lambda' + \lambda$. For example, consider the lattice partition $\mathbb{Z}/4\mathbb{Z}$, where $\mathbb{Z}$ is the integer lattice formed by the 1×1 identity matrix and $4\mathbb{Z}$ is a sublattice of $\mathbb{Z}$ that is formed by scaling the integer lattice by 4. Four disjoint cosets may be formed from $4\mathbb{Z}$ by adding the lattice points $\{0, 1, 2, 3\}$ to $4\mathbb{Z}$. Notice that the union of the four cosets is equal to $\mathbb{Z}$. One method of arriving at the four cosets of $4\mathbb{Z}$ is to use a partition tree, $\mathbb{Z}/2\mathbb{Z}/4\mathbb{Z}$. The first level of the tree is a partition of $\mathbb{Z}$ into two cosets that consist of the even and odd lattice points of $\mathbb{Z}$ (i.e., $2\mathbb{Z}$ and $2\mathbb{Z} + 1$). The next level of the partition tree further partitions $2\mathbb{Z}$ into $4\mathbb{Z}$ and $4\mathbb{Z} + 2$ and partitions $2\mathbb{Z} + 1$ into $4\mathbb{Z} + 1$ and $4\mathbb{Z} + 3$. A pictorial representation of the partition tree, $\mathbb{Z}/2\mathbb{Z}/4\mathbb{Z}$, is given in Figure 7.8. Each of the branches of the partition tree is labeled as either 0 or 1. This labeling defines a mapping between two-bit vectors and cosets of $4\mathbb{Z}$. For example, the coset $4\mathbb{Z} + 1$ corresponds to the bit label 10. Now, if we allow the output of a rate-$\frac{1}{2}$ convolutional code to index the labeling of the partition tree for each time instant, then a trellis code may be formed from $\mathbb{Z}/4\mathbb{Z}$ by searching all rate-$\frac{1}{2}$ convolutional codes of a given constraint length to find the convolutional code that maximizes the minimum Euclidean distance between codewords. Note that in the aforementioned, a finite subset of the lattice points must be used to form the trellis code to ensure that there is no ambiguity in decoding a sequence of lattice points to a bit sequence.

The performance of a TCM code is measured by the signal-to-noise ratio (SNR) that is needed to achieve a given probability of error. For high SNRs, it has been

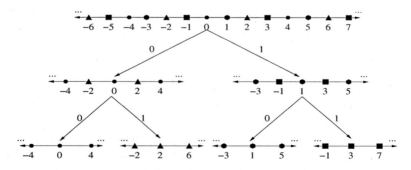

FIGURE 7.8: An example of the partition tree $\mathbb{Z}/2\mathbb{Z}/4\mathbb{Z}$. The branches of the tree are labeled by either 0 or 1 and represent a mapping from bits to cosets of $4\mathbb{Z}$.

shown that the probability of error for a TCM code can be approximated as

$$P_e \approx K_{\min} Q \left(\sqrt{\frac{d_{\min}^2}{4\sigma_N^2}} \right), \tag{7.14}$$

where Q is the Q function, $d_{\min}$ represents the minimum distance of the TCM code and $K_{\min}$ represents the number of codewords that have a distance of $d_{\min}$ from a given codeword. We use σ_N^2 to represent the variance of the channel noise. Though effective, the performance of TCM codes is considerably worse than information theoretic bounds.

7.3.3 Interleaving

While the codes described earlier are convenient for memoryless channels with small error rates, most of them are not suited to the protection against errors that occur in bursts. When errors occur in bursts, as in fading channels, a transmitted codeword is either free of errors or contains a large number of successive errors. The problem of burst errors can be alleviated with special codes (e.g., Fire codes [17]). An alternative is interleaving, which shuffles the symbols from different codewords before transmission. When a long burst error occurs, the erroneous symbols are distributed among many codewords where they appear as short burst errors. In block interleaving (Table 7.2), the channel codewords are placed in the rows of an array, and the codeword symbols are sent columnwise. In cross (or convolutional) interleaving, as shown in Figure 7.9, a set of ordered shift registers with linearly increasing memory size is used to separate the output symbols of the channel encoder.

7.3.4 Turbo Codes

In 1993, Berrou *et al.* [9,10] amazed the coding community by introducing a novel class of error-correcting codes, turbo codes, which, for a binary-input AWGN

Table 7.2: Block interleaver of size 4×7. To transmit four codewords of length 7, the codeword symbols are sent columnwise, in the order $1, 8, 15, 22, \ldots, 7, 14, 21, 28$. A burst error of length four produces no more than a single error in a transmitted codeword.

1. Codeword	1	2	3	4	5	6	7
2. Codeword	8	9	10	11	12	13	14
3. Codeword	15	16	17	18	19	20	21
4. Codeword	22	23	24	25	26	27	28

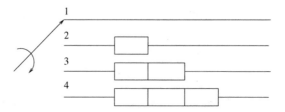

FIGURE 7.9: Cross interleaver with four shift registers. The memory sizes of the shift registers are 0, m, $2m$, and $3m$, respectively. At time unit i, a symbol is inserted into shift register i, which outputs its right-most symbol. Suppose that $m = 1$ and the input symbols are $0, 1, 2, 3, 4, 5, 6, 7, 8, \ldots$. After interleaving, the symbols are sent in the order $0, 4, 1, 8, 5, \ldots$.

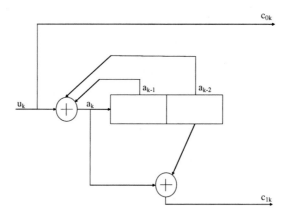

FIGURE 7.10: A recursive systematic convolutional code.

channel, achieved a BER of 10^{-5} with code rate $1/2$ and E_b/N_0 as close as 0.5 dB to the practical Shannon limit (see Section 7.2.4).

A turbo code is a parallel concatenation of two or more codes connected by pseudo-random interleavers. The constituent codes are usually identical, recursive systematic convolutional (RSC) codes of rate $1/2$. An example of an RSC encoder is shown in Figure 7.10. Its main property is the existence of a feedback in the shift-register realization.

Figure 7.11 shows a classical turbo encoder with two constituent RSC codes. In contrast to a serial code concatenation where the output of one encoder forms the input for the next one, in a parallel concatenation, both encoders operate on the same input block. In Figure 7.11, an input information block of length k bits,

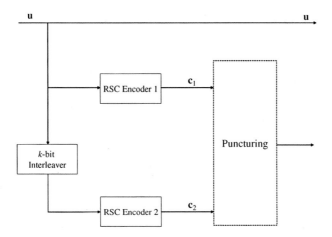

FIGURE 7.11:   A classical turbo encoder with two RSC codes.

$\mathbf{u} = (u_1, \ldots, u_k)$, is encoded by the first RSC encoder; at the same time, it is passed through a k-bit interleaver and fed into the second RSC encoder. For each input bit u_i, the output consists of that bit u_i and the two parity-check bits $c_{1,i}$ and $c_{2,i}$ from the two RSC encoders. The output corresponding to the input block $\mathbf{u}$ is the codeword $\mathbf{c} = (u_1, \ldots, u_k, c_{1,1}, \ldots, c_{1,k}, c_{2,1}, \ldots, c_{2,k})$. The code rate of the turbo code is 1/3. Higher code rates can be obtained by puncturing the output bits of the two encoders [1]. For example, rate 1/2 can be obtained by alternately puncturing the parity bits of the two RSC encoders. A turbo code is essentially a block code, thus encoding can be seen as a multiplication of the information block by a generator matrix.

One of the many novelties in the turbo code realization is the existence of a block interleaver between the two RSC coders. The interleaver introduces randomness to the code while leaving enough structure in it so that decoding is physically feasible. The size of the interleaver (the length of the information block) is usually very large (in the order of thousands bits) to ensure good performance. If the size is large enough, any pseudo-random interleaver will perform well. However, for short interleaver sizes, the performance of the code can be significantly enhanced by a clever design of the interleaver [5].

A typical turbo decoder consists of two soft-input soft-output decoders (see Section 7.3.2), two k-bit interleavers identical to the encoder interleaver, and a deinterleaver, as shown in Figure 7.12. The decoding is based on the symbol MAP rule (see Section 7.2.2). The a posteriori LLRs for the information bits $u_1, \ldots, u_k$ are estimated in an iterative way by exchanging information between the two constituent decoders. Suppose that the systematic part of the codeword, $\mathbf{c}_0 = (u_1, \ldots, u_k)$, is received as $\mathbf{y}_0$, while the two parity parts, $\mathbf{c}_1 = (c_{1,1}, \ldots, c_{1,k})$ and

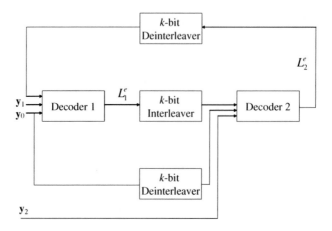

FIGURE 7.12:   Block scheme of a classical turbo decoder.

$\mathbf{c}_2 = (c_{2,1}, \ldots, c_{2,k})$, are received as $\mathbf{y}_1$ and $\mathbf{y}_2$, respectively. In the first iteration, the first decoder generates a reliability information $L_1^e(i)$ for each information bit u_i, $i = 1, \ldots, k$, based on its input, $(\mathbf{y}_0, \mathbf{y}_1)$. This soft-decision output, called extrinsic information, is interleaved and fed to the second decoder. Using its input $(\mathbf{y}_2$ and the interleaved version of $\mathbf{y}_0)$, the second decoder computes a reliability information $L_2^e(i)$ for each information bit. Next, the extrinsic information from the first decoder, the extrinsic information from the second decoder, and a channel log-likelihood ratio $\log \frac{Pr\{Y_i = y_{0,i} | U_i = 1\}}{Pr\{Y_i = y_{0,i} | U_i = 0\}}$ are summed to provide a first approximation of the a posteriori LLRs. In the second iteration, the extrinsic information $L_2^e(i)$ is deinterleaved and sent to the first decoder, which exploits this new information to update its extrinsic information. The procedure repeats until the a posteriori LLRs converge or a maximum number of iterations is reached.

Turbo coding with iterative decoding is currently one of the best error-correcting techniques. It significantly outperforms convolutional codes of the same constraint length. One of the key properties of turbo codes is the sharp performance improvement with the increase of the input block length. Thus, to achieve near-capacity performance, large block lengths are needed, which cause huge latency. Therefore, applications of turbo codes are currently limited to those that are not delay sensitive. For example, the new CCSDS telemetry channel coding standard for satellite and deep-space communications uses turbo codes. SMART-1, launched in September 2003 by the European Space Agency, is the first probe that exploits turbo codes. Turbo codes have also been adopted by the leading third-generation (3G) cellular standards, such as CDMA2000 and UMTS.

7.4 HIERARCHICAL MODULATION

Hierarchical modulation [19] is a digital modulation technique that enables transmission of two independent information bit streams with unequal priority on a single channel. As part of the digital terrestrial television standard DVB-T [18], it offers new possibilities in organizing scarce radio frequency bandwidth. In this section, we first outline the main concepts underlying hierarchical modulation and compare it to standard digital nonhierarchical modulation techniques; then, we give examples of possible applications.

Figure 7.13 shows constellations of four basic linear digital modulation techniques [38,39]. Each possible digital state (constellation point) in the phase diagram (represented by a dot in Figure 7.13) uniquely determines one phase of the carrier signal. Each transmitted bit stream is assigned to one constellation point. The performance of a digital modulation technique can be measured using its achieved data rate (or, equivalently, the number of bits assigned to each dig-

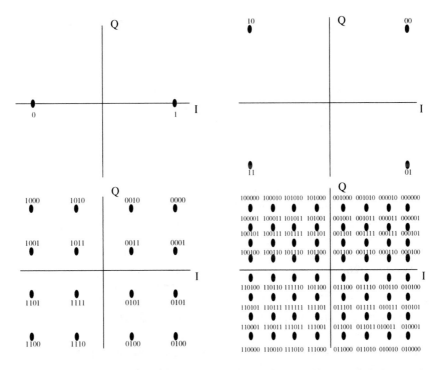

FIGURE 7.13:   Constellations of four standard digital modulation techniques: BPSK (top left), 4-QAM (top right), 16-QAM (bottom left), and 64-QAM (bottom right).

ital state) and minimum tolerated signal-to-noise ratio for reliable demodulation (which reflects robustness to channel noise). Normally, higher level modulation techniques achieve larger data rates at the expense of a lower robustness.

Binary Phase Shift Keying (BPSK) allows transmission of one bit per modulation signal. The phase of a carrier signal takes two possible values (separated by π) depending on the transmitted bit. 4-Quadrature Amplitude Modulation (4-QAM), also referred to as Quadrature Phase Shift Keying (QPSK or 4-PSK), transmits two bits on each carrier. Thus, it achieves twice the data rate of BPSK. In Figure 7.13, one possible constellation realization is presented, where the carrier phases are $\pi/4$, $3\pi/4$, $5\pi/4$, and $7\pi/4$. In 16-QAM and 64-QAM, because there are 4×4 and 8×8 different constellation points, respectively, four and six bits, respectively, can be sent per modulation signal. The assignment of the bit streams to the digital states is usually determined using Gray-code mapping so that the assignments of the closest constellation points differ in one bit. The data rate is increased compared to 4-QAM at the expense of a lower noise tolerance (due to smaller distances between neighboring states in the phase diagram). For example, compared to 4-QAM with the same code rate, the minimum tolerated signal-to-noise ratio is approximately 6 dB and 12 dB higher with 16-QAM and 64-QAM, respectively [19].

Note that in all modulation techniques discussed so far, a single information bit stream (possibly coded) is transmitted per one modulation signal. Hierarchical modulation, however, enables transmission of two separate information bit streams in a single modulation signal. One bit stream, called high-priority (HP) bit stream, is embedded within another, called low-priority (LP) bit stream. The main idea is to decouple the bit stream assigned to a digital state into two substreams: the first substream is HP, which determines the number of the quadrant (0, 1, 2, or 3) where the digital state is located; the second substream (LP) carries the information about the position of the digital state in the specified quadrant. As a result, hierarchical modulation can be viewed as a combination of 4-QAM (used for the HP bit stream) and either 4-QAM or 16-QAM (used for the LP bit stream).

Two hierarchical modulation constellations are shown in Figure 7.14. In the first constellation (the upper figure), 4-QAM is embedded in 16-QAM (thus, it is called "4-QAM in 16-QAM"); in the second one, 4-QAM is embedded in 64-QAM ("4-QAM in 64-QAM"). In both cases, the first two bits constitute the HP bit stream intended for an HP service/client; the remaining two or four bits are the LP bit stream intended for an LP service/client. In the example shown in Figure 7.14 (bottom), 10 is sent to the HP clients and 0101 to the LP clients.

Note that the HP bit stream is always modulated as 4-QAM. Thus, as in classic nonhierarchical 4-QAM, it carries two bits per modulation signal. However, because the LP bit stream can be seen at the receiver as an additional noise in the

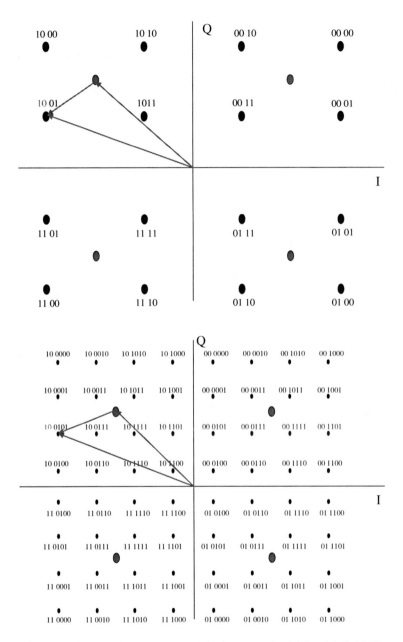

FIGURE 7.14: Hierarchical modulation: "4-QAM in 16-QAM" (top) and "4-QAM in 64-QAM" (bottom).

quadrant of the received signal, the HP bit stream is less robust than nonhierarchical 4-QAM (i.e., a higher minimum tolerated signal-to-noise ratio is needed).

The LP bit stream is essentially either 4-QAM [Figure 7.14 (top)] or 16-QAM
[Figure 7.14 (bottom)] modulated. Thus, it carries two or four bits and has the
same data rate as the corresponding nonhierarchical modulation method. The
noise sensitivity is comparable to that of the whole constellation [16-QAM in
Figure 7.14 (top) or 64-QAM in Figure 7.14 (bottom)]. Note that the total rate
of the HP and LP bit streams is equal to the rate of the whole nonhierarchical
constellation (16-QAM or 64-QAM).

The HP bit stream is obviously more robust to channel noise than the LP bit
stream; indeed, a transition of the carrier phase (due to channel noise) from one
digital state to the other within a quadrant is more likely to occur than a transition to a state in another quadrant. However, the robustness of the HP and LP bit
streams can be further improved by channel coding (i.e., by adding error protection) or by changing the constellation's α factor, as in Figure 7.15. The $\alpha = a/b$
factor [18] is defined as the ratio between a, the minimum distance separating
two constellation points that carry two different HP bit streams, and b, the minimum distance separating any two constellation points. Constellations with $\alpha > 1$
are called nonuniform constellations. The increase of α makes the HP bit stream
more robust at the expense of a less robustness of the LP bit stream. (The DVB-T
standard uses $\alpha \in \{1, 2, 4\}$.) Thus, hierarchical modulation splits the actual communication channel in two virtual channels whose characteristics depend on the

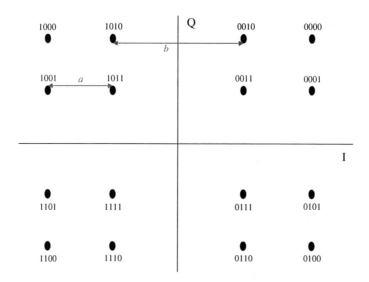

FIGURE 7.15:   A nonuniform 16-QAM constellation with $\alpha = b/a = 2$.

whole constellation (64-QAM), α factor, and code rates of the HP and LP bit streams.

Hierarchical modulation was originally proposed to enable two different coverage areas for a given transmitter in digital terrestrial TV. It offers great design flexibilities and simplifies network planning. Its value has become even more apparent with recent increasing demands for delivery of different services over heterogeneous networks, where communication channels between the sender and the clients are extremely diverse in available bandwidths and channel noise.

For example, suppose that two digital TV programs are to be transmitted simultaneously. With nonhierarchical modulation, the two programs must be broadcast over two separate frequency channels: 4-QAM can be used for the first channel (achieving a data rate of two bits per modulation signal) and 16-QAM for the second channel (with a data rate of four bits per modulation signal). With hierarchical modulation ("4-QAM in 64-QAM"), only one channel is needed: the first program can be transmitted as an HP bit stream (at a data rate of two bits per modulation signal), while the second TV program can be transmitted as an LP bit stream (at a data rate of four bits per modulation signal). Then, the coverage radius (which is determined by the noise tolerance) of the second TV program will be roughly the same as in the nonhierarchical case; the coverage radius of the first program, however, will be smaller than with nonhierarchical 4-QAM, but can be enlarged by increasing the α factor (at the expense of a smaller coverage radius of the second TV program) or by using error protection (at the expense of decreasing the information rate). Thus, one immediate advantage of hierarchical modulation over a nonhierarchical one is the savings in transmission channels because two streams with different data rates and different coverage areas can be transmitted on a single frequency channel.

Hierarchical modulation efficiently addresses the problem of heterogeneity in clients' available bandwidths, receiver resolution capabilities, and channel conditions. For example, a single frequency channel can be used to broadcast a video bit stream to mobile (or portable) receivers and fixed receivers. The mobile receivers will decode the HP bit stream, whereas the fixed receivers will be able, in addition, to decode the LP bit stream (due to their large roof top antenna gains).

Hierarchical modulation can be combined with quality/resolution scalable video coders. Then, the LP bit stream plays the role of the enhancement layer, which improves the quality/resolution of the HP (base layer) bit stream. Depending on transmission conditions, the receiver will be able to decode at the higher or lower quality/resolution level.

Another application is simulcast of the High Definition TV formats, together with the Standard Definition formats. (Transmitting the Standard Definition together with the High Definition formats is necessary because all the receivers do not have screens that support the latter formats.) Here, the HP bit stream carries the Standard Definition TV formats, and thus will be available to all receivers, whereas the LP bit stream carries the High Definition TV formats only.

Comparisons between hierarchical and nonhierarchical modulation in different scenarios can be found in [42].

7.5 AUTOMATIC REPEAT REQUEST, HYBRID FEC/ARQ

In this section, we present error protection techniques that use retransmissions. Here we assume the presence of a feedback channel from the receiver to the transmitter. We first describe pure ARQ techniques, which are based on error detection and retransmission of the corrupted packets. Then we explain type I hybrid ARQ protocols that combine error correction coding and ARQ techniques. Finally, we overview type II hybrid-ARQ protocols where the transmitter answers a retransmission request by sending additional parity symbols.

7.5.1 Pure ARQ Protocols

In a pure ARQ system, an information block of length k is encoded into a channel codeword of length n with an error-detecting code. The codeword is sent over the channel and the received word is decoded. If no errors are detected, the transmitted codeword is assumed to be received correctly and need not be retransmitted. Otherwise, the codeword must be sent again until it is received correctly. To send feedback information to the transmitter, the receiver can use a positive acknowledgment (ACK) to indicate that the codeword was received correctly or a negative acknowledgment (NACK) to indicate a transmission error. The efficiency of an ARQ scheme is measured by its reliability and throughput. The reliability is the probability that the receiver accepts a word that contains an undetectable error. The throughput is the ratio of the average number of bits successfully accepted per unit of time to the total number of bits that could be transmitted per unit of time [29]. In the following, we overview the most important ARQ schemes. Details can be found in [29] and [50].

7.5.1.1 Stop-and-Wait ARQ

In stop-and-wait ARQ, the transmitter sends a codeword and waits for an acknowledgment for that codeword. If an ACK is received, the next codeword is sent. If an NACK is received, the same codeword is retransmitted until it is received correctly, as in Figure 7.16. Stop-and-wait ARQ has a simple implementation. In particular, the codewords are not numbered. Its major drawback is the idle time spent by the transmitter waiting for an ACK.

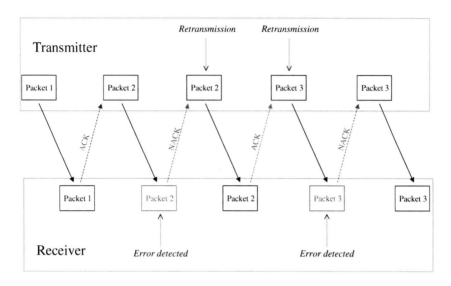

FIGURE 7.16:   Stop-and-wait ARQ.

7.5.1.2 Go-Back-N ARQ

In go-back-N ARQ, the transmitter sends the codewords continuously without waiting for an acknowledgment. Suppose that the acknowledgment for codeword c_i arrives after codewords $c_i, \ldots, c_{i+N-1}$ have been sent. If this acknowledgment is of the ACK type, the transmitter sends codeword c_{i+N}. Otherwise, the codewords $c_i, \ldots, c_{i+N-1}$ are sent again, as in Figure 7.17. On the receiver side, when an error is detected in a received word, this word and the $N-1$ subsequently received ones are ignored. Note that a buffer for N codewords is required at the transmitter side.

7.5.1.3 Selective-Repeat ARQ

Selective-repeat ARQ is similar to go-back ARQ. The difference is that when an NACK for codeword c_i is received, only c_i is retransmitted before the transmission proceeds where it stopped, as in Figure 7.18. In addition to the N-codeword buffer at the transmitter, a buffer is needed at the receiver so that the decoded codewords can be delivered in the correct order. This buffer must be large enough to avoid overflow. Selective-repeat ARQ with a finite-size buffer is presented in [29]. An alternative is to combine selective-repeat ARQ with go-back-N ARQ [29]. Here the transmitter switches from selective-repeat ARQ to go-back-N ARQ whenever μ retransmissions of a codeword have been done without receiving an

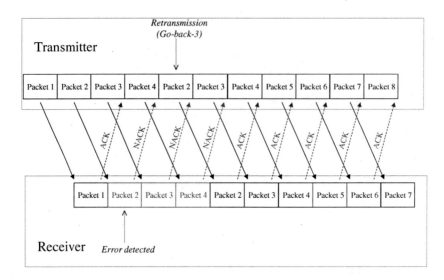

FIGURE 7.17: Go-back-N ARQ.

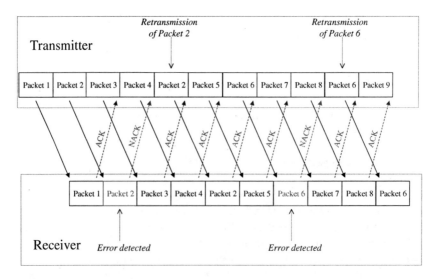

FIGURE 7.18: Selective-repeat ARQ.

ACK. It switches back to selective-repeat ARQ as soon as an ACK is received. In this way, the buffer size of the receiver can be limited to $\mu(N-1)+1$.

7.5.2 Hybrid ARQ Protocols

FEC and ARQ can be combined to provide for channels with high error rates better reliability than FEC alone and larger throughput than ARQ alone.

7.5.2.1 Type-I Hybrid ARQ Protocols

In a type-I hybrid ARQ system, each information block is encoded with a channel code with error detecting and error correcting capabilities. This can be a single linear code (see Section 7.3.1) or a concatenation of an error detection code as an outer code and an error correction code as an inner code. If the received word can be correctly decoded, then the decoded codeword is accepted. Otherwise, a retransmission is requested for the codeword.

7.5.2.2 Type-II Hybrid-ARQ Protocols

The basic difference between a type-I hybrid ARQ protocol and a type-II hybrid ARQ protocol is that in the latter the transmitter sends additional parity bits instead of the whole codeword when it receives a retransmission request for this codeword. The following example [50] illustrates the method. An (n, k) MDS code $\mathcal{C}$ is used to encode the information block. The resulting codeword is split in two. The first half can be seen as a codeword $\mathbf{c}_1$ from an $(n/2, k)$ code $\mathcal{C}_1$ and the second one as a codeword $\mathbf{c}_2$ from an $(n/2, k)$ code $\mathcal{C}_2$. Here the two codes $\mathcal{C}_1$ and $\mathcal{C}_2$ are obtained by puncturing the code $\mathcal{C}$. The transmitter starts by sending $\mathbf{c}_1$. If the received word $\mathbf{y}_1$ cannot be correctly decoded, a retransmission is requested. The transmitter then sends the codeword $\mathbf{c}_2$, which is received as $\mathbf{y}_2$. The receiver concatenates $\mathbf{y}_1$ and $\mathbf{y}_2$ and uses the stronger code $\mathcal{C}$ to decode the resulting word.

7.6 SUMMARY AND FURTHER READING

The first part of this chapter presented the fundamental results of information theory, which culminate in Shannon's joint source-channel coding theorem. While this theorem is useful in understanding the theoretical performance bounds for the communication of data over an unreliable channel, it does not explain how a practical communication system should be designed. Practical system design should consider source coding, channel control, and modulation. Practical source coding for media data is described in other chapters of this book (Chapter 5 for video coding and Chapter 6 for audio coding). State-of-the-art channel coding techniques are overviewed in the second part of the chapter. The main message is that channel coding techniques, in particular Turbo codes and LDPC codes, have reached a level of maturity that allows them to achieve performance close to the theoretical bounds announced by Shannon. Another important achievement in the area of channel coding is development of the class of digital fountain codes for protection against packet loss. The third part of the chapter discussed hierarchical modulation, an emerging modulation technique for digital video broadcasting. The last part of the chapter gave a brief survey of error control techniques that rely on data retransmission. These techniques, which require a two-way channel, can be used with error detection only or combined with error correcting codes.

We conclude this chapter with suggestions for further reading. A rigorous treatment of source coding can be found in [6] and [17]. Excellent descriptions of modern channel codes are given in [43] and [33]. The best reference for the latest advances in source and channel coding is the IEEE Transactions on Information Theory.

REFERENCES

[1] O. Acikel and W. Ryan. "Punctured turbo-codes for BPSK/QPSK channels," *IEEE Trans. Commun.*, vol. 47, pp. 1315–1323, September 1999.

[2] V. K. Agarwal and A. Ivanov. "Computing the probability of undetected error for shortened cyclic codes," *IEEE Trans. Commun.*, vol. 40, pp. 494–499, March 1992.

[3] R. B. Ash. *Information Theory*, Dover, New York, 1965.

[4] L. Bahl, J. Cocke, F. Jelinek, and J. Raviv. "Optimal decoding of linear codes for minimizing symbol error rate," *IEEE Trans. Inform. Theory*, pp. 284–287, March 1974.

[5] A. Barbulescu and S. Pietrobon. "Interleaver design for turbo codes," *Electronics Letters*, vol. 30, pp. 2107–2108, December 1994.

[6] T. Berger. *Rate Distortion Theory*, Prentice Hall, 1971.

[7] E. R. Berlekamp. *Algebraic Coding Theory*, McGraw-Hill, New York, 1968.

[8] E. R. Berlekamp, R. J. McEliece, and H. C. A. van Tilborg. "On the intractability of certain coding problems," *IEEE Trans. Inform. Theory*, vol. 24, pp. 384–386, May 1978.

[9] C. Berrou and A. Glavieux. "Near optimum error correcting coding and decoding: turbo-codes," *IEEE Trans. Commun.*, vol. 44, pp. 1261–1271, October 1996.

[10] C. Berrou, A. Glavieux, and P. Thitimajshima. "Near Shannon limit error-correcting coding and decoding: Turbo codes," *Proc. IEEE ICC-1993 International Conference on Communications*, pp. 1064–1070, Geneva, Switzerland, May 1993.

[11] S. A. Butman and R. J. McEliece. "The ultimate limits of binary coding for a wide-band Gaussian channel," JPL Deep Space Network Progress Report 42–22, pp. 78–80, 1974.

[12] L. N. Childs. *A Concrete Introduction to Higher Algebra*, Springer, New York, 1995.

[13] J. Conway and N. Sloane. *Sphere Packings and Error-Correcting Codes*, Springer-Verlag, New York, 1988.

[14] S.-Y. Chung, G. D. Forney, T. J. Richardson, and R. Urbanke. "On the design of low-density parity-check codes within 0.0045 dB of the Shannon limit," *IEEE Commun. Letters*, vol. 5, pp. 58–60, February 2001.

[15] T. M. Cover and J. A. Thomas. *Elements of Information Theory*, Wiley, 1991.

[16] D. Divsalar, H. Jin, and R. J. McEliece. "Coding theorems for 'turbo-like' codes," *Proc. 36th Allerton Conf. Communication, Control, and Computing*, pp. 201–210, Allerton, Illinois, September 1998.

[17] R. J. McEliece. *The Theory of Information and Coding*, Cambridge University Press, 2002.

[18] ETSI EN 300 744: Digital video broadcasting (DVB); framing structure, channel coding and modulation for digital terrestrial television, June 2004.

[19] ETSI: Digital video broadcasting (DVB); implementation guidelines for DVB terrestrial services; transmission aspects, Technical Report TR 101 190, December 1997.

[20] G. Forney. "Coset codes – part 1: Introduction and geometrical classification," *IEEE Trans. Inform. Theory*, vol. 34, pp. 1123–1151, September 1988.

[21] R. G. Gallager. *Low Density Parity-Check Codes*, MIT Press, Cambridge, 1963.

[22] R. Gray. *Entropy and Information Theory*, Springer-Verlag, New York, 1990.

[23] V. Guruswami and M. Sudan. "Improved decoding of Reed–Solomon and algebraic-geometry codes," *IEEE Trans. Inform. Theory*, vol. 45, pp. 1757–1767, September 1999.

[24] J. Hagenauer. "Rate-compatible punctured convolutional codes (RCPC codes) and their applications," *IEEE Trans. Commun.*, vol. 36, pp. 389–400, April 1988.

[25] J. Hagenauer and P. Hoeher. "A Viterbi algorithm with soft-decision outputs and its applications," *Proc. GLOBECOM*, vol. 3, pp. 1680–1686, Dallas, Texas, November 1989.

[26] J. Jiang and K. Narayanan. "Iterative soft decoding of Reed–Solomon codes," *IEEE Commun. Letters*, vol. 8, pp. 244–246, April 2004.

[27] H. Jin, A. Khandekar, and R. McEliece. "Irregular repeat-accumulate codes," *Proc. 2nd Int. Symposium. Turbo Codes*, pp. 1–8, Brest, France, September 2000.

[28] R. Koetter and A. Vardy. "Algebraic soft-decision decoding of Reed–Solomon codes," *IEEE Trans. Inform. Theory*, vol. 49, pp. 2809–2825, November 2003.

[29] S. Lin and D. Costello, Jr. *Error Control Coding*, 2nd ed., Prentice Hall, 2004.

[30] M. Luby. "LT codes," *Proc. 43rd Annual IEEE Symposium on Foundations of Computer Science*, pp. 271–282, 2002.

[31] M. Luby, M. Mitzenmacher, A. Shokrollahi, D. Spielman, and V. Stemann. "Practical loss-resilient codes," *29th ACM Symposium Theory Computation*, pp. 150–159, 1997.

[32] M. Luby, M. Mitzenmacher, A. Shokrollahi, and D. Spielman. "Efficient erasure correcting codes," *IEEE Trans. Inform. Theory*, vol. 47, pp. 569–584, February 2001.

[33] D. J. C. MacKay. *Information Theory, Inference and Learning Algorithms*, Cambridge University Press, 2003.

[34] D. J. C. MacKay and R. M. Neal. "Near Shannon limit performance of low density parity check codes," *Electronics Letters*, vol. 32, pp. 1645–1646, August 1996.

[35] D. J. C. MacKay. "Good error-correcting codes based on very sparse matrices," *IEEE Trans. Inform. Theory*, vol. 45, pp. 399–431, March 1999.

[36] M. MacWilliams and N. Sloane. *The Theory of Error-Correcting Codes*, Karlin, North-Holland, 1992.

[37] J. Pearl. "Fusion, propagation, and structuring in belief networks," *Artificial Intell.*, vol. 29, pp. 241–288, 1986.

[38] J. G. Proakis and M. Salehi. *Communication Systems and Engineering*, Prentice-Hall, New Jersey, 2002.

[39] T. S. Rappaport. *Wireless Communications*, Prentice-Hall, New Jersey, 1996.

[40] T. J. Richardson and R. Urbanke. "Efficient encoding of low-density parity-check codes," *IEEE Trans. Inform. Theory*, vol. 47, pp. 638–656, February 2001.

[41] M. Röder and R. Hamzaoui. "Fast tree-trellis list Viterbi algorithm," *IEEE Trans. Commun.*, vol. 54, pp. 453–461, March 2006.

[42] A. Schertz and C. Weck. "Hierarchical modulation," *EBU Technical Review*, April 2003.

[43] C. Schlegel. *Trellis Coding*, John Wiley & Sons, 1997.

[44] N. Seshadri and C.-E. W. Sundberg. "List Viterbi decoding algorithms with applications," *IEEE Trans. Commun.*, vol. 42, pp. 313–323, February–April 1994.

[45] C. E. Shannon. "A mathematical theory of communication," *Bell System Technical Journal*, vol. 27, pp. 379–423, 623–656, 1948.

[46] C. E. Shannon. "Coding theorems for a discrete source with a fidelity criterion," *I.R.E. Nat. Conv. Rec.*, part 4, pp. 142–163, 1959.

[47] A. Shokrollahi. "Raptor codes," *IEEE Trans. Inform. Theory*, vol. 52, pp. 2551–2567, June 2006.

[48] G. Ungerboeck. "Channel coding with multilevel/phase signals," *IEEE Trans. Inform. Theory*, vol. 28, pp. 55–67, January 1982.

[49] N. Wiberg, H.-A. Loeliger, and R. Kötter. "Codes and iterative decoding on general graphs," *Eur. Trans. Telecommun.*, vol. 6, pp. 513–525, September–October 1995.

[50] S. Wicker. *Error Control Systems for Digital Communication and Storage*, Prentice-Hall, New Jersey, 1995.

Channel Modeling and Analysis for the Internet

Hayder Radha and Dmitri Loguinov

8.1 INTRODUCTION

Performance modeling and analysis of channels and networks play a crucial role
in the design and development of multimedia applications. In particular, having
an insight into the expected number of packet losses, which could occur when
sending video or audio content over the Internet, provides multimedia application
designers an important premise for developing resilience techniques to protect
that content. Furthermore, real-time multimedia applications are sensitive to end-
to-end delay parameters, including delay jitter. These parameters influence the
particular techniques used for recovering lost packets. For example, depending
on the application and its level of tolerance for end-to-end delay, the application
designer may choose to adopt a strategy for recovering lost packets that is based
on retransmission, Forward Error Correction (FEC), or both.

This chapter covers fundamental analysis tools that are used to characterize
the loss performance of channels and networks that carry multimedia packets.
We focus on models and analysis tools for Internet multimedia applications. In
addition to performance analysis and modeling tools, experimental performance
studies are crucial for designing multimedia applications and services. Hence, this
chapter consists of two major parts. The first part emphasizes core and relatively
simple analysis tools that lead to key results and widely used formulas. Although
some of these results and formulas are basic, rather abstract, and generic in nature
(i.e., applicable to a variety of applications), their use for performance analysis of
multimedia applications is invaluable. The second part of this chapter describes a
comprehensive Internet video study conducted for gaining insight into a variety of
end-to-end performance parameters that are crucial for real-time multimedia applications. The study reveals many interesting and practical issues, and it provides

significant insight that is difficult (if not impossible) to gain based on pure analysis or modeling. The later (second) part also analyzes the performance parameters collected from the aforementioned Internet video study.

The analytical tools needed for characterizing channels and networks lie within basic concepts from probability theory, random processes, and information theory. Here, it is assumed that the reader has the appropriate background in probability theory and random processes. We later focus on some of the key, basic and relevant concepts and definitions from information theory that can be used for characterizing Internet links and routes. For popular Internet multimedia applications, packet losses represent the most crucial performance parameter. The information theory concepts covered in this chapter identify *performance bounds* for given loss measures.

8.2 BASIC INFORMATION THEORY CONCEPTS OF CHANNEL MODELS

Information theory [1–3] provides core channel models that are used to represent a wide range of communication and networking scenarios. We begin by highlighting the information-theoretic definition of a discrete memoryless channel (DMC) and then focus on simple DMC channel models applicable to basic links and routes over the Internet (Figure 8.1).

A DMC is characterized by the relationship between its input X and its output Y, where X and Y are two (hopefully) dependent random variables. Therefore, a DMC is usually represented by the conditional probability $p(y|x)$ of the channel output Y given the channel input X. Furthermore, and since X and Y are dependent on each other, their mutual information $I(X; Y)$ has a nonzero (i.e., strictly positive) value,

$$I(X; Y) = \sum_x \sum_y p(x, y) \log \frac{p(x, y)}{p(x)p(y)} > 0.$$

An important measure is the maximum amount of information that Y can provide about X for a given channel $p(y|x)$. This measure can be evaluated by maximizing the mutual information $I(X; Y)$ over all possible sources characterized by the marginal probability mass function $p(x)$ of the channel input X. This maximum measure of the mutual information is known as the "information" channel capacity C:

$$C = \max_{p(x)} I(X; Y).$$

Based on this definition, the channel capacity C is a function of the parameters that characterize the conditional probability $p(y|x)$ between the channel input X and the channel output Y. The following section focuses on a particular channel.

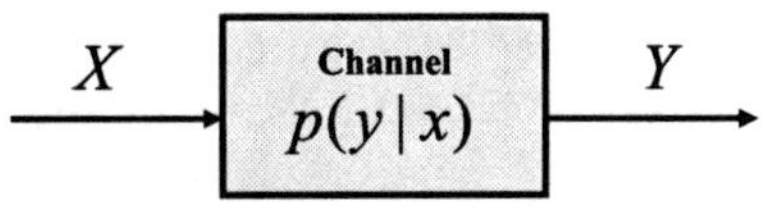

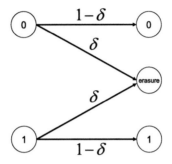

FIGURE 8.1:   A representation of a DMC channel.

FIGURE 8.2:   A representation of the Binary Erasure Channel.

8.2.1 The Binary Erasure Channel (BEC) Channel

The simplest DMC channel model that could be used for representing an Internet link or route is the Binary Erasure Channel (Figure 8.2). The BEC is characterized by the following.

- The input X is a binary (Bernoulli) random variable that can be either a zero or a one.
- A loss parameter δ, which represents the probability that the input is lost ("erased" or "deleted") when transmitted over the BEC channel.
- The output Y is a ternary random variable that could take on one of three possible values: zero, one, or "erasure." The latter output occurs when the channel loses the transmitted input X.

More specifically, a BEC is characterized by the conditional probability measures

$$\Pr\big[Y = \text{``}erasure\text{''} \mid X = 0\big] = \delta \quad \text{and} \quad \Pr\big[Y = \text{``}erasure\text{''} \mid X = 1\big] = \delta,$$
$$\Pr\big[Y = 0 \mid X = 0\big] = 1 - \delta \quad \text{and} \quad \Pr\big[Y = 1 \mid X = 1\big] = 1 - \delta,$$
$$\Pr\big[Y = 1 \mid X = 0\big] = 0 \quad \text{and} \quad \Pr\big[Y = 0 \mid X = 1\big] = 0.$$

Therefore, no errors occur over a BEC, as $\Pr[Y = 0 \mid X = 1] = \Pr[Y = 1 \mid X = 0] = 0$.

Due to the loss symmetry of the BEC (i.e., the conditional probability of losing a bit is independent of the bit value), it can be easily shown that the overall loss probability is also the parameter δ. In other words,

$$\Pr[Y = \text{``}erasure\text{''}] = \delta.$$

By using the definition of information channel capacity $C = \max_{p(x)} I(X; Y)$, it can be shown [1,2] that the channel capacity of the BEC is a rather intuitive expression,

$$C = 1 - \delta.$$

This capacity, which is measured in "bits" per "channel use," can be achieved when the channel input X is a uniform random variable with $\Pr[X = 0] = \Pr[X = 1] = 1/2$.

Despite its simplicity, the BEC provides a rough, yet very useful estimate of the maximum throughput one can achieve over an Internet link, or an end-to-end route between a server and a client. For example, if one measures the average packet loss probability over a link or route to be δ, then the throughput of the route is $1 - \delta$, which is the same as the capacity of a BEC with parameter δ. The next sections expand on the basic BEC channel in three aspects that provide more realistic modeling of practical links and routes: (1) cascaded channels, (2) channels with input vectors of bits (i.e., packets) rather than binary bits, and (3) channels with feedback from the receiver to the transmitter.

8.2.2 Cascaded BEC Channels

Packets that carry multimedia content usually traverse multiple links over a path between the source and the receiver. Hence, these links can be modeled as cascaded channels, and here we begin with cascaded BEC channels. First, let's assume that we have two BEC channels that are in cascade with each other. This, for example, could represent two Internet links over which multimedia packets are routed. The two BEC channels could have different loss probabilities,

$$\Pr[Y_1 = \text{``}erasure\text{''} \mid X_1] = \delta_1 \quad \text{and} \quad \Pr[Y_2 = \text{``}erasure\text{''} \mid X_2] = \delta_2,$$

where (X_1, Y_1) and (X_2, Y_2) are the input–output pairs for the first and second links, respectively. In this case, we know that the maximum throughput (as measured by the channel capacity) that can be received at the output Y_1 of the first channel is $C_1 = 1 - \delta_1$. Hence, the second link can be used only $(1 - \delta_1)$ fraction of the time. We also know that the maximum throughput of the second link is $C_2 = 1 - \delta_2$. Therefore, the overall throughput of the cascaded channel is

$C = (1 - \delta_1)(1 - \delta_2)$. This channel capacity assumes that the two channels are independent of each other and that both are DMC channels.

This result can be generalized to L cascaded links of BEC-independent channels. In this case, each link could have a different loss probability,

$$\Pr[Y_i = \text{"erasure"} \mid X_i] = \delta_i, \quad i = 1, 2, \ldots, L.$$

The overall channel capacity of the L cascaded BEC links is

$$C = \prod_{i=1}^{L}(1 - \delta_i).$$

This end-to-end path of L BEC channels is equivalent to a BEC channel with an effective end-to-end loss probability

$$\delta = 1 - \prod_{i=1}^{L}(1 - \delta_i).$$

Note that $C = 1 - \delta = 1 - (1 - \prod_{i=1}^{L}(1 - \delta_i))$. As in the single channel case, the capacity in this cascaded case is measured in bits per channel use. Moreover, the overall capacity C of the end-to-end route is bounded by the capacity $C_{\min}$ of the link with the smallest capacity among all cascaded channels in the route. In other words, $C \leq C_{\min} = \min_i(C_i)$. Hence, knowledge of the minimum capacity link provides an easy way for identifying the performance bound of the end-to-end route. As mentioned earlier, it is important to note that this bound is measured in terms of "per channel use." Therefore, $C_{\min}$ should not be confused by the "bottleneck" bandwidth $B_{\min}$ that is commonly referred to by the networking community. In this case, the bottleneck bandwidth usually represents the maximum transmission rate (e.g., 1.544 Megabits per second for a T1 line) that a particular link within the end-to-end path could support, and where this link has the minimum transmission rate: $B_{\min} = \min_i(B_i)$. Here, B_i can be thought of as the number of channel uses per second for link i. In general, a multimedia application must use a total rate R_{total} taking into consideration both the bottleneck bandwidth and the minimum end-to-end capacity. For example, let's assume that the transmission rates and link bandwidths are measured in bits per second. We also know that a BEC link is based on a "per channel use" where "channel use" is measured in bits (i.e., every time we use the BEC channel, we are transmitting a bit). Hence, the effective (maximum) throughput of a BEC link i in terms of bits per second can be expressed as $R_i = B_i C_i$. Hence, the total rate R_{total} used by an application should be bounded by the following effective performance throughput: $R_{\text{total}} \leq \min_i(R_i) = \min_i(B_i C_i)$ in bits per second.

8.2.3 The "Packet" Erasure Channel (PEC)

A simple generalization of the BEC is needed to capture the fact that multimedia content is usually packetized and transmitted over Internet links as "integrated vectors" of bits rather than individual bits. In other words, when a multimedia packet is lost, that packet is lost in its totality. Hence, for bits that belong to the same packet, these bits are 100% dependent on each other: either all the bits are transmitted successfully (usually without errors) or all the bits are erased (e.g., lost due to congestion).

We refer to this simple generalization as the Packet Erasure Channel. (In some literature, this type of channel may be referred to as an M-ary Erasure Channel as a generalization of the Binary Erasure Channel.) In this case, the input is a vector of random variables: $\overline{X} = (X_1, X_2, \ldots, X_n)$, where each element X_i is a binary random variable. The output of the channel includes the possible "erasure" outcome and all possible input vectors. In other words, we have the following conditional probability measures for the PEC:

$$\Pr\left[\,\overline{Y} = \text{``erasure''} \mid \overline{X}\,\right] = \delta \quad \text{and} \quad \Pr\left[\,\overline{Y} = \overline{X} \mid \overline{X}\,\right] = 1 - \delta.$$

Note that these conditional probability measures are independent of the particular input vector $\overline{X}$ (i.e., packet). Consequently, it is not difficult to show that the PEC has the same basic measures, such as channel capacity, as the BEC. Therefore, $C = 1 - \delta$. The capacity in this case is measured in "packets" per "channel use." Similarly, a cascade of L links of PEC channels has an effective loss probability $\delta = 1 - \prod_{i=1}^{L}(1 - \delta_i)$ and end-to-end capacity $C = 1 - \delta = 1 - (1 - \prod_{i=1}^{L}(1 - \delta_i)) = \prod_{i=1}^{L}(1 - \delta_i)$ in packets per channel use.

8.2.4 The BEC Channel with Feedback

It is quite common for many Internet applications, including multimedia ones, to support some form of feedback from the receiver to the transmitter. This could include feedback regarding requests for retransmissions of lost packets, a process that is commonly used in transport layer protocols such as TCP and in multimedia-specific variations of such protocols. For example, retransmissions of UDP/RTP packets carrying video or audio content are quite common over unicast Internet streaming sessions and are usually based on timely feedback from the receiver to the transmitter.

In this case, a crucial question is: what happens to the overall performance bounds of such channels with *feedback*? In particular, can we improve the maximum throughput or channel capacity C_{FB} by supporting feedback assuming that the feedback messages do not consume any of the capacity used in the forward direction (i.e., between the transmitter and the receiver)? Information theory provides an interesting and arguably a surprising answer [1,2]. For any discrete memoryless channel (DMC), including BEC and PEC channels, feedback does not improve (or worsen for that matter) the throughput/capacity performance of the channel: $C = C_{FB}$.

Therefore, the results listed earlier for the basic (without feedback) BEC and PEC channels are also applicable for these channels with feedback. For the scenario of cascaded BEC/PEC channels, this is true if the feedback is implemented on an end-to-end basis. Here, end-to-end feedback means that only the transmitter and the receiver are involved in the feedback (i.e., the final receiver node in the chain is providing feedback to the very first transmitter node without the involvement of any of the intermediate nodes in the feedback process). Hence, for cascaded BEC/PEC channels with feedback on an end-to-end basis, we have

$$C_{FB} = C = 1 - \delta = 1 - \left(1 - \prod_{i=1}^{L}(1 - \delta_i)\right) = \prod_{i=1}^{L}(1 - \delta_i).$$

However, if the feedback is done on a link-by-link basis, then the overall channel capacity of a cascaded set of links is bounded by the capacity of the "bottleneck" link. In other words, the capacity in this case is

$$C_{FB} = C_{\min} = \min_i(C_i) = \min_i(1 - \delta_i).$$

It is important to note that the relationship $C = C_{FB}$ (in the case of end-to-end feedback) does not imply that a multimedia application should not use feedback on an end-to-end basis. On the contrary, feedback is crucial for the following reason. End-to-end feedback helps an application achieve (or at least get close to) the end-to-end capacity $C_{FB} = \prod_{i=1}^{L}(1 - \delta_i)$, which may not be achievable "in practice" without feedback. It is well known, for example, that multimedia streaming applications could benefit from employing feedback to recover lost packets through retransmission. In particular, consider a case when a multimedia application is streaming a multimedia content that is coded with a (source) rate R packets per second. Let's assume that $R < BC$, where B is the available bandwidth (in packets per second) and C is the effective (end-to-end) capacity (in packets per use on an end-to-end basis). Hence, the probability of a packet loss is $\delta = 1 - C$. Therefore, without any feedback and retransmission, the effective throughput that the application can achieve is $R - \delta R = (1 - \delta)R$ packets per second. Naturally, $R > (1 - \delta)R$. However, if the application employs feedback with retransmission, then the application can recover the lost packets (assuming delay is not an issue), and consequently it can achieve a throughput of R packets per second (i.e., streaming the multimedia source reliably). In other words, feedback with retransmission can help the application use access bandwidth that is not being fully utilized by the application to achieve better reliability. Note that, in practice, even when the application (basic) source rate R is lower than the effective capacity, $R < BC$, packets will be lost, and therefore, retransmission can be very useful.

The aforementioned results for channel capacity with feedback are applicable to memoryless channels. Meanwhile, it has been well established that channels with memory could increase their capacity by employing feedback. The performance aspects of channels with memory are addressed next.

8.3 PACKET LOSSES OVER CHANNELS WITH MEMORY

Packet losses over Internet links and routes exhibit a high level of correlation and tend to occur in bursts. This observation, which has been well established by several Internet packet-loss studies, indicates that Internet links and routes exhibit memory. Consequently, although the DMC channel models discussed earlier could be useful for providing rough estimates of the loss behavior over the Internet, improved models are needed for more accurate estimates of the actual loss patterns. The most popular analysis and modeling tool used to capture memory is based on Markov chains. Channels that are modeled using Markov chains are sometimes referred to as Markov channels.

Bounds for the performance of channels with memory, including Markov channels, are significantly more difficult to derive and express as compared to DMC channels. In particular, performance bounds, such as capacity of channels with memory, do not have simple closed-form expressions as the case for DMC models. Recursive formulas for evaluating the channel capacity of general Markov channels have been developed though [4,5]. A special case of Markov channels is the Gilbert–Elliott channel, which consists of a two-state Markov chain. Recursive formulas for evaluating the channel capacity of the Gilbert–Elliott channel [4] and for (more general) finite-state Markov channels [5] have been developed.

This chapter focuses on the most basic (and probably most popular) Markov-based erasure channel model, which is the two-state Markov-state channel. This two-state Markov chain model of an erasure channel with memory is also known as the Gilbert model.

The Gilbert model of the two-state Markov chain is shown in Figure 8.3. Here, G and B represent the Good state and the Bad state, respectively. If the process (channel) is in the Good state, the transmitted packet is received without any errors; if the process is in the Bad state, the transmitted packets are lost (i.e., "erased"). At time zero, the system can start from the Good or the Bad state; this is known as the *initial state*. The system could also end in the Good or the Bad state.

This Gilbert channel is characterized by two parameters. A common parameter pair that is used for representing a Gilbert channel is the pair of transitional prob-

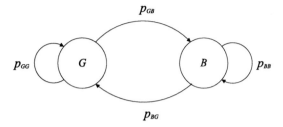

FIGURE 8.3:   State diagram of the Gilbert model.

abilities: p_{GB} and p_{BG}. These probabilities are conditional probabilities with the following interpretations. p_{GB} is the probability that the channel transits to the bad state given that the channel is in the good state. Similarly, p_{BG} is the probability that the channel transits to the good state given that the channel is in the bad state. From these two conditional probabilities, one can measure the other transitional probabilities of staying in the same state: $p_{GG} = 1 - p_{GB}$ and $p_{BB} = 1 - p_{BG}$.

From the transitional probabilities p_{GB} and p_{BG}, one can express the overall ("average") probability $\pi(G)$ of being in the good state and the overall probability $\pi(B)$ of being in the bad state:

$$\pi(G) = \frac{p_{BG}}{p_{GB} + p_{BG}} \quad \text{and} \quad \pi(B) = \frac{p_{GB}}{p_{GB} + p_{BG}}.$$

Note that the probability $\pi(B)$ of being in a bad state provides the average loss probability of the two-state Markov channel. In other words, $\pi(B)$ plays the same role as the loss probability δ of the BEC channel. However, while the BEC channel could be completely characterized by a single parameter (i.e., δ), the Gilbert model needs two parameters as highlighted earlier. Also note that $\pi(G) + \pi(B) = 1$.

An important performance measure for multimedia applications is the number of packets received given that the transmitter sends n packets over routes with memory. This measure, for example, could help application developers identify the level of resilience needed when transmitting a block of n video packets; this block of n packets may correspond to the number of packets in a Group of Pictures (GoP) of an MPEG stream. Another example could arise when the n packets may represent a Forward-Error-Correction (FEC) block with both k media data (e.g., video) packets and $(n - k)$ parity packets that are used to recover lost packets within the n-packet FEC block. Although there is no closed-form solution for the channel capacity of Markov channels, it is possible to derive closed-form expressions for certain probability measures of losses over these channels. We present a closed-form expression for the probability of receiving an arbitrary number i of packets when the transmitter sends n packets over a two-state Markov channel.

Let $\phi(n, i)$ be the probability that the sender transmits n packets over a Gilbert channel and the receiver correctly receives i packets. It can be shown [6,7] that this probability can be expressed as

$$\phi(n, i) = \pi(G)\left(\phi_{G_0 G_i}(n) + \phi_{G_0 B_i}(n)\right) + \pi(B)\left(\phi_{B_0 G_i}(n) + \phi_{B_0 B_i}(n)\right),$$

where

$$\phi_{G_0 G_i}(n) = \begin{cases} \sum_{m=1}^{i} \binom{i}{m}\binom{n-i-1}{m-1} p_{GB}^m p_{BG}^m p_{GG}^{i-m} p_{BB}^{n-i-m} & 0 < i < n, \\ 0 & i = 0, \\ p_{GG}^n & i = n, \end{cases}$$

$$\phi_{G_0 B_i}(n) = \begin{cases} \sum_{m=0}^{i} \binom{i}{m}\binom{n-i-1}{m} p_{GB}^{m+1} p_{BG}^m p_{GG}^{i-m} p_{BB}^{n-i-m-1} & 0 \le i < n, \\ 0 & i = n, \end{cases}$$

$$\phi_{B_0 G_i}(n) = \begin{cases} \sum_{m=0}^{i-1} \binom{i-1}{m}\binom{n-i}{m} p_{GB}^m p_{BG}^{m+1} p_{GG}^{i-m-1} p_{BB}^{n-i-m} & 0 < i \le n, \\ 0 & i = 0, \end{cases}$$

$$\phi_{B_0 B_i}(n) = \begin{cases} \sum_{m=0}^{i-1} \binom{i-1}{m}\binom{n-i}{m+1} p_{GB}^{m+1} p_{BG}^{m+1} p_{GG}^{i-m-1} p_{BB}^{n-m-i-1} & 0 < i < n, \\ p_{BB}^n & i = 0, \\ 0 & i = n. \end{cases}$$

Here, $\phi_{G_0 G_i}(n)$ is the probability that the sender transmits n packets and the receiver receives i packets given that the channel starts in a good state and ends in a good state. Similarly, interpretations can be inferred for $\phi_{G_0 B_i}(n)$, $\phi_{B_0 G_i}(n)$, and $\phi_{B_0 B_i}(n)$. For example, $\phi_{G_0 B_i}(n)$ is the probability that the sender transmits n packets and the receiver receives i packets given that the channel starts in a good state and ends in a bad state.

8.3.1 Packet Correlation over Channels with Memory

It is worth noting that the desired probability measure $\phi(n, i)$ can be completely evaluated using any two parameters that characterize the underlying Gilbert erasure channel. Traditionally, the transitional probabilities p_{GB} and p_{BG} (or $p_{GG} = 1 - p_{GB}$ and $p_{BB} = 1 - p_{BG}$) are used for such characterization.

A more useful insight and analysis can be gained by considering other parameter pairs. In particular, the average loss rate p and the *packet correlation* ρ can be used to represent the state transition probabilities, where $p_{GB} = p(1 - \rho)$ and $p_{BG} = (1 - p)(1 - \rho)$.

The steady-state probabilities are directly related to the average loss rate p: $\pi(G) = 1 - p$ and $\pi(B) = p$. The packet erasure correlation ρ provides an average measure of how the states of two consecutive packets are correlated to each other. In particular, when $\rho = 0$, the loss process is memoryless and the aforementioned probability measures reduce to the special case of a memoryless BEC. However, as the value of ρ increases, then the states of two consecutive packets become more and more correlated. Hence, we find that the parameters p and ρ provide an intuitive, insightful, and broad characterization for the impact of channel coding on networks with losses.

Figure 8.4 plots the probability that a receiver correctly receives i packets when the source send n packets over the Gilbert channel. Here, n is set to 30, the average loss rate p is set to 1%, and the packet correlation ρ is changed from 0 to 0.9. As compared with the Binomial model (where $\rho = 0$), we can see that as ρ increases, the probability of receiving a smaller number of packets increases. For a given ρ, as i increases, $\phi(n, i)$ increases exponentially; this increase slows down as ρ increases. When $\rho = 0.9$, we can see that $\phi(n, i)$ has a small spike at $i = 0$ and a big spike at $i = 30$. This observation is consistent with the analytical intuition; as the correlation is strong, once the process initially starts in a bad or a good state, it has the inertia to stay at that state. For $p = 0.01$ and $\rho = 0.9$, the transition probabilities are $p_{GG} = 0.999$, $p_{GB} = 0.001$, $p_{BG} = 0.099$, and $p_{BB} = 0.901$, respectively.

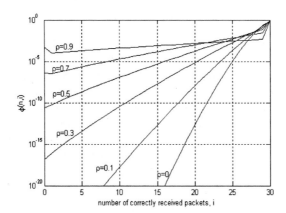

FIGURE 8.4: Probability of receiving i packets given that the transmitter sends $n = 30$ packets, for loss probability $p = 0.1$.

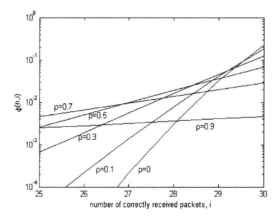

FIGURE 8.5:   A detailed view of the probability of receiving i packets given that the transmitter sends n packets.

Figure 8.5 is a detailed view when the received packets i changes from 25 to 30. Figure 8.5 shows that as the packet correlation increases, the probability of receiving a higher number of packets decreases.

8.3.2 Packet Losses over Cascaded Channels with Memory

As highlighted earlier, Internet routes and paths consist of multiple links that can be modeled as cascaded channels. Further, each of these links/channels usually exhibits memory. Hence, the case of cascaded channels with memory represents an important scenario for modeling the performance of Internet end-to-end paths. In this section, we extend the results of the aforementioned section while making the simplifying assumption that the cascaded links are independent of each other.

Let $\phi_j(n_j, i_j)$ be the probability of receiving i_j packets while transmitting n_j packets over a channel j with memory (e.g., a Markov channel). First, let's assume that we have only two channels that are cascaded with each other, and hence $j = 1, 2$. We are interested in measuring the probability $\phi(n, i)$ of receiving i packets at the output of these cascaded channels (i.e., the output of the second channel with index $j = 2$) when the transmitter sends n packets into the input of the first channel (i.e., the input of the first channel with index $j = 1$). Based on the notation adopted earlier, we have $n = n_1$, $i_1 = n_2$, and $i_2 = i$. Note that receiving $i_2 = i$ packets at the output of the second channel (which is the output of the overall two-cascaded channels) implies that the number of packets $n_2 = i_1$ transmitted into the input to the second channel, $j = 2$, must be at least $i_2 = i$; in other words, $n_2 = i_1 \geq i_2 = i$. Further, since $n \geq i_1$, $(n = n_1) \geq (n_2 = i_1) \geq (i_2 = i)$ (Figure 8.6).

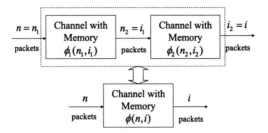

FIGURE 8.6:   A representation of the reception of i packets when transmitting n packets over two-cascaded channels with memory.

Hence, the desired probability $\phi(n, i)$ of receiving i packets at the output of these two cascaded channels when the transmitter sends n packets into the input of the first channel can be expressed as

$$\phi(n_1, i_2) = \sum_{i_1(=n_2)=i}^{n} \phi_1(n_1, i_1)\phi_2(n_2, i_2).$$

In other words,

$$\phi(n, i) = \sum_{i_1=i}^{n} \phi_1(n, i_1)\phi_2(i_1, i).$$

Hence, if the cascaded channels with memory are both Gilbert channels, then the desired probability of receiving i packets at the output of the second channel given that n packets are transmitted at the input of the first channel can be expressed as

$$\phi(n, i) = \sum_{i_1=i}^{n} \Big(\pi(G_1)\big(\phi_{1,G_0 G_{i_1}}(n) + \phi_{1,G_0 B_{i_1}}(n)\big)$$

$$+ \pi(B_1)\big(\phi_{1,B_0 G_{i_1}}(n) + \phi_{1,B_0 B_{i_1}}(n)\big)\Big)$$

$$\times \Big(\pi(G_2)\big(\phi_{2,G_0 G_i}(i_1) + \phi_{2,G_0 B_i}(i_1)\big)$$

$$+ \pi(B_2)\big(\phi_{2,B_0 G_i}(i_1) + \phi_{2,B_0 B_i}(i_1)\big)\Big).$$

Here, $\phi_{j,G_0 G_i}(n)$ $(\phi_{j,B_0 B_i}(n))$ is the probability that the transmitter sends n packets and the receiver receives i packets over the jth channel given that the channel begins and ends in a good (bad) state. Also, $\pi(G_j)$ $(\pi(B_j))$ is the probability that the jth channel is in a good (bad) state.

The aforementioned expressions for $\phi(n, i)$ over two-cascaded channels can be generalized to N channels with memory. In particular, one can infer the following probability of receiving i packets at the output of N cascaded channels with memory given that the transmitter sends n packets:

$$\phi(n, i) = \sum_{i_1=i} \sum_{i_2=i_1} \cdots \sum_{i_{N-1}=i_{N-2}} \phi_1(n, i_1)\phi_2(i_1, i_2) \cdots \phi_{N-1}(i_{N-2}, i_{N-1})$$
$$\times \phi_N(i_{N-1}, i).$$

A more compact representation of this probability is

$$\phi(n, i) = \sum_{i_1=i} \sum_{i_2=i_1} \cdots \sum_{i_{N-1}=i_{N-2}} \phi_1(n, i_1) \left(\prod_{j=2}^{N-1} \phi_j(i_{j-1}, i_j) \right) \phi_N(i_{N-1}, i).$$

8.4 WIDE-SCALE INTERNET STREAMING STUDY

8.4.1 Overview

The Internet is a complex interconnection of computer networks whose behavior and structure are usually challenging to measure. Numerous studies have attempted to shed light on the performance of the Internet; however, they traditionally examined backbone and campus-network characteristics and paid little attention to the conditions experienced by average home users during their daily activities. Among several traditional approaches, the Internet has been studied from the perspective of TCP connections by Paxson [27], Bolliger et al. [10], Caceres *et al.* [16], Mogul [25], and several others (e.g., [9]). Paxson's study included 35 geographically distributed sites in nine countries; Bolliger and colleagues employed 11 sites in seven countries and compared the throughput performance of various implementations of TCP during a 6-month experiment; whereas the majority of other researchers monitored transit TCP traffic at a single backbone router [8, 25] or inside several campus networks [16] for the duration ranging from several hours to several days. The methodology used in both large-scale TCP experiments [10,27] was similar and involved a topology where each participating site was paired with every other participating site for an FTP-like transfer. Although this setup approximates well the current use of TCP in the Internet, future entertainment-oriented streaming services, however, are more likely to involve a small number of backbone video servers and a large number of home users.

We should further mention that the Internet has been studied extensively by various researchers using ICMP `ping` and `traceroute` packets [8,17–19,26,27], UDP echo packets [11,14,15], and multicast backbone (MBone) audio packets

[35,36]. With the exception of the last one, similar observations apply to these studies—neither the setup nor the type of probe traffic represented realistic real-time streaming scenarios. Among the studies that specifically sent audio/video traffic over the Internet [12,13,20,21,32–34], the majority of experiments involved only a few Internet paths, lasted for a short period of time, and focused on analyzing the features of the proposed scheme rather than the impact of Internet conditions on real-time streaming.

In this work, we argue that studying network conditions observed by *regular users* is an important research topic and take a fundamentally different measurement approach that looks at Internet dynamics from the angle of Internet users rather than network operators. In our experiments, video streaming clients connect to the Internet through several dial-up ISPs in the United States and emulate the behavior of an average end user in the late 1990s and early 2000s.[1] In addition to choosing a different topological setup for the experiment, our work is different from the previous studies in the following three aspects. First, recall that the sending rate of a TCP connection is driven by its congestion control, which can sometimes cause increased packet loss and higher end-to-end delays in the path along which it operates (e.g., during slow start or after timeouts). In our experiment, we aimed to measure the *true* end-to-end path dynamics without the bias of congestion control applied to slow modem links. Our decision not to use congestion control was additionally influenced by the evidence that the majority of streaming traffic in the current Internet employs constant bit rate (CBR) video streams [30], where users explicitly select the desired streaming rate from content providers' Web pages. Second, TCP uses a positive ACK retransmission scheme, whereas current real-time applications (such as [30]) employ NACK-based retransmission to reduce the amount of traffic from users to streaming servers. As a consequence, end-to-end path dynamics perceived by a NACK-based protocol could differ from those sampled by TCP along the same path: real-time applications acquire samples of the round-trip delay (RTT) at rare intervals, send significantly less data along the path from the receiver to the sender, and bypass certain aspects of TCP's retransmission scheme (such as exponential timer backoff). Finally, TCP relies on window-based flow control, whereas real-time applications usually utilize rate-based flow control. In many video coding schemes, a real-time streaming server must maintain a certain target streaming rate for the decoder to avoid *underflow events*, which are caused by packets arriving after their decoding deadlines. As a result, a real-time sender may operate at different levels of packet

---

[1]Market research reports (e.g., [22,23,28]) show that in Q2 of 2001 approximately 89% of Internet-enabled U.S. households used dial-up access to connect to the Internet. As of March 2006, 34% of polled Americans used dial-up, many of whom had no plans or desire to switch to broadband [37]. Furthermore, countries with less developed network infrastructure are expected to experience dial-up-like (including high-latency satellite and cellular) Internet access for the foreseeable future.

burstiness and instantaneous sending rate than a TCP sender, as the sending rate of a TCP connection is governed by the arrival of positive ACKs from the receiver rather than by the application.

In what follows in the rest of this chapter, we present the methodology and analyze the results of a 7-month, large-scale, real-time streaming experiment that involved three nationwide dial-up ISPs, each with several million active subscribers in the United States. The topology of the experiment consisted of a backbone video server streaming MPEG-4 video sequences to unicast home users located in more than 600 major U.S. cities. The streaming was performed in real time (i.e., with a real-time decoder), utilized UDP for the transport of all messages, and relied on simple NACK-based retransmission to attempt recovery of lost packets before their decoding deadlines.

8.4.2 Methodology

8.4.2.1 Setup for the Experiment

We started our work by attaching a Unix video server to the UUNET backbone via a T1 link as shown in Figure 8.7. To support the clients' connectivity to the Internet, we selected three major nationwide dial-up ISPs: AT&T WorldNet, Earthlink, and IBM Global Network (which we call ISP_a, ISP_b, and ISP_c, respectively), each with at least 500 V.90 (i.e., 56 kb/s) dial-up numbers in the United States. Our experiment emulated the activity of hypothetical Internet users who dialed local access numbers to reach the Internet and streamed video sequences from a backbone server. Although the clients were physically located in our laboratory in the state of New York, they dialed long-distance phone numbers and connected to the Internet through ISPs' access points in each of the 50 states. Our database of phone numbers included 1813 different V.90 access numbers in 1188 major U.S. cities.

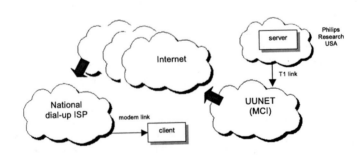

FIGURE 8.7:   Setup of the experiment.

After the phone database was in place, we designed and implemented special software, which we call the *dialer*, that dialed phone numbers from the database, connected to the ISPs using the point-to-point protocol (PPP), issued a *parallel traceroute* to the server, and, upon success, started the video client with the instructions to stream a 10-min video sequence from the server. Our implementation of traceroute (built into the dialer) used ICMP instead of the more traditional UDP, sent all probes in parallel instead of sequentially (hence the name "parallel"), and recorded the IP time-to-live (TTL) field of each returned "TTL-expired" message. The use of ICMP packets and parallel traceroute facilitated much quicker discovery of routers, and the analysis of the TTL field in the returned packets allowed the dialer to compute the number of hops in the reverse path from each intermediate router to the client machine using a simple fact that each router reset the TTL field of each generated "TTL-expired" packet to some default value. The majority of routers used the default TTL equal to 255, while some initialized the field to 30, 64, or 128. Subtracting the received TTL from the default TTL produced the number of hops along the reverse path. Using the information about the number of *forward* and *reverse* hops for each router, the dialer was able to detect asymmetric end-to-end paths, which is studied in Section 8.4.8.

In our analysis of data, we attempted to isolate clearly modem-related pathologies (such as packet loss caused by a poor connection over the modem link and large RTTs due to data-link retransmission) from those caused by congested routers of the Internet. Thus, connections that were unable to complete a traceroute to the server, those with high bit-error rates (BER), and those during which the modem could not sustain our streaming rates were all considered useless for our study and were excluded from the analysis in this section. In particular, we utilized the following methodology. We defined a streaming attempt through a given access number to be *successful* if the access point of the ISP was able to sustain the transmission of our video stream for its entire length at the stream's target IP bit rate r. Success was declared if the video client finished streaming while the *aggregate* (i.e., counting from the very beginning of a session) packet loss at all times t was below a certain threshold β_p and the *aggregate* incoming bit rate was above another threshold β_r. The experiments reported in this section used β_p equal to 15% and β_r equal to $0.9r$, whose combination was experimentally found to quite effectively filter out modem-related failures. The packet-loss threshold was activated after 1 min of streaming and the bit rate threshold after 2 min to make sure that slight fluctuations in packet loss and incoming bit rate at the beginning of a session were not mistaken for poor connection quality. After a session was over, the success or failure of the session was communicated from the video client to the dialer, the latter of which kept track of the time of day and the phone number that either passed or failed the streaming test.

In order to make the experiment reasonably short, we considered all phone numbers from the same state to be equivalent; consequently, we assumed that a successful streaming attempt through any phone number of a state indicated a successful coverage of the state regardless of which phone number was used. Furthermore, we divided each 7-day week into 56 three-hour timeslots (i.e., 8 time slots per day) and designed the dialer to select phone numbers from the database such that each state would be successfully covered within each of the 56 time slots at least once. In other words, each ISP needed to sustain exactly $50 \times 56 = 2800$ successful sessions before the experiment was allowed to end.

8.4.2.2 Real-Time Streaming

For the purpose of the experiment, we used an MPEG-4 encoder to create two 10-min QCIF (176×144) video streams coded at five frames per second (fps). The first stream, which we call S_1, was coded at the video bit rate of 14 kb/s, and the second steam, which we call S_2, was coded at 25 kb/s. The experiment with stream S_1 lasted during November–December 1999 and the one with stream S_2 was an immediate follow-up during January–May 2000.

During the transmission of each video stream, the server split it into 576-byte IP packets. Video frames always started on a packet boundary; consequently, the last packet in each frame was allowed to be smaller than others (in fact, many P [prediction-coded] frames were smaller than the maximum payload size and were carried in a single UDP packet). As a consequence of packetization overhead, the *IP bit rates* (i.e., including IP, UDP, and our special 8-byte headers) for streams S_1 and S_2 were 16.0 and 27.4 kb/s, respectively. The statistics of each stream are summarized in Table 8.1.

In our streaming experiment, the term *real time* refers to the fact that the video decoder was running in real time. Recall that each compressed video frame has a specific *decoding deadline*, which is usually based on the time of the frame's encoding. If a compressed video frame is not fully received by the decoder buffer at the time of its deadline, the video frame is discarded and an underflow event is registered. Moreover, to simplify the analysis of the results, we implemented a *strict* real-time decoder model, in which the playback of the arriving frames continued at the encoder-specified deadlines regardless of the number of underflow events (i.e., the decoding deadlines were not adjusted based on network conditions). Note that in practice, better results can be achieved by allowing the decoder to freeze the display and rebuffer a certain number of frames when underflow events become frequent (e.g., as done in [30]).

Table 8.1:   Summary of streams statistics.

Stream	Size, MB	Packets	Video bit rate, kb/s	Average frame size, bytes
S_1	1.05	4188	14.0	350
S_2	1.87	5016	25.0	623

In addition, many CBR video coding schemes include the notion of *ideal start-up delay* [29,30] (the delay is called "ideal" because it assumes a network with no packet loss and a constant end-to-end delay). This ideal delay must always be applied to the decoder buffer before the decoding process may begin. The ideal start-up delay is independent of the network conditions and solely depends on the decisions made by the encoder during the encoding process.[2] On top of this ideal start-up delay, the client in a streaming session must usually apply an *additional* start-up delay in order to compensate for delay jitter (i.e., variation in the one-way delay) and permit the recovery of lost packets via retransmission. This additional start-up delay is called the *delay budget* (D_{budget}) and reflects the values of the *expected* delay jitter and round-trip delay during the length of the session. Note that in the context of Internet streaming, it is common to call D_{budget} simply "start-up delay" and to completely ignore the ideal start-up delay (e.g., [21]). From this point on, we will use the same convention. In all our experiments, we used D_{budget} equal to 2700 ms, which was manually selected based on preliminary testing. Consequently, the total start-up delay (observed by an end user) at the beginning of each session was approximately 4 s.

8.4.2.3 Client–Server Architecture

For the purpose of our experiment, we implemented a client–server architecture for MPEG-4 streaming over the Internet. The server was fully multithreaded to ensure that the transmission of packetized video was performed at the target IP bit rate of each streaming session and to provide a quick response to clients' NACK requests. The streaming was implemented in bursts of packets (with the burst duration D_b varying between 340 and 500 ms depending on the bit rate) for the purposes of making the server as low overhead as possible (e.g., RealAudio servers have been reported to use $D_b = 1800$ ms [24]).

The second and the more involved part of our architecture, the client, was designed to recover lost packets through NACK-based retransmission and to collect extensive statistics about each received packet and each decoded frame. Furthermore, as it is often done in NACK-based protocols, the client was in charge of collecting round-trip delay samples. The measurement of RTTs involved the following two methods. In the first method, each successfully recovered packet provided a sample of the RTT, which was the duration between sending a NACK and receiving the corresponding retransmission. In our experiment, in order to avoid the ambiguity of which retransmission of the same packet actually returned to the client, the header of each NACK request and each retransmitted packet contained an extra field specifying the retransmission sequence number of the packet.

---

[2] We will not elaborate further on the ideal start-up delay, except to mention that it was approximately 1300 ms for each stream.

The second method of measuring the RTT was used by the client to obtain *additional* samples of the round-trip delay in cases where network packet loss was too low. The method involved periodically sending *simulated* retransmission requests to the server if packet loss was below a certain threshold. In response to these simulated NACKs, the server included the usual overhead of fetching the needed packets from the storage and sending them to the client.[3] In our experiment, the client activated simulated NACKs, spaced 30 seconds apart, if packet loss was below 1%.

We tested the software and the concept of a wide-scale experiment of this sort for 9 months before we felt comfortable with the setup, the reliability of the software, and the exhaustiveness of the collected statistics. In addition to extensive testing of the prototype, we monitored various statistics reported by the clients in real time (i.e., on the screen) during the experiments for sanity and consistency with previous tests. Overall, the work reported in this section took us 16 months to complete.

Our traces consist of six datasets, each collected by a different machine. Throughout this section, we use notation D_n^x to refer to the dataset collected by the client assigned to ISP$_x$ $(x = a, b, c)$ during the experiment with stream S_n $(n = 1, 2)$. Furthermore, we use notation D_n to refer to the combined set $\{D_n^a \cup D_n^b \cup D_n^c\}$.

8.4.3 Overview of Experimental Results

In dataset D_1, the three clients performed 16,783 long-distance connections to the ISPs' remote modems and successfully completed 8429 streaming sessions. Typical reasons for failing a session were PPP-layer connection problems, inability to reach the server (i.e., failed traceroute), high bit-error rates, and low (14.4–19.2 kb/s) modem connection rates. In D_2, the clients performed 17,465 connections and sustained 8423 successful sessions. In dataset D_1, the clients traced the arrival of 37.7 million packets, and in D_2, the arrival of an additional 47.3 million (for a total of 85 million). In terms of bytes, the first experiment transported 9.4 GB of video data and the second one transported another 17.7 GB (for a total of 27.1 GB).

Recall that each experiment lasted as long as it was needed to cover the entire United States. Depending on the success rate within each state, the access points used in the experiment comprised a subset of our database. In D_1, the experiment covered 962 dial-up points in 637 U.S. cities, and in D_2, it covered 880 dial-up points in 575 U.S. cities. Figure 8.8 shows the per-state distribution of the number

---

[3]Server overhead was below 10 ms for all retransmitted packets and did not have a major impact on our characterization of the RTT process later in this section.

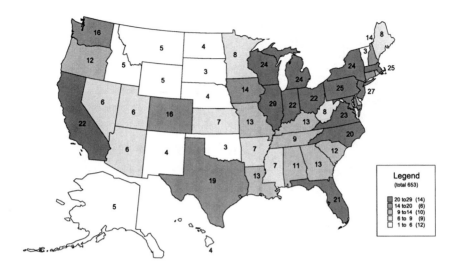

FIGURE 8.8:   The number of unique cities per state that participated in both experiments (i.e., in $\{D_1 \cup D_2\}$).

of distinct cities in each state covered by both experiments, which represents 1003 access points in 653 cities.

Analysis of the success rates observed during the experiment suggests that in order to receive real-time streaming material at 16 to 27.4 kb/s, an average U.S. end user equipped with a V.90 modem needs to make approximately two dialing attempts to his/her local ISPs. The success rate of streaming sessions during the different times of the day is illustrated in Figure 8.9 (top). Note the dip by a factor of two between the best (i.e., 12–3 a.m.) and the worst (i.e., 9 p.m.–12 a.m.) times of the day.

During this measurement study, each session was preceded by a parallel trace-route that recorded the IP addresses of all discovered routers (DNS and WHOIS lookups were done off-line after the experiments were over). The average time needed to trace an end-to-end path was 1731 ms, with 90% of the paths traced under 2.5 s and 98% under 5 s. Dataset D_1 recorded 3822 distinct Internet routers, D_2 recorded 4449 distinct routers, and both experiments combined produced the IP addresses of 5266 unique router interfaces. The majority of the discovered routers belonged to the ISPs' networks (51%) and UUNET (45%), which confirmed our intuition that all three ISPs had direct peering connections with UUNET. Interestingly, the traces showed approximately 200 routers that belonged to five additional Autonomous Systems (AS), indicating that certain end-to-end paths were routed across additional ISPs.

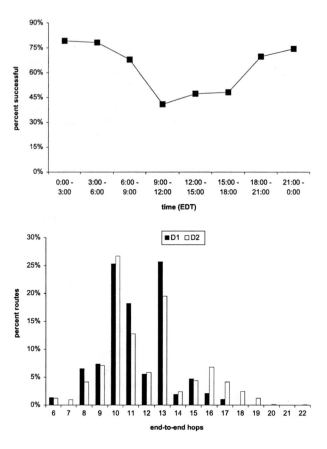

FIGURE 8.9:   Success of streaming attempts during the day (top). Distribution of the number of end-to-end hops (bottom).

The average end-to-end hop count was 11.3 in D_1 (6 minimum and 17 maximum) and 11.9 in D_2 (6 minimum and 22 maximum). Figure 8.9 (bottom) shows the distribution of the number of hops in the encountered end-to-end paths in each of D_1 and D_2. As Figure 8.9 shows, the majority of paths (75% in D_1 and 65% in D_2) contained between 10 and 13 hops.

Throughout the rest of the section, we restrict ourselves to studying only *successful* (as defined earlier) sessions in both D_1 and D_2. We call these new *purged* datasets with only successful sessions D_{1p} and D_{2p}, respectively (purged datasets D_{np}^x are defined similarly for $n = 1, 2$ and $x = a, b, c$). Recall that $\{D_{1p} \cup D_{2p}\}$ contains 16,852 successful sessions, which are responsible for 90% of the bytes and packets, 73% of the routers, and 74% of the U.S. cities recorded in $\{D_1 \cup D_2\}$.

8.4.4 Packet Loss

8.4.4.1 Overview

Numerous studies have focused on Internet packet loss; however, due to the enormous diversity of the Internet, only a few of them agree on the average packet loss rate or the average loss-burst length (i.e., the number of packets lost in a row). Among prior conclusions, the average Internet packet loss was reported to vary between 11 and 23% by Bolot [11] depending on the inter-packet transmission spacing, between 0.36 and 3.54% by Borella *et al.* [14,15] depending on the studied path, between 1.38 and 11% by Yajnik *et al.* [36] depending on the location of the MBone receiver, and between 2.7 and 5.2% by Paxson [27] depending on the year of the experiment. In addition, 0.49% average packet loss rate was reported by Balakrishnan *et al.* [9], who analyzed the dynamics of a large number of TCP Web sessions at a busy Internet server.

In dataset D_{1p}, the average recorded packet loss rate was 0.53% and in D_{2p}, it was 0.58%. Even though these rates are much lower than those traditionally reported by Internet researchers during the last decade due to the much lower transmission rates used in our study, they are still much higher than those advertised by backbone ISPs (i.e., 0.01–0.1%). We thus speculate that the majority of loss occurred at the "edges" of the Internet rather than at its core. Approximately 38% of the sessions in $\{D_{1p} \cup D_{2p}\}$ did not experience any packet loss, 75% experienced loss rates below 0.3%, and 91% experienced loss rates below 2%. However, 2% of the sessions suffered packet loss rates 6% or higher.

As expected, average packet loss rates exhibited a wide variation during the day. Figure 8.10 (top) shows the evolution of loss rates as a function of the time slot (i.e., the time of day), where each point represents the average of approximately 1000 sessions. As Figure 8.10 shows, the variation in loss rates between the best (3–6 a.m.) and the worst (3–6 p.m.) times of the day was by a factor of two in D_{1p} and by a factor of three in D_{2p}. The apparent discontinuity between time slots 7 (21:00–0:00) and 0 (0:00–3:00) is due to a coarse timescale in Figure 8.10 (top). On finer timescales (e.g., minutes), loss rates converge to a common value near midnight. A similar discontinuity in packet loss rates was reported by Paxson [27] for North American sites, where packet loss during time slot 7 was approximately twice as high as that during time slot 0.

The average *per-state* packet loss shown in Figure 8.10 (bottom) varied quite substantially from 0.2% in Idaho to 1.4% in Oklahoma, but virtually did not depend on the state's average number of end-to-end hops to the server (correlation coefficient ρ was -0.04) or the state's average RTT (correlation -0.16). However, as discussed later, the average per-state RTT and the number of end-to-end hops were, in fact, positively correlated.

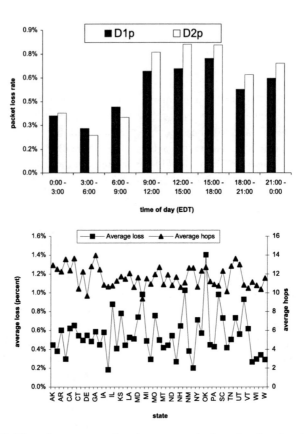

FIGURE 8.10:   Average packet loss rates during the day (top). Average per-state packet loss rates (bottom).

8.4.4.2 Loss Burst Lengths

We next attempt to answer the question of how bursty Internet packet loss was during the experiment. Figure 8.11 (top) shows the distribution (both the histogram and the CDF) of loss-burst lengths in $\{D_{1p} \cup D_{2p}\}$. Note that Figure 8.11 stops at burst length 20, which covers more than 99% of the bursts. Even though the upper tail of the distribution had very few samples, it was fairly long and reached burst lengths of over 100 packets.

Figure 8.11 (top) is based on 207,384 loss bursts and 431,501 lost packets. The prevalence of single-packet losses, given the fact that the traffic in our experiment was injected into the Internet in bursts at the T1 speed, leads to one possibility that router queues sampled in our experiment predominantly overflowed

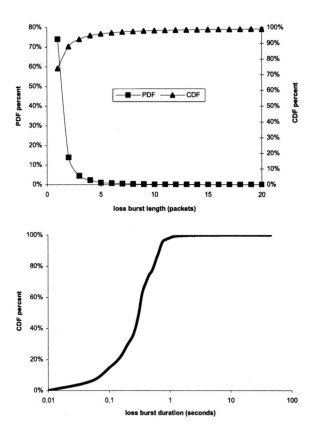

FIGURE 8.11: Histogram (PDF) and CDF functions of loss-burst lengths in $\{D_{1p} \cup D_{2p}\}$ (top). The CDF function of loss-burst durations in $\{D_{1p} \cup D_{2p}\}$ (bottom).

on timescales smaller than the time needed to transmit a single IP packet over a T1 link (i.e., 3 ms for the largest packets and 1.3 ms for the average-size packets). However, interference of cross-traffic between video packets at prebottleneck routers (i.e., which causes expansion of interpacket dispersion) or usage of RED makes it much more difficult to accurately assess the duration of loss events inside routers. To investigate the presence of RED in the Internet, we contacted several backbone and dial-up ISPs whose routers were recorded in our trace and asked them to comment on the deployment of RED in their backbones. Among the ISPs that responded to our request, the majority had purposely disabled RED and the others were running RED only for select customers at border routers, but not on the public backbone. Ruling out RED, another difficulty of computing the duration of congestion-related loss at routers is the fact that single-packet losses were underrepresented in our traces, as packets that were lost in bursts longer than one packet could have been dropped by *different* routers along the path from the server to the client. Therefore, using end-to-end measurements, an application cannot distinguish between n ($n \geq 2$) single-packet losses at n different routers from an n-packet bursty loss at a single router. Both types of loss events appear identical to an end-to-end application even though the underlying cause is quite different. Consequently, we conclude that even though the analysis of our datasets points toward transient (i.e., 1–3 ms) buffer overflows in the Internet routers sampled by our experiment, a more detailed study is needed to verify this finding and sample packet-loss durations at individual routers.

As previously pointed out by many researchers, the upper tail of loss-burst lengths usually contains a substantial percentage of all lost packets. In each of D_{1p} and D_{2p}, single-packet bursts contained only 36% of all lost packets, bursts 2 packets or shorter contained 49%, bursts 10 packets or shorter contained 68%, and bursts 30 packets or shorter contained 82%. At the same time, 13% of all lost packets were dropped in bursts at least 50 packets long.

Traditionally, the burstiness of packet loss is measured by the average loss-burst length. In dataset D_{1p}, the average burst length was 2.04 packets. In dataset D_{2p}, the average burst length was slightly higher (2.10), but not high enough to conclude that the higher bit rate of stream S_2 was clearly responsible for burstier packet loss. Furthermore, the *conditional probability* of packet loss, given that the previous packet was also lost, was 51% in D_{1p} and 53% in D_{2p}. These numbers are consistent with those previously reported in the literature. Bolot [11] observed the conditional probability of packet loss to range from 18 to 60% depending on interpacket spacing during transmission, Borella *et al.* [15] from 10 to 35% depending on the time of day, and Paxson [27] reported 50% conditional probability for *loaded* (i.e., queued behind the previous) TCP packets and 25% for *unloaded* packets. Using Paxson's terminology, the majority of our packets were *loaded* since the server sent packets in bursts at a rate higher than the bottleneck link's capacity.

8.4.4.3 Loss Burst Durations

To a large degree, the average loss-burst length depends on how closely the packets are spaced during transmission. Assuming that bursty packet loss comes from buffer overflows in drop-tail queues rather than from consecutive hits by RED or from bit-level corruption, it is clear that all packets of a flow passing through an overflown router queue will be dropped for the duration of the instantaneous congestion. Hence, the closer together the flow's packets arrive to the router, the more packets will be dropped during each queue overflow. This fact was clearly demonstrated in Bolot's [11] experiments, where UDP packets spaced 8 ms apart suffered larger loss-burst lengths (mean 2.5 packets) than packets spaced 500 ms apart (mean 1.1 packets). Yajnik *et al.* [36] reported a similar correlation between loss-burst lengths and the distance between packets. Consequently, instead of analyzing burst lengths, one might consider measuring burst durations in time units since the latter does not depend on interpacket spacing during transmission.

Using our traces, we can only infer an approximate duration of each loss burst because we do not know the *exact* time when the lost packets were supposed to arrive to the client. Hence, for each loss event, we define the *loss-burst duration* as the time elapsed between the receipt of the packet immediately preceding the loss burst and the packet immediately following it. Figure 8.11 (bottom) shows the distribution (CDF) of loss-burst durations in seconds. Although the distribution tail is quite long (up to 36 s), the majority (more than 98%) of loss-burst durations in both datasets D_{1p} and D_{2p} fall under 1 s. We speculate that some of this effect was caused by data-link retransmission on the modem link, which may also be responsible for large delays in modern wireless and satellite networks. Paxson's [27] study similarly observed large loss-burst durations (up to 50 s); however, only 60% of loss bursts studied by Paxson were contained below 1 s. In addition, our traces showed that the average distance between lost packets in the experiment was 172–188 good packets, or 21–27 s, depending on the streaming rate.

8.4.4.4 Heavy Tails

In conclusion of this section, it is important to note that packet losses sometimes cannot be modeled as independent events due to buffer overflows that last long enough to affect multiple adjacent packets. Consequently, future real-time protocols should expect to deal with bursty packet losses (Figure 8.11) and possibly heavy-tailed distributions of loss-burst lengths (see later). Several researchers reported a heavy-tailed nature of loss-burst lengths with shape parameter α of the Pareto distribution fitted to the length (or duration) of loss bursts ranging from 1.06 [8] to 2.75 [15]. However, Yajnik *et al.* [36] partitioned the collected data into empirically chosen stationary segments and reported that loss-burst lengths could be modeled as exponential (i.e., not heavy-tailed) within each stationary segment.

Using intuition, it is clear that packet loss and RTT random processes in both D_{1p} and D_{2p} are expected to be nonstationary. For example, the nonstationarity can be attributed to the time of day or the location of the client. In either case, we see three approaches to modeling such nonstationary data. In the first approach, one would analyze 16,852 CDF functions (one for each session) for stationarity and heavy tails. Unfortunately, an average session contained only 24 loss bursts, which was insufficient to build a good distribution function for statistical analysis.

The second approach would be to combine all sessions into groups that are intuitively perceived to be stationary (e.g., according to the access point or the time slot) and then perform similar tests for stationarity and heavy tails within each group. We might consider this direction for future work. The third approach is to assume that all data samples belong to some stationary process and are drawn from a single distribution, which is commonly performed by researchers for simplicity of analysis. Using the last approach, Figure 8.12 (top) shows a log–log plot of the complementary CDF function from Figure 8.11 (top) with a least-squares

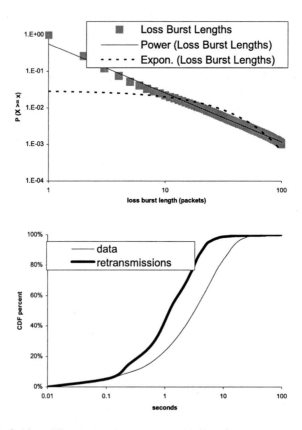

FIGURE 8.12: The complementary CDF of loss-burst lengths in $\{D_{1p} \cup D_{2p}\}$ on a log–log scale fitted with hyperbolic (straight line) and exponential (dotted curve) distributions (top). CDF functions of the amount of time by which retransmitted and data packets were late for decoding (bottom).

fit of a straight line representing a heavy-tailed distribution (the dotted curve is the exponential distribution fitted to data). The fit of a straight line is quite good (with correlation $\rho = 0.99$) and provides a strong indication that the distribution of loss-burst lengths in the combined dataset $\{D_{1p} \cup D_{2p}\}$ is heavy tailed. However, the exponential distribution in Figure 8.12 (top) decays too quickly to even remotely fit the data.

Finally, consider a Pareto distribution with CDF $F(x) = 1 - (\beta/x)^{\alpha}$ and PDF $f(x) = \alpha\beta^{\alpha}x^{-\alpha-1}$, where α is the shape parameter and β is the location parameter. Using Figure 8.12 (top), we establish that a Pareto distribution with $\alpha = 1.34$ (finite mean, but infinite variance) and $\beta = 0.65$ fits our data very well.

8.4.5 Underflow Events

The impact of packet losses on real-time applications is understood fairly well. Each lost packet that is not recovered before its deadline causes an underflow event. In addition to packet loss, real-time applications suffer from large end-to-end delays. However, not all types of delay are equally important to real-time applications. As shown later, one-way delay jitter was responsible for 90 times more underflow events in our experiment than packet loss combined with large RTTs.

Delays are important for two reasons. First, large round-trip delays make retransmissions late for their decoding deadlines. However, the RTT is important only to the extent of recovering lost packets and, in the worst case, can cause only *lost* packets to be late for decoding. However, delay jitter (i.e., one-way delay variation) can potentially cause each *data* (i.e., nonretransmitted) packet to be late for decoding. In $\{D_{1p} \cup D_{2p}\}$, packet loss affected 431,501 packets, out of which 159,713 (37%) were discovered to be missing *after* their decoding deadlines had passed. As a result, NACKs were not sent for these packets. Out of 271,788 remaining lost packets, 257,065 (94.6%) were recovered before their deadlines, 9013 (3.3%) arrived late, and 5710 (2.1%) were never recovered. The fact that more than 94% of "recoverable" lost packets were actually received before their deadlines indicates that retransmission is a very effective method of overcoming packet loss in real-time applications. Clearly, the success rate will be even higher in networks with smaller RTTs or applications with larger start-up delays. In fact, these results can be used to properly select D_{budget} for applications operating in similar network conditions to ensure the desired level of lost-packet recovery.

Before studying underflow events caused by delay jitter, we introduce two types of late retransmissions. The first type consists of packets that arrived after the decoding deadline of the last frame of the corresponding GoP. These packets were *completely* useless and were discarded. The second type of late packets, which we call *partially late*, consists of those packets that missed their *own* decoding deadline, but arrived before the deadline of the last frame of the same GOP. Since the video decoder in our experiment could decompress frames at a substantially higher rate than the target fps, the client was able to use partially late packets for motion-compensated reconstruction of the remaining frames from the same GOP before *their* corresponding decoding deadlines. Out of 9013 late retransmissions, 4042 (49%) were partially late. Using each partially late packet, the client was able to save on average 4.98 frames from the same 10-frame GOP in D_{1p} and 4.89 frames in D_{2p} by employing the catch-up technique described earlier (for more discussion, see [31]).

In contrast to 174,436 underflows caused by packet loss, one-way delay jitter was responsible for 1,167,979 underflows in *data* (i.e., nonretransmitted) packets. Hence, the total number of packets missing at the time of decoding was $174,436 + 1,167,979 = 1,342,415$ (1.7% of the number of sent packets), which means that 87% of underflow packets were produced by large one-way delay jitter rather than by packet loss. Even if the clients had not attempted to recover any of the 431,501 lost packets, 73% of the missing packets at the time of decoding would have been caused by large delay jitter. In terms of user-perceived metrics, 1.3 million underflow packets caused a freeze-frame effect on average for 10.5 s per 10-min session in D_{1p} and 8.6 s in D_{2p}, which can be considered excellent given the small amount of delay budget used in the experiments.

To further understand the phenomenon of late packets, Figure 8.12 (bottom) plots the CDFs of the amount of time by which late packets missed their deadlines (i.e., the amount of time that was needed to add to delay budget $D_{\text{budget}} = 2700$ ms in order to avoid a certain percentage of underflow events). As Figure 8.12 shows, 25% of late retransmissions missed their deadlines by more than 2.6 s, 10% by more than 5 s, and 1% by more than 10 s (the tail of the CDF extends up to 98 s). At the same time, one-way delay jitter had a more adverse impact on data packets: 25% of late data packets missed their deadlines by more than 7 s, 10% by more than 13 s, and 1% by more than 27 s (the CDF tail extends up to 56 s).

One common way of reducing the number of late packets caused by large RTTs and delay jitter is to apply a higher start-up delay D_{budget} at the beginning of a session. An additional approach is to freeze the display and effectively increase the start-up delay during the session as need arises. The final approach works for streaming prerecorded content and allows the receiver to request that the server transmit video traffic at a faster-than-ideal bit rate at certain times to compensate for delayed packets and to increase the amount of buffered frames at the decoder (available bandwidth permitting). Using a strict no-freeze model of this work, only the first approach was viable, which would require a 13-s total delay budget to save 99% of late retransmissions and 84% of late data packets under similar streaming conditions.

8.4.6 Round-Trip Delay

8.4.6.1 Overview

We should mention that circuit-switched long-distance links through PSTN between our clients and remote access points did not significantly influence the measured end-to-end delays because the additional delay on each long-distance link was essentially the propagation delay between New York and the location of the access point. Since the propagation delay is determined by the speed of light and geographic distance, most links experienced bias of no more than approximately 32 ms, which is the round-trip delay of a 3000-mile link. Clearly, this delay is negligible compared to the queuing and transmission delays experienced by our packets along the entire end-to-end path. Figure 8.13 (top) shows

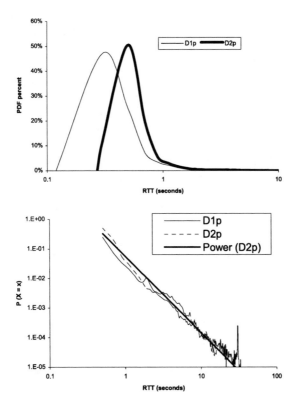

FIGURE 8.13: Histograms (PDF) of RTT samples in each of D_{1p} and D_{2p} (top). Log–log plot of the upper tails of the RTT histogram. The straight line is fitted to D_{2p} (bottom).

the histogram of round-trip delays in each of D_{1p} and D_{2p} (660,439 RTT samples in both datasets). Although the tail of the combined distribution reached the enormous values of 126 s for *simulated* and 102 s for *real* retransmissions, the majority (75%) of the samples were below 600 ms, 90% below 1 s, and 99.5% below 10 s. The average RTT was 698 ms in D_{1p} and 839 ms in D_{2p}. The minimum RTT was 119 and 172 ms, respectively. Although very rare, extremely high RTTs were found in all six datasets $D_{1p}^a - D_{2p}^c$. Out of more than 660,000 RTT samples in $\{D_{1p} \cup D_{2p}\}$, 437 were at least 30 s, 32 at least 50 s, and 20 at least 75 s.

Although pathologically high RTTs may seem puzzling at first, there is a simple explanation. Modem error correction protocols (i.e., the commonly used V.42) implement retransmission for corrupted blocks of data at the physical or data-link layer.[4] Error correction is often necessary if modems negotiated data compression (i.e., V.42bis) over the link and is desirable if the PPP Compression Control Protocol is enabled on the data-link layer. In all our experiments, both types of compression were enabled, imitating the typical setup of a home user. Therefore, if a client established a connection to a remote modem at a low bit rate (which was sometimes accompanied by a significant amount of noise in the phone line), each retransmission at the physical layer took a long time to complete before data were delivered to the upper layers. In addition, large IP-level buffers on either side of the modem link further delayed packets arriving to or originating from the client host.

Note that the purpose of classifying sessions into failed and successful in Section 8.4.2.1 was to avoid reporting pathological conditions caused by modem links. Since less than 0.5% of RTTs in $\{D_{1p} \cup D_{2p}\}$ were seriously affected by modem-level retransmission and bit errors (i.e., had RTTs higher than 10 s), we conclude that our heuristic was successful in filtering out the majority of pathological connections and that future application-layer protocols running over a modem link should be prepared to experience RTTs on the order of several seconds.

8.4.6.2 Heavy Tails

Mukherjee [26] reported that RTTs along certain Internet paths could be modeled by a shifted gamma distribution. Even though the shape of the PDF in Figure 8.13 (top) resembles that of a gamma function, the distribution tails in Figure 8.13 decay much slower than those of an exponential distribution (see later). Using our approach from Section 8.4.4.4 (i.e., assuming that each studied Internet random

---

[4]Since the telephone network beyond the local loop in the United States is mostly digital, we believe that dialing long-distance numbers had no significant effect on the number of bit errors during the experiment.

process is stationary), we extracted the upper tails of the PDF functions in Figure 8.13 (top) and plotted the results on a log–log scale in Figure 8.13 (bottom). Figure 8.13 shows that a straight line (without loss of generality fitted to the PDF of D_{2p} in the figure) provides a good fit to data (correlation 0.96) and allows us to model the upper tails of both PDF functions as a Pareto distribution with PDF $f(x) = \alpha \beta^\alpha x^{-\alpha-1}$, where shape parameter α equals 1.16 in dataset D_{1p} and 1.58 in D_{2p} (as before, the distribution has a finite mean, but an infinite variance).

8.4.6.3 Variation of the RTT

We conclude the discussion of the RTT by showing that it exhibited a variation during the day similar to that of packet loss shown previously in Figure 8.10 (top) and that the average RTT was correlated positively with the length of the corresponding end-to-end path. Figure 8.14 (top) shows the average round-trip

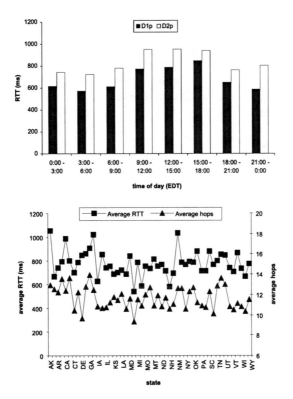

FIGURE 8.14: Average RTT as a function of the time of day (top). Average RTT and average hop count in each of the states in $\{D_{1p} \cup D_{2p}\}$ (bottom).

delay during each of the eight time slots of the day (as before, each point in Figure 8.14 represents the average of approximately 1000 sessions). Figure 8.14 confirms that the worst time for sending traffic over the Internet is between 9 a.m. and 6 p.m. EDT and shows that the increase in the delay during peak hours is relatively small (i.e., by 30–40%).

Figure 8.14 (bottom) shows the average RTT sampled by the clients in each of the 50 U.S. states. The average round-trip delay was consistently high (i.e., above 1 s) for three states: Alaska, New Mexico, and Hawaii. However, the RTT was consistently low (below 600 ms) also for three states: Maine, New Hampshire, and Minnesota. These results, except Minnesota, can be directly correlated with the distance from New York; however, in general, we found that the geographical distance of the access point from the East Coast had little effect on the average RTT. For example, certain states in the Midwest had small (600–800 ms) average round-trip delays and certain states on the East Coast had large (800–1000 ms) average RTTs. A more substantial link can be established between the number of end-to-end hops and the average RTT, as shown in Figure 8.14 (bottom). Even though the average RTT of many states did not exhibit a clear dependency on the average length of the path, the correlation between the RTT and the number of hops in Figure 8.14 (bottom) was reasonably high with $\rho = 0.52$. This result was intuitively expected, as the RTT is essentially the sum of queuing and transmission delays at intermediate routers.

8.4.7 Delay Jitter

As discussed earlier, in certain streaming situations round-trip delays are much less important to real-time applications than one-way delay jitter because the latter can potentially cause significantly more underflow events. In addition, due to asymmetric path conditions (i.e., uneven congestion in the upstream and downstream directions), large RTTs are not necessarily an indication of bad network conditions for a NACK-based application. In many sessions with high RTTs during the experiment, the outage was caused by the upstream path, while the downstream path did not suffer from extreme one-way delay variation and data packets were arriving to the client throughout the entire duration of the outage. Hence, we conclude that the RTT is not necessarily a good indicator of a session's quality during streaming and that one-way delay jitter should be used instead.

Assuming that delay jitter is defined as the difference between one-way delays of each two consecutively sent packets, an application can sample both positive and negative values of delay jitter. Negative values are produced by two types of packets—those that suffered a *packet compression event* (i.e., the packets' arrival spacing was smaller than their transmission spacing) and those that became reordered. The former case is of great interest in packet-pair bandwidth estimation studies and otherwise remains relatively unimportant. The latter case is studied in Section 8.4.8 under packet reordering. However, positive values of delay jitter represent *packet expansion events*, which are responsible for late packets. Consequently, we analyzed the distribution of only *positive* delay jitter samples and found that although the highest sample was 45 s, 97.5% of the samples were less than 140 ms and 99.9% under 1 s. As the aforementioned results show, large values of delay jitter were not frequent, but once a packet was significantly delayed by the network, a substantial number of the following packets were delayed as well, creating a "snowball" of underflows. This fact explains the large number of underflow events reported in previous sections, even though the overall delay jitter was relatively low.

8.4.8 Packet Reordering

8.4.8.1 Overview

Real-time protocols often rely on the assumption that packet reordering in the Internet is a rare and insignificant event for all practical purposes (e.g., [21]). Although this assumption simplifies the design of a protocol, it also makes the protocol poorly suited for use over the Internet. Certainly, there are Internet paths along which reordering is either nonexistent or extremely rare. At the same time, there are paths that are dominated by multipath routing effects and often experience reordering (e.g., Paxson [27] reported a session with 36% of packets arriving out of order).

Unfortunately, there is not much data documenting reordering rates experienced by IP traffic over modem links. Using intuition, we expected reordering in our experiments to be extremely rare given the low bit rates of streams S_1 and S_2. However, we were surprised to find out that certain paths experienced consistent reordering with a relatively large number of packets arriving out of order, although the average reordering rates in our experiments were substantially lower than those reported by Paxson [27].

For example, in dataset D_{1p}^a, we observed that out of every three missing[5] packets one was reordered. Hence, if users of ISP_a employed a streaming protocol that used a gap-based detection of lost packets [21] (i.e., the first out-of-order packet triggered an NACK), 33% of NACKs would be redundant and a large number of retransmissions would be unnecessary, causing a noticeable fraction of ISP's bandwidth to be wasted.

Since each missing packet is potentially reordered, the true frequency of reordering can be captured by computing the percentage of reordered packets relative to the total number of *missing* packets. The average reordering rate in our experiment was 6.5% of the number of *missing* packets, or 0.04% of the number

---

[5]Missing packets are defined as gaps in sequence numbers.

of *sent* packets. These numbers show that our reordering rates were at least by a factor of 10 lower than those reported by Paxson [27], whose average reordering rates varied between 0.3 and 2% of sent packets depending on the dataset. This difference can be explained by the fact that our experiment was conducted at substantially lower end-to-end bit rates, as well as by the fact that Paxson's experiment involved several paths with extremely high reordering rates.

Out of 16,852 sessions in $\{D_{1p} \cup D_{2p}\}$, 1599 (9.5%) experienced at least one reordering. Interestingly, the average session reordering rates in our datasets were very close to those in Paxson's 1995 data [27] (12% sessions with at least one reordering), despite the fundamental differences in sending rates. The highest reordering rate *per ISP* in our experiment occurred in D_{1p}^a, where 35% of missing packets (0.2% of sent packets) turned out to be reordered. In the same D_{1p}^a, almost half of the sessions (47%) experienced at least one reordering event. Furthermore, the maximum number of reordered packets in a single session occurred in D_{1p}^b and was 315 packets (7.5% of sent packets).

Interestingly, the reordering probability did not show any dependence on the time of day (i.e., the time slot) and was virtually the same for all states.

8.4.8.2 Reordering Delay

To further study packet reordering, we define two metrics that allow us to measure the extent of packet reordering. First, let *packet reordering delay* D_r be the delay from the time when a reordered packet was declared as *missing* to the time when the reordered packet arrived to the client. Second, let *packet reordering distance* d_r be the number of packets (including the very first out-of-sequence packet, but not the reordered packet itself) received by the client during reordering delay D_r. These definitions are illustrated in Figure 8.15, where reordering distance d_r is two packets and reordering delay D_r is the delay between receiving packets 3 and 2.

Figure 8.16 (top) shows the histogram of D_r in $\{D_{1p} \cup D_{2p}\}$. The largest reordering distance d_r in the combined dataset was 10 packets, and the largest reordering delay D_r was 20 s (however, in the latter case, d_r was only 1 packet). Although quite large, the maximum value of D_r is consistent with previously reported numbers (e.g., 12 s in Paxson's data [27]). The majority (90%) of samples

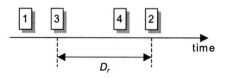

FIGURE 8.15:   The meaning of reordering delay D_r.

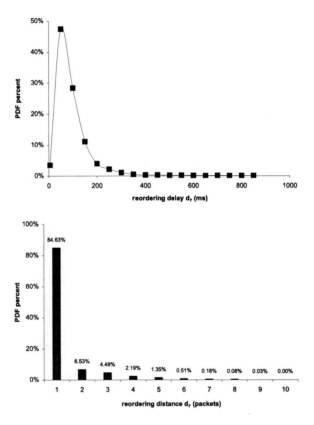

FIGURE 8.16:   Histogram of reordering delay D_r in $\{D_{1p} \cup D_{2p}\}$ (top). Histogram of reordering distance d_r in $\{D_{1p} \cup D_{2p}\}$ (bottom).

in Figure 8.16 (top) were below 150 ms, 97% below 300 ms, and 99% below 500 ms.

8.4.8.3 Reordering Distance

We next analyze the suitability of TCP's triple-ACK scheme in helping NACK-based protocols detect reordering. TCP's *fast retransmit* relies on *three* consecutive duplicate ACKs (hence the name "triple-ACK") from the receiver to detect packet loss and avoid unnecessary retransmissions. Therefore, if reordering distance d_r is either 1 or 2, the triple-ACK scheme successfully avoids duplicate packets; if d_r is greater than or equal to 3, it generates a duplicate packet. Figure 8.16 (bottom) shows the PDF of reordering distance d_r in both datasets.

Using Figure 8.16, we can infer that TCP's triple-ACK would be successful for 91.1% of the reordering events in our experiment, double-ACK for 84.6%, and quadruple-ACK for 95.7%. Note that Paxson's TCP-based data [27] show similar, but slightly better, detection rates, specifically 95.5% for triple-ACK, 86.5% for double-ACK, and 98.2% for quadruple-ACK.

8.4.9 Asymmetric Paths

Recall that during the initial executions of the traceroute, our dialer recorded the TTL field of each received "TTL-expired" packet. These fields allowed the dialer to compute the number of hops between the router that generated a particular "TTL-expired" message and the client. Suppose some router i was found at hop f_i in the *upstream* (i.e., forward) direction and at hop r_i in the *downstream* (i.e., reverse) direction. Hence, we can conclusively establish that an n-hop end-to-end path is *asymmetric* if a router exists for which the number of downstream hops is different from the number of upstream hops (i.e., $\exists i, 1 \le i \le n$: $f_i \ne r_i$). However, the opposite is not always true—if each router has the same number of downstream and upstream hops, we cannot conclude that the path is symmetric (i.e., it could be asymmetric as well). Hence, we call such paths *possibly symmetric*.

In $\{D_{1p} \cup D_{2p}\}$, 72% of the sessions sent their packets over *definitely* asymmetric paths. In that regard, two questions prompt for an answer. First, does path asymmetry depend on the number of end-to-end hops? To answer this question, we extracted path information from $\{D_{1p} \cup D_{2p}\}$ and counted each end-to-end path through a particular access point exactly once. Figure 8.17 shows the percentage of asymmetric paths as a function of the number of end-to-end hops in the path. As Figure 8.17 shows, almost all paths with 14 hops or more were asymmetric, as well as that even the shortest paths (with only 6 hops) were prone to asymmetry. This result can be explained by the fact that longer paths are more likely to cross over AS boundaries or intra-AS administrative domains. In both cases, "hot-potato" routing policies may cause path asymmetry.

The second question we attempt to answer is whether path asymmetry has anything to do with reordering. In $\{D_{1p} \cup D_{2p}\}$, 95% of all sessions with at least one reordered packet were running over an *asymmetric* path. Consequently, we can conclude that if a session in our datasets experiences a reordering event along a path, then the path is most likely asymmetric. However, a new question that arises is whether the opposite is true as well: if a path is asymmetric, will a session be more likely to experience a reordering? To answer the last question, we have the following numbers. Out of 12,057 sessions running over a definitely asymmetric path, 1522 experienced a reordering event, which translates into 12.6% reordering rate. However, out of 4795 sessions running over a possibly symmetric path, only 77 (1.6%) experienced a reordering event. Hence, an asymmetric

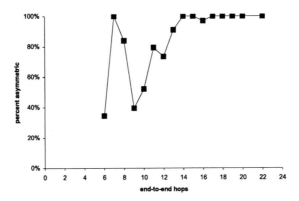

FIGURE 8.17: Percentage of asymmetric routes in $\{D_{1p} \cup D_{2p}\}$ as a function of the number of end-to-end hops.

path is eight times more likely to experience a reordering event than a possibly symmetric path.

Even though there is a clear link between reordering and asymmetry in our datasets, we speculate that the two could be related through the length of each end-to-end path. In other words, longer paths are more likely to experience reordering as well as be asymmetric. Hence, rather than saying that reordering causes asymmetry or vice versa, we can explain the result by noting that longer paths are more likely to cross AS-level routing boundaries during which both "hot-potato" routing (which causes asymmetry) and IP-level load balancing (which causes reordering) are apparently quite frequent.

Clearly, the findings in this section depend on the particular ISP employed by the end user and the autonomous systems that user traffic traverses. Large ISPs (such as the ones studied in this work) often employ numerous peering points (hundreds in our case), and path asymmetry rates found in this section may not hold for smaller ISPs. Nevertheless, our data allow us to conclude that home users in the United States experience asymmetric end-to-end paths with a much higher frequency than symmetric ones.

8.5 SUMMARY AND FURTHER READING

In this chapter, introductory information theory concepts that are related to characterizing packet losses over the Internet were presented. The most basic channel model that can be used to capture packet losses over network routes is the Binary Erasure Channel or its simple extension the Packet Erasure Channel. For a given probability δ of symbol loss (bit loss for a BEC and a packet loss for a

PEC), these channels have a capacity of $C = 1 - \delta$ in symbols (bits or packets) per channel use. Extensions of this basic and fundamental result to cascaded links and to routes with feedback were outlined. For excellent treatment of information theory concepts, the reader is referred to [1–3].

All of the results related to the BEC/PEC channels and their extensions are based on the assumption that the losses are memoryless. Meanwhile, deriving the capacity of channels with memory is beyond the scope of this introductory material. Methods for measuring information theory parameters, such as mutual information and capacity, for channels with memory can be found in [5]. An important measure for Internet multimedia applications that employ some form of channel coding is the probability of recovering a desired number of message (or data) packets when transmitting an FEC block of n packets [that include both k message and $(n - k)$ parity packets]. We outlined a set of closed form solutions of such measure for a basic channel with memory, namely the two-state Markov channel (i.e., the Gilbert channel). Some details for deriving these closed form solutions can be found elsewhere [6,7].

The second part of this chapter described a comprehensive Internet video study conducted for gaining insight into a variety of end-to-end performance parameters crucial for real-time multimedia applications. These performance parameters included packet loss, loss-burst lengths and durations, roundtrip delay, delay jitter, packet reordering and related delays due to reordering, and video underflow events. A great deal of work and research efforts has collected very valuable data regarding Internet performance. Some of these efforts focused on real-time and multimedia applications, including studies that specifically sent audio/video traffic over the Internet, such as the ones reported in [12,13,20,21,32–34]. The majority of these studies, however, involved only a few Internet paths, lasted for a short period of time, and focused on analyzing the features of the proposed scheme rather than the impact of Internet conditions on real-time streaming. However, the Internet video study reported in this chapter is quite comprehensive and covered a broad range of performance parameters that are important for Internet multimedia applications.

BIBLIOGRAPHY

[1] T. M. Cover and J. A. Thomas. *Elements of Information Theory*, Wiley, 1991.

[2] R. W. Yeung. *A First Course in Information Theory*, Kluwer Academic/Plenum Publishers, 2002.

[3] R. G. Gallager. *Information Theory and Reliable Communication*, Wiley, 1968.

[4] M. Mushkin and I. Bar-David. "Capacity and coding for the Gilbert–Elliot channels," *IEEE Trans. Inform. Theory*, vol. IT-35, no. 6, pp. 1277–1290, November 1989.

[5] A. J. Goldsmith and P. P. Varaiya. "Capacity, mutual information, and coding for finite-state Markov channels," *IEEE Trans. Inform. Theory*, vol. IT-42, no. 3, pp. 868–886, May 1996.

[6] M. Wu and H. Radha. "Network-Embedded FEC (NEF) Performance for Multi-Hop Wireless Channels with Memory," *IEEE International Conference on Communications (ICC)*, May 2005.

[7] M. Wu and H. Radha. "Network Embedded FEC for Overlay and P2P Multicast over Channels with Memory," *Conference on Information Sciences and Systems (CISS)*, Johns Hopkins University, March 2005.

[8] A. Acharya and J. Saltz. "A Study of Internet Round-trip Delay," *Technical Report CS-TR-3736*, University of Maryland, December 1996.

[9] H. Balakrishnan, V. M. Padmanablah, S. Seshan, M. Stemm, and R. H. Katz. "TCP Behavior of a Busy Internet Server: Analysis and Improvements," *IEEE INFOCOM*, March 1998.

[10] J. Bolliger, T. Gross, and U. Hengartner. "Bandwidth Modeling for Network-Aware Applications," *IEEE INFOCOM*, 1999.

[11] J. Bolot. "Characterizing End-to-End Packet Delay and Loss in the Internet," *Journal of High Speed Networks*, vol. 2, no. 3, pp. 289–298, September 1993.

[12] J. Bolot and T. Turletti. "A Rate Control Mechanism for Packet Video in the Internet," *IEEE INFOCOM*, pp. 1216–1223, June 1994.

[13] J. Bolot and T. Turletti. "Experience with Rate Control Mechanisms for Packet Video in the Internet," *ACM Computer Communication Review*, pp. 4–15, January 1998.

[14] M. S. Borella, D. Swider, S. Uludag, and G. B. Brewster. "Internet Packet Loss: Measurement and Implications for End-to-End QoS," *International Conference on Parallel Processing*, August 1998.

[15] M. S. Borella, S. Uludag, G. B. Brewster, and I. Sidhu. "Self-similarity of Internet Packet Delay," *IEEE ICC*, August 1997.

[16] R. Caceres, P. B. Danzig, S. Jamin, and D. Mitzel. "Characteristics of Wide-Area TCP/IP Conversations," *ACM SIGCOMM*, 1991.

[17] K. C. Claffy, G. C. Polyzos, and H.-W. Braun. "Measurement Considerations for Assessing Unidirectional Latencies," *Internetworking: Research and Experience*, vol. 4, pp. 121–132, 1993.

[18] K. C. Claffy, G. C. Polyzos, and H.-W. Braun. "Application of Sampling Methodologies to Network Traffic Characterization," *ACM SIGCOMM*, 1993.

[19] K. C. Claffy, G. C. Polyzos, and H.-W. Braun. "Traffic Characteristics of the T1 NSFNET Backbone," *IEEE INFOCOM*, 1993.

[20] B. Dempsey, J. Liebeherr, and A. Weaver. "A New Error Control Scheme for Packetized Voice over High-Speed Local Area Networks," *18th IEEE Local Computer Networks Conference*, September 1993.

[21] B. Dempsey, J. Liebeherr, and A. Weaver. "On retransmission-based error control for continuous media traffic in packet-switching networks," *Computer Networks and ISDN Systems*, vol. 28, no. 5, pp. 719–736, March 1996.

[22] ISP Planet and Cahners In-Stat Group. "Dial-Up Remains ISPs' Bread and Butter," http://isp-planet.com/research/2001/dialup_butter.html, 2001.

[23] ISP Planet and Telecommunications Research International. "U.S. Residential Internet Market Grows in Second Quarter," http://isp-planet.com/research/2001/us_q2.html, 2001.

[24] A. Mena and J. Heidemann. "An Empirical Study of Real Audio Traffic," *IEEE INFOCOM*, March 2000.

[25] J. C. Mogul. "Observing TCP Dynamics in Real Networks," *ACM SIGCOMM*, 1992.

[26] A. Mukherjee. "On the Dynamics and Significance of Low Frequency Components of Internet Load," *Internetworking: Research and Experience*, vol. 5, pp. 163–205, 1994.

[27] V. Paxson. "Measurements and Analysis of End-to-End Internet Dynamics," *Ph.D. dissertation*, Computer Science Department, University of California at Berkeley, 1997.

[28] S. P. Pizzo. "Why Is Broadband So Narrow?" *Forbes ASAP*, p. 50, September 2001.

[29] H. Radha, Y. Chen, K. Parthasarathy, and R. Cohen. "Scalable Internet Video Using MPEG-4," *Signal Processing: Image Communications Journal*, 1999.

[30] Real Player G2. Real Networks, http://www.real.com.

[31] I. Rhee. "Error Control Techniques for Interactive Low Bitrate Video Transmission over the Internet," *ACM SIGCOMM*, September 1998.

[32] S. Servetto and K. Nahrstedt. "Broadcast Quality Video over IP," *IEEE Transactions on Multimedia*, vol. 3, no. 1, March 2001.

[33] W. Tan and A. Zakhor. "Real-Time Internet Video Using Error Resilient Scalable Compression and TCP-Friendly Transport Protocol," *IEEE Transactions on Multimedia*, vol. 1, no. 2, June 1999.

[34] T. Turletti and G. Huitema. "Videoconferencing on the Internet," *IEEE/ACM Transactions on Networking*, vol. 4, no. 3, June 1996.

[35] M. Yajnik, J. Kurose, and D. Towsley. "Packet Loss Correlation in the MBone Multicast Network," *IEEE GLOBECOM*, November 1996.

[36] M. Yajnik, S. Moon, J. Kurose, and D. Townsley. "Measurement and Modelling of the Temporal Dependence in Packet Loss," *IEEE INFOCOM*, 1999.

[37] Pew Internet & American Life Project. "Home Broadband Adoption 2006," http://www.pewinternet.org/PPF/r/184/report_display.asp, May 2006.

9

Forward Error Control for Packet Loss and Corruption

Raouf Hamzaoui, Vladimir Stanković, and Zixiang Xiong

9.1 INTRODUCTION

Many techniques have been proposed to protect media data against channel errors. One possible approach is error-resilient source coding, which includes packetization of the information bit stream into independently decodable packets, exploitation of synchronization markers to control error propagation, reversible variable-length coding, and multiple description coding. Another approach is based on error concealment, where the lost or corrupted data is estimated at the receiver side with, for example, interpolation. Error control for media data may also exploit error detection and retransmission (ARQ, see Chapter 7). One further approach is forward error correction (FEC) with error correcting codes. Finally, one may combine any of the aforementioned methods. The choice of an appropriate error control method is not easy because it requires a deep understanding of both the source and the channel. In this respect, many important questions have to be answered: What is the type of the data? Is the data compressed? If yes, what is the compression scheme used? Is the data being transmitted over a wireline or a wireless network? Is there a feedback channel? What are the channel conditions? Moreover, the user requirements must also be taken into consideration. What is more important: reconstruction fidelity or transmission speed?

In this chapter, we present error control systems that rely on forward error correction only. While ARQ techniques have traditionally been the error control method of choice, there are many situations in which they are not suitable. For example, ARQ is not possible when there is no feedback channel. Also, in some applications, such as video multicasting or broadcasting, ARQ can overwhelm the sender with retransmission requests.

This chapter focuses on error control systems that were designed for embedded (or scalable) video bit streams (e.g., bit streams produced by MPEG-4 FGS, H.264/AVC MCTF, or some of the three-dimensional wavelet-based video coders described in Chapter 5). An overview of error control techniques for nonscalable video coders can be found in [33], in [32], and in Chapter 2. We describe several error protection systems and discuss their rate–distortion performance. When possible, we also provide efficient algorithms for optimizing this performance by adequately allocating the total transmission bit budget between the source coder and the channel coder.

This chapter is organized as follows. In Section 9.2, we present a class of transmission systems that are particularly well suited to the packet erasure channel, which as explained in Chapter 8, is a good model for the Internet. In Section 9.3, we describe a transmission system that was successfully used for bit error protection over a memoryless channel. Finally, Section 9.4 handles the more difficult case of channels with memory. Details about the channel codes mentioned in this chapter can be found in Chapter 7.[1]

9.2 PRIORITY ENCODING TRANSMISSION: CROSS-PACKET ERASURE CODING

In a packet network, the transmitted packets can be dropped, delayed, or corrupted (see Chapter 8). By ignoring delayed packets and discarding corrupted ones, one can model the channel as a packet erasure channel, which assumes that a transmitted packet is either correctly received or lost. In this section, we present transmission systems for this channel model. They share the feature that systematic maximum-distance separable (MDS) codes are applied across blocks of packets. Such codes could be Reed–Solomon (RS) codes, punctured RS codes, or shortened RS codes. For simplicity, we call them RS codes in this chapter. RS codes are used for two main reasons. First, as MDS codes, they are optimal in the sense that the smallest possible number of received symbols is used for full recovery of all information symbols. Second, both the encoding and the decoding are very fast when the length of the channel code word is not too large [18].

In Priority Encoding Transmission [1], the information bit stream is partitioned into segments with different priorities. Each segment is protected with a systematic RS code (Table 9.1). Since the packet number is indicated in the packet header, the receiver knows the location of the erased symbols in each codeword. Thus, if the RS code used for a given segment is known, the receiver is able to

---

[1] Parts of this work were previously published in [12].

Table 9.1: Priority encoding transmission with eight transmitted packets. The information bit stream is partioned into three segments with different priorities. Numbers denote information symbols and x denotes a redundant symbol. The first segment consists of the first 6 symbols of the message and is protected with an $(8, 2)$ systematic RS code. The second segment consists of the next 6 symbols of the message and is protected with an $(8, 3)$ systematic RS code. The third segment consists of the next 10 symbols of the message and is protected with an $(8, 5)$ systematic RS code.

Packet 1	1	2	3	7	8	13	14
Packet 2	4	5	6	9	10	15	16
Packet 3	x	x	x	11	12	17	18
Packet 4	x	x	x	x	x	19	20
Packet 5	x	x	x	x	x	21	22
Packet 6	x	x	x	x	x	x	x
Packet 7	x	x	x	x	x	x	x
Packet 8	x	x	x	x	x	x	x

reconstruct the segment when the number of packets lost does not exceed the number of parity symbols for this code. For example, if for the system of Table 9.1 two packets are lost, then the receiver can recover all information symbols. Given the length of the packet payload, the length of the information bit stream, the number of priority levels, the length of the bit stream in each priority level, and the RS code rate for each segment, the authors [1] provide an algorithm that computes the number of packets sent and the number of information packets in each segment.

In [15], priority encoding transmission was used for embedded information bit streams and extended by allowing the number of segments to be equal to the number of symbols in the packet payload. This is done as follows. Suppose that the encoded bit stream is to be sent as N packets of payload size L symbols each. Then the system builds L segments $S_1, \ldots, S_L$, each of which consists of $m_i \in \{1, \ldots, N\}$ information symbols and protects each segment S_i with an (N, m_i) systematic RS code (Table 9.2).

For each $i \in \{1, \ldots, L\}$, let $f_i = N - m_i$ denote the number of parity symbols that protect segment S_i. If n packets of N are lost during transmission, then the RS codes ensure that all segments that contain at most $N - n$ source symbols can be recovered. Thus, by adding the monotonicity constraint $f_1 \geq f_2 \geq \cdots \geq f_L$, if at most f_i packets are lost, then the receiver can recover at least the first i segments. This monotonicity constraint is justified by the fact that if a segment cannot be recovered, then all the next segments are useless. In the example of Table 9.2, suppose that any three packets are lost. Then the receiver can reconstruct the first four segments and thus decode the first eight information symbols.

Table 9.2: Block of packets. There are $N = 6$
packets of $L = 5$ symbols each. Numbers denote
information symbols of an embedded bit stream
and x denotes a parity symbol.

Packet 1	1	2	3	6	9
Packet 2	x	x	4	7	10
Packet 3	x	x	5	8	11
Packet 4	x	x	x	x	12
Packet 5	x	x	x	x	13
Packet 6	x	x	x	x	14

Denote by $\mathcal{F}_L$ the set of L-tuples $(f_1, \ldots, f_L)$ such that $f_i \in \{0, \ldots, N-1\}$
for $i = 1, \ldots, L$ and $f_1 \geq f_2 \geq \cdots \geq f_L$. Let ϕ be the operational distortion–
rate function of the source coder and X be the random variable whose value is the
number of packets lost when N packets are sent. For a given L-segment protection
$F = (f_1, \ldots, f_L) \in \mathcal{F}_L$, the expected distortion is

$$E[d](F) = \sum_{i=0}^{L} P_i(F)\phi(V_i(F)), \qquad (9.1)$$

where $V_0(F) = 0$, and for $i = 1, \ldots, L$, $V_i(F)$ is the number of information symbols in the first i segments, that is, $V_i(F) = \sum_{k=1}^{i} m_k = iN - \sum_{k=1}^{i} f_k$, and

$$P_i(F) = \begin{cases} Prob(X > f_1) & \text{for } i = 0; \\ Prob(f_{i+1} < X \leq f_i) & \text{for } i = 1, \ldots, L-1; \\ Prob(X \leq f_L) & \text{for } i = L. \end{cases}$$

Let $p_N(n)$ denote the probability that exactly n packets of N are lost. Then for
$i = 1, \ldots, L-1$, we have

$$P_i(F) = \begin{cases} 0 & \text{if } f_i = f_{i+1}; \\ \sum_{n=f_{i+1}+1}^{f_i} p_N(n) & \text{otherwise.} \end{cases}$$

An L-segment protection that minimizes (9.1) over $\mathcal{F}_L$ is called distortion optimal. We point out that the expected distortion (9.1) can also be expressed [9] in
the equivalent form

$$c_N(N)\phi(V_0(F)) + \sum_{i=1}^{L} c_N(f_i)(\phi(V_i(F)) - \phi(V_{i-1}(F))),$$

where $c_N(k) = \sum_{n=0}^{k} p_N(n)$, $k = 0, \ldots, N$. Thus, $c_N(f_i)$ is the probability that the receiver correctly recovers segment S_i.

Another way to look at the expected distortion was given in [17]. For any L-segment protection $F = (f_1, \ldots, f_L) \in \mathcal{F}_L$, there exists a unique N-tuple $\mathbf{R} = (R_1, \ldots, R_N)$ with $R_1 \leq \cdots \leq R_N$ such that for $i = 1, \ldots, N$, R_i denotes the number of successfully decoded information symbols if exactly i packets of N are received. For example, in Table 9.2, we have $R_1 = 2, R_2 = 2, R_3 = 8, R_4 = 8, R_5 = 8$, and $R_6 = 14$. The expected distortion for $\mathbf{R} = (R_1, \ldots, R_N)$ is $E[d](\mathbf{R}) = \sum_{j=0}^{N} q_N(j)\phi(R_j)$, where $R_0 = 0$ and $q_N(i) = 1 - p_N(i)$ is the probability that exactly i of N packets are received. It is easy to show that the total transmission rate (in symbols) is $R_t(\mathbf{R}) = \sum_{j=1}^{N} \alpha_j R_j$, where $\alpha_j = \frac{N}{j(j+1)}$, $j = 1, \ldots, N - 1$, and $\alpha_N = 1$.

9.2.1 Optimization

We now discuss algorithms for minimizing the expected distortion (9.1). Since the number of possible candidates $F \in \mathcal{F}_L$ is $\binom{L+N-1}{L}$, finding an optimal solution by brute force is infeasible in practice.

Puri and Ramchandran [17] noted that an optimal solution can be determined by finding $\mathbf{R} = (R_1, \ldots, R_N)$ that minimizes $E[d](\mathbf{R})$ subject to (1) $R_t(\mathbf{R}) \leq NL$, (2) $R_1 \leq R_2 \leq \cdots \leq R_N$, and (3) $R_i - R_{i-1} = k_i i$, $k_i \in \mathbf{N}$, $i = 2, \ldots, N$. Instead of this constrained discrete optimization problem, they first consider the relaxed problem of minimizing $E[d](\mathbf{R})$ for real variables $R_1, \ldots, R_N$ subject only to the first constraint $R_t(\mathbf{R}) \leq NL$. Assuming convexity and differentiability of the operational distortion–rate function, this is done by minimizing the Lagrangian

$$J(\mathbf{R}, \lambda) = \sum_{j=0}^{N} q_N(j)\phi(R_j) + \lambda\left(\sum_{j=1}^{N} \alpha_j R_j - NL\right) \tag{9.2}$$

giving the slopes of the distortion–rate function at the extremal points

$$\frac{d\phi(R_i)}{dR_i} = -\lambda\frac{\alpha_i}{q_N(i)}, \quad i = 1, \ldots, N. \tag{9.3}$$

After the Lagrange multiplier λ is eliminated via a bisectional search, further steps are carried out to handle constraints 2 and 3 [17]. The algorithm finds near-optimal solutions in practice and optimal ones subject to the convexity of ϕ and fractional bit allocation assignments. Its time complexity is $O(kN)$, where k is the number of iterations needed to determine the Lagrange multiplier that corresponds to the given transmission bit budget. Moreover, a preprocessing step that computes the vertices of the lower convex hull of LN distortion–rate points of the source coder is needed.

Mohr *et al.* [14] also determined a solution that is optimal if the operational distortion–rate function is convex and fractional bit allocation assignments are acceptable. The algorithm first computes the h vertices of the lower convex hull of LN distortion–rate points of the source coder and then finds a solution in $O(hN \log N)$ time.

Stockhammer and Buchner [29] presented an $O(N^2 L^2)$ dynamic programming algorithm that is almost exact in the general case and exact if the operational distortion–rate function is convex and the packet loss probability $p_N(n)$ is a monotonically decreasing function of the number of lost packets n. Dumitrescu *et al.* [9] independently found the same algorithm. However, they showed that its complexity can be reduced to $O(NL^2)$. Moreover, they gave an $O(N^2 L^2)$ algorithm that finds an optimal solution in the general case.

A fast local search algorithm that computes a near-optimal solution in practice was presented in [27]. The idea is to start from a *rate-optimal* solution and then iteratively improve it by searching for a better solution in its neighborhood (Figure 9.1). Here a rate-optimal solution is defined as an L-segment protection that maximizes over $\mathcal{F}_L$, the expected number of correctly reconstructed source symbols given by

$$E[r](F) = \sum_{i=0}^{L} P_i(F) V_i(F). \tag{9.4}$$

A rate-optimal L-segment protection is shown [27] to be the equal loss protection strategy $(f_r, \ldots, f_r)$, with

$$f_r = \arg \max_{i=0,\ldots,N-1} (N-i) \sum_{n=0}^{i} p_N(n).$$

Thus its computation is straightforward and can always be done in $O(N)$ steps. The local search (or iterative improvement) part needs at most $L(N-1)+1$ computations and $L(N-1)$ comparisons of cost function (9.1), bringing the overall worst-case time complexity to $O(NL)$.

9.2.2 Multiple Blocks of Packets (BOPs)

When the transmission rate budget R_T (in symbols) is large and the packet payload size L is small, the channel codeword length N has to be very large to guarantee that $LN = R_T$, making channel encoding and decoding very complex in software. A solution is to keep N small and use more than one block of packets (Table 9.3).

This problem is considered in [31], where a heuristic algorithm for efficiently determining the packet erasure protection in each block of packets is given. The

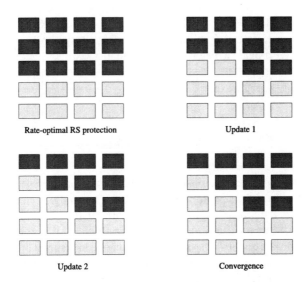

FIGURE 9.1: Illustration of the local search algorithm for $N = 5$ and $L = 4$. The neighbors of a solution (f_1, f_2, f_3, f_4) are $(f_1 + 1, f_2, f_3, f_4)$, $(f_1 + 1, f_2 + 1, f_3, f_4)$, $(f_1 + 1, f_2 + 1, f_3 + 1, f_4)$, and $(f_1 + 1, f_2 + 1, f_3 + 1, f_4 + 1)$. Either the current solution is updated with the best neighbor or the algorithm stops. Dark areas correspond to information symbols and light areas to parity symbols.

algorithm is iterative and converges to a local minimum. Dumitrescu and Wu [8] proposed a dynamic programming algorithm that finds an optimal solution to the problem. The time complexity of the algorithm is $O(K^2 L^2 N^2)$, where K is the number of transmitted BOPs.

9.2.3 Ensuring Quality of Service

One limitation of basing the protection strategy on minimizing the expected distortion (or maximizing the expected PSNR) is that no quality of service (QoS) is

Table 9.3: Multiple BOPs. The transmission rate budget is $R_T = 30$, the packet payload size is $L = 5$, the codeword length of the channel codes is $N = 3$, and $K = 2$ BOPs are sent.

Packet 1	1	2	4	6	9	Packet 4	12	13	14	16	19
Packet 2	x	3	5	7	10	Packet 5	x	x	15	17	20
Packet 3	x	x	x	8	11	Packet 6	x	x	x	18	21

Table 9.4:   Packet loss protection with QoS. Here $k' = 2$ and $L_1 = 3$. The first six symbols provide a distortion smaller than d_{min}.

Packet 1	1	3	5	7	10
Packet 2	2	4	6	8	11
Packet 3	x	x	x	9	12
Packet 4	x	x	x	x	13
Packet 5	x	x	x	x	14

guaranteed. Indeed, since the distortion is minimized on average, there may be transmissions where the distortion is too high for meaningful applications. One way to alleviate the problem is to add a constraint on the probability of such occurrences [10]. More precisely, for $F \in \mathcal{F}_L$, define $p(F)$ as the probability that the distortion is above a quality threshold d_{min}. Then one looks for a protection F that minimizes the expected distortion (9.1) subject to the constraint $p(F) < p_{max}$, where p_{max} is a probability threshold.

To reduce the complexity of the problem, a suboptimal algorithm is proposed in [10]. First one determines the largest integer k' such that the probability of receiving fewer than k' packets is smaller than p_{max}, that is, k' is the largest integer such that $\sum_{n=0}^{k'-1} q_N(n) < p_{max}$. Second, one determines the smallest integer L_1 such that $\phi(k'L_1) < d_{min}$. Then the first L_1 columns are protected with an (N, k') systematic RS code. The choice of k' ensures that the probability that the distortion is larger than d_{min} will be smaller than p_{max}. Finally, an optimal unequal error protection for the remaining $L - L_1$ columns is computed in the usual way (Table 9.4).

9.2.4 Layered Multiple Description Coding

In multicast applications, clients usually have differing transmission bandwidths. Instead of sending a separate block of packets to each client, Chou and colleagues [6] proposed to design a single block of packets consisting of a base layer and additional refinement layers. For example, when two clients are present, the low-bandwidth client receives only the base layer, while the high-bandwidth client additionally receives an enhancement layer (Table 9.5).

Unfortunately, this construction cannot offer to both clients the same quality performance as two separate, optimal, nonlayered multiple description schemes. A naive method to solve the problem by optimizing the protection for only one client usually leads to very high distortions for the nonoptimized client [6]. A better approach is to optimize the protection for the low-bandwidth client and reallocate a number of parity packets from the enhancement layer of the high-bandwidth client to the base layer to strengthen its protection [6]. However, the solution was

Table 9.5: The first three packets (base layer) are sent to both low-bandwidth and high-bandwidth clients. The remaining four packets are sent to the high-bandwidth client only. Numbers denote information symbols, x denotes a parity symbol. Packets 4 and 5 provide supplementary protection to the base layer.

Packet 1	1	2	4	6
Packet 2	x	3	5	7
Packet 3	x	x	x	8
Packet 4	x	x	x	x
Packet 5	x	x	x	x
Packet 6	9	10	11	12
Packet 7	x	x	x	13

optimized only for the low-bandwidth client, and the high-bandwidth client potentially suffered a significant performance loss. For example, for the Foreman video sequence encoded with MPEG-4 FGS, the expected distortion for the high-bandwidth client was 1.4 dB worse than the smallest possible distortion for this client [6].

A better trade-off between the distortions seen by the clients can be obtained by minimizing the largest performance loss experienced by any client [28]. Such a code tends to average the quality loss among the clients, ensuring that none of the clients suffers a significantly higher quality degradation than the others. Two fast heuristic algorithms for the setup with two clients were proposed in [28]. Experimental results show that the algorithms provide significant improvements in the quality trade-off over the results of [6]. Finding an optimal solution in polynomial time for the two-client case is still an open problem. Another open problem is to compute a fast optimal or near-optimal solution when there are more than two clients.

9.3 CRC+RCPC: WITHIN-PACKET ERROR DETECTION AND CORRECTION CODING

In this section, we present a transmission system based on a concatenation of an error detection code as an outer code and an error correction code as an inner code. Although this system was already known in the communications literature [20], it was Sherwood and Zeger [22] who first combined it with an embedded source coder for progressively transmitting images. The motivation for using the concatenated code is that it allows the receiver to stop the decoding as soon as the first noncorrectable error is detected. In this way, error propagation, which can

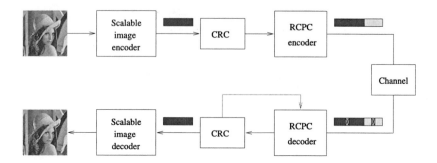

FIGURE 9.2: Schematic representation of the system of Sherwood and Zeger [22]. The dark areas correspond to information bits and the light areas to parity bits.

be catastrophic for variable-length source codes, is avoided. For illustration purposes, we will assume that the source coder is an embedded image coder; however, the reader should keep in mind that any embedded or scalable source coder can be used as well.

Figure 9.2 shows a schematic representation of the transmission system proposed in [22]. After an embedded coder is used to compress the source, the compressed bit stream is divided into consecutive information blocks. To each information block, CRC parity bits are appended, and the resulting block is encoded with an RCPC coder. The receiver uses a List Viterbi algorithm (LVA) to find a best maximum-likelihood decoding solution for a received packet. If an error is detected by the CRC decoder, the LVA is used again to find a next best solution, which is also checked for errors. This process is repeated until the CRC test is passed or a maximum number of solutions is reached. In the first case, the next received packet is considered, whereas in the second case, decoding is stopped and the image is reconstructed using only the correctly decoded packets.

In the following, we explain how to optimally allocate a transmission bit budget between the source coder and the channel coder for the system. Three different performance criteria are considered: the expected distortion, the expected PSNR (defined in decibels as $10 \log_{10} \frac{255^2}{MSE}$), and the expected number of correctly decoded information bits. In Section 9.3.1, we assume as in [22] that the lengths of all information blocks are fixed. In Section 9.3.2, we treat the case where the size of the channel codewords is fixed [2,25] (Figure 9.3).

9.3.1 Fixed-Length Information Blocks

Let N_p be the number of pixels in the image and L be the length of the information blocks. Suppose that the channel coder is given by a family $\mathcal{C} = \{c_1, \ldots, c_m\}$

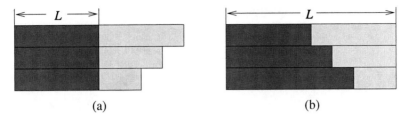

FIGURE 9.3: (a) Fixed-length information blocks and variable-length channel codewords. (b) Fixed-length channel codewords with variable-length information blocks. The dark areas correspond to information bits and the light areas to parity bits.

of error correction-detection codes. For $i = 1, \ldots, m$, let $r(c_i)$ and $p(c_i)$ denote the code rate and the probability of incomplete decoding for channel code c_i, respectively. It is assumed that all decoding errors can be detected. The protection of the information blocks is given by an error protection strategy (EPS) $\pi = (\pi_1, \ldots, \pi_{N(\pi)})$, where $N(\pi)$ is the number of transmitted information blocks, and for $i = 1, \ldots, N(\pi)$, $\pi_i \in C$ is the channel code used to protect the ith information block (Figure 9.3a).

For $k = 1, \ldots, N(\pi)$ and $i = k - 1, \ldots, N(\pi)$, let $P_{i|k-1}(\pi)$ denote the conditional probability that exactly the first i packets are decoded correctly given that the first $k - 1$ packets are decoded correctly. Since the channel is memoryless, we have

$$P_{i|k-1}(\pi) = \begin{cases} p(\pi_k) & \text{for } i = k - 1; \\ p(\pi_{i+1}) \prod_{j=k}^{i} (1 - p(\pi_j)) & \text{for } i = k, \ldots, N(\pi) - 1; \\ \prod_{j=k}^{N(\pi)} (1 - p(\pi_j)) & \text{for } i = N(\pi). \end{cases}$$

In particular, when $k = 1$, we have $P_{0|0}(\pi) = p(\pi_1)$ is the probability that the first packet is not correctly decoded, for $i = 1, \ldots, N(\pi) - 1$, $P_{i|0}(\pi) = p(\pi_{i+1}) \prod_{j=1}^{i} (1 - p(\pi_j))$ is the probability that the first i packets are correctly decoded while the next one is not, and $P_{N(\pi)|0}(\pi) = \prod_{j=1}^{N(\pi)} (1 - p(\pi_j))$ is the probability that all $N(\pi)$ packets are correctly decoded.

Let $\phi(r)$ be the operational distortion–rate function of the source coder with the rate r given in bpp. Then the expected distortion for an EPS π is

$$E[d](\pi) = \sum_{i=0}^{N(\pi)} P_{i|0}(\pi) \phi(iL/N_p). \tag{9.5}$$

The expected PSNR for the EPS π is

$$E[PSNR](\pi) = \sum_{i=0}^{N(\pi)} P_{i|0}(\pi) PSNR(iL/N_p). \tag{9.6}$$

Finally, the expected reconstructed source coding rate is

$$E[r](\pi) = \sum_{i=0}^{N(\pi)} P_{i|0}(\pi)(iL/N_p). \tag{9.7}$$

Ideally, one would like to minimize (9.5) or maximize (9.6). However, maximizing (9.7) is also reasonable for an efficient embedded coder because the expected distortion will generally decrease when the expected number of correctly decoded source bits increases. Note, however, that the optimization of (9.5), (9.6), and (9.7) does not necessarily yield the same solution, with one exception being the trivial case where ϕ is a linear function. One nice feature of maximizing (9.7) is that the solution is not dependent on the source contents or the source coder and thus can be computed off-line. Moreover, this solution can also be determined by the receiver and need not be transmitted over the channel.

For $k = 1, \ldots, N(\pi)$ let $\Delta(k, \pi) = \sum_{i=k}^{N(\pi)} (\sum_{j=k}^{i} \delta_j) P_{i|k-1}(\pi)$, where

$$\delta_i = \begin{cases} \phi((i-1)L/N_p) - \phi(iL/N_p) & \text{for the distortion;} \\ PSNR(iL/N_p) - PSNR((i-1)L/N_p) & \text{for the PSNR;} \\ 1, & \text{for the expected source rate.} \end{cases}$$

Then one can show [3] that an EPS that optimizes the performance of the system for a given total transmission bit rate r_T is a strategy $\pi^* = (\pi_1^*, \ldots, \pi_{N(\pi)}^*)$ that maximizes $\Delta(1, \pi)$ subject to $\sum_{i=1}^{N(\pi)} \frac{L}{N_p r(\pi_i)} \leq r_T$. This can be done with dynamic programming with complexity $O(r_T^2)$ if either the distortion or the PSNR is optimized, or $O(r_T)$ if the expected reconstructed source rate is maximized [3]. One can also show that for an EPS $\pi^* = (\pi_1^*, \ldots, \pi_{N(\pi)}^*)$ that maximizes the expected reconstructed source rate, we have $r(\pi_k^*) \leq r(\pi_{k+1}^*)$ for $k = 1, \ldots, N(\pi) - 1$ [3]. That is, the information blocks should be protected with increasingly weaker channel codes. However, this property does not necessarily hold if either the distortion or the PSNR is optimized. However, the property is satisfied if one assumes that the logarithm of the block decoding error probability is an affine function of the channel packet length [16].

Experimental results show that the solutions to maximizing the expected PSNR and maximizing the expected source rate yield a similar performance for the SPIHT coder and a CRC/RCPC channel coder (the difference in PSNR is less than 0.2 dB for the 512×512 gray-scale Lenna image [3]). This can be analytically confirmed under some theoretical assumptions, including an independent, identically distributed Gaussian source and a perfect progressive source coder that achieves the distortion–rate function [13].

A further nice feature of rate-based optimization is that if $\pi^* = (\pi_1^*, \ldots, \pi_N^*)$ is rate optimal for target transmission rate r_T, then the EPSs $(\pi_j^*, \ldots, \pi_N^*)$, $j = 2, \ldots, N$ are also rate optimal for target transmission rates $r_j = r_T - \frac{1}{N_p} \sum_{i=1}^{j-1} \frac{L}{r(\pi_i^*)}$ [3]. This result has an important application if rate-compatible channel codes are used. Indeed, in this case, the transmission of the sequence of bits can be organized such that rate-based optimality is guaranteed at the intermediate rates r_j, $j = 2, \ldots, N$ [3].

9.3.2 Fixed-Length Channel Codewords

We now consider the slightly different system of Figure 9.3b [2,25], where the size of the channel codewords is fixed, but the blocks of information bits have variable lengths. Compared to the system using information blocks of fixed length, the obvious advantage of having channel codewords of fixed length is that cross-layer design will be easier because other layers (e.g., the physical layer) do not have to deal with the issue of different channel codeword lengths. Denote the set of channel codes by $C = \{c_1, \ldots, c_m\}$ and the length of the channel codewords by L. Given a transmission rate budget B (in symbols), the system transforms $N = \lfloor B/L \rfloor$ successive blocks of the source coder output bit stream into a sequence of N channel codewords of fixed length L. Here we use an N-packet EPS $\pi = (\pi_1, \ldots, \pi_N)$, which encodes the kth information block with channel code $\pi_k \in C$. Like the system in Figure 9.3a with fixed-length information blocks, if the decoder detects an error, then the decoding is stopped, and the message is reconstructed from the correctly decoded packets.

For $i = 1, \ldots, m$, let $p(c_i)$ denote the probability of a decoding error of channel code c_i. We may assume without loss of generality that $p(c_1) < \cdots < p(c_m) < 1$. For the N-packet strategy π, the expected number of correctly decoded source bits is

$$E_N[r](\pi) = \sum_{i=0}^{N} P_{i|0}(\pi) V_i(\pi), \qquad (9.8)$$

where $V_0(\pi) = 0$ and for $i \geq 1$, $V_i(\pi) = \sum_{j=1}^{i} v(\pi_j)$ with $v(\pi_j) = \lfloor Lr(\pi_j) \rfloor$ being the number of source bits in the jth packet. The expected distortion is

$$E_N[d](\pi) = \sum_{i=0}^{N} P_{i|0}(\pi) \phi(V_i(\pi)), \qquad (9.9)$$

where $\phi(R)$ is the distortion associated to rate R (in bits).

As in Section 9.2.1, an EPS π^r that maximizes (9.8) is called rate optimal. A rate-optimal EPS can be computed in $O(mN)$ time [25]. This is essentially due to the property that if the N-packet EPS $(\pi_1, \ldots, \pi_N)$ is rate optimal, then for $1 \leq i \leq N - 1$ the $(N - i)$-packet EPS $(\pi_{i+1}, \ldots, \pi_N)$ must also be rate optimal [25]. An EPS π^d that minimizes (9.9) is called distortion optimal. However, in contrast to the fixed-information block setting, there is no known polynomial-time algorithm to compute a distortion-optimal EPS π^d. Assuming that the operational distortion–rate function $\phi(R)$ of the source coder is nonincreasing and convex, one can give a tight lower bound of $E_N[d](\pi^d)$ as $\phi(E_N[r](\pi^r))$ [11], which is computable with complexity $O(mN)$. Then if π^r is used as an approximation of π^d, a tight upper bound on the quality loss $E_N[d](\pi^r) - E_N[d](\pi^d)$ is $E_N[d](\pi^r) - \phi(E_N[r](\pi^r))$. In addition, it is conjectured in [11] that under the same assumptions for $\phi(R)$, the total number of information bits for π^d is smaller than or equal to that for π^r.

In [2], an approximation for π^d based on the Viterbi algorithm was proposed. It has a quadratic time complexity in the number of transmitted channel code words N. However, this result is guaranteed only for channel code rates that are a subset of $\{\frac{p}{q}, \frac{p+1}{q}, \ldots, \frac{q-1}{q}\}$, where p and q are positive integers with $p < q$. For channel codes that do not fulfill this condition, including rate-compatible punctured codes, the worst-case time complexity is exponential in N.

A fast local search algorithm was proposed in [11] to compute an approximation of π^d. The algorithm works by iterative improvement and has an $O(mN)$ worst-case complexity [11]. It starts from a rate-optimal solution π^r and then considers the first neighbor of π^r. If the expected distortion of this neighbor is smaller than that of the current solution, it updates the current solution and repeats the procedure; otherwise it considers the next neighbor and repeats the procedure. If there is no neighbor that is better than the current solution, the algorithm returns the current solution. Here a neighbor of an N-packet EPS π with nondecreasing rates is any N-packet EPS with nondecreasing rates, fewer information symbols than π, and differs in code rates from π on only one packet. For example, suppose $\mathcal{C} = \{c_1, c_2, c_3, c_4\}$, if $\pi = (c_1, c_2, c_4, c_4)$, then π has three neighbors, (c_1, c_2, c_3, c_4) being the first one, (c_1, c_2, c_2, c_4) the second, and (c_1, c_1, c_4, c_4) the third. Note how in observance of the conjecture in [11], all solutions tested by the local search algorithm have fewer information bits than π^r.

9.4 ERROR PROTECTION FOR WIRELESS NETWORKS

In fading channels, the transmitted packets experience different bit error rates: packets transmitted when the channel is in the bad state are exposed to much higher bit error rates than those transferred during the good state of the channel. Thus, to avoid decoding failures with the CRC/RCPC system of [22], the RCPC codes should be designed for the bit error rate in the channel's bad state. This causes overprotection during the good state of the channel (which usually lasts much longer) and bounds the achievable performance from the theoretical limits. In this section, we present three successful extensions of the CRC/RCPC system of [22] for fading channels. The first system [30] introduces interleaving. The two other systems [19,23] are based on product channel codes.

9.4.1 Using Interleaving

Interleaving tends to spread deep fade and to transform a memory channel into a memoryless one. It improves the performance during transmission over fading channels at the expense of increased complexity and time delay. A system that exploits block interleaving to alleviate the problems of channel burst errors during a deep fade is that of Stockhammer and Weiss [30]. As in the system of [22], an embedded bit stream is encoded with a punctured convolutional coder, and the decoding of the received bit stream is stopped when the first decoding error is detected. The convolutional coder has a strong systematic mother code of memory 96 and code rate 1/7. Channel decoding is done with the Fano algorithm. A distortion-optimal unequal error protection solution is determined using dynamic programming as in [3].

9.4.2 Product Code System

Sherwood and Zeger [23] proposed a transmission system based on a product channel code to protect the embedded information bit stream. The product code uses the concatenated CRC/RCPC code of [22] as the row code and a systematic RS code as the column code (Table 9.6). The main idea is to strengthen the protection of the CRC/RCPC code by using channel coding across the packets.

Table 9.6: EEP with the product code of Sherwood and Zeger [23]. There are $N = 6$ RCPC codewords, each of which has a payload of 11 symbols. Cells labeled by numbers contain successive information symbols of an embedded bit stream, x denotes a parity symbol of a $(3, 2)$ RS code, + a CRC parity symbol, and o an RCPC parity symbol. Each column contains two different RS codewords. The RCPC code need not be systematic.

Packet 1	1	2	3	4	5	+	+	o	o	o	o
Packet 2	6	7	8	9	10	+	+	o	o	o	o
Packet 3	x	x	x	x	x	+	+	o	o	o	o
Packet 4	11	12	13	14	15	+	+	o	o	o	o
Packet 5	16	17	18	19	20	+	+	o	o	o	o
Packet 6	x	x	x	x	x	+	+	o	o	o	o

Table 9.7:   Unequal error protection with the product code system of Sherwood
and Zeger [23]. The information symbols of the two blocks are protected with
a $(3, 2)$ RS code. Additionally, the information symbols of the first block are
protected with a $(4, 2)$ RS code, whose parity symbols are denoted by y.

Packet 1	1	2	3	4	5	+	+	o	o	o	o
Packet 2	6	7	8	9	10	+	+	o	o	o	o
Packet 3	x	x	x	x	x	+	+	o	o	o	o
Packet 4	11	12	13	14	15	+	+	o	o	o	o
Packet 5	16	17	18	19	20	+	+	o	o	o	o
Packet 6	x	x	x	x	x	+	+	o	o	o	o
Packet 7	y	y	y	y	y	+	+	o	o	o	o
Packet 8	y	y	y	y	y	+	+	o	o	o	o

The information bit stream is first partitioned into packets of equal length L,
which are then grouped into K blocks of k packets each. All k information packets
within a block are protected columnwise by an (n, k) systematic RS code. In
this way, $(n - k)$ parity packets are associated to each block, resulting in $N =
K \times n$ packets. Finally, each packet (information or parity) is fed to a CRC/RCPC
encoder. The transmitter first sends $k \times K$ information packets (more precisely,
RCPC codewords obtained by protecting information packets). Then, the parity
packets, which may be arbitrarily interleaved to improve performance during a
deep fade, are transmitted. Interleaving of the parity packets provides the desired
trade-off between performance quality and delay. In the example of Table 9.6,
$N = 6$, $L = 5$, $K = 2$, $k = 2$, and $n = 3$.

Finding an optimal RCPC code rate, an optimal RS code rate, and an optimal interleaver for the system is a very difficult problem. Moreover, no efficient
method that computes a near-optimal solution is known. Sherwood and Zeger [23]
suggest selecting RCPC code so that it can efficiently protect the transmitted data
while the channel is in the good state.

In addition to equal error protection, several ways of implementing unequal error protection were proposed in [23]. The most successful one protects the earliest
symbols of the embedded bit stream by additional RS codes (Table 9.7).

9.4.3 Another Product Code System

The system proposed by Sachs *et al.* [19] is also based on a product channel code
where each row code is a concatenated CRC/RCPC code and each column code
is a systematic RS code (Table 9.8).

The embedded information bit stream is first protected with RS codes of
length N as in the system of [15] (Table 9.2). Then the CRC parity symbols are
added to each row. Finally, each row is encoded with the same RCPC code of
length L. The resulting product code is sent as N packets of L symbols each.

Table 9.8: Product code of Sachs *et al.* [19]. There are $N = 6$ packets of $L = 11$ symbols each. Cells labeled by numbers contain successive information symbols of an embedded bit stream, x denotes an RS parity symbol, $+$ a CRC parity symbol, and o an RCPC parity symbol. The RCPC code need not be systematic.

Packet 1	1	3	6	10	15	+	+	o	o	o	o
Packet 2	2	4	7	11	16	+	+	o	o	o	o
Packet 3	x	5	8	12	17	+	+	o	o	o	o
Packet 4	x	x	9	13	18	+	+	o	o	o	o
Packet 5	x	x	x	14	19	+	+	o	o	o	o
Packet 6	x	x	x	x	20	+	+	o	o	o	o

Let $\mathcal{C} = \{c_1, \ldots, c_m\}$ be the set of available RCPC codes. For $c \in \mathcal{C}$, we denote by $L(c)$ the sum of the number of information symbols and RS parity symbols used in a packet protected with c. Thus, we have $L(c)$ information segments $S_1, \ldots, S_{L(c)}$, where segment S_j, $1 \leq j \leq L(c)$, consists of $m_j \in \{1, \ldots, N\}$ information symbols that are protected by $f_j = N - m_j$ RS symbols.

Packets are sent over the channel in the order in which they are generated. Since all packets are of equal importance, packet interleaving cannot improve the performance. Each received packet is decoded with the RCPC decoder. If the CRC code detects an error, then the packet is considered to be lost (we suppose that all errors can be detected). Suppose now that n packets of N are erased (i.e., either lost during transmission or discarded due to RCPC decoding failure), then the RS codes ensure that all segments that contain at most $N - n$ information symbols can be recovered. By adding the constraint $f_1 \geq \cdots \geq f_{L(c)}$, one guarantees that the receiver can decode at least the first j segments whenever at most f_j packets are erased.

In contrast to the system of [23], which puts the earliest symbols in the first rows, the product code system of [19] puts these symbols in the first columns. Consequently, the first system has a better progressive ability and a shorter decoding delay. However, experimental results [19] for a flat-fading Rayleigh channel and BPSK modulation indicate that the performance of the system of [19] is better than that of [23]. Finally, the performance of the first system depends on which packets are received, whereas in the second system, all packets are of equal importance. For example, suppose that the first two packets in Tables 9.6 and 9.8 are erased. Then, the first system cannot recover any information symbol, while the second system can successfully recover the first nine information symbols. However, if the second and fourth transmission packets are erased, the system in Table 9.6 reconstructs all 20 information symbols, while the system of Table 9.8 will be able to reconstruct only the first 10 symbols.

We now consider strategies for minimizing the expected distortion of the product code system of [19]. As in Section 9.1, we denote by $\mathcal{F}_{L(c)}$, $c \in \mathcal{C}$, the set of $L(c)$-tuples $(f_1, \ldots, f_{L(c)})$ such that $f_1 \geq \cdots \geq f_{L(c)}$ and $f_j \in \{0, \ldots, N-1\}$ for $j = 1, \ldots, L(c)$. Then a protection (c, F) for the product code is given by an RCPC code $c \in \mathcal{C}$ and an $L(c)$-segment RS protection $F \in \mathcal{F}_{L(c)}$.

A distortion-optimal product code solution (c^*, F^*) is given by an RCPC code $c^* \in \mathcal{C}$ and an $L(c^*)$-segment RS protection $F^* \in \mathcal{F}_{L(c^*)}$ that solve the minimization problem

$$\min_{c \in \mathcal{C}, F \in \mathcal{F}_{L(c)}} \sum_{k=0}^{L(c)} P_k(F)\phi\big(V_k(F)\big), \tag{9.10}$$

where P_k, ϕ, and $V_k(F)$ are defined as in Section 9.1. Solving (9.10) by brute force is impractical because the number of possible product codes is

$$\sum_{c \in \mathcal{C}} \binom{L(c) + N - 1}{L(c)}.$$

In [19], the authors use the Lagrange-based optimization algorithm of [17] to determine a near-optimal $L(c)$ segment RS protection for each $c \in \mathcal{C}$. Then the protection that yields the smallest expected distortion is selected. Even though the Lagrange-based optimization algorithm is fast, the overall optimization can be too expensive when the number of candidate RCPC codes is large.

A fast heuristic method for solving problem (9.10) was proposed in [27]. In contrast to [19], the method of [27] does not try to minimize (9.1) for each RCPC code. Instead, it starts from a rate-optimal product code solution, that is, one that solves the maximization problem

$$\max_{c \in \mathcal{C}, F \in \mathcal{F}_{L(c)}} \sum_{k=0}^{L(c)} P_k(F) V_k(F), \tag{9.11}$$

and then tries to improve this solution by progressively increasing the total number of parity symbols. This is done by alternately applying the local search algorithm of Section 9.2.1 and decreasing the RCPC code rate. The procedure is illustrated in Table 9.9, which is obtained by decreasing the RCPC code rate in Table 9.8. Note how the total number of parity symbols increases.

The method of [27] also exploits the fact that if F is the current RS protection, then one can exclude all RCPC code rates for which the expected distortion is greater than $E[d](F)$. This is because a distortion-optimal RS protection corresponding to one such code rate cannot be better than F. In the worst case, the algorithm computes $(N-1)L(c) + 1$ times the cost function (9.1) for each $c \in \mathcal{C}$.

Table 9.9: Product code obtained from Table 9.8 by decreasing the RCPC code rate. The new RS protection is (4, 3, 2, 1) whereas the old one is (4, 3, 2, 1, 0).

Packet 1	1	3	6	10	+	+	o	o	o	o	o
Packet 2	2	4	7	11	+	+	o	o	o	o	o
Packet 3	x	5	8	12	+	+	o	o	o	o	o
Packet 4	x	x	9	13	+	+	o	o	o	o	o
Packet 5	x	x	x	14	+	+	o	o	o	o	o
Packet 6	x	x	x	x	+	+	o	o	o	o	o

9.5 SUMMARY AND FURTHER READING

We presented FEC-based transmission systems for embedded media bit streams. We emphasized two optimization approaches for these systems. The first one maximizes the expected number of correctly decoded information bits. This approach has two desirable features: the optimization is independent of the source and it can be done very quickly. The second approach minimizes the expected distortion. While its optimization is more complex than that of the first approach, it can provide a significantly better rate–distortion performance in many situations.

We conclude this chapter with suggestions for further reading. FEC can be combined with other error-resilient techniques for robust media transmission. For example, Cosman *et al.* [7] combined FEC with error-resilient source coding. This was done by packetizing the compressed media bit stream into independently decodable packets before applying the CRC/RCPC system of Section 9.3. The system of [7] was later improved in [26]. Chande *et al.* [4] proposed a media transmission system for the binary symmetric channel that combines FEC with ARQ. The media data is first compressed with an embedded coder and encoded with the CRC/RCPC coder of Section 9.3. The receiver decodes the RCPC code and uses the CRC code to check for errors. If no errors are detected, the receiver sends an acknowledgment bit to the sender, which then proceeds with the next packet. If errors are detected, a no acknowledgment bit is sent to the sender, which then transmits additional parity bits of a stronger RCPC code. The procedure is repeated until the decoding of the packet is successful or no stronger RCPC code is available. In the latter case, packet decoding is stopped, and the media data is reconstructed from the correctly decoded packets only. The system of [4] was extended in [5] to the Gilbert–Elliot channel.

REFERENCES

[1] A. Albanese, J. Blömer, J. Edmonds, M. Luby, and M. Sudan. "Priority encoding transmission," *IEEE Trans. Inform. Theory*, vol. 42, pp. 1737–1744, November 1996.

[2] B. A. Banister, B. Belzer, and T. R. Fischer. "Robust image transmission using JPEG2000 and turbo-codes," *IEEE Signal Processing Letters*, vol. 9, pp. 117–119, April 2002.

[3] V. Chande and N. Farvardin. "Progressive transmission of images over memoryless noisy channels," *IEEE JSAC*, vol. 18, pp. 850–860, June 2000.

[4] V. Chande, H. Jafarkhani, and N. Farvardin. "Joint source-channel coding of images for channels with feedback," *Proc. IEEE Workshop Information Theory*, San Diego, February 1998.

[5] V. Chande, N. Farvardin, and H. Jafarkhani. "Image communication over noisy channels with feedback," *IEEE ICIP-99*, Kobe, October 1999.

[6] P. A. Chou, H. J. Wang, and V. N. Padmanabhan. "Layered multiple description coding," *Proc. 13th Intl. Packet Video Workshop*, Nantes, France, April 2003.

[7] P. Cosman, J. Rogers, P. G. Sherwood, and K. Zeger. "Combined forward error control and packetized zerotree wavelet encoding for transmission of images over varying channels," *IEEE Trans. Image Processing*, vol. 9, pp. 982–993, June 2000.

[8] S. Dumitrescu and X. Wu. "Globally optimal uneven erasure-protected multi-group packetization of scalable codes," *Proc. IEEE ICME 2005*, pp. 900–903, Amsterdam, July 2005.

[9] S. Dumitrescu, X. Wu, and Z. Wang. "Globally optimal uneven error-protected packetization of scalable code streams," *IEEE Trans. Multimedia*, vol. 6, pp. 230–239, April 2004.

[10] M. Grangetto, E. Magli, and G. Olmo. "Ensuring quality of service for image transmission: Hybrid loss protection," *IEEE Trans. Image Processing*, vol. 13, pp. 751–757, June 2004.

[11] R. Hamzaoui, V. Stanković, and Z. Xiong. "Fast algorithm for distortion-based error protection of embedded image codes," *IEEE Trans. Image Processing*, vol. 14, pp. 1417–1421, October 2005.

[12] R. Hamzaoui, V. Stanković, and Z. Xiong. "Optimized error protection of scalable image bitstreams," *IEEE Signal Processing Magazine*, vol. 22, pp. 91–107, November 2005.

[13] A. Hedayat and A. Nosratinia. "Rate allocation criteria in source-channel coding of images," *Proc. IEEE ICIP'01*, vol. 1, pp. 189–192, Thessaloniki, Greece, October 2001.

[14] A. E. Mohr, R. E. Ladner, and E. A. Riskin. "Approximately optimal assignment for unequal loss protection," *Proc. IEEE ICIP'00*, vol. 1, pp. 367–370, Vancouver, BC, September 2000.

[15] A. E. Mohr, E. A. Riskin, and R. E. Ladner. "Unequal loss protection: Graceful degradation of image quality over packet erasure channels through forward error correction," *IEEE JSAC*, vol. 18, pp. 819–828, June 2000.

[16] A. Nosratinia, J. Lu, and B. Aazhang. "Source-channel rate allocation for progressive transmission of images," *IEEE Trans. Commun.*, vol. 51, pp. 186–196, February 2003.

[17] R. Puri and K. Ramchandran. "Multiple description source coding using forward error correction codes," *Proc. 33rd Asilomar Conference on Signal, Systems, and Computers*, vol. 1, pp. 342–346, Pacific Grove, CA, October 1999.

[18] L. Rizzo, "On the feasibility of software FEC," DEIT Technical Report LR-970131.

[19] D. G. Sachs, R. Anand, and K. Ramchandran. "Wireless image transmission using multiple-description based concatenated code," *Proc. VCIP'00*, vol. 3974, pp. 300–311, San Jose, CA, January 2000.

[20] N. Seshadri and C.-E. W. Sundberg. "List Viterbi decoding algorithms with applications," *IEEE Trans. Commun.*, vol. 42, pp. 313–323, February–April 1994.

[21] P. G. Sherwood, X. Tian, and K. Zeger. "Channel code blocklength and rate optimization for progressive image transmission," *Proc. IEEE WCNC'99*, vol. 2, pp. 978–982, New Orleans, LA, 1999.

[22] P. G. Sherwood and K. Zeger. "Progressive image coding for noisy channels," *IEEE Signal Processing Letters*, vol. 4, pp. 189–191, July 1997.

[23] P. G. Sherwood and K. Zeger, "Error protection for progressive image transmission over memoryless and fading channels," *IEEE Trans. Commun*, vol. 46, pp. 1555–1559, December 1998.

[24] V. Stanković, R. Hamzaoui, Y. Charfi, and Z. Xiong. "Real-time unequal error protection algorithms for progressive image transmission," *IEEE JSAC*, vol. 21, pp. 1526–1535, December 2003.

[25] V. Stanković, R. Hamzaoui, and D. Saupe. "Fast algorithm for rate-based optimal error protection of embedded codes," *IEEE Trans. Commun.*, vol. 51, pp. 1788–1795, November 2003.

[26] V. Stanković, R. Hamzaoui, and Z. Xiong. "Efficient channel code rate selection algorithms for forward error correction of packetized multimedia bitstreams in varying chanels," *IEEE Trans. Multimedia*, vol. 6, pp. 240–248, April 2004.

[27] V. Stanković, R. Hamzaoui, and Z. Xiong. "Real-time error protection of embedded codes for packet erasure and fading channels," *IEEE Trans. Circuits and Systems for Video Tech.*, vol. 14, pp. 1064–1072, August 2004.

[28] V. Stanković, R. Hamzaoui, and Z. Xiong. "Robust layered multiple description coding of scalable media data for multicast," *IEEE Signal Proc. Letters*, vol. 12, pp. 154–157, February 2005.

[29] T. Stockhammer and C. Buchner. "Progressive texture video streaming for lossy packet networks," *Proc. 11th Intl. Packet Video Workshop*, Kyongju, May 2001.

[30] T. Stockhammer and C. Weiss. "Channel and complexity scalable image transmission," *Proc. IEEE ICIP'01*, vol. 1, pp. 102–105, Thessaloniki, Greece, October 2001.

[31] J. Thie and D. Taubman. "Optimal erasure protection assignment for scalable compressed data with small channel packets and short channel codewords," *EURASIP Journal on Applied Signal Processing*, no. 2, pp. 207–219, February 2004.

[32] Y. Wang, S. Wenger, J. Wen, and A. Katsaggelos. "Error resilient video coding techniques," *IEEE Signal Proc. Magazine*, pp. 61–82, July 2000.

[33] Y. Wang and Q.-F. Zhu. "Error control and concealment for video communication: A review," *Proc. IEEE*, vol. 86, pp. 974–997, May 1998.

10

Network-Adaptive Media Transport

Mark Kalman and Bernd Girod

10.1 INTRODUCTION

Internet packet delivery is characterized by variations in throughput, delay, and loss, which can severely affect the quality of real-time media. The challenge is to maximize the quality of audio or video at the receiver, while simultaneously meeting bit-rate limitations and satisfying latency constraints. For the best end-to-end performance, Internet media transmission must adapt to changing network characteristics; it must be *network adaptive*. It should also be *media aware*, so that adaptation to changing network conditions can be performed intelligently.

A typical streaming media system comprises four major components that should be designed and optimized in concert:

1. The *encoder application* compresses video and audio signals and uploads them to the media server.
2. The *media server* stores the compressed media streams and transmits them on demand, often serving hundreds of clients simultaneously.
3. The *transport mechanism* delivers media packets from the server to the client for the best possible user experience, while sharing network resources fairly with other users.
4. The *client application* decompresses and renders the video and audio packets and implements the interactive user controls.

The streaming media client typically employs error detection and concealment to mitigate the effects of lost packets. These techniques have been discussed in Chapter 2 for video and Chapter 3 for audio. To adapt to network conditions, the server receives feedback from the client, for example, as positive or negative acknowledgments. More sophisticated client feedback might inform about packet delay and jitter, link speeds, or congestion.

Unless firewalls force them to, streaming media systems do not rely on TCP but implement their own, application-layer transport mechanisms. This allows for protocols that are both network adaptive and media aware. A transport protocol may determine, for example, when to retransmit packets for error control and when to drop packets to avoid network congestion. If the protocol takes into consideration the relative importance of packets and their mutual dependencies, audio or video quality can be greatly improved.

The media server can implement intelligent transport by sending the right packets at the right time, but the computational resources available for each media stream are often limited because a large number of streams must be served simultaneously. Much of the burden of an efficient and robust system is therefore on the encoder application, which, however, cannot adapt to the varying channel conditions and must rely on the media server for this task. Rate scalable representations are therefore desirable to facilitate adaptation to varying network throughput without requiring computation at the media server. Switching among bit streams encoded at different rates is an easy way to achieve this task, and this method is widely used in commercial systems. Embedded scalable representations, as discussed in Chapter 5 for video and Chapter 6 for audio, are more elegant and are preferable, if the rate–distortion penalty often associated with scalable coding can be kept small.

This chapter begins in Section 10.2 with a review of the framework for rate–distortion optimized media streaming initially proposed by Chou and Miao [6]. In the sections that follow, we discuss extensions to the framework. Section 10.3 shows how rich acknowledgments can be incorporated. In Section 10.4, we discuss the importance of multiple deadlines for video packets. Section 10.5 discusses how the framework can be extended to include a more accurate statistical model for characterizing packet loss and delay. In Section 10.6, finally, we discuss an alternative to rate–distortion optimized streaming that directly minimizes congestion instead of rate.

10.2 RATE–DISTORTION OPTIMIZED STREAMING

We start by reviewing the seminal work by Chou and Miao on rate–distortion optimized (RaDiO) streaming [6]. They considered streaming as a stochastic control problem, with the goal of determining which packets to send and when to minimize reconstruction distortion at the client for a given average transmission rate. Our discussion serves as the starting point for the extensions and variations described in the later sections.

10.2.1 Basic RaDiO Framework

Let us assume that a media server has stored a compressed audio or video stream that has been packetized into data units. Each data unit l has a size in bytes B_l and a deadline by which it must arrive at the client in order to be useful for decoding. The importance of each data unit is captured by its *distortion reduction* ΔD_l, a value representing the decrease in distortion that results if the data unit is decoded. Often, distortion is expressed as mean-squared error, but other distortion measures might be used as well.

Whether a data unit can be decoded often depends on which other data units are available. In the RaDiO framework, these interdependencies are expressed in a directed acyclic graph. An example dependency graph is shown for SNR-scalable video encoding with Intra (I), Predicted (P), and Bidirectionally predicted (B) frames (Figure 10.1). Each square represents a data unit and the arrows indicate the order in which data units can be decoded.

The RaDiO framework can be used to choose an optimal set of data units to transmit at successive transmission opportunities. These transmission opportunities are assumed to occur at regular time intervals. Because of decoding dependencies among data units, the importance of transmitting a packet at a given transmission opportunity often depends on which packets will be transmitted in the near future. The scheduler therefore makes transmission decisions based on an entire optimized plan that includes anticipated later transmissions. Of course, to keep the system practical, only a finite time horizon can be considered.

The plan governing packet transmissions that will occur within a time horizon is called a *transmission policy*, π. Assuming a time horizon of N transmission opportunities, π is a set of length-N binary vectors π_l, with one such vector for each data unit l under consideration for transmission. In this representation, the N binary elements of π_l indicate whether, under the policy, the data unit l will

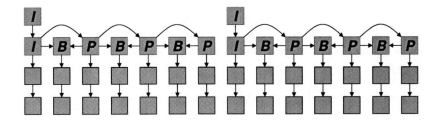

FIGURE 10.1: A directed acyclic graph captures the decoding dependencies for an SNR-scalable encoding of video with I-frames, P-frames, and B-frames. Squares represent data units and arrows indicate decoding order.

be transmitted at each of the next N transmission opportunities. The policy is understood to be contingent upon future acknowledgments that might arrive from the client to indicate that the packet has been received. No further transmissions of an acknowledged data unit l are attempted, even if π_l specifies a transmission for a future time slot.

Each transmission policy leads to its own *error probability*, $\varepsilon(\pi_l)$, defined as the probability that data unit l arrives at the client late, or not at all. Each policy is also associated with an expected number of times that the packet is transmitted under the policy, $\rho(\pi_l)$. The goal of the packet scheduler is to find a transmission policy π with the best trade-off between expected transmission rate and expected reconstruction distortion. At any transmission opportunity the optimal π minimizes the Lagrangian cost function

$$J(\pi) = D(\pi) + \lambda R(\pi), \tag{10.1}$$

where the expected transmission rate

$$R(\pi) = \sum_l \rho(\pi_l) B_l, \tag{10.2}$$

and the expected reconstruction distortion

$$D(\pi) = D_0 - \sum_l \Delta D_l \prod_{l' \preceq l} \left(1 - \varepsilon(\pi_{l'})\right). \tag{10.3}$$

The Lagrange multiplier λ controls the trade-off between rate and distortion. In (10.3) D_0 is the distortion if no data units arrive, ΔD_l is the distortion reduction if data unit l arrives on time and can be decoded, and the product term $\prod_{l' \preceq l} \left(1 - \varepsilon(\pi_{l'})\right)$ is the probability for this to occur. The notation $l' \preceq l$ is shorthand for the set of data units that must be present to decode data unit l.

In the aforementioned formulation, delays and losses experienced by packets transmitted over the network are assumed to be statistically independent. Packet loss is typically modeled as Bernoulli with some probability, and the delay of arriving packets is often assumed to be a shifted-Γ distribution. Expressions for $\varepsilon(\pi_l)$ and $\rho(\pi_l)$ can be derived in terms of the Bernoulli loss probabilities, the cumulative distribution functions for the Γ-distributed delays, the transmission policies and transmission histories, and the data units' arrival deadlines. These derivations are straightforward, but because the resulting expressions are cumbersome, they are omitted here.

The scheduler reoptimizes the entire policy π at each transmission opportunity to take into account new information since the previous transmission opportunity and then executes the optimal π for the current time. An exhaustive search to find the optimal π is generally not tractable; the search space grows exponentially with the number of considered data units, M, and the length of the policy vector, N [14]. Even though rates and distortion reductions are assumed to be additive, the graph of packet dependencies leads to interactions, and an exhaustive search would have to consider all 2^{MN} possible policies. Chou and Miao's RaDiO framework [6] overcomes this problem by using conjugate direction search. Their *Iterative Sensitivity Adjustment (ISA)* algorithm minimizes (10.1) with respect to the policy π_l of one data unit while the transmission policies of other data units are held fixed. Data units' policies are optimized in round-robin order until the Lagrangian cost converges to a (local) minimum.

Rewritten in terms of the transmission policy of one data unit, (10.1), (10.2) and (10.3) become

$$J_l(\pi_l) = \varepsilon(\pi_l) + \lambda' \rho(\pi_l), \tag{10.4}$$

where $\lambda' = \frac{\lambda B_l}{S_l}$ incorporates the rate–distortion trade-off multiplier λ from (10.1), the data unit size B_l, and S_l, a term that expresses the sensitivity of the overall expected distortion to the error probability $\varepsilon(\pi_l)$ of data unit l. The sensitivity term represents the relative importance of a particular data unit and incorporates the error probabilities of the other data units that l depends on. The sensitivity S_l changes with each iteration of the ISA algorithm to take into account the optimized policy for the other data units.

Figure 10.2 demonstrates improved video streaming performance achieved with RaDiO. Luminance PSNR versus transmitted bit rate is plotted for streaming simulations using an H.263+ two-layer SNR scalable encoding of the *Foreman* sequence. The frame rate is 10 fps; a Group of Pictures (GOP) consists of one I-frame followed by nine P-frames. The encoded source rate is 32 kbps for the base layer alone and 69 kbps when the enhancement layer is added. The results are for a simulated channel in which packet losses occur independently with a loss rate of 20%, and packet delays are drawn as independent, shifted-Γ random variables with a mean delay of 50 ms and a standard deviation of 25 ms. Figure 10.2 plots PSNR versus transmitted bit rate for a heuristic, prioritized ARQ system and for R–D optimized system. In the ARQ system, the client requests retransmissions for packets that do not arrive by a time interval after they are expected, and the server transmits these requested packets with priority as long as the requested packet may still reach the client in time for playout. When the capacity of the channel falls below the source rate for the enhanced stream, the ARQ system sends only the base layer packets. Both the ARQ and the R–D optimized system use an initial preroll delay of 400 ms. By continuously optimizing its packet transmission choices, the optimized system makes use of the SNR and temporal scalability of the source encoding to finely tune the source rate to the available channel capacity, yielding substantial gains.

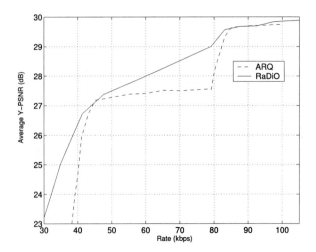

FIGURE 10.2:   PSNR vs. transmitted bit rate for a video streaming system that uses heuristic deadline-constrained prioritized ARQ and for a system that uses RaDiO transmission scheduling. The results are for an H.263+ SNR scalable encoding [9] of the *Foreman* sequence.

Several techniques have been proposed to further reduce the complexity of the basic RaDiO algorithm. Chou and Sehgal [7] have presented simplified methods to compute approximately optimized policies. The framework appears to be robust against simplifications of the algorithm and approximations to ΔD_l, the information characterizing the value of individual packets with respect to reconstruction distortion. An attractive alternative to ISA is a randomized algorithm recently developed by Setton in which heuristically and randomly generated candidate policies are compared at each transmission opportunity [15,17]. The best policy from the previous transmission opportunity is one of the candidates and thus past computations are efficiently reused. With a performance similar to ISA, the randomized algorithm usually requires much less computation.

10.2.2 Receiver-Driven Streaming

When transmitting many audio and video streams simultaneously, a media server might become computation limited rather than bandwidth limited. It is therefore desirable to shift the computation required for network adaptive media transport from the server to the client to the extent possible. Fortunately, rate–distortion optimized streaming can be performed with the algorithm running at the client so that very little computation is required at the server [7].

For *receiver-driven* streaming, the client is provided information about the sizes, distortion reduction values, and interdependencies of the data units available at the server ahead of time. The size of this *hint track* or *rate–distortion preamble* is small relative to the media stream. The receiver uses this information to compute a sequence of requests that specify the data units that the server should transmit. It is straightforward to adapt the algorithm discussed in Section 10.2.1 to compute a sequence of requests that yield an optimal trade-off between the expected transmission rate of the media packets that the server will send and the expected reconstruction distortion that will result [7]. Figure 10.3 illustrates the differences between sender-driven and receiver-driven streaming.

By combining sender-driven and receiver-driven techniques, the RaDiO framework can be applied to diverse network topologies. For example, RaDiO might be implemented in a proxy server placed between the backbone network and a last hop link (Figure 10.4) [3]. The proxy coordinates the communication between the media server and the client using a hybrid of receiver- and sender-driven stream-

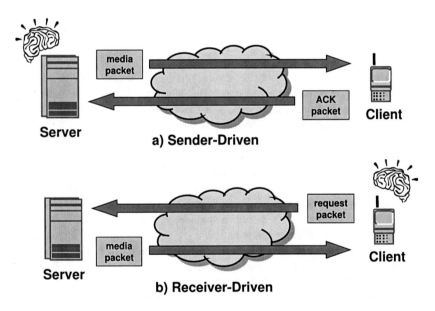

FIGURE 10.3:   In sender-driven streaming (a), the server computes an optimal sequence of media packet transmissions and the client acknowledges packets upon receipt. In receiver-driven streaming (b), the complexity is shifted to the client. The client computes an R–D optimized sequence of requests to send to the server and the server only needs to respond to the client's requests.

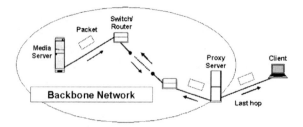

FIGURE 10.4: Proxy-driven RaDiO streaming. A proxy server located between the backbone network and a last hop link uses a hybrid of receiver- and sender-driven RaDiO streaming to jointly optimize requests to send to the server and media packets to forward to the client.

ing. End-to-end performance is improved compared to a sender- or receiver-driven RaDiO system because traffic created by retransmissions of media packets lost in the last hop to the client does not need to traverse and congest the backbone link.

10.3 RICH ACKNOWLEDGMENTS

In one extension to the RaDiO framework, streaming performance is improved through the use of *rich acknowledgments* [4]. In sender-driven RaDiO streaming using conventional acknowledgments, when a client receives a media packet, the client sends an acknowledgment packet (ACK) to the server. If the ACK packet is lost, the server may decide to unnecessarily retransmit the packet at the expense of other packets.

With rich acknowledgments, the client does not acknowledge each data unit separately. Instead, it periodically transmits a packet that positively acknowledges all packets that have arrived so far and negatively acknowledges (NACK) packets that have not yet arrived. A rich acknowledgment packet hence provides a snapshot of the state of the receiver buffer.

Rich acknowledgments require some changes to the basic RaDiO framework described in Section 10.2. As shown in [6], a transmission policy π_l for a data unit can be understood in terms of a Markov decision process. At discrete times t_i the server makes an observation o_i and then takes a transmission action a_i specifying *send* or *don't send*. Sequences of observation and action pairs (o_i, a_i) in time can be enumerated in a Markov decision tree. Each node q_i in the tree specifies a particular history of observations and actions $(a_0, o_0), (a_1, o_1), \ldots, (a_i, o_i)$. A transmission policy specifies what transmission action will be taken as a function of what state q_i is reached in the tree.

A Markov decision tree is shown in Figure 10.5. The tree enumerates the possible sequences of observation–action pairs for the transmission of a data unit using

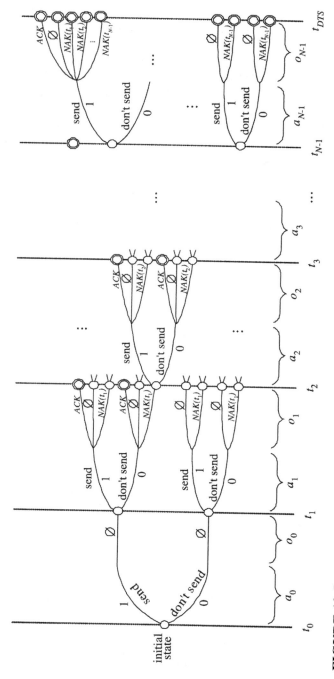

FIGURE 10.5: State space for the Markov decision process when *rich acknowledgments* are used.

the rich acknowledgment scheme. In the tree, possible actions *a* are *send* or *don't send*. Possible observations *o* are (∅), no relevant feedback has arrived, *ACK*, a feedback packet has acknowledged the reception of the data unit, or *NACK*, a feedback packet has indicated that the packet has not been received by the feedback packet's send time. NACKs with different time stamps are distinct observations. In contrast, in the conventional feedback scheme in which each packet is acknowledged individually upon receipt, there are only two possible observations, *ACK* and ∅. Regardless of the scheme, the optimization algorithm calculates the probabilities of each path through the tree given a policy and then chooses the policy that yields the best trade-off between expected number of transmissions $\rho(\pi_l)$ and loss probability $\varepsilon(\pi_l)$.

Figure 10.6 compares average PSNR versus transmitted bit rate for the 13-s *Foreman* sequence streamed using the rich feedback scheme and using the conventional acknowledgment scheme. Two-layer SNR-scalable H.263+ is used for the encoding [9]. The bit rate of the base layer alone is 32 kbps with an average PSNR of 27 dB. When the enhancement layer is added, the encoded rate becomes 69 kbps with an average PSNR of 30.5 dB. The results are for simulation experiments with a 10% loss rate for both media packets and feedback packets. Delays for packets not lost were distributed according to independent shifted-Γ distributions with shift $\kappa = 50$ ms, mean $\mu = 25$ ms, and standard deviation $\sigma = 35$ ms.

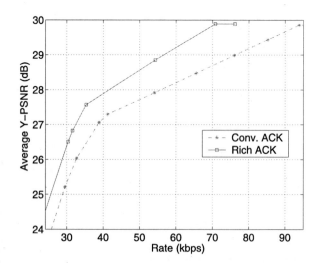

FIGURE 10.6:   Rich vs. conventional acknowledgments for rate–distortion optimized streaming of QCIF Foreman.

In Figure 10.6, the rich acknowledgment scheme outperforms the RaDiO scheme with conventional ACKs for all transmission rates. The maximum PSNR improvement is 1.3 dB at a transmitted bit rate of 70 kbps. The improved performance of the rich acknowledgment scheme is due to the robust transmission of the feedback information. With rich acknowledgments, the effect of a lost feedback packet is mitigated because subsequent feedback packets contain the same (updated) information. In addition, because rich acknowledgment packets also provide NACKs, there is less ambiguity for the server to resolve. In the case of conventional feedback, a nonacknowledged transmission may be due to a lost media packet or to a lost acknowledgment packet.

10.4 MULTIPLE DEADLINES

In the RaDiO framework described in Section 10.2, ΔD_l is the expected distortion reduction if data unit l is decodable by its deadline. It was assumed that a data unit l must arrive by its specific deadline in order for its distortion reduction ΔD_l to be realized and in order for data units dependent on l to be decoded. Late data units are discarded. Often, however, a data unit arriving after its deadline is still useful for decoding.

As an example, consider the case of bidirectional prediction with a sequence of frames I-B-B-B-P. In the RaDiO framework, the deadline for the P-frame would be determined by the decoding time of the first B-frame. If the P-frame arrives later, however, it should not be discarded. It may still be useful for decoding subsequent B-frames or at least for decoding and displaying the P-frame itself. Thus there are several deadlines associated with the P-frame, each with its own associated distortion reduction [18].

Another example where a data unit may be associated with multiple deadlines is the case of decoders that allow *Accelerated Retroactive Decoding* (ARD). This idea was initially proposed in the context of MPEG-2 transmission over ATM [8]. ARD makes use of the ability of many streaming clients to decode video faster than real time. With ARD, when late-arriving data units finally do arrive, the decoder goes back to the frames corresponding to the late-arriving packets and quickly again decodes the dependency chain up to the current playout time, but now without error. In this way the remaining pictures in the GOP can be decoded and displayed without degradation.

As shown in [12], the introduction of multiple deadlines results in changes to expressions used to calculate expected distortion $D(\pi)$ for R–D optimized streaming. For each data unit, there is no longer a single error probability, but a set of them, one for each of the frame deadlines associated with that data unit. This results in changes to (10.4) that express the Lagrangian cost (10.1) as a function of only the transmission policy of one data unit π_l while other policies are held fixed. With multiple deadlines, the expression in (10.4) becomes

$$J_l(\pi_l) = \rho(\pi_l) + \sum_{i \in \mathcal{W}_l} \nu_{t_i} \varepsilon(\pi_l, t_i), \tag{10.5}$$

where $\mathcal{W}_l$ is the set of frames that require data unit l for decoding, i is the frame index, and t_i is the decoding deadline for frame i. The quantity $\varepsilon(\pi_l, t_i)$ is the probability that data unit l does not arrive by deadline t_i. As before, $\rho(\pi_l)$ is the expected number of times data unit l is transmitted under policy π_l.

In (10.5) the quantity ν_{t_i}, given by $\nu_{t_i} = \frac{S_{l,t_i}}{\lambda B_l}$, is analogous to the reciprocal of λ' in (10.4). Note that the sensitivity term S_{l,t_i} is also indexed by the deadline. It is the sensitivity of the overall distortion to the arrival of data unit l by deadline t_i.

Figure 10.7 shows performance gains due to the multiple deadline formulation in the case when ARD is implemented in a streaming video client. PSNR-versus-rate results are shown for the *Foreman* sequence streamed in a low-latency application in which the preroll delay is 100 ms. In the simulation experiments, frames of video were due for decoding 100 ms after they became available for

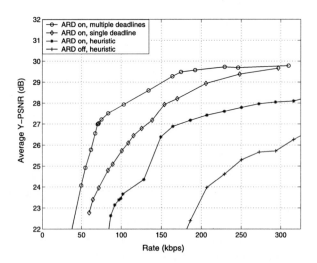

FIGURE 10.7: Rate–distortion performance of schedulers for the Foreman sequence streamed over a simulated channel with iid shifted-Γ-distributed packet delays and 20% Bernoulli loss. End-to-end latency $d = 100$ ms. A PSNR improvement of up to 3.15 dB is observed for the optimizing scheduler that considers multiple deadlines compared to the one that considers a single deadline.

transmission at the server. The packet loss rate was 20% in both directions, and delays for packets not lost were independent, identically distributed (iid) shifted-Γ with shift $\kappa = 10$ ms, mean $\mu = 40$ ms, and standard deviation $\sigma = 23$ ms. The sequence was encoded using a two-layer SNR-scalable H.263+ [9], at 10 fps with prediction structure I-P-P-P ... and GOP length of 20 frames. The base and enhancement layer bit rates and PSNRs were similar to those of the sequence in Section 10.3.

In Figure 10.7, PSNR-versus-rate curves compare the multiple-deadline schemes and the single-deadline scheme, as well as a heuristic scheme. The heuristic scheme uses prioritized, deadline-limited ARQ in which base layer retransmissions had highest priority, followed by base layer transmissions, enhancement layer transmission, and enhancement layer retransmissions. Retransmissions were triggered when packets were not acknowledged within the 0.90 point of the cumulative distribution function of the round-trip time. Figure 10.7 shows that the multiple-deadline formulation yields up to a 3-dB improvement over a single deadline. The single-deadline scheme does not recognize the utility of late packets and often misses opportunities to schedule valuable data units close to, or after, their original deadlines. The R–D optimizing schemes outperform the heuristic schemes regardless of whether the heuristic schemes are used with ARD-enabled clients.

10.5 DEPENDENT PACKET DELAYS

In the R–D optimized streaming algorithms discussed in Sections 10.2, 10.3, and 10.4, the delays of successive packets have been modeled as iid shifted-Γ random variables with loss also occurring independently as described in [6]. The iid model simplifies calculations for $\varepsilon(\pi_l)$, the error probability due to a transmission policy, and for $\rho(\pi_l)$, the expected number of transmissions that will result from a transmission policy. It fails to capture the dependence among delays, however. In the Internet, successive packets usually travel along the same path, might experience a similar backlog while waiting in the same queues, and rarely arrive out of order. This results in strongly dependent delays of successive packets.

In streaming simulations that employ measured Internet delay traces, we have observed that the iid model can lead to suboptimal scheduling performance. For example, Figure 10.8 shows simulation results when packets were delayed according to a delay trace measured over a 14-hop Internet path with a cable modem last hop, as described in [10]. At transmission rates above 80 kbps, the multideadline R–D optimizing formulation described in Section 10.4 is outperformed by the simple heuristic ARQ scheme (also described in Section 10.4). The suboptimal performance at high rates is due to the iid delay model assumed by the R–D optimization algorithm. With the iid model, policies that specify repeated

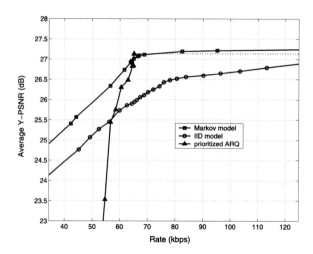

FIGURE 10.8:   Rate–distortion performance of schedulers for the *Foreman* sequence streamed over a measured Internet delay trace. End-to-end latency $d = 150$ ms. The RaDiO scheduler that models delays as iid is suboptimal at high rates where it is outperformed by a heuristic-prioritized ARQ scheduler. The scheduler that models delays as a first-order Markov random process yields PSNR improvement of up to 1.1 dB over the iid scheduler.

transmission of a data unit at successive opportunities yield lower calculated error probabilities for errors due to late loss. The algorithm mistakenly believes that if the data unit is delayed the first time it is transmitted, subsequent transmissions may arrive earlier and on time. Thus at higher rates, the algorithm sends packets multiple times even though in our measured trace the loss probability is very low (0.014%) and packets always arrive in the order they are transmitted.

Rate–distortion performance can be improved by modeling packet delays at successive transmission time slots as a first-order Markov random process [10]. In [11] we have presented an R–D optimization scheme that uses this model. In the scheme, feedback packets inform the server about the delay over the channel in the recent past. Using this feedback and a family of conditional delay distributions, the scheme can more accurately calculate the expected distortion $D(\pi)$ and the expected transmission rate $R(\pi)$ resulting from a transmission policy π.

Figure 10.8 shows that the RaDiO scheme using the Markov channel model outperforms the RaDiO scheduler that uses iid delay modeling by up to 1.1 dB and is not outperformed by the heuristic scheduler at low rates. We note that the mean PSNR for all experiments is limited because the delays in the 14-hop cable modem trace are often greater than the 150-ms preroll. Because the client uses the ARD scheme discussed in Section 10.4 and because the packet loss rate is nearly zero, the heuristic scheme, which uses time-out triggered retransmissions with the time-out set to $2 \cdot$ (estimated RTT), performs nearly optimally at high transmission bit rates.

10.6 CONGESTION–DISTORTION OPTIMIZED SCHEDULING

RaDiO streaming and its various extensions described do not consider the effect that transmitted media packets may have on the delay of subsequently transmitted packets. Delay is modeled as a random variable with a parameterized distribution; parameters are adapted slowly according to feedback information. In the case when the media stream is transmitted at a rate that is negligible compared to the minimum link speed on the path from server to client, this may be an acceptable model. In the case where there is a bottleneck link on the path from server to client, however, packet delays can be strongly affected by *self-congestion* resulting from previous transmissions.

In [16] a congestion–distortion optimized (CoDiO) algorithm is proposed, which takes into account the effect of transmitted packets on delay. The scheme is intended to achieve an R–D performance similar to RaDiO streaming but specifically schedules packet transmissions in a way that yields an optimal trade-off between reconstruction distortion and congestion, measured as average delay, on the bottleneck link. As with RaDiO, transmission actions are chosen at discrete transmission opportunities by finding an optimal policy over a time horizon. However, in CoDiO, the optimal policy minimizes the Lagrangian cost $D + \lambda \Delta$, where D is the expected distortion due to the policy and Δ is the expected end-to-end delay, which measures congestion.

CoDiO's channel model assumes a succession of high-bandwidth links shared by many users, followed by a bottleneck last hop used only by the media stream under consideration. CoDiO needs to know the capacity of the bottleneck, which can be estimated, for example, by transmitting back-to-back packets [13]. The overall delay experienced by packets is captured by a gamma pdf that is dynamically shifted by an extra delay that models the self-inflicted backlog at the bottleneck. Since the bottleneck is not shared and its capacity is known, the backlog can be accurately estimated. This channel model is used to calculate the expected distortion D due to packet loss and the expected end-to-end delay Δ.

The performance of the CoDiO scheme is illustrated using ns-2 simulation experiments [1,16]. The first hop is a high-bandwidth 45-Mbps link with 22-Mbps exponential cross-traffic. The second hop is a 50-kbps link that carries only the video traffic to be scheduled. The video encoding used is the same as that described in Section 10.4. The preroll delay for the experiments is 600 ms. Figure 10.9 plots luminance PSNR versus average end-to-end delay for the CoDiO

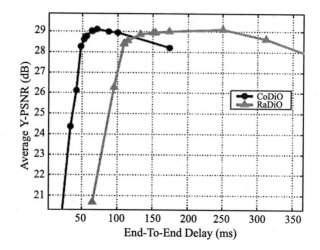

FIGURE 10.9: Performance comparison of RaDiO and CoDiO for video streaming over a bottleneck link. The horizontal axis shows the expected end-to-end delay due to the congestion caused by the video traffic. CoDiO causes much less congestion than RaDiO at the same PSNR. From [16].

and the RaDiO schemes. The various points on the curves were generated by varying λ, which trades-off congestion–distortion in the case of CoDiO and rate distortion in the case of RaDiO. The graphs show that the CoDiO scheme resulted in end-to-end delays that were approximately half of those measured for the RaDiO scheme at the same PSNR. Transmission rates versus PSNR for both schemes are almost identical (Figure 10.10).

CoDiO outperforms RaDiO because it distributes transmissions in time and attempts to send packets as late as safely possible. This reduces the backlog in the bottleneck queue and hence the average end-to-end delay. Other applications sharing the network experience less congestion. RaDiO, however, is less network-friendly. As the scheduler only considers average rate, its traffic tends to be more burst, relying more on the buffering in the network itself.

10.7 SUMMARY AND FURTHER READING

In this chapter we have discussed network adaptive media transport through the RaDiO framework for rate distortion optimized media streaming. After reviewing the basic framework as initially presented by Chou and Miao, we considered extensions and enhancements that have been proposed. The framework can be implemented in a media server or, alternatively, at the client. Rich acknowledgments

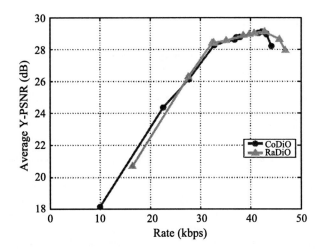

FIGURE 10.10:   Rate–distortion performance of RaDiO and CoDiO for video streaming over a bottleneck link. From [16].

are an easy way to improve resilience against losses in the feedback channel. For video streaming, it is useful to incorporate multiple deadlines for packets. Considerable gains are possible by accelerated retroactive decoding of packets, particularly if a multiple-deadline scheduler knows about this client capability and schedules accordingly. RaDiO typically assumes independent packet delays, but, in fact, Internet packet delays are highly dependent. In Section 10.5, an extension of RaDiO streaming that utilizes a Markov model of successive packet delays has been shown to rectify the poor performance that arises due to its simple iid channel model. Finally, we have considered self-congestion that might arise with streaming over a bottleneck link. Congestion–distortion optimized streaming, CoDiO, yields the same PSNR performance as RaDiO, but reduces the congestion, measured in terms of end-to-end delay.

Readers with further interest should first study Chou and Miao's seminal paper [6] in depth. The paper is based on a longer technical report [5], so readers might want to consult this document as well. Interestingly, numerous papers appeared during the review period of [6], inspired by this work, many of which are now referenced in [6] itself. Various extensions and the most comprehensive experiments applying RaDiO to streaming of H.264/AVC encoded video can be found in Chakareski's dissertation [2]. The best reference for CoDiO and low-complexity randomized scheduling algorithms so far is Setton's dissertation [15]. There are numerous research groups active in the area, and their publications might be of interest to those following the evolving state-of-the-art in network adaptive media transport.

REFERENCES

[1] The Network Simulator – ns-2. *www.isi.edu/nsnam/ns/*.

[2] J. Chakareski. *Rate-Distortion Optimized Packet Scheduling for Video Streaming.* Ph.D. thesis, Rice University, Houston, TX, 2005.

[3] J. Chakareski, P. A. Chou, and B. Girod. Rate-distortion optimized streaming from the edge of the network. In *IEEE Workshop on Multimedia Signal Processing*, St. Thomas, U.S. Virgin Islands, December 2002.

[4] J. Chakareski and B. Girod. Rate-distortion optimized video streaming with rich acknowledgments. In *Proceedings SPIE Visual Communications and Image Processing VCIP-2004*, Santa Clara, CA, January 2004.

[5] P. A. Chou and Z. Miao. Rate-distortion optimized streaming of packetized media. Technical report MSR-TR-2001-35, Microsoft Research, Redmond, WA, 2001.

[6] P. A. Chou and Z. Miao. Rate-distortion optimized streaming of packetized media. *IEEE Transactions on Multimedia*, 8(2):390–404, April 2006.

[7] P. A. Chou and A. Sehgal. Rate-distortion optimized receiver-driven streaming over best-effort networks. In *Packet Video Workshop*, Pittsburgh, PA, April 2002.

[8] M. Ghanbari. Postprocessing of late cells for packet video. *IEEE Transactions on Circuits and Systems for Video Technology*, 6(6):669–678, December 1996.

[9] ITU-T. Video coding for low bitrate communication: Recommendation H.263, Version 2, 1998.

[10] M. Kalman and B. Girod. Modeling the delays of successively-transmitted internet packets. In *IEEE Conference on Multimedia and Expo*, Taipei, Taiwan, June 2004.

[11] M. Kalman and B. Girod. Rate-distortion optimized video streaming using conditional packet delay distributions. In *IEEE Workshop on Multimedia Signal Processing*, Siena, Italy, September 2004.

[12] M. Kalman, P. Ramanathan, and B. Girod. Rate distortion optimized streaming with multiple deadlines. In *IEEE International Conference on Image Processing*, Barcelona, Spain, September 2003.

[13] V. Paxson. *Measurement and Analysis of End-to-End Internet Dynamics.* Ph.D. dissertation, UC Berkeley, Berkeley, CA, 1997.

[14] M. Podolsky, S. McCanne, and M. Vetterli. Soft ARQ for layered streaming media. Technical Report UCB/CSD-98-1024, University of California, Computer Science Department, Berkeley, CA, November 1998.

[15] E. Setton. *Congestion-Aware Video Streaming over Peer-to-Peer Networks.* Ph.D. dissertation, Stanford University, Electrical Engineering, 2006.

[16] E. Setton and B. Girod. Congestion-distortion optimized scheduling of video over a bottleneck link. In *IEEE Workshop on Multimedia Signal Processing*, Siena, Italy, September 2004.

[17] E. Setton, J. Noh, and B. Girod. Congestion-distortion optimized peer-to-peer video streaming. In *Proc. IEEE International Conference on Image Processing, ICIP-2006*, Atlanta, GA, October 2006.

[18] S. Wee, W. Tan, J. Apostolopoulos, and M. Etoh. Optimized video streaming for networks with varying delay. In *Proceedings of the IEEE International Conference on Multimedia and Expo 2002*, Lausanne, Switzerland, August 2002.

PART **D**

WIRELESS NETWORKING

CHAPTER 11 Performance Modeling and Analysis over Medium Access
Control Layer Wireless Channels
(Syed Ali Khayam and Hayder Radha)

CHAPTER 12 Cross-Layer Wireless Multimedia
(Mihaela van der Schaar)

CHAPTER 13 Quality of Service Support in Multimedia Wireless
Environments
(Klara Nahrstedt, Wanghong Yuan, Samarth Shah, Yuan Xue,
and Kai Chen)

11

Performance Modeling and Analysis over Medium Access Control Layer Wireless Channels

Syed Ali Khayam and Hayder Radha

11.1 INTRODUCTION

Wireless networks suffer from frequent bit errors due to their vulnerability to interference and transmission medium degradation. Errors not corrected by a wireless physical layer propagate to the medium access control (MAC) layer. Corrupted packets with bit errors are generally detected and dropped using a MAC layer checksum at a wireless receiver. Because users have little or no control over the hardware-based wireless physical layer, MAC layer bit errors constitute the higher layers' view of the wireless channel. Moreover, wireless standards generally adapt the physical layer to cater for new requirements, but the MAC and higher layers remain unchanged [1,2]. There has been significant research interest in analysis of wireless MAC layer packet losses and bit errors [3–9].

An accurate model of the MAC layer channel can render important insights into the underlying characteristics of an impairment (e.g., bit errors, packet losses) random process. This insight is essential for the design, performance evaluation, and parameter tuning of a wide range of wireless communication protocols, applications, and services. For instance:

- *Wireless congestion control protocols*, instead of relying on MAC layer retransmissions, can use accurate MAC layer error models to differentiate between losses due to congestion, medium degradation, or mobility. The inability of wired congestion control algorithms to differentiate between different types of losses (and the consequent bandwidth underutilization) has been repeatedly highlighted by wireless studies. Knowledge of losses due to channel errors is assumed in many wireless congestion control solutions and such knowledge can only be rendered by real-time MAC layer channel models. Understanding of error frequency and burstiness is also instrumental in parameter tuning of wireless congestion control protocols.

- *Cross-layer protocols* can use a real-time channel model to choose whether to use MAC layer retransmissions or to ignore data payload errors according to different application requirements.

- *Reliable routing protocols* for mobile networks can use MAC layer channel models to differentiate (and ultimately choose) reliable versus shortest routes to different destinations, provided that the model is able to provide real-time error characterization at different hops of the network.

- *MAC protocols* can decide when to increase/decrease the physical transmission data rate based on real-time channel estimation. An accurate channel model can predict future error characteristics, thereby saving the MAC layer protocol the overhead of switching to an inaccurate lower/higher data rate based on short-term observations.

- Real-time channel estimation provided by an accurate model can be employed by *rate-adaptive applications* to perform channel- and/or source-coding rate adaptation for efficient utilization of scarce wireless bandwidth.

- Design of effective *error-control schemes* for different wireless applications requires a thorough understanding of errors above the physical layer.

- Design of *error-resilience features* of contemporary multimedia codecs can benefit greatly from knowledge of MAC layer error characteristics.

Most benefits of a wireless MAC layer channel model can be realized when the model is able to provide real-time and online channel characterization and prediction. In complexity- and power-constrained wireless and mobile environments such channel characterization is only possible with a low-complexity model.

11.2 MARKOV CHAINS FOR WIRELESS CHANNEL MODELING

Markov chains have shown remarkable promise in modeling of many wireless error and loss processes [3–9]. Therefore, throughout the text we focus on analyzing and modeling wireless errors using Markov chains.

11.2.1 Discrete-Time Markov Chains

Let us consider a discrete-time stochastic process, X_n, that transits between states denoted as integers from a finite set $H = \{0, 1, \ldots, N - 1\}$. If $X_n = i$, then the process is said to be in state i at discrete time instance n. Whenever the process is in state i, there is a fixed probability that the next state of the process will be j. If that probability can be expressed

$$\Pr\{X_{n+1} = j \mid X_n = i, X_{n-1} = i_{n-1}, \ldots, X_0 = i_0\} = \Pr\{X_{n+1} = j \mid X_n = i\},$$
(11.1)

for all states $j, i, i_{n-1}, \ldots, i_0 \in H$ and for all $n \geq 0$, then such a stochastic process is known as a *discrete-time Markov chain* and (11.1) is called the *Markov property*. Thus, for a Markov chain the conditional distribution of any future state X_{n+1}, given the past state sequence $X_0, X_1, \ldots, X_{n-1}$ and the present state X_n, is independent of the past states and depends only on the present state X_n. Let us define $p_{i,j} = \Pr\{X_{n+1} = j \mid X_n = i\}$ as the probability of transiting to state i from j. Since $p_{i,j}$ represents a probability measure, it exhibits the following properties: (a) $p_{i,j} \geq 0$ for all i, j and (b) $\sum_{j=0}^{N-1} p_{i,j} = 1$ for $i = 0, 1, \ldots, N - 1$. The probability of transiting to the next state can be represented in a matrix form. This matrix is referred to as the one-step state transition probability matrix.

The steady-state or stationary probabilities of a Markov chain represent the long-run proportion of the time spent in each state. Once the transitional probabilities of a Markov chain are known, the steady-state probabilities of being in a particular state are the unique nonnegative solutions of the following linear system of equations:

$$\pi_j = \sum_{i=0}^{N-1} \pi_i p_{i,j}, \quad j = 0, 1, \ldots, N - 1$$

$$\sum_{j=0}^{N-1} \pi_j = 1.$$

A detailed treatment of the theory of Markov chains may be found in [10] and [11].

11.2.2 Memory Length of a Random Process

Consider a random process X_n that assumes values from a binary alphabet. Let us generically refer to the outputs of the process as *bits* belonging to $\{0, 1\}$. Observing the outputs of the random process will result in a binary time series. In the present channel modeling context, X_n represents the bit error data comprising *good* and *bad* bits. Correlation of the binary time series can reveal the amount of temporal dependence in the series. Specifically, one can obtain a general sense of the number of previous bits on which a particular bit of the time series depends. The value of the temporal dependence is referred to as the *memory length* or *order* of the random process.

It has been observed by previous studies that wireless impairment processes generally have a memory length greater than one. One the other hand, if we consider each bit to be an output of the random process, then the Markov property in (11.1) implies that a process correlated with more than one bit in the past cannot be characterized as a Markov chain. An obvious question here is: If a binary wireless impairment process has a memory length greater than one, then how does one use a Markov chain to model that process? The answer to this question is rather straightforward. We define a high-order Markov chain where each output of the process contains as many bits as the memory length. The output at each step is then a fixed number of bits referred to as the memory window. Since the size of the memory window is constant, at each step a new bit is added to the memory window and the oldest bit is dropped from the memory window. If the process adds new bits in the least significant bit position of the memory window, then at each step the process updates a shift register by (i) shifting the register one bit to the left to eliminate the most significant or the oldest bit and (ii) adding a new bit to the least significant bit position.

11.2.3 High-Order Markov Chains for Wireless Bit Errors

For a Markov chain with memory length k, one can represent the states of the process by 2^k possible combinations of k consecutive bits. Transition probabilities of a kth order Markov chain (k-MC) for wireless modeling are generally estimated by sliding a k bit memory window (bit by bit) over the wireless traces and by observing the frequency of a bit pattern $\underset{\rightarrow}{x} = [x_1 x_2 \cdots x_k]$ followed by a bit pattern $\underset{\rightarrow}{y} = [y_1 y_2 \cdots y_k]$ for all patterns $\underset{\rightarrow}{x}$ and $\underset{\rightarrow}{y}$.

11.3 PRACTICAL ISSUES

This section discusses some practical issues that arise when developing a high-order Markov chain model of a wireless channel.

11.3.1 Determining the Memory Length of a Markov Chain

Determining the memory length of a Markov chain has been explored in prior texts [13,14]. Autocorrelation of a process is a simple indication of the maximum memory length of a Markov chain to model the process. Let $X(n_1)$ and $X(n_2)$ be two random variables derived from a random process X_n. The sample correlation of these random variables is defined as [12]

$$\gamma(n_1, n_2) = \mathrm{E}\{X(n_1)X(n_2)\}, \tag{11.2}$$

where $E\{X\}$ represents the sample mean of the random variable X. Since both $X(n_1)$ and $X(n_2)$ are derived from realizations of the same random process, the correlation is often referred to as *autocorrelation*. Let n_1 and n_2 be separated in time by a lag η such that $n_1 = 0$ and $n_2 = n_1 + \eta = \eta$. In this case, the autocorrelation becomes a function of the lag η and a sample autocorrelation coefficient can be derived from (11.2) as

$$\rho(\eta) = \frac{E\{X(0)X(\eta)\} - E\{X(0)\}E\{X(\eta)\}}{\sigma_{X(0)}\sigma_{X(\eta)}}, \tag{11.3}$$

where σ_X represents the sample standard deviation of the random variable X. The sample autocorrelation function, when computed for different values of the lag, is a direct metric for the level of temporal dependence in the random process. Since there is a one-to-one correlation between the random variables at lag zero, the autocorrelation has its maximum value of one at this point. For a large range of statistical data, autocorrelation between two random variables decreases rapidly with an increase in the lag between them. Lag beyond which the autocorrelation coefficient drops to an insignificant value represents the memory length of the process. In slightly relaxed jargon, memory length represents the lag beyond which the random variables of a random process are uncorrelated.

11.3.2 Determining the Accuracy of a Wireless Channel Model

The accuracy of a wireless channel is generally quantified by synthesizing impairment traces from the model. The model-based traces are compared with traces collected over the channel to ascertain how closely the model is approximating the actual source. Such accuracy evaluation necessitates an appropriate statistical measure. We describe two such measures here.

11.3.2.1 Standard Error Between Cumulative Distributions

Let $p(X)$ and $q(X)$ be two probability mass functions (PMFs) of a random variable X defined over an alphabet set Ψ. Let $P(X)$ and $Q(X)$ denote the cumulative distribution functions (CDFs) of $p(X)$ and $q(X)$. The standard error between $P(X)$ and $Q(X)$ is then defined

$$S_{\text{err}}\big(P(X), Q(X)\big)$$

$$= \sqrt{\frac{1}{n(n-2)}\left(n\sum_{\Psi}(P(X))^2 - \left(\sum_{\Psi}P(X)\right)^2 - \frac{(n\sum_{\Psi}P(X)Q(X) - (\sum_{\Psi}P(X))(\sum_{\Psi}Q(X)))^2}{n\sum_{\Psi}(Q(X))^2 - (\sum_{\Psi}Q(X))^2}\right)},$$

$$\tag{11.4}$$

where n is the length of the CDF. The random variable X should capture a key statistic of the random process. Assume that $P(X)$ is a CDF provided by the actual random source (e.g., the MAC layer bit error process) and $Q(X)$ is a CDF provided by a model that approximates the random source. Then the standard error provides a measure of the error incurred by the model in approximating the actual source. Small values of S_{err} imply that a model is a good approximate of the actual source.

11.3.2.2 Entropy Normalized Kullback–Leibler Divergence

From a source coding perspective, entropy provides a measure of the average number of bits required to represent a source completely. For the random variable X defined earlier, entropy provides a weighted average of the minimum information of X, where *information* corresponds to the number of bits required to uniquely represent all possible outcomes of a random variable. Entropy is expressed as

$$H\big(p(X)\big) = - \sum_{X \in \Psi} p(X) \log\big(p(X)\big). \tag{11.5}$$

The Kullback–Leibler divergence [15] renders a measure of the statistical divergence between $p(X)$ and $q(X)$ as

$$D\big(p(X)\|q(X)\big) = \sum_{X \in \Psi} p(X) \log\big(p(X)/q(X)\big). \tag{11.6}$$

The Kullback–Leibler divergence provides a nonnegative statistical divergence measure, which is zero if and only if $p = q$ [15]. When a base-2 logarithmic measure is used, the Kullback–Leibler divergence gives the number of overhead bits incurred because a model (represented by $q(X)$) is used instead of the actual source (represented by $p(X)$).

In order to accurately judge the performance of a model, the Kullback–Leibler measure should be weighted with respect to the entropy. For example, let us assume that the entropy of the source is 20 bits whereas the overhead incurred by the model is 0.75 bits. The overhead is relatively insignificant since the source inherently requires a large number of bits to be represented. However, for the same overhead (of 0.75 bits), if the entropy of the source is low, say 1 bit, then an overhead of 0.75 bits is extremely high. Hence, for accurate performance evaluation of a model, both the entropy of the process (represented by some random variable X) and the Kullback–Leibler divergence should be taken into consideration.

In view of the aforementioned considerations, a new statistical divergence measure, the *entropy normalized Kullback–Leibler (ENK) divergence*, was proposed in [8]. The ENK divergence renders a measure of the source-coding-like over-head incurred by employing a model instead of the actual random source. The ENK divergence is defined as

$$ENK\big(p(X)\|q(X)\big) = \frac{D(p(X)\|q(X))}{H(p(X))}, \qquad (11.7)$$

where $D(p\|q)$ and $H(p)$ are defined in (11.6) and (11.5), respectively. A closer examination reveals that the ENK measure inherits basic properties of the Kullback–Leibler divergence: (i) nonnegativity, $ENK(p\|q) \geq 0$, (ii) nonsymmetry, $ENK(p\|q) \neq ENK(q\|p)$, and (iii) $ENK(p\|q) = 0 \Leftrightarrow p = q$.

Small values of ENK divergence indicate that the model renders a good approximate of the actual random source. Conversely, large values of the ENK imply that the source-coding-like overhead of the model is large, that is, the model is not a good approximate of the actual source. Note that we would expect the ENK between two realizations of a random source to be a small value. For instance, the ENK between two traces collected over a wireless medium under similar conditions should be quite small. This ENK value can be used as an evaluation reference for the ENK between the actual observations (i.e., traces collected over the wireless network) and the model-based observations (i.e., traces artificially synthesized by the model).

11.3.2.3 Random Variables for Performance Comparison

The performance evaluation measures described in preceding discussions are dependent on the choice of an appropriate random variable X to represent the stochastic process. Hence, X should capture a key statistic of the bit error random process. Wireless channel modeling studies generally employ two random variables to evaluate the performance of a model: (i) burst length of correctly received bits, referred to as *good bursts*; and (ii) burst length of bit errors, referred to as *bad bursts*. Both these random variables assume nonzero positive integer values. The burstiness of the bit error process is adequately characterized using these two random variables.

11.4 MODELING 802.11B BIT ERROR PROCESSES USING MARKOV CHAINS

Let us now model the bit errors at 2- and 5.5-Mbps data rates of an 802.11b local area network (LAN) [1,2] using kth order Markov chains (k-MCs). The traces used for results in this section were collected by positioning the wireless sender (server) and receivers (clients) in separate rooms to simulate a realistic business/classroom/home-network wireless setup.

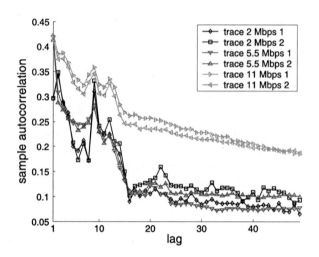

FIGURE 11.1:   Autocorrelation of bit error traces.

11.4.1 Autocorrelation of the Bit Error Traces

The sample autocorrelation coefficients of six traces collected at 2, 5.5, and 11 Mbps are illustrated in Figure 11.1. The autocorrelations at 2 and 5.5 Mbps exhibit a rapidly decaying trend as the level of temporal dependence decreases with time. From the examples provided in Figure 11.1, we assume that the memory length is determined by the lag beyond which the correlation is less than 0.15, an empirically determined threshold. Based on the threshold of 0.15, the maximum memory lengths of the 5.5-Mbps traces of Figure 11.1 are 12 and 14, respectively. The correlation of both 2-Mbps traces drops below 0.15 at the lag of 16. Thus, for the 5.5- and 2-Mbps bit error processes, maximum memory lengths of 14 and 16 are identified, respectively. (We observe later on that a bit-error process might be adequately characterized by a memory length that is slightly less than the maximum memory length identified here.)

Note that the correlation at 11 Mbps is really high even at large lags. Thus, the 11-Mbps bit error process has substantial memory. A k-MC model for such a highly correlated process will be unreasonably complex. Some models (e.g., the ones proposed in [16]) can be used to model the highly correlated 11-Mbps process. These models are out of the scope of this text.

11.4.2 Markov Chains for the 2-Mbps Bit Error Process

For both ENK and standard error performance evaluations, varying order Markov chains were trained using actual 2-Mbps bit error traces. The trained models were then used to synthesize artificial traces. The good- and bad-burst PMFs and CDFs were derived from both synthesized and actual traces. The ENK divergence between two actual traces is used as reference to quantify the performances of varying order Markov chains. Specifically, first the ENK divergence is computed by deriving $p(X)$ and $q(X)$ of (11.7) from two actual traces, say trace 1 and trace 2. This ENK value is used as a performance evaluation reference for Markov chains. To evaluate a Markov chain's accuracy, ENK divergence is computed by deriving $p(X)$ from trace 1 and $q(X)$ from a synthesized trace generated by the Markov chain. Similarly, for standard error-based performance evaluation, first $P(X)$ and $Q(X)$ of (11.4) are derived from trace 1 and trace 2, respectively. This value of standard error is used as a performance evaluation reference for Markov chains. To evaluate the accuracy of a Markov chain, standard error is computed by deriving $P(X)$ from trace 1 and $Q(X)$ from the synthesized trace generated by the Markov chain. Good- and bad-burst random variables are used for both ENK- and standard error-based performance evaluations.

The ENK-based performances of varying order Markov chains in modeling of the 2-Mbps bit error process are depicted in Figure 11.2. It is clear from Figure 11.2 that low-order Markov chains incur significant ENK overhead. Hence, low-order Markov chains cannot capture the 2-Mbps bit error behavior effectively. Nevertheless, as the order of the Markov chain increases, the ENK overhead decreases substantially and drops to a reasonable level. The accuracy of the order-10 Markov chain is comparable to the ENK divergence between two actual bit error traces. Figure 11.2 only provides analysis up to order 10, as the performance improvement saturates after the order-10 (1024 state) Markov chain. It can be observed that the 1024-state Markov chain renders a good approximate of the 2-Mbps MAC layer bit error process.

The standard errors of the good- and bad-burst CDFs rendered by the 1024-state Markov chain of the 2-Mbps process are given in Table 11.1. For comparison, standard errors of good- and bad-burst CDFs derived from two actual 2-Mbps traces are also given in Table 11.1. For both good- and bad-burst random variables, standard errors of the 1024-state Markov chain are very close to the standard errors of two actual traces. Thus, it can be concluded that a 1024-state Markov chain can adequately capture the bit error statistics of the 2-Mbps process.

11.4.3 Markov Chains for the 5.5-Mbps Bit Error Process

Performance of Markov chain models in modeling of the 5.5-Mbps bit error process is provided in Figure 11.3. High-order Markov chains perform remarkably well for the bad-burst random variable. Note that for the bad-burst random variable even smaller order chains perform quite adequately with low ENK

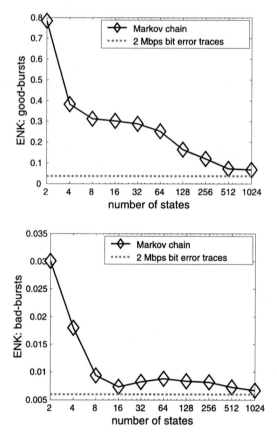

FIGURE 11.2:   ENK-based modeling accuracy of varying order Markov chains for the 2-Mbps MAC layer bit error process: (top) good bursts and (bottom) bad bursts.

Table 11.1:   Standard error of Markov chain-based cumulative densities at 2 and 5.5 Mbps.

	2 Mbps		5.5 Mbps	
	S_{err} between two actual traces	S_{err} between an actual trace and a trace synthesized by a 1024-state Markov chain	S_{err} between two actual traces	S_{err} between an actual trace and a trace synthesized by a 512-state Markov chain
Good bursts	0.003	0.014	0.004	0.006
Bad bursts	0.002	0.008	0.004	0.004

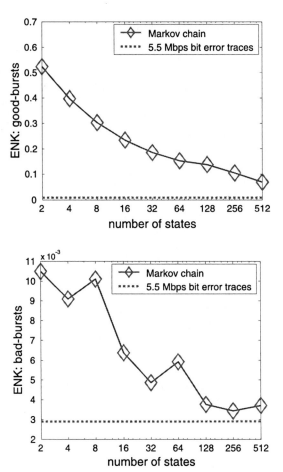

FIGURE 11.3: ENK-based modeling accuracy of varying order Markov chains for the 5.5-Mbps MAC layer bit error process: (top) good bursts and (bottom) bad bursts.

overhead for all cases. However, the good-burst random variable incurs significant overhead for low-order chains. For high-order chains, the overhead decreases and drops to a reasonable level, beginning at the order 9 (512 state) model.

The standard errors of good- and bad-burst CDFs at 5.5 Mbps are tabulated in Table 11.1. Clearly, the 512-state Markov chain provides standard errors that are comparable to the standard errors between actual 5.5-Mbps traces. Thus, a 512-state Markov chain can model the 5.5-Mbps process accurately.

11.5 REDUCING THE COMPLEXITY OF MARKOV CHAINS

The number of states in a k-MC is an exponential function of the memory length—2^k states for a process with memory-length k. This phenomenon, referred to as *state explosion*, constrains the applicability of a k-MC. For instance, a process with a memory-length 10 will result in $2^{10} = 1024$ states. Due to their high complexity, k-MCs cannot provide real-time channel characterization in resource-constrained wireless environments. Thus, despite their accuracy, the exponential complexity of Markov chains hampers their deployment in complexity-constrained wireless environments.

A natural alternative to reduce Markov chain complexity is to employ hidden Markov models (HMMs) [22]. However, in problem areas where HMMs are successful, well-defined characteristics of input data are available for preprocessing and training, for example, cepstral and linear-prediction features in speech. For wireless channel modeling, the corrupted trace regions exhibit highly random behavior, and it has been shown that simple features (e.g., energy) are not adequate to characterize error patterns in these corrupted regions [8]. Moreover, HMMs assume that the probability of staying in a state is distributed exponentially, which may not be an accurate assumption on practical wireless channels. An HMM trained using the exponential distribution assumption results in inaccurate parameterization, consequently leading to a model that is unable to approximate the bit error process [8].

Some studies have tried alternative approaches to approximate wireless bit error behavior [4–20]. This section outlines one such approach to reducing the complexity of Markov chains.

11.5.1 Observations About Markov Chains

Let us first state some important observations about k-MCs. These observations are employed in subsequent sections to derive properties of k-MCs. The first observation is a direct consequence of the binary nature of wireless impairment processes.

Observation 1. *For a binary process, if a bit-by-bit sliding window is used to compute the transition probabilities of a 2^k state Markov chain, then from a current state, $X_n = i$, in one transition the Markov chain can transit to only two possible states given by*

$$X_{n+1} = \begin{cases} (2i) \bmod 2^k, \\ (2i + 1) \bmod 2^k, \end{cases} \tag{11.8}$$

where k is the memory length of the Markov chain and $i \in \{0, 1, \ldots, 2^k - 1\}$ is an arbitrary state from the Markov state space.

An example given in Figure 11.4 clearly demonstrates this observation. A memory-length $k = 4$ is used in this example. The set of all possible Markov states is $\{0, 1, 2, \ldots, 2^4 - 1 = 15\}$. The current state is $X_n = (0110)_2 = (6)_{10}$ and, as the window slides by one bit, the 0 in the most significant bit position will be dropped and a bit will be added to the least significant bit position. Because the data are binary, the chain can transit to either $(1100)_2 = (12)_{10}$ or $(1101)_2 = (13)_{10}$. Thus, in essence, Observation 1 implies that at each slide of the memory window the process' current state i is subjected to three operations: left shift by one bit, which yields $2i$, followed by an addition of a zero $(2i + 0 = 2i)$ or an addition of a one $(2i + 1)$ at the least significant bit position (LSB), followed by a modulus operation that ensures that if the current state of the process is $X_n = 2^{k-1}$, then the next state wraps around to state 0 (for $X_{n+1} = 2i$) or state 1 (for $X_{n+1} = 2i + 1$). For instance, in the preceding example with $k = 4$, if $X_n = (1000)_2 = (8)_{10} = 2^{k-1}$, then the next state will be either $X_{n+1} = (2 \times 8) \bmod 2^4 = (0)_{10} = (0000)_2$ or $X_{n+1} = (2 \times 8 + 1) \bmod 2^4 = (1)_{10} = (0001)_2$. Since each Markov state has two transition possibilities, each row of the Markov transition probability matrix will have at most two nonzero entries, given by $p_{i,(2i) \bmod 2^k}$ and $p_{i,(2i+1) \bmod 2^k} = 1 - p_{i,(2i) \bmod 2^k}$.

Intuitively, one can argue that the number of error-free bits received over any reasonable wireless channel should be much more than the number of corrupted bits. The second observation stated next formulates this claim in terms of Markov chain parameters.

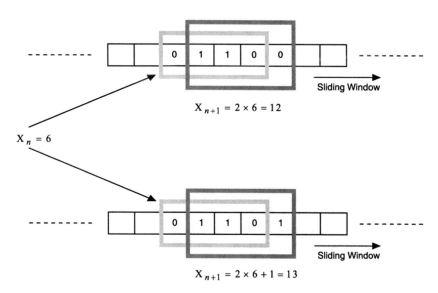

FIGURE 11.4:   Transition possibilities for a fourth-order Markov chain.

Table 11.2: Empirical evidence in support of Observation 2.

	2-Mbps bit error traces	5.5-Mbps bit error traces
π_0	0.997	0.974

Observation 2. *The steady-state probability of state 0 of a kth order Markov chain for wireless channels is much greater than the steady-state probabilities of all other states,*

$$\pi_0 \gg \sum_{j=1}^{2^k-1} \pi_j, \tag{11.9}$$

where k represents the memory length and π_i represents the steady-state probability of being in state i of the Markov chain.

This observation implies that the mean time spent in state 0 of the Markov chain (i.e., the state with no errors) is much greater than the mean time spent in all other states. As explained earlier, it can be intuitively argued that this observation holds for real-life wireless/mobile channels. Table 11.2 gives the steady-state probabilities of the 802.11b 2-Mbps bit error Markov chain of order 10 and the 5.5-Mbps bit error Markov chain of order 8. Since the steady-state probability of staying in the good (all-zero) state is very close to one for the two cases shown in Table 11.2, we can safely claim that Observation 11.2 holds for the wireless channels currently under consideration.

11.5.2 Markov Chain Good-Burst and Bad-Burst Distributions

The objective of the present analysis is to ascertain partitions of Markov state space. States in a particular partition will then be grouped together to form an aggregate state in the low-complexity approximating process. We want to define the Markov state space partitions such that the resulting aggregate process, while being less complex, closely matches the Markov chain characteristics.

Since bursts of good and bad bits on the channel are two fundamental (and arguably the most critical) characteristics that should be captured by an accurate model [7–9], the main Markov chain attribute that we focus on is how it captures bursts of good and bad bits. To that end, in this section we derive generalized probability distributions of good and bad bursts for a kth order Markov chain, where k is an arbitrary positive integer. The probability distributions are derived in terms of Markov chain transition and steady-state probabilities. These distributions render useful insights into important Markov characteristics, which are employed to develop guidelines for defining Markov state space partitions in the following sections.

Before proceeding further, we employ Observation 1 to prove a necessary condition for defining partitions of a Markov chain's state space. Let H and S denote the state spaces of a Markov chain and an aggregate (approximate) process, respectively. Let $i \in H$ and $S_i \in S$ denote two arbitrary states of the Markov and the approximate process, respectively. Then the following lemma imposes a necessary condition for defining aggregate states.

Lemma 1. *The next state in an aggregate process can be determined accurately only if Markov states $(2i) \bmod 2^k$ and $(2i + 1) \bmod 2^k$ do not belong to the same aggregate state,*

$$(2i) \bmod 2^k \in S_j \Rightarrow (2i + 1) \bmod 2^k \notin S_j, \tag{11.10}$$

where k is the memory length, $i \in H$, and $S_j \in S$.

PROOF. Lemma 1 is easily proven by contradiction. In essence, this lemma implies that both transition possibilities of a Markov state cannot be aggregated in a single state. As mentioned in Observation 1, $(2i) \bmod 2^k$ and $(2i + 1) \bmod 2^k$ are the only possible transitions for state i. Let there exist an aggregate state S_j that contains both states $(2i) \bmod 2^k$ and $(2i + 1) \bmod 2^k$. Also, let S_q represent an aggregate state that contains state i. Then, p_{S_q, S_j} does not give any information about whether a good or a bad bit should be added to the memory window.

To simplify notation, from this point forward we drop the $\bmod 2^k$ operation (where k is the memory length) on Markov states. Thus, state $i \bmod 2^k$ is simply written as state i. Let I and B denote the good- and bad-burst random variables. We want to derive closed-form expressions of I and B in terms of Markov chain parameters. The expressions for good- and bad-burst random variables render insights into how a Markov chain captures these random variables. The following theorem states the Markov probability distribution of good bursts.

Theorem 1. *The probability distribution of a good burst of length exactly l, $\Pr\{I = l\}$, for a kth order Markov chain is*

$$\Pr\{I = l\} = \sum_{i=0}^{2^{k-1}-1} \pi_{2i+1} \times \mu_i \times \prod_{j=0}^{\min\{k-2,l-2\}} P_{(2i+1)2^j,(2i+1)2^{j+1}},$$

$$\forall k,\, l > 0,\ \text{where } \mu_i = \begin{cases} P_{(2i+1)2^{l-1},(2i+1)2^l} \times P_{(2i+1)2^l,(2i+1)2^{l+1}+1}, & l < k, \\ P_{2^{k-1},0}(p_{0,0})^{l-k} p_{0,1}, & l \geq k. \end{cases}$$

$$\tag{11.11}$$

PROOF. Before proceeding with the proof, we recall that the subscripts of all transition and steady-state probabilities are modulo 2^k. Let us focus on the proof of the $l \geq k$ case, as the proof of the other case is much simpler and follows a similar procedure. Given any current state, a good burst (i.e., burst of 0's) will start if the current state has a 1 in the LSB position of the memory window, that is, the current state represents an odd-numbered Markov state $X_n = 2i + 1, 0 \leq i \leq 2^{k-1} - 1$.

Without loss of generality, consider the state path given in Figure 11.5. For a good burst of length l starting in the current odd-numbered state, the next $k - 1$ transitions will be $(2i + 1), (2i + 1)2, (2i + 1)2^2, \ldots, (2i + 1)2^{k-1}$. Note that $(2i + 1) \mod 2^{k-1} = 2^{k-1}$ and, based on the discussion in Observation 1, the process wraps around to state 0 at this point, that is, at point $X_{n+k-1} = 2^{k-1}$, the good burst continues and the process wraps around, $X_{n+k} = 0$. This transition sequence is followed by $l - k$ zero bits, that is, the next $l - k$ transitions are from state 0 to state 0, giving $X_{n+k} = X_{n+k+1} = X_{n+k+2} = \cdots = X_{n+l} = 0$. The good burst ends when a 1 bit is encountered at the $(l + 1)^{\text{st}}$ transition and the Markov process moves to $X_{n+l+1} = (00\ldots01)_2 = (1)_{10}$. When expressed in the form of probabilities, this state transition path will have to be summed over all possible odd-valued Markov states,

$$\Pr\{I = l\} = \pi_1 \begin{bmatrix} p_{1,(1)2} \times p_{(1)2,(1)2^2} \times \cdots \times p_{(1)2^{k-2},(1)2^{k-1}} \\ \times p_{(1)2^{k-1},0} \times (p_{0,0})^{l-k} \times p_{0,1} \end{bmatrix}$$

$$+ \pi_3 \begin{bmatrix} p_{3,(3)2} \times p_{(3)2,(3)2^2} \times \cdots \times p_{(3)2^{k-2},(3)2^{k-1}} \\ \times p_{(3)2^{k-1},0} \times (p_{0,0})^{l-k} \times p_{0,1} \end{bmatrix} + \cdots$$

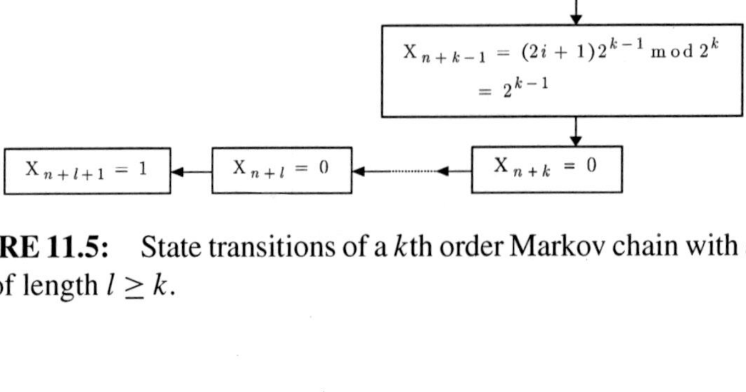

FIGURE 11.5: State transitions of a kth order Markov chain with a good burst of length $l \geq k$.

$$+ \pi_{2^k-1} \begin{bmatrix} P_{2^k-1,(2^k-1)2} \times P_{(2^k-1)2,(2^k-1)2^2} \\ \times \cdots \times P_{(2^k-1)2^{k-2},(2^k-1)2^{k-1}} \\ \times P_{(2^k-1)2^{k-1},0} \times (p_{0,0})^{l-k} \times p_{0,1} \end{bmatrix}.$$

Taking out common terms yields

$$\Pr\{I = l\} = p_{2^k-1,0}(p_{0,0})^{l-k} p_{0,1} \left[\sum_{i=0}^{2^{k-1}-1} \pi_{2i+1} \prod_{j=0}^{k-2} P_{(2i+1)2^j,(2i+1)2^{j+1}} \right],$$

which is the same as the expression in Theorem 1 for all $l \geq k$.

Similarly to Theorem 1, the probability distribution of a bad burst of length l is given in the following theorem.

Theorem 2. *The probability distribution of a bad burst of length exactly* l, $\Pr\{B = l\}$, *for a kth order Markov chain is*

$$\Pr\{B = l\} = \sum_{i=0}^{2^{k-1}-1} \pi_{2i} \times \mu_i \times \prod_{j=0}^{\min\{k-2,l-2\}} P_{(2i+1)2^j-1,(2i+1)2^{j+1}-1},$$

$$\forall k, l > 0, \ where \ \mu_i = \begin{cases} P_{(2i+1)2^{l-1}-1,(2i+1)2^l-1} \times P_{(2i+1)2^l-1,(2i+1)2^{l+1}-2}, & l < k, \\ P_{2^{k-1}-1,2^k-1} \times (p_{2^k-1,2^k-1})^{l-k} \times p_{2^k-1,2^k-2}, & l \geq k. \end{cases}$$

$$(11.12)$$

Proof of this theorem is similar to the proof of Theorem 1.

The expressions for good- and bad-burst probability distributions given in Equations (11.11) and (11.12) are rather convoluted. Hence in their present forms, these expressions neither offer any obvious insight into the random process' behavior nor are they amenable to further analysis. In the following section, we employ Observation 2 to simplify the probability distribution expressions of Equations (11.11) and (11.12). The simplification in turn leads us to the design guidelines that should be followed by a low complexity model.

11.5.3 Simplification of Good-Burst Distribution

Due to Observation 2 the steady-state probability of state 0 is very high and, consequently, the steady-state probabilities of odd states in the good-burst expression of (11.11) are negligible. Thus, the terms involving a transition to or from state 0 of the will dominate the good-burst probability distribution of (11.11). Moreover, since the channel usually stays in the good state for practical wireless networks, the good-burst length should in general be significantly greater than the memory length. Hence, an effective good-burst probability distribution $\Pr\{I = l\}$ should accurately capture the $l \geq k$ behavior. The good-burst probability distribution of (11.11) for $l \geq k$ can be rewritten

$$\Pr\{I = l\} \approx p_{2^{k-1},0}(p_{0,0})^{l-k} p_{0,1}, \quad \forall l \geq k > 0. \tag{11.13}$$

Although the aforementioned expression is an approximation of the Markov chain's good-burst probability distribution, it is clearly more tractable for analysis. A close look at (11.13) reveals that the parameter characterizing the (approximate) probability distribution is the probability of a good bit transmission followed by another good bit transmission ($p_{0,0}$) since this is the only parameter in (11.13) that involves the good-burst length (l). Hence, one important consideration while grouping states should be that the all-zero (i.e., no-error) state is not grouped with a large number of other states. This is also a natural consequence of Observation 2, which implies that the mean time spent in the all-zero (i.e., no-error) state is significantly higher than all other states.

Similarly, in addition to the state 0, two other important states are state 2^{k-1} and state 1 since $p_{2^{k-1},0}$ and $p_{0,1}$ are the only parameters, other than $p_{0,0}$, that appear in the approximate probability distribution given in (11.13). Hence, due to their relative importance in describing real-life wireless and mobile channels, a good model, in addition to state 0, should not group states 1 and 2^{k-1} with too many other states. This guideline will be employed to define a constant complexity model later.

11.5.4 Simplification of Bad-Burst Distribution

For the bad-burst probability distribution of (11.12), we again invoke Observation 2 and neglect the terms in (11.12) that are not multiplied with π_0. Using this approximation, the bad-burst distribution (11.12) can be written

$$\Pr\{B = l\} \approx \pi_0 \mu_0 \prod_{j=0}^{\min\{k-2, l-2\}} p_{2^j-1, 2^{j+1}-1},$$

$$\text{where } \mu_0 = \begin{cases} p_{2^{l-1}-1, 2^l-1} p_{2^l-1, 2^{l+1}-2}, & l < k, \\ p_{2^{k-1}-1, 2^k-1}(p_{2^k-1, 2^k-1})^{l-k} p_{2^k-1, 2^k-2}, & l \geq k. \end{cases} \tag{11.14}$$

The only terms appearing in (11.14) after the approximation involve states 0, $2^k - 2$, and $2^j - 1$, for any $1 \leq j \leq k$. From Observation 1 and the good-bursts approximation, we have already established that state 0 should not be aggregated with many other states. This deduction is reasserted here. Moreover, it is preferable not to aggregate state $2^k - 2$ with many other states. Also, if possible, all Markov states $2^j - 1$, where $1 \leq j \leq k$, should not be grouped with too many other states.

11.5.5 Guidelines for Approximating a kth Order Markov Chain

The analyses of preceding sections can be summarized in the following guidelines:

Guideline 1: Any state aggregation should satisfy the condition given in Lemma 1.

Guideline 2: State 0 should not be aggregated with other states.

Guideline 3: States 2^{k-1} and 1 should be aggregated with a minimal number of other states.

Guideline 4: States $2^k - 2$ and $2^j - 1$, for all $1 \leq j \leq k$, should be aggregated with a minimal number of other states.

Note that Guidelines 1 and 2 are more assertive than Guideline 3 and Guideline 4. This is due to the analysis provided in the previous section, which outlined that (i) Guideline 1 is necessary for an accurate model and (ii) Guideline 2, which is a consequence of Observation 2, is asserted by the approximate distributions of both good and bad bursts.

It can be observed that Guideline 1, Guideline 2, and Guideline 3 can be easily satisfied in a low-complexity model. However, Guideline 4 is somewhat problematic because putting each $2^j - 1$ state, for all $1 \leq j \leq k$, in a separate partition (i.e., separate aggregate state) makes the total number of states of the approximate model an increasing function of the memory-length k. Thus, satisfying Guideline 3 implies that the resultant complexity (i.e., number of states) of the aggregate model will at least be a linear function of the memory length. We, however, want to keep the number of states in the model independent of the underlying process' memory length. Nevertheless, if linear complexity is acceptable, then Guideline 4 should be incorporated into the design of future wireless channel models.

11.5.6 Constant Complexity Model

Based on the analysis of the last section, a *constant complexity model* (CCM) adhering to Guideline 1, Guideline 2, and Guideline 3 can be developed. The CCM keeps Markov states 0, 1, and 2^{k-1} each in a separate partition, while grouping all the remaining Markov states into two partitions. The resulting model always has five states irrespective of the memory length. The structure and transition possibilities of the CCM are illustrated in Figure 11.6. It is clearly outlined by Figure 11.6 that the CCM assigns separate (isolated) states to Markov states 0, 1, and 2^{k-1}, thereby adhering to Guideline 2 and Guideline 3. All remaining *even* Markov states are grouped in a single aggregate CCM state, while all remaining *odd* Markov states are grouped in another aggregate state. Note that none of the CCM states contain both an odd and an even state, that is, an aggregate state contains either even states or odd states. Thus, Guideline 1, which requires that

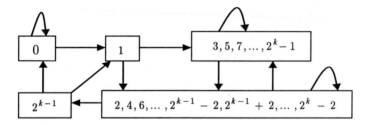

FIGURE 11.6:   State aggregation and transitions for the CCM.

Markov states $2i$ and $2i + 1$ are never aggregated together, is also satisfied by the CCM. Clearly, irrespective of the underlying process' memory length, the CCM always comprises five states. Based on our analysis, this five-state CCM should follow the behavior of the underlying 2^k state Markov process quite closely. This CCM efficacy is highlighted adequately in the next section where we compare its performance with Markov chains.

The Markov state space partitioning used by the CCM is only one of the many possible state assignments. Low-complexity channel models can also define other state partitions that should perform adequately as long as the aforementioned guidelines are followed.

11.5.7 Comparison of CCM with Markov Chains

11.5.7.1 Modeling Accuracy for the 2-Mbps Bit Error Process

Figure 11.7 provides ENK-based performance comparison of CCMs with varying memory lengths. Although the CCMs of Figure 11.7 have different memory lengths, the total number of states is five for all the CCMs. ENK overhead of the 1024-state Markov chain model formulates a criterion for performance evaluation of the CCMs. It is clear from Figure 11.7 (top) that for the good-burst random variable, CCMs with memory lengths of five and above perform as well as the 1024-state Markov model. Figure 11.7 (bottom) shows that the CCM ENK overhead for the bad-burst random variable is relatively higher than the Markov model. Nevertheless, in absolute terms the CCM ENK overhead is quite small. While keeping both good and bad bursts under consideration, the CCM model with a memory length of eight provides the best performance. The performance saturates after a memory length of eight, and therefore higher memory lengths are not shown in Figure 11.7. In conclusion, ENK divergence highlights that the CCM provides an accurate and low-complexity bit error model for 802.11b LANs operating at 2 Mbps. This performance substantiates the earlier analysis suggesting that a 5-state CCM can render a performance comparable to the respective 2^k-state Markov chain.

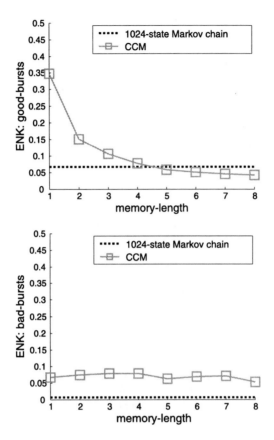

FIGURE 11.7: ENK-based modeling accuracy of the CCM for the 2-Mbps bit error process: (top) good bursts and (bottom) bad bursts.

Table 11.3:   Standard errors of CCM and Markov chains.

	2 Mbps		5.5 Mbps	
	1024-state Markov chain	5-state CCM	512-state Markov chain	5-state CCM
Good bursts	0.018	0.018	0.011	0.018
Bad bursts	0.007	0.007	0.009	0.01

Table 11.3 lists the standard error of good- and bad-burst CDFs generated by a 1024-state Markov model and a 5-state CCM with a memory length of eight. It can be clearly seen from Table 11.3 that the 5-state CCM perfectly matches the performance of the 1024-state Markov model for both good and bad bursts. Thus

it can be concluded that the 5-state CCM, while providing orders of magnitude reduction in complexity, renders a performance that is quite comparable to the 1024-state Markov model.

11.5.7.2 Modeling Accuracy for the 5.5-Mbps Bit Error Process

ENK-based performances of CCMs with varying memory lengths at 5.5 Mbps are outlined in Figure 11.8. For the good-burst random variable, performances of CCMs with memory lengths six and higher are comparable to the 512-state Markov chain. Thus, the CCM captures the good-burst behavior of the 5.5-Mbps

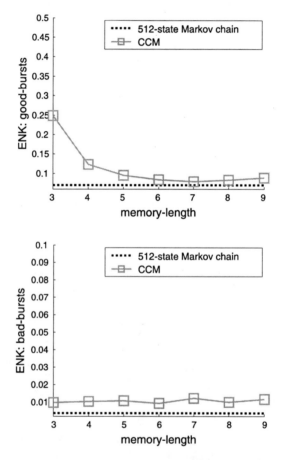

FIGURE 11.8: ENK-based modeling accuracy of the CCM for the 5.5-Mbps bit error process: (top) good bursts and (bottom) bad bursts.

channel very accurately. Similarly, Figure 11.8 (bottom) shows that the bad-burst ENK overhead of CCM is also very small for all memory lengths.

Table 11.3 compares the standard error-based performances of the 512-state Markov model and the 5-state CCM with a memory length of six. Table 11.3 reemphasizes that the CCM performance in modeling good and bad bursts is quite close to the Markov chain. Thus, it can be concluded that even for the 5.5-Mbps channel, the performance of the CCM is comparable to the exponential-complexity Markov model.

11.6 SUMMARY AND FURTHER READING

The objective of this chapter was to introduce the readers to the somewhat recent notion of analyzing and modeling bit errors at wireless MAC layers. This chapter discussed the theoretical aspects and practical issues involved in developing the widely used kth order Markov chain model for wireless MAC layer channels. It was highlighted that kth order Markov models, although very accurate, are too complex to be used in practical wireless systems. Consequently, we described a constant-complexity model that approximated the good- and bad-burst behavior of kth order Markov chains.

The kth order Markov chain models described in this chapter have been used to model many error and loss phenomena. Readers interested in packet-loss Markov models for reliable wireless protocols should refer to [6]. Similarly, read [7] to learn about Markov models of frame losses over cellular GSM networks. Refer to [9] to get insight into the impact of physical layer parameters (e.g., modulation type, antenna diversity) on MAC layer bit errors and channel models. Also note that mitigation of the exponential Markov chain complexity has been investigated by many studies, and the complexity reduction technique presented in this chapter is only one of the proposed methods. Another common complexity reduction technique is Markov chain lumpability [10]. Refer to [17] and [18] to understand how Markov chain lumpability can be employed to reduce modeling complexity over wireless channels. Other techniques that use data-driven heuristics to reduce Markov chain complexity have been proposed [4,19,20]. All of these approximate models (including the constant-complexity model derived earlier) invoke certain wireless channel assumptions to reduce Markov chain complexity. Thus to select the best-fit low-complexity model, one should evaluate the strengths and weaknesses of all relevant approximate channel models while taking the particular desired application(s) into consideration.

REFERENCES

[1] ISO/IEC 8802-11:1999(E). "Part 11: Wireless LAN Medium Access Control (MAC) and Physical Layer (PHY) Specifications," August 1999.

[2] IEEE Std. 802.11b-1999. "Part 11: Wireless LAN Medium Access Control (MAC) and Physical Layer (PHY) Specifications: Higher-Speed Physical Layer Extension in the 2.4 GHz band," September 1999.

[3] M. Zorzi and R. R. Rao. "On the Statistics of Block Errors in Bursty Channels," *IEEE Transactions on Communications*, vol. 45, no. 6, pp. 660–667, June 1997.

[4] S. A. Khayam and H. Radha. "Linear-Complexity Models for Wireless MAC-to-MAC Channels," *ACM Wireless Networks Journal (WINET)*, vol. 11, no. 5, pp. 533–545, September 2005.

[5] G. T. Nguyen, R. Katz, and B. Noble. "A Trace-Based Approach for Modeling Wireless Channel Behavior," *Winter Simulation Conference*, December 1996.

[6] H. Balakrishnan and R. Katz. "Explicit Loss Notification and Wireless Web Performance," *IEEE Globecom*, 1998.

[7] A. Konrad, B. Y. Zhao, A. D. Joseph, and R. Ludwig. "A Markov-Based Channel Model Algorithm for Wireless Networks," *ACM WINET*, vol. 9, pp. 189–199, 2003.

[8] S. A. Khayam and H. Radha. "Markov-Based Modeling of Wireless Local Area Networks," *ACM MSWiM*, September 2003.

[9] A. Willig, M. Kubisch, C. Hoene, and A. Wolisz. "Measurements of a Wireless Link in an Industrial Environment Using an IEEE 802.11-Compliant Physical Layer," *IEEE Trans. on Industrial Electronics*, vol. (49)6, pp. 1265–1282, December 2002.

[10] J. G. Kemeny and J. L. Snell. *Finite Markov Chains*, Springer-Verlag, New York, 1976.

[11] S. M. Ross. *Introduction to Probability Models*, Academic Press, 7th ed., February 2000.

[12] P. Brockwell and R. Davis. *Introduction to Time Series and Forecasting*, Springer-Verlag, New York, 1996.

[13] N. Merhav, M. Gutman, and J. Ziv. "On the Estimation of the Order of a Markov Chain and Universal Data Compression," *IEEE Trans. on Information Theory*, vol. 35, pp. 1014–1019, September 1989.

[14] M. J. Weinberger, J. J. Rissanen, and M. Feder. "A Universal Finite Memory Source," *IEEE Transactions on Information Theory*, vol. 41, no. 3, pp. 643–652, 1995.

[15] T. Cover and J. Thomas. *Elements of Information Theory*, Wiley, New York, 1991.

[16] R. J. Adler, R. E. Feldman, and M. S. Taqqu, eds. *A Practical Guide to Heavy Tails*, Birkhäuser, 1998.

[17] A. M. Chen and R. R. Rao. "Wireless Channel Models: Coping with Complexity," *Wireless Multimedia Network Technologies*, pp. 271–288, Kluwer Academic Publishers, 1999.

[18] A. M. Chen and R. R. Rao. "On Tractable Wireless Channel Models," *IEEE PIMRC*, September 1998.

[19] A. Willig. "A New Class of Packet- and Bit-Level Models for Wireless Channels," *IEEE PIMRC*, October 2001.

[20] A. Köpke, A. Willig, and H. Carl. "Chaotic Maps as Parsimonious Bit Error Models of Wireless Channels," *IEEE Infocom*, March 2003.

[21] P. Ji, B. Liu, D. Towsley, Z. Ge, and J. Kurose. "Modeling Frame-Level Errors in GSM Wireless Channels," *Performance Evaluation Journal*, vol. 55, nos. 1–2, pp. 165–181, January 2004.

[22] L. R. Rabiner. "A Tutorial on Hidden Markov Models and Selected Applications in Speech Recognition," *Proceedings of the IEEE*, vol. 77, no. 2, pp. 257–286, 1989.

12

Cross-Layer Wireless Multimedia

Mihaela van der Schaar

12.1 INTRODUCTION

Wireless networks are poised to enable a variety of existing and emerging applications due to their low cost and flexible infrastructure. Figure 12.1 shows the evolution of different wireless technologies with the X axis representing the throughput and the Y axis representing the mobility. The depicted classes of technologies are Wide Area Networks (WANs), Local Area Networks (LANs), and Personal Area Networks (PANs). Cellular networks belong to the class of WANs, Bluetooth and Ultra Wide Bands (UWBs) belong to PANs, and Wireless LANs (WLANs) and HiperLANs belong to LANs. WANs offer greater mobility, but lower data rates, while LANs offer higher bandwidths, but a limited coverage. PAN technologies are often deployed for cable replacement, whereas WLANs are envisioned as the wireless replacement of wired LANs. However, these wireless networks exhibit a large variation in channel conditions not only because of the different access technologies, but also due to multipath fading, cochannel interference, noise, mobility, handoff, and so on, as well as competing traffic from other wireless users. Thus, as the use of these wireless networks spreads beyond simple data transfer to bandwidth-intense, delay-sensitive, and loss tolerant multimedia applications (such as video-conferencing, emergency services, surveillance, telemedicine, remote teaching and training, augmented reality, and entertainment), addressing Quality of Service (QoS) issues becomes essential. Currently, a multitude of protection and adaptation strategies exists in the different layers of the Open Systems Interconnection (OSI) stack. Hence, an in-depth understanding and comparative evaluation of these strategies are necessary to effectively assess and enable the possible trade-offs in multimedia quality, power consumption, implementation complexity, and spectrum utilization that are provided by the various OSI

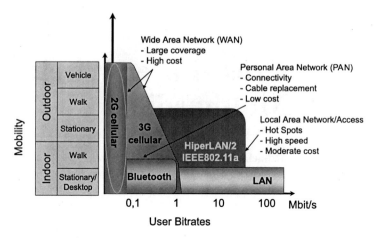

FIGURE 12.1:   Current wireless solutions space [72].

layers. This further opens the question of cross-layer optimization and its effectiveness in providing an improved solution with respect to the trade-offs just listed.

This chapter formalizes the cross-layer problem, discusses its challenges and relevant standards, presents several existing solutions, and highlights the key principles for cross-layer design. We discuss a cross-layer framework for *jointly* analyzing, selecting, and adapting the different strategies available at the various OSI layers in terms of multimedia quality, consumed power, and spectrum utilization. Developing such an integrated cross-layer framework is of fundamental importance, since it not only leads to improved multimedia performance over existing wireless networks, but it also provides valuable insights into the design of next-generation algorithms and protocols for wireless multimedia systems. Moreover, such a cross-layer approach does not necessarily require a redesign of existing protocols [4] and can be directly applied across existing application and lower layer standards and de facto solutions.

12.1.1 Challenges and Requirements for Wireless Transmission of Multimedia

Wireless networks are heterogeneous in bandwidth, reliability, and receiver device characteristics. In wireless channels, packets can be delayed (due to queuing, propagation, transmission, and processing delays), lost, or even discarded due to complexity/power limitations or display capabilities of the receiver. Hence, the experienced packet losses can be up to 10% or more, and the time allocated to the various users and the resulting goodput[1] for multimedia bit stream transmission can also vary significantly in time.

This variability of wireless resources has considerable consequences for multimedia applications and often leads to unsatisfactory user experience due to the following characteristics.

- High bandwidths—many consumer applications, for example, High-Definition TV, require transmission bit rates of several Mbps.
- Very stringent delay constraints—delays of less than 200 ms are required for interactive applications, such as videoconferencing and surveillance, while for multimedia streaming applications, delays of 1–5 s are tolerable. Packets that arrive after their display time are discarded at the receiver side or, at best, can be used for concealing subsequently received multimedia packets.

Fortunately, multimedia applications can cope with a certain amount of packet losses depending on the used sequence characteristics, compression schemes, and error concealment strategies available at the receiver (e.g., packet losses up to 5% or more can be tolerated at times). Consequently, unlike file transfers, real-time multimedia applications do not require a complete insulation from packet losses, but rather require the application layer *to cooperate* with the lower layers to select the optimal wireless transmission strategy that maximizes the multimedia performance.

Thus, to achieve a high level of acceptability and proliferation of wireless multimedia, in particular wireless video, several key requirements need to be satisfied by multimedia streaming solutions over such channels: (i) easy adaptability to wireless bandwidth fluctuations due to cochannel interference, multipath fading, mobility, handoff, competing traffic, and so on; (ii) robustness to partial data losses caused by the packetization of video frames and high packet error rates; and (iii) support for heterogeneous wireless clients with regard to their access bandwidths, computing capabilities, buffer availabilities, display resolutions, and power limitations.

12.1.2 Need for Cross-Layer Optimization

In recent years, to address the aforementioned requirements, the research focus has been to adapt existing algorithms and protocols for multimedia compression and transmission to the rapidly varying and often scarce resources of wireless networks [5]. For instance, network adaptive multimedia compression, bandwidth, and channel condition bit stream adaptation, prioritization and layering

---

[1] This is the correctly received bit-rate/bandwidth and represents the effective bandwidth that can be used by the application layer for video bitstream transmission.

mechanisms, error concealment strategies, rate–distortion modeling, joint source-channel coding, streaming strategies, multiuser resource management and allocation protocols and algorithms, distortion and channel aware scheduling, link layer adaptation, and power and system optimization strategies have been developed.

However, these solutions often do not provide adequate support for multimedia applications in crowded wireless networks, when the interference is high, or when the stations are mobile. This is because the resource management, adaptation, and protection strategies available in the lower layers of the OSI stack—Physical (PHY) layer, Medium Access Control (MAC) layer, and Network/Transport layers—are optimized without *explicitly* considering the specific characteristics of the multimedia applications, and conversely, multimedia compression and streaming algorithms do not consider the mechanisms provided by the lower layers for error protection, scheduling, resource management, and so on [5]. A set of relevant references discussing cross-layer optimization across lower layers of the protocol stack, without considering the multimedia communications requirements, can be found elsewhere [61–71]. This application-layer agnostic (or simplified) optimization leads to a simpler implementation, but can result in very poor performance (objective and perceptual quality) for real-time multimedia transmission when the available wireless resources are limited. As shown later in this chapter, improvements of up to 5 dB can be achieved in such cases through (often low-complexity) cross-layer optimizations that consider the unique features of multimedia applications.

12.1.3 Chapter Outline

To summarize the aim of this chapter is not to provide a complete single solution to the very complex problem of wireless multimedia transmission. Instead, the chapter is aimed at presenting a possible unified and formal approach to the difficult problem of real-time multimedia transmission over wireless networks by familiarizing the reader to several key principles for identifying optimized solutions for cross-layer transmission, efficient designs, and possible practical solutions.

Section 12.2 starts by presenting a short summary of the 802.11 WLAN standard's key features at the MAC and PHY layers and discusses their impact on wireless multimedia. In this chapter, we will mainly focus on WLAN networks to illustrate the design principles, fundamentals, and solutions for optimized multimedia transmission. However, these can be easily applied to other existing and emerging wireless networks, for example, 3G, 4G, and PAN wireless networks. Section 12.3 motivates the need for cross-layer optimization through a simple wireless video streaming example, where the ad hoc choices of lower layers parameters can have a significant impact on video quality. Section 12.4 formalizes the cross-layer design problem and discusses the challenges associated with solving this problem. Moreover, a categorization of the various cross-layer solutions is also presented. Next, to solve the cross-layer optimization problem, several different methods are proposed: Section 12.5 discusses a joint MAC–application-layer optimization for adaptive retransmission using queuing theory, while Section 12.6 presents a similar MAC–application-layer optimization for adaptive retransmission and packet size adaptation using Lagrangian optimization. Section 12.7 discusses the problem of efficient wireless resource allocation (i.e., allocation of transmission opportunities) using 802.11e. To enable the complex cross-layer optimization to be performed in real time, a low-cost solution relying on classification is outlined in Section 12.8. Section 12.9 discusses fairness strategies for dynamic multiuser wireless interaction. Section 12.10 presents a brief summary of the chapter and provides a list of relevant further reading.

It should be noted that the notation slightly varies across the various sections of the chapter and, for simplicity of notation, that the consistency of notation was only observed within an individual section. For instance, notations for retransmission limits, modulation strategies, packet sizes, and so on are adapted per section.

12.2 SHORT SUMMARY OF 802.11 WIRELESS LAN STANDARD AND IMPACT ON WIRELESS MULTIMEDIA

Before discussing the cross-layer design principles and solutions, we present several basic features of the IEEE 802.11 Wireless LANs [1–3], as this standard is used in the remainder of this chapter to illustrate the cross-layer design. However, note that the methodology for cross-layer design described in this chapter can similarly be applied to other WLAN, PAN, or WAN standards discussed in Figure 12.1. IEEE 802.11 is a wireless version of Ethernet that supports only best-effort services and that has enabled ubiquitous and low-cost broadband wireless access in home, enterprise, and public places such as airports, group meetings, and coffee shops. IEEE 802.11 has several working groups devoted to expanding the application domain of WLAN to include QoS provisioning, increased mobility support, security, and increased data rates. Figure 12.2 lists the various IEEE 802.11 focus areas. The IEEE 802.11a/b/g/n PHY layer provides data rates starting at 6 Mbps up to 54 Mbps, whereas IEEE 802.11b provide rates from 1 Mbps up to 11 Mbps. Alternatively, the emerging IEEE 802.11n standard uses Multiple Input Multiple Output (MIMO) antenna technology to increase data rates beyond 108 Mbps. IEEE 802.11 c/d/f define the bridging functions, international roaming, and interaccess point protocol, respectively, which are able to facilitate bridging function, fast roaming, and means to communicate between different WLAN access points. The IEEE 802.11e adapts the conventional 802.11a/b/g MAC protocol to accommodate QoS and is described in more detail later in this chapter. IEEE 802.11h/i/k define the dynamic frequency selection and transmit power control,

FIGURE 12.2:   Overview of IEEE 802.11 WLAN standards.

security, and radio resource measurement to increase the capabilities of WLAN when there is interference and to prevent others from entering into the network unnecessarily.

Next, we discuss some of the basic functionalities provided by 802.11 networks at the various layers that can significantly impact multimedia transmission.

- *PHY layer.* In the 802.11 WLAN standard, several modulation and coding schemes are available to a wireless station. Modulation schemes that have symbols closer to each other in the constellation diagram can result in erroneous decoding. Varying code rates can be employed within each modulation scheme to adapt to changing channel conditions by allowing more bits for channel coding (lower code rates) as conditions deteriorate. As the channel code rate decreases, the effective transmission rate reduces, and hence the achievable throughput for transmission reduces. The 802.11a PHY [1] is based on Orthogonal Frequency Division Multiplexing and provides eight different PHY modes with different modulation schemes and code rates, offering transmission data rates ranging from 6 to 54 Mbps (6, 9, 12, 18, 24, 36, 48, and 54 Mbps, respectively). Figure 12.3 depicts the bit error rate (BER) as a function of the channel condition represented here by the Signal-to-Noise Ratio (SNR) for the various modulation schemes in 802.11a. More details about the channel model can be found in [1,2,10,26].

Similarly, 802.11b also has various PHY modes that can be selected, but unlike 802.11a, the maximum throughput is only 15 Mbps and only four different PHY modes exist. It should also be noted that the aforementioned transmission data rates are at the PHY layer and do not include packetization and transmission overheads incurred at the PHY and MAC layers. Hence, the resulting application-layer rate for multimedia transmission is often significantly lower than the maximum PHY rate.

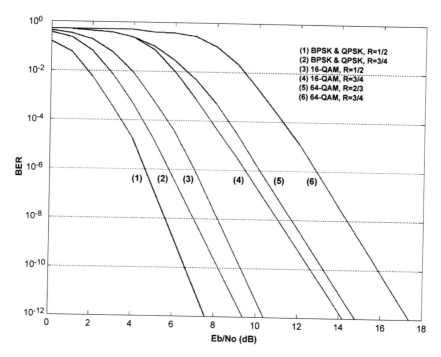

FIGURE 12.3:   BER vs. SNR for 802.11a WLAN networks [72].

- *MAC layer.* For a wireless device transmitting delay-sensitive multimedia content, periodic access to the shared wireless medium is paramount. In wireless networks, this access is controlled by the MAC layers. Hence, we briefly discuss the impact of the various existing WLAN MAC layer protocols on multimedia. We start by briefly presenting the 802.11a/b/g WLAN standard, which allows two different MAC mechanisms, namely the distributed coordination function (DCF) and the point coordination function (PCF). Subsequently, we discuss the 802.11e WLAN standard, which provides additional features to the conventional MAC to better enable multimedia streaming.

12.2.1 Distributed Coordination Function

DCF is the basic MAC mechanism, which is based on carrier sense multiple access with collision avoidance. In [54], a very good analytical model of the DCF protocol performance is presented.

In the DCF mode of operation, each station in the WLAN contends for the medium and relinquishes control after transmitting a single packet (MAC frame).

Hence, the DCF MAC strategy provides distributed, fair access to the wireless medium for competing wireless stations. With the DCF mechanism, over a long period of time all users will get equal access to the wireless network. This works well for traditional data applications such as ftp transfers, web browsing, and other delay-insensitive multimedia applications. However, this type of fairness is not appropriate when dealing with real-time multimedia applications that exhibit different delay deadlines and bandwidth requirements. For example, if a video streaming application does not gain timely access to the wireless medium while trying to transmit a very important portion of a compressed bit stream (e.g., the base layer or an "I" video frame) because it is being preempted by competing users, this will lead to unacceptable incurred delays and thus a significantly degraded video quality and a negative user experience. Due to these key disadvantages, this access mechanism is not very suitable for video streaming applications and is not discussed in much detail in this chapter.

12.2.2 Point Coordination Function

PCF is an optional channel access function in the 802.11 standard that is designed to support delay-sensitive applications such as multimedia streaming. Contention-free access to the wireless medium is controlled by a point coordinator (PC) collocated with the access point. PCF is based on a poll-and-response protocol to control access to the shared wireless medium and to eliminate contention among wireless stations. The PC is the central controller, which grants access to the medium. The PC gains control of the medium periodically. Once the PC gains control of the medium, it begins a contention-free period (CFP) during which access to the medium is completely controlled by the PC; after a CFP is finished, a contention period (CP) during which the mandatory DCF is used starts. During the CFP, the PC can deliver downlink traffic to the individual stations without any contention. The PC can also send a contention-free poll (CF-Poll) that allows the stations to send uplink traffic to the PC. If the station that is being polled has uplink traffic to send, it can transmit one packet (MAC frame) for each CF-Poll received. If the station does not have any pending packet, it responds with a data packet without any content, that is, a Null data packet. During the CFP, a wireless station can only transmit after being polled by the PC.

Since there is no contention, a certain QoS level is provided for multimedia applications (even though there is no actual guarantee provided about the actual goodput allocated to an application, which depends on the experienced packet-loss rate incurred due to interference, etc.). Hence, PCF is often used for wireless multimedia streaming, as it provides real-time applications a guaranteed transmission time (opportunity), that is, all stations are polled for a certain amount of time during a service interval.

12.2.3 Enhanced Distributed Channel Access (EDCA)

EDCA is a superset of the 802.11 DCF protocol adopted by the 802.11e standard. In DCF, all wireless stations compete for the wireless medium with the same priority. In EDCA, however, this mechanism is extended to four levels of priorities or access categories (AC). With a shorter maximum back-off time, the higher priority AC wins access to the medium more frequently than the lower priority AC. Therefore, statistically, packets with the highest AC are given access to the medium more frequently than those packets with a lower AC. However, EDCA can be viewed as a differentiated service (DiffServ) QoS that can assist multimedia applications by enabling them to map the various priority packets of the bit streams into various AC classes. Nevertheless, due to the nondeterministic nature of EDCA, it is not possible, except in very lightly loaded networks, to guarantee parameters such as bandwidth, jitter, and latency. The inefficiency arises due to contention and back-off mechanisms as in the DCF case and hence they are not suitable for multimedia streaming.

12.2.4 Hybrid Coordination Function (HCF) Controlled Channel Access (HCCA)

Similar to PCF, HCCA provides real-time applications a guaranteed transmission time (opportunity), that is, all stations are polled for a certain amount of time during a service interval. However, while HCCA provides multimedia streaming applications a certain level of QoS, there are no tight guarantees for parameters such as bandwidth, jitter, and latency, as is shown in Section 12.7

In conclusion, in this chapter we will assume a polling-based MAC for multimedia transmission such as PCF and HCCA. Hence, each service interval (SI) t_{SI} is divided among the various users based on a certain initial admission control policy. For instance, if there are M users in the network, the resource allocation is represented by the transmission opportunity time vector $[t_1, \ldots, t_M] \in \mathbb{R}_+^M$, where t_i $(0 \le t_i \le t_{SI})$ represents the transmission time allocated by the MAC to a user i every SI. Such time allocation for the various users is assumed in subsequent sections for discussion of the cross-layer optimized transmission. A detailed description of how the transmission opportunities are allocated to the users and how the stations are polled by the resource coordinator is given in Section 12.7.

However, it should be noted that none of the aforementioned MAC standards provides strict QoS guarantees for multimedia applications; also, the system-wide resource management is not always fair or efficient for such applications. This is due to the time-varying nature of the wireless channel and multimedia characteristics and to the lack of cross-layer awareness of the application and MAC layers about each other.

12.3 EXAMPLE OF CROSS-LAYER IMPACT ON THROUGHPUT EFFICIENCY AND DELAY FOR VIDEO STREAMING

To understand the possible impact of the cross-layer design, let us analyze the impact of the various layers of the protocol stack on the throughput efficiency and resulting delay performance. For illustration, let us assume that the polling-based mode of the 802.11a MAC standard (PCF) is used for video transmission. To protect video data, the adaptive deployment of retransmission at the MAC layer and that of Reed–Solomon (RS) codes at the application layer is considered in addition to the PHY layer modulation and coding strategies provided by 802.11a.

To analyze the overhead impact, the following simplified assumptions are made: (a) the video packets are of length L_a bytes and these packets are not fragmented in any of the lower layers and (b) the overhead of the higher layer protocols, such as RTP, UDP, and IP, is considered to be O bytes. The overhead of the MAC and PHY is not included in this. The average packet transmission duration computed in the following section accounts for the MAC and PHY overhead. The MAC-layer retransmission limit is denoted in this section as R.

12.3.1 Average Packet Transmission Duration

This section analyzes the average transmission duration of a MAC frame under different conditions. This is used later in the computation of application-layer throughput efficiency. Assuming that a packet with L-byte payload is transmitted using PHY mode m, the probability of a successful transmission is given by

$$P^m_{good\_cycle}(L) = \left(1 - P^m_{e,ack}\right)\left(1 - P^m_{e,data}(L)\right), \qquad (12.1)$$

where $P_{e,ack}$ is the CF-ACK packet error probability and $P_{e,data}$ is the data packet error probability. These can be calculated from the corresponding packet sizes (including the headers and the payload) and the BER. (See Figure 12.3 and [1] for more details on the various PHY modes and the resulting BER.) The average transmission duration for a good cycle, T^m_{good}, where neither the data packet nor the CF-ACK packet is in error, can be obtained from the timing intervals given in Figure 12.4. Similarly, the average transmission duration for a bad cycle, T^m_{bad}, in a cycle where either the data packet or the CF-ACK packet is in error can be computed from the timing intervals given in Figure 12.5. The average transmission duration for a packet with an L-byte payload, given that the transmission is successful with the retransmission limit of R, can be obtained as

$$D^m_{av,succ}(L, R) = \sum_{i=0}^{R} \frac{P^m_{succ}(i|L)}{P^m_{succ}(L, R)}\left[i T^m_{bad}(L) + T^m_{good}(L)\right], \qquad (12.2)$$

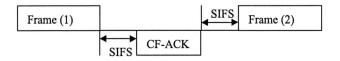

FIGURE 12.4: Successful downlink packet (MAC frame) transmission and associated timing (SIFS, Short Interframe Space; ACK, Acknowledgment).

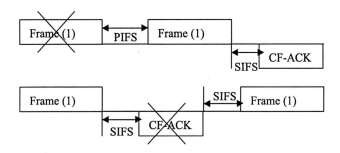

FIGURE 12.5: Retransmission due to packet or CF-ACK transmission error (SIFS, Short Interframe Space; PIFS, PCF Interframe Space).

where the probability that the packet with L-byte data payload is transmitted successfully after the ith retransmission using PHY mode m, is given by

$$P^m_{succ}(i|L) = \left[1 - P^m_{good\_cycle}(L)\right]^i P^m_{good\_cycle}(L), \qquad (12.3)$$

and the probability that the packet with an L-byte data payload is transmitted successfully within the R retransmission limit under PHY mode m is given by

$$P^m_{succ}(L, R) = 1 - \left[1 - P^m_{good\_cycle}(L)\right]^{R+1}. \qquad (12.4)$$

The average transmission duration for a packet with L-byte payload, given that the transmission is not successful with the retransmission limit R, is

$$D^m_{av,unsucc}(L, R) = (R + 1)T^m_{bad}(L). \qquad (12.5)$$

Now, the average transmission duration for a packet with L-byte payload and with a retransmission limit of R is

$$D^m_{av}(L, R) = D^m_{av,succ}(L, R)P^m_{succ}(L, R)$$
$$+ D^m_{av,unsucc}(L, R)\left(1 - P^m_{succ}(L, R)\right). \qquad (12.6)$$

12.3.2 Throughput Efficiency and Delay Analysis with Application-Layer RS Code

The throughput efficiency of 802.11a with the use of the (N, K) RS erasure code at the application layer can be computed based on the average packet transmission duration obtained earlier. Note that here the choice of N and K was determined empirically. However, a model-based joint source-channel coding approach can also be deployed to optimally determine these parameters. For more details, the interested reader is referred to [7–9,17] and the related error protection chapter in this book.

The RS decoder can correct up to $N - K$ packet erasures. If there are more than $N - K$ packet erasures, then this results in a decoding failure. Therefore, the probability of error after RS decoding is

$$P_{RS}^m = 1 - \sum_{i=0}^{N-K} \binom{N}{i} \left(P_r^m\right)^i \left(1 - P_r^m\right)^{N-i}, \qquad (12.7)$$

where the resulting residual error probability P_r^m of the data packet after R retransmissions is

$$P_r^m = 1 - P_{succ}(L, R). \qquad (12.8)$$

When a decoding failure happens, there are $N - i$ $(< K)$ correctly received packets, including both video and parity packets. These video packets can be utilized for video decoding and, on average, $(K/N)(N - i)$ packets out of $N - i$ correctly received packets are video packets. Therefore, the throughput efficiency, taking into the account the application-layer RS coding and the header overheads of the higher layer protocols, is

$$\begin{aligned} &E_{RS}^m(L_a, R, N, K) \\ &= \frac{8L_a\left(K(1 - P_{RS}^m) + \sum_{i=N-K+1}^{N}(N - i)\frac{K}{N}\binom{N}{i}(P_r^m)^i(1 - P_r^m)^{N-i}\right)}{N D_{av}^m(L_a + O, R)DR(m)}, \end{aligned}$$
$$(12.9)$$

where DR represents the maximum PHY data rates 6, 9, 12, 18, 24, 36, 48, and 54 Mbps for the various modes m. The numerator here corresponds to the average number of actually received video data bits, and the denominator corresponds to the total average number of bits that could have been transmitted in the time required to send those useful data bits successfully.

However, the impact of the various layers' overheads on the video quality is not only dependent on the throughput efficiency, but also on the overall delay incurred by the various packets, which need to be dropped if their deadline is exceeded. In this section, the total delay considered comprises different components: the delay due to buffering for RS coding at the transmitter, the RS encoding delay, the delay incurred in the transmission and the retransmission of packets, the buffering delay at the receiver for RS decoding, and the RS decoding delay. At the transmitter, there is no delay due to buffering and as each video packet is stored in the interleaver, it can be transmitted simultaneously, since the RS coding is applied across the video packets and the data transmission is along (not across) the video packets. (See the error protection chapter in this book for more details.) We assume that the process delay due to RS encoding or decoding is small and can be neglected compared to the transmission delay. In certain applications, such as the transmission of a video stored in a residential media server, it may be even possible to perform the (scalable) RS encoding before transmission. The maximum transmission delay depends on the length of a packet, the maximum number of retransmissions, and the specific 802.11a PHY mode m that is used. The worst-case delay[2] for R retransmissions is

$$D_{\max}(m, L) = (R + 1)\left(T_{data}^{m}(L) + T_{ack}^{m} + 2aSIFSTime\right). \tag{12.10}$$

If there are no packet erasures, then there is no buffering delay at the decoder. Each video packet can be delivered to the video decoder as soon it is received. In the presence of erasures out of the first k packets, the receiver needs to buffer up to n packets that belong to the current RS block before performing the erasure decoding. Therefore, the maximum buffering delay at the decoder is $N \times D_{\max}(m, L)$. Assuming a packet size of 2000 bytes, $R = 8$, and PHY mode 5, the value of $D_{\max}$ is 6.876 ms. Therefore, the total transmission delay for an RS code with $N = 63$ is 433.19 ms. To determine the acceptability of this delay for a particular video streaming application, the video encoding and decoding delay need to be further added on top of the transmission delay.

12.3.3 Impact of Cross-Layer Optimization on Video Quality

This section discusses the interaction between the various transmission strategies deployed by the different OSI layers and their impact on the resulting video quality, thereby highlighting the need for cross-layer optimization.

First, we will determine the optimal packet size that should be selected at the application layer to maximize the video quality Q for a given RS code and retransmission limit. Based on the previously computed [see (12.10)] throughput efficiency E_{RS}^{m} that takes into the account the application-layer RS coding and

---

[2]Note that the worst-case delay happens when all of the first R transmissions fail due to CF-ACK transmission failures, not data frame transmissions failures.

the header overheads of the higher layer protocols, the associated video quality $Q_{E_{RS}^m}$ can be computed using, for example, analytical rate–distortion models [17, 18]. The optimal packet size L_a^* can be then computed

$$L_a^* = \arg \max_{L_a} Q_{E_{RS}^m}. \tag{12.11}$$

Equation (12.11) can be solved by evaluating the E_{RS}^m function in (12.10) and determining the resulting $Q_{E_{RS}^m}$ for all possible values of L_a. In a practical implementation, we can use a look-up table by precomputing the values.

Figure 12.6 shows optimal packet sizes for a fixed APP-layer RS code (63,49) with three different numbers of maximum retransmissions, $R = 0$, 1, and 2. It can be seen that for low SNRs, the optimal packet size is the largest for the case corresponding to $R = 2$. For low SNRs, using the maximum allowed number of link layer retransmissions makes the link more reliable, and hence allows the use of larger packet sizes. As the SNR improves, the optimal packet size corresponding to the case of $R = 0$ increases rapidly. This is due to the fact that as the underlying link becomes more reliable at higher SNRs, the resultant packet erasures can be handled by the application-layer FEC even in the absence of any retransmissions.

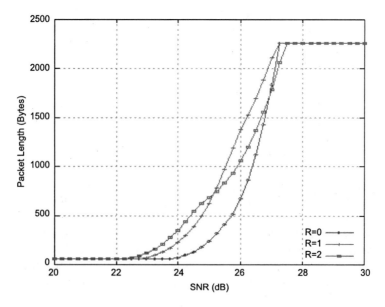

FIGURE 12.6: Comparison of optimal packet sizes for different retransmission limits.

Importantly, note that for an SNR of 26 dB, the difference in quality (PSNR) for the *Coastguard* video sequence is significant for various retransmission choices, varying from a very poor quality of PSNR = 28 dB for $R = 0$, and an acceptable quality of PSNR = 32 dB for $R = 2$, to a very good quality of PSNR = 35 dB for $R = 1$.

12.4 CROSS-LAYER DESIGN

12.4.1 Problem Definition

We formulate the cross-layer design problem as an optimization with the objective to select a joint strategy across multiple OSI layers. Initially, for simplicity, we limit our discussion to PHY, MAC, and Application (APP) layers. Hence, we mainly consider only one-hop wireless networks, where the network and transport layers play a less important role. Nevertheless, the proposed framework can easily be extended to include other layers. (For example, for an extension of the cross-layer design to multihop wireless networks, see [21,60].) For multimedia transmission over multihop wireless networks, the reader is referred to Section 12.10 for a list of related literature.

Let us consider M autonomous wireless stations (WSTAs) that are streaming video content in real time over a shared one-hop WLAN infrastructure. These WSTAs are competing for the available wireless resources $\mathcal{R}$ ($\mathcal{R} \in \mathbb{R}_+$). To use the resources effectively, the wireless stations adapt their cross-layer strategies.

We assume that the channel condition experienced by WSTA i can be characterized by the measured SNR, SNR_i, which varies over time.[3] The current state information for WSTA i is encapsulated in vector $\mathbf{x}_i$, which includes the channel condition SNR_i and the video source characteristics [19] ξ_i, that is, $\mathbf{x}_i = (SNR_i, \xi_i)$. We will refer to this vector as "private information" of the WSTA. Based on the private information, each WSTA jointly optimizes the various transmission strategies available at the different layers of the OSI stack. The PHY strategies may represent the various modulation and channel coding schemes existing for a particular wireless standard. The MAC strategies correspond to different packetization, retransmission, scheduling, admission control, and FEC mechanisms. At the APP layer, strategies may include adaptation of video compression parameters (including enabling spatio-temporal–SNR trade-offs), packetization, traffic shaping, traffic prioritization, scheduling, retransmission, and FEC mechanisms.

As mentioned in Section 12.2, in a typical resource allocation scenario, the resource allocation is represented by the transmission opportunity time vector

---

[3]Other metrics could also be incorporated in addition to SNR to characterize the channel condition (see, e.g., Chapter 13).

$\mathbf{T}(\mathcal{R}) = [t_1, \ldots, t_M] \in \mathbb{R}_+^M$, where t_i $(0 \leq t_i \leq t_{SI})$ represents the time allocation by the resource coordinator to a specific WSTA i. (The length of the SI, t_{SI}, is determined based on the channel conditions, source characteristics, and application-layer delay constraints [23], and is defined in more detail in the next sections.) This vector denotes the allocated time to WSTA i (with $\sum_{i=1}^M t_i \leq t_{SI}$) by either the polling-based MAC resource allocation (see Section 12.3 for details on various MAC strategies) or is obtained on average by a WSTA, through the contention process [54]. As highlighted in Section 12.3, the polling-based MAC is mostly used in practice for video transmission applications and forms the basis of the cross-layer design in this chapter.

Given a static time allocation, and the specific constraints of the WSTA (e.g., application-layer delay constraints), the cross-layer design problem can be formulated as an optimization with a certain objective (e.g., maximize goodput, minimize consumed power) based on which optimal joint strategy across the multiple OSI layers is selected. Let s_i represent a cross-layer strategy available to WSTA i, which lies in the set of feasible PHY, MAC, and APP layers strategies $\mathcal{S}_i$ for that station. The cross-layer strategy s_i is adopted in real time by the WSTA i. Then, given the private information $\mathbf{x}_i$ and the predetermined time allocation t_i, a cross-layer strategy s_i results in the utility $u_i(t_i, s_i, \mathbf{x}_i)$, which for video streaming applications represents the expected received video quality in terms of perceived quality or PSNR. Hence, the optimal cross-layer strategy can be found

$$s_i^{opt} = \arg\max_{s_i \in \mathcal{S}_i} u_i(t_i, s_i, \mathbf{x}_i),$$
$$\text{s.t. } Delay(t_i, s_i, \mathbf{x}_i) \leq Delay_i^{\max}. \tag{12.12}$$

In the formulation just given, $Delay_i^{\max}$ represents the delay constraint for the particular video transmitted by WSTA i and $Delay(t_i, s_i, \mathbf{x}_i)$ represents the delay incurred by the cross-layer strategy s_i for the specific private information $\mathbf{x}_i$ and resource allocation t_i. Importantly, note that, unlike multimedia communications over wired networks, which need to fulfill traditional optimizations in terms of rate and distortion [17], in the wireless multimedia transmission case, the constraint becomes meeting the strict deadlines of the video transmission $Delay_i^{\max}$ given the allocated transmission time t_i (i.e., transmission opportunities allocated or gained by a wireless user). Whenever these delay constraints are not met, the packets are not received in time by the decoder, thereby impacting the resulting utility u_i.

Figure 12.7 depicts a conceptual scheme of the aforementioned cross-layer optimization framework.

Finding the optimal solution to the aforementioned cross-layer optimization problem is difficult because:

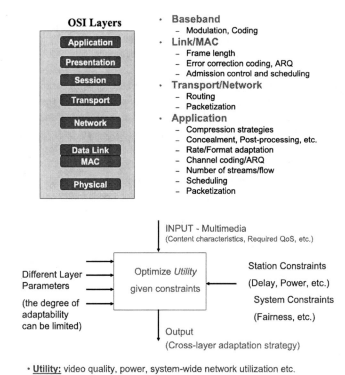

OSI Layers

- Application
- Presentation
- Session
- Transport
- Network
- Data Link
- MAC
- Physical

- **Baseband**
  - Modulation, Coding
- **Link/MAC**
  - Frame length
  - Error correction coding, ARQ
  - Admission control and scheduling
- **Transport/Network**
  - Routing
  - Packetization
- **Application**
  - Compression strategies
  - Concealment, Post-processing, etc.
  - Rate/Format adaptation
  - Channel coding/ARQ
  - Number of streams/flow
  - Scheduling
  - Packetization

INPUT - Multimedia
(Content characteristics, Required QoS, etc.)

Different Layer Parameters

(the degree of adaptability can be limited)

Optimize *Utility* given constraints

Station Constraints
(Delay, Power, etc.)

System Constraints
(Fairness, etc.)

Output
(Cross-layer adaptation strategy)

· <u>Utility:</u> video quality, power, system-wide network utilization etc.

FIGURE 12.7:   Conceptual framework of cross-layer optimization.

- Deriving analytical expressions for $u_i(t_i, s_i, \mathbf{x}_i)$ and $Delay(t_i, s_i, \mathbf{x}_i)$ as functions of channel conditions is very challenging, as these functions are nondeterministic (only worst case or average values can be determined), nonlinear, and there are dependencies between some of the strategies s_i [10,11].

- The algorithms and protocols at the various layers have often different objectives and have been traditionally optimized separately. Moreover, various layers operate on different units of the multimedia traffic and take as input different types of information. For instance, the PHY is concerned with symbols and depends heavily on the channel characteristics, whereas the application layer is concerned with the semantics and dependencies between flows and depends heavily on the multimedia content.

- The wireless channel conditions and multimedia content characteristics may change continuously, requiring constant updating of the parameters.

- Formal procedures are required to establish optimal *initialization*, *grouping* of strategies at different stages (i.e., which strategies should be optimized jointly), and *ordering* (i.e., which strategies should be optimized first) for performing the cross-layer adaptation and optimization.

- For the joint optimization of the strategies, one can use derivative and nonderivative methods (such as linear and nonlinear programming). Because this is a complex multivariate optimization with inherent dependencies (across layers and among strategies), an important aspect of this optimization is determining the best *procedure* for obtaining the optimal strategy s_i^{opt}. This involves determining the initialization, grouping of strategies at different stages, a suitable order in which the strategies should be optimized, and even which parameters, strategies, and layers should be considered based on their impact on multimedia quality, delay, or power. The selected procedure determines the rate of convergence and the values at convergence. The rate of convergence is extremely important, as the dynamic nature of the wireless channels requires rapidly converging solutions. Depending on the multimedia application, wireless infrastructure, and flexibility of the adopted WLAN standards, different approaches can lead to optimal performance. A categorization of the possible solutions is given in the next section.
- Finally, different practical considerations (e.g., buffer sizes, ability to change retry limits or modulation strategies at the packet level [11]) for the deployed wireless standard must be taken into account to perform the cross-layer optimization.

12.4.2 Categorization of Cross-Layer Solutions

To gain further insights into the principles that guide cross-layer design and to compare the various solutions, we propose the following classification of the possible solutions based on the order in which the cross-layer optimization is performed.

- Top-down approach—The higher layer protocols optimize their parameters and the strategies at the next lower layer. This cross-layer solution has been deployed in most existing systems, wherein the APP dictates the MAC parameters and strategies, while the MAC selects the optimal PHY layer modulation scheme. Section 12.6 presents such a cross-layer optimization approach.
- Bottom-up approach—The lower layers try to insulate the higher layers from losses and bandwidth variations. This cross-layer solution is not optimal for multimedia transmission due to incurred delays and unnecessary throughput reductions. The beginning of Section 12.6 presents such a cross-layer optimization approach.
- Application-centric approach—The APP layer optimizes the lower layer parameters one at a time in a bottom-up (starting from the PHY) or top-

down manner, based on its requirements. However, this approach is not always efficient, as the APP operates at slower timescales and coarser data granularities (multimedia flows or group of packets) than lower layers (that operate on bits or packets), and hence it is not able to instantaneously adapt their performance to achieve an optimal performance. Section 12.6 presents such a cross-layer optimization approach.

- MAC-centric approach—In this approach, the APP layer passes its traffic information and requirements to the MAC, which decides which APP layer packets/flows should be transmitted and with which delay or packet-loss requirement. The MAC also selects the PHY layer parameters based on the available channel information and higher layer requirements. The disadvantage of this approach resides in the inability of the MAC layer to perform adaptive source-channel coding trade-offs given the time-varying channel conditions and multimedia requirements. Section 12.5 presents such a cross-layer optimization approach.

- Integrated approach—In this approach, strategies are determined jointly across the various protocol layers. Unfortunately, exhaustively trying all the possible strategies and their parameters in order to choose the composite strategy leading to the best quality performance is impractical due to the associated complexity and incurred delay. A possible solution to solve this complex cross-layer optimization problem in an integrated manner is to use learning and classification techniques that use off-line training data to categorize the various channel conditions and application requirements and identify what are the optimal choices of cross-layer interactions for the various identified categories and, subsequently, use this information to drive the online cross-layer optimization. Section 12.8 presents such a cross-layer optimization approach.

The aforementioned cross-layer approaches exhibit different advantages and drawbacks for wireless multimedia transmission, and the best solution depends on the application requirements, used protocols, and algorithms at the various layers, complexity, and power limitations. Next, we will give several illustrative examples on how to perform the cross-layer optimization and highlight the improvements in multimedia quality and power consumption.

12.5 CROSS-LAYER MAC–APPLICATION-LAYER OPTIMIZATION FOR ADAPTIVE RETRANSMISSION USING QUEUING THEORY

This section illustrates how queuing theory can be used to model the transmission of video packets over an 802.11 WLAN network and how the joint MAC–application-layer interaction can be optimized based on the queuing models, while fulfilling complexity constraints (such as the MAC buffer limitation). We first design an optimal MAC retransmission limit adaptation strategy to maximize the achieved video quality and subsequently show that by jointly optimizing the MAC retransmission limit along with the application-layer rate adaptation and prioritized scheduling strategies, the decoded video quality can be improved significantly.

12.5.1 MAC-Layer Retransmission Limit Adaptation

First, we consider the optimization of the MAC-layer retransmission in isolation by aiming to maximize the resulting goodput. We assume that the MAC layer is aware of the packet-loss probability of the channel (after the PHY layer channel coding and modulation strategy was deployed), as well as the fixed multimedia traffic rate. This is a realistic assumption for existing 802.11-based wireless video solutions. (See Chapter 13.) Thus, we assume a very simple form of cross-layer parameter communication. However, because of this simplified cross-layer optimization, since the MAC is not aware of the video characteristics, the relative importance and dependencies between packets, the impact of losing specific packets on the quality, and so on, the problem of maximizing the video quality reduces to minimizing the MAC packet loss rate.

At the MAC, packet losses occur due to two reasons: link erasures and buffer overflows. While the loss due to link erasures decreases with an increasing retransmission limit R, the loss due to the buffer overflow increases with an increasing R. Thus, we need to have a strategy to optimally select the R that minimizes the overall MAC packet loss due to buffer overflow *and* link errors. We first show how an analytical solution for the optimal R can be obtained using a fluid model for the buffer queue under static channel error conditions and then illustrate the resulting improvements in multimedia quality using real-time retransmission limit adaptation [11].

A simplified analysis based on a fluid model for the queuing system is presented next. For this, a constant arrival rate λ of the multimedia packets with uniform (packet) size is assumed. Let P be the packet loss probability (controlled by the PHY layer) of the link without retransmission, p_B be the buffer overflow rate, and $p_L = P^{R+1}$ be the link packet erasure rate (i.e., the packet drop rate after R unsuccessful retransmissions). If C is the service rate of the link, the effective utilization factor of the link ρ may be defined as $\rho(P) = \lambda/C(1-P)$. The overall loss rate $p_T(R, P)$, which is defined as the sum of p_B and p_L,[4] may be derived [11]

---

[4]We assume both p_B and p_L are relatively small such that they can be added together to approximate the total loss rate.

$$p_T(R, P) = p_B(R, P) + p_L(R, P) = 1 - \frac{1}{\rho(P)} \frac{1}{1 - P^{R+1}} + P^{R+1}. \quad (12.13)$$

When P is fixed, $p_B(R)$ monotonically increases with R, while $p_L(R)$ decreases at the same time (see Figure 12.8). To minimize $p_T(R)$, we temporarily relax the discrete constraint on R, assuming it is a continuous variable. R can then be found by solving the equation $\frac{dp_T(R)}{dR} = 0$, which leads to

$$R = \log_P \left(1 - \frac{1}{\sqrt{\rho}}\right) - 1. \quad (12.14)$$

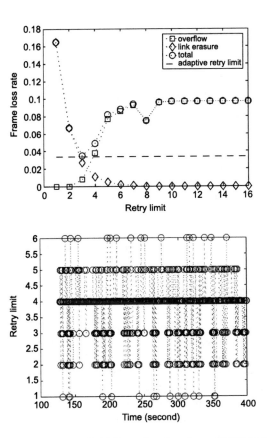

FIGURE 12.8:   (Top) MAC PLR under fixed- and RTRO-based retransmission strategies; (bottom) trace of retransmission limit adaptation.

Interestingly, it can be found that at this point $p_B(R) = p_L(R)$, implying that the optimal R is located at the intersection point of the two functions— $p_B(R)$ and $p_L(R)$. This can also be observed from Figure 12.8 (top). The optimized retransmission limit can then be obtained by rounding R to the closest integer. Therefore, we conjecture that we can determine the optimal R as $\arg\min_R |p_L(R) - p_B(R)|$. In other words, the optimal R is chosen as the one that can strike a balance between overflow loss and link loss. In [11], this conjecture was also proven using an M/G/1 queuing model for the video traffic, as well as using real video sequences and transmitting them using an NS-2 simulator-based implementation of the 802.11a/b/g MAC standard. The dependencies of the optimal R on the multimedia packet arrival rate, the experienced link packet loss rate (PLR), and multimedia traffic characteristics (CBR versus VBR) can also be found in [11].

This analysis resulted in the following simple iterative algorithm for *real-time retransmission limit optimization* (RTRO):

1. The network queue *and* the MAC layer monitor the overflow rate $p_B(R)$ and the packet error rate $p_L(R)$.
2. If $p_B < p_L$, then R is increased; if $p_B > p_L$, then R should be decreased.

In Figure 12.8 (top), one typical simulation result is presented based on [11] to show the effectiveness of the aforementioned RTRO strategy. From Figure 12.8, we can observe that an optimal static setting for R exists, depending on the channel conditions and traffic characteristics, which can minimize p_T. However, as illustrated in Figure 12.8, the optimal retransmission setting changes with channel conditions and traffic characteristics, and thus the MAC needs to continuously adapt (optimize) the retransmission limit. Fortunately, even a simple adaptive cross-layer strategy, such as the RTRO strategy, is able to quickly track the optimal retransmission limits, as shown in Figure 12.8 (bottom). See [11] for more details and results.

12.5.2 Joint Application–MAC Cross-Layer Optimization

The MAC-layer RTRO adaptation can also be jointly optimized with the application-layer rate adaptation and prioritized scheduling strategies by associating different retransmission limits to different priority packets. A synopsis of the discussed Application–MAC cross-layer transmission algorithm is given for illustration purposes. See [11] for more details.

The application layer can classify various packets/frames/layers of the compressed video bit stream into different priority classes having different delay requirements, dependencies, relative importance, and impact on the received video quality (see also next section). Let vector $\mathbf{P}_V = [P_{V1} \quad P_{V2} \quad \cdots \quad P_{VN}]$ specify the tolerable MAC packet loss rates of all the video layers (determined by the

QoS requirement of the scalable video). To maximize the video quality $\mathbf{Q}$, unequal error protection (UEP) needs to be provided: higher priority packets need to be transmitted first and with a lower PLR, as they have the highest impact on multimedia quality, while the lower priority packets can be discarded or transmitted with a higher PLR when the channel conditions worsen. To provide UEP, multiple priority queues are maintained at the interface between MAC and application layer [11] and different retransmission limits are used for each of the video layers. All the queues are managed by a common absolute Priority-Queuing (PQ) discipline. To achieve application-layer rate adaptation and prioritized scheduling, several new features can be added to conventional PQ. If c_i is the incoming rate of packets into priority queue i and C is the total available link capacity, then the perceived link capacity of queue j in the worst case[5] can be approximately expressed as $C_j = \max\{0, C - \sum_{i=1}^{j} c_i\}$, where queue priorities decrease with increasing i. As long as $c_j < C_j$, queue j will have few overflow losses. However, all queues will still be exposed to the same packet erasure rate.

The aforementioned analysis for the fluid model and M/G/1 model can be further extended to include a multiqueue system and, based on this, a systematic retry-limit configuration method for the MAC can be determined to optimize the video quality (see [11] for more details). Let $\mathbf{R} = [R_1 \quad R_2 \quad \cdots \quad R_N]$ be the set of the retransmission limits for the different priority layers/packets and $\mathbf{s} = [s_1(R_1, P) \quad s_2(R_2, P) \quad \cdots \quad s_N(R_N, P)]$ be the set of average number of link retransmissions given $\mathbf{R}$ and P. Given the departure rates from the queues to the link $\boldsymbol{\Lambda} = [\Lambda_1 \quad \Lambda_2 \quad \cdots \quad \Lambda_N]$, determined by the application-layer prioritized scheduling strategy, the overall average number of packet retransmissions can be calculated as

$$\bar{s}(\mathbf{R}, P) = \frac{\boldsymbol{\Lambda} \cdot \mathbf{s}^T(\mathbf{R}, P)}{\boldsymbol{\Lambda} \cdot \mathbf{1}}, \qquad (12.15)$$

where $\mathbf{1} = [1 \quad 1 \quad \cdots \quad 1]^T$.

We introduce a *shadow retry limit* (SRL) for the MAC, with a corresponding retransmission limit vector $\mathbf{R}^{\text{srl}}$ (all its elements are equal to SRL). This $\mathbf{R}^{\text{srl}}$ is maintained by the MAC but is not enforced on any of the queues. The optimal $\mathbf{R}^{\text{srl}}$ of a multiqueue system can be computed by lumping all the overflows and link erasures observed from different queues into a single overflow rate and link erasure rate and running the MAC-driven RTRO algorithm developed for a single-queue system. Meanwhile, by assuming the same average number of packet retransmissions as that of $\mathbf{R}^{\text{srl}}$, the MAC can compute the actual retransmission limit vector $\mathbf{R}^{\text{re}}$ (with unequal elements) that will be applied to the

---

[5]Worst case means that every arrival of queue j has to wait for the end of the service of a packet from a higher priority queue.

queues. The mapping from $\mathbf{R}^{srl}$ to $\mathbf{R}^{re}$ is performed using the following procedure.

1. Calculate vector $\mathbf{R}_V = [\lceil \log_P P_{V1} - 1 \rceil \quad \lceil \log_P P_{V2} - 1 \rceil \quad \cdots \quad \lceil \log_P P_{VN} - 1 \rceil]$, which specifies the minimum retransmission limit for the queues that can satisfy $\mathbf{P_v}$.
2. Set $i = 1$.
3. Construct $\mathbf{R}^{re} = [R_{V1} \quad \cdots \quad R_{Vi}0 \quad \cdots \quad 0]$.
4. If $\bar{s}(\mathbf{R}^{re}, P) < \bar{s}(\mathbf{R}^{srl}, P)$, go to step 5. Otherwise, continuously reduce the ith components retransmission limit R_i^{re} by 1 until $\bar{s}(\mathbf{R}^{re}, P) \leq \bar{s}(\mathbf{R}^{srl}, P)$ *again, and stop.*
5. If $i = N$, stop; otherwise, $i = i + 1$ and go to step 3.

More details about the deployed algorithm and its theoretical foundation can be found in [11].

To highlight the impact of this cross-layer optimization on the achieved multimedia quality we compare the following adaptation schemes:

- No optimized strategies are deployed at the MAC or application layers, that is, no RTRO.
- MAC-layer optimization (RTRO), but with no application-layer awareness.
- Application-layer optimization (rate adaptation and prioritized scheduling), but no MAC-layer optimization.
- Joint application–MAC cross-layer optimization.

The impact of these cross-layer strategies on the perceived video quality was evaluated by performing a visual experiment [11]. Since the experiments are conducted at relatively low bit rates and in the presence of packet losses, impairments are expected, and thus, the selected five scales are very annoying (1), annoying (2), slightly annoying (3), perceptible but not annoying (4), and imperceptible (5). The statistical scores summarized in Table 12.1 clearly illustrate the advantages of cross-layer optimization.

Table 12.1: Subjective video quality experiment.

Deployed strategies	Visual score
No optimization at MAC and application	1.4
MAC-layer optimization (RTRO)	1.9
Application-layer optimization	3.8
Joint application–MAC cross-layer optimization	4.6

12.6 CROSS-LAYER MAC–APPLICATION LAYER FOR ADAPTIVE RETRANSMISSION AND PACKETIZATION USING LAGRANGIAN OPTIMIZATION

This section illustrates a different optimization and modeling methodology (as opposed to the queuing-driven method discussed in the previous section) for the problem of cross-layer design for optimized wireless multimedia transmission, based on Lagrange multipliers.[6] We consider a similar cross-layer problem as before, namely the joint application-layer adaptive packetization and prioritized scheduling and MAC-layer retransmission strategy. The cross-layer problem is posed as a distortion minimization given delay constraints, and analytical solutions are derived based on the well-known Lagrangian optimization framework. In this process, we highlight an important aspect of wireless multimedia transmission: the need to convert conventional rate-constraint problems as conventionally considered by Lagrangian-based video optimizations into time-constrained problems based on the amount of time allocated by the resource moderator of the WLAN (i.e., access point) to a specific station. Moreover, we also discuss the difference between off-line optimizations as opposed to online solutions that can *explicitly* consider real-time available information about previously transmitted packets.

12.6.1 Motivation for Cross-Layer Optimization: A Simple Packetization Example

First, we highlight the need for joint application-MAC layer optimization by evaluating existing adaptive packetization algorithms currently deployed at the MAC layer, which do not explicitly consider the video applications delay constraints and distortions. Section 12.4 mentioned the overhead associated with the packetization and transmission protocols at the various layers of the OSI stack. We refer to this overhead (in terms of bits) discussed in the previous section as L^{Header}. (As before, L^{Header} reflects the packet header as well as the protocol overhead necessary to send a packet in a practical implementation.) Since the MAC is agnostic to the bit stream distortions or the video application delay constraints, the optimization at this layer is simply aimed at maximizing the throughput. Given the channel SNR and the PHY modes, the optimal packet size L^* that maximizes the goodput is computed analytically in [6,26] as

$$L^* = \frac{L^{Header}}{2} + \frac{1}{2}\sqrt{\left(L^{Header}\right)^2 - \frac{4b(L^{Header})^2}{\ln(1 - P_s)}}, \qquad (12.16)$$

---

[6]Note that Lagrangian optimization was already used successfully in other video system applications, such as rate-control optimization or joint source-channel coding.

Table 12.2:   Decoded PSNR for packet size optimized at the MAC layer.

p_e	Fixed packet size $L = 500$ bytes Decoded PSNR (dB)	Fixed packet size $L = 1000$ bytes Decoded PSNR (dB)	Optimized scheme L^* determined by MAC Decoded PSNR (dB)
6×10^{-6}	32.16	30.25	30.08 ($L^* = 2249$ bytes)
1×10^{-5}	30.45	28.32	27.90 ($L^* = 1738$ bytes)
3×10^{-5}	28.76	25.56	25.86 ($L^* = 997$ bytes)
5×10^{-5}	25.01	24.09	24.12 ($L^* = 768$ bytes)

where b is the number of bits per symbol and P_s is the probability of symbol error, which will depend on the modulation type and link SNR. However, this packet-size optimization mechanism does not consider either the distortion impact of the various packets or the video delay constraints. Illustrative results, comparing the decoded PSNR obtained with this optimal packet size versus alternative ad hoc schemes with fixed packet sizes, are summarized in Table 12.2 for the *Coast-guard* sequence (at CIF resolution 30 frames per second) that was compressed using a scalable codec [13,14] and for an application-layer delay constraint of 400 ms. Furthermore, the header overhead L^{Header} was 30 bytes (240 bits). In all scenarios, the retransmission limits have been set to 0.

From Table 12.2, it can be clearly concluded that the optimal packet size determined at the MAC layer results in a suboptimal performance in terms of the decoded video quality. This motivates the need for cross-layer optimization involving both channel conditions, but also *explicitly* considering the content characteristics and video encoder features, as well as the delay constraints, when determining the packet sizes and the associated retransmissions.

12.6.2 Formalizing the Joint Cross-Layer Optimization Problem Based on Delay Constraints

We consider a video bit stream that is first organized into separate layers based on the delay deadlines of the various video frames (e.g., I-, P-, and B-frames in conventional MPEG and H.26x predictive structures and L- and H-frames in the temporal pyramids of state-of-the-art wavelet scalable coders). In this way, data from different deadline layers are never jointly packetized, as this can lead to suboptimal scheduling strategies due to inefficient exploitation of the remaining transmission time. To facilitate *real-time adaptive* packetization, scheduling and cross-layer optimization with the lower layers based on instantaneous channel conditions and decoding deadlines (without actually requiring the reorganization of the bit stream) an abstraction layer "multitrack hinting" [45] can be adopted, which is an extension of the MP4 file format hinting mechanism [39]. Multitrack hinting can be used to structure the bit stream into multiple sub-layers with different distortion impacts and delay constraints, as illustrated in Figure 12.9. The

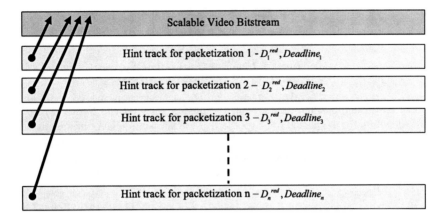

FIGURE 12.9:   Deployed multitrack rate–distortion hinting file format.

concept of multitrack hinting was developed in [45] and discussed in more detail in [15].

The multitrack concept is useful for wireless multimedia transmission because it enables (i) real-time adaptation of the packet sizes at transmission time, after the encoding has been performed, (ii) real-time prioritization of different packets based on distortion impacts and changing delay constraints, and (iii) real-time optimized scheduling of video packets based on their deadline and the transmission of the previous packets.

The goal of the cross-layer optimization discussed in this section is to determine the optimal packet size L_j and maximum number of times each packet j can be transmitted, m_j^{max}, such that the expected video distortion is minimized under a given delay constraint. Based on whether packet j is received or lost, the decoded video experiences distortion D_j^{quant} or D_j^{loss}. Hence, when a packet is received successfully, the decoded distortion decreases by an amount D_j^{red}, where $D_j^{red} = D_j^{loss} - D_j^{quant}$. This represents the utility (benefit) of receiving the packet and can be determined using encoding by empirical or analytical rate–distortion models [18]. The goal of the optimization strategy is to maximize the expected utility for a Group of Pictures (GOP),

$$D_{GOP} = \sum_{j=1}^{N_p} D_j^{red} P_j^{succ}, \qquad (12.17)$$

with N_p being the number of packets within a GOP and P_j^{succ} being the probability of successfully receiving packet j, given the bit error probability P_e, subject to a delay constraint,

$$\sum_{k=1}^{j} Time_k \leq Deadline_j, \quad 1 \leq j \leq N_p, \tag{12.18}$$

where $Time_j$ is the actual time it takes to transmit packet j and $Deadline_j$ is the time deadline for the packet to be received at the application layer of the client in order to be decoded and displayed.[7] The deadlines are determined based on the coding dependencies between the video frames (and thus, the encoding structure and parameters) and also include the maximum delay tolerated at the application layer $Delay_{max}$.

In the wireless video transmission scenario considered in this section, there are two reasons for discarding packets: packet loss from the BER in the wireless link and exceeded packet transmission deadlines. The impact of the buffer overflow or underflow was not considered. We define P_j^{succ} as the probability of successfully receiving the packet given bit errors in the network. With packet size L_j (bits) and bit error probability P_e (controlled by the physical layer, based on the channel SNR, channel coding and modulation strategy used, etc.), the packet loss probability is $P_{L_j} = 1 - (1 - P_e)^{L_j}$. Furthermore, if we assume that the wireless link is a memoryless packet erasure channel [26], such that the packets are dropped independently, the probability of success for packet j with an upper limit on the number of transmissions m_j^{max} (i.e., a retransmission limit $m_j^{max} - 1$) can be calculated

$$P_j^{succ} = \sum_{k=1}^{m_j^{max}} (P_{L_j})^{k-1}(1 - P_{L_j}) = 1 - (P_{L_j})^{m_j^{max}}. \tag{12.19}$$

The goal of the packetization and retransmission assignment policy is then to solve the delay-constrained optimization problem defined by Eqs. (12.18) and (12.19).

Importantly, two important differences exist between a conventional joint source-channel coding (JSCC) optimization [7–9] and the cross-layer optimization discussed here. First, in JSCC, the optimal channel codes are determined given channel rate constraints, while we are focusing on the delay-constrained transmission scenario for adaptive MAC retransmission and packetization. Second, as discussed in the previous sections, due to the MAC-layer feedback implemented within the 802.11 wireless protocol, we have access to timely informa-

---

[7]Note that we do not transmit any packets of the GOP beyond the deadline of the last packet within the GOP to avoid any impact on future GOPs, as GOPs are treated as independent entities in the SIV codec.

tion about the lost packets and the actual time that was needed for transmitting a packet $Time_{act}$. Hence, the cross-layer optimization can be performed successfully using online algorithms that combine real-time information with expected packet loss information, unlike in the conventional JSCC schemes that are deployed at the application layer. Furthermore, we rely on the implemented MAC retransmission strategies to consider the actual transmissions for cross-layer optimization rather than considering the current transmission and hypothetical future retransmission to optimize the expectation of a Lagrangian cost function. Hence, rather than modeling the effect of different transmission policies on the properties of a Markov decision process (as in [46,47]) and finding the strategy that maximizes the expectation of the video quality over all possible paths, the features of state-of-the-art wireless LAN protocols can consider determining an optimized cross-layer solution where

i. the feedback is considered to be immediate, such that coding dependencies are guaranteed to be satisfied, thereby avoiding the polynomial optimization objective encountered in [46,47]

ii. the approach is greedy in the sense that all resources can be consumed in transmitting data that has one deadline, before considering the transmission of data with a later deadline.

12.6.3 Packetizing and Retransmitting Data with Common Deadlines

Let us first consider the problem of solving the aforementioned cross-layer optimization for video layers with one common deadline. First, it can be shown that the problem of delay-constrained transmission can be mapped into a rate-constrained transmission. Assume that there are Q deadline layers with a common decoding deadline, which we label *Deadline*. Each deadline layer is partitioned into packets (one or more), and the optimal retransmission strategy is determined for this set of packets. Let one such partitioning lead to a total of $\hat{N}$ packets (for this set of deadline layers). Furthermore, consider that packet j, with packet size L_j,[8] is transmitted m_j times. Then, given the physical layer transmission rate $Rate_{PHY}$, the time to transmit this packet may be computed

$$Time_j = m_j \left(\frac{L_j}{Rate_{PHY}} + Time_O \right), \qquad (12.20)$$

where $Time_O$ is the timing overhead for the 802.11 MAC protocol (necessary to send a packet in a practical implementation), which can be approximated based

---

[8]Given that all bits within a deadline layer have roughly the same importance, we partition each deadline layer into equal parts for packetization. Hence packet sizes L_j are the same for all packets within one deadline layer. Furthermore, we assign the same retry limit to packets from the same deadline layer.

on [1,2,10] and includes the time of waiting for acknowledgments, duration of empty slots, expected back-off delays for transmitting a frame, and so on. Given that all packets have the same deadline, the delay constraint on the packet transmission can be rewritten

$$\sum_{j=1}^{\hat{N}} m_j \left(\frac{L_j}{Rate_{PHY}} + Time_O \right) \leq Deadline, \tag{12.21}$$

or, equivalently,

$$\sum_{j=1}^{\hat{N}} m_j \left(\frac{\hat{L}_j}{Rate_{PHY}} \right) \leq Deadline, \tag{12.22}$$

where the time overhead discussed in previous sections can be included as an equivalent packet length overhead. We can further rewrite this as

$$\sum_{j=1}^{\hat{N}} m_j \hat{L}_j \leq Rate_{PHY} \times Deadline = L_{\max}. \tag{12.23}$$

Hence, the delay constrained optimization becomes

$$\max \left[\sum_{j=1}^{\hat{N}} D_j^{red} P_j^{succ} \right] \quad \text{subject to} \quad \sum_{j=1}^{\hat{N}} m_j \hat{L}_j \leq L_{\max}. \tag{12.24}$$

Note that m_j corresponds to the redundancy rate associated with packet k. However, since the actual value of m_j cannot be determined analytically without actually transmitting the packet (it is a particular instance of an underlying random process), the *expected* redundancy rate, in terms of the expected number of transmissions of the packet, is considered. For packet j with a transmission limit $m_j^{\max}$ the expected number of times the packet is transmitted is

$$\overline{m}_j = \sum_{i=1}^{m_j^{\max}} i(1 - P_{L_j})(P_{L_j})^{i-1} + m_j^{\max}(P_{L_j})^{m_j^{\max}} = \frac{1 - (P_{L_j})^{m_j^{\max}}}{1 - P_{L_j}} = \frac{P_j^{succ}}{1 - P_{L_j}}. \tag{12.25}$$

Using a similar Lagrangian formulation, the optimization functional can be rewritten as

$$F = \sum_{j=1}^{\hat{N}} (D_j^{red} P_j^{succ} - \lambda \hat{L}_j \overline{m}_j), \tag{12.26}$$

where λ (≥ 0) is the Lagrange multiplier. The goal of the optimization is thus to maximize F. This problem may be further decomposed into a set of $\hat{N}$ independent optimizations for the packets, where the goal is to optimize the individual cost functional

$$F_j = \left(P_j^{succ} - \lambda_j \overline{m}_j\right), \quad \text{with } \lambda_j = \lambda \frac{\hat{L}_j}{D_j^{red}}. \tag{12.27}$$

The optimal solution may be obtained based on the convex hull of the probability of success P_j^{succ} versus the expected redundancy rate $\overline{m}_j$ curve. Note that the actual packet length L_j parameterizes this curve. In particular, the optimal solution $(m_j^{\max,opt}, L_j^{opt})$ is obtained on the curve at the point with the maximum redundancy, where the slope of the curve is larger (or equal) than the parameter λ_j. More details on determining the optimal λ using, for example, a bisection search, and the corresponding optimal retransmission limit and packet size can be obtained in [22].

Comparing the derived expressions for P_j^{succ} and $\overline{m}_j$ for the considered cross-layer optimization, we can clearly see that they have a linear relationship (with a slope $1 - P_{L_j}$). Hence, for such a linear curve, the optimal limit on the number of transmissions $m_j^{\max,opt}$ for packet j will be ∞, when $1 - P_{L_j} \geq \lambda_j$ and 0 otherwise, that is, either transmit a packet until it is received or do not transmit the packet at all. This is an important result, which indicates that the optimum retransmission policy is to retransmit as often as needed ($m_j^{\max,opt} = \infty$) the most important packets corresponding to high distortion impacts and to not transmit the less important packets at all.

Using the aforementioned analysis, a real-time algorithm can be developed to tune the retransmission limit based on the actual number of packet transmissions (instead of the expected redundancy rate). After analytically determining the optimal packet size[9] and the maximum number of packet transmissions (as ∞ or 0), we sort the set of packets in decreasing order of the fraction $(1 - P_{L_j^{opt}})/\lambda_j$. The packets are then transmitted in this order, where no packet is transmitted before all preceding packet transmissions are either completed or terminated. This ensures that coding dependencies between the layers are maintained and that the additive distortion model is not violated. Since in the delay-constrained wireless video transmission the maximum number of times a packet j can be transmitted cannot actually be ∞ and is bounded by the delay deadline *Deadline* (assumed here to be the same for all packets), the limit for each packet is tuned based on the

---

[9]Note that the packet size is upper bounded by the size of the deadline layers.

actual number of observed transmissions that occurred before it,

$$m_j^{\max,opt} = \left\lfloor \frac{Deadline - \sum_{k=1}^{j-1} m_k (L_k^{opt}/Rate_{PHY} + Time_o)}{L_j^{opt}/Rate_{PHY} + Time_o} \right\rfloor, \qquad (12.28)$$

where $\lfloor \cdot \rfloor$ is the floor operation. One additional advantage of computing this limit in real time is that we can recompute the retransmission limits (and also packet sizes if necessary) when the channel condition P_e or used PHY modulation strategy (that determines $Rate_{PHY}$) changes. Hence, for data belonging to different deadline layers with a common deadline, we can determine the optimal packet size as well as the retransmission limit using the aforementioned analysis. The next section shows how this approach can be extended to the case when we have deadline layers with different decoding deadlines for the real-time transmission scenario.

12.6.4 Real-Time Cross-Layer Algorithm for Wireless Video Streaming

This section extends the previous analysis to include sets of packets with different deadlines, as is the case in typical video streaming scenarios. One approach used to solve this cross-layer optimization is to formulate it as a joint optimization problem (optimization across different deadlines, quality layers, etc.) as performed in [47]. However, the complexity of such an algorithm increases rapidly with the number of different deadlines that need to be considered, especially as each transmission impacts all future transmissions and it is thus not practical. Additionally, such a joint optimization would require that assumptions are made about future channel conditions, modulation strategies employed, and so on.

Instead, a real-time greedy approach can be used, which is based on the analysis in the previous section, but which has the benefits of simplicity, as well as of enabling real time, instantaneous adaptation to varying channel conditions or PHY modulation strategies. In this greedy approach, the optimization problem (to determine the optimal packet size and the retransmission limit) can be solved independently for each set of deadline layers with a common deadline. Note that this approach does not consider the benefits of transmitting packets (deadline layers) with a late deadline before packets with an earlier deadline (which might be advantageous in some cases). However, a major advantage of three-dimensional wavelet video coders, as discussed in Chapter 5, is that packets with the largest distortion impact are mostly transmitted with an early decoding deadline due to the hierarchical temporal structure deployed, and hence the greedy algorithm is likely to perform close to the optimal solution. The real-time greedy algorithm is outlined in more detail in Table 12.3. In Table 12.3, the superscript k corresponds to a group of packets having the same deadline $Deadline^k$.

Table 12.3: Illustrative real-time greedy algorithm for adaptive packetization and MAC retransmission.

Set $Time_{cur} = 0$.

Compute the decoding deadlines for each subband, and hence each code block, based on the encoding parameters, and tolerable application delay. Let there be K separate deadlines (with values $Deadline^k$).

Reorganize (hint) the scalable bit stream into deadline layers.

Sort the deadlines in ascending order.

For $k = 1 : K$

   Gather all deadline layers with deadline ($Deadline^k$).

   Determine instantaneous channel conditions P_e and PHY modulation strategy $Rate_{PHY}$.

   Solve the equivalent rate-constrained optimization using the probability of success versus expected redundancy rate curve to determine optimal λ and determine optimal packet sizes and initial retransmission limits (as ∞ or 0).

   Packetize data using these obtained packet sizes $L_j^{opt,k}$.

   Sort the packets in descending order of $\left(1 - P_{L_j^{opt,k}}^k\right)/\lambda_j^k$.

   For $j = 1 : \hat{N}^k$

   Tune the actual retransmit limit $m_j^{max,opt,k} = \left\lfloor \dfrac{Deadline - Time_{cur}}{(L_j^{opt,k}/Rate_{PHY} + Time_o)} \right\rfloor$.

   Transmit the packet to determine the actual number of transmissions m_j^k ($m_j^k \leq m_j^{max,opt,k}$).

   Set $Time_{cur} \leftarrow Time_{cur} + m_j^k (L_j^{opt,k}/Rate_{PHY} + Time_o)$.

   If $Time_{cur} + \left(L_{j+1}^{opt,k}/Rate_{PHY} + Time_o\right) > Deadline^k$, break.

In summary, the main conclusions of the aforementioned cross-layer optimization case study are threefold. First, an analytical solution can be determined based on existing joint source channel coding research, for a special case of the considered cross-layer optimization problem, that is, when all packets have the same decoding deadline. Under such a scenario, the optimal cross-layer strategy results in retransmitting the most important packets (subbands) as often as needed and discarding the lesser important packets. Second, this analysis can be used to develop a real-time greedy algorithm to perform cross-layer optimization for the case when different sets of data have different decoding deadlines. This discussed greedy algorithm can successfully take advantage of the available feedback at the MAC about the actual number of times previous packets have been transmitted to correctly determine the number of times the current packet can be retransmitted.

Moreover, this algorithm can also successfully adapt on the fly to the changing channel conditions or physical layer modulation strategies. In [22], it was shown that the discussed algorithms can achieve significant improvements of 2 dB or more for a variety of video sequences, transmission bit rates, and delay constraints as opposed to simple algorithms based on only the packets' importance.

12.7 EFFICIENT RESOURCE RESERVATION MECHANISMS FOR WIRELESS MULTIMEDIA TRANSMISSION USING 802.11E

As mentioned in Section 12.1, in the 802.11e standard [3], a new wireless medium access method called Hybrid Coordination Function (HCF) is introduced, which combines the EDCA contention-based channel access mechanism with the polling-based channel access mechanism HCCA. Both EDCA and HCCA operate simultaneously and continuously. HCF enables differentiated treatment of traffic streams and can be tuned to meet QoS requirements of low latency and jitter. As such, its use for wireless multimedia streaming designs is an important cross-layer design issue. However, in order to achieve optimal transport of video over 802.11e HCCA, we need to accommodate application-layer constraints such as bandwidth variations due to variable bit rate (VBR) coding, delay constraints, and selective packet retransmission, as discussed in previous sections.

12.7.1 Background for Video Transmission over HCCA in IEEE 802.11e

The feasibility of the EDCA and HCCA mechanisms of HCF for multimedia transmission was addressed in [48–51]. In an attempt to optimize scheduling for VBR video traffic, in [49] an approach was presented for efficient scheduling by the resource manager (Hybrid Coordinator [HC]) based on the measured queue sizes of each traffic stream. HCCA was used, as it provides significant benefits over EDCF for applications requiring strict QoS. However, it is important to mention that all these approaches perform optimization at either the application layer or the MAC layer, thereby not benefiting from the advantages provided by the joint application-layer and MAC-layer optimization that can improve the overall system performance significantly.

HCCA-Based Admission Control for Video

HCCA is used to provide a parameterized QoS service. With HCCA, there is a negotiation of QoS requirements between the QoS enhanced wireless station and the HC. Once a stream for a WSTA is established, the HC allocates transmission opportunities (TXOPs) via polling to the WSTA in order to guarantee its QoS requirements. The HC enjoys free access to the medium during the contention-free period and uses the highest EDCA priority during the contention period in order to (1) send polls to allocate TXOPs and (2) send downlink parameterized traffic. It makes use of the priority interframe space to seize and maintain control of the medium. Once the HC has control of the medium, it starts to deliver parameterized downlink traffic to stations and issues QoS contention-free polls (QoS CF-Polls) to those stations that have requested parameterized services. QoS CF-Polls include the TXOP duration granted to the WSTA. If the station being polled has traffic to send, it may transmit several packets for each QoS CF-poll received respecting the TXOP limit specified in the poll. In order to utilize the medium more efficiently, it is possible to piggyback both the acknowledgment (CF-Ack) and the CF-Poll onto data packets. In contrast to the point coordination function of the IEEE 802.11-99 standard, HCCA operates during both the contention-free period and the contention period (see Figure 12.10).

The admission control and scheduling units enable HCCA to guarantee that the QoS requirements are met once a stream has been admitted in the network. Alternatively, EDCA only provides a QoS priority differentiation via a randomly distributed access mechanism.

To ensure user satisfaction, it is essential that, once admitted, a video stream is guaranteed QoS for its lifetime. Thus, there is a need to control how many streams are admitted to the system and what wireless resources should be allocated to each stream in order to obtain the optimal trade-off between a larger number of admitted stations and an acceptable video quality level for the admitted stations. In other words, a scalable admission control and adaptive protection strategy is necessary. Among the parameters defined in the traffic specification (TSPEC) element of IEEE 802.11e, we discuss the subset of parameters that influence the design of an efficient admission control algorithm for video applications. For each video flow i, these parameters are the peak data rate (P_i), the mean data rate (ρ_i), the maximum burst size (σ_i), the maximum permissible delay (d_i), the nominal MAC service data unit (packet) size (L_i), and the minimum physical-layer transmission rate (R_i).

In conventional video streaming mechanisms, P_i, ρ_i, and σ_i are part of a twin leaky bucket mechanism [52] and are supplied to the MAC by the application layer. Based on the twin leaky bucket analysis, the effective bandwidth for each video flow i can be computed[10]

$$g_i = \frac{P_i}{1 + d_i(P_i - \rho_i)\sigma_i^{-1}}. \tag{12.29}$$

---

[10]For the first part of the analysis presented in this section, we assume that channel or link state analysis is used in order to determine the additional percentage that needs to be reserved for the bandwidth to cover the losses that may occur in the wireless medium. Initially, we assume an ideal channel condition where no errors occur during the HCCA duration. Modifications imposed in the admission control in order to incorporate the effects of video packet retransmission due to channel errors are presented later.

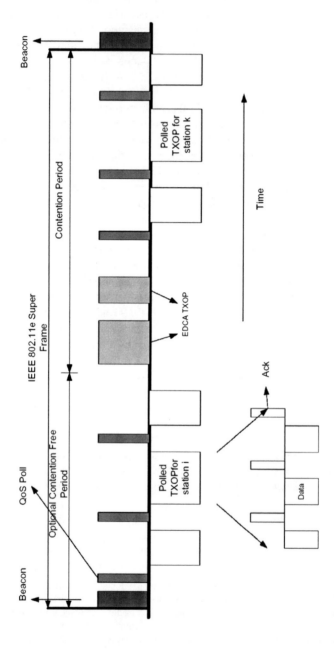

FIGURE 12.10:   Operation of the IEEE 802.11e HCF [3].

The previous bandwidth computation is "ideal" in the sense that it does not include overheads. As mentioned in previous sections, for the transmission of each packet there is an overhead in time based on the acknowledgment policy, the PIFS time, MAC-layer and physical-layer headers, and polling overhead. As a result, the scheduling policy has to determine and take into account these overheads, as different scheduling policies determine how many times one has to poll a WSTA in the duration of a service interval (SI), denoted as t_{SI}. Assuming that t_{SI} is known, the number of packets per SI is

$$N_i = \left\lceil \frac{g_i \cdot t_{\mathrm{SI}}}{L_i} \right\rceil \qquad (12.30)$$

and the modified guaranteed bandwidth including overheads is

$$g_i' = \frac{N_i(L_i + O_i)}{t_{\mathrm{SI}}}, \qquad (12.31)$$

where O_i represents the additional bits due to overheads for the transmission of a packet corresponding to video flow i. As a result, having already $i-1$ admitted flows in the network, the admission control for the ith video flow can be expressed

$$g_i' + \sum_{j=1}^{i-1} g_j' + g_{\mathrm{other}} \leq C, \qquad (12.32)$$

where g_{other} represents additional bandwidth allocated to nonvideo traffic (e.g., audio or other QoS-requiring media) and C is the total guaranteed bandwidth of the wireless medium. It is important to mention that a necessary condition for nonviolation of the initially negotiated QoS requirements is that $R_i \geq g_i'$. Based on the readjusted guaranteed bandwidth, the number of packets per SI is recalculated as in (12.30) with g_i replaced by g_i', and for each video flow i we denote the modified value by N_i'. The admission control unit can now calculate the TXOP duration required to service all these packets within t_{SI},

$$t_{\mathrm{TXOP},i} = N_i'\left(\frac{L_i}{R_i} + T_{\mathrm{overhead},i} \right), \qquad (12.33)$$

with $T_{\mathrm{overhead},i}$ the required overheads, as explained earlier. Similar to (12.32), we can express the admission control in terms of the TXOP duration for each video flow i:

$$\frac{t_{\mathrm{TXOP},i}}{t_{\mathrm{SI}}} + \sum_{j=1}^{i-1} \frac{t_{\mathrm{TXOP},j}}{t_{\mathrm{SI}}} + t_{\mathrm{TXOP,other}} \leq \frac{T - T_{\mathrm{CP}}}{T}, \qquad (12.34)$$

where $t_{\text{TXOP,other}}$ indicates the TXOP allocated to nonvideo traffic, T is the beacon interval illustrated in Figure 12.10, and T_{CP} is the time reserved for the contention period, that is, for EDCA traffic. Importantly, it should be noted that the $T_{\text{overhead,}i}$ and $t_{\text{TXOP,other}}$ have a significant impact on the number of admitted stations, as will be shown by the presented results.

The admission control expressed by (12.34) can be used for the construction of a round-robin, standard-compliant scheduler. In particular, the normative behavior set by the IEEE 802.11e standard [3] requires that the HC grants every flow i the negotiated time $t_{\text{TXOP,}i}$. Hence, for every video flow, the admission control described by (12.33) and (12.34) can be used. The remaining unknown parameter is t_{SI}, which is typically calculated [23,48] as

$$t_{\text{SI}} = 0.5 \min\{d_1, \ldots, d_n\} \tag{12.35}$$

for a total of n flows to be scheduled. Note that out of the n flows, several can be video flows, audio flows, or other delay-stringent applications. In addition, factor 0.5 is used to accommodate the jitter constraints demanded by the particular applications.

In order to better understand the challenges and limitations associated with deploying the previously described HCCA admission control for video, we consider the transmission of an MCTF scalable video coder,[11] whose particular architecture is outlined in Chapter 5. In typical MCTF-based video compression, the rate allocation for scalable bit stream extraction is performed with a maximum granularity of one GOP. This creates VBR characteristics for the compressed video content across the frames of each GOP. In addition, each decoded frame of every GOP has its own playback deadline determined by the frame rate. Note that, based on the MCTF structure, the decoding frame rate itself can be reduced dyadically by skipping the frames of the finer temporal levels [13]. Frame rate scalability will be useful in the cross-layer adaptation strategy that maximizes the number of admitted stations in the wireless network (see Chapter 5 for more details on how to perform spatio-temporal–SNR trade-offs).

12.7.2 A Scalable Video Admission Control Mechanism over IEEE 802.11e: The Sub-Flow Concept [16]

Implementation of the simple scheduler explained in Section 12.7.1 is easy, but it can be quite inefficient for real-time video streaming applications. This is be-

---

[11] However, it is important to emphasize that the cross-layer algorithms highlighted can be deployed with any video coding scheme. The essential part of the enhanced admission control mechanism is determination of the frame dependencies of the deployed video coder (and hence the frame/packet delays and traffic characteristics), which can be established based on the encoding parameters and modeled by direct acyclic graphs [47].

cause video traffic varies over time and consists of frames/packets with considerably varying sizes and different delay constraints. Conventionally, the video is considered as a single stream and the TSPEC parameters are set so that the MAC of IEEE 802.11e HCCA would do the admission control and scheduling as outlined previously. To improve the overall system utilization (number of admission stations), as well as the performance of the admitted stations, we introduce the sub-flow concept in which a video flow (bit stream) is divided into several subflows based on their delay constraints as well as on the relative priority in terms of the overall distortion of the decoded video. The application layer enables each sub-flow of the video to interface with the MAC as a separate flow. Each sub-flow has a different priority (determined by its distortion impact) and delay constraint. A sub-flow has its own TSPEC parameters and is admitted independently by the resource coordinator.

The goal is to use the sub-flow mechanism to provide a joint application–MAC optimization that maximizes the number of admitted wireless stations while optimizing the video quality for each admitted station. Given the channel conditions, the resource manager (coordinator) and the cooperating wireless stations have to determine for each application the number of sub-flows the application layer can transmit, as well as their protection strategies (e.g., MAC retry limits per subflow), while maximizing the number of wireless stations in the network. This section shows how the global flow traffic can be partitioned into sub-flows that are then shaped by multiple token leaky buckets to determine their individual QoS token rates.

For illustration, let us consider one GOP of 16 frames that is encoded using MCTF (see Figure 12.11). Frames with the same playback deadline are grouped

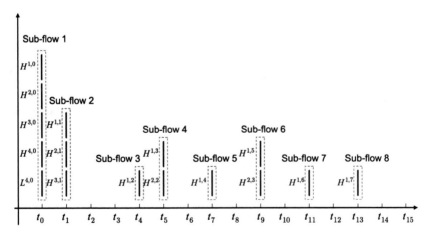

FIGURE 12.11: Example of sub-flow formation.

into the same sub-flow. The number of sub-flows depends on the temporal decomposition levels and the number of reference frames used for motion estimation. If we denote the number of sub-flows of one GOP as N_s we have

$$N_s = 2^{D-1}, \tag{12.36}$$

where D is the total number of temporal decomposition levels. Each sub-flow is regarded as an independent traffic flow passing through a twin leaky bucket to get its own QoS guaranteed bandwidth g_i as expressed by (12.29), with i indicating the sub-flow number, $1 \leq i \leq N_s$, and P_i, ρ_i, σ_i, and d_i the corresponding peak data rate, mean data rate, maximum burst size, and delay constraint of sub-flow i, respectively. As a result, each sub-flow has its own TSPEC parameters and thus there are multiple sets of TSPEC parameters corresponding to one global video flow. A WSTA uses these multiple sets of TSPEC parameters to negotiate with the resource coordinator.

The system performance gain that can be achieved by the discussed sub-flow concept can be quantified theoretically if we introduce the average transmission opportunity duration, $\overline{t_{TXOP}}$:

$$\overline{t_{TXOP}} = \frac{1}{N_s} \sum_{i=1}^{N_s} t_{TXOP,i}. \tag{12.37}$$

For a global video flow i, t_{TXOP} is equal to the definition given in (12.33). Following the admission control expressed in (12.34), if we assume only N_{QSTA} video flows for the HCCA transmission intervals, that is, $t_{TXOP,other} = 0$, by replacing the average transmission opportunity duration for each station by (12.37), we get the maximum number of admitted WSTA carrying video data as

$$N_{QSTA} = \left\lfloor \frac{t_{SI}(1 - T_{CP} \cdot T^{-1})}{t_{TXOP}} \right\rfloor. \tag{12.38}$$

In the following section, we determine the optimal allocated $t_{TXOP,i}$ for each sub-flow i (under predetermined delay constraints) such that the number of admitted stations (N_{QSTA}) is maximized.

12.7.3 Optimization of the Number of Admitted Stations

We discuss a mechanism that maximizes the number of simultaneously admitted wireless stations by optimizing the allocated transmission opportunity duration for each sub-flow. The solution can be obtained using linear programming. Given the allotted TXOP per sub-flow, as shown next, the maximum number of packet retransmissions can be determined in order to optimize the video quality under the presence of network errors. Subsequently, an algorithm is discussed for dynamic adaptation of packet retransmissions based on this derivation. Finally, we explain how link adaptation can be incorporated in the discussed framework to improve the overall performance for different channel conditions.

12.7.3.1 Optimized Multimedia Admission Control Under Delay Constraints

Although the use of sub-flows may increase the number of admitted stations in the HCCA traffic, if additional delay is permitted in the transmission of each sub-flow traffic, an optimal scheduling algorithm can yield further improvements. A visual example of such a case for one GOP of video data can be seen in Figure 12.12, where each increase in the transmission duration of each sub-flow i, $d_{s,i}$, provides the opportunity for traffic smoothing. In order to accommodate delay requirements, we have $\max\{d_{s,1}, \ldots, d_{s,2^{D-1}}\} \leq d_{\max}$ with $d_{\max}$ set by the chosen streaming scenario.

Each increase in the transmission duration of sub-flow i is reflected by a change in $t_{\text{TXOP},i}$. The optimization goal of maximizing N_{QSTA} given by (12.38) can be equivalently stated as minimizing $\overline{t_{\text{TXOP}}}$ since the other parameters in (12.38) are unaffected by changes in the transmission duration. As a result, if we limit

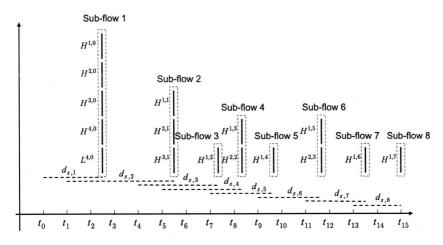

FIGURE 12.12:   Sub-flows with different transmission durations due to additional delay permitted. Each $d_{s,i}$, $1 \leq i \leq 2^{D-1}$ corresponds to additional transmission time for sub-flow i. For cases, we assume that an upper bound for the additional delay is set, denoted by $d_{\max}$, and we have $\max\{d_{s,1}, \ldots, d_{s,2^{D-1}}\} \leq d_{\max}$.

optimization to the duration of one GOP (since the video flow traffic is periodic for each GOP) by combining Eqs. (12.30)–(12.33), the minimization problem now becomes

$$\text{Primary problem:} \quad \{t^*_{s,1}, \ldots, t^*_{s,2^{D-1}}\} = \arg\min \sum_{i=1}^{2^{D-1}} g_{s,i}, \tag{12.39}$$

such that $\forall i : 1 \le i \le 2^{D-1}$ we have

$$\sum_{j=1}^{i} t^*_{s,j} \le \sum_{j=1}^{i} (t_{s,j} + d_{\max}). \tag{12.40}$$

In Eqs. (12.39) and (12.40), $\{t^*_{s,1}, \ldots, t^*_{s,2^{D-1}}\}$ are the optimal transmission durations corresponding to sub-flows $1 \le i \le 2^{D-1}$, $g_{s,i}$ is the effective bandwidth defined by $g_{s,i} = b_{s,i}/t_{s,i}$, with $b_{s,i}$ the size (in bits) of sub-flow i, and $t_{s,i}$ is the original transmission duration of sub-flow i. Note that this definition of $g_{s,i}$ corresponds to the generic definition of (12.29) if we assume that $P_i = \rho_i$, that is, under the assumption of CBR transmission for the transmission duration of sub-flow i. In order to facilitate the optimization process, the optimization problem stated in (12.39) and (12.40) can be expressed in a dual form [16] as

$$\text{Dual problem:} \quad \{b^*_{s,1}, \ldots, b^*_{s,2^{D-1}}\} = \arg\min \sum_{i=1}^{2^{D-1}} \frac{b_{s,i}}{t^{\max}_{s,i}}, \tag{12.41}$$

such that $\forall i : 1 \le i \le 2^{D-1}$ we have

$$\sum_{j=1}^{i} b^*_{s,j} \ge \sum_{j=1}^{i} b_{s,j}. \tag{12.42}$$

In Eqs. (12.41) and (12.42), $\{b^*_{s,1}, \ldots, b^*_{s,2^{D-1}}\}$ are the optimal sub-flow sizes, and $t^{\max}_{s,1} = t_{s,1} + d_{\max}$, $t^{\max}_{s,i} = t_{s,i}$ for $2 \le i \le 2^{D-1}$ represent the maximum permissible transmission durations for each sub-flow.

Under CBR transmission for each sub-flow, the Primary and Dual problems stated earlier provide the same solution. For example, by deriving the optimal sub-flow sizes we can establish the optimal transmission duration corresponding to the size of each sub-flow as

$$t^*_{s,i} = t^{\max}_{s,i} \frac{b_{s,i}}{b^*_{s,i}}. \tag{12.43}$$

Nevertheless, one difference of practical significance is that the Dual problem facilitates the application of linear programming techniques, namely the simplex minimization, for establishment of the optimal solution. This ensures optimality with low complexity, as the algorithm converges in a number of steps proportional to the total number of sub-flows, N_s. The simplex optimization scans through all the vertices of the N_s-dimensional simplex in order to establish the point corresponding to the minimum of (12.41) (see [16] for more details). It is important to mention that, in order to formulate a bounded problem for this purpose, we need to impose an upper bound to the maximum number of bits transmitted in the time interval corresponding to one GOP. Hence, we introduced an additional constraint to the problem,

$$\sum_{j=1}^{2^{D-1}-1} b_{s,j}^* \leq \sum_{j=1}^{2^{D-1}-1} R_j \cdot t_{s,j}^{\max}, \qquad (12.44)$$

which corresponds to the physical constraint that the maximum number of bits transmitted during the duration of one GOP, together with the packetization overhead introduced at the various layers, cannot exceed the mean amount of bits transmitted by the physical layer during this time.

Finally, although the optimization problem is defined and solved for the duration of one GOP, if access to additional sub-flows from consecutive GOPs is possible (e.g., in the case of off-line encoding), they can be included in the optimization problem of (12.41) and (12.42) following the same rationale. Experimental results with real video data utilizing the discussed optimization approach are presented in [16].

12.7.3.2 Packet Scheduling and Retransmissions Under the 802.11e HCCA Admission Control

For the admitted sub-flows of a WSTA, the application and MAC layers can cooperate to improve multimedia quality by adapting the retry limit. The discussions of retry limit adaptation in the previous section are not HCCA enabled and also they do not explicitly consider the delay bound set by the application for the various packets/flows. Here, the goal of packet scheduling and prioritized MAC retransmissions is to minimize the playback distortion for a video streaming session over an 802.11a/e HCCA WLAN, under delay constraints.

Due to limits imposed by link adaptation to different physical layer rates, as well as delay constraints, the retransmission bound for the earlier transmitted packets can be higher than the maximum retransmissions allowed for the remainder set of packets. Hence, under a scheme allowing for unequal video packet retransmissions, a higher probability for correct reception can be provided to the first subsets of video packets. This motivates packet prioritization at the application layer depending on the video data significance (incurred distortion due to losing the packet).

The optimal transmission duration for each sub-flow was already established in the previous section by linear programming. In this section, given the set of video packets for each sub-flow i, as well as the transmission duration $t_{s,i}^*$, we establish which subset should be transmitted, as well as the maximum permissible number of video packet retransmissions in case of errors.

Modeling approaches have been proposed for the establishment of substream significance in MCTF-based video compression [17,18]. Most of these models use dynamic computation of the expected distortion using signal statistics or precomputed distortion metadata in conjunction with models for the error propagation across the MCTF decoding structure. Although such solutions result in a model-optimized scheduling with the potential for high accuracy, they can also incur a high computational burden for online processing of many streams. In addition, if we define the number of retransmissions based only on the video packet significance, we will not be able to take advantage of the fact that the MAC layer can provide real-time feedback concerning the correct reception of each individual packet.

Once the ordering is complete, the video packets are placed in packets, which are passed to the MAC layer in the specified order. Although these rules are simply based on the compression architecture and the discussed sub-flow scheduling, the layering principle of fully scalable MCTF-based video coding ensures the optimality of such a scheduling approach. In addition, theoretical studies [18] have shown that the expected distortion–reduction obtained by decoding each video packet is proportional to the temporal and spatial level that the packet belongs to, according to the ordering expressed in the aforementioned rules. We remark that, similar to the previous section, the scheduling algorithm operates independently for each GOP, although extensions to multiple GOPs can be envisaged following similar principles.

Here, the transmission channel is assumed to be an independent, identically distributed error channel. Thus, the channel causes errors independently in each packet and the error probability is the same for all packets with the same length at all times. Let $p_b(m)$ be the bit error probability in physical-layer mode m. Then, the error probability of a packet of size L_i (belonging to sub-flow i) in physical-layer mode m is a function of bit error probability $p_b(m)$ and is defined

$$p_e(m, L_i) = 1 - \left[1 - p_b(m)\right]^{L_i}. \qquad (12.45)$$

Let $N_{\text{retry}}^{\max}(j)$ be the maximum number of retries of packet j belonging to sub-flow i. Note that the value of $N_{\text{retry}}^{\max}(j)$ depends on the position of the packet in the transmission queue (derived based on the criteria outlined earlier), as well as on the available transmission duration for the current sub-flow. The probability of unsuccessful transmission after $N_{\text{retry}}^{\max}(j)$ retransmissions is

$$P_e\big(m, L_i, N_{\text{retry}}^{\max}(j)\big) = \big[p_e(m, L_i)\big]^{N_{\text{retry}}^{\max}(j)+1}. \qquad (12.46)$$

In addition, based on $N_{\text{retry}}^{\max}(j)$, the average number of transmissions for the jth packet until the packet is transmitted successfully or the retransmission limit is reached can be found as discussed in the previous sections as

$$N_{\text{average}}(j) = \frac{1 - [p_e(m, L)]^{N_{\text{retry}}^{\max}(j)+1}}{1 - p_e(m, L)}. \qquad (12.47)$$

The corresponding average time to transmit the packet using the guaranteed channel rate g_i' for sub-flow i is

$$T_{\text{average}} = N_{\text{average}}(j)\left(\frac{L_i}{g_i'} + T_{\text{ACK}}\right), \qquad (12.48)$$

where T_{ACK} is the overhead for the transmission of the acknowledgment frame. Assuming that the maximum time before the packet expires is $T_{\max}$, we have

$$T_{\text{average}} \leq T_{\max}. \qquad (12.49)$$

Due to CBR transmission for the duration of each sub-flow, the packets are distributed evenly with an interval α_i (i.e., packet arrival interval for sub-flow i). Assuming that the transmission duration for sub-flow i is $t_{s,i}^*$ (estimated by the optimization of Section 12.7.3.1), for the jth packet of that sub-flow we have

$$T_{\max} = t_{s,i}^* - \alpha_i \sum_{k=1}^{j-1} N_{\text{retry}}^{\text{actual}}(k), \qquad (12.50)$$

where $N_{\text{retry}}^{\text{actual}}(k)$, $0 \leq N_{\text{retry}}^{\text{actual}}(k) \leq N_{\text{retry}}^{\max}(k)$, is the actual number of retries for each packet k that precedes packet j until an acknowledgment has been received, or the maximum number of retries has been performed. Note that $N_{\text{retry}}^{\text{actual}}(k)$ can be determined dynamically based on feedback from the MAC layer. The last equation can be used in conjunction with Eqs. (12.46) and (12.49) to establish the bound for the maximum-allowable number of retries for the current packet j:

$$N_{\text{retry}}^{\max}(j) \leq \log_{p_e(m, L_i)}\left[\left(1 - p_e(m, L_i)\right)\left(\frac{L_i}{g_i'} + T_{\text{ACK}}\right)^{-1}\right.$$

$$\left. \times \left(t_{s,i}^* - \alpha_i \sum_{k=1}^{j-1} N_{\text{retry}}^{\text{actual}}(k)\right)\right] - 1. \qquad (12.51)$$

Note that the estimated maximum number of retries determined by (12.51) can be negative, depending on whether we exceeded the available bandwidth for sub-flow i or not. In such a case, the remaining packets of the current sub-flow are simply discarded.

12.7.3.3 Scalable Sub-Flow Transmission with Dynamic Adaptation

We outline the steps performed during the actual streaming process for each sub-flow i in Table 12.4. Some of the last packets of each sub-flow will not be transmitted whenever the channel condition deteriorates, as the transmission duration (deadline) determined by the simplex optimization of the previous section does not take into account the retransmissions that will occur based on the algorithm of Table 12.4. This is checked in Step 2 of the algorithm of Table 12.4. Nevertheless, use of a scalable video coding and the prioritization rules for the transmission of the video packets specified before ensure that near-optimal adaptation of the video quality will occur based on the instantaneous channel capacity, as packets with the most important video data will be transmitted first.

An alternative design can be formulated by a priori calculating the maximum number of retransmissions for each packet j based on $p_b(m)$ and using (12.45) and (12.50) with the setting of $N_{\text{retry}}^{\text{actual}}(k) = N_{\text{retry}}^{\text{max}}(k)$ for every $1 \leq k < j$. Then the sub-flow sizes can be readjusted to include the estimated number of retransmissions. This allows for the optimization algorithm of Section 12.7.3.1 to derive optimal transmission durations that include the (worst-case) expected number of retransmissions for packets of the sub-flow. Overall, the latter case is expected to

Table 12.4: Transmission of packets of each sub-flow i.

- Initialization: Establish $p_b(m)$ based on the utilized physical-layer mode. Calculate $p_e(m, L_i)$ from (12.45).
- For each packet j:

     1. Establish T_{max} based on (12.50). Calculate $N_{\text{retry}}^{\text{max}}(j)$ based on (12.47)–(12.49). Set current_retries $= 0$.

     2. If $N_{\text{retry}}^{\text{max}}(j) \geq 0$
         - Set current_ACK $=$ FALSE; go to Step 3.
         else
         - Discard the current packet as well as the remaining sub-flow packets with the same deadline.

     3. While current_ACK $=$ FALSE AND current_retries $\leq N_{\text{retry}}^{\text{max}}$,
         - Transmit the current packet. Set: current_retries $\leftarrow$ current_retries $+ 1$.
         - Set current_ACK to TRUE or FALSE depending on MAC-layer feedback.

     4. Set $N_{\text{retry}}^{\text{actual}}(j) =$ current_retries.

overprovision bandwidth for each sub-flow, whereas the previous case can lead to some of the least-significant video packets being dropped, depending on the channel condition.

12.7.3.4 QoS Token Rate Adaptation for Link Adaptation

As mentioned earlier, IEEE 802.11a supports eight physical-layer rates from 6 to 54 Mbit/s. Link adaptation selects one appropriate physical-layer mode based on link conditions in order to improve the system goodput and throughput. WSTAs may adapt their physical-layer modulation and coding strategies depending on the link conditions. In particular, the physical-layer rate will be lowered dynamically when the link condition of one WSTA gets worse, that is, when the signal-to-interference noise ratio drops. The TXOP durations calculated by (12.33) will not take into account the new rate when the WSTA switches its default physical-layer rate mode and, as a result, the resource coordinator may deny the traffic stream of the WSTA whose physical rate turns out to be lower than the prenegotiated minimum rate.

In order to keep the number of admitted stations fixed and have graceful quality degradation, we can utilize the packet scheduling algorithm of Section 12.7.3.2 in order to drop packets containing less important video data such that the precalculated TXOP duration can still guarantee the QoS when the physical-layer mode is changed. For this purpose, we need to determine the new effective bandwidth for each sub-flow i, g_i'', under a change in the physical-layer transmission rate. If we assume that the modified rate for the duration of the sub-flow transmission is R_i', from (12.33) we have

$$N_i' = \frac{t_{\text{TXOP},i}}{L_i \cdot (R')^{-1} + T_{\text{overhead},i}}. \tag{12.52}$$

Then, from (12.30) we get

$$g_i' = \frac{N_i \cdot L_i}{t_{\text{SI}}}, \tag{12.53}$$

and because CBR transmission occurs for the duration of the sub-flow transmission, $t_{s,i}^*$, we can calculate the modified sub-flow size, $b_{s,i}'$, using (12.52) and (12.53) as

$$\rho_i' = \frac{b_{s,i}'}{t_{s,i}^*} = g_i' \Rightarrow b_{s,i}' = \frac{t_{s,i}^* \cdot t_{\text{TXOP},i} \cdot L_i}{[L_i \cdot (R')^{-1} + T_{\text{overhead},i}] \cdot t_{\text{SI}}}. \tag{12.54}$$

Note that in the cases where the link adaptation may change the physical layer rate more than once during the sub-flow transmission interval $t_{s,i}^*$, R_i' can be calculated based on the weighted sum of the different rates,

$$R' = \frac{1}{t_{s,i}^*} \sum_{k=1}^{w} \left[R_{\text{phy}}(k) \cdot t_{\text{phy}}(k) \right], \tag{12.55}$$

where $R_{\text{phy}}(k)$ and $t_{\text{phy}}(k)$ represent the rate and duration, respectively, corresponding to the kth link adaptation during time interval $t_{s,i}^*$ (out of w total adaptations).

The modified sub-flow size estimated by (12.54) may be used to restrict the number of video packets of each sub-flow; depending on the adaptive retransmission scheme of Table 12.4, once the amount of video packets sent reaches $b_{s,i}'$, the remaining packets in the prioritized transmission queue are discarded. Hence, similar to the case of Section 12.7.3.2, the prioritization mechanism ensures that the most significant packets receive the highest priority under link adaptation at the physical layer. An interesting extension of the link adaptation algorithm would be to optimize the chosen packet length depending on the chosen physical layer rate. This should be done having the application-layer packetization restrictions in mind in order not to affect the decoding dependencies.

12.7.4 Examples of Sub-Flow Transmission

In this section, several simple illustrative examples for video transmission over 802.11e are presented based on [16]. First, we highlight the importance of the (nonoptimized) sub-flow concept versus the conventional global flow scheduling. The experiment of Table 12.5 used a typical CIF video sequence—"Foreman," encoded at 30 frames per second (fps), although similar results have been obtained

Table 12.5: Sub-flow QoS token rates and $t_{\text{TXOP},i}$ with $d_{\max} = 200$ ms for the CIF-resolution sequence "Foreman" (2048 kbps, 30 fps).

Traffic name	Components	QoS token rate ρ_i (kbps)	t_{TXOP} (ms)[a]
Sub-flow $_1$	$H^{1,0}, H^{2,0}, H^{3,0}, H^{4,0}, L^{4,0}$	10,032	13.89
Sub-flow $_2$	$H^{1,1}, H^{2,1}, H^{3,1}$	2840	3.96
Sub-flow $_3$	$H^{1,2}$	184	0.26
Sub-flow $_4$	$H^{1,3}, H^{2,2}$	1064	1.46
Sub-flow $_5$	$H^{1,4}$	264	0.37
Sub-flow $_6$	$H^{1,5}, H^{2,3}$	728	1.00
Sub-flow $_7$	$H^{1,6}$	392	0.54
Sub-flow $_8$	$H^{1,7}$	440	0.61

[a]$\overline{t_{\text{TXOP}}} = 2.76$ msec, $N_{\text{QSTA}} = 7$.

with a variety of video content. The results of this section have been generated with the settings $T = 100$ ms, $T_{CP} = 60$ ms, and $t_{SI} = 50$ ms. The token rates reported in Table 12.5 were calculated based on a simulation with a twin leaky bucket traffic smoothing system [16], and the delay deadline was extended equally for all sub-flows, such that $d_{max} = 200$ ms. For the case of sub-flow scheduling we have $\overline{t_{TXOP}} = 2.76$ msec and, from (12.38), $N_{QSTA} = 7$. Similarly, for the global flow case we get $\overline{t_{TXOP}} = 13.89$ msec and $N_{QSTA} = 1$. The number of admitted stations can be increased if the optimization framework of Section 12.7.3.1 is used. This is shown by the results of Table 12.6, where the number of stations in the sub-flow case is increased to $N_{QSTA} = 10$. In addition, based on the priorities shown in Table 12.6, we can increase the number of admitted stations if the least-significant sub-flows are discarded. This is illustrated in Figure 12.13, where the number of admitted stations is plotted against the number of utilized sub-flows. Figure 12.13 demonstrates that under a progressive decrease in frame rate, resulting from the removal (drop) of the least-significant sub-flows (with the significance indicated in Table 12.6), the number of admitted stations can be increased further. In a collaborative framework, multiple stations may opt to decrease the video frame rate in order to allow for additional stations (or additional video flows) to utilize the wireless medium under HCCA. Also, the desired number of admitted sub-flows, as well as how these sub-flows are prioritized at the application layer, can be determined based on the channel resources, specific video application, and user preferences. For instance, different spatio-temporal resolutions (and corresponding sub-flows) should be selected for the best percep-

Table 12.6: Sub-flow QoS token rates and $t_{TXOP,i}$ with $d_{max} = 200$ ms for the CIF-resolution sequence "Foreman" (2048 kbps, 30 fps) with the optimization framework of Section 12.7.3.1. The "priority" indicates the importance (4, highest; 1, lowest) of each sub-flow in terms of incurred distortion at the receiver.

Traffic name	Components	QoS token rate ρ_i (kbps)	Priority	t_{TXOP} (ms)[a]
Sub-flow $_1$	$H^{1,0}, H^{2,0}, H^{3,0}, H^{4,0}, L^{4,0}$	4664	4	6.46
Sub-flow $_2$	$H^{1,1}, H^{2,1}, H^{3,1}$	2768	3	3.82
Sub-flow $_3$	$H^{1,2}$	216	1	0.31
Sub-flow $_4$	$H^{1,3}, H^{2,2}$	1376	2	1.90
Sub-flow $_5$	$H^{1,4}$	344	1	0.46
Sub-flow $_6$	$H^{1,5}, H^{2,3}$	880	2	1.24
Sub-flow $_7$	$H^{1,6}$	392	1	0.54
Sub-flow $_8$	$H^{1,7}$	440	1	0.61

[a]$\overline{t_{TXOP}} = 1.92$ msec, $N_{QSTA} = 10$.

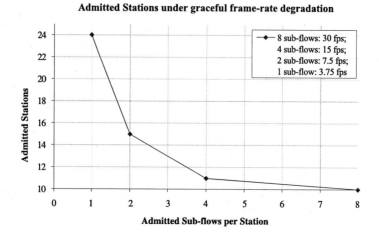

Admitted Stations under graceful frame-rate degradation

FIGURE 12.13: A reduction of the number of admitted sub-flows results in a dyadically reduced frame rate. However, the number of admitted stations increases. The utilized video sequences were encoded at 2048 kbps.

tual video quality for different channel conditions. This flexibility can be easily provided using the sub-flow concept.

In summary, we observe that a higher number of stations can be admitted given the same channel condition if the sub-flow case is used, as compared to the global flow case. Note that the same video bit streams are transmitted in both cases and that no losses are incurred due to the use of sub-flows.

For more details on optimized resource management for video transmission over 802.11e, the interested reader is referred to [3,16,23].

12.8 SIMPLIFYING THE REAL-TIME CROSS-LAYER OPTIMIZATION PROBLEM USING CLASSIFICATION

In previous sections, several joint optimizations across the various layers of the protocol stack have been discussed for improving the performance of real-time video transmission over wireless networks. However, the complexity associated with performing the cross-layer optimization in real time is very high. Thus, low complexity systems are required for determining the optimal cross-layer strategies in real time whenever a packet needs to be transmitted. Next, we discuss such a possible approach based on classification and machine learning techniques [19].

For illustration purposes, this section focuses on determining the optimal MAC retry limit for each video packet given the maximum available bit rate (R_{max}), the maximum tolerable delay $Delay_{\max}$, and the experienced bit error rate (P_e), similar to the problem investigated in Sections 12.5 and 12.6. However, classification techniques could also be used successfully to simplify other cross-layer optimizations.

12.8.1 Classification System for Cross-Layer Optimization

The classification-based wireless video transmission system is depicted in Figure 12.14. It consists of an off-line training module followed by online processing. The former includes modules for class definition and classifier learning, whereas the latter mainly involves classification and real-time cross-layer strategy prediction for video packets. The major steps in the approach are as follow.

Step 1: Generate ground truth (off-line)   First, a set of packets from a variety of video sequences is collected under different representative channel conditions and the entire set of cross-layer strategies available at the wireless station is identified. For each packet in this training set and collection of encoding parameters, the compressed-domain content features (CF) and packet types (PT) determined based on the specific encoder configuration/parameter set are extracted [32]. Used feature sets should also include the wireless channel conditions (WCC): $R_{\max}$[12] and P_e. Subsequently, the optimal strategy s^{opt} resulting in the best quality for the

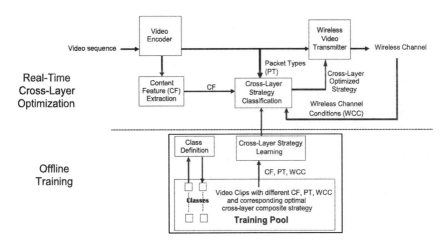

FIGURE 12.14:   Classification-based cross-layer system for wireless video.

---

[12] $R_{\max}$ can be determined based on the video encoding rate, delay constraint, and the PHY rate used for transmission (determined based on the modulation strategy, etc.) [26].

different training sequences, packet types, and channel conditions is determined using dynamic programming (see Section 12.6).

Step 2: Train classifier (off-line)   The key is to determine, for each packet j, a mapping from the composite feature vector $\mathbf{f}(j)$ to class label l_j, corresponding to a specific optimal strategy s^{opt}. During training, supervised clustering methods are used to map the composite features to the corresponding class label. Two different classification strategies aimed at minimizing the probability of misclassification and minimizing the cost of misclassification (in terms of video distortion), respectively, are discussed, for illustration purposes.

Step 3: Real-time strategy selection based on classification   The optimal strategy s^{opt} for a sequence of incoming video packets given the instantaneous wireless channel conditions/characteristics can be then determined, by the trained classifier, on a packet-by-packet basis using the composite feature vectors. The selected strategy is used to determine the optimized parameters and configurations of the wireless multimedia system.

The various steps just outlined are described in more detail in subsequent sections.

12.8.2 Feature Selection

For video packet j, a suitable feature vector $\mathbf{f}(j)$ needs to be identified that can predict the optimal decision with low complexity (i.e., with features that can be computed/extracted easily at run time). The WCC features P_e (equivalently P_L) and R_{max} can be determined in real time based on information that can be extracted easily from the wireless card driver. For example, the transmitter can use the received signal strength indicator (RSSI) of previously received MAC acknowledgment frames, as well as MAC acknowledgment reports to determine these features [22]. A more detailed description of the various features that can be extracted in real time from the lower layers of the transmission system can be found in Chapter 13.

Among CF, the packet energy can be selected, which may be used to distinguish among sequences with different levels of spatio-temporal detail. The energy for packet j is calculated by summing up the squared wavelet coefficients *coeff* belonging to the packet,

$$E_j = \sum_{i \in W_j} \left(coeff(i) \right)^2, \tag{12.56}$$

where W_j is the set of decoded coefficients (collected from all the decoding units within the packet) belonging to packet j. At encoding time, the energy of each decoding unit is computed for the various quality layers. During transmission, the packet energy can simply be computed by aggregating the relevant energies corresponding to the target bit rate.

The codec-specific (PT) features include the spatial and temporal level of the data in the packet. This is because packets belonging to distinct spatiotemporal bands have a different impact on the overall distortion and require different protection: the retry limit of the packet decreases with an increasing spatiotemporal level. Most ad hoc cross-layer strategies are based on this simple classification criterion for selecting the retry limit, that is, the spatiotemporal level (or frame type for conventional video coders). However, these schemes do not use either the content characteristics or the channel conditions, which directly impact the optimal retry limit. In order to test the suitability of the CF and PT features,[13] the correlation coefficient is computed between them and the optimal decision sequence (i.e., the choice of optimal retry limit per packet). If feature i from packet j is called $\mathbf{f}_i(j)$ and the optimal retry limit (decision) for this packet is $T^{opt}(j)$, then the correlation coefficient between the feature sequence and the decision sequence may be defined

$$\rho_i = \frac{\sum_{j=1}^{N_p} \mathbf{f}_i(j) T^{opt}(j)}{\sqrt{\sum_{j=1}^{N_p} (\mathbf{f}_i(j))^2 \sum_{j=1}^{N_p} (T^{opt}(j))^2}}, \tag{12.57}$$

where N_P is the number of packets in the GOP.

Table 12.7 shows the correlation coefficients for these different features with the optimal retry limit for the *Mobile* sequence. Similar results were obtained for other video sequences. The large values (close to 1) of the coefficients ρ_i in Table 12.7 show that for given channel conditions, the selected features are well correlated with the optimal decision sequence.

Table 12.7:   *Mobile*: Correlation coefficients ρ_i.

Feature	$R_{max} = 512$ kps			
	$P_L = 1\%$	$P_L = 3\%$	$P_L = 5\%$	$P_L = 10\%$
Packet energy	0.79	0.82	0.82	0.83
Temporal level	0.76	0.86	0.90	0.93
Spatial level	0.62	0.73	0.75	0.80
Feature	$R_{max} = 1024$ kps			
	$P_L = 1\%$	$P_L = 3\%$	$P_L = 5\%$	$P_L = 10\%$
Packet energy	0.75	0.80	0.81	0.81
Temporal level	0.72	0.82	0.85	0.89
Spatial level	0.60	0.67	0.73	0.76

---

[13]We exclude the WCC features as they are common to all the packets.

Table 12.8: Pair-wise MI for the chosen feature set.

	Packet energy	Temporal level	Spatial level	R_{max}	P_L
Packet energy	3.4	1.37	1.34	1.3	1.19
Temporal level	1.37	1.90	0.07	0.03	0
Spatial level	1.34	0.07	2.12	0.01	0
R_{max}	1.30	0.03	0.01	1.57	0
P_L	1.19	0	0	0	2

Table 12.9: Accuracy of the classifier based on a single feature.

	Packet energy	Temporal level	Spatial level	P_L	R_{max}
Percentage of accuracy	52%	58%	48%	52%	48%

In order to examine the redundancy in the feature set, metrics such as the mutual information[14] (MI) between pairs of features can be computed. An illustrative example is presented in Table 12.8. We can see from Table 12.8 that while there is some redundancy among the features, especially between packet energy and the rest of the features, each feature contains nonredundant information (for a majority of cases, the MI is significantly lower than the feature entropy). Allied with this is the fact that none of these features are computationally complex to determine, and hence we use the complete set of features in the system.

Finally, in order to validate these features for the actual classification task, we can also examine the classifier performance with each of these individual features. Table 12.9 shows the classifier accuracy results with each individual feature.

The temporal level feature leads to the best classification performance, whereas the video rate and the spatial level have the worst classification performance. This knowledge can be used to design an ad hoc strategy (similar to that used in [11, 33,34] but for different video coders) to determine the packet retransmission limits. Finally, since these features are used jointly, the classifier accuracy increases to ~83%. While additional features can be used (e.g., the motion vectors, available bits per frame, and number of bit planes per frame at various bit rates), these will increase the complexity of the real-time system with only limited possible improvement in the classification performance. See [19] for an extensive study.

In summarizing, the feature extraction step needs to be kept at a low complexity because it is also performed online. Consequently, content and encoder-specific features can be selected that are already computed during the encoding process (i.e., no additional complexity is needed for feature extraction). These features can be prestored in metadata files together with the video bit streams. Hence, at

---

[14]The MI between two random variables X and Y with distributions $p(x)$ and $p(y)$ and joint distribution $p(x, y)$ is defined as $MI(X, Y) = \sum_x \sum_y p(x, y) \log \frac{p(x, y)}{p(x)p(y)}$.

transmission time, only the channel features need to be determined based on the RSSI and MAC acknowledgment frames. These values can be accessed readily from device drivers of existing wireless cards (e.g., Intel PRO/Wireless 2915ABG Network Connection and Intel PRO/Wireless 2200BG Network Connection mini PCI adapters). A more detailed discussion on determining and monitoring the channel quality can be found in Chapter 13.

12.8.3 Classifier Design

The cross-layer optimization problem involves assigning a retry limit to each packet such that the expected overall decoded distortion is jointly minimized. Let us assume that there are M available retry limits $\{X_1, \ldots, X_M\}$ (i.e., an M-class classification problem) and N_t packets in the training set. From data within each packet j, we extract an F-dimensional feature vector $\mathbf{f}(j) \in \mathbb{R}^F$ (in this case $F = 5$). The classifier is then provided with feature vectors $\mathbf{f}(j)$, $1 \leq j \leq N_t$, and the associated optimal retry limit $T^{opt}(j) \in \{X_1, \ldots, X_M\}$ for each packet. The classifier then partitions the feature space $\mathbb{R}^F$ into M-nonoverlapping regions $G_1, \ldots, G_M$, with region G_i associated with a unique optimal retry limit X_i, such that the error in classification (i.e., probability of misclassification) on training data is minimized. This may be written

$$\{G_1, \ldots, G_M\}^{opt} = \arg\min_{G_1, \ldots, G_M} \sum_{j=1}^{N_t} [1 - B(\mathbf{f}(j) \in G_i \mid T^{opt}(j) = X_i)], \quad (12.58)$$

where $B(\mathbf{f}(j) \in G_i \mid T^{opt}(j) = X_i)$ is a binary-valued function that takes value 1 when vector $\mathbf{f}(j)$ is classified correctly, that is, if $\mathbf{f}(j)$, with optimal retry $T^{opt}(j)(= X_i)$ is inside region G_i, and zero otherwise.

While minimizing the previously defined classification error, the classifier views all feature vectors in the training set equivalently. However, in reality, the feature vectors do have different importance because misclassifying different feature vectors can lead to different penalties in the total distortion. Hence, since minimizing the decoded distortion is the final goal of the optimization, the classifier needs to be modified to take the distortion impact into account. Let the importance of packet j with feature vector $\mathbf{f}(j)$ be determined by the cost of misclassifying it $C(j)(\geq 0)$. We will discuss this cost in more detail later. Then, the classifier design problem may be written

$$\{G_1, \ldots, G_M\}^{opt} = \arg\min_{G_1, \ldots, G_M} \sum_{j=1}^{N_t} C(j)[1 - B(\mathbf{f}(j) \in G_i \mid T^{opt}(j) = X_i)]$$

$$(12.59)$$

or, alternatively,

$$\{G_1,\ldots,G_M\}^{opt} = \arg\min_{G_1,\ldots,G_M} \sum_{j=1}^{N_t} \sum_{k=1}^{C(j)} \left[1 - B\big(\mathbf{f}(j) \in G_i \mid T^{opt}(j) = X_i\big)\right].$$

(12.60)

This optimization has the same form as the one before, where instead of providing the classifier with vector $\mathbf{f}(j)$, we provide it vector $\mathbf{f}(j)$ repeated $C(j)$ times.[15] Hence, by modifying the training set in such a manner, the minimized classification error classifier can be used to minimize the cost of misclassification.

The cost of misclassification $C(j)$ in the cross-layer problem needs to be defined in terms of the increase in distortion when packet j is assigned the wrong retry limit. Hence, when instead of this optimal retry limit, a different, suboptimal, retry limit X_k is assigned, the corresponding increase in the incurred distortion is $(\bar{D}(X_k, j) - \bar{D}(T^{opt}(j), j)) \geq 0$. Hence, the total cost $C(j)$ of misclassifying the packet, in terms of distortion, may be computed

$$C(j) = \sum_{\substack{k=1 \\ X_k \neq T^{opt}(j)}}^{M} \big(\bar{D}(X_k, j) - \bar{D}(T^{opt}(j), j)\big).$$

(12.61)

For the classification, a supervised nonparametric classification technique, such as support vector machines, can be adopted.

12.8.4 Validation Experiments

In [19], the efficiency of the discussed classification-based system was validated using a real wireless streaming test bed. The performance of the classification-based cross-layer strategy is compared against the optimal exhaustive strategy for these real wireless channel traces in Table 12.10. Results demonstrate that under varying SNR, the cross-layer mechanism leads to a decrease in PSNR of ~0.7 dB as compared with the optimal strategy. The obtained classification-based results outperformed by 3–5 dB current ad hoc retransmission strategies available in the wireless card. A thorough validation study can be found in [19]. Also, a thorough description of how such real-time middleware systems can be designed and implemented can be found in Chapter 13.

---

[15]In general it is not necessary that all the costs $C(j)$ are integers; however, without loss of generality we can scale them appropriately to make them integers.

Table 12.10:   Decoded PSNR for real wireless packet loss traces.

Measured channel SNR	Foreman PSNR (dB)		Mobile PSNR (dB)	
	Classification	Exhaustive	Classification	Exhaustive
Poor channel conditions (12–15 dB)	33.81	34.29	26.31	26.50
Average channel conditions (15–20 dB)	35.90	36.06	28.48	29.26
Very good channel conditions (20–25 dB)	38.64	38.66	31.82	32.01

12.9 DYNAMIC AND FAIR MULTIUSER WIRELESS TRANSMISSION

In the previous sections, the time allocation among the various WSTAs was stati-
cally performed, that is, once for the entire duration of the flows (cf. Section 12.7,
where the TSPEC negotiation was only performed initially). This static resource
(transmission opportunities) management is inefficient because it does not scale
with the number of users, channel conditions, video characteristics, and so on.
Alternatively, a dynamic resource allocation enables the time allocation to be performed repeatedly, every SI or group of SIs depending on the channel condition,
cross-layer strategy, and used fairness policy. Moreover, as a result of the static TXOP allocation, until now, we only considered the problem of cross-layer
optimization in isolation, at each WSTA. However, in wireless multimedia transmission systems, the cross-layer strategies adopted by the various WSTAs impact
other competing stations. If a WSTA is adapting its transmission strategy, the delay and throughput of the competing stations are affected and, as a consequence,
they may need to adjust their own strategies. (See [12] for several such examples.)
Hence, the cross-layer strategies adopted by a station should not be optimized in
isolation, but should also consider the system-wide availability of resources and
"fairness" issues.

12.9.1 Why Are Current Fairness Strategies Not Suitable for Cross-Layer-Optimized Multimedia Transmission?

The objective of fair scheduling is to provide multimedia applications with different amounts of "work" (resources) proportional to their requirements in terms
of bandwidth, delay, and packet-loss rates. Usually, "work" is measured by the
amount of data transmitted (either in number of bytes or in packets/frames) during a certain period of time. Let $W_i(t_1, t_2)$ be the amount of video flow i's traffic
served in a time interval (t_1, t_2) and ϕ_i be its corresponding weight based on its
requirements. Then, an ideal fair scheduler (i.e., the Generalized Processor Sched-

uler [27]) for N WSTAs (and their flows) can be defined

$$\frac{W_i(t_1, t_2)}{W_j(t_1, t_2)} \geq \frac{\phi_i}{\phi_j}, \quad j = 1, 2, \ldots, N \qquad (12.62)$$

for any multimedia flow i that is continuously backlogged during (t_1, t_2). [Backlogged means that flow i has frames in its buffer during the specified time interval (t_1, t_2).] If all multimedia flows are transmitted at a fixed rate, we can obtain from (12.62),

$$\frac{W_i(t_1, t_2)}{t_2 - t_1} \geq \frac{\phi_i}{\sum_j \phi_j} r, \qquad (12.63)$$

where r is the physical transmission rate or the total channel capacity. Thus, each multimedia flow i is guaranteed to have the throughput given by (12.63) regardless of the states of the queues and frame arrivals of the other flows. However, the advantages of using GPS, such as the guaranteed throughput and independent service, cannot be preserved if the flows are deploying different cross-layer optimization, resulting in different transmission rates. Depending on the channel condition, or their distance from the access point, WSTAs may choose, as discussed in prior sections, different cross-layer transmission strategies (PHY modes, retry limits, packet sizes, etc.) to ensure optimized multimedia quality. Determining a *"fair share of resource"* among WSTAs in such a transmission scenario is a very challenging problem because serving an equal amount of traffic from individual stations deploying different strategies requires allocation of various amounts of airtime and results in different impacts on the multimedia quality.

12.9.2 Time Fairness

To obtain a better allocation of resources that explicitly considers the various deployed cross-layer strategies, time fairness was proposed in [12,28]. For this, the total throughput degradation due to WSTAs deploying different cross-layer strategies (e.g., different PHY rates) in the WLAN network can be computed. Given n WSTAs (with all stations having the same frame size), with $n_i (\sum_{i=1}^{8} n_i = n)$ operating at, for example, PHY mode $i (= 1, \ldots, 8)$, the throughput degradation can be determined

$$Throughput = \frac{1}{(1/n)\left(\sum_{j=1}^{8} n_j / R_j\right)}. \qquad (12.64)$$

WSTAs having different transmission rates R_j due to the different PHY modes or other deployed cross-layer optimization strategies cause this unwanted degradation. Time fairness tries to alleviate this problem by allocating each WSTA a fair share of time (i.e., a percentage of the SI), which is proportional to the requirements mentioned in their TSPEC (see Section 12.7), rather than guaranteeing a specific bandwidth (rate requirement). This proportional time allocation (e.g., allocated to a stream at admission time) removes part of the unfairness resulting from the deployment of different cross-layer strategies by the various WSTAs. Equation (12.62) can be thus rewritten to provide time fairness

$$\frac{T_i(t_1, t_2)}{T_j(t_1, t_2)} \geq \frac{\phi_i}{\phi_j}, \quad j = 1, 2, \ldots, N, \tag{12.65}$$

where T_i, and T_j represent the time allocated to the streams i and j, respectively.

The advantages of this airtime fair scheduler (AFS) as opposed to the conventional weighted fair queuing for multimedia transmission are analyzed in detail in [12]. AFS isolates the channel and differential transmission rates of the various WSTAs, thus guaranteeing a better multimedia performance across all participating stations.

12.9.3 Multimedia Quality Fairness

While time fairness is efficient for a variety of applications, multimedia users do require a different type of fairness, which quantifies the resulting resource allocation in terms of the utility impact rather than the consumed time resources. For instance, a resource manager (access point) can decide to implement a policy where the users derive either the same video quality or the same quality penalty, independent of the experienced channel conditions or deployed cross-layer strategies.

For this, bargaining solutions from game theory were deployed successfully in [25,57] to allocate utilities to selfish WSTAs fairly and optimally by *directly* considering the relationships in terms of utility resulting from various resource allocations according to different fairness policies. The Kalai–Smorodinsky bargaining solution, Egalitarian bargaining solution, and Nash bargaining solution were used in [25,57] in order to enforce different fairness policies among users.

Unlike traditional fairness approaches, such as the proportional fairness introduced by Kelly [58] and Kelly *et al.* [59] and the time fairness and GPS fairness solutions discussed earlier where the resulting relationships between the users' utilities cannot be guaranteed, utility-based bargaining solutions do ensure that certain relationships in terms of utilities are satisfied. For instance, as was shown in [25,57], the Kalai–Smorodinsky bargaining solution ensures that the participating WSTA incur the same drop in multimedia quality (PSNR drop) as compared to a maximum desirable video quality (see Figure 12.15 for a simple illustration of the feasible utility set of two WSTA and the resulting Kalai–Smorodinsky bargaining solution), whereas the Egalitarian bargaining solution guarantees that the

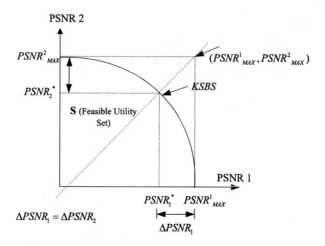

FIGURE 12.15: Utility-based fairness based on the Kalai–Smorodinsky bargaining solution.

users will have the same video quality independent of their cross-layer strategies or channel conditions. After a socially fair allocation in terms of utilities is derived using the bargaining solution, the corresponding resources (i.e., time opportunities) are determined and the user can start the actual transmission. The resource manager can also assign different bargaining powers to the various WSTAs.

Moreover, unlike conventional optimization solutions, the various bargaining solutions can be differentiated based on the axioms (properties) that they fulfill. These axioms are essential for a fair resource allocation among multimedia users. For instance, as shown in [25,57], the unique axiom of *individual monotonicity* of the Kalai–Smorodinsky bargaining solution guarantees that increasing the maximum achievable utility in a direction favorable to a WSTA (e.g., by deploying a more sophisticated cross-layer strategy) always benefits that WSTA. This property implicitly means that the Kalai–Smorodinsky bargaining solution encourages each WSTA to maximize its achievable utility and then allocates the resources based on its maximum achievable utility. This is especially useful for modeling the selfish user behavior of the WSTAs transmitting delay-sensitive multimedia.

12.9.4 Game-Theoretic Dynamic Resource Management

The static resource allocation discussed in Sections 12.4 and 12.7 represents the current, conventional approach for resource allocation. However, since the channel conditions, video characteristics, number of participating WSTAs, or even the user desired utility varies over time, the conventional resource allocation (e.g., 802.11e) does not exploit the network resources efficiently and does not provide adequate QoS support for multimedia transmission, especially when the network is congested. Also, importantly, the WSTA can untruthfully declare (exaggerate) its resource requirements during the initialization stage in order to obtain a longer transmission time t_i. Thus, in existing wireless networks, there is no mechanism available to prevent the WSTA from lying about the required t_i.

To eliminate the aforementioned limitations for multiuser wireless multimedia transmission, in [55,56] WSTAs were enabled to dynamically acquire wireless resources depending on the desired utility, their available cross-layer strategies, and private information. Specifically, in [55,56], the multiuser wireless communication is modeled as a noncollaborative resource management game regulated by the access point, referred to here as the Central Spectrum Moderator (CSM), where the WSTAs are allowed to dynamically compete for the available TXOPs by jointly adapting their cross-layer strategies and their willingness-to-pay and risk attitude. In this noncollaborative game, WSTAs are considered selfish (autonomous) users that solely aim at maximizing their own utilities by gathering as many resources as possible.

To prevent WSTAs from misusing the available resources, the CSM adopts a tool from mechanism design, referred to as *transfer*, to penalize WSTAs from exaggerating their resource requirements. Specifically, in [55,56], the Vickrey–Clarke–Groves (VCG) mechanism was used to implement and enforce the "rules" of the resource allocation game. In the VCG mechanism, the resource allocation is based on a "social decision," which maximizes the aggregated multiuser wireless system utility. To encourage the WSTAs to work in this social optimal way, the CSM charges WSTA a transfer corresponding to the inconvenience it causes to other WSTAs. In the noncollaborative wireless network of [55,56], the inconvenience caused by a WSTA is quantified as the utility penalty (drop) that the competing WSTAs incur due to the participation (resource usage) of that WSTA in the resource management game. In the formulation, the performance of each WSTA will depend on the private information, the adopted cross-layer strategy, and the WSTA willingness to pay for resources. The willingness to pay, denoted as w_i, will affect the ability of a WSTA i to transmit more or less video data during the current SI by accepting to pay a larger/lower transfer. Details of how the willingness-to-pay w_i affects the strategy with which the WSTA plays the resource game and its derived utility and incurred transfer can be found in [55,56], as well as the details of the VCG mechanism deployed at the CSM side.

Implementation of the resource allocation game is depicted pictorially in Figure 12.16. In the resource game, a *joint strategy* is defined for WSTA i that consists of selecting an *expected cross-layer strategy* $\bar{s}_i \in \mathcal{S}_i$ and a *revealing strategy* $\mu_i \in \mathcal{V}_i$, where $\mathcal{V}_i$ is the set of revealing strategies available to WSTA i. We denote the joint strategy as $\kappa_i = (\bar{s}_i, \mu_i), \kappa_i \in \mathcal{S}_i \times \mathcal{V}_i$. The purpose of the expected cross-layer strategy and the revealing strategy is outlined in subsequent paragraphs.

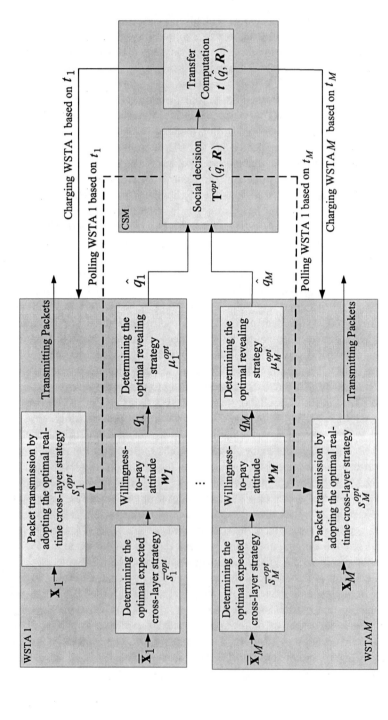

FIGURE 12.16:   Mechanism design framework for the multiuser wireless video resource allocation game.

The expected cross-layer strategy $\bar{s}_i$ is computed by the WSTA i *prior* to the transmission time in order to determine the *expected* benefit in terms of utility that it can derive by acquiring available resource during the upcoming SI. Note that the expected cross-layer strategy $\bar{s}_i$ is proactively decided at the beginning of every SI and will not be exactly the same as the actual real-time strategy s_i adopted at transmission time. The reason for this is that the strategy for playing the game also depends on the WSTA's private information $\mathbf{x}_i$. Unlike the real-time cross-layer strategy, which has precise information about $\mathbf{x}_i$, the expected cross-layer strategy will need to determine the modulation mode at the PHY layer, the number of retransmissions per packet at the MAC layer, the packet prioritization and scheduling at APP layer, and so on based on the expected private information $\bar{\mathbf{x}}_i$.

To play the resource management game, each WSTA i needs to announce its "type," denoted as $\theta_i(\bar{s}_i, \bar{\mathbf{x}}_i, \boldsymbol{w}_i)$, which represents the utility that can be derived from the potentially allocated resources (TXOPs). Based on the announced types, the CSM will determine the resources allocation and transfers for the participating WSTAs. We refer to the set of possible types available to WSTA i as Θ_i. The type is defined as a nominal vector that encapsulates the expected private information $\bar{\mathbf{x}}_i$, the expected cross-layer strategy $\bar{s}_i$, and the willingness-to-pay $\boldsymbol{w}_i$ for resources (transfers). The type profile for all WSTAs is defined as $\theta = (\theta_1, \ldots, \theta_M)$, with $\theta \in \Theta$, $\Theta = \Theta_1 \times \cdots \times \Theta_M$. For more details on this, the reader is referred to [55,56].

A revealing strategy μ_i is adopted by the WSTA i to determine which type should be declared to the CSM based on the derived real type θ_i. The type of WSTA i revealed to the CSM (referred to as announced type) can be computed as $\hat{\theta}_i = \mu_i(\theta_i)$. The announced type profile for all WSTAs is denoted as $\hat{\theta} = (\hat{\theta}_1, \ldots, \hat{\theta}_M)$. In other words, the joint strategy κ_i adopted by WSTA i determines the announced type $\hat{\theta}_i$, that is, $\hat{\theta}_i = \kappa_i(\bar{\mathbf{x}}_i, \boldsymbol{w}_i) = \mu_i(\theta_i(\bar{s}_i, \bar{\mathbf{x}}_i, \boldsymbol{w}_i))$.

For the dynamic resource allocation game, the outcome is denoted as $\mathbf{T}(\hat{\theta}, \mathcal{R})$, where $\mathbf{T} : \Theta \times \mathbb{R}_+ \to \mathbb{R}_+^M$ is a function of both the announced type profile $\hat{\theta}$ and the available resource $\mathcal{R}$. Thus, $\mathbf{T}(\hat{\theta}, \mathcal{R}) = [t_1, \ldots, t_M]$, where t_i denotes the allocated time to WSTA i within the current SI and $\sum_{i=1}^{M} t_i \leq t_{SI}$. Based on the dynamic resource allocation t_i and its derived type θ_i, WSTA i can derive utility $u_i(t_i, \theta_i)$. However, the utility computed at the CSM side for WSTA i is $u_i(t_i, \hat{\theta}_i)$, as this is determined based on the announced type $\hat{\theta}_i$. Note that t_i is decided by the CSM, which is a function of the announced type profile $\hat{\theta}$ and the available resource $\mathcal{R}$. Hence, note that the "real" utility derived by a WSTA and the utility that a CSM believes that the WSTA is obtaining can differ, as the CSM solely relies on the information announced by the WSTA. In the resource management game, the utility is computed not only based on the expected received video quality such as in the conventional cross-layer design, but also on the willingness to pay for resources of a WSTA, $\boldsymbol{w}_i$. The transfer computed by the CSM is represented by $\boldsymbol{\tau}(\hat{\theta}, \mathcal{R})$, where $\boldsymbol{\tau} : \Theta \times \mathbb{R}_+ \to \mathbb{R}_-^M$ is a function of both the announced type profile $\hat{\theta}$ and the available resource $\mathcal{R}$, and $\tau(\hat{\theta}, \mathcal{R}) = [\tau_1, \ldots, \tau_M]$, where τ_i denotes the transfer that WSTA i needs to pay during the current SI. By participating in the resource allocation game, WSTA i gains the "payoff" $\upsilon_i(\hat{\theta}, \theta_i, \mathcal{R}) = u_i(t_i, \theta_i) + \tau_i$, which is always nonnegative in the VCG mechanism.

In summary, the following dynamic, game-theoretic resource allocation at the CSM side can be implemented during each SI.

1. **Social decision**: After receiving the announced type profile $\hat{\theta} = (\hat{\theta}_1, \ldots, \hat{\theta}_M)$ from the WSTAs, the CSM decides the resource allocation $\mathbf{T}(\hat{\theta}, \mathcal{R})$ such that the multiuser wireless system utility (i.e., the sum of utilities of all WSTAs) is maximized.
2. **Transfer computation**: Next, it computes the transfers $\tau(\hat{\theta}, \mathcal{R})$ associated with this resource allocation to enforce the WSTA to reveal their real type truthfully.
3. **Polling WSTAs**: The CSM polls the WSTAs for packet transmission according to the allocated time.

At the WSTAs side, the subsequent steps are performed by WSTA i in order to play the resource management game.

1. **Private information estimation**: Each WSTA i estimates the expected private information $\bar{\mathbf{x}}_i$, which includes the expected video source characteristics $\bar{\xi}_i$ and channel conditions in terms of $\overline{SNR}_i$.
2. **Selection of optimal joint strategy and corresponding "type"**: Based on the private information, WSTA i determines the optimal joint strategy to play the resource allocation game, that is,

$$\kappa_i^{opt} = (\bar{s}_i^{opt}, \mu_i^{opt}) = \underset{\kappa_i=(\bar{s}_i,\mu_i)\in\mathcal{S}_i\times\mathcal{V}_i}{\arg\max} \upsilon_i(\hat{\theta}, \theta_i, \mathcal{R})$$
$$= \underset{\kappa_i=(\bar{s}_i,\mu_i)\in\mathcal{S}_i\times\mathcal{V}_i}{\arg\max} \{u_i(t_i, \theta_i) + \tau_i\} \quad (12.66)$$
$$\text{s.t.} \quad Delay(t_i, \theta_i) \leq Delay_i^{max}.$$

Note that the WSTA i cannot explicitly solve the optimization problem just given because both the resource allocation t_i and the transfer τ_i depend on the announced types of the other WSTAs, which are not known by this station. However, in [56] it was proven that whenever the VCG mechanism is used, *the optimal joint strategy* can be simply determined by first proactively selecting *the optimal expected cross-layer strategy* $\bar{s}_i^{opt}$ that maximizes the expected received video quality without considering the impact of the other WSTAs. Then, based on this, *the optimal revealing strategy* μ_i^{opt} through which the real (truthful) type (including willingness-to-pay attitude) is revealed, that is, $\hat{\theta}_i = \mu_i^{opt}(\theta_i) = \theta_i$. Details of the expected cross-layer strategy, revealing strategy and type computation, are presented in [56].

1. **Reveal the type to CSM**: The determined type $\hat{\theta}_i$ is declared by each WSTA to the CSM.

2. **Transmit video packets**: When polled by the CSM, each WSTA i determines and deploys the *optimal real-time cross-layer strategy* s_i^{opt} for video transmission that maximizes the expected received video quality. This cross-layer strategy is determined as discussed earlier.

Note that while the transfers are computed for each WSTA during every SI, the CSM can communicate and charge the WSTA the incurred (cumulative) transfer every couple of SIs. Various charging mechanisms and protocols can be used for this purpose.

In summarizing, to play the dynamic resource management game, WSTAs deploy three different types of strategies at different stages of the transmission: the optimal expected cross-layer strategies and the revealing strategies (prior to the actual transmission, in order to determine the announced type) and the optimal real-time cross-layer strategy (in real time, during the actual transmission). Hence, the cross-layer-optimized transmission strategies become the "smartness" with which WSTAs play the competitive, dynamic, resource management game.

12.10 SUMMARY AND FURTHER READING

Most existing wireless transmission algorithms and standards have been designed in an application agnostic fashion [1–3], as this guarantees their durability, adaptability, and generality. Research in cross-layer optimization has shown that the performance of existing wireless protocols can be improved by jointly optimizing the various layers; importantly, it was also shown that cross-layer optimization could catalyze the development of new protocols, with enhanced support for multimedia applications, while preserving these properties (e.g., 802.11e [3]).

This chapter showed that establishing communication mechanisms between OSI layers to convey application-layer information to lower layers (e.g., packet sizes, relative importance, different interrelationships, arrival rates, and delay constraints) and channel condition information to the application layer, as well as to enable resource and information exchanges among stations, can lead to an important improvement in the system efficiency and individual quality of the participating stations. We focused on multimedia applications that can operate at multiple quality levels and have different delay requirements, thereby enabling the study of different communication trade-offs. The cross-layer optimization problem was formulated, and several solutions based on queuing theory, Lagrange optimization, and classification were discussed. Moreover, the benefits in terms of multimedia quality of employing a cross-layer-optimized framework for different multimedia applications with different delay sensitivities and loss tolerances were quantified. However, the described cross-layer-optimized wireless multimedia paradigm is only recently emerging, and a variety of research topics need still to be addressed. A summary of such topics is presented together with a list of possible future reading.

Realistic integrated models for the delay, multimedia quality, and consumed power of various transmission strategies/protocols need to be developed. An example of such work can be found in [54].

An important extension of the cross-layer design principles, discussed in this chapter for the case of single-hop wireless transmission, is the extension to multiple hops. Video transmission over multihop wireless networks became recently of increasing interest, as such networks provide a flexible, low-cost infrastructure for the deployment of multimedia applications [20,21,24,38,43].

Another important topic of consideration when performing cross-layer optimization and considering its trade-offs is the resulting power. The interested reader is referred to [23,35–37] for several relevant works on this topic. Importantly, the design of the various cross-layer algorithms discussed in this chapter needs to be implemented into flexible, integrated middleware architectures. For more details on the principles, requirements, and solutions that guide such designs, the interested reader is referred to Chapter 13, which presents various designs for middle architectures.

We have also identified a new fairness paradigm for wireless multimedia transmission based on game-theoretic bargaining solutions, which can result in an improved utilization of wireless resources, as well as an enhanced multimedia performance by the participating stations. The interaction between various wireless stations and their cross-layer optimization strategies can be further analyzed based on economics principles such as bargaining and mechanism design. This is achieved by remodeling existing passive resource allocation problems as economics-driven interactions among selfish users competing for a common network resource "market" [25,55]. The outcome of various interactions among selfish users can be analyzed in terms of both dynamics and steady-state equilibrium(s), and mechanisms can be synthesized that achieve new measures of optimality, rationality, and fairness for multiuser communication systems [25,55]. Game-theoretic principles and tools (mechanism design, bargaining theory, equilibrium analysis, competitive analysis, and other microeconomic methods) can be used to model, analyze, and modify such interactions. However, this work is only at its inception and significant research still remains ahead.

ACKNOWLEDGMENTS

The author of this chapter thanks her previous colleagues at Philips Research—Dr. Deepak Turaga (IBM Research), Dr. Sai Shankar (Qualcomm), and Dr. Qiong

Li (Bayer)—and Dr. Yiannis Andreopoulos (postdoc, UCLA) and Mr. Fangwen Fu (Ph.D. student, UCLA) from her research group for their contributions to this chapter. Also, the author acknowledges the NSF Career Award, the Intel Research IT Grant, and, in particular, Dr. Dilip Krishnaswamy (Intel) for their support of the cross-layer optimized multimedia streaming research performed by the author and her students.

REFERENCES

[1] IEEE Std. 802.11-1999, Part 11: Wireless LAN Medium Access Control (MAC) and Physical Layer (PHY) specifications, Reference number ISO/IEC 8802-11:1999(E), IEEE Std. 802.11, 1999 edition, 1999.

[2] IEEE Std. 802.11b, Supplement to Part 11: Wireless LAN Medium Access Control (MAC) and Physical Layer (PHY) specifications: Higher-speed Physical Layer Extension in the 2.4 GHz Band, IEEE Std. 802.11b-1999, 1999.

[3] IEEE 802.11e/D8.0, Draft Supplement to Part 11: Wireless Medium Access Control (MAC) and Physical Layer (PHY) Specifications: Medium Access Control (MAC) Enhancements for Quality of Service (QoS), November 2003.

[4] V. Kawadia and P. R. Kumar. "A Cautionary Perspective on Cross Layer Design," *IEEE Wireless Communication Magazine*, July 2003.

[5] B. Girod, M. Kalman, Y. Liang, and R. Zhang. "Advances in Channel-Adaptive Video Streaming," *Wireless Communications and Mobile Computing*, vol. 2, no. 6, pp. 549–552, September 2002. (Invited)

[6] E. Setton, T. Yoo, X. Zhu, A. Goldsmith, and B. Girod. "Cross-Layer Design of Ad-Hoc Networks for Realtime Video Streaming," *IEEE Wireless Communication Magazine*, pp. 59–65, August 2005.

[7] P. Frossard. "FEC Performances in Multimedia Streaming," *IEEE Communications Letters*, vol. 5, no. 3, pp. 122–124, March 2001.

[8] P. Frossard and O. Verscheure. "Joint Source/FEC Rate Selection for Quality-Optimal MPEG-2 Video Delivery," *IEEE Transactions on Image Processing*, vol. 10, no. 12, pp. 1815–1825, December 2001.

[9] A. Nosratinia, J. Lu, and B. Aazhang. "Source-Channel Rate Allocation for Progressive Transmission of Images," *IEEE Transactions on Communications*, pp. 186–196, February 2003.

[10] M. van der Schaar, S. Krishnamachari, S. Choi, and X. Xu. "Adaptive Cross-Layer Protection Strategies for Robust Scalable Video Transmission over 802.11 WLANs," *IEEE Journal on Selected Areas of Communications (JSAC)*, vol. 21, no. 10, pp. 1752–1763, December 2003.

[11] Q. Li and M. van der Schaar. "Providing Adaptive QoS to Layered Video over Wireless Local Area Networks through Real-Time Retry Limit Adaptation," *IEEE Trans. on Multimedia*, vol. 6, no. 2, pp. 278–290, April 2004.

[12] M. van der Schaar and S. Shankar. "Cross-layer Wireless Multimedia Transmission: Challenges, Principles and New Paradigms," *IEEE Wireless Communications Magazine*, vol. 12, no. 4, pp. 50–58, August 2005.

[13] D. Turaga, M. van der Schaar, Y. Andreopoulos, A. Munteanu, and P. Schelkens. "Unconstrained Motion Compensated Temporal Filtering (UMCTF) for Efficient and Flexible Interframe Wavelet Video Coding," *EURASIP Signal Processing: Image Communication*, vol. 20, no. 1, pp. 1–19, January 2005.

[14] J. R. Ohm, M. van der Schaar, and J. Woods. "Interframe Wavelet Coding: Motion Picture Representation for Universal Scalability," *EURASIP Signal Processing: Image Communication*, Special issue on Digital Cinema, vol. 19, no. 9, pp. 877–908, October 2004.

[15] M. van der Schaar and Y. Andreopoulos. "Rate–Distortion-Complexity Modeling for Network and Receiver Aware Adaptation," *IEEE Trans. on Multimedia*, vol. 7, no. 3, pp. 471–479, June 2005.

[16] M. van der Schaar, Y. Andreopoulos, and Z. Hu. "Optimized Scalable Video Streaming over IEEE 802.11a/e HCCA Wireless Networks under Delay Constraints," *IEEE Trans. on Mobile Computing*, vol. 5, no. 6, pp. 755–768, June 2006.

[17] M. Wang and M. van der Schaar. "Model-Based Joint Source Channel Coding for Subband Video," *IEEE Signal Proc. Letters*, vol. 13, no. 6, pp. 341–344, June 2006.

[18] M. Wang and M. van der Schaar. "Operational Rate-Distortion Modeling for Wavelet Video Coders," *IEEE Trans. on Signal Processing,* vol. 54, no. 9, pp. 3505–3517, September 2006.

[19] M. van der Schaar, D. Turaga, and R. S. Wong. "Classification-Based System for Cross-Layer Optimized Wireless Video Transmission," *IEEE Trans. on Multimedia*, vol. 8, no. 5, pp. 1082–1095, October 2006.

[20] Y. Andreopoulos, R. Kelarapura, M. van der Schaar, and C. N. Chuah. "Failure-Aware, Open-Loop, Adaptive Video Streaming with Packet-Level Optimized Redundancy," *IEEE Trans. on Multimedia*, vol. 8, no. 6, pp. 1274–1290, December 2006.

[21] Y. Andreopoulos, N. Mastronade, and M. van der Schaar. "Cross-layer Optimized Video Streaming over Wireless Multi-hop Mesh Networks," *IEEE JSAC, special issue on "Multi-hop wireless mesh networks*," vol. 24, no. 11, pp. 2104–1215, November 2006.

[22] M. van der Schaar and D. Turaga. "Cross-layer Packetization and Retransmission Strategies for Delay-Sensitive Wireless Multimedia Transmission," *IEEE Trans. on Multimedia*, January 2007.

[23] S. Shankar and M. van der Schaar. "Performance Analysis of Video Transmission over IEEE 802.11a/e WLANs," *IEEE Trans. on Vehicular Technolog*, 2007.

[24] N. Mastronade, D. Turaga, and M. van der Schaar. "Collaborative Resource Exchanges for Peer-to-Peer Video Streaming over Wireless Mesh Networks," *IEEE JSAC*, Special issue on Peer-to-Peer communications and Applications, 2007.

[25] H. Park and M. van der Schaar. "Bargaining Strategies for Networked Multimedia Resource Management," *IEEE Trans. on Signal Proc.*, 2007.

[26] Daji Qiao, Sunghyun Choi, and Kang G. Shin. "Goodput Analysis and Link Adaptation for IEEE 802.11a Wireless LAN," *Proc. of IEEE Trans. on Mobile Computing*, vol. 1, no. 4, 2002.

[27] A. K. Parekh and R. G. Gallager. "A Generalized Processor Sharing Approach to Flow Control in Integrated Services Networks: The Single Node Case," *Proc. of IEEE/ACM Trans. on Networ.*, vol. 1, June 1993.

[28] M. van der Schaar and S. Shankar. "New Fairness Paradigms for Wireless Multimedia Communication," *Proc. IEEE ICIP*, Vol. 3, pp. 704–707, September 2005.

[29] Q. Zhang, W. Zhu, and Y. Zhang. "End-to-End QoS for Video Delivery over Wireless Internet," *Proc. IEEE*, 2005.

[30] C. Luna, L. Kondi, and A. K. Katsaggelos, "Maximizing User Utility in Video Streaming Applications," *IEEE Trans. Circuits and Systems for Video Technology*, vol. 13, no. 2, pp. 141–148, February 2003.

[31] G. Cheung and A. Zakhor. "Bit Allocation for Joint Source/Channel Coding of Scalable Video," *IEEE Trans. on Image Processing*, vol. 9, no. 3, pp. 340–357, March 2000.

[32] W. Tan and A. Zakhor. "Packet Classification Schemes for Streaming MPEG Video over Delay and Loss Differentiated Networks," Proc. Packet Video Workshop, 2001.

[33] Y. Shan and A. Zakhor. "Cross Layer Techniques for Adaptive Video Streaming over Wireless Networks," *IEEE ICME*, vol. 1, pp. 277–280, 2002.

[34] A. Majumdar, R. Puri, K. Ramchandran, and I. Kozintsev. "Robust Video Multicast under Rate and Channel Variability with Application to Wireless LANs," IEEE International Symposium on Circuits and Systems (ISCAS), Scottsdale, AZ, May 2002.

[35] F. Zhai, C.E. Luna, Y. Eisenberg, T.N. Pappas, R. Berry, and A.K. Katsaggelos. "Joint Source Coding and Packet Classification for Real-Time Video Streaming over Differentiated Services Networks," *IEEE Trans. Multimedia*, vol. 7, pp. 716–726, August 2005.

[36] A. K. Katsaggelos, Y. Eisenberg, F. Zhai, R. Berry, and T. N. Pappas. "Advances in Efficient Resource Allocation for Packet-Switched Video Transmission," *Proc. IEEE*, special issue on "Advances in Video Coding and Delivery," vol. 93, pp. 135–147, January 2005.

[37] Y. Eisenberg, C. Luna, T. N. Pappas, R. Berry, and A. K. Katsaggelos. "Joint Source Coding and Transmission Power Management for Energy Efficient Wireless Video Communications," *IEEE Tr. Circ. Sys. Video Techn.*, special issue on Wireless Video, vol. 12, pp. 411–424, June 2002.

[38] W. Wei and A. Zakhor. "Multipath Unicast and Multicast Video Communication over Wireless Ad Hoc Networks," *Proc. Int. Conf. Broadband Networks*, Broadnets, pp. 496–505, 2002.

[39] MPEG4IP: Open Source, Open Standards, Open Streaming [Online]. Available: http://mpeg4ip.net

[40] B. Awerbuch and T. Leighton. "Improved Approximation Algorithms for the Multicommodity Flow Problem and Local Competitive Routing in Dynamic Networks," *Proc. 26th ACM Symposium on Theory of Computing*, May 1994.

[41] S. Toumpis and A. J. Goldsmith. "Capacity Regions for Wireless Ad Hoc Networks," *IEEE Trans. Wireless Commun.*, vol. 2, no. 4, pp. 736–748, July 2003.

[42] A. Butala and L. Tong. "Cross-layer Design for Medium Access Control in CDMA Ad-Hoc Networks," *EURASIP Journal on Applied Signal Processing*, vol. 2005, no. 2, pp. 129–143, 2005.

[43] Y. Wu, P. A. Chou, Q. Zhang, K. Jain, W. Zhu, and S. Y. Kung. "Network Planning in Wireless Ad Hoc Networks: A Cross-Layer Approach," *IEEE Journal on Selected Areas in Communications*, vol. 23, no. 1, pp. 136–150, January 2005.

[44] D. S. J. De Couto, D. Aguayo, J. Bicket, and R. Morris. "A High Throughput Path Metric for Multi-hop Wireless Routing," *Proc. ACM Conf. Mob. Computing and Networking*, MOBICOM, pp. 134–146, 2003.

[45] Q. Li and M. van der Schaar. "A Flexible Streaming Architecture for Efficient Scalable Coded Video Transmission over IP Networks," in *ISO/IEC JTC 1/SC 29/WG 11/M8944*, October 2002.

[46] J. Thie and D. Taubman. "Optimal Erasure Protection Assignment for Scalable Compressed Data with Small Packets and Short Channel Codewords," *EURASIP Journal on Applied Signal Processing: Special issue on Multimedia over IP and Wireless Networks*, no. 2, pp. 207–219, February 2004.

[47] P. A. Chou and Z. Miao. "Rate–Distortion Optimized Streaming of Packetized Media," *Microsoft Research Technical Report MSR-TR-2001-35*, February 2001.

[48] A. Grilo, M. Macedo, and M. Nunes. "A Scheduling Algorithm for QoS Support in IEEE 802.11E Networks," *IEEE Wireless Commun. Mag.*, vol. 10, no. 3, pp. 36–43, June 2003.

[49] P. Ansel, Q. Ni, and T. Turletti. "An Efficient Scheduling Scheme for IEEE 802.11E," *Proc. IEEE Workshop on Model. and Opt. in Mob., Ad-Hoc and Wireless Net.* (WiOpt 2004), Cambridge, UK, March 2004.

[50] S. Mangold, S. Choi, G. Hiertz, O. Klein, and B. Walker. "Analysis of IEEE 802.11E for QoS Support in Wireless LANs," *IEEE Wireless Commun. Mag.*, vol. 10, no. 6, pp. 40–50, December 2003.

[51] P. Garg, R. Doshi, R. Greene, M. Baker, M. Malek, and X. Cheng. "Using IEEE 802.11E MAC for QoS over Wireless," *Proc. IEEE Internat. Conf. on Perform. Comp. and Commun.*, IPCCC 2003, vol. 1, pp. 537–542, April 2003.

[52] B. V. Patel and C. C. Bisdikian. "End-Station Performance over Leaky Bucket Traffic Shaping," *IEEE Network Mag.*, vol. 10, no. 5, pp. 40–47, September 1996.

[53] JPEG2000: Image Compression Fundamentals, Standards and Practice, D. Taubman and M. Marcellin, Kluwer Academic, 2002.

[54] G. Bianchi. "Performance Analysis of the IEEE 802.11 Distributed Coordination Function," *IEEE Journal on Selected Area in Comm.*, vol. 18, No. 3, March 2000.

[55] A. Fattahi, F. Fu, and M. van der Schaar, "Mechanism-Based Resource Allocation for Multimedia Transmission over Spectrum Agile Wireless Networks," *IEEE JSAC*, Special issue on Adaptive, Spectrum Agile and Cognitive Wireless Networks, 2007.

[56] F. Fu and M. van der Schaar. "Proactive Cross Layer Design for Optimized Resource Exchanges Using Mechanism Design," *IEEE Trans. On Multimedia*, accepted for publication.

[57] H. Park and M. van der Schaar. "Utility-Based Fairness for Multi-user Wireless Multimedia Resource Allocation Using Bargaining," submitted to *IEEE Trans. on Signal Processing*.

[58] F. Kelly. "Charging and Rate Control for Elastic Traffic," *Eur. Trans. Telecommun. "Focus on Elastic Services over ATM Networks,"* vol. 8, no. 1, pp. 33–37, 1997.

[59] F. Kelly, A. Maulloo, and D. Tan. "Rate Control for Communication Networks: Shadow Prices, Proportional Fairness and Stability," *Journal of the Operational Research Society*, vol. 49, no. 3, pp. 237–252, March 1998.

[60] H. P. Shiang and M. van der Schaar. "Multi-User Video Streaming over Multi-Hop Wireless Networks: A Distributed, Cross-Layer Approach Based on Priority Queuing," *IEEE Journal on Selected Area in Comm.*, May 2007.

[61] S. Shakkottai, T. S. Rappaport, and P. C. Karlsson. "Cross-layer Design for Wireless Networks," *IEEE Communications Magazine*, October 2003.

[62] A. Maharshi, L. Tong, and A. Swami. "Cross-layer Designs of Multichannel Reservation MAC under Rayleigh Fading," *IEEE Trans. Signal Processing*, vol. 51, no. 8, pp. 2054–2067, August 2003.

[63] I. Aad and C. Castelluccia. "Differentiation Mechanisms for IEEE 802.11," *Proceedings IEEE INFOCOM*, April 2001.

[64] C. Papadopoulos and G. Parulkar. "Retransmission Based Error Control for Continuous Media Applications," *Proceedings of the Sixth International Workshop on Network and Operating System Support for Digital Audio and Video*, 1996.

[65] R. Bhaskaran, P. Bhagwat, and S. Seshan. "Arguments for Cross-Layer Optimizations in Bluetooth Scatternets," *Proc. of Symposium on Applications and the Internet*, 2001.

[66] R. Kapoor, M. Cesana, and M. Gerla. "Link Layer Support for Streaming MPEG Video over Wireless Links," Conference on Computer Communications and Networks ICCCN'03, Dallas, TX, October 20–22, 2003.

[67] G. Pau, D. Maniezzo, S. Das, Y. Lim, J. Pyon, H. Yu, and M. Gerla. "A Cross-Layer Framework for Wireless LAN QoS Support," IEEE International Conference on Information Technology Research and Education, ITRE 2003, Newark, NJ, August 10–13, 2003.

[68] A. P. Butala and L. Tong. "Dynamic Channel Allocation and Optimal Detection for MAC in CDMA Ad Hoc Networks," in *Proc. 36th Asilomar Conf. Signals, Syst., Comput.*, Pacific Grove, CA, November 2002.

[69] R. Pan, C. Nair, B. Yang, and B. Prabhakar. "Packet Dropping Schemes, Some Examples and Analysis," *Proceedings of the 39th Annual Allerton Conference on Communication, Control and Computing*, pp. 563–572, October 2001.

[70] T. Yoo, R. Lavery, A. Goldsmith, and D. Goodman. "Throughput Optimization Using Adaptive Techniques," submitted for publication.

[71] G. Bianchi and A. Campbell. "A Programmable MAC Framework for Utility-based Adaptive Quality of Service Support," *IEEE Journal of Selected Areas in Communications*, Special Issue on Intelligent Techniques in High Speed Networks, vol. 18, no. 2, pp. 244–256, February 2000.

[72] S. Shankar and M. van der Schaar. "Multimedia Transmission over WLANs Using Cross Layer Design—Challenges, Principles and Standards," half-day tutorial at *IEEE Globecom 2003*.

13

Quality of Service Support in Multimedia Wireless Environments

Klara Nahrstedt, Wanghong Yuan, Samarth Shah, Yuan Xue, and Kai Chen

13.1 INTRODUCTION

Over recent years, there has been a strong proliferation in the use of multimedia wireless technology all over the world, creating new research and business opportunities for producers and consumers of these technologies. There are several reasons for this fast proliferation. First, wireless networking technologies such as cellular networks, wireless local area networking (WLAN), and Bluetooth are becoming an integral part of our communication environment. Second, new wireless devices such as cellular phones, PDAs, and laptops are emerging to assist people in their lives. Third, multimedia applications became popular, first in the Internet environment and now in wireless environments, due to (a) standardization of digital multimedia formats such as MPEG-2, MPEG-4, H.263, and others and (b) understanding of multimedia applications and user behaviors under different networking conditions. This allows service providers to build large-scale multimedia services such as video conferencing and video-on-demand and to offer them to the population at large. Fourth, new hardware opportunities are appearing such as multifrequency energy-efficient processors, allowing for more efficient use of energy in mobile devices.

However, these new opportunities bring with them also various challenges. We will concentrate on addressing two major challenges. First, mobile devices running distributed multimedia applications and communicating over wireless networks must deal with scarce and variable resources such as battery power, processor speed, memory, and wireless bandwidth. Hence the resource management problem for support of Quality of Service (QoS) must be solved. Second, multimedia applications running over wireless networks must achieve some level of performance QoS guarantees. Hence modeling of application QoS, QoS management and its connectivity to underlying resource management must be addressed.

In this chapter, we aim to answer these application QoS and resource management challenges and to describe some of the solutions that may contribute to solving these challenges. Since these two challenges are still very broad, we narrow their scope to address the following problems:

- The topic of multimedia applications and QoS is very broad and there is an extensive pool of solutions in the literature. We concentrate on modeling of conversational applications with strict delay requirements such as Voice over IP and retrieval applications with sensitive throughput requirements such as multimedia on demand using mobile multimedia devices. We consider three QoS metrics for multimedia distributed services: throughput, end-to-end delay, and application lifetime.
- The topic of resource management in wireless networks is also very broad and there are multiple techniques that optimize different resource usage. Furthermore, resource management is required for all types of wireless networks such as cellular networks, wireless LANs, mobile ad hoc networks, and sensor networks. In this chapter we concentrate on resource management schemes meant only for networks based on, or compatible with, the widely used network standard IEEE 802.11. Also, we consider four major resources to deliver application QoS: wireless network bandwidth, CPU bandwidth, memory, and energy. We provide algorithms, services, and protocols at the operating system and middleware layer with cross-layered access to selected information in lower level network solutions. We consider resource management in single mobile devices, in mobile devices connected via single hop ad hoc networks, and in mobile devices connected via access-point-based networks.

To design solutions that address the end-to-end QoS issues and corresponding resource management in 802.11 wireless single hop environments, we take the top-down approach in this chapter. First, we decide on multimedia applications and their models that will run in these environments. Section 13.2 discusses the modeling of these applications and their QoS requirements, especially the application task, connection and QoS (quality) models, and the cross-layer application-OS-network models that drive correct resource allocations in mobile nodes. Second, once it is clear what applications are primarily running in the 802.11 wireless environments, resource management techniques need to be chosen that execute according to QoS requirements. These resource management techniques must span within individual mobile nodes via their operating systems and across mobile nodes via the distributed network management. Therefore, the rest of the chapter addresses (a) operating-system-internal resource management techniques that help delivering application QoS requirements inside an individual mobile node and (b) network-specific resource management techniques to deliver QoS in end-to-end fashion from the sender(s) to the receiver(s).

The operating-system-internal techniques can be found in Section 13.3 and the network-specific techniques can be found in Section 13.4 as follows. Section 13.3 concentrates on the energy-efficient operating system (EOS) at mobile end points. The Linux-based EOS includes an integrated and cross-layer-optimized CPU/energy resource management to guarantee node delay and application lifetime QoS requirements. This end-point resource management must be addressed to achieve true end-to-end quality guarantees for any multimedia application [42]. Section 13.4 addresses the cross-layer-optimized network resource management to guarantee end-to-end delay and bandwidth QoS requirements in single hop wireless networks. The reason for concentrating on single hop wireless networks is that in commercial applications such as music on demand or phone conversations we believe there will be only a few hops before the multimedia stream reaches the wired infrastructure through which the information will be transported. Hence, what we need to ensure in wireless networks for these types of applications is that the multimedia data be transmitted over the first/last wireless mile in a quality-aware manner.

We have built multiple cross-layer QoS-aware systems that utilize techniques in Sections 13.3 and 13.4. The design principles and overall lessons learned from their design and development are summarized in Section 13.5. The chapter concludes with possible future directions with respect to wireless multimedia and the corresponding QoS support in Section 13.6.

13.2 APPLICATION MODELING

Wireless multimedia applications on various mobile devices are becoming an integral part of our life. Examples are music on demand using the Apple iPOD devices, short video clips on demand using cell phones, DVD players on laptops, and voice over IP using laptops and PDAs. We will first specify the common model of these applications so that we can then address them more easily in the resource management and design solutions that will serve these applications. We consider computational and communication requirements of multimedia applications to have comprehensive and expressive models for OS and network resource management and their support for QoS guarantees.

During their lifetimes, distributed multimedia applications use computational and communication resources on their mobile nodes. Hence when modeling multimedia applications, we need to consider requirements that these applications have on both resources and to include them into the overall application model.

Furthermore, we need to consider the overall quality goal of the end-to-end application. Therefore, the application model will consist of two parts: (a) application task, connection, and quality models and (b) cross-layer application model.

13.2.1 Application Task, Connection, and Quality Models

We consider multimedia distributed applications (video, voice, or music) as periodic tasks, running distributed application functions over single or multiple network connections between sender(s) and receiver(s). Each task consumes CPU time, energy, and network bandwidth resources and provides an output quality. Multimedia applications are adaptive tasks, which means that from the computational point of view they are *soft real-time tasks* that can operate at multiple application QoS (quality) levels. For example, a QoS level may correspond to a video frame rate in a video task. Each task i supports a discrete set of QoS levels, $q_{i1}, \ldots, q_{im}$ [7,43]. Each task can provide different quality levels, trading off quality with resource consumption or trading off consumption between different resources [37]. We aggregate all *best effort (nonmultimedia) applications* into one logical adaptive task. This logical task delivers either average (in lightly loaded environment) or no (in a heavily loaded environment) quality guarantees to individual best effort tasks.

Each connection connects multiple tasks to form a transmission medium between sender(s) and receiver(s) to exchange multimedia data and control information among mobile nodes. Also, each connection consumes through its distributed tasks CPU time, energy, and bandwidth resources, and based on the shared resource availability, especially the wireless channel, it provides an output quality. It is important to stress that from the 802.11 wireless networking point of view, multimedia distributed applications must be adaptive. This means that the end-to-end connections can yield only soft end-to-end guarantees and, in many cases, only statistical or best effort guarantees.

13.2.2 Cross-Layer Application-OS-Network Model

Each wireless multimedia application must have a strong relation to the underlying computing and communication layers that allocate resources to provide QoS guarantees q and utility $u(q)$. We will consider two layers where multimedia applications will interface to: (1) process management (representing the operating system and its access to processor hardware) with its soft real-time task scheduling and (2) middleware layer (representing entrance to the network protocol stack) with its connections/packets scheduling and bandwidth management.

Each application QoS level q has a utility $u(q)$, which measures the perceptual quality at a QoS level from the user's point of view and consumes $C(q)$ cycles and $B(q)$ network bytes per period $P(q)$. Furthermore, we assume that for each QoS level, the task has probability distribution of its cycle demand; that is, $F(x) = \mathcal{P}r(X \leq x)$ is the probability that the task demands no more than x cycles for each job. This distribution can be obtained with our previously developed kernel-based profiler [49,50]. Specifically, the operating system uses a profiling window to keep track of the number of CPU cycles each task has consumed for its recent jobs. The operating system then builds a histogram based on the result in the profiling window. The histogram estimates the probability distribution of the cycle demand of the task for each job. With respect to network connections, we assume two network models: the integrated service ("IntServ") model and the differentiated service ("DiffServ") model that determine the network bandwidth allocation in 802.11 wireless networks and will be discussed in detail in Section 13.4.1.

In the hardware layer, a multimedia application uses two adaptive resources: CPU and wireless network interface card (WNIC). The CPU can operate at multiple speeds (frequencies/voltages), $\{f_1, \ldots, f_{\max}\}$, trading off performance for energy. The power consumption of the CPU is $p(f)$ at speed f. The lower the speed is, the lower the power is. We assume that the overhead for adapting CPU speed is negligible.

The WNIC supports three operation modes: *active*, *idle*, and *sleep*, where the sleep mode has much less power. Power consumptions at the aforementioned states are p_{act}, p_{idl}, and p_{slp}, respectively. The overhead for switching the WNIC into sleep and from sleep is t_{slp}, which is not negligible (e.g., around 40 ms for the Lucent WaveLan card).

13.3 QoS SUPPORT IN MOBILE OPERATING SYSTEMS

In mobile wireless environments, QoS-aware operating system support for battery-powered mobile nodes is crucial in order to run multimedia applications. Such multimedia-enabled mobile systems need to save energy while supporting multimedia QoS requirements. There is a conflict in the design goals for QoS provisioning and energy saving. For QoS provisioning, system resources often need to provide high performance, typically resulting in high energy consumption. For energy saving, system resources should consume low energy. As a result, the operating system of mobile devices needs to manage resources in a QoS- and energy-aware manner and provides the flexibility to trade off QoS and energy based on the user's preferences.

Recently, a number of soft real-time operating systems has been proposed to support QoS for multimedia applications. These operating systems typically integrate predictable CPU allocation (such as proportional sharing [8,31] and reservation [18,36]) and real-time scheduling algorithms, such as earliest deadline first (EDF) and rate monotonic [21]. Energy management is also an important part of the operating system. For example, ECOSystem [52] and Nemesis [29] manage energy as a first-class OS resource. Vertigo [16] saves energy by monitoring application CPU usage and adapting the CPU speed correspondingly. More recently, there is some work on QoS and energy-aware cross-layer adaptation [27,33,34,50,51]. Pereira *et al.* [33] proposed a power-aware application programming interface that exchanges the information on energy and performance among the hardware, OS, and applications. Mohapatra *et al.* [27] proposed an approach that uses a middleware to coordinate the adaptation of hardware and applications at coarse time granularity (e.g., at the time of admission control). EQoS [34] is an energy-aware QoS adaptation framework, which formulates energy-aware QoS adaptation as a constrained optimization problem. GRACE [49–51] coordinates the adaptation of the CPU speed in the hardware layer, CPU scheduling in the OS layer, and multimedia quality in the application layer in response to system changes at both fine and coarse time granularity.

We next introduce the design of our operating system, which is a part of the GRACE project [50,51].

13.3.1 Design and Algorithm

The goal of the operating system is to maximize multimedia quality q of all concurrent tasks in the mobile device under the constraints of CPU, network bandwidth, and battery energy. Figure 13.1 shows the architecture of the operating system, which includes four major components: a coordinator, a soft real-time CPU scheduler, a CPU adapter, and a WNIC adapter. The coordinator coordinates tasks and the CPU and WNIC resources to determine the quality level and CPU allocation for each task and the average power consumption for the CPU and WNIC. The CPU scheduler enforces the coordinated allocation to support the coordinated QoS levels of individual tasks. Finally, the CPU and WNIC adapters dynamically adapt the CPU and network card to minimize their power consumption. We next describe each component in turn.

13.3.1.1 Coordination

The goal of the coordination is to maximize the aggregate utility of all concurrent tasks in the device subject to the constraints of CPU, network, and energy in the device. More formally, let's assume that (1) there are n tasks concurrently running in the device. Each task has multiple QoS levels, $\{q_{i1}, \ldots, q_{im}\}$. Each QoS level has a utility $u(q_{ij})$, consumes $C(q_{ij})$ cycles and $B(q_{ij})$ network bytes per period $P(q_{ij})$; (2) the remaining battery energy in the device is E; (3) the estimated operating time of the device is T; and (4) the available network bandwidth is BW. The coordination needs to determine a QoS level for each task, the CPU speed f and power $p(f)$, and the network power p_{net}. Intuitively, when tasks operate at a

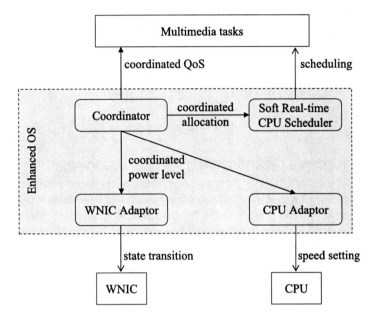

FIGURE 13.1:   The architecture of the OS.

higher QoS level, they demand more CPU and network resources; consequently, the CPU and WNIC perform at higher performance and hence consume more energy.

The coordination problem can be formulated as follows:

$$\text{maximize} \quad \sum_{i=1}^{n} u(q_{ij}) \qquad \text{(total utility)} \qquad (13.1)$$

$$\text{subject to} \quad \sum_{i=1}^{n} \frac{C(q_{ij})/f}{P(q_{ij})} \leq 1 \qquad \text{(CPU constraint)}, \qquad (13.2)$$

$$\sum_{i=1}^{n} \frac{B(q_{ij})}{P(q_{ij})} \leq BW \qquad \text{(network constraint)}, \qquad (13.3)$$

$$\left(p(f) + p_{\text{net}}\right) * T \leq E \quad \text{(energy constraint)}, \qquad (13.4)$$

$$q_{ij} \in \{q_{i1}, \ldots, q_{im_i}\} \qquad i = 1, \ldots, n \text{ (QoS levels)}, \quad (13.5)$$

$$f \in \{f_1, \ldots, f_{\text{max}}\} \qquad \text{(CPU speeds)}. \qquad (13.6)$$

The CPU power $p(f)$ is directly determined by the speed f. We determine the network power as follows: If the transmission speed for the WNIC is S, the WNIC needs to be in the active state for B/S and in idle state for $1 - B/S$ for every second, where B is the aggregate bandwidth requirement of all tasks, that is, $\sum_{i=1}^{n}(B(q_{ij})/P(q_{ij}))$. Then the network power is

$$p_{net} = p_{act} * \frac{B}{S} + p_{slp} * \left(1 - \frac{B}{S}\right). \tag{13.7}$$

Note that in (13.7), we switch the WNIC into sleep when it is idle.

The aforementioned constraint optimization happens at coarse time granularity, for example, when a task joins or leaves the system. The coordination problem is NP hard, since we can prove that the NP-hard Knapsack problem is an instance of the aforementioned constraint optimization problem. We therefore use the dynamically programming algorithm [28] that provides a heuristic solution. As a result of this solution, we determine the QoS level and CPU allocation for each task as well as the average CPU power and network power.

13.3.1.2 Soft Real-Time CPU Scheduling

Soft real-time scheduling is a common mechanism to support timing requirements of multimedia applications [8,11,30]. Here, we focus on the CPU scheduling. Previous soft real-time scheduling algorithms, however, often assume that the CPU runs at a constant speed. This assumption does not hold for our target mobile devices with a variable-speed CPU. As a result, we cannot directly use existing scheduling algorithms in our system. We therefore extend traditional real-time scheduling algorithms by adding another dimension—*speed*. That is, the scheduler also sets the CPU speed when executing a task and hence enforces the CPU allocation on a variable-speed CPU [48].

The operating system uses an energy-aware EDF scheduling algorithm, which enforces the globally coordinated CPU allocation on a variable-speed CPU [48]. Specifically, in this scheduling algorithm, each task has a deadline and a cycle budget:

- The deadline of the task equals the end of its current period. That is, when a task begins a new period, its deadline is postponed by the period.
- The budget of a task is recharged periodically. In particular, when a task begins a new period, its budget is recharged to the coordinated number of cycles.

The scheduler schedules all tasks based on their deadline and budget. In particular, the scheduler always dispatches the task that has the earliest deadline and a positive budget. As the task is executed, its budget is decreased by the number of cycles it consumes. When the budget of a task is decreased to 0, the task is preempted to run in best-effort mode until its budget is replenished again at the next period.

This preemption provides temporal and hence performance isolation among tasks; that is, a task's performance is not affected by the behavior of other tasks [11,18,30].

13.3.1.3 CPU Energy Saving

As the coordination problem just given shows, the coordinated CPU power consumption is $p(f)$, where $f = \sum_{i=1}^{n}(C(q_{ij})/P(q_{ij}))$. In other words, we expect the CPU to execute at a uniform speed for all concurrent tasks. If each task uses exactly $C(q_{ij})$ cycles per period $P(q_{ij})$, this uniform speed technique would consume minimum energy due to the convex nature of the CPU speed–power function [17]. However, the instantaneous cycle demand of multimedia tasks often varies greatly. In particular, a task may, and often does, complete a job before using up its allocated cycles. Such early completion often results in CPU idle time, thereby wasting energy. To avoid this energy waste, we dynamically adapt the CPU speed during each task's execution.

However, we cannot lower the speed too much, as the task may miss its deadline or cause other tasks to miss their deadlines. To do this, we allocate the task a time as follows: If there are n concurrent tasks and each task is allocated C_i cycles per period P_i, then the scheduler allocates the ith task CPU time $T_i = C_i / \sum_{i=1}^{n}(C_i/P_i)$ every period P_i. The reason for time allocation (in addition to cycle allocation) is to guarantee that each task executes for up to its allocated cycles within its allocated time, regardless of speed changes.

Without loss of generality, we focus on the speed adaptation for an individual task, which is allocated C cycles and T time per period and has a probability distribution of its cycle demand $F(x) = \mathcal{P}r(X \leq x), 1 \leq X \leq C$. Our goal is to minimize the expected energy consumption of each job of the task. To do this, we find a speed for each of the allocated cycles of this task, such that the total energy consumption of these allocated cycles is minimized while their total execution time is no more than the allocated time. More formally, if a cycle x executes at speed f_x, its execution time is $1/f_x$ and its expected energy consumption is $(1 - F(x)) \times 1/f_x \times p(f_x)$ [9]. We can then formulate the speed adaptation schedule problem as follows:

$$\min: \quad \underbrace{\sum_{x=1}^{C}(1 - F(x))\frac{1}{f_x}p(f_x)}_{\text{busy energy}} + \underbrace{\left(T - \sum_{x=1}^{C}(1 - F(x))\frac{1}{f_x}\right)p_{\text{idle}}}_{\text{idle energy}} \qquad (13.8)$$

subject to:

$$\sum_{x=1}^{C} \frac{1}{f_x} \leq T, \tag{13.9}$$

$$f_x \in \{f_1, \ldots, f_{max}\}, \tag{13.10}$$

where p_{idle} is the CPU idle power at the lowest speed. Note that the energy consists of two parts: The first part is the energy consumed when executing all allocated cycles. The second part is the energy consumed during the residual time (i.e., the time budget minus the expected execution time of all allocated cycles). During this residual time, the CPU is often idle since the process needs to wait until the next job is available. During this idle time, we set the CPU to the lowest speed during the idle slack.

We refer to the aforementioned optimization as a statistical Dynamic Voltage Scaling (DVS) approach. This optimization happens at fine time granularity, for example, within a multimedia frame execution. The optimization problem is NP hard. To provide an approximate solution, we develop a dynamic programming algorithm, based on the algorithm proposed by Pisinger [35]. Specifically, we first divide the allocated cycles into groups and find a speed for each group, rather than for each cycle. We then consider the combinations of all speed options for all cycle groups and sort them in the nondecreasing order of a *slope* that is defined as the ration of the increased energy to the decreased time by increasing a group's speed to the next higher speed. We initially set all cycle groups to the lowest speed and then visit the sorted slope list. For the currently visited slope, we try to increase the speed of its associated cycle group to the next higher speed. We finish the visit when the total execution time of all cycle groups is no more than its allocated time.

Each task has its own speed schedule and its speed schedule applies to all its jobs. In other words, the OS changes the CPU speed in three cases (Figure 13.2):

- **Context switch**. After a context switch, the OS sets the CPU speed based on the speed schedule of the switched-in task. This provides isolation of speed scaling among different tasks.
- **New job**. When the current task releases a new job, its execution speed is reset to the speed of its first cycle group.
- **Job progress**. The OS also monitors the progress of each job execution and changes the CPU speed when the job reaches its next cycle group.

13.3.1.4 Network Energy Saving

Dynamic power management (DPM) is a common technique used to save network energy by switching the WNIC into sleep when it is idle. DPM, however,

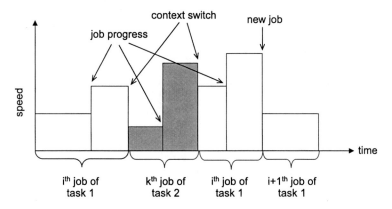

FIGURE 13.2:   The OS changes the CPU speed during job execution and at context switch.

cannot be directly applied in our target multimedia systems for the following reason. Multimedia applications are periodic and need to transmit or receive data in each period. Consequently, the idle interval of the WNIC is often shorter than the period. Since the period is often shorter than the DPM overhead, the WNIC cannot enter the lower-power sleep mode. To save network energy, we use a *buffering* approach. In this approach, each task still performs computation every period in a timely fashion, but delays the transmission by buffering frames and sending them in bursts at longer intervals (Figure 13.3).

Specifically, let's assume that the buffer size is k frames and each frame needs to transmit for t_{act} time. In each period P, the task processes a frame and stores it in the buffer. When the buffer has k frames (i.e., every k periods), the OS sends all buffered frames in batch. The buffering approach combines short WNIC idle intervals with length $(P - t_{act})$ into longer ones with length $k(P - t_{act})$. Such aggregate idle intervals are larger than the DPM overhead so the WNIC can enter sleep. The buffering approach saves more energy. That is, the network power in the k period is

$$p_{net} = \frac{p_{act} \times k t_{act} + p_{slp} \times k(P - t_{act})}{kP}$$

$$= p_{act} \times \frac{t_{act}}{P} + p_{slp} \times \left(1 - \frac{t_{act}}{P}\right), \tag{13.11}$$

which is equivalent to (13.7). That is, we enable the WNIC to consume the coordinated power.

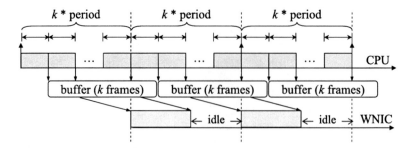

FIGURE 13.3:   The buffering approach.

13.3.2 Experimental Results

We have implemented a prototype of the OS. The hardware platform for our implementation is the HP Pavilion N5470 laptop with a single AMD Athlon 4 processor, which supports six different frequencies, 300, 500, 600, 700, 800, and 1000 MHz. The laptop has a Cisco Aironet 350 wireless card. The coordinator, scheduler, and CPU adapter are implemented as a set of patches and modules that hook into the Linux kernel 2.6.5. The WNIC adapter is implemented as a user-level process that switches the WNIC into the power-saving mode (PSM) when it is idle and into the continuous access mode (CAM) when it is active.

We next evaluate the OS prototype. Since the coordination requires the utility function for each task, which is application specific, we focus on our evaluation on energy saving. To measure energy, we remove the battery from the laptop and let it use the power from the AC adapter. The power consumption is the product of the input voltage and input current from the AC adapter. We use the Agilent 54621A oscilloscope to record the measurement. The sampling rate of the oscilloscope is 5 kHz, that is, making a sample every 200 μs. Figure 13.4 shows the setup for power measurement.

First, we analyze the impact of the CPU adaptation and WNIC adaptation together. To do this, we use an H263 encoder that encodes local raw images into frames in real time and sends the encoded frames to a receiver through a wireless network. The input pictures are `paris.cif`. The H263 encoder can process two or three frames per second in real time. We measure average energy consumption characteristics for three different system scenarios:

- *no adapt*: the CPU always runs at the highest speed and the WNIC always runs at the CAM mode.
- *CPU only*: the CPU runs at a uniform speed that meets the total average demand of applications.
- *CPU+NW*: The CPU and WNIC both adapt.

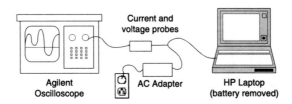

FIGURE 13.4:   Setup for power measurement.

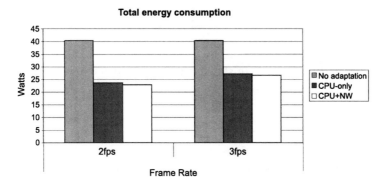

FIGURE 13.5:   Benefits of CPU adaptation and WNIC adaptation.

This gives us an idea of the energy saving resulting from CPU speed adaptation and wireless card mode changing.

Figure 13.5 shows the energy consumption of the laptop. We note that the CPU speed adaptation reduces base energy consumption of the laptop by about 34% at 3 fps, and the network card mode-changing reduces the energy consumption of the network interface by about 42% at the same frame rate. However we find that the total energy saving in the CPU+NW case over the CPU-only case is only 2–3% with the HP Pavilion laptop. The reason is that the WNIC consumes much less energy than the CPU in the HP laptop.

Second, we evaluate the benefits of our proposed CPU energy-saving technique. To do this, we disable the wireless connection and let the H263 encode three frames per second in real time and store the encoded frames in a local file. We run the stand-alone H263 encoder under the following DVS techniques:

- *No DVS*. This is the baseline technique that always runs the CPU at the highest speed.
- *Uniform DVS*. It sets the CPU speed based on the average CPU demand of the H263 encoder.

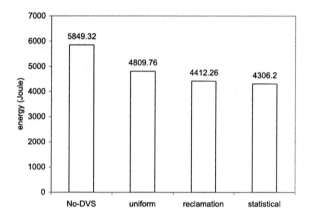

FIGURE 13.6:   Benefits of statistical DVS compared to other DVS techniques.

- *Reclamation DVS.* It first sets a uniform speed and sets to the lowest speed when the H263 encoder completes a job early.
- *Statistical DVS.* It adjusts the execution speed for each task job based on its demand distribution.

Figure 13.6 shows the energy results. Compared to the baseline algorithm without DVS, all DVS techniques save energy significantly. In particular, the statistical DVS reduces energy by 26.4% compared to the no-DVS approach. The reason is that the CPU does not need to always run at the highest speed. This clearly shows the benefits of energy saving by dynamically adapting the CPU speed. Compared to other DVS techniques, the statistical DVS further reduces the total energy by 2 to 10%. This clearly shows the benefits of adapting the CPU speed based on demand distribution of tasks.

13.4 QoS SUPPORT IN MOBILE WIRELESS NETWORKS

To achieve end-to-end QoS guarantees in multimedia wireless networks, a strong QoS-aware cross-layer networking system support for wireless multimedia applications must be present. We will present a complete cross-layer networking system support for a *single-hop ad hoc network* based on the IEEE 802.11 MAC layer. In this network, all the nodes are within one-hop transmission range of each other. They are able to talk to each other in a peer-to-peer fashion. They all share the same wireless medium and hence need to cooperate with each other in satisfying their QoS needs.

The nodes in our network use the IEEE 802.11 MAC protocol's Distributed Coordination Function (DCF) mode for communication. The IEEE 802.11 standard specifies two operating modes: Point Coordination Function (PCF) and DCF. The former requires a single coordinator to arbitrate access to the shared wireless channel. The latter mode allows peers to arbitrate channel access without any centralized coordinator using a CSMA/CA protocol. Wireless nodes using the DCF mode carrier sense the medium. If the channel is busy, transmissions are deferred. When the channel is clear, nodes back off for collision avoidance. A node that captures the channel for transmission uses a RTS-CTS-DATA-ACK cycle to transmit a MAC frame. The RTS/CTS handshake is used mainly to deal with the hidden terminal effect.

Multimedia applications running over this 802.11 DCF network need to pay attention to the following conditions: (1) interference of wireless communications between different flows within the network and (2) dynamics of the network environment where resource usage patterns and wireless signals may vary with time. As a result, multimedia applications need to adapt to these conditions with proper system support.

To date, most of the existing work has been proposed within the context of an individual layer, such as the routing and MAC layer. Much less progress has been made in addressing the overall system support for running multimedia applications over wireless networks. One solution for overall system support for wireless multimedia applications is to adopt a *cross-layer* system architecture among MAC, transport, middleware and application layers. All these layers communicate and coordinate with each other to support QoS for multimedia applications.

13.4.1 QoS Models

Before discussing details of our cross-layer networking system architecture, we first revisit the QoS models proposed in the Internet and review their applicability in the wireless environment. There are two different QoS models: (1) the integrated service ("IntServ") model and (2) the differentiated service ("DiffServ") model.

The IntServ QoS model defines two types of services: *guaranteed* and *best effort*. In guaranteed service, each *flow* can request a certain level of QoS from the network, such as minimum bandwidth and maximum delay. Over the Internet, IntServ is usually implemented by per-flow resource reservation in the routers. To apply the IntServ model to a wireless network, admission control must be designed to work with imprecise and time-varying resources information. Furthermore, the reserved resources of a flow may have to change in response to wireless resource fluctuations. As a result, in wireless networks, multimedia applications often specify their QoS requirements over a *range*, for example, minimum and maximum bandwidths, and the granted resource can be a QoS level within that range.

In the DiffServ model, flows are aggregated into multiple traffic *classes*. A router needs to provide certain per-hop forwarding behavior for each class of packets. In particular, we are interested in the *relative DiffServ* model [12], which assures the relative quality ordering between different classes. *No* guarantee is provided for any of those classes. This QoS model is appealing, especially in wireless networks because it does not need to provide any bandwidth guarantees for any class of packets. Instead, it relies on the end-host's adaptation behavior to dynamically select an appropriate service class for each of its applications.

These two QoS models address different needs of multimedia applications. IntServ is more stringent in resource provisioning. An application has a better level of QoS guarantee but at the same time there is a higher probability that the QoS request may be rejected in admission or terminated due to resource fluctuations. The relative DiffServ model has less guarantee for each application, but each application is always allowed to send out packets, although with different levels of QoS.

In the following subsections, we discuss in detail our design of two cross-layer architectures that realize the QoS models mentioned earlier. There have been several other cross-layer architectures for dynamic bandwidth management and adaptation, such as INSIGNIA [20], SWAN [2], TIMELY [6], dRSVP [26], and, most recently, MPARC [47] and PBRA [46]. These cross-layer architectures assume different QoS models and network topologies, but the underlying mechanisms (subtasks) implemented in order to manage bandwidth are, with some exceptions, similar: available bandwidth monitoring at the MAC, soft state reservation, application adaptation to network variations, and fair bandwidth allocation. QoS research for wireless networks has also addressed fair scheduling at the MAC layer [4,15,19,22–24,44] and new transport mechanisms [3,25,40,46] to improve application performance.

13.4.2 IntServ: Bandwidth Management

13.4.2.1 Bandwidth Management Architecture

Bandwidth Management architecture [38] arbitrates the bandwidth requests of all the flows in a single-hop wireless network. In this architecture, every host in the network monitors its MAC layer transmissions to observe wireless channel fading and interference effects. These observations are fed into a *central* network arbiter, which takes the bandwidth requirements and channel effects pertaining to each multimedia stream in the network into account to decide how much *channel time* each stream gets to access the network to ensure that its requirements are met.

An overview of the architecture is shown in Figure 13.7. It consists of a middleware agent for each host, which obtains channel quality updates from the MAC

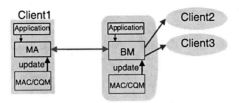

MA: Middleware Agent
CQM: Channel Quality Monitor
MAC: Medium Access Control
BM: Bandwidth Manager

FIGURE 13.7:   Bandwidth management architecture: overview.

layer monitor and application throughput requirements from each application, including the media application. It translates the throughput requirements into *channel time* requirements, using channel quality. The channel time requirement represents the fraction of unit time that the media stream must have access to the wireless channel of the observed quality in order to satisfy its throughput requirement. The channel time required thus depends on the throughput required as well as the channel quality observed. The middleware agent feeds these channel time fractions required by a particular stream to a central network arbiter, called the *Bandwidth Manager* (BM), which resides on one of the hosts in the network. The BM allocates the unit channel time resource among the various media streams in the network. It can be configured with any logical policy to distribute the resource among the streams, taking into account their requirements, for example, by using a fair, utility-based or price-based policy.

The BM returns to the middleware agent at each wireless host the *channel fraction* allocated to each application running on the host. When there is some change in application throughput requirement or channel quality observed, the BM must reallocate resources. This may involve *revoking* partially the resources previously allocated to an application and reallocating them based on the new network conditions.

Each host also has a *rate-control system* (i.e., traffic shaper) comprising leaky-bucket queues. It is configured to ensure that each application injects no more traffic than can occupy the channel for the fraction of time the application was allotted. The sequence of events within each wireless host is shown in Figure 13.8.

The centralized architecture shown in Figure 13.7 is flexible enough to work with any single-hop wireless topology. It can be used for single-hop peer-to-peer ad hoc networks and for access-point (AP)-based networks. Furthermore, it can be extended to a network consisting of multiple APs that cover a large area with overlapping frequency bands. In such networks, the BM must also keep track

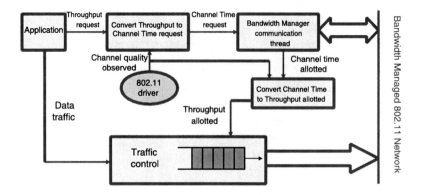

FIGURE 13.8:   Bandwidth management architecture: host.

of spatial reuse of the channel resource, apart from tracking the channel time requirements [39]. The channel quality monitor that we describe later is powerful enough to help a host using one AP to detect the presence of interference from a host using a different one.

13.4.2.2 Channel Quality Monitoring

In the BM architecture, a key component is the monitoring of the channel quality. We monitor the channel quality at the MAC layer, that is, we observe how fading and interference phenomena affect MAC frame transmissions. We observe the delay in MAC frame transmission and observe the loss rate of MAC frames. We explain in this section how fading and interference phenomena are manifested in the MAC frame delay and loss rate. We do not change the IEEE 802.11 protocol in any way in constructing the channel quality monitor. We merely observe the MAC layer transmissions of data packets in drawing our inferences.

Interference on the network can be estimated by the amount of time a transmitting host senses the channel busy, and must hence back-off and wait before being able to transmit its RTS or DATA frame. Thus the delay $t_r - t_s$ in Figure 13.9 (top) reflects the interference levels in the network. Signal fading effects cause bit errors in individual frame transmissions, thus requiring the frame to be retransmitted. If ultimately the RTS-CTS-DATA-ACK cycle is successfully completed, then the interval $t_r - t_s$ also measures signal fading effects, since delays due to retransmissions are also accounted for in the interval. In case the RTS or DATA retransmission limit is exceeded, then the frame is dropped at the MAC layer, despite a time T_w wasted in trying to send it. Thus measuring this time wasted T_w in Figure 13.9 (bottom) and the frame loss rate is also crucial in estimating signal fading effects.

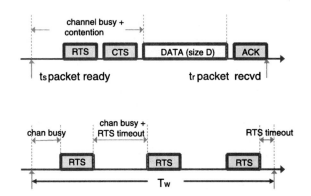

FIGURE 13.9:   Successful and unsuccessful transmissions in 802.11.

Our channel quality monitoring scheme also accounts for hidden-terminal effects that might occur in networks spread out over a larger area. Hidden terminal effects cause the CTS frame to be suppressed. This is because the transmitter of the RTS does not know about the transmissions in the receiver's neighborhood. But these transmissions prevent the intended receiver from responding with a CTS. This may result in multiple RTS retransmissions, as would be the case if there were bit errors in the individual frames, and even result in the RTS retransmission limit being exceeded. Both of these scenarios are accounted for when we measure the delay in Figure 13.9 (top) and the time wasted and frame loss rate in Figure 13.9 (bottom).

The channel quality monitoring mechanism measures, over a time interval T, the number of frames successfully transmitted, the delay $t_r - t_s$ incurred in transmitting them, the number of frames lost, and the time wasted in attempting to transmit them T_w. These four measures comprise our channel quality metric. They give us an indication of how many higher layer packets can be transmitted in unit time and how many will be lost in the process. The channel fraction required for a media stream to obtain its required throughput depends on this information.

Note that we have described earlier only the principle behind our channel quality monitoring mechanism. We have omitted the details pertaining to how different higher layer packet sizes affect the monitor and also considerations pertaining to packet-header overhead consuming some channel fraction. Details on dealing with these issues can be found in [38].

13.4.2.3 Illustrative Example

We now demonstrate using the network simulator ns-2 the performance of our channel quality monitoring and rate-control schemes that together constitute our bandwidth management solution. We assume a network topology shown in

Figure 13.10 with two APs, node mobility, handoff, and hidden node effects. The transmission range of a wireless node is 250 m and the carrier-sense range is 550 m.

Note that there is no spatial reuse of the channel, that is, two transmissions are not simultaneously possible on the wireless channel. In order to create the hidden node effect, and illustrate how our scheme deals with it, we assume both APs use the same wireless frequency, although in practice adjacent 802.11 APs tend to use noninterfering frequencies in the 2.4-GHz band. The BM is located in the backbone distribution system and is not shown in Figure 13.11.

Figure 13.11 shows the observed throughput in the absence of any bandwidth management. Figure 13.12 shows the observed throughput when using our bandwidth management architecture. Our scheme provides weighted fairness in throughput to each flow accessing the shared channel. Note that we are able to

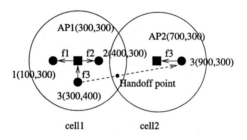

FIGURE 13.10:   Illustrative example: no spatial reuse.

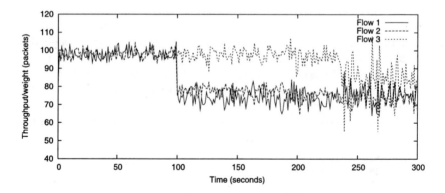

FIGURE 13.11:   Observed weighted throughput without bandwidth management.

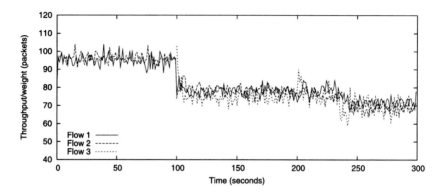

FIGURE 13.12:   Observed weighted throughput with bandwidth management.

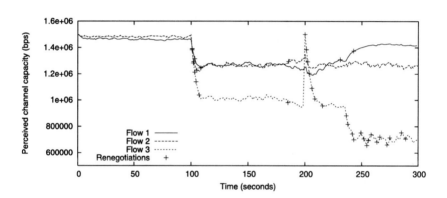

FIGURE 13.13:   Perceived channel capacity for each flow.

provide weighted fairness in an extended LAN with multiple APs *without* changing the MAC protocol in any way. Figure 13.13 shows the channel capacity perceived (which takes into account time wasted) by each flow in the network. Figure 13.14 shows the fraction of unit time each flow is permitted to be active on the wireless channel. Flows with lower perceived channel capacity (i.e., worse channel quality) are allowed to spend more time on the channel, and vice versa. The accuracy of our channel quality estimation, even in the presence of hidden node effects, is illustrated by the fact that the allotted channel fractions exactly compensate channel quality variations and the result is a high degree of fairness in throughput among flows.

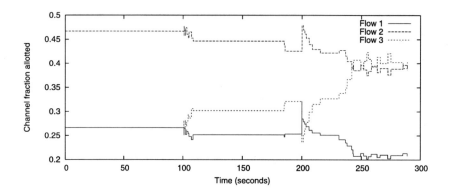

FIGURE 13.14:   Channel fraction allotted to each flow.

Of course, throughput fairness is only one notion of fairness. Another notion of fairness is channel-time fairness, wherein all flows get equal access to the channel, and flows with better channel quality end up transmitting more packets successfully. Since we provide flows with worse channel quality more access to the channel, we use the channel less efficiently as a result. (In the ideal case, for maximum efficiency, only one flow should transmit on a completely clear channel, but obviously this starves all other flows and is hence not a practical solution.) In our scenario given earlier, we observe up to 15% drop in overall channel efficiency as compared to the baseline case without bandwidth management.

In cases with spatial reuse of the channel, the BM must arbiter *multiple* resources. It must identify the flows in a particular region that shares the wireless channel in that region of the network, and arbiter the channel among them. In another area of the network, a different set of nodes shares the wireless channel, and channel arbitration must be performed separately for that set of nodes. Details on identifying the flow sets that shares the channel, and on the bandwidth management in a scenario with spatial reuse, can be found in [39].

13.4.3 DiffServ: Proportional Delay Differentiation

13.4.3.1 Delay Management Architecture

Our second cross-layer design is a DiffServ QoS architecture that provides different delays for packets in different service classes [45]. The cross-layer architecture in Figure 13.15 operates from the MAC layer up to the application layer. At the network level, packets from different service classes are processed differently via per-hop forwarding mechanisms (e.g., packet scheduling and queue manage-

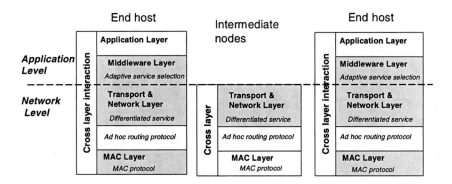

FIGURE 13.15:   Delay management QoS architecture: overview.

ment). At the middleware level, a monitor component monitors the performances of applications. Based on the monitored results, it performs appropriate service class adaptation so that different applications are able to meet their required QoS specifications.

A detailed diagram of our delay management QoS architecture, which shows the key components of this architecture, is illustrated in Figure 13.16. In order to provide QoS support in the wireless networking environment, these components interact in the following way.

1. *At application level in the end hosts*:

   - The application notifies the *Adapter* in the middleware that it wishes to set up a flow between two end hosts. It also provides its QoS specification and adaptation policy to the *Adapter* in the middleware layer.

2. *At middleware level in the end hosts*:

   - Based on the previous performance of the service classes and the QoS specifications of the applications, the *Adapter* decides the appropriate service class for each application and notifies the *Classifier*. Adaptation is an application-specific process. Based on application-specific adaptation policy, actions are taken to adapt the application's service class.
   - The packets from applications are delivered through the middleware layer, where the *Classifier* marks the packets with their corresponding service class.
   - The *Monitor* monitors the performance of each service class and notifies the *Adapter* of the observed changes and QoS violations.

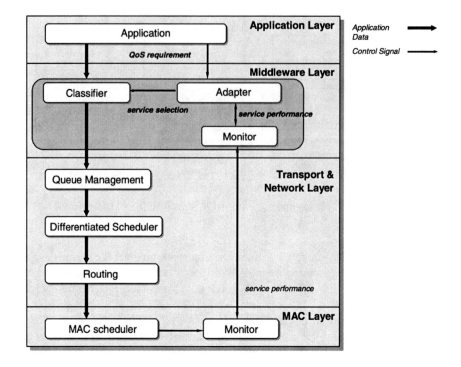

FIGURE 13.16:   Delay management QoS architecture: details.

3. *At network level in routing nodes*:

- The *Queue Management* component allocates buffer spaces and marks or drops packets. It deals with packet loss rate differentiation.
- The *Differentiated Scheduler* selects a packet to transmit. It performs packet-level QoS enforcement, allocates bandwidth for different flows, and provides delay differentiation.

This architecture balances very well between architectural flexibility and scalability. At the network level, the service differentiation mechanisms work to bring scalability with per-class packet scheduling and queue management. At the middleware level, the individual QoS requirement of each application is met via the application-specific adaptation process.

In the following, we discuss details of the cross-layer proportional delay differentiation scheduler and the adaptation service at the middleware layer.

13.4.3.2 Cross-Layer Proportional Delay Differentiation Scheduler

The model of the proportional service differentiation was first introduced as a per-hop-behavior (PHB) for DiffServ in wireline networks [12]. It states that certain class performance metrics should be proportional to the differentiation parameters. In particular, if we consider the case of delay differentiation in a network with C service classes, the proportional delay differentiation model imposes the following constraints for all pairs of classes:

$$\frac{\bar{d}_i(t, t + \tau)}{\bar{d}_j(t, t + \tau)} = \frac{\delta_j}{\delta_i}, \quad \text{for all } i \neq j \text{ and } i, j \in \{1, 2, \ldots, C\}, \tag{13.12}$$

where δ_i is the service differentiation parameter for class i and $\bar{d}_i(t, t + \tau)$ is the average delay for class i, $(i = 1, 2, \ldots, C)$ in the time interval $(t, t + \tau)$, where τ is the monitoring timescale.

The basic idea of proportional differentiation is that even though the actual quality level of each class may vary with traffic loads, the quality ratio between classes should remain constant in various timescales. In addition, such a quality ratio can be controlled by setting the service differentiation parameters, which provide flexible class provisioning and management. Under certain conditions (i.e., the network is well provisioned), applications with absolute delay requirements can select appropriate service classes to meet their requirements [13], even though the network offers only relative differentiation.

One of the packet scheduling algorithms that can realize the proportional delay differentiation model in a short timescale is the *waiting time priority* (WTP) scheduler [14]. In this algorithm, a packet is assigned with a weight, which increases proportionally to the packet's waiting time. Service classes with higher differentiation parameters have larger weight-increase factors. The packet with the largest weight is served first in nonpreemptive order. Formally, if $wt_{pkt}(t)$ is the waiting time of a packet pkt of class i at time t, define its *normalized waiting time* $\hat{wt}_{pkt}(t, i)$ at time t to be

$$\hat{wt}_{pkt}(t, i) = wt_{pkt}(t) \cdot \delta_i. \tag{13.13}$$

The normalized waiting time is then used as the weight for scheduling. The packet with the largest weight is then selected by the WTP scheduler for transmission. Formally, at time t it will transmit the packet pkt that satisfies

$$pkt = \arg \max_{pkt \in \mathcal{P}} \hat{wt}_{pkt}(t, i), \tag{13.14}$$

where $\mathcal{P}$ is the set of backlogged packets. It is shown that the WTP scheduler is able to approximate the proportional delay differentiation model in wireline networks under heavy traffic condition [14].

Here we introduce the *proportional service differentiation model* into the domain of wireless LANs. In contrast to wireline networks, in which flows through a router contend with each other on the outgoing link, in wireless LANs, not only do flows originating from a node contend with each other, but they also contend with flows originating from other nodes. To extend the concept of proportional service differentiation to wireless LANs, flows originating from different nodes must be considered. To address this, our proportional delay differentiation model for wireless LANs states that the relation (13.12) holds for all flows within the wireless LAN no matter whether they originate from the same node or not.

As a result of the distributed medium sharing, packet scheduling needs cooperation among all the nodes. This is in contrast to wireline networks where packets that need to be scheduled originate from the same router, and hence the packet scheduling decision can be made by the router itself only considering its own packets. We argue that delay differentiation in wireless LANs can only be achieved through a *joint packet scheduling* at the network layer and distributed coordination at the MAC layer. Therefore, we present a *cross-layer waiting time priority scheduling (CWTP) algorithm* that is able to achieve proportional delay differentiation in wireless LANs.

The CWTP algorithm divides the scheduling task into two parts, which are performed at two layers in the network stack. At the network layer, *intra-node* scheduling at node n selects a packet pkt_n^* with the longest normalized waiting time, that is, a packet pkt_n^* that satisfies

$$pkt_n^* = \arg \max_{pkt \in \mathcal{P}_n} \hat{wt}_{pkt}(t, i), \qquad (13.15)$$

where $\mathcal{P}_n$ is the set of all backlogged packets at node n. At the MAC layer, *inter-node* scheduling selects a packet pkt^* among the packets pkt_n^*, which satisfies

$$pkt^* = \arg \max_{pkt_n^* \ n \in \mathcal{N}} \hat{wt}_{pkt_n^*}(t, i), \qquad (13.16)$$

where $\mathcal{N}$ is the set of wireless nodes.

Such an intra- and inter-node scheduling algorithm can fit well the environment of wireless LANs. In particular, the intra-node scheduling can be implemented via network layer packet scheduling at each individual node and the inter-node scheduling can be implemented via medium access control that coordinates packet transmissions among nodes. Figure 13.17 illustrates such a cross-layer scheduling architecture. In this architecture, the packet scheduler at the network layer

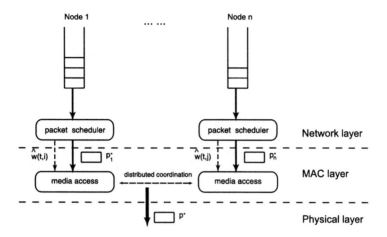

FIGURE 13.17:   Cross-layer architecture.

and the distributed coordination function at the MAC layer are coordinated using normalized packet waiting time $\hat{w}t$ as a cross-layer signal.

At the MAC layer, in order to transmit the packet with the largest normalized waiting time before ones with smaller normalized waiting times, we map the normalized waiting time $\hat{w}t$ to the backoff time b via function $b = \Phi(\hat{w}t)$. In [45], we present two mapping schemes, namely linear mapping and piecewise linear mapping to implement the function $\Phi(\hat{w}t)$.

In the linear mapping scheme, the normalized waiting time of a packet is mapped to its MAC layer backoff time via a linear function. Formally, let us consider a linear function $\phi(x) : \mathfrak{R}^+ \to \mathfrak{R}$,

$$\phi(x) = \beta - \alpha \cdot x, \tag{13.17}$$

where $\alpha, \beta > 0$ are parameters of this linear function. To ensure it is a nonnegative integer, the backoff time b (in numbers of time slots) of a packet with normalized waiting time $\hat{w}t$ is chosen as

$$b = \Phi(\hat{w}t) = \left\lceil [\phi(\hat{w}t)]^+ \right\rceil, \tag{13.18}$$

where $[x]^+ = \max(0, x)$ and $\lceil \cdot \rceil$ is the ceiling operation. These two operations round up the value of $\phi(\hat{w}t)$ to a nonnegative integer. It is obvious that α and β determine the effectiveness of the mapping function, and thus the performance of the cross-layer scheduling algorithm. We present a dynamic tuning algorithm for α and β. Let $\overline{cw}$ be the expected value of the contention window under

IEEE 802.11 DCF without differentiation. The backoff time b is uniformly chosen from $[0, \overline{cw})$. Let $\hat{wt}_{max}$ and $\hat{wt}_{min}$ be the maximum and minimum normalized waiting times, respectively. Preferably, the maximum normalized waiting time $\hat{wt}_{max}$ can be mapped to the smallest backoff time (0) for efficient channel utilization, and $\hat{wt}_{min}$ can be mapped to $\overline{cw}$ for similar contention behavior as IEEE 802.11 without differentiation.

The linear mapping scheme neglects the fact that the distribution of the normalized waiting time can be nonuniform. If there is a higher density over a certain interval of time, then it will increase the possibility of packets with different normalized waiting times being mapped into the same backoff time. It can also increase the possibility of packet collision at the MAC layer. To address these problems, we present a piecewise linear mapping scheme that considers the effect of the normalized waiting time distribution. In the piecewise linear mapping scheme, the normalized waiting times $\hat{wt}$ are divided into L intervals of equal lengths defined by points $\hat{wt}_{min} = \hat{wt}_0, \hat{wt}_1, \hat{wt}_2, \ldots, \hat{wt}_L = \hat{wt}_{max}$. During each interval, a function $\Phi_i(\hat{wt}) = \lceil [\beta_i - \alpha_i \cdot \hat{wt}]^+ \rceil$ will be used for the mapping. Figure 13.18 compares these two mapping algorithms.

We simulate the CWTP algorithm under both linear mapping and piecewise linear mapping schemes on a variety of network settings in ns-2 [41]. In the simulation, the number of nodes (N) is a parameter to show how CWTP scales to the network size. Each node in the wireless LAN sets up a connection. The transmission rate of each flow is configured to give the network an aggregated load of about 1500 Kbps.

We first show the impact of network size on the CWTP algorithm. In this experiment, two service classes with $\delta_2/\delta_1 = 2$ are supported in the network. Figure 13.19 shows the differentiation index I with different numbers of nodes in the network. The differentiation index (I) is defined as the ratio of the average delay of the two service classes. That is,

$$I = \frac{\bar{d}_1}{\bar{d}_2}, \qquad (13.19)$$

where $\bar{d}_i$ is the expected packet delay of service class i. This metric shows the effectiveness of the service differentiation—how close the differentiation result matches the differentiation goal. Ideally, in these experiments $I = 2$. We observe that both linear mapping and piecewise linear mapping schemes can lead the CWTP scheduling algorithm to achieve a delay differentiation index very close to the target value, when the network size is relatively small (the number of nodes $N < 20$). When the network size is large (e.g., $N = 50$), the piecewise linear mapping scheme performs much better than the linear mapping scheme.

In Figure 13.20, we show the instantaneous delay behaviors under these two schemes when $N = 10$. From these results, we observe that the piecewise linear

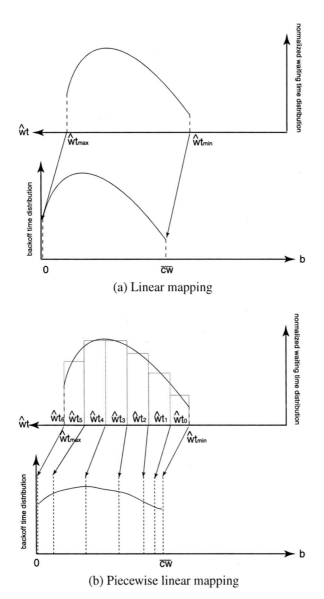

(a) Linear mapping

(b) Piecewise linear mapping

FIGURE 13.18:   Linear mapping and piecewise linear mapping: a comparison.

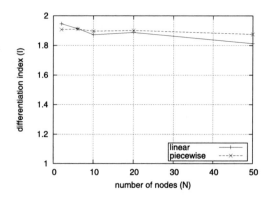

FIGURE 13.19:   Differentiation index.

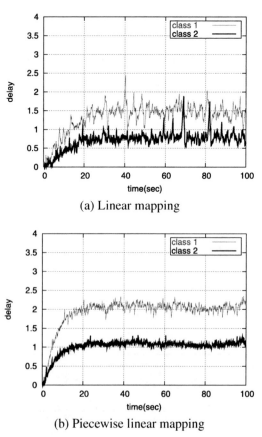

(a) Linear mapping

(b) Piecewise linear mapping

FIGURE 13.20:   Instantaneous delay behavior.

mapping scheme gives much more consistent and smooth delay behavior than the linear mapping scheme. This is because with the consideration of the normalized waiting time distribution, piecewise linear mapping significantly reduces the possibility of packet collision at the MAC layer.

13.4.3.3 Middleware-Based Adaptation Services

Now we describe the adaptation services to be provided by the middleware framework. The adaptation services work with the network level service differentiation mechanism to provide an *absolute* QoS level for applications. At the network level, service differentiation provides differentiated quality for packets from different classes. However, applications usually require a QoS level with an absolute value; hence the middleware is responsible for mapping the required QoS level to the correct service class. Our middleware achieves this goal by continually monitoring the performances of the applications and adaptively adjusting their service classes to meet their required QoS levels.

The design of our middleware adaptation framework is based on a task control model as shown in Figure 13.21a. Within the middleware control framework, the *Adaptation Task* and the *Observation Task* are represented in two respective components: the *Adapter* and the *Monitor*. The *Target System* is the differentiated network, represented by the *Classifier* in the middleware layer, as shown in Figure 13.21b. The *Control Action* is the service class selection, and *Task States* are the end-to-end performance of the multimedia application. In particular, the *Adapter* takes the end-to-end delay observed by the *Monitor* as its input, makes the service class selection decision based on the input values, and sets the service class at the classifier as its output. It is controlled by a set of conditional statements in the form of if-then rules. In [32], we presented the detailed design of rules. An example rule is illustrated as follows, where d is the current observed delay of the application, d^* is its delay bound, and $\delta(t)$ is its service differentiation parameter

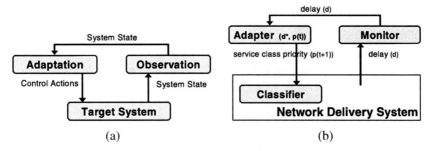

FIGURE 13.21:   Middleware control framework.

at time t:

$$\text{If} \quad (d > 2.5d^*) \tag{13.20}$$

$$\text{then} \quad \delta(t+1) = 2\delta(t). \tag{13.21}$$

We show the performance of the adaptation service integrated with the delay differentiation service over an IEEE 802.11-based wireless ad hoc test bed implementation. In the experiment, we first start an audio application that has a QoS requirement in terms of maximum packet delivery delay. Then background UDP traffic with 15,000 Bytes/s is started. From the results in Figure 13.22, we see that the average delay increases quickly from 70 to 800 ms without service differentiation and adaptation. Using the service adaptation policy in the example and the underlying delay differentiation support, we observe that the average delay for the audio application was successfully bounded to < 150 ms.

13.4.4 Comparison of QoS Architectures

The two QoS architectures described earlier support different QoS models. BM supports the IntServ model by admission control, bandwidth reservation, traffic shaping, and bandwidth renegotiations. Proportional delay differentiation supports the DiffServ model by a special per-hop forwarding behavior that relies on a joint scheduling algorithm at the MAC and network layers.

Each of these QoS architectures has its own strength and weakness. For example, it is convenient for BM to provide a per-flow "soft" bandwidth guarantee, but a flow may be rejected in admission or terminated during transmission. In the delay differentiation architecture, every flow can always send out packets, but the quality protection between different classes of packets is only "relative." Each application takes the risk and burden of choosing an appropriate service class to meet its own needs. Therefore, BM is more suitable for a small number of concurrent flows with stringent QoS requirements, whereas delay differentiation is better for a large number of flows where a few of them are QoS sensitive while the rest are not.

Despite differences in their QoS models, there is a common trait in these two architectures, which is the *cross-layer* design principle. In both architectures, there is a close interaction among application, middleware, network, and MAC layers. Together they provide an agile adaptation framework for QoS applications in wireless networks.

13.4.5 Beyond Single-Hop Wireless Networks

The two QoS architectures discussed earlier assume a single-hop ad hoc network (or wireless LAN) where each node can talk to each other directly. In this section

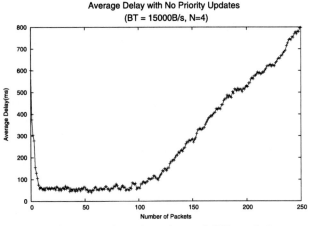

(a) Without service adaptation and differentiation

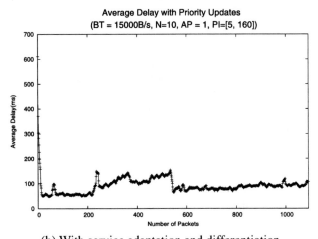

(b) With service adaptation and differentiation

FIGURE 13.22:   Performance comparison.

we discuss how to support multimedia applications in a *multi-hop* ad hoc network (or "MANET").

   Running multimedia applications over a MANET has even more challenges: (1) the network topology is dynamic, which often results in route breakage and rerouting and (2) wireless resource usage is very dynamic and complex due to location-dependent wireless contention and spatial reuse. Examples of QoS support architectures in this network include INSIGNIA [20] and SWAN [2].

INSIGNIA supports the IntServ model by reserving bandwidth over a multi-hop path and continually renegotiating the reservations via signaling. SWAN supports the DiffServ model by differentiating two classes of traffic: real time and best effort. Real-time traffic needs to go through a distributed admission control process at a flow's start-up and needs to monitor the available bandwidth of the path continuously.

Due to the dynamic nature of the multi-hop ad hoc network, robust QoS support is very difficult. Hence we ask another interesting question: how can we better support multimedia flows as part of the *best-effort* traffic in MANET? We are not concerned about any QoS model, but we are interested in how flow control at the transport layer can facilitate the transmission of multimedia traffic. Traditional flow control such as TCP relies on "probing" the network until packet lost is observed. This is certainly not an appealing method to carry multimedia traffic because frequent and large rate fluctuations are inevitable, especially in a wireless environment.

To this end, we study a special *explicit* flow control scheme called "EX-ACT" [10] where the transport layer gives explicit rate signals to the application layer. Its design rationale is as follows:

- *Router-Assisted Flow Control*: In our framework, the router explicitly gives rate signals to the flows that are currently passing it, since routers are in a better position to react to network bandwidth variations and route changes in MANET.
- *Rate-Based Transmission*: In our framework, the sender follows the rate information set by the routers, and hence the packet transmission is rate based.
- *Feasibility in MANET*: Our framework incurs additional complexity and overhead at the routers. It is *not* targeted for the large-scale Internet (where core routers have to process huge numbers of concurrent flows), but rather as a solution for the smaller scale MANET environment.

13.4.5.1 Overview

An overview of the EXACT framework is shown in Figure 13.23a. Each data packet carries a special IP header, called a *flow control header*, which is modified by the intermediate routers to signal the flow's allowed sending rate. When the packet reaches the destination, the explicit rate information is returned to the sender in a feedback packet. As a result, any bandwidth variation along the path will be returned to the sender within one RTT.

In the event of rerouting (Figure 13.23b), the first data packet traveling through the new path (R_1, R_2, R'_3) collects the new allowed rate of the flow. As a result, the sender learns the exact sending rate after only one RTT of delay after rerouting, without having to go through the additive probing phase of TCP.

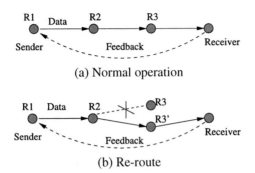

(a) Normal operation

(b) Re-route

FIGURE 13.23:   Overview of the EXACT flow control scheme.

A packet's flow control header includes two fields: *Explicit Rate* (ER) and *Current Rate* (CR). ER is the allowed sending rate of a flow. It is initially set at the sender as its maximum requested rate and is subsequently reduced by the intermediate routers to signal its allowed data rate. CR is initially set at the sender as its current sending rate and is modified by the intermediate routers to signal possible rate reduction along the path. Each router remembers the CR of the current flows in its *flow table* in order to compute each flow's fair share of bandwidth.

13.4.5.2 Router's Behavior

A router plays the central role in EXACT. A router has four major tasks: (1) keep track of current flows and their sending rates; (2) measure the current bandwidth of the outgoing wireless links; (3) compute rates for the current flows; and (4) update the header of each passing data packet.

The core part of each router is its rate computation algorithm to allocate sending rates for the competing flows. The rate computation, performed locally, is based on the current measured bandwidths of the outgoing links, as well as the current rates of the flows going through the router. Efficiency is achieved by making sure that the flows can fully occupy the outgoing wireless links. Fairness can be achieved by allocating the bandwidth "fairly" to each flow. A common fairness criterion is *max–min fairness* [5]. In max–min fairness, flows with minimum requests are granted their requests first; the remaining bandwidth resource is then divided evenly among the higher demanding flows.

Here we propose to maintain fairness among competing flows according to their *channel time* demands to access the wireless channel. The wireless link's bandwidth at the MAC layer is measured using the monitor as described earlier. To represent a flow's resource request, we normalize a flow's requested rate to its next-hop link's bandwidth as $TF_i = r_i/b_i$, where r_i is the flow's data rate and b_i is the current bandwidth of the link. The max–min allocation is then performed on top of the requests of the flows: TF_i, $i = 1$ to N. Since each flow obtains a throughput proportional to its next-hop link's bandwidth, we call it *bandwidth-proportional max–min fair*. For details of rate computation, interested readers are referred to [10].

13.4.5.3 Multimedia Streaming Using EXACT

EXACT provides explicit rate signals for the flows, but these rate signals may be fluctuating. In order to support multimedia streaming on top of EXACT, our framework supports *split-level* adaptations. At the transport layer, EXACT provides explicit rate signals to the upper applications. It serves as the upper bound of the application's sending rate. Within this upper bound, each application may adjust its own sending rate based on its adaptation policies, for example, to maintain smooth rate changes for multimedia flows.

Such *informed* adaptation is possible only with EXACT's explicit rate signals. Although all the flows are treated as best effort at the transport layer, using EXACT as the flow control scheme facilitates running multimedia applications over MANET.

13.4.5.4 Evaluations

Here we show the efficiency of EXACT compared to traditional TCP flow control. Using the ns-2 simulator, we create a MANET with 30 nodes moving in a 1500-m by 300-m space with a maximum speed of 20 m/s and different pause times (0, 5, 10, 15, and 20 s) to create different levels of network dynamics. Under these mobility patterns, we compare EXACT with TCP-Reno and TCP-SACK. For each scenario, we average the total number of reliably transmitted packets over 10 runs for each scheme. The results in Figure 13.24 show that under all mobility

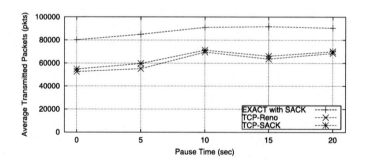

FIGURE 13.24:   Comparison of EXACT with TCP under different mobility patterns.

scenarios, EXACT overall outperforms TCP-Reno and TCP-SACK by 42 and 36% more packets, respectively. This demonstrates the effectiveness of the EX-ACT flow control scheme in a dynamic MANET environment.

13.5 DESIGN PRINCIPLES LEARNED

In this section we summarize various design principles we have learned in our study.

13.5.1 Cross-Layer Strategies

Cross-layer resource management strategies in wireless networks have attracted increasing attention in recent years.[1] The need for cross-layer design is based on two characteristics of wireless networks. First, the wireless medium is a shared medium. Sending a packet from one node to another creates interference to other nodes in the same neighborhood. Therefore, in designing network packet scheduling algorithms, we have to consider the interaction between the network layer and the MAC layer due to wireless interference. At the network layer, only packets within the same host are scheduled; interhost packet transmissions can only be enabled at the MAC layer.

Second, resources are generally scarce and variable in wireless environments, and hence they must be managed carefully. For example, we translate multimedia application requirements into bandwidth and CPU resource requirements and use controllers at the lower level to monitor the load on the resource. The feedbacks from the controllers are then used to tune the network and CPU schedulers so as to satisfy multimedia application requirements. In this picture, the control flow of resource management is two way. Variations in the load on the resource are fed by the lower-level controllers to the application so that the application can adapt. The chosen operating quality level of the multimedia application is fed to the lower-level controllers so that the schedulers can be tuned accordingly.

13.5.2 Tightly Coupled Resources

In wireless networks, resources are tightly coupled with each other. Therefore, we need to adopt *coordinated* resource management strategies because resources cannot be managed independently of each other.

---

[1] Interested readers are referred to [1] for more research results in cross-layer design for wireless networks.

For example, if a lot of bandwidth is available, a bandwidth management scheme may allot a high operating quality level to a media streaming application. However, if CPU resources are scarce, a CPU management scheme will allot the same application a lower operating quality level. Obviously, this is a contradictory scenario, hence the resource management strategy must be coordinated between resources.

A direct result of the tight coupling of resources means that we need a multilevel resource management strategy. For example, some resources are global to the hosts (nodes) in a wireless network, for example, network bandwidth. Other resources are global within a single host, for example, energy. Thus, a multilevel resource management strategy is to let the network-wide resource management constrain the host's resource availability and let the host-wide resource management constrain each application's resource availability.

13.5.3 Adaptation of Both Software and Hardware

Resource adaptation should not be limited to software only. To achieve greater flexibility, the middleware layer needs to consider the adaptability of both software and hardware. For example, adaptive hardware such as adaptive CPU and wireless network interface cards can trade off performance for energy consumption; multimedia applications can trade off quality for resource demand.

Software and hardware adaptation and optimization can take place at different time granularities. At a coarse time granularity, for example, when an application starts, we can optimize to achieve high application utility and desired battery lifetime. At a finer time granularity, for example, when the application renders a frame, we can optimize to save more energy.

13.5.4 Suitable QoS Model

Selecting a suitable QoS model is the most important step in designing a QoS support architecture because it has a fundamental impact on the overall architecture. This is especially true in wireless networks due to the scarcity of bandwidth resources.

While selecting a QoS model, we need to keep in mind the unique characteristics of wireless networks. The QoS models in the Internet, such as IntServ and DiffServ, should be carefully re-examined. For example, the main challenge of deploying IntServ over the Internet is the scalability problem in keeping per-flow state at the Internet routers. In contrast, the challenge of adopting IntServ in wireless networks is not the scalability problem; instead, it is the time-varying resource availability problem, which may result in repeated QoS setups. Relative DiffServ may be a more suitable QoS model here since it does not require the QoS setup phase and hence avoids the difficulty and overhead in doing repeated admission control and resource signaling.

13.6 SUMMARY AND FURTHER READING

In this chapter we discussed QoS support in mobile operating systems and mobile wireless networks for multimedia applications. We have shown that with careful OS design with respect to scheduling and dynamic voltage scaling, we can achieve deadline guarantees for wireless multimedia applications as well as energy efficiency of mobile nodes to extend the application lifetime. Furthermore, we have shown two cross-layer networking architectures that support statistical bandwidth and delay guarantees in cooperative wireless single-hop environments. The bandwidth management architecture realizes the IntServ QoS model, while the proportional delay differentiation architecture realizes the DiffServ model. We have shown that by leveraging the cross-layer design principle, both of them can achieve different levels of QoS protection and are suitable in many situations in wireless networks.

Wireless networks are at the critical junction of being widely accepted into everyday life by the proliferation of small wireless devices such as smart phones, as well as the maturation of VoIP software. Now many municipal governments are planning to roll out city-wide mesh 802.11 networks to the general public. Such networks are owned by a single entity, for example, the city government, so that cooperation among the nodes can be assumed. It is likely that the IntServ QoS model can be implemented by per-user bandwidth provisioning based on their subscriptions, considering the fact that the number of users and flows should be manageable for a city-scale network. Higher speed 802.11 standards such as 802.11n using MIMO are also going to alleviate the scarcity of wireless bandwidth. Wireless multimedia may become the next killer application, and QoS is certainly an important enabler in this picture.

Beyond the references cited in this chapter, the reader is recommended to read Chapter 4 on Bandwidth Adaptation Mechanisms, Chapter 10 on Network-Adaptive Media Transport, and Chapter 12 on Cross-Layer Wireless Multimedia.

REFERENCES

[1] *IEEE Transactions on Vehicular Technology, Special Issue on Cross-layer Design in Mobile Ad hoc Networks and Wireless Sensor Networks*, 55(3), May 2006.

[2] G.-S. Ahn, A. T. Campbell, A. Veres, and L.-H. Sun. "SWAN: Service Differentiation in Stateless Wireless Ad Hoc Networks." In *IEEE INFOCOM 2002*, New York, NY, June 2002.

[3] H. Balakrishnan, V. N. Padmanabhan, S. Seshan, and R. H. Katz. "A Comparison of Mechanisms for Improving TCP Performance over Wireless Links," in *ACM Sig-Comm*, Stanford, CA, 1996.

[4] B. Bensaou, Y. Wang, and C. Ko. "Fair Medium Access in 802.11 Based Wireless Ad Hoc Networks," in *IEEE MobiHoc*, Boston, MA, 2000.

[5] D. Bertsekas and R. Gallager. *Data Networks (2nd Ed.)*. Prentice-Hall, 1992.

[6] V. Bharghavan, K. W. Lee, S. Lu, S. Hu, J. R. Li, and D. Dwyer. "The Timely Adaptive Resource Management Architecture," *IEEE Personal Communication Magazine*, 5(4), August 1998.

[7] S. Brandt. "Performance Analysis of Soft Real-Time Systems," in *20th IEEE International Performance, Computing and Networking Conference (IPCCC 2001)*, April 2001.

[8] A. Chandra, M. Adler, P. Goyal, and P. Shenoy. "Surplus Fair Scheduling: A Proportional-Share CPU Scheduling Algorithm for Symmetric Multiprocessors," in *Proceedings of 4th Symposium on Operating System Design and Implementation*, San Diego, CA, October 2000.

[9] A. Chandrakasan, S. Sheng, and R. W. Brodersen. "Low-power CMOS Digital Design," *IEEE Journal of Solid-State Circuits*, 27:473–484, April 1992.

[10] K. Chen, K. Nahrstedt, and N. Vaidya. "The Utility of Explicit Rate-Based Flow Control in Mobile Ad Hoc Networks," in *Proc. of IEEE Wireless Communications and Networking Conference (WCNC 2004)*, Atlanta, GA, March 2004.

[11] H. H. Chu and K. Nahrstedt. "CPU Service Classes for Multimedia Applications," in *Proceedings of IEEE International Conference on Multimedia Computing and Systems*, pages 296–301, Florence, Italy, June 1999.

[12] C. Dovrolis and P. Ramanathan. "A Case for Relative Differentiated Services and the Proportional Differentiation Model," *IEEE Network*, 13(5):26–34, 1999.

[13] C. Dovrolis and P. Ramanathan. "Dynamic Class Selection: From Relative Differentiation to Absolute QoS," in *IEEE International Conference on Network Protocols*, 2001.

[14] C. Dovrolis, P. Ramanathan, and D. Stiliadis. "Proportional Differentiated Services: Delay Differentiation and Packet Scheduling," *IEEE/ACM Transactions on Networking*, 10:12–26, February 2002.

[15] D. Eckhardt and P. Steenkiste. "Effort-Limited Fair (elf) Scheduling for Wireless Networks," in *IEEE InfoCom*, Tel Aviv, Israel, March 2000.

[16] K. Flautner and T. Mudge. "Vertigo: Automatic Performance-Setting for Linux," in *Proceedings of 5th Symposium on Operating Systems Design and Implementation*, Boston, MA, December 2002.

[17] T. Ishihara and H. Yasuura. "Voltage Scheduling Problem for Dynamically Variable Voltage Processors," in *Proceedings of International Symposium on Low-Power Electronics and Design*, Monterey, CA, 1998.

[18] M. Jones, D. Rosu, and M. Rosu. "CPU Reservations and Time Constraints: Efficient, Predictable Scheduling of Independent Activities," in *Proceedings of 16th Symposium on Operating Systems Principles*, St-Malo, France, October 1997.

[19] V. Kanodia, C. Li, A. Sabharwal, B. Sadeghi, and E. Knightly. "Distributed Multi-hop Scheduling and Medium Access with Delay and Throughput Constraints," in *ACM MobiCom*, Rome, Italy, 2001.

[20] S.-B. Lee, G.-S. Ahn, X. Zhang, and A. T. Campbell. "INSIGNIA: An IP-Based Quality of Service Framework for Mobile Ad Hoc Networks," *Journal of Parallel and Distributed Computing*, 60(4):374–406, 2000.

[21] C. L. Liu and J. W. Layland. "Scheduling Algorithms for Multiprogramming in a Hard Real-Time Environment," *JACM*, 20(1):46–61, January 1973.

[22] S. Lu, T. Nandagopal, and V. Bharghavan. "Design and Analysis of an Algorithm for Fair Service in Error-Prone Wireless Channels," *ACM Wireless Networks*, 6(4), 2000.

[23] H. Luo, P. Medvedev, J. Cheng, and S. Lu. "A Self-Coordinating Approach to Distributed Fair Queuing in Ad Hoc Wireless Networks," in *IEEE InfoCom*, Anchorage, AK, 2001.

[24] H. Luo, S. Lu, and V. Bharghavan. "A New Model for Packet Scheduling in Multihop Wireless Networks," in *ACM MobiCom*, Boston, MA, August 2000.

[25] L. Magalhaes and R. Kravets. "Mmtp: Multimedia Multiplexing Transport Protocol," in *Workshop on Data Communication in Latin America and Caribbean (SIGCOMM-LA)*, 2001.

[26] M. Mirhakkak, N. Schult, and D. Thomson. "Dynamic Bandwidth Management and Adaptive Applications for a Variable Bandwidth Wireless Environment," *IEEE Journal of Selected Areas in Communications*, 19(10), October 2001.

[27] Shivajit Mohapatra, Radu Cornea, Nikil Dutt, Alex Nicolau, and Nalini Venkatasubramanian. "Integrated Power Management for Video Streaming to Mobile Devices," in *Proceedings of ACM Multimedia*, Berkeley, CA, November 2003.

[28] M. Moser, D. Jokanovi, and N. Shiratori. "An Algorithm for Multidimensional Multiple-Choice Knapsack Problem," *IEEE Transactions on Fundamentals*, 80(2), March 1997.

[29] R. Neugebauer and D. McAuley. "Energy Is Just Another Resource: Energy Accounting and Energy Pricing in the Nemesis OS," in *Proceedings of 8th IEEE Workshop on Hot Topics in Operating Systems (HotOS-VIII)*, Schloss Elmau, Germany, May 2001.

[30] J. Nieh and M. S. Lam. "The Design, Implementation and Evaluation of SMART: A Scheduler for Multimedia Applications," in *Proceedings of 16th Symposium on Operating Systems Principles*, St-Malo, France, October 1997.

[31] Jason Nieh and Monica S. Lam. "A Smart Scheduler for Multimedia Applications," *ACM Transaction on Computer Systems*, 21(2):117–163, 2003.

[32] C. S. Ong, Y. Xue, and K. Nahrstedt. "A Middleware for Service Adaptation in Differentiated 802.11 Wireless Networks," in *Proc. of The Workshop on Coordinated Quality of Service in Distributed Systems (COQODS), held in conjunction with IEEE International Conference on Networks (ICON)*, Singapore, November 2004.

[33] C. Pereira, R. Gupta, P. Spanos, and M. Srivastava. "Power-Aware API for Embedded and Portable Systems." In R. Graybill and R. Melhem, editors, *Power Aware Computing*, pages 153–166. Plenum/Kluwer Publisher, 2002.

[34] P. Pillai, H. Huang, and K. G. Shin. "Energy-Aware Quality of Service Adaptation." Technical report CSE-TR-479-03, University of Michigan, 2003.

[35] D. Pisinger. "A Minimal Algorithm for the Multiple-Choice Knapsack Problem," *European Journal of Operational Research*, 83:94–410, 1995.

[36] R. Rajkumar, K. Juvva, A. Molano, and S. Oikawa. "Resource Kernels: A Resource-Centric Approach to Real-Time Systems," in *Proceedings of SPIE Multimedia Computing and Networking Conference*, January 1998.

[37] R. Rajkumar, C. Lee, J. Lehoczky, and D. Siewiorek. "A Resource Allocation Model for QoS Management," in *Proceedings of 18th IEEE Real-Time Systems Symposium*, San Francisco, CA, December 1997.

[38] S. H. Shah, K. Chen, and K. Nahrstedt. "Dynamic Bandwidth Management for Single-Hop Ad Hoc Wireless Networks," *ACM/Kluwer Mobile Networks and Applications (MONET) Journal*, 10(1), 2005.

[39] S. H. Shah and K. Nahrstedt. "Channel-Aware Throughput Fairness in Multi-cell Wireless Lans," in *Proc. IEEE VTC'04-Fall*, Los Angeles, California, September 2004.

[40] P. Sinha, T. Nandagopal, N. Venkitaraman, R. Sivakumar, and V. Bharghavan. "WTCP: A Reliable Transport Protocol for Wireless Wide-Area Networks," in *ACM MobiCom*, Seattle, WA, August 1999.

[41] Web Site. The network simulator ns-2. *http://www.isi.edu/nsnam/ns/*, 2005.

[42] R. Steinmetz and K. Nahrstedt. *Multimedia Systems*. Springer Verlag, Heidelberg, 2004.

[43] H. Tokuda and T. Kitayama. "Dynamic qos Control Based on Real-Time Threads," in *3rd International Workshop on Network and Operating Systems Support for Digital Audio and Video (NOSSDAV)*, November 1993.

[44] N. Vaidya, P. Bahl, and S. Gupta. "Distributed Fair Scheduling in a Wireless Lan," in *ACM MobiCom*, Boston, MA, August 2000.

[45] Y. Xue, K. Chen, and K. Nahrstedt. "Achieving Proportional Delay Differentiation in Wireless LAN via Cross-Layer Scheduling," *Journal of Wireless Communications and Mobile Computing, special issue on Emerging WLAN Technologies and Applications*, 4(8):849–866, 2004.

[46] Y. Xue, B. Li, and K. Nahrstedt. "Optimal Resource Allocation in Wireless Ad Hoc Networks: A Price-Based Approach," *IEEE Transactions on Mobile Computing*, 5(4):347–364, April 2006.

[47] Y. Yang and R. Kravets. "Throughput Guarantees for Multi-priority Traffic in Ad Hoc Networks," in *IEEE MASS*, Fort Lauderdale, FL, October 2004.

[48] W. Yuan and K. Nahrstedt. "Integration of Dynamic Voltage Scaling and Soft Real-Time Scheduling for Open Mobile Systems," in *Proceedings of 12th International Workshop on Network and OS Support for Digital Audio and Video*, Miami Beach, FL, May 2002.

[49] W. Yuan and K. Nahrstedt. "Energy-Efficient Soft Real-Time CPU Scheduling for Mobile Multimedia Systems," in *Proceedings of 19th Symposium on Operating Systems Principles*, Bolton Landing, NY, October 2003.

[50] W. Yuan and K. Nahrstedt. "Energy-Efficient CPU Scheduling for Multimedia Applications," *ACM Transactions on Computer Systems*, 24(3):1–40, 2006.

[51] W. Yuan, K. Nahrstedt, S. Adve, D. Jones, and R. Kravets. "Grace-1: Cross-Layer Adaptation for Multimedia Quality and Battery Energy," *IEEE Transactions on Mobile Computing*, 5(7):799–815, 2006.

[52] H. Zeng, X. Fan, C. Ellis, A. Lebeck, and A. Vahdat. "ECOSystem: Managing Energy as a First Class Operating System Resource," in *Proceedings of 10th Intl. Conf. on ASPLOS*, pages 123–132, San Jose, CA, October 2002.

PART E

SYSTEMS

CHAPTER   14 Streaming Media on Demand and Live Broadcast
              (Philip A. Chou)

CHAPTER   15 Real-Time Communication: Internet Protocol Voice and Video
              Telephony and Teleconferencing
              (Yi Liang, Yen-Chi Lee, and Andy Teng)

CHAPTER   16 Adaptive Media Playout
              (Eckehard Steinbach, Yi Liang, Mark Kalman, and
              Bernd Girod)

14

Streaming Media on Demand and Live Broadcast

Philip A. Chou

14.1 INTRODUCTION

Media on demand is a user scenario epitomized by playing back audio or video locally from a CD or DVD, whereas *live broadcast* is a user scenario epitomized by tuning in to a radio or television program. In the former scenario, the user has control over the start time for specific content, and in addition may have various other interactive controls (fast forward, pause, seek, etc.). In the latter scenario, the user simply joins an ongoing session and has little control except the ability to leave. While in the session, the user hears and sees the same content at the same time as other users in the session.

Today it is common to see both of these scenarios fulfilled by content delivered over the Internet. A subscriber to any of a number of music services, for example, can click on any of millions of songs and hear them on demand. Numerous Internet radio stations have sprung up, offering broadcast content either free or by subscription. Video content is also popular, offering news shorts, movie trailers, and so forth on demand, as well as live news feeds available at various web sites.

How are these scenarios enabled, technically? This chapter pulls together components from the previous chapters, while adding fundamental elements such as buffering, to outline the construction of systems for streaming media on demand and live broadcast over the Internet and over other IP networks such as wireless networks within the home.

Section 14.2 provides an overview of architectures, protocols, and format issues. Section 14.3 covers buffering and timing fundamentals. Section 14.4 details how media data may be communicated in a system for streaming media on demand. Section 14.5 details how media data may be communicated in a system for live broadcast.

14.2 ARCHITECTURES, PROTOCOLS, AND FILE FORMATS

In this section, we review the basic architectures of systems for streaming media on demand and live streaming, covering the roles of the encoder, media file, server, network, buffer, and client. We introduce basic elements of the communication protocols required for streaming media on demand. These elements come in layers and include (from top to bottom) content discovery; file specification and interactive control (start, stop, pause, fast forward, seek); stream selection and coding rate control; congestion control (transmission rate control); and the transport protocol. We mention the continuum between sender-driven and receiver-driven protocols, and we discuss some of the related standards (RTP, RTSP, etc.). Finally we cover the basic elements of file formats: header information, streams, data units, and indexing, and we comment on some of the related standards (MPEG4, QuickTime, ASF, etc.). We also discuss content format in general terms: multi bit rate (MBR) coding vs. scalable coding, the details for which we refer to Chapters 5 and 6.

14.2.1 Architectures

Streaming media on demand and live broadcast require somewhat different architectures, as depicted in Figure 14.1. Figure 14.1a pertains to streaming media on demand, while Figure 14.1b pertains to live broadcast. In streaming media on demand, a source of media is encoded off line and the encoded source is placed into a media file. The format of the media file may be specialized to support various modes of streaming, as discussed in Section 14.2.3. The media file is placed

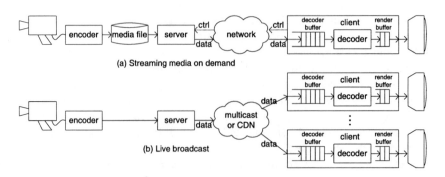

FIGURE 14.1:   (a) Streaming media on demand. (b) Live broadcast.

in a location on the server from which it can be streamed. Various protocols between the server and the client, as discussed in Section 14.2.2, are used to stream the media across the network to the client. During streaming, the client temporarily buffers the encoded media data in a *decoder buffer* before decoding and then temporarily buffers the decoded media data in a *render buffer* before rendering the media, or presenting the media to the user. The render buffer is usually fairly short—a frame or two—and is used to buffer the relatively large decoded frames after a variable amount of decoder computation time. The decoder buffer, however, is usually relatively long and is used for a variety of purposes: network jitter compensation, error recovery, bandwidth management, and variable rate coding. Indeed the decoder buffer is a key element in streaming media on demand and is usually simply called the *client buffer*. In some client devices, such as desktop computers, the client buffer can be quite large, indeed, large enough to store the entire media content, such as a movie. In other client devices, such as mobile phones and consumer electronics, the client buffer may be fairly limited, capable of storing at most only a few seconds of encoded media content. In all cases, the user is generally able to control the experience through VCR-like commands such as play, fast forward, stop, and seek. Communication between the server and the client can be tailored to the resources of the client and to the network connection between the server and the client.

In streaming media on demand, because the entire file is available to the server ahead of time and because the server can individualize streaming to each client, there is great flexibility in which parts of the media file are transmitted at any given time. For example, if the client buffer is sufficiently large and the network bandwidth to the client is sufficiently large, then the server can look arbitrarily far ahead, streaming the media to the client faster than real time, essentially downloading the media file to the client while the client is simultaneously playing back the content in real time. This is sometimes called *progressive downloading* instead of streaming, although it is really just an extreme case of streaming with a large client buffer and a network bandwidth that is larger than the bit rate at which the content is encoded—the latter henceforth is known as the *source coding rate*. If the file format satisfies some basic properties, such as the ability to be decoded sequentially, then progressive downloading can be accomplished using any of a number of simple file transfer protocols, such as FTP over TCP/IP or HTTP over TCP/IP. Thus, progressive downloading can often be done using an ordinary FTP or web server. Even if the client has a limited media buffer, progressive downloading over TCP/IP can be done using simple TCP flow control. Specifically, the client can accept data from its TCP connection if and only if there is space in its media buffer. This technique was popularized by SHOUTcast, an early streaming music service [30].

Progressive downloading is a special case of streaming media on demand, which works only if the network bandwidth (specifically, the TCP fair share of the path between the server and the client) is larger than the source coding rate, on average. Of course, the network bandwidth may fluctuate widely, as competing communication processes begin and end or even (if wireless networks are involved) when there are interfering elements, such as people walking near an antenna, turning on a microwave oven, or picking up a cordless phone. Furthermore, a user generally wants an average quality commensurate with the highest possible source coding rate, not a source coding rate less than the worst-case network bandwidth. Hence, it is generally desirable or necessary to adapt the source coding rate to the available transmission rate. Herein lie many of the intricacies of streaming media on demand, affecting the communication protocol between the client and the server (covered in Section 14.2.2), file format (covered in Section 14.2.3), and rate control (covered in Section 14.4).

In contrast, in live broadcast, as depicted in Figure 14.1b, the encoder may be directly connected to the server through an encoder buffer. To maintain a fixed and acceptably short end-to-end delay, the encoder buffer must contain only a limited amount of data. Thus the server can access data only so far ahead of the client's playback point, rather than access arbitrary data in a file. This restricts adaptivity of what the server can transmit to the client. Furthermore, in live broadcast, the server ordinarily communicates to multiple clients simultaneously through a multicast or content distribution network of some kind. (See Chapter 19 for more information on infrastructure-based content distribution systems.) Thus, in live broadcast, it is generally not possible for the server to give clients VCR-like interactive access to the media.[1] Furthermore, in live broadcast, it is generally difficult for the server to adapt its transmission rate to the bandwidths of particular clients. However, some adaptation is possible, using, for example, receiver-driven layered multicast (RLM) [28,29]. Finally, in live broadcast, it is generally difficult for the server to use retransmission-based error control due to the so-called negative acknowledgment (NAK) implosion problem, in which the server would potentially have to handle retransmissions to a huge number of clients. Hence, error control becomes an especially acute issue for live broadcast. Section 14.5 is dedicated to all of these issues. Thus, in the following, up until Section 14.5 we will consider only streaming media on demand.

There has been a fair amount of work on video "on demand" systems that, rather than devoting a unique stream to each user, multicast a relatively small number of time-staggered streams to an unlimited number of users who may start the video on demand or nearly on demand [4]. Such systems work by, for example, devoting some of the multicast streams to enabling users to "catch up" to one of the main multicast streams. VCR-like functionalities such as fast forward are not

---

[1] Of course, it is always possible for clients to cache the broadcasts and then enable local playback of the cached content with VCR-like functionality, as is done with many personal video recorders (e.g., TiVo, Replay TV) and set top boxes (e.g., Comcast) today.

generally available, although of course some of these can be partially recovered through client-side caching. These systems have been mainly of interest to the cable/satellite TV industry, who may be able to afford a dozen full-bandwidth multicast channels flowing simultaneously into a set top box to enable a single movie on demand. However, this approach is not generally possible when the bandwidth into a client is at a premium and the client wishes to make full use of that bandwidth for the highest possible quality. Hence we will not address this approach further in this chapter, but rather leave the subject to further reading.

14.2.2 Communication Protocols

Streaming media on demand requires a large number of communication protocols at different levels. At the topmost level are protocols for content discovery and connection to a specific streaming media server. Typically, content discovery is done "out of band," for example, by browsing a web page or receiving a link to the content in an email message. In either case the link would typically have a form such as

```
http://www.microsoft.com/directory/contentname.asx
http://www.realnetworks.com/directory/contentname.ram
http://www.apple.com/directory/contentname.mov
```

which are, respectively, representative of links to content from Microsoft Windows Media, RealNetworks RealMedia, and Apple QuickTime. These uniform resource locators (URLs) point, actually, to small auxiliary, metadata, or reference files typically located on a web server rather than to the media file itself. An asx file, for example, is actually an XML file describing the URL of the media server and the specific name of the media file on the server, including the protocol and potentially other parameters and content presentation instructions [17]. RealMedia uses a similar format, called ram. Figure 14.2 provides examples of such auxiliary files.[2] QuickTime accomplishes a similar task with a small reference movie file in the QuickTime mov format.

Once an auxiliary file is retrieved from a web server or other location, its file name extension and MIME type indicate that the default client software (e.g., media player) should be launched, and the auxiliary file is then read by the client application or embedded object or control (known hereafter simply as the client).

---

[2]The auxiliary file can provide minor scripting of the presentation, such as insertion of advertisements and player background color. However, if more complex scripting is needed, an alternative or additional level of indirection, the SMIL file, can be used. SMIL is a variant of HTML capable of describing fairly complex multimedia presentations involving, for example, fading from one piece of content into another at a particular time in the presentation, integrating with images and text, etc. Originally promulgated by RealNetworks, it was substantially reworked by a number of interested parties and is now a W3C recommendation [3].

```
<ASX Version="3.0">
<ENTRY>
<REF HREF="mms://streamingmedia/studios/0505/24721/MTV_XBOX_preview_160k.wmv" />
</ENTRY>
<ENTRY>
<REF HREF="mms://winmedianw/studios/0505/24721/MTV_XBOX_preview_160k.wmv" />
</ENTRY>
</ASX>
```

(a)

```
# First URL that opens a related info pane.
rtsp://helixserver.example.com/video3.rm?rpcontextheight=350
&rpcontextwidth=300&rpcontexturl="http://www.example.com/relatedinfo2.html"
&rpcontexttime=5.5&rpvideofillcolor=rgb(30,60,200)
#
# Second URL that keeps the same related info pane,
# but changes the media playback pane's background color.
rtsp://helixserver.example.com/video4.rm?rpcontexturl=_keep &rpvideofillcolor=red
```

(b)

FIGURE 14.2:   Auxiliary files describing where to find streaming media content. (a) An ASX file, from Microsoft. (b) A RAM file, from RealNetworks.

At the appropriate time, the client contacts the server using the URL for the content, for example,

```
rtsp://wms.microsoft.com/directory/contentname.wmv
rtsp://helixserver.example.com/audio1.rm?start=55&end=1:25
rtsp://qtserver.apple.com/directory/contentname.mov
```

where the prefix indicates the streaming protocol used, and various optional suffixes can pass information to the server, such as seek point and play speed.

The "streaming protocol" is a high-level control protocol enabling the client to interactively control playback using VCR-like functions, including start, stop, pause, fast forward, and seek. These commands are typically communicated reliably over a TCP connection. Although various roughly equivalent proprietary protocols are used here, one protocol that is now widely adopted is the Real Time Streaming Protocol (RTSP), which is codified by the Internet Engineering Task Force (IETF) Request for Comments (RFC) 2326 [37]. RTSP is an HTTP-like protocol, including commands to play and stop. Sample commands are shown in Table 14.1. Although the commands appear very basic, extensions can be defined using the SET_PARAMETER command, for example, to allow dynamic selection of particular streams from the media file. As discussed in the next section, a media file generally offers several streams, not only an audio stream and a video stream, but potentially several audio and video streams, for example, for different languages, subtitles, source coding rates, etc. Some of these, such as languages

Table 14.1:   RTSP protocol.

DESCRIBE	Retrieves description of presentation, usually in Session Description Protocol (SDP) format [19], together with all initialization information.
SETUP	Causes server to allocate resources for a stream; specifies transport protocol; starts an RTSP session.
SET_PARAMETER	Specifies stream bit rate, etc.
PLAY	Starts data transmission of a stream from a specified time point at a specified speed.
PAUSE	Temporarily halts stream without freeing server resources.
TEARDOWN	Frees resources associated with the stream; ends an RTSP session.

and subtitles, must ultimately be user-selectable, while others, such as source coding rate, may be automatically selectable by the server and/or client. The SET_PARAMETER command can be used to pass information from the client to the server to enable dynamic stream selection.

The "streaming protocol" also enables the client to specify which lower level data transport protocol to use. The data transport protocol is usually either RTP over UDP or RTP over TCP (the only two transport protocols that are standardized with RTSP) or HTTP over TCP (which can be specified with nonstandardized streaming protocols). Systems such as Windows Media and Helix implement multiple transport protocols and use whichever protocol is most appropriate for a given situation. For example, HTTP over TCP may be used when there are firewall issues to be avoided. RTP over UDP or RTP over TCP is usually preferred for bandwidth efficiency. However, when RTP over UDP is used, there must be a proprietary means of transmission rate control (i.e., congestion control) and error control (i.e., packet loss recovery). To date, there is no standard means of transmission rate control and error control for RTP (Real Time Transport Protocol, IETF RFC 3550 [36]). RTP is essentially only a packet format that adds a timestamp, a sequence number, a contributing source identifier, and a payload type and format on top of an ordinary UDP packet. As with UDP, the application is left to perform transmission rate control and error control. RTCP (Real Time Control Protocol, IETF RFC 3551 [35]) is often paired with RTP, but provides only a format with which receivers may provide statistical feedback to the sender. There is no standard protocol by which receivers may provide timely feedback to the sender. This makes RTP+RTCP over UDP inherently *not interoperable*, proprietary, and hence (in the author's opinion) of limited use as a standard. However, the IETF is currently at work trying to change this.

The Windows Media system uses a particular form of transmission rate control and error control for RTP over UDP. Transmission rate control is currently based on constant bit rate transmission from the server, at the source coding rate of the content. By monitoring its buffer, the client can determine whether congestion is occurring and, if so, can signal to the server to change to a stream with a lower source coding rate. Roughly, if the client buffer duration drops below an adaptive theshold or if the packet loss rate rises above an adaptive threshold, then congestion is detected and the stream transmission or source coding rate is switched down. The extended absence of congestion allows the stream transmission/source coding rate to be switched up.

An alternative method of transmission rate control would be to use, for example, either a TCP-friendly rate control (TFRC) algorithm [13,18] or a TCP-like congestion control algorithm (i.e., window-based additive increase and multiplicative decrease without retransmission or in-order delivery). Both TFRC and a TCP-like congestion control are being standardized as two profiles in the umbrella Datagram Congestion Control Protocol (DCCP) [14,15,25]. However, such a transmission rate control protocol must be paired with a source coding rate control protocol, since the source coding rate of the content must also, at least over the long run, rise and fall with the transmission rate and yet it may not be possible or desirable to make the source coding rate always equal to the transmission rate. A potential source coding rate control algorithm that can be paired with an arbitrary transmission rate protocol is the rate-distortion optimized (RaDiO) scheduling algorithm described in Chapter 10. Section 14.4 presents an alternative method based on optimal control theory.

Error control in Windows Media is currently based on selective retransmission. If the client detects gaps in the packet sequence numbers, it sends a NAK to the server, which retransmits the missing packet(s). The number of packets requested for retransmission is limited to a percentage of the overall bandwidth. Audio packets are given highest priority, while video packets closest to their playout deadlines are given lowest priority, on the presumption that if the client is scrambling to recover packets in a bandwidth-limited situation, then these packets are the most likely to miss their playback deadlines even if they are retransmitted. A more precise way of prioritizing retransmissions, of course, is using the rate-distortion optimized scheduling algorithm, as described in Chapter 10. Rate-distortion optimized scheduling will optimize user quality under deadline pressure. Regardless of the scheduling and retransmission algorithm, some packets may remain missing at their playback deadlines. Hence in such cases the client must ultimately decide whether to stall playback until the packets can be recovered or conceal the missing packets. The Windows Media player chooses to stall until all audio packets can be recovered, while skipping lost video packets. Lost video packets can be dealt with by some form of error concealment, as discussed in Chapter 2. A rudimentary form of error concealment is to freeze until the next I frame.

14.2.3 File Formats

The greatest challenge for streaming media on demand is adapting the content of a fixed media file to various network and client conditions. Unlike so-called *real-time communication* (RTC), such as telephony, conferencing, and online gaming (covered in Chapter 15), in streaming media on demand the encoder must encode its content off line, possibly years before it is actually streamed. Thus it cannot have direct knowledge of the communication channel selected (including the capacity and loss rate of the network path and the capacity of the client buffer) nor can it have direct knowledge of the instantaneous communication state (including the level of network congestion or interference and the state of the client buffer). Instead, the encoder must build a certain degree of flexibility into the media file and leave it to the server to adapt the media file to the network and client conditions.

As an extreme case, the media file may be simply a raw, uncompressed recording of the content, and the server may spawn an online encoder to adaptively compress the content for each connected client. However, this is usually infeasible, both because of the high storage requirements for uncompressed media and the high computational requirements for real-time encoding for multiple simultaneous clients. As a somewhat less extreme case, the media file may be a high bit rate encoding of the content, and the server may spawn an online transcoder, or *transrater*, to adaptively recompress the content for each connected client. At the opposite end of the spectrum, the media file may contain an immutable encoding of the content, which the server simply copies onto the network connection (such as in the progressive download scenario). Usually, however, a better engineering trade-off involves making the media file format flexible enough for the server to simply index into the file and extract the content that it wants for specific users. For this, the format of the file, and possibly the format of its encoded bit streams, must be thoughtfully designed.

There are a number of streaming file formats available, from international standards such as the MPEG-4 file format [38] to *de facto* industry standards such as Apple's QuickTime format [10] (on which the MPEG-4 file format is based), RealNetworks' RealMedia format [33], and Microsoft's Advanced Streaming Format (ASF) [11]. All files in these formats have some common characteristics. First, they are able to contain, or multiplex, not only multiple media, but also multiple versions of each medium. Each version is recorded in a *track* (in MPEG-4/QuickTime parlance) or a *stream* (in ASF parlance). Each track or stream is decomposed into a sequence of *chunks* (in MPEG-4/QuickTime parlance) or packets (in ASF parlance), which contain actual encoded media data. In this chapter we will call these *data units*. In each file, header structures contain static metadata relating to the overall file as well as to specific tracks or streams. These metadata may include, for example, title, author, and date of composition, encryption and rights management information, table of contents, track/stream enumeration, and descriptions of their relationships, as well as individual track/stream properties such as start time, duration, bit rate, buffer size, sampling rate, picture size, and scalability capabilities. Time-varying metadata are associated with each track/stream. These metadata may include, for example, network packetization information, decoding and presentation time stamps, SMPTE time codes, key frame, switch frame, or other clean point information, and fine grain scalability information, such as a set of cut points and associated distortion or RD-slope information for each chunk or data unit. How these time-varying metadata are associated with individual chunks or data units, however, reveals one of the few philosophical differences between formats. MPEG-4/QuickTime uses separate tracks, called *hint tracks*, to add time-varying metadata to a track, whereas ASF uses extensible side structures (which may be called *hints*) associated with each data unit in a stream. A final type of metadata common to all formats is an index to allow seeking to particular time locations in each track/stream. One way to create such an index so that it can be efficiently searched (given, e.g., a SMPTE time code) is to arrange the index as a sequence of fixed-length records, each record corresponding to a unit of time (say, a 1-s interval), and each record containing a pointer into each track or stream. In all these formats, the structures are, in principle, highly extensible, by assigning new 32-bit (four-character) codes ("fourCC"s), by assigning new 128-bit globally unique identifiers (GUIDs), or by defining new structures in areas for opaque data. In practice, however, such extensions are limited in utility by the availability of servers and clients that understand the extensions.

Some of the metadata in a streaming media file is intended for consumption by the server only, while other metadata must be transmitted across the network for consumption by the client. For example, the hint and index information is usually used only at the server and is not transmitted across the network. If the end user wishes to seek to a particular time in a presentation, then the client will send a seek command and time to the server (see the previous section, Section 14.2.2), which will then use the seek time to look up in the index an appropriate starting offset within each stream[3] (e.g., at the last key frame before the seek time), and then will begin streaming from that point.

Other metadata, such as the descriptions and relationships of the streams, are usually transmitted over the network to the client so that the end user (and/or the client application on the user's behalf) can choose an appropriate set of streams for transmission, whether the selection has to do with the content (e.g., language of the audio track, optional subtitles) or the encoding of the content (e.g., bit rate, picture size, number of audio channels). As a rule of thumb, static metadata, whose size is independent of the length of the data, are relatively inexpensive to

---

[3] Henceforth for simplicity we will use only the *stream* terminology.

transmit over the network, whereas time-varying metadata, whose size grows with the length of the data, are relatively expensive to transmit over the network.

The encoded media data in the data units, of course, are generally intended to be transmitted over the network to the client. However, in a given session, usually only a fraction of all the encoded media data in a file is actually transmitted. Indeed, perhaps the main purpose of a streaming media file format is to provide a structure in which metadata can be used to easily select an appropriate subset of the data for transmission. Selection of an appropriate subset may be either *coarse grained* or *fine grained*. In coarse-grained selection, data units are selected on a per-stream basis. Thus, at any given time, the server is streaming only a particular subset of streams to the client. The subset of selected streams may change over time, but in coarse-grained selection this subset changes only on a timescale that is long compared to a data unit. In fine-grained selection, not only may a subset of streams be selected, but also some fraction of data within a stream may be selected for transmission. This fine-grained selection may be either at the data unit level (in which some data units in a stream are transmitted, while others are not) or below the data unit level, in which a portion of each data unit may be selected for transmission.

Multibit rate (MBR) coding and scalable coding are two means of encoding media data into a streaming media file that allow computationally simple selection of data for transmission based on the source coding rate. In MBR coding, multiple independent encodings of the same media content, each at a different source coding rate, are stored in different streams in the same file. Adaptation is based on stream selection. For example, as discussed in Section 14.2.2, if the client detects congestion based on buffer fullness, it can ask the server to switch to a stream with a lower source coding rate. In scalable coding, as described in detail in Chapters 4–6, encoded bit streams at different source coding rates are embedded, like layers of an onion. In coarse-grained scalability, if the client detects congestion, it can ask the server simply to drop the stream corresponding to the currently uppermost layer for a medium. In fine-grained scalability (FGS), in contrast, the client may instead send a parameter (such as a Lagrange multiplier) related to the desired source coding rate for a medium, with which the server may adjust the source coding rate for the medium using fine-grained selection of the data in the medium's streams. This would typically be done using a simple threshold. For example, if each data unit is tagged with metadata that sets a collection of breakpoints in the data unit along with a Lagrange multiplier corresponding to each breakpoint (in a decreasing sequence), then the server could use the Lagrange multiplier given to it by the client to threshold each data unit to determine where to truncate the data unit. Those segments of the data unit with Lagrange multipliers higher than the Lagrange multiplier specified by the client are transmitted, while those segments of the data unit with Lagrange multipliers below are not transmitted.

The data units (or portions of data units) selected for transmission are packetized into network data units, or *packets*, for transmission over the network. In the parlance of ITU H.264/ISO MPEG-4 AVC, the file format is a Network Adaptation Layer (NAL), which is an encapsulation layer below the encoded bit stream layer at the same level as, say, RTP and other network transport protocols. Thus packetization can be regarded as re-encapsulations of the encoded media data from one transport protocol (the file format) into another (e.g., RTP).

It can now be appreciated that media file formats designed for local playback and storage are not suitable for streaming, in general. Even QuickTime, which was originally designed for local playback of media but which is highly flexible, adds metadata in "hint tracks" for the purposes of streaming and restricts its many levels of indirection and indexing both to allow the file to be used for progressive downloading and to allow the server maximal access efficiency. Furthermore, even "streaming" formats, such as the MPEG-2 transport stream, which was designed for streaming data over isochronous cable, terrestrial radio, and satellite channels, is not very suitable as a file format for adaptive streaming over packet networks, since it is not very easy for a server to adaptively extract selected portions of the stream, nor does it have an indexing mechanism to allow a user to randomly access (i.e., seek to) arbitrary points in the stream. Thus streaming media file formats must be carefully designed to fit their purposes.

14.3 FUNDAMENTAL ABSTRACTIONS

In this section, we lay out the fundamental abstractions of streaming media on demand. In particular, we cover leaky bucket models of the bit streams, constant bit rate (CBR) vs. variable bit rate (VBR) streams, compound (multiple media) streams, preroll delay, playback speed, timing, clocks, and decoder and presentation timestamps. At the end of this section, the reader will know, for example, for streaming multiple media over an ideal (isochronous) network, when it is safe for the client to begin playback after streaming begins, at any playback speed.

14.3.1 Buffering and Leaky Bucket Models

We first consider the constant bit rate scenario in which both the encoder and the decoder communicate over a dedicated isochronous noiseless communication channel.[4] In this scenario, to match the instantaneous coding rate of the source to the constant transmission rate of the channel, an *encoder buffer* is required between the encoder and the channel and a *decoder buffer* is required between the

---

[4]An isochronous channel is one, such as a telephone modem, in which equal amounts of data are communicated in equal amounts of time (from the Greek *iso*, "same," plus *chronos*, "time"). Information flows through an isochronous channel as fluid through a pipe.

channel and the decoder, as illustrated in Figure 14.3. A *schedule* is the sequence
of times at which successive bits in the coded bit stream pass a given point in the
communication pipeline. Figure 14.4 illustrates the schedules of bits passing the
points A, B, C, and D in Figure 14.3. Schedule A is the schedule at which captured
frames are instantaneously encoded and put into the encoder buffer. This schedule
is a staircase in which the nth step rises by $b(n)$ bits at time $\tau(n)$, where $\tau(n)$ is
the time at which frame n is encoded, and $b(n)$ is the number of bits in the resulting encoding. Schedules B and C are the schedules at which bits, respectively,
enter and leave the channel. The slope of these schedules is R bits per second,
where R is the transmission rate of the channel. Schedule D is the schedule at
which frames are removed from the decoder buffer and instantaneously decoded
for presentation. Note that Schedule D is a right shift of Schedule A, assuming
constant end-to-end delay and to zero encoding and decoding delay, including al-
gorithmic delay. (These assumptions will be relaxed in Section 14.4.) Note also
that Schedule B is a lower bound to Schedule A, while Schedule C is an upper
bound to Schedule D. Indeed the gap between Schedules A and B represents, at
any point in time, the fullness in bits of the encoder buffer, while the gap between Schedules C and D likewise represents the fullness of the decoder buffer.
Thus it is clear that the source coding schedule (either A or D) can be contained
within a *buffer tube*, as illustrated in Figure 14.5, having slope R bits per second,
some height B bits, and some initial offset F_e bits from the bottom of the tube
or, equivalently, some initial offset $F_d = B - F_e$ bits from the top of the tube.
The buffer tube characterizes with three parameters (R, B, F_e) or, equivalently,
(R, B, F_d)—the variability of the instantaneous rate of the source coding sched-

FIGURE 14.3:   Communication pipeline.

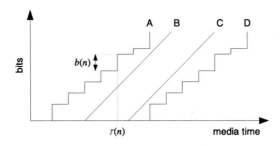

FIGURE 14.4:   Schedules at which bits in the coded bit stream pass the
points A, B, C, and D in the communication pipeline.

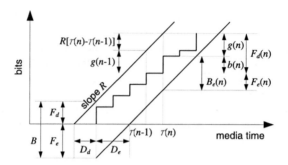

FIGURE 14.5:   Buffer tube containing a coding schedule.

ule around an average rate R. In some sense, the buffer tube paints with a broad brush stroke the source coding schedule (a possibly infinite sequence of step sizes and times $(b(n), \tau(n))$, $n = 0, 1, 2, \ldots$) as a straight line with slope R, thickness B, and offset F_e.

Traditionally, the buffer tube is used by an online source encoder to ensure that its output will not cause the decoder buffer to underflow or overflow. It is clear that at any given frame, the fullness of the encoder buffer and the fullness of the decoder buffer are complementary, adding up to B bits, after an appropriate delay. Thus, if the encoder and decoder buffers each have capacity B bits, an overflow of the encoder buffer is equivalent to an underflow of the decoder buffer, and vice versa. The online source encoder traditionally uses a "rate control" algorithm to assign a number of bits $b(n)$ to each frame n to ensure that its B-bit buffer neither underflows nor overflows, when beginning with initial fullness F_e bits. (Beginning with initial fullness F_e bits means simply that the first bit inserted into the buffer by the encoder will be delayed $D_e = F_e/R$ seconds before it enters the channel.) Thus any B-bit decoder buffer will not overflow or underflow if it begins with initial fullness $F_d = B - F_e$. (Beginning with initial fullness F_d bits means simply that the first bit entering the buffer from the channel will be delayed $D_d = F_d/R$ seconds before it is extracted by the decoder.) The decoder buffer delay $D_d = F_d/R$ is thus complementary to the encoder buffer delay, with overall buffer delay equal to B/R seconds. The end-to-end delay is thus B/R plus any transmission delay. The resulting bit stream is called a CBR bit stream with average rate R even though, unlike the rate at which bits enter the channel, the rate that the online source encoder produces bits is obviously not constant over timescales shorter than one frame period.

For off-line source encoding, such as for streaming media on demand, the encoder often produces a CBR bit stream in exactly the same way—assuming a decoder buffer with size B. However, unlike the online case in which it is important to keep the overall buffer delay B/R low, in the off-line case it is important

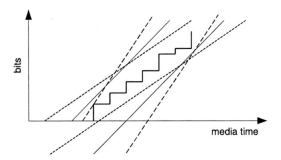

FIGURE 14.6:   Multiple buffer tubes containing a given bit stream.

only to keep the decoder buffer delay $D_d = F_d/R$ low. The encoder buffer delay portion of the overall buffer delay is not important. The *decoder buffer delay*, also loosely known as the *preroll delay*, is usually the largest component in the *start-up delay*, or the time between a user pushing "play" and seeing or hearing the first frame (during which media players usually display a "Buffering . . ." message).[5] The encoder can produce a CBR bit stream minimizing the decoder buffer delay by starting the encoder buffer in a full state (F_e close to B), although this would mean that the initial frame would get very few bits. This is a reflection of a fundamental trade-off, at any given transmission rate, between preroll delay and initial quality, which we will explore further in Section 14.4.

It is also possible for off-line source encoders to ignore all buffer constraints. A typical such scenario is the scenario where the encoder tries to produce a constant distortion bit stream (e.g., with equal quantization stepsizes for all frames). The resulting bit stream is usually called a variable bit rate stream. Ultimately, there is no firm distinction between VBR and CBR streams, although they may be produced in different ways. The distinction, if any, is one of degree. Both CBR and VBR streams have schedules that can be represented by finite sequences of step sizes and times, $\{(b(n), \tau(n))\}_{n=0}^{N}$. Thus, both can be contained in buffer tubes with some appropriate slope, width, and offset. However, VBR streams tend to require wider buffer tubes than CBR streams. This usually means that VBR streams require a larger start-up delay.

It is clear that any given finite-duration bit stream is containable by an infinite number of buffer tubes, as illustrated in Figure 14.6. The slope R, the width B, and the offset F_e are not unique. This implies, in particular, that the average bit rate of a stream, whether VBR or CBR, is not well defined by the bit rate of a

---

[5]The start-up delay includes, in addition to the decoder buffer delay, usually much smaller delays such as the round trip delay between client and server, server processing delays, and decoding and presentation delays, if any.

constant bit rate channel over which the stream may flow with sufficient buffering. Of course, there are ways to define the average bit rate of a stream uniquely. One possible definition is the slope of parallel lines bounding the stream's schedule $\{(b(n), \tau(n))\}_{n=0}^{N}$, clamped together by a vice as tightly as possible (so to speak), to make the buffer tube unique. Another possible definition is the total number of bits in the stream divided by the duration of the stream. These are approximately equal if the stream is long enough. Furthermore they will be approximately equal to the slope R of any buffer tube (R, B, F_e) containing the stream as long as the duration of the stream is long compared to the buffer size B. Thus any reasonable definition of average bit rate will suffice as long as we are given a corresponding buffer tube.

We now extend the original online scenario to the case in which the encoder does not use the channel continuously. In this case, the channel has a peak transmission rate R higher than the average bit rate of the stream. When the encoder has bits to send, it sends them at rate R. Otherwise it does not use the channel and the channel may be used to transmit other information during this time. This is a realistic setting for shared channels such as packet networks. As far as the encoder is concerned, the channel time shares between transmitting at rate R and transmitting at rate 0, such that the time average of these two instantaneous channel rates is approximately the average bit rate of the stream.

In this scenario, the encoder buffer is best modeled by a *leaky bucket*. The encoder dumps $b(n)$ bits into the leaky bucket at time $\tau(n)$, and the bits leak out of the bucket (into the channel) at rate R. When the leak rate R is higher than the average bit rate, the bucket will occasionally become empty. Thus the encoder buffer fullness $F_e(n)$ immediately before frame n is added to the bucket and the encoder buffer fullness $B_e(n)$ immediately after frame n is added to the bucket evolve from an initial encoder buffer fullness $F_e(0) = F_e$ according to the dynamical system

$$B_e(n) = F_e(n) + b(n), \qquad (14.1)$$

$$F_e(n + 1) = \max\{0, B_e(n) - R[\tau(n + 1) - \tau(n)]\}, \qquad (14.2)$$

for $n = 0, 1, 2, \ldots$. As described earlier, a leaky bucket can be specified by three parameters: its leak rate R, its capacity B, and its initial fullness F_e. A leaky bucket (R, B, F_e) is said to *contain* a bit stream with schedule $\{(b(n), \tau(n))\}_{n=0}^{N}$ if the bucket does not overflow, that is, $B_e(n) \le B$ for all $n = 0, 1, \ldots, N$ in the dynamical system (14.1) and (14.2).

It is of interest to find among all leaky buckets containing a stream the one that leads to the smallest decoder buffer size and also the one that leads to the smallest decoder buffer delay. For a given stream, define the minimum bucket capacity given leak rate R and initial fullness F_e as

$$B^{\min}(R, F_e) = \min_n B_e(n), \tag{14.3}$$

and define the corresponding initial decoder buffer fullness as

$$F_d^{\min}(R, F_e) = B^{\min}(R, F_e) - F_e. \tag{14.4}$$

Denote the minimum of each of these over F_e as

$$B^{\min}(R) = \min_{F_e} B^{\min}(R, F_e), \tag{14.5}$$

$$F_d^{\min}(R) = \min_{F_e} F_d^{\min}(R, F_e). \tag{14.6}$$

It is shown in [34, Proposition 2] that remarkably, these are each minimized by the same value of F_e, which is hence equal to

$$F_e^{\min}(R) \triangleq B^{\min}(R) - F_d^{\min}(R). \tag{14.7}$$

Thus given a bit stream with schedule $\{(b(n), \tau(n))\}_{n=0}^{N}$, for each bit rate R there is a *tightest leaky bucket* containing the stream that has the minimum buffer capacity B as well as the minimum decoder buffer delay $D_d = F_d/R$, provided it begins with initial fullness $F_e = F_e^{\min}(R)$.

These formulae work for any $R > 0$, even for R less than the average bit rate of the stream. However, when R is less than the average bit rate of the stream, the leaky bucket accumulates bits faster than they leak out, causing the required bucket capacity to grow linearly as R goes to zero, up to the size of the entire stream. In a like manner, the preroll delay that is required to ensure that the decoder buffer does not underflow during playback grows linearly up to the playback time of the entire stream as R goes to zero. However, when R is above the average bit rate of the stream, bits leak out of the bucket faster than they are put in, causing the bucket to become empty on occasion. This provides another possible definition of average bit rate of a stream: the average bit rate of a stream, henceforth called the *source coding rate* R_c of a stream, is the maximum leak rate R such that a leaky bucket (R, B, F_e) containing the stream does not underflow when starting with initial fullness $F_e = F_e^{\min}(R)$.

It is intuitively clear from the leaky bucket metaphor that the larger the leak rate R, the smaller the required capacity. It is also true that the decoder buffer delay can be lower. Indeed, it can be shown using results from Ribas-Corbera *et al.* [34, using Lemmas 3, 5, 6, 11, 12] that both $B^{\min}(R)$ and $F_d^{\min}(R)$ are decreasing, piecewise linear, convex functions of R, as shown in Figure 14.7. Hence if the

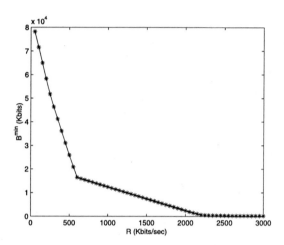

FIGURE 14.7: Plot of $B^{\min}(R)$ for a VBR video clip compressed by H.264/AVC with QP=26.

transmission rate R is greater than the source coding rate R_c, the decoder buffer size $B = B^{\min}(R)$ can be reduced compared to $B = B^{\min}(R_c)$ and the decoder buffer delay $D_d = F_d^{\min}(R)/R$ can be reduced compared to $D_d = F_d^{\min}(R_c)/R_c$. Figure 14.7 shows, for a typical video bit stream with average source coding rate $R_c \approx 600$ Kbps, the minimum buffer size $B^{\min}(R)$ as a function of the peak channel transmission rate R. Observe that the function is piecewise constant and can be characterized by a small number of points.

In the off-line scenario, the client is generally connected to the server across a channel whose transmission rate is different than the source coding rate R_c of the bit stream. The client can determine the required buffer size and preroll delay from the functions $B^{\min}(R)$ and $F_d^{\min}(R)$. These functions can be computed off-line at a selected set of channel transmission rates R, say $R_1 < R_2 < \cdots < R_L$ and stored in the bit stream header as a set of leaky bucket parameters (R_i, B_i, F_i), $i = 1, 2, \ldots, L$, where $B_i = B^{\min}(R_i)$ and $F_i = F_d^{\min}(R_i)$, which can be communicated to the client upon initialization. Typically, the first such leaky bucket can be a buffer tube representing the source coding rate, that is, $R_1 = R_c$, and the remaining leaky buckets can be located at other significant breakpoints in the piecewise linear functions $B^{\min}(R)$ and $F_d^{\min}(R)$. Then, given any channel transmission rate R between R_i and R_{i+1}, the client can estimate $B^{\min}(R)$ and $F_d^{\min}(R)$ by the linear interpolations

$$\hat{B}^{\min}(R) \triangleq \frac{R_{i+1} - R}{R_{i+1} - R_i} B_i + \frac{R - R_i}{R_{i+1} - R_i} B_{i+1} \geq B^{\min}(R), \qquad (14.8)$$

$$\hat{F}_d^{\min}(R) \triangleq \frac{R_{i+1} - R}{R_{i+1} - R_i} F_i + \frac{R - R_i}{R_{i+1} - R_i} F_{i+1} \geq F_d^{\min}(R). \qquad (14.9)$$

The inequalities follow from the convexity of the functions $B_e^{\min}(R)$ and $F_d^{\min}(R)$ in R, and they guarantee that a buffer size B and a preroll delay F_d/R are sufficient to ensure glitch-free playback when the channel has peak transmission rate R and the client can use flow control to ensure that the buffer does not overflow. Extrapolation at the low and high ends is also possible. For $R < R_1$,

$$\hat{B}^{\min}(R) \triangleq B_1 + (R_1 - R)T \geq B^{\min}(R), \qquad (14.10)$$

$$\hat{F}_d^{\min}(R) \triangleq F_1 + (R_1 - R)T \geq F_d^{\min}(R), \qquad (14.11)$$

where T is the duration of the bit stream, while for $R > R_L$,

$$\hat{B}^{\min}(R) \triangleq B_L \geq B^{\min}(R), \qquad (14.12)$$

$$\hat{F}_d^{\min}(R) \triangleq F_L \geq F_d^{\min}(R). \qquad (14.13)$$

Thus, a small set of leaky buckets $\{(R_i, B_i, F_i)\}_{i=1}^L$ stored in the bit stream header can be used to derive a fairly tight leaky bucket (R, B, F) for any channel transmission rate $R \geq 0$.

14.3.2 Compound Streams

A streaming media file often contains multiple independently encoded media streams, such as an audio stream, a video stream, and perhaps other streams, intended to be streamed concurrently.

When multiple media streams are selected for concurrent transmission, it is convenient to consider them as a single *compound stream* having an aggregate source coding rate and set of leaky buckets. Happily, a leaky bucket (B, F, R) for a compound stream can be easily derived as the sum of leaky buckets for its component streams. For example, if (R^a, B^a, F^a) and (R^v, B^v, F^v) are leaky buckets containing the component (say audio and video streams) streams, then the parameters

$$R = R^a + R^v, \qquad (14.14)$$

$$B = B^a + B^v, \qquad (14.15)$$

$$F = F^a + F^v \qquad (14.16)$$

characterize a leaky bucket containing the compound stream. This is because, as is intuitively clear from the leaky bucket metaphor, if the separate leaky buckets contain the component streams without overflowing, then the combined leaky bucket will contain the combination of the streams without overflowing. (However, the combined bucket is, in general, not the tightest leaky bucket that is able to contain the compound stream.) It is simple to show this mathematically, although we will not do so here.

If the component streams each have multiple leaky buckets, then any combination of their leaky buckets will suffice to contain the compound stream. For example, if $\{(R_i^a, B_i^a, F_i^a)\}_{i=1}^{L^a}$ and $\{(R_j^v, B_j^v, F_j^v)\}_{j=1}^{L^v}$ are, respectively, sets of leaky buckets containing an audio stream and a video stream, then $\{(R_{i,j}, B_{i,j}, F_{i,j}) : (i, j) \in [1, \ldots, L^a] \times [1, \ldots, L^v]\}$ is a set of leaky buckets containing the compound audio and video stream, where $R_{i,j} = R_i^a + R_j^v$, $B_{i,j} = B_i^a + B_j^v$, and $F_{i,j} = F_i^a + F_j^v$. However, it turns out that not all $L^a \times L^v$ leaky buckets in this set are useful for characterizing the compound stream. In fact, at most $L^a + L^v$ index pairs (i, j) have the property that $(R_{i,j}, B_{i,j})$ lies on the lower convex hull of the set $\{(R_{i,j}, B_{i,j}) : (i, j) \in [1, \ldots, L^a] \times [1, \ldots, L^v]\}$ used to estimate $B_e^{\min}(R)$ and $F_d^{\min}(R)$. Indices for pairs on the lower convex hull can be found easily by minimizing a Lagrangian for some positive Lagrange multiplier $\lambda > 0$, namely

$$(i_\lambda, j_\lambda) = \arg\min_{(i,j)}\{B_{i,j} + \lambda R_{i,j}\} \tag{14.17}$$

$$= \arg\min_{(i,j)}\{B_i^a + B_j^v + \lambda[R_i^a + R_j^v]\} \tag{14.18}$$

$$= \left(\arg\min_i\{B_i^a + \lambda R_i^a\}, \arg\min_j\{B_j^v + \lambda R_j^v\}\right). \tag{14.19}$$

Thus, as λ is swept from 0 to ∞, a sequence of L^a audio leaky buckets indexed by i_λ can be chosen by minimizing the Lagrangian $B_i^a + \lambda R_i^a$, and *independently* a sequence of L^v video leaky buckets indexed by j_λ can be chosen by minimizing the Lagrangian $B_j^v + \lambda R_j^v$. These can be paired by matching their Lagrange multipliers λ to find the (at most) $L^a + L^v$ leaky buckets for the compound stream.

This approach can be easily extended to more media than just audio and video. For example, suppose there are M concurrent media streams in a streamed video game and $m = 1, 2, \ldots, M$ indexes the media, and suppose that for each medium m, there is a set of leaky buckets indexed by $i^m = 1, \ldots, L^m$. Then following the aforementioned arguments it is easy to see that for each medium m, one can select for each $\lambda > 0$ a leaky bucket index $i_\lambda^m = \arg\min_i\{B_i^m + \lambda R_i^m\}$, where (R_i^m, B_i^m, F_i^m) is the ith leaky bucket for medium m. These can then be aligned by λ to choose the component leaky buckets for the (at most) $\sum_m L^m$ leaky buckets for the compound stream. Even further simplifications accrue when $L^m = 2$ for all m, for example, when there are leaky buckets (R_1^m, B_1^m, F_1^m) and (R_2^m, B_2^m, F_2^m) for only average and peak bit rates for each component stream. In that case, as λ goes from 0 to ∞, for each m there is a simple threshold, namely $\lambda^m = [B_1^m - B_2^m]/[R_2^m - R_1^m]$, such that when $\lambda \geq \lambda^m$ we have $i_\lambda^m = 1$ (choose the LB for average bit rate) and when $\lambda < \lambda^m$ we have $i_\lambda^m = 2$ (choose the LB for peak bit rate). Thus a set of $M + 1$ leaky buckets $\{(R_k, B_k, F_k)\}_{k=0}^M$ for the compound stream can be obtained by sorting the media on λ^m and successively flipping the chosen component leaky buckets from average to peak bit rate, namely $R_k = \sum_{m=1}^k R_1^m + \sum_{m=k+1}^M R_2^m$ (and similarly for B_k and F_k).

14.3.3 MBR and Scalable Streams

In MBR and scalable streaming, in addition to the possibility of streaming multiple *concurrent* media streams such as audio and video, each concurrent media stream is generally selected from a list of *mutually exclusive* media streams, each encoded at a different source coding rate. Combining all possible mutually exclusive audio streams with all possible mutually exclusive video streams can lead to a large number of compound streams, each having a different aggregate source coding rate and set of leaky buckets. In principle, each of the (say) N^a mutually exclusive audio streams can be matched with each of the N^v mutually exclusive video streams, producing all possible $N^a \times N^v$ combinations. However, most of these combinations are not desirable. In fact, typically there are only on the order of $N^a + N^v$ desirable combinations. For example, if audio quality is more important than video quality, then during network congestion it may be desirable to reduce video quality through N^v levels before reducing audio quality through an additional N^a level. However, it may instead be desirable to reduce the audio and video bit rates together. A principled way to decide which of the $N^a \times N^v$ combinations are desirable is to take a distortion–rate approach such as the following. Assign a distortion D_i^a and a source coding rate R_i^a to each audio stream $i = 0, 1, \ldots, N^a$ (which includes the empty stream $i = 0$) and a corresponding distortion D_j^v and source coding rate R_j^v to each video stream $j = 0, 1, \ldots, N^v$. Define for each combined stream (i, j) an overall distortion and an overall source coding rate,

$$D_{i,j} = \alpha D_i^a + D_j^v \qquad (14.20)$$

$$R_{i,j} = R_i^a + R_j^v, \qquad (14.21)$$

allowing the audio distortion to be arbitrarily weighted by a parameter α relative to the video distortion. Select a "desirable" subset of the audio/video substream combinations (i, j) such that for each (i, j) in the subset, $D_{i,j} \le D_{i',j'}$ for all (i', j') such that $R_{i',j'} \le R_{i,j}$. That is, desirable combinations have the property that they have the lowest total distortion among all combinations with the same or lower total bit rate. One such desirable subset consists of the combinations (i, j) whose rate–distortion pairs $(R_{i,j}, D_{i,j})$ lie on the lower convex hull of the set of rate–distortion pairs for all possible combinations. Similar to the methodology described in the previous subsection, pairs on this lower convex hull can be easily found by minimizing a Lagrangian for some positive Lagrange multiplier $\lambda > 0$. That is,

$$(i_\lambda, j_\lambda) = \arg\min_{(i,j)}\{D_{i,j} + \lambda R_{i,j}\}, \qquad (14.22)$$

$$= \arg\min_{(i,j)}\{\alpha D_i^a + D_j^v + \lambda[R_i^a + R_j^v]\}, \qquad (14.23)$$

$$= \left(\arg\min_i\{D_i^a + (\lambda/\alpha)R_i^a\}, \arg\min_j\{D_j^v + \lambda R_j^v\}\right). \quad (14.24)$$

Thus, as λ is swept from 0 to ∞, a sequence of $N^a + 1$ audio streams i_λ (including the empty substream $i = 0$) can be chosen by minimizing the Lagrangian $D_i^a + (\lambda/\alpha)R_i^a$, and (independently) a sequence of $N^v + 1$ video streams j_λ can be chosen by minimizing the Lagrangian $D_j^v + \lambda R_j^v$. These can be paired by matching their Lagrange multipliers λ. Note that it is a simple matter to repair them if the relative audio weight α changes, possibly under user control.

Also similar to the methodology in the previous section, this approach can be easily extended to more media than just audio and video. For example, suppose there are M concurrent media streams in a streamed video game and $m = 1, 2, \ldots, M$ indexes the media, and suppose that for each medium m, there is a set of mutually exclusive streams $i^m = 0, 1, \ldots, N^m$ (including the empty stream $i^m = 0$), one of which can be combined with streams from other media to form a compound stream. It is easy to see that for each medium m, one can select for each $\lambda > 0$ a substream $i_\lambda^m = \arg\min_i\{D_i^m + \lambda R_i^m\}$, where (R_i^m, D_i^m) is the rate–distortion pair for the ith stream of medium m. These can then be aligned by λ to choose the components of the "desirable" compound streams, a process that is linear in M instead of exponential in M. Even further simplifications accrue when $N^m = 1$ for all m. In that case, as λ goes from 0 to ∞, for each m there is a simple threshold, namely $\lambda^m = [D_0^m - D_1^m]/R_1^m$, such that when $\lambda \leq \lambda^m$ we have $i_\lambda^m = 1$ (i.e., medium m is included in the compound stream) and when $\lambda > \lambda_m$ we have $i_\lambda^m = 0$ (i.e., medium m is not included in the compound stream). Thus the set of desirable compound streams can be obtained by sorting the media elements on λ^m and including them, in order, into the compound streams.

14.3.4 Temporal Coordinate Systems and Timestamps

Timestamps are generally associated with each encoded frame to instruct the client when to extract the frame from the decoder buffer and (instantaneously) decode it. These timestamps are known as *decoder timestamps* (DTS) in MPEG terminology and are the primary timestamps that we consider here. They can also be considered *decoding deadlines* by which the frame must arrive at the client in order to be decoded on time. It is fair for the client to decode received frames ahead of their decoding deadlines, if there is sufficient room in the presentation buffer between the decoder and the renderer. The presentation buffer holds decoded frames. Decoded frames are also associated with timestamps, known as *presentation timestamps* (PTS) in MPEG terminology. These timestamps instruct the renderer when to render the frame and are critical to achieving synchronization between separate streams such as audio and video. Presentation timestamps lie at a layer above decoding timestamps and hence do not need to be visible to the client system until after decoding. In fact the decoder may generate most presentation timestamps from the decoding timestamps on the fly, for example, using a fixed delay. Presentation timestamps need to be explicitly different from decoding timestamps only in situations where frames must be presented out of decoding order. For example, MPEG frames $I_0, B_1, B_2, P_3, B_4, B_5, P_6, \ldots$ (in presentation order) must be decoded in the order $I_0, P_3, B_1, B_2, P_6, B_4, B_5, \ldots$. In the sequel we assume that frames are timestamped at the encoder with both decoder and presentation timestamps. They are inserted into the bit stream in decoding order. Henceforth in this chapter we will be concerned only with decoding timestamps.

It will pay to distinguish between the *clocks*, or temporal coordinate systems, in which timestamps are expressed. We use *media time* to refer to the clock running on the device used to capture and timestamp the original content, while *client time* refers to the clock running on the client used to play back the content. We assume that media time is real time (i.e., one second of media time elapses in one second of real time) at the time of media capture, while client time is real time at the time of media playback. We use the symbol τ to express media time and the symbol t to express client time, with subscripts and additional arguments to indicate corresponding events. For example, we use $\tau_{DTS}(0), \tau_{DTS}(1), \tau_{DTS}(2), \ldots$ to express the decoding deadlines of frames $0, 1, 2, \ldots$ in media time, while we use $t_{DTS}(0), t_{DTS}(1), t_{DTS}(2), \ldots$ to express the decoding deadlines of frames $0, 1, 2, \ldots$ at the client. The subscripts and/or arguments may be dropped or shortened if they are understood.

Content may be played back at a rate ν times real time. If $\nu = 2$, for example, the content is played back at twice real time (i.e., fast forward). The conversion from media time to client time can be expressed

$$t = t_0 + \frac{\tau - \tau_0}{\nu}, \qquad (14.25)$$

where t_0 and τ_0 represent the time of a common initial event, such as the decoding time of frame 0 (or the decoding time of the first frame after a seek or rebuffering event) in media and client coordinate systems, respectively. Using (14.25), the leaky bucket update (14.2) becomes

$$F_e(n+1) = \max\{0, B_e(n) - R'[t(n+1) - t(n)]\}, \qquad (14.26)$$

where $R' = R\nu$ is the arrival rate of bits into the client in bits per client time. Hence $R = R'/\nu$ is the rate that must be used to compute the required buffer size $B_e^{\min}(R)$ and initial decoder buffer fullness $F_d^{\min}(R)$. The preroll delay is thus $F_d^{\min}(R)/R' = F_d^{\min}(R)/R/\nu$. The larger the playback speed, the smaller the preroll delay.

14.4 STREAMING MEDIA OVER PACKET NETWORKS

In this section, we deal with streaming media over packet networks, such as the Internet. Unlike the idealized channel models of Section 14.3, packet networks are neither isochronous nor lossless, and they are shared by multiple communication processes, whose actions cause the network to have time-varying behavior. Hence, the major technical problem in streaming media on demand over packet networks is the need to maintain a good user experience in the face of time-varying network conditions. Users expect that regardless of the network conditions, the start-up delay will be low, playback will be continuous, and quality will be as high as possible given the average network bandwidth.

Buffering at the client is the key to meeting these user expectations. Technically, buffering serves several distinct but simultaneous purposes. First, as we have seen in Section 14.3, it allows the media to be coded with a variable instantaneous bit rate. Second, it allows the client to compensate for short-term variations in packet transmission delay (i.e., "jitter"). Third, it allows the client to continue playing back the media during lapses in network bandwidth. Finally, it gives the client time to perform packet loss recovery if needed. These last three purposes require additional buffer space at the client beyond the minimal buffer size $B^{\min}(R)$ computed in Section 14.3. However, a single buffer at the client can be shared among all four purposes. This section is primarily about how to keep the client buffer sufficiently full, on average, to serve all four purposes, and yet permit a low start-up delay, in the face of varying network conditions.

14.4.1 Source Coding, Channel Coding, Sending, Transmission, and Arrival Rates

In Section 14.3, we took pains to define the *source coding rate* R_c of a media stream as the slope of a tight buffer tube containing its schedule, measured in bits per second of media time.

Distinct from the source coding rate R_c is the *sending rate* R_s or the rate at which the server application injects bits into a reliable transport layer, measured in bits per second of client time.

Distinct from both the source coding rate R_c and the sending rate R_s is the *transmission rate* R_x, which is the rate at which the server injects bits into the network layer, again measured in bits per second of client time. The transmission rate is limited, preferably, by the congestion control mechanism in either standard TCP or a TCP-friendly rate control (TFRC) mechanism [13] such as DCCP [25] or a nonstandard transmission rate control mechanism over UDP that adapts the transmission rate to the degree of network congestion. However, a simple transmission rate control mechanism could also set R_x to be constant, for example, irrespective of the level of network congestion. This could be appropriate if the channel is dedicated.

The sending rate R_s is limited, in turn, by the transmission rate R_x. In fact the difference between R_s and R_x can be attributed to the error control overhead, or redundancy, needed for reliable communication over the network, as described in Chapters 7–10. The fraction R_s/R_x is known as the *channel coding rate*, or the rate of the error control code in source bits per channel bit, which can be no greater than the Shannon capacity of the channel. The channel coding rate R_s/R_x is determined by the retransmission mechanism in TCP or by any other error control layer, which typically adapts the channel coding rate to the loss rate of the channel. TFRC and DCCP do not define an error control mechanism and hence an explicit mechanism must be provided for reliable communication, just as one must be provided for any nonstandard transmission rate control mechanism used over raw UDP or RTP/UDP. This is illustrated in Figure 14.8a.

Since all bits injected into a reliable transport layer eventually arrive at the client application, the sending rate R_s is over the long run equal to the *arrival rate R_a*, or the rate at which bits emerge at the client application. Since relatively little data can be buffered in the network and error control layer compared to the client buffer, we generally assume that R_a and R_s are essentially equivalent at any

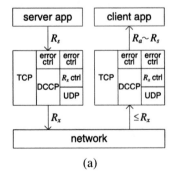
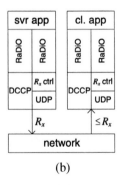

(a)   (b)

FIGURE 14.8:   (a) Both error control and transmission rate control are factored out of the streaming application, which then deals only with source coding rate control. (b) Only transmission rate control-factored out of the streaming application, which performs joint source-channel coding such as in RaDiO (Chapter 10).

given time. In this chapter we will speak primarily in terms of the arrival rate R_a since it is from the client's point of view.

Many streaming media practitioners assume that once the user determines the playback speed v, then the source coding rate R_c and the arrival rate R_a must be locked together by the relation $R_a = vR_c$ (except during the initial buffering period, during which $v = 0$ and $R_a > 0$). For example, if $v = 1$, a stream encoded at 100 Kbps must be communicated reliably at 100 Kbps (resulting in a raw transmission rate higher than 100 Kbps if retransmissions become necessary). However, this need not be the case, and in fact unlocking R_c and R_a can lead to important advantages.

The major advantage of decoupling the source coding and sending or arrival rates is that it makes possible continuous control of the number of seconds of content in the client buffer, known as the client buffer *duration*. The client buffer duration tends to increase or decrease depending on whether the arrival rate R_a (the average number of bits per second that arrive into the client buffer) is greater or less than the source coding rate R_c times the playback speed v (the average number of bits per second that play out of the client buffer). That is, if $R_a > R_c v$ then the buffer duration increases; otherwise it decreases. For a given R_a and R_c, it is possible to adjust the playback speed v to control the buffer duration. This approach is explored in detail in Chapter 16. On the one hand, in the long run, v cannot remain very much different from the user's preferred playback speed. On the other hand, the arrival rate R_a is essentially limited by the network capacity. Hence, if the network capacity drops dramatically for a sustained period, reducing the source coding rate R_c is the only appropriate way to maintain the buffer duration and prevent an underflow leading to a rebuffering event. Adjusting the source coding rate in the face of time-varying network conditions is the problem of *source coding rate control*.

By continuously controlling the client buffer duration using source coding rate control, it is possible to begin playback after only $F_d^{\min}(R_a)/R_a$ seconds—when there is just enough data in the buffer to guarantee continuous playback under ideal, predictable conditions—then to continuously grow the client buffer duration to provide, over time, the necessary robustness to packet loss, jitter, and variations in network capacity—and finally to maintain, in the long run, a roughly constant buffer duration to ensure that playback quality is as high as the network capacity will allow. This helps meet the user expectations of low startup delay, continuous playback, and quality as high as possible given the average network bandwidth.

Being able to control R_c independently of R_s (or R_a) also makes efficient streaming possible with arbitrary transports, such as TCP, DCCP, or other proprietary transport protocols. Such protocols typically have their own error control and transmission rate control mechanisms, whose rates generally fluctuate according to network conditions and hence cannot be locked to a fixed source coding rate unless they are locked well below the average network capacity, resulting in obvious inefficiency.

It is well worth mentioning here that if compatibility with TCP is not required, then it is possible for the source coding rate control and the error control modules illustrated in Figure 14.8a to be combined into a single module, as illustrated in Figure 14.8b. The transmission rate control module is not changed and still determines the frequency of transmission opportunities based on network congestion. In this way, the source coding and error control mechanisms can *jointly* determine whether a source packet or an error control packet (such as a retransmission of a previously transmitted packet, or a parity packet) should be put onto the wire at the next transmission opportunity. This is a joint source-channel coding problem sometimes known as the *scheduling* problem and is treated in detail in Chapter 10, using the RaDiO framework.

In this chapter, however, we will adopt the more classical approach of building a source coding layer on top of a reliable transport.

14.4.2 Source Coding Rate Control

In this section we detail an approach to source coding rate control based on the classical theory of optimal linear quadratic control [2]. The goal is to control the client buffer duration to a target, despite variations in the arrival rate R_a. This will be accomplished by choosing the source coding rate R_c as a function of R_a and the client buffer duration and its history (i.e., whether it is growing or shrinking). In order to choose an appropriate source coding rate R_c, we assume the existence at the server of multiple (or scalable) compound media streams at a variety of average bit rates $R^{(1)}$, $R^{(2)}$, $R^{(3)}$, ..., each having a schedule contained in an appropriately tight buffer tube $(R^{(i)}, B^{(i)}, F_e^{(i)})$, as illustrated in Figure 14.5.

14.4.2.1 Control Theoretic Model

Assume for the moment that bits arrive at the client at a constant rate R_a. Then frame n (having size $b(n)$, as illustrated in Figure 14.5) arrives at the client $b(n)/R_a$ seconds after frame $n - 1$. Indeed, dividing the vertical scale of the schedules in Figure 14.5 by R_a, we obtain the schedules in terms of client time, rather than bits, as shown in Figure 14.9. The coding schedule divided by R_a becomes the *arrival schedule*, which provides for each n the time $t_a(n)$ of arrival of frame n at the client. The buffer tube upper bound (in bits) divided by R_a becomes the buffer tube upper bound (in time), which provides for each n the time $t_b(n)$ by which frame n is guaranteed to arrive. For continuous playback, it is sufficient that the buffer tube upper bound $t_b(n)$ be ahead of the *playback deadline* $t_d(n)$, which is the time at which frame n is scheduled to be instantaneously decoded

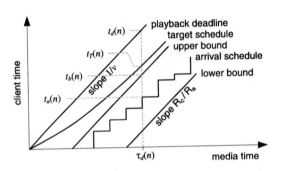

FIGURE 14.9: Arrival schedule and its upper bound in client time. The upper bound is controlled to the target schedule, which is increasingly in advance of the playback deadline to provide greater robustness over time.

and played. Note that the gap between a frame's arrival time $t_a(n)$ and its playback deadline $t_d(n)$ is the client buffer duration at the time of the frame's arrival. This must be nonnegative to allow continuous playback.

In reality the arrival rate is not constant. At any moment, the arrival rate may suddenly drop due to an increase in competing traffic, for example. Then each frame would take longer to be transmitted, the frame arrival times would become increasingly delayed, and the whole arrival schedule and its buffer tube would veer upward, threatening to cross over the playback schedule. To guard against such an event, if the buffer duration is too low, the buffer duration can be increased by switching to a lower source coding rate R_c, thereby reducing the slope of the buffer tube.

To see how, let $t_a(n-1)$ and $t_a(n)$ be the arrival times of frames n and $n-1$, respectively, and define

$$R_a(n) = \frac{b(n)}{t_a(n) - t_a(n-1)} \tag{14.27}$$

to be the *instantaneous arrival rate* at frame n. In practice, the average arrival rate at frame n will be estimated by a moving average $\tilde{R}_a(n)$ of previous values of $R_a(n)$, as detailed in the Appendix. Hence using (14.27) the arrival time of frame n can be expressed in terms of the arrival time of frame $n-1$ as

$$t_a(n) = t_a(n-1) + \frac{b(n)}{R_a(n)} \tag{14.28}$$

$$= t_a(n-1) + \frac{b(n)}{\tilde{R}_a(n)} + v(n), \tag{14.29}$$

where the $v(n)$ term is an error term that captures the effect of using the slowly moving average $\tilde{R}_a(n)$ instead of the instantaneous arrival rate $R_a(n)$.

How does the source coding rate R_c fit into all this? From Figure 14.5 it is clear that the decoder buffer fullness $F_d(n) = B - F_e(n)$ can also be expressed

$$F_d(n) = b(n) + g(n) = g(n-1) + \frac{R_c(n)}{f(n)}, \qquad (14.30)$$

where

$$f(n) = \frac{1}{\tau(n) - \tau(n-1)} \qquad (14.31)$$

is the instantaneous frame rate and the source coding rate $R_c(n)$ is now indexed by n, to take into account that different frames may lie in different buffer tubes with different coding rates as coding rate control is applied and streams are switched. Now from (14.30), we have

$$b(n) = \frac{R_c(n)}{f(n)} + g(n-1) - g(n), \qquad (14.32)$$

whence [substituting (14.32) into (14.29)] we have

$$t_a(n) = t_a(n-1) + \frac{R_c(n)}{f(n)\tilde{R}_a(n)} + \frac{g(n-1)}{\tilde{R}_a(n)} - \frac{g(n)}{\tilde{R}_a(n)} + v(n). \qquad (14.33)$$

Now defining the buffer tube upper bound (in time) of frame n as

$$t_b(n) = t_a(n) + \frac{g(n)}{\tilde{R}_a(n)}, \qquad (14.34)$$

so that

$$t_b(n) - t_b(n-1) = t_a(n) - t_a(n-1) + \frac{g(n)}{\tilde{R}_a(n)} - \frac{g(n-1)}{\tilde{R}_a(n-1)}, \qquad (14.35)$$

we obtain the following update equation:

$$t_b(n) = t_b(n-1) + \frac{R_c(n)}{f(n)\tilde{R}_a(n)} + w(n-1), \qquad (14.36)$$

where

$$w(n-1) = \frac{g(n-1)}{\tilde{R}_a(n)} - \frac{g(n-1)}{\tilde{R}_a(n-1)} + v(n) \qquad (14.37)$$

is again an error term that captures variations around a locally constant arrival rate.

Using (14.34), the client can compute $t_b(n-1)$ from the measured arrival time $t_a(n-1)$, the estimated arrival rate $\tilde{R}_a(n-1)$, and $g(n-1)$ [which can be transmitted to the client along with the data in frame $n-1$ or computed at the client from $g(n-2)$ and $R_c(n-1)$ using (14.30)]. Then using (14.36), the client can control the coding rate $R_c(n)$ so that $t_b(n)$ reaches a desired value, assuming the frame rate and arrival rate remain roughly constant. From this perspective, (14.36) can be regarded as the state transition equation of a feedback control system and it is thus possible to use a control-theoretic approach to regulate the coding rate.

14.4.2.2 Control Objective

With the state transition equation defined in (14.36), uninterrupted playback can be achieved by regulating the coding rate so that the client buffer does not underflow. To introduce a margin of safety that increases over time, we introduce a *target schedule*, illustrated along with the buffer tube in Figure 14.9, whose distance from the playback deadline grows slowly over time. By regulating the coding rate, we attempt to control the buffer tube upper bound so that it tracks the target schedule. If the buffer tube upper bound is close to the target schedule, then the arrival times of all frames will certainly be earlier than their playback deadlines and thus uninterrupted playback will be ensured. Note that controlling the actual arrival times (rather than their upper bounds) to the target would result in an approximately constant number of bits per frame, which would in turn result in very poor quality overall. By taking the leaky bucket model into account, we are able to establish a control that allows the instantaneous coding rate to fluctuate naturally according to the encoding complexity of the content, within previously established bounds for a given average coding rate.

Although controlling the upper bound to the target schedule is our primary goal, we also wish to minimize quality variations due to large or frequent changes to the coding rate. This can be achieved by introducing into the cost function a penalty for relative coding rate differences.

Letting $t_T(n)$ denote the target schedule for frame n, we use the following cost function to reflect both of our concerns:

$$I = \sum_{n=0}^{N}\left(\left(t_b(n) - t_T(n)\right)^2 + \sigma\left(\frac{R_c(n+1) - R_c(n)}{\tilde{R}_a(n)}\right)^2 \right), \qquad (14.38)$$

where the first term penalizes the deviation of the buffer tube upper bound from the target schedule and the second term penalizes the relative coding rate difference between successive frames. N is the control window size and σ is a Lagrange multiplier or weighting parameter to balance the two terms.

14.4.2.3 Target Schedule Design

Figure 14.10 shows an illustrative target schedule. The gap between the playback deadline and the target schedule is the desired minimum client buffer duration. If the gap is small at the beginning of streaming, then it allows a small start-up delay, whereas if the gap grows slowly over time, it gradually increases the client's ability to counter jitter, delays, and throughput changes.

The slope of the target schedule relates the average source coding rate to the average arrival rate. Let $t_T(n)$ be the target for frame n. As illustrated in Figure 14.10, the slope of the target schedule at frame n is

$$s(n) = \frac{t_T(n+1) - t_T(n)}{\tau(n+1) - \tau(n)}. \tag{14.39}$$

If the upper bound $t_b(n)$ aligns perfectly with the target schedule [i.e., $t_b(n) = t_T(n)$] and the arrival rate R_a is constant [i.e., the $w(n-1)$ term vanishes], we get from (14.36)

$$s(n) = \frac{t_b(n+1) - t_b(n)}{\tau(n+1) - \tau(n)} = \frac{R_c(n+1)}{R_a}. \tag{14.40}$$

Thus initially, if the slope is low, that is, $s(n)$ is less than $1/v$, then R_a is greater than $R_c v$, causing the client buffer to grow. Over time, as the slope approaches $1/v$, R_a approaches $R_c v$, and the buffer remains relatively constant, except for changes due to variations in the instantaneous coding rate.

A reasonable way to choose the target schedule t_T is to have the client buffer duration grow logarithmically over time. Specifically, if t_d is the playback dead-

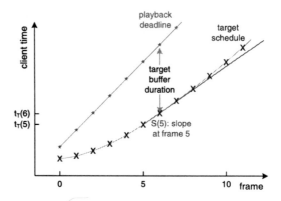

FIGURE 14.10:   Target schedule design.

line, then for each t_d greater than some start time t_{d0},

$$t_T = t_d - \frac{b}{a}\ln\big(a(t_d - t_{d0}) + 1\big). \qquad (14.41)$$

Since $t_d = t_{d0} + (\tau_d - \tau_{d0})/v$ by (14.25), we have

$$s = \frac{dt_T}{d\tau_d} = \frac{dt_T}{dt_d}\frac{dt_d}{d\tau_d} = \frac{1}{v} - \frac{b}{a(\tau_d - \tau_{d0}) + v}, \qquad (14.42)$$

and hence the initial slope at frame 0 (when $t_d = t_{d0}$) is $s(0) = (1-b)/v$. Setting $b = 0.5$ implies that initially $R_c/R_a = 0.5/v$, causing the client buffer to grow initially at two times real time. Further setting $a = 0.15$ implies that the client buffer duration will be 7.68 s after 1 min, 15.04 s after 10 min, and 22.68 s after 100 min, regardless of v.

14.4.2.4 Controller Design

Recall from (14.36) the fundamental state transition equation, which describes the evolution of the buffer tube upper bound $t_b(n)$ in terms of the source coding rate $R_c(n)$:

$$t_b(n + 1) = t_b(n) + \frac{R_c(n + 1)}{f \tilde{R}_a} + w(n). \qquad (14.43)$$

Here we now assume that the frame rate f and the average arrival rate $\tilde{R}_a$ are relatively constant. Deviations from this assumption are captured by $w(n)$.

We wish to control the upper bound by adjusting the source coding rate. As each frame arrives at the client, a feedback loop can send a message to the server to adjust the source coding rate. Note, however, that by the time frame n arrives completely at the client, frame $n + 1$ has already started streaming from the server. Thus the coding rate $R_c(n + 1)$ for frame $n + 1$ must already be determined by time $t_a(n)$. Indeed, at time $t_a(n)$, frame $n + 2$ is the earliest frame for which the controller can determine the coding rate. Hence at time $t_a(n)$, the controller's job must be to choose $R_c(n + 2)$. We must explicitly account for this one-frame delay in our feedback loop.

For simplicity, we linearize the target schedule around the time that frame n arrives. The linearization is equivalent to using a line tangent to the original target schedule at a particular point as an approximate target schedule. Thus we have

$$t_T(n + 1) - 2t_T(n) + t_T(n - 1) = 0. \qquad (14.44)$$

Rather than directly control the evolution of the upper bound, which grows without bound, for the purposes of stability we use an error space formulation.

By defining the error

$$e(n) = t_b(n) - t_T(n), \qquad (14.45)$$

we obtain

$$e(n+1) - e(n) = \big(t_b(n+1) - t_T(n+1)\big) - \big(t_b(n) - t_T(n)\big) \quad (14.46)$$
$$= \big(t_b(n+1) - t_b(n)\big) - \big(t_T(n+1) - t_T(n)\big) \quad (14.47)$$
$$= \frac{R_c(n+1)}{f \tilde{R}_a} - \big(t_T(n+1) - t_T(n)\big) + w(n), \quad (14.48)$$

from which we obtain in turn

$$\big(e(n+1) - e(n)\big) - \big(e(n) - e(n-1)\big)$$
$$= \big[R_c(n+1) - R_c(n)\big]/f \tilde{R}_a$$
$$\quad - \big(t_T(n+1) - 2t_T(n) + t_T(n-1)\big)$$
$$\quad + \big(w(n) - w(n-1)\big) \qquad (14.49)$$
$$= \frac{R_c(n+1) - R_c(n)}{f \tilde{R}_a} + \big(w(n) - w(n-1)\big). \qquad (14.50)$$

We next define the control input

$$u(n) = \frac{R_c(n+2) - R_c(n+1)}{\tilde{R}_a}, \qquad (14.51)$$

and we define the disturbance

$$d(n) = w(n) - w(n-1). \qquad (14.52)$$

Then (14.50) can be rewritten

$$e(n+1) = 2e(n) - e(n-1) + \frac{u(n-1)}{f} + d(n). \qquad (14.53)$$

Therefore, defining the state vector

$$\mathbf{e}(n) = \begin{bmatrix} e(n) \\ e(n-1) \\ u(n-1) \end{bmatrix} = \begin{bmatrix} t_b(n) \\ t_b(n-1) \\ \frac{R_c(n+1)}{\tilde{R}_a} \end{bmatrix} - \begin{bmatrix} t_T(n) \\ t_T(n-1) \\ \frac{R_c(n)}{\tilde{R}_a} \end{bmatrix}, \qquad (14.54)$$

the error space representation of the system can be expressed

$$
\mathbf{e}(n+1) = \begin{bmatrix} 2 & -1 & \frac{1}{f} \\ 1 & 0 & 0 \\ 0 & 0 & 0 \end{bmatrix} \mathbf{e}(n) + \begin{bmatrix} 0 \\ 0 \\ 1 \end{bmatrix} u(n) + \begin{bmatrix} 1 \\ 0 \\ 0 \end{bmatrix} d(n), \qquad (14.55)
$$

or $\mathbf{e}(n+1) = \Phi\mathbf{e}(n) + \Gamma u(n) + \Gamma_d d(n)$ for appropriate matrices Φ, Γ, and Γ_d.

Assuming the disturbance $d(n)$ is a pure white noise, and assuming *perfect state measurement* (i.e., we can measure all components of $\mathbf{e}(n)$ without using an estimator), the disturbance $d(n)$ does not affect the controller design. Thus we can use a linear controller represented by

$$
u(n) = -G\mathbf{e}(n), \qquad (14.56)
$$

where G is a vector *feedback gain*. By the time frame n is completely received, all elements of $\mathbf{e}(n)$ are available at the client and $u(n)$ can thus be computed. The ideal coding rate for frame $n+2$ can then be computed as

$$
R_c(n+2) = R_c(n+1) - G\mathbf{e}(n)\tilde{R}_a. \qquad (14.57)
$$

Finding the optimal linear controller amounts to finding the feedback gain G^* that minimizes the quadratic cost function (14.38). Before continuing with the design, we first check the system *controllability matrix* C,

$$
C = [\,\Gamma \quad \Phi\Gamma \quad \Phi^2\Gamma\,] = \begin{bmatrix} 0 & \frac{1}{f} & \frac{2}{f} \\ 0 & 0 & \frac{1}{f} \\ 1 & 0 & 0 \end{bmatrix}, \qquad (14.58)
$$

which has full rank for any frame rate f. Thus, the system is *completely controllable* [16] and the state $\mathbf{e}(n)$ can be regulated to any desirable value. Now recall that the cost function (14.38) is

$$
I = \sum_{n=0}^{N} \left\{ \left(t_b(n) - t_T(n) \right)^2 + \sigma \left(\frac{R_c(n+1) - R_c(n)}{\tilde{R}_a} \right)^2 \right\} \qquad (14.59)
$$

$$
= \sum_{n=0}^{N} \{ \mathbf{e}(n)^T Q\mathbf{e}(n) + u(n-1)^T Ru(n-1) \}, \qquad (14.60)
$$

where $Q = C^T C$ (with $C = [1\ 0\ 0]$) and $R = \sigma$. Then, the original control problem of tracking the target schedule while smoothing the coding rate fluctuations (i.e., minimizing the cost function I) is converted to a standard regulator problem in the error space. Letting $N \to \infty$, the infinite horizon optimal control problem can be solved by applying the results in [2, Section 3.3] to obtain an optimal regulator in two steps: (1) solving, to get S, the discrete algebraic Riccati equation

$$S = \Phi^T \left\{ S - S\Gamma \left[\Gamma^T S\Gamma + R \right]^{-1} \Gamma^T S \right\} \Phi + Q, \qquad (14.61)$$

and (2) computing the optimal feedback gain

$$G^* = \left[\Gamma^T S\Gamma + R \right]^{-1} \Gamma^T S\Phi. \qquad (14.62)$$

The existence and uniqueness of S (and in turn of G^*) are guaranteed when Q is nonnegative definite and R is positive definite, which is straightforward to verify in our case.

14.4.2.5 Effect of Frame Rate

In the derivation given earlier, we assumed that the frame rate is constant. This assumption is reasonable when streaming a single medium, such as video without audio. However, usually video and audio are streamed together, and their merged coding schedule may have no fixed frame rate. Even if there is a fixed frame rate f, we may wish to operate the controller at a rate lower than f to reduce the feedback rate, for example.

To address these issues, in practice we use the notion of a *virtual frame rate*. We choose a virtual frame rate f, for example, $f = 1$ frame per second (fps); we partition media time into intervals of size $1/f$; and we model all of the (audio and video) frames arriving within each interval as a *virtual frame* whose decoding and playback deadline is the end of the interval.

This approach has several advantages. First, it allows us to design off line a universal feedback gain, which is independent of the actual frame rate of the stream or streams. Second, it allows us to reduce the rate of feedback from the client to the server. Finally, since the interval between virtual frames is typically safely larger than a round trip time (RTT), a one-frame delay in the error space model (as described in the previous section) is sufficient to model the feedback delay. Otherwise we would have to model the feedback delay with approximately RTT/f additional state variables to represent the network delay using a shift register of length RTT/f.

In the sequel we therefore use a virtual frame rate $f = 1$ fps, and we refer to this simply as the frame rate. With $f = 1$ and $\sigma = 50$ (chosen empirically for good damping), we can solve for $G^* = [0.6307, -0.5225, 0.5225]$.

14.4.2.6 Controller Interpretation

With the aforementioned coefficients for G^*, we are now able to give an intuitive explanation of the source coding rate control (14.57). Plugging the coefficients of G^* into (14.57), we obtain

$$R_c(n+2) = R_c(n+1)$$

$$- 0.1082e(n)\tilde{R}_a \tag{14.63}$$

$$- 0.5225\big[e(n) - e(n-1)\big]\tilde{R}_a \tag{14.64}$$

$$- 0.5225\big[R_c(n+1) - R_c(n)\big]. \tag{14.65}$$

Focusing on the first term (14.63), it can be seen that the source coding rate R_c tends to decrease if the current error $e(n) = t_b(n) - t_T(n)$ is positive, and it tends to increase if $e(n)$ is negative, in proportion to $e(n)$ with proportionality constant 0.1082 times the estimated arrival rate $\tilde{R}_a$. This has the effect of moving the upper bound t_b toward the target t_T, whether it is above or below the target. At the same time, from the second term (14.64), it can be seen that the source coding rate tends to decrease if the current error $e(n)$ is numerically greater than the previous error $e(n-1)$, whether $e(n)$ is positive or negative. This has the effect of either strengthening the compensation or preventing the controller from overcompensating, since if $e(n)$ is positive then $e(n) > e(n-1)$ indicates that the magnitude of the error is still growing, whereas if $e(n)$ is negative then $e(n) > e(n-1)$ indicates that the magnitude of the error is shrinking too fast to be sustainable. The proportionality constant for this second effect is 0.5225 times $\tilde{R}_a$, which is even larger than that for the first effect. Finally, from the third term (14.65), it can be seen that the source coding rate tends to decrease if it had previously increased, with proportionality constant 0.5225. This ensures appropriate damping and smoothing of the source coding rate.

It is important to emphasize that the optimal feedback gain G^* is completely determined given σ and f, and that it is independent of the arrival rate and the source coding rate. Thus, G^* can be obtained off line, and only a linear calculation is required to compute the source coding rate $R_c(n+2)$ on the fly.

Figure 14.11 shows results of a simulation in which FTP cross traffic reduces the fair share for streaming from 800 to 200 Kbps and back again over 180 s. Figure 14.11a shows the fair share bandwidth, as well as the rate of arrival of reliable information over TCP and the resulting source coding rate. The source coding rate starts at about half the arrival rate to build up the client buffer duration and approaches the arrival rate over the first 45 s. Subsequently the source coding rate tends to track the arrival rate, but with less variation. Figure 14.11b shows the associated client buffer duration $t_d(n) - t_a(n)$, as well as the target $t_d(n) - t_T(n)$

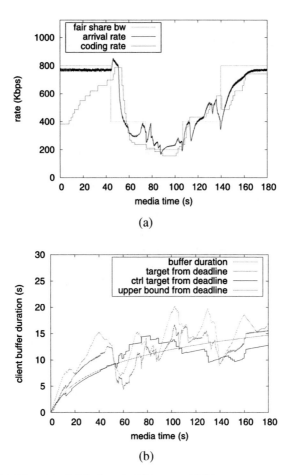

(a)

(b)

FIGURE 14.11:   Variable bandwidth over TCP.

and the buffer tube upper bound $t_d(n) - t_b(n)$ relative to the deadline. Despite sudden large changes in the TCP arrival rate (e.g., at the 50-s mark), the buffer duration remains safely positive and recovers quickly to the target.

14.5 LIVE BROADCAST

Section 14.2 covered the architectural differences between live broadcast and streaming media on demand. In live broadcast, the encoder is online, but communicates through the server to multiple clients simultaneously. Thus even though the encoder is online, it is still not feasible to know the channel conditions between the server and each client separately. In general, the clients experience different channels, such as different rates of packet loss, different patterns of packet loss, and different limitations on bit rate. Thus a major issue in live broadcast is dealing with the *heterogeneity of channels* across clients, in terms of both error and bit rate characteristics.

Another issue in live broadcast is dealing with the *heterogeneity of devices* across clients, in terms of resolution and computational power. Mobile phones have limited screen real estate, a limited number of audio channels, and limited computational power for decoding. In contrast, home media centers may have high-definition projection monitors, multichannel surround sound, multigigahertz, multicore computational engines, and specialized hardware or firmware decoders. Because of such heterogeneity in both devices and channels, the encoder cannot generally produce a single encoding that is satisfactory to all clients.

A time-honored means of broadcasting to heterogeneous clients is *simulcast*. Terrestrial television broadcast in North America, for example, is currently simulcasting (simultaneously broadcasting) standard definition and high-definition programs. This is analogous to multibit rate files for streaming media on demand. As a result, it is always possible to address heterogeneous client populations by simulcasting streams with different bit rates, error protection, source resolutions, and decoding requirements. Each client can "tune in" to the appropriate "channel" depending on its needs. In the case of IP multicast, each "channel" is represented by an IP multicast group address (or simply *multicast address*) [31]. Once these addresses and the descriptions of their contents are known (using an out-of-band mechanism such as the session announcement and description protocols [19,20]), it is possible for a client to subscribe to the appropriate multicast address to obtain an appropriate stream.

A means of broadcasting to heterogeneous clients that makes more efficient use of network resources is based on scalable coding rather than multibit rate coding. In *layered multicast*, each layer of a scalable encoding is multicast to a different address. Each client subscribes to the appropriate set of addresses to obtain the appropriate layers of the encoding. This idea was first operationalized by McCanne [28], although the idea itself precedes McCanne's work. In McCanne's protocol, called *receiver-driven layered multicast*, each client continually probes for bandwidth by subscribing to and unsubscribing from (i.e., adding and dropping) the client's current topmost enhancement layer. This is an effective way to adapt the bit rate and to provide congestion control in bandwidth-heterogeneous IP multicast networks.

McCanne's work did not address error control. As noted earlier, different clients generally experience different packet loss rates and packet loss patterns, in addition to different bit rate limitations. Unfortunately, the standard error control technique of end-to-end packet retransmission, used so effectively in streaming media on demand to control packet loss adaptively, cannot be used in the broadcast scenario because of limitations on feedback to the server. Timely feedback of either positive or negative acknowledgments from the clients to the server would cause a *feedback implosion* at the server, and hence would not scale to large numbers of clients.

However, *statistical feedback*, as opposed to timely feedback, is possible. The common example of statistical feedback is RTCP receiver reports [35], which can be periodically sent from the client to each server to inform the server of the average packet loss rate. In multicast situations, the clients can send the receiver reports at random intervals with a frequency inversely proportional to the number of clients in the session. In this way, the rate at which receiver reports arrive at the server remains approximately constant regardless of the number of clients. The server can use such statistical feedback to understand its client population and to tailor one or more streams to the population.

Because timely feedback is generally not feasible in multicast settings, error control is usually based on feedforward rather than feedback mechanisms. Forward error correction (FEC) coding [27] or, more precisely, forward erasure coding is typically used to control packet loss in multicast settings. The Windows Media Server, for example, uses a systematic Reed–Solomon style erasure code, as described in Chapter 7, to generate and transmit $N - K$ parity packets after every block of K source packets when broadcasting over IP multicast. (IP multicast is widely used on the Microsoft campus to broadcast lectures, meetings, etc.) Thus every "source block" of K source packets maps to a "code block" of N source and parity packets. If at least K out of N packets in a code block are received (i.e., if no more than $N - K$ packets in a code block are lost), then the corresponding K source packets can still be recovered. The parameters (N, K) can be optimized to match the packet loss characteristics of the client population, as can be determined by RTCP receiver reports. Typically, $(N - K)/N$ is set close to the worst-case error rate.

More efficient than FEC, however, to protect scalable media is *priority encoded transmission* (PET) [1], as described in Chapter 9. FEC tends to degrade sharply if more than $N - K$ packets in a code block are lost—a "cliff" effect. In contrast, PET degrades gracefully as more packets are lost in a code block. This is because in PET, the number of layers that can be recovered by the client in the scalable source encoding is equal to the number of packets that are received, as illustrated in Figure 14.12. Figure 14.13 shows video quality as a function of the number of packets received per code block. Like FEC, PET can be optimized as a function of the packet loss characteristics of the client population. If $q_0, q_1, \ldots, q_N$ is the probability distribution of the number of packets received by a client in any block of N code packets, then the procedures detailed in Chapter 9 can be used to optimize the PET parameters $\mathbf{R} = (R_0, R_1, \ldots, R_N)$ to minimize (subject to a rate constraint) the average distortion $D = \sum_{n=0}^{N} q_n D(R_n)$ over the population. The resulting bit stream can be packetized as described in [26].

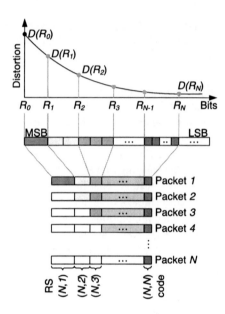

FIGURE 14.12: PET packetization. An embedded bit stream with distortion–rate function $D(R)$ is partitioned into N layers and poured into N packets. Layer K is protected with an (N, K) RS code such that if any K out of N packets are received, the first K layers are recoverable.

Optimizing the FEC or PET parameters for a heterogeneous client population may result in a stream that is far from optimal for any homogeneous sub-population. In this situation, it may pay to provide multiple streams, each one targeted to a sub-population. Relatively homogeneous sub-populations can be identified by clustering, as follows. Suppose $q_{\theta,0}, q_{\theta,1}, \ldots, q_{\theta,N}$ is the probability distribution of the number of packets received by client $\theta \in \Lambda$ in any block of N code packets, where Λ represents the overall population of clients. Let $m(\theta) : \Lambda \to \{1, \ldots, M\}$ be the assignment of client θ to one of M sub-populations $\Lambda_m \subseteq \Lambda$ and let $\mathbf{R}(m) = (R_{m,0}, R_{m,1}, \ldots, R_{m,N})$ be the PET parameters for sub-population Λ_m. Clearly, the optimal assignment for each client θ is the one that maps θ to the sub-population Λ_m whose PET parameters $\mathbf{R}(m)$ result in the lowest distortion for client θ, that is,

$$m(\theta) = \arg \min_m \sum_{n=0}^{n} q_{\theta,n} D(R_{m,n}). \qquad (14.66)$$

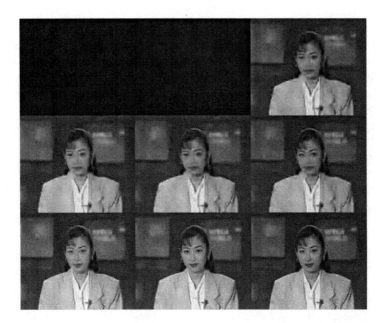

FIGURE 14.13: PET quality as a function of number of packets received. From top to bottom, left to right: zero to eight packets received (out of eight transmitted).

However, the optimal PET parameters for each sub-population Λ_m minimize the average distortion for the sub-population, that is,

$$\mathbf{R}(m) = \arg \min_{\mathbf{R}} \sum_{n=0}^{N} q_{m,n} D(R_n), \tag{14.67}$$

where $q_{m,n}$ is the average of $q_{\theta,n}$ over $\theta \in \Lambda_m$. The minimization (14.67) can be performed with the algorithms in Chapter 9. The minimizations (14.66) and (14.67) can be repeated until the distortion averaged over the entire population Λ converges to a minimum, determining both the clustering and the PET parameters for each cluster [8].

Using FEC or PET for error control can be combined with either simulcast or layered multicast. The simulcast case is straightforward. As usual, the client population is partitioned into sub-populations according to bit rate. Then for each bit rate, FEC or PET is applied to make a loss-resilient stream at that bit rate. Multiple loss-resilient streams for a given bit rate are also possible, as described earlier, if the clients at that bit rate are heterogeneous in terms of loss.

Combining FEC or PET with layered multicast is trickier because insufficient protection of a lower (e.g., base) layer will render a higher (e.g., enhancement) layer irrelevant. Thus in general the lower layers need more error protection than the higher layers. Furthermore, the optimum amount of protection of any given layer increases as the overall bit rate increases. Therefore, as enhancement layers are added, stronger error protection must also be added for each of the preceding layers. Hence the error protection itself must be layered. In addition, the available bit rate must be optimally allocated to the various layers.

A natural approach to this problem is given in [7,40]. Suppose that all the source layers have an equal rate, say one packet per group of frames (GOF). As illustrated in Figure 14.14, partition the packets in each source layer into blocks having K packets per block, where the block size K is constant across all source layers and the block boundaries are synchronized across layers. For each block of K source packets in a source layer, generate $N - K$ parity packets using a systematic (N, K) Reed–Solomon style erasure code, where the "code length" N is determined by the maximum amount of redundancy that will be needed by any client to protect the source layer. Place each of the parity packets so generated in its own multicast stream so that each source layer is accompanied by $N - K$ parity layers, each at $1/K$ the rate of the source layer. In this way, a client now has many layers to which it can subscribe. It can subscribe to any collection of source layers and any collection of parity layers associated with those source layers.

The problem now is to determine the layers to which a client should subscribe to minimize the expected distortion given a total bit rate constraint and a packet loss rate. Let N_l be the number of code packets (i.e., source packets plus parity packets) for source layer l to which the client subscribes, $l = 1, \ldots, L$. Then N_l takes the value 0 if the client does not subscribe to source layer l or any of its associated parity layers; it takes the value K if the client subscribes to source layer

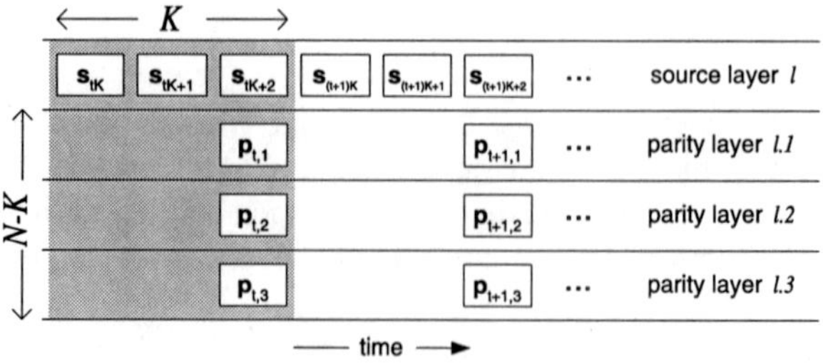

FIGURE 14.14: Generation of parity packets: block each source layer into K packets per block; produce $N - K$ parity packets per block with a systematic RS-style code; and send each parity packet to a different multicast address.

l but to none of its associated parity layers; and it takes the values $K + 1, \ldots, N$ if the client subscribes to source layer l and $1, \ldots, N - K$ of its associated parity layers, respectively. Let the redundancy $\pi_l = N_l / K$ be the number of packets per GOF transmitted to the client in layer l. (This is the inverse of the code rate.) The vector $\pi = (\pi_1, \ldots, \pi_L)$, called the *transmission policy*, specifies which source layers to subscribe to and also which parity layers to subscribe to for each source layer. Any given transmission policy π induces a total bit rate and an expected distortion. The total bit rate, in terms of transmitted packets per GOF, is

$$R(\pi) = \sum_l \pi_l, \tag{14.68}$$

whereas the expected distortion per GOF is

$$D(\pi) = D_0 - \sum_l \Delta D_l \prod_{l' \preceq l} \bigl(1 - \varepsilon(\pi_{l'})\bigr), \tag{14.69}$$

as shown in [7]. Here, D_0 is the distortion if no packets in a GOF can be decoded, ΔD_l is the distortion reduction if the packet in layer l can be decoded, and the product $\prod_{l' \preceq l}(1 - \varepsilon(\pi_{l'}))$ is the probability for this to occur, as described in Chapter 10. The notation $l' \preceq l$ is shorthand for the set of layers l' on which layer l depends for decoding, and $\varepsilon(\pi_l)$ is the residual probability of packet loss after channel decoding under the transmission policy. In [7] this is shown to be $1 - M(N_l, K)/K$, where

$$M(N_l, K) = \sum_{i=0}^{N_l} \binom{N_l}{i} \varepsilon^{N_l - i} (1 - \varepsilon)^i M(N_l, K \mid i) \tag{14.70}$$

is the expected number of source packets that can be recovered after channel decoding with a (N_l, K) code. Here $M(N_l, K \mid i)$ equals K if $i \geq K$ and equals iK/N_l if $i < K$, and ε is the packet loss rate for the client in question.

Chande and Farvardin [5] provide a dynamic programming algorithm to find the transmission policy π that minimizes $D(\pi)$ subject to $R(\pi) \leq R_{\max}$ when the dependencies between layers are sequential. When the dependencies are given more generally by a directed acyclic graph, then the transmission policy can be optimized by the Iterative Sensitivity Adjustment algorithm [6,7], as discussed in Chapter 10.

An alternative approach to combining error control with layered coding is based on PET, as described in [9,39]. However, this approach gets quite complicated with any more than two source layers.

In the aforementioned discussion, we assumed a dumb network such as an IP network, in which the network nodes can only copy and forward data. However, if the network nodes are more intelligent, for example, if the network is an overlay network of servers or peers, then much more can be done. As a simple example, if the network nodes are computers, then communication between nodes can be made reliable by using sufficient buffering and retransmission (e.g., using TCP), thus eliminating the problem of error control altogether (although rate control remains a problem). For example, today's CoolStreaming and PPLive applications [41,42] deliver IP television peer to peer with essentially no glitching as long as the available bandwidth is high enough.

14.6 SUMMARY AND FURTHER READING

In this chapter, we treated both streaming media on demand and live broadcast. An attempt was made, more than in any other book we know, to formalize these systems and to show how they can be optimized.

Much of Section 14.3, on leaky bucket models, is based on [34]. Another primary source of information on leaky buckets is [21]. Much of Section 14.4, on rate control, is based on [22–24]. Much of Section 14.5, on multicast, is based on [7,8]. Please see these primary sources for more detailed information.

For more general information on streaming media, see the excellent books by Crowcroft *et al.* [12] and Perkins [32]. Of course an amazing amount of information is freely available through the web.

ACKNOWLEDGMENTS

The author is indebted to Anders Klemets, Cheng Huang, Jordi Ribas-Corbera, Shankar Regunathan, and Albert Wang for their contributions to this chapter.

RealMedia and Helix are registered trademarks of RealNetworks, Inc. QuickTime is a registered trademark of Apple Computer Corporation. Windows is a registered trademark of Microsoft Corporation.

APPENDIX: RATE ESTIMATION

This section details our exponential averaging algorithm for the arrival rate, the preferred algorithm in any context in which a bit rate must be estimated from a sequence of variable-sized packets with variable inter-packet intervals.

Let $\tilde{R}_a(k)$ and $R_a(k)$ be the average arrival rate and the instantaneous arrival rate, respectively, when packet k is received. Note that unlike the controlling operation, the rate averaging operation may be performed after the arrival of every *packet* rather than after the arrival of every *frame*. Hence we use the discrete packet index k rather than the frame index n. Instead of using the widely adopted exponentially weighted moving average (EWMA)

$$\tilde{R}_a(k) = \beta(k)\tilde{R}_a(k-1) + \left(1 - \beta(k)\right)R_a(k) \tag{14.71}$$

with constant $\beta(k) = \beta$, we perform the exponential averaging more carefully. In our algorithm, the factor $\beta(k)$ is not constant, but varies according to the packets' interarrival gaps. Our algorithm has several advantages over the EWMA algorithm with constant $\beta(k)$. First, the estimate of the average arrival rate $\tilde{R}_a(k)$ goes to zero naturally as the gap since the last packet goes to infinity, rather than being bounded below by $\beta\tilde{R}_a(k-1)$. Second, the estimate of the average arrival rate $\tilde{R}_a(k)$ does not go to infinity as the gap since the last packet goes to zero. This is especially important, as packets often arrive in bursts, causing extremely high instantaneous arrival rates. Finally, the estimate of the average arrival rate $\tilde{R}_a(k)$ does not overweight the initial condition, as if it represented the infinite past. This is especially important in the early stages of estimation.

As in (14.27), we define the instantaneous arrival rate after packet k as

$$R_a(k) = \frac{b(k)}{t_a(k) - t_a(k-1)}, \tag{14.72}$$

where here $b(k)$ denotes the size of packet k and $t_a(k)$ denotes the arrival time of packet k. We extend the discrete time function $R_a(k)$ to the piecewise constant continuous time function $R_a(t)$ by

$$R_a(t) = R_a(k) \quad \text{for all } t \in \left[t_a(k-1), t_a(k)\right], \tag{14.73}$$

as illustrated in Figure 14.15. Then we filter the function $R_a(t)$ by the exponential impulse response $\alpha e^{-\alpha t}$, $t \geq 0$, for some time constant $1/\alpha$:

$$\tilde{R}_a(k) = \frac{\int_{t(0)}^{t(k)} R_a(t')\alpha e^{-\alpha(t(k)-t')}dt'}{\int_{t(0)}^{t(k)} \alpha e^{-\alpha(t(k)-t')}dt'}. \tag{14.74}$$

[Here and in the remainder of the Appendix we suppress the subscript from the arrival time $t_a(k)$.] Noting that $\int_t^\infty \alpha e^{-\alpha t'}dt' = e^{-\alpha t}$, the denominator integral can be expressed $1 - e^{-\alpha(t(k)-t(0))}$. Now, we split the range of the numerator integral into ranges $[t(0), t(k-1)]$ and $[t(k-1), t(k)]$ to obtain a recursive expression for $\tilde{R}_a(k)$ in terms of $\tilde{R}_a(k-1)$ and $R_a(k)$,

$$\tilde{R}_a(k) = \frac{1 - e^{-\alpha[t(k-1)-t(0)]}}{1 - e^{-\alpha[t(k)-t(0)]}}e^{-\alpha[t(k)-t(k-1)]}\tilde{R}_a(k-1)$$

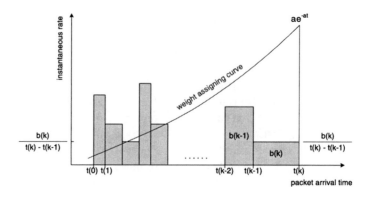

FIGURE 14.15: Exponential averaging.

$$+ \frac{1 - e^{-\alpha[t(k)-t(k-1)]}}{1 - e^{-\alpha[t(k)-t(0)]}} R_a(k) \tag{14.75}$$

$$= \beta(k)\tilde{R}_a(k-1) + (1 - \beta(k))R_a(k), \tag{14.76}$$

where

$$\beta(k) = \frac{e^{-\alpha[t(k)-t(k-1)]} - e^{-\alpha[t(k)-t(0)]}}{1 - e^{-\alpha[t(k)-t(0)]}}. \tag{14.77}$$

Note that $\beta(k)$ is numerically stable as k goes to infinity. However, as the gap $\delta = t(k) - t(k-1)$ goes to zero, $1 - \beta(k)$ goes to zero while $R_a(k)$ goes to infinity. Their product, however, is well behaved. Indeed,

$$\tilde{R}_a(k) = \frac{1 - e^{-\alpha[t(k-1)-t(0)]}}{1 - e^{-\alpha[\delta+t(k-1)-t(0)]}} e^{-\alpha\delta} \tilde{R}_a(k-1)$$

$$+ \frac{1 - e^{-\alpha\delta}}{1 - e^{-\alpha[t(k)-t(0)]}} \frac{b(k)}{\delta} \tag{14.78}$$

$$\rightarrow \tilde{R}_a(k-1) + \frac{\alpha b(k)}{1 - e^{-\alpha[t(k)-t(0)]}} \tag{14.79}$$

as $\delta \rightarrow 0$, using l'Hôpital's rule. Thus (14.79) is the update rule in the case when $t(k) = t(k-1)$.

REFERENCES

[1] A. Albanese, J. Blömer, J. Edmonds, M. Luby, and M. Sudan. "Priority Encoding Transmission," *IEEE Trans. Information Theory*, 42:1737–1744, November 1996.

[2] B. D. O. Anderson and J. B. Moore. *Optimal Control: Linear Quadratic Methods.* Prentice Hall, 1990.

[3] D. Bulterman, G. Grassel, J. Jansen, A. Koivisto, N. Layaïda, T. Michel, S. Mullender, and D. Zucker. Synchronized multimedia integration language (SMIL 2.1). Recommendation REC-SMIL2-20051213, W3C, December 2005. http://www.w3.org/AudioVideo/.

[4] S. W. Carter, D. D. E. Long, and J.-F. Pâris. "Video-on-Demand Broadcasting Protocols." In J. D. Gibson, editor, *Multimedia Communications: Directions and Innovations*, chapter 11, pages 179–190. Academic Press, 2001.

[5] V. Chande and N. Farvardin. "Progressive Transmission of Images over Memoryless Noisy Channels," *IEEE J. Selected Areas in Communications*, 18(6):850–860, June 2000.

[6] P. A. Chou and Z. Miao. "Rate-Distortion Optimized Streaming of Packetized Media," *IEEE Trans. Multimedia*, 8(2):390–404, April 2006.

[7] P. A. Chou, A. E. Mohr, A. Wang, and S. Mehrotra. "Error Control for Receiver-Driven Layered Multicast of Audio and Video," *IEEE Trans. Multimedia*, 3(1):108–122, March 2001.

[8] P. A. Chou and K. Ramchandran. "Clustering Source/Channel Rate Allocations for Receiver-Driven Multicast with Error Control under a Limited Number of Streams," in *Proc. Int'l Conf. Multimedia and Exhibition*, volume 3, pages 1221–1224, New York, NY, July 2000.

[9] P. A. Chou, H. J. Wang, and V. N. Padmanabhan. "Layered Multiple Description Coding," in *Proc. Int'l Packet Video Workshop*, Nantes, France, April 2003.

[10] Apple Computer Corporation. QuickTime reference library. http://developer.apple.com/referencelibrary/QuickTime.

[11] Microsoft Corporation. Advanced systems format (ASF) specification. http://www.microsoft.com/windows/windowsmedia/forpros/format/asfspec.aspx.

[12] J. Crowcroft, M. Handley, and I. Wakeman. *Internetworking Multimedia.* UCL Press, December 1998. http://www.cs.ucl.ac.uk/staff/jon/mmbook/book/book.html.

[13] S. Floyd, M. Handley, J. Padhye, and J. Widmer. "Equation-Based Congestion Control for Unicast Applications," in *Proc. Data Communication, Ann. Conf. Series (SIGCOMM)*, Stockholm, Sweden, August 2000. ACM.

[14] S. Floyd and E. Kohler. Profile for datagram congestion control protocol (DCCP) congestion control ID 2: TCP-like congestion control. Proposed standard RFC 4341, IETF, http://www.ietf.org/rfc/rfc4341, March 2006.

[15] S. Floyd, E. Kohler, and J. Padhye. Profile for datagram congestion control protocol (DCCP) congestion control ID 3: TCP-friendly rate control (TFRC). Proposed standard RFC 4342, IETF, http://www.ietf.org/rfc/rfc4342, March 2006.

[16] G. Franklin, J. Powell, and M. Workman. *Digital Control of Dynamic Systems.* Addison-Wesley, 3rd edition, 1997.

[17] T. Gill and B. Birney. *Microsoft Windows Media Resource Kit.* Microsoft Press, February 2003.

[18] M. Handley, S. Floyd, J. Padhye, and J. Widmer. TCP friendly rate control (TFRC): Protocol specification. Proposed standard RFC 3448, IETF, http://www.ietf.org/rfc/rfc3448, January 2003.

[19] M. Handley, V. Jacobson, and C. Perkins. SDP: Session Description Protocol. Proposed standard RFC 4566, IETF, http://www.ietf.org/rfc/rfc4566, July 2006. Obsoletes RFC2327.

[20] M. Handley, C. Perkins, and E. Whelan. Session announcement protocol. Experimental RFC 2974, IETF, http://www.ietf.org/rfc/rfc2974, October 2000.

[21] C.-Y. Hsu, A. Ortega, and A. Reibman. "Joint Selection of Source and Channel Rate for VBR Video Transmission under ATM Policing Constraints," *IEEE Journal on Selected Areas in Communications*, 15(5):1016–1028, August 1997.

[22] C. Huang, P. A. Chou, and A. Klemets. "Optimal Coding Rate Control for Scalable Streaming Media," in *Proc. Int'l Packet Video Workshop*, Irvine, CA, December 2004. IEEE.

[23] C. Huang, P. A. Chou, and A. Klemets. "Optimal Control of Multiple Bit Rates for Streaming Media," in *Proc. Picture Coding Symposium*, San Francisco, CA, December 2004.

[24] C. Huang, P. A. Chou, and A. Klemets. "Optimal Coding Rate Control of Scalable and Multi Bit Rate Streaming Media." Technical Report MSR-TR-2005-47, Microsoft Research, Redmond, WA, April 2005.

[25] E. Kohler, M. Handley, and S. Floyd. Datagram Congestion Control Protocol (DCCP). Proposed standard RFC 4340, IETF, http://www.ietf.org/rfc/rfc4340, March 2006.

[26] G. Leibl, T. Stockhammer, M. Wagner, J. Pandel, G. Baese, M. Nguyen, and F. Burkert. An RTP payload format for erasure-resilient transmission of progressive multimedia streams. Internet Draft draft-ieft-avt-uxp-00.txt, IETF, February 2001. Expired.

[27] S. Lin and D. J. Costello, Jr. *Error Control Coding: Fundamentals and Applications*. Prentice-Hall, Englewood Cliffs, NJ, 1984.

[28] S. R. McCanne. *Scalable Compression and Transmission of Internet Multicast Video*. Ph.D. thesis, The University of California, Berkeley, CA, December 1996.

[29] S. R. McCanne, V. Jacobson, and M. Vetterli. "Receiver-Driven Layered Multicast," in *Proc. SIGCOM*, pages 117–130, Stanford, CA, August 1996. ACM.

[30] NullSoft, Inc. Shoutcast. http://www.shoutcast.com, 1999.

[31] S. Paul. *Multicasting on the Internet and Its Applications*. Kluwer, 1998.

[32] C. Perkins. *RTP: Audio and Video for the Internet*. Addison-Wesley, June 2003.

[33] RealNetworks, Inc. Content production and authoring documentation. http://service.real.com/help/library/encoders.html.

[34] J. Ribas-Corbera, P. A. Chou, and S. Regunathan. "A Generalized Hypothetical Reference Decoder for H.264/AVC," *IEEE Trans. Circuits and Systems for Video Technology*, 13(7), July 2003.

[35] H. Schulzrinne. RTP profile for audio and video conferences with minimal control. Standard RFC 3551, IETF, http://www.ietf.org/rfc/rfc3551, July 2003. Obsoletes RFC1890.

[36] H. Schulzrinne, S. Casner, R. Frederick, and V. Jacobson. RTP: A transport protocol for real-time applications. Standard RFC 3550, IETF, http://www.ietf.org/rfc/rfc3550, July 2003. Obsoletes RFC1889.

[37] H. Schulzrinne, A. Rao, and R. Lanphier. Real time streaming protocol (RTSP). Proposed standard RFC 2326, IETF, http://www.ietf.org/rfc/rfc2326, April 1998.

[38] D. Singer, W. Belkap, and G. Franceschini. ISO media file format specification. Technical report, ISO/IEC JTC1/SC29/WG11 MPEG01/N4270-1, 2001.

[39] V. Stanković, R. Hamzaoui, and Z. Xiong. "Robust Layered Multiple Description Coding of Scalable Media Data for Multicast," *IEEE Signal Processing Letters*, 12:154–157, February 2005.

[40] W.-T. Tan and A. Zakhor. "Video Multicast Using Layered FEC and Scalable Compression," *IEEE Trans. Circuits and Systems for Video Technology*, 11(3):373–387, March 2001.

[41] Wikipedia. Coolstreaming. http://en.wikipedia.org/wiki/CoolStreaming.

[42] Wikipedia. PPLive. http://en.wikipedia.org/wiki/PPLive.

15

Real-Time Communication: Internet Protocol Voice and Video Telephony and Teleconferencing

Yi Liang, Yen-Chi Lee, and Andy Teng

15.1 INTRODUCTION

Internet Protocol (IP)-based real-time communication, including voice-over IP (VoIP), video telephony, and teleconferencing, has been gaining popularity in recent years. One example is VoIP, which has been competing with the traditional public switched telephone network (PSTN) for years and now enjoys increased market share. This is due to the many advantages of IP-based communication, including lower cost as well as the capability of providing integrated data, voice, and video, a larger variety of features, and more value-added services.

Despite rapid expansion and improvement of the underlying infrastructure, quality-of-service (QoS) is still one of the major challenges of real-time communication over IP networks. The unreliable and stateless nature of today's Internet protocol results in a best-effort service, that is, packets may be delivered with an arbitrary delay or may even be lost. Transmitted over the best-effort network and suffering from variable throughput, delay, and loss, data packets have to be delivered by a deadline to become useful. Excessive delay severely impairs communication interactivity; packet loss results in glitches in audio and poor picture quality and frozen frames in video. The heterogeneity of today's Internet also poses a major challenge for media delivery to users with various connection speeds, where scalability is highly desirable.

The challenges that the industry faces, in conjunction with the commercial promise of the technology, have attracted considerable effort in research and product development. In this chapter, we will first describe an architecture for real-time communication, followed by topics on how to improve the QoS. In Section 15.2, we will describe the basic system architecture as well as two categories of the most important protocols: signaling and transport. In Section 15.3, we will address QoS issues, especially minimizing latency, combating loss, adapting to available bandwidth, and audio–video synchronization.

15.2 ARCHITECTURE AND FUNDAMENTALS

15.2.1 Systems

Figure 15.1 shows the setup of a typical VoIP system. An IP phone or a sufficiently equipped PC connects to the Internet to be able to make VoIP calls. For traditional phones in the PSTN network, a gateway is needed for the interoperation between the PSTN and the Internet. After introducing signaling and transport protocols later in this section, we will illustrate the process of setting up a call using corresponding protocols in more detail (Figure 15.8).

Figure 15.2 shows a typical architecture for real-time audio and video communication over IP networks. Transport protocols, including UDP, TCP, and Real-Time Transport (RTP)/Real-Time Transport Control Protocols (RTCP) are built on top of the IP layer. Audio and video codecs are applied on the content encapsulated or to be encapsulated in the payload. The upper-layer applications call audio and video codecs to perform data compression. Signaling protocols, such as session initiation protocol (SIP), are used for call setup and control. The signaling and transport protocols are described in more detail in the following sections.

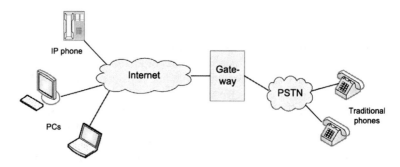

FIGURE 15.1: A typical configuration for a VoIP system with both IP-based devices and traditional PSTN phones.

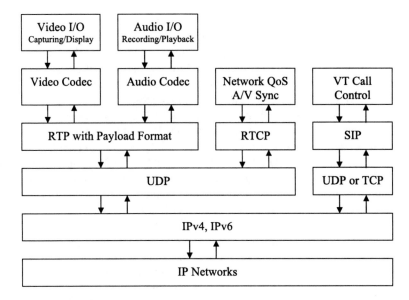

FIGURE 15.2: A typical architecture for an IP-based video and audio communication system.

15.2.2 Signaling Protocols

The SIP, originally developed by the IETF Multi-Party Multimedia Session Control Working Group, is the most widely used signaling protocol for real-time conversational applications over IP networks. As a signaling protocol, SIP provides the following functions:

- Call setup and tear down;
- Advanced features, such as call hold, call waiting, call forwarding, and call transfer;
- Capability exchange;
- Interoperability between different types of networks (e.g., PSTN) and different signaling protocols (e.g., H.323);
- Multicasting.

Moreover, SIP has been designed to be scalable enough to support simultaneous calls for a substantial number of users and to be extensible enough to include more features and functions in the future.

SIP may be transported by either TCP or UDP. TCP provides a reliable, connection-oriented transport, while UDP provides a best-effort, connectionless transport across the Internet. Port numbers 5060 and 5061 are the default ports for SIP, although any number above 49172 may be used. The protocol stack for SIP-based IP phone service is shown in Figure 15.3.

There are two types of SIP messages: request and response. The request message is initiated by a user agent client (UAC) for registering, call setup, tear down, acknowledgment, etc., while the response message is generated by a user agent server (UAS) or a SIP server in response to the request.

The request message in SIP, as with the other IETF protocols (e.g., RTSP), is called a "method." There are six fundamental SIP methods considered as basic signaling for call setup and tear down, which are defined in IETF RFC 3261 [1]: INVITE, ACK, BYE, REGISTER, CANCEL, and OPTIONS. Specifically, the INVITE method is used to initiate a call. The ACK method is used by the call originator to acknowledge the final response to the INVITE request. The BYE method is used to terminate a call. The REGISTER method is used by a user agent (UA) to register itself to a SIP server with the addressing information (contact URI). The CANCEL method is used to cancel the request sent earlier. The OPTIONS method is used to query a SIP server/client capability. In addition to the six methods defined in RFC 3261, other methods were added later as SIP extensions and specified in different RFCs. Examples include INFO (RFC 2976 [2]), MESSAGE (RFC 3428 [3]), NOTIFY (RFC 3265 [4]), PRACK (RFC 3262 [5]), REFER (RFC 3515 [6]), SUBSCRIBE (RFC 3265 [4]), and UPDATE (RFC 3311 [7]).

The response message is called the "response code" in SIP. The SIP response codes are inherited from HTTP/1.1, except for the 6xx class, which is defined by SIP itself (RFC 3261). The six classes of SIP response codes are described briefly here.

1xx (provisional response): information to indicate current status before a definitive response. The 1xx response is designed such that an ACK is never triggered by it and thus the reliability for 1xx transmission is not critical. 180 Ringing is an example of a 1xx response, which is used to inform the originator that the UA has already received the INVITE request.

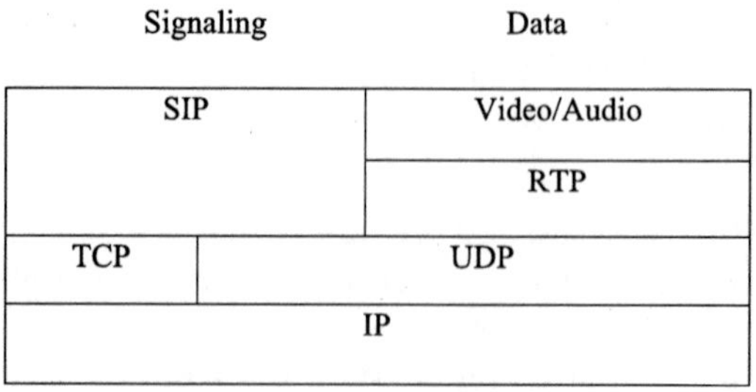

Signaling		Data
SIP		Video/Audio
		RTP
TCP	UDP	
IP		

FIGURE 15.3:   Protocol stack (signaling flow and data flow).

2xx (successful response): a response used to indicate that the request has been successfully received. Example: 200 OK.

3xx (redirectional response): information used to indicate the user's new location or alternative services.

4xx (request failure): a response used by a UAS or a server to indicate that the request cannot be processed due to authorization failure, authentication failure, account issue, requesting itself, or other problems not related to the server. Example: 400 Bad Request indicates that the server does not understand the request.

5xx (server failure): a response used by a UAS or a server to indicate that the request cannot be processed due to the server's problem. Examples include 500 Server Internal Error and 501 Not Implemented.

6xx (global failure): a response used to indicate that the response will fail in all locations and thus the request should not be delivered.

A simple message flow for call setup and tear down is illustrated in Figure 15.4. The SIP request message is composed as follows: method name (e.g., INVITE), address, header fields, and message body. Each response message consists of a

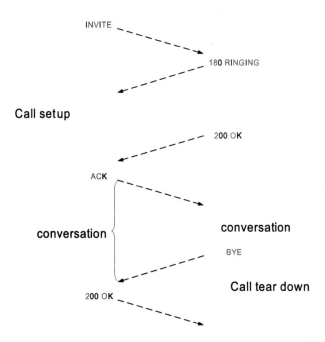

FIGURE 15.4: Simple message flow for call setup and tear down.

code (e.g., 200 OK), header fields, and message body. Note that the header fields and the message body may not appear in all messages.

15.2.2.1 Address

SIP supports a variety of addressing schemes, including SIP URI (Uniform Resource Identifiers), secure SIP URI, telephone URI, and e-mail URL (Uniform Resource Locator). SIP URI is usually represented as `sip:<userinfo>@<host>:<port>`.

15.2.2.2 Header Fields

A header field is composed as `<header>:<field>`. There are 44 header fields defined in RFC 3261: Accept, Accept-Encoding, Accept-Language, Alert-Info, Allow, Authentication-Info, Authorization, Call-ID, Call-Info, Contact, Content-Disposition, Content-Encoding, Content-Language, Content-Length, Content-Type, CSeq, Date, Error-Info, Expires, From, In-Reply-To, Max-Forwards, Min-Expires, MIME-Version, Organization, Priority, Proxy-Authenticate, Proxy-Authorization, Proxy-Require, Record-Route, Reply-To, Require, Retry-After, Route, Server, Subject, Supported, Timestamp, To, Unsupported, User-Agent, Via, Warning, and WWW-Authenticate. The most common ones are introduced here:

> *Call-ID*: used to uniquely identify a call. Example: `CALL-ID: t315fde3-68te-33uyr@test.com`
> *Contact*: used to carry a URI that identifies the resource requested or the request originator. Example: `Contact: sip:johnsmith@test.com`
> *CSeq*: a decimal number used to uniquely identify a request. All responses corresponding to a request use the same CSeq as the request. The CSeq number is usually increased by one for a new request.
> *From*: used to specify the originator. Example: `From: "John Smith" <sip:johnsmith@test.com>`
> *Max-Forwards*: an integer in the range of 0–255 used to specify the maximum number of hops that a message can take. The recommended initial value is 70. It is decreased by one as the message passes through a proxy or gateway. The proxy/gateway discards the message when the value is dropped to zero.
> *To*: used to specify the recipient of the request.
> *Via*: used to record the path the request has been traveled. The response walks through the same path in the reverse order.

The mandatory headers for the six fundamental requests are shown in Table 15.1.

Table 15.1: Mandatory header fields for six fundamental SIP methods, where M denotes *mandatory*.

Header/Requests	INVITE	ACK	BYE	REGISTER	CANCEL	OPTIONS
Call-ID	M	M	M	M	M	M
Contact	M					
CSeq	M	M	M	M	M	M
From	M	M	M	M	M	M
Max-Forwards	M	M	M	M	M	M
To	M	M	M	M	M	M
Via	M	M	M	M	M	M

15.2.2.3 Message Body

Although any format can be used as a message body, the Session Description Protocol (SDP) [8] is the most popular one. SDP specifies media information such as media type, codec, author, title, encryption key, bandwidth, start time, and end time. SDP can be used for capability exchange at the call set-up stage. An example of SDP message is shown here

```
m = audio 49170 RTP/AVP 102
a = rtpmap:102 AMR/8000
a = fmtp:102 maxptime=60; octect-align=1; mode-set=4
m = video 49350 RTP/AVP 110
a = rtpmap:110 MP4V-ES/90000
a = fmtp:110 profile-level-id=0; config=000001B.....
```

The SDP message just given specifies the following information. Audio is transported by the RTP/AVP protocol through port 49170, with payload number 102. The RTP timestamp resolution is 1/8000 s. The audio is coded by AMR with the maximum bit rate of 7.4 kbps. Three-frame bundling is used, three audio frames are bundled together to form an RTP packet. Audio packetization should follow the rules defined in RFC 3267 [9]. Video is transported by the RTP/AVP protocol through port 49350, with payload number 110. The RTP timestamp resolution is 1/90,000 s. The video is coded by MPEG-4 video SVP L0 (simple visual profile level 0). Video packetization should follow the rules defined in RFC 3016 [10].

SIP is an IP telephony signaling protocol developed by the IETF, which competes with the H.323 protocol developed by the ITU-T for the same application. The fundamental difference between the two protocols is that SIP is a text-based protocol and inherits the rich set of the IETF protocols, such as SDP, whereas H.323 is binary encoded and utilizes many features from other ITU-T protocols, for example, H.245. Comparisons between the two protocols on features,

Table 15.2:   Comparisons between SIP and H.323.

Comparisons	SIP	H.323
Encoding method	Text	Binary
Family	IETF	ITU-T
Transport	TCP or UDP	TCP
Packet loss recovery	Through SIP itself	Through TCP
Capability exchange	SDP (simple but limited)	H.245 (rich but complicated)
Security	Through other IETF; protocols for encryption, authentication, etc.	Not very good
Features	Call holding, call transfer, call forwarding, call waiting, conferencing, instant messaging	Call holding, call transfer, call forwarding, call waiting, conferencing

packet loss recovery, security mechanism, and capability exchange are listed in Table 15.2. A more detailed comparison can be found in [11].

15.2.3 Media Transport and Control Protocols

The commonly used media transport and control protocols in IP voice and video telephony applications are RTP and RTCP, as defined in RFC 3550. RTP and RTCP are designed to be independent of the underlying transport and network layers. Applications usually run RTP and RTCP on top of UDP and IP, as shown in Figure 15.3.

15.2.3.1 Real-Time Transport Protocols

RTP provides end-to-end delivery services for media data that have real-time characteristics. It defines useful information such as timestamp, sequence number, and marker, to allow receivers to keep the order of the packets, and to play out media at the proper pace. This is due to the fact that IP networks often introduce jitter in packets' arrival time and sometimes packet reordering. RTP itself, however, does not provide any mechanism to ensure timely delivery or to provide another quality of service.

Figure 15.5 shows the format of an RTP packet and its RTP header. Typically, in one-to-one telephony applications, the size of the RTP header is 12 bytes (no CSRC). V is a 2-bit field that identifies the version of the RTP. P is 1-bit information used to indicate if there are any padding octets at the end that are not part of the payload. X is a 1-bit field used to tell if there is any header extension information. CC means CSRC count, which uses 4 bits in the header and contains the number of CSRC identifiers that follow the header with fixed size. If an RTP session is one to one, such as in a video telephony application, the CSRC count should be set to zero. PT indicates payload type in 7 bits. It tells the format of the payload that an RTP packet carries.

M is a 1-bit marker and its interpretation is defined by a profile or payload format. For example, RFC 3016 is the payload format used for MPEG-4 audio and video. It specifies that if an encoded video frame is carried in multiple RTP packets, the marker bit of the last packet should be set to one to indicate the end of the frame. This is particularly useful for the RTP receiver to signal the video decoder to decode a video frame as soon as the last packet arrives.

SN specifies the sequence number of the RTP packet. It increases by one when one RTP data packet is sent. The initial sequence number of the first RTP packet for an RTP session should be randomly generated. For different media, the initial value may be different. For real-time telephony applications, the receiver can use the sequence numbers to detect any lost packets.

The timestamp TS reflects the sampling time of the first octet in the RTP packet payload. The sampling time should be calculated from a clock that increases monotonically and linearly in time to allow synchronization and jitter calculations. The timestamp may increase at a different pace for different media. For example, speech data are usually sampled at 8000 Hz and each speech frame can typically have 160 samples. Each RTP packet for speech will have a timestamp increment of 160. For video data sampled at 15 frames per second, the timestamp increment is 6000, based on a 90,000-Hz clock. If an encoded video frame is packetized into several RTP packets, each RTP packet will have the same timestamp as the data in each RTP packet are sampled at the same time instant.

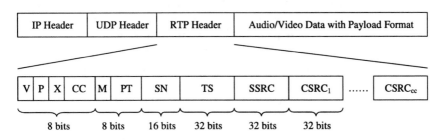

FIGURE 15.5:   RTP header format.

A timestamp is particularly useful for media playout control at the receiver. The IP networks usually introduce packet interarrival jitter. In addition, for video encoding, it is possible that a video frame will be skipped in order to maintain a predefined fixed encoding bit rate. By looking at the timestamp, the receiver can properly play out the media at the pace when they were originally sampled. Timestamp information can also be used to synchronize the playout of different media, such as audio and video, with the help of RTCP. We will describe audio and video synchronization in more detail in Section 15.3.4.

SSRC specifies the synchronization source and has 32 bits. RTP packets generated from the same source, such as a camera or microphone, should have the same SSRC. SSRC can be used to help the receiver group RTP packets of the same media for playback. CSRC is also a 32-bit field. It indicates the source of a stream of RTP packets that have contributed to the combined stream produced by an RTP mixer. For one-to-one video telephony and VoIP applications, there is no CSRC present in the RTP header.

15.2.3.2 Real-Time Control Protocols

RTCP is used in conjunction with RTP to allow RTP session participants to monitor the quality of data delivery. It is based on the periodic transmission of control packets. There are five control packets defined in RFC 3550:

- SR: Send Report. This is sent by an RTP participant that sends and receives the RTP packets;
- RR: Receiver Report. This is sent by an RTP participant that only receives the RTP packets;
- SDES: Source DEScription, including CNAME;
- BYE: This is to indicate the end of the RTP participation;
- APP: Application-specific functions.

Both SR and RR control packets contain reception statistics such as interarrival jitter and packet loss rate. Each SR control packet further includes the sender's wallclock time and the corresponding RTP timestamp when it is generated, as well as transmission statistics, such as how many packets and bytes have been transmitted since the beginning of the RTP session. SR control packets can also be used to synchronize the playout of different media data.

SR and RR reports are also often used for flow and congestion control. For example, by analyzing the interarrival jitter field of the sender report, we can measure the jitter over a certain interval and indicate congestion. As defined in RFC 3550, when Packet i is received, the interarrival Jitter $J(i)$ is calculated as

$$J(i) = J(i-1) + \frac{|D(i-1,i)| - J(i-1)}{16}, \tag{15.1}$$

where

$$D(i - 1, i) = \big(R(i) - R(i - 1)\big) - \big(TS(i) - TS(i - 1)\big), \qquad (15.2)$$

and $R(i)$ and $TS(i)$ are the arrival time and the timestamp of Packet i, respectively. Both are in RTP timestamp units. It is up to the implementation to decide what action to take when congestion occurs. A typical solution is to reduce the transmission rate until congestion becomes alleviated.

The round-trip time can also be estimated using last SR timestamp (LSR) and the delay since last SR (DLSR) information in both RR and SR control packets. Figure 15.6 demonstrates one example of a round-trip time calculation. Assume that the RTP sender sends one SR packet at time 10:20:30.250. The RTP receiver receives this SR and, after 5 s, sends an RR packet. In the RR control packet, LSR is the timestamp in SR(i) and the DLSR is 5 s. When the RTP sender receives this RR packet at time 10:20:36.750, it can calculate the round-trip time by subtracting the sending time of SR(i) and the DLSR from the arrival time of RR(i), which is 1.5 s as shown in Figure 15.6.

The fraction of loss in SR and RR control packets can also be used for the video encoder to perform error control. The packet loss rate is defined as the number of packets lost over the total number of received packets since the last SR or RR packet was sent.

The transmission interval of RTCP packets is often specified in proportion to the session bandwidth. It is recommended that the fraction of the session bandwidth added for RTCP be fixed at 5%. Some applications may specify the minimal transmission interval to be, for example, 5 s.

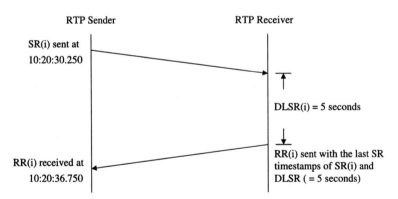

Round-trip time = 10:20:36.750 – 10:20:30.250 – 5 = 1.5 (seconds)

FIGURE 15.6:   An example of a round-trip time calculation.

15.2.3.3 Video Payload Format

The purposes of using a video payload format are to specify an efficient way to encapsulate data to form a standard-compliant bit stream and to enhance the resilience against packet losses. The payload here means media data that are packed in an RTP packet. Forming the media payload can be done in a thin layer between the media encoder and the RTP transport layer. Currently, payload formats defined in RFC 3016 and RFC 2429 for encapsulating MPEG-4 and H.263 video data into individual packets are most commonly used.

The RTP payload formats are designed such that (i) a payload format should be devised so that the stream being transported is still useful even in the presence of a moderate amount of packet loss and (ii) ideally, each packet should possibly be decoded and played out irrespective of whether the preceding packets have been lost or arrived late.

Figure 15.7 shows examples of RTP packets generated for MPEG-4 video based on RFC 3016. Among these examples, Figure 15.7(b) shows one of the most commonly used packetization methods that have the best error-resilience capability. With this packetization method, one RTP packet contains one video packet. A video packet contains resynchronization marker information at the beginning of the video payload. When the RTP packet containing the VOP header is lost, the other RTP packets can still be decoded due to the use of the Header Extension Code information in the video packet header. No extra RTP header field is necessary.

For H.263 video, similar to MPEG-4 video described in Figure 15.7(b), RFC 2429 specifies that the PSC and slice header have to be at the beginning of each RTP packet. It also specifies that the picture header information can be repeated in

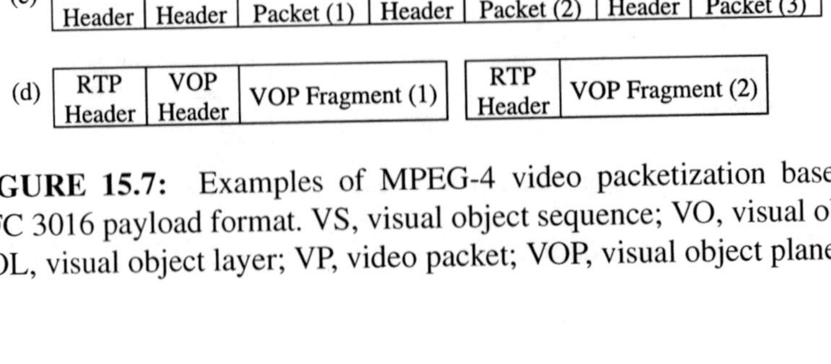

FIGURE 15.7: Examples of MPEG-4 video packetization based on RFC 3016 payload format. VS, visual object sequence; VO, visual object; VOL, visual object layer; VP, video packet; VOP, visual object plane.

each RTP packet. This can significantly reduce the number of frames that cannot be decoded due to picture header corruption. H.263 Annex W also provides a similar header protection mechanism, but this repeated header information can only be embedded once in the current picture header or the one in the previous or next frame. Thus, it has lower error resilience and may introduce delay due to waiting for the next frame.

Another purpose of using payload format is for interoperation between two video telephony users that use different applications. A certain video payload format for different codecs has to be supported and implemented to provide a unified video payload encapsulation.

15.2.3.4 An Example of a Call Setup Process

Before moving to the next section, we provide an example and illustrate the process of setting up a call using SIP. As illustrated in Figure 15.8, the caller PC, which is a SIP user agent, initiates a call by sending an INVITE request to the called party. The message has to go through the SIP server that serves the domain of the called party. The SIP server is responsible for locating the addressee via a location service and routing the message to the called party. Once the called party receives the INVITE request, it responses with 200 OK, which is sent back to the caller. Then the caller sends an ACK directly to the called party, so that the call is set up, and an RTP pipe is established for audio and video transmission.

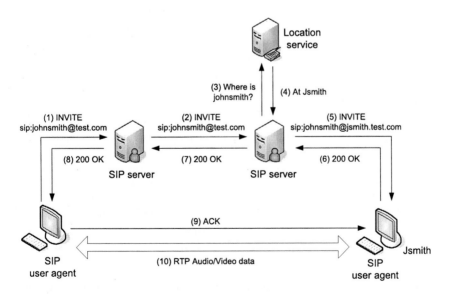

FIGURE 15.8: A call setup process using SIP.

SIP, being a signaling protocol, is only responsible for initiating and establishing the session, but the actual communication is directly between the caller and the called party.

15.3 QUALITY OF SERVICE

15.3.1 Minimizing Latency

To achieve toll quality for real-time communication, it is typically required that the round-trip delay be lower than 300 ms. Many factors contribute to the packet delay in a real-time communication system. The total end-to-end delay, D, can be divided into the following components:

$$D = d_{enc} + d_{pack} + d_{net} + d_{buf} + d_{dec}, \qquad (15.3)$$

where d_{enc} is the encoding delay, d_{pack} is the packetization delay, d_{net} is the delay introduced by the network, d_{buf} is the buffering delay, and d_{dec} is the decoding delay (Figure 15.9). To minimize the end-to-end latency, each delay component has to be minimized and trade-offs have to be considered in optimizing the overall system design.

Encoding delay is introduced during the data compression process. For speech coders, encoding delay usually includes the frame size and look-ahead delay. Look-ahead delay is the time spent in processing part of the next frame so that a correlation between successive frames can be exploited. Typically, more advanced codecs achieve higher compression efficiency at the cost of higher encoding delays. Decoding delay is introduced during the data decompression process. Table 15.3 lists the coding delays for some common speech coders.

Packetization delay is the time spent in collecting sufficient data frames to form the payload of an IP packet. Since the packet headers have a fixed size, a larger payload size reduces the header overhead and improves the transmission efficiency. However, due to the stringent latency requirement, the payload can

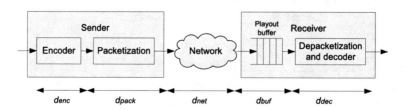

FIGURE 15.9:   Total end-to-end delay in a typical real-time communication system.

Table 15.3:   Coding delays for sample speech coders.

Speech coder	Encoded bit rate (kbit/s)	Frame size (ms)	Look-ahead delay (ms)	Decoding delay (ms)
G.711	64	0.125	0	0
G.729A	8	10	5	7.5
G.723.1	5.3/6.4	30	7.5	18.75

usually contain only a limited number of frames in order to reduce the packetization delay.

The network delay comprises the propagation delay and the queuing delay across all links in the transmission path. The propagation delay, which is a constant for a fixed path, depends on the packet size and the speed of links, as well as the length of the links. The queuing delay occurs when a packet is queued behind some other packets waiting to be transmitted over the same link. The queuing delay is a random variable depending on the packet size, traffic load and characteristics of the route, and the scheduling scheme. Advanced resource allocation and scheduling schemes such as Resource Reservation Protocol and Differentiated Services enable prioritization of audio and video packets and can efficiently reduce queuing delay for these real-time data streams.

Varying queuing delay, typically caused by congestions of links in the route and related to the queuing mechanisms, introduces delay jitter, which is usually unknown and random. Due to delay jitter, IP packets are sent periodically but are received in irregular patterns. For this reason, a playout buffer, also referred to as a dejitter buffer, is employed at the receiver to absorb the delay jitter before media are output. When using a playout buffer, packets are not played out immediately after being received but are held in a buffer until their scheduled playout time (playout deadline) arrives. Although this introduces additional delay for packets arriving early, this mechanism ensures continuous media playback. The buffering delay is the time a packet is held in the buffer before it is played out.

Note that a trade-off exists between the average buffering delay and the number of packets that have to be dropped because they arrive too late (late loss). Scheduling a later deadline increases the possibility of playing out more packets and results in a lower loss rate, but at the cost of a higher buffering delay. Vice versa, it is difficult to decrease the buffering delay without significantly increasing the loss rate. Therefore, packet loss in delay-sensitive, real-time applications is a result of not only a packet being dropped over the network, but also delay jitter, which impairs communication quality greatly.

Due to the aforementioned buffering delay—late loss rate trade-off—it is desirable to design smart playout scheduling mechanisms to reduce the buffering delay. Fixed scheduling poses a limitation for this trade-off. In real-time speech communication, more advanced mechanisms use a playout buffer to completely absorb delay jitter within talkspurts and dynamically adjust the schedule between talkspurts [12–16]. Adaptive playout scheduling is proposed to allow adaptive schedules even within talkspurts [17], and this idea has also been extended to video streaming [18,19]. An adaptive playout schedule is able to reduce the latency and the effective packet loss rate at the same time. Interested readers may refer to Chapter 16 for more details.

15.3.2 Combating Losses

In real-time communications, losses are a result of not only packets dropping over the network, but also late arrival for packets. We introduce different loss-resilient techniques for both audio and video in two categories: client-side techniques and active techniques, depending on whether they require any encoder involvement.

15.3.2.1 Client-Side Techniques

One category of loss techniques is passive methods that are implemented at the client side, which do not require any cooperation of the sender or increase the cost of transmission. Client-side techniques impose low overhead for the communication system but can be highly efficient in enhancing the quality of the rendered media.

To combat channel losses, the client typically employs error-detection and loss-concealment techniques to mitigate the effect of lost data. For speech and audio coded techniques based on waveform, most client-side schemes take advantage of the data received adjacent to the lost packet and interpolate the missing information by exploiting the redundancy in the signal. In particular, waveform repetition simply repeats the information contained in the packets prior to the lost one [20, 21]. A more advanced loss-concealment technique using timescale modification is described in [22] and [23] and can be used in conjunction with adaptive playout scheduling in a low-latency scenario [17]. Waveform repetition typically does not introduce any algorithm delay as timescale modification typically does. However, it does not provide as good a sound quality [24]. Interested readers may further refer to Chapter 3 for error-resilient techniques for various codecs.

For video communication, postprocessing is typically applied at the client side for error concealment and loss recovery. Techniques to recover the damaged areas based on characteristics of image and video signals have been reviewed in [25]. Interested readers may further refer to Chapter 2 for more detailed descriptions on error-resilient video.

15.3.2.2 Active Techniques

A different category of error-resilience techniques requires the encoder to play a primary role. They are able to provide even higher robustness for media communication over best-effort networks. We refer to these techniques as "active" to differentiate them from those only employed at the client side.

For speech communication, one widely accepted way to reduce the effective packet loss observed by the receiver is to add redundancy to the data stream at the sender. This is possible without imposing too much extra network load since the data rate of the voice traffic is very low when compared with other types of multimedia and data traffic. A common method to add redundancy is forward error correction (FEC), which transmits redundant information across packets, where loss recovery is performed at the cost of higher latency. The efficiency of FEC schemes is largely limited by the bursty nature of the channel losses. In order to combat burst losses, redundant information has to be added into temporally distant packets, which introduce higher delay.

Another sender-based loss recovery technique, interleaving, does not increase the data rate of transmission but still introduces delay at both encoder and decoder sides. The efficiency of loss recovery depends on over how many packets the source packet is interleaved and spread over. Again, the wider the spread, the higher the introduced delay. For low-latency speech communication, path diversity techniques, presented in [26] as well as in Chapter 17, have been demonstrated to be very powerful in combating losses.

Video communication typically requires much higher data transmission rates than audio. A variety of active schemes has been proposed not only to increase the robustness of communication, but also to take the data rate efficiency into consideration [27–29]. Many of the recent algorithms use rate–distortion (R–D) optimization techniques to improve the compression efficiency [30–32], as well as to improve the error-resilient performance over lossy networks [33,34]. The goal of the R–D optimization algorithms is to minimize the expected distortion due to both compression and channel losses subject to the bit-rate constraint.

One example of this area is Intra/Inter-mode switching [35–38], where Intra-coded macroblocks are updated according to the network condition to mitigate temporal error propagation. Another approach is to modify the temporal prediction dependency of motion-compensated video coding in order to mitigate or stop error propagation. Example implementations include reference picture selection [27,39–41] and NEWPRED in MPEG-4 [42,43], where channel feedback is used to efficiently stop error propagation due to any transmission error. Another example is video redundancy coding (VRC), where the video sequence is coded into independent threads (streams) in a round-robin fashion [27,44]. A Sync-frame is encoded by all threads at regular intervals to start a new thread series and stop error propagation. If one thread is damaged due to packet loss, the remaining threads can still be used to predict the Sync-frame. VRC provides improved error resilience, but at the cost of a much higher data rate. Dynamic control of the prediction dependency can also be used by employing long-term memory prediction to achieve improved R–D performance [33,45,46].

Typically a channel coding module in a robust video communication system may involve FEC and automatic retransmission on request (ARQ). Similar to their applications in speech communication, when FEC is employed across packets, missing packets can be recovered at the receiver as long as a sufficient number of packets is received [47–50]. FEC is widely used as an unequal error protection scheme to protect prioritized transmissions. In addition to FEC codes, data randomization and interleaving are also employed for enhanced protection [51–55].

ARQ techniques incorporate channel feedback and employ the retransmission of erroneous data [56–60]. Unlike FEC schemes, ARQ intrinsically adapts to the varying channel conditions and tends to be more efficient in transmission. However, for real-time communication and low-latency streaming, the latency introduced by ARQ is a major concern. In addition, like all feedback-based error control schemes, ARQ is not appropriate for multicasting.

15.3.3 Adapting to the Available Bandwidth

Due to the lack of a QoS guarantee over most commercially deployed networks, it is expected that the condition, as well as the available bandwidth of the network, varies during a real-time communication session. It is beneficial to employ bandwidth adaptation mechanisms to control the rate at which the media are transmitted. This helps avoid a potential penalty on overuse of bandwidth, which usually leads to quality degradation and even service interruption. Typical bandwidth adaptation techniques include rate control, transcoding, scalable coding, and bit stream switching. Readers may refer to Chapter 4 for details of various bandwidth adaptation techniques, and further refer to Chapters 5 and 6 for scalable coding for video and audio, respectively.

15.3.4 Audio–Video Synchronization

RTP timestamps from different media streams may advance at different rates and usually have independent and random offsets. Therefore, although these timestamps are sufficient to reconstruct the timing of a single stream, directly comparing RTP timestamps from different media is not effective for synchronization. Instead, for each medium the RTP timestamp is related to the sampling instant by pairing it with a timestamp from a reference clock (wallclock) that represents the time when the medium was sampled. The reference clock is shared by all media to be synchronized.

Synchronizing audio and video can be achieved by playing out audio and video according to their original sampled time. By doing so, the receiver can play back audio and video at a proper pace by mapping their original sampled time to the receiver's local time. RTCP SR control packets provide useful information to help

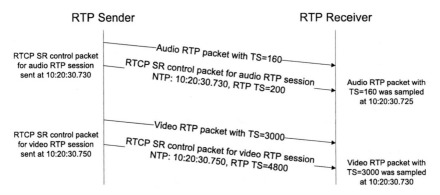

FIGURE 15.10:   An example of audio and video synchronization.

the receiver calculate the sampled time of the audio and the video at the sender. Figure 15.10 illustrates an example of audio and video synchronization by using RTCP SR control packets. When an RTCP SR control packet is generated, it will carry the wallclock time (NTP) and the RTP timestamp using its corresponding media reference time. In Figure 15.10, the RTCP SR control packet for the audio RTP session is generated at time 10:20:30.730 and the corresponding timestamp is 200. When receiving this SR packet, the receiver is able to calculate when all the audio RTP packets are sampled at the sender. For the example in Figure 15.10, the audio packet with timestamp 160 is actually generated at time 10:20:30.725, assuming that a 8000-Hz clock is used for audio timestamping. Similarly, for video packets, the receiver can also calculate when each video frame is sampled. In this way, the receiver can easily find out which part of audio data and video data should be played back at the same time.

15.4 SUMMARY AND FURTHER READING

In this chapter, we have described the system and architecture for real-time communication, including two categories of the most important protocols, signaling and transport, respectively. We have also addressed the QoS issues, especially on minimizing latency, combating losses, adapting to available bandwidth, and audio–video synchronization. Beyond the references cited in this chapter, the reader is recommended to read Chapter 2, on error-resilient video, and Chapter 3, on error-resilient audio. Interested readers are further recommended to read Chapter 16, on adaptive media playout, as well as Chapter 17, on path diversity, for enhanced QoS performance.

REFERENCES

[1] J. Rosenberg, H. Schulzrinne, G. Camarillo, A. Johnston, J. Peterson, M. Hardley, and E. Schooler. "SIP: Session Initiation Protocol," *RFC 3261*, June 2002.

[2] S. Donovan. "The SIP INFO Method," *RFC 2976*, Oct. 2000.

[3] B. Campbell et al. "Session Initiation Protocol (SIP) Extension for Instant Messaging," *RFC 3428*, December 2002.

[4] A. B. Roach. "Session Initiation Protocol (SIP): Specific Event Notification," *RFC 3265*, June 2002.

[5] J. Rosenberg and H. Schulzrinne. "Reliability of Provisional Responses in the Session Initiation Protocol," *RFC 3262*, June 2002.

[6] R. Sparks. "The Session Initiation Protocol (SIP) Refer Method," *RFC 3515*, April 2003.

[7] J. Rosenberg. "The Session Initiation Protocol (SIP) UPDATE Method," *RFC 3311*, September 2002.

[8] M. Handley and V. Jacobson. "SDP: Session Description Protocol," *RFC 2327*, April 1998.

[9] S. Sjoberg, M. Westerlurd, A. Lakaniemi, and Q. Xie. "Real-Time Transport Protocol (RTP) Payload Format and File Storage Format for the Adaptive Multi-Rate (AMR) and Adaptive Multi-Rate Wideband (AMR-WB) Audio Codec," *RFC 3267*, June 2002.

[10] Y. Kikuchi, T. Nomura, S. Fukunaga, Y. Matsui, and H. Kimata. "RTP Payload Format for MPEG-4 Audio/Visual Streams," *RFC 3016*, November 2000.

[11] I. Dalgic and H. Fang. "Comparison of H.323 and SIP for IP Telephony Signaling," in *Proc. of Photonics East*, Boston, MA, September 1999.

[12] R. Ramjee, J. Kurose, D. Towsley, and H. Schulzrinne. "Adaptive Playout Mechanisms for Packetized Audio Applications in Wide-Area Networks," in *Proceedings IEEE INFOCOM '94*, vol. 2, pp. 680–688, June 1994.

[13] S. B. Moon, J. Kurose, and D. Towsley. "Packet Audio Playout Delay Adjustment: Performance Bounds and Algorithms," *Multimedia Systems*, vol. 6, no. 1, pp. 17–28, January 1998.

[14] J. Pinto and K. J. Christensen. "An Algorithm for Playout of Packet Voice Based on Adaptive Adjustment of Talkspurt Silence Periods," in *Proceedings 24th Conference on Local Computer Networks*, pp. 224–231, October 1999.

[15] P. DeLeon and C. J. Sreenan. "An Adaptive Predictor for Media Playout Buffering," in *Proceedings of the IEEE International Conference on Acoustics, Speech, and Signal Processing (ICASSP-99)*, vol. 6, pp. 3097–3100, March 1999.

[16] J. Rosenberg, L. Qiu, and H. Schulzrinne. "Integrating Packet FEC into Adaptive Voice Playout Buffer Algorithms on the Internet," in *Proceedings IEEE INFOCOM 2000*, vol. 3, pp. 1705–1714, Tel Aviv, Israel, March 2000.

[17] Y. J. Liang, N. Färber, and B. Girod. "Adaptive Playout Scheduling and Loss Concealment for Voice Communication over IP Networks," *IEEE Transactions on Multimedia*, vol. 5, no. 4, pp. 532–543, December 2003.

[18] E. Steinbach, N. Färber, and B. Girod. "Adaptive Playout for Low-Latency Video Streaming," in *IEEE International Conference on Image Processsing ICIP-01*, vol. 1, pp. 962–965, Thessaloniki, Greece, October 2001.

[19] M. Kalman, E. Steinbach, and B. Girod. "Adaptive Playout for Real-Time Media Streaming," in *IEEE International Symposium on Circuits and Systems*, vol. 1, pp. 1–45–8, Scottsdale, AZ, May 2002.

[20] D. J. Goodman, G. B. Lockhart, O. J. Wasem, and W.-C. Wong. "Waveform Substitution Techniques for Recovering Missing Speech Segments in Packet Voice Communications," *IEEE Transactions on Acoustics, Speech, and Signal Processing*, vol. 34, no. 6, pp. 1440–1448, December 1986.

[21] O. J. Wasem, D. J. Goodman, C. A. Dvorak, and H. G. Page. "The Effect of Waveform Substitution on the Quality of PCM Packet Communications," *IEEE Transactions on Acoustics, Speech, and Signal Processing*, vol. 36, no. 3, pp. 342–348, March 1988.

[22] A. Stenger, K. Ben Younes, R. Reng, and B. Girod. "A New Error Concealment Technique for Audio Transmission with Packet Loss," in *Proc. European Signal Processing Conference*, vol. 3, pp. 1965–1968, September 1996.

[23] H. Sanneck, A. Stenger, K. Ben Younes, and B. Girod. "A New Technique for Audio Packet Loss Concealment," in *IEEE GLOBECOM*, pp. 48–52, November 1996.

[24] C. Perkins, O. Hodson, and V. Hardman. "A Survey of Packet Loss Recovery Techniques for Streaming Audio," *IEEE Network*, vol. 12, no. 5, pp. 40–48, September–October 1998.

[25] Yao Wang and Qin-Fan Zhu. "Error Control and Concealment for Video Communication: A Review," *Proceedings of the IEEE*, vol. 86, no. 5, pp. 974–997, May 1998.

[26] Y. J. Liang, E. G. Steinbach, and B. Girod. "Real-Time Voice Communication over the Internet Using Packet Path Diversity," in *Proceedings ACM Multimedia 2001*, pp. 431–440, Ottawa, Canada, October 2001.

[27] S. Wenger, G. D. Knorr, J. Ott, and F. Kossentini. "Error Resilience Support in H.263+," *IEEE Transactions on Circuits and Systems for Video Technology*, vol. 8, no. 7, pp. 867–877, November 1998.

[28] R. Talluri. "Error-Resilient Video Coding in the ISO MPEG-4 Standard," *IEEE Communications Magazine*, pp. 112–119, June 1998.

[29] W. Tan and A. Zakhor. "Real-time Internet Video Using Error Resilient Scalable Compression and TCP-Friendly Transport Protocol," *IEEE Trans. Multimedia*, pp. 172–186, June 1999.

[30] G. J. Sullivan and T. Wiegand. "Rate-Distortion Optimization for Video Compression," *IEEE Signal Processing Magazine*, vol. 15, no. 6, pp. 74–90, November 1998.

[31] A. Ortega and K. Ramchandran. "From Rate-Distortion Theory to Commercial Image and Video Compression Technology," *IEEE Signal Processing Magazine*, vol. 15, no. 6, pp. 20–122, November 1998.

[32] T. Wiegand, X. Zhang, and B. Girod. "Long-Term Memory Motion-Compensated Prediction," *IEEE Transactions on Circuits and Systems for Video Technology*, vol. 9, no. 1, pp. 70–84, February 1999.

[33] T. Wiegand, N. Färber, and B. Girod. "Error-Resilient Video Transmission Using Long-Term Memory Motion-Compensated Prediction," *IEEE Journal on Selected Areas in Communications*, vol. 18, no. 6, pp. 1050–1062, June 2000.

[34] P. A. Chou, A. E. Mohr, A. Wang, and S. Mehrotra, "Error Control for Receiver-Driven Layered Multicast of Audio and Video," *IEEE Transactions on Multimedia*, vol. 3, no. 1, pp. 108–122, March 2001.

[35] J. Y. Liao and J. D. Villasenor. "Adaptive Intra Update for Video Coding over Noisy Channels," in *Proceedings IEEE International Conference on Image Processing*, Lausanne, Switzerland, vol. 3, pp. 763–766, September 1996.

[36] R. O. Hinds, T. N. Pappas, and J. S. Lim. "Joint Block-Based Video Source/Channel Coding for Packet-Switched Networks," in *Proceedings of the SPIE VCIP 98*, vol. 3309, pp. 124–133, San Jose, CA, October 1998.

[37] G. Cote and F. Kossentini. "Optimal Intra Coding of Blocks for Robust Video Communication over the Internet," *Signal Processing: Image Communication*, vol. 15, no. 1-2, pp. 25–34, September 1999.

[38] R. Zhang, S. L. Regunathan, and K. Rose. "Video Coding with Optimal Inter/Intra-mode Switching for Packet Loss Resilience," *IEEE Journal on Selected Areas in Communications*, vol. 18, no. 6, pp. 966–976, June 2000.

[39] S. Fukunaga, T. Nakai, and H. Inoue. "Error Resilient Video Coding by Dynamic Replacing of Reference Pictures," in *Proc. of the IEEE Global Telecommunications Conference*, vol. 3, pp. 1503–1508, London, UK, November 1996.

[40] ITU-T Recommendation H.263 Version 2 (H.263+), *Video Coding for Low Bitrate Communication*, January 1998.

[41] ITU-T Recommendation H.264, *Advanced Video Coding (AVC) for Generic Audio-visual Services*, May 2003.

[42] International Organisation for Standardisation, ISO/IEC JTC1/SC29/WG11 Final Committee Draft 14496-2, *Information Technology – Coding of Audio-Visual Objects: Visual (MPEG-4)*, March 1998.

[43] International Organisation for Standardisation, ISO/IEC JTC1/SC29/WG11 Final Committee Draft 14496-2, *Information Technology – Coding of Audio-Visual Objects: Visual (MPEG-4)*, March 1998.

[44] S. Wenger. "Video Redundancy Coding in H.263+," in *Proc. of the Workshop on Audio-Visual Services for Packet Networks*, September 1997.

[45] M. Budagavi and J.D Gibson. "Multiframe Video Coding for Improved Performance over Wireless Channels," *IEEE Transactions on Image Processing*, vol. 10, no. 2, pp. 252–265, February 2001.

[46] Y. J. Liang and B. Girod. "Network-Adaptive Low-Latency Video Communication over Best-Effort Networks," *IEEE Transactions on Circuits and Systems for Video Technology*, vol. 16, no. 1, pp. 72–81, January 2006.

[47] Internet Engineering Task Force. "RTP Payload Format for MPEG-1/MPEG-2 Video," *RFC 2250*, January 1998.

[48] A. Albanese, J. Blömer, J. Edmonds, M. Luby, and M. Sudan. "Priority Encoding Transmission," *IEEE Transactions on Information Theory*, vol. 42, no. 6, pp. 1737–1744, November 1996.

[49] P. C. Cosman, J. K. Rogers, P. G. Sherwood, and K. Zeger. "Image Transmission over Channels with Bit Errors and Packet Erasures," in *Proceedings of the Thirty-Second Asilomar Conference on Signals, Systems and Computers*, vol. 2, pp. 1621–1625, Pacific Grove, CA, November 1998.

[50] W. Tan and A. Zakhor. "Video Multicast Using Layered Fec and Scalable Compression," *IEEE Transactions on Circuits and Systems for Video Technology*, vol. 11, no. 3, pp. 373–387, March 2001.

[51] J.-Y. Cochennec. *Method for the Correction of Cell Losses for Low Bit-Rate Signals Transport with the AAL Type 1*. ITU-T SG15 Doc. AVC-538, July 1993.

[52] Q.-F. Zhu, Y. Wang, and L. Shaw. "Coding and Cell-Loss Recovery in DCT-Based Packet Video," *IEEE Transactions on Circuits and Systems for Video Technology*, vol. 3, no. 3, pp. 248–258, June 1993.

[53] T. Kinoshita, T. Nakahashi, and M. Maruyama, "Variable-Bit-Rate HDTV Codec with ATM-Cell-Loss Compensation," *IEEE Transactions on Circuits and Systems for Video Technology*, vol. 3, no. 3, pp. 230–237, June 1993.

[54] K. Stuhlmüller, N. Färber, M. Link, and B. Girod. "Analysis of Video Transmission over Lossy Channels," *IEEE Journal on Selected Areas in Communications*, vol. 18, no. 6, pp. 1012–1032, June 2000.

[55] Y. J. Liang, J. G. Apostolopoulos, and B. Girod, "Model-Based Delay-Distortion Optimization for Video Streaming Using Packet Interleaving," in *Proceedings of the 36th Asilomar Conference on Signals, Systems and Computers*, Pacific Grove, CA, November 2002.

[56] S. B. Wicker. *Error Control Systems for Digital Communication and Storage*, Prentice Hall, 1995.

[57] M. Khansari, A. Jalali, E. Dubois, and P. Mermelstein. "Low Bit-Rate Video Transmission over Fading Channels for Wireless Microcellular Systems," *IEEE Transactions on Circuits and Systems for Video Technology*, vol. 6, no. 1, pp. 1–11, February 1996.

[58] B. Dempsey, J. Liebeherr, and A. Weaver. "On Retransmission-Based Error Control for Continuous Media Traffic in Packet-Switching Networks," *Computer Networks and ISDN Systems Journal*, vol. 28, no. 5, pp. 719–736, March 1996.

[59] C. Papadopoulos and G. M. Parulkar. "Retransmission-Based Error Control for Continuous Media Applications," in *Proc. Network and Operating System Support for Digital Audio and Video (NOSSDAV)*, Zushi, Japan, July 1996.

[60] H. Liu and M. El Zarki. "Performance of H.263 Video Transmission over Wireless Channels Using Hybrid ARQ," *IEEE Journal on Selected Areas in Communications*, vol. 15, no. 9, pp. 1775–1786, December 1999.

16

Adaptive Media Playout

Eckehard Steinbach, Yi Liang, Mark Kalman,
and Bernd Girod

16.1 INTRODUCTION

This chapter discusses Adaptive Media Playout (AMP) as a method of reducing the user-perceived latencies that are inherent in systems that send packetized media over best-effort packet networks. These systems strive to allow the immediate display of media data as it is delivered from a remote sender. In practice, however, the systems must buffer an amount of media at the client to prevent packet losses and delays from constantly interrupting the playout of the stream. While the likelihood of a playout interruption decreases as more data is buffered, the delays that buffering introduces increase.

Adaptive media playout allows the client to buffer less data and, thus, introduces less delay to achieve a given playout reliability. In this scheme, the client varies the rate at which it plays out audio and video according to the state of its playout buffer. Generally, when the buffer occupancy is below a desired level, the client plays media slowly to reduce its data consumption rate. Faster-than-normal playout may be used during good channel periods to eliminate any excess latency accumulated with slowed playout. By manipulating playout speeds AMP can reduce initial buffering delays in the case of prestored streams and reduce the user-perceived latency of live streams, all without sacrificing playout reliability.

To control the playout speed of media, the client scales the duration that each video frame is shown and processes audio to scale it in time without affecting its pitch. Variations in the media playout rate are subjectively less irritating than playout interruptions and long delays. How much the media signal can be stretched or compressed depends on the application. In this chapter AMP is discussed using two popular applications. Internet Telephony (VoIP) is used as a representative for bidirectional conversational applications with strict end-to-end delay requirements. Video streaming is selected as an application with comparatively relaxed end-to-end delay requirements.

This chapter is organized as follows. We first discuss the receiver buffer in combination with fixed playout as the traditional means of adapting the application to varying transmission characteristics. We then introduce AMP using Internet Telephony and Video Streaming as example applications. Next, algorithms for duration scaling of audio, speech, and video segments are discussed. Toward the end of the chapter we touch on advanced deployment of AMP in the context of multipath transmission.

16.2 SENDER AND RECEIVER CURVES

The end-to-end delay encountered when transmitting digital media signals over a packet switched or circuit switched network is the accumulation of various delay contributions (see also Chapter 15.3). End-to-end delay is considered to be the time difference between capturing the media signal at the sender and displaying the signal at the receiver. Figure 16.1 shows a block diagram of the individual steps involved. The sender sampling curve $p_s(t)$ describes the amount of media data (e.g., in bytes) captured up to a certain time instant t. Without loss of generality we can assume that $t = T_{start} = 0$ s is our starting point. The digital media signal may be fed into an encoder with the purpose of data compression. Typically multiple samples of the sender signal are compressed jointly, for example, a block of speech samples or a digital video frame.

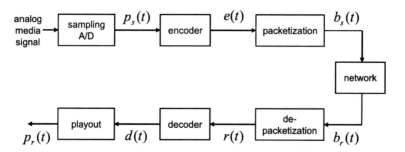

FIGURE 16.1: Processing and transmission of digital media signals. Each step introduces constant or variable delay, which accumulates to the total end-to-end delay. End-to-end delay is the time difference between capturing a media data sample at the sender side and displaying it at the receiver.

The encoder curve $e(t)$ describes the length of the bitstream output by the encoder up to time t. During packetization a certain number of data units is put into one data packet, which is then injected into the network. Packet size can be fixed or dynamically adapted. Once the encoder has output enough data units to fill the next packet we assume that the packet is immediately sent out on the network. The sender packet curve $b_s(t)$ describes the number of data units injected into the network up to time instant t. Depending on whether the network is circuit switched or packet switched, the delivery time, that is, the time it takes the packet to reach the receiver side, is either fixed or variable. The receiver packet curve $b_r(t)$ describes the amount of continuous packet payload data that has been received up to time instant t. Next, the payload is extracted from the packets and the depacketization curve $r(t)$ describes the input to the decoder. The output of the decoder is described by the decoder curve $d(t)$, which corresponds to the amount of decoded data ready for display. The playout process then decides which data to play at what time instant. The data played up to time t is described by the receiver playout curve $p_r(t)$.

The meaning of these various curves and their relationship can be best understood when looking at specific examples. The two examples discussed in the following are the transmission of a digital speech signal over a circuit-switched network and the transmission of a digital video signal over a packet-switched network. For additional discussion of buffering and timing fundamentals, see also Section 14.3.

Example 1: Sender and Receiver Curves for Transmission of a Digital Speech Signal

In this example the transmission of a digital speech signal over a circuit-switched network is considered. The digital speech signal is obtained by A/D conversion of an analog microphone signal. The sampling frequency is assumed to be $f_s = 8$ KHz and the signal amplitude resolution in our example is 8 bit/sample. Figure 16.2 illustrates possible sender and receiver curves. The sender sampling curve $p_s(t)$ is a straight line with slope 64 kbit/s. In this example it is assumed that the encoder does not perform data compression on the digital speech signal, which leads to $e(t) = p_s(t)$. The signal is partitioned into blocks or packets of 20 ms, which corresponds to a payload of 160 byte. The sender packet curve $b_s(t)$ hence becomes a step curve with step height 160 byte and step width 20 ms. The speech signal is transmitted over a circuit-switched network and the constant packet delivery time is assumed to be 100 ms. The receiver packet curve $b_r(t)$ in Figure 16.2 therefore becomes simply a shifted version of $b_s(t)$. Depacketization is assumed to be of negligible duration and decoding does not have to be performed for uncompressed data, which leads to $d(t) = r(t) = b_r(t)$. Playout is initiated by the receiver 20 ms after the arrival of the first packet. Playout is therefore started at $t = 140$ ms. This time instant is called the initial playout

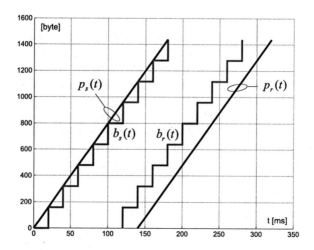

FIGURE 16.2: Example sender and receiver curves for transmission of a constant bit-rate signal (a digital speech signal with 64 kbit/s) over a circuit-switched network.

delay $T_{initial}$. The receiver playout curve $p_r(t)$ becomes a shifted version of the sender playout curve with a constant end-to-end delay of $T_{e2e} = 140$ ms.

Example 2: Sender and Receiver Curves for Transmission of a Digital Video Signal

For digital video we capture individual frames at a certain frame rate (e.g., 25 frames/second). After acquisition, the digital video frames are compressed and the encoder produces an encoder curve $e(t)$ that deviates from a uniform step curve as the output of the encoder is a variable bit rate stream (VBR stream). Let us consider a video sequence with a spatial resolution of 176×144 pixels, 25 frames/second, and an amplitude resolution of 12 bit/pixel. This leads to a raw data rate of $176 \times 144 \times 25 \times 12$ bit/s or 37.125 Kbyte/frame. The sender sampling curve $p_s(t)$ is a step curve with a step width of 40 ms, which corresponds to the inter-frame spacing. The step height corresponds to the frame size in bytes, in this example 37.125 Kbyte. After compression, every video frame has a different size, which leads to the varying step height of the encoder curve $e(t)$ shown in Figure 16.3. The video is transmitted over the Internet and for simplicity it is assumed that one encoded video frame is transmitted as the payload of one IP packet. This leads to variable size packets. The packetizer waits until the encoder outputs the encoded bit stream for a new video frame and then injects one packet into the network. Neglecting the packetization time leads to $b_s(t) = e(t)$. The packets are transmitted over a packet-switched network, which leads to a receiver

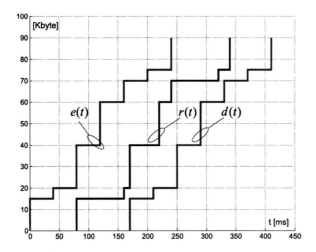

FIGURE 16.3: Example sender and receiver curves for the transmission of compressed video over a packet-switched network. The sender sampling curve is replaced by the encoder curve $e(t)$ and the receiver playout curve by the decoding curve $d(t)$ assuming that encoding and decoding times are negligible.

packet curve that is no longer a shifted version of the sender packet curve $b_s(t)$. Every packet encounters a different delivery time. Depacketization time is again neglected, which leads to a receiver curve $r(t)$ that is identical to the receiver packet curve $b_r(t)$. Once the bit stream portion of a video frame is available, the decoder can decode and display the frame. Because data compression reduces the amount of data per frame it is difficult to show the sender sampling and receiver playout curves in Figure 16.3. If we assume that the encoding time of a video frame is negligible we can replace the sender sampling curve $p_s(t)$ by the encoder curve $e(t)$. Please note that they are not the same but the steps in both curves happen at the same time. The step height, however, is different because of compression. Similarly, we can assume that the decoding of a frame starts when the frame is to be displayed and decoding time is negligible. Then, the receiver playout curve can be replaced by the decoder curve $d(t)$. Again, they are not identical but the steps in both curves happen at the same time instant. They only differ in step height. Most of the time we are only interested in identifying if enough data has been received by the client to display a certain media unit. Given the assumptions made earlier, we can draw the same conclusions about delay and playout interruptions from $e(t)$ and $d(t)$ that we would obtain when looking at $p_s(t)$ and $p_r(t)$.

In Figure 16.3, the receiver starts playout at time $T_{initial} = 170$ ms. Every 40 ms a new frame has to be displayed. It can be seen from Figure 16.3 that this selection of the initial playout time $T_{initial}$ leads to a successful decoding process as the decoding curve $d(t)$ is always to the right of the receiver packet curve $b_r(t)$. This means that the decoder always has sufficient data to decode the video frames before their scheduled display time.

16.3 CLIENT BUFFERING

The standard way of dealing with the VBR nature of both the source bit stream and the network data delivery is by using a receiver buffer. The main purpose of this buffer is to store media data after the server starts sending the packets. For low delay applications, the client buffer mainly absorbs packet delay jitter. For applications with moderate delay requirements, the client buffer additionally provides time for the retransmission of lost packets. The amount of data prebuffered before the playout starts influences the initial waiting time and the late loss rate. Both quantities significantly influence user satisfaction.

16.3.1 Buffer Size versus Initial Delay

After a certain initial waiting time or once the buffer occupancy has reached a predefined target level, the client initiates the playout process, that is, the first media unit is played at $T_{initial}$. The size of the buffer determines the initial delay $T_{initial}$ observed by the user. For live media streams the initial delay is the time difference between the sampling instant of the first media sample at the sender and display of this sample at the receiver. For pre-encoded media content, for example, in video streaming scenarios, $T_{initial}$ is the time it takes between sending a request to the streaming server and displaying the first media unit at the client.

If we select the receiver buffer to be large, we are able to smooth significant delay variations. An extreme case is file download, where the buffer target fullness corresponds to the file size and playout only starts once the entire file has been completely transferred. If our aim is to keep the perceived end-to-end delay small, prebuffering has to be used carefully. This is particularly true for conversational applications where the end-to-end delay is critical for user satisfaction. For bidirectional conversational services involving speech and video, the tolerable end-to-end delay is typically given in the range of 150–250 ms. There is obviously a trade-off between robustness against network quality variations and initial delay.

16.3.2 Late Loss Rate versus End-to-End Delay

Once the client receives the first packets from the sender, in principle the playout process can be started. In order to allow a continuous playout at the receiver it is, however, wise to wait some additional time to fill up the receiver buffer. The playout process at the receiver works without interruptions as long as the decoder curve $d(t)$ always stays to the right and below the receiver packet curve $b_r(t)$. If the two curves intersect, the decoder has to decode data that has not yet been received. In this case some of the packets arrive after their scheduled decoding time, which results in so-called late loss. Typically, regular packet loss and late loss can be jointly considered, as a true packet loss is simply a late loss where the delivery time is infinitely large. The influence of late loss on the reconstruction quality is application dependent. While speech applications where speech segments are encoded individually typically tolerate late loss rates of up to about 5%, video applications where the error-free decoding of one frame depends on the successful decoding of previous frames typically do not tolerate packet loss. The receiver therefore has the difficult task of deciding the initial playout delay $T_{initial}$ such that the tolerable late loss rate is not exceeded. A large value of $T_{initial}$ reduces late loss but at the same time increases the user perceived latency of the application.

Figure 16.4 shows sender and receiver curves for the transmission of voice packets over a packet-switched network and two example selections of $T_{initial}$. In the top plot of Figure 16.4 the playout process is started at $T_{initial} = 130$ ms, which leads to late loss of two out of nine packets. In the bottom plot of Figure 16.4 $T_{initial}$ is reduced to 120 ms, which leads to late loss of four out of nine packets. In the lower plot of Figure 16.4 the played signal part is shown as a thick line on top of the desired decoding curve and it can be observed that three playout interruptions happen.

The resulting loss rate is determined by counting the packets that are not available at their decoding deadline and dividing this number n_{late} by the total number of packets of the session $n_{session}$,

$$p_{loss} = \frac{n_{late}}{n_{session}}. \tag{16.1}$$

Depending on the selection of $T_{initial}$ the receiver has to prebuffer different amounts of data. The larger $T_{initial}$, the larger the required buffer capacity at the receiver side. If the buffer is not large enough to hold all the data, buffer overflow occurs and media packets are lost despite their successful and timely arrival at the receiver. In practical applications we can typically assume that the receiver buffer capacity is large enough to hold all received packets before they are decoded. Our main concern is buffer underflow caused by late arrival of information.

Example 3: Late Loss Rate versus End-to-End Delay for VoIP

Figure 16.5 and Figure 16.6 show an example of late loss rate versus initial delay for a VoIP scenario where 20-ms voice packets are transmitted from a host located

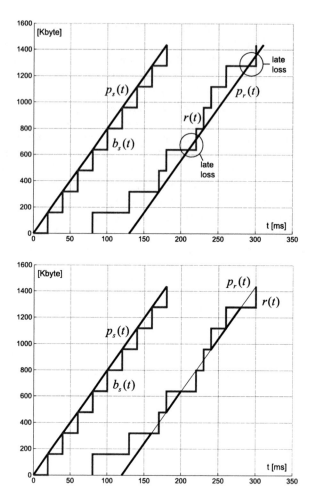

FIGURE 16.4:   Sender and receiver curves for the transmission of voice packets over a packet-switched network. (Top) The initial playout time is $T_{\text{initial}} = 130$ ms, which leads to two late packets. (Bottom) The initial playout time is reduced to 120 ms, which leads to four out of nine packets being late for the playout process.

at the West Coast of the United States to a host at the East Coast. Figure 16.5 shows the measured delay values for 250 packets, and Figure 16.6 shows the resulting late loss rate as a function of the initial playout delay T_{initial}. The larger the end-to-end delay, the smaller the late loss rate. However, the larger the user-perceived application latency.

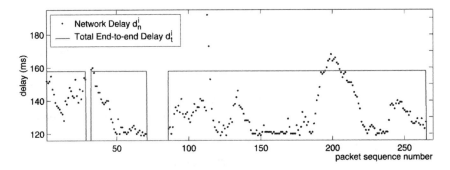

FIGURE 16.5:   Measured packet delivery times for VoIP.

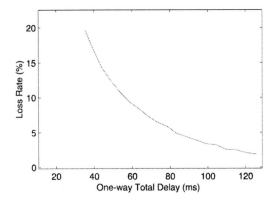

FIGURE 16.6:   Late loss rate versus user-perceived end-to-end delay.

16.4 ADAPTIVE MEDIA PLAYOUT

Adaptive Media Playout allows the client to buffer less data and thus introduce less delay to achieve a given playout reliability. When using AMP, the receiver varies the rate at which it plays out audio and video. The playout speed can, for instance, be controlled by the state of the receiver buffer. In this case, when the buffer occupancy is below a desired level, the client plays media slowly to reduce its data consumption rate. For conversational services or streaming of live content, slowed playout causes the user-perceived latency to increase. Faster-than-normal playout is used in this case during good channel periods in order to eliminate or re-duce excess latency accumulated with slowed playout. Faster-than-normal playout is unnecessary in the case of streaming of prestored programs however. Prestored programs that are slowed during bad channel periods will simply last longer at the client. By manipulating playout speed, AMP can reduce initial buffering delays in the case of prestored streams and reduce the viewing latency (end-to-end delay) of live streams—all without sacrificing playout reliability. Figure 16.7 revisits the scenario introduced in the top plot of Figure 16.4 where two out of nine voice packets could not be played because of their late arrival. Adaptive Media Playout copes with this situation by stretching the playout duration of some voice packets. In Figure 16.7 the third voice segment is played twice as long as normal, which delays the playout deadline of all following packets by 20 ms. Hence, the receiver playout curve changes from $p_r(t)$ to $p_r^{AMP}(t)$. It can be seen from Figure 16.7 that now all packets are available at their playout deadlines. The playout curve $p_r^{AMP}(t)$ is always below and to the right of the receiver curve $r(t)$, which was not the case before. From a user perspective, playout interruptions are avoided. The end-to-end latency, however, increases by 20 ms after stretching the third packet.

To control the playout speed of media, the client scales the duration of one or more media units. For video signals this corresponds to changing the display duration of video frames. For audio or speech signals the duration of segments has to be changed without affecting its pitch [9,24]. Section 16.5 discusses algorithms for media duration scaling in detail.

It is interesting to note that playout speed modification has a precedent in traditional media broadcasting. Motion pictures shot at a frame rate of 24 fps are

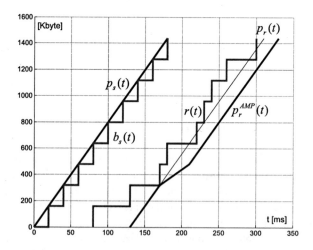

FIGURE 16.7: Adaptive Media Playout for the speech transmission scenario introduced in Figure 16.4. The third packet is played at half the speed at the receiver. This leads to a change of the playout curve and the deadline of all following packets is shifted to the right. Buffer underflow and hence playout interruption are avoided.

shown on European PAL/SECAM broadcast television at 25 fps. Video frames are displayed 1000/25 ms instead of 1000/24 ms, which corresponds to a media unit dilation of 4% and it is typically done without audio timescale modification.

16.4.1 Adaptive Media Playout for Low-Delay Conversational Services

In low-delay conversational services (e.g., video conferencing, Internet Telephony) excessive end-to-end delay impairs the interactivity of communication (see also Chapter 15). The latency experienced when completely absorbing delay jitter and eliminating late loss by receiver buffering can be very high. With Adaptive Media Playout, packet delay variations are compensated by playout speed variations.

The receiver has to decide when to start the playout of the media data once a session has been established. One way to decide the start of playout is to wait for the first speech packet to come in and then wait some additional time (safety margin) before playing this packet. Once the first packet is played, the playout deadlines for all following packets are fixed. If the safety margin was too conservative because the first packet was delayed exceptionally, the end-to-end delay is bigger than necessary. If the first packet arrives exceptionally early, the buffer will be selected too small and the late loss rate of the following packets might become too high.

Adaptive Media Playout addresses this issue by adaptively modifying the end-to-end delay using a playout scheduler that slows down playout if packet delivery times are increasing and speeds up playout if packet delivery times are decreasing. The basic operation of the playout scheduler is to set the playout time for each packet. As a result, network jitter is smoothed and mean end-to-end delay can be minimized. The actual end-to-end delay experienced by the user is continuously changing. As long as this variation stays within certain limits it is not impairing the quality of the communication. Only if the end-to-end delay increases significantly, bidirectional conversations become unnatural and participants start interrupting each other.

For low-delay conversational services the amount of media data available in the receiver buffer and therefore the number of packets available for playout scaling at any time are typically very limited due to the stringent end-to-end delay requirements. This means that the playout scheduler might have to significantly increase the playout duration of single packets in case of sudden changes in packet delay. In extreme situations, the scaling of the current media packet has to be decided without knowing the arrival time of the next packet. In order to keep the current packet concatenated with the next one at output, the arrival time of the next packet has to be estimated. If the delay estimation of the next packet is accurate and the current packet is scaled accordingly, the next packet should arrive and be ready by the end of playback of the current packet. A reliable estimation of the net-

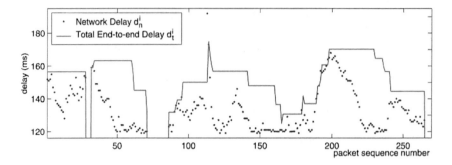

FIGURE 16.8: Adaptive Media Playout for VoIP. The playout schedule is adjusted within talkspurts. Gaps in solid lines correspond to silence periods between talkspurts.

work delay is therefore an important component for adaptive playout scheduling in low-delay conversational services.

Example 4: Adaptive Media Playout for VoIP

When using Adaptive Media Playout for Voice over IP, the playout schedule may not only be adjusted during silence periods but also within talkspurts, as illustrated in Figure 16.8. Each individual packet may have a different playout schedule, which is set according to the varying network condition. With Adaptive Media Playout, the interval between playout times or the length of each voice packet is no longer a constant, although the packetization period is. Continuous output of audio can be achieved by scaling the voice packets using the signal processing techniques described in Section 16.5. For the same delay trace as shown in Figure 16.5, the adaptive scheme is able to effectively reduce average delay and mitigate late loss by adjusting the playout schedule in a more dynamic way. The trade-off between buffering delay and late loss can hence be improved, as shown in Figure 16.9.

16.4.2 Adaptive Media Playout for Nonconversational Services with Moderate-Delay Requirements

Section 16.4.1 described Adaptive Media Playout for low-delay conversational services where due to stringent end-to-end delay requirements typically only very few packets are in the receiver buffer at any time. The main challenge for low-delay applications is to accurately estimate the arrival time of the following packets in order to be able to decide the playout duration of the current packet. The limit on the end-to-end delay is strict, which requires that additional delay intro-

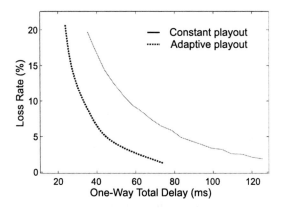

FIGURE 16.9: Trade-off between average end-to-end delay and late loss rate for constant and adaptive playout. The trade-off curve for constant playout is identical to the one shown in Figure 16.6.

duced by slow playout has to be compensated at a later time by faster-than-normal playout. In addition, the required changes in playout duration may be substantial if sudden changes in packet delivery time occur. Some packets may have to be scaled by 100% or more in order to follow network delay variations quickly enough.

The situation is very different for applications that can prebuffer significant amounts of data in their receiver buffer as a result of their moderate latency requirements. Internet Video Streaming is a popular application that falls into this category. This application will be used in the following to describe the use of Adaptive Media Playout for applications with moderate-delay requirements.

Video streaming over the Internet is an example for VBR traffic over a VBR channel. In video streaming, a client requests a pre-encoded media stream from a media server. The pre-encoded video stream is typically encoded at a variable bit rate so the encoder curve $e(t)$ is similar to the one shown in Figure 16.3. The media server packetizes the pre-encoded media stream and sends the packet stream $b_s(t)$ over the Internet to the client. Following the argument in Section 16.2 we use the encoder curve $e(t)$ and decoder curve $d(t)$ instead of the sender sampling curve $p_s(t)$ and receiver playout curve $p_r(t)$ as the video frames are compressed. The decoder curve $d(t)$ tells us at what time a certain media unit (video frame) has to be decoded and displayed at the decoder. This time is relative to the decoding and playout time of the first video frame and for constant playout simply becomes a shifted version of the encoder curve $d(t) = e(t - T_{\text{initial}})$.

Adaptive Media Playout can again be used to reduce the perceived latency while maintaining a desired playout reliability [19]. From a user perspective there

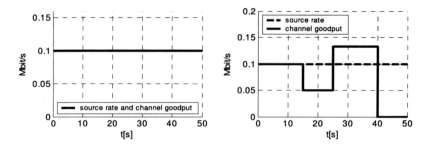

FIGURE 16.10: The source rate is fixed at 100 kbit/s. Two examples of transmission goodput are used in the following. (Left) Constant goodput that matches the source rate. (Right) Variable goodput in the range from 0 to 133 kbit/s.

are two buffering delays that are noticeable. Start-up delay is the time that it takes for the client buffer to fill to a desired level so that playout can begin after a user request. Viewing latency, noticeable in the case of live streams, is the time interval separating a live event and its viewing time at the client. To explain how AMP can be used to reduce these delays, we distinguish among three separate modes of operation [8], illustrated in Figures 16.11–16.13. These modes are called AMP-Initial, AMP-Robust, and AMP-Mean.

For illustrative purposes we will base our discussion in the following on the two specific transmission scenarios shown in Figure 16.10. On the left-hand side of Figure 16.10 a constant bit-rate source stream is transmitted over a constant bit-rate channel. The source and the channel rate match and are both 100 kbit/s. On the right hand side of Figure 16.10 the constant bit-rate source stream is sent over a channel with variable goodput. The goodput varies as a function of time. The maximum goodput $g(t)$ reaches 133 kbit/s.

16.4.2.1 Initial Playout Delay Reduction (AMP-Initial)

AMP-Initial is used to decrease the start-up delay. In this mode, the client initiates the playout process before the buffer is filled to the usual target level. Despite this early start of playout the buffer is able to fill to the target level over time by initially playing the media slower than normal. The buffer fills over time since the data consumption rate during slowed playout is smaller than the arrival rate of the media packets, assuming that during normal playout the source rate and the channel goodput match the data consumption rate at the decoder. Once the target level is reached, the playout speed returns to normal. This technique allows fast switching between different programs or channels without sacrificing protection against adverse channel conditions, after the initial buffer is built up.

Figure 16.11 illustrates AMP-Initial. The source rate and channel goodput correspond to the left-hand side of Figure 16.10. The consumption rate of the playout process at normal playout speed is 0.1 Mbit/s and hence matches the source rate. The second plot in Figure 16.11 shows the client buffer occupancy as a function of time for the case of nonadaptive playout. The target buffer level is assumed to be 1 Mbit, yielding a preroll time of 10 s in this example. The third plot illustrates the client buffer occupancy for the AMP-Initial scheme in which playout starts when the buffer occupancy is only half the target level. This happens after 5 s. The client slows playout initially to allow the buffer occupancy to increase over time. The

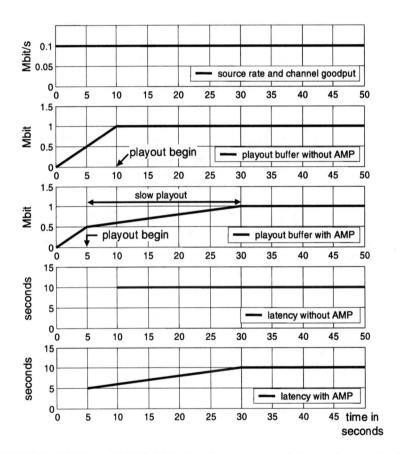

FIGURE 16.11:   AMP-Initial: For low start-up delays, playout begins after a reduced number of frames are buffered at the client. Slowed playout allows the buffer occupancy to grow to a safer target level over time. In this example, frame periods are stretched by 20% during slow playout periods.

media units are stretched by 20% during slowed playout and hence after a total of 30 s the target buffer level is reached. The two lower plots in Figure 16.11 show the viewing latency with and without AMP-Initial. While the latency remains constant for the nonadaptive case, for the AMP-Initial scheme latency increases from 5 s initially to 10 s when the target buffer level is reached.

16.4.2.2 Improved Robustness Against Network Variations (AMP-Robust)

As illustrated in Figure 16.12, AMP-Robust increases the robustness of the playout process with respect to variations of goodput. In this mode the playout speed is

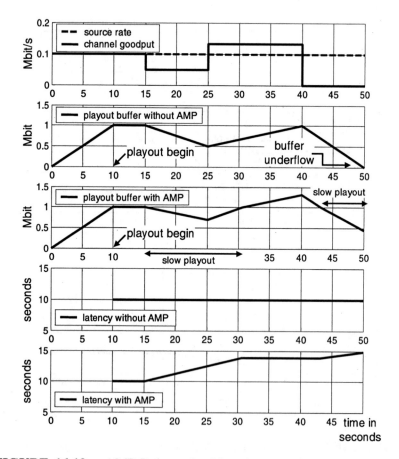

FIGURE 16.12: AMP-Robust: In this scheme, suitable for prestored programs where viewing latency is not important, slowed playout is used to keep the buffer occupancy at a desired level.

simply reduced whenever the buffer occupancy falls below the target level. Now, the transmission scenario shown on the right-hand side of Figure 16.10 is considered. As before, the source rate is a constant 0.1 Mbit/s. The channel goodput varies over time with a reduction to 0.05 Mbit/s at $t = 15$ s, an improvement to 0.133 Mbit/s at $t = 25$ s, and a complete channel outage at $t = 40$ s. The second plot of Figure 16.12 shows the buffer occupancy as a function of time for nonadaptive playout. The target buffer level is again 1 Mbit, which leads to a playout start at $t = 10$ s. Playout is interrupted, however, after 50 s, when reductions in the channel goodput lead to a buffer underflow. The third plot in Figure 16.12 shows the buffer occupancy for the AMP-Robust scheme in which the client stretches frame periods by 25% whenever the buffer occupancy falls below the target level. In this example, buffer underflow is averted with AMP. The lower two plots in Figure 16.12 show the viewing latency as a function of time. For nonadaptive playout, latency is constant. For the adaptive case, the latency increases whenever playout is slowed, which is fine for a prestored program. Note that playout starts at $t = 10$ s for both cases. AMP-Robust can be combined with AMP-Initial to also allow reduced start-up time.

16.4.2.3 Live Media Streaming (AMP-Live)

AMP-Live is suitable for the streaming of live programs. In this mode, the client slows playout during bad channel periods but also plays media faster than normal during good channel periods to reduce additional viewing latency that has accumulated during periods of slowed playout. By playing the media faster and slower than normal, the mean viewing latency can be reduced for a given probability of buffer underflow. An example of the application of AMP-Live is given in Figure 16.13 for the transmission scenario introduced in the right-hand side of Figure 16.10.

Whenever the buffer occupancy falls below the target level, playout is slowed. When the occupancy is greater than the target level, media is played faster than normal to eliminate excess latency. In Figure 16.13, during faster playout the client reduces frame periods by 25%, which corresponds to a 33% increase in the data consumption rate. Therefore, the buffer remains at the target level in the third plot of Figure 16.13 during fast playout. Latency, shown in the lower two plots of Figure 16.13, decreases during faster-than-normal playout.

16.5 SIGNAL PROCESSING FOR ADAPTIVE MEDIA PLAYOUT

16.5.1 Time Compression and Dilation of Speech and Audio Signals

When Adaptive Media Playout is used, the duration of the audio or speech signal has to be scaled without impairing quality. The scaling of a voice or audio

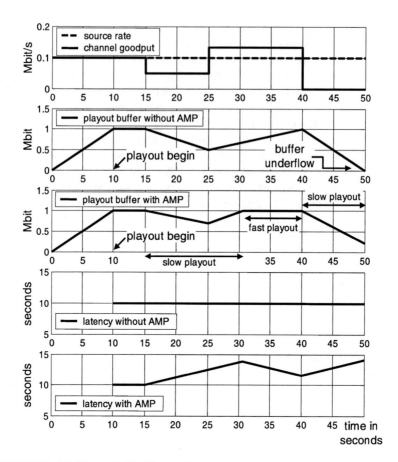

FIGURE 16.13: AMP-Live: For live streams, low viewing latency is desirable. The client slows playout when poor channel conditions threaten to starve the client buffer. During good channel periods, however, faster-than-normal playout is used to reduce or even eliminate latency accumulated during periods with slowed playout.

segment may be realized by *timescale modification* based on the *Waveform Similarity Overlap-Add* (WSOLA) algorithm, which is an interpolation-based method operating in the time domain. This technique was used in [21] to scale long audio blocks and was modified and improved in [20] and [17] for loss concealment by expanding a block of several packets. For a detailed discussion on error concealment for audio communication, refer to Chapter 3.

The basic idea of WSOLA is to decompose the input into overlapping segments of equal length, which are then realigned and superimposed to form the output with equal and fixed overlap. The realignment leads to modified output length. For those segments to be added in overlap, their relative positions in the input are found through the search of the maximum correlation between them so that they have the maximum similarity and the superposition will not cause any discontinuity in the output. Weighting windows are applied to the segments before they are superimposed to generate smooth transitions in the reconstructed output. For speech processing, WSOLA has the advantage of maintaining the pitch period, which results in improved quality compared to resampling.

Since the goal of Adaptive Media Playout is to reduce delay, low processing delay is desirable. The conventional WSOLA algorithm can be tailored and improved to work on only *one* packet. In other words, an incoming packet can be scaled immediately and independently, without introducing any additional processing delay. To scale a voice packet, a *template segment* of constant length is first selected in the input. Then a *similar segment* that exhibits maximum similarity to the template segment is being searched. The start of the similar segment is searched in a *search region*, as shown in Figure 16.14. When working on a single packet, the search for a similar segment is more constrained, as the realignment of the similar segments must be made in units of pitch periods and there are fewer pitch periods available in one short packet. For a 20-ms packet, depending on the speaker's gender and voice pitch, there could be fewer than two pitch periods included, which makes it difficult to extract the target segments with similarity. To overcome this problem, the conventional WSOLA algorithm has to be modified to decrease the segment length for correlation calculation, and the first template segment is positioned at the beginning of the input packet, as shown in Figure 16.14a. To expand short packets, the search region for the first similar segment is moved to the prior packet in order to have a larger range to look for similar waveforms. In Figure 16.14a, although the input packet starts in Pitch Period 2, the similar segment is found within Pitch Period 1. Although the prior packet might already be played out at the time of scaling, similar waveforms can still be extracted from it to construct new output without delaying the prior packet. Once the similar segment is found, it is weighted by a rising window and the template segment is weighted by a symmetric falling window. The similar segment followed by the rest of the samples in the packet is then shifted and superimposed with the template segment to generate the output. The resulting output is longer than the input due to the relative position of the similar segment found and the shift of the similar segment, as shown in Figure 16.14a. The amount of expansion depends on the position and the size of the defined search region.

In Figure 16.14, complete pitch periods in the waveform are separated by vertical dashed lines and marked with sequential numbers. For example, in Figure 16.14a, it is observed from the output waveform that one extra pitch period

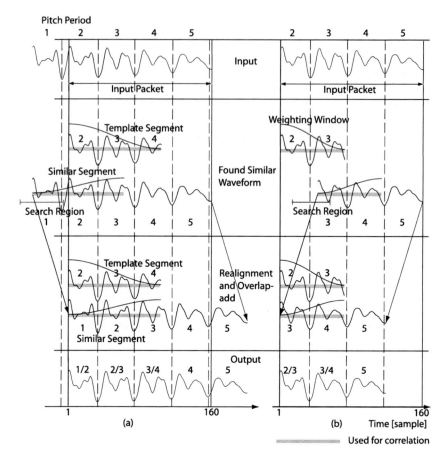

FIGURE 16.14:   Extension (a) and compression (b) of single voice packets using timescale modification.

is created and added as a result of realignment and superposition of the extracted segments from the input. However, the extra pitch period is not just a simple replication of any pitch period from the input, but the interpolation of several pitch periods instead. For the output in Figure 16.14a, the first three pitch periods are the weighted superposition of Pitch Periods 1/2, 2/3, and 3/4, respectively. This explains why the sound quality using timescale modification is better than that of pitch repetition (described in [4,13]). The same is true for compressing a packet, where the information carried by a chopped pitch period is preserved and distributed among the remaining ones. The operations of searching for a similar segment and extending the packet by multiple pitch periods, as described earlier, constitute one *iteration* in the scheme. If the output speech has not met the target length after such operations, additional iterations are performed. In a subsequent iteration, a new template segment of the same length is defined that immediately follows the template in the last iteration. All the defined template segments and the remaining samples following the last template in the input should cover the entire output with the target length. Packet compression is done in a similar way, as depicted in Figure 16.14b. The only difference is that the search region for the similar segment should not be defined in the prior packet in order to generate an output shorter in length.

Since the scaling of packets has to be performed in integer multiples of pitch periods, it is unlikely to achieve the exact packet length as targeted by the adaptive scheduler. However, as the resulting output packet length is fed into the scheduler, this inaccuracy will be absorbed and corrected in potential scaling of the following packets so that the overall schedule is maintained as targeted.

Comparing the input and output waveforms in Figure 16.14, it becomes obvious that the operation preserves the pitch frequency of the input speech. Only the packet length and hence the rate of speech are altered. Subjective listening tests show that infrequent scaling of the packets does not degrade speech quality, even if the scaling ratio is occasionally high [12]. Note that the scheme is speech codec independent. The operations can be applied on the PCM output.

One advantage of working with a short packet is that the input is divided into fewer template segments so that typically only one or two iterations will yield the output with the target length. Another important feature of the algorithm observed in Figure 16.14 is that the beginning and the end of each packet are not altered. As a result, when concatenating modified packets, no overlap or merging is needed to obtain smooth transitions. Hence, packets can be modified independently and sent to the output queue back to back. This type of operation is ideally suited for a highly adaptive playout scheduler.

16.5.2 Time Compression and Dilation of Video Signals

While changing the display duration of audio and speech signals requires the use of special timescale modification algorithms as described in the previous section, for video the situation is much easier. Time compression or dilation of a video signal can be achieved by simply changing the display duration of individual video frames. If the display process supports only fixed duration display of video frames, repetition or dropping of video frames can be used instead. As an example let us assume that we want to scale the playout of the video signal by 20% for a video sequence with 25 frames per second and a fixed display duration of 40 ms per frame. Repetition of every 5th frame makes 30 frames or 1.2 s out of an original 1-s segment of the video signal. For a fixed display duration of 40 ms per frame the playout duration is now 1.2 s, which corresponds to the desired 20% playout dilation.

16.5.3 Time Compression and Dilation of Silence Periods

As mentioned previously, scaling of up to 100% is tolerable if applied infrequently to short segments of speech. Continuous scaling of speech or audio signals for longer segments, as needed for AMP in video streaming scenarios, however, becomes noticeable and practical scaling factors are much lower. In these cases typically scaling of up to 25% can be used. However, if we detect silence within the packets in our client buffer, then we can overproportionally stretch or compress the silence periods without significantly impairing the perceived quality.

16.6 PLAYOUT SPEED CONTROL MECHANISMS

Playout speed control is a key issue when using Adaptive Media Playout and, in general, the playout scheduler has to be designed individually for a particular application. While, for example, a simple heuristic that chooses a playout speed from a small set of discrete values depending on the occupancy of the playout buffer is suitable for Internet Media Streaming, low-delay conversational services as described in Section 16.4.1 require more sophisticated schemes. Advanced playout speed control mechanisms may, for instance, operate in a way that meets a constraint on expected distortion or finds an optimal trade-off among the distortion due to playout speed variation and the distortion due to expected decoding errors, and latency. In the following we discuss a selection of playout speed control mechanisms.

16.6.1 Heuristic Playout Speed Control for Video Streaming

A simple adaptive playout strategy for video streaming controls the playout frame rate by examining the number of frames of media in the playout buffer. Let $\mu(n)$ be the playout frame rate dictated by the scheme, where n is the number of frames that occupy the playout buffer. In the nonadaptive case this rate is constant and given by $1/t_F$, where t_F is the frame period. With Adaptive Media Playout, $\mu(n)$ varies with n. For example, a simple playout policy for AMP-Live (introduced in Section 16.4.2) is

$$\mu(n) = \begin{cases} \dfrac{1}{s \cdot t_F} & n < N_{\text{low}}, \\[2ex] \dfrac{1}{f \cdot t_F} & n > N_{\text{high}}, \\[2ex] \dfrac{1}{t_F} & \text{otherwise,} \end{cases} \qquad (16.2)$$

where $s \geq 1$ represents a decrease in playout speed, $f \leq 1$ is an increase in playout speed, n is the number of contiguous frames in the playout queue, and N_{high} and N_{low} are threshold values. When there are fewer than N_{low} frames in the playout queue, each frame plays for $s \cdot t_F$ seconds. When the number in the queue exceeds N_{high}, each frame plays for $f \cdot t_F$ seconds.

In general, functions $\mu(n)$ can be defined depending on goals with respect to robustness, mean latency, buffer size, initial preroll delay, and playout speed variability. For instance, in the case of AMP-Initial and AMP-Robust, the controller in (16.2) can be used with $N_{\text{high}} = \infty$. Alternative heuristic controllers may, for example, allow playout speed to vary continuously as a function of buffer occupancy.

16.6.2 Distortion-Latency Optimized Playout Speed Control

This section discusses a scheme [7] that controls playout in a way that attempts to yield an optimal trade-off among distortion of decoded media, distortion due to playout variation, and latency.

In this scheme, a scaling factor for the playout speed of a frame is determined by an algorithm that jointly optimizes a vector of scaling factors $v \in \Re^M$ for the playout speed of a window of M future frames. The scheme finds a v that gives an approximately optimal trade-off between the expected distortion $D(v)$ and functions $G_i(v)$ that assess perceptual costs due to playout speed and latency variation. The optimal trade-off is determined to be the one that minimizes the Lagrangian cost function

$$J(v) = D(v) + \sum_i \lambda_i G_i, \tag{16.3}$$

where the λ_i are user-defined weights for the perceptual costs. Cost functions $G_i(v)$ that assess the perceptual impact of playout speed and latency variation can be defined, for example, as

$$G_1(v) = \sum_{i=1}^{M} (v_i - 1)^2, \tag{16.4}$$

$$G_2(v) = \sum_{i=1}^{M} (v_i - v_{i-1})^2, \tag{16.5}$$

$$G_3(v) = \left(t_F \sum_{i=1}^{M} (v_i - 1) + t_{\text{accum}} \right)^2, \tag{16.6}$$

where M is the length of vector v. In these examples, G_1 assesses a cost for deviation of the frame-period scaling factors from 1, G_2 assesses a cost on variations in the playout rate from one frame to the next, and G_3 assigns a cost to latencies that do not match the initial buffering delay. G_3 is useful in cases such as live or interactive streams in which latency must be constrained. In (16.6), t_{accum} is the amount of delay that will have accumulated by the end of the currently playing frame, less the initial buffering delay.

16.6.3 Adaptive Media Playout and R–D Optimized Media Streaming

The control scheme described in Section 16.6.2 can be integrated with the framework for rate-distortion optimized streaming described in Chapter 10.2.1 [7].

The scheme uses receiver-driven streaming in which the receiver calculates optimal requests to transmit to the sender and the sender simply transmits the requested packets.

If we combine Adaptive Media Playout with receiver-driven RD optimized streaming, transmission requests and playout speeds have both to be computed at the receiver and can therefore be computed jointly. In this case, the Lagrangian optimization objective of (16.3) is augmented to be a function not only of the playout speeds v, but also of the transmission policy π. The goal in this case is to minimize the Lagrangian

$$J(\pi, v) = D(\pi, v) + \lambda R(\pi, v) + \lambda_1 G_1(v) + \lambda_2 G_2(v) + \lambda_3 G_3(v), \qquad (16.7)$$

where $R(\pi, v)$ is the expected transmission rate as a function of the transmission policy and playout speeds. The iterative descent algorithm used to minimize the Lagrangian with respect to the transmission policy π remains mostly as described in Section 10.2.1 of this book. The Lagrangian is iteratively minimized one variable at a time while the others are held fixed. The step of minimizing the Lagrangian with respect to the playout speed vector while the transmission policy variable is held fixed is added, however.

16.6.4 Playout Speed Control for Low-Delay Applications

As discussed in Section 16.4.1 the success of Adaptive Media Playout for low-delay conversational services mainly depends on how accurately the receiver can estimate the arrival time of future packets. A key component of playout speed control for this kind of application is therefore packet transfer delay estimation. Several delay estimation techniques have been proposed, including linear recursive filtering with stochastic gradient algorithms [16], histogram-based approaches [14,18], normal approximation [3], and event counting [23]. The playout speed control mechanism used for VoIP shown in Figure 16.8 is based on the delay of the most recent packets [12]. In this scheme, the user specifies a desired rate ε_l of errors due to late loss. The algorithm estimates the late loss probability of a packet as a function of its playout deadline by examining the delays of a window of recent transmissions. The algorithm scales the playout speed of each frame so that the next packet's deadline yields an expected loss probability that meets the constraint set by the user.

To find the expected loss probability for a packet as a function of its deadline, the algorithm makes use of order statistics compiled from the delays of a window of the last w received packets. Let $D^1, D^2, \ldots, D^w$ denote the delays of the last w received packets in ascending order such that $D^1 \leq D^2 \leq \cdots \leq D^w$. Let the random network delay of a packet be denoted d_n. The expected cumulative distribution function (CDF) for the delay can be written as

$$E\left[\Pr\{d_n \leq D^r\}\right] = \frac{r}{w+1}, \quad r = 1, 2, \ldots, w \tag{16.8}$$

and represents the expected probability that a packet with the same delay statistics can be received with delay D^r or less. Interpolation can be used to evaluate the expected CDF at values between the D^r.

Using this estimate for the delay CDF, the deadline for a packet can be chosen so as to meet the late loss rate constraint ε_l. The playout speed of a speech segment is scaled to control the deadline of the packet containing the following segment.

One important feature of this history-based estimation is that the user can specify the acceptable loss rate, and the algorithm adjusts the playout schedule accordingly. Therefore, the trade-off between buffering delay and late loss can be controlled explicitly.

Over IP networks, it is common to observe sudden high delays ("spikes") incurred by voice packets, as shown by packets 113–115 in Figure 16.8. Delay spikes usually occur when new traffic enters the network and a shared link becomes congested, in which case past statistics are not useful to predict future delays. In this case, the scheduler switches from a normal mode to the *rapid adaptation mode* when the current delay exceeds the previous one by more than a threshold value. In rapid adaptation mode, the first packet with an unpredictable high delay has to be discarded. Following that, the delay estimate is set to the last "spike delay" without considering or further updating the order statistics. The rapid adaptation mode is switched off when delays drop to the level before the spike and the scheduler returns to its normal operation, reusing the state of order statistics before the spike occurred. This rapid adaptation helps to mitigate burst loss as illustrated in Figure 16.8.

16.7 ADAPTIVE MEDIA PLAYOUT AND PACKET PATH DIVERSITY

In Chapter 17, path diversity is described for reliable communication over lossy networks using multiple description coding. It has been observed that for multipath transmission the end-to-end application sees a virtual average path, which exhibits a smaller variability in quality than any of the individual paths. In this section, packet path diversity is revisited for low-delay applications when Adaptive Media Playout is employed.

16.7.1 Packet Path Diversity for Low-Delay Conversational Services

In the context of delay-sensitive applications, such as interactive VoIP, the largely uncorrelated characteristics of the delay jitter on multiple network paths can be exploited using Adaptive Media Playout techniques [10]. The multiple streams to be delivered via different paths are formed by multiple description coding (MDC), which generates multiple descriptions of the source signal of equal importance. These descriptions can be decoded independently at the receiver. If all descriptions are received, the source signal can be reconstructed in full quality. If only a subset of the descriptions is received, the quality of the reconstruction is degraded, but is still better than the quality resulting from losing all descriptions. Depending on the MDC scheme selected, the overall data rate of the payload does not necessarily increase as a result of transmitting multiple streams. The data rate only increases if redundancy is introduced between the multiple streams.

In order to maximize the benefits of multipath transmission, paths that exhibit largely uncorrelated jitter and loss characteristics are preferred. Sending streams along different routers from source to destination naturally leads to path diversity, which could include streams traversing different ISPs or even streams being sent in different directions around the globe. For a detailed discussion on how to practically realize multipath transmission, refer to Chapter 17.

16.7.2 Adaptive Two-Stream Playout Scheduling

To exploit the characteristics of multipath transmission, the playout scheduler is again a key component, as in the previous discussion in this chapter. An adaptive scheduler for two-stream playout is similar to the single stream case described in Section 16.4.1. Before the arrival of each packet i, the playout deadline for that packet has to be set according to the most recent delays recorded. The playout deadline of packet i is denoted by d_{play}^i, which is the time from the moment the packet is delivered to the network until it has to be played out. When determining the playout deadlines, the trade-off among delay, losing both MDC descriptions (referred to as *packet erasure*), and losing only one description has to be considered. This trade-off can be stated as the following constrained problem: given a certain acceptable signal distortion, minimize the average delay $\mathcal{E}\{d_{\text{play}}^i\}$. This constrained problem can be formulated as an unconstrained problem by introducing a Lagrange cost function for packet i,

$$C^i = d_{\text{play}}^i + \lambda_1 \cdot Pr(\text{both descriptions lost})$$
$$+ \lambda_2 \cdot Pr(\text{only one description lost})$$
$$= d_{\text{play}}^i + \lambda_1 \hat{\varepsilon}_{S_1}^i \hat{\varepsilon}_{S_2}^i + \lambda_2 \left(\hat{\varepsilon}_{S_1}^i \left(1 - \hat{\varepsilon}_{S_2}^i \right) + \hat{\varepsilon}_{S_2}^i \left(1 - \hat{\varepsilon}_{S_1}^i \right) \right), \qquad (16.9)$$

where $\hat{\varepsilon}_{S_1}^i$ and $\hat{\varepsilon}_{S_2}^i$ are the estimated loss probabilities of the descriptions in Streams 1 and 2, respectively, given a certain d_{play}^i. The estimate of $\hat{\varepsilon}_{S_1}^i$ and $\hat{\varepsilon}_{S_2}^i$ can be based on past delay values recorded for the two streams. The higher d_{play}^i is, the lower the loss probabilities since the likelihood of playing out delayed packets is higher. The Lagrange multipliers λ_1 and λ_2 are predefined parameters used to trade off delay and the two loss probabilities.

The playout deadline can be optimized by searching for the d_{play}^i that minimizes the cost function (16.9). Multiplier λ_1 is used to trade off total delay and packet erasure probability. Greater λ_1 results in a lower erasure rate at the cost of higher delay. Multiplier λ_2 is introduced to penalize distortion as a result of playing out only one description. The greater λ_2 is, the better the quality of the reconstructed signal at the cost of higher delay. Note that although packet erasure [the second term in (16.9)] and quality degradation due to the loss of one MDC description [the third term in (16.9)] are different perceptual experiences, they are not independent measures. From (16.9), increasing λ_2 also leads to lower erasure probability. However, with zero or very small λ_2, only packet erasure is considered. In this case, good reconstruction quality is not a priority, but lower latency is given more emphasis, with the trade-off between delay and erasure rate determined mainly by λ_1.

When switching between streams during speech playout, the playout schedule has to be dynamically adjusted and adapted to the delay statistics of each individual stream. Adaptive Media Playout in combination with packet path diversity has first been demonstrated in [10] for two-stream VoIP. The experimental results in [10] demonstrate that this combination has the potential to significantly reduce the application latency of low-delay conversational services over the Internet while preserving the user-perceived signal quality.

16.8 SUMMARY AND FURTHER READING

This chapter discussed Adaptive Media Playout as a receiver-based technique to adapt multimedia communication applications to varying transmission conditions.

The main idea of AMP is to consider the time axis as a rubber band that can be locally stretched or compressed. In the context of video streaming delivery, AMP can successfully be employed to decrease the initial as well as the average latency of the application. For VoIP the flexibility to adjust the playout duration of individual speech segments allows us to adjust playout deadlines even within talkspurts and to dynamically optimize the trade-off between latency and late loss rate. While for video the change of playout duration is straightforward, for audio and speech signals special signal processing techniques have to be employed, which lead to noticeable quality impairments if the scaling factor becomes too large. Finally, it should be mentioned that AMP is particularly beneficial in multicast or broadcast scenarios where every user sees a different channel and can individually adapt to the current transmission properties without getting the sender involved.

REFERENCES

[1] J. G. Apostolopoulos. "Reliable Video Communication over Lossy Packet Networks Using Multiple State Encoding and Path Diversity," *Proceedings Visual Communication and Image Processing*, pp. 392–409, January 2001.

[2] David G. Andersen, Hari Balakrishnan, M. Frans Kaashoek, and Robert Morris. "The Case for Resilient Overlay Networks," *Proceedings of the 8th Annual Workshop on Hot Topics in Operating Systems (HotOS-VIII)*, Online at: http://nms.lcs.mit.edu/projects/ron/, May 2001.

[3] J. F. Gibbon and T. D. C. Little. "The Use of Network Delay Estimation for Multimedia Data Retrieval," *IEEE Journal on Selected Areas in Communications*, vol. 14, no. 7, pp. 1376–1387, September 1996.

[4] David J. Goodman, Gordon B. Lockhart, Ondria J. Wasem, and Wai-Choong Wong. "Waveform Substitution Techniques for Recovering Missing Speech Segments in Packet Voice Communications," *IEEE Transactions on Acoustics, Speech, and Signal Processing*, vol. 34, no. 6, pp. 1440–1448, December 1986.

[5] M. Kalman, B. Girod, and E. Steinbach. "Adaptive Playout for Real-Time Media Streaming," *International Symposium on Circuits and Systems, ISCAS 2002*, Scottsdale, Arizona, May 2002.

[6] M. Kalman, E. Steinbach, and B. Girod. "R-D Optimized Media Streaming Enhanced with Adaptive Media Playout," *International Conference on Multimedia and Expo, ICME 2002*, Lausanne, August 2002.

[7] M. Kalman, E. Steinbach, and B. Girod. "Rate-Distortion Optimized Video Streaming with Adaptive Playout," *International Conference on Image Processing, ICIP 2002*, Rochester, New York, September 2002.

[8] M. Kalman, E. Steinbach, and B. Girod. "Adaptive Media Playout for Low Delay Video Streaming over Error-Prone Channels," *IEEE Transactions on Circuits and Systems for Video Technology*, vol. 14, no. 6, pp. 841–851, June 2004.

[9] Y. Liang, N. Faerber, and B. Girod. "Adaptive Playout Scheduling Using Time-Scale Modification in Packet Voice Communications," *Proc. IEEE Intern. Conf. Acoustics, Speech, and Signal Processing, ICASSP-2001*, Salt Lake City, UT, May 2001.

[10] Yi J. Liang, E. Steinbach, and B. Girod. "Real-Time Voice Communication over the Internet Using Packet Path Diversity," *Proc. ACM Multimedia 2001*, pp. 431–440, Ottawa, Canada, September/October 2001.

[11] Yi J. Liang, E. Steinbach, and B. Girod. "Multi-Stream Voice over IP Using Packet Path Diversity," *Proc. IEEE Workshop on Multimedia Signal Processing*, pp. 555–560, Cannes, France, October 2001.

[12] Yi. J. Liang, N. Faerber, and B. Girod. "Adaptive Playout Scheduling and Loss Concealment for Voice Communication over IP Networks," *IEEE Transactions on Multimedia*, vol. 5, no. 4, pp. 532–543, December 2003.

[13] Wen-Tsai Liao, Jeng-Chun Chen, and Ming-Syan Chen. "Adaptive Recovery Techniques for Real-Time Audio Streams," *Proceedings IEEE INFOCOM 2001*, vol. 2, pp. 815–823, Anchorage, AK, April 2001.

[14] S. B. Moon, J. Kurose, and D. Towsley. "Packet Audio Playout Delay Adjustment: Performance Bounds and Algorithms," *Multimedia Systems*, vol. 6, no. 1, pp. 17–28, January 1998.

[15] C. Perkins, O. Hodson, and V. Hardman. "A Survey of Packet Loss Recovery Techniques for Streaming Audio," *IEEE Network*, vol. 12, no. 5, pp. 40–48, September/October 1998.

[16] R. Ramjee, J. Kurose, D. Towsley, and H. Schulzrinne. "Adaptive Playout Mechanisms for Packetized Audio Applications in Wide-Area Networks," *Proceedings IEEE INFOCOM '94*, vol. 2, pp. 680–688, June 1994.

[17] H. Sanneck, A. Stenger, K. Ben Younes, and B. Girod, "A New Technique for Audio Packet Loss Concealment," *IEEE GLOBECOM*, pp. 48–52, November 1996.

[18] Cormac J. Sreenan, Jyh-Cheng Chen, Prathima Agrawal, and B. Narendran. "Delay Reduction Techniques for Playout Buffering," *IEEE Transactions on Multimedia*, vol. 2, no. 2, pp. 88–100, June 2000.

[19] E. Steinbach, N. Faerber, and B. Girod. "Adaptive Playout for Low-Latency Video Streaming," *Proc. International Conference on Image Processing, ICIP-2001*, pp. 962–965, Thessaloniki, Greece, October 2001.

[20] A. Stenger, K. Ben Younes, R. Reng, and B. Girod. "A New Error Concealment Technique for Audio Transmission with Packet Loss," *Proc. EUSIPCO '96*, Trieste, Italy, September 1996.

[21] W. Verhelst and M. Roelands. "An Overlap-Add Technique Based on Waveform Similarity (WSOLA) for High Quality Time-Scale Modification of Speech," *Proc. ICASSP '93*, pp. 554–557, April 1993.

[22] Ondria J. Wasem, David J. Goodman, Charles A. Dvorak, and Howard G. Page. "The Effect of Waveform Substitution on the Quality of PCM Packet Communications," *IEEE Transactions on Acoustics, Speech, and Signal Processing*, vol. 36, no. 3, pp. 342–348, March 1988.

[23] Y. Xie, C. Liu, M. Lee, and T. N. Saadawi. "Adaptive Multimedia Synchronization in a Teleconference System," *Multimedia Systems*, vol. 7, no. 4, pp. 326–337, July 1999.

[24] M. C. Yuang, S. T. Liang, and Y. G. Chen. "Dynamic Video Playout Smoothing Method for Multimedia Applications," *Multimedia Tools and Applications*, vol. 6, pp. 47–59, 1998.

[25] ITU-T Recommendation P.862. "Perceptual Evaluation of Speech Quality (PESQ), an Objective Method for End-to-End Speech Quality Assessment of Narrow-Band Telephone Networks and Speech Codecs, February 2001.

PART **F**

ADVANCED TOPICS

CHAPTER   17 Path Diversity for Media Streaming
(John Apostolopoulos, Mitchell Trott, and Wai-Tian Tan)

CHAPTER   18 Distributed Video Coding and Its Applications
(Abhik Majumdar, Rohit Puri, Kannan Ramchandran, and
Jim Chou)

CHAPTER   19 Infrastructure-Based Streaming Media Overlay Networks
(Susie Wee, Wai-Tian Tan, and John Apostolopoulos)

17

Path Diversity for Media Streaming

The Use of Multiple Description Coding

John Apostolopoulos, Mitchell Trott, and Wai-Tian Tan

17.1 INTRODUCTION

Media streaming over best-effort packet networks such as the Internet is quite challenging because of the dynamic and unpredictable delay, loss rate, and available bandwidth. Streaming over multiple paths to provide path diversity, coupled with careful co-design of the media coding and packetization to exploit path diversity, has emerged as an approach to help overcome these problems. This chapter provides an overview of path diversity, of complementary media coding techniques such as multiple description coding, and of their benefits and uses for improved media streaming.

Path diversity is a transmission technique that sends data through two or more paths in a packet-based network. A path diversity system may use multiple paths at the same time or may perform path selection to switch between them. This is in contrast to the conventional approach where all packets are sent over a single path between sender and receiver, and this path does not vary with time under the direct or indirect control of the application. The paths may originate from single or multiple sources. An example of the single-source case in a video streaming application is shown in Figure 17.1. A more complex multiple-source scenario is illustrated in Figure 17.2.

Using multiple paths through the transport network for streaming can help overcome the loss and delay problems that afflict streaming media and low-latency communication. In addition, it has long been known that multiple paths can improve fault tolerance and link recovery for data delivery, as well as provide larger

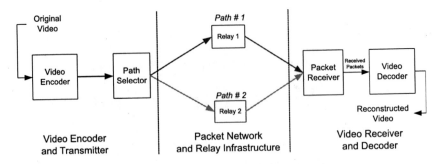

FIGURE 17.1: Media packets are sent over multiple paths in a packet network. In this case packets from a single source are directed over different paths via relays.

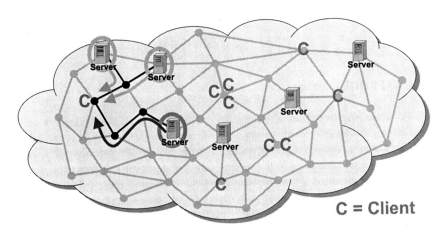

C = Client

FIGURE 17.2: Path diversity in a content delivery network using multiple sources. A basic question: which two of the three circled servers should be selected to stream to the client? The two nearby servers that share a link or a nearby server and the more distant server?

aggregate bandwidth, load balancing, and faster bulk data downloads. The benefits of path diversity are examined in detail in Section 17.3.

Diversity techniques have been studied for many years for wireless communication, for example, frequency, time, and spatial diversity. However, path diversity over packet networks has received limited attention until relatively recently. The early work in this area, for example, [4,5,22], focuses on reliable data delivery through error correction coding or retransmission and is generally performed in the context of multiple virtual circuits on connection-oriented systems such as ATM.

A number of thorough experimental studies, for example, [29], have demonstrated the great variability in the end-to-end performance observed over the Internet. This variability is analogous to the variability of wireless links and motivates the application of wireless diversity techniques to wired and wireless Internet communication. Further motivation for the use of multiple paths is that the default (single) path between two nodes on a network is often not the best path. For example, the measurement study [35] comparing the paths between two hosts on the Internet found that "in 30–80% of the cases, there is an alternate path with significantly superior quality" to the default path, where quality is measured in terms of metrics such as round-trip time, loss rate, and bandwidth.

This chapter provides a survey of the benefits, architectures, system design issues, and open problems associated with streaming media delivery using path diversity. Complementary media coding techniques such as multiple description coding are also reviewed. We begin in Section 17.2 by describing two basic components of the path diversity systems we consider: media streaming and media coding. Section 17.3 surveys the benefits of path diversity in a streaming-media context. Many of these benefits accrue only for media streaming applications and have no direct analogy, for example, to benefits associated with classical wireless diversity. Section 17.4 provides an overview of multiple description (MD) coding and its application to different types of media, including speech, audio, image, and video. Section 17.5 examines the design, analysis, and operation of media streaming systems that use path diversity and highlights some techniques for analyzing and modeling path diversity that are beneficial for selecting the best paths or best servers in a path diversity system. In Section 17.6 we describe various architectures that support and benefit from path diversity, including overlay networks, low-delay applications, peer-to-peer networks, and wireless networks. Finally, Section 17.7 provides a summary and pointers for further reading.

17.2 BUILDING BLOCKS FOR MEDIA STREAMING

In this section we introduce the basic components of media streaming, independent of any path diversity enhancements. We first describe how media streams differ from ordinary file transfer. We then describe how source material, such as audio or video streams, is transformed into a sequence of packets for transmission over a network. This encoding architecture is used in essentially all nondiversity applications and is extended in subsequent sections to support path diversity.

17.2.1 Media Streaming Characteristics

The problem of streaming media such as voice and video over best-effort packet networks is complicated by a number of factors. Unlike static content delivery or file download, streaming involves the simultaneous delivery and playback of media and is characterized by delay constraints on each transmitted packet. Packets that arrive after their decoding or display deadline are generally useless. These inevitable packet losses are not necessarily fatal; most media streams have some tolerance to packet loss, albeit limited by the use of temporally predictive compression. Delay constraints and tolerance to loss are primary factors that distinguish media streaming from ordinary data transport. Conversational or interactive applications have particularly tight delay constraints, typically 100 ms or less.

Conventional approaches for overcoming packet loss and network congestion in data delivery, such as reliable transport via TCP, generally are not possible for streaming because the persistent retransmissions cause too much delay and the rate adaptation is inappropriate for a constant-rate streaming source. Moreover, many applications (e.g., multicast or broadcast) lack a back channel or other means for retransmissions. Thus, meeting tight delay constraints in the presence of packet losses, queuing delays and network outages is quite challenging and provides motivation for some of the path diversity techniques that follow.

17.2.2 From Media to Packets

A representative packetization scheme is depicted in Figure 17.3. In most applications, the "media encoder and packetizer" module operates by first compressing the media frames into blocks of data, where the block boundaries are selected in some sensible manner to limit catastrophic parsing errors and error propagation at the decoder if blocks are lost. The media codec is optionally followed by some combination of forward error correction coding (FEC) and interleaving into transport packets. As the transport packets traverse the network some are lost or

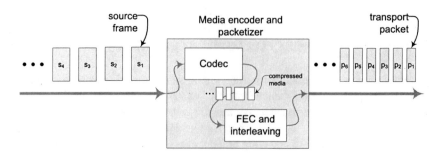

FIGURE 17.3:   Generic media coding and packetization scheme.

delayed. The client must reconstruct and play out each frame of the source media by its play out deadline using the packets it has received thus far.

The separation of source and channel coding shown in Figure 17.3 is tremendously convenient for a host of reasons. For example, separate coder and error correction modules can be implemented in different hardware, can be designed by different standardization teams, can be upgraded, replaced, or reused separately, and so on. Even if the modules are implemented separately, however, significant benefits can accrue from designing them jointly. In particular, the precise manner in which coded media is distributed across multiple transport packets greatly impacts the quality of the reconstructed media after packet erasures. This point will be amplified in Section 17.4.

From a theoretical standpoint it's known that fully separating source and channel coding can hurt performance in some circumstances. The rather general scheme in Figure 17.3 has therefore already compromised potential performance to arrive at a simpler architecture. Nevertheless, essentially all modern packet streaming systems follow the block diagram shown in Figure 17.3, which is the structure on which we will concentrate.

17.3 BENEFITS OF PATH DIVERSITY

Streaming over multiple paths can mitigate three basic problem areas in networks: bandwidth, loss, and delay. In this section we characterize these benefits.

Path diversity to a single receiver can arise when streaming from one source or when streaming from several sources. Examples of the latter include streaming from multiple servers in a content delivery network or from multiple peers in a peer-to-peer system. In addition to path diversity, these applications also provide something that can be termed "source diversity," the benefits of which persist even on an uncongested network. For example, if hosts in a peer-to-peer system enter and exit then source diversity reduces the probability of service outage. Similarly, source diversity provides a load balancing benefit that can be important when the hosts are disk or CPU limited. Therefore, the use of multiple hosts, and associated multiple paths, leads to both host diversity and path diversity, where the largest benefit depends on where the bottleneck is: paths or hosts. While the discussion that follows is framed in terms of path diversity, it's useful to keep in mind the complementary benefits that can arise from using multiple hosts.

Leaving aside questions of fairness and resource consumption for the moment, a straightforward way to realize performance gains with multiple paths is to use all of them at once. For example, if in a peer-to-peer system the hosts are connected via cable modems or DSL connections with limited uplink bandwidth, path diversity with multiple sources provides much-needed bandwidth aggregation. This is shown in Figure 17.4a. Bandwidth aggregation can also be achieved with a single

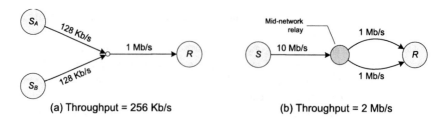

(a) Throughput = 256 Kb/s   (b) Throughput = 2 Mb/s

FIGURE 17.4: (a) Bandwidth is aggregated across paths using two streaming sources S_A and S_B. (b) Bandwidth is aggregated using one source and a mid-network relay. Paths are labeled with their available bandwidths.

source node, as in Figure 17.4b. A complementary benefit to bandwidth aggregation is traffic load balancing, that is, decreased per-path bandwidth by splitting a stream across multiple paths.

If bandwidth is not a primary concern, delay and loss may be reduced by replicating each packet across the paths. The receiver then sees the minimum of the path delays (effectively chopping off the long tails in the end-to-end delay distribution) and is immune to packet losses unless they occur on all paths simultaneously.

A more challenging problem—and the main focus of this chapter—is to realize performance gains in the presence of delay and loss without doubling the number of packets transmitted. How this is done depends on the amount of information the sender has about prevailing link conditions.

Perhaps the simplest way to realize gains without consuming extra bandwidth is through path selection. Selection diversity arises when there are multiple paths available, when the sender knows which path has the most favorable characteristics, and when the sender can respond in a timely manner to direct packets along the currently most favorable path. A simple example is shown in Figure 17.5a. The benefits of selection diversity are often quite large, so large that even approximate knowledge of link conditions suffices to realize gains. Thus, when a single-path system is unreliable, selection diversity should be one of the first techniques considered.

Often, however, either the sender does not have detailed knowledge about the current state of the paths or it cannot take advantage of its knowledge. This occurs in a variety of situations, including:

1. time-invariant paths that lack feedback,
2. time-varying paths where the path measurement system lags the variation, and

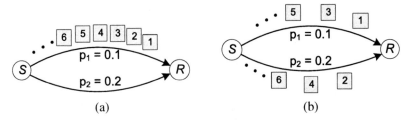

(a)   (b)

FIGURE 17.5: (a) Selection diversity directs packets over the path with the smallest loss rate. (b) The sender responds to its uncertainty by sending odd packets on the upper path and even packets on the lower path. The average loss rate is more predictable than the loss rate in a single-path system that selects a path at random.

3. broadcast or multicast scenarios in which a single transmission strategy serves all users at once.

Selection diversity alone is not a viable approach in these cases, and the sender can take advantage of path diversity only through more sophisticated approaches.

An example of path diversity in which two time-invariant paths have differing loss rates is shown in Figure 17.5b. If the sender is unsure about which path is best it can hedge its bets by dispersing media packets across the paths. The receiver then sees the average $(p_1 + p_2)/2$ of the loss rates.

Averaging loss rates illustrates a significant benefit of path diversity: reduced uncertainty. Reduced uncertainty enables methods for combating losses, such as forward error correction, to become more effective [25,26]. FEC adds specialized inter-packet redundancy that enables data recovery up to a loss threshold. Compared to a single-path system that selects from a set of paths at random, averaging loss rates improves the probability that the overall loss rate lies below the critical threshold (in most cases of interest).

For time-varying links, for example, links that shift between periods of no loss and high loss that are common on the Internet, the amount of redundancy can be adjusted dynamically to compensate for changes in the loss rate. However, adaptation is problematic when the network changes quickly: the FEC is inevitably overdesigned and therefore inefficient or underdesigned and therefore ineffective. Combining FEC with long interleaving also helps combat loss variability, but the added delay often makes interleaving unsatisfactory for media streaming. When used with FEC, path diversity provides benefits similar to time interleaving with a smaller associated delay.

Path diversity can dramatically decrease the probability of outage, where an *outage* is an extreme form of time variation in which all communication along a network path is lost for a sizable length of time. A single-path system necessarily fails during an outage. However, with two-path diversity the average loss rate becomes 50%, which is tolerable for certain codecs (see Section 17.4). A service outage then occurs only if both paths fail at once. In heuristic terms, path diversity improves the probability of outage from p to p^2.

Problems of delay and delay jitter may also be addressed using path diversity. If the sender distributes packets across paths the receiver sees the mixture of the delay distributions of the paths. This effect is termed *queue diversity* because network delays are often due to backlogged queues, and to emphasize the benefit of multiple parallel queues. Queue diversity offers little benefit for loss-intolerant data because the receiver must wait for all packets from all paths. In contrast, loss-tolerant delay-intolerant voice or video streams remain useful when only some packets arrive promptly. Similar to loss-rate averaging, queue diversity is helpful for time-invariant paths that have different but unknown delay characteristics. It's also helpful when the paths are time varying, for example, when cross traffic causes episodes of high delay that strike the paths at independent times. A typical application of queue diversity is to allow end-to-end delay constraints to be tightened while maintaining quality. Examples of such delay reductions may be found in voice over IP (VoIP) [20], as described in Chapter 16, and video over 802.11 wireless networks [23], as described in 17.6.4.

Path diversity can also reduce the length of burst losses, that is, losses of consecutive packets. Distributing packets across multiple paths increases the inter-packet spacing on each path, and therefore for a network congestion event of a given duration fewer packets are lost. This is illustrated in Figure 17.6. If all paths

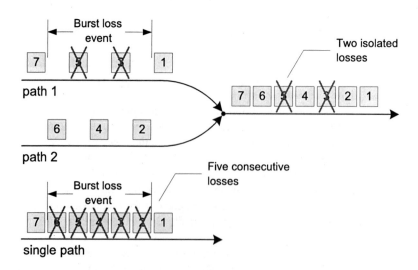

FIGURE 17.6: Path diversity reduces the length of burst losses.

are subject to burst losses, however, long burst events are in effect replaced with a larger number of shorter events. Whether this trade-off is advantageous depends on the media coding. If latency is not critical, then using FEC over a sufficiently long block will make the decoder largely indifferent to burst vs. isolated losses. In contrast, we will see in Section 17.4.3 an example of a simple low-latency speech coding strategy that is resistant to isolated but not burst losses. In addition, for video codecs it can sometimes be easier to recover from multiple isolated losses than from an equal number of consecutive losses [1]; for example, a gain of 0.5–1.0 dB in video quality is achievable in certain situations [23]. Still greater gains are possible by carefully codesigning the encoder, decoder, and path diversity system, as we shall see in Section 17.4.6.

17.4 MULTIPLE DESCRIPTION CODING

In this section we introduce multiple description coding, a media coding technique that is quite appealing when multiple transport paths are available. An excellent review of MD coding, both history and theory, is given in [13].

Multiple description coding produces two or more sets of compressed data, referred to as *descriptions*, as in Figure 17.7. In broad terms, MD coding permits a usable reproduction of the original signal to be reconstituted when only some of the descriptions are available, at the decoder. The more descriptions available, the better the quality of the reproduction. For example, a simple MD video coder can be achieved by splitting a video stream into even and odd frames and coding them separately.

One way to apply multiple description coding to packet networks is for each packet to contain one of the descriptions in the MD code. The resulting system can be tuned to exhibit a graceful degradation of media quality with the number

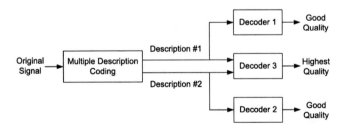

FIGURE 17.7: A basic type of MD coder produces two descriptions of roughly equal importance. If a decoder receives either description it can reconstruct a good quality signal, whereas if it receives both it can reconstruct the highest quality signal.

of packets lost. Used in this manner, MD coding exemplifies a design philosophy that treats unpredictable variations in packet loss rate as inevitable and aims to make systems robust to a range of loss conditions. A contrasting approach, which does not employ MD coding, is to compress media into a loss-sensitive packet stream and use retransmission or forward error correction to recover from losses. The MD approach is particularly advantageous when the loss rate is varying or unknown and when latency constraints hinder the use of retransmissions.

MD coding is also useful for systems that employ path diversity. The source is coded into two or more data streams and each stream is viewed as a description to be sent along a different path. With this approach, the coding system may be designed to tolerate losses that differentially impact one stream, for example, where one stream experiences 20% packet losses while the other is largely loss free. Examples illustrate MD codes that are effective in this scenario.

Note that in some contexts a "description" implies a single packet, while in other contexts it refers to an entire stream of packets. Both cases exist in the literature. In the case of path diversity, the two viewpoints can be unified by treating each packet as a description while recognizing that the packet loss patterns have a special structure. In particular, for path diversity, packet losses are concentrated on the subset of packets transmitted over a failing path, while for systems with a single path, packet losses are distributed more uniformly.

We continue by providing a high-level comparison of MD coding versus conventional single description (SD) and scalable coding techniques, which were described in detail in Chapters 2–6. We then give an overview of the information theory results that apply to MD coding, all of which take the one-description-per-packet approach. We next examine the salient features of several practical examples of MD coding for speech, audio, image, and video. These examples illustrate how the one-description-per-packet and one-description-per-stream approaches lead to different coding techniques. We will also see that MD coding can be implemented through special source codecs, through a joint design of the source codec with interleaving, or through a joint design of codec, interleaver, and FEC.

17.4.1 Comparing MD Coding with SD and Scalable Coding

Conventional SD coding algorithms, such as MPEG-1/2/4 and H.261/3/4 video coding standards, compress media into a single bit stream. In scalable (also called layered) coding, media is coded into multiple bit streams, beginning with a base layer that provides low but usable quality, and one or more enhancement layers that improve quality. The scalable coding bit streams are partially ordered, and different subsets can, for example, represent video at different spatial, temporal, or amplitude resolutions and fidelities.

Applications and networks that support prioritization can exploit scalable coding by assigning higher delivery priorities to coding layers that are more important. However, in best-effort networks, such as the Internet, all packets are equally likely to be lost or delayed. This fundamental mismatch—prioritized data on a nonprioritized network—makes scalable coding by itself difficult to exploit using the Internet. One solution to this problem is to combine scalable coding with channel coding. For example, erasure-correction coding can be used to make the base layer more tolerant to packet loss than the enhancement layer(s). This approach will be described in more detail in Section 17.4.4.

Multiple description coding differs from scalable coding in at least one important way: scalable coding has a base layer that is critically important and if lost renders the other bit stream(s) useless. MD coding enables a useful reproduction of the signal when any description is received (when following the one-description-per-stream approach) or when any sufficiently large set of descriptions is received (when following the one-description-per-packet approach).

17.4.2 MD Coding: Information Theory Perspective

The multiple description coding problem has received significant attention in the information theory literature, beginning in 1980 with [27,44–46]. For recent perspectives and comprehensive bibliographies, see, for example, [13,18,30,31].

The basic information theory problem in multiple description coding is that of compressing a block of independent identically distributed (i.i.d.) random variables, typically Gaussian or binary, into a set of packets for transmission over an erasure channel. The simplest case, which turns out to be far from trivial, encodes into just two packets. Encoding and decoding are done without regard to delay, hence the theory is more directly relevant to problems such as still image compression than to streaming media. The generalization of multiple description information theory to problems that incorporate delay constraints is an important (and challenging) area for future research.

A general theme of multiple description information theory research is to characterize the achievable distortion as a function of erasure patterns. In the case of a source encoded into two packets—or equivalently, into two descriptions—we'd like the quality of the recovered source to be good when just one of the two packets survives the network and to improve when both packets survive. One bound on this problem comes from classical rate-distortion theory: the distortion–rate function $D(R)$ for the source gives the minimum achievable average distortion D when the source is described using R bits per source symbol. For example, the distortion–rate function for a unit variance i.i.d. Gaussian source where distortion is measured by mean-squared error is $D(R) = 2^{-2R}$. Applied to the multiple description problem with two packets, assuming each packet contains R bits per source symbol, the best that can be achieved when one packet survives is 2^{-2R}. The best that can be achieved when both packets survive is 2^{-4R}.

But are these naive bounds useful? That is, can a multiple description compression algorithm simultaneously achieve both single- and dual-description upper bounds $D(R)$ and $D(2R)$? The answer is no: these bounds are wildly optimistic when the rate R is large (i.e., much above 1 bit per symbol). For example, if in the Gaussian case the single description meets the $D(R)$ bound, the joint description can be no better than roughly $D(R + 1/2)$, which is quite a bit worse than $D(2R)$ at high rates.

A sensible engineering compromise in this situation is to leave some slack in the system. Rather than trying to meet either the $D(R)$ or the $D(2R)$ bounds exactly, one should instead aim for reasonable but not ideal performance for both single- and dual-description cases. The exact set of available trade-offs in the Gaussian case with mean-squared distortion was determined by Ozarow [27]; useful plots of this trade-off and a more detailed discussion may be found in Goyal [13].

The Gaussian case is noteworthy for being the only nontrivial example where the multiple description trade-off curve is known exactly. Even for the apparently simple case of binary source with Hamming distortion the exact curve is unknown. Simple arguments suggest, however, that real-world sources will have the same characteristic trade-offs as the Gaussian source, hence the Gaussian case remains a useful benchmark.

Generalizations of multiple description coding from two descriptions to many descriptions are treated in [30,31,39]. A complete solution to this problem would allow us to answer the following type of question: suppose a channel has either 30% packet erasures or 60% packet erasures, but the encoder doesn't know which. How should the source be coded to prepare for these two contingencies, and what distortions can be achieved? Broadly speaking, a system designed aggressively to do as best as possible with 30% erasures will fare quite poorly when confronted with 60% erasures. Conversely, a conservative design that does as well as possible with 60% erasures will see only modest performance improvements when there are only 30% erasures. The achievable trade-offs for this problem have been bounded but are not precisely known.

The relative lack of theoretical results about the trade-offs inherent in multiple description coding presents no obstacle to a practical exploration of the space. There is growing literature on practical schemes for multiple description media coding for both streaming and nonstreaming applications, as discussed next. While many of these schemes have good performance or insightful architectures, one should keep in mind that they represent particular achievable points in the space of trade-offs; only in special scenarios is the ideal performance known, let alone approached closely. Thus there remain many interesting opportunities to find improved solutions.

17.4.3 MD Speech and MD Audio Coding

The earliest MD coders were applied to speech signals. For example, in [16,17] speech is partitioned into speech frames of (say) 16 ms duration, and each speech frame is split into even and odd samples, which are then coded independently and sent in separate packets. This coding method protects better against certain loss patterns than others. For example, losing both the even and the odd packet from one speech frame is likely to sound worse than losing an even and an odd packet from different frames. The even/odd coding strategy is therefore most effective when the two packet streams are sent along different paths that suffer independent outages.

A variety of other simple MD techniques exist. For example, each packet can contain the current speech frame and a low-quality copy of the previous speech frame, as in Figure 17.8. In another variation, a packet containing the coded even (odd) samples may also contain a coarsely coded version of the odd (even) samples. This is illustrated in Figure 17.9, where the packets containing the even samples are sent over one path and the packets containing the odd samples are sent over a second path. In this way, as long as either of the two packets for each speech frame is received the decoder can reconstruct a good version of half of the samples and a degraded version of the other half. Further discussion on the use of MD speech coding is given in Chapter 16 and in [20].

In most speech and audio coders the source frames (as in Figure 17.3) are coded largely independently of the neighboring speech or audio frames. This is true for most SD, scalable, and MD speech and audio coders. The loss of one speech or

| 7 | 8 | | 6 | 7 | | 5 | 6 | | 4 | 5 | | 3 | 4 |

FIGURE 17.8:   Packets for audio frames 4–8 contain low-quality copies of frames 3–7, respectively. Loss of audio frame 5 will not cause a playback gap if frame 6 is received. However, a playback gap will result if both frames 5 and 6 are lost.

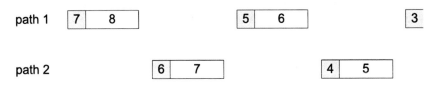

FIGURE 17.9:   Burst loss in either path 1 or path 2 alone will not cause a gap in playback. This is an example in which path diversity does not reduce loss rate, but provides a more usable set of data for the application.

audio frame therefore affects a small portion of the reconstructed signal. This is in contrast to conventional video coding where temporal prediction is applied between video frames, and a single packet loss can lead to significant error propagation, which affects many frames.

17.4.4 MD Image Coding

MD codes for images can be constructed using methods from source coding or by combining source coding with FEC. A common source coding approach is to subsample in the spatial or frequency domains. Straightforward subsampling, however, provides no control over the trade-off between single- vs. multiple-description image quality. In MD transform coding (e.g., [41]) a correlating transform introduces controlled redundancy between the subsets of coefficients, which enables such trade-offs.

MD codes may also be created by coupling a scalable coder with FEC to provide unequal error protection (UEP) for the scalable layers, in a manner sometimes referred to as MD-FEC [32]. While MD-FEC was first proposed in the context of MD image coding and is appealing in this context because high-quality scalable image coders such as JPEG-2000 are available, it's applicable to any type of media that's scalably coded. In this technique, the source coder does not produce multiple descriptions directly, but the combination of scalable coding and UEP produces a set of packets that have the MD property. This allows one to turn a scalable, prioritized bit stream into a nonprioritized one that is better matched to a best-effort packet network such as the Internet.

An example of MD-FEC is shown in Figure 17.10. In Figure 17.10 a scalable code with two layers—a base layer and a single enhancement layer—is used to construct an M-description MD code. Each of the M descriptions is contained in a separate packet. The base layer is split into m equal-sized blocks, and $M - m$ parity blocks are computed using, for example, an (M, m) systematic Reed–Solomon code. In this manner the base layer is expanded into M descriptions, any m of which allow the receiver to recover the layer perfectly. The enhancement layer in this example has no FEC, hence all M descriptions are needed to recover it perfectly. An important feature of MD-FEC is its flexibility: it can be used with any number of scalable layers, variable amounts of FEC per layer, and an arbitrary number of descriptions.

17.4.5 MD Video Coding

Multiple description video coding has some attributes of the audio coding and image coding cases considered earlier. As with audio, coded video consists of a sequence of packets, and the manner in which burst losses interact with this sequence has important consequences for encoder and decoder design. As with

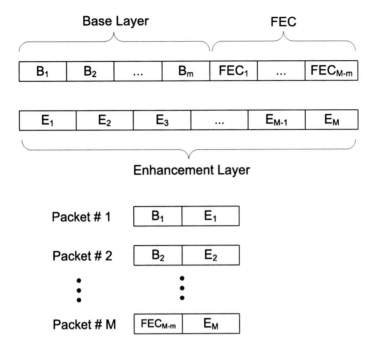

FIGURE 17.10: In MD-FEC a signal is scalably coded into two or more layers that are spread across M packets, with unequal cross-packet FEC for each layer. In this example, if any m packets are received, the base layer can be recovered perfectly; if all M packets are received, both layers can be recovered perfectly.

images, each packet can be thought of as a description, and one can trade off performance when few descriptions are lost vs. performance when many descriptions are lost.

Video sequences do, however, have special characteristics not present in image and audio sources. Consecutive video frames tend to be similar, and the most common approach to exploit this redundancy for compression is to apply some form of predictive coding along the temporal direction. For example, the MPEG-1/2/4 and H.261/3/4 video compression standards all employ motion-compensated prediction between frames. Predictive coding is based on the assumption that the encoder and decoder are able to maintain the same state, that is, that the frames used for forming the prediction are the same at the encoder and decoder. However, packet losses can cause a mismatch between the states at the encoder and decoder. This mismatch can lead to significant error propagation into subsequent frames, even if the packets corresponding to those frames are correctly received.

For example, a single lost packet can impair the video quality of tens or hundreds of subsequent frames, until the prediction is reinitialized with an I frame.

The design of an MD video codec depends on the loss patterns one expects to encounter. In the case of path diversity, a conservative design goal is to maintain good quality even when half the data is lost, for example, when a path permanently fails. A more aggressive target that leads to greater compression efficiency is to provide resilience to burst or isolated losses, provided they do not occur on all paths at the same time. The latter scenario commonly arises when the paths have independent losses or when the loss statistics on the paths are different, for example, when one suffers isolated 1% packet loss while another suffers burst losses at an overall rate of 10%.

A variety of MD video coding techniques suitable for these and other packet loss scenarios are based on varying the prediction between frames, for example, [1,33,40,43], where these techniques are motivated by the importance of predictive coding in most video coders today. MD video coding techniques that apply motion-compensated filtering between frames, as often used for scalable video coding, have been proposed, and these techniques can provide the advantages of both MD and scalable coding, for example, [38]. An excellent review of MD video coding is given in [42]. For simplicity, the following discussion assumes that we code the video into two packet streams to be transmitted over two paths in a packet network.

One type of predictive MD coding emphasizes the case where a packet stream decodes with reasonable quality even when the other stream is completely lost. This can be accomplished by using independent prediction loops for each stream. For example, two separate prediction loops may be used so that even frames are predicted based on past even frames and odd frames are predicted based on past odd frames. (A standard-compliant way to achieve this is to use multiple reference frames, as supported in H.263v2, MPEG-4, and H.264.) Independence between streams can also be achieved by having a single prediction loop, but duplicating the information required to form the prediction in each stream to ensure that if packets from either stream are received the receiver can form the required prediction. These approaches allow a good quality reconstruction when one packet stream is received and one is lost (e.g., the video is reconstructed at half the original frame rate); however, they suffer a sizable penalty in compression performance since the two streams are coded independently of each other.

On the other extreme are predictive MD coders that try to maximize the coding efficiency when both packet streams are received. In particular, they use a single prediction loop in a manner similar to single description coding. If both streams are received they provide excellent quality; however, the prediction requires information from both packet streams and if either is lost then mismatch occurs with subsequent error propagation. There are also predictive MD coders that try to operate between these two extremes, providing the ability to trade off compression efficiency (when both streams are received) versus resilience to the full or partial loss of a stream. An active area of research is designing MD coders that automatically adjust the compression efficiency versus resiliency as a function of the channel characteristics to maximize the expected quality at the receiver, for example, [15,40].

Video, like audio, is frequently used in situations that require low latency. If latency is not a primary concern, one approach to MD video coding is to carefully combine a scalable video coder with UEP in a manner analogous to MD image coding (Section 17.4.4). This technique provides a straightforward way to produce many packet streams. In contrast, the predictive MD video coding methods described earlier are generally limited to a small number of description streams (typically two) because compression efficiency decreases with the number of streams. It is worth noting that while predictively coded video has historically provided significant compression benefits over scalable coding, and hence the widespread use of predictive coded video for both practical applications and MD video coder design, this may change in the future with some of the emerging scalable video coding techniques, as discussed in Chapter 5.

17.4.6 Repairable MD Coding

Repairable MD coding (also known as *state recovery* in MD coding) is an extension of conventional MD coding beneficial for temporally predictively coded media such as video [1]. Predictive coding causes errors in one frame, due, for example, to lost packets, to propagate to potentially many subsequent frames. In repairable MD coding the decoder attempts to stop error propagation by repairing the corrupted frames in one description using uncorrupted frames from the other description. This technique can maintain usable quality even when *both* descriptions suffer losses, as long as both descriptions are not simultaneously lost.

Figure 17.11 illustrates the impact of packet loss on a conventional SD MPEG-type video coder and on a repairable MD coder. The particular MD video coder in Figure 17.11 forms the first description by predicting even frames from previously coded even frames and forms the second description likewise from odd frames. For both SD and MD examples, the packet(s) that describes how frame 3 is used to predict the subsequent coded frame is assumed lost. For SD, the packet that predicts frame P_4 from P_3 is lost, and the decoder estimates the missing frame 4 using the last correctly decoded frame (frame 3), where the inaccuracy leads to error propagation that continues until the next I frame. The repairable MD decoder estimates the lost frame by bidirectionally predicting it (that is, interpolating it) from neighboring frames in both descriptions. The use of both previous and future frames to estimate the lost frame provides significant improvements in accuracy as compared to the use of only previous frames.

Conventional MPEG-Type Video Coder

Example MD Video Coder Illustrating Concept of "Repairing"

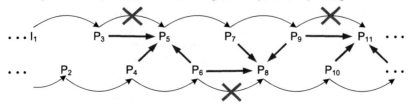

FIGURE 17.11: Benefits of repairable MD coding to reduce error propagation. The arrows show the prediction dependencies between frames, and each "X" denotes packet loss that leads to an error in the following predicted frame. The conventional SD coder exhibits error propagation that continues until the next I frame. The repairable MD decoder limits error propagation by repairing the missing or damaged frame by estimating it using neighboring previous and future frames from both descriptions.

Repairable MD coding and path diversity complement each other to improve the effectiveness of MD coding: the path diversity transmission system reduces the probability that both descriptions are simultaneously lost, and the MD decoder enables recovery from losses as long as both descriptions are not simultaneously lost [1]. This is illustrated in Figure 17.11 where the MD coder is afflicted by three losses affecting both descriptions—without repairing then both descriptions would be corrupted and the MD video quality would likely be no better than the SD quality. This example also highlights the importance of considering the effect of partial losses of both descriptions, in particular since even a single lost packet can lead to significant error propagation that corrupts a description for a long length of time. This comparatively recent decoder-side optimization is complementary to the ongoing efforts to improve the rate vs. quality trade-off of MD encoders, which typically do not consider partial losses of both descriptions.

17.4.7 Comments on SD, Scalable, and MD Coding for Media

The relative compression efficiencies of SD, scalable, and MD coding depend on the media type. For image and audio sources, scalable coding can be as efficient as SD coding, and many recent coding standards, for example, JPEG-2000, are scalable. In addition, scalable image or audio coding may be combined with unequal error protection to provide an efficient MD-like system: more redundancy is allocated to high-priority data relative to low-priority data, improving the probability that high-priority data are correctly received. For video sources both scalable coding and MD coding are currently less efficient than SD coding; however, they provide valuable properties for streaming and, as a result, there is intense research underway to improve their performance and reduce the compression efficiency gap.

17.5 DESIGN, ANALYSIS, AND OPERATION OF MULTIPATH STREAMING SYSTEMS

The prior sections discuss the potential benefits of path diversity for media streaming and describe media coding techniques useful for path diversity. This section discusses issues that arise in effectively designing and using path diversity in streaming media systems.

17.5.1 Joint and Disjoint Paths

Multiple paths are not guaranteed in practice to be independent and may, for example, share links. The benefits of path diversity do not depend on whether paths are completely disjoint, but rather on whether bottlenecks occur on shared or disjoint portions. Shared bottlenecks reduce the impact of path diversity, while disjoint bottlenecks do not. Identifying bottlenecks and avoiding them if possible are important elements in effective use of path diversity. Joint bottleneck detection is an active area of research, for example, [34].

17.5.2 How Many Paths to Use?

How do diversity benefits scale with the number of paths and when is it worthwhile to use more than one path? These complicated questions depend on the specifics of the application, the path diversity benefits that one is trying to exploit, and the characteristics of the available paths. For example, for repairable MD video coding, the improved error recovery arises with two paths, and while increasing the number of paths helps there are no further jumps in performance.

End-to-end network characteristics improve in different ways with the number of paths. Total aggregated bandwidth (in principle) increases additively with the number of paths. Probability of outage decreases exponentially with the number of independent paths. Delay variability, measured in terms of standard deviation, decreases as $1/\sqrt{N}$ where N is the number of independent paths. For media streaming in a real-world scenario with reasonably reliable networks and servers, we would expect that typically a small number of paths would provide a good balance between complexity and performance. In a peer-to-peer scenario in which hosts frequently enter and leave, a much larger number of paths could prove useful.

17.5.3 Selecting the Best Paths or Best Servers

As discussed earlier, the effectiveness of using multiple paths depends less on their lengths than on their shared vs. disjoint topology. Of still greater importance is whether bottlenecks occur on shared portions. Thus, it may be preferable to have longer paths or longer shared portions of paths if the resulting bottlenecks are not shared. This observation hints at the complexity of the important basic question: How to select the best paths to use?

Determining the best paths is important for point-to-point multipath streaming, but its impact becomes even more apparent when streaming from multiple servers. Which of several available servers should be selected? For a single-path system one typically selects a server that is in some sense nearby. However, a multiple server system requires fundamentally different metrics: minimizing distance from the client to multiple servers while maximizing path diversity, two generally conflicting objectives. Accurately evaluating these metrics is necessary for designing and operating a multiple server system that uses path diversity. In addition, the server selection problem must be solved for every client request, necessitating efficient solutions. Further characteristics of multiple server systems are provided in Section 17.6.2.

17.5.4 Modeling Path Diversity Performance

The aforementioned discussion highlights the importance of accurately modeling the performance of a path diversity system. An accurate model is needed for selecting the best subset of paths from a set of possible paths, selecting the best subset of servers from a set of possible servers, comparing path diversity scenarios, or simply evaluating the merits of a path diversity system relative to a conventional single path system. Determining an appropriate performance model depends on the benefits (reviewed in Section 17.3) one intends to capture and on the particular characteristics of the media and the network.

In the following we describe a model for predicting SD and MD video quality over a lossy packet network as a function of path diversity and loss characteristics. The model has two parts, one that provides a probabilistic model of the loss patterns that occur in the network and another that quantifies how packet losses reduce video quality. See [2,3] for complete details.

The sender(s) and receiver in a path diversity system may be connected through a wide range of complex topologies that include joint and disjoint links. It can be shown, however, that under certain assumptions the end-to-end properties of the network are captured using the dramatically simplified three-link topologies shown in Figure 17.12. The bursty losses on each link are modeled using, for example, a two-state Gilbert model.

Packet losses affect SD and MD video differently. The model must therefore distinguish among isolated packet losses, burst losses of various lengths, and for MD whether the loss(es) occurs on one or both descriptions at the same time. For example, for SD we may have a finite-state model that accounts for the packet loss burst length, and for MD a four-state model that represents for each pair of packets transmitted whether both descriptions are correctly received, one is correctly received and one is lost, or both are simultaneously lost. Each state transition causes an incremental change in video quality determined by the details of the particular codec. The state transition probabilities are derived from the loss model described in the previous paragraph.

An application-level performance model of this form provides insights into fundamental questions in path diversity, for example, the relative performance of conventional SD over a single path versus MD with two-path diversity. Using the model, one can determine that MD with path diversity is beneficial for video streaming when the packet losses fall predominantly on disjoint links, while SD sometimes performs better when the losses are on joint links (see [2,3]).

Additional work includes [10], which investigates rate-distortion optimized packet transmission schedules across multiple paths, [8], where fast heuristics are presented for quickly performing path selection when a large number of candidate path pairs are available while accounting for the loss and on-time arrival probability of each path, and [42], which provides an overview of MD video coding and its transport over multiple paths.

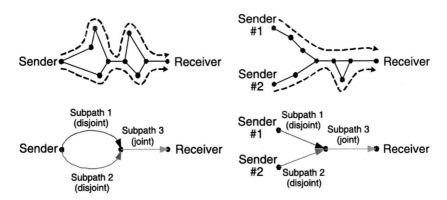

FIGURE 17.12: Complex path diversity topologies (top) and the simplified network models (bottom), which preserve the end-to-end characteristics important for accurately predicting video distortion.

17.5.5 Streaming and Packet Scheduling Across Asymmetric Paths

Different paths may offer different bandwidths, loss rates, and delay characteristics. A path diversity system should compensate for and exploit these asymmetries. The first step is to estimate the characteristics of each path. Path measurement is an active area of research, and many techniques developed for single paths may be applied to the multiple path case.

When paths have different, potentially time-varying, available bandwidths, it is important to adapt the rate across paths. In the point-to-point case, rate adaptation can be performed in a centralized manner. However, in the multipoint-to-point case, a distributed algorithm is generally required. The distributed rate allocation should not only perform the appropriate adaptation, but also for SD coding should ensure that the different senders send disjoint sets of packets (no duplication) to the receiver [25].

Paths with different packet loss rates or delays provide the opportunity to perform packet scheduling across the paths [10]. For example, more important packets may be sent over the path with the lower packet loss rate. Similarly, packets with tighter delay constraints may be sent over the path with shorter delay. Furthermore, real-time video encoding can be adapted to react to the time-varying path characteristics and losses [19].

17.6 APPLICATIONS AND ARCHITECTURES

In this section we examine a variety of application areas for which path diversity provides performance benefits: low-delay applications, content delivery networks, peer-to-peer networks, and wireless networks. These application areas also illustrate architectures for realizing path diversity, for example, by using mid-network relays, distributed content, or explicit routing control. We summarize these architectures at the end of the section.

17.6.1 Low-Delay Applications

Many applications, such as video conferencing and VoIP, require low latency for effective interactive communication. One possible approach used to achieve a latency guarantee is through network quality-of-service mechanisms. Nevertheless, schemes such as Skype [7] that operate over best-effort networks have shown to be effective most of the time. As illustrated in Figure 17.13, in order to bypass firewalls and network address translators (NAT), Skype uses relay nodes in the public Internet. The existence of multiple available relay nodes improves its ability to choose a low-latency relay path. This scheme exploits the existence of multiple paths via *selection*, or choosing a good or the best path. Generally, knowledge of network states is imprecise, and selection works best when network statistics

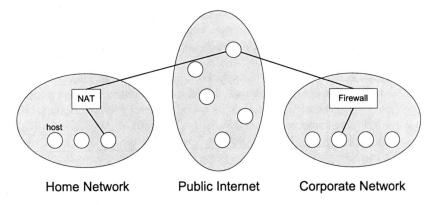

FIGURE 17.13:   Skype uses nodes in the public Internet to bypass firewalls and NATs. Multiple relay paths are available for selection.

do not change rapidly. These issues are discussed in more detail in Sections 17.3 and 17.5.

Another consequence of low-latency requirement is the limitation in choices of error recovery mechanisms. Specifically, common and effective techniques such as retransmissions, interleaving, and forward error correction tend to introduce additional latency and may be unacceptable. One practical approach for error recovery in voice communication is to append to each voice packet a low-quality version of the previous packet, as illustrated in Figure 17.8. This technique avoids gaps in audio playback for isolated losses; however, by itself it is ineffective for burst losses. By simply alternating packets across multiple paths, or transmitting the low-quality version on a separate path, burst losses can be effectively reduced to isolated losses. This scheme exploits the *independence* of multiple paths. Notice that from the network's perspective, the total number of packets sent and delivered remains the same. However, from the application's perspective, the set of received packets from multiple paths is far more usable. Chapter 16 examines the problem of low-latency communication in more depth and shows how the combination of path diversity and adaptive media playout, where the media playout rate is varied as a function of the receiver's playout buffer fullness, can lead to sizable improvements in user-perceived quality.

17.6.2 Content Delivery Networks

A content delivery network (CDN) is a set of hosts inside a network that cooperate to improve content delivery by performing functions such as caching, content serving, and traffic relaying. CDNs have been widely used to provide low latency, scalability, fault tolerance, and load balancing for the delivery of web content and more recently streaming media. Figure 17.14 illustrates the operation of a CDN. By locating content close to the users, a CDN improves access latency, lowers packet loss rate, and reduces traffic demand. CDNs are described in detail in Chapter 19.

The replication of content at multiple servers at different locations provides a number of benefits. First, it eliminates the bandwidth bottleneck associated with a single server or the network at a single location, thereby improving scalability to support a large number of clients. Second, it naturally allows delivery of content using multiple paths from multiple servers. Unlike the relay example, where multiple paths are provided between a single sender and a single receiver via multiple relays, in the context of a CDN, the different paths correspond to different senders, as shown in Figure 17.2.

The currently prevalent manner in which CDNs exploit multiple paths is via selection, that is, choosing a good or best server. Nevertheless, simultaneous use of independent paths may provide additional gains. For example, appropriately coupling MD coding with a CDN can provide improved reliability to packet losses, link outages, and temporary server overload or server failures. This system is referred to as a Multiple Description Streaming Media Content Delivery Network or an MD-CDN for short.

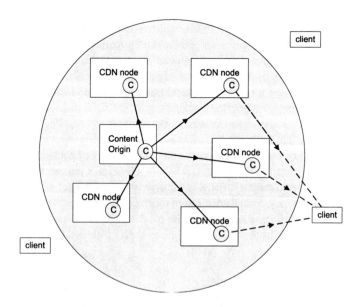

FIGURE 17.14:   Content C is distributed to multiple CDN nodes. As a result, a client has the benefits associated with closer access, as well as the benefits of choosing one or more locations and paths to serve the content.

An MD-CDN operates in the following manner [3]. The media is coded into multiple complementary descriptions, which are distributed across different servers in the CDN. When a client requests a stream, complementary descriptions are simultaneously sent from different nearby servers through different network paths to the client. This architecture simultaneously reaps the benefits of path diversity, of source diversity, and of CDNs.

The multiple servers in a CDN can also provide path diversity with SD coding and FEC [25]. In this case, the content is replicated on multiple mirror servers and multiple servers stream disjoint sets of SD and FEC packets to the client. As discussed earlier, the reduced variability of losses afforded by path diversity makes FEC more efficient.

It is worth noting that the fundamental problems that arise when designing and operating a CDN are changed in important ways when using multipath streaming. Three key CDN problems are:

1. Where to deploy the servers? (Server placement problem)
2. How to distribute the content? (Content distribution across server problem)
3. How to select the best server for each client? (Server selection problem)

In a conventional CDN where each client receives a stream from a single server over a single path, the problems just given are solved by minimizing some notion of distance between a client and a server. In contrast, an MD-CDN should use a different metric that accounts for both distance and path diversity as discussed in Section 17.5.3. MD-CDN design and operation is discussed in [3].

17.6.3 Peer-to-Peer Networks

Peer-to-peer systems such as BitTorrent [11] are widely used for the distribution of large data files. The use of such systems for streaming is starting to appear in large-scale deployments (e.g., [47]) and is an active area of research.

Similar to a CDN, in a peer-to-peer distribution system every piece of content is stored by multiple peers. This allows scalability: the number of peer servers and peer clients increases at the same rate, overcoming the bottleneck of a single central server or a fixed number of CDN servers. Unlike the typical CDN, peers or locations may only have a portion of the content. This complicates the mechanism needed to locate content and generally necessitates communication with multiple peers to complete a transfer. Also, unlike a CDN, successful peer-to-peer systems usually enforce fairness constraints that enable peers who contribute more serving bandwidth to receive more in return.

Streaming using a peer-to-peer system, and in particular streaming of live events, is more difficult than distributing large data files. The essential challenge lies in providing an uninterrupted flow of data to each client for the duration of the streaming session. In comparison, for file distribution the data can flow in fits and starts, and the users are broadly tolerant of fluctuations in total transfer time so long as visible progress occurs.

Various structures may be imposed on the relationships between peers to improve performance, for example, to reduce the end-to-end system delay or to increase robustness to peer failures. Peers may be taken as nodes in tightly organized distribution structures such as trees, sets of trees, or directed acyclic graphs (DAGs) (e.g., [6,28,37]) or in more flexible distribution nets (e.g., [47]). A comparison of various tree-based and DAG-based systems can be found in [6].

The critical need to avoid service outages in the face of uncertain peer and network conditions makes path diversity particularly relevant to peer-to-peer streaming. In many applications the peers are dispersed geographically and are unlikely to share bottlenecks (such as a DSL or cable modem uplink), hence an environment suitable for path diversity arises automatically. A system using path diversity with MD coding for peer-to-peer streaming is described in [28].

17.6.4 Path Diversity over Wireless Networks

Wireless networks are quite challenging for streaming since they generally offer time-varying and unpredictable behavior caused by multiple users, interference, propagation effects, and mobility. At the network level, these effects appear as variable delays, losses, and bandwidth. Wireless links, rather than the wired infrastructure, are typically the bottlenecks. As mentioned in the introduction, various forms of diversity have been used for decades to overcome these problems, for example, in the cellular environment.

Wireless LANs such as IEEE 802.11 are becoming widespread as they provide simple connectivity and data delivery. One approach to reliable streaming over 802.11 connections, in particular for low-latency or interactive communication, is to exploit the potential path diversity between each mobile client and multiple 802.11 access points (APs) in the infrastructure [23,24]. A mobile 802.11 wireless client is often in range of multiple APs, each offering a different relationship to the client with respect to distance, obstructions, multipath, signal strength, contention, available bandwidth, neighboring interferers, and potential hidden nodes. Figure 17.15 illustrates the variability seen by a mobile client in an 802.11 network with two access points.

If a router on the wired side of the network were clever enough to select the best access point for each packet at each time—or, more boldly, to schedule all the traffic flowing to all clients through the entire wireless system—significant performance gains would result. This is in fact the goal of some of the "switched WLAN" products currently on the market (e.g., those of Meru Networks and others). The scheduling in switched WLANs cannot, of course, be ideal because the current state of the wired and wireless network cannot be perfectly known even

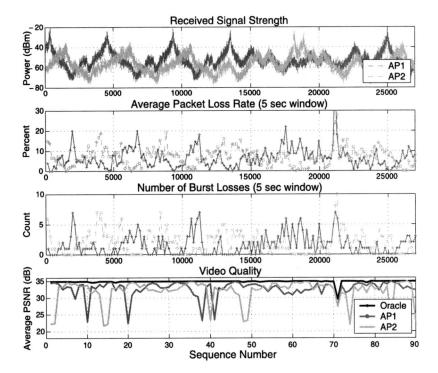

FIGURE 17.15: Performance statistics for path diversity between a mobile 802.11 wireless client and two APs in the distributed infrastructure [23]: received packet signal strength variation (top), average packet loss rate (second), and number of loss events of burst length ≥ 2 (third) as a function of packet sequence number for a 15-min packet trace. The bottom plot illustrates video quality when using only AP1 or only AP2, and the upper bound on achievable performance by selecting the best AP for every packet.

with a centralized controller. When some uncertainty about the best path at any given moment exists, path diversity techniques become useful.

By using multiple paths simultaneously or by switching between multiple paths (site selection) as a function of channel characteristics, results indicate that significant benefits may be achieved by using a wireless path diversity system compared to a conventional single access point system. In addition, these benefits may be achieved using a single client radio on a single channel [23]; there is no need to perform physical layer combining or multichannel operation or require multiradios.

Path diversity is also beneficial in ad-hoc wireless networks, where the topology may change or nodes may come or go. Many ad-hoc routing protocols identify multiple paths between the sender and the receiver, and the use of multiple paths can improve the reliability of the connection between the two wireless hosts. The effectiveness of path diversity over an ad-hoc wireless network for image and video communication is examined in [12] and [21].

17.6.5 Controlling Packet Routes

Path diversity requires, by definition, that packets destined for a receiver traverse different paths through the network. Even if the set of all possible paths was known (which would require learning the underlying network topology) and all the links in these paths were statistically characterized (another difficult measurement problem) and it was known how to both generate and apportion packets across paths to maximize some measure of performance (the subject of previous sections), there remains the problem of achieving the required degree of control over packet routing.

Indeed, the end-to-end structure of IP network is designed to achieve the opposite effect: packets are routed independently based on the destination address and reach their destination at the whim of a variety of midnetwork routers. It would seem that path diversity requires this structure to be circumvented, for example, using source routing. As shown earlier this turns out to be partially but not entirely true; there are a variety of scenarios where path diversity arises "for free" as a consequence of other architectural features of the system. For example, path diversity occurs naturally when the desired content is available in multiple physical locations. As discussed previously, this can be arranged in a distributed caching infrastructure such as in a content delivery network or in a peer-to-peer delivery system.

When the content is available at only one location and cannot be cached, for example, real-time speech or video, path diversity must be realized using network or infrastructure support. One approach for directing different streams over different paths is to send each stream to a different relay host placed at a strategic (or merely convenient) node in the network. The relays forward the streams to their final destination(s) [1]. In a large corporation, for example, the relay hosts can be installed at the corporation's various points of presence scattered throughout the country or the world. The relay infrastructure forms an application-specific overlay network on top of the conventional Internet, thereby providing a service of improved reliability while leveraging the infrastructure of the Internet.

Source routing, when available, can be an attractive option for achieving path diversity. In certain circumstances it is possible for the packet source to specify the set of nodes or "source route" for each packet to traverse. Path diversity can then be achieved by explicitly specifying different source routes for different subsets of packets. While IP source routing is theoretically straightforward, there are a number of problems that limit its use in the current Internet, although it may be useful within a private network. It has been argued that IPv6 may allow source routing to be adopted more widely.

17.7 SUMMARY AND FURTHER READING

Media streaming with path diversity has gained significant interest in the last few years, as it provides valuable benefits for overcoming some of the challenges that afflict best-effort packet networks, including dynamic and unpredictable available bandwidth, delay, and loss rate. Studies have shown promise for both the single sender to single receiver case and the multiple sender to single receiver case as in a streaming media CDN, as well as for both wired and wireless networks. A media streaming system may use multiple paths at the same time or may perform path selection where it chooses the best path to use at any point in time. Multiple description coding combined with path diversity can enhance the benefits of each and, in certain circumstances, can lead to sizable improvements over media coded with single description coding and sent over a single path. Path diversity helps us take a step closer to feedback-free video streaming, which could simplify a range of applications from low-latency communication to multicast or broadcast streaming. The combination of media streaming and path diversity provides significant promise, and it is likely to see continued evolution and adoption in the future.

A variety of excellent sources exist for further reading. For a description of the early work on path diversity for data delivery see [4,5,22] and the overview paper [14]. The idea that multiple paths can improve fault tolerance and link recovery for data delivery, as well as provide larger aggregate bandwidth and load balancing, has long been known. The combination of using multiple paths and sophisticated rateless FEC codes can provide faster bulk data downloads, without the transmission of redundant data [9]. The use of path diversity for media streaming gained attention more recently. The paths may originate from a single source (e.g., [1,8, 12,19–21,23]) or from multiple sources (e.g., [3,10,25]). Dynamic path selection for streaming, from a set of possible paths, is also an important problem [36]. While path diversity can be exploited with many different types of media coding, the combination of multiple description coding and path diversity is conceptually particularly appealing. Excellent reviews of MD coding, both history and theory, and of MD video coding are available in [13] and [42], respectively.

REFERENCES

[1] J. G. Apostolopoulos. "Reliable Video Communication over Lossy Packet Networks Using Multiple State Encoding and Path Diversity," *Visual Communications and Image Processing (VCIP)*, January 2001.

[2] J. G. Apostolopoulos, W. Tan, S. J. Wee, and G. W. Wornell. "Modeling Path Diversity for Multiple Description Video Communication," *IEEE ICASSP*, May 2002.

[3] J. G. Apostolopoulos, T. Wong, W. Tan, and S. J. Wee. "On Multiple Description Streaming with Content Delivery Networks," *IEEE INFOCOM*, June 2002.

[4] E. Ayanoglu, C.-L. I, R. D. Gitlin, and J. E. Mazo. "Diversity Coding: Using Error Control for Self-Healing in Communication Networks," *Proc. IEEE INFOCOM'90*, 1:95–104, June 1990.

[5] A. Banerjea. "Simulation Study of the Capacity Effects of Dispersity Routing for Fault-Tolerant Real-Time Channels," *Computer Communications Review (ACM SIG-COMM'96)*, 26(4):194–205, October 1996.

[6] M. Bansal and A. Zakhor. "Path Diversity Based Techniques for Resilient Overlay Multimedia Multicast," in *Picture Coding Symposium*, December 2004.

[7] S. Baset and H. Schulzrinne. "An Analysis of the Skype Peer-to-Peer Internet Telephony Protocol," *Columbia University Technical Report CUCS-039-04*, September 15, 2004.

[8] A. Begen, Y. Altunbasak, and O. Ergun. "Fast Heuristics for Multi-Path Selection for Multiple Description Encoded Video Streaming," *IEEE ICME*, July 2003.

[9] J. Byers, M. Luby, and M. Mitzenmacher. "Accessing Multiple Mirror Sites in Parallel: Using Tornado Codes to Speed up Downloads," *IEEE INFOCOM*, 1999.

[10] J. Chakareski and B. Girod. "Rate-Distortion Optimized Packet Scheduling and Routing for Media Streaming with Path Diversity," *IEEE DCC*, April 2003.

[11] B. Cohen. "Incentives Build Robustness in BitTorrent," in *1st Workshop on Economics of Peer-to-Peer Systems*, May 2003.

[12] N. Gogate, D. Chung, S. S. Panwar, and Y. Wang. "Supporting Image/Video Applications in a Mobile Multihop Radio Environment Using Route Diversity and Multiple Description Coding," *IEEE Trans. Circuits and System for Video Technology*, September 2002.

[13] V. Goyal. "Multiple Description Coding: Compression Meets the Network," *IEEE Signal Processing Magazine*, September 2001.

[14] E. Gustafsson and G. Karlsson. "A Literature Survey on Traffic Dispersion," *IEEE Network Magazine*, 1997.

[15] B. Heng, J. G. Apostolopoulos, and J. S. Lim. "End-to-End Rate-Distortion Optimized MD Mode Selection for Multiple Description Video Coding," *EURASIP Journal on Applied Signal Processing special issue on Video Analysis and Coding for Robust Transmission*, 2006.

[16] N. S. Jayant. "Subsampling of a DPCM Speech Channel to Provide Two 'Self-contained' Half-Rate Channels," *Bell Syst. Tech. J.*, 60(4):501–509, April 1981.

[17] N. S. Jayant and S. W. Christensen. "Effects of Packet Losses in Waveform Coded Speech and Improvements Due to an Odd-Even Sample-Interpolation Procedure," *IEEE Transactions on Communications*, COM-29(2):101–109, February 1981.

[18] J. N. Laneman, E. Martinian, G. W. Wornell, and J. G. Apostolopoulos. "Source-Channel Diversity for Parallel Channels," *IEEE Transactions on Information Theory*, October 2004.

[19] Y. Liang, E. Setton, and B. Girod. "Channel-Adaptive Video Streaming Using Packet Path Diversity and Rate-Distortion Optimized Reference Picture Selection," *IEEE Fifth Workshop on Multimedia Signal Processing*, December 2002.

[20] Y. J. Liang, E. G. Steinbach, and B. Girod. "Real-Time Voice Communication over the Internet Using Packet Path Diversity," *Proc. ACM Multimedia*, September/October 2001.

[21] S. Mao, S. Lin, S. Panwar, Y. Wang, and E. Celebi. "Video Transport over Ad Hoc Networks: Multistream Coding with Multipath Transport," *IEEE Journal on Selected Areas in Communications*, pages 1721–1737, December 2003.

[22] N. F. Maxemchuk. *Dispersity Routing in Store and Forward Networks*. Ph.D. thesis, University of Pennsylvania, May 1975.

[23] A. Miu, J. Apostolopoulos, W. Tan, and M. Trott. "Low-Latency Wireless Video Over 802.11 Networks Using Path Diversity," *IEEE ICME*, July 2003.

[24] A. Miu, G. Tan, H. Balakrishnan, and J. G. Apostolopoulos. "Divert: Fine-Grained Path Selection for Wireless LANs," *ACM MobiSys*, June 2004.

[25] T. Nguyen and A. Zakhor. "Distributed Video Streaming with Forward Error Correction," *Packet Video Workshop*, April 2002.

[26] T. Nguyen and A. Zakhor. "Path Diversity with Forward Error Correction (pdf) System for Packet Switched Networks," *IEEE INFOCOM*, April 2003.

[27] L. Ozarow. "On a Source Coding Problem with Two Channels and Three Receivers," *Bell Syst. Tech. J.*, 59:1909–1921, December 1980.

[28] V. N. Padmanabhan, H. J. Wang, P. A. Chou, and K. Sripanidkulchai. "Distributing Streaming Media Content Using Cooperative Networking," *ACM NOSSDAV*, May 2002.

[29] V. Paxson. "End-to-End Internet Packet Dynamics," *Proc. of the ACM SIGCOMM*, pages 139–152, September 1997.

[30] S. Pradhan, R. Puri, and K. Ramchandran. "n-Channel Symmetric Multiple Descriptions. Part I: (n, k) Source-Channel Erasure Codes," *IEEE Transactions on Information Theory*, pages 47–61, January 2004.

[31] R. Puri, S. Pradhan, and K. Ramchandran. "n-Channel Symmetric Multiple Descriptions. Part II: An Achievable Rate-Distortion Region," *IEEE Transactions on Information Theory*, April 2005.

[32] R. Puri and K. Ramchandran. "Multiple Description Source Coding Using Forward Error Correction Codes," *IEEE Asilomar Conference on Signals, Systems, and Computers*, October 1999.

[33] A. R. Reibman, H. Jafarkhani, Y. Wang, M. T. Orchard, and R. Puri. "Multiple Description Video Coding Using Motion-Compensated Temporal Prediction," *IEEE Trans. Circuits and Systems for Video Technology*, March 2002.

[34] D. Rubenstein, J. Kurose, and D. Towsley. "Detecting Shared Congestion of Flows Via End-to-End Measurement," *ACM SIGMETRICS*, 2000.

[35] S. Savage, A. Collins, E. Hoffman, J. Snell, and T. Anderson. "The End-to-End Effects of Internet Path Selection," *ACM SIGCOMM*, October 1999.

[36] S. Tao and R. Guerin. "Application-Specific Path Switching: A Case Study for Streaming Video," *ACM Multimedia*, October 2004.

[37] D. Tran, K. Hua, and T. Do. "ZIGZAG: An Efficient Peer-to-Peer Scheme for Media Streaming," in *IEEE INFOCOM*, April 2003.

[38] M. van der Schaar and D. S. Turaga. "Multiple Description Scalable Coding Using Wavelet-Based Motion Compensated Temporal Filtering," *IEEE ICIP*, September 2003.

[39] R. Venkataramani, G. Kramer, and V. Goyal. "Multiple Description Coding with Many Channels," *IEEE Transactions on Information Theory*, 49(9):2106–2114, September 2003.

[40] Y. Wang and S. Lin. "Error Resilient Video Coding Using Multiple Description Motion Compensation," *IEEE Trans. Circuits Systems for Video Tech*, June 2002.

[41] Y. Wang, M. T. Orchard, V. Vaishampayan, and A. R. Reibman. "Multiple Description Coding Using Pairwise Correlating Transforms," *IEEE Transactions on Image Processing*, pages 351–366, March 2001.

[42] Y. Wang, A. Reibman, and S. Lin. "Multiple Description Coding for Video Communications," *Proceedings of the IEEE*, January 2005.

[43] S. Wenger, G. Knorr, J. Ott, and F. Kossentini. "Error Resilience Support in H.263+," *IEEE Transactions on Circuits and Systems for Video Technology*, pages 867–877, November 1998.

[44] H. Witsenhausen. "On Source Networks with Minimal Breakdown Degradation," *Bell Syst. Tech. J.*, 59:1083–1087, July–August 1980.

[45] H. Witsenhausen and A. D. Wyner. "Source Coding for Multiple Descriptions II: A Binary Source," Technical Report TM-80-1217, Bell Labs, December 1980.

[46] J. Wolf, A. Wyner, and J. Ziv. "Source Coding for Multiple Descriptions," *Bell Syst. Tech. J.*, 59:1417–1426, October 1980.

[47] X. Zhang, J. Liu, and B. Li. "On Large-Scale Peer-to-Peer Live Video Distribution: CoolStreaming and Its Preliminary Experimental Results," in *IEEE Multimedia Signal Processing Workshop*, October 2005.

18

Distributed Video Coding and Its Applications

Abhik Majumdar, Rohit Puri, Kannan Ramchandran, and Jim Chou

18.1 INTRODUCTION

Contemporary digital video coding architectures have been driven primarily by the "downlink" broadcast model of a complex encoder and a multitude of light decoders. However, with the current proliferation of video devices ranging from hand-held digital cameras to low-power video sensor networks to camera-equipped cellphones, the days of typecasting digital video transmission as a downlink experience are over. We expect future systems to use multiple video input and output streams captured using a network of distributed devices and transmitted over a bandwidth-constrained, noisy wireless transmission medium, to either a peer (as in a peer-to-peer network) or a central location for processing. This new emerging class of "uplink"-rich media applications places a new set of architectural requirements that include:

- robustness to packet/frame loss caused by channel transmission errors;
- low-power and light-footprint encoding due to limited battery power and/or device memory; and
- high compression efficiency due to both bandwidth and transmission power limitations.

In addition, certain applications may impose very stringent end-to-end delay requirements. Current video coding paradigms fail to simultaneously address these requirements well. Predictive or full-motion inter-frame video coding approaches that are part of popular standards, such as H.26x and MPEGx [1,3,4,10] achieve state-of-the-art compression efficiency, but fail to meet the other two criteria, as they are fragile to packet losses[1] while being computationally heavy at the encoder (primarily due to motion search). Alternatively, intra-frame video coding (motion-JPEG) methods, where individual frames are encoded as still images, are robust to packet drops and have low computational complexity but they take a high hit in compression efficiency.

One approach to overcoming these limitations and designing a new video coding solution that has *inbuilt robustness* to channel losses, a *flexible distribution of computational complexity between encoder and decoder*[2] depending upon the device constraints and the channel conditions, and *high compression efficiency* is to have a more *statistical* rather than a *deterministic* mindset. It is in this context that we introduce PRISM, a video coding paradigm founded on the principles of distributed source coding (also called source coding with side information) [38, 40]. Recently, there has been a spate of research activity in the area of video coding based on the ideas of distributed source coding (see Section 18.3.6). In this chapter, however, we will limit our discussion to the PRISM codec [32].

This chapter is organized as follows. Sections 18.2 and 18.3 provide background information motivating the PRISM framework. Section 18.4 lists the key architectural goals underlying the proposed PRISM framework. With a view to quantify the key architectural traits of PRISM, we present the information–theoretic performance limits of prediction-based and side information-based video codecs in Section 18.5. These theoretical insights guide the practical implementation of PRISM described in detail in Sections 18.6 and 18.7 along with experimental results presented in Section 18.8.

With the continued expansion of high-speed wireless networks, such as third-generation cellular networks, 802.11a/b/g (WiFi), and 802.16 (WiMAX), we expect the proliferation of "video sensor networks" in the near future. Typical video sensor networks would be made up of multiple cameras with varying degrees of spatially and temporally overlapping coverage, generating correlated signals that need to be processed, compressed, and exchanged in a loss-prone wireless environment in order to facilitate real-time decisions. Since there would be a high degree of spatiotemporal correlation in the data gathered by a video sensor network, distributed source coding principles can provide useful tools for efficiently exploiting this correlation. In Section 18.9 we discuss briefly how the PRISM architecture can be scaled to scenarios involving multicamera applications.

---

[1] The loss of predictor information in inter-frame coding renders the residue information useless from the point of view of decoding leading to fragility.

[2] In this work, by complexity we refer to motion search complexity.

18.2 CONVENTIONAL VIDEO CODING BACKGROUND

This section quickly overviews the conventional video inter-frame motion-compensated predictive coding (MCPC) architecture that underlies current video coding standards such as the MPEGx and H.26x. Video is a temporal sequence of two-dimensional images (also called frames). For the purpose of encoding, each of these frames is partitioned into regular spatial blocks. These blocks are encoded primarily in the following two modes.

1. **Intra-Coding (I) Mode:** The intra-coding mode exploits the spatial correlation in the frame that contains the current block by using a block transform such as the Discrete Cosine Transform. It typically achieves *poor compression*, since it does not exploit the temporal redundancies in video.

2. **Inter-Coding or Motion-Compensated Predictive (P) Mode:** This mode exploits both spatial and temporal correlations present in the video sequence, resulting in *high compression*. The *high-complexity* motion estimation operation uses the frame memory to infer the best predictor block for the block being encoded. Motion compensation provides the residue between the predictor block and the block in question, which is then transformed and encoded. Inter-coding is illustrated in Figure 18.1.

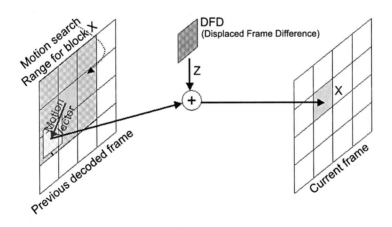

FIGURE 18.1: P-Frame coding (motion-compensated predictive video coding): The current frame is divided up into blocks of n pixels. $\mathbf{X}$ is the current block being encoded. $\mathbf{Y}_1, \ldots, \mathbf{Y}_M$ are M candidate predictor blocks for $\mathbf{X}$ in the previous decoded frame within a search range. $\mathbf{Y}_T$ is the best predictor for $\mathbf{X}$. $\mathbf{Z}$ corresponds to the prediction error (or innovations noise).

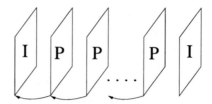

FIGURE 18.2:   A Group of Frames. I, intra-mode coded frames; P, motion-compensated predictive mode coded frames.

Typically, the video sequence is grouped into a Group of Frames (see Figure 18.2) where the first frame in the group is coded in Intra-mode only while the remaining frames in the group are usually coded in Inter-mode.

Intra-coding has *low encoding complexity* and *high robustness* (being a self-contained description of the block being encoded) but has *poor compression efficiency*. To offset this, the MPEGx and H.26x standards use MCPC to achieve the compression needed to communicate over bandwidth-constrained networks. However, MCPC suffers from two major drawbacks.

(a)   Fragility to synchronization or "drift"[3] between encoder and decoder in the face of prediction mismatch, primarily due to channel loss, is a major drawback of the current paradigms. This is a major problem in wireless communication environments, which are characterized by noise and deep fades.

(b)   These frameworks are hampered by a rigid computational complexity partition between encoder (heavy) and decoder (light) where the encoding complexity is dominated by the motion search operation.

18.3 BACKGROUND ON SOURCE CODING WITH SIDE INFORMATION

We now introduce the concept of source coding with side information (distributed source coding) by examining the following illustrative example [31] (see Figure 18.3).

---

[3]Difference in frame memories at the encoder and the decoder results in the residue error being encoded at the encoder off some predictor and decoded at the decoder off some other predictor causing drift. Scenarios such as transmission losses can lead to nonidentical encoder and decoder frame memories.

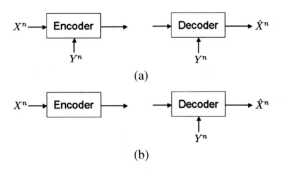

(a)

(b)

FIGURE 18.3: (a) Source coding with side information at both encoder and decoder. (b) Source coding with side information only at the decoder.

18.3.1 Example for Source Coding with Side Information

Let X and Y be length 3-bit binary data that can equally likely take each of eight possible values. However, they are correlated such that the Hamming distance between them is at most 1. That is, given Y (e.g., [0 1 0]), X is either the same as Y ([0 1 0]) or different in the first ([1 1 0]) or the middle ([0 0 0]) or the last bit ([0 1 1]). The goal is to efficiently encode X in the following two scenarios (see Figure 18.3) so that it can be perfectly reconstructed at the decoder.

Scenario 1: In the first scenario (see Figure 18.3a), Y is present both at the encoder and at the decoder. Here X can be predicted from Y. The residue $(X \oplus Y)$ or the error pattern of X with respect to Y takes four distinct values and hence can be encoded with 2 bits. The decoder can combine the residue with Y to obtain X. We note that X is analogous to the current video block that is being encoded, Y is analogous to the predictor from the frame memory, the correlation between X and Y is analogous to the temporal correlation, hence this method corresponds to **predictive coding** (Section 18.2).

Scenario 2: Here Y is made available to the decoder but the encoder for X does not have access to Y as illustrated in Figure 18.3b. However, it does know the correlation structure and also knows that the decoder has access to Y. This scenario being necessarily no better than the first scenario, its performance is limited by that of the first scenario. However, even in this seemingly worse case, we can achieve the same performance as in the first scenario (i.e., encode X using 2 bits)!

This can be done using the following approach. The space of codewords of X is partitioned into four sets each containing two codewords, namely **Coset1** ([0 0 0] and [1 1 1]), **Coset2** ([0 0 1] and [1 1 0]), **Coset3** ([0 1 0] and [1 0 1]), and **Coset4** ([1 0 0] and [0 1 1]). The encoder for X identifies the set containing the codeword for X and sends the index for the set (which can be described in 2 bits), also called syndrome, instead of the individual codeword. The decoder, in turn, on the reception of the coset index (syndrome), uses Y to disambiguate the correct X from the set by declaring the codeword that is closest to Y as the answer. Note that the distance between X and Y is at most 1, and the distance between the two codewords in any set is 3. Hence, decoding can be done perfectly.

Such an encoding method, where the decoder has access to correlated side information, is known as **coding with side information** (also called distributed source coding). We note that **Coset1** in the aforementioned example is a repetition channel code [27] of distance 3 and the other sets are cosets [12,13] of this code in the codeword space of X. In channel coding terminology, each coset is associated with a unique *syndrome*. We have used a channel code that is "matched" to the correlation distance (equivalently, noise) between X and Y to partition the source codeword space of X (which is the set of all possible 3 bit words) into cosets of the 3-bit repetition channel code. The decoder here needs to perform *channel decoding* since it needs to guess the source codeword from among the list of possibilities enumerated in the coset indicated by the encoder. To do so, it finds the codeword in the indicated coset closest to Y. Since the encoder sends the label or *syndrome* for the coset containing the codeword for X to the decoder, we sometimes refer to this operation as **syndrome coding**.

The general source coding with side-information problem, where the source X and decoder side information Y are discrete random variables and X is to be communicated losslessly to the decoder (as in the aforementioned example), has been solved in literature [38] and is known as the Slepian–Wolf theorem. This result, which gives the smallest rate required for communicating X, is summarized in Section 18.3.2.

18.3.2 Source Coding with Side Information: Lossless Case

Consider the problems depicted in Figure 18.3. In Figure 18.3a, the side-information Y^n is available only to the decoder, while in Figure 18.3b it is available to both encoder and decoder. In both cases, let $\{X_i, Y_i\}_{i=1}^n$ be i.i.d. $\sim p(x, y)$, where X and Y are discrete random variables drawn from finite alphabets $\mathcal{X}$ and $\mathcal{Y}$, respectively. The decoder is interested in recovering X^n perfectly with high probability, that is,

$$P_e^{(n)} = P\left(\hat{X}^n \neq X^n\right) \to 0 \quad \text{as } n \to \infty.$$

Now, from information theory [11] we know that the rate region for the problem of Figure 18.3b, when the side information is available to both encoder and decoder, is $R \geq H(X|Y)$. The surprising result of Slepian and Wolf [38] is that the rate region for the problem of Figure 18.3a, when the side information is only available to the decoder, is also $R \geq H(X|Y)$.[4] *Thus one can do as well when the side information is available only to the decoder as when it is available to both encoder and decoder.*

We now turn to the case when we are interested in recovering X^n at the decoder to within some distortion. This is the subject matter of the Wyner–Ziv theorem [40] presented later (see Section 18.3.3), which extends distributed source coding to the more general case of lossy coding with a distortion measure, which is the case of interest for video.

18.3.3 Source Coding with Side Information: Lossy Case

Consider again the problem of Figure 18.3a. We now remove the constraint on X and Y to be discrete and allow them to be continuous random variables as well. We are now interested in recovering X^n at the decoder to within a distortion constraint D for some distortion measure $d(x, \hat{x})$. Let $\{X_i, Y_i\}_{i=1}^{n}$ be i.i.d. $\sim p(x, y)$ and let the distortion measure be $d(x^n, \hat{x}^n) = \frac{1}{n} \sum_{i=1}^{n} d(x_i, \hat{x}_i)$. Then the Wyner–Ziv theorem [40] states that the rate–distortion function for this problem is

$$R(D) = \min_{p(u|x)p(\hat{x}|u,y)} I(X; U) - I(Y; U),$$

where

$$p(x, y, u) = p(u|x)p(x, y)$$

and the minimization is under the distortion constraint

$$\sum_{x,u,y,\hat{x}} p(\hat{x} \mid u, y)p(u|x)p(x, y)d(x, \hat{x}) \leq D.$$

Here U is the active source codeword and the term $I(Y; U)$[5] is the rate rebate due to the presence of side information at the decoder. For the case when X and Y are jointly Gaussian and the mean-squared error (MSE) is the distortion measure, it can be shown [40], using the Wyner–Ziv theorem, that the rate–distortion performance for coding X^n is the same whether or not the encoder has access to Y^n (i.e., the encoder cannot use the knowledge of Y^n for improving the rate–distortion performance in coding X^n). Later in [30] it was shown that this also holds true for the case of $\mathbf{X} = \mathbf{Y} + \mathbf{Z}$, where $\mathbf{Z}$ is independent and identically distributed Gaussian, and the distortion measure is the MSE. In general, however,

---

[4]The notation $H(A)$ stands for the Shannon entropy of random variable A [11].
[5]The notation $I(A; B)$ stands for the Shannon mutual information between two random variables A and B [11].

when compared with a predictive coding approach, the side information-based approach has a small loss in performance [42]. This loss is often termed *Wyner–Ziv rate loss*. Let us now consider the following illustrative example from [23] for the Wyner–Ziv problem.

18.3.4 Illustrative Example for Wyner–Ziv Coding

In this example, X is a real-valued number. The encoder will first quantize X to $\hat{X}$ with a scalar quantizer with step size δ (Figure 18.4). Clearly, the distance between X and $\hat{X}$ is bounded as $|X - \hat{X}| \leq \delta/2$. We can think of the quantizer as consisting of three interleaved quantizers (cosets), each of step size 3δ. In Figure 18.4 we have labeled the reconstruction levels of the three quantizers as 'A', 'B', and 'C', respectively. The encoder, after quantizing X, will note the label of $\hat{X}$ and send this label to the decoder, which requires $\log_2(3)$ bits on average.

The decoder has access to the label transmitted by the encoder and the side information Y. In this example, we assume that X and Y are correlated such that $|Y - X| < \delta$. Thus, we can bound the distance between $\hat{X}$ and Y as

$$\left|\hat{X} - Y\right| \leq \left|\hat{X} - X\right| + |X - Y| < \frac{\delta}{2} + \delta = \frac{3\delta}{2}.$$

Because $\hat{X}$ and Y are within a distance of $\frac{3\delta}{2}$ of each other and the reconstruction levels with the same label are separated by 3δ, the decoder can correctly find $\hat{X}$ by selecting the reconstruction level with the label sent by the encoder that is closest to Y. This can be seen in Figure 18.4, which shows one realization of X and Y.

In this example, the encoder has transmitted only $\log_2(3)$ bits per sample, and the decoder can correctly reconstruct $\hat{X}$, an estimate within $\delta/2$ of the source X. In the absence of Y at the decoder, the encoder would need to quantize X on an m-level quantizer of step-size δ. Thus, by exploiting the presence of Y at the

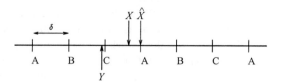

FIGURE 18.4: Distributed compression example: The encoder quantizes X to $\hat{X}$ and transmits the label of $\hat{X}$, an 'A'. The decoder finds the reconstruction level labeled 'A' that is closest to the side information, which is equal to $\hat{X}$.

decoder, the encoder saves $(\log_2(m) - \log_2(3))_+$ bits—this can be quite large if m is large, which should be the case if the variance of X is large.

Intuitively, what is happening here is that the source quantizer is partitioned into cosets of a channel code. We can think of the side-information Y as a free (but noisy) version of the source X available at the decoder. The decoder decodes this noisy version of X in a channel codebook (the specific codebook used will be the coset specified by the encoder). Just as in channel coding, the decoder needs to guess the source codeword from among a set of possible codewords. If the channel code is strong enough, Y will be decoded correctly to $\hat{X}$. Thus, *the goal is to partition a source codebook into good channel codes.* We see that the Wyner–Ziv problem requires a combination of source and channel coding. Note that this was also true for the lossless case (the Slepian–Wolf problem) as illustrated in the example of Section 18.3.1.

Let us now take a more formal look at Wyner–Ziv encoding and decoding.

18.3.5 Wyner–Ziv Encoding and Decoding

As in regular source coding, encoding proceeds by first designing a rate–distortion codebook of rate R' (containing $2^{nR'}$ codewords) constituting the space of quantized codewords for X. Each n-length block of source samples $\mathbf{X}$ is first quantized to the "nearest" codeword in the codebook. As in the illustrative example given earlier, the quantized codeword space (of size $2^{nR'}$ codewords) is further partitioned into 2^{nR} cosets or bins ($R < R'$) so that each bin contains $2^{n(R'-R)}$ codewords. This can be achieved by the information theoretic operation of random binning. The encoder only transmits the index of the bin in which the quantized codeword lies and thereby only needs R bits/sample.

The decoder receives the bin index and disambiguates the correct codeword in this bin by exploiting the correlation between the codeword and the matching n-length block of side-information samples $\mathbf{Y}$. This operation is akin to channel decoding. Once the decoder recovers the codeword, if MSE is the distortion measure, it forms the minimum MSE estimate of the source to achieve an MSE of D.

The optimal codec structure for this problem is illustrated in Figure 18.5 and can be briefly described as follows. The reader is referred to [11] for details.

- Codebook Construction: As in regular source coding, we first construct a codebook for quantization of source X to a random variable U. This is done by drawing $2^{nR'}$ n-length vectors, each of whose components is independent and identically distributed according to the marginal distribution $p_U(u)$, where $p_{U,X}(u,x) = p(x)p(u|x)$. For $\mathbf{X} = \mathbf{Y} + \mathbf{Z}$, where $\mathbf{Z}$ is independent and identically distributed Gaussian of variance σ_Z^2, and MSE distortion measure, we have $p(u|x) = \mathcal{N}(\alpha x, D\alpha)$, and $\alpha := \frac{1}{D}(\sigma_Z^2 - D)$.

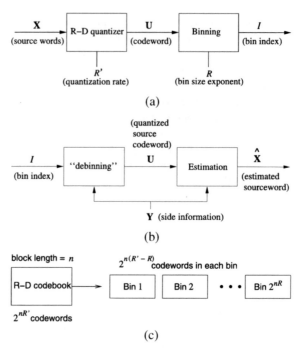

FIGURE 18.5: (a) Structure of distributed encoders. Encoding consists of quantization followed by a binning operation. (b) Structure of distributed decoders. Decoding consists of "de-binning" followed by estimation. (c) Structure of the codebook bins. The R–D codebook containing approximately $2^{nR'}$ codewords is partitioned into 2^{nR} bins each with approximately $2^{n(R'-R)}$ codewords.

This constitutes the space of quantized codewords for X. As in the illustrative example given earlier, this quantized codeword space (of size $2^{nR'}$ codewords) is further partitioned into 2^{nR} cosets or bins ($R < R'$) so that each bin contains $2^{n(R'-R)}$ codewords. This can be achieved by the information theoretic operation of random binning.

- Encoding: Each n-length block of source samples X is first quantized to the "nearest" codeword in the codebook. By standard rate–distortion theory arguments [11], this can be ensured by choosing a rate $R' = I(X; U)$. The encoder then transmits the index of the bin in which the quantized codeword lies and thereby only needs R bits/sample.

- Decoding: The decoder receives the bin index and attempts to disambiguate the correct codeword in this bin by exploiting the correlation between the codeword and the matching n-length block of side-information samples $\mathbf{Y}$. This operation succeeds (with high probability) if the bin size is not too large to cause irrecoverable confusion: quantitatively, if $R' - R \le I(U; Y)$. Hence, $R \ge I(X; U) - I(U; Y)$. For the choice of $p(u|x)$ given earlier, it can be shown that for $\mathbf{X} = \mathbf{Y} + \mathbf{Z}$, where $\mathbf{Z}$ is independent and identically distributed Gaussian, and the MSE distortion measure, this is the same rate distortion function as would be obtained if the side-information $\mathbf{Y}$ was available to both encoder and decoder. As mentioned earlier, *the decoding operation is akin to channel decoding since the decoder needs to guess the correct source codeword from all the possible codewords in the bin.*

• Reconstruction: Once the decoder recovers the codeword, it forms the best estimate of the source word using the recovered codeword and the side information. For the MSE distortion case, the decoder forms the minimum MSE estimate of the source-word $\hat{X}(j)$ to achieve a distortion D, where $\hat{X}(j) = f(U(j), Y(j)) := E[X(j) \mid U(j), Y(j)]$, $j = 1, \dots, n$. Here $f(u, y) = u + (1 - \alpha)y$ and the MSE is $E(X - f(U, Y))^2 = D$.

Thus, we see that Wyner–Ziv encoding is an interplay of both source and channel coding, requiring us to design a good source codebook that can be partitioned into cosets of a good channel code.

18.3.6 Related Work

Before we describe the PRISM video compression framework, we briefly describe some of the related research activity. As mentioned before, PRISM is founded on the principles of distributed source coding, the information theory for which was established in the Slepian–Wolf [38] and the Wyner–Ziv [40] theorems for lossless and lossy cases, respectively. In fact, PRISM represents a generalization of the latter to the case where there is uncertainty in side information [20].

The first instance of distributed compression ideas for video coding can be found in [39], which pointed out the feasibility of distributed compression for video coding. However, [39] merely offers a conceptual treatment; there are no codec details and it does not address critical issues such as motion compensation. More recently, [32–34] proposed the PRISM distributed video codec system based on the framework of [20] in a block-level setup with motion search at the decoder. The distributed video coding problem was also independently studied in [6]. Further, [22,37] study the robustness property associated with distributed source coding and its application to video.

The idea of moving the computational burden away from the encoder was first presented in [35] in an MCPC setup, where the task of motion estimation was essentially transferred from the video encoder to the network terminal. In the distributed video coding context, the concept of moving motion estimation to the decoder was first presented in PRISM [32] and later in [17].

Further, there has been a spate of research activity in the area of distributed video coding addressing issues such as standards-compatible distributed video coding architectures [29,37] and scalability in the distributed video coding framework [36,41]. Finally, extensions of the PRISM framework from the point-to-point single camera case (as in the distributed video coding application) to the multicamera case (as in the video sensor network application) have been considered in [16,19,43].

18.4 ARCHITECTURAL GOALS OF PRISM

We now discuss the three major architectural goals of PRISM.

18.4.1 Compression Performance

As discussed before, it has been shown that in general, source coding with a side–information-based approach can have a small loss in compression performance when compared with a predictive coding approach [42]. However, it was shown in [30,38,40] that in many situations of interest, the performance of a side-information coding system can match that of one based on predictive coding, as in the example given in Section 18.3.1.

We note that **Coset1** in this example is a repetition channel code [27] of distance 3 and the other sets are cosets [12,13] of this code in the codeword space of X. We have thus used a channel code that is "matched" to the unit correlation distance (equivalently, noise) between X and Y to partition the source codeword space of X into cosets. This reduces the encoding rate for X and enables a side–information encoding system to give a **high compression** performance, comparable to a predictive coding system.

We now revisit the video coding problem. Let $\mathbf{X}$ denote the current macro-block to be encoded. Let $\mathbf{Y}$ denote the best (motion-compensated) predictor block for $\mathbf{X}$ and let $\mathbf{Y} = \mathbf{X} + \mathbf{N}$. Using the insight from the aforementioned example, we can encode X by finding a channel code that is matched to the correlation noise $\mathbf{N}$ (also called innovations process from $\mathbf{X}$ to $\mathbf{Y}$) and use that to partition the codeword space of $\mathbf{X}$.

18.4.2 Robustness

A major goal of PRISM is in-built robustness to packet and frame drops in contrast to what is possible with today's video codecs. PRISM targets this by using the "universally robust" side–information-based coding framework. The partitioning of X in the example of Section 18.3.4 is *universal*, that is, the same partitioning of X works for all Y regardless of the value of Y as long as both X and Y satisfy the correlation structure. Note that in this example, as long as $|Y - X| < \delta$, the decoder is guaranteed to recover the correct $\hat{X}$.

Essentially, in the predictive coding framework the encoding for the current unit hinges on a *single* deterministic predictor, the loss of which results in erroneous decoding and error propagation. A side-information coding-based paradigm encodes the current unit, in principle, with respect to the correlation statistics between the current unit and the predictor only. At the decoder, the availability of *any* predictor that satisfies the correlation statistics enables correct decoding. A valid question to ask is: how does PRISM differ from the conventional use of Forward Error Correction (FEC) codes [27] on top of a MCPC compressed bit stream? Primarily, we note that FEC-based solutions serve to minimize the probability of error, thereby reducing the likelihood of mismatch between the encoder and the decoder *but they cannot fix the mismatch when there is one* (which is almost inevitable). Second, FEC-based solutions usually need large block lengths of data for attaining good performance, thus adding to the overall end-to-end delay while PRISM offers a low-latency solution.

18.4.3 Moving Motion-Search Complexity to the Decoder

Another architectural goal is to allow for a much more flexible distribution of the computational complexity (motion search) between encoder and decoder, depending upon device constraints, than is possible today. For example, in uplink-rich media applications, it is desirable to move the bulk of the complexity from the battery-power constrained encoder to the more capable decoder. PRISM facilitates this by allowing for partly or wholly *moving the computationally intensive motion search module to the decoder*. That is, in addition to the conventional high-complexity encoder and low-complexity decoder setting, PRISM also allows for the reverse possibility comprising a low-complexity encoder and a high-complexity decoder. The underlying theoretical paradigm for this is based on a generalization of the Wyner–Ziv side-information coding framework to the case where there is uncertainty at the receiver about the exact state of the side information [20], as will be described in Section 18.5.1.

In this context, we would like to point out that in conventional MCPC systems (where only the encoder performs motion search), a low-complexity encoding solution can be realized by limiting the amount of motion estimation performed at the encoder. This, however, decreases the overall compression efficiency of the system. In the case of PRISM, while in theory motion complexity can be completely moved to the decoder with little loss of compression performance (as is detailed in Section 18.5.1), in practice, however, we observe a similar complexity-compression trade-off in the PRISM video codec with a no-motion PRISM encoder generally taking a hit in compression performance relative to an inter-frame codec (see Section 18.8).

However, when we consider the end-to-end performance of PRISM for the case of transmission over a loss-prone channel, we can show that (see Section 18.5.3) as the channel noise increases, doing a motion search at the encoder gives diminishing marginal utility. At the same time, as the channel degrades, the decoder will need to search more among the list of available predictors to find one that enables successful decoding.

18.5 A THEORY FOR DISTRIBUTED VIDEO CODING

In Section 18.4, we proposed the distributed compression paradigm as a feasible approach for addressing the architectural goals of PRISM. In this section, we first describe a generalization of the concepts of lossy source coding with side information to the case when there is uncertainty in the side information at the decoder [20] (Section 18.5.1). This corresponds to the exact theoretical paradigm that underlies the PRISM framework. We then present an analysis that showcases the advantages of the side–information-based framework over the predictive coding framework when transmitting over a lossy channel (Section 18.5.2). We also discuss the complexity performance trade-offs for a side–information-based video codec when there are losses on the transmission channel (Section 18.5.3).

While the relatively simple models used in the following do not capture the rich and complex video phenomenon in its entirety, they are powerful enough to capture the essence of the problem at hand and offer valuable insights into developing the practical PRISM solution.

18.5.1 Sharing Motion Complexity Between Encoder and Decoder

In [20], it was shown that for an interesting class of signal models, motion complexity can be arbitrarily shared between encoder and decoder. Specifically, in [20] the information-theoretic rate–MSE performance of encoding X when the encoder *does not have access* to the decoded blocks in the previous frame(s), that is, motion compensation *is not possible* at the encoder, is compared with the performance when the encoder *has access* to all the correlated decoded blocks in the previous frame(s) to encode X, as is done in contemporary video codecs that are based on MCPC. The surprising answer is that both systems have the same performance (when the innovations process has Gaussian statistics). In this section we give a short overview of the results of [20].

18.5.1.1 A Motion-Compensated Video Model

A model for video signals is depicted in Figures 18.1 and 18.6. Here, a block of pixels X in the current frame is modeled as the sum of a block of pixels Y_T in the previous decoded frame that is spatially close to X and a block of independent

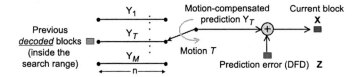

FIGURE 18.6: Motion-indexed additive–innovations model for video signals. $\mathbf{X}$ denotes a block of size n pixels in the current frame to be encoded and $\{\mathbf{Y}_i\}_{i=1}^{M}$ the set of blocks (each of size n) in the previous decoded frame corresponding to different values of the motion vector indexed by T.

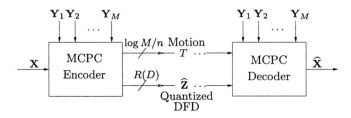

FIGURE 18.7: Motion-Compensated Predictive Coding (MCPC). Encoder sends motion using $\frac{1}{n}\log M$ bpp and the quantized residual $\mathbf{Z}$ using $R(D)$ bpp.

and identically distributed (i.i.d.) white Gaussian "innovations noise" $\mathbf{Z}$. That is, $\mathbf{X} = \mathbf{Y}_T + \mathbf{Z}$ where the parameter $T \in \{1, \dots, M\}$ (called motion index) accounts for any motion that has occurred in consecutive frames.

18.5.1.2 Motion-Compensated Predictive Coding

We first derive the rate–MSE performance for the MCPC approach. Conventional MCPC is done in the following two steps (see Figure 18.7).

(a) The encoder estimates and transmits the index of the estimated motion vector to the decoder. The rate (bits per pixel or bpp) needed to specify T is given by $\frac{\log M}{n}$.

(b) Once the decoder knows T, the video coding problem is reduced to the problem of compressing the "source" $\mathbf{X}$ using the correlated side-information $\mathbf{Y}_T$ now available to *both* the encoder and the decoder. The solution to this problem is well known: for a target MSE value of D, the minimum rate $R(D)$ (in bpp) needed to encode $\mathbf{X}$ is given by the smallest rate that is needed to quantize $\mathbf{Z}$ to the nearest codeword $\widehat{\mathbf{Z}}$ within a distortion D. That is, $R(D)$ is given by [11]

$$R(D) = \min\left(0, 0.5 \log_2(\sigma_Z^2/D)\right). \tag{18.1}$$

The decoder receives the quantized codeword and reconstructs the source block as $\mathbf{Y}_T + \widehat{\mathbf{Z}}$ whose MSE is D. The total rate needed is $\frac{\log M}{n} + R(D)$ bpp.

18.5.1.3 Distributed Video Coding

In this case, due to severely limited processing capability (or some other reason), the encoder is disallowed from performing the complex motion-compensated prediction task. This is in effect pretending that the encoder does not have access to the previous decoded blocks $\mathbf{Y}_1, \ldots, \mathbf{Y}_M$.

Help from an Oracle:

As an intermediate step, consider the situation depicted in Figure 18.8 where an oracle reveals the true value of T only to the decoder (the encoder still does not know T). This is precisely the setup of the source coding with the decoder side information problem [40]. As mentioned in Section 18.3.3, for the special case of i.i.d. Gaussian statistics for $\mathbf{Z}$, the performance in the coding with side–information case is identical to MCPC, that is, the minimum bit rate needed to achieve an MSE D is given by (18.1). The encoding and decoding operations are as described in Section 18.3.3.

Reality: no oracle is available:

In the absence of the oracle, T is not available to the decoder and represents an additional source of uncertainty (see Figure 18.9). However, it turns out that this additional uncertainty can be overcome by decreasing the size of the bins or equivalently by having more bins. *This incurs an additional bit budget of $\frac{1}{n} \log M$ bpp, which is precisely the bit budget needed by motion-compensated predictive video codecs to convey the motion index to the decoder.* The encoder uses the same rate–distortion codebook as before. Whereas earlier each bin contained $2^{n(R'-R)}$

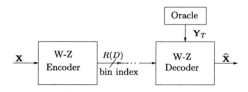

FIGURE 18.8: Wyner–Ziv codec with Oracle. Oracle reveals $\mathbf{Y}_T$ to the decoder only. Encoder does not have access to or is constrained from using $\mathbf{Y}_1, \ldots, \mathbf{Y}_M$.

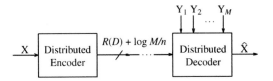

FIGURE 18.9: Low encoding complexity-distributed video codec. The encoder is incapable of using the previous decoded blocks. The decoder does not know the hidden motion index T.

codewords, now each bin will contain $2^{n(R'-R-\frac{1}{n}\log M)}$ codewords. Upon receiving a bin index, the decoder tries each $\mathbf{Y}_i$ in turn and stops as soon as it has found a codeword in the bin with which it is "sufficiently strongly correlated" according to the joint component statistics expected of $\mathbf{Y}_T$ and the quantized representation of $\mathbf{X}$.[6] This is like a "block-matching" motion-compensation operation but done at the decoder. It can be rigorously demonstrated that this algorithm not only finds the correct quantized codeword of $\mathbf{X}$, but also recovers the correct motion index T with high probability [20].

We have thus summarized an information-theoretic construction that enables shifting the motion complexity to the decoder without losing any performance relative to MCPC.

18.5.2 Robustness to Transmission Errors

In this section, we present an information-theoretic analysis for a very simple mismatched side-information problem that clarifies the nature of the drift problem associated with predictive coding and the value of distributed coding. This will highlight the superior robustness properties of the distributed video coding approach.

Consider the setup depicted in Figure 18.10. Here, $X = Y + Z$ stands for the data source that needs to be transmitted, Y denotes the predictor for X available at the encoder with associated independent innovations Z, and $Y' = Y + W$ is the predictor for X available at the destination. Here, W denotes the accumulated drift noise that cannot be observed at the encoder. We shall compare the performance of the predictive and distributed approaches for communicating X to the destination for two cases detailed later. In this analysis, we will consider that the encoder does a motion search and finds the best block to use from the previous frame(s) (which is the predictor Y) and sends the motion vector to the decoder. Hence, the decoder knows what side information to use, unlike in Section 18.5.1.3. At the end of this

---

[6]This is also referred to as "jointly typical decoding" [11].

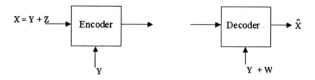

FIGURE 18.10: Problem setup: The encoder needs to compress the source $X = Y + Z$. Y is the predictor available to the encoder while $Y' = (Y + W)$ is the "drifted" predictor available to the decoder.

section, we will return to the model of Section 18.5.1.3, where the decoder needs to perform a motion search to find the correct side information to use.

18.5.2.1 Discrete Data, Lossless Recovery

The encoder does not have access to the realization of the drift random variable W, only to the joint statistics of Y, Z, and W. We assume that Z is independent of Y and Y'. The goal is to ensure that $\hat{X}$ is equal to X with high probability. It can be shown (see [28]) that the optimal solution is to ignore Y at the encoder and hence, using the Slepian–Wolf theorem [38], the smallest encoding rate in bits per sample needed to convey X losslessly to the decoder is given by

$$R_{dsc} = H\left(X|Y'\right).$$

Here the subscript "dsc" stands for distributed source coding.

We now outline the derivation of a lower bound on the rate required by a predictive coding system. The predictive coding system first forms the innovations Z and sends it to the decoder, incurring a total rate of $H(Z)$ bits per sample. If there is no drift between the encoder and the decoder ($W = 0$), the decoder can recover Z and use Y to recover X. However, with a nonzero drift between the encoder and the decoder, an additional drift correction rate needs to be incurred. But the encoder does not have access to the realization of the drift random variable W. To correct for the drift, the best that the encoder can do is to use a distributed source coding approach to convey the missing information needed to recover X. This incurs an extra rate of $H(X|Z, Y')$ bits per sample. Note, however, that this method of using distributed source coding to correct for the drift is *not* followed by the MPEGx or H.26x standards and so we can term this extra rate to correct for drift as a *lower bound* for the extra rate required by the predictive coding system to correct the drift. Hence, the predictive coding approach needs a total bit rate not smaller than

$$R_{pc}^{lb} = H(Z) + H\left(X \mid Z, Y'\right) = H(Z) + H\left(Y + Z \mid Z, Y'\right) = H(Z) + H\left(Y|Y'\right),$$

where the subscripts "pc" and "lb" stand, respectively, for predictive coding and lower bound. The last equality follows from the fact that Z is independent of Y. The last expression suggests an alternative interpretation for R_{pc}. The term $H(Y|Y')$ can be interpreted as the rate required to "correct" the side information, that is, resynchronize the encoder and the decoder frame memories.

Note that $H(Z|Y') = H(Z)$ since Z is independent of Y'. So, we have

$$
\begin{aligned}
R_{pc}^{lb} &= H(Z) + H\big(X \mid Z, Y'\big) \\
&= H\big(Z|Y'\big) + H\big(X \mid Z, Y'\big) \\
&= H\big(Z, X \mid Y'\big) \\
&= H\big(X|Y'\big) + H\big(Z \mid X, Y'\big) \\
&= R_{dsc} + H\big(Z \mid X, Y'\big).
\end{aligned}
$$

The rate penalty due to drift for the predictive coding approach over the distributed source coding approach is then

$$
R_{pc}^{lb} - R_{dsc} = H\big(Z \mid X, Y'\big) = H\big((X - Y) \mid X, Y'\big) = H\big(Y \mid X, Y'\big),
$$

which is always nonnegative and zero only when $Y = Y'$ (i.e., $W = 0$) or if $Z = 0$.

The rate penalty $R_{pc}^{lb} - R_{dsc}$ evaluated earlier is significant only if the "innovations" component $H(Z)$ and the "channel noise" component $H(Y|Y')$ are both large [since $H(Z \mid X, Y') \leq H(Z)$ and $H(Y \mid X, Y') \leq H(Y|Y')$]. This is not surprising since when $H(Z)$ is small the two-step approach is not "wasting" a lot of rate by sending $H(Z)$ simply because it does not require a lot of bits to send $H(Z)$. However, when $H(Y|Y')$ is small, the drift is small and it does not take too many bits to correct it (in the extreme case when there is no drift, predictive coding is, of course, optimal). However, the interesting case is really when the drift *is* significant and it is in this case that the aforementioned rate penalty is also significant. Hence, when there is significant drift, the predictive coding framework can be quite suboptimal.

18.5.2.2 Jointly Gaussian Data, Recovery with MSE $\leq D$

We now present a rate–distortion analysis for the two approaches in a jointly Gaussian setting. Random variables Y, Z, W are jointly Gaussian and mutually independent Gaussian random variables with variances $\sigma_y^2, \sigma_z^2, \sigma_w^2$, respectively. Let U denote the quantization random variable (the output of the encoder) and $\hat{X}$ the reconstruction random variable. We are interested in recovering X to a target distortion D.

It can be shown [28] that the optimal solution here is to ignore Y at the encoder and hence, using the Wyner–Ziv theorem [40], the smallest encoding rate in bits per sample needed is

$$R_{dsc}(D) = \min_{p(u|x)p(\hat{x}|u,y')} I(X; U \mid Y') = \min_{p(u|x)p(\hat{x}|u,y')} I(X; U) - I(Y; U),$$

where $Y' = Y + W$ and the minimization is under the constraint that the overall expected distortion is at most D where MSE is the distortion measure. Then we have the following theorem:

Theorem 18.5-1. *For jointly Gaussian and mutually independent random variables, Y, Z, W with variances $\sigma_y^2, \sigma_z^2, \sigma_w^2$, respectively, and an MSE distortion measure, let $X = Y + Z$ be the source to be encoded with Y available at the encoder and $Y' = Y + W$ available at the decoder. Then the rate–distortion function for the distributed source coding approach is*

$$R_{dsc}(D) = \max\left(0, \frac{1}{2}\log_2 \frac{\sigma_z^2 + \sigma_y^2\sigma_w^2/(\sigma_y^2 + \sigma_w^2)}{D}\right). \tag{18.2}$$

For the proof of Theorem 18.5-1 please refer to [28].

As in Section 18.5.2.1, we lower bound the rate required by the predictive coding system using a two-step approach. The predictive coding system quantizes Z to $\hat{Z}$ with a distortion D. We assume $D < \sigma_z^2$ since otherwise the predictive coding system will not encode the innovations at all. If the encoder and the decoder use identical predictor information, $\hat{X}$ can be recovered from $\hat{Z}$ as $\hat{X} = \hat{Z} + Y$. In the general case, however, there is a drift between the encoder and the decoder. As in Section 18.5.2.1, the encoder needs to spend an additional rate (using distributed coding techniques) to correct for the drift, thus resulting in a total rate

$$R_{pc}^{lb}(D) = I(Z; \hat{Z}) + \min_{p(u|x)p(\hat{x}|u,y',\hat{z})} I(X; U \mid Y', \hat{Z}), \tag{18.3}$$

where $Y' = Y + W$ and the minimization is under the constraint that the overall expected distortion is at most D where MSE is the distortion measure. The rate required to correct the drift (using Wyner–Ziv techniques) is given by $\min_{p(u|x)p(\hat{x}|u,y',\hat{z})} I(X; U|Y', \hat{Z})$. Then we have the following theorem.

Theorem 18.5-2. *For jointly Gaussian and mutually independent random variables, Y, Z, W with variances $\sigma_y^2, \sigma_z^2, \sigma_w^2$, respectively, and an MSE distortion measure, let $X = Y + Z$ be the source to be encoded with Y available at the encoder and $Y' = Y + W$ available at the decoder. Then for target distortion*

$D < \sigma_z^2$, *the rate distortion function for the two-step predictive coding and drift correction method is*

$$R_{pc}^{lb}(D) = \frac{1}{2} \log_2 \frac{\sigma_z^2(D + \sigma_y^2 \sigma_w^2/(\sigma_y^2 + \sigma_w^2))}{D^2}. \tag{18.4}$$

For the proof of Theorem 18.5-2 please refer to [28].

Note that when $D < \sigma_z^2$,

$$R_{dsc}(D) = \frac{1}{2} \log_2 \frac{\sigma_z^2 + \sigma_y^2 \sigma_w^2/(\sigma_y^2 + \sigma_w^2)}{D}.$$

The rate penalty due to drift for the predictive coding approach over the distributed source coding approach is then

$$R_{pc}^{lb} - R_{dsc} = \frac{1}{2} \log_2 \frac{1 + A/D}{1 + A/\sigma_z^2},$$

where $A = \sigma_y^2 \sigma_w^2/(\sigma_y^2 + \sigma_w^2)$. For the range of interest $D < \sigma_z^2$, the difference is positive. In fact, $R_{pc}^{lb} \geq R_{dsc}$, with $R_{pc}^{lb} = R_{dsc}$ if $D \geq \sigma_z^2$, or $\sigma_y^2 = 0$, or $\sigma_w^2 = 0$. In the context of video coding, $D \geq \sigma_z^2$ is akin to the case of not sending the block at all (the "skip" mode), $\sigma_y^2 = 0$ is like not having any useful predictor available (the "intra" mode), and $\sigma_w^2 = 0$ implies that the encoder and decoder are in sync (no drift). For all other cases, $R_{pc}^{lb} > R_{dsc}$.

Further, we note in the high-quality regime (i.e., $D \to 0$), we have

$$\lim_{D \to 0} \frac{R_{pc} - R_{dsc}}{R_{dsc}} \to 1, \tag{18.5}$$

that is, *the predictive coding system needs nearly double the rate as compared to the distributed coding system.*[7]

The analysis of this section is readily extended to the multiple predictors case of Section 18.5.1 where the side information at the decoder is not known exactly and is only known to be one among a set of predictors $\{Y_i\}_{i=1}^n$.

To see this, note that the rate–distortion functions for the case when the side information is known at the decoder (the motion vector is known) and the case when it is not (the motion vector is unknown) are identical (as $n \to \infty$) [20]. That is, the problems depicted in Figures 18.9 and 18.8 have the same rate–distortion function. Thus it is sufficient to consider the case when the side information is known at the decoder, which is the case considered here.

---

[7]Equation (18.5) can be proved using L'Hospital's rule.

18.5.3 Complexity Performance Trade-Offs

In the previous sections of this chapter, we had assumed perfect knowledge of the correlation statistics at both the encoder and the decoder. However, real-world video encoding algorithms involve an "online" learning of the correlation statistics through the process of motion estimation. Typically, the more the complexity invested in the motion estimation process, the more accurate is the estimate of the statistics leading to better compression performance. While this is true for the case of transmission over a clean channel, in the following we show that, using a distributed video coding approach over a lossy channel, the *marginal value* of accurately learning the correlation statistics at the encoder diminishes as the channel noise increases.

Let X be the block to be encoded. Let $\mathbf{Y} = (Y_1, Y_2, \ldots, Y_M)$ be the set of predictors available to the encoder for the block X. Let $\mathbf{Y}' = (Y_1', Y_2', \ldots, Y_M')$ be the set of predictors available to the decoder for the same block. Here $\mathbf{Y}'$ is a noisy version of $\mathbf{Y}$ (due to previous transmission errors). We assume that $X \leftrightarrow \mathbf{Y} \leftrightarrow \mathbf{Y}'$ form a Markov chain, that is, the set of predictors $\mathbf{Y}'$ is a degraded version of the set of predictors $\mathbf{Y}$. As in Section 18.5.2.1, we are interested in communicating X losslessly to the decoder.

Note that the minimum rate required to losslessly communicate X to the decoder is $R_{dsc} = H(X|\mathbf{Y}')$, since $\mathbf{Y}'$ is the side information available to the decoder. It can be shown [21] that this rate is

$$R_{dsc} = H\big(X|\mathbf{Y}'\big) = H\big(\mathbf{Y}|\mathbf{Y}'\big) + H(X|\mathbf{Y}) - H\big(\mathbf{Y} \mid X, \mathbf{Y}'\big).$$

Since we are interested in observing the effect of channel noise, we will upper bound R_{dsc} by neglecting the last term (since $H(\mathbf{Y} \mid X, \mathbf{Y}')$ can at most increase to $H(\mathbf{Y}|X)$ as the noise increases). So

$$R_{dsc} \leq H\big(\mathbf{Y}|\mathbf{Y}'\big) + H(X|\mathbf{Y}). \tag{18.6}$$

Note that the term $H(X|\mathbf{Y})$ is a measure of the source correlation while $H(\mathbf{Y}|\mathbf{Y}')$ is a measure of the effect of channel noise. Further, also note that

$$H(X|Y_1) \geq H(X \mid Y_1, Y_2) \geq \cdots \geq H(X|\mathbf{Y}).$$

$H(X|Y_1)$ can be thought of as the encoder estimate of $H(X|\mathbf{Y})$ if the encoder only looked at one predictor from the previous frame. Similarly, $H(X \mid Y_1, Y_2)$ would be the encoder estimate of $H(X|\mathbf{Y})$ if it looked at two predictors from the previous frame, and so on. Thus, we will get better estimates of $H(X|\mathbf{Y})$ as we search the list of predictors (motion search). However, as (18.6) shows, the rate R_{dsc} depends on the sum of the correlation noise and the channel noise. For a fixed correlation noise, the reduction in R_{dsc}, as we find the correlation noise more accurately (through more motion search), diminishes as we increase the channel noise.

18.6 PRISM: ENCODING

We have thus summarized a system-level information theory for distributed video coding with the goal of addressing the feasibility of the architectural goals of PRISM. In extending these methods to the real-world video scenario, we recognize that we are dealing with sources having complex correlation noise structures that are imprecisely known, requiring estimation models. In this context, we would like to point out a principal reason underlying the success of current video coding standards (H.26x and MPEGx), namely their ability to model, estimate, and process motion as a *local block-level phenomenon*. Realizing that accurate motion modeling is the key to success, we have based our implementation of the PRISM on the local block-motion, block-DCT, block-coding framework.

We now list the main aspects of the PRISM encoding process. We note that the video frame to be encoded is divided into nonoverlapping spatial blocks (we choose blocks of size 8×8 in our implementation).

18.6.1 Decorrelating Transform

We first apply a DCT on the source block. The transformed coefficients $\mathbf{X}$ are then arranged in a one-dimensional order (size 64) by doing a zig-zag scan on the two-dimensional block (size 8×8).

18.6.2 Quantization

Following this, we apply a scalar quantizer. The transformed coefficients are quantized with a target quantization step size chosen based on the desired reconstruction quality (as in [10]).

18.6.3 Classification

The next step involves the design of a Wyner–Ziv codebook in order to exploit the correlation between the source and the side information. In this context, it is convenient to view individual quantized coefficients in a block in terms of bit planes, as shown in Figure 18.11. Correlation between a source coefficient X_i ($i \in \{0, 1, \ldots, 63\}$) and the corresponding side-information Y_i can be interpreted in terms of the number of most-significant bit planes of the quantized representation of X_i that can be inferred from side-information Y_i (Figure 18.11 illustrates this with the bits corresponding to the white color being predictable using the

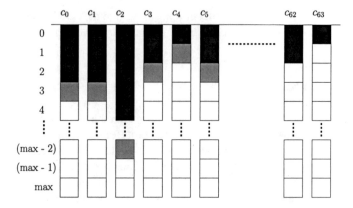

FIGURE 18.11: A bit plane view of a block of 64 coefficients. Bit planes are arranged in increasing order with 0 corresponding to the least-significant bit.

decoder side information). The remaining least-significant bit planes (shown in gray and black in Figure 18.11) are not inferable at the decoder and need to be encoded. These bits constitute the Wyner–Ziv encoding (syndrome) for source coefficient X_i.

This is also illustrated in Figure 18.12. Here U_i corresponds to the quantized representation for X_i with a target step-size δ. Starting from the least-significant bit plane of U_i, each successive bit plane identifies a partition of codewords containing U_i. The number of least-significant bits that need to be communicated to the decoder is given by the tree depth for which the distance between successive codewords in the partition is greater than twice the correlation noise magnitude between U_i and Y_i. This would enable correct decoding (in other words, inferring the remaining most-significant bit planes) of U_i at the decoder using Y_i. Clearly, the higher the correlation, the smaller the correlation noise, the greater the number of most-significant bit planes that can be predicted from the side information. The Wyner–Ziv encoding of a source block $\mathbf{X}$ thus corresponds to a suitable number of least-significant bit planes for each coefficient X_i such that the remaining (most-significant) bit planes can be inferred at the decoder.

While the previous paragraph describes the method for Wyner–Ziv encoding of source block $\mathbf{X}$, one important difference between the aforementioned description and the problem at hand is that the aforementioned description assumes knowledge of the correlation structure between $\mathbf{X}$ and $\mathbf{Y}$ at the encoder. In practice, however, this structure is not known precisely and needs to be estimated for better compression performance. It is for this reason that we use a classification module in our approach, with the goal of estimating the correlation noise between each

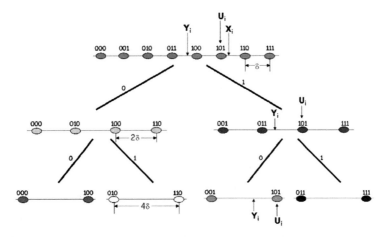

FIGURE 18.12: Partitioning of the quantization lattice into levels. X_i is the source, U_i is the (quantized) codeword, and Y_i is the side information. The number of levels in the partition tree depends on the effective noise between U_i and Y_i.

video block and its temporal predictor from frame memory, as measured in number of most-significant bits that are predictable at the decoder for every quantized coefficient.

Real-world video sources exhibit a spatiotemporal correlation noise structure with highly varying statistics. Spatial blocks that are a part of the scene background or relate to previous frames via simple/regular motion exhibit high correlation with their temporal predictor blocks (i.e., they are associated with correlation noise **N** that is "small"). However, blocks that are a part of a scene change, occlusion, or arise from irregular motion have little correlation with their temporal predictor blocks ("large" **N**). Our classification module deploys block-motion estimation to infer the correlation noise between the current 8 × 8 spatial block and its temporal predictors. As discussed in Section 18.5.3, depending on the available complexity budget, as well as the prevailing channel conditions, the classification module can perform varying degrees of motion search, ranging from an exhaustive motion search to a coarse motion search to no motion search at all. We now discuss our implementation of the classification module for two extreme configurations—one corresponding to little motion search and the other corresponding to an exhaustive motion search. The compression/robustness performance of these schemes is presented later in Section 18.8.

(a) **No motion search:** In this case, we use the residue information between the current block (considered in the pixel domain) and the colocated block in the previous frame (corresponding to zero motion) to infer the correlation noise $\mathbf{N}$ and, consequently, the number of least-significant bits that need to be communicated to the decoder. We use a combination of online measurements and off-line training to accomplish this objective.

- We first determine the scalar mean-squared error E corresponding to the residue information between the current block and its zero-motion predictor.

- The appropriate "class" for the current block is then determined by thresholding E using a set of predetermined threshold values. We use a set of 15 thresholds (T_i where $i \in \{0, \ldots, 14\}$) in our implementation corresponding to 16 classes labeled 0 through 15. Class i is chosen when $T_{i-1} \leq E < T_i$.

- Each class i is associated with a block correlation noise $\mathbf{N}^i$ whose statistics were determined using off-line training.[8] The inferred block correlation noise is used to determine the number of least-significant bits for individual coefficients that need to be communicated to the decoder.

- Note that by following this procedure, we have made a conservative determination of the correlation noise between the current block and its best motion-compensated temporal predictor block. As a result of this, due to the need to communicate more bit planes to the decoder, we can incur excessive bit rate. We treat this inefficiency by jointly encoding the most-significant bit planes of individual coefficients that need to be communicated to the decoder with a coset channel code. These bit planes correspond to the gray color in Figure 18.11. The remaining least-significant bit planes, shown in black in Figure 18.11, are encoded using a suitable entropy code. This is further detailed in Section 18.6.4.

(b) **High-complexity motion search:** Similar to conventional video encoders, in this case, we make a precise determination of the correlation noise between the current block and its best motion-compensated temporal predictor. The residue information between the current block and its motion-compensated temporal predictor is used to obtain the number of least-significant bits for individual coefficients that need to be communicated to the decoder. In terms of Figure 18.11, these bit planes correspond to black color (there is no gray color in this case) and are encoded using a suitable entropy code. Optionally, we can also indicate the chosen motion vector at the encoder as a part of the bitstream.

---

[8]We consider $\mathbf{N}^i$ in the transform domain where the absolute values of its components were modeled as a set of independent Laplacian random variables $\{N_0^i, N_1^i, N_2^i, \ldots, N_{63}^i\}$. The parameters corresponding to the various Laplacian random variables (a Laplacian random variable is completely characterized by its mean value) belonging to different classes were obtained by off-line training. We used a long news clip from the "Euronews" TV channel to derive these statistics. The choice of the Laplacian model was based on its success as reported in the literature [6] and by our experiments on statistical modeling of residue coefficients in the transform domain.

18.6.4 Syndrome Encoding

The syndrome encoding step is assigned the task of encoding the least-significant bits of individual coefficients in a block (as determined by the classification step) in an efficient manner. As described in Section 18.6.3, the least-significant bit planes for individual coefficients in a block fall under two cases—bit planes corresponding to black in Figure 18.11 are encoded using an entropy code and bit planes corresponding to gray are encoded using a coset channel code.

(a) **Entropy Coding:** We note that contemporary video compression standards including [1,3,10] use a (**run, level, sign, last**) 4-tuple[9]-based alphabet for entropy coding the residue information. Given the alphabet, the actual entropy coding is then accomplished by using Huffman coding [11] or arithmetic coding [25].

In our implementation, we use a variant of this method for defining the alphabet used for entropy coding of the least-significant bit planes shown in black in Figure 18.11. Our entropy coding alphabet consists of (**run, depth, path, last**) 4-tuple. Here **run** indicates the number of coefficients prior to the current coefficient for which no bit planes are encoded, **depth** indicates the number of least-significant bit planes encoded for the current coefficient, and **path** indicates the bit path in the binary tree that specifies the coset containing the current coefficient. The number of values taken by **path** is given by $2^{\mathbf{depth}}$. The entry **last** has identical meaning to the corresponding term used in contemporary video compression standards. We use an arithmetic coding engine that operates on this alphabet to efficiently code the syndrome information.

(b) **Coset Channel Coding:** As mentioned in Section 18.6.3, for the case of an encoder with no motion search, we make a conservative determination of correlation noise between the current block and its best motion-compensated temporal predictor block. As a result of this, due to the need to communicate more bit planes to the decoder, we can incur excessive bit rate. We treat this inefficiency by jointly encoding the topmost least-significant bit planes (corresponding to gray in Figure 18.11) using a coset channel code. These bits are encoded using the parity check matrix [27] of an (n, k_i) linear error correction code. $\mathbf{s}_i = H_i \mathbf{b}_i$, where $\mathbf{s}_i$ and H_i represent the syndrome and parity check matrix corresponding to the ith linear channel code and $\mathbf{b}_i$ represents the corresponding input bits. The encoding rate for this case is given by $(n - k_i)/n$ bits per coefficient.

---

[9] A block of quantized residue coefficients is interpreted as a set of (**run, level, sign, last**) tuples where **run** indicates the number of coefficients with a value equal to zero before a nonzero coefficient residue, **level** indicates the absolute value of the nonzero coefficient residue, **sign** indicates the sign associated with the nonzero coefficient residue, and the binary-valued **last** indicates whether the nonzero coefficient is the last in the block.

Since we have small block lengths at our disposal (640 samples for an 8×8 block), we use the relatively simple BCH [27] block codes, which work well even at reasonably small block lengths (unlike more sophisticated channel codes, such as LDPC codes [15] and turbo codes [7]). The parameter k_i associated with the ith channel code is a function of the class i (see Section 18.6.3) to which the block belongs. The parameters for each class were chosen by using the error probability versus SNR performance curves of the various BCH codes.

18.6.5 Hash Generation

When the encoder is of low complexity and/or the channel is lossy, we require the decoder to perform motion search. For this case, unlike the classical Wyner–Ziv coding setup, we have several side-information candidates Y_i at the decoder corresponding to various motion-predictor choices (as described in Section 18.5.1). The decoder does not know the "best" predictor for the block $\mathbf{X}$. In theory (see Section 18.5.1), it is possible to find the best predictor and decode the block $\mathbf{X}$ through joint-typical decoding. In practice, however, joint-typical decoding is not feasible given the short block lengths and the complexity constraints at the decoder. Accordingly, the encoder needs to transmit not only the syndrome for the side–information-encoded coefficients, but also a hash signature (of sufficient strength) for the quantized sequence codewords.

For this purpose, we use a cyclic redundancy check (CRC) checksum as a "signature" of the quantized codeword sequence. In contrast to the conventional paradigm, it is the decoder's task to do motion search here, and it searches over the space of candidate predictors one by one to decode a sequence from the set labeled by the syndrome. When the decoded sequence matches the CRC check, decoding is declared to be successful. Note that the CRC needs to be sufficiently strong so as to act as a reliable signature for the codeword sequence. For this reason, we use a 16-bit checksum, which has a reasonable error performance, in our implementation.

18.6.6 Summary

The bit stream associated with a block is illustrated in Figure 18.13. Depending on the scenario at hand, different subsets of these fields are used to represent the block. For instance, for the case when we are interested in pure compression

Class Label	Motion Vector	Syndrome	Hash

FIGURE 18.13:   Bit stream associated with a block.

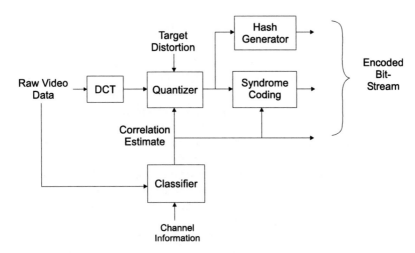

FIGURE 18.14:   Functional block diagram of the encoder.

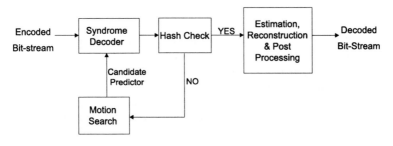

FIGURE 18.15:   Functional block diagram of the decoder.

performance, since there is no need for motion search at the decoder, we do not indicate the hash signature associated with a block. Instead, like conventional video compression standards, we indicate the motion vector information for the current block, as determined by the encoder.

Figure 18.14 summarizes the encoding process through the overall encoder block diagram.

18.7 PRISM: DECODING

The block diagram of the PRISM decoder is shown in Figure 18.15. We note that when the decoder does not have to do a motion search, the encoder sends the motion vector that points to the correct side-information block to use and hence the motion search and CRC check modules in Figure 18.15 are unnecessary. We now describe the main decoder modules.

1. **Generation of Side Information (Motion Search):** The decoder does a motion search to generate candidate predictors, which are tried one by one to decode the sequence of quantized codewords from the set labeled by the received syndrome. In our current implementation, a half-pixel motion search is used to obtain various candidate predictors, as is also done at the encoding side in the standard video algorithms [1,4,10]. We reiterate that the framework is very general so as to accommodate any other sophisticated motion estimation procedures, such as multiframe prediction [18], variable block-sized motion estimation [4], and optical flow [24]. The choice of a more sophisticated algorithm can only serve to enhance the performance of the PRISM paradigm.

2. **Syndrome Decoding:** Each of the candidate predictors generated by the motion search module forms the side-information ($\mathbf{Y}$) for the syndrome decoding step. The syndrome decoding consists of two steps. In the first step, the bits that were entropy coded (the black-colored bit planes in Figure 18.11) are run through an entropy decoder to recover the source bits. If there are no coset channel-coded bit planes (the gray-colored bit plane in Figure 18.11), then the entropy-decoded bits uniquely identify the coset in which the side-information $\mathbf{Y}$ must be decoded. If there is a coset channel-coded bit plane, then the syndrome from the coset channel encoding operation, together with the entropy-decoded bits, specifies the coset in which $\mathbf{Y}$ must be decoded. In the second step, soft decision decoding is performed on the side information, $\mathbf{Y}$, to find the closest codeword within the specified coset. In general, soft decision decoding is computationally intensive for block codes. To reduce the computational burden, we chose to use ordered-statistics decoding [14]. Soft decision decoding based on [14] is near optimal with a loss in performance on the order of 0.2–0.3 dB.

3. **Hash Check:** Since for every candidate predictor, we will decode one codeword sequence from the set of sequences labeled by the syndrome that is nearest to it, the hash signature mechanism is required to infer the codeword sequence intended by the encoder. Thus for every decoded sequence we check if it matches the transmitted hash. If so, then the decoding is declared to be successful. Else using the motion search module, the next candidate predictor is obtained and then the whole procedure is repeated. When correct, the syndrome decoding process recovers the base quantization intervals for the coefficients that are syndrome encoded.

4. **Estimation and Reconstruction:** Once the quantized codeword sequence is recovered, it is used along with the predictor to obtain the best reconstruction of the source. In our current implementation, we use the best mean-squared estimate from the predictor and the quantized codeword

to obtain the source reconstruction. However, any sophisticated signal processing algorithm (e.g., spatiotemporal interpolation) or post processing mechanism can be deployed in this framework, which can only serve to improve the overall performance.

5. **Inverse Transform:** Once all the transform coefficients have been dequantized, the zig-zag scan operation carried out at the encoder is inverted to obtain a two-dimensional block of reconstructed coefficients. The transformed coefficients are then inverted using the inverse transform so as to give reconstructed pixels.

18.8 SIMULATION RESULTS

In this section, we present some preliminary simulation results that illustrate the various features of PRISM. As mentioned earlier, we use the block size 8×8 processing primitives for the motion search, DCT, and entropy coding, same as in the H.263+ codec [10] when used in the advanced prediction mode. Thus for the purpose of a fair comparison, we use the H.263+[10] codec as our reference system.

Compression Performance Tests: For tests on pure compression performance, both PRISM and the reference predictive codec use a full-motion search at the encoder. Figure 18.16 shows a comparison of the compression performance of the PRISM video coding algorithm and H.263+ for the first 15 frames of the Football (352×240, 15 fps) and Stefan (176×144, 15 fps) sequences. As can be seen from Figure 18.16, the performance of the proposed scheme nearly matches that of H.263+. This shows that distributed source coding-based video coding can approach the performance of prediction-based coders when it can estimate the correlation structure accurately through the use of good-motion models.

Robustness tests: For robustness tests, PRISM uses the frame difference-based low-complexity classifier. The objective here is to show that even with a low-complexity encoder PRISM can outperform a predictive codec when there are channel losses.

For these robustness tests we used a wireless channel simulator obtained from Qualcomm Inc. This simulator adds packet errors to multimedia data streams transmitted over wireless networks conforming to the CDMA2000 1X standard [2]. (The packet error rates are determined by computing the carrier to interference ratio of the cellular system.) We tested PRISM, H.263+, H.263+ protected with FEC codes (Reed–Solomon codes used, 20% of total rate used for parity bits), and H.263+ with intra-refresh over this simulated wireless channel. Figure 18.17 shows the performance comparison of these four schemes over

---

[10]Obtained from the University of British Columbia, Vancouver.

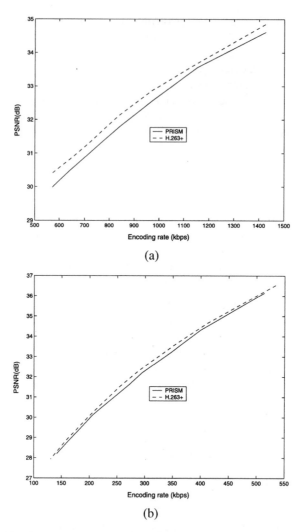

FIGURE 18.16: Lossless channel results: Comparison of proposed Distributed Video Coding (DVC) algorithm and H.263+ for (a) the Football sequence (352 × 240, 15 fps) and (b) the Stefan sequence (176 × 144, 15 fps).

a range of error rates for the Football (352 × 240, 15 fps, 1700 kbps), Stefan (176 × 144, 15 fps, 720 kbps), Football (176 × 128, 15 fps, 160 kbps), and Flower Garden (176 × 128, 15 fps, 700 kbps) sequences. Figure 18.17 clearly demon-

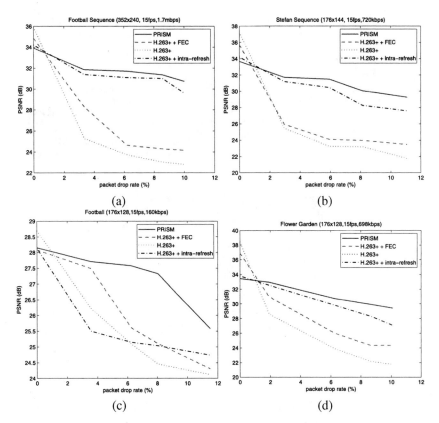

FIGURE 18.17:   Lossy channel results: Comparison of the PRISM Distributed Video Coding algorithm, H.263+, H.263+ protected with Forward Error Correcting (FEC) codes (Reed–Solomon codes used, 20% of total rate used for parity bits), and H.263+ with intra-refresh over a simulated CDMA2000 1X channel for (a) the Football sequence (352 × 240, 15 fps, 1700 kbps), (b) the Stefan sequence (176 × 144, 15 fps, 720 kbps), (c) the Football sequence (176 × 128, 15 fps, 160 kbps), and (d) the Flower Garden sequence (176 × 128, 15 fps, 700 kbps).

strates the superior robustness properties of PRISM. While the decoded quality for the H.263+ system decreases drastically with an increase in packet error rate and saturates at a low value, the decoded quality for PRISM degrades in a graceful fashion.

Figure 18.18 shows the decoded visual quality for the three schemes for the Football (352 × 240, 15 fps, 1700 kbps) sequence at 8% average error rate. As

(H.263+)

(H.263+ with FEC)

(PRISM)

FIGURE 18.18: Decoded visual quality of the 9th frame of the Football sequence (352 × 240, 15 fps, 1700 kbps) encoded using PRISM, H.263+, and H.263+ protected with Forward Error Correcting (FEC) codes (Reed–Solomon codes used, 20% of total rate used for parity bits). In each case 15 frames were encoded and then sent over a simulated CDMA2000 1X channel. Note that there are very noticeable artifacts for both H.263+ and H.263+ protected with FECs while PRISM has been able to recover from past errors.

can be seen in Figure 18.18, PRISM is able to recover from past errors while error propagation continues to occur for both H.263+ and H.263+ protected with FECs.

As mentioned earlier, PRISM does not do any motion search at the encoder and so loses to H.263+ at a 0% loss rate due to inaccurate modeling of the DFD statistics. However, as channel noise increases, the importance of such accurate modeling diminishes (as described in Section 18.5.3) and the robustness advantages of distributed video coding start to dominate, leading to significant performance gains (over even H.263+ protected with FEC and H.263+ with intra-refresh), as highlighted in Figure 18.17.

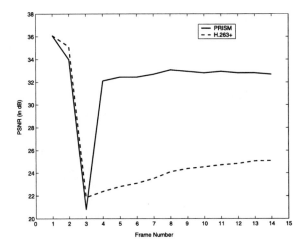

FIGURE 18.19: Effect of frame drops: Comparison of PRISM and H.263+ for the Football sequence (352 × 240, 15 fps, 1700 kbps) when the third frame was dropped.

Figure 18.19 shows the effect on quality when an entire frame is dropped. For this test the two comparison systems were PRISM and H.263+ and the sequence used was Football (352 × 240, 15 fps, 1700 kbps). For both PRISM and H.263+, the third frame was dropped. As can be seen from Figure 18.19, the decoded quality in both cases drops drastically for the third frame. However, while the PRISM system recovers quickly and is still able to deliver high quality for subsequent frames, the H.263+ system can only recover to a small extent. This indicates that PRISM can quickly recover from errors.

18.9 SUMMARY AND FURTHER READING

While the simulation results described earlier fuel optimism about the promise of PRISM for uplink-rich media applications, much work remains before a complete codec system can be endorsed. We envisage a scale of effort similar to what has gone into current commercial standards for video compression to make the concepts of PRISM a reality for practical and ubiquitous deployment. There are numerous promising directions for future research.

- More sophisticated motion models need to be integrated into PRISM.
- More sophisticated channel codes based on turbo codes [7,8] and low-density parity check (LDPC) codes [9,15] need to be integrated into the

PRISM fold while keeping intact the block-level motion modeling philosophy of PRISM.

- The classification phase of the codec in estimating the temporal correlation (innovations) noise variance is critical to the performance of PRISM. We plan to direct our future study toward more robust and sophisticated approaches to classification, keying on the complexity versus performance trade-off benefits. The work of [26] on fast motion search appears to be a promising hunting ground for this.

We would like to point out that we have described the PRISM framework primarily in a point-to-point single-camera single receiver setup. Our proposed paradigm, however, scales naturally to scenarios involving multiple-camera applications that we believe will form the cornerstone of emerging video sensor networks. Section 18.9.1 describes an exciting application of multicamera video sensor networks.

18.9.1 Scene Super-Resolution Through the Network

Imagine a dense configuration of cameras conducting surveillance in the parking lot of your office building. These cameras have overlapping coverage and each of these individual cameras is an inexpensive low-resolution device. For instance, each of these cameras can offer a low frame rate (low temporal resolution). An interesting question that arises here is whether all these low-resolution observations can be synergistically combined, providing a "virtual super-resolution" system that allows for enhanced capabilities ranging from novel spatiotemporal viewpoint generation/rendering with robustness to individual camera failures? This is indeed feasible, as is demonstrated by Figure 18.20, which shows three consecutive video frames from two adjacent cameras: A (middle row) and B (top row). Even though the middle frame in stream A (bordered) is missing (e.g., when A operates at half the frame rate of B), sophisticated processing based on camera motion (between A and B), as well as object-motion modeling, enables a near-perfect reconstruction of the missing scene (bottom row).

Additionally, we can also ask if these correlated data can be efficiently compressed for the purpose of archiving/storage. The increasing relevance of this problem can be gauged from the fact that an industry-wide initiative [5] has been launched in the International Standards Organization MPEG group with the purpose of addressing this question.

The caveat here is that our sophisticated processing/compression algorithms require all the frames to be present at one central location. While this is easy to resolve in the high-bandwidth wired network case, where the individual cameras can communicate their respective streams (uncompressed or marginally compressed) to the central processing location, this can be a real daunting task in the low-bandwidth, harsh transmission environment wireless network case. It is here

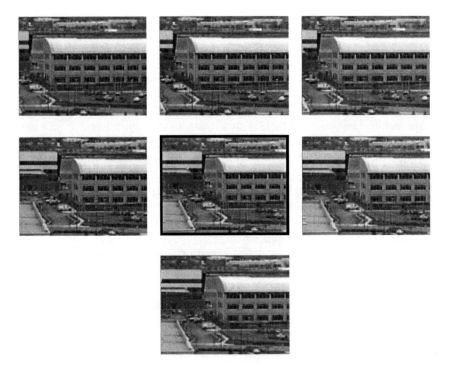

FIGURE 18.20:   Top row: video stream from camera B. Middle row: video stream from camera A, including the missing "original" middle frame (bordered). Bottom row: reconstructed missing middle frame from camera A.

that we can use distributed compression algorithms to reduce our transmission bandwidth, as well as provide natural robustness to the vagaries of the wireless transmission environment.

We realize that this problem requires an interdisciplinary approach leveraging the latest advances in the areas of signal and video processing, computer vision, and wireless networking. However, the fundamental architectural features of PRISM, which include robustness as well as an ability to share computational complexity between different network nodes, offer the necessary building blocks that form the core of the solution for this problem. While this problem remains an ongoing challenge for the video networking community at large at this time, promising preliminary efforts are already under way in the research community. The interested reader is referred to [16,19,43] for an overview of the same.

18.9.2 Conclusions

We have introduced PRISM, a practical video coding framework built on distributed source coding principles. Based on a generalization of the classical Wyner–Ziv setup, PRISM is characterized by an inherent system uncertainty about the "state" of the relevant side information that is known at the decoder. The two main architectural goals of PRISM that make it radically different from existing video codecs are (i) flexible distribution of complexity between encoder and decoder (including the special case of reversal of complexities with the decoder picking up the expensive task of motion search, as has been detailed in this work), and (ii) naturally in-built robustness to drift between encoder and decoder caused by a lack of synchronization due to channel loss (as has been demonstrated successfully through simulations in this work). This renders PRISM as an attractive candidate for wireless video applications.

The fundamental architectural traits of PRISM are also well suited for the multicamera regime. Indeed, as the scale of video sensor networks increases in the future, the architectural benefits of PRISM will be magnified. The full potential of large-scale ubiquitous video sensor networks of the future will require an interdisciplinary approach involving signal and video processing, computer vision, multiterminal information theory, and wireless networking. The work presented here represents an important first step toward this goal.

To conclude, our work represents but a tip of the surface of what we believe is an exciting new direction for video coding for a large class of emerging uplink-rich media applications (including broadband wireless video sensor networks). We are optimistic that our work represents a promising start to this exciting journey.

REFERENCES

[1] Information Technology—Generic Coding of Moving Pictures and Associated Audio Information: Video (MPEG-2), 2nd edition. *ISO/IEC JTC 1/SC 29 13818-2*, 2000.

[2] TIA/EIA Interim Standard for CDMA2000 Spread Spectrum Systems. May 2002.

[3] Information Technology—Coding of Audio-Visual Objects – Part 2: Visual (MPEG-4 Visual). *ISO/IEC JTC 1/SC 29 14496-2*, 2004.

[4] Information Technology—Coding of Audio-visual Objects – Part 10: Advanced Video Coding (H.264). *ISO/IEC JTC 1/SC 29 14496-10*, 2005.

[5] Preliminary call for proposals on multi-view video coding. In *ISO/IEC JTC1/SC29/WG11 N7094*, Busan, Korea, April 2005.

[6] A. Aaron, R. Zhang, and B. Girod. "Wyner-Ziv Coding of Motion Video," *36th Asilomar Conference on Signals, Systems, and Computers*, Pacific Grove, CA, November 2002.

[7] C. Berrou, A. Glavieux, and P. Thitimajshima. "Near Shannon Limit Error-Correcting Coding and Decoding: Turbo-codes (1)," *IEEE International Conference on Communications*, 2:1064–1070, May 1993.

[8] J. Chou, S. S. Pradhan, and K. Ramchandran. "Turbo and Trellis-Based Constructions for Source Coding with Side Information," *Proceedings of Data Compression Conference (DCC)*, Snowbird, UT, March, 2003.

[9] S. Y. Chung, G. D. Forney, T. J. Richardson, and R. Urbanke. "On the Design of Low-Density Parity-Check Codes within 0.0045 dB of the Shannon Limit," *IEEE Communications Letters*, 5:58–60, February 2001.

[10] G. Cote, B. Erol, M. Gallant, and F. Kossentini. "H.263+: Video Coding at Low Bit Rates," *IEEE Transactions on Circuits and Systems for Video Technology*, 8(7):849–866, November 1998.

[11] T. M. Cover and J. A. Thomas. *Elements of Information Theory*, John Wiley and Sons, New York, 1991.

[12] G. D. Forney. "Coset Codes-Part I: Introduction and Geometrical Classification," *IEEE Transactions on Information Theory*, 34(5):1123–1151, September 1988.

[13] G. D. Forney. "Coset Codes-Part II: Binary Lattices and Related Codes," *IEEE Transactions on Information Theory*, 34(5):1152–1187, September 1988.

[14] M. P. C. Fossorier and S. Lin. "Soft Decision Decoding of Linear Block Codes Based on Order Statistics," *IEEE Transactions on Information Theory*, 41(5):1379–1396, September 1995.

[15] R. G. Gallager. "Low Density Parity Check Codes," Ph.D. Thesis, MIT, Cambridge, MA, 1963.

[16] N. Gehrig and P. L. Dragotti. "Different-Distributed and Fully Flexible Image Encoders for Camera Sensor Network," in *International Conference on Image Processing*, Genova, Italy, September 2005.

[17] B. Girod, A. Aaron, S. Rane, and D. Rebollo-Monedero. "Distributed Video Coding," in *Proceedings of IEEE*, January 2005.

[18] B. Girod and T. Wiegand. *Multiframe Motion-Compensated Prediction for Video Transmission*. Kluwer Academic Publishers, 2001.

[19] D. A. Hazen, R. Puri, and K. Ramchandran. "Multi-Camera Video Resolution Enhancement by Fusion of Spatial Disparity and Temporal Motion Fields," in *IEEE International Conference on Computer Vision Systems*, New York City, NY, January 2006.

[20] P. Ishwar, V. M. Prabhakaran, and K. Ramchandran. "Towards a Theory for Video Coding Using Distributed Compression Principles," *Proceedings of IEEE International Conference on Image Processing (ICIP)*, Barcelona, Spain, September 2003.

[21] P. Ishwar, R. Puri, A. Majumdar, and K. Ramchandran. "Analysis of Motion-Complexity and Robustness for Video Transmission," in *Proceedings of WirelessCom*, 2005.

[22] A. Jagmohan, A. Sehgal, and N. Ahuja. "Predictive Encoding Using Coset Codes," *Proceedings of IEEE International Conference on Image Processing (ICIP)*, Rochester, NY, September 2002.

[23] M. Johnson, P. Ishwar, V. Prabhakaran, D. Schonberg, and K. Ramchandran. "On Compressing Encrypted Data," *IEEE Transactions on Signal Processing*, 52:2992–3006, October 2004.

[24] R. Krishnamurthy, J. M. Woods, and P. Moulin. "Frame Interpolation and Bidirectional Prediction of Video Using Compactly-Encoded Optical Flow Fields and Label Fields," *IEEE Transactions on Circuits and Systems for Video Technology*, 9(5):713–726, August 1999.

[25] G. G. Langdon, Jr. "An Introduction to Arithmetic Coding," *IBM Journal of Research and Development*, 28(2):135–149, March 1984.

[26] K. Lengwehasatit and A. Ortega. "Probabilistic Partial Distance Fast Matching for Motion Estimation," *IEEE Transactions on Circuits and Systems for Video Technology*, 11(2):139–152, February 2001.

[27] F. J. Macwilliams and N. J. A. Sloane. *The Theory of Error Correcting Codes*, Elseiver-North-Holland, 1977.

[28] A. Majumdar. "PRISM: A Video Coding Paradigm Based on Source Coding with Side Information," Ph.D. Thesis, Department of Electrical Engineering and Computer Sciences, University of California, Berkeley, December 2005.

[29] A. Majumdar, J. Wang, K. Ramchandran, and H. Garudadri. "Drift Reduction in Predictive Video Transmission Using a Distributed Source Coded Side-Channel," *Proceedings of ACM Multimedia*, New York, NY, September 2004.

[30] S. S. Pradhan, J. Chou, and K. Ramchandran. "Duality between Source Coding and Channel Coding and Its Extension to the Side Information Case," *International Transactions on Information Theory*, 49(5):1181–2003, July 2003.

[31] S. S. Pradhan and K. Ramchandran. "Distributed Source Coding Using Syndromes (DISCUS): Design and Construction," *Proceedings of Data Compression Conference (DCC)*, Snowbird, UT, March 1999.

[32] R. Puri and K. Ramchandran. "PRISM: A New Robust Video Coding Architecture Based on Distributed Compression Principles," *40th Allerton Conference on Communication, Control and Computing*, Allerton, IL, October 2002.

[33] R. Puri and K. Ramchandran. "PRISM: A 'Reversed' Multimedia Coding Paradigm," *IEEE International Conference on Image Processing*, Barcelona, Spain, September 2003.

[34] R. Puri and K. Ramchandran. "PRISM: An Uplink-Friendly Multimedia Coding Paradigm," *IEEE International Conference on Acoustics, Speech and Signal Processing (ICASSP)*, Hong Kong, April 2003.

[35] W. Rabiner and A. P. Chandrakasan. "Network-Driven Motion Estimation for Wireless Video Terminals," *IEEE Transactions on Circuits and Systems for Video Technology*, 7(4):644–653, August 1997.

[36] A. Sehgal, A. Jagmohan, and N. Ahuja. "Scalable Video Coding Using Wyner–Ziv Codes," *Proceedings of Picture Coding Symposium (PCS)*, San Francisco, CA, December 2004.

[37] A. Sehgal, A. Jagmohan, and N. Ahuja. "Wyner-Ziv Coding of Video: An Error-Resilient Compression Framework," *IEEE Transactions on Multimedia*, 6(2): 249–258, April 2004.

[38] D. Slepian and J. K. Wolf. "Noiseless Coding of Correlated Information Sources," *IEEE Transactions on Information Theory*, 19: 471–480, July 1973.

[39] H. S. Witsenhausen and A. D. Wyner. Interframe coder for video signals. *United States Patent* (4191970), March 1980.

[40] A. D. Wyner and J. Ziv. "The Rate-Distortion Function for Source Coding with Side Information at the Decoder," *IEEE Transactions on Information Theory*, 22(1): 1–10, January 1976.

[41] Q. Xu, V. Stankovic, and Z. Xiong. "Layered Wyner–Ziv Video Coding with IRA Codes for Noisy Channel," in *Proceedings of Visual Communications and Image Processing*, Beijing, China, July 2005.

[42] R. Zamir. "The Rate Loss in the Wyner–Ziv Problem," *IEEE Transactions on Information Theory*, 42(6):2073–2084, November 1996.

[43] X. Zhu, A. Aaron, and B. Girod. "Distributed Compression for Large Camera Arrays," in *IEEE Workshop on Statistical Signal Processing*, St. Louis, Missouri, September 2003.

19

Infrastructure-Based Streaming Media Overlay Networks

Susie Wee, Wai-Tian Tan, and John Apostolopoulos

19.1 INTRODUCTION

Technology advances are giving people increasingly immersive multimedia experiences in their home entertainment systems, on their portable media players, on their desktop and laptop computers, and even on their mobile phones. While IP networks provide unprecedented connectivity between people and devices for data applications, even today, large fractions of the network are not suitable for the high bandwidths and real-time streaming requirements of multimedia applications. For example, the Internet provides connectivity between any two end nodes on the Internet; however, it only provides best-effort service and therefore provides no guarantees on the available bandwidth, maximum delay or delay jitter, or loss rates. Thus, there remains a challenge for providing high-quality media between people and devices over large portions of the network, and these problems are amplified as the number of people trying to use the network increases.

In this chapter, we describe the basic concepts and architecture of a media overlay, which adds resources to an existing network infrastructure to enhance the media capability of the network. A media overlay can enable new media capabilities in the network, while improving the end-user media performance and the system-wide efficiency of the network for both its media and nonmedia traffic. This is achieved by leveraging the underlying resources and existing connectivity provided by the original network, while enhancing it to improve its ability to deliver real-time media to end users and scaling to support a large number of users.

The term "overlay" refers to the approach of adding resources on top of an existing network infrastructure, as shown in Figure 19.1. This has the advantage

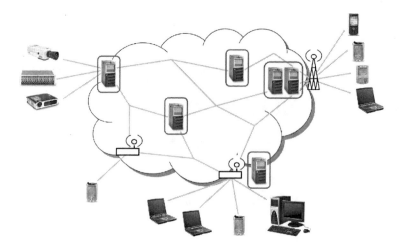

FIGURE 19.1:   Media overlays add resources to an existing network to enable new media capabilities and to improve end-user media performance, scaling to support large numbers of users, and system-wide efficiency.

of leveraging the attributes of the existing infrastructure, such as its existing deployment, widespread connectivity, and built-in network services such as domain name services (DNS) and system management. While the existing network has some inherent capabilities, the overlay provides additional capabilities to achieve an extended set of goals, such as enhancing the media capabilities of a network, improving the operational efficiency and system-wide performance of the network itself, and improving the user-perceived performance of media applications.

  The benefit of an overlay can be illustrated with a simple example. Consider a corporation that wants to stream corporate webcasts to their employees over their existing corporate intranet. In most cases, the existing intranet will not have the capacity to support a centralized streaming service for all their employees, where a single server would stream a separate unicast stream for each employee. In this case, a media overlay can provide distributed caching to replicate the webcast content at overlay nodes close to large employee sites. The employee requests would then be served by streaming the replica on the nearest overlay node rather than from the centralized server. In this example, the media overlay allowed the webcast application to be provided on an existing corporate intranet using the overlay capabilities of media caching and streaming, and it was performed in a manner that significantly reduced the network load on the corporate intranet.

19.1.1 Comparing Client–Server, Overlay, and Peer-to-Peer Models

To better understand media overlays, it is helpful to consider the traditional capabilities provided by current networks and the relative contributions of a media overlay to its alternatives. In this chapter we focus on infrastructure-based overlay systems. Some peer-to-peer systems can be considered as client-based overlays [11], but to simplify terminology we use the term overlay to refer to infrastructure-based overlays.

A challenge to all successful networks is the possibility of having usage demand outgrow the original capacity or design. In order to maintain or improve the performance of existing services or to provide new services, enhancement mechanisms need to be added in a fashion transparent to existing clients, without prolonged disruption to the services. One example of such evolution includes Intelligent Networks (IN) in telecommunications networks, which provide functions such as three-way calling and call waiting for a network originally designed for point-to-point voice communications. Another example is Content Distribution Networks (CDN) for the Internet, which provide reduced access latency for end users and improves scalability to a larger number of users by having multiple caches near the end users [20]. With an ever-increasing growth of multimedia access, especially for video, in both cellular networks and the Internet, it is becoming important to examine mechanisms to provide improved performance and added features for multimedia communications. In this chapter, similar to what INs have done for telephone networks and CDNs for the Internet, our focus will be on improvement in the existing delivery infrastructure itself, rather than developing a completely new infrastructure or assuming a peer-to-peer architecture.

The traditional approach to supporting streaming media and Web traffic alike is to use the Client–Server model of Figure 19.2a where a single server is in charge of serving all clients. As the client population grows, this model hits two limitations. First, a single server cannot scale to serve an ever-increasing number of clients. This problem is sometimes solved by implementing a logical server by multiple physical servers. Second, since a server cannot be simultaneously close to all clients, access latency for some clients is bound to be long. The use of an overlay infrastructure, as shown in Figure 19.2b, is one possible solution to the limitations of the client–server approach. An overlay network is a logical network that relies on a physical network for connectivity service. Specifically, in Figure 19.2b, having nodes A and B inside the infrastructure allows content to be served from multiple possible servers, and specifically for each requesting client we can choose the "closest" server to serve the content. A key point is that an overlay infrastructure is designed based on the underlying network, as well as expected client demands and desired services. An important example of commercially deployed overlay infrastructure are CDNs for Web traffic. So far, we have only discussed the use of an overlay infrastructure for caching purposes.

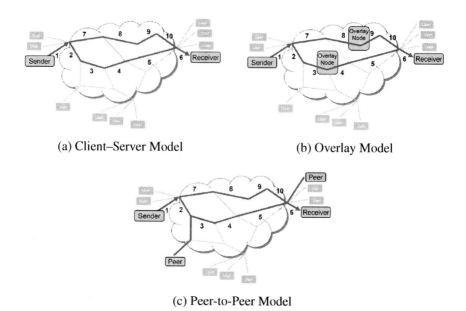

(a) Client–Server Model   (b) Overlay Model

(c) Peer-to-Peer Model

FIGURE 19.2:   (a) The classical Client–Server Model assumes only basic connectivity service from the network. (b) The Overlay Model uses the
same connectivity service, but also has overlay nodes inside the infrastructure to provide computation and storage inside the infrastructure. (c) The
Peer-to-Peer Model, however, relies on peer nodes outside the infrastructure to provide storage and computation.

Other benefits include the possibility of performing additional services and the
provisioning of multiple paths. For example, the minimum-hop path between the
client and the server in Figure 19.2 traverses links 1, 2, 3, 4, 5, and 6 and involves
a bottleneck link 3. Using an overlay infrastructure for relaying, it is possible to
effectively use another path 1, 7, 8, 9, 10, 6 even when the physical network does
not offer routing choices.

   Another approach used to overcome the limitations of the client–server model
is the peer-to-peer model (P2P) of Figure 19.2c. Common for file-swapping applications in which a large number of clients want to receive the same piece of content, the P2P architecture allows every client to access the already-downloaded
portions of other clients. In return, every client would make available the portion
of content it has downloaded. A P2P network is therefore self-scaling in the sense
that the number of requesting nodes and potential serving nodes is equal. Therefore, P2P architectures have the advantage of supporting potentially very large
active client populations. In addition, for popular content it is possible for a client

Table 19.1: Comparison among client–server, overlay infrastructure, and peer-to-peer systems for three different classes of metrics.

	Metric	Client–server	Overlay	Peer-to-peer
User-centric performance	Availability	Bad	Good	Good–poor
	Latency	Bad	Good	Good–poor
	Streaming quality	Bad	Good	Average
	File transfer quality	Bad	Good	Best
System-wide efficiency	Low control overhead	Best	Good	Poor
	Bandwidth usage	Bad	Good	Good
	Control/manageability	Good	Good	Bad
Service extensibility	Ease to add services and capabilities	Good	Good	Poor

to download from a closer location under P2P than is possible under infrastructure overlay. In P2P systems the peers view network and infrastructure as a black box providing connectivity, and the P2P intelligence resides at the end hosts. One major disadvantage of P2P is the lack of control of *peers* in terms of population size, availability, and actions, making it difficult to provide predictable quality of service. For example, P2P networks are typically afflicted by sizable churn where the peers may come and go. Another disadvantage is the large amount of control traffic necessary in a typical implementation to maintain the distribution structure. Furthermore, fairness is a difficult problem in P2P systems. An overview of when P2P systems or infrastructure solutions are preferred based on desired application attributes is given in [31].

In this chapter, we focus on infrastructure-based overlay networks that are designed and deployed with the underlying network resources in mind [18]. A simplistic overlay network can be constructed, for example, by using the system shown in Figure 19.2c, where content distribution is performed in a way that the server streams to P, which in turns relays to P'. In this case, P is a new physical resource that enables an overlay relaying service to P', but is impractical due to the lack of resource planning.

In Table 19.1, we compare the relative merits of the client–server model, the overlay model, and the P2P model in the following three classes of metrics. The first class is user centric and involves access latency and availability for a single user. The second class relates to system-wide performance. The third class focuses on the ability to introduce new services. We see that the overlay infrastructure provides a useful balance among the three classes of objectives.

19.1.2 Overview of a Streaming Media Overlay

A streaming media overlay is designed to provide a number of basic capabilities, such as media streaming, caching, content distribution, resource monitoring, resource management, and signaling. These capabilities are discussed in Section 19.2. An overlay may also have advanced capabilities that can perform session management of streaming media sessions, request redirection, load balancing, caching, and relaying media streams. Furthermore, an overlay can perform media processing operations such as transcoding to adapt media streams for different display sizes and network capacities, perform logo insertion to personalize media streams for individuals or locations, or voice/video activity detection to enable applications such as multiuser conferencing, which is discussed in Sections 19.2 and 19.5. These capabilities can be upgraded over time to provide new media services.

Existing network infrastructure can be viewed as a number of layers, as shown in Figure 19.3. At the base level, there is a base-wired/wireless IP network that, for example, could be a telecom network, an enterprise, the open Internet, a hot spot network, or a home network. Any of these networks may have a series of elementary network services in them. For example, a telecom network may have a home location registry that tracks client movements. The next layer may contain a number of overlay network subsystems. The media overlay and media service network reside at this layer. Finally, a system and network management layer may exist to monitor and manage the entire network and systems.

Since the overlay becomes an integral part of the infrastructure, it is important that it respects the existing network applications and perhaps even improves them. Thus, manageability is critical to an overlay's success. Thus, the overlay nodes perform a valuable distributed network monitoring function to make network and system measurements based on their observations of network and system load

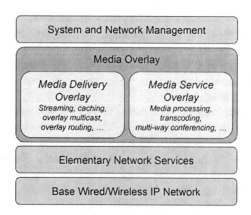

FIGURE 19.3:   A media overlay is an integrated part of an extended system architecture. It exploits the base network and elementary network services for data delivery, but may itself be managed by other entities.

and client requests. These measurements can be aggregated and analyzed to make decisions on how to handle media streams in the overlay. For example, it may decide to cache popular content at overlay nodes closer to end users, reroute streams to avoid congestion points, or transcode media streams to adapt them for lower bandwidth links.

The overlay can be architected in a manner that provides the benefits of incremental deployment and upgradeability. Thus, a small overlay deployment can be used to provide an initial media service or application. Then, more resources can be deployed over time based on the measured usage of the application. Furthermore, the capabilities of the overlay can be upgraded to provide new services or new capabilities. This can be done by adding additional overlay resources or upgrading the existing resources with new capabilities.

19.1.3 Chapter Outline

This chapter continues in Section 19.2 by examining the basic capabilities that may be provided by a streaming media infrastructure, including an example to illustrate the use of these capabilities. The architectural and design considerations that arise when designing and operating this infrastructure are discussed in Section 19.3. More advanced functions that may be provided by a streaming media infrastructure are then discussed in Section 19.4. The benefits of such streaming media overlays are discussed in Section 19.5. The chapter concludes by providing a summary and pointers for further reading in Section 19.6.

19.2 CAPABILITIES OF A STREAMING MEDIA OVERLAY

A streaming media overlay infrastructure can enable large-scale media delivery on an existing network infrastructure. A media overlay can improve the performance of a media delivery system in a number of ways. For example, if a requested media stream is cached on the overlay, the request can be served from the overlay, thereby reducing the latency of the streaming session. Also, since the overlay server can be colocated at the network edge, it can quickly adapt the streaming session to the rapid variations of the last link; for example, it can be colocated at a wireless base station to adapt to a rapidly varying wireless channel. In addition, since overlay servers are located at intermediate locations in the network, they can act as monitoring points in the network and provide system and network load information that can be used to improve the performance of the overall system.

19.2.1 Media Overlay Server Capabilities

A media overlay adds resources on top of an existing network to enhance its media capabilities. These added resources can include overlay servers and managers that can be placed in the middle and at the edge of the network, as shown in Figure 19.4. Overlay servers are the basic building block of a media overlay, and they can have capabilities of streaming, caching and content distribution, resource monitoring and management, signaling, and possibly media processing [26]. They can be used to store or cache media streams in the network and to relay media streams across the network. Furthermore, overlay servers can monitor and log the conditions of their surroundings and gather valuable network health information.

The overlay server's basic *streaming* capabilities allow it to send and receive media streams to and from streaming servers and clients. The overlay server is capable of handling many simultaneous input and output streams; it uses a scheduler to coordinate the streaming of these sessions. Furthermore, the overlay server is able to start, stop, and pause its outgoing streaming media sessions and record its incoming streaming media sessions. Handoff capabilities during streaming sessions can also be an important capability for streaming media overlay servers, in particular because of the long-lived nature of streaming media sessions.

The overlay server has *caching* capabilities that allow it to store requested media content for future requests. An overlay server can obtain media data to be cached via data transfer or streaming modes. The resulting cached media streams can then be transmitted as data transfers or streaming sessions as well.

Media content can also be distributed across the overlay infrastructure using the overlay's *content distribution* capabilities. This allows the overlay servers to transfer media streams to other overlay servers, web servers, and media servers. Cached media content can be possibly locked for a specified period of time to prevent premature eviction.

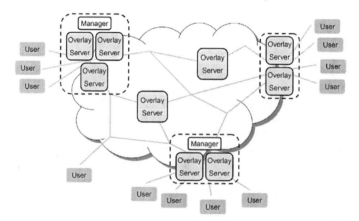

FIGURE 19.4: Overlay resources are placed at strategic locations in a network. Each location may contain one or more overlay servers and/or managers.

The overlay server has *resource monitoring and management* capabilities that allow it to monitor and log its observations over time and to share these logs with other overlay servers and managers through the control/management interface. Overlay servers can track user requests as well as server load and observed network conditions over time. These logs can be gathered and analyzed to improve the performance of the media overlay.

Overlay servers have *coordination* capabilities that allow them to query or track the contents of other overlay servers for requests that are not in its cache. It can have parent/child or sibling relationships with other overlay servers, which can be set or changed through the management and control interface.

These capabilities are discussed in more detail in the following sections.

19.2.2 Media Transport and Streaming

Media overlay servers must be able to transport media to and from sources, other overlay servers, and clients. Media transport can be performed in different ways depending on the needs of the application and the capabilities of the origin servers and clients.

Sending media to clients: A media overlay must be able to deliver media to clients using protocols that the clients understand. Download media clients receive media streams in a file or data transfer mode using protocols such as TCP/IP or HTTP. These clients download the entire media file and store them on a local disk and then allow a user to play the locally stored media content at any time after the download. Streaming media clients receive packetized media content in a streaming mode using protocols such as UDP or RTP streaming or HTTP streaming. These clients store the received media packets in a receiver buffer and then decode and play back these media packets after a short delay. Note that when protocols such as UDP or RTP are used, it is possible that some packets will be lost before reaching the client. In this case, it is important that the media client has error-resilience capabilities to be able to deal with lost packets effectively [40]. Further discussion on error-resilience can be found in Chapters 2 and 3.

Receiving media from media sources: A media overlay must be able to receive media from various media sources that are not part of the media overlay using protocols that the media sources understand. Media sources such as web servers and content servers and media upload clients often use file and data transfer protocols such as TCP/IP, HTTP, or even FTP for reliable media transport. Media sources also include streaming servers and live media recorders that use streaming protocols such as UDP or RTP streaming and HTTP streaming. Note that if UDP or RTP streaming is used and an overlay server wants to cache or store the stream, then it is possible that some media packets will be lost and the stored media content will have some errors. In this case, the overlay server needs to know how to handle these streams by only transferring these streams to clients with error-resilience capabilities or by repairing the stream into a recognizable media stream format before sending the media content to clients that do not have error-resilience capabilities.

Media transport between overlay servers: In addition to delivering media to and from media clients and sources, media overlay servers can also transport streams with each other. This can be done in data or file transport modes to perform operations such as content distribution, prefetching, and caching. This can also be done using streaming connections to perform operations such as stream redirection, stream relay, and stream splitting.

Stream relay: Overlay servers that can send and receive media streams through streaming connections allow the overlay to perform stream relay tasks. Stream relay can be used to explicitly route or redirect streams in the network, for example, to avoid network bottlenecks that are detected by the overlay. Routing streams through overlay servers can improve operational efficiency of the network by exploiting routes with underutilized resources, while allowing health monitoring of the network or media stream by detecting packet loss or performing bandwidth and latency measurements using the media packets.

Note that the overlay can be designed so that it is transparent as to whether the media is going to or coming from a media source, another overlay server, or a media client. This design allows media streams to be relayed through any number of overlay servers, allowing for various degrees of precision in stream routing and network health monitoring.

Stream splitting: A key problem in networked multimedia is supporting popular events with many users and supporting one-to-many communication [17]. While IP Multicast is a possible solution to this problem, difficulties arise when media streams must traverse networks that do not have IP Multicast support. In these cases, stream splitting, also referred to as overlay or application-level multicast, can be used to increase the scalability of the system and improve network efficiency.

Stream splitting is also useful if a sending device is capable of serving only one stream but many clients are interested in receiving that stream. In that case, the original stream can be sent to an overlay server, which can relay it to multiple downstream devices, as shown in Figure 19.5. This is called stream splitting, overlay multicast, or application-layer multicast. Stream splitting has the advantage that it can be used to provide multicast-like capabilities on networks that do not have native IP multicast support.

19.2.3 Media Distribution and Caching

Media distribution across overlay infrastructure: Placing media content on an overlay server close to a requesting client can lead to the media being streamed over a shorter network path, thus reducing the start-up latency of a streaming ses-

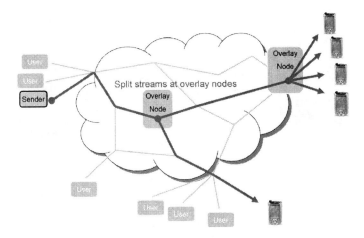

FIGURE 19.5: Stream relay and stream multicast capabilities allow overlay nodes to form flexible media distribution paths, as illustrated here in the form of a multicast tree. Other benefits include the ability to route or redirect media streams around failed links, perform network health monitoring operations by analyzing the media packets, and efficiently deliver media streams to many users.

sion, the probability of packet loss, and the total network usage. This motivates the need for media distribution algorithms that optimize system performance based on the predicted demand. These optimizations can be performed by aggregating measured statistics and developing predictive prefetching algorithms based on statistical analysis. Specifically, the prediction can be based on the content request patterns monitored, logged, and reported by the overlay servers through control and management interfaces. Therefore, important issues relate to the number of caching nodes, their placement in the network based on traffic demands, the predistribution of media content across the caching infrastructure, and the dynamic cache allocation within a single node as described next [27].

Media caching: Closely related is the problem of media caching on the overlay servers. The goal of improving the cache hit rate makes it desirable to store large numbers of media streams on the overlay servers. However, since media streams can require large amounts of storage, storing entire media streams in a cache is clearly inefficient. Thus, the media caching problem involves determining which media streams [23] to cache. These decisions can be based on a number of factors, such as media popularity, size, cacheability, and other factors such as premium content versus free content. Media distribution and caching are critical

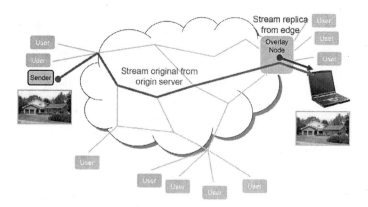

FIGURE 19.6:   A media overlay improves network efficiency by allowing a cached replica of the media to be streamed from the edge rather than from the origin.

components of a streaming media infrastructure as they can lead to considerable improvements in resource utilization and system reliability (Figure 19.6).

Media segmentation: Another interesting overlay capability is media segmentation, where a long media stream is divided into media segments that can then be distributed across the network and cached in various overlay servers [8,34]. These segments can be cached in a manner that is aligned with user-viewing statistics. For example, an overlay may stream a live sporting event to many users. At the same time, it may record and store the stream for users who wish to view the event at a later time. However, it may turn out that the most viewed segments of a sporting event are where the goals and highlights occur. The overlay can track this behavior and then cache the various segments according to the user-viewing statistics. For example, the most watched highlight segments can be replicated more frequently than the less viewed segments.

19.2.4 Client Request Handling

There are a number of ways a client can gain access to the services in a media overlay. In the simplest model, a client directly accesses a service portal that is part of the media overlay. Examples discussed in further details later include recording and retrieval of multimedia messages. Alternatively, if a client is attempting to access portals outside the overlay, additional mechanisms are necessary in order to invoke overlay services. If a request always traverses the overlay network, explicit detection and redirection are possible. Otherwise, common techniques include explicit proxy configuration at the clients or DNS-based redirection [5].

After a request reaches a portal in an overlay node, the client needs to be redirected to a server with appropriate capability to satisfy the request. This requires determining which is the "best" overlay server for serving the client, where best is determined by a number of metrics, including which server(s) has the desired content, as well as the server and network loads and capabilities such as transcoding. To evaluate the suitability of each server requires a system monitoring and management component for gathering and processing this information in a timely manner. An example of an architecture designed for monitoring the server and network load of overlay servers and assigning requests to the least-loaded, available edge server is given in [32]. Once the best server is determined the client redirection to that server can be achieved through a number of mechanisms, such as techniques based on DNS [5]. Alternatively, redirection to an appropriate server can happen through mechanisms such as dynamic SMIL rewriting [46].

19.2.5 System Monitoring and Management

System monitoring: Monitoring is an important capability in an overlay network. As mentioned before, statistics such as server and network load allow selection of appropriate servers for satisfying a particular request. Generally, monitoring enables other adaptation on a finer or coarser timescale. For example, real-time network and server statistics can guide short timescale adaptations such as transcoding or other media adaptation, and server handoffs. Longer timescale statistics, however, facilitate resource planning, such as reservation of resources for "flash crowds."

The application awareness of a media overlay allows collection of semantically meaningful statistics, such as the response time of a request to retrieve a stored multimedia message. Furthermore, the location of overlay nodes inside the infrastructure and its application awareness allow collection of better statistics than is possible between end points only. For example, in a traditional client–server streaming setting, a server has limited visibility for the state of the network since it can only observe aggregate conditions along the entire path, and only from traffic originating from itself. An overlay node, however, can observe statistics for a segment shorter than the end-to-end path, and it can observe flows from all servers traversing through it. By observing the network statistics on shorter network path segments, the overlay can achieve improved streaming performance by providing functions such as network-adaptive streaming, as discussed in Section 19.4.1. Furthermore, an overlay can collect certain useful statistics that are not possible without application awareness. For example, an overlay node can differentiate adaptive UDP flows from nonadaptive UDP flows, which are generally difficult to differentiate [14].

System management: Management is another important feature of a media overlay. While monitoring allows the overlay to gather system statistics, management allows the overlay to analyze the gathered data and assert control on various parts of the overlay and system as a whole. Management capabilities allow managers and overlay servers to query other media overlay components for their monitored information, such as content usage statistics, server load, and network congestion, and to give commands to other media overlay components. This allows the overlay servers to cooperate and act as a system to collect and analyze statistics, predict behaviors from these statistics, and perform tasks to serve predicted user requests in a resource-efficient manner. Furthermore, this allows the overlay servers to work cooperatively to handle the media delivery load in response to changing user patterns and time-varying network and system loads.

An overlay's control and management capabilities also allow the media overlay to receive information from other layers of the network, as shown in Figure 19.3. For example, the control interface can allow a home location registry to pass client mobility information to the overlay server to trigger a streaming server handoff. Furthermore, it allows the overlay to perform operational roles, such as adding or reconfiguring overlay servers and shutting them down for maintenance.

19.2.6 Media Processing Services

Up to this point, this chapter has discussed how an overlay can be used for delivering media streams across a network. In this section, we discuss another important capability that the overlay can provide, namely performing media processing operations on the media streams that are transported by the overlay. We refer to networked media processing operations performed by overlay servers as *media processing services* or, more simply, *media services* provided by the overlay.

Media processing: An overlay server may be able to perform a media service such as media transcoding to adapt media streams for diverse client capabilities and changing network conditions [6,19,36,43]. For example, Figure 19.7 shows a high-resolution, high-bandwidth media stream being simultaneously delivered to two clients with different display capabilities and network connections. The first client may be able to receive and decode the entire high-resolution, high-bandwidth media stream. However, a second client with a lower display resolution and slower network connection may not be able to receive and decode the entire stream. In this case, the overlay can transcode the media stream to a lower resolution and bit rate and then relay the transcoded stream to the low-resolution client.

Other media processing services that an overlay can provide include video and audio processing operations such as VCR functionalities, speed-up/slow-down, logo insertion, background removal, and noise reduction. Overlays can also provide conferencing services such as video tiling, speaker detection, and speaker focus.

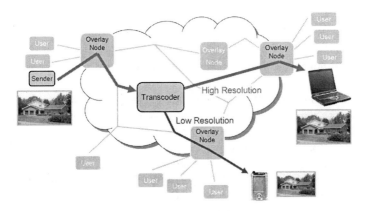

FIGURE 19.7: Performing live transcoding inside an overlay simplifies requirements on both clients and senders. To support the multicast application shown, the clients and senders need only support one stream and do not need the resource or algorithm to perform transcoding.

For mobile multimedia applications, it may be useful for overlay servers to be able to perform midstream handoffs of streaming sessions to adapt to user movements across cell sites. If a transcoding service is provided in a mobile overlay network, it may also be useful for overlay servers to be able to perform midstream handoffs of live transcoding sessions [33].

Notice that when an overlay performs media processing services in the middle of the network, it often operates on input compressed media streams and produces output compressed media streams. Some of these processing operations can be compute-intensive. Since an overlay server may need to process many media streams at once, it is useful to develop computationally efficient algorithms for processing compressed streams [44]. This is a research area that has been examined for many years, and technology advances are now allowing these media processing services to be performed in real time.

Media services architecture: In addition to being able to perform media processing operations, the overlay must be able to manage the media services. Thus, it is important to have a *media services architecture* that allows the media services to be deployed, operated, and managed in the overlay [16] in a manner that works smoothly with the media delivery capabilities of the overlay. This requires the overlay to be able to deploy new media service capabilities on existing overlay servers, track which servers have which media service capabilities, and redirect media streams to the appropriate overlay servers for a streaming session. In addition, the overlay should be able to track the load of the various overlay servers to ensure that a chosen server is capable of handling the additional stream-ing task.

19.2.7 Example Walk-Through of Media Overlay Usage

Figure 19.8 shows an illustration of one possible way in which different functions discussed in Sections 19.2.3 to 19.2.5 can act together. Other choices are possible and are discussed further in Section 19.3.

In Figure 19.8, two events happen before a client can access a piece of con-tent from a media overlay. First, information such as availability of contents and server load are continuously collected, as shown by step 0 in Figure 19.8. In Fig-ure 19.8, the information is collected centrally by a *Location Manager*. Such ex-changes can be conveniently implemented using standardized protocols such as the Simple Object Access Protocol, and possibly *digests* [30] of server contents are exchanged to reduce communication cost. Second is the media distribution described in Section 19.2.3, which is indicated by step 1 in Figure 19.8. In our example, media is predelivered to one or more servers before the first request ar-rives; however, it is also possible to perform delivery following the initial request. The preferred mode of operation depends on the prediction or measurement of the content's demand, as well as the relative demand for other content, which may be

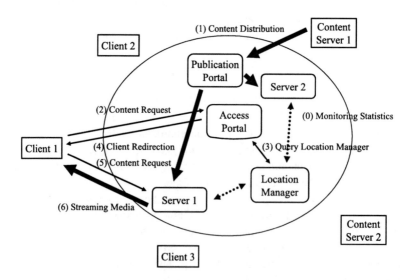

FIGURE 19.8: Various parts of a media overlay, shown in rounded boxes and enclosed, function together to allow access of media content from *Content Server 1* to *Client 1*.

cached in the same servers, etc. One possible implementation of media transport for step 1 is HTTP, which is widely used for data transport.

When a client wishes to retrieve a content, it would contact an *Access Portal* using common mechanisms such as the Real-Time Streaming Protocol (RTSP) or Synchronized Multimedia Integration Language (SMIL). Further details on some common streaming protocols can be found in Chapter 15. In the case of RTSP, step 2 of Figure 19.8 may be an RTSP SETUP message, upon receiving which the *Access Portal* would consult the *Location Manager* in step 3 for the name of an appropriate server. The requesting client can be redirected to the appropriate server through the use of an RTSP REDIRECT message, although it can be more convenient to simply return an error of "moved temporarily" to *Server 1* in response to the SETUP message. This would instruct the client to contact the intended server in step 5 using another RTSP SETUP message, which eventually leads to streaming of media in step 6, possibly using RTP transport.

When using the SMIL-based approach, described in further detail in [46], the request in step 2 may assume the form of an HTTP GET message to retrieve an SMIL file. After consulting with the *Location Manager* in step 3, the *Access Portal* would dynamically rewrite the content of the SMIL to use the intended server. Step 4 then becomes the HTTP transport of the (rewritten) SMIL file, which contains instructions on how to access and compose the media content. In particular, it may contain instruction to access the desired content using RTSP to *Server 1*. An RTSP SETUP message would then be generated in step 5, which results in media streaming in step 6. In both the RTSP and SMIL examples, the client is not aware of the complex operations between the overlay entities and assumes the simple client–server model.

Figure 19.9 shows a possible implementation of messages in steps 2 and 4 of Figure 19.8 when RTSP is used by the client. Note that the *Location Manager* determines that the desired server is *Server 1* and specifies the redirected location for the content in the response to the RTSP SETUP message. Example content of an SMIL file for client redirection is given in Figure 19.10. Note that the address of the desired server, *Server 1*, is specified in the body of the file. As a reminder,

```
SETUP rtsp://Access-Portal:554/content.3gp RTSP/1.0
CSeq: 2
Transport: RTP/AVP;unicast;client_port=8322-8323

RTSP/1.0 302 Moved Temporarily
CSeq: 2
Location: rtsp://Server_1:554/content.3gp
```

FIGURE 19.9:   Example content of messages in steps 2 (top) and 4 (bottom) of Figure 19.8 when client makes an RTSP request.

```
<smil xmlns="http://www.w3.org/2001/SMIL20/Language">
    ...
    <body>
        <audio src="rtsp://Server_1:554/content.3gp/Track1"/ >
        <video src="rtsp://Server_1:554/content.3gp/Track2"/ >
    </body>
</smil>
```

FIGURE 19.10:   Example content of an SMIL file for client redirection.

the SMIL file may be rewritten for each client's request based on network and server load.

So far, our media overlay example illustrates how a client can be redirected to a desired server to obtain the *same* piece of content. A media overlay can perform media processing functions as well. For instance, through various client capability exchanges, a streaming server may determine that it is necessary to transcode a content to a reduced frame size for proper display on a client. Clearly, other content transformations are possible, and further discussion about incorporation of media processing functions is given in Section 19.2.6.

19.3 ARCHITECTURE AND DESIGN PRINCIPLES

Media overlays must have a very modular and robust design and architecture to meet the demands of large-scale, streaming media delivery. This section describes the architecture and design principles of an infrastructure-based media overlay network.

19.3.1 Modular Media Overlay Design

A modular design allows a media overlay to be scaled over time in a manner that adapts to user demand and network and system load. For example, as seen in Figure 19.11, an initial deployment of a media overlay network can include a number of overlay servers at a couple of network nodes in different locations in the network. As the number of users increases, additional overlay servers can be added in those locations to satisfy the user demand. As the number of users further increases, the network resource usage may become prohibitive. At this stage, a new overlay server location can be added to improve the network efficiency. A well-architected media overlay with a modular design can allow for this type of scalability over time.

The philosophy of the overlay is that if even just one overlay server is deployed, it should work *independently* to improve the media delivery performance of the system, and if more and more overlay servers are deployed they should work

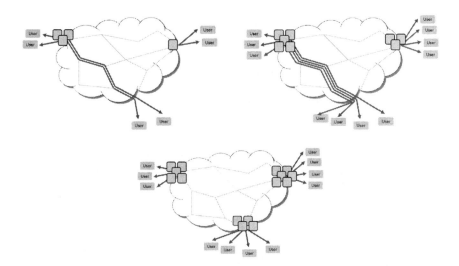

FIGURE 19.11: Media overlays should be designed and architected in a manner that allows them to be scaled to adapt to user demand and system and network load over time. An initial deployment (upper left) can add basic media capabilities to the network. As usage increases, additional resources can be deployed to satisfy the increased user demand (upper right) and improve resource efficiency (bottom).

cooperatively so that their combined performance is greater than the sum performance of the individual components. Also, overlay servers should have *peering* capabilities so that they can be grouped with other overlay servers.

The media overlay architecture should allow for the *incremental deployment* of overlay servers. Since the peering relationships can be controlled, the process of adding a new overlay server can be as simple as putting the new overlay server in place and then setting a peering relationship with an existing overlay server. Likewise, user requests can now be directed to the new overlay server, which can act in isolation as a cache or can be peered with other overlay servers as well.

Furthermore, the system should be *scalable and adaptable* to load in a number of ways. For example, if an overlay server receives many requests, additional overlay servers can be added to increase the cluster size of the existing overlay server. Also, if new areas of the network start experiencing high loads, new overlay servers can be added to those areas. If neighboring areas start seeing lots of correlation between their requests, they can be peered to share content usage statistics and content data between them. If the correlation patterns change, the peering relationships between servers can also be changed. This adaptability makes the media overlay well suited for campus and enterprise environments and cellular and 802.11 wireless environments.

19.3.2 Media Overlay System Management

Manageability was a key design goal of the media overlay. Media overlay management can be divided into two functions: (1) system monitoring, measurement, and analysis (through queries) and (2) system control (through commands). Both these functions can be performed between components through a management/control interface. The control interface allows the system to accept and give requests and commands. Since each overlay server tracks its own statistics, it can respond to queries for content usage, server load, and network conditions. Also, overlay servers can respond to commands for moving content, beginning and ending streaming sessions, and processing streams. These commands and requests can be from other overlay servers or managers. It is this modular design that allows the media overlay to be configured in many different modes of operation.

A number of specific notes can be made about media overlay system management. First, since overlay servers are constantly monitoring and logging statistics, they can be configured to periodically report their statistics to a specified entity or to reply to queries for these statistics received through the management/control interface. Next, it should be noted that overlay servers can be turned on or off for administrative needs such as system maintenance. Also, overlay servers can be added to the media overlay to facilitate incremental deployment, and they can be moved between nodes to adapt to evolving request patterns and system and network load patterns. In addition, as overlay servers get loaded with streaming sessions or as overlay network links become congested, it may become necessary to change servers during midsession. This can be done with the overlay server's streaming handoff capabilities. Thus, management can influence active streaming sessions. Finally, managers can change the peering relationships of overlay servers through the management interface. Peered overlay servers can be in the same overlay node or in different overlay nodes, and different overlay servers within a single overlay node do not necessarily have to be peered with each other.

19.3.3 Media Overlay Design Choices

The flexibility and modularity of the media overlay architecture allow it to be used in a number of modes of operation and customized for a number of deployment scenarios. We discuss a few of these modes and scenarios.

The modular components and interfaces of the media overlay allow it to work in a *centralized or distributed* mode of operation (Figure 19.12). In centralized mode, a central manager can collect statistics from all the overlay servers, analyze these statistics, determine the best strategy for delivering media streams, and

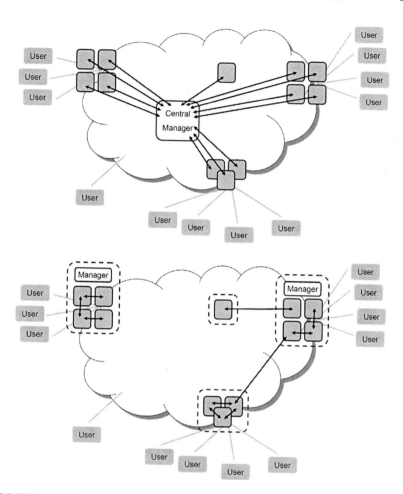

FIGURE 19.12:   Centralized vs. distributed management: a media overlay can be managed centrally (top) where all overlay servers report to and are controlled by a central manager. A media overlay can also be operated in a more distributed fashion (bottom) where overlay servers are peered to share statistics and make more rapid, local decisions.

send commands to the overlay servers to carry out this strategy. In distributed mode, each overlay server can analyze its own statistics and perhaps collect and analyze statistics from neighboring overlay servers, and then make decisions on how best to serve mobile streaming requests. The centralized operation has the advantage of having a global view of the statistics, but may be better suited to longer timescale adjustments, whereas the distributed operation may allow quicker data collection and analysis and allow quicker reactions to rapidly changing user patterns and system and network load patterns. Of course, hybrid combinations may be advantageous for a number of scenarios.

A media overlay network can have a *single owner* responsible for its operation. In this case, system management becomes much simpler because the owner can track the deployment of each overlay server and monitor the server and network load. Alternatively, a media overlay can have *multiple owners* who must agree to how their overlay resources should cooperate to deliver the media streams between end points. Finally, a media overlay can have *no defined owner*, in which case each of the overlay servers must be able to operate independently and cooperatively using standard compliant protocols for its interfaces.

The system can act in *push* or *pull* mode. In pull mode, content distribution can be triggered by user requests, for example, by caching the content with the highest number of requests. In push mode, the content can be distributed based on an analysis of user requests and network and system load performed by an overlay's management capabilities. In other words, content can be prefetched by the various overlay servers. Also, the push to overlay servers can be explicitly configured, for example, by an operator or content owner to ensure high-quality access to specific content.

19.4 ADVANCED TOPICS

A variety of more advanced capabilities can also be incorporated in a media overlay to improve the media delivery performance for end users or to improve the network utilization. This section briefly highlights some of the advanced capabilities that have been developed in recent years.

19.4.1 Network-Adaptive Media Streaming

Once media distribution and client request redirection are performed, the streaming session itself can begin. Streaming involves the delivery of long, continuous media streams and desires highly predictable bandwidths, low delay, and preferably no losses. In particular, midstream disruption of a streaming session can be highly distracting. There are a variety of important opportunities in overlay nodes for performing adaptive streaming for improving system performance, for example, see [37].

Stream scheduling: A number of opportunities lie in the general area of stream scheduling, where the basic idea is scheduling the packet transmissions for a media stream over a channel that may exhibit time-varying available bandwidth, loss rate, and delay. These scheduling problems have a number of flavors, including scheduling delivery of a single stream over a rate-constrained, time-varying channel, shared scheduling of many streams across a shared channel, and shared scheduling of many streams of a single server itself. While basic streaming systems simply transmit media packets in consecutive order without regard to the importance of individual packets, significant benefits can be obtained by exploiting the natural priority of each packet, for example, I, P, or B frames or scalable layer [1]. Further benefits result from rate-distortion optimized packet scheduling, which decides which packet should be transmitted at each transmission opportunity, as a function of each packet's importance and coding dependencies, estimated channel conditions, and feedback from the client on prior received/lost packets (see [10,15] and Chapters 4, 10, and 14). In addition, low-complexity stream scheduling algorithms can exploit periodic coding structures in the encoded video [45].

Wireless streaming: Wireless channels are a shared, highly dynamic medium, leading to unpredictable, time-varying available bandwidth, delay, and loss rates [13]. A key opportunity lies in optimizing wireless streaming algorithms from the overlay nodes to the mobile client. The streaming algorithm must adapt to time-varying network conditions and must be resilient to packet loss over error-prone wireless channels, as described in Chapters 11–13.

When an overlay server is colocated with a wireless base station and has accurate and timely information about the channel conditions, it can more readily adapt the streaming to the wireless channel variations. If an overlay server is not serving a stream but merely relaying content to a wireless client, there are still several beneficial functions that it can perform. First, it provides an additional observation point for packet reception statistics. When combined with reception statistics observed at the client, this allows the determination of whether packet losses are due to congestion or wireless link corruption. Such information is important for congestion control purposes. Second, in wireless wide-area networks, wireless link delay is typically very high, making adaptation inefficient. The overlay node could provide feedback on a much shorter timescale to make media adaptation more effective [9].

Adaptive streaming for multiple clients: Streaming applications may need to stream media to clients with different network bandwidths. These clients require different bit rate versions of the same content. This can be supported by using scalable coding and sending different layers on different multicast trees—each receiver joins the appropriate multicast tree(s) based on the desired content [22]. Similarly, multiple multicast trees can provide different amounts of forward error correction (FEC) for error control, where each client selects the desired amount of FEC [38].

19.4.2 Real-Time Media Adaptation and Transcoding

A streaming system must be able to deliver media streams to a diverse range of clients over heterogeneous, time-varying networks. In many scenarios, the downstream network conditions and client capabilities are not known in advance, and the network conditions may be time varying based on cross traffic. To overcome these obstacles requires dynamically matching the streaming media to the available bandwidth and capabilities of the specific client device. A number of approaches can be used to solve this problem. Multiple file switching switches between media files coded at different data rates [12]. Scalable coding stores base and enhancement streams that can be sent in a prioritized fashion [28]. Transcoding adapts precompressed streams into formats better suited for downstream conditions. These methods provide different trade-offs in terms of flexibility, compression efficiency, and complexity [6,19,36,39,43,44].

Mid-network stream adaptation: Media adaptation or transcoding may be performed at the sender or at a mid-network node. For example, for pre-encoded content it is customary to adapt the pre-encoded content at the sender for the current delivery situation. However, it is often valuable to transcode at a mid-network node—a node in the middle of the network between the sender and the receiver. A practical reason is that it is unlikely that every content source will have transcoding capability, and a transcoding-capable overlay is arguably the simplest solution. There are technical advantages in other situations as well. Another example is multicast video, where a single input stream is adapted to create multiple streams of different bit rates. Note that mid-network node transcoding is important for both pre-encoded and live content. Therefore, mid-network transcoding is a generally useful capability for overlay nodes to transcode streams according to downstream network conditions, such as lower bandwidth channels, congested network nodes, and time varying wireless channels. Since an overlay node may have to transcode many streams at once, both quality and computational efficiency are of importance.

19.4.3 Media Security

There are a number of important issues that relate to media security in the context of streaming media infrastructure. These include security issues related to the media itself, such as providing confidentiality of the media content or limiting access to the content to only those with appropriate access rights. Digital rights management becomes more involved since centralized solutions at the origin server must be extended to the distributed infrastructure where caching and streaming may occur at overlay nodes. For example, the policies for certain content may specify that it should not be cached. There is a need to control malicious attacks, such as Denial of Service attacks. Many of the aforementioned security issues are not specific to media and are not discussed further here due to limited space. One security problem that does directly relate to media processing is the question of how to transcode encrypted content.

End-to-end security and mid-network secure transcoding: A practically important problem involves how to provide end-to-end security for a streaming session, while also supporting mid-network transcoding. End-to-end security corresponds to encrypting the content at the sender, decrypting at the receiver, and having the content in encrypted form everywhere in between. Mid-network transcoding is therefore challenging because the content is encrypted. The conventional approach is to give the transcoder the key so that it can decrypt/transcode/re-encrypt the content, but this breaks the end-to-end security. To be more specific, giving the transcoder the key raises the key distribution problem, and the transcoder may also be untrustworthy. While end-to-end security and mid-network transcoding appear to be mutually exclusive, a careful codesign of the compression, encryption, and packetization can enable mid-network transcoding while preserving end-to-end security—referred to as *secure transcoding* to emphasize that the transcoding is performed without compromising end-to-end security [3,42].

19.4.4 Path and Server Diversities

Routing around failures: The ability of an overlay node to relay traffic provides flexibility in selecting the network path. Path selection, whereby a path of best or good quality is chosen among a set of candidate paths, is an obvious way to improve streaming quality. In particular, selection allows routing around failed links, which may otherwise render parts of a network inaccessible.

Robust streaming using distributed infrastructure and diversity: The distributed infrastructure of the overlay network also provides an opportunity to explicitly achieve *path diversity* and *server diversity* between each client and multiple nearby overlay servers. For example, multiple servers can send different streams over different paths (partially shared and partially not) to each client, thereby providing various forms of diversity that can overcome congestion or outage along a single path and improved fault tolerance. This may be achieved using multiple description (MD) coding as an MD-CDN [4] (using various MD codecs, e.g. [2, 29,41]) or single description or scalable coding with FEC [7,21,25]. It can also be achieved by using multiple wireless base stations or 802.11 access points [24]. A more detailed discussion of the benefits and use of path diversity is given in Chapter 17.

19.4.5 Mid-Session Streaming Handoff

Handoff of streaming sessions: Streaming media delivery differs from webpage delivery in that streaming sessions are often long lived. The long-lived nature of streaming sessions, combined with user mobility, raises the possible need of midstream handoffs of streaming sessions between overlay servers. This handoff should be transparent to the receiving client. Handoff of video sessions between overlay servers is challenging since the receiving client is highly sensitive to any interrupts. Furthermore, when the streaming session involves transcoding, mid-session handoff of the transcoding session may also be required between overlay nodes [33].

Dynamic load balancing of long-lived streaming sessions: The midstream handoff capability is also useful for enabling improved dynamic load balancing and fault tolerance. As more streaming or transcoding sessions are started, it may be useful to rebalance the streaming or transcoding sessions. For example, the overlay nodes can be used to explicitly route streams by using application-level forwarding where the overlay servers act as relays. By combining this with midstream handoff capability, streams can be dynamically rerouted to alleviate network congestion and improve load balancing.

19.5 MEDIA OVERLAY USES AND BENEFITS

In this section, we discuss some example applications enabled by a media overlay infrastructure. The advantages of media overlay can be examined from several perspectives: (1) improvement for the end user, (2) improvement for system scalability and performance, and (3) new capabilities. For each of the examples discussed in the remainder of this section we highlight important advantages along these three perspectives.

19.5.1 Media Delivery

The most basic function of a network is the delivery of data. In this section, we discuss how media delivery can be improved with a media overlay.

Consider an end user who is employing streaming media for entertainment and communication. The user's primary concerns (cost not withstanding) are ease of content access, smooth media playback, and acceptable latency for interactive communication. We next examine how a media overlay can help achieve these objectives.

Similar to how CDNs reduce access latency for web access, a media overlay improves latency when accessing media by physically locating the content closer to the user. By using multiple distributed servers, and selecting the "closest" server for each requesting client, improved responsiveness can be achieved as compared to using a single, likely distant server. The shorter distance from server to user also reduces the likelihood of encountering a network bottleneck that causes packet losses and throughput degradation, thereby improving user streaming experience.

Media overlays provide unique features for streaming media that have no correspondence in CDNs for web access. These are needed to accommodate the continuous requirement to have streaming media delivered on time to end users. One important feature that provides many advantages is media multicast or splitting; this is discussed further in Section 19.5.2.

In addition, the overlay can provide the feature of adapting media content on a real-time basis. One example of such adaptation is prioritized dropping, where packets that are more disposable are preferentially discarded when needed. Such dropping of data is best performed inside the infrastructure for a number of reasons. First, while a transmitting source can best prioritize its own traffic, it cannot optimize across the different media flows that are sharing the resource bottleneck. Second, real-time information for the resource bottleneck may be difficult to obtain due to large physical separation or impossible to obtain due to the presence of administrative boundaries.

Another example of media adaptation by a media overlay is transcoding a media stream to a lower bit rate in response to, for example, throughput degradation. Traditional approaches to address throughput variation in networks include adaptive live encoding or rate transcoding at the transmitting source for live content and switching between multiple copies of the same content at different bit rates for stored content. A media overlay is superior for the former by being able to perform adaptation closer to the bottleneck. For stored content, it is often economical to produce multiple copies only for content that is popular, and even then, only very limited bit rate options are available. Live transcoding inside a media overlay provides the option of a customized stream whenever necessary.

One key benefit of a media overlay architecture is the possibility of having path diversity, which is the subject of Chapter 17. Path diversity can be exploited in several ways, including selection and aggregation. Under selection, a good or best path is selected for a media stream, while multiple paths are used for a single stream under aggregation. The advantages afforded by path diversity include improved reliability. This is achieved by the ability to bypass network failures via alternative paths and by the potential to exploit underutilized paths to improve throughput stability.

From a system perspective, a media overlay enables a number of advantages, which we shall discuss shortly. Similar to CDN for web traffic, by locating content close to the user, a media overlay is efficient in that the network resources needed to achieve a task are typically reduced compared to using a single distant server. This is achieved by the caching functions of a media overlay. In addition, the possibility of using multiple paths and servers allows a more efficient use of resources via balancing of network and server loads. One benchmark for an efficient delivery infrastructure is that every packet traverses every link at most once. The combination of caching and routing functions of a media overlay provides the key components for realizing this ideal.

19.5.2 Multicast or "Splitting" Service

A well-known overlay application is point-to-multipoint communication or multicast, under which overlay architectures are used to form distribution trees for relaying a single content to multiple recipients [11,17]. These overlays effectively emulate a multicast service in an otherwise point-to-point network. Since an overlay node may receive one copy of a packet and relay it to multiple recipients, the operation is sometimes called "splitting." This is achieved by the flexible delivery path afforded by a media overlay discussed in Section 19.4.4.

Traditionally in a point-to-point network, the only way to achieve multicast communications is to employ multiple independent transmissions of the same data. Clearly, such repetition can be wasteful for large group sizes and poses heavy loads for servers and networks alike. Nevertheless, repetition allows the preservation of the simple client–server model of Figure 19.2a, which is of practical importance for compatibility with capability-constrained devices or older devices. In the other extreme, it is possible to establish relaying infrastructure using end hosts only, as is done in many peer-to-peer systems. For example, in Figure 19.2c, it is possible for "Server" to stream to client P, which is then responsible for relaying data to P'. When each client relays data to only one other client, we have a distribution chain, but more general distribution structures are clearly possible. The use of end-host systems can surely relieve the server load and, to a certain extent, relieve network load as well, depending on the particular distribution structure employed. Nevertheless, these all come at the expense of higher complexity and resource requirements for the clients. For example, the simple client–server model is no longer valid, and a client has to maintain communications with multiple end hosts and change these connections based on end-host churning. Furthermore, end hosts now need to perform data transmission in addition to reception.

By strategically placing the "splitting" function in the overlay nodes, the overlay multicast solution allows clients to assume the simple client–server model, while relieving the high server and network loads associated with using multiple independent transmissions. End-user video quality is improved with reduced server and network load, and the possibility of having "local" retransmissions between overlay nodes. For the operator, the reduction of network traffic associated with multicast greatly reduces network cost, and the simple client–server model guarantees support for a wide range of clients, as well as simpler problem diagnosis.

Many multicast communications with large client population are scheduled in advance. Examples include major sports events for entertainment and CEO announcements for corporate communications in a large enterprise. In Figure 19.4, overlay resources are represented as overlay nodes inside the infrastructure and edge servers near the clients. One possible approach to affect multicast is then to use the *push* mode of operation discussed in Section 19.3.3. Under push mode, the overlay nodes and edge nodes form a distribution tree, with edge nodes assuming the additional duty of streaming to clients. A client can be redirected to an appropriate edge node via one of several mechanisms discussed in Section 19.4.

Application-level multicast or "splitting" architectures are particularly relevant for video content due to the high volume of data involved. However, many technical issues remain. For example, in the dense client situation (when the expected number of clients per nearby edge server is large) it is sensible to push the content to an edge server. This design provides two advantages. First, the edge server serves as a rendezvous point for clients to access the content. Second, a relatively static distribution structure can be used to connect the edge servers, each of which individually handles joining and leaving of clients. When clients are sparsely distributed, two corresponding problems arise. First, it may no longer be efficient to involve an edge server, and an entry point into the overlay system is required, for example, via a portal. Second, the distribution structure may need to evolve as clients join and leave, which is typically challenging due to the relatively unpredictable behavior of individual clients.

19.5.3 Multi-Way Conferencing

A media overlay allows new capabilities to be introduced incrementally to an existing network without modifying existing clients or requiring global infrastructure upgrades. For example, consider a network that supports point-to-point video communication. In this example, client devices have a video conferencing application that can receive, decode, and play back one audio/video stream and that can capture, encode, and send one audio/video stream. Normally, clients can communicate directly with one another to establish a two-way conference, as shown in the upper left of Figure 19.13. Three-way or multi-way video conferencing can be achieved, as shown in the upper right of Figure 19.13, where all the streams are sent to all the clients, but this approach requires upgrading all the clients and requires each client to have the ability to receive and process multiple streams. However, the question that we now consider is how to support three-way or, more generally, multi-way video conferencing using existing applications designed for two-way conferencing? We show how the media overlay can enable this improved functionality without requiring any changes in the client, as shown in the lower right of Figure 19.13.

Since the client is able to send and receive a single audio/video stream, the key capability that the media overlay must provide is the ability to combine the audio/video streams from all the other clients in the video conferencing session into a single audio/video stream that can be decoded by the client. This single audio/video stream should contain the appropriate view from one or more of the various session participants. This can be achieved in a number of ways. First, the media overlay can turn the remote participants' streams into a single stream by

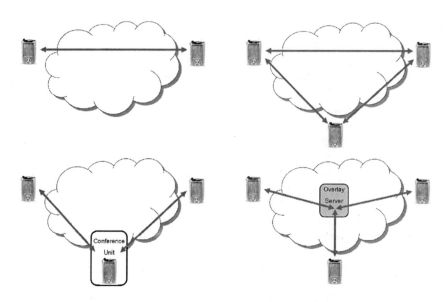

FIGURE 19.13: Conferencing. (Upper left) Two-way conferencing. (Upper right) Three-way conferencing can be accomplished by sending all streams to all other users, but this requires each participant to be able to receive all the clients to be upgraded and capable of receiving and playing multiple streams. (Lower left) Multi-way conferencing can also be achieved by upgrading only one client with conferencing capabilities and having all the clients send and receive to this client. (Lower right) Multi-way conferencing can be achieved transparently to all clients with the overlay approach. All the clients interact with an overlay server as if it were a single client. The overlay then combines the streams into the appropriate single stream for each client. The overlay can be upgraded over time to provide improved conferencing capabilities in a manner that is transparent to clients.

performing a video transcoding operation that downscales all the video streams and stitches or tiles them together into a single video stream and by performing an audio processing operation that combines all the audio streams into a single audio stream. Another option for combining multiple downscaled video streams is selecting the video of the active speaker. The media overlay can achieve this by applying an activity detection algorithm to the audio and/or video streams and selecting the video of the active participant. The media overlay can perform other options as well, such as combining the first two approaches where all the video

streams are transcoded, but done in a manner so that the active remote participant is displayed with a larger display size than the nonactive participants. In all
these examples, since the media overlay performs the multistream transcoding in a
manner that produces a single audio/video stream that is accepted by the two-way
video conferencing client application, multiuser conferencing is a new capability
that is seamlessly provided by the media overlay.

To further understand the advantages provided by an overlay approach as compared to end-host approaches, the next few paragraphs further examine the trade-
offs that arise with different end-host approaches to multi-way conferencing. If the
video conferencing client application could be upgraded, then one way to achieve
multi-party conferencing is for each client to send to and receive from all other
participants as shown in the upper left of Figure 19.13. Analogous client-side operations to achieve the features described earlier, such as video downscaling and
audio mixing, are then performed locally. This is most flexible, but also requires
the largest amount of network and system resources both in the infrastructure and
at the clients. Therefore, this approach is not scalable to large conference sizes.
In addition, this solution presumes appropriate network support: it may not be
possible to get a new multi-party conferencing phone to work with the existing
telephone network.

For tiling display of multiple participants, the scheme presented earlier can be
improved by allowing participants to downscale their video streams to an appropriate size before sending them to the other participants. This requires coordination and signaling between the various clients to determine the size that each
participant's video must be reduced to. For display of active speaker only, the
scheme presented earlier can be improved by locally performing activity detection. Coordination and signaling for selecting an active sender are also required.

To allow Alice, Bob, and Carol to participate in three-way conferencing, it is
possible for Alice alone to have an updated application, while Bob and Carol
use their legacy application to call Alice. This is shown in the lower left of Figure 19.13. Alice then plays the role of the central aggregator and performs all media processing for the entire conference. Compared to the overlay solution, this
end-host only solution has four limitations. First, it is not applicable to networks
such as telephone networks that only allow a single point-to-point communication. Second, at least one participant must have an upgraded application that is
known to all participants. Third, the limit on maximum number of participants is
likely to be much lower for an end host than an overlay infrastructure. Finally,
Alice, the central aggregator, cannot leave the conference without ending the conference.

For end users, overlay conferencing allows existing applications to be used, and
simple logic for joining and leaving a conference that is likely to translate into
fewer disturbances for other participants. It can also support greater customiza-
tion, where each client decides, for example, on the desired viewing size for each

stream. From a systems perspective, the overlay solution is attractive due to the lower amount of traffic corresponding to a central aggregation point.

19.5.4 Additional Overlay-Based Media Features

Recording and retrieval of multimedia messages: In addition to data delivery, the recording and retrieval of voice and video messages have evolved to become common features in many networks. An overlay infrastructure of Figure 19.4 is well equipped for this task because of its storage and streaming capabilities. The recording and retrieval of multimedia messages can be implemented in the client if it is permanently attached to a network, as is the case in land-line telephones. Nevertheless, the overlay implementation offers several advantages. For the user, it provides higher service availability, as the client no longer needs to be always turned on and attached to a network. The user also benefits from easier access to the content from other devices. From a systems perspective, the economy of scale allows such recording and retrieval functions to be more economically implemented in the infrastructure than in the end clients.

Enhanced media access: With new media formats being created, and the capability of network and client devices being improved continuously, the range of available media content becomes highly diversified in terms of codec types and options, bit rates, and picture sizes. This clearly poses a nightmare for interoperability. While updating applications on clients to support new codecs is arguably possible, although administratively difficult, a high bit rate or high complexity content may always be incompatible with a constrained client. A media overlay is in an ideal position to bridge the gap. Since a media overlay is involved in the delivery of the media content, it can exploit its available computation resources to transcode the media content to a format that a client is capable of handling, where format subsumes relevant parameters such as codec types and options, bit rate, and frame size. For the user, the benefit is access to content that would otherwise be unaccessible. While there may be slight quality degradations associated with transcoding, for a large class of content whose purpose is communication rather than visual entertainment, such a trade-off is well justified. From a systems perspective, the overlay solution provides a single point of upgrading for new capabilities, such as a new codec. In addition, it is impossible to predict and impractical to encode, at content creation time, all possible configurations required by different clients. The overlay solution effectively provides a way of dynamically creating a custom stream only when necessary. The possibility of caching transcoded content makes the solution more competitive in terms of computation requirements [35].

Content sharing: In an example given earlier, the overlay infrastructure stores the multimedia message boxes for users. Generally, the infrastructure can store other content for the user and allow playback not only to a device, but to a conference of participants as well. This allows an enhanced version of the multi-way conferencing discussed earlier, where the display options are expanded from scaled and tiled video of participants, and the active speaker, to include a document under discussion or vacation video being shared. Again, the overlay solution does not require any clients to be modified. An equivalent system implemented in the end host would require all clients wishing to share content to be upgraded, along with other drawbacks outlined in Section 19.5.2. While the necessary media processing may be held in an overlay server, the content to be shared may reside in another server inside or outside the overlay infrastructure. Therefore, this application cannot be realized without the media processing and content distribution functions of the overlay infrastructure.

Content adaptation for improved usability: Similar to transcoding of media discussed earlier, there are a number of other media processing that could be incorporated in a media overlay infrastructure without requiring client changes. We will discuss here two examples for improving usability of media content. The first example is "camera stabilization." Many mobile devices are equipped with cameras, but shooting usable video requires a trained and stable hand. When incorporation of image stabilization in the end devices is not computationally practical, the media overlay provides a natural place for such algorithms, especially when the content is stored in the overlay. The second example relates to the rendering of speech as text overlayed onto the video. This is important for viewing content in public places, such as libraries, or in noisy places, such as trains and restaurants. In noisy environments, visual text may be more comprehensible than listening to the original audio through an earphone. While the overlaying of text onto video is not a difficult task and may be performed at the client, speech recognition may prove too complex for most client devices. Again, the media overlay infrastructure is conveniently involved in the delivery of content and can perform the aforementioned processing to render an appropriate stream to be delivered to the client.

Additional possible services: There are many other potentially important media services, including video or audio processing operations, such as speed up/slow down of playback, VCR functionalities, logo insertion, background removal, enhancing resolution, and deblurring and noise reduction. In addition, and very importantly, an overlay infrastructure provides a convenient and highly flexible platform for introducing new services and gradually expanding the services based on the number of users or improved functionalities, and it provides this capability while generally enabling backward compatibility with older client devices.

19.6 SUMMARY AND FURTHER READING

This chapter introduces the basic concepts, capabilities, and operations of a media overlay. The media overlay is an extension of an existing network infrastructure and improves upon the basic network by having strategically located overlay nodes with processing, storage, and relaying capabilities. This is in contrast to the traditional client–server approach, where all intelligence and processing reside in the two end points, and the peer-to-peer model, where the intelligence and processing are distributed across multiple end points without being integrated with the basic network.

The benefits of the infrastructure approach assumed by a media overlay can be examined in many different respects, including (1) improved availability, latency, and quality of service for end users, (2) improved operational efficiency and manageability for network operators, and (3) ease of adding new services and capabilities. All of these benefits are achieved with minimal changes to existing clients and network infrastructure and allow incremental introduction of new features and scaling of existing features to a larger audience.

Many capabilities are central to the operations of a media overlay. For media delivery, these include media distribution, caching, multicast, media serving, and security. For maintenance and management, these include resource monitoring, management, and handoffs functions. For media services, these include operations that adapt the content of the media being delivered. For example, transcoding can be used to adapt a media stream's display resolution for a particular client device or bit rate for a congested network.

Since the overlay is a part of a larger infrastructure, design and architectural considerations are important. Some important design considerations for media overlay design discussed in this chapter include modular design with well-defined interfaces for data and control, push and pull delivery of media, and centralized and distributed modes of operation for the media overlay. Some architectural considerations discussed in this chapter include the system and network monitoring capabilities of the overlay and the manageability of the overlay, which includes allowing incremental deployment and upgradeability over time.

By properly designing a media overlay, an existing network infrastructure can be evolved to handle multimedia applications. This chapter discusses a number of overlay-enabled applications, including media delivery, overlay multicast, multiway conferencing, and other media services, including multimedia messaging, enhanced media access, content sharing, and content adaptation.

Evolution of networked media services: Many networked media services such as multimedia messaging, streaming media, video conferencing, mobile television, multiplayer gaming, and video blogging and podcasting are beginning to emerge. We foresee widespread adoption in the coming decade, and we believe that two key ingredients are giving users compelling media services and high-quality media experiences. This requires a flexible infrastructure that allows new services to be incrementally deployed, since it is difficult to predict user response to new services, and allows its media delivery capabilities to be upgraded in an evolutionary manner, since there are costs associated with infrastructure improvements and network owners are hesitant to upgrade their infrastructure until they see signs of high adoption and associated revenue.

Media overlays are a likely path to the widespread adoption of networked multimedia services because they provide a highly flexible platform for introducing and trying new services and are a means for gradually expanding the service deployment as the number of users increases. It also allows the infrastructure's media capabilities to be upgraded in an evolutionary manner. Furthermore, over time we believe that many of these media overlay capabilities will eventually be built into the base network itself, but on the path to widespread deployment, media overlays will provide the vehicle through which these capabilities and new services will first be developed and deployed.

Comparisons of infrastructure-based overlays to other approaches are given in [11,17,20,31]. In [20], the design issues and choices of an infrastructure-based overlay are discussed. In [17], the trade-offs among several approaches for video-on-demand applications are evaluated. A readable account of when to adopt peer-to-peer systems is given in [31], while [11] presents an approach in which an overlay is formed by clients rather than by infrastructure nodes. Readers interested in problems relating to server placement or content placement may consult [27], while [4] discusses the use of media overlays for streaming of video coded in a multiple-description fashion. A detailed example of SMIL-based redirection, as well as the use of segmented video, is discussed in [46]. Further discussion on how media processing services, such as transcoding, may be implemented in a media overlay is given in [16]. An example of possible media adaptation inside an overlay infrastructure to improve transport over wireless networks is given in [9]. Further readings on several topics can be found in other chapters in this book. For example, bandwidth adaptation techniques are discussed in Chapters 4 and 10, streaming media on demand in Chapter 14, and media streaming protocols in Chapter 15.

REFERENCES

[1] A. Albanese, J. Blomer, J. Edmonds, M. Luby, and M. Sudan. "Priority Encoding Transmission," in *Proceedings of IEEE Symposium on Foundations of Computer Science*, pages 604–612, November 1994.

[2] J. Apostolopoulos. "Reliable Video Communication over Lossy Packet Networks Using Multiple State Encoding and Path Diversity," *Proceedings of Visual Communications and Image Processing (VCIP)*, January 2001.

[3] J. Apostolopoulos. "Secure Media Streaming and Secure Adaptation for Nonscalable Video," *Proceedings of IEEE International Conference on Image Processing*, October 2004.

[4] J. Apostolopoulos, T. Wong, W. Tan, and S. Wee. "On Multiple Description Streaming with Content Delivery Networks," *Proceedings of IEEE INFOCOM*, June 2002.

[5] A. Barbir, B. Cain, F. Douglis, M. Green, M. Hofmann, R. Nair, D. Potter, and O. Spatscheck. "Known Content Network (CN) Request-Routing Mechanisms," *Internet Engineering Task Force*, RFC 3568, July 2003.

[6] N. Bjork and C. Christopoulos. "Transcoder Architectures for Video Coding," in *Proceeedings of IEEE International Conference on Acoustics, Speech, and Signal Processing*, Seattle, WA, May 1998.

[7] J. Chakareski and B. Girod. "Rate-Distortion Optimized Packet Scheduling and Routing for Media Streaming with Path Diversity," *Proceedings of IEEE Data Compression Conference*, April 2003.

[8] S. Chen, B. Shen, S. Wee, and X. Zhang. "Segment-Based Streaming Media Proxy: Modeling and Optimization," *IEEE Transactions on Multimedia*, 8(2):243–256, April 2006.

[9] G. Cheung, W. Tan, and T. Yoshimura. "Double Feedback Streaming Agent for Real-Time Delivery of Media over 3G Wireless Networks," *IEEE Transactions on Multimedia*, 6(2):304–314, April 2004.

[10] P. Chou and Z. Miao. "Rate-Distortion Optimized Streaming of Packetized Media," *IEEE Transactions on Multimedia*, 8(2):390–404, April 2006.

[11] Y. Chu, S. Rao, S. Seshan, and H. Zhang. "A Case for End System Multicast," *IEEE Journal on Selected Areas Communications*, 20(8):1456–1471, October 2002.

[12] G. Conklin, G. Greenbaum, K. Lillevold, A. Lippman, and Y. Reznik. "Video Coding for Streaming Media Delivery on the Internet," *IEEE Transactions on Circuits and Systems for Video Technology*, March 2001.

[13] S. Dawkins, M. Kojo, V. Magret, and N. Vaidya. "Long Thin Networks," *Internet Engineering Task Force*, RFC 2757, January 2000.

[14] S. Floyd and K. Fall. "Promoting the Use of End-to-End Congestion Control in the Internet," *IEEE/ACM Transactions on Networking*, 7(4):458–472, August 1999.

[15] B. Girod, J. Chakareski, M. Kalman, Y. Liang, E. Setton, and R. Zhang. "Advances in Network-Adaptive Video Streaming," *Tyrrhenian International Workshop on Digital Communications*, September 2002.

[16] M. Harville, M. Covell, and S. Wee. "An Architecture for Componentized, Network-Based Media Services," in *Proceedings of IEEE International Conference on Multimedia and Expo*, Baltimore, Maryland, July 2003.

[17] K. Hua, M. Tantaoui, and W. Tavanapong. "Video Delivery Technologies for Large-Scale Deployment of Multimedia Applications," *Proceedings of IEEE*, September 2004.

[18] R. Katz and E. Brewer. "The Case for Wireless Overlay Networks," in Tomasz Imielinski and Henry F. Korth, editors, *Mobile Computing*, pages 621–650. Kluwer Academic Publishers, 1996.

[19] G. Keesman, R. Hellinghuizen, F. Hoeksema, and G. Heideman. "Transcoding MPEG Bitstreams," *Signal Processing: Image Communication*, 8(6), September 1996.

[20] L. Kontothanassis, R. Sitaraman, J. Wein, D. Hong, R. Kleinberg, B. Mancuso, D. Shaw, and D. Stodolsky. "A Transport Layer for Live Streaming in a Content Delivery Network," *Proceedings of IEEE*, September 2004.

[21] A. Majumdar, R. Puri, and K. Ramchandran. "Distributed Multimedia Transmission from Multiple Servers," *Proceedings of IEEE International Conference on Image Processing*, September 2002.

[22] S. McCanne, V. Jacobsen, and M. Vetterli. "Receiver-Driven Layered Multicast," *ACM SIGCOMM*, August 1996.

[23] M. Miao and A. Ortega. "Scalable Proxy Caching of Video under Storage Constraints," *IEEE Journal on Selected Areas Communications*, September 2002.

[24] A. Miu, J. Apostolopoulos, W. Tan, and M. Trott. "Low-Latency Wireless Video over 802.11 Networks Using Path Diversity," *Proceedings of IEEE International Conference on Multimedia and Expo*, July 2003.

[25] T. Nguyen and A. Zakhor. "Distributed Video Streaming over Internet," *SPIE Multimedia Computing and Networking 2002*, January 2002.

[26] C. Patrikakis, Y. Despotopoulos, A. Rompotis, N. Minogiannis, A. Lambiris, and A. Salis. "An Implementation of an Overlay Network Architecture Scheme for Streaming Media Distribution," in *29th Euromicro Conference (EUROMICRO'03)*, September 2003.

[27] L. Qiu, V. Padmanabhan, and G. Voelker. "On the Placement of Web Server Replicas," *Proceedings of IEEE INFOCOM*, April 2001.

[28] H. Radha, M. van der Schaar, and Y. Chen. "The MPEG-4 Fine-Grained Scalable Video Coding Method for Multimedia Streaming over IP," *IEEE Trans. on Multimedia*, March 2001.

[29] A. Reibman, H. Jafarkhani, Y. Wang, M. Orchard, and R. Puri. "Multiple Description Video Coding Using Motion-Compensated Temporal Prediction," *IEEE Trans. Circuits and Systems for Video Technology*, March 2002.

[30] A. Rousskow and D. Wessels. "Cache Digests," *Computer Networks and ISDN Systems*, 30(22–23):2155–2168, November 1998.

[31] M. Roussopoulos, M. Baker, D. Rosenthal, T. Giuli, P. Maniatis, and J. Mogul. "2 P2P or Not 2 P2P," *Proceedings of 3rd International Workshop on Peer-to-Peer Systems (IPTPS)*, February 2004.

[32] S. Roy, M. Covell, J. Ankcorn, and S. Wee. "A System Architecture for Managing Mobile Streaming Media Services," in *Proceedings of IEEE International Workshop on Mobile Distributed Computing*, May 2003.

[33] S. Roy, B. Shen, V. Sundaram, and R. Kumar. "Application Level Handoff Support for Mobile Media Transcoding Sessions," *ACM NOSSDAV*, May 2002.

[34] S. Sen, J. Rexford, and D. Towsley. "Proxy Prefix Caching for Multimedia Streams," in *Proceedings of IEEE INFOCOM*, March 1999.

[35] B. Shen, S. J. Lee, and S. Basu. "Caching Strategies in Transcoding-Enabled Proxy Systems for Streaming Media Distribution Networks," *IEEE Transactions on Multimedia*, 6(2):375–386, April 2004.

[36] H. Sun, W. Kwok, and J. Zdepski. "Architectures for MPEG Compressed Bitstream Scaling," *IEEE Transactions on Circuits and Systems for Video Technology*, 6(2), April 1996.

[37] M. Sun and A. Reibman, editors. *Compressed Video over Networks*. Marcel Dekker, 2001.

[38] W. Tan and A. Zakhor. "Video Multicast Using Layered FEC and Scalable Compression," *IEEE Transactions on Circuits and Systems for Video Technology*, March 2001.

[39] A. Vetro, C. Christopoulos, and H. Sun. "Video Transcoding Architectures and Techniques: An Overview," *IEEE Signal Processing Magazine*, March 2003.

[40] Y. Wang, M. Hannuksela, V. Varsa, A. Hourunranta, and M. Gabbouj. "The Error Concealment Feature in the H.26L Test Model," in *Proceedings International Conference on Image Processing*, pages II-729–II-732, September 2002.

[41] Y. Wang and S. Lin. "Error Resilient Video Coding Using Multiple Description Motion Compensation," *IEEE Transactions on Circuits and Systems for Video Technology*, June 2002.

[42] S. Wee and J. Apostolopoulos. "Secure Scalable Streaming Enabling Transcoding without Decryption," *Proceedings of IEEE International Conference on Image Processing*, October 2001.

[43] S. Wee, J. Apostolopoulos, and N. Feamster. "Field-to-Frame Transcoding with Spatial and Temporal Downsampling," in *Proceedings of IEEE International Conference on Image Processing*, Kobe, Japan, October 1999.

[44] S. Wee, B. Shen, and J. Apostolopoulos. "Compressed-Domain Video Processing," *HP Labs Tech Report (HPL-2002-282)*, October 2002.

[45] S. Wee, W. Tan, J. Apostolopoulos, and M. Etoh. "Optimized Video Streaming for Networks with Varying Delay," in *Proceedings of IEEE International Conference on Multimedia and Expo*, Lausanne, Switzerland, August 2002.

[46] T. Yoshimura, Y. Yonemoto, T. Ohya, M. Etoh, and S. Wee. "Mobile Streaming Media CDN Enabled by Dynamic SMIL," in *Proceedings of the International World Wide Web Conference*, Honolulu, Hawaii, May 2002.

INDEX

Accelerated retroactive decoding (ARD), 303, 304

Access Portal, 649

ACK. *See* Positive acknowledgment

Adaptation points, 88, 90, 110

Adaptation Task, 439

Adapter, 439

Adaptive codebook gains, 64

Adaptive intra updates, 44

Adaptive Media Playout (AMP), 527, 535–543, 536f, 548, 550
  for low-delay conversational services, 537–538
  for nonconversational services, 538–540
  packet path diversity and, 552–553
  signal processing for, 543–548
  two-stream scheduling, 552–553
  for VoIP, 538

Adaptive Multi-Rate, 63

Adaptive packetization, real-time greedy algorithm for, 369t

Adaptive Stream Management (ASM), 92–93

Adaptive temporal and spatial Error Concealment (AEC), 37

Additional startup delay, 247

Additive white Gaussian noise (AWGN), 195, 196, 202

Admission control, optimized multimedia, 377–379

Admitted stations, 376–377

Advanced Simple Profile (ASP), 21

AEC. *See* Adaptive temporal and spatial Error Concealment

Aggregates, 245
  bandwidth, 564f

Agilent 54621A oscilloscope, 420

AMP. *See* Adaptive Media Playout

AMP-initial. *See* Initial playout delay reduction

AMP-live. *See* Live media streaming

AMP-robust. *See* Improved robustness against network variations

AMR-WB. *See* Wideband Adaptive Multirate codec

AMR-WB codec, 78

Analysis tools, 229–230

Application modeling, 411–413
  cross-layer, 412–413
  task, connection, and quality, 412

Application-layer RS code, throughput efficiency and delay analysis with, 348–349

ARD. *See* Accelerated retroactive decoding

Arithmetic coder, 180

ARQ. *See* Automatic repeat request

Arrival rates, 476–479

Arrival schedule, 479, 480f

ASM. *See* Adaptive Stream Management

ASP. *See* Advanced Simple Profile

Asymmetric paths, 266–267
  in multipath streaming systems, 580
  percentage of, 267f

AT&T, 245

Audio transform, 163–165

Audio-video synchronization, 520–522

Auditory masking threshold, 167f
  implicit, 169–171
  temporal masking, 168, 169f

Automatic repeat request (ARQ), 188, 222–225, 271, 297, 519
  Go-Back-N, 223, 224f
  pure, 222–223
  selective repeat, 223–224, 224f
  stop and wait, 222–223

$AVE_{i,k}$, 168

AWGN. *See* Additive white Gaussian noise

B frames, 26, 27
Backward Error Correction (BEC), 19
Bad-burst distributions
  Markov chain, 326–329
  simplification of, 330
Bandwidth, 4, 339
  aggregation, 564f
  available, 86, 520
  granularity, 89
Bandwidth adaptation mechanisms, 82,
    87–98
  bit stream switching in, 104–105
  classification of, 110
  client driven decisions in, 92–93
  clients in, 91–92
  coding techniques for, 98–109
  complexity in, 96
  criteria and constraints, 94
  end-to-end delay in, 95–96
  examples of, 96–97
  flexibility and reaction time, 90f
  information overhead in, 96
  latency in, 95–96
  media quality in, 94–95
  multiple bit rate coding in, 105–107
  optimization techniques for, 108–109
  proxies in, 92
  proxy driven decisions in, 93
  rate control for, 98–99
  reaction time in, 95–96
  scalability in, 90f
  scalable coding in, 103–104
  senders in, 91
  server driven decisions in, 93–94
  SI-frames in, 107
  SP-frames in, 107
  storage in, 96
  stream morphing in, 107–108
  trade-offs, 88–90
  transcoding in, 101–103
Bandwidth management architecture,
    424–426
  host, 426f
  overview of, 425f
  weighted throughput with, 429f
  weighted throughput without, 428f
Bandwidth managers (BM), 425
Bandwidth-proportional max-min fairness,
    444
Barbell lifting scheme, 139f, 140

Base layer (BL), 120
Basic Information Theory, 230–231
Bayesian estimation, 180–181
BEC. *See* Backward Error Correction;
    Binary erasure channel
BER. *See* Bit error rate
Bernoulli loss probabilities, 296
Bernoulli process, 75
Bernoulli random variables, 231
Best effort, 32
B-frames, 295f
Binary erasure channel (BEC), 193, 214,
    231–232, 233, 267–268
  cascaded, 232–233
  with feedback, 234–235
  representation of, 231f
Binary repetition code, 200–201
Binary symmetric channel (BSC), 192, 194
Bit error rate (BER), 194, 245
  channel coding and, 196–217
  SNR v., in 802.11, 343f
Bit error traces, autocorrelation of, 320
Bit planes, 614f
  approximation quantization of, 124–127
  structure of, 129
Bit redundancy, 74
Bit stream assembler, 181–182
Bit stream switching, 106f
  in bandwidth adaptation, 104–105
Bit stream syntax, 181
  EAC, 182f
Bit stream transmission, 8–9
Bit streams associated with blocks, 618f
Bits, 73
BitTorrent, 3, 5
BL. *See* Base layer
Block codes, 204
  performance of, 196
Block diagonal structure, 69
Block diagrams, 64f, 619f
Block interleavers, 213t
Block scheme of turbo decoders, 216f
Block significance pass, 126–127
Block-based motion-compensated
    prediction, 135–136
Blocking artifacts, 66
Blocks of packets (BOPs), 277
Bluetooth, 337, 409
BM. *See* Bandwidth managers
BOPs. *See* Blocks of packets

Bottlenecks, 235
Boundary-matching criteria, 35f
BPSK modulation, 287
Broadcast, 7
  downlink model, 591
  Internet, 97
  live, 6, 453, 489–496
BSC. *See* Binary symmetric channel
Buffer tubes, 465
  containing coding schedules, 466f
  multiple, 467f
Buffering approach, 419, 420f
Buffering model, 464–471
Buffers. *See* Buffer tubes; Client buffers;
    Decoder buffers; Encoder
    buffers; Render buffers
Burst errors, 16

Caching, 642–644
Call setup
  using SIP, 515f
  VoIP, 515–516
Call-ID, 508
CAM. *See* Continuous access mode
CANCEL method, 506
Cascaded BEC channels, 232–233
Cascaded channels with memory, packet
    losses over, 240–241
CBP. *See* Coded block pattern
CBR. *See* Constant bit rate
CBR transmission, 378–379
CCM. *See* Constant complexity model
CDF functions, 253f, 255, 257, 258, 321,
    323
  complementary, 256f
CDMA2000, 217, 621
CDN. *See* Content Distribution Networks
Cell phones, 81
CELP. *See* Codebook Excited Linear
    Prediction
Central Spectrum Moderator (CSM), 397,
    401
Centralized management, 653f
CF-ACK transmission error, 347f
CFP. *See* Contention-free period
Channel capacity, 192–193, 233, 429f
  information, 232
Channel codewords, 187–188

Channel coding, 192, 476–479
  for bit errors and packet losses, 196–217
  rates, 477
Channel decoders, 187–188, 596
Channel fraction, 425
  allotted to each flow, 430f
Channel mixers (MIX), 161
  scale by number of audio channels,
    162–163
Channel models, basic information theory
    concepts of, 230–231
Channel quality monitoring, 426–427
Chunks, 461
CIF. *See* Common Intermediate Formate
Cisco Aironet, 420
Classical communication systems, 187
Classifiers, accuracy of, 390t
Client application, 293
Client buffers, 532–534
  duration, 478
  loading, 85, 455
Client time, 475
Clients, 84, 93
  adaptive streaming for multiple, 655
  in bandwidth adaptation mechanisms,
    91–92
  request handling, 644–645
  user agent, 506
Client–server architecture, 247–248,
    635–637
Clocks, 475
CNN.com, 3
Coarse grained selection, 463
Coastguard sequence, 362
Codebook(s), 198f
  construction of, 599–600
Codebook Excited Linear Prediction
    (CELP), 60, 63–65, 79
  block diagram of, 64f
Coded block pattern (CBP), 129
Coded video data, 15–16
Codewords, 189, 198f, 209
Coding delay, 517f
Coding schedules, buffer tubes containing,
    466f
Coding techniques, 88, 98–109
CoDiO. *See* Congestion-distortion optimized
    scheduling
Coefficient significance pass, 127
Combined source-channel coding, 78

Common Intermediate Formate (CIF), 52
Completely controllable systems, 486
Complexity in bandwidth adaptation
    mechanisms, 96
Compound streams, 471–473
Compression, 8
    efficiency, 594
    performance tests, 621
    PRISM, 602
    ratios, 160
Concurrent media streams, 473
Conditional entropy, 189
Conditional probabilities, 255
Congestion-distortion optimized scheduling
    (CoDiO), 307–308
    RaDiO and, 308f, 309f
Constant bit rate (CBR), 243, 464
Constant complexity model (CCM),
    331–332
    Markov chains compared with, 332–334
    standard errors of, 333t
    state aggregation and transitions for, 332f
Content Distribution Networks (CDN),
    581–583, 635, 658, 659
    MD, 582–583
Content sharing, 664–665
Contention-free period (CFP), 344
Context adaptive entropy coder, 177–178
Context switches, 418
Continuity, 32
Continuous access mode (CAM), 420
Control Action, 439
Control objective, 482
Control theoretic model, 479–482
Controllability matrix, 486
Controller design, 484–487
Controller interpretation, 488–489
Conventional acknowledgments, Rich
    acknowledgments v., 302f
Conversational services
    adaptive media playout for, 537
    packet path diversity for, 552
Convex rate-distortion functions, 76–77
Convolutional codes, 196, 206–213
    example of, 207f
    expression of, 208
    generation of, 211
    LFSM of, 207f
    trellis representation of, 209f
CoolStreaming, 3

Correlation coefficients, 389t
Coset channel coding, 617–618
Cosets, 212
CPU adaptation, 421
CPU energy saving, 417–418
CR. See Current Rate
CRC. See Cyclic redundancy check
Critical bands, encoding, 174–175
Cross interleavers, 214f
Cross-layer applications, 412–413
Cross-layer architecture, 435f
Cross-layer design, 351–355, 440
Cross-layer impact on throughput efficiency,
    346–351
Cross-layer MAC-application layer, using
    Lagrangian optimization,
    361–370
Cross-layer optimization
    classification system for, 387–388
    classifier design, 391–392
    conceptual framework of, 353f
    fairness strategies, 393–394
    formalizing joint, 362–365
    initialization, 353–354
    joint application-MAC, 358–360
    ordering, 354
    using queuing theory, 356–361
    validation experiments, 392
    video quality and, 349–351
Cross-layer problem, 338
    optimization, 339–340
Cross-layer proportional delay
        differentiation scheduler,
        433–439
Cross-layer protocols, 314
Cross-layer solutions
    application-centric approach, 354–355
    bottom-up, 354
    categorization of, 354–355
    integrated approach, 355
    MAC-centric approach, 355
    top-down, 354
Cross-layer strategy, 397, 445
Cross-layer waiting time priority scheduling
    (CWTP), 434, 436
Cross-packet erasure coding, 272–279
CSM. See Central Spectrum Moderator
Current Rate (CR), 443
CWTP. See Cross-layer waiting time priority
    scheduling

Cyclic redundancy check (CRC), 196, 289, 618
  codes, 201
  within-packet error detection and correction coding, 279–284

Data
  discrete, 608–609
  jointly Gaussian, 609–610
  loss, 16–17
  partitioning, 24–25
  requests, 85
  units, 461
Datagram Congestion Control Protocol (DCCP), 460
DCCP. See Datagram Congestion Control Protocol
DCF. See Distributed coordination function
DCT. See Discrete Cosine Transform
DCT-IV. See Discrete Cosine Transform type IV
Deadlines, 369
  decoding, 474–475
  packetizing/retransmitting data with common, 365–368
  playback, 479
Decision agents, 88
Decoder buffers, 455, 464
  delay, 87, 467
  underflow, 86
Decoder timestamps (DTS), 29, 474–475
Decoding deadlines, 474–475
Decoding delay, 87
  buffer, 87
Decorrelating transform, 613
Delay, 4, 5
  additional startup, 247
  budget, 247
  coding, 517f
  constraints, 339
  decoder buffer, 87
  decoding, 87
  encoder buffer, 86–87
  encoding, 86
  end-to-end, 86, 95, 308f, 516f, 532–533, 536, 539f
  FEC and, 73
  ideal startup, 247
  initial, 532

jitter, 257, 262–263, 566
  positive, jitter, 263
  preroll, 467
  reordering, 264–265, 265f
  spike, 551
  transmission channel, 87
Delay management architecture, 430–432
  at application level, 431
  details, 432f
  at middleware level, 431
  at network level, 432
  overview, 431f
Delay-constrained transmission, 86–87
Demodulators, 187–188
Dependent packet delays, 305–307
Deployed multitrack rate-distortion hinting file format, 363f
Design principles, 445–446
Deterministic mindset, 592
Dialers, 245
Differentiation index, 438f
DiffServ model, 413, 430–439
  cross-layer proportional delay differentiation scheduler, 433–439
  delay management architecture in, 430–432
  relative, 424
Digital communication systems, basic components of, 189f
Digital fountain codes, 196, 204
Digital media signals, processing and transmission of, 528f
Digital modulation techniques, standard, 218f
Digital speech signal, sender and receiver curves for, 529–530
Digital video signal, sender and receiver curves for, 530–532
Dilation
  of speech and audio signals, 543–547
  of video signals, 547–548
Discrete Cosine Transform (DCT), 66, 68, 69, 99, 102, 108
Discrete Cosine Transform type IV (DCT-IV), 164
Discrete data, 608–609
Discrete memoryless channel (DMC), 230, 235
Discrete sources, 188–189

Discrete wavelet signals (DWT), 150
Discrete-Time Markov chain, 314–315
Disjoint paths, 577
Distortion, 14, 75, 109
Distortion-latency optimized playout speed control, 549–550
Distributed compression, 598f
Distributed coordination function (DCF), 343–344, 423
Distributed decoders, 600f
Distributed encoders, 600f
Distributed management, 653f
Distributed video coding
    complexity performance trade-offs, 612
    motion complexity, 604
    robustness to transmission errors in, 607–608
    theory for, 604–613
DMC. See Discrete memoryless channel
DNS. See Domain name services
Domain name services (DNS), 249, 634
Downlink broadcast model, 591
Downlink packet, 347f
Downloading
    progressive, 455
    streaming v., 5–6, 85–86
DPM. See Dynamic power management
Drift effect, 124
dRSVP, 424
DTS. See Decoder timestamps
DVB-T, 217, 221
DVS. See Dynamic Voltage Scaling
DWT. See Discrete wavelet signals
Dynamic adaptation, 82
    scalable sub-flow transmission with, 382–383
Dynamic load balancing, 658
Dynamic power management (DPM), 418–419
Dynamic Voltage Scaling (DVS), 418
    benefits of, 422f
    reclamation, 422
    statistical, 422

EAC. See Embedded audio coder
Earthlink, 245
EBCOT, 141, 143
ECOSystem, 414
ECU. See Embedded coding units

EDCA. See Enhanced distributed channel access
EDU. See Energy distributed update
Egalitarian bargaining solution, 395
802.11B bit error processes, 320–323
EL. See Enhancement layer
Elias coder, 178–179, 180
    bit stream output, 179
    initialization, 179
    probability interval subdivision, 178f, 179
Embedded audio coder (EAC), 161–162, 181–182
    bit stream syntax, 182f
    framework, 161f
    subbit plane coders in, 172
Embedded bit streams, 24
Embedded coders, 160
Embedded coding units (ECU), 166, 171–172
    marking identity of, 173–174
Embedded entropy coders, 162
Embedded subbit plane entropy coding, 166–181
Embedded zerotree wavelet (EZW), 160
EMFGS. See Enhanced mode-adaptive FGS
Encoder application, 293
Encoder buffers, 464, 468
Encoder-decoder mismatch, 20
Encoding
    buffer delay, 86–87
    delay, 86
    online v. off-line, 6
End-to-end delay, 86, 95, 308f, 516f, 532–533, 536, 539f
End-to-End video transmission, 14–15
Energy distributed update (EDU), 140
Energy saving
    CPU, 417–418
    network, 418–419
Energy-efficient operating systems (EOS), 411
Enhanced distributed channel access (EDCA), 345
Enhanced mode-adaptive FGS (EMFGS), 134
Enhancement layer (EL), 120
ENK. See Entropy normalized Kullback–Leibler divergence
Entropy coding, 617

Entropy normalized Kullback-Leibler divergence (ENK), 318–319, 320, 321
modeling, 322f, 323f, 333f, 334f
Entropy of discrete memoryless source, 189
lossless source coding, 189–190
source coding, 189
Entropy of stationary sources, 195–196
EOS. *See* Energy-efficient operating systems
EPS. *See* Error protection strategy
ER. *See* Explicit Rate
Erasure channels, 236
Error concealment, 17, 20, 29–41, 31–32, 82
adaptive, 37
hybrid, 37
multihypothesis, 36
nonnormative, 31–32
performance of, 38f
spatial, 31–32, 33f
temporal, 34–37
Error control systems, 271–272
Error correction, 201
Error detection, 19, 201
packet, 279–284
Error mitigation, 41–53
motivation, 41–42
Error probability, 296
Error propagation, 17
Error protection strategy (EPS), 281, 282
N-packet, 284
rate-optimal, 284
unequal, 286t
for wireless networks, 284–289
Error Tracking, 46
Error vector, 199–200
Error-control schemes, 314
Error-resilience features, 314
Error-resilient entropy coding, 21
Error-resilient video transmission, 18–29
data partitioning in, 24–25
design principles, 19–20
error control methods, 20
FMO and, 23–24
redundant slices in, 25–26
scalability, 24
slice structured coding and, 21–22
system overview, 18–19
video compression tools in, 20–21
ETSI. *See* European Telecommunications Standard Institute

Euclidean distance, 198, 206, 209
code, 211
Euclidean metrics, 197
European Space Agency, 217
European Telecommunications Standard Institute (ETSI), 63
EWMA. *See* Exponentially weighted moving averages
EXACT framework, 442
flow control scheme, 443f
multimedia streaming using, 444
router behavior in, 443–444
TCP and, 444f
Explicit Rate (ER), 443
Exponential averaging, 498f
Exponentially weighted moving averages (EWMA), 497
EZBC, 141
EZW. *See* Embedded zerotree wavelet

Fairness strategies
for cross-layer optimized media transmission, 393–394
multimedia quality, 395–396
time, 394–395
Fano algorithm, 211
Fast retransmit, 265
FEC. *See* Forward Error Correction
Feedback channels, 271–272
Feedback gain, 485
Feedback implosion, 491
Feedback modes, 47–50
BEC channel with, 234–235
operation of, 48f
regular prediction with limited error propagation, 50–51
synchronized reference frames, 50
unrestricted reference areas with expected distortion update, 51
FGS. *See* Fine granularity scalability
FGS Temporal (FGST) pictures, 130–131
FGST pictures. *See* FGS Temporal
Fine grained selection, 463
Fine granularity scalability (FGS)
enhanced mode-adaptive, 134
motion-compensated, 133
MPEG-4, 127–135
nonstandard, 132–135

Fine granularity scalability (FGS)
  (continued)
  progressive, 133
  robust, 133
Finite fields, 197
Finite precision arithmetic operation, 180
Fixed codebook gains, 64
Fixed rate distortion functions, 75
Fixed-length channel codewords, 281f,
    283–284
Fixed-length information blocks, 280–281
Flexibility, in bandwidth adaptation
    mechanisms, 90f
Flexible distribution, 592
Flexible Macroblock Ordering (FMO),
    23–24, 30, 33
Flexible reference frame concept, 26–27
Flow control header, 442
FMO. *See* Flexible Macroblock Ordering
Foreman, 39, 49f, 52f, 279, 302, 304, 306f
Forward Error Correction (FEC), 9, 19, 59,
    78, 188, 229, 237, 271, 289, 491,
    519, 565
  with 4:3 redundancy, 73f
  delay and, 73
  MDC, 573f
  media-dependent, 73–78
  PET and, 493–494
  for speech, 72–78
Forward hops, 245
4-QAM, 217, 218f, 219f, 220, 221
Four-level hierarchical-B prediction
    structure, 152f
Frame(s), 42f, 60, 61
  drops, 625f
  rates, 487
  virtual, 487
Frequency-domain concealment techniques,
    38
FS-1016, 63
FTP, 5, 242
(PDF) functions, 253f
Fundamental abstractions, 464–476

G.711, 61, 62–63, 79
G.722.1, 74, 79
G.729, 65
Gain predictors, 65
Galois fields, 197

Game-theoretic dynamic resource
    management, 396–401
Gaussian source, 283
GDR. *See* Gradual Decoding Refresh
Generator matrix, 205, 215
  expression of, 208
Geometric structure, 34
Gilbert channels, 238, 239, 241
Gilbert model, 236
  state diagram of, 237f
Gilbert-Elliott channel, 236
Global failure, 507
Global System for Mobile Communications
    (GSM), 63
GOB. *See* Group of blocks
Go-Back-N ARQ, 223, 224f
GOF. *See* Group of frames
Golomb coder, 178
Good-burst distributions
  Markov chain, 326–329
  simplification of, 329–330
GOP. *See* Group of pictures
GRACE, 414
Graceful degradation, 24
Gradual Decoding Refresh (GDR), 288
Granularity, bandwidth, 89
Group of blocks (GOB), 22, 26, 46
Group of frames (GOF), 123, 135, 594f
  temporal Haar wavelet decomposition of,
    136f
Group of pictures (GOP), 237, 257, 297,
    305, 363–364, 377, 378, 379
GSM. *See* Global System for Mobile
    Communications

H.261, 20–21, 22, 46
H.263, 20, 22, 26, 30, 46, 118, 409, 420,
    515, 624f
H.263++, 21, 25f, 46
H.264, 20, 53, 118, 146
  formalization, 29–30
H.264/AVC, 13, 15, 21, 22, 25, 27f, 28, 36,
    42, 54
H.323, SIP v., 510t
Haar decomposition, 139
Haar multiresolution analysis, 138
Haar transform, 135–151, 147
  shift variance of, 150f

Hamming distance, 193–194, 197–198, 206, 209
  code, 211
Hamming metrics, 197
Hardware adaptation, 446
Hash generation, 618
HCCA. *See* HCF controlled channel access
HCF. *See* Hybrid coordination function
HCF controlled channel access (HCCA), 345
  video transmission over, 370–374
HDTV, 15
Header fields, 508, 509t
  RTP, 511f
Heavy tails, 255–257, 260–261
Heterogeneity of channels, 490
Heterogeneity of devices, 490
Heuristic playout speed control, 548–549
Hexagonal lattice, 206f
Hidden Markov models (HMMs), 324
Hierarchical modulation, 217–222, 219f
Hierarchical-B, 152
High compression efficiency, 592
High Definition TV, 222, 339
High-order Markov chains, 316
High-priority bit streams, 218, 220, 221
Hint track, 299, 462
HiperLANs, 337
HMMs. *See* Hidden Markov models
Home surveillance cameras, 81
HPHR, 133–134
HPLR, 133–134
Human auditory masking, 167–169
Hybrid ARQ protocols, 225
  type I, 225
  type II, 225
Hybrid concealment, 37
Hybrid coordination function (HCF), 345
Hybrid video coding system, 17f

IBM Global Network, 245
ICMP packets, 245
Ideal startup delay, 247
Identity matrices, 70
IDR frames, 28f
IEEE 802.11, 341–345, 410, 423, 436, 440
  operation of, 372f
  overview of, 342f
  packet scheduling and retransmission
    under, 379–382

resource reservation mechanisms for, 370–386
  scalable video admission control
    mechanisms over, 374–376
  SNR v. BER in, 343f
  transmissions in, 427f
IETF. *See* Internet Engineering Task Force
I-frames, 105, 295f
iid model, 305
Implicit auditory masking, 169–171
  encoding using, 170f
Improved robustness against network
    variations (AMP-robust), 542–543
IN. *See* Intelligent Networks
In-band prediction, 149f
In-band temporal filtering, 148
Inbuilt robustness, 592
Incremental deployment, 651
Independent Segment Decoding (ISD), 46
Individual monotonocity, 396
Information bits, 280f
Information overhead, in bandwidth
    adaptation mechanisms, 96
Informed adaptation, 444
Initial delay, 532
Initial playout delay reduction (AMP-initial), 540–542
Initial state, 236
Input audio channels, 163
INSIGNIA, 424, 441
Instantaneous arrival rate, 480
Instantaneous delay behavior, 438f
Intelligent Networks (IN), 635
Intelligent Streaming, 83
INTER mode, 99, 100, 133, 134f
Interactive error control, 45–47
Inter-coding mode, 593
Interleaving, 213–214, 285
  block, 213t
  cross, 214f
International Telecommunications Union
    (ITU), 60
Internet, 4–5, 187
  broadcast, 97
  test conditions, 51–52
Internet Engineering Task Force (IETF), 458, 506
Internet Telephony. *See* Voice over IP
Inter-node scheduling, 434

Intra information coding, 28–29
INTRA mode, 99, 100
Intra mode, 28
Intra-coding mode, 593
Intra/Inter-mode switching, 519
Intra-node scheduling, 434
IntServ model, 413, 423, 424–430
    bandwidth management architecture in,
        424–426
    illustrative example of, 427–430
Inverse transform, 621
INVITE method, 506, 515
IP bit rates, 246
iPod, 3, 411
IRA codes. *See* Irregular repeat-accumulate
Irregular repeat-accumulate (IRA) codes,
    203
ISA. *See* Iterative Sensitivity Adjustment
ISD. *See* Independent Segment Decoding
Iterative decoding, 216
Iterative Sensitivity Adjustment (ISA), 297,
    495
ITU. *See* International Telecommunications
    Union
ITU G.722.2, 65, 66
iTunes, 3

Jitter delay, 257, 262–263, 566
JND. *See* Just noticeable distortion
Joint application-MAC cross-layer
    optimization, 358–360
Joint packet scheduling, 434
Joint paths, 577
Joint source-channel coding (JSCC), 364
Joint strategy, 397
Jointly Gaussian data, 609–610
JPEG2000, 142, 143, 160
JSCC. *See* Joint source-channel coding
Just noticeable distortion (JND), 167, 168,
    170, 172, 174
    in subbit plane-embedded entropy coding,
        175

Kaiser–Bessel Derived (KbD) window, 164
Kalai–Smorodinsky bargaining solution,
    395, 396f
KbD window. *See* Kaiser–Bessel Derived
Kullback–Leibler divergence, 318–319

Lagrange-based optimization algorithm, 288
Lagrangian multiplier techniques, 43, 76–77,
    275, 296, 474
Lagrangian optimization, 100
    cross-layer MAC-application layer using,
        361–370
LANs. *See* Local Area Networks
Lapped transform codecs, loss concealment
    for, 65–72
Late loss rate, 532–533
    end-to-end delay and, 539f
    for VoIP, 534–535
Latency, 95–96
    playback, 85
    in VoIP, 516–518
Lattice codes, 196, 204–205
Layered coding, 120. *See also* Scalable
        coding
    global structure of, 121f
    SNR scalability, 125f
    spatial scalability, 122f
    temporal scalability, 123f
Layered multicast, 490
Layered multiple description coding,
    278–279
LDPC code. *See* Low-density parity-check
Leaky bucket model, 464–471
Least-significant bits (LSBs), 126, 129,
    171–172
LFSM. *See* Linear finite state machine
Lifting scheme
    Barbell, 139f, 140
    basic steps of, 138f
    spatiotemporal motion-compensated, 138f
    three-band, 146f
Lifting-like schemes, 147f
Limited efficiency spatial scalability, 148
Limited motion-estimation efficiency, 148
Limited spatiotemporal decomposition
        structure, 148
Line Spectral Pairs (LSP), 64
Linear block codes, 196–197
Linear finite state machine (LFSM), 206
    representation of convolutional code, 207f
Linear mapping, 437f
Linear Prediction (LP), 63
Link adaptation, QoS token rate adaptation
    for, 383–384

Linux, 411
List Viterbi algorithm (LVA), 280
Live broadcast, 6, 453, 489–496
Live media streaming (AMP-live), 543, 544f
Live transcoding, 647f
LLR. *See* Log-likelihood ratios
Loaded packets, 254
Local Area Networks (LANs), 337
Local search algorithms, 275–276
Location Managers, 648, 649
Log-likelihood ratios (LLR), 211
Loss, 4
Loss burst duration, 254–255
Loss burst lengths, 252–254
Loss concealment, 75–76
    algorithms for, 62–63
    for CELP speech codecs, 63–65
    for lapped transform codecs, 65
    for waveform speech codecs, 60–63
Lossless recovery, 608–609
Lossless source coding, 189–190, 596–597
Lossy source coding, 190–191, 597–598
Low encoding complexity-distributed video
        codec, 607f
Low-density parity-check (LDPC) code,
        196, 202–203
Low-priority bit streams, 218, 220, 221
LP. *See* Linear Prediction
LPC Synthesis Filter, 63, 71
LPLR, 133–134
LSBs. *See* Least-significant bits
L-segment protection, 275, 277
LSP. *See* Line Spectral Pairs
LT codes. *See* Luby Transform
Luby Transform (LT) codes, 204
LVA. *See* List Viterbi algorithm

MAC. *See* Medium access control
MAC-centric channel models, 9
Macroblock-based PFGS (MPFGS),
        133–134
Macroblocks (MBs), 16, 23f, 26, 31f, 34f, 99
Magnitude Refinement, 143
MANET. *See* Multi-hop ad hoc networks
MAP rule. *See* Maximum a posteriori rule
Markov chain model, 236, 335
    for 2-Mbps bit error process, 320–321
    for 5.5-Mbps bit error process, 321–322
    approximating, 331

CCM compared with, 332–334
discrete-time, 314–315
good-burst and bad-burst distributions,
        326–329
high-order, 316
observations about, 324–326
performance evaluation, 319
practical issues, 316–319
reducing complexity of, 324–335
standard errors of, 322t, 333t
transition possibilities for fourth-order,
        325f
for wireless channel modeling, 314–316
Markov channel model, 306
Markov channels, 236, 237
Markov decision tree, 300, 301f
Markov property, 315
Markov Random Field (MRF), 38
Masking thresholds, 168
Maximum a posteriori decoding, 193
Maximum a posteriori (MAP) rule, 194
Maximum distance decoding, 193
Maximum-distance separable (MDS) codes,
        199, 272
Maximum-likelihood decoding, 193
M-band filter banks, 146
MBR streaming, 473–474
MBs. *See* Macroblocks
MC-FGS. *See* Motion-Compensated FGS
MCP. *See* Motion-Compensated Prediction
MCPC. *See* Motion-Compensated Predictive
        Coding
MCP-coded video, 16–17
    in packet lossy environment, 18f
MCTF. *See* Motion-Compensated Temporal
        Filtering
MDA. *See* Multidimensional adaptation
MDC. *See* Multiple Description Coding;
        Multiple description coding
MDCT. *See* Modified discrete cosine
        transform
m-dimensional integer, 205
MDS codes. *See* Maximum-distance
        separable codes
Mean square error (MSE), 597–598, 599
    recovery with, 609–610
Media awareness, 293
Media distribution, 642–644
Media on demand, 453
    architectures, 454–457

Media on demand *(continued)*
  buffering model, 464–471
  communication protocols, 457–460
  compound streams, 471–473
  control objective, 482
  controller design, 484–487
  controller interpretation, 488–489
  file formats, 461–464
  frame rates, 487
  fundamental abstractions, 464–476
  leaky bucket model, 464–471
  target schedule design, 483–484
Media overlays, 633–634, 635–637
  adaptive streaming for multiple clients,
      655
  advanced topics, 654–658
  architecture and design, 650–654
  caching, 642–644
  capabilities of, 639–641
  client request handling, 644–645
  content adaptation, 665
  content sharing, 664–665
  design choices, 652–653
  enhanced media access, 664
  in extended system architecture, 638f
  in media delivery, 658–659
  media distribution, 642–644
  media security, 656–657
  mid-session streaming handoff, 657–658
  modular, 650–652
  multi-way conferencing, 661–664
  network-adaptive media streaming,
      654–655
  overview of streaming, 637–639
  path and server diversities, 657
  processing services, 646–648
  real-time media adaptation and
      transcoding, 655–656
  receiving media, 641–642
  recording and retrieving multimedia
      messages, 664
  sending media, 641
  server capabilities of, 640–641
  splitting service, 660–661
  stream relay, 642
  system monitoring and management,
      645–646, 652
  transport and streaming, 641–642
  uses and benefits, 658–665
  walk-through, 648–650

Media processing services, 646–648
Media quality, 86, 94–95
Media server, 293
Media services architecture, 647–648
Media time, 475
Media transport and control protocols, 510
Media-dependent FEC, 73–78
Medium access control (MAC), 313, 325,
      335, 340, 343–344, 435, 436
  in cross-layer solutions, 355
  PLR, 357f
  protocols, 314
MELP. *See* Mixed excitation linear
      prediction
Memory length of Markov chains, 316–317
Memory lengths, 315–316
Memoryless sources, 188–189
Meshes, 136
Message flow, 507f
Metrics for quantifying performance, 7–8
Microsoft Messenger, 79
Middleware control framework, 439f
Middleware-based adaptation services,
      439–440
MIL-STD-3005, 63
MIME, 457
MIMO. *See* Multiple Input Multiple Output
Minimal real-time processing, 128
Minimum distance coding, 193
Mismatch, 17
MIX. *See* Channel mixers
Mixed excitation linear prediction (MELP),
      63
MLT. *See* Modulated Lapped Transform
Mobile operating systems
  architecture of, 415f
  coordination in, 414–416
  CPU energy saving in, 417–418
  CPU speed changing in, 419f
  design and algorithms of, 414
  experimental results, 420–422
  network energy saving in, 418–419
  QoS in, 413–422
  soft real-time CPU scheduling in, 416–417
Mobile sequence, 389
Model based coders, 144
Modem error correction protocols, 260
Modified discrete cosine transform (MDCT),
      163–164, 181
  with switching window, 165f

Modulated Lapped Transform (MLT), 66,
  67f, 68, 163–164
Modulators, 187–188
Modulo-2 addition, 208
Monitor, 439
Moore-Penrose generalized inverse, 70
Most significant bit (MSB) plane, 129,
  171–172
Motion complexity, in DVC, 604
Motion search, 615–616
  high complexity, 616–617
  no, 615–616
Motion vector (MV), 24, 132, 154
  scalability, 120
Motion-Compensated FGS (MC-FGS), 133
Motion-Compensated Prediction (MCP), 13,
  104, 593
Motion-Compensated Predictive Coding
  (MCPC), 605–606
Motion-Compensated Temporal Filtering
  (MCTF), 135–140, 153–154
  2D + t, 150, 151f
  t + 2D, 150, 151f
  unconstrained, 145–147
  wavelet, 139
Motion-Compensated Video Model,
  604–605
Motion-compensated wavelet video codecs,
  135–151
Motion-search complexity, 603–604
MP3, 5, 66, 159
MPARC, 424
MPEG-1, 20
MPEG-2, 8, 26, 30, 118, 409
MPEG-4, 5, 13, 15, 20, 21, 46, 53, 118, 159,
  409, 519
  AVC/H.264 scalable extension, 152–153
  FGS coding, 127–135, 279
  FGS encoders, 128f
  FGS two-layer bit stream, 130f
  hybrid temporal-SNR scalability with
    FGS structure, 129–132
  SNR FGS structure in, 127–129
  video packetization, 515f
MPFGS. See Macroblock-based PFGS
MRF. See Markov Random Field
MSB plane. See Most significant bit
MSE. See Mean square error
MSNBC.com, 3

Multicast, 7, 97. See also Receiver-driven
    layered multicast
  address, 490
  backbone, 242–243
  layered, 490
Multidimensional adaptation (MDA), 153
Multi-hop ad hoc networks (MANET),
    441–442
  best effort traffic in, 442
Multimedia codecs, 83
Multimedia communication, 4–8
  applications, 4–5
  sender and receiver curves for, 528–532
Multimedia quality fairness, 395–396
Multipath streaming systems
  analysis, 577–580
  asymmetric paths in, 580
  design, 577–580
  joint and disjoint paths, 577
  number of paths, 577–578
  operation, 577–580
  path selection in, 578
Multiple bit rate coding, 463
  in bandwidth adaptation, 105–107
Multiple deadlines, 303–305
Multiple Description Coding (MDC), 79,
    104, 567–577
  audio coding, 571–572
  basic, 567f
  benefits of, 576f
  CDN, 582–583
  FEC, 573f
  image coding, 572
  information theory perspective on,
    569–570
  for media, 576–577
  packet losses and, 579
  predictive, 574
  repairable, 575–576
  scalable coding v., 568–569
  SD coding v., 568–569
  speech coding, 571–572
  video coding, 572–573
Multiple description coding (MDC), 552
Multiple Input Multiple Output (MIMO),
    341
Multiresolution motion compensation coder,
    149f
Multiuser wireless video resource allocation
    game, 398f

Mutual information, 189
 pair-wise, 390t
Mutually exclusive media streams, 473
MV. *See* Motion vector

NACK, 53
NAK. *See* Negative acknowledgment
NAL. *See* Network abstraction layer
Napster, 3
Nash bargaining solution, 395
n-dimensional vector, 205
Negative acknowledgment (NAK), 47, 50,
    222, 243, 247, 257, 262, 301,
    302, 456
Nemesis, 414
Network abstraction layer (NAL), 15
Network adaptive transmission, 293
Network energy saving, 418–419
Network layer, 340
New Prediction (NEWPRED), 46, 519
NEWPRED. *See* New Prediction
$N_{MB/DU}$, 30
NMR, 181
No excitation response, 70–71
Nonconversational services, AMP for,
    538–540
Nonsignificance pass, 126
Normalization, 143
Normalized waiting time, 433

Observation Task, 439
ODWT. *See* Overcomplete discrete wavelet
    data
Offline encoding, 6
Online encoding, 6
Open Systems Interconnection (OSI), 337
Open-loop architecture, 101
Operation encoder control, 42–44
Operational coder control, 42, 43f
Optimal expected cross-layer strategy, 400
Optimal joint strategy, 400
Optimal real-time cross-layer strategy, 401
Optimal revealing strategy, 400
Optimization complexity, 109
Optimization procedure, 76f, 77
Optimum rate allocation, 77–78
OPTIONS method, 506
Oracle, 606

Orthogonal Frequency Division
    Multiplexing, 342
OSI. *See* Open Systems Interconnection
Overall probabilities, 237
Overcomplete discrete wavelet data
    (ODWT), 150
Overcomplete wavelet domain, motion
    estimation and compensation in,
    148–151
Overlapped block motion compensation, 36
Overlapped transforms, 66–67

P frames, 26
P2P networks. *See* Peer-to-peer networks
Packet(s), 74, 75, 279
 blocks of, 274t
 error detection, 279–284
 loaded, 254
 media to, 562–563
 partially late, 257
 unloaded, 254
 useless, 257
Packet compression event, 262
Packet correlation
 over channels with memory, 238–240
 probabilities and, 239f, 240f
Packet Data Unit (PDU), 39, 40
Packet erasure channel (PEC), 234, 267–268
Packet expansion events, 263
Packet losses, 236–238, 358
 average, 252f
 burst durations, 254–255
 burst lengths, 252–254
 channel coding and, 196–217
 heavy tails, 255–257
 over cascaded channels with memory,
    240–241
 over channels with memory, 236–238
 overview of, 251–252
 per-state, 251
 protection with QoS, 278
 SD and MD video, 579
 in Wide Scale Internet streaming study,
    251–257
Packet path diversity, 552–553
 for low-delay conversational services, 552
Packet reception, 241f
Packet reordering, 263–266
 distance, 264

Packet routes, controlling, 586–587
Packet transmission duration, 346–349
Packetization modes, 31f
Packetization scheme, 562f
PAL, 537
PANs. *See* Personal Area Networks
Parallel traceroutes, 245
Pareto distribution, 257, 261
Parity bits, 280f
Parity check matrix, 199, 201
Parity packets, generation of, 495
Parity symbols, 273
Partition tree, 212f
Path diversity, 559, 560f
    applications and architectures, 580–587
    benefits of, 563–567
    content delivery networks, 581–583
    controlling packet routes, 586–587
    low-delay applications for, 580–581
    in media overlays, 657
    modeling, 578–579
    over peer-to-peer networks, 583–584
    over wireless networks, 584–586
    selection of, 565f
    topologies, 580f
PBRA, 424
PBx, 3–4
PCF. *See* Point coordination function
PCM. *See* Pulse Code Modulation
PDF, 257
PDU. *See* Packet Data Unit
Peak Signal-to-Noise Ratio (PSNR), 8, 39,
        41f, 48, 49f, 50, 51, 52f, 95, 282
    decoded, 362t, 393t
    plot of, 40f
    rate curves v., 305
    transmitted bit rate v., 298f, 302
PEC. *See* Packet erasure channel
Peering, 651
Peer-to-peer (P2P) networks, 84, 635–637
    path diversity over, 583–584
Perfect state measurement, 486
Performance bounds, 230
Per-hop-behavior (PHB), 433
Personal Area Networks (PANs), 337, 340
PET. *See* Priority encoding transmission
PFC. *See* Previous Frame Concealment
PFGS. *See* Progressive FGS
P-frames, 105, 106, 295f
    coding, 593f

PHB. *See* Per-hop-behavior
PHY. *See* Physical layer
Physical layer (PHY), 340, 342, 349, 352
Piecewise linear mapping, 437f
PIFS time, 373
Pitch period, 62, 545–547
Playback, 85
    deadline, 479
    latency, 85
Playout speed control mechanisms, 548–551
    distortion-latency optimized, 549–550
    heuristic, 548–549
    for low-delay applications, 550–551
PMFs. *See* Probability mass functions
PN. *See* Predicted insignificance
Podcasting, 3, 5
Point coordination function (PCF), 344
Point-to-point protocol (PPP), 245
    Compression Control Protocol, 260
Positive acknowledgment (ACK), 47, 222,
        243, 265–266, 506
Power measurement, 421f
Power-saving mode (PSM), 420
PPLive, 3
PPP. *See* Point-to-point protocol
Predicted insignificance (PN), 173
Predicted significance (PS), 173
Prediction across frames, 109
Predictive coding, 595
Predictive video coding scheme, 119f
Preroll delay, 467
Presentation Time Stamp (PTS), 47, 475
Previous Frame Concealment (PFC), 34–35
Prioritization methods, 19
Priority encoding transmission (PET),
        272–279, 491
    BOPs in, 277
    with eight transmitted packets, 273t
    FEC and, 493–494
    optimization, 275–276
    packetization, 492f
    QoS of, 277–278
    quality, 493f
PRISM, 601, 628
    architectural goals of, 602–604
    classification, 613–614
    compression performance of, 602
    decoding, 619–621
    decorrelating transform, 613
    encoding, 613–619

PRISM *(continued)*
  future research in, 625–626
  lossless channel results, 622f
  lossy channel results, 623f
  motion-search complexity, 603–604
  quantization, 613
  robustness, 602–603
  simulation results, 621–625
Private information estimation, 400
Probability estimation, 180–181
Probability mass functions (PMFs), 317–318
Product code system, 285, 286–287, 287t, 289t
Progressive downloading, 455
Progressive FGS (PFGS), 133
  macroblock-based, 133–134
Proportional service differentiation model, 434
Protocol stack, 506f
Provisional response, 506
Proxy, 84
  in bandwidth adaptation mechanisms, 92
PS. *See* Predicted significance
PSM. *See* Power-saving mode
PSNR. *See* Peak Signal-to-Noise Ratio
PTS. *See* Presentation Time Stamp
Pulse Code Modulation (PCM), 60, 61, 74
Pure ARQ protocols, 222–223
Purged datasets, 250–251

QCIF. *See* Quarter Common Intermediate Format
QM coder, 178
QoS. *See* Quality-of-Service
QP. *See* Quantization step size
QPSK. *See* Quadrature Phase Shift Keying
Quadrature Phase Shift Keying (QPSK), 217
Quality-of-Service (QoS), 13, 20, 81, 337, 371, 503
  architectures, 440
  end-to-end, 410
  in mobile operating systems, 413–422
  in mobile wireless networks, 422–445
  models, 423–424, 446
  priority encoding transmission and, 277–278
  sub-flow, token rates, 384t, 385t

token rate adaptation for link adaptation, 383–384
VoIP, 516–522
Quantization
  lattice, 615f
  section split and, 165–166
Quantization step size (QP), 99, 100
Quarter Common Intermediate Format (QCIF), 39
Queue diversity, 566
QuickTime, 457

RA codes. *See* Repeat-accumulate codes
RaDiO. *See* Rate-distortion optimized streaming
Radio Link Control (RLC), 39, 40
Random process, memory lengths of, 315–316
Rapid adaptation mode, 551
Raptor codes, 204
Rate, 14
Rate compatible punctured convolutional (RCPC) codes, 196, 211, 285, 288
  decoders, 287
  decreasing, 289t
  encoders, 286
  within packet error detection, 279–284
Rate control, 102, 110
  for bandwidth adaptation, 98–99
Rate distortion (RD), 98
  preamble, 89, 299
Rate estimation, 496–498
Rate-adaptive applications, 314
Rate-based optimization, 282–283
Rate-Based Transmission, 442
Rate-control system, 425
Rate-distortion function, 191
Rate-distortion optimized streaming (RaDiO), 294–300, 460
  basic framework, 295–298
  CoDiO and, 308f, 309f
  multiple deadlines in, 303–305
  proxy driven streaming, 300f
  receiver-driven streaming, 298–300
Rate-distortion performance, 304f, 306f
Rate-optimal solutions, 276–277

Rate-priority points in subbit plane-embedded entropy coding, 175
Rayleigh channel, 287
RCPC codes. *See* Rate compatible punctured convolutional codes
RD. *See* Rate distortion
R-D curves, 76, 100
R-D optimization algorithm, 305
R-D optimized system, 297, 305, 550
R-D value pairs, 144
Reaction time in bandwidth adaptation mechanisms, 95–96
Real Audio, 159
Real Time Streaming Protocol (RTSP), 458, 459t, 649
RealMedia, 457
RealNetworks, 457
RealPlayer, 83
RealSystem, 97
Real-time adaptive packetization, 362
Real-time algorithms, 367
Real-time communication, 6, 59, 461
Real-time cross-layer algorithm for wireless video streaming, 368–370
Real-time cross-layer optimization, 386–393
feature selection, 388–391
Real-time greedy algorithm for adaptive packetization, 369t
Real-time retransmission limit optimization (RTRO), 358, 360
Real-time strategy selection, 388
Real-time streaming, 246–247
Real-time Transport Control Protocol (RTCP), 44, 504
VoIP, 512–513
Real-time Transport Protocol (RTP), 44, 504, 510–512, 511
header format, 511f
Receiver curves
for digital speech signal transmission, 529–530
for digital video signal transmission, 530–532
for multimedia communication, 528–532
for voice packets, 534f
Receiver devices, 7
Receiver driven streaming, 298–300
Receiver-driven layered multicast (RLM), 456, 490

Recursive Optimal per-Pixel Estimate (ROPE), 45
RED, 253
Redirectional response, 507
Redundancy, 82, 187
rates, 366–367
Redundant slices, 25–26
Reed–Solomon codes, 196, 202, 272, 346
REF. *See* Refinement
Reference areas with expected distortion update, 51
Reference frames, synchronized, 50
Reference Picture Selection (RPS), 26
Refinement (REF), 173
context, 176
subbit plane, 173
Refinement bit, context for, 176
Refinement pass, 127
Region of Interest (ROI), 23
REGISTER method, 506
Regular prediction with limited error propagation, 50–51
Regular users, 243
Reliable routing protocols, 314
Render buffers, 455
Reordering delay, 264–265
histogram of, 265f
Reordering distance, 265–266
Repeat-accumulate (RA) codes, 204
Replacement excitation, 64–65
Request failure, 507
Request for Comments (RFC), 458
Resource monitoring, 641
Resynchronization, 29–41
Retransmission schemes, 244
optimal packet sizes for, 350f
Revealing strategy, 397
Reverse hops, 245
Reversible Variable Length Coding (RVLC), 21
RFC. *See* Request for Comments
RFGS. *See* Robust FGS
RIch acknowledgments, 300–303
conventional acknowledgments v., 302f
RLC. *See* Radio Link Control
RLM. *See* Receiver-driven layered multicast
Robust FGS (RFGS), 133
Robustness tests, 621–622
ROI. *See* Region of Interest

ROPE. *See* Recursive Optimal per-Pixel
        Estimate
Round-trip delay (RTT), 243, 259–262, 487
    average, 261f
    calculation, 513f
    heavy tails, 260–261
    histograms of, 259f
    overview of, 259–260
    variation of, 261–262
Router-Assisted Flow Control, 442
RPS. *See* Reference Picture Selection
RSC encoders, 214
RTCP. *See* Real-Time Control Protocol;
        Real-time Transport Control
        Protocol
RTP. *See* Real-Time Transport Protocol
RTRO. *See* Real-time retransmission limit
        optimization
RTSP. *See* Real Time Streaming Protocol
RTT. *See* Round-trip delay
RVLC. *See* Reversible Variable Length
        Coding

SAD. *See* Sum of Absolute Differences
Scalability, 24, 91, 117, 651
    in bandwidth adaptation mechanisms, 90f
    complex, 127
    content, 127
    in current video coding standards,
        118–127
    fine granularity, 103, 463
    frequency, 127
    hybrid temporal-SNR, 129–132
    layered SNR, 125f
    layered spatial, 122f
    layered temporal, 123f
    motion vector, 120
    multilayer FGS-temporal, 132f
    SNR, 103, 124
    spatial, 103, 120
    temporal, 103, 123
Scalable audio coding framework, 161–162
Scalable coding, 160. *See also* Layered
        coding
    in bandwidth adaptation, 103–104
    MDC v., 568–569
    for media, 576–577
Scalable streaming, 473–474

Scalable video admission control
        mechanisms, over IEEE 802.11,
        374–376
Scene super-resolution, 626–627
SDP. *See* Session Description Protocol
Search regions, 545
Secondary SP (SSP), 29
Section split, quantization and, 165–166
Security, 656–657
Selective-Repeat ARQ, 223–224, 224f
Self-congestion, 307
Sender curves
    for digital speech signal transmission,
        529–530
    for digital video signal transmission,
        530–532
    for multimedia communication, 528–532
    for voice packets, 534f
Sender-driven streaming, 299f
Senders, 84, 110
    in bandwidth adaptation mechanisms, 91
Sending rates, 476–479
Server failure, 507
Service intervals (SI), 373
Session Description Protocol (SDP), 509
    MDC v., 568–569
    for media, 576–577
    packet losses and, 579
Session initiation protocol (SIP), 504,
        505–508
    call setup using, 515f
    H.323 v., 510t
    Uniform Resource Identifiers, 508
S-frames, 106
Shadow retry limit (SRL), 359
Shannon information theory, 178
Shannon's channel theorem, 188–196
    source channel coding, 194
Shannon's noiseless coding theorem, 190
    lossy source coding, 190–191
Shannon's source theorem, 188–196
    channel coding, 192
Shannon's source-channel coding theorem,
        194–195
Shift registers, 214f
Shift variance of Haar transform, 150f
SI. *See* Service intervals; Switching Intra
Side information, source coding with,
        595–596
SI-frames in bandwidth adaptation, 107

Sign bits, 176
Sign coding, 176
  sign and context for, 177f
Sign count, 177f
Signaling protocols, VoIP, 505–508
Signal-to-noise ratio (SNR), 213, 350
  BER v., in 802.11, 343f
  subjectively weighted, 78f
Significance identification, context for, 177f
Significance Propagation, 143
Silence periods, 548
Simple Object Access Protocol, 648
Simplified systems, 84
Simulated retransmission, 248
Simulcast, 117–118, 490
Single rate distortion functions, 75
Single voice packets, extension and
          compression of, 546f
Single-hop ad hoc network, 422
Single-hop wireless networks, 440–442
SIP. See Session initiation protocol
16-QAM, 217, 218f, 219f, 220
  nonuniform, 220f
64-QAM, 218f, 219f, 220, 221
Skype, 3–4
Slice groups, 23
Slice structured coding, 21–22
  example of, 22f
SMIL. See Synchronized Multimedia
          Integration Language
SMPTE, 361
SNR. See Signal-to-noise ratio
SNR coding structure, 118–124
Social decisions, 400
Soft IP switches, 3–4
Soft real-time CPU scheduling, 416–417
Soft real-time tasks, 412
Software adaptation, 446
Source coding, 455, 470, 476
  background, 594–602
  control, 478, 479
  with side information, 595–596
Source encoders, 187
SP pictures. See Switching-Predictive
Spatial coding structure, 118–124
Spatial reuse, 428f
Spatial transforms, 126
  temporal transforms and, 147–148
Spatial wavelet transform, 148

Spatiotemporal decomposition,
          parent-offspring relationship in,
          142f
Spatiotemporal error propagation, 17
Spatiotemporal motion-compensated lifting
          scheme, 138f
Spatiotemporal SNR, visual performance
          and, 153
Speech codecs, 68–72
Speech signal, 61f, 67f
  FEC for, 72–78
SP-frames, in bandwidth adaptation, 107
SPIHT, 141, 144, 145, 282
Spike delay, 551
Split-level adaptation, 444
Splitting function, 660–661
SRL. See Shadow retry limit
SSD. See Sum of Squared Differences
SSP. See Secondary SP
Stack algorithm, 211
Standard array, 200f
  tabulating, 201
Standard error, between cumulative
          densities, 317–318
Stationary sources, entropy of, 195–196
Statistical feedback, 491
Statistical mindset, 592
Steady-state probabilities, 239
Stop-and-wait ARQ, 222–223
Storage in bandwidth adaptation
          mechanisms, 96
Stream morphing in bandwidth adaptation,
          107–108
Stream relay, 642, 643f
Streaming, 303–305. See also
          Rate-distortion optimized
          streaming
  building blocks for, 561–563
  characteristics, 562
  on demand, 6
  downloading v., 5–6, 85–86
  MBR, 473–474
  over packet networks, 476–489
  overlays, 637–639
  protocol, 459
  real-time, 246–247
  receiver-driven, 298–300
  scalable, 473–474
  sender-driven, 299f
  statistics, 246t

Streaming *(continued)*
    video, 368–370, 548–549
Subbit plane context adaptive entropy coder,
        175–177
Subbit plane-embedded entropy coding, 172f
    encoding critical bands in, 174–175
    finding current gap in, 174
    initialization of, 174
    recording rate-priority points in, 175
    updating JND threshold in, 175
Sub-flow concept, 374–376
    with different transmission durations, 378f
    examples of transmission, 384–386
    formation, 375f
    frame rates and, 386f
    QoS token rates, 384, 385t
    scalable, with dynamic adaptation,
        382–383
    transmission of packets of, 382t
Suboptimal algorithms, 278
Subsequences, 26
Successful response, 507
Successive packets, 305
Successive refinement, 24
Sum of Absolute Differences (SAD), 36
Sum of Squared Differences (SSD), 36
Supplementary materials, 10
Surestream, 83, 97
SWAN, 424, 441
Switching Intra (SI), 29
Switching pictures, 29
Switching windows, MDCT with, 165f
Switching-Predictive (SP) pictures, 29
Synchronized Multimedia Integration
        Language (SMIL), 649, 650f
Syndrome coding, 596
Syndrome decoding, 200, 620
Syndrome vector, 199–200
Syntax-constrained rate-distortion
        optimization, 42–43
Synthesis filter parameters, 64
System management, 645–646
System monitoring, 645–646

Tanner graphs, 202, 203f
Target schedule design, 483–484
Target System, 439
Task States, 439
TCM codes. *See* Trellis-coded modulation

TCP. *See* Transmission Control Protocol
TCP-friendly rate control (TFRC), 460, 477
TDA. *See* Time domain aliasing
Template segments, 545
Temporal coding structure, 118–124
Temporal coordinate systems, 474–476
Temporal decomposition, 136–137
Temporal Haar wavelet decomposition, 136f
Temporal masking, 168, 169f
Temporal MC Haar filtering, 137f
Temporal transforms, spatial transforms and,
        147–148
Ternary random variables, 231
TFRC. *See* TCP-friendly rate control
$TH\_INTER_{i,k}$, 168
$TH\_INTRA_{i,k}4$, 168
Third Generation Partnership Project. *See*
        3GPP
3D ESCOT, 142–144
    neighbors of sample in, 143f
3D EZBC, 144–145, 145f
    quad tree decomposition, 145f
3D SPIHT, 141–142
3D-wavelet coefficients coding, 140–141
    separable, 140f
3GPP (Third Generation Partnership
        Project), 63, 65
Three-band lifting scheme, 146f
Three-band lifting-like scheme, 147f
Throughput efficiency
    with application-layer RS code, 348–349
    cross-layer impact on, 346–351
Tightest leaky bucket, 469
Tightly coupled resources, 445–446
Time compression
    dilation of speech and audio signals and,
        543–547
    dilation of video signals, 547–548
    of silence periods, 548
Time domain aliasing (TDA), 164
Time fairness, 394–395
TIMELY, 424
Timescale modification, 544
Timestamps, 474–476
    decoder, 474–475
    presentation, 47, 475
Time-to-live (TTL), 245
Tornado codes, 196, 204
Traditional auditory masking, 170f
Traffic specification (TSPEC), 371, 375, 376

Train classifiers, 388
Transcaling (TS), 134
Transcoding
  in bandwidth adaptation, 101–103
  for bit rate reductions, 102f
Transfer computations, 399
Transmission channel delay, 87
Transmission Control Protocol (TCP), 20,
        234, 242
  EXACT and, 444f
  variable bandwidth over, 489f
Transmission opportunities (TXOPs), 370,
        373–374, 383, 397, 399
Transmission policy, 295–296, 495
Transmission rates, 476–479
Transport layer, 340
Transport mechanisms, 293
Trellis, 208–209, 210
  of convolutional code, 209f
Trellis-coded modulation (TCM) codes,
        212–213
Truncation points, 181
TS. See Transcaling
TS 26.190, 65
TSPEC. See Traffic specification
TTL. See Time-to-live
Turbo codes, 196, 214–217
  block scheme of, 216f
  classical, 215f
TXOPs. See Transmission opportunities

UA. See User agent
UAC. See User agent client
UAS. See User agent server
UDP. See User Datagram Protocol
UEP. See Unequal Error Protection
Ultra Wide Bands (UWBs), 337
UMCTF. See Unconstrained MCTF
UMTS, 217
Unconstrained MCTF (UMCTF), 145–147
Underflow events, 244, 257–260
Unequal Error Protection (UEP), 25, 359
Unicast, 7
Uniform resource locators (URLs), 457
Uniquely decodable sources, 190
Unloaded packets, 254
Upstream, 266, 267
Urge, 3
URLs. See Uniform resource locators

User agent (UA), 506
User agent client (UAC), 506
User agent server (UAS), 506
User Datagram Protocol (UDP), 16, 234
UUNET, 244, 249
UWBs. See Ultra Wide Bands

V.42, 260
Variable bandwidth over TCP, 489f
Variable bit rate (VBR), 464, 470f
Variable-length channel codewords, 281f
VBR. See Variable bit rate
VCG. See Vickrey-Clarke-Groves
VCI, 13
Vector-matrix products, 208
Vickrey-Clarke-Groves (VCG), 397
Video applications, 15
Video coding techniques, 109
  conventional, 593–594
Video communication systems, 14–18
Video data units, 31
Video packetization modes, 30–31
Video payload format, in VoIP, 514–515
Video quality, subjective experiment, 360t
Virtual frames, 487
Visual performance, spatiotemporal SNR
        and, 153
Viterbi decoding algorithm, 209, 210, 211,
        284
Voice over IP (VoIP), 3–4, 60, 82, 503
  active techniques in, 518–519
  address, 508
  AMP for, 538
  architecture, 504–516
  audio-video synchronization, 520–522
  available bandwidth, 520
  call setup, 515–516
  client-side techniques in, 518
  combating losses in, 518
  end-to-end delay for, 534–535
  header fields, 508, 509t
  late loss rate for, 534–535
  latency in, 516–518
  media transport and control protocols, 510
  message body, 509–510
  packet delivery times for, 535f
  QoS, 516–522
  real-time transport protocols, 510–512
  RTCP in, 512–513

Voice over IP (VoIP) *(continued)*
  signaling protocols, 505–508
  systems, 504
  typical configuration for, 504f
  video payload format in, 514–515
VoIP. *See* Voice over IP
Voronoi region, 205

Waiting time priority (WTP), 433
WANs. *See* Wide Area Networks
Waveform Similarity Overlap-Add
      (WSOLA), 544, 545
Waveform speech codecs, loss concealment
      for, 60–63
WCC. *See* Wireless channel conditions
WHOIS, 249
Wide Area Networks (WANs), 337
Wideband Adaptive Multirate codec
      (AMR-WB), 65
Wide-scale Internet streaming study,
      242–267
  asymmetric paths in, 265–266
  cities participating in, 249f
  client-server architecture in, 247–248
  experimental results of, 248–250
  methodology of, 244–248
  overview of, 242–244
  packet loss in, 251–257
  packet reordering, 263–266
  purged datasets in, 250
  real-time streaming in, 246–247
  setup for, 244–246
  success of streaming attempts in, 250f
  underflow events, 257–260

WiFi, 4
Windows Media Audio (WMA), 66, 159,
      457
Windows Media Player, 83
Wireless channel conditions (WCC), 387,
      414, 415
Wireless channel model, accuracy of, 317
Wireless congestion control protocols,
      313–314
Wireless LANs (WLANs), 337, 340, 409
Wireless network interface cards (WNIC),
      413
  adaptation, 421f
Wireless solutions space, 338f
Wireless stations (WSTA), 351, 352, 370,
      373, 376, 394, 399
  polling, 400
Wireless Test Conditions, 39–41
Wireless transmission, 338–339
  multiuser, 401
WLANs. *See* Wireless LANs
WMA. *See* Windows Media Audio
WNIC. *See* Wireless network interface cards
WSOLA. *See* Waveform Similarity
      Overlap-Add
WSTA. *See* Wireless stations
WTP. *See* Waiting time priority
Wyner-Ziv coding, 598–599, 606
Wyner-Ziv decoding, 599–601
Wyner-Ziv encoding, 599–601, 614
Wyner-Ziv rate loss, 598

YouTube, 3

Lightning Source UK Ltd.
Milton Keynes UK
UKOW04n0606161013

219123UK00007B/123/P